GEORGETTE HEYER GEORGETTE HEYER GEORGETTE HEYER GEORGETTE HEYER GEORGETTE HEYER GEORGETTE HEYER GEORGETTE HEYER GEORGETTE HEYER GEORGETTE HEYER GEORGETTE HEYER GEORGETTE HEYER

Georgette Heyer

Georgette Heyer

These Old Shades

Sprig Muslin

Sylvester

The Corinthian

The Convenient Marriage

Heinemann/Octopus

These Old Shades first published in Great Britain in 1926
Sprig Muslin first published in Great Britain in 1956
Sylvester first published in Great Britain in 1957
The Corinthian first published in Great Britain in 1940
The Convenient Marriage first published in Great Britain in 1934

This edition first published
in 1977 by
William Heinemann Limited
15–16 Queen Street
London W1

in association with

Octopus Books Limited
59 Grosvenor Street
London W1

ISBN 0 905712 19 6

© Georgette Heyer 1957

Printed in Great Britain by
Jarrold & Sons Ltd, Norwich

Contents

These
Old
Shades

Georgette
Heyer

THESE OLD SHADES

'. . . This Age I grant (and grant with pride),
  Is varied, rich, eventful:
But if you touch its weaker side,
  Deplorably resentful:

Belaud it, and it takes your praise
  With air of calm conviction:
Condemn it, and at once you raise
  A storm of contradiction.

Whereas with these old shades of mine,
  Their ways and dress delight me;
And should I trip by word or line,
They cannot well indict me. . . .'

AUSTIN DOBSON
Epilogue to Eighteenth-Century Vignettes

I

His Grace of Avon Buys a Soul

A gentleman was strolling down a side street in Paris, on his way back from the house of one Madame de Verchoureux. He walked mincingly, for the red heels of his shoes were very high. A long purple cloak, rose-lined, hung from his shoulders and was allowed to fall carelessly back from his dress, revealing a full-skirted coat of purple satin, heavily laced with gold; a waistcoat of flowered silk; faultless small clothes; and a lavish sprinkling of jewels on his cravat and breast. A three-cornered hat, point-edged, was set upon his powdered wig, and in his hand he carried a long beribboned cane. It was a little enough protection against footpads, and although a light dress sword hung at the gentleman's side its hilt was lost in the folds of his cloak, not quickly to be found. At this late hour, and in this deserted street, it was the height of foolhardiness to walk unattended and flaunting jewels, but the gentleman seemed unaware of his recklessness. He proceeded languidly on his way, glancing neither to left nor to right, apparently heedless of possible danger.

But as he walked down the street, idly twirling his cane, a body hurled itself upon him, shot like a cannon-ball from a dark alley that yawned to the right of the magnificent gentleman. The figure clutched at that elegant cloak, cried out in a startled voice, and tried to regain his balance.

His Grace of Avon swirled about, gripping his assailant's wrists and bearing them downwards with a merciless strength belied by his foppish appearance. His victim gave a whimper of pain and sank quivering to his knees.

'M'sieur! Ah, let me go! I did not mean—I did not know—I would not—Ah, m'sieur, let me go!'

His Grace bent over the boy, standing a little to one side so that the light of an adjacent street lamp fell on that white agonized countenance. Great violet-blue eyes gazed wildly up at him, terror in their depths.

'Surely you are a little young for this game?' drawled the Duke. 'Or did you think to take me unawares?'

The boy flushed, and his eyes grew dark with indignation.

'I did not seek to rob you! Indeed, indeed I did not! I—I was running away! I—oh, m'sieur, let me go!'

'In good time, my child. From what were you running, may I ask? From another victim?'

'No! Oh, please let me go! You—you do not understand! He will have started in pursuit! Ah, please, please, milor'!'

The Duke's curious, heavy-lidded eyes never wavered from the boy's face. They had widened suddenly, and become intent.

'And who, child, is "he"?'

'My—my brother. Oh, please—'

Round the corner of the alley came a man, full-tilt. At sight of Avon he checked. The boy shuddered, and now clung to Avon's arm.

'Ah!' exploded the newcomer. 'Now, by God, if the whelp has sought to rob you, milor' he shall pay for it! You scoundrel! Ungrateful brat! You shall be sorry, I promise you! Milor', a thousand apologies! The lad is my young brother. I was beating him for his laziness when he slipped from me—'

The Duke raised a scented handkerchief to his thin nostrils.

'Keep your distance, fellow,' he said haughtily. 'Doubtless beating is good for the young.'

The boy shrank closer to him. He made no attempt to escape, but his hands twitched convulsively. Once again the Duke's strange eyes ran over him, resting for a moment on the copper-red curls that were cut short and ruffled into wild disorder.

'As I remarked, beating is good for the young. Your brother, you said?' He glanced now at the swarthy, coarse-featured young man.

'Yes, noble sir, my brother. I have cared for him since our parents died, and he repays me with ingratitude. He is a curse, noble sir, a curse!'

The Duke seemed to reflect.

'How old is he, fellow?'

'He is nineteen, milor'.'

The Duke surveyed the boy.

'Nineteen. Is he not a little small for his age?'

'Why, milor', if—if he is it is no fault of mine! I—I have fed him well. I pray you, do not heed what he says! He is a viper, a wild-cat, a veritable curse!'

'I will relieve you of the curse,' said his Grace calmly.

The man stared, uncomprehending.

'Milor'—?'

'I suppose he is for sale?'

A cold hand stole into the Duke's, and clutched it.

'Sale, milor'? You—'

'I believe I will buy him to be my page. What is his worth? A louis? Or are curses worthless? An interesting problem.'

The man's eyes gleamed suddenly with avaricious cunning.

'He is a good boy, noble sir. He can work. Indeed, he is worth much to me. And I have an affection for him. I—'

'I will give you a guinea for your curse.'

'Ah, but no, milor'! He is worth more! Much, much more!'

'Then keep him,' said Avon, and moved on.

The boy ran to him, clinging to his arm.

'Milor', take me! Oh please take me! I will work well for you! I swear it! Oh, I beg of you, take me!'

His Grace paused.

'I wonder if I am a fool?' he said in English. He drew the diamond pin from his cravat, and held it so that it winked and sparkled in the light of the lamp. 'Well, fellow? Will this suffice?'

The man gazed at the jewel as though he could hardly believe his eyes. He rubbed them, and drew nearer, staring.

'For this,' Avon said, 'I purchase your brother, body and soul. Well?'

'Give it me!' whispered the man, and stretched out his hand. 'The boy is yours, milor'.'

Avon tossed the pin to him.

'I believe I requested you to keep your distance,' he said. 'You offend my nostrils. Child, follow me.' On he went, down the street, with the boy at a respectful distance behind him.

They came at last to the Rue St.-Honoré, and to Avon's house. He passed in with never a glance behind him to see whether his new possession followed or not, and walked across the courtyard to the great nail-studded door. Bowing lackeys admitted him, looking in surprise at the shabby figure who came in his wake.

The Duke let fall his cloak, and handed his hat to one of the footmen.

'Mr Davenant?' he said.

'In the library, your Grace.'

Avon sauntered across the hall to the library door. It was opened for him, and he went in, nodding to the boy to follow.

Hugh Davenant sat by the fire, reading a book of poems. He glanced up as his host came in, and smiled.

'Well, Justin?' Then he saw the shrinking child by the door. 'Faith, what have we here?'

'You may well ask,' said the Duke. He came to the fire, and stretched one elegantly shod foot to the blaze. 'A whim. That dirty and starved scrap of humanity is mine.' He spoke in English, but it was evident that the boy understood, for he flushed, and hung his curly head.

'Yours?' Davenant looked from him to the boy. 'What mean you, Alastair? Surely—you cannot mean—your son?'

'Oh, no!' His Grace smiled in some amusement. 'Not this time, my dear Hugh. I bought this little rat for the sum of one diamond.'

'But—but why, in heaven's name?'

'I have no idea,' said his Grace placidly. 'Come here, rat.'

The boy came to him timidly, and allowed Justin to turn his face to the light.

'Quite a pretty child,' the Duke remarked. 'I shall make him my page. So entertaining to possess a page, body and soul.'

Davenant rose, and took one of the boy's hands in his.

'I suppose you will explain, some time or another,' he said. 'For the present, why not feed the poor child?'

'You are always so efficient,' sighed the Duke. He turned to the table, on which a cold supper was laid, awaiting him. 'Wonderful. You might almost have known that I should bring home a guest. You may eat, little rat.'

The boy looked up at him shyly.

'Please, milor', I can wait. I—I would not eat your supper. I would rather wait, if—if you please.'

'I do not please, my child. Go and eat.' He sat down as he spoke, twirling his quizzing glass. After a moment's hesitation the boy went to the table and waited for Hugh to carve him a leg of chicken. Having supplied his wants, Hugh came back to the fire.

'Are you mad, Justin?' he asked, faintly smiling.

'I believe not.'

'Then why have you done this? What do you, of all men, want with a child of his age?'

'I thought it might be an amusement. As you doubtless know, I am suffering from *ennui*. Louise wearies me. This—' he waved one white hand towards the famished boy—'is a heaven-sent diversion.'

Davenant frowned.

'You surely do not intend to adopt the child?'

'He—er—adopted me.'

'You are going to make him as your son?' persisted Hugh incredulously.

The Duke's eyebrows rose, rather superciliously.

'My dear Hugh! A child from the gutter? He shall be my page.'

'And what interest will that afford you?'

Justin smiled, and his glance travelled to the boy.

'I wonder?' he said softly.

'You have some special reason?'

'As you so sapiently remark, my dear Hugh, I have some special reason.'

Davenant shrugged his shoulders, and allowed the subject to drop. He sat watching the child at the table, who presently finished his repast, and came to the Duke's side.

'If you please, sir, I have finished.'

Avon put up his eyeglass.

'Have you?' he said.

The boy knelt suddenly and, to Davenant's surprise, kissed the Duke's hand.

'Yes, sir. Thank you.'

Avon disengaged himself, but the boy knelt still, looking up into the handsome face with humble eyes. The Duke took a pinch of snuff.

'My esteemed child, there sits the man you had best thank.' He waved his hand towards Davenant. 'I should never have thought of feeding you.'

'I—I thanked you for saving me from Jean, milor',' the boy answered.

'You are reserved for a worse fate,' said the Duke sardonically. 'You now belong to me—body and soul.'

'Yes, sir. If you please,' murmured the boy, and sent him a swift glance of admiration from beneath his long lashes.

The thin lips curled a little.

'The prospect is no doubt pleasing?'

'Yes, sir. I—I would like to serve you.'

'But then, you do not know me very well,' said Justin, with a slight chuckle. 'I am an inhuman taskmaster, eh, Hugh?'

'You are not the man to care for a child of his age,' said Hugh quietly.

'True, very true. Shall I give him to you?'

A trembling hand touched his great cuff.

'Please, sir—'

Justin looked across at his friend.

'I do not think I shall, Hugh. It is so entertaining, and so—er—novel, to be a gilded saint in the eyes of—er—unfledged innocence. I shall keep the boy for just so long as he continues to amuse me. What is your name, my child?'

'Léon, sir.'

'How delightfully brief!' Always a faint undercurrent of sarcasm ran beneath the surface of the Duke's smooth voice. 'Léon. No more, no less. The question is—Hugh will of course have the answer ready—what next to do with Léon?'

'Put him to bed,' said Davenant.

'Naturally—And do you think—a bath?'

'By all means.'

'Ah yes!' sighed the Duke, and struck a handbell at his side.

A lackey came in answer to the summons, bowing deeply.

'Your Grace desires?'

'Send me Walker,' said Justin.

The lackey effaced himself, and presently a neat individual came in, grey-haired and prim.

'Walker! I had something to say to you. Yes, I remember. Walker, do you observe this child?'

Walker glanced at the kneeling boy.

'Ay, your Grace.'

'He does. Marvellous,' murmured the Duke. 'His name, Walker, is Léon. Strive to bear it in mind.'

'Certainly, your Grace.'

'He requires several things, but first a bath.'

'Ay, your Grace.'

'Secondly, a bed.'

'Yes, your Grace.'

'Thirdly, a nightgown.'

'Yes, your Grace.'

'Fourthly, and lastly, a suit of clothes. Black.'

'Black, your Grace.'

'Severe and funereal black, as shall befit my page. You will procure them. No doubt you will prove yourself equal to this occasion. Take the child away, and show him the bath, the bed, and the nightgown. And then leave him alone.'

'Very good, your Grace.'

'And you, Léon, rise. Go with the estimable Walker. I shall see you to-morrow.'

Léon came to his feet, and bowed.

'Yes, Monseigneur. Thank you.'

'Pray, do not thank me again,' yawned the Duke. 'It fatigues me.' He watched Léon go out, and turned to survey Davenant.

Hugh looked full into his eyes.

'What does this mean, Alastair?'

The Duke crossed his legs, and swung one foot.

'I wonder?' he said pleasantly. 'I thought that you would be able to tell me. You are always so omniscient, my dear.'

'Some scheme you have in mind, I know,' Hugh said positively. 'I have known you long enough to be sure of that. What do you want with that child?'

'You are sometimes most importunate,' complained Justin. 'Never more so than when you become virtuously severe. Pray spare me a homily.'

'I have no intention of lecturing you. All I would say is that it is impossible for you to take that child as your page.'

'Dear me!' said Justin, and gazed pensively into the fire.

'For one thing, he is of gentle birth. One can tell that from his speech, and his delicate hands and face. For another—his innocence shines out of his eyes.'

'How very distressing!'

'It would be very distressing if that innocence left him—because of you,' Hugh said, a hint of grimness in his rather dreamy voice.

'Always so polite,' murmured the Duke.

'If you wish to be kind to him—'

'My dear Hugh! I thought you said you knew me?'

Davenant smiled at that.

'Well, Justin, as a favour to me, will you give me Léon, and seek a page elsewhere?'

'I am always sorry to disappoint you, Hugh. I desire to act up to your expectations on all possible occasions. So I shall keep Léon. Innocence shall walk behind Evil—you see, I forestall you—clad in sober black.'

'Why do you want him? At least tell me that?'

'He has Titian hair,' said Justin blandly. 'Titian hair has ever been one of—my—ruling—passions.' The hazel eyes glinted for a moment, and were swiftly veiled. 'I am sure you will sympathize with me.'

Hugh rose and walked to the table. He poured himself out a glass of burgundy, and sipped it for a time in silence.

'Where have you been this evening?' he asked at length.

'I really forget. I believe I went first to De Touronne's house. Yes, I remember now. I won. Strange.'

'Why strange?' inquired Hugh.

Justin flicked a grain of snuff from his great cuff.

'Because, Hugh, in the days, not so long since, when it was—ah—common knowledge that the noble family of Alastair was on the verge of ruin—yes, Hugh, even when I was mad enough to contemplate marriage with the present—er—Lady Merivale—I could only lose.'

'I've seen you win thousands in a night, Justin.'

'And lose them the following night. Then, if you remember, I went away with you to—now, where did we go? Rome! Of course!'

'I remember.'

The thin lips sneered a little.

'Yes. I was the—ah—rejected and heart-broken suitor. I should have blown my brains out to be quite correct. But I was past the age of drama. Instead I proceeded—in due course—to Vienna. And I won. The reward, my dear Hugh, of vice.'

Hugh tilted his glass, watching the candle-light play on the dark wine.

'I heard,' he said slowly, 'that the man from whom you won that fortune—a young man, Justin—'

'—with a blameless character.'

'Yes. That young man—so I heard—*did* blow his brains out.'

'You were misinformed, my dear. He was shot in a duel. The reward of virtue. The moral is sufficiently pointed, I think?'

'And you came to Paris with a fortune.'

'Quite a considerable one. I bought this house.'

'Yes. I wonder how you reconcile it with your soul?'

'I haven't one, Hugh. I thought you knew that.'

'When Jennifer Beauchamp married Anthony Merivale you had something approaching a soul.'

'Had I?' Justin regarded him with some amusement.

Hugh met his look.

'And I wonder too what Jennifer Beauchamp is to you now?'

Justin held up one beautiful white hand.

'Jennifer Merivale, Hugh. She is the memory of a failure, and of a spell of madness.'

'And yet you have never been quite the same since.'

Justin rose, and now the sneer was marked.

'I told you half an hour ago, my dear, that it was my endeavour to act up to your expectations. Three years ago—in fact, when I heard from my sister Fanny of Jennifer's marriage—you said with your customary simplicity that although she would not accept my suit, she had made me. *Voilà tout.*'

'No.' Hugh looked thoughtfully across at him. 'I was wrong, but—'

'My dear Hugh, pray do not destroy my faith in you!'

'I was wrong, but not so much wrong. I should have said that Jennifer prepared the way for another woman to make you.'

Justin closed his eyes.

'When you become profound, Hugh, you cause me to regret the day that saw me admit you into the select ranks of my friends.'

'You have so many, have you not?' said Hugh, flushing.

'*Parfaitement.*' Justin walked to the door. 'Where there is money there are also—friends.'

Davenant set down his glass.

'Is that meant for an insult?' he said quietly.

Justin paused, his hand on the door-knob.

'Strange to say, it was not. But by all means call me out.'

Hugh laughed suddenly.

'Oh, go to bed, Justin! You are quite impossible!'

'So you have often told me. Good night, my dear.' He went out, but before he had shut the door bethought himself of something, and looked back, smiling. '*A propos*, Hugh, I have got a soul. It has just had a bath, and is now asleep.'

'God help it!' Hugh said gravely.

'I am not sure of my cue. Do I say amen, or retire cursing?' His eyes mocked, but the smile in them was not unpleasant. He did not wait for an answer, but shut the door, and went slowly up to bed.

2

Introducing the Comte de Saint-Vire

Shortly after noon on the following day Avon sent for his page. Léon came promptly, and knelt to kiss the Duke's hand. Walker had obeyed his master's commands implicitly, and in place of the shabby, grimy child of the evening before was a scrupulously neat boy, whose red curls had been swept severely back from his brow, and whose slim person was clad in plain black raiment, with a starched muslin cravat about his neck.

Avon surveyed him for a moment.

'Yes. You may rise, Léon. I am going to ask you some questions. I desire you will answer them truthfully. You understand?'

Léon put his hands behind him.

'Yes, Monseigneur.'

'You may first tell me how you come to know my language.'

Léon shot him a surprised glance.

'Monseigneur?'

'Pray do not be guileless. I dislike fools.'

'Yes, Monseigneur. I was only surprised that you knew. It was at the inn, you see.'

'I do not think I am obtuse,' said Avon coldly, 'but I see naught.'

'Pardon, Monseigneur. Jean keeps an inn, and very often English travellers come. Not—not noble English, of course.'

'I see. Now you may relate your history. Begin with your name.'

'I am Léon Bonnard, Monseigneur. My mother was the Mère Bonnard, and my father—'

'—was the Père Bonnard. It is not inconceivable. Where were you born, and when did your worthy parents die?'

'I—I do not know where I was born, Monseigneur. It was not in Anjou, I think.'

'That is of course interesting,' remarked the Duke. 'Spare me a list of the places where you were not born, I beg of you.'

Léon coloured.

'You do not understand, Monseigneur. My parents went to live in Anjou when I was a baby. We had a farm Bassincourt, *auprès de Saumur*. And—and we lived there until my parents died.'

'Did they die simultaneously?' inquired Justin.

Léon's straight little nose wrinkled in perplexity.

'Monseigneur?'

'At one and the same time.'

'It was the plague,' explained Léon. 'I was sent to Monsieur le Curé. I was twelve then, and Jean was twenty.'

'How came you to be so much younger than this Jean?' asked Justin, and opened his eyes rather wide, so that Léon looked full into them.

A mischievous chuckle escaped Léon; he returned the piercing stare frankly.

'Monseigneur, my parents are dead, so I cannot ask them.'

'My friend—' Justin spoke softly. 'Do you know what I do to impertinent pages?'

Léon shook his head apprehensively.

'I have them whipped. I advise you to have a care.'

Léon paled, and the laugh died out of his eyes.

'Pardon, Monseigneur. I—I did not mean to be impertinent,' he said contritely. 'My mother had once a daughter who died. Then—then I came.'

'Thank you. Where did you learn to speak as a gentleman?'

'With M. le Curé, Monseigneur. He taught me to read and to write and to know Latin a little, and—and many other things.'

Justin raised his eyebrows.

'And your father was a farmer? Why did you receive this extensive education?'

'I do not know, Monseigneur. I was the baby, you see, and the favourite. My mother would not have me work on the farm. That is why Jean hates me, I think.'

'Possibly. Give me your hand.'

Léon extended one slender hand for inspection. Justin took it in his, and surveyed it through his eyeglass. It was small, and finely made, with tapering fingers roughened by toil.

'Yes,' said the Duke. 'Quite a pretty member.'

Léon smiled engagingly.

'*Quant à ça*, you have very beautiful hands, Monseigneur, I think.'

The Duke's lips quivered.

'You overwhelm me, my child. As you were saying, your parents died. What then?'

'Oh, then Jean sold the farm! He said he was made for greater things. But I do not know.' Léon tilted his head to one side, considering the point. The irrepressible dimple appeared, and was swiftly banished. Léon eyed his master solemnly, and a little nervously withal.

'We will leave Jean's capabilities out of the discussion,' said Justin smoothly. 'Continue your story.'

'Yes, Monseigneur. Jean sold the farm, and took me away from M. le Curé.' Léon's face clouded over. 'Monsieur wanted to keep me, but Jean would not have it so. He thought I should be useful. So of course monsieur could do naught. Jean brought me to Paris. That was when he made me—' Léon stopped.

'Go on!' said Justin sharply. 'That was when he made you—?'

'Work for him,' said Léon lamely. He encountered a searching glance, and his big eyes fell before it.

'Very well,' said Justin at last. 'We will leave it that. *Et puis?*'

'Then Jean bought the inn in the Rue Sainte-Marie, and–and after a time he met Charlotte, and–and married her. Then it was worse, because Charlotte hated me.' The blue eyes flashed. 'I tried to kill her once,' said Léon naïvely. 'With the big carving-knife.'

'Her hatred is not incomprehensible,' said Justin dryly.

'N-no,' replied Léon doubtfully. 'I was only fifteen then. I remember I did not have anything to eat all day–besides the beating. And–and that is all, Monseigneur, till you came, and took me away.'

Justin picked up a quill and passed it through his fingers.

'May I ask why you tried to kill this Charlotte–er–with the carving-knife?'

Léon flushed, and looked away.

'There–there was a reason, Monseigneur.'

'I do not doubt it.'

'I–oh, I think she was very unkind and cruel and she–she made me angry. That was all.'

'I am both cruel and unkind, but I do not advise you to try and kill me. Or any of my servants. You see, I know what the colour of your hair denotes.'

The long dark lashes lifted again, and the dimple showed.

'*Colère de diable,*' Léon said.

'Precisely. You will do well to hide it with me, my child.'

'Yes, Monseigneur. I do not seek to kill those whom I love.'

Justin's lip curled rather sardonically.

'I am relieved. Now listen to me. You will henceforth be my page; you will be clothed and fed, and well provided for, but in return I will have obedience from you. You understand?'

'But yes, Monseigneur.'

'You will learn that my word is law with my servants. And this is my first command: if anyone should question you as to who you are, or from where you come, you will answer only that you are Avon's page. You will forget your past until I give you leave to remember it. You see?'

'Yes, Monseigneur.'

'And you will obey Walker as you would myself.'

The firm chin was tilted at that; Léon looked speculatively at the Duke.

'If you do not'–the soft voice grew softer still–'you will find that I too know how to punish.'

'If it is your will that I obey this Walker,' said Léon with dignity, 'I will do it, *y-your-r-r Gr-r-race*!'

Justin looked him over.

'Certainly you will do so. And I prefer that you call me Monseigneur.'

The blue eyes twinkled wickedly.

'This Walker, he has told me that when I speak to you, Monseigneur, I must say "your-r-r" ah, bah! I cannot, *enfin*!'

For one moment Justin stared haughtily at his page. Instantly the twinkle disappeared. Léon stared back gravely.

'Be very careful,' Justin warned him.

'Yes, Monseigneur,' Léon said meekly.

'You may go now. This evening you will accompany me out.' The Duke dipped his quill in the inkhorn, and started to write.

'Where, Monseigneur?' inquired the page with great interest.

'Is that your affair? I dismissed you. Go.'

'Yes, Monseigneur. Pardon!' Léon departed, carefully closing the door behind him. Outside he met Davenant, coming slowly down the stairs. Hugh smiled.

'Well, Léon? Where have you been all the morning?'

'Dressing myself, in these new clothes, m'sieu'. I think I look nice, *n'est-ce pas?*'

'Very nice. Where are you going now?'

'I do not know, m'sieu'. Perhaps there is something I may do for Monseigneur?'

'If he gave you no orders there is nothing. Can you read?'

'But yes! I was taught. Ah, I have forgotten, m'sieu'!'

'Have you?' Hugh was amused. 'If you come with me, child, I'll find you a book.'

Twenty minutes later Hugh entered the library to find the Duke still writing, as Léon had left him.

'Justin, who and what is Léon? He is a delightful child; certainly no peasant!'

'He is a very impertinent child,' said Justin, with the ghost of a smile. 'He is the first page I have had who ever dared to laugh at me.'

'Did he laugh at you? A very wholesome experience for you, Alastair. How old is the child?'

'I have reason to believe that he is nineteen,' said Justin placidly.

'Nineteen! Faith, it's not possible! He is a babe!'

'Not entirely. Do you come with me to Vassaud's tonight?'

'I suppose so. I've no money to lose, but what matter?'

'You need not play,' said Justin.

'If one does not play, why visit a gaming-house?'

'To talk to the *monde*. I go to Vassaud's to see Paris.' He resumed his writing, and presently Hugh strolled away.

At dinner that evening Léon stood behind the Duke's chair, and waited upon him. Justin seemed hardly to notice him, but Hugh could not take his eyes from that piquant little face. Indeed, he stared so hard that at last Léon stared back, with great dignity, and some reproach. Observing his friend's fixed regard, Justin turned, and put up his glass to look at Léon.

'What are you doing?' he asked.

'Monseigneur, only looking at M. Davenant.'

'Then do not.'

'But he looks at me, Monseigneur!'

'That is another matter.'

'I do not see that that is fair,' remarked Léon, *sotto voce*.

Some time after dinner the two men set out for Vassaud's. When Hugh realized that Léon was to accompany them he frowned, and took Avon aside.

'Justin, have done with this affectation! You can have no need of a page at Vassaud's, and it's no place for such a child!'

'My very dear Hugh, I do wish you would allow me to know my own mind,' answered Justin sweetly. 'The page goes with me. Another whim.'

'But why? The child should be in bed!'

Justin flicked a speck of snuff from his coat.

'You force me to remind you, Hugh, that the page is mine.'

Davenant compressed his lips, and swung out of the door. Nonchalantly his Grace followed.

Vassaud's was crowded, early in the evening though it was. The two men left their cloaks with the lackey in the vestibule, and proceeded, with Léon in their wake, across the hall to the broad stairway which led to the gaming-rooms on the first floor. Hugh saw a friend, standing at the foot of the stairs, and paused to exchange a greeting, but Avon swept on, bowing slightly to right and left as some chance acquaintance hailed him. He did not stop to speak to anyone, although several called to him as he passed, but went on his regal way with just a faint smile in his lips.

Léon followed him close, his blue eyes wide with interest. He attracted some attention, and many were the curious glances cast from him to the Duke. He flushed delicately when he encountered such a glance, but his Grace appeared to be quite unaware of the surprise he had created.

'What ails Alastair now?' inquired the Chevalier d'Anvau, who was standing with one De Salmy in a recess on the staircase.

'Who knows?' De Salmy shrugged elegantly. 'He must ever be unusual. Good evening, Alastair.'

The Duke nodded to him.

'I rejoice to see you, De Salmy. A hand of piquet later?'

De Salmy bowed.

'I shall be delighted.' He watched Avon pass on, and shrugged again. 'He bears himself as though he were the king of France. I mislike those strange eyes. Ah, Davenant, well met!'

Davenant smiled pleasantly.

'You here? A crowd, is it not?'

'All Paris,' agreed the Chevalier. 'Why has Alastair brought his page?'

'I have no idea, Justin is never communicative. I see Destourville is back.'

'Ah yes, he arrived last night. You have no doubt heard the scandal?'

'Oh, my dear Chevalier, I never listen to scandal!' Hugh laughed, and went on up the stairs.

'*Je me demande*,' remarked the Chevalier, watching Hugh's progress through his eyeglass, 'why it is that the good Davenant is a friend of the bad Alastair?'

The salon on the first floor was brilliantly lighted, and humming with gay, inconsequent conversation. Some were already at play, others were gathered about the buffet, sipping their wine. Hugh saw Avon through the folding doors that led into a smaller salon, the centre of a group, his page standing at a discreet distance behind him.

A muttered exclamation near him made him turn his head. A tall, rather carelessly dressed man was standing beside him, looking across the room at Léon. He was frowning, and his heavy mouth was shut hard. Through the powder his hair glinted red, but his arched brows were black, and very thick.

'Saint-Vire?' Hugh bowed to him. 'You are wondering at Alastair's page? A freak, is it not?'

'Your servant, Davenant. A freak, yes. Who is the boy?'

'I do not know. Alastair found him yesterday. He is called Léon. I trust Madame your wife is well?'

'I thank you, yes. Alastair found him, you say? What does that mean?'

'Here he comes,' answered Hugh. 'You had best ask him.'

Avon came up with a swish of silken skirts, and bowed low to the Comte de Saint-Vire.

'My dear Comte!' The hazel eyes mocked. 'My very dear Comte!'

Saint-Vire returned the bow abruptly.

'M. le Duc!'

Justin drew forth his jewelled snuff-box, and presented it. Tall as he was, Saint-Vire was made to look insignificant beside this man of splendid height, and haughty bearing.

'A little snuff, dear Comte? No?' He shook the foaming ruffles back from his white hand, and very daintily took a pinch of snuff. His thin lips were smiling, but not pleasantly.

'Saint-Vire was admiring your page, Justin,' Davenant said. 'He is exciting no little attention.'

'No doubt.' Avon snapped his fingers imperiously, and Léon came forward. 'He is almost unique, my dear Comte. Pray look your fill.'

'Your page is of no interest to me, m'sieur,' Saint-Vire answered shortly, and turned aside.

'Behind me.' The command was given coldly, and at once Léon stepped back. 'The so worthy Comte! Comfort him, Hugh.' Avon passed on again, and in a little while was seated at a card table, playing lansquenet.

Davenant was called to another table presently, and proceeded to play at faro, with Saint-Vire as his partner. A foppish gentleman sat opposite him, and started to deal.

'*Mon cher*, your friend is always so amusing. Why the page?' He glanced towards Avon's table.

Hugh gathered up his cards.

'How should I know, Lavoulère? Doubtless he has a reason. And—forgive me—I am weary of the subject.'

'He is so—so arresting,' apologized Lavoulère. 'The page. Red hair—oh, but of a radiance!—and blue, blue eyes. Or are they purple-black? The little oval face, and the patrician nose—! Justin is wonderful. You do not think so, Henri?'

'Oh, without doubt!' Saint-Vire answered. 'He should have been an actor. *Quant à moi*, I would humbly suggest that enough notice has been taken of the Duc and his page. Your play, Marchérand.'

At Avon's table one of the gamblers yawned, pushing back his chair.

'*Mille pardons*, but I thirst! I go in search of refreshment.'

The game had come to an end, and Justin was toying with his dice-box. He glanced up now, and waved to Château-Mornay to keep his seat.

'My page will fetch wine, Louis. He is not only to be gazed upon. Léon!'

Léon slipped from behind Avon's chair, from where he had been an intent spectator of the game.

'Monseigneur?'

'Canary and burgundy, at once.'

Léon withdrew, and nervously threaded his way between the tables to the buffet. He returned presently with a tray, which he presented to Justin, on one knee. Justin pointed silently to where Château-Mornay sat, and, blushing for his mistake, Léon went to him, and again presented the tray. When he had served each one in turn he looked inquiringly up at his master.

'Go to M. Davenant, and ask him if he has commands for you,' said Justin languidly. 'Will you hazard a throw with me, Cornalle?'

'Ay, what you will.' Cornalle pulled a dice-box from his pocket. 'Two ponies? Will you throw?'

Justin cast his dice carelessly on the table, and turned his head to watch Léon. The page was at Davenant's elbow. Davenant looked up.

'Well, Léon? What is it?'

'Monseigneur sent me, m'sieur, to see if you had commands for me.'

Saint-Vire shot him a quick look, leaning back in his chair, one hand lying lightly clenched on the table.

'Thank you, no,' Hugh replied. 'Unless—Saint-Vire, will you drink with me? And you, messieurs?'

'I thank you, Davenant,' said the Comte. 'You have no thirst, Lavoulère?'

'At the moment, no. Oh, if you all must drink, then so will I!'

'Léon, will you fetch burgundy, please?'

'Yes, m'sieur,' bowed Léon. He was beginning to enjoy himself. He walked away again, looking about him appreciatively. When he returned he made use of the lesson just learned at Avon's table, and presented the silver tray first to Saint-Vire.

The Comte turned in his chair and, picking up the decanter, slowly poured out a glassful, and handed it to Davenant. He poured out another, his eyes on Léon's face. Conscious of the steady regard Léon looked up, and met Saint-Vire's eyes frankly. The Comte held the decanter poised, but poured no more for a long minute.

'What is your name, boy?'

'Léon, m'sieur.'

Saint-Vire smiled.

'No more?'

The curly head was shaken.

'*Je ne sais plus rien, m'sieur.*'

'So ignorant?' Saint-Vire went on with his work. As he picked up the last glass he spoke again. 'Methinks you have not been long with M. le Duc?'

'No, m'sieur. As m'sieur says.' Léon rose, and looked across at Davenant. 'M'sieur?'

'That is all, Léon, thank you.'

'So you have found a use for him, Hugh? Was I not wise to bring him? Your servant, Lavoulère.'

The soft voice startled Saint-Vire, and his hand shook, so that a little liquid was spilled from his glass. Avon stood at his side, quizzing-glass raised.

'A very prince of pages,' smiled Lavoulère. 'How is your luck to-night, Justin?'

'Wearisome,' sighed the Duke. 'For a week it has been impossible to lose. From the dreamy expression on Hugh's face I infer that it is not so with him.' He went to stand behind Hugh's chair, laying a hand on his shoulder. 'Belike, my dear Hugh, I shall bring you better luck.'

'I have never known you do that yet,' retorted Davenant. He set down his emptied glass. 'Shall we play again?'

'By all means,' nodded Saint-Vire. 'You and I are in a sad way, Davenant.'

'And shall soon be in a sadder,' remarked Hugh, shuffling the pack. 'Remind me, Lavoulère, that in future I only play with you as my partner.' He dealt the cards round, and, as he did so, spoke quietly to the Duke, in

English. 'Send the child downstairs, Alastair. You have no need of him.'

'I am as wax in your hands,' replied his Grace. 'He has served his turn. Léon, you will await me in the hall.' He stretched out his hand to pick up Hugh's cards. 'Dear me!' He laid them down again, and watched the play in silence for a while.

At the end of the round Lavoulère spoke to him.

'Where is your brother, Alastair? The so charming youth! He is quite, quite mad!'

'Lamentably so. Rupert, for all I know, is either languishing in an English sponging house, or living upon my hapless brother-in-law's bounty.'

'That is Miladi Fanny's husband, yes? Edward Marling, *n'est-ce pas*? You have only one brother and sister?'

'They more than suffice me,' said his Grace.

Lavoulère laughed.

'*Voyons*, it amuses me, your family! Is there no love between you at all?'

'Very little.'

'And yet I have heard that you reared them, those two!'

'I have no recollection of it,' said Justin.

'Come now, Justin, when your mother died you kept a hand on the reins!' expostulated Davenant.

'But lightly, my dear. Enough only to make both a little afraid of me; no more.'

'Lady Fanny is very fond of you.'

'Yes, I believe she is occasionally,' agreed Justin calmly.

'Ah, Miladi Fanny!' Lavoulère kissed his finger-tips. 'Behold! how she is *ravissante*!'

'Also behold that Hugh wins,' drawled his Grace. 'My compliments, Davenant.' He shifted his position slightly, so that he faced Saint-Vire. 'Pray how is Madame, your charming wife, dear Comte?'

'Madame is well, I thank you, m'sieur.'

'And the Vicomte, your so enchanting son?'

'Also.'

'Not here to-night, I think?' Avon raised his glass, and through it surveyed the room. 'I am desolated. No doubt you deem him too young for these delights? He is but nineteen, I believe?'

Saint-Vire laid his cards face downwards on the table, and looked angrily up at that handsome, enigmatic countenance.

'You are most interested in my son, M. le Duc!'

The hazel eyes widened and narrowed again.

'But how could it be otherwise?' asked the Duke politely.

Saint-Vire picked up his cards again.

'He is at Versailles, with his mother,' he said curtly. 'My play, Lavoulère?'

3

Which tells of a Debt Unpaid

When Davenant returned to the house in the Rue St-Honoré, he found that although Léon had long since come in, and was now in bed, his Grace was still out. Guessing that Avon had gone from Vassaud's to visit his latest light o' love, Hugh went into the library to await him. Soon the Duke sauntered in, poured himself out a glass of canary wine, and came to the fire.

'A most instructive evening. I hope my very dear friend Saint-Vire recovered from the sorrow my early departure must have occasioned him?'

'I think so,' smiled Hugh. He rested his head back against the cushions of his chair, and looked at the Duke with rather a puzzled expression on his face. 'Why do you so hate one another, Justin?'

The straight brows rose.

'Hate? I? My dear Hugh!'

'Very well, if you like it better I will say why does Saint-Vire hate you?'

'It is a very old tale, Hugh; almost a forgotten tale. The–er–*contretemps* between the amiable Comte and myself took place in the days before I had the advantage of possessing your friendship, you see.'

'So there was a *contretemps*? I suppose you behaved abominably?'

'What I admire in you, my dear, is your charming candour,' remarked his Grace. 'But in this instance I did not behave abominably. Amazing, is it not?'

'What happened?'

'Very little. It was really quite trivial. So trivial that nearly every one has forgotten it.'

'It was a woman, of course?'

'Even so. No less a personage than the present Duchesse de Belcour.'

'Duchesse de Belcour?' Hugh sat upright in surprise. 'Saint-Vire's sister? That red-haired shrew?'

'Yes, that red-haired shrew. As far as I remember, I admired her–er–shrewishness–twenty years ago. She was really very lovely.'

'Twenty years ago! So long! Justin, surely you did not—'

'I wanted to wed her,' said Avon pensively. 'Being young and foolish. It seems incredible now; yet so it was. I applied for permission to woo her–yes, is it not amusing?–to her worthy father.' He paused, looking into the fire. 'I was–let me see! twenty–a little more; I forget. My father and her father had not been the best of friends. Again a woman; I believe my sire won that encounter. I suppose it rankled. And on my side there were, even at that age, my dear, some trifling intrigues.' His shoulders shook. 'There always are–in my family. The old Comte refused to give me leave to woo his daughter. Not altogether surprising, you think? No, I did not elope with her. Instead I received a visit from Saint-Vire. He was then Vicomte de Valmé. That visit was almost humiliating.' The lines about Justin's mouth were grim. 'Al-most hu-miliating.'

'For you?'

Avon smiled.

'For me. The noble Henri came to my lodging with a large and heavy whip.' He looked down as Hugh gasped, and the smile grew. 'No, my dear, I was not thrashed. To resume: Henri was enraged; there was a something between us, maybe a woman—I forget. He was very much enraged. It should afford me some consolation, that. I had dared to raise my profligate eyes to the daughter of that most austere family of Saint-Vire. Have you ever noticed the austerity? It lies in the fact that the Saint-Vire amours are carried on in secrecy. Mine, as you know, are quite open. You perceive the nice distinction? *Bon!*' Avon had seated himself on the arm of a chair, legs crossed. He started to twirl his wine glass, holding the narrow stem between thumb and finger. 'My licentious—I quote his very words, Hugh—behaviour; my entire lack of morals; my soiled reputation; my vicious mind; my—but I forget the rest. It was epic—all these made my perfectly honourable proposal an insult. I was to understand that I was as the dirt beneath the Saint-Vire feet. There was much more, but at length the noble Henri came to his peroration. For my impudence I was to receive a thrashing at his hands. I! Alastair of Avon!'

'But, Justin, he must have been mad! It was not as though you were low-born! The Alastairs—'

'Precisely. He was mad. These red-haired people, my dear Hugh! And there was something between us. No doubt I had at some time or other behaved abominably to him. There followed, as you may imagine, a short argument. It did not take me long to come to my peroration. In short, I had the pleasure of cutting his face open with his own whip. Out came his sword.' Avon stretched out his arm, and the muscles rippled beneath the satin of his coat sleeve. 'I was young, but I knew a little of the art of the duello, even in those days. I pinked him so well that he had to be carried home in my coach, by my lackeys. When he had departed I gave myself up to thought. You see, my dear, I was, or fancied that I was, very much in love with that—er—red-haired shrew. The noble Henri had told me that his sister had deemed herself insulted by my court. It occurred to me that perhaps the lady had mistaken my suit for a casual intrigue. I visited the Hôtel Saint-Vire to make known mine intentions. I was received not by her father, but by the noble Henri, reclining upon a couch. There were also some friends of his. I forget. Before them, before his lackeys, he informed me that he stood in—er—*loco parentis*, and that his sister's hand was denied me. Further that if I so much as dared to accost her his servants would whip me from her presence.'

'Good God!' cried Hugh.

'So I thought. I retired. What would you? I could not touch the man; I had wellnigh killed him already. When next I appeared in public I found that my visit to the Hôtel Saint-Vire had become the talk of Paris. I was compelled to leave France for a time. Happily another scandal arose which cast mine into the shade, so Paris was once more open to me. It is an old, old story, Hugh, but I have not forgotten.'

'And he?'

'He has not forgotten either. He was half mad at the time, but he would not apologize when he came to his senses; I don't think I expected him to do so. We meet now as distant acquaintances; we are polite—oh, scrupulously!—but he knows that I am still waiting.'

'Waiting. . .?'

Justin walked to the table and set down his glass.

'For an opportunity to pay that debt in full,' he said softly.

'Vengeance?' Hugh leaned forward. 'I thought you disliked melodrama, my friend?'

'I do; but I have a veritable passion for–justice.'

'You've nourished thoughts of–vengeance–for twenty years?'

'My dear Hugh, if you imagine that the lust for vengeance has been my dominating emotion for twenty years, permit me to correct the illusion.'

'Has it not grown cold?' Hugh asked, disregarding.

'Very cold, my dear, but none the less dangerous.'

'And all this time not one opportunity has presented itself?'

'You see, I wish it to be thorough,' apologized the Duke.

'Are you nearer success now than you were–twenty years ago?'

A soundless laugh shook Justin.

'We shall see. Rest assured that when it comes it will be–so!' Very slowly he clenched his hand on his snuffbox, and opened his fingers to show the thin gold crushed.

Hugh gave a little shiver.

'My God, Justin, do you know just how vile you can be?'

'Naturally Do they not call me–Satanas?' The mocking smile came; the eyes glittered.

'I hope to heaven Saint-Vire never puts himself in your power! It seems they were right who named you Satanas!'

'Quite right, my poor Hugh.'

'Does Saint-Vire's brother know?'

'Armand? No one knows save you, and I, and Saint-Vire. Armand may guess, of course.'

'And yet you and he are friends!'

'Oh, Armand's hatred for the noble Henri is more violent than ever mine could be.'

In spite of himself Hugh smiled.

'It is a race betwixt you, then?'

'Not a whit. I should have said that Armand's is a sullen detestation. Unlike me, he is content to hate.'

'He, I suppose, would sell his soul for Saint-Vire's shoes.'

'And Saint-Vire,' said Avon gently, 'would sell his soul to keep those shoes from Armand.'

'Yes, one knows that. It was common gossip at the time that that was his reason for marrying. One could not accuse him of loving his wife!'

'No,' said Justin, and chuckled as though at some secret thought.

'Well,' Hugh went on, 'Armand's hopes of the title were very surely dashed when Madame presented Saint-Vire with a son!'

'Precisely,' said Justin.

'A triumph for Saint-Vire, that!'

'A triumph indeed,' suavely agreed his Grace.

4

His Grace of Avon Becomes Further Acquainted with his Page

For Léon the days passed swiftly, each one teeming with some new excitement. Never in his life had he seen such sights as now met his eyes. He was dazzled by the new life spread before him; from living in a humble, dirty tavern, he was transported suddenly into gorgeous surroundings, fed with strange foods, clad in fine clothes, and taken into the midst of aristocratic Paris. All at once life seemed to consist of silks and diamonds, bright lights, and awe-inspiring figures. Ladies whose fingers were covered with rings, and whose costly brocades held an elusive perfume, would stop to smile at him sometimes; great gentlemen with powdered wigs and high heels would flip his head with careless fingers as they passed. Even Monseigneur sometimes spoke to him.

Fashionable Paris grew accustomed to see him long before he became accustomed to his new existence. After a while people ceased to stare at him when he came in Avon's wake, but it was some time before he ceased to gaze on all that met his eyes, in wondering appreciation.

To the amazement of Avon's household, he still persisted in his worship of the Duke. Nothing could shake him from his standpoint, and if one of the lackeys vented his outraged feelings below-stairs in a tirade against Avon, Léon was up in arms at once, blind rage taking possession of him. Since the Duke had ordained that none should lay violent hands on his page, save at his express command, the lackeys curbed their tongues in Léon's presence, for he was over-ready with his dagger, and they dared not disobey the Duke's orders. Gaston, the valet, felt that this hot partisanship was sadly wrong; that any should defend the Duke struck forcibly at his sense of propriety, and more than once he tried to convince the page that it was the duty of any self-respecting menial to loathe the Duke.

'*Mon petit*,' he said firmly, 'it is ridiculous. It is unthinkable. *Même*, it is outrageous. It is against all custom. The Duke, he is not human. Some call him Satanas, and, *mon Dieu*, they have reason!'

'I have never seen Satan,' answered Léon, from a large chair where he sat with his feet tucked under him. 'But I do not think that Monseigneur is like him.' He reflected. 'But if he is like the devil no doubt I should like the devil very much. My brother says I am a child of the devil.'

'That is shame!' said fat Madame Dubois, the housekeeper, shocked.

'Faith, he has the devil's own temper!' chuckled Gregory, a footman.

'But listen to me, you!' insisted Gaston. 'M. le Duc is of a hardness! Ah, but who should know better than I? I tell you, *moi qui vous parle*, if he would but be enraged all would go well. If he would throw his mirror at my head I would say naught! That is a gentleman, a noble! But the Duc! Bah! he speaks softly—oh, so softly!—and his eyes they are al-most shut, while his voice—*voilà*, I shudder!' He did shudder, but revived at the murmur of applause. 'And you, *petit*! When has he spoken to you as a boy? He speaks to you as his dog! Ah, but it is imbecile to admire such a man! It is not to be believed!'

'I am his dog. He is kind to me, and I love him,' said Léon firmly.

'Kind! Madame, you hear?' Gaston appealed to the housekeeper, who sighed, and folded her hands.

'He is very young,' she said.

'Now I will tell you of a thing!' Gaston exclaimed. 'This Duc, what did he do, think you, three years ago? You see this hôtel? It is fine, it is costly! *Eh bien*! Me, I have served the Duke for six years, so you may know that I speak truth. Three years ago he was poor! There were debts and mortgages. Oh, we lived the same, *bien sûr*; the Alastairs are always thus. We had always the same magnificence, but there were only debts behind the splendour. Me, I know. Then we go to Vienna. As ever, the Duc he play for great stakes: that is the way of his house. At first he loses. You would not say he cared, for still he smiles. That too is his way. Then there comes a young nobleman, very rich, very joyous. He plays with the Duc. He loses; he suggests a higher stake; the Duc, he agrees. What would you? Still that young noble loses. On and on, until at last—pouf! It is over! That fortune, it has changed hands. The young man he is ruined—*absolument*! The Duc, he goes away. He smiles—ah, that smile! The young man fights a duel with pistols a little later, and he fires wide, wide! Because he was ruined he chose Death! And the Duc—' Gaston waved his hands—'he comes to Paris and buys this hôtel with that young noble's fortune!'

'Ah!' sighed Madame, and shook her head.

Léon tilted his chin a little.

'It is no such great matter. Monseigneur would always play fair. That young man was a fool. *Voilà tout*!'

'*Mon Dieu*, is it thus you speak of the wickedness? Ah, but I could tell of things! If you knew the women that the Duc has courted! If you knew—'

'Monsieur!' Madame Dubois raised protesting hands. 'Before me?'

'I ask pardon, madame. No, I say nothing. Nothing! But what I know!'

'Some men,' said Léon gravely, 'are like that, I think. I have seen many.'

'*Fi donc*!' Madame cried. 'So young, too!'

Léon disregarded the interruption, and looked at Gaston with a worldly wisdom that sat quaintly on his young face.

'And when I have seen these things I have thought that it is always the woman's fault.'

'Hear the child!' exclaimed Madame. 'What do you know, *petit*, at your age?'

Léon shrugged one shoulder, and bent again over his book.

'Perhaps naught,' he answered.

Gaston frowned upon him, and would have continued the discussion had not Gregory forestalled him.

'Tell me, Léon, do you accompany the Duke to-night?'

'I always go with him.'

'Poor, poor child!' Madame Dubois sighed gustily. 'Indeed, it is not fitting.'

'Why is it not fitting? I like to go.'

'I doubt it not, *mon enfant*. But to take a child to Vassaud's, and to Torquillier's—*voyons*, it is not *convenable*!'

Léon's eyes sparkled mischievously.

'Last night I went with Monseigneur to the Maison Chourval,' he said demurely.

'What!' Madame sank back in her chair. 'It passes all bounds!'

'Have you been there, Madame?'

'I? *Nom de Dieu*, what next will you ask? Is it likely that I should go to such a place?'

'No, Madame. It is for the nobles, is it not?'

Madame snorted.

'And for every pretty slut who walks the streets!' she retorted.

Léon tilted his head to one side.

'Me, I did not think them pretty. Painted, and vulgar, with loud voices, and common tricks. But I did not see much.' His brow wrinkled. 'I do not know—I *think* perhaps I had offended Monseigneur, for of a sudden he swept round, and said "Await me below!" He said it as though he were angered.'

'Tell us, Léon, what is it like, the Maison Chourval?' asked Gaston, unable to conceal his curiosity.

'Oh, it is a big hôtel, all gold and dirty white, and smelling of some scent that suffocates one. There is a card-room, and other rooms; I forget. There was much wine, and some were drunk. Others, like Monseigneur, were just bored. The women—ah, they are just nothing!'

Gaston was rather disappointed; he opened his mouth to question Léon further, but madame's eye was upon him, and he shut it again. A bell was heard in the distance, and at the sound of it Léon shut his book, and untucked his legs, waiting expectantly. A few minutes later a footman appeared with a summons for him. The page sprang up delightedly, and ran to where a cracked mirror hung. Madame Dubois watched him smooth his copper curls, and smiled indulgently.

'*Voyons, petit*, you are as conceited as a girl,' she remarked.

Léon flushed, and left the mirror.

'Would you have me present myself to Monseigneur in disorder? I suppose he is going out. Where is my hat? Gaston, you have sat upon it!' He snatched it from the valet, and, hurriedly twitching it into shape, went out in the wake of the footman.

Avon was standing in the hall, talking to Hugh Davenant. He twirled a pair of soft gloves by their tassels, and his three-cornered hat was under one arm. Léon sank down on to one knee.

The hard eyes travelled over him indifferently.

'Well?'

'Monseigneur sent for me?'

'Did I? Yes, I believe you are right. I am going out. Do you come with me, Hugh?'

'Where?' asked Davenant. He bent over the fire, warming his hands.

'I thought it might be amusing to visit La Fournoise.'

Hugh made a grimace of distaste.

'I like actresses on the stage, Justin, but not off it. La Fournoise is too opulent.'

'So she is. You may go, Léon. Take my gloves.' He tossed them to the page, and his hat after them. 'Come and play at piquet, Hugh.' He strolled away to the salon, yawning, and with a tiny shrug of his shoulders Hugh followed.

At the Comtesse de Marguéry's ball that night Léon was left to await his master in the hall. He found a chair in a secluded corner, and settled down quite contentedly to watch the arrival of the guests. As it was the Duke's custom to make his appearance as late as possible, he was not very hopeful of seeing many arrivals. He pulled a book out of his capacious pocket, and started to read.

For a while only the desultory conversation of the lackeys came to his ears, as they lounged against the stair-rail. Then suddenly they sprang to attention, and the idle chatter stopped. One flung open the door, while another stood ready to relieve this late-comer of his hat and cloak.

Léon raised his eyes from his book in time to see the Comte de Saint-Vire enter. He was becoming familiar with the notables of town, but even had this not been so Saint-Vire would have been hard to mistake. In these days of fastidiousness in all matters of dress the Comte was conspicuous for the carelessness with which he bore himself, and the slight disorder of his clothes. He was tall, and loose-limbed, with a heavy face, and beak-like nose. His mouth had a sullen curve, and his eyes a latent fierceness in their dark pupils. As usual his thick hair, rather grizzled now, was inadequately powdered, so that here and there a gleam of red showed. He wore many jewels, seemingly chosen at random, and with no regard to the colour of his coat.

His coat was revealed now, as he allowed the attendant lackey to take his long cloak. Purple velvet met Léon's critical eye; a salmon-pink vest with embroidering in gold and silver; purple small clothes with white stockings loosely rolled above the knee, and red-heeled shoes with large jewelled buckles. The Comte shook out his ruffles, and put up one hand to straighten his tumbled cravat. As he did so he cast a quick glance about him, and saw the page. A frown came, and the heavy mouth pouted a little. The Comte gave the lace at his throat an impatient twist, and walked slowly towards the stairs. With his hand on the rail he paused and, half-turning, jerked his head as a sign that he wished to speak to Léon.

The page rose at once, and went to him.

'M'sieur?'

The spatulate fingers on the rail drummed methodically; Saint-Vire looked the page over broodingly, and for a moment did not speak.

'Your master is here?' he said at last, and the very lameness of the question seemed to indicate that it was but an excuse to call Léon to him.

'Yes, m'sieur.'

The Comte hesitated still, tapping his foot on the polished floor.

'You accompany him everywhere, I believe?'

'When Monseigneur wishes it, m'sieur.'

'From where do you come?' Then, as Léon looked puzzled, he changed the question, speaking sharply. 'Where were you born?'

Léon let fall the long lashes over his eyes.

'In the country, m'sieur,' he said.

The Comte's thick brows drew together.

'What part of the country?'

'I do not know, m'sieur.'

'You are strangely ignorant,' said Saint-Vire sarcastically.

'Yes, m'sieur.' Léon glanced up, chin firmly set. 'I do not know why m'sieur should take so great an interest in me.'

'You are impertinent. I have no interest in peasant-children.' The Comte went on up the staircase, to the ballroom.

In a group by the door stood his Grace of Avon, clad in shades of blue, with his star on his breast, a cluster of blazing diamonds. Saint-Vire paused for a moment before he tapped that straight shoulder.

'If you please, m'sieur . . .!'

The Duke turned to see who accosted him, eyebrows raised. When his eyes alighted on Saint-Vire the haughty look faded, and he smiled, bowing with the exaggerated flourish that made a veiled insult of the courtesy.

'My dear Comte! I had almost begun to fear that I should not have the felicity of meeting you here to-night. I trust I see you well?'

'I thank you, yes.' Saint-Vire would have passed on, but again his Grace stood in the way.

'Strange to say, dear Comte, Florimond and I were but this instant speaking of you—your brother, rather. Where is the good Armand?'

'My brother, m'sieur, is this month in attendance at Versailles.'

'Ah? Quite a family gathering at Versailles,' smiled the Duke. 'I trust the Vicomte, your so charming son, finds court life to his taste?'

The man who stood at the Duke's elbow laughed a little at this, and addressed Saint-Vire.

'The Vicomte is quite an original, is he not, Henri?'

'Oh, the boy is young yet!' Saint-Vire answered. 'He likes court well enough.'

Florimond de Chantourelle tittered amiably.

'He so amused me with his megrims and his sighs! He told me once that he liked best to be in the country, and that 'twas his ambition to have a farm under his own management at Saint-Vire!'

A shadow crossed the Comte's face.

'A boy's fancy. When at Saint-Vire he pines for Paris. Your pardon, messieurs—I see Madame de Marguéry.' He brushed past Avon as he spoke, making his way towards his hostess.

'Our friend is always so delightfully brusque,' remarked the Duke. 'One wonders why he is tolerated.'

'He has moods,' answered Chantourelle. 'Sometimes he is very agreeable, but he is not much liked. Now Armand is another matter. Of a gaiety—! You know that there is enmity between them?' He lowered his voice mysteriously, agog to relate the tale.

'The dear Comte is at pains to show us that it is so,' said Avon. 'My esteemed friend!' He waved one languid hand to a lavishly powdered and painted individual. 'Did I see you with Mademoiselle de Sonnebrune? Now that is a taste I find hard to cultivate.'

The painted gentleman paused, simpering.

'Oh, my dear Duc, she is the *dernier cri*! One must worship at her feet; it is *de rigueur*, I assure you.'

Avon put up his glass the better to observe Mademoiselle.

'H'm! Is Paris so devoid of beauties, then?'

'You do not admire her, no? It is a stately beauty, of course.' He was silent for a while, watching the dancers; then he turned again to Avon. '*A propos*, Duc, is it true that you have acquired a most striking page? I have been out of Paris this fortnight, but I hear now that a red-haired boy goes everywhere in your wake.'

'Quite true,' said Justin. 'I thought that the violent but fleeting interest of the world had died?'

'No, oh no! It was Saint-Vire who spoke of the boy. It seems there is some mystery attached to him, is it not so? A nameless page!'

Justin turned his rings round, smiling faintly.

'You may tell Saint-Vire, my friend, that there is no mystery. The page has a very good name.'

'I may tell him?' The Vicomte was puzzled. 'But why, Duc? 'Twas but an idle conversation.'

'Naturally.' The enigmatical smile grew. 'I should have said that you may tell him if he asks again.'

'Certainly, but I do not suppose–Ah, there is Davenant! *Mille pardons, Duc!*' He minced away to meet Davenant.

Avon smothered a yawn in his scented handkerchief, and proceeded in his leisurely fashion to the card-room, where he remained for perhaps an hour. Then he sought out his hostess, complimented her in his soft voice, and departed.

Léon was half asleep downstairs, but he opened his eyes as the Duke's footfall sounded, and jumped up. He assisted the Duke into his cloak, handed him his hat and gloves, and asked whether he was to summon a chair. But the Duke elected to walk, and further commanded his page to keep step beside him. They walked slowly down the street and had turned the corner before Avon spoke.

'My child, when the Comte de Saint-Vire questioned you this evening, what did you answer?'

Léon gave a little skip of surprise, looking up at his master in frank wonderment.

'How did you know, Monseigneur? I did not see you.'

'Possibly not. No doubt you will answer my question in your own good time.'

'Pardon, Monseigneur! M. le Comte asked me where I was born. I do not understand why he should wish to know.'

'I suppose you told him so?'

'Yes, Monseigneur,' nodded Léon. He looked up, twinkling. 'I thought you would not be angered if I spoke just a little rudely to that one?' He saw Avon's lips curl, and flushed in triumph at having made the Duke smile.

'Very shrewd,' remarked Justin. 'And then you said—?'

'I said I did not know, Monseigneur. It is true.'

'A comforting thought.'

'Yes,' agreed the page. 'I do not like to tell lies.'

'No?' For once Avon seemed disposed to encourage his page to talk. Nothing loth, Léon continued.

'No, Monseigneur. Of course it is sometimes necessary, but I do not like it. Once or twice I lied to Jean because I was afraid to tell the truth, but that is cowardly, *n'est-ce pas*? I think it is not so wicked to lie to your enemy, but one could not lie–to a friend, or–or to somebody one loved. That would be a black sin, would it not?'

'As I cannot remember ever having loved anyone, I am hardly fitted to answer that question, my child.'

Léon considered him gravely.

'No one?' he asked. 'Me, I do not love often, but when I do it is for ever. I loved my mother, and the Curé, and–and I love you, Monseigneur.'

'I beg your pardon?' Avon was a little startled.

'I–I only said that I loved you, Monseigneur.'

'I thought that I could not have heard aright. It is, of course, gratifying, but I do not think you have chosen too wisely. I am sure they will seek to reform you, below-stairs.'

The big eyes flashed.

'They dare not!'

The quizzing-glass was raised.

'Indeed? Are you so formidable?'

'I have a very bad temper, Monseigneur.'

'And you use it in my defence. It is most amusing. Do you fly out upon—my valet, for instance?'

Léon gave a tiny sniff of scorn.

'Oh, he is just a fool, Monseigneur!'

'Lamentably a fool. I have often remarked it.'

They had come to Avon's hôtel by now, and the waiting lackeys held the door for them to pass through. In the hall Avon paused, while Léon stood expectantly before him.

'You may bring wine to the library,' said the Duke, and went in.

When Léon appeared with a heavy silver tray Justin was seated by the fire, his feet upon the hearth. Beneath drooping lids he watched his page pour out a glass of burgundy. Léon brought it to him.

'Thank you.' Avon smiled at Léon's evident surprise at the unusual courtesy. 'No doubt you imagined that I was sadly lacking in manners? You may sit down. At my feet.'

Léon promptly curled up on the rug, cross-legged, and sat looking at the Duke, rather bewildered, but palpably pleased.

Justin drank a little wine, still watching the page, and then set the glass down on a small table at his elbow.

'You find me a trifle unexpected? I desire to be entertained.'

Léon looked at him seriously.

'What shall I do, Monseigneur?'

'You may talk,' Avon said. 'Your youthful views on life are most amusing. Pray continue.'

Léon laughed suddenly.

'I do not know what to say, Monseigneur! I do not think I have anything interesting to talk about. I chatter and chatter, they tell me, but it is all nothing. Madame Dubois lets me talk, but Walker—ah, Walker is dull and strict!'

'Who is Madame—er—Dubois?'

Léon opened his eyes very wide.

'But she is your housekeeper, Monseigneur!'

'Really? I have never seen her. Is she a stimulating auditor?'

'Monseigneur?'

'No matter. Tell me of your life in Anjou. Before Jean brought you to Paris.'

Léon settled himself more comfortably, and as the arm of Avon's chair was near enough to be an inviting prop, he leaned against it, unaware that he was committing a breach of etiquette. Avon said nothing, but picked up his glass and started to sip the wine it held.

'In Anjou—it is all so very far away,' sighed Léon. 'We lived in a little house, and there were horses and cows and pigs—oh, many animals! And my father did not like it that I would not touch the cows or the pigs. They were dirty, you understand. Maman said I should not work on the farm, but she made me care for the fowls. I did not mind that so much. There was one speckled hen, all mine. Jean stole it to tease me. Jean is like that, you know. Then there was M. le Curé. He lived a little way from our farm, in a tiny house next the church. And he was very, very good and kind. He gave me sweetmeats when I learned my lessons well, and sometimes he told stories—oh, wonderful stories of fairies and knights! I was only a baby then, but I can still remember them. And my father said it was not seemly that a priest should tell of things that are not, like fairies. I was not very fond of my father. He was like Jean, a little. . . . Then there was the plague, and people died. I went to the Curé, and–but Monseigneur knows all this.'

'Tell me of your life in Paris, then,' said Justin.

Léon nested his head against the arm of the chair, looking dreamily into the fire. The cluster of candles at Avon's elbow played softly over the copper curls so that they seemed alive and on fire in the golden light. Léon's delicate profile was turned towards the Duke, and he watched it inscrutably; each quiver of the fine lips, each flicker of the dark lashes. And so Léon told his tale, haltingly at first, and shyly, hesitating over the more sordid parts, his voice fluctuating with each changing emotion until he seemed to forget to whom he spoke, and lost himself in his narration. Avon listened in silence, sometimes smiling at the quaint philosophy the boy unfolded, but more often expressionless, always watching Léon's face with narrowed keen eyes. The hardships and endurances of those years in Paris were revealed more by what was left unsaid than by any complaint or direct allusion to the petty tyrannies and cruelties of Jean and his wife. At times the recital was that of a child, but every now and then a note of age and experience crept into the little deep voice, lending a strange whimsicality to the story, which seemed to invest the teller with a Puck-like quality of old and young wisdom. When at last the rambling tale was finished Léon moved slightly, and put up a timid hand to touch the Duke's sleeve.

'And then you came, Monseigneur, and you brought me here, giving me everything. I shall never forget that.'

'You have not seen the worst of me yet, my friend,' answered Justin. 'I am really not the hero you think me. When I bought you from your estimable brother it was not, believe me, from any desire to save you from bondage. I had a use for you. If it should chance that you are after all of no use to me I am quite likely to cast you forth. I say this that you may be warned.'

'If you send me away I will drown myself!' said Léon passionately. 'When you are tired of me, Monseigneur, I will serve in your kitchen. But I will never leave you.'

'Oh, when I am tired of you I shall give you to Mr Davenant!' Avon chuckled a little. 'It should be amusing–Dear me, speak of angels—!'

Hugh came quietly in, but paused on the threshold, staring at the two by the fire.

'Quite a touching picture, eh, Hugh? Satanas in a new rôle.' He flicked Léon's head with one careless finger. 'Bed, my child.'

Léon rose at once, and reverently kissed the Duke's hand. With a little bow to Davenant he went out.

Hugh waited until he had closed the door; then he strode forward to the fire, frowning. Resting his elbow on the mantelpiece, his other hand thrust deep into his pocket, he stood looking down at his friend with a good deal of severity in his glance.

'When are you going to end this folly?' he demanded.

Justin tilted his head back, returning the angry stare with one of amused cynicism.

'What ails you now, my good Hugh?'

'Seeing that child at your feet fills me with–disgust!'

'Yes, I thought that you seemed perturbed. It must tickle your sense of the ridiculous to observe me upon a pinnacle of heroism.'

'It sickens me! The child worshipping at your feet! I hope his admiration stings you! If it could make you realize your own unworthiness it were to some purpose!'

'Unhappily it does not. May I ask, my dear Hugh, why you take so great an interest in—a page?'

'It is his youth and innocence that command my pity.'

'Curiously enough he is by no means as innocent as you imagine.'

Davenant turned impatiently on his heel. He walked to the door, but as he opened it Avon spoke again.

'By the way, my dear, I am relieving you of my company to-morrow. Pray hold me excused from going with you to Lourdonne's card-party.'

Hugh looked back.

'Oh? Where are you going?'

'I am going to Versailles. I feel that it is time I again paid homage to King Louis. I suppose it is useless to ask your company?'

'Quite, I thank you. I've no love for Versailles. Is Léon to go with you?'

'I have really not given the matter a thought. It seems probable. Unless you wish to take him to Lourdonne's?'

Hugh left the room without a word.

5

His Grace of Avon Visits Versailles

The Duke's light town coach, with its four grey horses, stood at the door of his house shortly before six on the following evening. The horses champed at their bits and tossed their beautiful heads in impatience, and the paved courtyard rang with the sound of their stamping. The postilions, liveried in black and gold, stood to their heads, for the Duke's horses were not chosen for their docility.

In the hall Léon awaited his master, aglow with excitement. His Grace had issued certain orders earlier in the day; in accordance with them the page was dressed in black velvet, with real lace at his throat and wrists. He carried his tricorne beneath his arm, and in his other hand he held his master's beribboned cane.

Avon came slowly down the stairs, and seeing him Léon drew in a quick breath of wonderment. The Duke was always magnificent, but to-night he had surpassed himself. His coat was made of cloth-of-gold, and on it the blue ribbon of the Garter lay, and three orders blazed in the light of the candles. Diamonds nestled in the lace of his cravat, and formed a solid bar above the riband that tied back his powdered hair. His shoes had jewelled heels and buckles, and below his knee he wore the Garter. Over his arm he carried a long black cloak, lined with gold, which he handed to Léon; and in his hand was his snuff-box, and scented handkerchief. He looked his page over in silence, and frowned at last, and turned to his valet.

'You may perhaps call to mind, my good Gaston, a golden chain studded with sapphires, presented to me by I forget whom. Also a sapphire clasp in the shape of a circle.'

'Y-yes, Monseigneur?'

'Fetch them.'

Gaston hurried away, presently to reappear with the required ornaments. Avon took the heavy sapphire chain and threw it over Léon's head so that it lay across his breast, glowing with an inward fire, yet no brighter or more liquid than the boy's eyes.

'Monseigneur!' gasped Léon. He put up his hand to feel the precious chain.

'Give me your hat. The clasp, Gaston.' Unhurriedly he fixed the diamond and sapphire circle on the upturned brim of the page's hat. Then he gave it to Léon, and stepped back to observe the effect of his handiwork. 'Yes, I wonder why I never thought of sapphires before? The door, my infant.'

Still dazed by his master's unexpected action, Léon flew to open the door for him. Avon passed out, and climbed into the waiting coach. Léon looked up at him inquiringly, wondering whether he was to mount the box or enter with his master.

'Yes, you may come with me,' said Avon, answering the unspoken question. 'Tell them to let go the horses.'

Léon delivered the order, and sprang hurriedly into the coach, for he knew the ways of Avon's horses. The postilions mounted quickly, and in a trice the fretting horses leaped forward in their collars, and the coach swerved round towards the wrought-iron gates. Out they swept, and down the narrow street as swiftly as was possible. But the very narrowness of the street, the slippery cobblestones, and the many twists and turns, made their progress necessarily slow, so that it was not until they came out on the road to Versailles that the speed and power of the horses could be demonstrated. Then they seemed to spring forward as one, and the coach bowled along at a furious pace, lurching a little over the worst bumps in the road, but so well sprung that for the most part the surface of the road might have been of glass for all the jolting or inconvenience that the occupants felt.

It was some time before Léon could find words to thank the Duke for his chain. He sat on the edge of the seat beside the Duke, fingering the polished stones in awe, and trying to squint down at his breast to see how the chain looked. At length he drew a deep breath and turned to gaze at his master, who lay back against the velvet cushions idly surveying the flying landscape.

'Monseigneur—this is—too precious for—*me* to wear,' he said in a hushed voice.

'Do you think so?' Avon regarded his page with an amused smile.

'I—I would rather not wear it, Monseigneur. Suppose—suppose I were to lose it?'

'I should then be compelled to buy you another. You may lose it an you will. It is yours.'

'Mine?' Léon twisted his fingers together. '*Mine*, Monseigneur? You cannot mean that! I—I have done nothing—I could do nothing to deserve such a present.'

'I suppose it had not occurred to you that I pay you no wage? Somewhere in the Bible—I don't know where—it says that the labourer is worthy of his hire. A manifestly false observation for the most part, of course, but I choose to give you that chain as—er—hire.'

Léon pulled his hat off at that, and slipped the chain over his head, almost throwing it at the Duke. His eyes burned dark in a very pale face.

'I do not want payment! I would work myself to death for you, but payment—*no*! A thousand times no! You make me angry!'

'Evidently,' murmured his Grace. He picked up the chain, and began to play with it. 'Now I had imagined you would be pleased.'

Léon brushed his hand across his eyes. His voice shook a little as he answered.

'How could you think that? I—I never looked for payment! I served you for love, and—and out of gratitude, and—you give me a chain! As if—as if you thought I should not continue to work well for you without payment!'

'If I had thought that I should not have given it to you,' yawned his Grace. 'It may interest you to know that I am not accustomed to being spoken to in this fashion by my pages.'

'I—I am sorry, Monseigneur,' whispered Léon. He turned his face away, biting his lips.

Avon watched him for a time in silence, but presently the mixture of forlornness and hurt dignity in his page drew a soft laugh from him, and he pulled one of the bright curls admonishingly.

'Do you expect me to apologize, my good child?'

Léon jerked his head away, and still stared out of the window.

'You are very haughty.' The mocking note in that gentle voice brought a wave of colour to Léon's cheeks.

'I—you are not—kind!'

'So you have just discovered that? But I do not see why I should be called unkind for rewarding you.'

'You do not understand!' said Léon fiercely.

'I understand that you deem yourself insulted, infant. It is most entertaining.'

A tiny sniff, which was also a sob, answered him. Again he laughed, and this time laid a hand on Léon's shoulder. Under the steely pressure Léon came to his knees, and stayed there, eyes downcast. The chain was flung over his head.

'My Léon, you will wear this because it is my pleasure.'

'Yes, Monseigneur,' said Léon stiffly.

The Duke took the pointed chin in his hand, and forced it up.

'I wonder why I bear with you?' he said. 'The chain is a gift. Are you satisfied?'

Léon pressed his chin down quickly to kiss the Duke's wrist.

'Yes, Monseigneur. Thank you. Indeed I am sorry.'

'Then you may sit down again.'

Léon picked up his hat, gave a shaky laugh, and settled himself on the wide seat beside the Duke.

'I think I have a very bad temper,' he remarked naïvely. 'M. le Curé would have made me do penance for it. He used to say that temper is a black sin. He talked to me about it—oh, often!'

'You do not appear to have profited unduly from his discourse,' replied Avon dryly.

'No, Monseigneur. But it is difficult, you understand. My temper is too quick for me. In a minute it is up, and I cannot stop it. But I am nearly always sorry afterwards. Shall I see the King to-night?'

'Quite possibly. You will follow me close. And do not stare.'

'No, Monseigneur, I will try not to. But that is difficult too.' He looked round confidingly as he spoke, but the Duke, to all outward appearance, was asleep. So Léon snuggled into one corner of the coach, and prepared to enjoy the drive in silence. Occasionally they passed other vehicles, all bound for Versailles, but not once did a coach pass them. The four English thoroughbreds swept by their French brethren time and again, and those within the coaches that were left behind leaned out to see who it was that drove at such a pace. The crest on the door of Avon's coach, seen in the light of their own lanterns, told them surely enough, and the black and gold livery was unmistakable.

'One might have known,' said the Marquis de Chourvanne, drawing in his head. 'Who else would drive at such a pace?'

'The English Duc?' asked his wife.

'Of course. Now I met him last night and he spoke no word of coming to the levée to-night.'

'Theodore de Ventour told me that no one knows from one moment to the next where the Duc will be.'

'*Poseur!*' snorted the Marquis, and put up the window.

The black and gold coach rolled on its way, scarcely checking till Versailles was reached. Then it slowed to enter the gates, and Léon sat forward to peer interestedly out into the gloom. Very little met his eyes, save when the coach passed under a lamp, until they entered the Cour Royale. Léon stared first this way and then that. The three-sided court was a blaze of light, shining from every unshuttered window that gave on to it, and further supplemented by great flambeaux. Coaches were streaming in a long line to the entrance, pausing there to allow their burdens to alight, then passing on to allow others to take their place.

Not until they finally drew up at the door did the Duke open his eyes. He looked out, dispassionately surveying the brilliant court, and yawned.

'I suppose I must alight,' he remarked, and waited for his footman to let down the steps. Léon climbed down first, and turned to assist his Grace. The Duke stepped slowly out, paused for a moment to look at the waiting coaches, and strolled past the palace lackeys with Léon at his heels, still holding the cloak and cane. Avon nodded to him to relinquish both to an expectant servant, and proceeded through the various antechambers to the Marble Court, where he was soon lost in the crowd. Léon followed as best he might while Avon greeted his friends. He had ample opportunity for taking stock of his surroundings, but the vast dimensions of the court, and its magnificence, dazzled him. After what seemed to be an interminable time, he found that they were no longer in the Marble Court, having moved slowly but surely to the left. They stood now before a great marble staircase, heavily encrusted with gold, up which a stream of people were wending their way. Avon fell in with a very much painted lady, and offered his arm. Together they mounted the broad stairs, crossed the hall at the top, and traversed various chambers until they came to the old Œil de Bœuf. Restraining an impulse to clutch the whaleboned skirts of Avon's coat, Léon followed him as closely as he dared into a room beside which all the others through which he had passed faded to nothingness. Some one had said downstairs that the levée was being held in the Galerie des Glaces; Léon realized that this was it. It seemed to him that the huge gallery was even double its real size, filled with a myriad candles in scintillating chandeliers, peopled by thousands of silk-clad ladies and gentlemen, until he discovered that one entire side was covered by gigantic mirrors. Opposite were as many windows; he tried to count them but ceased presently in despair, for groups of people from time to time obscured his view. The room was stuffy, yet cold, covered by two great Aubusson carpets. There were very few chairs, he thought, for this multitude of people. Again the Duke was bowing to right and left, sometimes stopping to exchange a few words with a friend, but always working his way to one end of the gallery. As they neared the fireplace the crowd became less dense, and Léon was able to see more than the shoulders of the man in front of him. A stout gentleman in full court dress and many orders sat in a gilded chair by the fire, with various gentlemen standing about him, and a fair lady in a chair by his side. The wig of this gentleman was almost grotesque, so large were the rolling curls that adorned it. He wore pink satin with gold lacing; he was bejewelled and painted, with black patches on his florid face, and a diamond-hilted sword at his side.

Avon turned his head to speak to Léon, and smiled faintly at the look of astonishment on the page's face.

'You have seen the King. Await me now over there.' He waved his hand towards an embrasure, and Léon started to retrace his steps, feeling very much as though his one support and guide in this vast place had deserted him.

The Duke paid homage to King Louis the Fifteenth, and to the pale Queen beside him, stayed for a few minutes to speak to the Dauphin, and proceeded in a leisurely fashion to where stood Armand de Saint-Vire, in attendance on the King.

Armand clasped his hands in warm welcome.

'*Mon Dieu*, but it is refreshing to see your face, Justin! I did not know even that you were in Paris. Since when have you returned, *mon cher*?'

'Nearly two months ago. Really, this is most fatiguing. I am thirsty already, but I suppose it is quite impossible to obtain any burgundy?'

Armand's eyes sparkled in sympathy.

'In the Salle de Guerre!' he whispered. 'We will go together. No, wait, *mon ami*, La Pompadour has seen you. Ah, she smiles! You have all the luck, Justin.'

'I could find another name for it,' said Avon, but he went to the King's mistress, and bowed exceedingly low as he kissed her hand. He remained at her side until the Comte de Stainville came to claim her attention, and then made good his escape to the Salle de Guerre. There he found Armand, with one or two others, partaking of light French wines, and sugared sweetmeats.

Someone handed the Duke a glass of burgundy; one of the footmen presented a plate of cakes, which he waved aside.

'A welcome interlude,' he remarked. '*A ta santé, Joinlisse*! Your servant, Tourdeville. A word in your ear, Armand.' He took Saint-Vire aside to where a couch stood. They sat down, and for a time talked of Paris, court-life, and the trials of a gentleman-in-waiting. Avon allowed his friend to ramble on, but at the first pause in Armand's rather amusing discourse, he turned the subject.

'I must make my bow to your charming sister-in-law,' he said. 'I trust she is present to-night?'

Armand's round good-humoured face became marred all at once by a gloomy scowl.

'Oh yes. Seated behind the Queen, in an obscure corner. If you are *épris* in that direction, Justin, your taste has deteriorated.' He snorted disdainfully. 'Curds and whey! How Henri could have chosen her passes my comprehension!'

'I never credited the worthy Henri with much sense,' answered the Duke. 'Why is he in Paris and not here?'

'Is he in Paris? He was in Champagne. He fell into slight disfavour here.' Armand grinned. 'That damnable temper, you understand. He left Madame, and that clodhopping son.'

Avon put up his eyeglass.

'Clodhopping?'

'What, have you not seen him, then? A boorish cub, Justin, with the soul of a farmer. And that is the boy who is to be Comte de Saint-Vire! *Mon*

Dieu, but there must be bad blood in Marie! My beautiful nephew did not get his boorishness from us. Well, I never thought that Marie was of the real nobility.'

The Duke looked down at his wine.

'I must certainly see the young Henri,' he said. 'They tell me that he is not very like his father or his mother.'

'Not a whit. He has black hair, a bad nose, and square hands. It is a judgment on Henri! First he weds a puling, sighing woman with no charm and less beauty, and then he produces–that!'

'One would almost infer that you are not enamoured of your nephew,' murmured his Grace.

'No, I am not! I tell you, Justin, if it had been a true Saint-Vire I could have borne it better. But this–this half-witted bumpkin! It would enrage a saint!' He set down his glass on a small table with a force that nearly smashed the frail vessel. 'You may say that I am a fool to brood over it, Alastair, but I cannot forget! To spite me Henri marries this Marie de Lespinasse, who presents him with a son after three fruitless years! First it was a still-born child, and then, when I had begun to think myself safe, she astonishes us all with a boy! Heaven knows what I have done to deserve it!'

'She astonished you with a boy. I think he was born in Champagne, was he not?'

'Ay, at Saint-Vire. Plague take him. I never set eyes on the brat until three months later when they brought him to Paris. Then I was well-nigh sick with disgust at Henri's fatuous triumph.'

'Well, I must see him,' repeated the Duke. 'How old is he?'

'I neither know nor care. He is nineteen,' snapped Armand. He watched the Duke rise, and smiled in spite of himself. 'Where's the good of growling, eh? It's the fault of this damned life I lead, Justin. It's all very well for you who come on a visit to this place. You think it very fine and splendid, but you've not seen the apartments they give to the gentlemen-in-waiting. Airless holes, Justin, I give you my word! Well, let's go back into the gallery.'

They went out, and paused for a moment just within the gallery.

'Yes, there she is,' said Armand. 'With Julie de Cornalle over there. Why do you want her?'

Justin smiled.

'You see, *mon cher*,' he explained sweetly, 'it will afford me much satisfaction to be able to tell the dear Henri that I spent a pleasant half-hour with his fascinating wife.'

Armand chuckled.

'Oh, if that is your will—! You so love the dear Henri, do you not?'

'But of course,' smiled the Duke. He waited until Armand had melted into the crowd before he beckoned to Léon, who, in obedience to his commands, still stood in the embrasure. The page came to him slipping between two groups of chattering ladies, and followed him across the gallery to the couch on which sat Madame de Saint-Vire.

Avon swept the lady a magnificent leg.

'My dear Comtesse!' He took her thin hand, and holding it with the tips of his fingers just brushed it with his lips. 'I had hardly dared hope for this joy.'

She inclined her head, but out of the corner of her eye she was watching Léon. Mademoiselle de Cornalle had moved away, and Avon seated himself in her place. Léon went to stand behind him.

'Believe me, Comtesse,' continued the Duke, 'I was desolated not to see you in Paris. How is your delightful son?'

She answered nervously, and under pretence of arranging her skirt changed her position on the couch, so that she almost faced Avon, and thus was able to see the page behind him. Her eyes fluttered up to the boy's face, and widened for an instant before they fell. She became aware of Avon's smiling scrutiny, and coloured deeply, unfurling her fan with fingers that trembled slightly.

'My—my son? Oh, Henri is well, I thank you! You see him over there, m'sieur, with Mademoiselle de Lachère.'

Justin's gaze followed the direction of her pointing fan. He beheld a short, rather stocky youth, dressed in the height of fashion and seated mumchance beside a sprightly lady who was with difficulty restraining a yawn. The Vicomte de Valmé was very dark, with brown eyes heavy-lidded now from weariness and boredom. His mouth was a trifle wide, but well curved; his nose, so far from following the Saint-Vire aquiline trend, showed a tendency to turn up.

'Ah yes!' said Justin. 'I should hardly have recognized him, madame. One looks usually for red hair and blue eyes in a Saint-Vire, does not one?' He laughed gently.

'My son wears a wig,' answered Madame rather quickly. Again she sent a fleeting glance towards Léon. Her mouth twitched slightly, uncontrollably. 'He—he has black hair. It often happens so, I believe.'

'Ah, no doubt,' agreed Justin. 'You are looking at my page, madame? A curious combination, is it not?—his copper hair and black brows.'

'I? No, why should I—?' With an effort she collected her wits. 'It is an unusual combination, as you say. Who—who is the child?'

'I have no idea,' said his Grace blandly. 'I found him one evening in Paris and bought him for the sum of a jewel. Quite a pretty boy, is he not? He attracts no little attention, I assure you.'

'Yes—I suppose so. It seems hard to believe that—that hair is—is natural.' Her eyes challenged him, but again he laughed.

'It must seem quite incredible,' he said. 'It is so seldom that one sees that—particular—combination.' Then as the Comtesse stirred restlessly, opening and shutting her fan, he deftly turned the subject. 'Ah, behold the Vicomte!' he remarked. 'His fair companion has deserted him.'

The Comtesse looked across at her son, who was standing irresolute a few paces away. He saw his mother's eyes upon him, and came to her, heavy-footed and deliberate, glancing curiously at the Duke.

'My—my son, m'sieur. Henri, the Duc of Avon.'

The Vicomte bowed, but although his bow was of just the required depth, and the wave of his hat in exact accordance with the decrees of fashion, the whole courtesy lacked spontaneity and grace. He bowed as one who had been laboriously coached in the art. Polish was lacking, and in its place was a faint suggestion of clumsiness.

'Your servant, m'sieur.' The voice was pleasant enough if not enthusiastic.

'My dear Vicomte!' Avon flourished his handkerchief. 'I am charmed to make your acquaintance. I remember you when you were still with your tutor, but of late years I have been denied the pleasure of meeting you. Léon, a chair for m'sieur.'

The page slipped from his place behind the couch, and went to fetch a low chair which stood against the wall, some few paces away. He set it down for the Vicomte, bowing as he did so.

'If m'sieur will be seated?'

The Vicomte looked him over in surprise. For a moment they stood shoulder to shoulder, the one slim and delicate, with eyes that matched the sapphires about his neck; and glowing curls swept back from a white brow beneath whose skin the veins showed faintly blue. The other was thickset and dark, with square hands and short neck; powdered, perfumed, and patched, dressed in rich silks and velvet, but in spite of all rather uncouth and awkward. Avon heard Madame draw in her breath swiftly, and his smile grew. Then Léon went back to his original place, and the Vicomte sat down.

'Your page, m'sieur?' he asked. 'You were saying that you had not met me, I think? You see, I do not love Paris, and when my father permits I stay in Champagne, at Saint-Vire.' He smiled, casting a rueful glance at his mother. 'My parents do not like me to be in the country, m'sieur. I am a great trial to them.'

'The country . . .' The Duke unfobbed his snuff-box. 'It is pleasing to the eye, no doubt, but it is irrevocably associated in my mind with cows and pigs–even sheep. Necessary but distressing evils.'

'Evils, m'sieur? Why—'

'Henri, the Duc is not interested in such matters!' interposed the Comtesse. 'One–does not talk of–of cows and pigs at a levée.' She turned to Avon, smiling mechanically. 'The boy has an absurd whim, m'sieur: he would like to be a farmer! I tell him that he would very soon tire of it.' She started to fan herself, laughing.

'Yet another necessary evil,' drawled his Grace. 'Farmers. You take snuff, Vicomte?'

The Vicomte helped himself to a pinch.

'I thank you, m'sieur. You have come from Paris? Perhaps you have seen my father?'

'I had that felicity yesterday,' replied Avon. 'At a ball. The Comte remains the same as ever, madame.' The sneer was thinly veiled.

Madame flushed scarlet.

'I trust you found my husband in good health, m'sieur?'

'Excellent, I believe. May I be the bearer of any message you may wish to send, madame?'

'I thank you, m'sieur, but I am writing to him–to-morrow,' she answered. 'Henri, will you fetch me some negus? Ah, madame!' She beckoned to a lady who stood in a group before them.

The Duke rose.

'I see my good Armand yonder. Pray give me leave, madame. The Comte will be overjoyed to hear that I found you well–and your son.' He bowed, and left her, walking away into the dwindling crowd. He sent Léon to await him in the Œil de Bœuf, and remained for perhaps an hour in the gallery.

When he joined Léon in the Œil de Bœuf he found him almost asleep, but making valiant efforts to keep himself awake. He followed the Duke downstairs, and was sent to retrieve Avon's cloak and cane. By the time he had succeeded in obtaining these articles the black and gold coach was at the door.

Avon swung the cloak over his shoulders and sauntered out. He and Léon entered the luxurious vehicle and with a sigh of content Léon nestled back against the soft cushions.

'It is all very wonderful,' he remarked, 'but very bewildering. Do you mind if I fall asleep, Monseigneur?'

'Not at all,' said his Grace politely. 'I trust you were satisfied with the King's appearance?'

'Oh yes, he is just like the coins!' said Léon drowsily. 'Do you suppose he likes to live in such a great palace, Monseigneur?'

'I have never asked him,' replied the Duke. 'Versailles does not please you?'

'It is so very large,' explained the page. 'I feared I had lost you.'

'What an alarming thought!' remarked his Grace.

'Yes, but you came after all.' The deep little voice was getting sleepier and sleepier. 'It was all glass and candles, and ladies, and—*Bonne nuit, Monseigneur,*' he sighed. 'I am sorry, but everything is muddled, and I am so very tired. I do not think I snore when I sleep, but if I do, then of course you must wake me. And I might slip, but I hope I shall not. I am right in the corner, so perhaps I shall remain here. But if I slip on to the floor—'

'Then I suppose I am to pick you up?' said Avon sweetly.

'Yes,' agreed Léon, already on the borderland of sleep. 'I won't talk any more now. Monseigneur does not mind?'

'Pray do not consider me in the slightest,' answered Avon. 'I am here merely to accommodate you. If I disturb you I beg you will not hesitate to mention it. I will then ride on the box.'

A very sleepy chuckle greeted this sally, and a small hand tucked itself into the Duke's.

'I wanted to hold your coat because I thought I should lose you,' murmured Léon.

'I presume that is why you are holding my hand now?' inquired his Grace. 'You are perhaps afraid lest I should hide myself under the seat?'

'That is silly,' replied Léon. 'Very silly. *Bonne nuit, Monseigneur.*'

'*Bonne nuit, mon enfant.* You will not lose me—or I you—very easily, I think.'

There was no answer, but Léon's head sank against his Grace's shoulder, and remained there.

'I am undoubtedly a fool,' remarked the Duke. He pushed a cushion under Léon's relaxed arm. 'But if I wake him he will begin to talk again. What a pity Hugh is not here to see! . . . I beg your pardon, my infant?' But Léon had muttered only in his sleep. 'If you are going to converse in your sleep I shall be compelled to take strong measures of prevention,' said his Grace. He leaned his head back against the padded seat, and, smiling, closed his eyes.

6

His Grace of Avon Refuses to Sell his Page

When Davenant met his Grace at breakfast next morning he found that the Duke was in excellent spirits. He was more than usually urbane, and whenever his eye alighted on Léon he smiled, as if at some pleasant thought.

'Was the levée well attended?' asked Hugh, attacking a red sirloin. Unlike the Duke, who never ate more than a roll for breakfast, he made a hearty meal of eggs and bacon, and cold meats, washed down by English ale, especially imported by the Duke for his delectation.

The Duke poured himself out a second cup of coffee.

'Crowded, my dear Hugh. It was in honour of some birthday, or saint's day, or something of the sort.'

'Did you see Armand?' Hugh reached out his hand for the mustard.

'I saw Armand, and the Comtesse, and the Vicomte, and everybody I least wished to meet.'

'One always does. I suppose La Pompadour was delighted to see you?'

'Oppressively so. The King sat on his throne and smiled benignantly. Just like a coin.'

Hugh suspended his fork in mid-air.

'Just like a what?'

'A coin. Léon will explain. Or possibly he has forgotten.'

Hugh looked inquiringly at the page.

'What is the joke, Léon? Do you know?'

Léon shook his head.

'No, m'sieur.'

'Ah, I thought perhaps you would not remember,' said his Grace. 'Léon was quite satisfied with the King, Hugh. He confided to me that he was just like the coins.'

Léon blushed.

'I—I am afraid I was asleep, Monseigneur.'

'Very nearly so. Do you always sleep as one dead?'

'N-no. That is—I do not know, Monseigneur. I was put to bed in all my clothes.'

'Yes, I did that. Having wasted ten minutes in endeavouring to rouse you, I thought that the simplest plan would be to carry you up to bed. You are not all joy, my infant.'

'I am very sorry, Monseigneur; you should have made me wake up.'

'If you would tell me how that may be done I shall do so on the next occasion. Hugh, if you must eat beef, pray do not brandish it in my face at this hour.'

Davenant, whose fork was still suspended midway between his plate and mouth, laughed, and went on eating.

Justin began to sort the letters that lay beside his plate. Some he threw away, others he slipped into his pocket. One had come from England, and spread over several sheets. He opened them and started to decipher the scrawl.

'From Fanny,' he said. 'Rupert is still at large, it seems. At Mistress Carsby's feet. When I saw him last he was madly in love with Julia Falkner. From one extreme to another.' He turned over the page. 'Now, how interesting! Dear Edward has given Fanny a chocolate-coloured coach with pale blue cushions. The wheels are picked out in blue.' He held the sheet at arm's length. 'It seems strange, but no doubt Fanny is right. I have not been in England for such a time— Ah, I beg her pardon! You will be relieved to hear, my dear Hugh, that the wheat in England still grows as ever it did. Ballentor has fought another duel, and Fanny won fifty guineas at play the other night. John is in the country because town air does not suit him. Now, is John her lap-dog or her parrot?'

'Her son,' said Davenant.

'Is he? Yes, I believe you are right. What next? If I can find her a French cook she vows she will love me more than ever. Léon, tell Walker to find me a French cook.—She wishes she could visit me as I suggested some time ago— how rash of me!—but it is quite impossible as she cannot leave her darling Edward alone, and she fears he would not accompany her to my hovel.

Hovel. Not very polite of Fanny. I must remember to speak to her about it.'

'Hôtel,' suggested Hugh.

'Once more you are right. Hôtel it is. The rest of this enthralling communication concerns Fanny's toilettes. I will reserve it. Oh, have you finished?'

'Finished and gone,' answered Davenant, rising. 'I am riding out with D'Anvau. I shall see you later.' He went out.

Avon leaned his arms on the table, resting his chin on the back of his clasped hands.

'Léon, where does your remarkable brother live?'

Léon started, and fell back a pace.

'Mon–Monseigneur?'

'Where is his inn?'

Suddenly Léon fell on his knees beside Avon's chair, and clutched the Duke's sleeve with desperate fingers. His face was upturned, pale and agonized, the great eyes swimming in tears.

'Oh no, no, no, Monseigneur! You would not–Oh, please not that! I–I will never go to sleep again! Please, please forgive me! Monseigneur! Monseigneur!'

Avon looked down at him with upraised brows. Léon had pressed his forehead against his master's arm, and was shaking with suppressed sobs.

'You bewilder me,' complained the Duke. 'What is it that I am not to do, and why will you never sleep again?'

'Don't–don't give me back to Jean!' implored Léon, clinging tighter still. 'Promise, promise!'

Avon loosened the clasp on his sleeve.

'My dear Léon, I beg you will not weep over this coat. I have no intention of giving you to Jean, or to anyone else. Stand up, and do not be ridiculous.'

'You must promise! You shall promise!' Léon shook the arm he held almost fiercely.

The Duke sighed.

'Very well: I promise. Now tell me where I may find your brother, my child.'

'I won't! I won't! You–he–I won't tell you!'

The hazel eyes became hard.

'I have borne much from you in patience, Léon, but I will not brook your defiance. Answer me at once.'

'I dare not! Oh, please, please do not make me tell! I–I do not mean to be defiant! But perhaps Jean is sorry now that–that he let me go, and–and will try to m-make you give me back!' He was plucking at the Duke's sleeve now, and again Avon removed the frenzied fingers.

'Do you think Jean could make me give you back?' he asked.

'N-no–I don't know. I thought perhaps because I went to sleep you were angered, and–and—'

'I have already told you that it is not so. Strive to have a little sense. And answer my question.'

'Yes, Monseigneur. I–I am sorry. Jean–Jean lives in the Rue Sainte-Marie. There is only one inn–the Crossbow. Oh, what are you going to do, Monseigneur?'

'Nothing at all alarming, I assure you. Dry your tears.'

Léon hunted through his various pockets.

'I–I have lost my handkerchief,' he apologized.

'Yes, you are very young, are you not?' commented his Grace. 'I suppose I must give you mine.'

Léon took the fine lace handkerchief which the Duke held out, wiped his eyes, blew his nose, and gave it back again. The Duke received it gingerly, and eyed the crumpled ball through his quizzing glass.

'Thank you,' he said. 'You are nothing if not thorough. I think you had better keep it now.'

Léon pocketed it cheerfully.

'Yes, Monseigneur,' he said. 'Now I am happy again.'

'I am relieved,' said the Duke, and rose. 'I shall not want you this morning.' He strolled out, and in half an hour's time was in his coach, driving towards the Rue Sainte-Marie.

The street was very narrow, with refuse in the kennels on either side of the road; the houses were mostly tumbledown, projecting outward from the first storey. Hardly one had all its windows intact; there were cracked and missing panes on all sides, and where curtains hung they were ragged and dirty. Half a dozen partly clothed children were playing in the road, and scattered to right and left as the coach drove up, standing on the footway, and watched the progress of this fine equipage with astonished eyes, and many startled comments.

The tavern of the Crossbow was situated midway down the squalid street, and from its open door issued a smell of cooking, and of cabbage water, thrown carelessly out into the kennel. The coach drew up outside the inn, and one of the footmen sprang down to open the door for his Grace to alight. His countenance was quite impassive, and only by the lofty tilt of his chin did he betray his emotions.

His Grace came slowly down from the coach, his handkerchief held to his nose. He picked his way across the filth and garbage to the inn door, and entered what appeared to be the taproom and the kitchen. A greasy woman was bending over the fire at one end, a cooking-pot in her hand, and behind the counter opposite the door stood the man who had sold Léon to the Duke a month ago.

He gaped when he saw Avon enter, and for a moment did not recognize him. He came forward cringingly, rubbing his hands together, and desired to know Monseigneur's pleasure.

'I think you know me,' said his Grace gently.

Bonnard stared, and suddenly his eyes dilated, and his full-blooded countenance turned a sickly grey.

'Léon! Milor'—I—'

'Precisely. I want two words with you in private.'

The man looked at him fearfully, passing his tongue between his lips.

'I swear by God—'

'Thank you. In private I said.'

The woman, who had watched the encounter open-mouthed, came forward now, arms akimbo. Her soiled dress was in disorder, cut low across her scraggy bosom, and there was a smudge of dirt on her cheek.

'Now, if the little viper has said aught against us,' she began shrilly, but was cut short by Avon's lifted hand.

'My good woman, I have no desire to speak with you. You may return to your stew-pots. Bonnard, in private!'

Charlotte would have interrupted again, but her husband hustled her back to the stove, whispering to her to hold her tongue.

'Yes, milor', indeed yes! If milor' will follow me?' He pushed open the crazy, rat-eaten door at the other end of the room, and ushered his Grace into the parlour. The room was scantily furnished, but it was not so dirty as the taproom. Avon went to the table that stood by the window, flicked the dust from its surface with a corner of his cloak, and sat down on the edge of the rickety structure.

'Now, my friend. That you may not misunderstand me, or seek to evade me, let me tell you that I am the Duke of Avon. Yes, I thought that you would be surprised. You realize, I am sure, that it would be very dangerous to play with me. I am going to ask you one or two questions about my page. I wish to know first where he was born.'

'I–I think in the north, Monseigneur. In–Champagne, but I am not sure. Our–our parents never spoke of that time, and I can scarce remember–I—'

'No? It seems strange that you do not know why your worthy parents went so suddenly to live in Anjou.'

Bonnard looked at him helplessly.

'My–my father told me that he had come into money! Indeed, I know no more, Monseigneur! I would not lie. I swear I would not.'

The fine lips curled sardonically.

'We will pass over that. How comes it that Léon is so unlike you in face and form?'

Bonnard rubbed his forehead. There was no mistaking the perplexity in his eyes.

'I do not know, Monseigneur. I have often wondered. He was ever a weakly child, petted and cosseted when I was made to work on the farm. My mother cared nothing for me beside him. It was all Léon, Léon, Léon! Léon must learn to read and write, but I–the eldest–must tend the pigs! A sickly, pert lad he was ever, Monseigneur! A viper, a—'

Avon tapped the lid of his snuff-box with one very white finger.

'Do not let us misunderstand one another, my friend. There never was a Léon. A Léonie, perhaps. I want that explained.'

The man shrank.

'Ah, Monseigneur! Indeed, indeed I did it for the best! It was impossible to have a girl of that age here, and there was work to be done. It was better to dress her as a boy. My wife–Monseigneur will understand–women are jealous, milor'. She would not have a girl here. Indeed, indeed, if the boy–girl–has said aught against us, he lies! I could have turned him out into the streets, for he had no claim on me. Instead, I kept him, clothed him, fed him, and if he says he was ill-treated it is a lie! He is a wicked brat with a vicious temper. You could not blame me for hiding his sex, Monseigneur! It was for his sake, I swear! He liked it well enough. Never did he demand to be a girl!'

'No doubt he had forgotten,' said Avon dryly. 'Seven years a boy . . . Now—' He held up a louis. 'Mayhap this will refresh your memory. What do you know of Léon?'

The man looked at him in a puzzled way.

'I–do not understand, Monseigneur. What do I know of him?'

Avon leaned forward slightly, and his voice became menacing.

'It will not serve you to feign ignorance, Bonnard. I am very powerful.'

Bonnard's knees shook.

'Indeed, Monseigneur, I do not understand! I cannot tell you what I do not know! Is–is aught amiss with Léon?'

'You never thought that he was, perhaps, not your parents' child?'

Bonnard's jaw dropped.

'Not—Why, Monseigneur, what do you mean? Not my parents' child. But—'

Avon sat back.

'Does the name Saint-Vire convey aught to you?'

'Saint-Vire . . . Saint-Vire . . . no. Stay, the name has a familiar ring! But—Saint-Vire—I do not know.' He shook his head hopelessly. 'It may be that I have heard my father speak the name, but I cannot remember.'

'A pity. And when your parents died was there no document found belonging to them which concerned Léon?'

'If there was, milor', I never saw it. There were old accounts and letters—I cannot read, Monseigneur, but I have them all.' He looked at the louis, and licked his lips. 'If Monseigneur would care to see for himself? They are here, in that chest.'

Avon nodded.

'Yes. All of them.'

Bonnard went to the chest and opened it. After some search he found a sheaf of papers, which he brought to the Duke. Avon went through them quickly. For the most part they were, as Bonnard had said, farm accounts, with one or two letters amongst them. But at the bottom of the pile was a folded slip of paper, addressed to Jean Bonnard, on the estate of M. le Comte de Saint-Vire, in Champagne. It was only a letter from some friend, or relation, and it held nothing of importance, save the address. The Duke held it up.

'This I will take.' He tossed the louis to Bonnard. 'If you have lied to me, or deceived me, you will be sorry. At present I am willing to believe that you know nothing.'

'I have spoken naught but the truth, Monseigneur, I swear!'

'Let us hope that it is so. One thing, however—' he produced another louis—'you can tell me. Where shall I find the curé at Bassincourt, and what is his name?'

'M. de Beaupré, Monseigneur, but he may be dead now, for aught I know. He was an old man when we left Bassincourt. He used to live in a little house beside the church. You cannot mistake it.'

Avon threw the louis into his eager hand.

'Very well.' He went to the door. 'Be advised by me, my friend, and strive to forget that you ever had a sister. For you had not, and it might be that if you remembered a Léonie there would be a reckoning to be paid for your treatment of her. I shall not forget you, I assure you.' He swept out, and through the taproom to his coach.

That afternoon, when Avon sat in the library of his house, writing to his sister, a footman came to him and announced that M. de Faugenac wished to see him.

The Duke raised his head.

'M. de Faugenac? Admit him.'

In a few minutes' time there entered a tubby little gentleman with whom his Grace was but slightly acquainted. Avon rose as he came in and bowed.

'Monsieur!'

'Monsieur!' De Faugenac returned the bow. 'Pardon the unseemly hour of this intrusion, I beg!'

'Not at all,' answered the Duke. 'Fetch wine, Jules. Pray be seated, m'sieur.'

'No wine for me, I thank you! The gout, you understand. A sad affliction!'

'Very,' agreed his Grace. 'Is there something I can do for you, I wonder?'

De Faugenac stretched his hands to the fire.

'Yes, I come on business, m'sieur. Bah, the ugly word! M'sieur will pardon the interruption, I am sure! A splendid fire, Duc!'

Avon bowed. He had seated himself on the arm of a chair, and was looking at his visitor in mild surprise. He drew out his snuff-box and offered it to De Faugenac, who helped himself to a liberal pinch and sneezed violently.

'Exquisite!' he said enthusiastically. 'Ah, the business! M'sieur, you will think I come upon a strange errand, but I have a wife!' He beamed at Avon, and nodded several times.

'I felicitate you, m'sieur,' said Avon gravely.

'Yes, yes! A wife! It will explain all.'

'It always does,' answered his Grace.

'Aha, the pleasantry!' De Faugenac broke into delighted laughter. 'We know, we husbands, we know!'

'As I am not a husband I may be excused my ignorance. I am sure you are about to enlighten me.' His Grace was becoming bored, for he had remembered that De Faugenac was an impoverished gentleman usually to be found at the heels of Saint-Vire.

'Indeed yes. Yes indeed. My wife. The explanation! She has seen your page, m'sieur!'

'Wonderful!' said the Duke. 'We progress.'

'We—? You said progress? We? Progress?'

'It seems I erred,' Avon sighed. 'We remain at the same place.'

De Faugenac was puzzled for a moment, but all at once his face broke into fresh smiles.

'Another pleasantry! Yes, yes, I see!'

'I doubt it,' murmured Avon. 'You were saying, m'sieur, that your wife had seen my page.'

De Faugenac clasped his hands to his breast.

'She is ravished! She is envious! She pines!'

'Dear me!'

'She gives me no peace!'

'They never do.'

'Aha! No, never, never! But you do not take my meaning, m'sieur, you do not take my meaning!'

'But then, that is hardly my fault,' said Avon wearily. 'We have arrived at the point at which your wife gives you no peace.'

'That is the matter in a nutshell! She eats out her heart for your so lovely, your so enchanting, your so elegant—'

Avon held up his hand.

'M'sieur, my policy has ever been to eschew married women.'

De Faugenac stared.

'But—but—what do you mean, m'sieur? Is it another pleasantry? My wife pines for your page.'

'How very disappointing!'

'Your page, your so elegant page! She plagues me day and night to come to you. And I am here! Behold me!'

'I have beheld you for the past twenty minutes, m'sieur,' said Avon rather tartly.

'She begs me to come to you, to ask you if you would part with your page! She cannot rest until she has him to hold her train for her, to carry her gloves and fan. She cannot sleep at night until she knows that he is hers!'

'It seems that madame is destined to spend many sleepless nights,' said Avon.

'Ah no, m'sieur! Consider! It is said that you bought your page. Now, is it not truly said that what may be bought may be sold?'

'Possibly.'

'Yes, yes! Possibly! M'sieur, I am as a slave to my wife.' He kissed the tips of his fingers. 'I am as the dirt beneath her feet.' He clasped his hands. 'I must bestow on her all that she desires, or die!'

'Pray make use of my sword,' invited his Grace. 'It is in the corner behind you.'

'Ah no! M'sieur cannot mean that he refuses! It is impossible! M'sieur, you may name your own price and I will give it!'

Avon stood up. He picked up a silver hand-bell, and rang it.

'M'sieur,' he said silkily, 'you may bear my compliments to the Comte de Saint-Vire, and tell him that Léon, my page, is not for sale. Jules, the door.'

De Faugenac rose, very crestfallen.

'M'sieur?'

Avon bowed.

'M'sieur. You mistake! You do not understand!'

'Believe me, I understand perfectly.'

'Ah, but you have no soul thus to thwart a lady's wish!'

'My misfortune entirely, m'sieur. I am desolate that you are unable to stay longer. M'sieur, your very obedient!' So he bowed De Faugenac out.

No sooner had the door closed behind the little man than it opened again to admit Davenant.

'Who in the name of all that's marvellous was that?' he asked.

'A creature of no account,' replied his Grace. 'He wished to buy Léon. An impertinence. I am going into the country, Hugh.'

'Into the country? Why?'

'I forget. No doubt I shall call the reason to mind some time. Bear with me, my dear; I am still moderately sane.'

Hugh sat down.

'You never were sane. 'Pon rep, you're a casual host!'

'Ah, Hugh, I crave your pardon on my knees! I encroach on your good nature.'

'Damme, you're very polite! Is Léon to accompany you?'

'No, I leave him in your charge, Hugh, and I counsel you to have a care for him. While I am away he will not leave the house.'

'I thought there was some mystery. Is he in danger?'

'N-no. I can hardly say. But keep him close, and say naught, my dear. I should not be pleased if harm came to him. Incredible as it may seem, I am becoming fond of the child. I must be entering upon my dotage.'

'We are all fond of him,' said Hugh. 'But he is an imp.'

'Undoubtedly. Do not allow him to tease you; he is an impertinent child. Unhappily he cannot be brought to realize that fact. And here he is.'

Léon came in and smiled confidingly as he met the Duke's eyes.

'Monseigneur, you told me to be ready to accompany you out at three, and it is now half-past the hour,' he said.

Hugh's shoulders shook with suppressed laughter; he turned away, coughing.

'It would appear that I owe you an apology,' said his Grace. 'Pray hold me excused for once. I am not going out after all. Come here.'

Léon approached.

'Yes, Monseigneur?'

'I am going into the country for a few days, my infant, from to-morrow. Oblige me by looking on M. Davenant as master in mine absence, and do not, on any account, leave the house until I return.'

'Oh!' Léon's face fell. 'Am I not to come with you?'

'I am denying myself that honour. Please do not argue with me. That is all that I wished to say.'

Léon turned away and went with lagging steps to the door. A small sniff escaped him, and at the sound of it Avon smiled.

'Infant, the end of the world has not come. I shall return, I hope, within the week.'

'I wish—oh, I wish that you would take me!'

'That is hardly polite to M. Davenant. I do not think he is likely to ill-use you. I am not going out to-night, by the way.'

Léon came back.

'You—you won't go to-morrow without saying goodbye, will you, Monseigneur?'

'You shall hand me into my coach,' promised the Duke, and gave him his hand to kiss.

7

Satan and Priest at One

The village of Bassincourt, which lay some six or seven miles to the west of Saumur, in Anjou, was a neat and compact place whose white houses were for the most part gathered about its hub, a square market-place paved by cobblestones as large as a man's fist. On the north the square was flanked by various houses of the more well-to-do inhabitants; on the west by smaller cottages, and by a lane that led into the square at right-angles to this side, and which stretched out into the open country, winding this way and that to touch each of the three farms that lay to the west of Bassincourt. On the south side was the small grey church, within whose square tower a cracked bell was wont to ring out its summons to the villagers. The church stood back from the market-place with its burial ground all about it and beyond, on one side, the Curé's modest house, squatting in its own garden, and seeming to smile across the square in gentle rulership.

The east side of the square was closed-packed by shops, a blacksmith's yard, and a white inn, over whose open door hung a gay green shield, with a painting of the Rising Sun thereon. The sign swung to and fro with every wind that blew, creaking a little if the gale were fierce, but more often sighing only on its rusted chains.

On this particular day of November the square was a-hum with voices, and echoing occasionally to a child's shrill laugh, or to the stamp of a horse's hoofs on the cobbles. Old Farmer Mauvoisin had driven into Bassincourt with three pigs for sale in his cart, and had drawn up at the inn to exchange the time of day with the landlord, and to quaff a tankard of thin French ale while his pigs grunted and snuffled behind him. Close by, gathered about a stall where La Mère Gognard was selling vegetables, was a group of women, alternately haggling and conversing. Several girls in stuff gowns kilted high above their ankles, their feet in clumsy wooden sabots, stood chattering beside the ancient porch which led into the graveyard; in the centre of the square, near to the fountain, some sheep were herded, while a party of possible buyers picked their way amongst them, prodding and inspecting at will. From the blacksmith's yard came the ring of hammer on anvil, mingled with spasmodic snatches of song.

Into this busy, contented scene rode his Grace of Avon, upon a hired horse. He came trotting into the market-place from the eastern road that led to Saumur, dressed all in sombre black, with lacing of gold. As soon as his horse's hoofs struck the uneven cobblestones he reined in, and sitting gracefully at ease in the saddle, one gloved hand resting lightly on his hip, cast a languid glance round.

He attracted no little attention. The villagers stared at him from his point-edged hat to his spurred boots, and back again. One tittering girl, remarking those cold eyes, and the thin, curling lips, whispered that it was the devil himself come amongst them. Although her companion scoffed at her for a foolish maid, she crossed herself surreptitiously, and drew back into the shelter of the porch.

The Duke's glance swept all round the square, and came to rest at last on a small boy, who watched him with goggling eyes, and his thumb in his mouth. One hand in its embroidered gauntlet beckoned imperiously, and the small boy took a hesitating step forward in answer to the Duke's summons.

His Grace looked down at him, faintly smiling. He pointed to the house beside the church.

'Am I right in thinking that that is the abode of your Curé?'

The boy nodded.

'Yes, milor'.'

'Do you think that I shall find him within?'

'Yes, milor'. He came back from the house of Madame Tournaud an hour since, if you please, milor'.'

Avon swung himself lightly down from the saddle, and twitched the bridle over his horse's head.

'Very well, child. Be so good as to hold this animal for me until I return. You will thus earn a louis.'

The boy took the bridle willingly.

'A whole louis, milor'? For holding your horse?' he said breathlessly.

'Is it a horse?' The Duke eyed the animal through his quizzing glass. 'Perhaps you are right. I thought it was a camel. Take it away and water it.' He turned on his heel, and sauntered up to the Curé's house. The wondering villagers saw M. de Beaupré's housekeeper admit him, and started to propound their views on this strange visitation, one to the other.

His Grace of Avon was led through a tiny spotless hall to the Curé's sanctum, a sunny room at the back of the house. The rosy-cheeked housekeeper ushered him into her master's presence with unruffled placidity.

'Here, *mon père*, is a gentleman who desires speech with you,' she said, and then withdrew, without another glance at the Duke.

The Curé was seated at a table by the window, writing on a sheet of paper. He looked up to see who was his visitor, and, perceiving a stranger, laid down his quill and rose. He was slight, with thin, beautiful hands, calm blue eyes, and aristocratic features. He wore a long soutane, and his head was uncovered. For an instant Avon thought that the milky white hair was a wig, so ordered were the soft waves, and then he saw that it was natural, brushed smoothly back from a broad low brow.

'M. de Beaupré, I believe?' His Grace bowed deeply.

'Yes, m'sieur, but you have the advantage of me.'

'I am one Justin Alastair,' said the Duke, and laid his hat and gloves on the table.

'Yes? You will pardon me, monsieur, if I do not at once recognize you. I have been out of the world for many years, and for the moment I cannot call to mind whether you are of the Alastairs of Auvergne, or of the English family.' De Beaupré cast him an appraising look, and put forward a chair.

Justin sat down.

'The English family, monsieur. You perhaps knew my father?'

'Slightly, very slightly,' answered De Beaupré. 'You are the Duc of Avon, I think? What may I have the honour of doing for you?'

'I am the Duke of Avon, m'sieur, as you say. Am I right in thinking that I address a relative of the Marquis de Beaupré?'

'His uncle, m'sieur.'

'Ah!' Justin bowed. 'You are the Vicomte de Marrillon, then.'

The Curé seated himself at the table again.

'I renounced that title years ago, m'sieur, deeming it empty. My family will tell you that I am mad. They do not mention my name.' He smiled. 'Naturally, I have disgraced them. I chose to work amongst my people here when I might have worn a cardinal's hat. But I suppose you did not come all the way to Anjou to hear that. What is it I may do for you?'

Justin offered his host some snuff.

'I hope, m'sieur, that you may be able to enlighten me,' he said.

De Beaupré took a pinch of snuff, holding it delicately to one nostril.

'It is hardly probable, m'sieur. As I said, I have long since withdrawn from the world, and what I knew of it I have wellnigh forgotten.'

'This, *mon père*, has naught to do with the world,' replied his Grace. 'I want you to cast your mind back seven years.'

'Well?' De Beaupré picked up his quill and passed it through his fingers. 'Having done that, *mon fils*, what then?'

'Having done that, m'sieur, you may perhaps recall a family living here by the name of Bonnard.'

The Curé nodded. His eyes never wavered from Avon's face.

'More particularly the child—Léonie.'

'One wonders what the Duc of Avon knows of Léonie. I am not likely to forget.' The blue eyes were quite inscrutable.

His Grace swung one booted leg gently to and fro.

'Before I go further, *mon père*, I would have you know that I speak in confidence.'

The Curé brushed his quill lightly across the table.

'And before I consent to respect the confidence, my son, I will learn what it is you want of a peasant girl, and what that peasant girl is to you,' he answered.

'At the moment she is my page,' said Avon blandly.

The Curé raised his brows.

'So? Do you usually employ a girl as your page, M. le Duc?'

'It is not one of my most common practices, *mon père*. This girl does not know that I have discovered her sex.'

The quill brushed the table again, rhythmically.

'No, my son? And what comes to her?'

Avon looked haughtily across at him.

'M. de Beaupré, you will pardon me, I am sure, for pointing out to you that my morals are not your concern.'

The Curé met his look unflinchingly.

'They are your own, my son, but you have seen fit to make them all the world's. I might retort: Léonie's welfare is not your concern.'

'She would not agree with you, *mon père*. Let us understand one another. Body and soul she is mine. I bought her from the ruffian who called himself her brother.'

'He had reason,' said De Beaupré calmly.

'Do you think so? Rest assured, m'sieur, that Léonie is safer with me than with Jean Bonnard. I have come to ask your help for her.'

'I have never before heard that—Satanas—chose a priest for his ally, m'sieur.'

Avon's teeth showed white for a moment in a smile.

'Withdrawn as you are from the world, *mon père*, you yet have heard that?'

'Yes, m'sieur. Your reputation is well known.'

'I am flattered. In this case my reputation lies. Léonie is safe with me.'

'Why?' asked De Beaupré serenely.

'Because, my father, there is a mystery attached to her.'

'It seems an insufficient reason.'

'Nevertheless it must suffice. My word, when I give it, is surety enough.'

The Curé folded his hands before him, and looked quietly into Avon's eyes. Then he nodded.

'It is very well, *mon fils*. Tell me what became of *la petite*. That Jean was worthless, but he would not leave Léonie with me. Where did he take her?'

'To Paris, where he bought a tavern. He dressed Léonie as a boy, and a boy she has been for seven years. She is my page now, until I end that comedy.'

'And when you end it, what then?'

Justin tapped one polished finger-nail against the lid of his snuff-box.

'I take her to England—to my sister. I have some vague notion of—ah—adopting her. As my ward, you understand. Oh, she will be chaperoned, of course!'

'Why, my son? If you desire to do good to *la petite* send her to me.'

'My dear father, I have never desired to do good to anyone. I have a reason for keeping this child. And, strange to say, I have developed quite a keen affection for her. A fatherly emotion, believe me.'

The housekeeper entered at this moment, bearing a tray with wine and glasses upon it. She arranged the refreshment at her master's elbow, and withdrew.

De Beaupré poured his visitor out a glass of canary.

'Proceed, my son. I do not yet see how I can aid you, or why you have journeyed all this way to see me.'

The Duke raised the glass to his lips.

'A most tedious journey,' he agreed. 'But your main roads are good. Unlike ours in England. I came, my father, to ask you to tell me all that you know of Léonie.'

'I know very little, m'sieur. She came to this place as a babe, and left it when she was scarce twelve years old.'

Justin leaned forward, resting one arm on the table.

'From where did she come, *mon père?*'

'It was always kept secret. I believe they came from Champagne. They never told me.'

'Not even—under the seal of the confessional?'

'No. That were of no use to you, my son. From chance words that the Mère Bonnard from time to time let fall I gathered that Champagne was their native country.'

'M'sieur,' Justin's eyes widened a little, 'I want you to speak plainly. Did you think when you saw Léonie grow from babyhood into girlhood that she was a daughter of the Bonnards?'

The Curé looked out of the window. For a moment he did not answer.

'I wondered, monsieur. . .'

'No more? Was there nothing to show that she was not a Bonnard?'

'Nothing but her face.'

'And her hair, and her hands. Did she remind you of no one, my father?'

'It is difficult to tell at that age. The features are still unformed. When the Mère Bonnard was dying she tried to say something. That it concerned Léonie I know, but she died before she could tell me.'

His Grace frowned quickly.

'How inconvenient!'

The Curé's lips tightened.

'What of *la petite*, sir? What became of her when she left this place?'

'She was, as I told you, compelled to change her sex. Bonnard married some shrewish slut, and bought a tavern in Paris. Faugh!' His Grace took snuff.

'It was perhaps as well then that Léonie was a boy,' said De Beaupré quietly.

'Without doubt. I found her one evening when she was flying from punishment. I bought her, and she mistook me for a hero.'

'I trust, *mon fils*, that she will never have cause to change her opinion.'

Again the Duke smiled.

'It is a hard rôle to maintain, my father. Let us pass over that. When first I set eyes on her it flashed across my brain that she was related to—someone I know.' He shot the Curé a swift glance, but De Beaupré's face was impassive. 'Someone I know. Yes. On that fleeting conviction I acted. The conviction has grown, *mon père*, but I have no proof. That is why I come to you.'

'You come in vain, monsieur. There is nothing to tell whether Léonie be a Bonnard or not. I too suspected, and because of that I took pains with *la petite*, and taught her to the best of mine ability. I tried to keep her here when the Bonnards died, but Jean would not have it so. You say he ill-treated her? Had I thought that I would have done more to retain the child. I did not think it. True, I had never an affection for Jean, but he was kind enough to *la petite* in those days. He promised to write to me from Paris, but he never did so, and I lost trace of him. Now it seems that Chance has led you to Léonie, and you suspect what I suspected.'

Justin set down his wine-glass.

'Your suspicion, *mon père?*' It was spoken compellingly.

De Beaupré rose, and went to the window.

'When I saw the child grow up in a delicate mould; when I saw those blue eyes, and those black brows, coupled with hair of flame, I was puzzled. I am an old man, and that was fifteen or more years ago. Yet even then I had been out of the world for many years, and I had seen no one of that world since the days of my youth. Very little news reaches us here, monsieur; you will find me strangely ignorant. As I say, I watched Léonie grow up, and every day I saw her become more and more like to a family I had known before I was a priest. It is not easy to mistake a descendant of the Saint-Vires, m'sieur.' He turned, looking at Avon.

The Duke lay back in his chair. Beneath his heavy lids his eyes glittered coldly.

'And thinking that—suspecting that, my father—you yet let Léonie slip through your fingers? You knew also that the Bonnards came from Champagne. It is to be supposed that you remembered where the Saint-Vire estate lay.'

The Curé looked down at him in surprised hauteur.

'I fail to understand you, m'sieur. It is true that I thought Léonie a daughter of Saint-Vire, but what could that knowledge avail her? If Madame Bonnard wished her to know she could have told her. But Bonnard himself recognized the child as his. It was better that Léonie should not know.'

The hazel eyes opened wide.

'*Mon père*, I think we are at cross-purposes. In plain words, what do you think Léonie?'

'The inference is sufficiently obvious, I think,' said the Curé, flushing.

Avon shut his snuff-box with a click.

'We will have it in plain words, nevertheless, my father. You deemed Léonie a base-born child of the Comte de Saint-Vire. It is possible that you have never appreciated the situation between the Comte and his brother Armand.'

'I have no knowledge of either, m'sieur.'

'It is manifest, *mon père*. Listen to me a while. When I found Léonie that night in Paris a dozen thoughts came into my head. The likeness to Saint-Vire is prodigious, I assure you. At first I thought as you. Then there flashed before mine eyes a picture of Saint-Vire's son as last I had seen him. A raw clod, my father. A clumsy thick-set yokel. I remembered that between Saint-Vire and his brother had ever been a most deadly hatred. You perceive the trend of the matter? Saint-Vire's wife is a sickly creature; it was common knowledge that he married her simply to spite Armand. Now behold the irony of fate. Three years pass. Madame fails to present her lord with anything but a still-born child. Then—miraculously a son is born, in Champagne. A son who is now nineteen years old. I counsel you, my father, to put yourself in Saint-Vire's place for one moment, not forgetting that the flame of the Saint-Vire hair is apt to enter the Saint-Vire head. He is determined that there shall be no mistake this time. He carries Madame into the country, where she is brought to bed, and delivered of—let us say—a girl. Conceive the chagrin of Saint-Vire! But, my father, we will suppose that he had prepared for this possibility. On his estate was a family of the name of Bonnard. We will say that Bonnard was in his employ. Madame Bonnard gives birth to a son some few days before the birth of—Léonie. In a fit of Saint-Vire madness the Comte exchanged the children. Evidently he bribed Bonnard very heavily, for we know that the Bonnard family came here and bought a farm, bringing with them Léonie de Saint-Vire, and leaving their son to become—Vicomte de Valmé. *Eh bien?*'

'Impossible!' said De Beaupré sharply. 'A fairy tale!'

'Nay, but listen,' purred his Grace. 'I find Léonie in the streets of Paris. *Bien*. I take her to my hôtel, I clothe her as my page. She accompanies me everywhere, and thus I flaunt her under the nose of Saint-Vire. That same nose quivers with apprehension, *mon père*. That is nothing, you say? Wait! I take Léon—I call her Léon—to Versailles, where Madame de Saint-Vire is in attendance. One may always trust a woman to betray a secret, monsieur. Madame was agitated beyond all words. She could not drag her eyes from Léon's face. A day later I receive an offer from one of Saint-Vire's satellites to buy Léon. You see? Saint-Vire dare not show his hand in the matter. He sends a friend to work for him. Why? If Léon is a base-born child of his what is simpler—if he wants to rescue her from my clutches—than to approach me, telling me all? He does not do that. Léonie is his legitimate daughter, and he is afraid. For aught he knows I may have proof of that fact. I should tell you, *mon père*, that he and I are not the closest of friends. He fears me, and he dare not move one way or the other lest I should suddenly disclose some proof of which he knows nothing. It may also be that he is not sure that I know, or even suspect, the truth. I do not quite think that. I have something of a reputation, my father, for—uncanny omniscience. Whence, in part, my *sobriquet*.' He smiled. 'It is my business to know everything, father. I am thus a personality in polite circles. An amusing pose. To return: You perceive that M. le Comte de Saint-Vire finds himself in something of a quandary?'

The Curé came slowly to his chair, and sat down.

'But, m'sieur—what you suggest is infamous!'

'Of course it is. Now I had hoped, *mon père*, that you would know of some document to prove the truth of my conviction.'

De Beaupré shook his head.

'There was none. I went through all the papers with Jean, after the plague.'

'Saint-Vire is more clever than I had imagined, then. Nothing, you say? It seems that this game must be carefully played.'

De Beaupré was hardly listening.

'Then—at her death, when Madame Bonnard tried so hard to speak to me, it must have been that!'

'What did she say, *mon père*?'

'So little! "*Mon père—écoutez donc—Léonie n'est pas—je ne peux plus—!*" No more. She died with those words on her lips.'

'A pity. But Saint-Vire shall think that she made confession—in writing. I wonder if he knows that the Bonnards are dead? M. de Beaupré, if he should come here, on this same errand, allow him to think that I bore away with me—a document. I do not think he will come. It is probable that he purposely lost trace of the Bonnards.' Justin rose, and bowed. 'My apologies for wasting your time in this fashion, my father.'

The Curé laid a hand on his arm.

'What are you going to do, my son?'

'If she is indeed what I think her I am going to restore Léonie to her family. How grateful they will be! If not—' He paused. 'Well, I have not considered that possibility. Rest assured that I shall provide for her. For the present she must learn to be a girl again. After that we shall see.'

The Curé looked full into his eyes for a moment.

'My son, I trust you.'

'You overwhelm me, father. As it chances, I am to be trusted this time. One day I will bring Léonie to see you.'

The Curé walked with him to the door, and together they passed out into the little hall.

'Does she know, m'sieur?'

Justin smiled.

'My dear father, I am far too old to place my secrets in a woman's keeping. She knows nothing.'

'The poor little one! Of what like is she now?'

Avon's eyes gleamed.

'She is something of an imp, *mon père*, with all the Saint-Vire spirit, and much impudence of which she is unaware. She has seen much, as I judge, and at times I espy a cynicism in her that is most entertaining. For the rest she is wise and innocent by turn. An hundred years old one minute, a babe the next. As are all women!'

They had come to the garden gate now, and Avon beckoned to the boy who held his horse.

Some of the anxious lines were smoothed from De Beaupré's face.

'My son, you have described the little one with feeling. You speak as one who understands her.'

'I have reason to know her sex, my father.'

'That may be. But have you ever felt towards a woman as you feel towards this—imp?'

'She is more a boy to me than a girl. I admit I am fond of her. You see, it is so refreshing to have a child of her age—and sex—in one's power, who thinks no ill of one, nor tries to escape. I am a hero to her.'

'I hope that you will ever be that. Be very good to her, I pray you.'

Avon bowed to him, kissing his hand with a gesture of half-ironical respect.

'When I feel that I can no longer maintain the heroic pose I will send Léonie—by the way, I am adopting her—back to you.'

'*C'est entendu*,' nodded De Beaupré. 'For the present I am with you. You will take care of the little one, and perhaps restore her to her own. *Adieu, mon fils.*'

Avon mounted, tossed the small boy a louis, and bowed again, low over his horse's withers.

'I thank you, father. It seems that we understand one another very well—Satan and priest.'

'Perhaps you have been misnamed, my son,' said De Beaupré, smiling a little.

'Oh, I think not! My friends know me rather well, you see. *Adieu, mon père!*' He put on his hat, and rode forward across the square, towards Saumur.

The small boy, clutching his louis, raced to his mother's side.

'*Maman, maman*! It was the Devil! He said so himself!'

8

Hugh Davenant is Amazed

A week after Avon's departure for Saumur, Hugh Davenant sat in the library, endeavouring to amuse the very disconsolate Léon with a game of chess.

'I would like to play cards, if you please, m'sieur,' said Léon politely, on being asked his pleasure.

'Cards?' repeated Hugh.

'Or dice, m'sieur. Only I have no money.'

'We will play chess,' said Hugh firmly, and set out the ivory men.

'Very well, m'sieur.' Léon privately thought Hugh a little mad, but if he wished to play chess with his friend's page he must of course be humoured.

'Do you think Monseigneur will return soon, m'sieur?' he asked presently. 'I remove your bishop.' He did so, to Hugh's surprise. 'It was a little trap,' he explained. 'Now it is check.'

'So I see. I grow careless. Yes, I expect Monseigneur will return quite soon. Farewell to your rook, my child.'

'I thought you would do that. Now I move a pawn forward, so!'

'Much ado about nothing, *petit*. Where did you learn to play this game? Check.'

Léon interposed one of his knights. He was not taking a very keen interest in the game.

'I forget, m'sieur.'

Hugh looked across at him shrewdly.

'You've a surprisingly short memory, have you not, my friend?'

Léon peeped at him through his lashes.

'Yes, m'sieur. It—it is very sad. And away goes your queen. You do not attend.'

'Do I not? Your knight is forfeit, Léon. You play a monstrous reckless game.'

'Yes, that is because I like to gamble. Is it true, m'sieur, that you leave us next week?'

Hugh hid a smile at the proprietary 'us'.

'Quite true. I am bound for Lyons.'

Léon's hand hovered uncertainly over the board.

'I have never been there,' he said.

'No? There is time yet.'

'Oh, but I do not wish to go!' Léon swooped down upon a hapless pawn, and took it. 'I have heard that Lyons is a place of many smells, and not very nice people.'

'So you won't go there? Well, perhaps you're wise. What's toward?' Hugh raised his head, listening.

There was some slight commotion without; the next moment a footman flung open the library door, and the Duke came slowly in.

Table, chessboard, and men went flying. Léon had sprung impetuously out of his chair, and had almost flung himself at Avon's feet, all etiquette and decorum forgotten.

'Monseigneur, Monseigneur!'

Over his head Avon met Davenant's eyes.

'He is mad, of course. I beg you will calm yourself, my Léon.'

Léon gave his hand a last kiss, and rose to his feet.

'Oh, Monseigneur, I have been miserable!'

'Now, I should never have suspected Mr Davenant of cruelty to infants,' remarked his Grace. 'How are you, Hugh?' He strolled forward, and just touched Hugh's outstretched hands with his finger-tips. 'Léon, signify your delight at seeing me by picking up the chessmen.' He went to the fire, and stood with his back to it, Hugh beside him.

'Have you had a pleasant time?' Hugh asked.

'A most instructive week. The roads here are remarkable. Allow me to point out to your notice, Léon, that an insignificant pawn lies under that chair. It is never wise to disregard the pawns.'

Hugh looked at him.

'What may that mean?' he inquired.

'It is merely advice, my dear. I should have made an excellent father. My philosophy is almost equal to Chesterfield's.'

Hugh chuckled.

'Chesterfield's conversation is marvellous.'

'A little tedious. Yes, Léon, what now?'

'Shall I bring wine, Monseigneur?'

'Mr Davenant has certainly trained you well. No, Léon, you shall not bring wine. I trust he has been no trouble, Hugh?'

Léon cast Davenant an anxious glance. There had been one or two slight battles of will between them. Hugh smiled at him.

'His behaviour has been admirable,' he said.

His Grace had seen the anxious look, and the reassuring smile.

'I am relieved. May I now have the truth?'

Léon looked up at him gravely, but volunteered no word. Hugh laid his hand on Avon's shoulder.

'We have had a few small disputes, Alastair. That is all.'

'Who won?' inquired his Grace.

'We reached the end by a compromise,' said Hugh solemnly.

'Very unwise. You should have insisted on utter capitulation.' He took Léon's chin in his hand, and looked into the twinkling blue eyes. 'Even as I should have done.' He pinched the chin. 'Should I not, infant?'

'Perhaps, Monseigneur.'

The hazel eyes narrowed.

'Perhaps? What is this? Are you so demoralized during this one short week?'

'No, oh no!' Léon's dimples quivered. 'But I am very obstinate, Monseigneur, sometimes. Of course I will always try to make myself do as you wish.'

Avon released him.

'I believe you will,' he said unexpectedly, and waved one white hand to the door.

'I suppose it is useless to ask where you have been?' said Hugh, when Léon had gone.

'Quite.'

'Or where you intend to go next?'

'No, I believe I can answer that. I am going to London.'

'London?' Hugh was surprised. 'I thought you intended to remain here some months?'

'Did you, Hugh? I never have intentions. That is why mothers of lovely daughters eye me askance. I am constrained to return to England.' He drew from his pocket a fan of dainty chicken-skin, and spread it open.

'What constrains you?' Hugh frowned upon the Duke's fan. 'Why that new affectation?'

Avon held the fan at arm's length.

'Exactly what I ask myself, dear Hugh. I found it awaiting me here. It comes from March, who begs—' He searched in his pocket for a folded sheet of paper, and, putting up his glass, read the scrawled lines aloud. 'Begs—yes, here we are. "I send you this pretty trifle, which I give you my word is now become the rage here, all men who aspire to be beaux using them both in warm weather and cold, so that we rival the ladies now in this matter. I beg you will make use of it, my dear Justin; it is cunningly painted, you will agree, and was procured by me from Geronimo, expressly for you. The golden sticks should please you, as I hope they will do."' Avon raised his eyes from the letter to observe the fan, which was painted black, with a gold design, and gold sticks and tassels. 'I wonder if I do like it?' he said.

'Foppery!' answered Hugh shortly.

'Undoubtedly. Natheless it will give Paris something fresh to talk about. I shall purchase a muff for March. Of miniver, I think. You perceive that I must return to England forthwith.'

'To give March a muff?'

'Precisely.'

'I perceive that you will make that an excuse. Léon goes with you?'

'As you say, Léon goes with me.'

'I had meant to ask you once again to give him to me.'

The Duke fanned himself with an air, handling the chicken-skin like a woman.

'I really could not permit it, my dear; it would be most improper.'

Hugh looked sharply up at him.

'Now, what mean you by that, Justin?'

'Is it possible that you have been hoodwinked? Dear, dear!'

'You'll explain, if you please!'

'I had come to think you omniscient,' sighed his Grace. 'You have had Léon in your care for eight days, and you are as innocent of his deception as you were when I first introduced him to your notice.'

'You mean?'

'I mean, my dear, that Léon is Léonie.'

Davenant threw up his hands.

'You knew, then!'

His Grace stopped fanning himself.

'I knew? I knew from the first. But you?'

'Perhaps a week after he came here. I hoped that you knew nothing.'

'Oh, my dear Hugh!' Avon shook with gentle laughter. 'You thought me guileless! I forgive you only because you have restored my faith in your omniscience.'

'I never dreamed that you suspected!' Hugh took a few quick steps across the room and back again. 'You've hidden it well!'

'So also have you, my dear.' Avon resumed his fanning.

'What was your object in allowing the deception to go on?'

'What was yours, oh worthy Hugh?'

'I dreaded lest you should discover the truth! I wanted to take the child away from you.'

His Grace smiled slowly, eyes nearly shut.

'The fan expresses my emotions. I must kiss March's hands and feet. Metaphorically speaking.' He waved the fan gently to and fro.

Davenant glared at him for a moment, annoyed at his nonchalance. Then an unwilling laugh broke from him.

'Justin, pray put that fan away! If you know that Léon is a girl what will you do? I beg that you will give her to me—'

'My dear Hugh! Bethink you, you are but thirty-five—quite a child still. It would be most improper. Now, I—I am over forty. A veteran, and therefore harmless.'

'Justin—' Hugh came to him, and laid a hand on his arm. 'Will you sit down, and talk this over—quietly and reasonably?'

The fan paused.

'Quietly? But did you imagine that I wished to bawl at you?'

'No. Don't be flippant, Justin. Sit down.'

Avon went to a chair, and sat upon its arm.

'When you become excited, my dear, you remind me of an agitated sheep. Quite irresistible, believe me.'

Hugh controlled a quivering lip, and seated himself opposite the Duke. Avon stretched out his hand to where a small spindle-legged table stood and pulled it into place between himself and Davenant.

'So. I am now reasonably safe. Continue, Hugh.'

'Justin, I am not jesting—'

'Oh, my dear Hugh!'

'—and I want you also to be serious. Put away that damned fan!'

'It incites you to wrath? If you assault me I shall summon assistance.' But he shut the fan, and held it so, between his hands. 'I am all attention, beloved.'

'Justin, you and I are friends, are we not? Let us for once have plain speaking!'

'But you always speak plainly, dear Hugh,' murmured his Grace.

'You've been kind—ay, I admit that—to little Léon; you've permitted him to take many liberties with you. At times I've hardly recognized you with him. I thought—well, never mind that. And all the while you knew he was a girl.'

'You are becoming rather involved,' remarked Avon.

'She, then. You knew she was a girl. Why have you allowed her to keep up the pretence? What do you mean by her?'

'Hugh—' Avon tapped the table with his fan. 'Your painful anxiety impels me to inquire—what do *you* mean by her?'

Davenant looked his disgust.

'My God, do you think you are amusing? I mean this: That I will have her away from you if it costs me my life.'

'This becomes interesting,' said Avon. 'How will you have her away from me, and why?'

'You can ask that? I never thought you were a hypocrite, Justin.'

Avon unfurled his fan.

'If you were to ask me, Hugh, why I permit myself to bear with you I could not tell you.'

'My manners are atrocious. I know it. But I've an affection for Léon, and if I allowed you to take her, innocent as he is—'

'Careful, Hugh, careful!'

'Oh, *she*, then! If I allowed that—I—'

'Calm yourself, my dear. If I did not fear that you would mutilate it I would lend you my fan. May I make known mine intentions.'

'It's what I want!'

'I should not have guessed that, somehow. Strange how one may be mistaken. Or even how two may be mistaken. It will surprise you to hear that I am fond of Léon.'

'No. She will make a beautiful girl.'

'Remind me one day to teach you how to achieve a sneer, Hugh. Yours is too pronounced, and thus is but a grimace. It should be but a faint curl of the lips. So. But to resume. You will at least be surprised to hear that I had not thought of Léonie in the light of a beautiful girl.'

'It amazes me.'

'That is much better, my dear. You are an apt pupil.'

'Justin, you are impossible. This is no laughing matter!'

'Certainly not. You see in me–a strict guardian.'

'I don't understand.'

'I am taking Léonie to England, where I shall place her 'neath my sister's wing until I have found some discreet lady who will act the part of duenna to my ward, Mademoiselle Léonie de Bonnard. Again the fan expresses my emotions.' He performed a sweep in the air with it, but Hugh was staring in open-mouthed wonderment.

'Your–your ward! But–why?'

'Oh, my reputation!' mourned his Grace. 'A whim, Hugh, a whim!'

'You'll adopt her as your daughter?'

'As my daughter.'

'For how long? If it be a whim only—'

'It is not. I have a reason. Léonie will not leave me until–let us say until she finds a more fitting home.'

'Until she marries, you mean?'

The thin black brows twitched suddenly together.

'I did not mean that, but let it stand. All that signifies is that Léonie is as safe in my care as she would be in–I will say yours, for want of a better simile.'

Hugh rose.

'I–you–Good God, Justin, are you jesting?'

'I believe not.'

'You seriously mean what you say?'

'You seem dazed, my dear.'

'More like a sheep than ever, then,' retorted Hugh, with a quick smile, and held out his hand. 'If you are honest now–and I think you are—'

'You overwhelm me,' murmured his Grace.

'—you are doing something that is—'

'—quite unlike anything I have ever done before.'

'Something that is damned good!'

'But then you do not know my motives.'

'I wonder if you yourself know your motives?' Hugh said quietly.

'Very obscure, Hugh. I flatter myself that I do know–full well.'

'I am not so certain.' Hugh sat down again. 'Ay, you've amazed me. What now? Does Léon know that you have discovered his–her–fiend seize it, I am becoming involved again!–sex?'

'She does not.'

Hugh was silent for a few moments.

'Perhaps she will not wish to remain with you when you tell her,' he said at last.

'It is possible, but she is mine, and she must do as I bid her.'

Suddenly Hugh rose again, and went to the window.

'Justin, I don't like it.'

'May I ask why you do not like it?'

'She–she is too fond of you.'

'Well?'

'Would it not be kinder to make some arrangement–send her away?'

'Whither, my conscientious one?'

'I don't know.'

'How helpful! As I do not know either I think we may safely banish that notion.'

Hugh turned, and came back to the table.

'Very well. I trust no harm will come of this, Justin. When shall you—put an end to her boyhood?'

'When we arrive in England. You see, I am deferring that moment as long as may be.'

'Why?'

'One reason, my dear, is that she might feel shy of me in her boy's raiment when once I knew the secret. The other—the other—' He paused, and studied his fan, frowning. 'Well, let us be honest. I have grown fond of Léon, and I do not want to exchange him for Léonie.'

'I thought so,' Hugh nodded. 'Be kind to Léonie, Justin.'

'It is my intention,' bowed the Duke.

9

Léon and Léonie

Early in the next week Davenant left Paris for Lyons. On the same day Avon summoned his *maître d'hôtel*, Walker, to his presence, and informed him that he was leaving France on the morrow. Well accustomed to his master's sudden decisions, Walker felt no surprise. He was a discreet personage with an unyielding countenance. For many years he had been in the Avon employ, and as he had proved himself to be scrupulously honest and trustworthy, the Duke had placed him in charge of his Paris establishment. As his Grace owned another establishment in St James's Square, London, and kept both open and staffed with servants, this post was one of considerable importance. It was Walker's duty to keep the Hôtel Avon in such strictness and order that it should always be ready for the Duke or for his brother.

When Walker left the library he went below-stairs to inform Gaston, the valet, Meekin, the groom, and Léon, the page, that they must hold themselves in readiness to depart from Paris to-morrow morning. He found Léon seated on the table in the housekeeper's room, swinging his legs and munching a slice of cake. Madame Dubois was sitting in a large chair before the fire, dolefully regarding him. She welcomed Walker with a coy smile, for she was a comely woman, but Léon, having cast one glance towards the prim figure in the doorway, tilted his head a little, and went on eating.

'*Eh bien, m'sieur!*' Madame smoothed her gown, smiling upon the *maître d'hôtel*.

'I crave pardon thus to have disturbed you, madame.' Walker bowed. 'I came but to find Léon.'

Léon wriggled round to face him.

'You perceive me, Walker,' he said.

A slight spasm contracted Walker's features. Alone amongst the staff Léon never gave him a prefix to his name.

'His Grace sent for me a few moments back to tell me that he is leaving for London to-morrow. I come to warn you, Léon, that you must be ready to accompany him.'

'Bah! He had told me that this morning,' said Léon scornfully.

Madame nodded.

'Yes, and he comes to eat a last cake with me, *le petit.*' She sighed gustily. 'Indeed, my heart is heavy to think I must lose thee, Léon. But thou–thou art glad, little ingrate!'

'I have never been to England, you see,' apologized Léon. 'I am so excited, *ma mère.*'

'*Ah, c'est cela!* So excited that you will forget fat old Madame Dubois.'

'No, I swear I will not! Walker, will you have some of Madame's cake?' Walker drew himself up.

'No, I thank you.'

'*Voyons,* he insults your skill, *ma mère!*' chuckled Léon.

'I assure you, madame, it's no such thing.' Walker bowed to her and withdrew.

'He is like a camel,' remarked the page placidly.

He repeated this observation to the Duke next day, as they sat in the coach, bound for Calais.

'A camel?' said his Grace. 'Why?'

'We-ll . . .' Léon wrinkled his nose. 'I saw one once, a long time ago, and I remember it walked along with its head very high, and a smile on its face, just like Walker. It was so full of dignity, Monseigneur. You see?'

'Perfectly,' yawned his Grace, leaning farther back into the corner.

'Do you think that I shall like England, Monseigneur?' asked Léon presently.

'It is to be hoped that you will, my infant.'

'And–and do you think that I shall feel sick upon the ship?'

'I trust not.'

'So do I,' said Léon devoutly.

As it chanced, the journey was quite uneventful. They spent one night on the road to Calais, and embarked next day on a night boat. Much to Léon's disgust, the Duke sent him into his cabin, with orders to remain there. For perhaps the first time in all his Channel crossings Avon remained on deck. Once he went down to the tiny cabin, and, finding Léon fast asleep in a chair, lifted him, and put him gently into a bunk, covering him with a fur rug. Then he went out again to pace the deck until morning.

When Léon appeared on deck next morning he was shocked to find that his master had remained there all night, and said so. Avon pulled one of his curls, and, having breakfasted, went below to sleep until Dover was reached. Then he emerged, and with becoming languor went ashore, Léon at his heels. Gaston had disembarked one of the first, and by the time the Duke arrived at the inn on the quay had roused the landlord to activity. A private parlour awaited them, with lunch set out on the table.

Léon eyed the meal with some disapproval and not a little surprise. A sirloin of English beef stood at one end of the table, flanked by a ham and some capons. A fat duck was at the other end, with pasties and puddings. There was also a flagon of burgundy, and a jug of foaming ale.

'Well, my Léon?'

Léon turned. His Grace had entered the room, and stood behind him, fanning himself. Léon looked sternly at the fan, and seeing the condemnation in his eyes Avon smiled.

'The fan does not find favour with you, infant?'

'I do not like it at all, Monseigneur.'

'You distress me. What think you of our English meats?'

Léon shook his head.

'Terrible, Monseigneur. It is—it is *barbare!*'

The Duke laughed, and came to the table. At once Léon went to him, intending to stand behind his chair.

'Child, you will observe that two places are laid. Seat yourself.' He shook out his napkin, and picked up the carving-knife and fork. 'Will you essay the duck?'

Léon sat down shyly.

'Yes, please, Monseigneur.' He was served, and began to eat, rather nervously, but daintily, as Avon saw.

'So—so this is Dover,' remarked Léon presently, in a politely conversational tone.

'You are right, infant,' replied his Grace. 'This is Dover. You are pleased to approve?'

'Yes, Monseigneur. It is queer to see everything English, but I like it. I should not like it if you were not here, of course.'

Avon poured some burgundy into his glass.

'I fear you are a flatterer,' he said severely.

Léon smiled.

'No, Monseigneur. Did you remark the landlord?'

'I know him well. What of him?'

'He is so little, and so fat, with such a bright, bright nose! When he bowed to you, Monseigneur, I thought he would burst! It looked so droll!' His eyes twinkled.

'A horrible thought, my child. You would appear to have a slightly gruesome sense of humour.'

Léon gave a delighted chuckle.

'Do you know, Monseigneur,' he said, wrestling with a stubborn joint, 'I had never seen the sea until yesterday! It is very wonderful, but just for a little while it made the inside of me go up and down. Like that.' He described the motion with his hand.

'My dear Léon! Really, I cannot have that topic discussed at meal time. You make me feel quite ill.'

'Well, it made me feel ill, Monseigneur. But I was not sick. I shut my mouth very tightly—'

Avon picked up his fan and dealt Léon a smart rap with it across the knuckles.

'Continue to keep it shut, infant, I beg of you.'

Léon rubbed his hand, looking at the Duke in aggrieved wonderment.

'Yes, Monseigneur, but—'

'And do not argue.'

'No, Monseigneur. I was not going to argue. I only—'

'My dear Léon, you are arguing now. I find you most wearisome.'

'I was trying to explain, Monseigneur,' said Léon, with great dignity.

'Then please do not. Confine your energy to the duck.'

'Yes, Monseigneur.' Léon continued eating in silence for perhaps three minutes. Then he looked up again. 'When do we begin to go to London, Monseigneur?'

'What an original way of putting it!' remarked his Grace. 'We begin in about an hour's time.'

'Then when I have finished my *déjeuner* may I go for a walk?'

'I am desolated to have to refuse my permission. I want to talk to you.'

'To talk to me?' echoed Léon.

'Madness, you think? I have something of import to say. What is the matter now?'

Léon was examining a black pudding with an expression akin to loathing on his face.

'Monseigneur, this—' he pointed disdainfully at the pudding—'this is not for *people* to eat! Bah!'

'Is aught amiss with it?' inquired his Grace.

'Everything!' said Léon crushingly. 'First I am made to feel sick upon that ship, and then I am made to feel sick again by an evil—pudding, you call it? *Voyons*, it is a good name! Pig-pudding! Monseigneur, you must not eat it! It will make you—'

'Pray do not describe my probable symptoms as well as your own, infant. You have certainly been prodigiously ill-used, but endeavour to forget it! Eat one of those sweetmeats.'

Léon selected one of the little cakes, and started to nibble it.

'Do you always eat these things in England, Monseigneur?' he asked, pointing to the beef and the puddings.

'Invariably, my infant.'

'I think it would be better if we did not stay very long here,' said Léon firmly. 'I have finished now.'

'Then come here.' His Grace had moved to the fire, and was sitting on the oaken settle. Léon sat beside him obediently.

'Yes, Monseigneur?'

Avon started to play with his fan, and his mouth was rather grim. He was frowning slightly, and Léon racked his brains to think how he could have offended his master. Suddenly Avon clasped his hand on Léon's and held it in a cool, strong clasp.

'My infant, it has become necessary for me to put an end to the little comedy you and I have been playing.' He paused, and saw the big eyes grow apprehensive. 'I am very fond of Léon, my child, but it is time he was Léonie.'

The little hand in his quivered.

'Mon-seigneur!'

'Yes, my child. You see, I have known from the very first.'

Léonie sat rigid, staring up into his face with the look of a stricken creature in her eyes. Avon put up his free hand to pat her white cheek.

'It is no such great matter after all, infant,' he said gently.

'You—you won't send me—away?'

'I will not. Have I not bought you?'

'I—I may still be your page?'

'Not my page, child. I am sorry, but it is not possible.'

All the rigidity went out of the slight frame. Léonie gave one great sob, and buried her face in his coat sleeve.

'Oh please! oh please!'

'Infant, sit up! Come, I object to having my coat ruined. You have not heard all yet.'

'I won't, I won't!' came the muffled voice. 'Let me be Léon! Please let me be Léon!'

His Grace lifted her.

'Instead of my page you shall be my ward. My daughter. Is it so terrible?'

'I do not want to be a girl! Oh please, Monseigneur, please.' Léon slipped from the settle to the floor, and knelt at his feet, gripping his hand. 'Say yes, Monseigneur! Say yes!'

'No, my babe. Dry your tears and listen to me. Don't tell me you have lost your handkerchief.'

Léonie drew it from her pocket, and mopped her eyes.

'I don't w-want to be—a girl!'

'Nonsense, my dear. It will be far more pleasant to be my ward than my page.'

'No!'

'You forget yourself,' said his Grace sternly. 'I will not be contradicted.'

Léonie gulped down another sob.

'I—I am sorry, Monseigneur.'

'It's very well. As soon as we have come to London I am going to take you to my sister—no, do not speak—my sister, Lady Fanny Marling. You see, infant, you cannot live with me until I have found some lady to act as—ah—duenna.'

'I will not! I will not!'

'You will do as I say, my good child. My sister will clothe you as befits your new position, and teach you to be—a girl. You will learn these things—'

'I will not! Never, never!'

'—because I command it. Then, when you are ready, you shall come back to me, and I will present you to Society.'

Léonie tugged at his hand.

'I won't go to your sister! I will be just Léon! You cannot make me do as you say, Monseigneur! I will *not*!'

His Grace looked down at her in some exasperation.

'If you were still my page I should know how to deal with you,' he said.

'Yes, yes! Beat me, if you like, and let me still be your page! Ah, please, Monseigneur!'

'Unhappily it is impossible. Recollect, my infant, that you are mine, and must do as I say.'

Léonie promptly collapsed into a crumpled heap beside the settle, and sobbed into the hand she held. Avon allowed her to weep unrestrainedly for perhaps three minutes. Then he drew his hand away.

'You want me to send you away altogether?'

'Oh!' Léonie started up. 'Monseigneur, you would not! You—oh no, no!'

'Then you will obey me. It is understood?'

There was a long pause. Léonie stared hopelessly into the cold hazel eyes. Her lip trembled, and a large tear rolled down her cheek.

'Yes, Monseigneur,' she whispered, and drooped her curly head.

Avon leaned forward, and put his arm about the childish figure, drawing it close.

'A very good infant,' he said lightly. 'You will learn to be a girl to please me, Léonie.'

She clung to him, her curls tickling his chin.

'Will—will it please you, Monseigneur?'

'Above all things, child.'

'Then—I'll try,' said Léonie, a heartbroken catch in her voice. 'You won't l-leave me with y-your sister for l-long, will you?'

'Only until I can find someone to take care of you. Then you shall go to my house in the country, and learn to curtsy, to flirt with your fan, to simper, to have the vapours—'

'I—won't!'

'I hope not,' said his Grace, smiling faintly. 'My dear child, there is no need for such misery.'

'I have been Léon for so—so long! It will be so very, very hard!'

'I think it will,' said Avon, and took the crumpled handkerchief from her. 'But you will try to learn all that you are taught, that I may be proud of my ward.'

'Could you be, Monseigneur? Of—of *me*?'

'It is quite possible, my infant.'

'I should like that,' said Léonie, more happily. 'I will be very good.'

The Duke's fine lips twitched.

'So you may be worthy of me? I wish Hugh could hear.'

'Does—does he know?'

'It transpired, my child, that he always knew. Allow me to suggest that you rise from your knees. So. Sit down.'

Léonie resumed her place on the settle, and gave a doleful sniff.

'I must wear petticoats, and not say bad words, and always be with a woman. It is very hard, Monseigneur. I do not like women. I wish to be with you.'

'And I wonder what Fanny will say to you?' remarked his Grace. 'My sister, Léonie, is all a woman.'

'Is she like you?' asked Léonie.

'Now how am I to take that?' inquired his Grace. 'She is not like me, infant. She is golden-haired and blue-eyed. I beg your pardon?'

'I said Bah!'

'You seem partial to that observation. It is not at all ladylike, my dear. You will obey Lady Fanny, and you will not flout and scorn her because of her golden hair.'

'Of course I shall not. She is your sister, Monseigneur,' answered Léonie. 'Will she like me, do you think?' She looked up at him with a troubled gleam in her eyes.

'Why not?' said his Grace flippantly.

A little smile flitted across Léonie's mouth.

'Oh—oh, I don't know, Monseigneur!'

'She will be kind to you for my sake.'

'Thank you,' said Léonie meekly, and with eyes downcast. Then, as Avon said nothing, she peeped up, and the roguish dimple appeared. Seeing it Avon ruffled her curls as though she still had been a boy.

'You are refreshing,' he said. 'Fanny will try and make you like the rest of your sex. I believe that I do not want that.'

'No, Monseigneur. I will be just myself.' She kissed his hand, and her lip trembled. She controlled it, and smiled through her tears. 'You have taken my handkerchief, Monseigneur.'

IO

Lady Fanny's Virtue is Outraged

Lady Fanny Marling, reposing on a settee, found life monotonous. She pushed away the book of poems, over which she had been yawning, and started to play with one golden curl that had strayed over her shoulder and lay glistening on the lace of her wrapper. She was *en déshabillé*, her fair hair unpowdered, and loosely dressed beneath a Mechlin cap whose blue ribands were tied under her chin in a coquettish bow. She wore a blue taffeta gown, with a broad fichu about her perfect shoulders, and as the room in which she sat was furnished in gold and blue and white she had reason to be pleased with herself and her setting. She was pleased, but she would have liked it better had there been someone with her to share the aesthetic pleasure. So when she heard the clang of her front-door bell her china-blue eyes brightened, and she stretched out her hand for her mirror.

In a few minutes her black page tapped upon the door. She put the mirror down, and turned her head to look at him.

Pompey grinned and bobbed his woolly head.

'Genelman to see ma'am!'

'His name?' she asked.

A soft voice spoke from behind the page.

'His name, my dear Fanny, is Avon. I am fortunate to find you at home.'

Fanny shrieked, clapped her hands, and flew up to greet him.

'Justin! You! Oh, how prodigiously delightful!' She would not permit him to kiss her finger-tips, but flung her arms about his neck, and embraced him. 'I declare, 'tis an age since I have seen you! The cook you sent is a marvel! Edward will be so pleased to see you! Such dishes! And a sauce at my last party which I positively cannot describe!'

The Duke disengaged himself, shaking out his ruffles.

'Edward and the cook would appear to have become entangled,' he remarked. 'I trust I find you well, Fanny?'

'Yes, oh yes! And you? Justin, you cannot imagine how glad I am that you have come back! I vow I have missed you quite too dreadfully! Why, what is this?' Her eyes had alighted on Léonie, wrapped in a long cloak, her tricorne in one hand, a fold of the Duke's coat in the other.

His Grace loosened the tight hold on his garment, and allowed Léonie to clutch his hand.

'This, my dear, was, until yesterday, my page. It is now my ward.'

Fanny gasped, and fell back a pace.

'Your—your ward! This boy? Justin, have you taken leave of your senses?'

'No, my dear, I have not. I solicit your kindness for Mademoiselle Léonie de Bonnard.'

Fanny's cheeks grew crimson. She drew her small figure up, and her eyes became haughtily indignant.

'Indeed, sir? May I ask why you bring your—your ward here?'

Léonie shrank a little, but spoke never a word. Very silky became Avon's voice.

'I bring her to you, Fanny, because she is my ward, and because I have no duenna for her. She will be glad of you, I think.'

Fanny's delicate nostrils quivered.

'You think so? Justin, how dare you! How dare you bring her here!' She stamped her foot at him 'You have spoiled everything now! I hate you!'

'You will perhaps accord me a few minutes' private conversation?' said his Grace. 'My infant, you will await me in this room.' He went to one end of the room and opened a door, disclosing an antechamber. 'Come, child.'

Léonie looked up at him suspiciously.

'You'll not go?'

'I will not.'

'Promise! Please, you must promise!'

'This passion for oaths and promises!' sighed Avon. 'I promise, my infant.'

Léonie released his hand then, and went into the adjoining room. Avon shut the door behind her, and turned to face his wrathful sister. From his pocket he drew his fan, and spread it open.

'You are really very foolish, my dear,' he said, and came to the fire.

'I am at least respectable! I think it very unkind and insulting of you to bring your–your—'

'Yes, Fanny? My—?'

'Oh, your *ward*! It's not decent! Edward will be very, very angry, and I hate you!'

'Now that you have unburdened yourself of that sentiment no doubt you will allow me to explain.' His Grace's eyes were nearly shut, and his thin lips sneered.

'I do not want an explanation! I want you to take that creature away!'

'When I have told my story, and if you still wish it, I will take her away. Sit down, Fanny. The expression of outraged virtue is entirely wasted on me.'

She flounced into a chair.

'I think you are very unkind! If Edward comes in he will be furious.'

'Then let us hope that he will not come in. Your profile is enchanting, my dear, but I would sooner see both your eyes.'

'Oh, Justin!' She clasped her hands, anger forgotten. 'You think it enchanting still? I vow, I thought I looked a positive fright when I looked in the mirror this morning! 'Tis age, I suppose. Oh, I am forgetting to be angry with you! Indeed, I am so thankful to see you again I cannot be cross! But you must explain, Justin.'

'I will start mine explanation, Fanny, with an announcement. I am not in love with Léonie. If you will believe that it will make matters more simple.' He tossed the fan on the couch, and drew out his snuff-box.

'But–but if you are not in love with her, why–what–Justin, I don't understand! You are most provoking!'

'Pray accept my most humble apologies. I have a reason for adopting the child.'

'Is she French? Where did she learn to speak English? I wish you would explain!'

'I am endeavouring to do so, my dear. Allow me to say that you give me very little opportunity.'

She pouted.

'Now you are cross. Well, start, Justin! The child is pretty enough, I grant you.'

'Thank you. I found her in Paris one evening, clad as a boy, and fleeing from her unpleasant–er–brother. It transpired that this brother and his inestimable wife had made the child masquerade as a boy ever since her twelfth year. She was thus of more use to them. They kept a low tavern, you see.'

Fanny cast up her eyes.

'A tavern-wench!' She shuddered, and raised her scented handkerchief to her nose.

'Precisely. In a fit of–let us say–quixotic madness, I bought Léonie or Léon, as she called herself, and took her home with me. She became my page. I assure you she created no little interest in polite circles. It pleased me to keep her a boy for a time. She imagined that I was in ignorance of her sex. I became a hero to her. Yes, is it not amusing?'

'It is horrid! Of course the girl hopes to intrigue you. La, Justin, how can you be such a fool?'

'My dear Fanny, when you know Léonie a little better you will not accuse her of having designs upon me. She is in very truth the infant I call her. A gay, impertinent, and trusting infant. I have a notion that she regards me in the light of a grandparent. To resume: as soon as we arrived at Dover I told her that I knew her secret. It may surprise you to hear, Fanny, that the task was damnably hard.'

'It does,' said Fanny, frankly.

'I was sure it would. However, I did it. She neither shrank from me nor tried to coquette. You can have no idea how refreshing I found it.'

'Oh, I make no doubt you found it so!' retorted Fanny.

'I am glad that we understand one another so well,' bowed his Grace. 'For reasons of mine own I am adopting Léonie, and because I will have no breath of scandal concerning her I bring her to you.'

'You overwhelm me, Justin.'

'Oh, I trust not! I believe you told me some months ago that our cousin by marriage, the unspeakable Field, had died?'

'What has that to do with it?'

'It follows, my dear, that our respected cousin, his wife, whose name I forget, is free. I have a mind to make her Léonie's chaperon.'

'Lud!'

'And as soon as may be I will send her and Léonie down to Avon. The infant must learn to be a girl again. Poor infant!'

'That is all very well, Justin, but you cannot expect me to house the girl! I vow 'tis preposterous! Think of Edward!'

'Pray hold me excused. I never think of Edward unless I can help it.'

'Justin, if you are minded to be disagreeable—'

'Not at all, my dear.' The smile faded from his lips. Fanny saw that his eyes were unwontedly stern. 'We will be serious for once, Fanny. Your conviction that I had brought my mistress to your house—'

'Justin!'

'I am sure you will forgive my plain speaking. That conviction, I say, was pure folly. It has never been my custom to compromise others by my numerous affairs, and you should know that I am sufficiently strict where you are concerned.' There was peculiar meaning in his voice, and Fanny, who had once been famed for her indiscretions, dabbed at her eyes.

'How c-can you be *s-so* unkind! I do not think you are at all nice to-day!'

'But I trust I have made myself plain? You realize that the child I have brought you is but a child?—an innocent child?'

'I am sorry for her if she is!' said her ladyship spitefully.

'You need not be sorry. For once I mean no harm.'

'If you mean her no harm how can you think to adopt her?' Fanny tittered angrily. 'What do you suppose the world will say?'

'It will be surprised, no doubt, but when it sees that my ward is presented by the Lady Fanny Marling its tongue will cease to wag.'

Fanny stared at him.

'I present her? You're raving! Why should I?'

'Because, my dear, you have a kindness for me. You will do as I ask. Also, though you are thoughtless, and occasionally exceedingly tiresome, I never found you cruel. 'Twere cruelty to turn my infant away. She is a very lonely, frightened infant, you see.'

Fanny rose, twisting her handkerchief between her hands. She glanced undecidedly at her brother.

'A girl from the back streets of Paris, of low birth—'

'No, my dear. More I cannot say, but she is not born of the *canaille*. You have but to look at her to see that.'

'Well, a girl of whom I know naught—foisted on me! I declare 'tis monstrous! I could not possibly do it! What would Edward say?'

'I am confident that you could, if you would, cajole the worthy Edward.'

Fanny smiled.

'Yes, I could, but I do not want the girl.'

'She will not tease you, my dear. I wish you to keep her close, to dress her as befits my ward, and to be gentle with her. Is it so much to ask?'

'How do I know that she will not ogle Edward, this innocent maid?'

'She is too much the boy. Of course, if you are uncertain of Edward—'

She tossed her head.

'Indeed, 'tis no such thing! 'Tis merely that I've no wish to house a pert, red-headed girl.'

His Grace bent to pick up his fan.

'I crave your pardon, Fanny. I'll take the child elsewhere.'

Fanny ran to him, penitent all at once.

'Indeed and you shall not! Oh, Justin, I am sorry to be so disobliging!'

'You'll take her?'

'I—yes, I'll take her. But I don't believe all you say of her. I'll wager my best necklet she's not so artless as she would have you think.'

'You would lose, my dear.' His Grace moved to the door into the antechamber, and opened it. 'Infant, come forth!'

Léonie came, her cloak over her arm. At sight of her boy's raiment Fanny closed her eyes as though in acute pain.

Avon patted Léonie's cheek.

'My sister has promised to care for you until I can take you myself,' he said. 'Remember, you will do as she bids you.'

Léonie looked shyly across at Fanny, who stood with primly set lips and head held high. The big eyes noted the unyielding pose, and fluttered up to Avon's face.

'Monseigneur—please do not—leave me!' It was a despairing whisper, and it amazed Fanny.

'I shall come to see you very soon, my babe. You are quite safe with Lady Fanny.'

'I don't—want you to go away! Monseigneur, you—you do not understand!'

'Infant, I do understand. Have no fear; I shall come back again!' He turned to Fanny, and bowed over her hand. 'I have to thank you, my dear. Pray convey my greetings to the excellent Edward. Léonie, how often have I forbidden you to clutch the skirts of my coat?'

'—I am sorry, Monseigneur.'

'You always say that. Be a good child, and strive to bear with your petticoats.' He held out his hand, and Léonie dropped on one knee to kiss it. Something sparkling fell on to those white fingers, but Léonie turned her head away, surreptitiously wiping her eyes.

'F-Farewell, Mon—monseigneur.'

'Farewell, my infant. Fanny, your devoted servant!' He made a profound leg, and went out, shutting the door behind him.

Left alone with the small but forbidding Lady Fanny, Léonie stood as though rooted to the ground, looking hopelessly towards the shut door, and twisting her hat in her hands.

'Mademoiselle,' said Fanny coldly, 'if you will follow me I will show you your apartment. Have the goodness to wrap your cloak about you.'

'Yes, madame.' Léonie's lip trembled. 'I am—very sorry, madame,' she said brokenly. A tiny sob escaped her, valiantly suppressed, and suddenly the icy dignity fell from Fanny. She ran forward, her skirts rustling prodigiously, and put her arms about her visitor.

'Oh, my dear, I am a shrew!' she said. 'Never fret, child! Indeed, I am ashamed of myself! There, there!' She led Léonie to the sofa, and made her sit down, petting and soothing until the choked sobs died away.

'You see, madame,' Léonie explained, rubbing her eyes with her handkerchief. 'I felt so—very lonely. I did not mean to cry, but when—Monseigneur—went away—it was so very dreadful!'

'I wish I understood!' sighed Fanny. 'Are you fond of my brother, child?'

'I would die for Monseigneur,' said Léonie simply. 'I am here only because he wished it.'

'Oh, my goodness gracious me!' said Fanny. 'Here's a pretty coil! My dear, be warned by me, who knows him! Have naught to do with Avon: he was not called Satanas for no reason.'

'He is not a devil to me. And I do not care.'

Fanny cast up her eyes.

'Everything is upside down!' she complained. Then she jumped up. 'Oh, you must come up to my chamber, child. 'Twill be so droll to clothe you! See!' She measured herself against Léonie. 'We are very much of a height, my love. Perhaps you are a little taller. Not enough to signify.' She fluttered to where Léonie's cloak had fallen, caught it up, and wrapped it about her charge. 'For fear lest the servants should see and chatter,' she explained. 'Now come with me.' She swept out, one arm about Léonie's waist, and, meeting her butler on the stairs, nodded condescendingly to him. 'Parker, I have my brother's ward come unexpectedly to visit me. Be good enough to bid them prepare the guest-chamber. And send my tirewoman to me.' She turned to whisper in Léonie's ear. 'A most faithful, discreet creature, I give you my word.' She led the girl into her bedroom, and closed the door. 'Now we shall see! Oh, 'twill be most entertaining, I dare swear!' She kissed Léonie again, and was wreathed in smiles. 'To think I was so dull! 'Pon rep, I owe my darling Justin a debt of gratitude. I shall call you Léonie.'

'Yes, madame.' Léonie recoiled slightly, fearing another embrace.

Fanny tripped to her wardrobe.

'And you must call me Fanny, my dear. Off with those—those dreadful clothes!'

Léonie glanced down at her slim figure.

'But, madame, they are very fine clothes! Monseigneur gave them to me.'

'Indelicate creature! Off with them, I say! they must be burned.'

Léonie sat down plump upon the bed.

'Then I will not take them off.'

Fanny turned, and for a moment they stared at one another. Léonie's chin was tilted, her dark eyes flashed.

'You are very tiresome,' pouted Fanny. 'What can you want with man's attire?'

'I will not have them burned!'

'Oh, 'tis very well, my dear! Keep them if you will!' said Fanny hastily, and wheeled about as the door opened. 'Here is Rachel! Rachel, this is

Mademoiselle de Bonnard, my brother's ward. She—she wants some clothes.'

The tirewoman gazed at Léonie in horrified wonder.

'So I should think, my lady,' she said austerely.

Lady Fanny stamped her foot.

'Wicked, insolent woman! Don't dare to sniff! And if you say a word below-stairs, Rachel—'

'I would not so demean myself, your ladyship.'

'Mademoiselle—has come from France. She—she was compelled to wear those garments. It does not matter why. But—but now she wants to change them.'

'No, I do not,' said Léonie truthfully.

'Yes, yes, you do! Léonie, if you are disagreeable, I shall lose my temper!'

Léonie looked at her in some surprise.

'But I am not disagreeable. I only said—'

'I know, I know! Rachel, if you look like that, I vow I will box your ears!'

Léonie crossed one leg under her.

'I think I will tell Rachel everything,' she said.

'My dear! Oh, as you please!' Fanny flounced to a chair, and sat down.

'You see,' said Léonie gravely, 'I have been a boy for seven years.'

'Lawks, miss!' breathed Rachel.

'What is that?' inquired Léonie, interested.

'It is nothing!' said Fanny sharply. 'Go on, child.'

'I have been a page, Rachel, but now Monseign—I mean, the Duc of Avon—wants to make me his—his ward, so I have to learn to be a girl. I do not want to, you understand, but I must. So please will you help me?'

'Yes, miss. Of course I will!' said Rachel, whereupon her mistress flew up out of her chair.

'Admirable creature! Rachel, find linen! Léonie, I implore you, take off those breeches!'

'Don't you like them?' inquired Léonie.

'Like them!' Fanny waved agitated hands. 'They are monstrous improper! Take them off!'

'But they are of an excellent cut, madame.' Léonie proceeded to wriggle out of her coat.

'You must not—you positively must not speak of such things!' said Fanny earnestly. ''Tis most unseemly.'

'But, madame, one cannot help seeing them. If men did not wear them—'

'*Oh!*' Fanny broke into scandalized laughter. 'Not another word!'

For the next hour Léonie was bundled in and out of garments, while Fanny and Rachel twisted and turned her, laced her and unlaced her, and pushed her this way and that. To all their ministrations she submitted patiently, but she displayed no interest in the proceedings.

'Rachel, my green silk!' commanded her ladyship, and held out a flowered petticoat to Léonie.

'The green, my lady?'

'The green silk that became me not, stupid girl! Quickly! 'Twill be ravishing with your red hair, my love!' She seized a brush, and proceeded to arrange the tumbled curls. 'How could you cut it? 'Tis impossible to dress your hair now. No matter. You shall wear a green riband threaded through, and—oh, hasten, Rachel!'

Léonie was put into the green silk. It was cut low across the chest, to her evident confusion, and spread over a great hoop below the waist.

'Oh, said I not that 'twould be ravishing?' cried Fanny, stepping back to look at her handiwork. 'I cannot bear it! Thank goodness Justin is to take you into the country! You are far, far too lovely! Look in the mirror, ridiculous child!'

Léonie turned to see herself in the long glass behind her. She seemed taller, all at once, and infinitely more beautiful, with her curls clustering about her little pointed face, and her big eyes grave and awed. Her skin showed very white against the apple-green silk. She regarded herself in wonder, and between her brows was a troubled crease. Fanny saw it.

'What! Not satisfied?'

'It is very splendid, madame, and—and I look nice, I think, but—' she cast a longing glance to where her discarded raiment lay. 'I want my breeches!'

Fanny flung up her hands.

'Another word about those breeches, and I burn them! You make me shudder, child!'

Léonie looked at her solemnly.

'I do not at all understand why you do not like—'

'Provoking creature! I insist on your silence! Rachel, take those—those garments away this instant! I declare I will not have them in my room.'

'They shall not be burned!' said Léonie challengingly.

Fanny encountered the fierce glance, and gave vent to a little titter.

'Oh, as you will, my love! Put them in a box, Rachel, and convey them to Mistress Léonie's apartment. Léonie, I will have you look at yourself! Tell me, is it not a modish creation?' She went to the girl and twitched the heavy folds of silk into position.

Léonie regarded her reflection again.

'I think I have grown,' she said. 'What will happen if I move, madame?'

'Why, what should happen?' asked Fanny, staring.

Léonie shook her head dubiously.

'I think something will burst, madame. Me perhaps.'

Fanny laughed.

'What nonsense! Why, 'tis laced so loosely that it might almost fall off you! Nay, never pick your skirts up so! Oh, heaven, child, you must not show your legs! 'Tis positively indecent!'

'Bah!' said Léonie, and, gathering up her skirts, walked carefully across the room. 'Certainly I shall burst,' she sighed. 'I shall tell Monseigneur that I cannot wear women's clothes. It is as though I were in a cage.'

'Don't say you'll—*burst*—again!' implored Fanny. ''Tis a most unladylike expression.'

Léonie paused in her perambulations to and fro.

'Am I a lady?' she inquired.

'Of course you are! What else?'

The roguish dimple peeped out for the first time, and the blue eyes danced.

'Well, what now? Is it so funny?' asked Fanny, a trifle peevishly.

Léonie nodded.

'But yes, madame. And—and very perplexing.' She came back to the mirror, and bowed to her own reflection. '*Bonjour, Mademoiselle de Bonnard! Peste, qu'elle est ridicule!*'

'Who?' demanded Fanny.

Léonie pointed a scornful finger at herself.

'That silly creature.'

''Tis yourself.'

'*No!*' said Léonie with conviction. 'Never!'

'You are most provoking!' cried Fanny. 'I have been at pains to dress you in my prettiest gown–yes, the very prettiest, though, to be sure, it became me not–and you say 'tis silly!'

'But no, madame. It is I who am silly. Could I not keep my breeches just for to-night?'

Fanny clapped her hands to her ears.

'I positively will not listen! Don't dare to mention that word to Edward, I implore you!'

'Edward? Bah, what a name! Who is it?'

'My husband. A dear creature, I give you my word, but I faint to think of what he would feel an you spoke of breeches in his hearing!' Fanny gave a little gurgle of laughter. 'Oh, how entertaining 'twill be to buy clothes for you! I quite love Justin for bringing you to me! And whatever will Rupert say?'

Léonie withdrew her gaze from the mirror.

'That is Monseigneur's brother, *n'est-ce-pas?*'

'The most provoking creature,' nodded Fanny. 'Quite mad, you know. But then we Alastairs are all of us that. No doubt you have observed it?'

The big eyes twinkled.

'No, madame.'

'What! And you have–have lived with Avon for three months?' Fanny cast up her eyes. The sound of a shutting door somewhere below roused her to sudden activity. 'There! That is Edward returned from White's already! I think I will go down and–and talk to him while you rest. Poor child, I dare swear you are dreadfully fatigued?'

'N-no,' said Léonie. 'But you will tell Mr Marling that I have come, is it not so? And if he does not like it–and I do not think that he will–I can—'

'Fiddle!' said Fanny, blushing faintly. 'No such thing, my love, I assure you. Edward will be enchanted! Of course he will, stupid child! A pretty thing 'twould be an I could not twist him round my finger. 'Twas only that I wanted you to rest, and indeed you shall! I vow you are nigh dropping with fatigue! Don't try to argue with me, Léonie!'

'I am not arguing,' Léonie pointed out.

'No, well, I thought you might, and it makes me so cross! Come with me, and I will take you to your chamber.' She led Léonie to a blue guest-chamber, and sighed. 'Ravishing!' she said. 'I wish you were not quite so lovely. Your eyes are like those velvet curtains. I got them in Paris, my dear. Are they not exquisite? I forbid you to touch your dress while I am gone, mind!' She frowned direfully, patted Léonie's hand, and was gone in a whirl of silks and laces, leaving Léonie alone in the middle of the room.

Léonie walked to a chair, and sat down carefully, heels together, and hands demurely clasped in her lap.

'This,' she told herself, 'is not very nice, I think. Monseigneur has gone away, and I could never find him in this great, horrible London. That Fanny is a fool, I think. Or perhaps she is mad, as she said.' Léonie paused to consider the point. 'Well, perhaps she is just English. And Edward will *not* like me to be here. *Mon Dieu*, I suppose he will think I am just *une fille de joie*. That is very possible. I wish Monseigneur had not gone.' This thought occupied her mind for some moments, and led to another. 'I wonder what he will think of me when he sees me? That Fanny said I was lovely. Of course that is just silly, but I think I look a little pretty.' She rose, and planted her chair down before the mirror. She frowned upon her reflection, and shook her head. 'You are not Léon: that is very certain. Only one little bit of you is Léon.' She bent forward to look at her feet, shod still in Léon's shoes. '*Hélàs*! Only yesterday I was Léon the page, and now I am Mademoiselle de Bonnard. And I am very uncomfortable in these clothes. I think too that I am a *little* frightened. There is not even M. Davenant left. I shall be forced to eat pudding, and that woman will kiss me.' She heaved a large sigh. 'Life is very hard,' she remarked sadly.

I I

Mr Marling's Heart is Won

Lady Fanny found her husband in the library, standing before the fire and warming his hands. He was a medium-sized man, with regular features, and steady grey eyes. He turned as she entered the room, and held out his arms to her. Lady Fanny tripped towards him.

'Pray have a care for my gown, Edward. 'Tis new come from Cerisette. Is it not elegant?'

'Prodigious elegant,' agreed Marling. 'But if it means that I must not kiss you I shall think it hideous.'

She raised china-blue eyes to his face.

'Just one then, Edward. Oh, you are greedy, sir! No, Edward, I'll not be held. I've a monstrous exciting thing to tell you.' She shot him a sidelong glance, wondering how he would take her news. 'Do you remember, my love, that I was so *ennuyée* to-day that I could almost have cried?'

'Do I not!' smiled Marling. 'You were very cruel to me, sweet.'

'Oh no, Edward! I was not cruel! 'Twas you who were so very provoking. And then you went away, and I was so dull! But now it is all over, and I have something wonderful to do!'

Edward slipped an arm about her trim waist.

'Faith, what is it?'

''Tis a girl,' she answered. 'The most beautiful girl, Edward!'

'A girl?' he repeated. 'What new whim is this? What do you want with a girl, my dear?'

'Oh, I didn't want her! I never thought about her at all. How could I, when I'd not set eyes on her? Justin brought her.'

The clasp about her waist slackened.

'Justin?' said Marling. 'Oh!' His voice was polite, but not enthusiastic. 'I thought he was in Paris.'

'So he was, until a day or two ago, and if you are minded to be disagreeable, Edward, I shall cry. I am very *fond* of Justin!'

'Ay, dear. Go on with your tale. What has the girl, whoever she is, to do with Avon?'

'That is just the astonishing part of it!' said Fanny, her brow clearing as if by magic. 'She is Justin's adopted daughter! Is it not interesting, Edward?'

'*What*?' Marling's arm fell away from her. 'Justin's what?'

'Adopted daughter,' she answered airily. 'The sweetest child, my dear, and so devoted to him! I declare I quite love her already, although she is so lovely, and—oh, Edward, don't be cross!'

Edward took her by the shoulders, and made her look up at him.

'Fanny, do you mean to tell me that Alastair had the effrontery to bring the girl here? And you were mad enough to take her in?'

'Indeed, sir, and why not?' she demanded. 'A pretty thing 'twould be an I turned away my brother's ward!'

'Ward!' Marling almost snorted.

'Yes, sir, his ward. Oh, I'll not deny I thought the same as you when first I saw her, but Justin swore 'twas not so. And Edward, you know how strict Justin is with me. You can't be cross! Why, 'tis but a child, and half a boy at that!'

'Half a boy, Fanny? What mean you?'

'She has been a boy for seven years,' said Fanny triumphantly. Then, as the lines about his mouth hardened, she stamped her foot angrily. 'You're very unkind, Edward! How dare you suppose that darling Justin would bring his light o' love to my house? 'Tis the stupidest notion I ever heard! He wants me to chaperon the child until he can prevail upon Madam Field to come. What if she has been a boy? Pray what has that to say to anything?'

Marling smiled unwillingly.

'You must admit that for Justin to adopt a girl—'

'Edward, I truly believe that he means no ill! Léonie has been his page—Oh, now you are shocked again!'

'Well, but—'

'I won't hear a word!' Fanny put up her hands to his mouth. 'Edward, you'll not be angry, and hard?' she coaxed. 'There's some mystery about Léonie, I feel sure, but—oh, my dear, you have only to look in her eyes! Now listen to me, dear Edward!'

He imprisoned her hands in his, drawing her to the couch.

'Very well, my dear, I'll listen.'

Fanny seated herself.

'Dearest Edward! I knew you'd be kind! You see, Justin came here to-day with Léonie, dressed as a boy. I was so enchanted! I never imagined that Justin was in England! Oh, and he has a fan! You cannot conceive anything so absurd, dear! Though indeed I believe they are become quite the most fashion—'

'Ay, Fanny, but you were to explain about this girl—Léonie.'

'I was explaining,' she protested, pouting. 'Well, he sent Léonie into another room—my dear, I think she positively worships him, poor child—and he begged me to keep her with me for a few days because he does not want there to be a shadow of scandal attached to her. And I am to clothe her, and oh, Edward, will it not be entertaining? She has red hair, and black eyebrows, and I have given her my green silk. You cannot imagine how quite too tiresomely lovely she is, though perhaps she would look better in white.'

'Never mind that, Fanny. Go on with your story.'

'To be sure. It seems that Justin found her in Paris—only then he thought she was a boy—and she was being ill-treated by some tavern-keeper. So Justin bought her and made her his page. And he says that he has a fondness for her, and will make her his ward. And oh, Edward, I have just thought how wonderfully romantic 'twould be an he married her! But she is only a child, and dreadfully boyish. Only fancy!—she insisted on keeping her breeches! Now Edward, say that you will be nice to her, and that I may keep her! Say it, Edward, say it!'

'I suppose you must keep her,' he said reluctantly. 'I cannot turn her out. But I do not like it.'

Fanny embraced him.

'It doesn't signify in the least, Edward. You will fall in love with her, and I shall be jealous.'

'There's no fear of that, you little rogue,' he said, and gave her hand a quick squeeze.

'No, and I am so glad. And now go and put on that new puce coat. 'Tis prodigious modish, and I want you to look very nice tonight.'

'Are we not dining out?' he asked. 'I thought—'

'Dining out! Good gracious, Edward, and that child a visitor, and only just arrived! No indeed!' With that she rustled out of the room, full of a new importance.

An hour later when Marling sat in the withdrawing-room awaiting his wife, the door was flung open, and Fanny sailed in. Behind her came Léonie, hesitantly. Edward rose quickly, staring.

'My love,' said Fanny, 'this is my husband, Mr Marling. Edward, Mademoiselle de Bonnard.'

Marling bowed; so also did Léonie, but paused in the act of doing so.

'I must curtsy, is it not so? Bah, what skirts!' She smiled shyly up at Edward. 'Please pardon me, m'sieur. I have not learned to curtsy yet.'

'Give him your hand, child,' commanded Fanny.

The small hand was extended.

'Please, why?' asked Léonie.

Marling kissed her finger-tips punctiliously, and released them. Léonie's cheeks were tinged with colour, and she looked doubtfully up at him.

'*Mais, m'sieur*'—she began.

'Mademoiselle?' In spite of himself Marling smiled.

'*C'est peu convenable*,' explained Léonie.

'No such thing,' said Fanny briskly. 'Gentlemen do always kiss the lady's hands. Remember that, my love. And now my husband will give you his arm to the dining-room. Lay but the tips of your fingers on it, like that. What ails you now, child?'

'It is nothing, madame. Only that I am not at all myself. I think that I look very strange.'

'Tell the silly child that it is not so, Edward,' sighed her ladyship.

Edward found that he was patting Léonie's hand.

'My dear, 'tis as my lady says. You look very proper and charming.'

'Ah bah!' said Léonie.

12

His Grace of Avon's Ward

A fortnight later, when Léonie was practising a court curtsy before the mirror in her room, Fanny entered with the announcement that Avon had come at last. Léonie arose from her curtsy with more haste than grace.

'Monseigneur!' she cried, and would have flown from the room, had it not been for Fanny, who resolutely barred her passage. 'Let me go, let me go! Where is he?'

''Pon rep, Léonie, that is no way to receive a gentleman!' said her ladyship. 'To run downstairs like a hoydenish miss, with your hair in a tangle, and your gown caught up! Come back to the mirror.'

'Oh, but—'

'I insist!'

Léonie came reluctantly and was passive while Fanny arranged her gown of primrose silk, and combed out the unruly curls.

'Léonie, you tiresome creature, where is your riband?'

Léonie fetched it meekly.

'I do not like to feel a riband in my hair,' she complained. 'I would rather—'

'It is of no consequence at all,' said Fanny severely. 'I am determined you shall look your best. Shake out your petticoat, and pick up your fan. And if you dare to run forward in an unmaidenly way I shall be so mortified—'

'Let me go now! Please, I am ready!'

'Then follow me, child, so!' Out swept Fanny, and down the stairs, 'Remember! A decorous curtsy, my love, and give him your hand to kiss.' As she spoke she opened the door into the withdrawing-room.

'Bah!' said Léonie.

His Grace was standing by the window, looking out.

'So my sister has not induced you to stop saying "bah"?' he said, and turned. For a moment he said nothing, but stood looking at his ward. 'Infant, it is very well,' he said at last, slowly.

Léonie sank into a curtsy, talking all the time.

'I must do this because madame says so, and you bade me do as she told me, Monseigneur, but oh, I would rather bow to you!' She rose gracefully, and danced forward. 'Monseigneur, Monseigneur, I thought that you would never come! I am so very pleased to see you!' She caught his hand to her lips. 'I have been good and patient, and now will you take me, please?'

'Léonie!'

'Well, but madame, I want so much for him to take me.'

Avon raised his eyeglass.

'Stand still, child. Fanny, I kiss your hands and feet. I am almost surprised at the miracle you have wrought.'

'Monseigneur, do you think that I am nice?' asked Léonie, tiptoeing before him.

'It's an inadequate word, child. You are no longer Léon.'

She sighed, shaking her head.

'I wish I were Léon still. Monseigneur, do *you* understand what it is to be put into petticoats?'

Fanny started, and frowned direfully.

'Naturally I do not, my beautiful ward,' Justin answered gravely. 'I can imagine that, after the freedom of your breeches, petticoats are a little cramping.'

Léonie turned triumphantly to Fanny.

'Madame, he said it! You heard him? He spoke of breeches!'

'Léonie—Justin, I'll not have you let her bewail her—her breeches—as she is for ever doing! And don't, don't say bah, Léonie!'

'She has fatigued you, my dear? I believe I warned you that she was something of a rogue.'

Fanny relented.

'Indeed, and we love her dearly! I could wish that you would leave her with us longer.'

Léonie took a firm hold on Avon's coat sleeve.

'You won't, will you, Monseigneur?'

He disengaged himself.

'My infant, you must strive to be more polite. One would infer that you had been unhappy with Lady Fanny.'

'Yes, Monseigneur, very unhappy. It is not because she is not kind, for she has been very kind to me, but I belong to you.'

Over her head Justin looked mockingly at his sister.

'It distresses you, my dear? I believe you are right, Léonie. I have come to fetch you.'

She was all smiles at once.

'*Voyons*, now I am happy! Where will you take me, Monseigneur?'

'Into the country, child. Ah, the worthy Edward! Your devoted servant, Edward.'

Marling had entered quietly. Stiffly he returned Avon's bow.

'I would have a word with you an it please you, Alastair,' he said.

'But does it please me?' wondered his Grace. 'No doubt you wish to speak concerning my ward?'

Edward looked annoyed.

'In private, sir.'

'Quite unnecessary, my dear Edward, I assure you.' He flicked Léonie's cheek with one careless finger. 'Mr Marling has no doubt warned you that I am no fit companion for the young and—ah—innocent, infant?'

'No-no.' Léonie tilted her head. 'I know all about that, you see. Me, I am not very innocent, do you think?'

'That will do, Léonie!' hastily interposed Fanny. 'You'll drink a dish of Bohea with me, Justin? Léonie shall be ready to accompany you to-morrow. Léonie, my love, I have left my handkerchief in your room. Be so good as to fetch it for me. And Edward may go too. Yes, Edward, please!' So she drove them out, and turned again to her brother. 'Well, Justin, I've done as you desired me.'

'Admirably, my dear.'

Her eyes twinkled.

'At no small cost, Justin.'

'It is no matter, Fanny.'

She eyed him irresolutely.

'What now, Justin?'

'Now I take her to Avon.'

'With Cousin Field?'

'But could you doubt it?' He bowed.

'Easily.' She curled her lip. 'Justin, what is it you intend? You've some scheme, I know. I'll believe you mean no ill by Léonie.'

'It is always wise to believe the worst of me, Fanny.'

'I confess I don't understand you, Justin. 'Tis most provoking.'

'It must be,' he agreed.

She drew nearer, coaxing him.

'Justin, I do wish that you would tell me what is in your mind!'

He took a pinch of snuff, and shut the box with a snap.

'You must learn, my dear Fanny, to curb your curiosity. Suffice it that I am as a grandfather to that child. It should suffice.'

'It does, in part, but I do so want to know what scheme you have in your head!'

'I am sure you do, Fanny,' he said sympathetically.

'You are very horrid,' she pouted. A sudden smile came. 'Justin, what new whim is this? Léonie speaks of you as of a strict governor. 'Tis for ever "Monseigneur would not like me to do that," or "Do you think that Monseigneur would mind?" It's not like you, my dear.'

'An I knew less of the world's ways I should no doubt be a more lenient guardian,' he said. 'As it is, Fanny—' He shrugged, and drew his fan from one of his great pockets.

Léonie came back into the room, holding up her gown with one little hand.

'I could not find your handkerchief, madame,' she began, and then saw Avon's fan. A look of disapproval came over her face; there was a measure of reproof in the candid blue eyes. Avon smiled.

'You will grow accustomed to it, my child.'

'Never,' said Léonie positively. 'It does not please me at all.'

'But then,' murmured his Grace, 'I do not use it to please you.'

'*Pardon, Monseigneur!*' she answered contritely, and peeped at him through her lashes. The irresistible dimple quivered.

'She'll snare him,' thought Fanny. 'She is all too fascinating.'

Justin took his ward down to Avon by coach the following day, in company with Madam Field, on whose amiable vapidity Léonie looked with scant respect. Justin was quick to read her opinion of the lady, and when they arrived at Avon, took her aside.

'This,' said Léonie buoyantly, 'is a nice house. I like it.'

'I am rejoiced to hear you say so,' replied his Grace ironically.

Léonie looked round the panelled hall, with its carven chairs, its paintings, and tapestry, and the gallery above.

'Perhaps it is a little sombre,' she said. 'Who is this gentleman?' She went to a suit of armour, and regarded it with interest.

'It is not a gentleman at all, my infant. It is the armour one of my ancestors wore.'

'*Vraiment?*' She wandered away to the foot of the stairs, and inspected an ancient portrait. 'Is this another ancestor, this foolish woman?'

'A very famous one, my dear.'

'She has a stupid smile,' Léonie remarked. 'Why was she famous? What for?'

'Principally for her indiscretions. Which reminds me, child, that I want to speak to you.'

'Yes, Monseigneur?' Léonie was staring now at a shield which hung above the fireplace. '"*J'y serai*". That is French.'

'Your intelligence is remarkable. I wish to speak to you of my cousin, Madam Field.'

Léonie looked at him over her shoulder, grimacing.

'May I say what I think, Monseigneur?'

He sat down on the great carved table, swinging his eyeglass.

'To me, yes.'

'She is just a fool, Monseigneur.'

'Indubitably. And therefore, my infant, you must not only bear with her folly, but you must be at pains to cause her no trouble.'

Léonie seemed to debate within herself.

'Must I, Monseigneur?'

Justin looked at her, and recognized the naughty twinkle in her eye.

'Because I will it so, my child.'

The little straight nose wrinkled.

'Oh, *eh bien!*'

'I thought so,' remarked Avon beneath his breath. 'It is a promise, Léonie?'

'I do not think that I will promise,' Léonie temporized. 'I will *try*.' She came and stood before him. 'Monseigneur, it is very kind of you to bring me to this beautiful place, and to give me everything just as though I were not the sister of an innkeeper. Thank you very much.'

Justin looked at her for a moment, and his lips twisted in a curious smile.

'You think me a paragon of all the virtues, don't you, *ma fille?*'

'Oh no!' she answered candidly. 'I think it is only to me that you are kind. With some women you are not good at all. I cannot help knowing these things, Monseigneur!'

'And yet, child, you are content to remain with me?'

'But of course!' she answered in some surprise.

'You are full of trust,' he remarked.

'Of course,' she said again.

'This,' said Avon, looking at the rings on his hand, 'is a new experience. I wonder what Hugh would say?'

'Oh, he would pull down his mouth, so! and shake his head. I think he is sometimes not very wise.'

He laughed, and laid a hand on her shoulder.

'I never thought, *ma fille*, to take unto me a ward so much after mine own heart. I beg you will be careful not to shock Madam Field.'

'But with you I may say what I please?'

'You always do,' he replied.

'And you will stay here?'

'For the present. I have to attend to your education, you see. There are things you have to learn that I can best teach you.'

'What, *par example?*'

'To ride?'

'On a horse? *Vraiment?*'

'The prospect pleases you?'

'Yes, oh yes! And will you teach me to fight with a sword, Monseigneur?'

'It's not a ladylike occupation, *ma fille*.'

'But I do not always want to be a lady, Monseigneur! If I may learn to fight with a sword I will try very hard to learn the other silly things.'

He looked down at her, smiling.

'I believe you are trying to drive a bargain with me! What if I will not teach you to fence?'

She dimpled.

'Why, then I fear I shall be very stupid when you teach me to curtsy, Monseigneur. Oh, Monseigneur, say you will! Please say it quickly! Madame is coming.'

'You force my hand,' he bowed. 'I will teach you, imp.'

Madam Field entered the hall in time to see her charge execute a neat step-dance. She murmured expostulations.

13

The Education of Léonie

The Duke remained at Avon for over a month, during which time Léonie applied herself energetically to the task of becoming a lady. Madam Field's ideal of this estate was luckily not Avon's. He had no wish to see his ward sitting primly over her stitchery, which was just as well, perhaps, for after the first attempt Léonie declared that nothing would induce her to ply a needle. Madam Field was a little flustered by this defection, and by Léonie's taste for sword-play, but she was far too good-natured and indefinite to do more than murmur nervous remonstrances. She stood very much in awe of her cousin, and although she was by birth an Alastair she felt herself to be a wholly inferior creature. She had been happy enough with her husband, an obscure gentleman with a taste for farming, but she knew that in the eyes of her family she had disgraced herself by marrying him. This had not troubled her much while he lived, but now that he was dead, and she had returned to what had once been her own *milieu*, she was uncomfortably conscious of the step downwards that she had taken in her foolish youth. She was rather frightened of Avon, but she liked to live in his house. When she looked about her, at faded tapestries, at stretches of velvet lawns, at portraits innumerable, and crossed swords above the doorway, she remembered anew the glory of past Alastairs, and some almost forgotten chord stirred within her.

Léonie was enchanted by Avon Court, and demanded to know its history. She walked with Justin in the grounds, and learned how Hugo Alastair, coming with the Conqueror, settled there, and built himself a fair dwelling, which was destroyed in the troublous times of King Stephen; how it was built again by Sir Roderick Alastair; how he was given a barony, and prospered, and how the first Earl, under Queen Mary, pulled down the old building and erected the present house. And she learned of the bombardment that partially destroyed the West Wing, when Earl Henry held all for the King against the usurper Cromwell, and was rewarded for it at the Restoration by a dukedom. She saw the sword of the last Duke, the same that he had used in tragic '15, for King James III, and heard a small part of Justin's own adventures, ten years ago, for King Charles III. Justin touched but lightly on this period of his life; his work in that attempt, Léonie guessed, had been secret and tortuous, but she learned that the true King was Charles Edward Stuart, and learned to speak of the little war-like man on the throne as Elector George.

Her education at Justin's hands was a source of interest and amusement to her. Up in the long picture gallery he taught her to dance, with an eagle eye for the smallest fault, or the least hint of awkwardness in her bearing. Madam Field came to play on the spinet for them, and watched with an indulgent smile while they trod each stately measure. She reflected that she had never seen her unapproachable cousin so human, as with this laughing sprite of a girl. They danced the minuet, and the long lines of ancestors gazed down upon them indulgently.

Avon made Léonie practise her curtsy, and made her combine her pretty roguishness with some of the haughtiness that characterized my Lady Fanny. He showed her how to extend her hand for a man to kiss, how to use her fan, and how to place her patches. He would walk with her in the pleasaunce, teaching every rule of deportment until she was word perfect. He insisted that she should cultivate certain queenliness of bearing. She soon learned, and would rehearse her newest lesson before him, enjoying herself hugely, radiant if she earned a word of praise.

She could already ride, but astride only. She was disgusted with the side-saddle, and for a while rebelled against it. For the space of two days her will held fast against Avon's, but his frigid politeness disarmed her, and on the third day she came to him with head hanging, and faltered:

'I am sorry, Monseigneur. I—I will ride as you wish.'

So they rode together in the grounds until she had mastered this new art, and then they went out over the countryside, and those who saw the Duke beside this beautiful girl cast knowing glances at each other, and shook their heads wisely, for they had seen other beautiful girls with Avon.

Bit by bit the Court, so long bereft of a mistress, began to wear a more cheerful air. Léonie's glad young spirit pervaded it; she flung back heavy curtains, and consigned ponderous screens to the lumber room. Windows were opened to let in the wintry sun, and bit by bit the oppressive solemnity of the place disappeared. Léonie would have none of the stern neatness that was wont to reign there. She tumbled prim cushions, pushed chairs out of place, and left books lying on odd tables, caring nothing for Madam Field's shocked protests. Justin permitted her to do as she pleased; it amused him to watch her gyrations, and he liked to hear her give orders to his expression-less lackeys. Clearly she had the habit of command: unusual she might be, but never did she exhibit any lack of breeding.

Her lessons were soon put to the test. On one occasion he said suddenly:

'We will suppose, Léonie, that I am the Duchess of Queensbury, and that you have just been presented to me. Show me how you would curtsy.'

'But you cannot be a duchess, Monseigneur,' she objected. 'That is ridiculous. You don't *look* like a duchess! Let us pretend you are the Duke of Queensbury.'

'The Duchess. Show me the curtsy.'

Léonie sank down and down.

'Like this: low, but not so low as to the Queen. This is a very good curtsy I am doing, *n'est-ce pas?*'

'It is to be hoped you would not talk all the time,' said his Grace. 'Spread out your skirts, and do not hold your fan like that. Show me again.'

Léonie obeyed meekly.

'It is very difficult to remember everything,' she complained. 'Now let us play at piquet, Monseigneur.'

'Presently. Curtsy now to—Mr Davenant.'

She swept her skirts right regally, and with head held high extended one small hand. Avon smiled.

'Hugh is like to be amazed,' he remarked. 'It's very well, *ma fille*. Curtsy now to me.'

At that she sank down with bent head, and raised his hand to her lips.

'No, my child.'

She rose.

'That is the way I do it, Monseigneur. I like it.'

'It is incorrect. Again, and the proper depth. You curtsied then as to the King. I am but an ordinary mortal, remember.'

Léonie searched in her mind for a fitting retort.

'Lawks!' she said vaguely.

His Grace stiffened, but his lips twitched.

'I—beg—your—pardon?'

'I said lawks,' said Léonie demurely.

'I heard you.' His Graces's voice was cold.

'Rachel said it,' Léonie ventured, peeping up at him. 'She is Lady Fanny's maid, you know. You do not like it?'

'I do not. I should be glad if you would refrain from modelling your conversation on that of Lady Fanny's maid.'

'Yes, Monseigneur. Please, what does it mean?'

'I have not the slightest idea. It is a vulgarity. There are many sins, *ma belle*, but only one that is unforgivable. That is vulgarity.'

'I won't say it again,' promised Léonie. 'I will say instead—*tiens*, what is it?—Tare an' ouns!'

'I beg you will do no such thing, *ma fille*. If you must indulge in forceful expressions confine them to 'pon rep, or merely Lud!'

'Lud? Yes, that is a pretty one. I like it. I like Lawks best, though. Monseigneur is not angry?'

'I am never angry,' said Avon.

At other times he fenced with her, and this she enjoyed most of all. She donned shirt and breeches for the pastime, and displayed no little aptitude for the game. She had a quick eye and a supple waist, and she very soon mastered the rudiments of this manly art. The Duke was one of the first swordsmen of the day, but this in no wise discomposed Léonie. He taught her to fence in the Italian manner, and showed her many subtle passes which he had learned abroad. She experimented with one of them, and since his Grace's guard, at that moment, was lax, broke through. The button of her foil came to rest below his left shoulder.

'*Touché*,' said Avon. 'That was rather better, infant.'

Léonie danced in her excitement.

'Monseigneur, I have killed you! You are dead! you are dead!'

'You display an unseemly joy,' he remarked. 'I had no notion you were so bloodthirsty.'

'But it was so clever of me!' she cried. 'Was it not, Monseigneur?'

'Not at all,' he said crushingly. 'My guard was weak.'

Her mouth dropped.

'Oh, you let me do it!'

His Grace relented.

'No, you broke through, *ma fille*.'

Sometimes he talked to her of personalities of the day, explaining who this was, and who that, and how they were related.

'There is March,' he said, 'who will be Duke of Queensbury. You have heard me speak of him. There is Hamilton, who is famous for his wife. She was one of the Miss Gunnings—beauties, my dear, who set London by the ears not so many years ago. Maria Gunning married Coventry. If you want wit, there is Mr Selwyn, who has quite an inimitable way with him: he would hate to be forgotten. He lives in Arlington Street, child, and wherever you go you may be sure of meeting him. In Bath I believe Nash still reigns. A parvenu, infant, but a man of some genius. Bath is his kingdom. One day I will take you there. Then we have the Cavendish–Devonshire, my dear; and the Seymours, and my Lord Chesterfield, whom you will know by his wit, and his dark eyebrows. Whom else? There is my Lord of Bath, and the Bentincks, and his Grace of Newcastle, of some fame. If you want the Arts you have the tedious Johnson: a large man, with a larger head. He is not worth your consideration. He lacks polish. There is Colley Cibber, one of our poets, Mr Sheridan, who writes plays for us, and Mr Garrick, who acts them; and a score of others. In painting we have Sir Joshua Reynolds, who shall paint you, perhaps, and a great many others whose names elude me.'

Léonie nodded.

'Monseigneur, you must write their names down for me. Then I shall remember.'

'*Bien.* We come now to your own country. Of the Blood Royal we have the Prince de Condé, who is now, as I reckon, twenty years of age–*à peu près.* There is the Comte d'Eu, son of the Duc de Maine, one of the bastards, and the Duc de Penthièvre, son of yet another bastard. Let me see. Of the nobility there is M. de Richelieu, the model of true courtesy, and the Duc de Noailles, famed for the battle of Dettingen, which he lost. Then we have the brothers Lorraine-Brionne, and the Prince d'Armagnac. My memory fails me. Ah yes, there is M. de Belle-Isle, who is the grandson of the great Fouquet. He is an old man now. *Tiens*, almost I had forgot the estimable Chavignard–Comte de Chavigny, child–a friend of mine. I might go on for ever, but I will not.'

'And there is Madame de Pompadour, is there not, Monseigneur?'

'I spoke of the nobility, *ma fille*,' said his Grave gently. 'We do not count the cocotte amongst them. La Pompadour is a beauty of no birth, and wit–a little. My ward will not trouble her head with any such.'

'No, Monseigneur,' said Léonie abashed. 'Please tell me some more.'

'You are insatiable. Well, let us essay. D'Anvau you have seen. A little man, with a love of scandal. De Salmy you have also seen. He is tall and indolent, and hath somewhat of a reputation for sword-play. Lavoulère comes of old stock, and doubtless has his virtues even though they have escaped my notice. Machérand has a wife who squints. I need say no more. Château-Mornay will amuse you for half an hour, no longer. Madame de Marguéry's salons are world-famous. Florimond de Chantourelle is like some insect. Possibly a wasp, since he is always clad in bright colours, and always plagues one.'

'And M. de Saint-Vire'

'My very dear friend Saint-Vire. Of course. One day, infant, I will tell you all about the so dear Comte. But not to-day. I say only this, my child–you will beware of Saint-Vire. It is understood?'

'Yes, Monseigneur, but why?'

'That also I will tell you one day,' said his Grace calmly.

14

When Avon left the country Léonie was at first disconsolate. Madam Field was not an exhilarating companion, as her mind ran on illness and death, and the froward ways of the younger generation. Fortunately the weather became warmer, and Léonie was able to escape from the lady into the park, well-knowing that Madam was not fond of any form of exercise.

When she rode out Léonie was supposed to have a groom in attendance, but she very often dispensed with this formality, and explored the countryside alone, revelling in her freedom.

Some seven miles from Avon Court lay Merivale Place, the estate of my Lord Merivale, and his beautiful wife, Jennifer. My lord had grown indolent of late years, and my lady, for two short seasons London's toast, had no love for town life. Nearly all the year they lived in Hampshire, but sometimes they spent the winter in Bath, and occasionally, my lord being smitten with a longing for the friends of his youth, they journeyed to town. More often my lord went alone on these expeditions, but he was never away for long.

It was not many weeks before Léonie rode out in the direction of the Place. The woods that lay about the old white house lured her, and she rode into them, looking around with great interest.

The trees were sprouting new leaves, and here and there early spring flowers peeped up between the blades of grass. Léonie picked her way through the undergrowth, delighting in the wood's beauty, until she came to where a stream bubbled and sang over the rounded stones on its bed. Beside this stream, on a fallen tree-trunk, a dark lady was seated, with a baby playing on the rug at her feet. A small boy, in a very muddied coat, was fishing hopefully in the stream.

Léonie reined in short, guiltily aware of trespass. The youthful fisherman saw her first, and called to the lady on the tree-trunk.

'Look, mamma!'

The lady looked in the direction of his pointing finger, and raised her brows in quick surprise.

'I am very sorry,' Léonie stammered. 'The wood was so pretty—I will go.'

The lady rose, and went forward across the strip of grass that separated them.

'It's very well, madam. Why should you go?' Then she saw that the little face beneath the hat's big brim was that of a child, and she smiled. 'Will you not dismount, my dear, and bear me company a while?'

The wistful, uncertain look went out of Léonie's eyes. She dimpled, nodding.

'S'il vous plaît, madame.'

'You're French? Are you staying here?' inquired the lady.

Léonie kicked her foot free of the stirrup, and slid to the ground.

'But yes, I am staying at Avon. I am the—bah, I have forgotten the word!—the—ward of Monseigneur le Duc.'

A shadow crossed the lady's face. She made a movement as though to stand between Léonie and the children. Léonie's chin went up.

'I am not anything else, madame, *je vous assure*. I am in the charge of Madame Field, the cousin of Monseigneur. It is better that I go, yes?'

'I crave your pardon, my dear. I beg that you will stay. I am Lady Merivale.'

'I thought you were,' confided Léonie. 'Lady Fanny told me of you.'

'Fanny?' Jennifer's brow cleared. 'You know her?'

'I have been with her two weeks, when I came from Paris. Monseigneur thought it would not be *convenable* for me to be with him until he had found a lady suitable to be my *gouvernante*, you see.'

Jennifer, in the past, had had experience of his Grace's ideas of propriety, and thus she did not see at all, but she was too polite to say so. She and Léonie sat down on the tree-trunk while the small boy stared round-eyed.

'No one likes Monseigneur, I find,' Léonie remarked. 'Just a few perhaps. Lady Fanny, and M. Davenant, and me, of course.'

'Oh, you like him, then?' Jennifer looked at her wonderingly.

'He is so good to me, you understand,' explained Léonie. 'That is your little son?'

'Yes, that is John. Come and make your bow, John.'

John obeyed, and ventured a remark:

'Your hair is quite short, madam.'

Léonie pulled off her hat.

'But how pretty!' exclaimed Jennifer. 'Why did you cut it?'

Léonie hesitated.

'Madame, please will you not ask me? I am not allowed to tell people. Lady Fanny said I must not.'

'I hope 'twas not an illness?' said Jennifer, with an anxious eye to her children.

'Oh no!' Léonie assured her. Again she hesitated. 'Monseigneur did not say I was not tell. It was only Lady Fanny, and she is not always very wise, do you think? And I do not suppose that she would want me not to tell you, for you were at the convent with her, *n'est-ce pas*? I have only just begun to be a girl, you see, madame.'

Jennifer was startled.

'I beg your pardon, my dear?'

'Since I was twelve I have always been a boy. Then Monseigneur found me, and I was his page. And—and then he discovered that I was not a boy at all, and he made me his daughter. I did not like it at first, and these petticoats still bother me, but in some ways it is very pleasant. I have so many things all my own, and I am a lady now.'

Jennifer's eyes grew soft. She patted Léonie's hand.

'You quaint child! For how long do you think to stay at Avon?'

'I do not quite know, madame. It is as Monseigneur wills. And I have to learn so many things. Lady Fanny is to present me, I think. It is nice of her, is it not?'

'Prodigious amiable,' Jennifer agreed. 'Tell me your name, my dear.'

'I am Léonie de Bonnard, madame.'

'And your parents made the—the Duke your guardian?'

'N-no. They have been dead for many years, you see. Monseigneur did it all himself.' Léonie glanced down at the babe. 'Is this also your son, madame?'

'Yes, child, this is Geoffrey Molyneux Merivale. Is he not beautiful?'

'Very,' said Léonie politely. 'I do not know babies very well.' She rose, and picked up her plumed hat. 'I must go back, madame. Madame Field will have become agitated.' She smiled mischievously. 'She is very like a hen, you know.'

Jennifer laughed.

'But you'll come again? Come to the house one day, and I will present my husband.'

'Yes, if you please, madame. I should like to come. *Au revoir, Jean; au revoir, bébé*!'

The baby gurgled, and waved an aimless hand. Léonie hoisted herself into the saddle.

'One does not know what to say to a baby,' she remarked. 'He is very nice, of course,' she added. She bowed, hat in hand, and, turning, made her way back along the path down which she had come, to the road.

Jennifer picked up the baby, and, calling to John to follow, went through the wood and across the gardens to the house. She relinquished the children to their nurse, and went in search of her husband.

She found him in the library, turning over his accounts, a big, loose-limbed man, with humorous grey eyes, and a firm-lipped mouth. He held out his hand.

'Faith, Jenny, you grow more lovely each time I look upon you,' he said.

She laughed, and went to sit on the arm of his chair.

'Fanny thinks us unfashionable, Anthony.'

'Oh, Fanny—! She's fond enough of Marling at heart.'

'Very fond of him, Anthony, but she is modish withal, and likes other men to whisper pretty things in her ear. I fear that I shall never have the taste for town ways.'

'My love, if I find "other men" whispering in your ear—'

'My lord!'

'My lady?'

'You are monstrous ungallant, sir! As if they—as if I would!'

His hold about her tightened.

'You might be the rage of town, Jenny, an you would.'

'Oh, is that your will, my lord?' she teased. 'Now I know that you are disappointed in your wife. I thank you, sir!' She slipped from him, and swept him a mock curtsy.

My lord jumped up and caught her.

'Rogue, I am the happiest man on earth.'

'My felicitations, sir. Anthony, you have had no word from Edward, have you?'

'From Edward? Nay, why should I?'

'I met a girl to-day in the woods who has stayed with the Marlings. I wondered whether he had written to tell you.'

'A girl? Here? Who was she?'

'You'll be surprised, my lord. She is a very babe, and—and she says she is the Duke's ward.'

'Alastair?' Merivale's brow wrinkled. 'What new whim can that be?'

'I could not ask, of course. But is it not strange that—that man—should adopt her?'

'Perchance he is a reformed character, my love.'

She shivered.

'He could never be that. I feel so sorry for this child—in his power. I asked her to come and see me one day. Was it right of me?'

He frowned.

'I'll have no dealings with Alastair, Jenny. I am not like to forget that his Grace saw fit to abduct my wife.'

'I wasn't your wife then,' she protested. 'And—and this child—this Léonie—is not like that at all. I should be so pleased if you would let her come.'

He made her a magnificent leg.

'My lady, you are mistress in your own house,' he said.

So it was that when next Léonie rode over to Merivale she was received gladly both by Jennifer and her lord. She was rather shy at first, but her nervousness fled before Merivale's smile. Over a dish of Bohea she made gay conversation, and presently turned to her host.

'I wanted to meet you, milor',' she said cheerfully. 'I have heard much—oh, much—about you!'

Merivale sat bolt upright.

'Who in the world—?' he began uneasily.

'Lady Fanny, and Monseigneur, a little. Tell me, m'sieur, did you really stop Lord Harding's coach—?'

'For a wager, child, for a wager!'

She laughed.

'Aha, I knew. And he was very angry, was he not? And it had to be kept secret, because in—in dip-lo-mat-ic circles it—'

'For heaven's sake, child!'

'And *now* you are called The Highwayman!'

'No, no, only to my intimates!'

Jennifer shook her head at him.

'Oh, my lord! Go on, Léonie. Tell me some more. The wretch has grossly deceived me, I'll have you know.'

'Mademoiselle,' said Merivale, wiping his heated brow, 'have pity!'

'But tell me,' she insisted. 'Was it not very exciting to be a highwayman for one night?'

'Very,' he said gravely. 'But not at all respectable.'

'No,' she agreed. 'One does not always want to be respectable, I think. Me, I am a great trial to everybody, because I am not respectable at all. It seems that a lady may do many bad things and still be respectable, but if one speaks of such things as breeches then one is unladylike. I find it very hard.'

His eyes danced. He tried to suppress a laugh, and failed.

'Faith, you must come often to see us, mademoiselle! 'Tis not often we meet such a charming little lady.'

'You must come to see me next,' she answered. 'That is right, is it not?'

'I am afraid—' began Jennifer uncomfortably.

'His Grace and I do not visit,' ended Merivale.

Léonie flung up her hands.

'Oh, *parbleu*! Every one I meet is the same! It does not surprise me that sometimes Monseigneur is wicked when everybody is so unkind to him.'

'His Grace has a way of making it difficult for one to be—er—kind to him,' said Merivale grimly.

'M'sieur,' answered Léonie with great dignity, 'it is not wise to speak thus of Monseigneur to me. He is the only person in the whole world who cares what happens to me. So you see I will not listen to people who try to warn me against him. It makes something inside me get all hot and angry.'

'Mademoiselle,' said Merivale, 'I crave your pardon.'

'I thank you, m'sieur,' she said gravely.

She came often to Merivale after that, and once dined there with Madam Field, who had no knowledge of the rift between Avon and Merivale.

A fortnight passed, bringing no word from Justin, but at the end of it a travelling coach, loaded with baggage arrived at Merivale, and a tall young exquisite leaped out. He was admitted into the house and met by Jennifer, who laughed when she saw him, and held out both her hands.

'Why, Rupert! Have you come to stay?'

He kissed her hands, and then her cheek.

'Devil take it, Jenny, you're too lovely, 'pon my soul you are! Lord, here's Anthony! I wonder if he saw?'

Merivale gripped his hand.

'One of these days, Rupert, I'll teach you a lesson,' he threatened. 'What's to do? You've brought enough baggage for three men.'

'Baggage? Nonsense, man! Why, there's only a few things there, I give you my word! One must dress, y'know, one must dress. Anthony, what's this fandangle about Justin? Fanny's devilish mysterious, but the tale's all over town that he's adopted a girl! Stap me, but that's—' He broke off, remembering Jennifer's presence. 'I've come down to see for myself. God knows where Justin is! I don't.' He looked sharply at Merivale, consternation in his face. 'He's not at Avon, is he?'

'Calm yourself,' soothed Merivale. 'He is not here.'

'Praise the Lord for that. Who is the girl?'

'A pretty child,' Merivale answered guardedly.

'Ay, I'd have guessed that. Justin had ever a nice taste in—' Again he stopped. 'Thunder an' turf, I beg your pardon, Jenny! I'd forgot! Demmed careless of me!' He looked ruefully at Merivale. 'I must always be saying the wrong thing, Tony. It's this rattle-pate of mine, and what with the bottle—well, well!'

Merivale led him into the library, where a lackey came to them presently, bringing wine. Rupert settled his long length in a chair and drank deeply.

'Truth to tell, Tony,' he said confidently, 'I'm more at ease when the ladies are not present. My tongue runs away with me, burn it! Not but what Jenny's a devilish fine woman,' he added hastily. 'The wonder is that you admit me into your house. When one thinks 'twas my brother ran off with Jenny—' He shook his head comically.

'You're always welcome,' smiled Merivale. 'I've no fear that you'll seek to abduct Jenny.'

'Lord, no! I'm not saying that I haven't trifled somewhat with women now and then—one has to, y'know. Honour of the name, my boy—but I've no real taste for 'em, Tony, none at all.' He refilled his glass. ''Tis a queer thing, when you come to think on't. Here am I, an Alastair, with never an intrigue to my name. I feel it sometimes,' he sighed, ''tis as though I were no true Alastair. Why, there's never been one of us—'

'I'd not crave the vice, Rupert,' said Merivale dryly.

'Oh, I don't know! There's Justin, now, and wherever he is there is sure to be some wench. I'm not saying aught against him, mind you, but we don't love one another overmuch. I'll say one thing for him, though: he's not mean. I daresay you'll not believe me, Tony, but since he came into that fortune of his I've not been in a sponging house once.' He looked up with some pride. 'Not once.'

'It's marvellous,' Merivale agreed. 'And have you really come down to see Léonie?'

'Is that her name? Ay, what else?'

The grey eyes began to twinkle.

'I thought mayhap 'twas to see myself and Jennifer?'

'Oh, of course, of course!' Rupert assured him, sitting up hurriedly. He saw the twinkle, and sank back again. 'Devil take you, Tony, you're laughing at me! Ay, I'd a mind to see Justin's latest. Is she alone at the Court?'

'No, with a cousin of yours. Madam Field.'

'What, not old cousin Harriet? Lud, what will Justin be at next? He's got his eye fixed to the proprieties this time, eh?'

'I believe it's true that she is no more than his ward.'

Rupert cocked one incredulous eyebrow.

'For which reason, my dear fellow, you'll either treat her with becoming respect, or journey back to town.'

'But, Tony—Damn it, you know Justin!'

'I wonder if any of us do? I know this child.'

'I'll see for myself,' said Rupert. He chuckled. 'I'd give something to see Justin's face when he finds I've been poaching on his land! Not that I want to anger him; he's devilish unpleasant when he's crossed.' He paused, frowning prodigiously. 'You know, Tony, I often wonder what he feels about me. He's fond of Fanny, I'll swear. He was devilish strict with her in the old days—never think it, would you?—But me—He gives me a handsome allowance these days, yet it's seldom he has a friendly word for me.'

'Do you want a friendly word from him?' inquired Merivale, smoothing a wrinkle from his satin sleeve.

'Oh well! He's my brother, y'know! Queer part of it is he used to take precious good care what happened to me when I was a youngster. He was always a damned smooth-tongued icicle, of course. I don't mind telling you, Tony, I'm still something nervous of him.'

'I don't pretend to understand him, Rupert. I used to think there was good in him somewhere. The child—Léonie—worships him. Have a care to what you say in her presence!'

'My dear fellow, it's not likely I'd say aught—'

'It's more than likely,' retorted Merivale. 'Addlepated young scamp!'

'Now stap me, that's not fair!' cried Rupert, heaving himself up. 'Scamp, did you say? What about the High Toby, my boy, eh?'

Merivale flung up his hand.

'*Touché*! For the love of heaven, Rupert, don't spread that tale about town!'

Rupert smoothed his ruffled hair, and managed to assume an expression of vast superiority.

'Oh, I'm not such a fool as you think, Tony, I assure you!'

'Well, thank God for that!' answered Merivale.

15

Rupert rode over to the Court the very next day and heralded his arrival by a prolonged peal on the door bell, accompanied by several resounding knocks. Léonie was seated by the fire in the hall, and the commotion startled her a little. When the butler came to admit the visitor she rose, and peeped round the corner of the screen to see who it was. A gay, boisterous voice met her ears.

'Hey, Johnson! Not dead yet? Where's my cousin?'

'Oh, it's you, my lord?' said the old man. ''Tis no one else would make such a thundering on the door, to be sure. Madam's within.'

Rupert strode past him into the hall. At sight of Léonie regarding him in some trepidity from the fireplace he swept off his hat and bowed.

'Your pardon, mamzelle. Thunder an' turf, what's come over the place?' He cast an astonished glance about him. 'It's been like a tomb for centuries, and now—!'

'It's my Lord Rupert, madam,' explained Johnson, apologetically. He frowned severely at his young master. 'Ye can't stay here, my lord. This is his Grace's ward. Mistress Léonie de Bonnard.'

'I'm at Merivale, old sobersides,' said the graceless Rupert. 'If you say I'm to go, mamzelle, I will.'

Léonie's nose wrinkled in perplexity.

'Rupert? Oh, you are the brother of Monseigneur!'

'Mon—? Oh, ay, ay! That's it!'

Léonie skipped forward.

'I am very pleased to see you,' she said politely. 'Now I curtsy and you kiss my hand, *n'est-ce pas?*'

Rupert stared.

'Ay, but—'

'*Eh bien!*' Léonie sank, and rose, and held out her small hand. Rupert kissed it punctiliously.

'I never before was told by a lady to kiss her hand,' he remarked.

'I should not have said it?' she asked anxiously. '*Voyons*, these things are very difficult to learn! Where is Monseigneur, please?'

'Lord, I don't know, my dear! Ours is no united household, I give you my word!'

Léonie looked at him gravely.

'You are the young Rupert. I know. I have heard tell of you.'

'Not a might of good, I'll be bound. I'm the scapegrace of the family.'

'Oh no! I have heard people speak of you in Paris, and I think they like you very much.'

'Do they, by Gad? Do you come from Paris, my dear?'

She nodded.

'I was Monseigneur's pa—' She clasped her hands over her mouth, and her eyes danced.

Rupert was greatly intrigued. He cast a shrewd glance at her short curls. 'Pa—?'

'I must not say. Please do not ask me!'

'You were never his *page*?'

Léonie stared down at her toes.

'Here's a romance!' said Rupert, delighted. 'His page, by all that's marvellous!'

'You must not tell!' she said earnestly. 'Promise!'

'Mum as a corpse, my dear!' he answered promptly. 'I never thought to stumble on such a fairy tale! What are you doing cooped up here?'

'I am learning to be a lady, milor'.'

'Milor' be damned, saving your presence! My name's Rupert.'

'Is it *convenable* for me to call you that?' she inquired. 'I do not know these things, you see.'

'*Convenable*, my dear? I pledge you my word it is! Are you not my brother's ward?'

'Y-es.'

'*Eh bien*, then, as you'd say yourself! Fiend seize it, here's my cousin!'

Madam Field came down the stairs, peering out of her short-sighted eyes.

'Well, to be sure! And is it indeed you, Rupert?' she exclaimed.

Rupert went forward to meet her.

'Ay, cousin, it's myself. I hope I see you in your customary good health?'

'Save for a trifling touch of the gout. Léonie! You here?'

'I presented myself, cousin. I believe I am something in the nature of an uncle to her.'

'An uncle? Oh no, Rupert, surely not!'

'I will not have you for an uncle,' said Léonie with her nose in the air. 'You are not enough respectable.'

'My love!'

Rupert burst out laughing.

'Faith, I'll none of you for a niece, child. You are too saucy.'

'Oh no, Rupert!' Madam assured him. 'Indeed, she is very good!' She looked at him doubtfully. 'But Rupert, do you think you should be here?'

'Turning me from mine own roof, cousin?'

'I protest, I did not mean—'

'I am come to make the acquaintance of my brother's ward, cousin, as is fitting.' His voice was convincing. Madam's brow cleared.

'If you say so, Rupert—Pray where are you staying?'

'At Merivale, cousin, by night, but here, an it please you, by day.'

'Does—does Justin know?' ventured Madam.

'Do you suggest that Alastair would object to my presence, cousin?' demanded Rupert in righteous indignation.

'Oh no, indeed! You misunderstood me! I make no doubt 'tis monstrous dull for Léonie to have only me to bear her company. Perhaps you will sometimes ride out with her? The child will leave her groom at home, which is vastly improper, as I have told her many times.'

'I'll ride with her all day!' promised Rupert jovially. 'That is if she will have me.'

'I should like it, I think,' said Léonie. 'I have never met anyone *tout comme vous*.'

'If it comes to that,' said Rupert, 'I've never met a girl like you.'

Madam Field sighed, and shook her head.

'I fear she will never become quite as I should wish,' she said sadly.

'She'll be the rage of town,' Rupert prophesied. 'Will you walk with me to the stables, Léonie?'

'I will get a cloak,' she nodded, and ran lightly upstairs.

When she returned Madam Field had delivered a short lecture to Rupert, and extracted a promise from him that he would behave with suitable decorum towards Léonie.

As soon as they had left the house, Léonie, dancing along beside Rupert with little excited steps, looked up at him with her confiding smile.

'I have thought of a plan,' she announced. 'Suddenly it came to me! Will you please fight me with a sword?'

'Will I do what?' ejaculated Rupert, stopping short.

She stamped an impatient foot.

'Fight with swords! Fence!'

'Thunder an' turf, what next? Ay, I'll fence with you, rogue.'

'Thank you *very* much! You see, Monseigneur began to teach me, but then he went away, and Madam Field does not fence at all. I asked her.'

'You should ask Anthony Merivale to teach you, my dear. Justin's good, I'll admit, but Anthony nearly worsted him once.'

'Aha! I knew there was a mystery! Tell me, did Monseigneur intrigue himself with miladi Jennifer?'

'Ran off with her in Anthony's teeth, my dear!'

'*Vraiment*? She would not like that, I think.'

'Lord no! But what woman would?'

'I should not mind,' said Léonie calmly. 'But Lady Merivale—ah, that is another thing! Was she married then?'

'Devil a bit. Justin's not often in an affair with a married woman. He wanted to marry her.'

'It would not have done,' she said wisely. 'She would have wearied him. Milor' then came to the rescue?'

'Ay, and tried to fight Justin *à outrance*. Marling stopped it. Never was there such a scene! They don't speak now, y'know. Damned awkward, seeing that we've known Merivale since we were children. Marling don't love Justin overmuch either.'

'Oh!' Léonie was scornful. 'He is a kind man, that one, but of a dullness!'

'Ay, but 'tis enough to make a man sober to be wedded to Fanny, I can tell you.'

'I think your family is very strange,' she remarked. 'Everyone in it hates everyone else. Oh no, Lady Fanny sometimes loves Monseigneur!'

'Well, you see, we'd a spitfire for mother,' Rupert explained. 'And the old Duke was no saint, the Lord knows! 'Tis no wonder we grew up like snarling dogs.'

They had arrived at the stables, where Rupert's horse had been taken. He spoke to one of the grooms, hailing him good-naturedly, and went to inspect the few horses that were there. By the time they returned to the house he and Léonie might have know one another for years. Rupert was delighted with his brother's ward, and had already decided to remain some time at Merivale. A girl who was as outspoken as a boy, and who evidently did not expect him to make love to her, was something quite new to Rupert. A month ago he had danced attendance on Mistress Julia Falkner; he was weary of the pastime, and had determined to eschew feminine company. But Léonie, with her friendliness and her quaint ways, would be a pleasant amusement, he thought. She was very young, too, and his loves had hitherto been older than himself. He promised himself a few weeks' gaiety unspoiled by any fear that he would be entrapped into marriage.

He came again next day, and was informed by the lackey who admitted him that Léonie awaited him in the picture gallery. Thither went he, and found her wandering round in coat and breeches, inspecting his ancestors.

'By Gad!' he exclaimed. 'You—you rogue!'

She turned quickly, and laid a finger in her lips.

'Where is madame?'

'Cousin Harriet? I've not seen her. Léonie, you should always wear those clothes. They suit you, 'pon my soul they do!'

'I think so too,' she sighed. 'But if you tell madame she will be agitated, and she will say that it is unmaidenly. I brought the foils up.'

'Oh, we're to fence, are we, Amazon?'

'You said you would!'

'As you will, as you will! Damme, I'd like to see Julia's face an she knew!' He chuckled impishly.

She nodded. He had told her of Mistress Falkner already.

'I do not suppose that she would like me,' she observed. She swept a hand round, indicating the many portraits. 'There are a great number of people in your family, are there not? This one is nice. He is like Monseigneur, a little.'

'Lord, child, that's old Hugo Alastair! Devilish rake-helly fellow! They're a damned gloomy lot, all of 'em, and everyone has a sneer on his face for all the world like Justin himself. Come and look at this one; it's my respected parent.'

Léonie looked up into Rudolph Alastair's dissipated countenance.

'He does not please me at all,' she said severely.

'Never pleased anyone, my dear. Here's her Grace. She was French like yourself. Lord, did you ever see such a mouth? Fascinating, y'know, but a temper like the fiend.'

Léonie moved on to where the last picture hung. An awed look came into her eyes.

'And this is—Monseigneur.'

'It was done a year ago. Good, eh?'

The hazel eyes under their drooping lids looked mockingly down on them.

'Yes, it is good,' said Léonie. 'He does not always smile just so. I think he was not in a nice humour when that was painted.'

'Fiendish, ain't he? Striking, of course, but Lord, what a damned mask of a face! Never trust him, child, he's a devil.'

The swift colour flooded Léonie's cheeks.

'He is not. It is you who are a gr-r-reat stupid!'

'But it's true, my dear. I tell you he's Satan himself. Damme, I ought to know!' He turned just in time to see Léonie seize one of the foils. 'Here! What will you be at—?' He got no further, but leaped with more speed than dignity behind a chair, for Léonie, her eyes flaming, was bearing down upon him with the rapier poised in a distinctly alarming manner. Rupert hoisted the chair, and held it to keep Léonie at arm's length, a look of comical dismay on his face. Then, as Léonie lunged across the chair he took to his heels and fled down the gallery in laughing panic, Léonie close behind. She drove him into a corner, where he had perforce to stay, using his chair as a protection.

'No, no! Léonie, I say! Hey, you nearly had me! The button'll come off for a certainty! Devil take it, it's monstrous! Put it down, you wild-cat! Put it down!'

The wrath died out of Léonie's face. She lowered the foil.

'I wanted to kill you,' she said calmly. 'I *will* if you say things to me like that of Monseigneur. Come out. You are cowardly!'

'I like that!' Rupert put the chair down cautiously. 'Put that damned foil down, and I'll come.'

Léonie looked at him, and suddenly began to laugh. Rupert came out of the corner, smoothing his ruffled hair.

'You looked so very funny!' gasped Léonie.

Rupert eyed her gloomily. Words failed him.

'I would like to do it again, just to see you run!'

Rupert edged away. A grin dawned.

'For the Lord's sake don't!' he begged.

'No, I won't,' Léonie said obligingly. 'But you are not to say those things—'

'Never again! I swear I won't! Justin's a saint!'

'We will fence now, and not talk any more,' said Léonie regally. 'I am sorry I frightened you.'

'Pooh!' said Rupert loftily.

Her eyes twinkled.

'You *were* frightened! I saw your face. It was so fun—'

'That'll do,' said Rupert. 'I was taken unawares.'

'Yes, that was not well done of me,' she said. 'I am sorry, but you understand I have a quick temper.'

'Yes, I understand that,' grimaced Rupert.

'It is very sad, *n'est-ce pas*? But I am truly sorry.'

He became her slave from that moment.

16

The Coming of the Comte de Saint-Vire

The days sped past, and still the Duke did not come. Rupert and Léonie rode, fenced, and quarrelled together like two children, while, from afar, the Merivales watched, smiling.

'My dear,' said his lordship, 'she reminds me strangely of someone, but who it is I cannot for the life of me make out.'

'I don't think I have ever seen anyone like her,' Jennifer answered. 'My lord, I have just thought that 'twould be a pretty thing if she married Rupert.'

'Oh, no!' he said quickly. 'She is a babe, for sure, but, faith, she's too old for Rupert!'

'Or not old enough. All women are older than their husbands, Anthony.'

'I protest I am a staid middle-aged man!'

She touched his cheek.

'You are just a boy. I am older by far.'

He was puzzled, and a little worried.

'I like it so,' she said.

Meanwhile at Avon Léonie and her swain made merry together. Rupert taught Léonie to fish, and they spent delightful days by the stream and returned at dusk, tired and wet, and unbelievably dirty. Rupert treated Léonie as a boy, which pleased her, and he told her endless tales of Society which also pleased her. But most of all she liked him to remember scraps of recollection of his brother. To these she would listen for hours at a time, eyes sparkling, and lips parted to drink in every word.

'He is—he is grand *seigneur!*' she said once, proudly.

'Oh, ay, every inch of him! I'll say that. He'll count no cost, either. He's devilish clever, too.' Rupert shook his head wisely. 'Sometimes I think there's nothing he don't know. God knows how he finds things out, but he does. All pose, of course, but it's damned awkward, I give you my word. You can't keep a thing secret from him. And he always comes on you when you least expect him—or want him. Oh, he's cunning, devilish cunning.'

'I think you do like him a little,' Léonie said shrewdly.

'Devil a bit. Oh, he can be pleasant enough, but it's seldom he is! One's proud of him, y'know, but he's queer.'

'I wish he would come back,' sighed Léonie.

Two days later Merivale, on his way to Avon village, met them, careering wildly over the country. They reined in when they saw him and came to him. Léonie was flushed and panting, Rupert was sulky.

'He is a great stupid, this Rupert,' Léonie announced.

'She has led me a fine dance this day,' Rupert complained.

'I do not want you with me at all,' said Léonie, nose in air.

Merivale smiled upon their quarrel.

'My lady said a while ago that I was a boy, but 'fore Gad you make me feel a greybeard,' he said. 'Farewell to ye both!' He rode on to the village, and there transacted his business. He stopped for a few minutes at the Avon Arms, and went into the coffee-room. In the doorway he ran into a tall gentleman who was coming out.

'Your pardon, sir,' he said, and stared in amazement. 'Saint-Vire! Why, what do ye here, Comte? I'd no notion—'

Saint-Vire had started back angrily, but he bowed now, and if his tone was not cordial, at least he was polite.

'Your servant, Merivale. I had not thought to see you here.'

'Nor I you. Of all the queer places in which to meet you! What brings you here?'

Saint-Vire hesitated for a moment.

'I am on my way to visit friends,' he said, after a while. 'They live—a day's journey north of this place. My schooner is at Portsmouth.' He spread out his hands. 'I am forced to break my journey to recover from a slight indisposition which attacked me *en route*. What would you? One does not wish to arrive *souffrant* at the house of a friend.'

Merivale thought the story strange, and Saint-Vire's manner stranger still, but he was too well-bred to show incredulity.

'My dear Comte, it's most opportune. You will give me the pleasure of your company at dinner at Merivale? I must present you to my wife.'

Again it seemed that Saint-Vire hesitated.

'Monsieur, I resume my journey to-morrow.'

'Well, ride out to Merivale this evening, Comte, I beg of you.'

Almost the Comte shrugged.

'*Eh bien*, m'sieur, you are very kind, I thank you.'

He came that evening to Merivale and bowed deeply over Jennifer's hand.

'Madame, this is a great pleasure. I have long wished to meet the wife of my friend Merivale. Is it too late to felicitate, Merivale?'

Anthony laughed.

'We are four years married, Comte.'

'One has heard much of the beauty of Madame la Baronne,' Saint-Vire said.

Jennifer withdrew her hand.

'Will you be seated, monsieur? I am always glad to see my husband's friends. For where are you bound?'

Saint-Vire waved a vague hand.

'North, madame. I go to visit my friend—er—Chalmer.'

Merivale's brow creased.

'Chalmer? I don't think I know—'

'He lives very much in seclusion,' explained Saint-Vire, and turned again to Jennifer. 'Madame, I think I have never met you in Paris?'

'No, sir, I have not been outside mine own country. My husband goes there sometimes.'

'You should take madame,' Saint-Vire smiled. 'You we see often, *n'est-ce pas?*'

'Not so often as of yore,' Merivale answered. 'My wife has no taste for town life.'

'Ah, one understands then why you stay not long abroad these days, Merivale!'

Dinner was announced, and they went into the adjoining room. The Comte shook out his napkin.

'You live in most charming country, madame. The woods here are superb.'

'They are finer about Avon Court,' said Anthony. 'There are some splendid oaks there.'

'Ah, Avon! I am desolate to hear that the Duc is away. I hoped—but it is not to be.'

In the recesses of Merivale's brain memory stirred. Surely there had been some scandal, many years ago?'

'No, Avon, I believe, is in London. Lord Rupert is staying with us—he is at the Court now, dining with Madame Field, and Mademoiselle de Bonnard, the Duke's ward.'

Saint-Vire's hand, holding the wine-glass, shook a little.

'Mademoiselle de—?'

'Bonnard. You knew that Avon had adopted a daughter?'

'I heard some rumour,' the Comte said slowly. 'So she is here?'

'For a time only. She is to be presented soon, I think.'

'*Vraiment?*' The Comte sipped his wine. 'No doubt she is *ennuyée* here.'

'I think she is well enough,' Merivale answered. 'There is much to amuse her at Avon. She and that scamp, Rupert, have taken to playing at hide-and-seek in the woods They are naught but a pair of children!'

'Aha?' Saint-Vire slightly inclined his head. 'And the Duc is, you say, in London?'

'I cannot say for sure. None ever knows where he will be next. Léonie expects him daily, I think.'

'I am sorry to have missed him,' said Saint-Vire mechanically.

After dinner he and Merivale played at piquet together and soon Rupert came striding in, and stopped dead upon the threshold at sight of the visitor.

'Thun—Your very devoted, Comte,' he said stiffly, and stalked over to where Jennifer was seated. 'What's that fellow doing here?' he growled in her ear.

She laid a finger on her lips.

'The Comte was just saying that he is sorry to have missed seeing your—your brother, Rupert,' she said clearly.

Rupert stared at Saint-Vire.

'Eh? Oh, ay! My brother will be heartbroken, I assure you, sir. Did you come to pay him a visit?'

A muscle quivered beside the Comte's heavy mouth.

'No, milor'. I am on my way to visit friends. I thought maybe to see M. le Duc on my way.'

'Pray let me be the bearer of any message you may wish to send him, sir,' said Rupert.

'*Cela ne vaut pas la peine, m'sieur*,' said the Comte politely.

No sooner had he taken his leave of them than Rupert scowled upon his host.

'Devil take you, Tony, why did you ask that fellow here? What's he doing in England? 'Pon my soul, it's too bad that I should have to meet him, and be civil!'

'I noticed no civility,' remarked Merivale. 'Was there some quarrel between him and Alastair?'

'Quarrel! He's our worst enemy, my dear! He insulted the name! I give you my word he did! What, don't you know? He hates us like the devil! Tried to horse-whip Justin years ago.'

Enlightenment came to Merivale.

'Of course I remember! Why in the world did he pretend he wanted to meet Alastair?'

'I don't like him,' Jennifer said, troubled. 'His eyes make me shiver. I think he is not a good man.'

'What puzzles me,' said Rupert, 'is why he should be the living spit of Léonie.'

Merivale started up.

'That is it, then! I could not think where I had seen her like! What does it all mean?'

'Oh, but she is not like him!' protested Jennifer. ''Tis but the red hair makes you say so. Léonie has a sweet little face!'

'Red hair *and* dark eyebrows,' said Rupert. 'Damme, I believe there's more in this than we think! It's like Justin to play a deep game, stap me if it isn't!'

Merivale laughed at him.

'What game, rattle-pate?'

'I don't know, Tony. But if you'd lived with Justin for as many years as I have you wouldn't laugh. Justin hasn't forgot the quarrel, I'll swear! He never forgets. There's something afoot, I'll be bound.'

17

Of a Capture, a Chase, and Confusion

'Oh, *parbleu*!' Léonie said in disgust. 'This Rupert he is always late, the *vaurien*!'

'My dearest love,' Madam Field reproved her. 'That expression! Indeed, it is not becoming in a young lady! I must beg of you—'

'To-day I am not a lady at all,' said Léonie flatly. 'I want Monseigneur to come.'

'My dear, it is hardly proper in you to—'

'Ah, bah!' said Léonie, and walked away.

She went to her own apartment, and sat disconsolately down at the window.

'It is two weeks since Monseigneur wrote,' she reflected. 'And then he said, I come soon now. *Voyons*, this is no way to keep that promise! And Rupert is late again.' A sparkle came into her eyes. She jumped up. 'I will have a game with Rupert,' she said.

With this intention she pulled her boy's raiment out of the cupboard, and struggled out of her skirts. Her hair had grown, but it was not yet long enough to be confined in the nape of her neck by a riband. It clustered about her head still in a myriad soft curls. She brushed it back from her forehead, dressed herself in shirt and breeches and coat, and, catching up her tricorne, swaggered downstairs. Luckily Madam Field was nowhere to be seen, so she escaped without let or hindrance into the garden. It was the first time she had ventured out of doors in her boy's gear, and since it was an illicit pleasure her eyes twinkled naughtily. Rupert, with all his laxity, had in him a quaint streak of prudery, as she knew.

He would of a certainty be shocked to see her parading the grounds thus clad, and as this was precisely what she wanted she set out in the hope of meeting him, making for the woods that ran down towards the road.

Half-way across the big meadow that separated her from the woodland she espied Rupert coming from the stables, carrying his hat under his arm, and whistling jauntily. Léonie cupped her hands about her mouth.

'Ohé, Rupert!' she called gleefully.

Rupert saw her, stood still a moment, and then came striding towards her.

'Fiend seize it, what will you be at next?' he shouted. ''Pon my soul, it's scandalous, stap me if it's not! Home with you, you hoyden!'

'I shall not, Milor' Rupert!' she cried tauntingly, and danced away. 'You cannot make me!'

'Can I not, then?' called Rupert, and, dropping his hat, broke into a run.

Léonie straightway dived into the wood, and fled as for her life, for she knew very well that if he caught her Rupert would have no hesitation in picking her up and carrying her back to the house.

'Wait till I catch you!' threatened Rupert, crashing through the undergrowth. 'Damme, I've torn my ruffle, and the lace cost me fifteen guineas! Plague take it, where are you?'

Léonie sent a mocking cry echoing through the wood, and ran on, listening to Rupert's blundering progress behind her. She led him in and out of trees, through bushes, round in circles, and over the stream, always keeping just out of sight, until she found herself coming out into the road. She would have turned and doubled back, had she not chanced to see a light travelling coach standing near by. She was surprised, and tiptoed to peep at it over a low thorn-bush. In the distance she heard Rupert's voice, half-exasperated, half-laughing. She threw back head to call to him, and, as she did so, saw to her amazement the Comte de Saint-Vire, walking quickly up one of the paths that led through the wood. He was frowning, and his heavy mouth pouted. He looked up, and as his glance fell upon her the frown went from his face, and he came hurrying towards her.

'I give you good morrow, Léon the Page,' he said, and the words bit. 'I had hardly hoped that I should find you thus soon. The luck is with me this round, I think.'

Léonie retreated a little. Avon's warning was in her mind.

'*Bon jour, m'sieur,*' she said, and wondered what he was doing in the Duke's grounds, or why he was in England at all. 'Did you go to see Monseigneur?' she asked, with wrinkled brow. 'He is not here.'

'I am desolated,' said Saint-Vire sarcastically, and came right up to her. She shrank, and, in a fit of inexplicable panic, called to Rupert.

'Rupert, Rupert, *à moi!*'

Even as she cried Saint-Vire's hand was over her mouth and his other arm about her waist. Struggling madly she was swept from the ground and borne at a run to where the coach stood waiting. Without compunction she bit deeply into the hand over her mouth. There was a muttered oath, the hand flinched a little, and she jerked her head away to shriek again.

'Rupert, Rupert, *on m'enporte! A moi, à moi, à moi!*'

His voice came to her, nearer at hand.

'Who—what—? What the devil—?'

She was flung then into the coach, sprang up like a small fury, but was thrust roughly back again. She heard Saint-Vire give an order to the coachman; then he jumped in beside her, and the coach lurched forward.

Rupert came plunging into the road, hot and dishevelled, just in time to see the coach disappear round the bend in the road, in the direction of the village.

He had suspected at first that Léonie was only teasing him, but her second cry had held a note of genuine alarm, while now there was no sign of her. With characteristic impetuosity he went headlong down the road in pursuit of the coach, never stopping to consider the wisdom of returning to the stables for his horse. Full-tilt he went, hatless, with torn ruffles, and wig askew. The coach was out of sight, but he ran on until he was blown. Then he dropped into a walk. When he had got his breath back he ran again, and had a grin for the comic figure he knew he must be cutting. He had no idea who had seized Léonie, or why, but he felt certain that she was in that coach. His fighting spirit was aroused, and, incidently, his love of adventure: he determined to catch the coach if it cost him his life. So, alternately running and walking, he came at last to the straggling village, three miles distant, and, seeing the first cottage, broke once more into a weary jog-trot.

The blacksmith was working in his yard and looked up in astonishment as Rupert's well-known figure approached.

'Hey, there!' Rupert panted. 'A coach—passed this way. Where went—it?'

The smithy rose and touched his forelock.

'Yes, my lord.'

'Devil take you! The coach!'

'Yes my lord, yes,' said the puzzled smith.

Did—it—pass here?' demanded Rupert in stentorian tones.

Light broke upon the smith.

'Why, yes, your lordship, and stopped at the Arms. 'Tis gone this twenty minutes.'

'Curse it! Whither?'

The smith shook his head.

'Beg pardon, your lordship, but I was not watching.'

'You're a fool,' said Rupert, and plodded on.

The landlord of the Avon Arms was more communicative. He came bustling out to meet his young lordship, and threw up his hands at the sight of him.

'My lord! Why, your lordship has lost his hat! Your coat, sir—'

'Never mind my coat,' said Rupert. 'Where went that coach?'

'The French gentleman's coach, sir?'

Rupert had collapsed on to the settle, but he sat bolt upright now.

'French? *French?* So that's it, is it? Oho, M. le Comte! But what the deuce does he want with Léonie?'

The landlord looked at him sympathetically, and waited for him to explain.

'Ale!' said Rupert, sinking back again. 'And a horse, and a pistol.'

The landlord was more perplexed than ever, but he went off to fetch ale in a large tankard. Rupert disposed of it speedily, and drew a deep breath.

'Did the coach stop here?' he demanded. 'Did you see my brother's ward in it?'

Mistress Léonie, my lord? No, indeed! The French gentleman did not alight. He was in a mighty hurry, sir, seemingly.'

'Scoundrel!' Rupert shook his fist, scowling.

Mr Fletcher retreated a pace.

'Not you, fool,' said Rupert. 'What did the coach stop for?'

'Why, sir, the reckoning was not paid, and the moossoo had left his valise. The servant jumps off the box, comes running in here to settle the reckoning with me, snatches up the valise, and was out of the place before I'd time to fetch my breath. They're queer people, these Frenchies, my lord, for there was me never dreaming the gentleman proposed to leave to-day. Driving hell for leather, they was, too, and as good a team of horses as ever I see.'

'Rot his black soul!' fumed Rupert. 'The devil's in it now, and no mistake. A horse, Fletcher, a horse!'

'Horse, sir?'

'Burn it, would I want a cow? Horse, man, and quickly!'

'But, my lord—'

'Be hanged to your buts! Go find me a horse and a pistol!'

'But, my lord, I've no riding horses here! Farmer Giles hath a cob, but—'

'No horse? Damme, it's disgraceful! Go and fetch the animal the smith's shoeing now! Away with you!'

'But, my lord, that is Mr Manvers' horse, and—'

'Devil take Mr Manvers! Here, I'll go myself! No, stay! A pistol, man.'

The landlord was upset.

'My lord, it's a touch of the sun must have got into your head!'

'Sun at this time of the year?' roared Rupert, thoroughly exasperated.

'Go find me a pistol, sirrah!'

'Yes, my lord, yes!' said Fletcher, and retreated in haste.

Rupert set off down the road to the blacksmith's, and found him whistling to himself as he worked.

'Coggin! Coggin, I say!'

The blacksmith paused.

'Yes, my lord?'

'Hurry with that shoe, my man! I want the horse.'

Coggin stared, open-mouthed.

'But—but 'tis not one of his Grace's horses, sir—'

'Tare an' 'ouns, would his Grace own such a brute? Do ye take me for a fool?'

'But 'tis Mr Manvers' roan, your lordship!'

'I don't care if 'tis the devil's own chestnut!' cried Rupert. 'I want it, and that's enough! How long before you have that shoe on?'

'Why, sir, twenty minutes, or maybe longer.'

'A guinea for you if you hasten!' Rupert searched in his pockets and produced two crowns. 'And ask it of Fletcher,' he added, stowing the crowns away again. 'Don't sit staring at me, man! Hammer that shoe on, or I'll take the hammer to knock sense into your head withal! Stap me if I won't!'

Thus adjured, the smith set to with a will.

'The groom's walked on to Fawley Farm, my lord,' he ventured presently. 'What will your honour have me say to him when he comes back?'

'Tell him to present Lord Rupert Alastair's compliments to Mr Manvers—who the devil *is* Mr Manvers?—and thank him for the loan of his horse.' Rupert walked round the animal, inspecting its points. 'Horse, is it? Cow-hocked bag of bones! A man's no right to own a scarecrow like this! You hear me, Coggin?'

'Yes, my lord. Certainly, sir!'

'Hurry with that shoe, then, and fetch the animal up to the Arms.' Away went Rupert up the road again to the inn, where he found Fletcher awaiting him with a large pistol.

''Tis loaded, sir,' Fletcher warned him. 'Indeed, my lord, and are you sure your lordship is well?'

'Never mind! Which way did the coach go?'

'Making for Portsmouth, sir, as I judge. But surely to goodness your lordship isn't of a mind to chase it?'

'What else, fool? I want a hat. Produce me one.'

Fletcher resigned himself to the inevitable.

'If your lordship would condescend to take my Sunday beaver—'

'Ay, 'twill suffice. Make out the reckoning and I'll pay—er—when I return. Damn that fellow Coggin! Will he be all night at his work? They've nigh on an hour's start of me already!'

But Coggin came presently, leading the roan. Rupert stowed his pistol away in the saddle holster, tightened the girths, and sprang into the saddle. The smith gave vent to a last appeal.

'My lord, Mr Manvers is a testy gentleman, and indeed—'

'To hell with Mr Manvers, I'm sick of the fellow!' said Rupert, and rode off at a canter.

The borrowed horse was no fiery charger, as Rupert soon discovered. It cherished its own ideas as to a suitable pace to maintain, and managed to do so for the most part, to its own satisfaction and Rupert's disgust. Thus it was close on four in the afternoon when he came at last into Portsmouth, and both he and his mount were very weary.

He rode at once to the quay, and learned that the private schooner anchored there for the past three days had set sail not an hour ago. Rupert dashed Mr Fletcher's hat on the ground.

'Blister me, I'm too late!'

The harbour-master eyed him in polite surprise, and picked up the hat.

'Tell me now,' said Rupert, dismounting. 'Was it a French scoundrel embarking?'

'Ay, sir, 'twas a foreign gentleman with red hair, and his son.'

'Son?' ejaculated Rupert.

'Ay, sir, a sick lad it was. The moossoo said he was suffering from a fever. He carried him on board like one dead, all muffled up in a great cloak. I said to Jim here, "Jim," I said, "it's a shame to take the boy on board, ill as he is, that it is." '

'Drugged, by Gad!' exclaimed Rupert. 'I'll have his blood for this! Taken her to France, has he! Now, what in thunder does he want with her? Hi, you! When does the next packet sail for Le Havre?'

'Why, sir, there's no boat for the likes of you till Wednesday,' said the harbour-master. Rupert's ruffles might be torn, and his coat muddied, but the harbour-master knew a gentleman when he saw one.

Rupert glanced ruefully down his person.

'The likes of me, eh? Well, well!' He pointed with his whip to a ram-shackle vessel laden with bales of cloth. 'Where is she bound for?'

'For Le Havre, sir, but 'tis only a trading ship, as your honour sees.'

'When does she sail?'

'To-night, sir. She's lain here two days too long already, waiting for the wind to turn, but she'll be away with the tide soon after six.'

'That's the ship for me,' said Rupert briskly. 'Where's her master?'

The harbour-master was perturbed.

''Tis but a dirty old boat, sir, and never a—'

'Dirty? So am I dirty, damn it!' said Rupert. 'Go find me the master, and tell him I want a passage to France this night.'

So off went the harbour-master, to return anon with a burly individual in homespun, with a great black beard. This gentleman eyed Rupert stolidly, and, removing the long clay pipe from his mouth, rumbled forth two words.

'Twenty guineas.'

'What's that?' said Rupert. 'Not a farthing more than ten, you rogue!'

The bearded gentleman spat deliberately into the sea, but vouchsafed no word. A dangerous light came into Rupert's eyes. He tapped the man on the shoulder with his riding-whip.

'Fellow, I am Lord Rupert Alastair. You shall have ten guineas off me and for the rest I'll see you damned.'

The harbour-master pricked up his ears.

'I was hearing, my lord, that his Grace has the *Silver Queen* anchored in Southampton Water.'

'The devil fly away with Justin!' exclaimed Rupert wrathfully. 'He was always wont to have her here!'

'Maybe, sir, if you was to ride to Southampton—'

'Ride to hell! I'd find them painting her, like as not. Come now, fellow, ten guineas!'

The harbour-master took his colleague aside, and whispered urgently. Presently he turned, and addressed Rupert.

'I am saying, my lord, as how fifteen guineas is a fair price.'

'Fifteen guineas it is!' said Rupert promptly, thinking of the two crowns in his pocket. 'I shall have to sell the horse.'

'Six o'clock we sets sail, and don't wait for nobbut,' growled the captain, and walked off.

Rupert rode into the town, and by good fortune was able to sell Mr Manvers' roan for the sum of twenty guineas. The sale being accomplished he went to the inn on the quayside, and refreshed himself with a wash, and a bowl of punch. Thus fortified he boarded the sailing vessel, and sat him down on a coil of rope, thoroughly enjoying the adventure, and not a little amused.

''Fore Gad, I never was in such a mad chase!' he remarked to the sky. 'Here's Léonie spirited off by Saint-Vire, the Lord knows why, or where, for that matter—and myself hot on the scent with five crowns in my pocket, and the landlord's hat on my head. And what am I going to do when I find the chit?' He pondered deeply. 'It's a plaguey queer business, so it is,' he decided. 'Justin's at the back of it, I'll be bound. And where the devil is Justin?' Suddenly he flung back his head and laughed. 'Damme, I'd give something to see old cousin Harriet's face when she finds me gone off with Léonie! Hey, hey, here's a pretty coil, to be sure, for, faith, I don't know where I am, and I don't know where Léonie is, nor she where I am, and at Avon they don't know where any of us are!'

18

The Indignation of Mr Manvers

Madam Field was worried, for it was six in the evening and neither Léonie nor Rupert had returned. Considerably flustered at length Madam sent a messenger to Merivale to inquire whether the truants were there. Half an hour later the lackey returned, with Merivale riding beside him. Merivale went swiftly to the withdrawing-room, and as soon as he entered Madam Field sprang up.

'Oh, Lord Merivale! Oh, and have you brought the child home? I have been in such a taking, for I never saw her after eleven in the morning, or maybe 'twas later, or perhaps a little earlier—I cannot say for sure. And never a sign of Rupert, so I thought mayhap they were with you—'

Merivale broke into the flood of words.

'I've not seen either of them since this morning when Rupert set out to come here,' he said.

Madam's jaw dropped. She let fall her fan, and began to cry.

'Oh dear, oh dear, and Justin telling me to have a care to her! But how could I tell, for sure 'twas his own brother! Oh, my lord, can they—can they have eloped?'

Merivale laid his hat and whip on the table.

'Eloped? Nonsense, madam!' Impossible!'

'She was ever a wild piece,' wept Madam. 'And Rupert so scatterbrained! Oh, what shall I do, my lord? What shall I do?'

'Pray madam, dry your tears!' begged Merivale. 'I am convinced there's naught so serious in this as an elopement. For God's sake, madam, calm yourself.'

But Madam, to his dismay, went into a fit of the vapours. My lord turned to the servant.

'Ride back to Merivale, my man, and request my lady to join me here,' he ordered, with an uneasy eye on the prostrate lady. 'And—and send madam's abigail here! Mayhap the children are playing some trick on us,' he muttered to himself. 'Madam, I beg you will not alarm yourself unduly!'

Madam Field's maid came running with salts, and presently the lady recovered somewhat, and lay upon the couch calling on heaven to witness that she had done her best. To all Merivale's questions she could only reply that she had had no notion of such wickedness, and what Justin would say she dared not think. Came my Lady Merivale, in her chaise, and was ushered into the withdrawing-room.

'Madam! Why, madam, what is this? Anthony, have they not returned? Fie, they are trying to frighten us! Depend upon it, that is it! Never fret, madam, they'll return soon.' She went to the agitated chaperon, and began to chafe her hands. 'Pray, madame, hush. It's no such great matter, I am sure. Mayhap they have lost their way somewhere, for they are out riding you may be sure.'

'My dear, Rupert knows every inch of the country,' Merivale said quietly. He turned again to the lackey. 'Be good enough to send to the stables and see whether my lord and Mistress Léonie have taken the horses.'

Ten minutes later the man returned with the news that Lord Rupert's horse was in a loose-box, and had been there all day. Whereupon Madam had a fresh attack of the vapours, and Merivale frowned.

'I don't understand this,' he said. 'If they had eloped—'

'Oh, Anthony, can they have done that?' Jennifer cried aghast. 'Oh no, surely! Why, the child can think of no one but the Duke, and as for Rupert—'

'Listen!' said my lord sharply, and raised his hand.

Outside they heard horses, and the scrunch of wheels on gravel. Madam started up.

'Heaven be praised, they have come back!'

With one accord Anthony and Jennifer deserted the ailing lady, and hurried into the hall. The great front-door stood open, and into the house stepped his Grace of Avon, elegant in a coat of fine purple velvet, laced with gold, a many-caped greatcoat, over all, worn carelessly open, and polished top-boats on his feet. He paused on the threshold and raised his eyeglass to survey the Merivales.

'Dear me!' he said languidly. 'An unexpected honour. Your ladyship's devoted servant.'

'Oh lord!' said Merivale, for all the world like a rueful boy.

His Grace's lips quivered, but Jennifer blushed fiery red. Merivale went forward.

'You must deem this an unwarranted intrusion, Duke,' he began stiffly.

'Not at all,' bowed his Grace. 'I am charmed.'

Merivale returned the bow.

'I was summoned to Madam Field's assistance,' he said. 'Otherwise I should not be here, believe me.'

Leisurely the Duke divested himself of his greatcoat, and shook out the ruffles.

'But shall we not repair to the withdrawing-room?' he suggested. 'You are saying, I think, that you came to my cousin's assistance?' He led the way to the withdrawing-room, and bowed them in. Madam Field, seeing him, gave a shriek, and fell back upon her cushions.

'Oh, mercy, 'tis Justin!' she cried.

Jennifer went to her.

'Hush, madam! Calm yourself!'

'You appear to be strangely afflicted, cousin,' remarked his Grace

'Oh Justin—oh cousin! I had no notion! So innocent they seemed! I can scarce believe—'

'Innocent! Of course they were!' snorted Merivale. 'Have done with this elopement foolery! It's mere child's talk!'

'Oh Anthony, do you think so indeed?' said Jennifer thankfully.

'I do not wish to seem importunate,' said the Duke, 'but I should like an explanation. Where, may I ask, is my ward?'

'That,' said Merivale, 'is the very root of the matter.'

The Duke stood very still.

'Indeed!' he said softly. 'Pray continue. Cousin, I must request you to cease your lamentations.'

Madam's noisy sobs abated. She clutched Jennifer's hand, and sniffed dolefully.

'I know nothing more than this,' said Merivale. 'She and Rupert have been absent since eleven of the clock this morning.'

'Rupert?' said his Grace.

'I should have told you that Rupert has been staying with us these past three weeks.'

'You amaze me,' said Avon. His eyes were as hard as agates. He turned, and put his snuff-box down on the table. 'The mystery would seem to be solved,' he said evenly.

'Sir!' It was Jennifer who spoke. His Grace looked at her indifferently. 'If you are thinking that—that they have eloped, I am sure—oh, I am sure that 'tis not so! Such a notion was never in either of their heads!'

'So?' Avon looked from one to the other. 'Pray enlighten me!'

Merivale shook his head.

'Faith, I cannot. But I would stake mine honour that there's been no thought of love between them. They are the veriest children and even now I suspect they may be playing a trick on us. More than that—' He paused.

'Yes?' said Avon.

Jennifer broke in.

'Sir, the child can talk of no one but yourself!' she said impetuously. 'You have all her—her adoration!'

'So I thought,' answered Avon. 'But one may be mistaken. I believe there is a saying that youth will to youth.'

'It's no such thing,' Merivale averred. 'Why, they are for ever quarrelling! Moreover they have taken no horses. Mayhap they are hiding somewhere to frighten us.'

A footman came to them.

'Well?' Avon spoke without turning his head.

'Mr Manvers, your Grace, who desires speech with my Lord Rupert.'

'I have not the pleasure of Mr Manvers' acquaintance,' said the Duke, 'but you may admit him.'

Entered a little wiry gentleman with red cheeks, and bright, angry eyes. He glared at the assembled company, and, singling out the Duke, rapped forth a question.

'Are you Lord Rupert Alastair, sir?'

'I am not,' said his Grace.

The irate little man rounded on Merivale.

'You, sir?'

'My name is Merivale,' Anthony replied.

'Then where is Lord Rupert Alastair?' demanded Mr Manvers, in a voice of baffled rage.

His Grace took snuff.

'That is what we should all like to know,' he said.

'Damme, sir, do you think to play with me?' fumed Mr Manvers.

'I have never played with anyone,' said the Duke.

'I am come here to find Lord Rupert Alastair! I demand speech with him! I want an explanation of him!'

'My dear sir,' said Avon. 'Pray join our ranks! We all want that.'

'Who the devil are you?' cried the exasperated little man.

'Sir,' bowed his Grace. 'I believe I *am* the devil. So they say.'

Merivale was shaken with silent laughter. Mr Manvers turned to him.

'Is this a mad-house?' he asked. 'Who is he?'

'He is the Duke of Avon,' said Merivale unsteadily.

Mr Manvers pounced on Avon again.

'Ah! Then you are Lord Rupert's brother!' he said vindictively.

'My misfortune, sir, believe me.'

'What I demand to know is this!' said Mr Manvers. '*Where is my roan?*'

'I haven't the least idea,' said his Grace placidly. 'I am not even sure that I know what you are talking about.'

'Faith, I'm sure I don't!' chuckled Merivale.

'My roan horse, sir! Where is it? Answer me that!'

'I fear you will have to hold me excused,' said the Duke. 'I know nothing about your horse. In fact, I am not, at the moment, interested in your horse—roan or otherwise.'

Mr Manvers raised his fists heavenwards.

'Interested in it!' he spluttered. 'My horse has been stolen!'

'You have all my sympathy,' yawned his Grace. 'But I fail to see what concern it is of mine.'

Mr Manvers thumped the table.

'Stolen, sir, by your brother, Lord Rupert Alastair, this very day!'

His words brought about a sudden silence.

'Continue!' requested his Grace. 'You interest us now exceedingly. Where, when, how, and why did Lord Rupert steal your horse?'

'He stole it in the village, sir, this morning! And I may say, sir, that I consider it a gross impertinence! A piece of insolence that infuriates me! I am a calm man, sir, but when I receive such a message from a man of birth, of title—'

'Oh, he left a message, did he?' interposed Merivale.

'With the blacksmith, sir! My groom rode over on the roan to the village, and, the horse casting a shoe, he took him to the smith, very properly! While Coggin was shoeing the animal my fellow walked on to Fawley to execute my commands.' He breathed heavily. 'When he returned, the horse was gone! The smith—damn him for a fool!—tells me that Lord Rupert insisted on taking the horse—*my* horse, sir!—and left his compliments for me and his—his *thanks* for the loan of my horse!'

'Very proper,' said his Grace.

'Damme, sir, it's monstrous!'

A gurgling laugh came from Jennifer.

'Oh, was there ever such a boy?' she cried. 'What in the world should he want with your horse, sir?'

Mr Manvers scowled at her.

'Exactly, madam! Exactly! What did he want with my horse? The man's mad, and should be clapped up! Coggins tells me he came running into the village like one demented, with no hat on his head! And not one of those gaping fools had the sense to stop him from seizing my horse! A set of idiots, sir!'

'I can well believe it,' said Avon. 'But I do not yet see how your information can help us.'

Mr Manvers fought with himself.

'Sir, I am not come here to help you!' he raged. 'I have come to demand my horse!'

'I would give it you had I it in my possession,' said his Grace kindly. 'Unfortunately Lord Rupert has your horse.'

'Then I want its recovery!'

'Do not distress yourself!' Avon advised him. 'No doubt he will return it. What I wish to know is, why did Lord Rupert want your horse, and where did he go?'

'If that dolt of a landlord is to be believed,' said Mr Manvers, 'he has gone to Portsmouth.'

'Fleeing the country, evidently,' murmured his Grace. 'Was there a lady with Lord Rupert?'

'No, there was not! Lord Rupert went off at a disgraceful pace in pursuit of a coach, or some such nonsense.'

The Duke's eyes widened.

'Almost I begin to see daylight,' he said. 'Proceed.'

Merivale shook his head.

'I'm all at sea,' he confessed. 'The mystery grows.'

'On the contrary,' his Grace replied gently. 'The mystery is very nearly solved.'

'I don't understand you—any of you!' exploded Mr Manvers.

'That was not to be expected,' said Avon. 'Lord Rupert, you say, went to Portsmouth in pursuit of a coach. Who was in that coach?'

'Some damned Frenchman, Fletcher said.'

Merivale started; so also did Jennifer.

'Frenchman?' Merivale echoed. 'But what did Rupert—'

His Grace was smiling grimly.

'The mystery,' he said, 'is solved. Lord Rupert, Mr Manvers, borrowed your horse to go in pursuit of M. le Comte de Saint-Vire.'

Merivale gasped.

'You knew he was here, then?'

'I did not.'

'Then how a' God's name—?'

Again the Duke took snuff.

'Shall we say—intuition, my dear Anthony?'

'But—but why did Rupert pursue Saint-Vire? And—and what was Saint-Vire doing on the road to Portsmouth? He told he was journeying north to visit a friend! This goes beyond me!'

'What I want to know,' Jennifer said, 'is, where is Léonie?'

'Ay, that's the question,' nodded Merivale.

'Your pardon, sir,' interjected Mr Manvers, 'but the question is, where is my horse?'

They turned to the Duke for enlightenment.

'Léonie,' said the Duke, 'is by now on the way to France, in company with the Comte de Saint-Vire. Rupert, I imagine, is also on his way to France, for I do not suppose he was in time to intercept them. Mr Manvers' horse is in all probability at Portsmouth. Unless, of course, Rupert has taken it to France with him.'

Mr Manvers collapsed into the nearest chair.

'Taken—taken my horse to France, sir? Oh, it's monstrous! it's monstrous!'

'For God's sake, Avon, be more explicit!' begged Merivale. 'Why has Saint-Vire run off with Léonie? He had not even seen her!'

'On the contrary,' said Avon, 'he has seen her many times.'

Jennifer rose to her feet.

'Oh, sir, he will not harm her?'

'No, he will not harm her, my lady,' Avon replied, and there was a glint in his eyes. 'You see, there will be no time for that. He has Rupert hard on his heels—and me.'

'You'll go?'

'Of course I shall go. Follow my example, and place your trust in Rupert. It seems I shall live to be grateful to him yet.'

'Alastair, what in God's name does all this mean?' demanded Merivale. 'Rupert himself swore there was a mystery as soon as he saw Léonie's likeness to Saint-Vire.'

'So Rupert saw that? I appear to have underrated Rupert's intelligence. I believe I can satisfy your curiosity. Come with me into the library, my dear Merivale.'

Past enmity was forgotten. Anthony went to the door. Mr Manvers sprang up.

'But all this doesn't help me to my horse!' he said bitterly.

With his hand on the door Avon paused, and looked back.

'My good sir,' he said haughtily, 'I am weary of your horse. It has served its turn, and shall be restored to you.' He went out with Merivale, and shut the door behind him. 'So. One moment, Anthony. Johnson!'

The butler came forward.

'Your Grace?'

'Bid them harness Thunderbolt and Blue Peter to the curricle at once, place my large valise in it, and tell one of the women to pack some clothes for Mistress Léonie. Within half an hour, Johnson.'

'Very good, your Grace,' bowed the old man.

'And now, Merivale, this way.'

'By Gad, you're a cool devil!' exclaimed Merivale, and followed him to the library.

His Grace went to his desk and extracted from it a brace of gold-mounted pistols.

'Briefly, Anthony, the matter is this: Léonie is Saint-Vire's daughter.'

'I never knew he had a daughter!'

'No one knew. You thought he had a son, perhaps?'

'Yes. Well, naturally! I've seen the boy many times.'

'He is no more Saint-Vire's son than you are,' said his Grace, snapping the breech of one of his pistols. 'His name is Bonnard.'

'Good God, Alastair, do you mean to tell me that Saint-Vire had the audacity to exchange the children? Because of Armand?'

'I am delighted to find that you understand the situation so well,' said the Duke. 'I beg you will let it go no further, for the time is not yet.'

'Very well, but what a piece of villainy! Does he know that you know?'

'I had best tell you the whole story,' sighed Avon.

When they at length emerged from the library Merivale's face was a study of mingled emotions, and he appeared to be speechless. Jennifer met them in the hall.

'You are going, sir. You—you will bring her back?'

'That I cannot say,' Avon replied. 'She will be safe with me, my lady.'

Her eyes fell.

'Yes, sir, I feel that that is so.'

His Grace looked at her.

'You surprise me,' he said.

She put her hand out, hesitating.

'She has told me so much. I cannot but be sure of your—kindness.' She paused. 'Sir, what—what lies between you and me is past, and should be forgotten.'

His Grace bowed over her hand; his lips were smiling.

'Jenny, if I said that I had forgotten you would be offended.'

'No,' she answered, and a laugh trembled in her voice. 'I should be glad.'

'My dear, I desire nothing better than to please you.'

'I think,' she said, 'that there is one now who holds a greater place in your heart than ever I held.'

'You err, Jenny. I have no heart,' he replied.

A silence fell. It was broken by a lackey.

'Your Grace, the curricle waits.'

'How will you cross?' Merivale asked.

'In the *Silver Queen*. She lies in Southampton Water. Unless Rupert has already commandeered her. If that should chance to be so, I suppose I must hire a vessel.'

Mr Manvers came up.

'Sir, I will not stay with that woman who has the vapours,' he said. 'It is very well for you to say you are weary of my horse, but I want its instant recovery!'

The Duke had donned his great-cloak, and now he picked up his hat and gloves.

'My Lord Merivale will be charmed to assist you,' he said, with the glimmering of a smile. He bowed low to them all, and was gone.

19

Lord Rupert Wins the Second Trick

Léonie awoke, sighing. Nausea threatened to overwhelm her, and for a few minutes she lay with closed eyes, in semi-consciousness. By degrees she shook off the effects of the drug, and struggled up, a hand to her head. She looked about her in bewilderment, and found that she was on a couch in a strange apartment, alone. Bit by bit memory came, and she got up, and went to the window.

'*Tiens!*' she said, looking out. 'Where am I now? I do not know this place. It is the sea.' She stared at the harbour in bewilderment. 'That man gave me an evil drink, I remember. And I went to sleep, I suppose. Where is this wicked Comte? I think that I bit him very hard, and I know that I kicked him. And then we came to that inn—where was it?—miles and miles from Avon—and he brought me coffee.' She chuckled. 'And I threw it at him. *How* he did swear! Then he brought more coffee and he made me drink it. Faugh! Coffee, he called it? Pig-wash! What then? *Peste*, I do not know anything more!' She turned to look at the clock on the mantel-piece, and frowned. '*Mon Dieu*, what is this?' She went to the clock, and regarded it fixedly. '*Sotte!*' she addressed it. 'How can you be noon? It was noon when he made me drink that evil pig-wash. *Tu ne marches pas.*'

The steady ticking gave her the lie. She put her head on one side.

'*Comment? Voyons*, I do not understand this at all. Unless—' her eyes widened—'Am I in to-morrow?' she wondered. 'I *am* in to-morrow! That man made me go to sleep, and I have slept all day and night! *Sacré bleu*, but I am angry with that man! I am glad that I bit him. Doubtless he means to kill me, but why? Perhaps Rupert will come and save me, but I think that I will save myself, and not wait for Rupert, for I do *not* want to be killed by this Comte.' She considered. 'No, mayhap he does not want to kill me. But if he does not—*Grand Dieu*, can it be that he elopes with me? No, that is not possible, because he believes I am a boy. And I do not think that he can love me very much.' Her eyes twinkled impishly. 'Now I will go,' she said.

But the door was fast, and the windows too small to allow her to escape through them. The twinkle died, and the small mouth set mutinously.

'*Parbleu, mais c'est infame!* He locks me in, *enfin!* Oh, I am *very* angry!' She laid her finger on her lips. 'If I had a dagger I would kill him, but I have no dagger, *tant pis*. What then?' She paused. 'I am a little frightened, I think,' she confessed. 'I must escape from this wicked person. It will be better, perhaps, if I am still asleep.'

Footsteps sounded. Quick as thought Léonie returned to her couch, covered herself with her cloak, and lay down, with closed eyes. A key grated in the lock, and someone entered. Léonie heard Saint-Vire's voice.

'Bring *déjeuner* here, Victor, and do not let any enter. The child still sleeps.'

'*Bien, m'sieur.*'

'Now, who is Victor?' wondered Léonie. 'It is the servant, I suppose. *Dieu me sauve!*'

The Comte came to her side, and bent over her, listening to her breathing. Léonie tried to still the uncomfortably hard beating of her heart. Evidently the Comte noticed nothing unusual, for he moved away again. Presently Léonie heard the chink of crockery.

'It is very hard that I must listen to this pig-person eating, when I am so hungry,' she reflected. 'Oh, but I will make him very sorry!'

'When will m'sieu have the horses put to?' inquired Victor.

'Oho!' thought Léonie. 'We travel further, then!'

'There is no need for haste now,' Saint-Vire answered. 'That young fool, Alastair, would not follow us to France. We will start at two.'

Léonie's eyes nearly flew open. She restrained herself with an effort.

'*Le misérable!*' she thought savagely. 'Am I in Calais? No, for this is of a certainty not Calais. Perhaps I am at Le Havre. I do not immediately see what I am to do, but certainly I will go on being asleep. We went to Portsmouth, then. I think that Rupert *will* come, if he saw the way we went, but I must not wait for him. I would like to bite that man again. *Diable*, I am in great danger, it seems! I have a very cold feeling in my inside, and I wish that Monseigneur would come. That is foolishness, of course. He does not know that anything has happened to me. Ah, bah! Now this pig-person eats, while I starve! Certainly I will make him sorry.'

'The lad sleeps overlong, m'sieur,' Victor said. 'He should wake soon now.'

'I do not expect it,' Saint-Vire replied. 'He is young, and I gave him a strong dose. There is no cause for alarm, and it suits my purpose better if he sleeps for a while yet.'

'*Sans doute!*' thought Léonie. 'So that was it! He drugged me! He is of a wickedness! I must breathe more heavily.'

Time went lagging by, but at length there came some commotion without, and Victor entered the room again.

'The coach awaits, m'sieur. Shall I take the boy?'

'I will. You have paid the reckoning?'

'Yes, m'sieur.'

Saint-Vire went to Léonie and lifted her. She was limp in his hold.

'I must let my head fall back, so! And my mouth open a little, thus! *Voyons*, I am being very clever! But I do not in the least know what comes to me. This man is a fool.'

She was carried out, and put into the coach, and propped up with cushions.

'You will make for Rouen,' Saint-Vire said. '*En avant!*'

The door was shut, Saint-Vire settled himself beside Léonie, and the coach rolled forward.

Léonie set her wits to work.

'This becomes more and more difficult. I do not see that I can do anything but continue to sleep while this man sits beside me. Presently we shall stop to change horses, for these are not good, I think. Perhaps this pig-person will get out then. If he thinks I am asleep he will do that, for he will want to eat again. But *still* I do not see how I am to escape. I will say a prayer to the *Bon Dieu* to show me a way.'

Meanwhile the coach travelled on at a fair rate, and the Comte took a book from his pocket and began to read it, glancing occasionally at the inert figure beside him. Once he felt Léonie's pulse, and seemed to be satisfied, for he sank back into his corner and resumed his reading.

They must have been over an hour on the road when it happened. There was a terrific bump, a lurch, shouts and the stamping of frightened horses, and the coach toppled slowly into the ditch, so that the door by Léonie was only a yard from the hedge. She was flung violently against the side of the coach, with Saint-Vire atop of her, and it was only by a supreme effort of will that she refrained from throwing out a hand to save herself.

Saint-Vire struggled up, and wrenched at the off-side door, calling to know what was the matter. Victor's voice answered.

'The near back wheel, m'sieur! We have one of the horses down, and a trace broken!'

Saint-Vire swore roundly, and hesitated, glancing at his captive. Once more he bent over her, listening to her breathing and then jumped down into the road, shutting the door behind him. Léonie heard him join in the mêlée without, and scrambled up. Cautiously she opened the door that leaned drunkenly to the hedge, and slipped out, crouching low. The men were at the horses' heads, and Saint-Vire was hidden from her sight by one of the plunging leaders. Bent almost double she fled down the road, keeping to the ditch, and, coming presently upon a gap in the high hedge, pushed her way through it into the field beyond. She was hidden now from the road, but she knew that at any moment Saint-Vire might discover her escape, and she ran on, dizzy and trembling, back along the way they had come, looking wildly round for some hiding-place. The field stretched away on either side; the bend in the road was some hundred yards further on, and there was no sign of human habitation, or friendly woodland.

Then in the distance she heard the sound of a horse's hoofs on the hard road, galloping from the direction of Le Havre. She peeped through the hedge, wondering whether she dared call upon this furious rider to stop and assist her. The horse came round the bend. She saw a familiar blue coat, muddied over, a torn ruffle, and a dark handsome young face, flushed and excited.

She tore her way through the hedge, flew out into the road, and waved her hands.

'*Rupert, Rupert, j'y suis!*' she shrieked.

Rupert pulled up, wrenching his horse back upon its haunches, and let out a whoop of triumph.

'Quick! Oh, quick!' Léonie panted, and ran to his stirrup.

He hoisted her up before him.

'Where is he? Where's that black scoundrel?' he demanded. 'How did you—'

'Turn, turn!' she commanded. 'He is there, with that coach, and there are three others! Oh, quickly, Rupert!' She pulled the horse round, but Rupert held it in still.

'No, damme, I'll have his blood, Léonie. I've sworn—'

'Rupert, there are three with him, and you have no sword! Now he has seen! *Nom de Dieu, en avant!*'

He looked over his shoulder, undecided. Léonie saw Saint-Vire snatch a pistol from his pocket, and drove her heels into the horse's flanks with all her might. The animal leaped forward; something sang past Léonie's cheek, scorching it; there was a terrific oath from Rupert, and the horse bolted with them down the road. A second explosion came, and Léonie felt Rupert lurch in the saddle, and heard the quick intake of his breath.

'*Touché*, b'gad!' he gasped. 'On with you, you mad-cap!'

'*Laisse moi, laisse moi!*' she cried, and snatched the bridle from him, urging the frightened horse round the bend. 'Hold to me, Rupert, it is well now.'

Rupert could still laugh.

'Well, is it? Gad—what a—chase! Steady, steady! There's—lane—further down—turn into it—never reach—Le Havre.'

She twisted the bridle round her little hands, and pulled gallantly.

'He will mount one of those horses,' she said, thinking quickly. 'And he will ride to Le Havre. Yes, yes, we will turn down the lane; Rupert, *mon pauvre*, are you badly hurt?'

'Right shoulder—'tis naught. There—should be—village. There's the lane! Steady him, steady him! Good girl! Hey, what an adventure!'

They swept into the lane, saw cottages ahead, and a farm. Of impulse Léonie pulled up her mount, turned aside to the hedge, and made the horse push through into the fields. Then on she drove him, cross-country, at a canter.

Rupert was swaying in the saddle.

'What—will you be at?' he said hoarsely.

'*Laisse moi!*' she repeated. 'That is too near the road. He would be sure to look for us. I go further.'

'Damme, let him look for us! I'll put a bullet through his black heart, so I will!'

Léonie paid no heed, but rode on with a wary eye on the look-out for shelter. Rupert, she knew, was losing blood fast, and could not long endure. To the right, in the distance, she saw a church spire, and made for it, a cold fear in her heart.

'Have courage, Rupert! Hold to me, and it will be very well!'

'Ay, I'm well enough,' said Rupert faintly. 'Courage be damned! It's not I who'd run away! Burn it, I can't get my hand to the hole he's made in me! Gently, gently, and 'ware rabbit-holes!'

A mile further the village was reached, a little peaceful haven, with its church sitting placidly by. Men working on the fields stared in amazement at the fleeing couple, but they rode on into the cobbled street, and up it till they came upon a tiny inn, with a swinging board over the door, and stables lying tumble-down about the yard.

Léonie reined in, and the horse stood quivering. An ostler gaped at them, mop in hand.

'You there!' Léonie called imperiously. 'Come and help m'sieur to the ground! Quickly, great fool! He is wounded by—by highwaymen!'

The man looked fearfully down the road, but, seeing no dread footpad, came to do Léonie's bidding. Then the landlord bustled out to see what was toward, an enormous man with a scratch wig on his head, and a twinkle in his eye. Léonie held out her hand to him.

'Ah, *la bonne chance!*' she cried. 'Aid, m'sieur, I beg of you! We were travelling to Paris, and were set upon by a party of footpads.'

'Tare an' ouns!' said Rupert. 'Do you think I'd run from a parcel of greasy footpads? Think of another tale, for the love of God!'

The landlord slipped an arm about his lordship, and lifted him down. Léonie slid to the ground, and stood trembling.

'*Mon Dieu*, what an escape!' said the landlord. 'These footpads! You, Hector! Take m'sieur's legs, and help me bear him to a guest-chamber.'

'Devil take you, leave my legs alone!' swore Rupert. 'I can—I can walk!'

But the landlord, a practical man, saw that he was almost fainting, and bore him without more ado up the stairs to a little chamber under the eaves. He and the ostler laid his lordship on the bed, and Léonie fell on her knees beside him.

'Oh, but he is wounded to death!' she cried. 'Help me with his coat!'

Rupert opened his eyes.

'Fiddle!' he said, and sank into unconsciousness.

'Ah, an Englishman!' cried the landlord, struggling with his lordship's tight-fitting coat.

'An English milor',' nodded Léonie. 'I am his page.'

'*Tiens!* One would know it was a great gentleman. Ah, the fine coat so spoiled! The shirt we must tear.' He proceeded to do so, and, turning my lord to his side, laid bare the wound. 'It needs a surgeon, *bien sûr*. Hector shall ride to Le Havre. These highwaymen!'

Léonie was busy staunching the blood.

'Yes, a surgeon!' She started. 'Ah, but Le Havre! He will be–they will pursue us there!' She turned to the landlord. 'Hector must know naught of us if he is questioned!'

The landlord was bewildered.

'No, no, they would not dare! The highwaymen keep to the open country, my child.'

'It–they were not–highwaymen,' Léonie confessed, blushing. 'And I am not really Lord Rupert's page.'

'*Hein?* What is this?' demanded the landlord.

'I–I am a girl,' said Léonie. 'I am the ward of the English Duc of Avon, and–and Lord Rupert is his brother!'

The landlord stared from one to the other, and a mighty frown came.

'Ah, I see well! It is an elopement! Now I will tell you, mademoiselle, that I do not—'

'But no!' Léonie said. 'It is that the–the man who pursues us stole me from the house of Monseigneur le Duc, and he drugged me, and brought me to France, and I think he would have killed me. But Milor' Rupert came swiftly, and our coach lost a wheel, and I slipped out, and ran and ran and ran! Then milor' came, and the man who stole me fired at him, and–and that is all!'

The landlord was incredulous.

'*Voyons*, what tale is this you tell me?'

'It is quite true,' sighed Léonie, 'and when Monseigneur comes you will see that it is as I say. Oh, please, you must help us!'

The landlord was not proof against those big, beseeching eyes.

'Well, well!' he said. 'You are safe here, and Hector is discreet.'

'And you won't let–that man–take us?'

The landlord blew out his cheeks.

'I am master here,' he said. 'And I say that you are safe. Hector shall ride to Le Havre for a surgeon, but as for this talk of Ducs!' He shook his head indulgently, and sent a wide-eyed serving maid to fetch Madame, and some linen.

Madame came swiftly, a woman as large about as her husband, but comely withal. Madame cast one glance at Lord Rupert, and issued sharp orders, and began to rend linen. Madame would listen to nobody until she had tightly bound my Lord Rupert.

'*Hé, le beau!*' she said. 'What wickedness! That goes better now.' She laid a plump finger to her lips, and stood billowing, her other hand on her hip. 'He must be undressed,' she decided. 'Jean, you will find a nightshirt.'

'Marthe,' interposed her husband. 'This boy is a lady!'

'*Quel horreur!*' remarked Madame placidly. 'Yes, it is best that we undress him, *le pauvre*!' She turned and drove the peeping maid out, and Léonie with her, and shut the door on them.

Léonie wandered down the stairs and went out into the yard. Hector was already gone on his way to Le Havre; there was no one in sight, so Léonie sank wearily on to a bench hard by the kitchen windows, and burst into tears.

'Ah, bah!' she apostrophized herself fiercely. '*Bête! Imbécile! Lâche!*'

But the tears continued to flow. It was a damp, drooping little figure that met Madame's eye when she came sailing out into the yard.

Madame, having heard the strange story from her husband, was properly shocked and wrathful. She stood with arms akimbo, and began severely:

'This is a great wickedness, mademoiselle! I would have you know that we—' She broke off, and went forward. 'But no, but no, *ma petite!* There is nothing to cry about. *Tais toi, mon chou!* All will go well, trust Maman Marthe!' She enfolded Léonie in a large embrace, and in a few minutes a husky voice said, muffled:

'I am *not* crying!'

Madame shook with fat chuckles.

'I am *not!*' Léonie sat up. 'But oh, I think I am very miserable, and I wish Monseigneur were here, for that man will surely find us, and Rupert is like one dead!'

'It is true then that there is a Duc?' Madame asked.

'Of course it is true!' said Léonie indignatly. 'I do not tell lies!'

'An English Duc, *alors?* Ah, but they are of a wildness, these English! But thou—thou art French, little cabbage!'

'Yes,' said Léonie. 'I am so tired I cannot tell you all now.'

'It is I who am a fool!' Madame cried. 'Thou shalt to bed, *mon ange*, with some hot *bouillon*, and the wing of a fowl. That goes well, *hein?*'

'Yes, please,' Léonie answered. 'But there is Milor' Rupert, and I fear that he will die!'

'Little foolish one!' Madame scolded. 'I tell thee—*moi qui te parle*—that it is well with him. It is naught. A little blood lost; much weakness—and that is all. It is thou who art nigh dead with fatigue. Now thou shalt come with me.'

So Léonie, worn out with the terrors and exertions of the past two days, was tucked up between cool sheets, fed, crooned over, and presently left alone to sleep.

When she awoke, the morning sun streamed in at the window, and sounds of bustle came from the street below. Madame was smiling at her from the doorway.

She sat up and rubbed her eyes.

'Why—why it is morning!' she said, 'Have I slept so long?'

'Nine of the clock, little sluggard. It is better now?'

'Oh, I am very well to-day!' Léonie said, and threw back the blankets. 'But Rupert—the doctor—'

'*Doucement, doucement*, said I not that it was naught? The doctor came when thou wert asleep, my cabbage, and in a little minute the bullet was out, and no harm done, by the grace of the good God. Milor' lies on his pillows, and calls for food, and for thee.' Madame chuckled. 'And when I bring him good broth he snatches the wig from his head, and demands red beef, as they have it in England. *Dépêches toi, mon enfant.*'

Twenty minutes later Léonie went dancing into Rupert's chamber, and found that wounded hero propped up by pillows, rather pale, but otherwise himself. He was disgustedly spooning Madame's broth, but his face brightened at the sight of Léonie.

'Hey, you madcap! Where in thunder are we now?'

Léonie shook her head.

'That I do not know,' she confessed. 'But these people are kind, *n'est-ce pas?*'

'Deuced kind,' Rupert agreed, then scowled. 'That fat woman won't bring me food, and I'm devilish hungry. I could eat an ox, and this is what she gives me!'

'Eat it!' Léonie commanded. 'It is very good, and an ox is not good at all. Oh, Rupert, I feared you were dead!'

'Devil a bit!' said Rupert cheerfully. 'But I'm as weak as a rat, confound it. Stap me if I know what we're at, the pair of us! What happened to you? And why by all that's queer did Saint-Vire run off with you?'

'I do not know. He gave me an evil drug, and I slept for hours and hours. He is a pig-person. I hate him. I am glad that I bit him, and threw the coffee over him.'

'Did you, b'gad? Blister me if I ever met such a lass! I'll have Saint-Vire's blood for this, see if I don't!' He wagged his head solemnly, and applied himself to the broth. 'Here am I chasing you to God knows where, with never a sou in my pocket, nor a sword at my side, and the landlord's hat on my head! And what they'll be thinking at home the Lord knows! I don't!'

Léonie curled herself up on the bed, and was requested not to sit on his lordship's feet. She shifted her position a little, and related her adventures. That done she demanded to know what had befallen Rupert.

'Blessed if I know!' said Rupert. 'I went haring after you as far as the village, and learned the way you went. So I got me a horse, and set off for Portsmouth. But the luck was against me, so it was! You'd set sail an hour since, and the only boat leaving the harbour was a greasy old tub—well, well! What did I do then? 'Pon my soul I almost forget! No, I have it! I went off to sell the horse. Twenty meagrely guineas was all he fetched, but a worse—'

'Sold one of Monseigneur's horses?' exclaimed Léonie.

'No, no, 'twas a brute I got at the blacksmith's owned by—burn it, what's the fellow's name—Manvers!'

'Oh, I see!' said Léonie, relieved. 'Go on. You did very well, Rupert!'

'Not so bad, was it?' said Rupert modestly. 'Well, I bought a passage on the old tub, and we got in at Le Havre at one, or thereabouts.'

'We did not leave Le Havre until two! He thought you would not follow, and he said that he was safe enough now!'

'Safe, eh? I'll show him!' Rupert shook his fist. 'Where was I?'

'At Le Havre,' Léonie prompted.

'Oh, ay, that's it! Well, by the time I'd paid this fee and that, my guineas were all gone, so off I went to sell my diamond pin.'

'Oh! It was such a pretty pin!'

'Never mind that. The trouble I had to get rid of the damned thing you'd scare believe. 'Pon my soul, I believe they thought I'd stolen it!'

'But did you sell it?'

'Ay, for less than half its worth, rot it! Then I skipped off to the inn to inquire of you, and to get me something to eat. Thunder and turf, but I was hungry!'

'So was I!' sighed Léonie. 'And that pig-person ate and ate!'

'You put me out,' said Rupert severely. 'Where was I? Oh yes! Well, the landlord told me that Saint-Vire was gone off by coach to Rouen at two o'clock, so the next thing I had to do was to hire a horse to be after you again. That's all there is to it, and devilish good sport it was! But where we are now, or what we're to do, beats me!'

'The Comte will come, do you not think?' Léonie asked anxiously.

'I don't know. He can't very well snatch you when I'm here. I wish I knew what the plague he wants with you. Y'know, this is mighty difficult, for we haven't either of us a notion what the game is we're playing.' He frowned, thinking. 'Of course, Saint-Vire may come to steal you again. He'll have ridden back to Le Havre first, depend on't, and when he finds we've not been there he may scour the countryside, for he knows he hit me, and it's likely we'd be hiding somewhere near.'

'What are we to do?' asked Léonie, with pale cheeks.

'What, not afraid, are you? Damn it, he can't walk off with you under my very nose!'

'Oh, he can, Rupert, he can! You are so weak you cannot help me!'

Rupert made an effort to hoist himself up, and failed dismally. He lay fuming.

'Well, damme, I can fire!'

'But we have no gun!' objected Léonie. 'At any moment he may come, and these people will never be able to keep him out.'

'Pistol, child, pistol! Lord, what will you say next? Of course we have one! D'ye take me for a fool? Feel in the pockets of my coat.'

Léonie jumped down from the bed, and dragged my lord's coat from the chair. She produced Mr Fletcher's unwieldy pistol from one of its pockets, and brandished it gleefully.

'Rupert, you are very clever! Now we can kill that pig-person!'

'Hi, put it down!' commanded Rupert in some alarm. 'You know naught of pistols, and we'll have an accident if you fiddle with it! The thing's loaded and cocked!'

'I *do* know about pistols!' said Léonie indignantly. 'You point it, so! And pull this thing.'

'For God's sake, put it down!' cried Rupert. 'You're levelling the damned thing at me, silly chit! Put it on the table beside me, and find my purse. It's in my breeches pocket.'

Léonie laid the pistol down reluctantly, and rummaged anew for the purse.

'How much have we?' Rupert asked.

Léonie emptied the guineas on to the bed. Three rolled on to the floor, and one dropped into Rupert's broth with a splash.

''Pon my soul, you are a careless minx!' said Rupert, fishing for the coin in his bowl. 'There's another gone now, under the bed!'

Léonie dived after the errant guineas, retrieved them, and sat down on the bed to count them.

'One, two, four, six, and a louis—oh, and another guinea, and three sous, and—'

'That's not the way! Here, give 'em to me! There's another gone under the bed, burn it!'

Léonie was grovelling under the bed in search of the coin when they heard the clatter of wheels outside.

'What's that?' said Rupert sharply. 'Quick! To the window!'

Léonie extricated herself with difficulty, and ran to the window.

'Rupert, 'tis he! *Mon Dieu, mon Dieu*, what are we to do?'

'Can you see him?' Rupert demanded.

'No, but there is a coach, and the horses are steaming! Oh listen, Rupert!'

Voices were heard below, expostulating. Evidently Madame was guarding the staircase.

'Saint-Vire, I'll bet a monkey!' said Rupert. 'Where's that pistol? Plague take this broth!' He threw the bowl and the rest of its contents on to the floor, settled his wig straight, and reached out a hand for the pistol, a very grim look on his drawn young face.

Léonie darted forward and seized the weapon.

'You are not enough strong!' she said urgently. 'See you have exhausted yourself already! Leave me! I will shoot him dead!'

'Here, no, I say!' expostulated Rupert. 'You'll blow him to smithereens!'

Give it to me! Fiend seize it, do as I say!'

The commotion below had subsided a little, and footsteps could be heard mounting the stairs.

'Give that pistol to me, and get you to the other side of the bed,' ordered Rupert. 'By Gad, we'll see some sport now! Come *here!*'

Léonie had backed to the window, and stood with the pistol levelled at the door, her finger crooked about the trigger. Her mouth was shut hard, and her eyes blazed. Rupert struggled impatiently to rise.

'For God's sake, give it to me! We don't want to kill the fellow!'

'Yes, we do,' said Léonie. 'He gave me an evil drug.'

The door opened.

'If you come one step into the room I will shoot you dead!' said Léonie clearly.

'And I thought that you would be pleased to see me, *ma fille,*' said a soft drawling voice. 'I beg you will not shoot me dead.' Great-coated, booted and spurred, not a hair of his elegant wig out of place, his Grace of Avon stood upon the threshold, quizzing glass raised, a faint smile curling his thin lips.

Rupert gave a shout of laughter, and collapsed on to his pillows.

'Thunder and turf, but I never thought I'd live to be thankful for the sight of you, Justin!' he gasped. 'Stap me if I did!'

20

His Grace of Avon Takes Command of the Game

The colour came flooding back to Léonie's cheeks.

'Monseigneur!' she gasped, and flew across the room towards him, laughing and crying at once. 'Oh, Monseigneur, you have come, you have come!' She landed breathless in his arms, and clung to him.

'Why, *ma fille!*' said his Grace gently. 'What is all this? Did you doubt I should come?'

'Take that pistol from her,' recommended Rupert faintly, but with a smile.

The pistol was pressed to his Grace's heart. He removed it from Léonie's clutch, and pocketed it. He looked down at the curly head with a curious smile, and presently stroked it.

'My dear infant, you must not cry. Come, it is in very truth Monseigneur! There is nothing to frighten you.'

'Oh, I am n-not *frightened!*' said Léonie. 'I am so very glad!'

'Then I beg you will signify your gladness in a more becoming manner. May I ask what you are doing in those clothes?'

Léonie kissed his hand, and mopped her eyes.

'I like them, Monseigneur,' she said, with a twinkle.

'I doubt it not.' Avon went past her to the bed, and bent over it, laying his cool white hand over Rupert's galloping pulse. 'You are hurt, boy?'

Rupert managed to smile.

'It's naught. A hole in my shoulder, plague take it!'

His Grace produced a flask from one pocket, and put it to Rupert's lips.

Rupert drank, and the blue shade went from about his mouth.

'I believe I have to thank you,' said the Duke, and removed a pillow. 'You did well, my child. In fact, you have surprised me. I am in your debt.'

Rupert flushed.

'Pooh, 'twas nothing! I did precious little. 'Twas Léonie got us off. 'Fore Gad, I'm devilish pleased to see you, Justin!'

'Yes, so you remarked.' His Grace put up his quizzing glass and eyed the coins that lay scattered over the bed. 'What, may I ask, is all this wealth?'

'Oh, that's our money, Monseigneur!' said Léonie. 'We were counting it when you came.'

'*Our* money!' ejaculated Rupert. 'That's rich, 'pon my soul it is! There's some on the floor still.'

'And what,' said his Grace, turning to the broken bowl, 'is this?'

'Rupert did it,' said Léonie. 'It is his broth, but when we heard you coming he threw it on the floor.'

'My appearance seems to have produced a strange effect upon you,' remarked his Grace. 'Can either of you tell me where is my very dear friend Saint-Vire?'

Rupert struggled up on his elbow.

'Tare an' ouns, how did you know 'twas he?'

His Grace put him back on his pillows.

'It is my business always to know, Rupert.'

'Well, I always swore you were at the bottom of it! But how the deuce did you find out that he'd got Léonie? Where were you? How did you guess I was after them?'

'Yes, and how did you know where to find us?' asked Léonie. 'Why did he take me?'

The Duke took off his greatcoat, and smoothed a wrinkle from the velvet sleeve beneath.

'You bewilder me, my children. One question at a time, I beg of you.'

'How did you know who had run off with Léonie?'

The Duke sat down by the bed, and snapped his fingers to Léonie, who came at once to sit at his feet.

'It was really quite simple,' he said.

'Simple, was it, egad! Then for the love of God, Justin, tell us what we've been doing, for I'll be hanged if I know!'

Avon twisted his rings.

'Oh, I think you do!' he said. 'Léonie was abducted by a very pretty rogue, and you rescued her.'

'She rescued herself,' chuckled Rupert.

'Yes. I did,' Léonie nodded. 'When the wheel came off I slipped out of the coach, and ran down the road. *Then* Rupert came.'

'Yes, but there's more to it than that,' interrupted Rupert. 'What did Saint-Vire want with Léonie? Do you know that?'

'I do, my dear boy.'

'Well, *I* think it was a great impudence,' said Léonie. 'Why did he want me?'

'My children, you cannot expect me to tell you all my secrets.'

'But, Monseigneur, I do *not* see that that is fair! We have been on a big adventure, and we have done it all by ourselves, and we do not know what it is about in the very least, and now you will not tell us!'

'I think you might tell us, Justin,' said Rupert. 'We can be discreet, you know.'

'No, my children. My opinion of your discretion is not so great as my opinion of your courage and resource. By the way, what did you do with Mr Manvers' roan?'

Rupert stared.

'Lord, is there anything you don't know? Who told you that?'

'Mr Manvers himself,' replied the Duke. 'I arrived at Avon on the evening of the day you—er—left. Mr Manvers came to retrieve his property.'

'Curse his impudence!' said Rupert. 'I left him a message! Does the fellow think I'm not to be trusted with a horse?'

'That was rather the impression he gave me,' said his Grace. 'What did you do with it?'

'Well, to tell the truth, I sold it,' replied Rupert, grinning.

The Duke lay back in his chair.

'Then I very much fear that Mr Manvers will be satisfied with nothing less than our lives,' he sighed. 'Pray do not imagine that I disapprove of your action, but I should like to know why you disposed of this roan thus speedily?'

'Well, you see, I'd no money,' explained Rupert. 'I forgot I'd my pin to sell. Besides, what else could I do with the animal? I didn't want to bring it to France.'

The Duke looked at him in some amusement.

'Did you set out on this venture penniless?' he inquired.

'No, I'd a couple of crowns in my pocket,' Rupert answered.

'You make me feel incredibly old,' complained his Grace. He smiled down at Léonie. 'What happened to you, my infant?'

'Oh, I was just teasing Rupert!' Léonie replied buoyantly. 'That is why I am in these clothes. I put them on to make him angry. And I ran away from him into the wood, and that pig-person was there—'

'One moment, my infant. You will pardon my ignorance, but I do not know who the—er—pig-person is meant to be.'

'Why, the wicked Comte!' said Léonie. 'He is a pig-person, Monseigneur.'

'I see. I do not think I admire your choice of adjective, though,'

'Well, I think it is a very good name for him,' said Léonie, unabashed. 'He seized me, and threw me into his coach, and I bit him till there was blood.'

'You distress me, child. But proceed.'

'I called to Rupert as loud as I could, and I kicked the pig-person—'

'The Comte de Saint-Vire.'

'Yes, the pig-person—on his leg a great many times. He did not like it at all.'

'That,' said his Grace, 'does not altogether surprise me.'

'No. If I had had my dagger I would have killed him, for I was very angry—oh, but *very* angry! But I had no dagger, so I could only call to Rupert.'

'The Comte de Saint-Vire has yet something to be thankful for,' murmured his Grace. 'He little knows the temper of my ward.'

'Well, but would not you have been angry, Monseigneur?'

'Very, infant; but continue.'

'Oh, you know the rest, Monseigneur! He gave me an evil drink—pig-wash! He called it coffee.'

'Then let us also call it coffee, child, I beg of you. I can support "Pig-person", but "Pig-wash" I will not endure.'

'But it *was*, Monseigneur! I threw it at him, and he swore.'

His Grace regarded her inscrutably.

'You seem to have been a pleasant travelling companion,' he remarked. 'What then?'

'*Then* he brought more pig—coffee, and he made me drink it. It was drugged, Monseigneur, and it made me go to sleep.'

Poor infant!' His Grace tweaked one curl. 'But a most indomitable infant withal.'

'There is nothing more to tell you, Monseigneur. I woke up next day at the inn at Le Havre, and I pretended to be asleep. Then the coach broke, and I escaped.'

'And what of Rupert?' The Duke smiled across at his brother.

'Faith, I don't think I stopped running till I came here!' said Rupert. 'I am still something out of breath.'

'Oh, Rupert was very clever!' Léonie struck in. 'Monseigneur, he even sold his diamond to follow me, and he came to France in a dirty old boat, without a hat or a sword!'

'Nonsense, silly chit, Fletcher gave me his Sunday beaver. You talk too much, Léonie. Stop it!'

'I do not talk too much, do I, Monseigneur? And it is as I say. I do not know what would have happened to me but for Rupert.'

'Nor I, *ma fille*. We owe him a very big debt of gratitude. It is not often that I put my faith in another, but I did so these last two days.'

Rupert blushed and stammered.

''Twas Léonie did it all. She brought me here, wherever we are. Where are we, Justin?'

'You are at Le Dennier, some ten miles from Le Havre, my children.'

'Well, that's one mystery solved at all events!' said Rupert. 'Léonie went 'cross country till the head turned on my shoulders. Oh, she diddled Saint-Vire finely, I give you my word!'

'But if you had not come I could not have got away,' Léonie pointed out.

'If it comes to that,' said Rupert, 'The Lord alone knows what would have happened if you'd not caught us, Justin.'

'I understand that my bloodthirsty ward would have shot the so dear Comte—er—dead.'

'Yes, I would,' Léonie averred. '*That* would have taught him a lesson!'

'It would indeed,' agreed his Grace.

'Will you shoot him for me, please, Monseigneur?'

'Certainly not, infant. I shall be delighted to see the dear Comte.'

Rupert looked at him sharply.

'I've sworn to have his blood, Justin.'

His Grace smiled.

'I am before you, my dear, by some twenty years, but I bide my time.'

'Ay, so I guessed. What's your game, Avon?'

'One day I will tell you, Rupert. Not to-day.'

'Well, I don't envy him if you've your claws on him,' said Rupert frankly.

'No, I think he is not to be envied,' said his Grace. 'He should be here soon now. Infant, a trunk was been carried to your chamber. Oblige me by dressing yourself once more *à la jeune fille*. You will find a package sent by my Lady Fanny, which contains, I believe, a sprigged muslin. Put it on: it should suit you.'

'Why, Monseigneur, did you bring my clothes?' cried Léonie.

'I did, my child.'

'By Gad, you're an efficient devil!' remarked Rupert. 'Come, Justin! Tell us your part in the venture.

'Yes, Monseigneur, please!' Léonie seconded.

'There is very little to tell,' sighed his Grace. 'My share in the chase is woefully unexciting.'

'Let's have it!' requested Rupert. 'What brought you down to Avon so opportunely? Damme, there's something uncanny about you, Satanas, so there is!'

Léonie fired up at that.

'You shall not call him by that name!' she said fiercely. 'You only dare to do it because you are ill and I cannot fight you!'

'My esteemed ward, what is this lamentable talk of fighting? I trust you are not in the habit of fighting Rupert?'

'Oh no, Monseigneur, I only did it once! He just ran and hid behind a chair. He was afraid!'

'Small wonder!' retorted Rupert. 'She's a wild-cat, Justin. It's Have-at-you! before you know where you are, 'pon my oath it is!'

'It seems I stayed away too long,' said his Grace sternly.

'Yes, Monseigneur, much, much too long!' said Léonie, kissing his hand. 'But I was good—oh, many times!'

His Grace's lips twitched. At once the dimple peeped out.

'I knew you were not really angry!' Léonie said. 'Now tell us what you did.'

The Duke flicked her cheek with one finger.

'I came home, my infant, to find my house invaded by the Merivales, your duenna being prostrate with the vapours.'

'Bah, she is a fool!' said Léonie scornfully. 'Why was Milor' Merivale there?'

'I was about to tell you, my dear, when you interrupted me with your stricture upon my cousin. My Lord and Lady Merivale were there to help find you.'

'Faith, it must have been a merry meeting!' put in the irrepressible Rupert.

'It was not without its amusing side. From them I learned of your disappearance.'

'Did you think we had eloped?' Rupert inquired.

'That explanation did present itself to me,' admitted the Grace.

'Eloped?' Léonie echoed. 'With *Rupert?* Ah, bah, I would as soon elope with the old goat in the field!'

'If it comes to that, I'd as soon elope with a tigress!' retorted Rupert. 'Sooner, by Gad!'

'When this interchange of civilities is over,' said his Grace languidly, 'I will continue. But do not let me interrupt you.'

'Ay, go on,' said Rupert. 'What next?'

'Next, my children, Mr Manvers bounced in upon us. I fear that Mr Manvers is not pleased with you, Rupert, or with me, but let that pass. From him I gathered that you, Rupert, had gone off in pursuit of a coach containing a French gentleman. After that it was easy. I journeyed that night to Southampton—you did not think to board the *Queen*, boy?'

'I remembered her, but I was in no mood to waste time riding to Southampton. Go on.'

'For which I thank you. You would undoubtedly have sold her had you taken her to France. I crossed in her yesterday, and came into Le Havre at sundown. There, my children, I made sundry inquiries, and there also I spent the night. From the innkeeper I learned that Saint-Vire had set off with Léonie by coach for Rouen at two in the afternoon, and further that you, Rupert, had hired a horse half an hour or more later—by the way, have you still that horse, or has it already gone the way of its fellow?'

'No, it's here right enough,' chuckled Rupert.

'You amaze me. All this, I say, I learned from the innkeeper. It was rather too late then for me to set out in search of you, and, moreover, I half expected you to arrive at Le Havre. When you did not arrive I feared that you, Rupert, had failed to catch my very dear friend Saint-Vire. So this morning, my children, I took coach along the road to Rouen, and came upon a derelict.' His Grace produced his snuff-box, and opened it. 'My very dear friend's coach, with his arms blazoned upon the door. It was scarcely wise of my very dear friend to leave his coach lying for me to find, but it is possible, of course, that he did not expect me.'

'He is a fool, Monseigneur. He did not know even that I was pretending to be asleep.'

'According to you, my infant, the world is peopled by fools. I believe you have reason. To resume. It seemed probable that Léonie had escaped; further it seemed probable that she had escaped towards Le Havre. But since neither of you had arrived at that port I guessed that you were concealed somewhere on the road to Le Havre. Therefore, *mes enfants*, I drove back along the road until I came to a lane that gave on to it. Down this lane I proceeded.'

'We went across the fields,' Léonie cut in.

'A shorter way, no doubt, but one could hardly expect a coach to take it. At the hamlet I came upon they knew nothing of you. I drove on, and came at length, by devious ways, to this place. The luck, you see, favoured me. Let us hope that my very dear friend will be equally fortunate. Infant, go and change your clothes.'

'Yes, Monseigneur. What are we going to do now?'

'That remains to be seen,' said Avon. 'Away with you!'

Léonie departed. His Grace looked at Rupert.

'My young madman, has a surgeon seen your wound?'

'Ay, he came last night, confound him!'

'What said he?'

'Oh, naught! He'll come again to-day.'

'From your expression I am led to infer that he prophesied some days in bed for you, child.'

'Ten, plague him! But I shall be well enough by to-morrow.'

'You will remain there, nevertheless, until the worthy surgeon permits you to arise. I must send for Harriet.'

'Lord, must you? Why?'

'To chaperon my ward,' said his Grace calmly. 'I hope my letter will not bring about a fresh attack of the vapours. Gaston had best start for Le Havre at once.' He rose. 'I want pen, ink, and paper. I suppose I shall find them downstairs. You would be better for an hour's sleep, my dear.'

'But what of Saint-Vire?' Rupert asked.

'The so dear Comte is in all probability scouring the country-side. I hope to see him soon.'

'Ay, but what will you do?'

'I? I shall do precisely nothing.'

'I'd give a pony to see his face when he finds you here!'

'Yes, I do not think he will be pleased,' said his Grace, and went out.

2I

The Discomfiture of the Comte de Saint-Vire

Mine host and hostess of the Black Bull at Le Dennier had never before entertained such quality at their humble inn. Madame sent a serving man running hot-foot to her neighbour, Madame Tournoise, and presently the lady came hurrying in with her daughter to aid Madame in her preparations. When she heard that no less a personage than an English Duke, with his entourage, had arrived at the inn, she was round-eyed in wonderment, and when his Grace came slowly down the stairs clad in a coat of palest lavender, with lacing of silver, and a silver waistcoat, amethysts in his lace, and on his fingers, she stood staring open-mouthed.

His Grace went to the little parlour, and sent for writing materials. Mine host came bustling with the inkhorn, and desired to know whether Monseigneur would take any refreshment. His Grace bespoke a bottle of canary wine, and three glasses, and sat him down to write to his cousin. A faint smile hovered about his lips

> My very dear Cousin,—
> I Trust that by the Time you Receive this Missive you will have recovered from the Sad Indisposition which had overtaken you when I had the Pleasure of seeing you, three Days since. I am Desolat'd to be Oblig'd to put you to Added Inconvenience, but I believe I must Request you to Join me here as soon as may be. Gaston, who brings this letter, will Escort you. Pray pack your Trunks for a long stay, for I have some notion of Proceeding in due Course to Paris. My Ward, you will be Reliev'd to hear, is with me in this charming Village, in company with my Lord Rupert.
> I have the Honour, my dear Cousin, to be
> Yr most devot'd, humble, and obedient servant
> Avon

His Grace signed his name with a flourish, still smiling. The door opened, and Léonie came in, all in foaming white muslin, with a blue sash about her waist, and a blue riband in her hair.

'Monseigneur, is it not kind of Lady Fanny to send me this pretty dress? I look nice, do you not think?'

The Duke put up his glass.

'My child, you look charming. Lady Fanny's taste is unimpeachable.' He rose, and picked up a flat velvet case from the table. 'I beg you will accept this trifling mark of my affection for you, infant.'

Léonie skipped up to him.

'*Another* present, Monseigneur? I think you are very kind to me! What is it, I wonder?'

His Grace opened the case. Léonie's lips formed a soundless Oh!

'Mon-seigneur!'

The Duke lifted the pearls from their bed of velvet, and clasped them about her neck.

'Oh, Monseigneur, thank you!' she said in a gasp, and held the long string between her fingers. 'They are beautiful! I love them, oh, much! Would you like me to curtsy to you, or may I just kiss your hand?'

His Grace smiled.

'You need do neither, infant.'

'I will do both,' said Léonie, and sank down with skirts outspread and one little foot peeping from beneath the muslin flounces. Then she kissed the Duke's hand, and rose. Lastly she inspected his Grace's clothes.

'That is a nice dress, I think,' she said.

Avon bowed.

'I like it,' Léonie said. 'Monseigneur, I feel very brave now. What will you do to that pig-person when he comes?'

'I shall have the honour of presenting you, my dear,' Avon answered. 'Let him have your haughtiest curtsy. It is a little game we play.'

'Yes? But I do not want to curtsy to him. I want to make him sorry.'

'Believe me, he will be very sorry, but the time is not yet. Bear in mind, *ma fille*, that you have not till now set eyes on my dear friend.'

'Ah, bah, what is this?' she demanded. 'I know him well, and he knows me!'

'Strive to cultivate a little imagination,' sighed his Grace. 'The so dear Comte stole my page, Léon. You are my ward, Mademoiselle de Bonnard.'

'Oh!' said Léonie doubtfully. 'I must be polite, *enfin?*'

'Very polite, child. And remember, you and I are here for our health. We know naught of abductions, or evil drinks, or even–er–pig-persons. Can you play the game of pretence?'

'But yes, Monseigneur! Will he pretend, do you think?'

'I have reason to think, child, that he will follow my lead.'

'Why, Monseigneur?'

'Because, child, he has a secret which he suspects I share. But since it is a highly discreditable secret he would not like me to think that he had any knowledge of it. We fence, you see, but whereas I see my way clearly, he moves in darkness.'

'Oh, I see!' she said. 'He will be surprised to find you, *n'est-ce pas?*'

'I rather think he will,' agreed his Grace. He went to the table and poured out two glasses of canary. One of them he gave to Léonie. 'My dear, I drink to your safe deliverance.'

'Oh, I thank you, Monseigneur! What shall I drink to?' She put her head on one side. '*Voyons*, I will just drink to *mon cher seigneur!*'

'Quite neat,' said the Duke. 'Gaston? *A la bonne heure!* You will journey back to Avon, Gaston, at once.'

Gaston's face fell.

'But yes, Monseigneur.'

'Bearing with you this letter to my cousin. She will accompany you to France again.'

Gaston brightened perceptibly.

'Further, you will go to Milor' Merivale and obtain from him the clothes of Milor' Rupert. It is understood?'

'All Milor' Rupert's clothes, Monseigneur?' asked Gaston aghast.

'All of them. If he is there, bring milor's valet also. I had wellnigh forgot Mademoiselle Léonie's maid. Instruct her to pack the rest of mademoiselle's clothes, and bring her–and them–to me here.'

Gaston blinked rapidly.

'Yes, Monseigneur,' he said with an effort.

'You will board the *Silver Queen,* of course, and you will convey your charges by coach to Portsmouth.' His Grace tossed a fat purse to him. 'At Portsmouth, on your way to Avon, you will seek out a certain roan horse.'

'*Bon Dieu!*' muttered Gaston. 'A roan horse, Monseigneur, yes.'

'A roan horse belonging to one Mr Manvers of Crosby Hall, sold by Milor' Rupert on Monday. You will buy it back.' Another purse followed the first. 'The price is of no moment. You will have the animal conveyed to Crosby Hall, with Milor' Rupert's compliments and–er–thanks. That also is understood?'

'Yes, Monseigneur,' said Gaston dismally.

'*Bien.* This is, I think, Wednesday. You will be here again no later than Monday. Send Meekin to me now. You may go.'

The groom came speedily.

'Your Grace sent for me?'

'I did. You will start for Paris, my friend, within the hour.'

'Ay, your Grace.'

'To apprise the admirable Walker of my coming. You will bring back with you the large berline, the smaller travelling coach, and a light chaise for my Lord Rupert's baggage. You will arrange for change of horses to await me at Rouen, at Tign, and at Pontoise. I shall rest at the Coq d'Or at Rouen for one night.'

'Very good, your Grace. Which day am I to tell the landlord?'

'I have not the least idea,' said the Duke. 'But when I come I shall require four bedchambers, a private parlour, and quarters for my servants. I trust I make myself plain?'

'Yes, your Grace.'

'That is all,' said Avon.

Meekin bowed, and went out.

'*Voyons*,' said Léonie from her seat by the fire. 'It gives me great pleasure to hear you say Do this–do that! I like to hear them answer only, "Yes, Monseigneur," and go so quickly to do your bidding.'

Avon smiled.

'I have only once in my life had a servant in mine employ who dared to question my commands,' he said.

'Oh?' Léonie looked up in all innocence. 'Who was that, Monseigneur?'

'A page I had, my dear, by name–er–Léon.'

Her eyes sparkled, but she folded her hands demurely.

'*Tiens!* I wonder he dared, Monseigneur.'

'I believe there was nothing he would not dare,' said Avon.

'Truly? Did you like him, Monseigneur?'

'You are a minx, my dear.'

She laughed, blushed and nodded.

'It is not a compliment,' said his Grace, and came to the fire, and sat down. 'I have sent for your duenna, you hear.'

'Yes.' She grimaced. 'But she will not come till Monday, will she? Why are we going to Paris?'

'As well Paris as anywhere else,' Avon replied. 'Your education is nearly complete. You are going to make your curtsy to the Polite World.'

'Am I, Monseigneur? *Vraiment?* I think it will be *fort amusant*. Shall I go to Vassaud's?'

The Duke's brows twitched together.

'No, *ma fille*, you will not. Vassaud's is one of those places which you will strive to forget.'

Léonie peeped at him.

'And—and the Maison Chourval?'

'Did I take you there?' His Grace was still frowning.

'But yes, Monseigneur, only you sent me to wait for you in the vestibule.'

'I had that much decency left, then. You will most assuredly forget the Maison Chourval. It would be interesting to know what you made of it?'

'Very little, Monseigneur. It is not a nice place, I think.'

'No, infant, you are right. It is not a nice place, nor was I—nice—to take you there. That is not the world you shall enter.'

'Tell me!' begged Léonie. 'Shall I go to balls?'

'Certainly, *ma belle*.'

'And will you dance with me?'

'My dear, there will be gallants enough to claim your hand. You will have no need of me.'

'If you will not dance with me I won't dance at all,' she announced. 'You will, Monseigneur, won't you?'

'Perhaps,' he said.

'I do not like perhaps,' she said. 'Promise!'

'You are really very *exigeante*,' he complained. 'I am past the age of dancing.'

'*Eh bien!*' Léonie tilted her chin. 'Me, I am too young to dance. *Nous voilà!*'

'You, my infant,' said his Grace severely, 'are a very naughty, wilful child. I do not know why I bear with you.'

'No, Monseigneur. And will you dance with me?'

'Quite incorrigible,' he murmured. 'Yes, infant.'

A horse came clattering up the street, and paused at the inn-door.

'Monseigneur—do you think—is it—*he?*' Léonie asked nervously.

'It seems likely, my dear. The game begins.'

'I am not feeling—*quite* so brave, Monseigneur.'

He rose, and spoke softly.

'You will not disgrace yourself, or me, infant. There is naught to fear.'

'N-no, Monseigneur.'

The landlord entered.

'Monseigneur, it is M. le Docteur to see milor'.'

'How disappointing,' said his Grace. 'I will come. Stay here, child, and if my very dear friend should come, remember that you are my ward, and behave with proper courtesy.'

'Yes, Monseigneur,' she faltered. 'You will come back soon, won't you?'

'Assuredly.' His Grace went out with a swish of silken skirts. Léonie sat down again, and regarded her toes. Overhead, in Rupert's chamber, she heard footsteps, and the muffled sound of voices. These signs of the Duke's proximity reassured her a little, but when again she heard the clatter of hoofs on the cobbled street some of the delicate colour left her cheeks.

'This time it is in very truth that pig-person,' she thought. 'Monseigneur does not come—he wants me to play the game a little by myself, I think. *Eh bien, Léonie, courage!*'

She could hear Saint-Vire's voice upraised in anger outside. Then came a quick, heavy tread, the door was flung open, and he stood upon the threshold. His boots were caked with mud, and his coat bespattered; he carried a riding-whip and gloves, and his cravat and hair were in disorder. Léonie looked at him in some hauteur, copying Lady Fanny's manner to a nicety. For an instant it seemed that the Comte did not recognize her; then he came striding forward, his face dark with passion.

'You thought you had tricked me, madame page, did you not? I am not so easily worsted. I do not know where you obtained those fine clothes, but they avail you nothing.'

Léonie came to her feet, and let her eyes wander over him.

'M'sieur is in error,' she said. 'This is a private room.'

'Very prettily played,' he sneered, 'but I am no fool to be put off by those airs and graces. Come, where's your cloak! I've no time to waste!'

She stood her ground.

'I do not understand you, m'sieur. This is an intrusion.' She rolled the word off her tongue, and was pardonably pleased with it.

The Comte grasped her arm, and shook it slightly.

'Your cloak! Quickly, now, or it will be the worse for you.'

Much of her icy politeness left Léonie.

'Bah! Take your hand away from my arm!' she said fiercely. 'How dare you touch me?'

He pulled her forward, an arm about her waist.

'Have done! The game is up, my dear. You will do better to submit quietly. I shall not hurt you if you do as I say.'

From the doorway came the faint rustle of silk. A cool haughty voice spoke.

'You mistake, m'sieur. Have the goodness to unhand my ward.'

The Comte jumped as though he had been shot, and wheeled about, a hand to his sword hilt. Avon stood just inside the room, quizzing glass raised.

'*Sacré mille diables*,' swore Saint-Vire. '*You!*'

A slow and singularly unpleasant smile curved his Grace's lips.

'Is it possible?' he purred. 'My very dear friend Saint-Vire!'

Saint-Vire tugged at his cravat as though it choked him.

'You!' he said again. His voice was hardly above a whisper. 'Are you in very truth your namesake? Even–here–I find you!'

Avon came forward. An elusive perfume was wafted from his clothes as he walked; in one hand he held a lace handkerchief.

'Quite an unexpected *rencontre*, is it not, Comte?' he said. 'I have to present my ward, Mademoiselle de Bonnard. I believe she will accept your apologies.'

The Comte flushed dark, but he bowed to Léonie, who swept him a magnificent curtsy, and muttered a few incoherent words.

'No doubt you mistook her for someone else?' said his Grace urbanely. 'I do not think you have met her before?'

'No. As m'seiur says–I mistook her–*Mille pardons, mademoiselle.*'

His Grace took snuff.

'Strange how one may be mistaken,' he said. 'Likenesses are so inexplicable, are they not, Comte?'

Saint-Vire started.

'Likenesses. . .?'

'You do not find it so?' His Grace drew a fan of lavender silk mounted on silver sticks from his pocket, and waved it languidly. 'One wonders what can have brought the Comte de Saint-Vire to this unsophisticated spot.'

'I came on business, M. le Duc. One also wonders what can have brought the Duc of Avon here.'

'But business, dear Comte, business!' said Avon, gently.

'I have come to retrieve some–property–I lost at–Le Havre!' said the Comte wildly.

'How singular!' remarked Avon. 'I came on precisely the same errand. Our paths seem fated to–er–cross, my dear Comte.'

Saint-Vire set his teeth.

'Yes, m'sieur? On–on the same errand, you say?' He forced a laugh. 'Singular indeed!'

'Quite remarkable, is it not! But, unlike yours, my property was stolen from me. I hold it in–er–trust.'

'Indeed, m'sieur?' The Comte's mouth was unpleasantly dry, and it was evident that he was at a loss to know what to say.

'I trust, dear Comte, that you have found your property?' Avon's tone was silky.

'Not yet,' Saint-Vire answered slowly.

His Grace poured out the third glass of wine, and offered it to him. Mechanically the Comte accepted it.

'Let us hope that I may be able to restore it to you,' said his Grace, and sipped meditatively at his wine.

Saint-Vire choked.

'M'sieur?'

'I shall spare no pains,' continued his Grace. 'The village is not a large hunting-ground, to be sure. You know that it is here, I suppose?'

'Yes–no–I do not know. It is not worth your trouble, m'sieur.'

'Oh, my dear Comte!' protested his Grace, 'if it is worth so much endeavour—' his eyes flickered to those mud-caked boots–'so much endeavour on your part, I am sure it is also worth my attention.'

The Comte seemed to choose his words carefully.

'I have reason to think, m'sieur, that it is one of those jewels that contain–a flaw.'

'I trust not,' answered Avon. 'So it was a jewel? Now that which was stolen from me is in the nature of a weapon.'

'I hope you have had the good fortune to find it,' said Saint-Vire, goaded, but holding fast to his self-control.

'Yes, my dear Comte, yes. Chance favours me nearly always. Strange. Let me assure you that I shall do my utmost to restore your–jewel, I think you said it was?–your jewel to you.'

'It–is not likely that you will find it,' said Saint-Vire, between his teeth.

'You forget the element of Chance, dear Comte. I am a great believer in my luck.'

'My property can hardly interest you, M. le Duc.'

'On the contrary,' sweetly replied his Grace, 'it would afford me great pleasure to be able to assist you in the matter.' He glanced towards Léonie, who stood by the table, listening with a puzzled frown to the quick give and take of words. 'I have quite a happy–shall we say, knack?–of finding lost–er–property.'

Saint-Vire turned livid. His hand shook as he raised his glass to his lips. Avon regarded him in exaggerated concern.

'My dear Comte, surely you are unwell?' Again his eyes went to Saint-Vire's boots. 'You must have come a long way, dear Comte,' he said solicitously. 'No doubt you are sadly fatigued.'

The Comte spluttered and set down his glass with a snap.

'As you say. I–I am not entirely myself. I have been suffering from a–slight indisposition, which has confined me to my room for these last three days.'

'It is really most remarkable,' marvelled his Grace. 'My brother–I think you know him? Yes, quite so–is at this very moment above-stairs, also suffering from a slight indispostion. I fear there must be something unhealthy in the air of this place. You find it a trifle sultry, perhaps?'

'Not at all, m'sieur!' snarled Saint-Vire.

'No? These annoying disorders, I believe, have a way of overtaking one in any climate.'

'As my lord Rupert found,' said Saint-Vire harshly. 'I trust his–indisposition has not given him a distaste for my country.'

'Quite the reverse,' said his Grace blandly. 'He is agog to proceed to Paris. He and I, dear Comte, believe firmly in that old remedy: the hair of the dog.'

The veins stood out on Saint-Vire's forehead.

'Indeed? It is to be hoped that my lord does not act rashly.'

'You must not be concerned for him, dear Comte. I stand–as it were–behind him, and I have a wonderfully cool head. So they tell me. But you–ah, that is another matter! You must have a care to yourself, Comte. Let me implore you to relinquish your–search–until you are more yourself.'

Saint-Vire's hand clenched.

'You are too good, m'sieur. My health is not your concern.'

'You mistake, dear Comte. I take a most lively interest in your–er–health.'

'I believe I shall do very well, m'sieur. My complaint is not so serious, I am glad to say.'

'Nevertheless, my dear Comte, it is always well to proceed cautiously, is it not? One never knows when these trifling ailments may not grow suddenly to quite large proportions. I have known a mere chill creep to the lungs, and strike a man down in the very prime of life.' He smiled pleasantly upon the Comte, who sprang suddenly to his feet, overturning his chair.

'Curse you, you've no proof!' he cried.

Up went his Grace's brows. His eyes mocked.

'I assure you, dear Comte, I have known such a case.'

Saint-Vire pulled himself together with an effort.

'It will not happen–to me, I think,' he said thickly.

'Why, we will hope not,' agreed the Duke. 'I believe that no one is–struck down–before the appointed hour.'

The Comte groped for his whip, and stood wrenching the lash between his hands.

'With your permission, m'sieur, I will leave you. I have wasted enough time already. Mademoiselle, your servant!' He spat the words out, snatched up his gloves, and went blindly to the door.

'So soon?' mourned his Grace. 'I shall hope to have the felicity of seeing you in Paris. I must present my ward to your so charming wife.'

Saint-Vire flung open the door, and twisted the handle viciously. He looked back with a sneer.

'You are full of plans, m'sieur. We will hope that none of them go awry.'

'Certainly,' bowed Avon. 'Why should they?'

'There is sometimes–a flaw!' snapped Saint-Vire.

'You bewilder me,' said his Grace. 'Are we speaking of your lost jewel, or my plans–or both? I should warn you that I am something of a judge of precious stones, dear Comte.'

'Yes, m'sieur?' The flush mounted to Saint-Vire's face again. 'It is possible that you are labouring under a delusion, M. le Duc. The game is not played out yet.'

'By no means,' said the Duke. 'Which reminds me that I have not inquired after your so charming son. Pray how does he?'

The Comte showed his teeth.

'He is very well, m'sieur. I feel no anxiety on his behalf. Your servant!' The door shut with a slam.

'The so dear Comte!' murmured Avon.

'Monseigneur, you did not do anything to him!' cried Léonie. 'I thought that you would punish him!'

'*Ma fille*, the day comes when I shall punish him,' answered Avon, and threw down his fan. His voice had changed, and sounded harsh in Léonie's ears. 'And there will be no mercy for him at my hands.'

Léonie looked at him in awe and some admiration.

'You look quite angry, Monseigneur!'

His glance came to rest on her face. He went to her, and, taking her chin in his hands, looked deep into her eyes. They smiled trustfully up at him. Abruptly he released her.

'I have reason, child. You have seen a villain to-day.'

'Yes, a pig-person,' she nodded. 'You won't let him take me again, will you, Monseigneur?'

'No, my infant. He shall never again have you in his clutches. That I swear.'

She frowned, watching him.

'You seem different, Monseigneur, I think. You are not angry with *me?*'

The grimness left his mouth, and he smiled.

'It would be impossible, my dear. We will go now and solace Rupert's boredom.'

22

The Arrival of Another Player in the Game

Monday came and went with no sign of Gaston or his charges. His Grace frowned, but Léonie danced with delight, and offered the suggestion that Madam Field had died of agitation.

'It does not seem to worry you over-much,' said Avon dryly.

'No, Monseigneur. I think we are very happy without her. What shall we do to-day?'

But the Duke was not pleased. Rupert looked up at him with a grin.

'Never known you so mindful of the proprieties before, Justin, stap me if I have!'

He encountered a cold glance, and was instantly solemn.

'No offence, Avon, no offence! You can be as prudish as you like for aught I care. But she's not.'

'Léonie,' said his Grace crushingly, 'is as feather-brained as you, or nearly so.'

'Egad,' said Rupert irrepressibly, 'I thought we'd not bask much longer in the sunshine of your approval.'

Léonie spoke aggrievedly.

'I am not as feather-brained as Rupert. You are very unkind to say so, Monseigneur.'

Rupert looked at her admiringly.

'That's it, Léonie. Stand up to him, and hit out from the shoulder. It's more than I ever did in my life!'

'I am not afraid of Monseigneur,' said Léonie, elevating her small nose. 'You are just a coward, Rupert.'

'My child—' the Duke turned his head—'you forget yourself. You owe some gratitude to Rupert.'

'Hey, up I go, and down go you!' said Rupert. 'Ecod, it's a see-saw we're on!'

'Monseigneur, I have been grateful to Rupert all the morning, and now I am not going to be grateful any longer. It makes me cross.'

'So I observe. Your manners leave much to be desired.'

'I think that you are very cross too,' Léonie ventured. '*Voyons*, what does it matter that Gaston does not come? He is silly, and fat, and Madame Field is like a hen. We do not want them.'

'Here's a fine philosophic spirit!' cried Rupert. 'You used to be much the same yourself, Justin. What's come over you?'

Léonie turned to him in triumph.

'I told you he was different, Rupert, and you would only laugh! I never saw him so disagreeable before.'

'Lud, it's easy to see you've not lived with him long!' said Rupert, audaciously.

His Grace came away from the window.

'You are an unseemly pair,' he said. 'Léonie, you were wont to respect me more.'

She saw the smile in his eyes, and twinkled responsively.

'Monseigneur, I was a page then, and you would have punished me. Now I am a lady.'

'And do you think I cannot still punish you, my child?'

'Much she'd care!' chuckled Rupert.

'I should care!' Léonie shot at him. 'I am sorry if Monseigneur only frowns!'

'The Lord preserve us!' Rupert closed his eyes.

'A little more,' said his Grace, 'and you will not get up to-day, my son.'

'Oh, ay! You've the whip-hand!' sighed Rupert. 'I'm silenced!' He shifted his position, and winced a little.

The Duke bent over him to rearrange the pillows.

'I am not sure that you will get up at all to-day, boy,' he said. 'Is is easier?'

'Ay—I mean, I hardly feel it now,' lied his lordship. 'Damme, I won't stay abed any longer, Justin! At this rate we'll never start for Paris!'

'We shall await your convenience,' said Avon.

'Mighty condescending of you,' smiled Rupert.

'You are not to be impertinent to Monseigneur, Rupert,' said Léonie sternly.

'I thank you, infant. It needs for someone to support my declining prestige. If you are to rise to-day you will rest now, Rupert. Léonie, an you wish to ride out I am at your disposal.'

She jumped up.

'I will go and put on my riding-dress at once. *Merci, Monseigneur.*'

'I'd give something to come with you,' said Rupert wistfully, when she had gone.

'Patience, child.' His Grace drew the curtains across the window. 'Neither the doctor nor I keep you in bed for our amusement.'

'Oh, you're a damned good nurse! I'll say that for you,' grimaced Rupert. He smiled rather shyly up at his brother. 'I'd not ask for a better.'

'In truth, I surprise myself sometimes,' said his Grace, and went out.

'Ay, and you surprise me, damme you do!' muttered Rupert. 'I'd give something to know what's come over you. Never was there such a change in anyone!'

And indeed his Grace was unusually kind during these irksome days and the biting sarcasm which had withered Rupert of yore was gone from his manner. Rupert puzzled over this inexplicable change for some time, and could find no solution to the mystery. But that evening when he reclined on the couch in the parlour, clad in his Grace's clothes, he saw Avon's eyes rest on Léonie for a moment, and was startled by their expression. He pursed his lips in a soundless whistle.

'Thunder an' turf!' he told himself. 'He's fallen in love with the chit!'

Tuesday brought no Gaston, and Avon's frown grew blacker.

'Of a certainty Madame has died,' Léonie said wickedly. '*Tiens, c'est bien drôle!*'

'You have a perverted sense of humour, child,' said his Grace. 'I have often remarked it. We start for Paris on Friday, Gaston or no Gaston.'

But soon after noon on Wednesday there was some bustle in the village street, and Rupert, seated by the parlour window, craned his neck to see if it were Gaston at last.

A hired coach of large dimensions drew up at the door, followed by another, piled high with baggage. From this vehicle Gaston leaped nimbly down, and ran to the door of the first coach. One of the lackeys let down the steps, the door was opened, and a serving maid climbed out. Behind her came a little lady enveloped in a large travelling cloak. Rupert stared, and burst out laughing.

'Egad, 'tis Fanny! Lord, who'd have thought it?'

Léonie ran to the window.

'It is! it is! *Mon Dieu, que c'est amusant!* Monseigneur, it is Lady Fanny!'

His Grace went in a leisurely fashion to the door.

'So I understand,' he said placidly. 'I fear your unfortunate duenna is indeed dead, infant.' He opened the door. 'Well, Fanny?'

Lady Fanny came briskly in, embraced him, and let fall her cloak to the ground.

'La, what a journey I have had! My sweetest love, are you safe indeed?' She embraced Léonie. 'I have been in a fever of curiosity, I give you my word! I see you are wearing the muslin I sent you. I knew 'twould be ravishing, but never tie your sash like that, child! Oh, and there is Rupert! Poor boy, you look quite too dreadfully pale!'

Rupert held her off.

'Have done, Fan, have done! What in thunder brought you over?'

Lady Fanny stripped off her gloves.

'Since my cousin was nigh dead with the vapours, what would you?' she protested. 'Besides, 'twas so monstrous exciting I declare I could not be still!'

The Duke put up his glass.

'May I ask whether the worthy Edward is aware that you have joined us?' he drawled

My lady dimpled.

'I am so tired of Edward!' she said. 'He has been most provoking of late. I doubt I have spoiled him. Only fancy, Justin, he said I must not come to you!'

'You astonish me,' said his Grace. 'Yet I observe that you are here.'

'A pretty thing 'twould be an I let Edward think he could order me as he chooses!' cried her ladyship. 'Oh, we have had a rare scene. I left a note for him,' she added naïvely.

'That should console him, no doubt,' said his Grace politely.

'I do not think it will,' she answered. 'I expect he will be prodigious angry, but I *pine* for gaiety, Justin, and Gaston said you were bound for Paris!'

'I do not know that I shall take you, Fanny.'

She pouted.

'Indeed and you shall! I won't be sent home. What would Léonie do for a chaperon if I went? For Harriet is in bed, my dear, and vows she can no more.' She turned to Léonie. 'My love, you are vastly improved, 'pon rep you are! And that muslin becomes you sweetly. La, who gave you those pearls?'

'Monseigneur gave them to me,' Léonie said. 'They are pretty, *n'est-ce pas?*'

'I would sell my eyes for them.' said her ladyship frankly, and shot a curious glance at her impassive brother. She sank down into a chair with much fluttering of skirts. 'I implore you, tell me what happened to you, for Harriet is such a fool, and so taken up with her vapours that she can tell me naught but enough to whet my curiosity. I am nigh dead with it, I vow.'

'So,' said his Grace, 'are we. Where do you come from, Fanny, and how have you had speech with Harriet?'

'Speech with her?' cried my lady. 'Oh lud, Justin! "My head, my poor head!" she moans, and: "She was ever a wild piece!" Never a word more could I get from her. I was near to shaking her, I give you my word!'

'Be hanged to you, Fan, for a chatterbox!' exclaimed Rupert. 'How came you to Avon?'

'Avon, Rupert? I protest I've not seen the place for nigh on a twelve-month, though indeed I took some notion to visit my dearest Jennifer the other day. But it came to naught, for there was my Lady Fountain's rout, and I could scarce leave—'

'Devil take Lady Fountain's rout! Where's my cousin?'

'At home, Rupert. Where else?'

'What, not with Edward?'

Fanny nodded vigorously.

'She should suit his humour,' murmured the Duke.

'I doubt she will not,' said Fanny pensively. 'What a rage he will be in, to be sure! Where was I?'

'You were not, my dear. We are breathlessly awaiting your arrival.'

'How disagreeable of you, Justin! Harriet! Of course! Up she came to town in Gaston's charge, and was like to expire in my arms. Some rigmarole she wept down my best taffeta, and at last held out your letter, Justin. She vowed she'd not come to France, do what you would. Then I had more wailings of her sickness did she so much as set eyes on the sea. Oh, I had a pretty time with her, I do assure you! She could but moan of an abduction, and Rupert's hat found in Long Meadow, hard by the wood, and of some man come to find a horse, and you setting off for Southampton, Justin. 'Twas like the threads of a sampler with naught to stitch 'em to. Gaston could tell me little more—la, Justin, why will you have a fool to valet?—and the end of it was that I was determined to come and see for myself and find what 'twas all about. Then, if you please, what says Edward but that I am not to go! 'Pon rep, things have come to a pretty pass between us, thought I! So when he went away to White's—no, it was the Cocoa Tree, I remember, for he was to meet Sir John Cotton there—I set Rachel to pack my trunks, and started off with Gaston to come to you. *Me voici,* as Léonie would say.'

'*Voyons!*' Léonie's eyes sparkled. 'I think it was very well done of you, madame! Will you come to Paris too? I am to make my curtsy to the World, Monseigneur says, and go to balls. Please come, madame!'

'Depend upon it, I shall come, my love. 'Tis the very thing for which I have been pining. My sweetest life, there is a milliner in the Rue Royale who has the most ravishing styles! Oh, I will teach Edward a lesson!'

'Edward,' remarked his Grace, 'is like to follow you demanding my blood. We must await his coming.'

'Dear Edward!' sighed my lady. 'I do hope that he will not come, but I dare swear he will. And now for the love of heaven let me have your story! I shall die of curiosity else.'

So Léonie and Rupert poured forth the tale of their adventures once more into a most sympathetic ear. Fanny interspersed the recital with suitable exclamations, flew up and embraced Rupert before he could save himself when she heard of his narrow escape, and at the end of it all stared in amazement at his Grace, and burst out laughing.

The Duke smiled down at her.

'It makes you feel middle-aged, my dear? Alas!'

'No indeed!' My lady fanned herself. 'I felt an hundred in my boredom, but this adventure—faith, 'tis the maddest ever I heard—throws me back into my teens, 'pon rep it does! Justin, you should have cut him to pieces with your small-sword, the villain!'

'That is what I think,' Léonie struck in. 'I wanted to make him sorry, madame. It was a great impertinence.'

'A very proper spirit, my love, but if you in sooth flung a cup of hot coffee over him I'll wager you made him sorry enough. La, what a hoyden you are, child! But I vow I envy you your courage. Saint-Vire? Ay, I know him well. A head of hair that could set six hayricks ablaze, and the most unpleasant eyes of any I know. What did he want with you, sweet?'

'I do not know,' Léonie answered. 'And Monseigneur will not tell.'

'Oh, so you know, Justin? I might have guessed it! Some fiendish game you will be playing.' My lady shut her fan with a click. 'It's time I took a hand indeed! I'll not have this child endangered by your mad tricks, Justin. Poor angel, I shudder to think of what might have befallen you!'

'Your solicitude for my ward's safety is charming, Fanny, but I believe I am able to protect her.'

'Of course he is!' said Léonie. 'Do I not belong to him?' She put her hand on his Grace's arm, and smiled up at him.

My lady looked, and her eyes narrowed. On Rupert's face she surprised a knowing grin, and of a sudden jumped up, saying that she must see to the bestowal of her boxes.

'Faith, the inn won't hold them!' chuckled Rupert. 'Where are you to sleep, Fan?'

'I do not care an I sleep in an attic!' said my lady. ''Deed, I almost expect to sleep in the stables! It would be fitting in such a venture.'

'I believe we need not put that upon you,' said his Grace. 'Gaston shall remove my trunks into Rupert's chamber. Thus you may have my room.'

'My dear, 'twill do excellently well! You shall show me the way, Léonie. 'Pon rep, child, you grow more lovely each day!' She put her arm about Léonie's waist, and went out with her.

'Egad, here's a fine muddle!' said Rupert, when the door was shut behind the ladies. 'Fan's in a mighty good humour, but lord! is she to come with us?'

'I imagine that the worthy Edward will have a word to say to that,' Avon replied.

'How Fan could have chosen such a dull dog, and you abetted her, I don't know!' said Rupert.

'My dear boy, I abetted her because he was dull enough to sober her. And he has money.'

'There's that, of course, but, faith, he'd turn the milk sour if he smiled at it! Will you take Fan alone?'

'I almost think that I shall,' said Avon. 'I could find no better hostess.'

Rupert stared.

'Are you going to entertain, Justin?'

'Lavishly, Rupert. It will be most fatiguing, but I have a duty as Léonie's guardian which I must endeavour to perform.'

Rupert sat up in his chair, and spoke briskly.

'You may count on my presence for the season, Justin.'

'I am honoured, of course,' bowed his Grace.

'Ay, but–but will you let me join your party?' Rupert asked.

'You will add quite a *cachet* to my poor house,' Avon drawled. 'Yes, child, you may join us, provided you behave with proper circumspection, and refrain from paying my very dear friend back in his own coin.'

'What, am I not to call him out?' demanded Rupert.

'It is so clumsy,' sighed his Grace. 'You may leave him to my–er–tender mercies–with a clear conscience. The hole in your shoulder is added to the debt he owes me. He shall pay–in full.'

'Poor devil!' said Rupert feelingly. He saw into his brother's eyes, and ceased to smile. 'My God, Justin, do you hate him so?'

'Bah!' said his Grace. '–I borrow the word from my infant's vocabulary–does one hate an adder? Because it is venomous and loathsome one crushes it underfoot, as I shall crush this Comte.'

'Because of what happened twenty years ago–to you?' Rupert asked, greatly daring.

'No, boy. Not that, though it weighs also in the scale.'

'Because of what he did to Léonie, then?'

'Because of what he did to my infant,' softly echoed his Grace. 'Yes, child.'

'There's more to this than meets the eye,' said Rupert with conviction.

'Much more,' agreed his Grace. The unaccustomed harshness went from his face, and left it inscrutable as ever. 'Remind me, boy, that I owe you a diamond pin. It was a single stone, I think, of a peculiar beauty?'

'Ay, you gave it me, years ago.'

'I wonder what can have possessed me?' said his Grace. 'No doubt you were–er–"basking in the sunshine of my approval".'

23

Mr Marling Allows himself to be Persuaded

Lady Fanny partook of breakfast in bed next morning, and was sipping her hot chocolate when Léonie scratched on the door. My lady put up her hands to her pretty night-cap and patted her golden curls before she called 'Come in!'

'Oh, 'tis you, child! Mercy, are you riding out so early?'

Léonie was in riding dress, with polished boots, and leathern gauntlets, tasselled, and a big black beaver on her head with a long feather that swept her shoulder.

'Yes, madame, but only if you do not need me. Monsiegneur said that I must ask you.'

Lady Fanny nibbled at a sweet biscuit and regarded the bed-post with rapt interest.

'No, child, no. Why should I need you? Lud, what roses you have, I'd give my best necklet for your complexion. To be sure, I had it once. Go, my love. Don't keep Justin waiting. Is Rupert up?'

'His valet dresses him, madame.'

'I'll bear him company in the parlour,' said her ladyship, and pushed her cup and saucer away. 'Away with you, child! Stay! Send Rachel to me, my love, if you will be so good.'

Léonie went with alacrity. Half an hour later my lady, having bustled exceedingly, came tripping into the parlour dressed in a flowered muslin, and her fair hair unpowdered beneath a becoming cap. Rupert looked up as she entered, and put down the book over which he had been yawning.

'Lord, you're up early, Fan!'

'I came to bear you company,' she cooed, and went to sit by him, at the window.

'Wonders'll never cease,' Rupert said. He felt that this amiability on Fanny's part ought not to go unrewarded. 'You look twenty this morning, Fan, 'pon my soul you do!' he said handsomely.

'Dear Rupert! Do you really think so?'

'Ay,–that'll do, though! Léonie has gone riding with his Grace.'

'Rupert,' said my lady.

'Ay, what?'

Fanny looked up.

'I have made up my mind to it Justin shall marry that child.'

Rupert was unperturbed.

'Will he, do you think?'

'My dear boy, he's head over ears in love with her!'

'I know that–I'm not blind, Fan. But he's been in love before.'

'You are most provoking, Rupert! Pray what has that to do with it?'

'He's not married any of 'em,' said my lord.

Fanny affected to be shocked.

'Rupert!'

'Don't be prudish, Fanny! That's Edward's doing, I know.'

'Rupert, if you are minded to be unkind about dear Edward—'

'Devil take Edward!' said Rupert cheerfully.

Fanny eyed him for a moment in silence, and suddenly smiled.

'I am not come to quarrel with you, horrid boy. Justin would not take Léonie as his mistress.'

'No, damme, I believe you're right. He's turned so strict you'd scarce know him. But marriage—! He'd not be so easily trapped.'

'Trapped?' cried my lady. 'It's no such thing! The child has no notion of wedding him. And that is why he will want her to wife, mark my words!'

'He might,' Rupert said dubiously. 'But—Lord, Fanny, he's turned forty, and she's a babe!'

'She is twenty, my dear, or near it. 'Twould be charming! She will always think him wonderful, and she'll not mind his morals, for she's none herself; and he—oh, he will be the strictest husband in town, and the most delightful! She will always be his infant, I dare swear, and he "Monseigneur". I am determined he shall wed her. Now what do you say?'

'I? I'd be pleased enough, but—egad, Fanny, we don't know who she is! Bonnard? I've never met the name, and it hath a plaguey bourgeois ring to it, damme, so it has! And Justin—well, y'know, he's Alastair of Avon, and it won't do for him to marry a nobody.'

'Pooh!' said my lady. 'I'll wager my reputation she does not come of common stock. There's some mystery, Rupert.'

'Any fool could tell that,' Rupert said frankly. 'And if you asked me, Fan, I'd say she was related to Saint-Vire.' He leaned back in his chair and looked for surprise in his sister. It did not come.

'Where would be my wits if I'd not seen that?' demanded Fanny. 'As soon as I heard that 'twas Saint-Vire who carried her off I felt positive she was a base-born child of his.'

Rupert spluttered.

'Gad, would you have Justin marry any such?'

'I should not mind at all,' said my lady.

'He won't do it,' Rupert said with conviction. 'He's a rake, but he knows what's due to the family, I'll say that for him.'

'Pho!' My lady snapped her fingers. 'If he loves her he'll not trouble his head over the family. Why, what did I care for the family when I married Edward?'

'Steady, steady! Marling has his faults, I'm not saying he hasn't, but there's no bad blood in his family, and you can trace him back to—'

'Stupid creature, could I not have had Fonteroy for the lifting of a finger? ay, or my Lord Blackwater, or his Grace of Cumming? Yet I chose Edward, who beside them was a nobody.'

'Damn it, he's not base-born!'

'I would not have cared, I give you my word!'

Rupert shook his head.

'It's lax, Fanny, 'fore Gad it's lax. I don't like it.'

My lady pulled a face at him.

'Oh, tell Justin you do not like it, my dear! Tell him—'

'I'm not meddling in Justin's affairs, I thank you. He'll do as he likes, but I'll lay you a monkey he weds no bastard.'

'Done!' said my lady. 'Oh, Rupert! I lost my big emerald at play last week! I could have cried my eyes out, and Edward could only say that it must be a lesson to me!'

'That's Edward all over,' nodded Rupert. 'Don't I know it!'

'No, you do not, tiresome boy! He will give me another emerald.' She blinked rapidly. 'Indeed, he is very good to me. I wonder if he will come here? I vow I shall be miserable if he does not!'

Rupert's eyes were on the street.

'Well, he has come, and mighty *à propos*, too.'

'What! Is it really he, Rupert? You're not teasing me?'

'No, it is he, right enough, and in a thundering rage by the look of him.'

Lady Fanny sighed ecstatically.

'Darling Edward! He will be very angry with me, I am sure.'

Marling came quickly in. He was travel-stained, and heavy-eyed from lack of sleep, and his mouth was set in an uncompromising fashion. He looked his pretty wife over in silence.

'That's the last of us,' said Rupert jovially. 'We've all the family now, glory be! Give you good morrow, Edward!'

Lady Fanny rose, and held out her hand.

'Edward, I protest this is foolish of you.'

He ignored the outstretched hand.

'You'll return with me to-day, Fanny. I don't brook your defiance.'

'Whew!' spoke Rupert under his breath. 'Sa-sa— Have at you!'

Lady Fanny tittered.

'Oh sir, you are ungallant! Pray have you looked at yourself in the mirror? You come to me muddied and in disorder! And I who so love a man to be *point de vice*!'

'We'll leave my appearance out of it, if you please. I've borne enough of your whims, Fanny. You'll return with me to England.'

'Indeed, sir, do you think I shall?' The light of battle was in my lady's eyes.

'You are my wife, madam.'

'But not your chattel, sir. Pray take that frown from your face! It likes me not.'

'Ay, do!' Rupert put in. 'How did you leave my cousin, Marling?'

'Yes, sir, and *why* did you leave poor dear Harriet? It was not well done of you, Edward.'

'Fanny, have you done? I warn you, I am in no mood for these tricks!'

'Now, careful, Fan, careful!' said Rupert, enjoying himself hugely. 'He'll disown you, so he will!'

Marling swung round to face him.

'Your pleasantries are ill-timed, Alastair. I believe we shall do better if you leave us.'

'How dare you, Edward? And the poor boy just out of his bed, with a wound in his shoulder that only escaped the lung by a bare inch!'

'I am not concerned with Rupert's hurts,' said Marling cuttingly. 'He will survive without my sympathy.'

'Ay, but damme, I shall suffer a relapse if I have to look on your gloomy countenance much longer!' retorted Rupert. 'For God's sake, smile, man!'

'Oh yes, Edward, do smile!' begged her ladyship. 'It gives me a headache to see you frowning so.'

'Fanny, you will give me five minutes in private.'

'No, sir, I shall not. You are prodigious ill-natured to talk to me in this vein, and I protest I want no more of it.'

'There's for you, Marling!' Rupert said. 'Go and bespeak some breakfast.

You'll be better for it, I swear! 'Tis the emptiness of you makes you feel jaundiced: I know the feeling well. A ham, now, and some pasties, with coffee to wash it down will make a new man of you, stap me if it won't!'

Lady Fanny giggled. Marling's brow grew blacker, his eyes harder.

'You'll regret this, madam. You've trifled with me once too often.'

'Oh sir, I'm in no mood for your heroics! Pray keep them for Harriet! She has the taste for them, no doubt!'

'Try 'em on Justin,' suggested Rupert. 'Here he is, with Léonie. Lord, what a happy gathering!'

'For the last time, Fanny—I shall not ask again—will you accord me a few minutes alone?'

'Alone?' echoed Rupert. 'Ay, of course she will, as many as you like! Solitude's the thing, so it is! Solitude, and a fat ham—'

'My dear Marling, I hope I see you well?' His Grace had come quietly in.

Marling picked up his hat.

'I am in excellent health, I thank you, Avon.'

'But his spirits!' said Rupert. 'Oh, lud!'

'I confess,' Marling said steadily, 'my spirits are a little—bruised.'

'Never say so!' Rupert feigned astonishment. 'You've had a bad crossing, Edward, and your liver's upside down.'

Avon turned.

'Your conversation is always so edifying, Rupert. Yet I believe we can dispense with it.'

Rupert collapsed promptly. My lady tossed her head. Avon went to the side-table, and poured out a glass of burgundy, and offered it to Marling, who waved it aside.

'I came, sir, to fetch my wife home. As she declines to accompany me there is no more to be said. I'll take my leave of you.'

Avon put his quizzing glass, and through it regarded my lady.

'Yes, Justin. I do. I am coming to Paris with you.'

'I am gratified, of course,' said his Grace. 'Nevertheless, my dear, you will go with your husband.'

'I thank you!' Marling laughed harshly. 'I do not take her an she comes at your bidding! She must come at mine.'

'I w-won't go at anyone's b-bidding!' Lady Fanny's face puckered like that of a child about to cry. 'You are very unkind!'

Marling said nothing. She dabbed at her eyes.

'You come—bullying, and—and scowling—I won't go with you. I hate you, Edward!'

'It needed only that,' said Marling, and turned to the door.

There was a rustle of silks as my lady fled across the room.

'Oh, Edward, I didn't mean it, you know I didn't!'

He held her away from him.

'You will return with me?'

She hesitated, then looked up into his face. Two large tears stole down her cheeks. Marling took her hands, and pressed them.

'In truth,' he said gently, 'I cannot bear to see you weep, love. Go with Justin.'

At that she cast herself into his arms, and sobbed.

'Oh Edward, I will come! I truly will! You must f-forgive me!'

'My dear!' He caught her to him.

'I am decidedly *de trop*,' remarked his Grace, and poured out another glass of burgundy.

'I'll come, Edward, but I do—oh, I do want to go to Paris!'

'Then go, sweetheart. I'd not deny you your pleasure.'

'But I c-can't bear to leave you!' sobbed Fanny.

'May I be allowed to make a suggestion?' His Grace came slowly forward. 'There is really no occasion for these heart-burnings. The matter is very simple.' He swept Marling a magnificent leg. 'Pray come with us to Paris, my dear Edward.'

'Oh, I thank you, but—'

'Yes, I know,' said Avon languidly. 'You would prefer not to enter the unhallowed portals of my abode.'

Marling flushed.'

'I protest—'

'It is quite unnecessary, believe me. I would not propose such a distasteful plan were it not for the fact that I have need of Fanny.'

'I don't understand why you should need her, Avon.'

His Grace was incredulous.

'My very dear Edward, I should have thought that with your strict sense of propriety the reason must positively leap to your understanding.'

'Léonie! I had forgot.' Marling stood irresolute. 'Can you find no other lady to chaperon her?'

'I could doubtless find an hundred, but I require a hostess.'

'Then Fanny had best stay with you. I will go back to England.'

Fanny sighed.

'Edward, if you will not come to Paris I must return with you. But I do wish that you would come!'

At that moment Léonie appeared, and clapped her hands at sight of Marling.

'*Parbleu,* it is M. Marling! *Bonjour, m'sieur!*'

He smiled, and kissed her hand.

'I hope I see you well, child? Your pretty colour answers me.'

'My infant finds favour in the austere eyes,' murmured his Grace. 'Infant, I am trying to prevail upon Mr Marling to honour my poor house with his presence. Pray add your entreaties to mine.'

'Yes?' Léonie looked from one to the other. 'Please will you come, m'sieur? I shall ask Monseigneur to invite M. Davenant also.'

In spite of himself Avon smiled.

'A happy thought, *ma fille.*'

'Why, child, I believe I must not,' Marling said. 'You shall take her ladyship, and let me go home.'

'Ah, bah!' said Léonie. 'It is because you do not like Monseigneur, is it not?'

'My infant is nothing if not outspoken,' remarked Avon. 'That is the matter in a nutshell, child.'

'You do not think he is enough respectable. But indeed he is very respectable now, *je vous assure!*'

A choking sound came from Rupert; my lady's shoulders shook, and Marling collapsed into helpless laughter. Léonie looked at the convulsed trio in disgust, and turned to the Duke.

'What is the matter with them, Monseigneur? Why do they laugh?'

'I have no idea, infant,' replied Avon gravely.

'They are silly, I think. Very silly.'

But the laughter cleared the air. Marling looked at the Duke, and said unsteadily:

'I confess—it's your lack of—of respectability that sticks—somewhat in my gullet!'

'I am sure it must,' said his Grace. 'But you shall have Davenant to support you. He will be delighted to join you in mourning over my departed morals.'

'The prospect is most alluring,' Marling said. He glanced uncertainly at his wife. 'But I do not think I fit well in this mad venture.'

'My dear, Edward, do I fit well in it?' asked his Grace, pained. 'I count upon you to aid me in lending a note of sobriety to the party.'

Marling regarded his Grace's coat of dull crimson velvet quizzically.

'I might lend sobriety, but you, Avon? You supply the magnificence, I think.'

'You flatter me,' Avon bowed. 'I am to understand that you will join us?'

'Yes, Edward, yes! Oh please!'

'*Voyons,* it will be *fort amusant, m'sieur.* You must come.'

Rupert ventured to uplift his voice.

'Ay, join us, Marling. The more the merrier.'

'In face of such kind entreaties what can I say?' Marling took his wife's hand. 'I thank you, Avon. I will come.'

'Gaston, then, had best return to London for your baggage,' said his Grace.

Léonie chuckled.

'He will die, Monseigneur. I know it.'

'As you observe,' remarked his Grace to Marling, 'death and disaster are a source of never-failing amusement to my infant.'

Marling laid a hand on Léonie's head.

'She is a rogue, Avon, is she not? But a pretty rogue.'

Léonie opened wide her eyes.

'*Vraiment?* Am I pretty, Monseigneur? Do you think so?'

'Passable, my infant, passable.'

Her face fell.

'I was afraid you would not think so, Monseigneur.'

Avon pinched her chin.

'Child, do I not call you *"ma belle"*?'

Léonie caught his hand to her lips.

'*Merci, Monseigneur!* You make me very happy, *enfin!*'

Marling looked suddenly at his wife. She smiled, and cast down her eyes. Marling turned to Rupert.

'I think I'll take your excellent—though ill-timed—advice, my boy.'

Rupert grinned.

'What, the ham? Ay, 'twas good advice, stap me it was! But I'll not deny 'twas said to enrage you, Edward.'

'It succeeded in doing so, scamp. Avon, I'll not ask you to send Gaston back to England. I can return there myself, and join you in Paris next week.'

'My dear Edward, it is good for Gaston to bestir himself. He grows fat and lazy. He shall meet us in Paris.'

'You are very good,' Marling bowed.

'That is not my reputation,' said his Grace, and rang the bell.

On the following morning the whole party set out for Paris. Lady Fanny was flustered, Marling amused, Rupert flippant, Léonie excited, and the Duke leisurely and placid as ever. The entire population of Le Dennier turned out to see the passing of this cavalcade, and marvelled at the chaise piled high with baggage, at the great berline with his Grace's arms blazoned on the door, and at the two smaller coaches that followed it.

The Marlings occupied one of these, while Avon, Léonie and Rupert travelled in the berline. Rupert was propped up with cushions to alleviate the discomfort of the jolting, and whiled away the time by playing cards with Léonie. His Grace lay back in his corner and watched them in some amusement.

24

Hugh Davenant is Agreeably Surprised

They rested at Rouen over the week-end, and came to Paris on Tuesday. Walker awaited them in the hall of the Hôtel Avon, and not by the flicker of an eyelid did he betray that he recognized Léonie. All was in order for his Grace's coming, and Lady Fanny immediately took charge of the establishment. Having seen to the unpacking of her trunks, and scattered her orders broadcast, she repaired to his Grace in the library, what time Léonie went to see Madame Dubois the housekeeper.

'Well, Justin, what now?' said my lady, sitting down opposite him at his desk. 'Are we to make some noise?'

'Decidedly, Fanny. As much noise as possible. I await your suggestions.'

'A ball,' she said briskly. ''Twill do for a beginning.' She bit her finger-tip reflectively. 'I must equip the child first, and myself. I declare I have scarce a rag to my back! A white brocade for Léonie, I think, or a certain shade of green. With that flaming head—'

'My dear, I desire she shall be *poudrée*.'

'As you will, Justin. Yes, it might be pretty. We shall see. I dare swear you have your reasons for wishing it. I shall send the invitations for—a fortnight hence. It's a little enough time, to be sure, but I don't despair of acceptances. Your name and mine, my dear—' Her eyes sparkled. 'I vow I'll have all Paris here! And then?'

'Then, my dear Fanny, Versailles,' he said.

Lady Fanny nodded.

'It's very well. You'll make some stir with her, Justin.'

'It is my intention,' he said. 'Send out your cards, my dear.'

'Expense?' She cocked her head to one side.

'You will not consider it. I think we will have the young Condé and De Penthièvre. The Duc de Richelieu also.'

'I leave them to you. There must be Madame du Deffand, of course, and the Duchesse de la Roque.' Lady Fanny half-closed her eyes. 'My dearest Justin, there is no one who is anyone who will not come to the ball, I pledge you my word! But la, what a work I have before me! They'll come out of curiosity, depend upon it!' She rustled to the door. 'The child's toilettes, Justin?'

'I never quarrel with your taste, Fanny.'

'How droll 'twill be! 'Tis as though I had a daughter, though thank heaven I have not! She's to be richly clad?'

'As befits my ward, Fanny, but *à la jeune fille*.'

'Oh, never fear! You'll not complain. Dear me, I have not been so excited since my girlhood, when you took me to Versailles, Justin. The whole house must be thrown open. I vow some of the rooms are postively thick with dust. 'Twill need an army to set all in order. The Ball but starts my activities, I assure you.' She laughed delightedly. 'We will have *soirées*, and card-parties, a rout, maybe, and–oh, we shall make some stir!' She hurried away, full of business-like determination.

His Grace sat down to write a letter to Hugh Davenant.

From then onward the Hôtel Avon was plunged into bustling activity. Milliners and mantua-makers came and went, dancing masters and *coiffeurs*; and the servants invaded every shut room, and threw it open, and swept and garnished it. His Grace was hardly ever at home. He was at pains to show himself abroad, circulating the news of his return. Rupert he set to promote an ever-ready curiosity, so my lord as soon as he was well enough, sallied forth to the gaming houses, and to the abodes of his cronies, and characteristically spread the tale of his brother's latest whim. Léonie's beauty lost nothing in his description of it; he hinted at dark mystery, and assured all and sundry that Avon counted on the presence of the Prince de Condé at his ball, and that also of M. de Richelieu. Paris began to hum, and Fanny sat in her boudoir with notes of acceptance scattered about her.

'Oh, we shall do famously!' she cried. 'Said I not all Paris should come?'

But Léonie slipped away, escaping from dancing-masters and dress-makers alike, and stole into the library where the Duke was usually to be found. She stood in the doorway regarding him wistfully. He looked up, laid down his quill, and stretched out a hand to her.

'Well, *ma fille*?'

She ran to him, and sank on to her knees beside his chair.

'Monseigneur, it frightens me.'

He stroked her bright curls caressingly.

'What frightens you, child?'

She made a comprehensive gesture.

'This–all of it! There are so many grand people coming, and everyone is so busy. I myself have no time to talk to you, Monseigneur.'

'You do not like it, child?'

She wrinkled her nose. '*Ah, quant à ca*–! It excites me, Monseigneur, and–yes, I like it very well. But it is as it was at Versailles. You remember I lost you. It was so big and brilliant.'

'Child–' He looked down into her eyes. 'I am always here.' He smiled a little. 'I think, infant, it is I shall be in danger of losing you when you are launched into the world. You will no longer wish to sit with me then.'

She shook her head vehemently.

'Always, always! *Voyons, Monseigneur*, I am going round and round in all this gaiety that comes to me, and for a little while I like it. But always I want to run away to you. Then I am safe, and–and things do not bewilder me. You see?'

'Perfectly,' said his Grace. 'I shall not fail you, infant.'

'No, Monseigneur.' She nestled her hand in his, and gave a tiny sigh. 'Why do you do all this for me?'

'I have many reasons, infant. You will not bother your head with them.'

'No, Monseigneur,' she said again, obediently. 'It is very far away now, that time with Jean and Charlotte.'

'I desire you will forget it, *ma mie*. It was an evil dream no more.'

'*Bien, Monseigneur.*' She rested her head against his arm, and stayed so a long time.

That very evening Davenant arrived, and was told that the Duke was at dinner. He gave his greatcoat and hat to a lackey, and waving the man aside went alone to the dining-room, whence a babel of talk came.

The long room was lit by candles that stood in gold clusters on the table. Silver winked, and cut glass, and the mellow light was thrown over all. At the foot of the table my Lady Fanny sat, with Marling on her right, hot in argument with Rupert, opposite. Beside Marling was Léonie, dressed in dull yellow gold, and old lace. She was saying something to his Grace, at the head of the table, as Davenant came in, but she looked up at the sound of the opening door and suddenly clapped her hands.

'*Tiens*, it is M. Davenant! He is come, then! See, Monseigneur!'

His Grace rose, and put down his napkin.

'My dear Hugh! You come most opportunely. Jacques, lay for monsieur.'

Davenant clasped his hand for a moment, nodding to Rupert, and to Marling.

'I could not resist your invitation—or was it a summons?' he said. He bowed low to Fanny. 'My lady?'

She gave him her hand, in high good-humour.

'I declare I am prodigious glad to see you, Hugh! I vow 'tis an age since I met you last!'

'As beautiful as ever,' he said, kissing her hand. But his eyes were on Léonie.

'Oh!' Lady Fanny pouted. 'I am put in the shade, Hugh, yes, positively I am put in the shade—by this chit! It is so mortifying!' She smiled at Léonie, and beckoned.

Léonie came forward in her best manner, and swept a curtsy. A wicked little smile hovered about her mouth; she fixed Davenant with wide, innocent eyes.

'Is it possible?' he said, and bent over her fingers.

'You are dazzled, in fact?' His Grace came to stand beside his ward.

'Completely! I would not have believed it could be! You are to be congratulated, Alastair.'

'Why, so I think,' said the Duke.

Léonie made a quaint little bow.

'Sometimes, m'sieur, I am still Léon.'

'Ay, that is Léon,' Hugh smiled. 'Do you like being Léonie?'

'At first it did not please me at all,' she answered. 'But now I think it is very agreeable. You have pretty things if you are a girl, and go to balls. There is to be a ball here next week, m'sieur.'

'So I hear,' he said. 'Who comes to it?'

They sat down again at the table, Davenant opposite Léonie. It was Fanny who answered.

'Everyone, Hugh. I give you my word! 'Pon rep, I have worked over this ball!'

'Ay, and made the house a veritable wasps' nest,' grumbled Rupert. 'How are you, Hugh?'

'The same as ever, Rupert. And you?'

'Well enough,' Rupert said. 'We're all of us reformed, as you see. Never was there such a united family, and all of us so amiable one to the other—God knows how long 'twill last.'

Davenant laughed across the table at Marling.

'I learn that I am to bear you company in this disreputable establishment, Marling!'

'We are invited to supply a note of sobriety,' nodded Marling. 'It was Léonie's notion. How did you leave your brother?'

'As long as you did leave him, Hugh, I'm satisfied,' grimaced Rupert.

'Ah yes!' said his Grace. 'The deplorable Frederick! How does he?'

'Oh, there never was a man so tedious as Colehatch!' cried my lady. 'Only fancy, Hugh, he loved me once! The great Lord Colehatch. La! I should be honoured!'

'He is just as deplorable as ever, I fear,' Hugh replied. 'He was not pleased to hear that I intended to visit this house again.'

'Lord, did he want you, Fan?' exclaimed Rupert. 'Well, I always knew the man was a fool.'

'I thank you, my lord!' Davenant made him a mock bow. 'You are all of you vastly complimentary towards my respected brother.'

'Oh, and to me!' said my lady. 'Horrid boy! Do you remember that Colehatch wanted me, Justin?'

'My memory fails me when I try to disentangle your suitors, my dear. Was he the one who demanded you of me with a pistol at my head, as it were? No, I believe that was Fonteroy. Colehatch, I think, wrote me a correct application for your hand which I still cherish. He said that he was willing to overlook such trifling faults in you, my dear, as your levity and your extravagance.'

'Fanny, I make you my apologies on his behalf!' laughed Hugh.

Marling helped himself to a peach.

'What an ardent lover!' he remarked. 'I hope I did not say that I would overlook your faults?'

'Dearest Edward, you said that you adored me from my heels to my topmost curl!' sighed her ladyship. 'Lud, what days they were! Cumming– dear soul–fought John Drew because he disparaged my eyebrows, and Vane–do you remember Vane, Justin?–wanted to fly with me!'

Léonie was greatly interested.

'And did you?' she inquired.

'La, child, what will you ask next? He had not a penny, poor darling, and was mad into the bargain.'

'I should like people to fight over me,' Léonie said. 'With swords.'

Davenant was amused.

'Would you Léon–Léonie!'

'But yes, m'sieur! It would be so exciting. Did you see them fight, madame?'

'Good gracious, no, child! Of course I did not. One never does.'

'Oh!' Léonie was disappointed. 'I thought you watched.'

Davenant looked at the Duke.

'The lady would appear to have a taste for bloodshed,' he remarked.

'A veritable passion for it, my dear. Nothing pleases her more.'

'You are not to encourage her, Justin!' said my lady. 'I vow it's scandalous!'

Léonie twinkled merrily.

'There is one thing I made Monseigneur teach me that is very blood-thirsty,' she said. 'You do not know!'

'What is it, puss?'

'Aha, I will not tell!' She shook her head wisely. 'You would say it is unladylike.'

'Oh, Justin, what have you been at? Some hoydenish trick it is, I dare swear!'

'Tell us!' said Marling. 'You've whetted our curiosity, child, and soon we shall begin to guess.'

'Ecod, do you mean—' began Rupert.

Léonie waved agitated hands.

'No, no, *imbécile! Tais toi!'* She pursed her mouth primly. 'M. Marling would be shocked, and madame would say it is not at all respectable. Monseigneur, he is not to tell!'

'One would infer that it was some disgraceful secret,' said his Grace. 'I believe I have several times requested you not to call Rupert "*imbécile*", infant.'

'But Monseigneur, he is an *imbécile!*' she protested. 'You know he is!'

'Undoubtedly, *ma fille*, but I do not tell the whole world so.'

'Then I do not know what I am to call him,' said Léonie. 'He calls *me* spitfire, Monseigneur, and wildcat.'

'And so she is, by Gad!' exclaimed his lordship.

'I am *not*, Rupert, I am a lady. Monseigneur says so.'

'A manifestly false assertion,' said his Grace. 'But I cannot remember ever having said anything of the kind, infant.'

She peeped naughtily up at him, through her lashes. It was one of her most captivating little tricks.

'But, Monseigneur, you said only a minute ago that your memory is not at all good.'

There was a shout of laughter; Avon's own eyes were alight with it. He picked up his fan and dealt Léonie a rap across the knuckles. She chuckled, and turned jubilantly to the others.

'*Voyons*, I have made you all laugh!' she said. 'And I *meant* to make you laugh! I am a wit, *enfin!*'

Davenant was looking at Avon, dawning wonder on his face, for Avon's eyes rested on his ward with such tender amusement in them that Davenant could hardly believe it was the Duke that he looked on.

'Oh lud, what a child it is!' said my lady, dabbing at her eyes. 'I vow I would never have dared speak so to Justin at your age!'

'Nor I!' said Rupert. 'But there's nothing she won't dare, damme, there's not!' He turned to Davenant. 'Never was there such a girl, Hugh! Do you know she's even been abducted?'

'Abducted?' Davenant looked round, half-incredulous. 'What's this?'

'Oh, that pig-person!' said Léonie scornfully.

'My love!' Lady Fanny jumped. '*What* did I hear you say?'

'Well, but, madame, Monseigneur allows me to say pig-person. You do not mind, do you, Monseigneur?'

'My infant, it is not a beautiful expression, nor am I in any way enamoured of it, but I believe that I did say I could support it as long as you refrained from talking of pig–er–wash.'

'Yes, you did,' she said triumphantly.

'But what do you mean?' demanded Davenant. 'Who abducted Léonie? Is it true?'

Marling nodded to him across the table.

'As pretty a piece of villainy as ever I heard.'

'But who did it? Who is the–the pig-person?'

'The bad Comte de Saint-Vire!' said Léonie. 'He gave me an evil drink, and brought me to France, and Rupert saved me!'

Davenant started, and stared at his Grace.

'Saint-Vire!' he said, and again, beneath his breath, 'Saint-Vire.'

His Grace cast a quick look round, but the lackeys had left the room.

'Yes, Hugh, Yes. The so dear Comte.'

Davenant opened his mouth to speak, and then shut it again.

'Quite so,' said his Grace.

'But, Avon—' it was Marling who spoke—'Fanny tells me that cards for the ball have been sent to Saint-Vire and his wife. Why did you do that?'

'I believe I had a reason,' said his Grace pensively. 'No doubt it will return to my mind some time or other.'

'If the fellow comes I'll never be able to contain myself!' Rupert said.

'I do not imagine that he will come, my child. Hugh, if you have finished, I suggest we repair to the library. It is the only room that Fanny has left undisturbed.'

Fanny rose, and shook her finger at him.

'I shall throw it open on the night of the ball, never fear! I have a mind to set card-tables there.'

'No,' said Léonie firmly. 'It is our very own room, Monseigneur. You are not to let her!' She laid her finger-tips on his crooked arm, and prepared to go out with him. Hugh heard an urgent whisper. 'Monseigneur, not that room! We always sit there. You brought me to it the very first night.'

Avon turned his head.

'You hear, Fanny?'

'It's most tiresome!' said her ladyship, in a long-suffering manner. 'What odds can it make, child? What's your reason?'

'Madam, I cannot think of the word. It is what Monseigneur says when you ask him why he does a thing?'

Rupert opened the door.

'Faith, I know what she means! A whim!'

'*C'est cela!*' Léonie gave a little skip. 'You are very clever to-night, Rupert, I think.'

The ladies retired early to bed, and as Rupert dragged the unwilling Marling out to Vassaud's, Avon and Hugh were left alone in the quiet library. Hugh looked round with a little smile.

'Egad, it's like old times, Justin!'

'Three months ago, to be precise,' said his Grace. 'I am becoming something of a patriarch, my dear.'

'Are you?' Davenant said, and smiled to himself. 'May I compliment you on your ward?'

'Pray do! You find her to your taste?'

'Infinitely. Paris will be enchanted. She is an original.'

'Something of a rogue,' conceded his Grace.

'Justin, what has Saint-Vire to do with her?'

The thin brows rose.

'I seem to remember, my dear, that your curiosity was always one of the things I deplored in you.'

'I've not forgot the tale you told me—in this very room, Justin. Is Léonie the tool with which you hope to crush Saint-Vire?'

His Grace yawned.

'You fatigue me, Hugh. Do you know, I have ever had a fancy to play my game—alone.'

Davenant could make nothing of him, and gave up the attempt. Marling came in presently, and remarked that Rupert was not like to return until the morning.

'Who was there?' Davenant asked.

'The rooms were crowded, but I know so few people.' Marling said. 'I left Rupert dicing with one Lavoulère.' He looked at the Duke. 'The lad's incorrigible, Avon. He will dice his soul away one of these days.'

'Oh, I trust not!' said Avon. 'I suppose he is losing?'

'He is,' Marling replied. 'It is not my affair, Justin, but I think you should strive to check this gambling fever in him.'

'I agree,' Davenant said. 'The boy is too thoughtless.'

Avon strolled to the door.

'Beloved, I leave you to your moralities,' he said softly, and went out.

Hugh laughed, but Marling frowned.

'Impossible Satanas!' said Hugh.

'He seems not to trouble his over Rupert's welfare.' Marling spoke heavily. 'He should have some hold over the boy.'

'Oh, my dear Marling, Rupert will come to heel whenever Avon chooses to lift his finger.'

'It's very well, Hugh, but I have yet to see him lift it.'

'I have seen it,' Davenant answered. He drew his chair nearer the fire. 'I see also a vast change in our Satanas.'

'Ay,' Marling admitted. 'It's the child's influence. My lady dreams of a bridal.'

'I would it might be so,' Hugh crossed his legs. 'There is that in Avon's eyes when he looks on Léonie—'

'I do not trust him.'

'Why, I think I do for once.' Hugh laughed a little. 'When last I saw Léonie–Léon she was then–it was "Yes, Monseigneur" and "No, Monseigneur." Now it is "Monseigneur, you must do this," and "Monseigneur, I want that!" She twists him round her little finger, and, by Gad, he likes it!'

'Oh, but there's naught of the lover in his manner, Hugh! You have heard him with her, scolding, correcting.'

'Ay, and I have heard the note in his voice of–faith, of tenderness! This wooing will be no ordinary one, methinks, but there is a bridal in the air.'

'She is twenty years behind him!'

'Do you think it signifies? I would not give Justin a bride his own age. I'd give him this babe who must be cherished and guarded. And I'll swear he'd guard her well!'

'It may be. I do not know. She looks up to him, Davenant! She worships him!'

'Therein I see his salvation,' Hugh said.

25

Léonie Curtsies to the Polite World

Lady Fanny stepped back to obtain a better view of her handiwork.

'I cannot make up my mind,' she said. 'Shall I put a riband in your hair, or–no, I have it!–a single white rose!' She picked one up from the table at her side. 'You can well spare it from your corsage, my dear. Where is the little buckle Justin gave you?'

Léonie, seated before the mirror, held out the pearl and diamond ornament. My lady proceeded to fasten the rose with it above Léonie's left ear, so that it nestled amongst the powdered curls that were skilfully arranged to resemble a coiffure. The *friseur* had worked wonders. The curls clustered thickly about the queenly little head, and just one had been coaxed to fall to the shoulder.

'It could not be better!' said my lady. 'Give me the haresfoot, wench!'

Léonie's maid handed it to her, and stood ready with the various pots.

'Just a touch of rouge, I think,' said Fanny. 'The veriest suspicion—so! The lip-stick, girl! ... Keep still, my love; I must not overdo it. There! Powder, girl!' The haresfoot fluttered over Léonie's face. My lady studied the effect intently. 'It's very well. Now for the patches! Two, I think. Don't wriggle, child!' Expert fingers pressed the patches on: one below the dimple, one above the cheekbone. 'Famous!' cried my lady. 'Mercy, look at the time! I must hurry! Stand up, Léonie, and you, girl, hand me the dress!'

Léonie stood up in her under-dress of lace, ruffle upon ruffle of it falling over a great hoop to her ankles, and watched my lady shake out the folds of soft white brocade. Fanny flung it deftly over her head, so that not a hair was disturbed, pulled it over the hoop, twitched it into place, and told the maid to lace it up. Léonie's feet peeped from beneath the lace petticoat in shoes of white satin with heels that were studded with tiny diamonds. Buckles flashed on them—yet another present from Avon. Léonie pointed her toe, and regarded the effect gravely.

Fanny came to arrange a lace fichu about Léonie's shoulders. Out of the lace they rose, sloping and very white. Fanny shook out the ruffles, tied ribbons, and fastened the two other roses into place over the knot with a pearl pin.

'Why, madame, what is that?' asked Léonie quickly. 'It is not mine, I know!'

Fanny kissed her lightly.

'Oh, it is naught but a trifle, my love, that I had a mind to give you! I beg you will not heed it!'

Léonie flushed.

'Madame, you are *very* good to me! Thank you!'

Someone scratched on the door; the abigail went to open it, and came back into the room with a small silver tray, on which were two packages, and white roses in a silver holder.

'For mademoiselle,' smiled the maid.

Léonie ran forward.

'For me? Who sent them?' She bent over the tray to read the cards. 'Rupert—M. Marling—M. Davenant! But how they are kind! Why do you all give me presents, madame?'

'My sweet, 'tis your first appearance. I suspect Hugh asked Justin what flowers he should send.' She picked up the bouquet. 'See, child, the holder is so cunningly wrought! What says the card?'

Léonie held it between her fingers.

'"To Léon, from Hugh Davenant." *Voyons*, I am not Léon to-night, but Mademoiselle de Bonnard! What can this be?—from M. Marling—oh, the little ring! Madame, look!' She slipped the wrappings from the last package, and disclosed a fan of delicately painted chicken-skin mounted on ivory sticks. 'Oh, this clever Rupert! Madame, how did he know I wanted a fan?'

Fanny shook her head mysteriously.

'La, child, don't ask me! Stop skipping round the room, stupid! Where are Justin's pearls?'

'Oh, the pearls!' Léonie ran to the dressing-table, and extracted the long, milky string from one of the boxes there.

Fanny twisted it twice round her neck, cast another distracted glance at the clock, sprinkled scent on to a handkerchief, and over Léonie, gave a last twitch to the brocade gown, and hurried to the door.

'You will be so late!' Léonie cried. 'All because you dressed me. I will wait for you, madame, shall I?'

'Yes, child, of course! I want to be there when Jus—when they see you. Come and sit with me while I finish my toilette.'

But Léonie was in no mood to sit still. She paraded in front of the mirror, curtsied to herself, fluttered her fan, and sniffed at her roses.

Rachel worked swiftly to-night, and soon my lady stood up in a gown of rose silk, with a petticoat of silver lace, and the most enormous hoop Léonie had ever seen. My lady whisked the haresfoot across her face again, slipped bracelets on to her arms, and fixed nodding feathers into her marvellous coiffure.

'Oh madame, it is very fine, I think!' said Léonie, pausing in her perambulations to and fro.

My lady pulled a face at her own reflection.

'It matters naught what I look like to-night,' she said. 'Do you like the silver lace, child? And the shoes?' She lifted her skirts and showed a pretty ankle.

'Yes, madame. I like it—oh, much! Now let us go downstairs and show Monseigneur!'

'I am with you in a moment, my sweet life. Rachel, my fan and gloves! Léonie, hold your bouquet in the other hand, and slip the riband of your fan over your wrist. Yes, that is excellent. Now I am ready.'

'I am so excited I feel as though I should burst!' said Léonie.

'Child! Remember you are to put a guard on your tongue! Let me hear no "bursts" or "pig-persons" on your lips to-night, as you love me.'

'No, madame, I will remember. And not "breeches" either!'

'Certainly not!' tittered Fanny, and sailed out to the staircase. At the head of it she paused, and stood aside. 'Go before me, child. Slowly, slowly! Oh dear, you will break hearts, I know!' But this she said to herself.

Léonie went sedately down the broad stairway that was brilliantly lit to-night with branches of tall candles set in the niches of the wall. Below, in the hall, gathered about the fire, the gentlemen were waiting, his Grace with orders glittering on a coat of purple satin; Lord Rupert in a pale blue, with much rich lacing, and an elegant flowered waistcoat; Marling in puce; and Davenant in maroon. Léonie paused half-way down the stairs and unfurled her fan.

'But look at me!' she said reprovingly.

They turned quickly at the sound of her voice, and saw her with candles on either side, a little figure, all white, from the ordered curls to the jewelled heels: white brocade cut low across the shoulders, white lace to form a petticoat, white roses at her breast and in her hand. Only her eyes were deep, sparkling blue, and her parted lips like cherries, her cheeks faintly flushed.

'You beauty!' gasped Rupert. 'By—Gad, you beauty!'

His Grace went forward to the foot of the stairs, and held out his hands. 'Come, *ma belle*!'

She ran down to him. He bowed low over her hand, whereat she blushed, and curtsied a little way.

'I am nice, Monseigneur, do you not think? Lady Fanny did it all, and see, Monseigneur, she gave me this pin, and Rupert gave me the flow–no, the fan. It was M. Davenant gave me the flowers, and M. Marling this pretty ring!' She danced over to where they stood, just staring at her. 'Thank you *very* much, all of you! Rupert, you are very grand to-night! I have never seen you so–so tidy, and *tout à fait beau!*'

Lady Fanny came down the stairs.

'Well, Justin? Have I succeeded?'

'My dear, you have surpassed yourself.' His eyes ran over her. 'Your own toilette leaves nothing to be desired.'

'Oh!' She shrugged her shoulders. 'I am naught to-night.'

'You are *très grande dame,* my dear,' he said.

'That, perhaps,' she nodded. 'It was my intention.'

Rupert lifted his quizzing glass.

'You always look a beauty, Fan, I'll say that for you.'

The lackeys about the great doorway suddenly sprang to attention.

'La, are they arriving already?' cried my lady. 'Come, child!' She led the way into the big ballroom, that ran the length of the house. Léonie looked about her appreciatively.

'*Voyons*, this pleases me!' she said, and went up to one of the great baskets of flowers to inspect the frail blooms. 'We are all very grand, and so is the house. Monseigneur, Rupert is beautiful, is he not?'

Avon surveyed his tall, rakish young brother.

'Would you call him beautiful?' he drawled.

'Devil take you, Justin!' spluttered his lordship.

A footman stood in the wide doorway, and rolled forth names. Rupert effaced himself, and Lady Fanny went forward.

An hour later it seemed to Léonie that the whole house was full of gaily dressed ladies and gentlemen. She had curtsied a hundred times; she still could hear my lady's voice saying: 'I have the honour to present you to Mademoiselle de Bonnard, madame, my brother's ward.'

Very early in the evening Avon had come to her with a young man beside him: a young man dressed in the height of fashion, with orders on his breast, and a marvellous wig upon his head. Avon had said:

'My ward, Prince. Léonie, M. le Prince de Condé desires an introduction.'

She curtsied very low; Condé bent over her hand.

'But, mademoiselle is *ravissante*!' he murmured.

Léonie rose from her curtsy, and smiled shyly. M. le Prince laid a hand over her heart.

'Mademoiselle will honour me for this first dance?' he said.

She thought him a charming boy, no more. She put her hand on his arm, and smiled sunnily up at him.

'Yes, please, m'sieur. It is my very own ball! Is it not exciting?'

'Condé, accustomed to débutantes who were properly bored, was enchanted with this frank enjoyment. The fiddlers struck up, the couples took their places behind him and Léonie.

'Must we go first?' she asked confidentially.

'But yes, mademoiselle, surely!' he smiled. 'You lead your very own ball.'

Lady Fanny, standing by the door, touched Rupert's arm.

'Who has the child got for partner? It should be a prince of the Blood at least, by the orders! Who is it?'

'Young Condé,' Rupert answered. 'You wouldn't know him, Fan. He's only twenty or so.'

'La, how did Justin get him here so early?' gasped my lady. 'He to lead her out! She's made for life! Look, he's laughing! Oh, she has captivated him, never fret!' She turned her head to find Avon behind her. 'Justin, *how* did you contrive to get Condé here so early? You're a wizard, I vow!'

'Yes, it was well thought of, was it not?' said his Grace. 'You will present her next to De Brionne. He is just come. Who is that child with the silver roses on her gown?'

'My dear, I don't know! There are so many new faces I protest I cannot remember to whom they all belong! Justin, Condé is enchanted! There's not a man in the room will not hasten to Léonie's side having seen him so enraptured! Ah, madame!' She rustled away to greet a late-comer.

'I think I'll go to the card-room and take charge there,' said Rupert ingenuously, and prepared to depart.

'Quite unnecessary, my child,' said his Grace, barring the way. 'Hugh has it well in hand. You, boy, will lead out Mademoiselle de Vauvallon.'

'Oh, lud!' groaned Rupert, but he moved away to where Mademoiselle was seated.

When next Fanny had leisure to observe Léonie she saw her seated on a couch in an alcove, drinking negus with her partner. The two seemed to be enjoying themselves hugely. Fanny watched, well pleased, and presently, evading the group of young men who were one and all clamouring for an introduction, she took the Comte de Brionne over to the alcove, and presented him. Condé rose, and made a leg.

'Oh, mademoiselle, you must save one little minute for me later!' he said. 'When may it be?'

'We will meet somewhere,' said Léonie. 'I know! Under the big palm over there, at–at ten minutes past eleven!' She twinkled. 'That is like an adventure!'

'Mademoiselle, I shall be there!' Condé promised, laughing.

Fanny stepped forward.

'My brother's ward, m'sieur. M. de Brionne, Léonie.'

Léonie set down her glass, rose, and curtsied. Her brow was wrinkled. Inexorably Fanny bore Condé away.

'Mademoiselle looks worried?' De Brionne gave her her glass again.

She turned to him, and smiled engagingly.

'M'sieur, I am very stupid. I cannot remember who you are!'

De Brionne was taken aback for a moment. It was not thus that young ladies were wont to address the son of Louis de Lorraine. But he could not resist the fascination of Léonie's eyes. Moreover, where Condé had been pleased De Brionne would certainly not be affronted. He returned the smile.

'You are new come to Paris, mademoiselle?'

She nodded.

'Yes, m'sieur. Now let me think. *I* know! You are the son of the Comte d'Armagnac–M. le Grand!'

The Comte was much amused. It was probable that he had never before met a lady who pondered thus naïvely over his genealogy. He settled down to enjoy himself, and found that he was required to name most of the people who passed, for Léonie's edification.

'*Voyons, m'sieur*, you know everybody!' she said presently. 'You are being very useful to me. Now tell me who it is dancing with Monseigneur?'

'Monseigneur?'

'Yes, the Duc–my–my guardian.'

'Oh—! That is Madame du Deffand.'

'Truly?' Léonie regarded the lady intently. 'She amuses him, I think.'

'She is a very amusing lady,' said De Brionne gravely. 'Did Condé point our notables out to you?'

'No–no.' Léonie dimpled. 'We found such a lot of other things to talk about, m'sieur. He told me about duels, and what it is like to be a royal prince.'

De Brionne began to laugh.

'Did you ask him, mademoiselle?'

'Yes, m'sieur,' said Léonie innocently.

In the doorway Fanny was curtsying low to the Duc de Penthièvre, who had just arrived. He kissed her hand with pretty gallantry.

'My dear Lady Fanny! One was *bouleversé* when one learned of the return of the so charming Lady Fanny!'

'Ah, m'sieur!' She smiled, and spread out her fan.

Avon came up with Madame du Deffand on his arm.

'My dear Penthièvre, I am rejoiced to see you.'

'*Mon cher Duc! Madame, votre serviteur!*' He swept a bow. 'Tell me, Alastair, where is this ward one hears tell of?'

'My ward . . . let me see, she was with De Brionne a moment ago. No, she is dancing now with my brother. In white, with the rose in her hair.'

De Penthièvre looked across the room to where Léonie was circling gracefully with Rupert. Their hands were held high, her foot was pointed, and she was laughing.

'So!' said de Penthièvre. 'Our débutantes will tear their powdered locks, Duc!'

The rooms grew more crowded. Some time later Lady Fanny, proceeding to the refreshment room, met her husband in the hall, and said radiantly:

'My dearest love, what a success! Have you seen the child? De Penthièvre has danced with her, and Condé! Where's Justin?'

'Gone into the little salon. You're satisfied, sweet?'

'Satisfied! Paris will talk of naught but this ball and Léonie for weeks to come! I shall keep them talking, I promise you!' She hurried away to the refreshment room, found it crowded, with Léonie the centre of a delighted and admiring group. Fanny took a forlorn lady under her wing, and bore her off in search of a cavalier.

In the card-room they discussed the Duke's latest whim.

'*Mon Dieu*, Davenant, but what a beauty! What colouring! What wonderful eyes!' cried Lavoulère. 'Who is she?'

The Chevalier d'Anvau cut in before Hugh could reply.

'Ah, he is proud of her, is Satanas! One sees it clearly.'

'He has reason,' remarked Marrignard, toying with a dice-box. 'She has not only beauty, but also *espiéglerie*! I was amongst the fortunate who obtained her hand. Condé is greatly *épris*.'

The Chevalier looked at Hugh.

'She is like someone. I cannot think who it may be. I have racked my brains, but it eludes me.'

'Yes, it is true,' nodded Lavoulère. 'When I set eyes on her it came to me in a flash that I had met her before. Is it possible that I have done so, Davenant?'

'Quite impossible,' Hugh said fervently. 'She has but just come from England.'

Madame de Marguéry, playing at lansquenet at an adjacent table, looked up.

'But she is French, surely? Who were her parents?'

'I do not know, madame,' said Hugh with truth. 'As you know, Justin is never communicative.'

'Oh!' Madame cried. 'He loves to make a mystery! It is to intrigue us all! The child is quite charming, and well-born, of course. That naïve innocence should make her success assured. I would my daughters had it.'

Meanwhile Lady Fanny had sent Rupert to extricate Léonie from the refreshment room. She came back on my lord's arm, and chuckled gleefully.

'Madame, M. le Prince says I have eyes like stars, and another man said that a shaft from my eyes had slain him, and—'

'Fie, child!' said my lady. 'Never tell me all that here! I am going to present you to Madame de la Roque. Come!'

But at midnight Léonie escaped from the ballroom, and wandered into the hall. Condé, coming from one of the other salons, met her there.

'The little butterfly! I went to look for you, mademoiselle, and could not find you.'

Léonie smiled upon him.

'Please, have you seen Monseigneur, m'sieur?'

'A dozen monseigneurs, little butterfly! Which one do you want?'

'My own Monseigneur,' said Léonie. 'The Duc of Avon, of course.'

'Oh, he is in the farthest salon, mademoiselle, but shall not I do as well?'

She shook her head.

'But no, m'sieur. I want him.'

Condé took her hand, and smiled down at her.

'You are unkind, Fairy Princess! I thought you liked me just a little?'

'Yes, I do. I like you very much,' Léonie assured him. 'But now I want Monseigneur.'

'Then I'll fetch him for you at once,' Condé said gallantly.

'But no! I will go to him, m'sieur. You take me!'

Condé presented his arm promptly.

'Now you are a little kinder, mademoiselle! Is this monseigneur going to bring you to Versailles, I wonder?'

'Yes, I think so. Will you be there? Please do, m'sieur!'

'Of a certainty I shall be there. Then, at Madame de Longchamps' rout I shall meet you, surely?'

'I do not know,' she said. 'I think I am going to a great many routs, but Monseigneur has not told me which ones yet. Oh, there he is!' She released Condé's arm, and ran forward to where his Grace was standing. 'Monseigneur, I have been looking for you. The Prince brought me. Thank you very much, m'sieur!' She held out a friendly hand. 'Now you will go and dance with—with—oh, with somebody! I do not know the names!'

Condé kissed the small hand.

'You will bring her to court, Duc?'

'To the levée next week,' said his Grace.

'Then I am satisfied,' Condé said, bowed, and left them.

The Duke looked down at his ward in some amusement.

'You dismiss Royalty very summarily, Babe.'

'Oh, Monseigneur, he is quite young, and very like Rupert! He did not mind, do you think?'

'He did not appear to mind,' said the Duke. 'What do you want with me, infant?'

'Nothing, Monseigneur. But I thought I would come to find you.'

'You are tired, infant.' He led her to a couch. 'You shall sit quietly with me awhile.'

'Yes, please, Monseigneur. It is a *very* nice dance, I think. I have danced with a great many grand people, and they were all very kind to me indeed.'

'I am glad to hear it, child,' he said gravely. 'How does your Prince please you?'

'Oh, he is *fort amusant*! He told me ever so many things about court, Monseigneur, and he explained who the people were—oh no! it was M. de Brionne who did that. I said "Bah" to the Prince, I am afraid, but he liked it, and he laughed. And I danced with Rupert—and oh, Monseigneur, with M. d'Anvau! He said he was sure he had met me before!' Her eyes danced. 'I wanted to say, "But yes, m'sieur. I brought you wine at Vassaud's one night!"'

'I sincerely trust you did not, infant?'

'Oh no, I was very discreet, Monseigneur. I said *"Tiens!* Me, I do not think I have met m'sieur before." It was not at all true, was it?'

'Never mind, child, it was a very proper reply. And now I am going to present you to a very old friend of mine who desires speech with you. Come, infant!'

'*Qui est-ce?*' she asked.

He walked slowly with her through the salons to the hall.

'It is M. de Richelieu, my child. You will be very polite to him.'

'Yes, Monseigneur,' she said docilely, and nodded her head to a young exquisite who was smiling at her and trying to catch her eye. 'I have been very polite to everyone to-night. Except Rupert, of course.'

'That goes without saying,' said his Grace, and took her back into the ballroom.

A middle-aged exquisite was standing by the fire at one end, holding animated converse with a plump lady of some beauty. Avon waited until others had gathered about this lady, and then he went forward.

Richelieu saw him, and came to meet him.

'Ah, Justin, the promised introduction! Your beautiful ward!'

Léonie took her hand from Avon's arm, and curtsied. Richelieu bowed to her, and took her hand, and patted it.

'Child, I envy Justin. Justin, go away! I shall look after mademoiselle very well without you.'

'I don't doubt it,' said his Grace, and went away to find Lady Fanny.

Armand de Saint-Vire pounced on him as he crossed the hall.

'My friend, who is that girl?' he demanded. 'I craved an introduction. Miladi Fanny was good enough to present me. I talked with the sprite—*mon Dieu, qu'elle est jolie!*—and all the time I asked myself: Who is she? who is she?'

'And did you obtain an answer from yourself?' inquired his Grace.

'No, Justin, I did not! Therefore I ask you: Who is she?'

'She is my ward, dear Armand,' smiled his Grace, and passed on as Mademoiselle de la Vogue came up.

Fanny was in the refreshment room, with Davenant. She waved to Justin as he entered.

'I have earned a moment's repose!' she said gaily. 'Lud, Justin, I've presented a score of children to each other and never caught one of their names! Where's Léonie?'

'With Richelieu,' he said. 'No, Fanny, you need not be alarmed. He is under oath to be discreet. Hugh, you have been a godsend to me this night.'

My lady began to fan herself.

'We have all of us worked a little,' she said. 'My poor Edward is with the dowagers, playing at ombre, and Rupert has scarce been inside the card-room.'

'You have worked the hardest of us all,' said Hugh.

'Oh, but I have enjoyed myself so prodigiously!' she said. 'Justin, I don't know how many young beaux have not been making love to Léonie! Condé is ravished, he tells me. Do I not make a famous chaperon? When I present Léonie I feel fifty–yes, Hugh, positively I do!–but when I meet Raoul de Fontanges again–ah, then I am back in my teens!' She cast up her eyes.

But presently people began to take their leave, and at last they were alone again in the hall, tired but triumphant.

Rupert yawned prodigiously.

'Lord, what an evening? Burgundy, Hugh?' He poured out several glasses. 'Fan, you've torn your lace.'

Fanny sank into a chair.

'My dear, I do not care if 'tis in ribbons. Léonie, my pet, you look worn out! Oh, my poor Edward, you did nobly with the dowagers!'

'Ah yes!' said his Grace. 'I have to thank you, Edward. You were quite untiring. Infant, can you still hold your eyes open?'

'Yes, Monseigneur. Oh, madame, M. le Prince said that my dress was ravishing!'

'Ay—' Rupert shook his head at her. 'I'd give something to know what you've been at this night, rogue! Did old Richelieu make love to you?'

'Oh no!' Léonie was surprised. 'Why, he is quite an old man!'

'Alas, poor Armand!' said his Grace. 'Don't tell him so, infant, I implore you.'

'Nor anyone, my love,' said her ladyship. 'It would fly round Paris! He would be so chagrined!'

'Well, who did make love to you?' asked Rupert. 'Besides Condé.'

'He didn't, Rupert! No one did.' Léonie looked round innocently. 'He only said I was a Fairy Princess. Yes, and he said that about my eyes.'

'If that's not making—' Rupert encountered a glance from his brother, and broke off. 'Oh, ay! I'm dumb, never fear!'

'Monseigneur,' Léonie said. 'I kept thinking it was a dream! If they knew I had been a page I do not think they would have been so kind to me. They would have thought I was not enough respectable!'

26

The Presentation of Léonie

After the ball invitations came swiftly to the Hôtel Avon. More than one lady begged that Miladi Fanny would forgive the shortness of the notice and honour her on such-and-such a night, at ball, or rout, or card-party. Fanny went carefully through the pile of little cards, and was triumphant.

'My dearest Justin!' she cried. 'We shall not be above three nights at home, I give you my word! Here is a card from Madame du Deffand, for next month—a soirée. This is from the Comtesse de Meuilly—a ball. And here we have one from my dear Madame de Follemartin, for Saturday! And this one—'

'Spare us, Fanny!' said his Grace. 'Accept and decline as you will, but let us have no lists. Infant, what have you there?'

Léonie had come dancing in with a bouquet in her hand, to which a card was attached.

'Monseigneur, are they not pretty? They come from the Prince de Condé. I think he is very kind to me!'

Fanny looked at her brother.

'So we begin,' she said. 'Where are we like to end, I wonder?'

'I shall end in a debtors' prison, never fear!' said Rupert, from the depths of an arm-chair. 'Two hundred cool guineas last night, and—'

'Rupert, it's wanton!' exclaimed Marling. 'Why do you play so high?'

Rupert deigned no reply, deeming the question beneath contempt. It was Davenant who filled the breach.

'I believe it's in the family,' he said. 'Rupert, of course, is a scamp.'

'Oh no!' said Léonie. 'He is very silly, but he is not a scamp! Monseigneur, tell me what I am to wear at Versailles to-morrow! Madame says blue, but I want to wear my white dress again.'

'No, infant. To wear the same frock twice running would create almost a scandal. You shall wear gold, and dull yellow, and the sapphires I once gave you. And your hair shall be unpowdered.'

'Oh?' said my lady. 'Why, Justin?'

Hugh walked to the fireplace.

'Is it, Justin, because Titian hair has always been one of your ruling passions?'

'Exactly,' bowed his Grace. 'What an excellent memory you have, my dear!'

'I don't understand,' complained Fanny. 'What do you mean?'

'I am not quite sure,' said Avon. 'I suggest you ask Hugh. He is omniscient.'

'Now you are being disagreeable!' Fanny pouted. 'Dull yellow—ay, 'twill do. Léonie, my love, we must order a petticoat of gold net from Cerise; they are quite the rage now, I hear.' She became absorbed in modes and fashions.

She and Avon and Rupert accompanied Léonie to Versailles. Marling and Davenant were alike in their distaste for courts, and they refused to join the party, preferring to spend a quiet evening playing at piquet, and perusing the latest copy of the *Adventurer*, which had come that day from London.

So Léonie and her escort left them to their devices, and sped away in the light coach to Versailles. The drive provoked in Léonie a reminiscent mood. She sat beside Lady Fanny, whose skirts billowed about her, and addressed herself to the Duke, opposite.

'Monseigneur, do you remember that when we went to Versailles before you gave me this chain?' She touched the sapphires that lay across her white breast.

'I do, infant. I also remember that on our return you went to sleep, and would not wake up.'

'Yes, that is true,' she nodded. 'It seems very strange to be going to court again, like this!' She indicated her petticoats, and spread out her fan. 'M. le

Prince was at Madame de Cacheron's party last night, Monseigneur.'

'So I have heard,' said Avon, who had not been present.

'And danced twice with the chit!' said my lady. ''Twas positively unseemly!'

'Ay, so it was,' agreed Rupert. 'If you were to ask me I should say he came to see Léonie and none other.'

'Yes, he did,' said Léonie ingenuously. 'He told me so. I like him.'

Rupert looked at her severely.

'Well, you ought not to sit with him talking God knows what,' he said magisterially. 'When I wanted to lead you out you were nowhere to be found.'

Léonie pulled a face at him.

'You are talking like that because you have all your best clothes on,' she told him. 'They make you feel grand, and very important. *I* know!'

Rupert burst out laughing.

'Faith, that's good! But I'll not deny this is a devilish fine coat.' He regarded his rich claret-coloured sleeve with some affection.

'It is not so—so *distingué* as Monseigneur's grey and pink,' said Léonie. 'Monseigneur, whom shall I see to-night?'

'Why, child, I thought you had a dozen assignations made!' remarked her ladyship.

'Yes, madame, but I meant new people.'

'Oh, she's insatiable!' murmured Rupert. 'She'll boast a wonderful collection of hearts before the month's out, mark my words!'

'You will see the King, infant, and the Queen, and possibly the Dauphin,' said his Grace.

'And Madame de Pompadour. I want to see her, because I have heard that she is very beautiful.'

'Very,' said his Grace. 'You will also see her favourite, de Stainville, and Monsieur, and the Comte d'Eu.'

'*Tiens!*' said Léonie.

When they had come to Versailles she went presently up the marble stairway, in Lady Fanny's wake, to the Galerie des Glaces, and, looking about her, drew a deep breath.

'*How* I remember!' she said.

'For goodness' sake, child, never say so!' begged Fanny' 'You have never been here before. Let me hear no more of your recollections!'

'No, madame,' said Léonie abashed. 'Oh, there is M. de la Valaye!'

La Valaye came to talk to them, and stole a curious glance at Léonie's unpowdered head. Rupert slipped away into the crowd, in search of a kindred spirit, and was seen no more for some time.

Many people were turning to look at Léonie.

'*Dis donc,*' said de Stainville, 'who is this beautiful little red-head? I do not recognize her.'

His friend, de Sally, took snuff.

'Have you not heard?' he asked. 'That is the very latest beauty! She's Avon's ward.'

'Oho! Yes, one has heard,' nodded de Stainville. 'It is Condé's new toy, *hein?*'

'No, no, my friend!' De Sally shook his head vehemently. 'Condé's new goddess!'

Léonie was curtsying to the Duchess de la Roque; de Stainville saw my Lady Fanny.

'So Alastair has brought his so charming sister! *Madame, votre serviteur!*'
Fanny turned.

'La, so 'tis you, m'sieur.' She held out her hand. 'I declare 'tis an age since
I have seen you!'

'Madame, the years fly back when I look upon you,' de Stainville said,
kissing her hand. 'But surely it was Etienne once, and not that cold
M'sieur?'

My lady hid behind her fan.

'I vow I have no recollection of it!' she said. 'No doubt I was very foolish—
so long ago!'

De Stainville drew apart, and they fell to talking of bygone days.
Perceiving that his sister was fully occupied, Avon rescued Léonie from her
growing circle of admirers, and bore her off to curtsy to the Comte d'Eu,
who was passing down the gallery. Soon Fanny left de Stainville, and came
to Avon's side. The Comte bowed to her.

'Madame, I may compliment you upon your charge?' He waved one
jewelled hand towards Léonie, who was speaking to a shy débutante who
had been present at her ball.

Fanny nodded.

'She pleases you, m'sieur?'

'It could not be otherwise, madame. She is *éclatante*! That hair, and those
eyes! I prophesy a *succès enorme*!' He bowed, and moved away on the arm of
a friend.

Léonie came back to Avon.

'Monseigneur, I think very young men are silly,' she said flatly.

'Undoubtedly, infant. Who has had the misfortune to incur your
disapproval?'

'It was M. de Tanqueville, Monseigneur. He says I am cruel. And I am
not, am I?'

'Of course you are, child!' said my lady. 'All young ladies must be cruel.
It is *de rigueur*!'

'Ah, bah!' said Léonie. 'Monseigneur, where is the King?'

'By the fire, infant. Fanny, take her to the King.'

My lady furled her fan.

'You arranged, Justin?'

'Certainly, my dear. You are expected.'

So Fanny led Léonie down the room, and curtsied low to Majesty, who
was pleased to be gracious. Behind Majesty, with Monsieur, and one or two
others, Condé stood. Léonie encountered his gaze, and dimpled mischievously. Majesty was pleased to compliment my Lady Fanny on
Mademoiselle de Bonnard; the Queen murmured praise of such beauty, and
my lady passed on to make way for the next presentation.

'*Bon!*' said Léonie. 'Now I have spoken to the King.' She turned to Avon,
and the twinkle was in her eyes. 'Monseigneur, it is as I said! He is just like
the coins.'

Condé made his way to her side, and Lady Fanny withdrew discreetly.

'Oh, Fairy Princess, you flame in our hearts to-night!'

Léonie put her hand to her curls.

'But it is not at all kind of you to speak of my red hair!' she protested.

'Red?' Condé cried. 'It is the colour of copper, Princess, and your eyes are
like the violets you wear at your breast. As a white rose you enchanted me,
and now as a golden rose you strengthen your spell.'

'M'sieur,' said Léonie severely, 'that is how M. de Tanqueville talks. I do not like it at all.'

'Mademoiselle, I am at your feet! Tell me what I may do to regain your favour!'

Léonie looked at him speculatively. He laughed.

'Oh la, la! It is to be some great venture of chivalry, *enfin*?'

Her eyes danced.

'It is just that I am so very thirsty, m'sieur,' she said plaintively.

A gentleman standing a few paces from them looked at her in astonishment, and turned to a friend.

'*Mon Dieu*, did you hear that, Louis? Who is this beauty who has the audacity to send Condé to fetch her refreshment?'

'Why, do you not know?' exclaimed his friend. 'It is Mademoiselle de Bonnard, the English Duc's ward! She is an original, and Condé is captivated by her so unusual behaviour.'

Condé had given Léonie his arm. Together they passed an adjoining salon, where he procured a glass of ratafie for her. A quarter of an hour later Lady Fanny found them there, both in high fettle, Condé trying to illustrate for Léonie's benefit a fencing trick, with his quizzing glass as foil.

'Lud, child, what will you be at?' demanded my lady. She curtsied low to Condé. 'M'sieur, you will not let her weary you, I beg.'

'Oh, but I am not wearying him, madame, truly!' said Léonie. 'He was thirsty too! Oh, here is Rupert!'

Rupert came in with the Chevalier d'Anvau. When the Chevalier saw Léonie his brow creased.

'Who? who? *who? M'sieur, on vous demande.*'

Condé waved him aside.

'Mademoiselle, the promised guerdon?'

Léonie gave him the violets at her breast, and smiled prettily as she did so. Condé kissed her hand, and then the flowers and went back into the gallery with the fragrant bunch worn on his coat.

'Well!' said Rupert. ''Pon my soul!'

'Come along, Rupert!' said Léonie. 'Take me to find Madame de Pompadour now.'

'No, damme, that I won't!' said my lord gracefully. 'I've but this moment escaped, with d'Anvau here. It's a plaguey dull affair, so it is!'

'Child, I want you,' said Fanny, and took her back to the gallery and left her with her very dear friend Madame de Vauvallon, while she herself went in search of Avon.

She found him at length near the Œil de Bœuf, with de Richelieu and the Duc de Noailles. He came to her at once.

'Well, Fanny, where is my infant?'

'With Clothilde de Vauvallon,' she answered. 'Justin, she has given Condé her violets, and he is wearing them! Whither shall this lead?'

'Nowhere, my dear,' said his Grace placidly.

'But, Justin, 'tis not well to ensnare Royalty thus! Too great favour shown spells ruin as surely as too little.'

'I beg you will not distress yourself, my dear. Condé is not in love with the infant, nor she with him.'

'In love! 'Pon rep, I hope not indeed! But all this coquetting and—'

'Fanny, you are sometimes very blind. Condé is amused, no more.'

'Oh, 'tis very well!' shrugged my lady. 'What now?'

His Grace's quizzing glass swept the gallery.

'Now, my dear, I desire you will take Léonie and present her to Madame de Saint-Vire.'

'Why?' asked my lady, watching him.

'Oh, I think she might be interested!' said his Grace, and smiled.

When Lady Fanny led Léonie to Madame de Saint-Vire, Madame's hand clenched in her fan, and under all her paint she whitened.

'Madame!' Lady Fanny saw the clenched hand, and heard the quick intake of breath. 'It is so long since we met! I trust I see you well?'

'I am very well, madame. You are with—with your brother in—Paris?' Madame spoke with an effort.

'Yes, I am this child's chaperon!' said Fanny. 'Is it not ridiculous? I may present my brother's ward? Mademoiselle de Bonnard, Madame de Saint-Vire!' She stood back.

Madame's hand went out involuntarily.

'Child—' she said, and her voice trembled. 'Sit with me a while, I beg!' She turned to Fanny. 'Madame, I will have a care to her. I should—I should like to talk to her.'

'But certainly!' said Fanny, and walked away at once.

Léonie was left looking into her mother's face. Madame took her hand, and patted it, and stroked it.

'Come, my little one!' she faltered. 'There is a couch by the wall. You will stay with me a few—just a few—minutes?'

'Yes, madame,' said Léonie politely, and wondered why this faded lady should be so agitated. She was not at all pleased at being left with Saint-Vire's wife, but she went with her to the couch, and sat down beside her.

Madame seemed to be at a loss. She held Léonie's hand still, and her eyes devoured the girl.

'Tell me, *chérie*,' she said at last. 'Are you—are you happy?'

Léonie was surprised.

'But yes, madame. Of course I am happy!'

'That man—' Madame pressed her handkerchief to her lips—'That man—is good to you?'

'You speak of Monseigneur, my guardian, madame?' Léonie spoke stiffly.

'Yes, *petite*, yes. Of him.' Madame's hand trembled.

'*Naturellement* he is good to me,' Léonie answered.

'Ah, you are offended, but indeed, indeed— Child you are so young! I—I might be—your mother!' She laughed rather wildly. 'So you will not mind what I say to you, will you? He—your guardian—is not a good man, and you—you—'

'Madame—' Léonie drew her hand away—'I do not want to be rude to you, you understand, but I will not let you speak thus of Monseigneur.'

'You are so fond of him?'

'Yes, Madame, I love him *de tout mon cœur*—.'

'Ah, *mon Dieu*!' Madame whispered. 'And he—does he love you?'

'Oh no!' said Léonie. 'At least, I do not know, madame. He is just very kind to me.'

Madame's eyes searched her face.

'It is well,' she said, on a sigh. 'Tell me, child, how long have you lived with him?'

'Oh—oh *depuis longtemps*!' Léonie said vaguely.

'Child, don't tease me! I—I would not tell your secrets! Where did the Duc find you?'

'Pardon, madame. I have forgotten.'

'He told you to forget!' Madame said quickly. 'That is so, is it not?'

Someone came to the couch; Madame shrank a little and was silent.

'Well met, mademoiselle,' said Saint-Vire. 'I trust I see you in good health?'

Léonie's chin tilted.

'M'sieur?' she said blankly. 'Ah, *je me souviens!* It is M. de Saint-Vire!' She turned to Madame. 'I met m'sieur at–*peste*, I forget! Ah yes!–at Le Dennier, near Le Havre, madame.'

Saint-Vire's brow darkened.

'You have a good memory, mademoiselle.'

Léonie looked him between the eyes.

'Yes, m'sieur. I do not forget people–ever!'

Not ten paces from them Armand de Saint-Vire was standing, as though rooted to the ground.

'*Nom d'un nom d'un nom d'un nom!*' he gasped.

'That,' said a soft voice behind him, 'is an expression which I have never admired. It lacks–er–force.'

Armand swung round to face the Duke.

'My friend, you shall tell me now who is this Mademoiselle de Bonnard!'

'I doubt it,' said his Grace, and took a pinch of snuff.

'But look at her!' said Armand urgently. 'It is Henri! Henri to the life now that I see them side by side!'

'Do you think so?' asked his Grace. 'I find her more beautiful than the so dear Comte, and more refined in type.'

Armand shook his arm.

'Who is she?'

'My dear Armand. I have not the slightest intention of telling you, so pray do not grip my arm thus violently.' He removed Armand's hand from his sleeve, and smoothed the satin. 'So. You will do well, my friend, to be blind and dumb concerning my ward.'

'Aha?' Armand looked at him inquisitively. 'I wish I knew what game you are playing. She's his daughter, Justin. I would swear to it!'

'It will be much better if you do no such thing, my dear,' said his Grace. 'Leave me to play this game to a close. You shall not then be disappointed.'

'But I do not understand! I cannot imagine what you think to do with—'

'Then pray do not try, Armand. I have said that you shall not be disappointed.'

'I am to be dumb? But all Paris will be talking of it soon!'

'So I think,' agreed his Grace.

'Henri won't like it,' pondered Armand. 'But I do not see that it can harm him. So why do you—'

'My dear, the game is more intricate than you think. You are better out of it, believe me.'

'Well!' Armand bit his finger. 'I can trust you to deal with Henri, I suppose. You love him as much as I do, *hein?*'

'Less than that,' said his Grace, and went slowly to the couch where Léonie sat. He bowed to Madame de Saint-Vire. 'Your servant, madame. Once again we meet in this exceedingly draughty salon. My very dear Comte!' He bowed to Saint-Vire. 'You renew your acquaintance with my ward?'

'As you see, Duc.'

Léonie had risen, and stood now beside his Grace. He took her hand, and looked mockingly at the Comtesse.

'I had the felicity of meeting my very dear friend in the most unexpected spot only a month ago,' he told her. 'We were both, as I remember rightly, in search of—er—lost property. Quite a curious coincidence, was it not? It seems there are some sad rogues in this delightful country.' He pulled out his snuff-box, and saw Comte redden.

Then the Vicomte de Valmé came up, smothering a yawn behind his broad hand.

'Your so charming son,' purred Avon.

Madame rose quickly, and one of the sticks of her fan snapped under her restless fingers. Her lips moved soundlessly; she met her husband's eyes, and stood silent.

The Vicomte bowed to his Grace, and looked admiringly at Léonie.

'Your servant, Duc.' He turned to Saint-Vire. 'Will you present me, sir?'

'My son, Mademoiselle de Bonnard!' Saint-Vire said brusquely.

Léonie curtsied, looking closely at the Vicomte.

'You are *ennuyé*, Vicomte, as usual?' Avon fobbed his snuff-box. 'You pine for the country, and—a farm, was it not?'

The Vicomte smiled.

'Oh, m'sieur, you must not speak of that foolish wish of mine! In truth, it grieves my parents.'

'But surely a most—ah—praiseworthy ambition?' drawled Avon. 'We will hope that you may one day realize it.' He inclined his head, offered his arm to Léonie, and walked away with her down the long gallery.

Léonie's fingers gripped his sleeve.

'Monseigneur, I have remembered! It came to me in a flash!'

'What, my infant, is "it"?'

'That young man. Monseigneur, we met him before, when I was a page, and I could not think who he was like. But just now it came to me! He is like Jean. It is ridiculous, is it not?'

'Most ridiculous, *ma fille*. I desire you will not repeat that to anyone.'

'No, Monseigneur, of course not. I am very discreet now, you know.'

Avon saw Condé in the distance, with the violets pinned to his coat, and smiled a little.

'I did not know it, infant, nor have I observed signs of discretion in you, but let that pass. Where, I wonder, is Fanny?'

'She is talking to M. de Penthièvre, Monseigneur. I think he likes her—oh much! Here she is! She looks very pleased, so I expect M. de Penthièvre has told her that she is just as beautiful as she was when she was nineteen.'

Avon put up his glass.

'My infant, you are becoming positively shrewd. Do you know my sister so well?'

'I am very fond of her, Monseigneur,' Léonie hastened to add.

'I do not doubt it, *ma fille*.' He looked towards Fanny, who had paused to speak to Raoul de Fontanges. 'It is most surprising, nevertheless.'

'But she is so kind to me, Monseigneur. Of course she is sometimes very s—' Léonie stopped, and peeped up at the Duke uncertainly.

'I entirely agree with you, infant. Very silly,' said his Grace imperturbably. 'Well, Fanny, can we now depart?'

'That was exactly what I had a mind to ask you!' said my lady. 'What a crush! Oh, my dear Justin, de Penthièvre has been saying such things to me! I vow I am all one blush! What are you smiling at? My love, what had Madame de Saint-Vire to say to you?'

'She is mad,' said Léonie, with conviction. 'She looked as though she were going to cry, and I did not like it at all. Oh, here is Rupert! Rupert, where have you been?'

Rupert grinned.

'Faith, asleep, in the little salon over there. What, are we going at last? God be praised!'

'Asleep! Oh, Rupert!' Léonie cried. 'It has been *fort amusant*! Monseigneur, who is that pretty lady over there?'

'La, child, that is La Pompadour!' whispered Fanny. 'Will you present her, Justin?'

'No, Fanny, I will not,' said his Grace gently.

'Here's a haughtiness,' remarked Rupert. 'For the Lord's sake let us be gone before all these young pups crowd round Léonie again.'

'But, Justin, will it serve?' asked my lady. 'She will take offence, belike.'

'I am not a French satellite,' said his Grace. 'And therefore I shall not present my ward to the King's mistress. I believe Léonie can dispense with the lady's smiles or frowns.'

'But, Monseigneur, it would please me to—'

'Infant, you will not argue with me, I think.'

'Oh, won't she!' said Rupert, *sotto voce*.

'No, Monseigneur. But I did want to—'

'Silence, my child.' Avon led her to the door. 'Content yourself with having been presented to their Majesties. They are not, perhaps, so powerful as La Pompadour, but they are infinitely better born.'

'For heaven's sake, Justin!' gasped my lady. 'You'll be heard!'

'Think of us!' Rupert besought him. 'You'll have the lot of us clapped up, if you're not careful, or hounded out of the country.'

Avon turned his head.

'If I thought that there was the smallest chance of getting you clapped up, child, I would shout my remarks to the whole of this very overcrowded room,' he said.

'I think you are not at all in a nice humour, Monseigneur,' said Léonie reproachfully. 'Why may I not be presented to La Pompadour?'

'Because, infant,' replied his Grace, 'she is not—er—enough respectable.'

27

The Hand of Madame de Verchoureux

And Paris began to talk, in whispers at first, then gradually louder, and more openly. Paris remembered an old, old scandal, and said that the English Duc had adopted a base-born daughter of Saint-Vire in revenge for past injuries. Paris thought that it must irk Saint-Vire considerably to see his offspring in the hands of his greatest enemy. Then Paris wondered what the English Duc meant to do with Mademoiselle de Bonnard, and found no solution to the riddle. Paris shook its head, and thought that the ways of Avon were inscrutable and probably fiendish.

Meanwhile Lady Fanny swept through the town with Léonie, and saw to it that her social activities this season should not easily be forgotten. Léonie enjoyed herself very much, and Paris enjoyed her even more. In the mornings she rode out with Avon, and two factions sprang up thereafter amongst her admirers. One faction held that the divine Léonie was seen at her best in the saddle; the other faction was firm that in the ballroom she was incomparable. One excitable young gentleman challenged another on this score, but Hugh Davenant was present, and he took both young hotheads severely to task for bandying Léonie's name about over their cups, and the affair came to naught.

Others tried to make love to Léonie, whereat she was angry, and turned a cold shoulder on their enthusiasms. She could be dignified when she chose, and her admirers were speedily abashed. Learning of their discomfiture one evening when she was helping Léonie to dress, Lady Fanny forgot herself, and exclaimed:

'Oh, splendidly done, my love! What a duchess you will make, to be sure!'

'A duchess, madame?' Léonie said. 'How could I be that?'

Lady Fanny looked at her, and then at a new bracelet that lay on the table.

'Don't tell me you don't know, puss!'

Léonie was trembling now.

'Madame—'

'Oh, my dear, he's head over ears in love with you, as all the world must know! I have watched it grow, and—my dearest life, there is no one I would sooner have for my sister than you, I do assure you!'

'Madame, you—you must be mistaken!'

'Mistaken? I? Trust me to read the signs, my love! I have known Justin many years, and never have I seen him as he is now. Silly child, why does he give you all these jewels?'

'I—I am his ward, madame.'

'Pooh!' My lady snapped her fingers. 'A fig for that! Tell me why he made you his ward?'

'I—I do not know, madame. I—did not think.'

My lady kissed her again.

'You will be a duchess before the year is out, never fear!'

Léonie pushed her away.

'It's not true! You shall not say these things!'

'Why, here's a heat! Is there ever a man you have liked as you like "Monseigneur"?'

'Madame—' Léonie pressed her hands together. 'I am very ignorant, but I know—I have heard what people say when such as Monseigneur wed—wed ladies of no birth. I am only a tavern-keeper's sister. Monseigneur could not marry me. I—I had not thought of it.'

''Tis I who am a fool to have put the idea into your head!' said Fanny remorsefully.

'Madame, I beg you will not say it to anyone.'

'Not I, child, but everyone knows that you have Avon in your toils.'

'I have not! I hate you when you talk like that!'

'Oh, my dear, we are but two women. What matter? Justin will count no cost, believe me. You may be born as low as you please, but will he care once he looks into your eyes?'

Léonie shook her head stubbornly.

'I know I am not a fool, madame. It would be a disgrace for him to marry me. One must be born.'

'Fiddle, child! If Paris accepts you without question shall not Avon too?'

'Madame, Monseigneur had no love for those who are low-born. Many, many times I have heard him say so.'

'Never think of it, child.' Lady Fanny wished that she had not allowed her tongue to run away with her. 'Come, let me tie your ribands!' She bustled about Léonie, and presently whispered in her ear: 'My sweet, do you not love him?'

'Oh, madame, madame, I have always loved him, but I did not think–until you made me see—'

'There, child, there! Do not cry, I implore you! You will make your eyes red.'

'I do not care about my eyes!' said Léonie, but she dried her tears, and permitted Lady Fanny to powder her face again.

When they went downstairs together Avon stood in the hall, and the sight of him brought the colour to Léonie's cheeks. He looked at her closely.

'What ails you, infant?'

'Nothing, Monseigneur.'

He pinched her chin caressingly.

'It is the thought of your princely admirer that makes you blush, *ma fille*?'

Léonie recovered herself at this.

'Ah, bah!' she said scornfully.

Condé was not present at Madame de Vauvallon's rout that night, but there were many others who had come to see Léonie, and not a few who had come early in the hope of securing her hand for a dance. Avon arrived late, as ever, and Madame de Vauvallon, who had no daughter of marriageable age, greeted him with a laugh, and a gesture of despair.

'My friend, I have a score of young beaux who give me no peace until I promise to present them to *la petite*! Fanny, Marchérand is back! Let me find–oh, la la! I should say choose–a gallant for Léonie, and I'll tell you the scandal! Come, little one!' She took Léonie's hand, and led her into the room. 'How you have set Paris by the ears! Were my daughters older I should be so jealous! Now, child, who will you have to lead you out?'

Léonie looked round the room.

'I do not mind, madame. I will have–oh, oh, oh!' She let go Madame's hand, and ran forward. 'Milor' Merivale, Milor' Merivale!' she cried joyfully.

'Léonie! Well, child, and how do you go on?' He kissed her hand. She was radiant. 'I hoped I might see you here to-night.'

Madame de Vauvallon bore down upon them.

'Fie, what behaviour!' she said indulgently. 'Is this your cavalier? Very well, *petite*. You need no introduction, it seems.' She smiled benignantly upon them, and went back to Fanny's side.

Léonie tucked her hand in Merivale's.

'M'sieur, I am very pleased to see you. Is Madame here too?'

'No, child, I am on one of my periodical visits. Alone. I won't deny that I was drawn hither by certain rumours that reached us in London.'

She put her head on one side.

'What rumours, m'sieur?'

His smile grew.

'Faith, rumours of the *sucès fou* that has been achieved by—'

'Me!' she cried, and clapped her hands. 'Milor', I am *le dernier cri*! *Vraiment*, it is so! Lady Fanny says it is. *C'est ridicule, n'est-ce pas?*' She saw Avon coming towards them, and beckoned with pretty imperiousness. 'Monseigneur, see whom I have found!'

'Merivale?' His Grace made a leg. 'Now why?'

'We have heard things in London,' said Merivale, 'Egad, I could not but come!'

'Oh, and we are very glad!' Léonie said enthusiastically.

His Grace offered Merivale snuff.

'Why, I believe my infant speaks for us all,' he said.

'Hey, is it you, Tony, or am I in my cups?' demanded a jovial voice. Lord Rupert came up, and wrung Merivale's hand. 'Where are you staying? When did you come?'

'Last night. I am with De Châtelet. And—' he looked from one to the other—'I am something anxious to hear what befell you all!'

'Ay, you were in our escapade, weren't you?' said Rupert. 'Gad, what a chase! How does my friend–stap me if I have not forgot his name again!–Manvers! That's the fellow! How does he?'

Merivale flung out a hand.

'I beg you'll not mention that name to me!' he said. 'All three of you fled the country, and, faith, it's as well you did!'

'I suggest we repair to the smaller salon,' Avon said, and led the way there. 'I trust you were able to satisfy Mr Manvers?'

Merivale shook his head.

'Nothing less than your blood is like to satisfy him,' he said. 'Tell me all that happened to you.'

'In English,' drawled his Grace, 'and softly.'

So once again the tale was told of Léonie's capture and rescue. Then Madame de Vauvallon came in search of Léonie, and bore her away to dance with an ardent youth. Rupert wandered away to the card-room.

Merivale looked at the Duke.

'And what does Saint-Vire say to Léonie's success?' he inquired.

'Very little,' replied his Grace. 'But he is not pleased, I fear.'

'She does not know?'

'She does not.'

'But the likeness is striking, Alastair. What says Paris?'

'Paris,' said his Grace, 'talks in whispers. Thus my very dear friend Saint-Vire lives in some dread of discovery.'

'When do you intend to strike?'

Avon crossed his legs, and eyed one diamond shoe-buckle pensively.

'That, my dear Merivale, is still on the knees of the gods. Saint-Vire himself must supply the proof to my story.'

'It's awkward, damned awkward!' Merivale commented. 'You've no proof at all?'

'None.'

Merivale laughed.

'It does not seem to worry you!'

'No,' sighed his Grace, 'no. I believe I can trap the Comte through his so charming wife. I play a waiting game, you see.'

'I am glad that I am not Saint-Vire. Your game must be torture to him.'

'Why, so I think,' agreed Avon pleasantly. 'I am not anxious to put an end to his agonies.'

'You're very vindictive!'

There was a moment's silence; then Avon spoke.

'I wonder if you have realized to the full my friend's villainy. Consider for a moment, I beg of you. What mercy would you show to a man who could condemn his own daughter to the life my infant has led!'

Merivale straightened in his chair.

'I know nothing of her life. It was bad?'

'Yes, my dear, it was indeed bad. Until she was twelve years old she, a

Saint-Vire, was reared as a peasant. After that she lived among the *canaille* in Paris. Conceive a tavern in a mean street, a bully for master, a shrew for mistress, and Vice, in all its lowest forms, under my infant's very nose.'

'It must have been—hell!' Merivale said.

'Just so,' bowed his Grace. 'It was the very worst kind of hell, as I know.'

'The wonder is that has come through it unscathed.'

The hazel eyes lifted.

'Not quite unscathed, my dear Anthony. Those years have left their mark.'

'It were inevitable, I suppose. But I confess I have not seen the mark.'

'Possibly not. You see the roguery, and the dauntless spirit.'

'And you?' Merivale watched him curiously.

'Oh, I see beneath, my dear! But then, I have had experience of the sex, as you know.'

'And you see—what?'

'A certain cynicism, born of the life she has led; a streak of strange wisdom; the wistfulness behind the gaiety; sometimes fear; and nearly always the memory of loneliness that hurts the soul.'

Merivale looked down at his snuff-box, and fell to tracing the pattern on it with one finger.

'Do you know,' he said slowly, 'I think that you have grown, Alastair?'

His Grace rose.

'Quite a reformed character, in fact,' he said.

'You can do no wrong in Léonie's eyes.'

'No, it is most amusing, is it not?' Avon smiled, but there was bitterness in his smile, which Merivale saw.

Then they went back into the ballroom, and learned from Lady Fanny that Léonie had disappeared some time ago on Rupert's arm, and had not since been seen.

She had indeed gone out with Rupert to a small salon where he brought her refreshment. Then had come towards them one Madame de Verchoureux, a handsome termagant who had been all things to Avon when Léonie had first come to him. She looked at Léonie with hatred in her eyes, and paused for a moment beside her couch.

Rupert came to his feet, and bowed. Madame swept a curtsy.

'It is—Mademoiselle de Bonnard?' she said.

'Yes, madame.' Léonie got up, and curtsied also. 'I am very stupid, but I cannot at once recall madame's name.'

Rupert, supposing the lady to be one of Fanny's friends, lounged back into the ballroom; Léonie was left looking up at Avon's slighted mistress.

'I felicitate you, mademoiselle,' said the lady sarcastically. 'You are more fortunate than I was, it seems.'

'Madame?' The sparkle was gone from Léonie's eyes. 'Have I the honour of madame's acquaintance?'

'I am one Henriette de Verchoureux. You do not know me.'

'Pardon, madame; but I know of you—much,' Léonie said swiftly. Madame had steered clear of open scandal, but she was somewhat notorious. Léonie remembered the days when Avon had visited her so often.

Madame flushed angrily.

'Indeed, mademoiselle? And of Mademoiselle de Bonnard is also known—much. Mademoiselle is very clever, *sans doute,* but to those who know Avon the so strict chaperon is a poor disguise.'

Léonie raised her eyebrows.

'Is it possible that madame imagines that I have succeeded where she failed?'

'Insolent!' Madame's hand clenched her fan.

'Madame?'

Madame stared down at Youth, and knew the pangs of jealousy.

'Brazen it out!' she said shrilly. 'You hope to marry in all honour, little fool, but be advised by me, and leave him, for Avon will wed no base-born girl!'

Léonie's eyelids flickered, but she said nothing. Madame changed her tactics suddenly, and stretched out her hand.

'My dear, I protest I pity you! You are so young; you do not know the ways of this world of ours. Avon would not be fool enough to wed with one of your blood, believe me. He were surely lost an he dared!' She laughed, covertly watching Léonie. 'Even an English Duke would not be received were he wedded to such as you,' she said.

'*Tiens*, am I so base?' Léonie said with polite interest. 'I think it is not possible that madame should have known my parents.'

Madame shot her a piercing look.

'Can it be that you do not know?' she asked, and flung back her head, and laughed again. 'Have you not heard the whispers? Have you not seen that Paris watches you, and wonders?'

'But yes, madame, I know that I am quite the rage.'

'Poor child, is that all you know? Why, where is your mirror? Where are your eyes? Have you never looked at that fiery head of yours, never asked whence came your black brows and lashes? All Paris knows, and you are ignorant?'

'*Eh bien!*' Léonie's heart beat fast, but she maintained her outward composure. 'Enlighten me, madame! What does Paris know?'

'That you are a base-born child of the Saint-Vire, my child. And we—*nous autres*—laugh to see Avon all unconsciously harbouring a daughter of his dearest enemy!'

Léonie was as white as her ruffle.

'You lie!'

Madame laughed tauntingly.

'Ask your fine father if I lie!' She gathered her skirts about her and made a gesture of disdain. 'Avon must know soon, and then what comes to you? Little fool, best leave him now while you may do so of your own choice!' She was gone on the word, leaving Léonie to stand alone in the salon, her hands clasped together tightly, her face set and rigid.

Gradually she relaxed her taut muscles, and sank down again upon the couch, trembling. Her impulse was to seek shelter at Avon's side, but she restrained herself, and stayed where she was. At first she was incredulous of Madame de Verchoureux's pronouncement, but little by little she came to see the probability of the story's truth. Saint-Vire's attempt to kidnap her was thus explained, as was also the interest he had always taken in her. Sick disgust rose in her.

'*Bon Dieu*, what a father I have!' she said viciously. 'Pig-person! Bah!'

Disgust gave way to a feeling of horror, and of fright. If Madame de Verchoureux had spoken the truth, Léonie could see the old loneliness stretching ahead, for it was clearly unthinkable that such a one as Avon could marry, or even adopt, a girl of her birth. He came of the nobility; she felt herself to be of mongrel blood. Lax he might be, but Léonie knew that if he married her he would disgrace the ancient name he bore. Those who knew him said that he would count no cost, but Léonie would count the cost for him, and because she loved him, because he was her seigneur, she would sacrifice everything sooner than drag him down in the eyes of his world.

She bit hard on her lip; it was better by far to think herself of peasant blood than a bastard daughter of Saint-Vire. Her world was toppling about her ears, but she rose up, and went back into the ballroom.

Avon came to her soon, and gave her his arm.

'I believe you are tired, my infant. We will find Lady Fanny.'

Léonie tucked her hand in his arm, and gave a little sigh.

'Monseigneur, let us go, and leave Lady Fanny, and Rupert. I do not want them.'

'Very well, infant.' Avon beckoned to Rupert across the room, and when he came to them, said languidly: 'I am taking the child home, Rupert. Oblige me by waiting to escort Fanny.'

'I'll take Léonie home,' offered Rupert with alacrity. 'Fanny won't come away for hours!'

'That is why I am leaving you to look to her,' said his Grace. 'Come, *ma fille*.'

He took Léonie home in his light town chaise, and during the short drive she forced herself to talk gaily of the rout they had left, of this man and that, and a thousand other trivialities. Arrived at the Hôtel Avon she went at once to the library. His Grace followed.

'Well, *ma mie*, what now?'

'Now it is just as it used to be,' Léonie said wistfully, and sat down on a low stool beside the Duke's chair.

His Grace poured out a glass of wine, and looked down at Léonie with a questioning lift to his brows.

Léonie clasped her hands about her knees, and stared deep into the fire.

'Monseigneur, the Duc de Penthièvre was there tonight.'

'As I saw, infant.'

'You do not mind him, Monseigneur?'

'Not at all, infant. Why should I?'

'Well, Monseigneur, he is not—he is not well-born, is he?'

'On the contrary, child, his father was a royal bastard, and his mother a de Noailles.'

'That was what I meant,' said Léonie. 'It does not matter that his father was a bastard prince?'

'*Ma fille*, since the Comte de Toulouse's father was the King, it does not matter at all.'

'It would matter if his father were not the King, would it not? I think it is very strange.'

'It is the way of the world, infant. We forgive the peccadilloes of a king, but we look askance on those of a commoner.'

'Even you, Monseigneur. And—and you do not love those who are base-born.'

'I do not, infant. I deplore the modern tendency to flaunt an indiscretion before the eyes of Society.'

Léonie nodded.

'Yes, Monseigneur.' She was silent for a moment. 'M. de Saint-Vire was also there to-night.'

'I trust he did not seek to abduct you again?' His Grace spoke flippantly.

'No, Monseigneur. Why did he try to do it before?'

'Doubtless because of your *beaux yeux*, infant.'

'Bah, that is foolish! What was his real reason, Monseigneur?'

'My child, you make a great mistake in thinking me omniscient. You confuse me with Hugh Davenant.'

Léonie blinked.

'Does that mean you do not know, Monseigneur?'

'Something of the sort, *ma fille.*'

She raised her head, and looked at him straightly.

'Do you suppose, Monseigneur, that he did it because he does not like you?'

'Quite possibly, infant. His motives need not worry us. May I now be permitted to ask you a question?'

'Yes, Monseigneur?'

'There was at the rout to-night a lady of the name of Verchoureux. Did you have speech with her?'

Léonie was gazing into the fire again.

'Verchoureux?' she said musingly. 'I do not think . . .'

'It's very well,' said his Grace.

Then Hugh Davenant came into the room, and his Grace, looking at him, did not see the tell-tale blush that crept on Léonie's cheeks.

28

The Comte de Saint-Vire Discovers an Ace in his Hand

The comment that Léonie was exciting in the Polite World reduced Madame de Saint-Vire to a state of nervous dread. Her mind was in a tumult; she watered her pillow nightly with useless, bitter tears and was smitten alike with fear, and devastating remorse. She tried to hide these sensations from her husband, of whom she was afraid, but she could hardly bring herself to speak to her pseudo-son. Before her eyes, day and night, was Léonie's image, and her poor cowed spirit longed for this daughter, and her arms ached to hold her. Saint-Vire spoke roughly when he saw her red eyes, and wan looks.

'Have done with these lamentations, Marie! You've not seen the girl since she was a day old, so you can have no affection for her.'

'She is *mine*!' Madame said with trembling lips. 'My own daughter! You do not understand, Henri. You cannot understand.'

'How should I understand your foolish megrims? You'll undo me with your sighing and your weeping! Have you thought what discovery would mean?'

She wrung her hands, and her weak eyes filled again with tears.

'Oh, Henri, I know, I know! It's ruin! I—I would not betray you, but I cannot forget my sin. If you would but let me confess to Father Dupré!'

Saint-Vire clicked his tongue impatiently.

'You must be mad!' he said. 'I forbid it! You understand?'

Out came Madame's handkerchief.

'You are so hard!' she wept. 'Do you know that they are saying she is—she is—your base-born child? My little, little daughter.'

'Of course I know it! It's a loophole for escape, but I do not yet see how I can turn it to account. I tell you, Marie, this is not the time for repentance, but for action! Do you want to see our ruin? Do you know how complete it would be?'

She shrank from him.

'Yes, Henri, yes! I–I know, and I am afraid! I scarce dare show my face abroad. Every night I dream that it is all discovered. I shall go mad, I think.'

'Calm yourself, madame. It may be that Avon plays this waiting game to fret my nerves so that I confess. If he had proof he would surely have struck before.' Saint-Vire bit his finger-nail, scowling.

'That man! That horrible, cruel man!' Madame shuddered. 'He has the means to crush you, and I know that he will do it!'

'If he has no proof he cannot. It's possible that Bonnard confessed, or that his wife did. They must both be dead, for I'll swear Bonnard would not have dared let the girl out of his keeping! *Bon Dieu*, why did I not inquire whither they went when they left Champagne?'

'You thought–you thought it would be better not to know,' Madame faltered. 'But where did that man find my little one? How could he know—'

'He is the devil himself. I believe there is naught he does not know. But if I can only get the girl out of his hands he can do nothing. I am convinced he has no proof.'

Madame began to pace the room, twisting her hands together.

'I cannot bear to think of her in his power!' she exclaimed. 'Who knows what he will do to her? She's so young, and so beautiful—'

'She's fond enough of Avon,' Saint-Vire said, and laughed shortly. 'And she's well able to care for herself, little vixen!'

Madame stood still, hope dawning in her face.

'Henri, if Avon has no proof how can he know that Léonie is my child? Does he not perhaps think that she is–what they are saying? Is that not possible?'

'It is possible,' Saint-Vire admitted. 'And yet, from things he has said to me, I feel sure that he has guessed.'

'And Armand!' she cried. 'Will he not guess? *Oh mon Dieu, mon Dieu,* what can we do? Was it worth it, Henri? Oh, was it worth it, just to spite Armand?'

'I don't regret it!' snapped Saint-Vire. 'What I have done I have done, and since I cannot now undo it I'll not waste my time wondering if it was worth it! You'll be good enough to show your face abroad, madame. I do not desire to give Avon more cause for suspicion.'

'But what will he do?' Madame asked. 'Why does he wait like this? What is in his mind?'

'*Sangdieu*, madame, if I knew do you suppose that I should stand thus idle?'

'Does–does she know, think you?'

'No, I'd stake mine honour she does not know.'

Madame laughed wildly.

'Your honour! your honour! *Grand Dieu*, you can speak of that?'

He took an angry step towards her; her fingers were about the door-handle.

'It was dead when you made me give up my child!' she cried. 'You will see your name dragged in the mud! And mine! and mine! Oh, can you do nothing?'

'Be silent, madame!' he hissed. 'Do you want the lackeys to hear you?'

She started, and cast a quick, furtive glance round.

'Discovery—will kill me, I think,' she said, quite quietly, and went out.

Saint-Vire flung himself into a chair, and stayed there, frowning. To him came presently a lackey.

'Well?' Saint-Vire shot the word out.

'Monsieur, there is a lady who desires speech with you.'

'A lady?' Saint-Vire was surprised. Who?'

'Monsieur, I do not know. She awaits you in the smaller salon, and she says that she will see you.'

'Of what like is she?'

'Monsieur, she is veiled.'

'And intrigue, *enfin*!' Saint-Vire rose. 'In the smaller salon?'

'Yes, Monsieur.'

Saint-Vire went out, and crossed the hall to the little withdrawing-room. A lady was standing by the window, enveloped in a cloak, and with a veil hanging down over her face. She turned as Saint-Vire came in, and put back the veil with a small, resolute hand. Saint-Vire looked into his daughter's dark eyes.

'Oho!' he said softly, and looked for the key to the door.

'I have it,' Léonie said calmly. 'And I will tell you, m'sieur, that my maid waits for me in the street. If I do not come to her in half an hour she will go at once to Monseigneur and tell him that I am here.'

'Very clever,' Saint-Vire said smoothly. 'What is it that you want from me? Are you afraid to put yourself in my power?'

'Bah!' said Léonie, and let him see her little gold-mouthed pistol.

Saint-Vire came further into the room.

'A pretty toy,' he sneered, 'but I know what women are with such playthings.'

'*Quant à ca*,' said Léonie frankly, 'I should like very much to kill you, because you gave me an evil drink, but I won't kill you unless you touch me.'

'Oh, I thank you, mademoiselle! To what am I indebted for this visit?'

Léonie fixed her eyes on his face.

'Monsieur, you shall tell me now if it is true that you are my father.'

Saint-Vire said nothing, but stood very still, waiting.

'Speak, you!' Léonie said fiercely. 'Are you my father?'

'My child—' Saint-Vire spoke softly. 'Why do you ask me that?'

'Because they are saying that I am your base-born daughter. Tell me, is it true?' She stamped her foot at him.

'My poor child!' Saint-Vire approached, but was confronted by the nozzle of the pistol. 'You need not fear, *petite*. It has never been my intention to harm you.'

'Pig-person!' Léonie said. 'I am not afraid of anything, but if you come near me I shall be sick. Is it true what they say?'

'Yes, my child,' he said, and achieved a sigh.

'*How* I hate you!' she said with fervour.

'Will you not be seated?' he asked. 'It grieves me to hear you say that you hate me, but indeed I understand what you must feel. I am very sorry for you, *petite*.'

'I will not be seated,' Léonie said flatly, 'and it makes me feel worse when you call me *petite*, and say you are sorry for me. More than ever I want to kill you.'

Saint-Vire was rather shocked.

'I am your father, child!'

'I do not care at all,' she replied. 'You are an evil person, and if it is true that I am your daughter you are more evil than even I thought.'

'You do not understand the ways of the world we live in,' he sighed. 'A youthful indiscretion—you must not think too hardly of me, child. I will do all in my power to provide for you, and indeed I am greatly exercised over your welfare. I believed you to be in the charge of some worthy people once in mine employ. You may judge of my feelings when I found you in the Duc of Avon's clutches.' Before the look on Léonie's face he recoiled a little.

'If you speak one word against Monseigneur I will shoot you dead,' said Léonie softly.

'I do not speak against him, child. Why should I? He is no worse than any of us, but it grieves me to see you in his toils. I cannot but take an interest in you, and I fear for you when it becomes common knowledge that you are my daughter.'

She said nothing. After a moment he continued.

'In our world, child, we dislike open scandal. That is why I tried to rescue you from Avon a while back. I wish that I had told you then why I carried you off, but I thought to spare you that unpleasant knowledge.'

'How you are kind!' marvelled Léonie. 'Of a truth it is a great thing to be the daughter of M. de Saint-Vire!'

He flushed.

'You thought me brutal, I know, but I acted for the best. You outwitted me, and I saw that it would have been wiser to have told you of your birth. The secret cannot be kept, for you resemble me too greatly. We are like to be plunged in a scandal now that will hurt us all.'

'It seems that most people know who I am,' Léonie answered, 'but I am very well received, *je vous assure*.'

'At the moment you are, but when I openly acknowledge you—what then?'

'*Tiens!*' Léonie stared at him. 'Why should you do that!'

'I have no cause to love your—guardian,' Saint-Vire said, and kept a wary eye on the pistol. 'And I do not think that he would be pleased if the world knew he had adopted a base-born child of mine. His pride would be humbled, I think.'

'What if he knows already?' Léonie asked. 'If others know, so must he.'

'Do you think he does?' Saint-Vire said.

She was silent.

'He might suspect,' he went on. 'Perhaps he does; I do not know. Yet I think if he had done so he would hardly have brought you to Paris. He would not like Society to laugh at him as Society will laugh when it learns who you are. I can harm him greatly in this matter.'

'How can you harm him, you—you pig-person?'

Saint-Vire smiled.

'Were you not his page, *ma fille*? It is not *convenable* for young girls to masquerade as boys in the house of an Alastair. Think of the scandal when I tell that tale! Be very sure that I shall take care to set Paris about M. le Duc's ears. His morals are well known, and I do not think that Paris will believe in his innocence, or yours.'

Léonie curled her lip.

'*Voyons*, am I a fool? Paris would not care that Monseigneur had made a bastard his mistress.'

'No, child, but would not Paris care that Avon had had the audacity to take his base-born mistress into Society? You have queened it right royally, and I hear that you even have Condé in your toils. That will not make Paris more lenient. You have been too great a success, my dear. You are a masquerader, and Avon has cheated Society with you. Do you think Society will forgive that? I think we shall not see M. le Duc in France again, and it is possible the scandal might spread to London. His reputation would not aid him to kill the scandal, I assure you.'

'I wonder if it would be better that I kill you now?' Léonie said slowly. 'You shall not harm Monseigneur, pig-person. That I swear.'

'I have no great wish to harm him,' Saint-Vire said indifferently. 'But I cannot see my child in his care. Some paternal feeling you will allow me. Put yourself in my hands, and Avon has nothing to fear from me. All my wish is to see you safely disposed in life. There need be no scandal if you disappear from Society, but if you remain under Avon's roof scandal must come. And since I am like to be involved in it, I prefer to head the cry.'

'And if I go you will say nothing?'

'Not a word. Why should I? Let me make provision for you. I can find a home for you. I will send you money. And perhaps you will—'

'I do not put myself in the hands of a pig-person,' Léonie said crushingly. 'I will disappear, *bien entendu*, but I will go to one who loves me, not to you, who are without doubt a villain.' She swallowed hard, and her hand clutched on the pistol. 'I give you my word that I will disappear.'

He held out his hand.

'Poor child, this is a sad day for you. There is nothing I can say, but that I am sorry. It is for the best, as you will see. Where do you go?'

She held her head high.

'I do not tell you or anyone that,' she said. 'I make just one prayer to the good God that I may never see you again.' Words choked in her throat; she made a gesture of loathing, and went to the door. There she turned. 'I forget. You will swear to me that you will say nothing that may harm Monseigneur. Swear it on the Bible!'

'I swear,' he said. 'But there is no need. Once you are gone there will be no occasion for me to speak. I want no scandal.'

'*Bon!*' she said. 'I do not trust your oath, but I think you are a great coward, and you would not like to make scandal. I hope you will be punished one day.' She flung the door-key down on the floor, and went quickly out.

Saint-Vire passed his handkerchief across his brow.

'*Mon Dieu*,' he whispered. 'She showed me how to play my ace! Now, Satanas, we shall see who wins!'

29

The Disappearance of Léonie

Lord Rupert yawned mightily, and heaved himself up in his chair.

'What do we do to-night?' he asked. ''Pon my soul, I've never been to so many balls in my life! It's no wonder I'm worn out.'

'Oh, my dear Rupert, I am nigh dead with fatigue!' Fanny cried. 'At least we have this one evening quiet! To-morrow there is Madame du Deffand's soirée.' She nodded to Léonie. 'You will enjoy that, my love, I assure you. A few poems to be read, discussion, all the wit of Paris present—oh, 'twill be a most amusing evening, I vow! There is no one who will not be there.'

'What, so we have respite to-day, have we?' said Rupert. 'Now, what shall I do?'

'I thought you said you were worn out?' Marling remarked.

'So I am, but I can't sit at home all the evening. What do you do?'

'Hugh and I are bound for de Châtelet's, to visit Merivale. Will you accompany us?'

Rupert considered for awhile.

'No, I believe I'll go to this new gaming-house I hear tell of.'

Avon put up his glass.

'Oh? What, and where, is the novelty?'

'In the Rue Chambéry. It's like to kill Vassaud's if what they say is true. I'm surprised you'd not heard of it.'

'Yes, it is not in keeping with the part,' Avon said. 'I believe I will go with you there this evening, child. It will not do for Paris to think I did not know of it.'

'What, will you all be out?' Fanny asked. 'And I had promised to dine with my dear Julie! Léonie, I am sure that she will be pleased if you come with me.'

'Oh madame, I am so tired!' Léonie protested. 'I would like to go to bed early to-night.'

Rupert stretched his long legs out before him.

'Tired at last!' he said. 'Faith, I thought you'd never be wearied out!'

'My dearest life, I will tell the servants to take a tray to your room,' Fanny said. 'You must not be tired to-morrow, for I am determined you shall come to Madame de Deffand's soirée. Why, Condé is sure to be there!'

Léonie smiled rather wanly, and encountered Avon's scrutiny.

'My infant, what has happened to trouble you?' he asked.

She opened wide her eyes.

'But nothing, Monseigneur! It is just that I have a touch of the *migraine*.'

'To be sure, I am not surprised.' My lady shook her head wisely. 'We have been abroad late every night this week. It is I who am at fault to have permitted it.'

'Oh, but madame, it has been *fort amusant*!' Léonie said. 'I have enjoyed myself so much!'

'Egad, and so have I!' Rupert remarked. 'It has been a mad two months, and I scarce know whether I am standing on my head or my heels. Are you off already, Hugh?'

'We are dining with de Châtelet at four,' Hugh explained. 'I'll say good night, Léonie. You'll be abed when we return.'

She gave him her hand; her eyes were downcast. Both he and Marling kissed the slender fingers. Hugh made some joke to Rupert, and they went out.

'Do you dine at home, Justin?' asked my lady. 'I must go change my gown, and order the light chaise to take me to Julie.'

'I will bear my infant company at dinner,' said Avon. 'And then she shall go to bed. Rupert?'

'No, I'm off at once,' said Rupert. 'I've a little matter to talk over with d'Anvau. Come, Fan!'

They went out together. Avon crossed over to the couch where Leonie sat, and tweaked one of her curls.

'Child, you are strangely silent.'

'I was thinking,' she said gravely.

'Of what, *ma mie?*'

'Oh, I shall not tell you that, Monseigneur!' she said, and smiled. 'Let us—let us play at piquet until it is time for dinner!'

So they played at piquet, and presently Lady Fanny came in to say good night, and was gone again in a minute, having adjured Léonie to be sure and retire to bed immediately after dinner. She kissed Léonie, and was surprised to receive a quick hug from her. Rupert went away with Fanny, and Léonie was left alone with the Duke.

'They are gone,' she said in a curious voice.

'Yes, child. What of it?' His Grace dealt the cards with an expert hand.

'Nothing, Monseigneur. I am stupid to-night.'

They played on until dinner was served, and then went into the big dining-room, and sat down together at the table. Avon soon sent the lackeys away, whereat Léonie gave a sigh of relief.

'That is nice,' she remarked. 'I like to be alone again. I wonder whether Rupert will lose much money to-night?'

'We will hope not, infant. You will know by his expression to-morrow.'

She did not reply, but began to eat a sweetmeat, and did not look at his Grace.

'You eat too many sweetmeats, *ma fille*,' he said. 'It's no wonder you are growing pale.'

'You see, Monseigneur, I had never eaten any until you bought me from Jean,' she explained.

'I know, child.'

'So now I eat too many,' she said. 'Monseigneur, I am very glad that we are alone together to-night, like this.'

'You flatter me,' he bowed.

'No. Since we came back to Paris we have hardly ever been alone, and I have wanted—oh, many times!—to thank you for being so very kind to me.'

He frowned down at the walnut he was cracking.

'I pleased myself, infant. I believe I told you once before that I am no hero.'

'Did it please you to make me your ward?' she asked.

'Evidently, *ma fille*, else I had not done so.'

'I have been very happy, Monseigneur.'

'If that is so it is very well,' he said.

She rose, and put down her napkin.

'I am growing more and more tired,' she said. 'I hope Rupert wins to-night. And you.'

'I always win, child.' He opened the door for her, and went with her to the foot of the stairs. 'I wish you a good night's rest, *ma belle*.'

She dropped suddenly on one knee, and pressed his hand to her lips and held it there for a moment.

'*Merci, Monseigneur. Bonne nuit!*' she said huskily. Then she rose again, and ran up the stairs to her chamber.

Her maid was there, agog with excitement. Léonie shut the door carefully, brushing past the girl, and flung herself on to the bed, and cried as though her heart would break. The abigail hovered over her, soothing and caressing.

'Oh, mademoiselle, why will you run away like this? Must we go to-night indeed?'

Downstairs the great front door shut; Léonie clasped her hands over her eyes.

'Gone! Gone! Ah, Monseigneur, Monseigneur!' She lay battling with her sobs, and presently rose, quiet and resolute, and turned to her maid. 'The travelling-coach, Marie?'

Yes, mademoiselle, I hired one this morning, and 'tis to await us at the corner of the road in an hour's time. But it has cost you the best part of six hundred francs, mademoiselle, and the man did not like to start so late. We shall not reach farther than Chartres to-night, he says.'

'It's no matter. I have enough money left to pay for everything. Bring me paper now, and ink. Are you sure—are you *sure* that you wish to come with me?'

'But yes, mademoiselle!' the girl averred. 'M. le Duc would be wroth with me an I let you go alone.'

Léonie looked at her drearily.

'I tell you we shall never, never see him again.'

Marie shook her head sceptically, but merely said that she had quite made up her mind to go with mademoiselle. Then she fetched ink and paper, and Léonie sat down to write her farewell.

Upon her return Lady Fanny peeped into Léonie's room to see whether she slept. She held her candle high so that the light fell on the bed, and saw that it was empty. Something white lay upon the coverlet; she darted forward, and with a trembling hand held two sealed notes to the candlelight. One was addressed to herself; the other to Avon.

Lady Fanny felt suddenly faint, and sank down into a chair, staring numbly at the folded papers. Then she set her candle down upon the table, and tore open the note that was for her.

My dear Madame, (*she read*),—
I write this to say Fare Well, and Because I want to Thank you for your Kindness to me. I have told Monseigneur why I must go. You have been so very Good to me, and I Love you, and indeed, indeed I am sorry thatt I can only write to you. I shall never forget you.

Léonie

Lady Fanny flew up out of her chair.

'Oh, good God!' she cried. 'Léonie! Justin! Rupert! Oh, is *no* one here? Heavens, what shall I do?' Down the stairs she ran, and, seeing a lackey by the door, hurried up to him. 'Where's mademoiselle? When did she go out? Answer me, dolt!'

'Madame? Mademoiselle is abed.'

'Fool! Imbecile! Where's her maid?'

'Why, madame, she went out just before six, with—Rachel, I think it was.'

'Rachel is in my chambers!' snapped her ladyship. 'Oh, what in God's name shall I do! Is his Grace returned?'

'No, madame, not yet.'

'Send him to me in the library as soon as he comes in!' Lady Fanny commanded, and went there herself, and read Léonie's note again.

Twenty minutes later his Grace entered.

'Fanny? What's to do?'

'Oh, Justin, Justin!' she said on a sob. 'Why did we leave her? She's gone! Gone, I tell you!'

His Grace strode forward.

'Léonie?' he said sharply.

'Who else?' demanded my lady. 'Poor, poor child! She left this for me, and one for you. Take it!'

His Grace broke the seal of his note, and spread out the thin sheet. Lady Fanny watched him while he read, and saw his mouth set hard.

'Well?' she said. 'What does she write to you? For heaven's sake tell me!'

The Duke handed the note to her, and went to the fire, and stared down into it.

> Monseigneur,—
>
>   I have run away from you because I have discovered thatt I am not what you Think me. I told you a Lie when I said thatt Madame de Verchoureux had not Spoken to me the other Night. She told me thatt Every One knows I am a Base-born daughter of Saint-Vire. It is Quite True, Monseigneur, for on Thursday I slipped out with my Maid, and went to his House, and asked him if it were indeed so. Monseigneur, it is not convenable thatt I stay with you. I cannot bear thatt I should bring Scandal to you, and I know that I must do this if I stay with you, for M. de Saint-Vire will say thatt I am his Bastard, and your Mistress. I do not want to go, Monseigneur, but it is best thatt I should. I tried to Thank You To-night, but you would not let me. Please, you must not be anxious for me. I wanted at first to Kill myself, but then I saw thatt thatt is cowardly. I am Quite Safe, and I am going very far away to Some One who will be good to me, I know. I have left all my Things, except the Money you gave me, which I must take to pay my journey, and the Sapphire Chain which you gave me when I was your Page. I thought you would not Mind if I took thatt, because it is the only thing I have kept which you gave me. Marie goes with me, and Please you must not be Angry with the lackeys for letting me go, for they thought I was Rachel. I leave for Rupert, and M. Davenant, and M. Marling, and Milor' Merivale my so Great Love for them. And for you, Monseigneur. I cannot write it. I am Glad thatt we were Alone to-night.
>
> > A Dieu.
> >
> > Infant

Lady Fanny's face worked for a minute, then she whisked out her handkerchief and cried into it, regardless of paint and powder. His Grace picked up the note, and read it through again.

'Poor little infant!' he said softly.

'Oh, Justin, we must find her!' sniffed her ladyship.

'We shall find her,' he answered. 'I think I know where she has gone.'

'Where? Can you go after her? Now? She is such a babe, and she has only a foolish abigail with her.'

'I believe that she has gone to—Anjou.' His Grace folded the note and put it into his pocket. 'She has left me because she fears to endanger my—reputation. It is somewhat ironic, is it not?'

Lady Fanny blew her nose vigorously, and gave yet another watery sniff.

'She loves you, Justin.'

He was silent.

'Oh Justin, do you not care? I felt so certain that you loved her!'

'I love her—too well to marry her, my dear,' said his Grace.

'Why?' Lady Fanny put away her handkerchief.

'There are so many reasons,' sighed his Grace. 'I am too old for her.'

'Oh, fiddle!' said my lady. 'I thought that maybe 'twas her birth you cavilled at.'

'Her birth, Fanny, is as good as yours. She is Saint-Vire's legitimate daughter.'

Lady Fanny gaped at him.

'In her place he has put the clod you know as de Valmé. His name is Bonnard. I have waited too long, but I strike now.' He picked up a handbell, and rang it. To the lackey who came he said: 'You will go at once to the Hôtel de Châtelet, and request M. Marling and M. Davenant to return at once. Ask Milor' Merivale to accompany them. You may go.' He turned to his sister. 'What did the child write to you?'

'Only farewell!' Lady Fanny bit her lip. 'And I wondered why she kissed me so sweetly to-night! Oh dear, oh dear!'

'She kissed my hand,' Avon said. 'We have all been fools this day. Do not distress yourself, Fanny. I shall bring her back if I have to search the world for her. And when she comes she will come as Mademoiselle de Saint-Vire.'

'But I don't understand how—oh, here is Rupert! Yes, Rupert, I have been crying, and I do not care. Tell him, Justin.'

Avon showed his young brother Léonie's letter. Rupert read it, exclaiming at intervals. When he came to the end he snatched his wig from his head, threw it upon the floor, and stamped on it, saying various things beneath his breath that made Lady Fanny clap her hands over her ears.

'If you don't have his blood for this, Justin, I shall!' he said at last, picked up his wig, and put it on his head again. 'May he rot in hell for a black scoundrel! Is she his bastard?'

'She is not,' said Avon. 'She is his legitimate daughter. I have sent for Hugh and Marling. It is time that you all knew my infant's story.'

'Left her love for me, bless her!' choked Rupert. 'Where is she? Are we to set off at once? Only give the word, Justin, and I'm ready!'

'I do not doubt it, child, but we do not start to-day. I believe I know whither she has gone; she will be safe enough. Before I bring her back she shall be righted in the eyes of the world.'

Rupert glanced down at the letter in his hand.

'*I cannot bear thatt I should bring Scandal to you,*' he read. 'Burn it, your life's one long scandal! And she—Devil take it, I could cry like a woman, so I could!' He gave the letter back to the Duke. 'She's made a cursed idol of you, Justin, and you're not fit to kiss her little feet!' he said.

Avon looked at him.

'That I know,' he said. 'My part ends when I bring her back to Paris. It is better so.'

'So you do love her.' Rupert nodded to his sister.

'I have loved her for a long time. And you, my son?'

'No, no, I'm no suitor of hers, I thank you! She's a darling, but I'd have none of her to wife. It's you she wants, and it's you she'll have, mark my words!'

'I am "Monseigneur",' Avon replied with a crooked smile. 'There is glamour attached to me, but I am too old for her.'

Then the others came in in a state of liveliest curiosity.

'What's to do, Justin?' asked Hugh. 'Has there been a death in the house?'

'No, my dear. Not a death.'

Lady Fanny sprang up.

'Justin—she—she would not have killed herself, and—and said that in her letters so that you should not guess her intention? I never thought of that? Oh, Edward, Edward, I am so unhappy!'

'She?' Marling put an arm about Fanny. 'Do you mean—Léonie?'

'She has not killed herself, Fanny. You forget that she has her maid with her,' Avon said reassuringly.

Davenant shook him by the arm.

'Speak out, man, for God's sake! What has happened to the child?'

'She has left me,' Avon said, and put Léonie's note in his hand.

With one accord Merivale and Marling went to look over Hugh's shoulder.

'God's truth!' exploded Merivale, and clapped a hand to his sword hilt as he read. 'Oh, what a villain! *Now*, Justin, you shall have at him, and I'm with you to the death!'

'But—' Marling looked up with puckered brows. 'Poor, poor child, is it true?'

Hugh came to the end, and said huskily:

'Little Léon! 'Fore Gad, it's pathetic!'

Rupert, at this juncture, relieved his feelings by throwing his snuff-box at the opposite wall.

'Oh, we'll send him to hell between us, never fear!' he stormed. 'Cur! Dastardly cur! Here, give me some burgundy, Fan! I'm in such a heat— Swords are too good for the rogue, damme they are!'

'Much too good,' agreed his Grace.

'Swords!' Merivale exclaimed. 'It's too quick. You or I, Justin, could kill him in less than three minutes.'

'Too quick, and too clumsy. There is more poetry in the vengeance I take.'

Hugh looked up.

'But explain?' he begged. 'Where is the child? What are you talking about? You have found a way to pay your debt in full, I suppose, but how have you found it?'

'Curiously enough,' said his Grace, 'I had forgotten that old quarrel. You remind me most opportunely. The scales weigh heavily against M de Saint-Vire. Give me your attention for one minute, and you shall know Léonie's story.' Briefly, and with none of his accustomed suavity, he told them the truth. They listened in thunder-struck silence, and for some time after he had finished could find no words to speak. It was Marling who broke the silence.

'If that is true the man is the biggest scoundrel unhung!' he said. 'Are you sure, Avon?'

'Perfectly, my friend.'

Rupert shook his fist, and muttered darkly.

'Good God, do we live in the Dark Ages?' cried Hugh. 'It's almost incredible!'

'But the proof!' Fanny cut in. 'What can you do, Justin?'

'I can stake everything on the last round, Fanny. I am going to do that. And I think—yes, I really think that I shall win.' He smiled unpleasantly. 'For the present my infant is safe, and I believe I may put my hand on her when I wish.'

'What do you intend to do?' shouted Rupert.

'Oh yes, Justin, please tell us!' besought my lady. 'It is so dreadful to know nothing. To have to sit idle!'

'I know, Fanny, but once more I must ask you all to be patient. I play my games best alone. One thing I may promise you: You shall be in at the death.'

'But when will it be?' Rupert poured out another glass of burgundy. 'You're too devilish tricky for me, Justin. I want a hand in the affair.'

'No.' Hugh shook his head. 'Let Avon play his game to a close. There are too many of us to join with him, and there's a proverb that says "Too many cooks spoil the broth." I'm not usually bloodthirsty, but I do not want Saint-Vire's broth to be spoiled.'

'I want to see him crushed,' said Merivale. 'And that soon!'

'You shall, my dear Anthony. But for the present we will behave as ever. If any ask for Léonie she is indisposed. Fanny, did you say that Madame du Deffand gives a soirée to-morrow?'

'Yes, but I've not the heart to go,' sighed my lady. 'It will be so brilliant too, and I did want Léonie to be there.'

'Nevertheless, my dear, you will go, with us all. Calm yourself, Rupert. Your part was played, and played well, at Le Havre. Now it is my turn. Fanny, you are tired out. Go to bed now; you cannot do anything yet.'

'I must go back to de Châtelet,' said Merivale. He gripped Avon's hand. 'Act up to your name now, Satanas, if ever you did! We are all with you.'

'Even I,' said Marling with a smile. 'You may be as devilish as you please, for Saint-Vire is the worst kind of villain I have had the ill-luck to meet.'

Rupert, hearing, choked in the act of drinking his third glass of burgundy.

'Damme, I boil with rage when I think of him!' he swore. 'Léonie called him pig-person, but 'fore God he's worse than that! He's—'

Fanny fled incontinently from the room.

30

His Grace of Avon Trumps the Comte's Ace

The Marlings came early to Madame du Deffand's house, and were followed shortly by Merivale and Hugh Davenant. Madame du Deffand wanted to know what had become of Léonie, and was informed that she was indisposed, and had remained at home. Rupert presently arrived in company with d'Anvau and Lavoulère, and was twitted by several people, Madame du Deffand included, on his appearance at such a function.

'Doubtless you are come to read us a madrigal or a rondeau,' Madame teased him. '*Faites voir*, milor', *faites voir!*'

'I? No, b'Gad!' Rupert said. 'I've never written a verse in my life! I'm come to listen, madame.'

She laughed at him.

'You will be bored, my poor friend! Bear with us!' She moved away to greet a fresh arrival.

Under the wail of the violins which played at one end of the room, Merivale spoke to Davenant.

'Where's Avon?'

Hugh shrugged.

'I've scarce set eyes on him all day. He starts for Anjou immediately after this party.'

'Then he means to strike to-night.' Merivale looked round. 'I saw Armand de Saint-Vire a moment ago. Is the Comte here?'

'Not yet, I think, but I am told that both he and his wife are coming. Justin will have a large audience.'

The rooms were filling speedily. Merivale presently heard a footman announce Condé. Behind the Prince came the Saint-Vires, and the Marchérands, and the Duc and Duchesse de la Roque. A young exquisite approached Fanny and demanded Mademoiselle de Bonnard. On being told that she was not present his face fell considerably, and he confided mournfully to my lady that he had written a madrigal to Léonie's eyes which he had intended to read to-night. My lady commiserated him, and turned to find Condé at her elbow.

'Madame!' He bowed. 'But where is *la petite?*'

Lady Fanny repeated Léonie's excuses, and was requested to bear a graceful message to her charge. Then Condé moved away to join in a game of *bouts-rhymés*, and the wail of the violins died down to a murmur.

It was just as Madame du Deffand had called upon M. de la Douaye to read his latest poems that some slight stir arose by the door, and his Grace of Avon came in. He wore the dress he had once worn in Versailles, cloth of gold, shimmering in the candlelight. A great emerald in the lace at his throat gleamed balefully, another flashed on his finger. At his side was a light dress sword; in one hand he carried his scented handkerchief, and a snuff-box studded with tiny emeralds, and from one wrist hung a fan of painted chicken-skin mounted upon gold sticks.

Those who were near the door drew back to let him pass, and for a moment he stood alone, a tall, haughty figure, dwarfing the Frenchmen about him. He was completely at his ease, even a little disdainful. He raised his quizzing glass, and swept a glance round the room.

'By Gad, he's a magnificent devil, 'pon my soul he is!' said Rupert to Merivale. 'Damme if I've ever seen him look more regal!'

'What a dress!' said Fanny, in her husband's ear. 'You cannot deny, Edward, that he is truly handsome.'

'He has a presence,' conceded Marling.

Avon went forward across the room, and bowed over his hostess's hand.

'Late as usual!' she scolded him. 'Oh, and you still have a fan, I see! *Poseur!* You are just in time to hear M. de la Douaye read to us his poems.'

'The luck always favours me, madame,' he said, and inclined his head to the young poet. 'May we beg m'sieur to read us his lines addressed to the Flower in her Hair!'

La Douaye flushed with pleasure, and bowed.

'I am honoured that that so poor trifle should still be remembered,' he said, and went to stand before the fireplace with a roll of papers in his hand.

His Grace crossed slowly to the Duchesse de la Roque's couch, and sat down beside her. His eyes flickered to Merivale's face, and from thence to the door. Unostentatiously Merivale linked his arm in Davenant's and moved with him to a sofa that stood by the door.

'Avon makes me feel nervous,' murmured Davenant. 'An impressive entrance, a striking dress, and that in his manner that sends a chill down one's back. You feel it?'

'I do. He means to hold the stage to-night.' Merivale spoke lower still, for La Douaye's liquid voice sounded in the first line of his poem. 'He sent me to sit here. If you can catch Rupert's eye signal to him go to the other door.' He crossed his legs, and fixed his attention on La Douaye.

A storm of applause greeted the verses. Davenant craned his neck to see where Saint-Vire was, and caught a glimpse of him by the window. Madame de Saint-Vire was at some distance from him, and several times she looked across at him with wide apprehensive eyes.

'If Saint-Vire's seen that Léonie's not here he'll be feeling that chill down his back too, methinks,' said Merivale. 'I wish I knew what Avon means to do. Look at Fanny! Egad, Avon's the only one of us who's at his ease!'

La Douaye began to read again; followed praise, and elegant discussion. Avon complimented the poet, and moved away to the adjoining salon, where some were still playing at *bouts-rhymés*. In the doorway he met Rupert. Merivale saw him pause for an instant, and say something. Rupert nodded, and lounged over to the two by the main door. He leaned over the back of the couch, and chuckled gleefully.

'Mysterious devil, an't he?' he said. 'I've orders to watch the other door. I'm agog with excitement, stap me if I'm not. Tony, I'll lay you a monkey Justin wins this last round!'

Merivale shook his head.

'I'll not bet against a certainty, Rupert,' he said. 'Before he came I was assailed by doubts, but, faith, the sight of him is enough to end them! The sheer force of his personality should carry the day. Even I feel something nervous. Saint-Vire, with the knowledge of his own guilt, must feel a thousand times more so. Rupert, have you any idea what he means to do?'

'Devil a bit!' answered Rupert cheerfully. He lowered his voice. 'I'll tell you something, though. This is the last soirée I'll attend. Did you hear that fellow mouthing out his rhymes?' He shook his head severely. 'Y'know, it ought not to be allowed. An under-sized little worm like that!'

'You'll agree that he is something of a poet nevertheless?' smiled Hugh.

'Poet be damned!' said Rupert. 'He's walking about with a rose in his hand! A rose, Tony!' He snorted indignantly, and saw to his horror that a portly gentleman was preparing to read an essay on Love. 'God save us all, who's this old Turnip-Top?' he demanded irreverently.

'Hush, child!' whispered Lavoulère, who was standing near by. 'It is the great M. de Foquemalle!'

M. de Foquemalle began to roll forth impressive periods. Rupert edged along the wall towards the smaller salon, with a look of comical dismay on his face. He came upon the Chevalier d'Anvau, who pretended to bar his passage.

'What, Rupert?' The Chevalier's shoulders shook. 'Whither away, *mon vieux*?'

'Here, let me pass!' whispered Rupert. 'Damme if I can stand this! The last one kept snuffing at a rose, and this old ruffian's got a nasty look in his eye which I don't like. I'm off!' He winked broadly at Fanny, who was sitting with two or three ladies in the middle of the room, soulfully regarding M. de Foquemalle.

In the other salon Rupert found an animated party gathered about the fire. Condé was reading his stanza amid laughter, and mock applause. A lady beckoned to Rupert.

'Come, milor', and join us! Oh, is it my turn to read?' She picked up her paper and read out her lines. 'There! It goes not well when one has heard M. le Duc's verse, I fear. Do you leave us, Duc?'

Avon kissed her hand.

'My inspiration fails, madame. I believe I must go speak with Madame du Deffand.'

Rupert found a seat beside a lively brunette.

'Take my advice, Justin, and keep away from the other room. There's an ill-favoured old rascal reading an essay on Love or some such nonsense.'

'De Foquemalle, I'll lay a pony!' cried Condé, and went to peep through the doorway. 'Shall you brave it, Duc?'

M. de Foquemalle came at last to his peroration; Madame du Deffand headed the compliments that showered upon him; de Marchérand started a discussion on M. de Foquemalle's opinions. A lull fell presently, and lackeys came in with refreshments. Learned arguments gave way to idle chatter. Ladies, sipping negus and ratafie, talked of toilettes, and the new mode of dressing the hair; Rupert, near the door he guarded, produced a dice-box, and began surreptitiously to play with a few intimates. His Grace strolled over to where Merivale stood.

'More commands?' inquired my lord. 'I see Fanny has Madame de Saint-Vire in close conversation.'

His Grace waved his fan languidly to and fro.

'But one more command,' he sighed. 'Just keep our amiable friend away from his wife, my dear.' He passed on to speak to Madame de Vauvallon, and was presently lost in the crowd.

Lady Fanny was complimenting Madame de Saint-Vire on her gown.

'I declare, that shade of blue is positively ravishing!' she said. 'I searched the town for just such a taffeta not so long ago. La, there is that lady in puce again! Pray who may she be?'

'It is—I believe it is Mademoiselle de Cloué,' Madame replied. The Vicomte de Valmé came up. 'Henri, you have seen your father?'

'Yes, madame, he is with de Châtelet and another, over there.' He bowed to Fanny. 'It is Milor' Merivale, I think. Madame, may I be permitted to fetch you a glass of ratafie?'

'No, I thank you,' said my lady. 'Madame, my husband!'

Madame gave her hand to Marling. Up came Madame du Deffand.

'Now where is your brother, Lady Fanny? I have asked him to entertain us with some of his so amusing verses, and he says that he has another form of entertainment for us!' She rustled on, looking for Avon.

'Is Avon to read us his verses?' asked someone near by. 'He is always so witty! Do you remember the one he read at Madame de Marchérand's rout last year?'

A gentleman turned his head.

'No, not verse this time, d'Orlay. I heard d'Aiguillon say that it was to be some kind of story.'

'*Tiens!* What will he be at next, I wonder?'

Young de Chantourelle came up with Mademoiselle de Beaucour on his arm.

'What's this I hear of Avon? Is it a fairy tale he means to tell us?'

'An allegory, perhaps,' suggested d'Anvau. 'Though they are not now in fashion.'

Madame de la Roque gave him her wine-glass to take away.

'It is so strange to tell us a story,' she remarked. 'If it were not Avon one would go away, but since it is he one stays, full of curiosity. Here he comes!'

His Grace made his way across the room with Madame du Deffand. People began to seat themselves, and those gentlemen who could find no chairs ranged themselves along the wall, or stood in small groups by the doors. Out of the tail of her eye Lady Fanny saw Saint-Vire seated in a small alcove near the window, with Merivale perched on the edge of a table beside him. Madame de Saint-Vire made a movement as though to get to him. Lady Fanny took her arm affectionately.

'My dear, do sit with me! Now where shall we go?' Avon was at her side.

'You lack a chair, Fanny? Madame, your most devoted servant!' He raised his eyeglass, and beckoned to a lackey. 'Two chairs for mesdames.'

'There is not the need,' said Madame hurriedly. 'My husband will give me his—'

'Oh no, madame, you must not leave me thus alone!' said Fanny gaily. 'Ah, here are chairs! I vow we have the best place in the room!' She whisked Madame into a spindle-legged chair that had been brought by the lackey, so that she sat by the fireplace, to one side, able to see the room, and to be seen by nearly everyone. On the same side, but withdrawn a little into the alcove, her husband sat, and could only see her profile. She turned to look at him imploringly; he sent her a warning glance, and set his teeth. Merivale swung one leg gently, and smiled across at Davenant, leaning against the doorpost.

Madame du Deffand settled herself beside a small table, and laughed up at Avon.

'Now, my friend, let us hear your fairy tale! I hope it is exciting?'

'Of that, madame, I shall leave you to judge,' Avon replied. He took up his stand before the fire, and opened his snuff-box, and helped himself delicately to a pinch of snuff. The firelight and the candlelight played upon him; his face was inscrutable, except that the strange eyes held a mocking gleam.

'There's something afoot, I'll swear!' d'Anvau confided to his neighbour. 'I mislike that look on our friend's face.'

His Grace shut his snuff-box, and flicked a speck of snuff from one great cuff.

'My story, madame, begins as all good stories should,' he said, and though he spoke softly his voice carried through the room. 'Once upon a time—there were two brothers. I have forgotten their names, but since they detested each other, I will call them Cain and—er—Abel. I have no idea whether the original Abel detested the original Cain, and I beg that no one will enlighten me. I like to think that he did. If you ask me whence sprang this hatred between the brothers I can only suggest that it may have originated in the heads of each. Their hair was so fiery that I fear some of the fire must have entered into the brain.' His Grace spread open his fan, and looked serenely down into Armand de Saint-Vire's face of dawning wonderment. 'Quite so. The hatred grew and flourished until I believe there was nothing one brother would not do to spite the other. It became a veritable obsession with Cain, a madness that recoiled on him in the most disastrous manner as I shall show you. My tale is not without a moral, you will be relieved to hear.'

'What in the world does all this mean?' whispered Lavoulère to a friend. 'Is it a fairy tale, or does something lie behind.'

'I don't know. How does he manage to hold his audience so still, I wonder?'

His Grace went on, speaking very slowly and dispassionately.

'Cain, being the elder of these two brothers, succeeded in due course to his father, who was a Comte and went the way of all flesh. If you imagine that the enmity now subsided between him and Abel, I beg you will permit me to disabuse your minds of so commonplace a thought. Cain's succession but added fuel to the fire of hatred, and whereas our friend Abel was consumed of a desire to stand in his brother's shoes, Cain was consumed of a like desire to keep him out of them. A situation fraught with possibilities, you perceive.' He paused to survey his audience; they watched him in mingled bewilderment and curiosity. 'With this life-ambition in view, then, our single-minded friend Cain took a wife unto himself and doubtless thought himself secure. But Fate, capricious jade, evidently disliked him, for the years went by, and still there came no son to gladden Cain's heart. You conceive the chagrin of Cain? Abel, however, grew more and more jubilant, and I fear he did not hesitate to make—er—a jest of his brother's ill-luck. It was perhaps unwise of him.' His Grace glanced at Madame de Saint-Vire, who sat rigid, and very pale, beside Lady Fanny. His Grace began to wave his fan rhythmically to and fro. 'I believe Cain's wife presented him once with a still-born child. It began to seem unlikely that Cain would realize his ambition, but, contrary to Abel's expectations, Madame la Comtesse raised her husband's hopes once more. This time Cain determined that there should be no mistake. Possibly he had learned to mistrust his luck. When madame's time was upon her he carried her off to his estates, where she was delivered of—a daughter.' Again he paused, and looked across the room at Saint-Vire. He saw the Comte cast a furtive glance towards the door, and colour angrily at sight of Rupert lounging there. His Grace smiled, and swung his eyeglass on its riband. 'Of a daughter. Now observe the cunning of Cain. On his estate, possibly in his employ, there dwelt a farm-labourer, as I judge, whose wife had just presented him with a second son. Fate, or Chance, thus set a trap for Cain, into which he walked. He bribed this peasant to give him his lusty son in exchange for his daughter.'

'But what infamy!' exclaimed Madame de Vauvallon comfortably. 'You shock me, Duc!'

'Strive to bear with me, madame. There is always the moral. This exchange, then, was affected, none being the wiser save the parents of each child, and of course the midwife who attended Madame la Comtesse. What became of her I do not know.'

'*Mon Dieu,* what a tale!' remarked Madame du Deffand. 'I do dislike these villains!'

'Go on, Justin!' said Armand sharply. 'You interest me extraordinarily!'

'Yes, I thought that I should,' nodded his Grace pensively.

'What became of—Cain's daughter?'

'Patience, Armand. Let us first dispose of Cain and his supposed son. Cain presently brought his family back to Paris—did I tell you that this tale takes place in France?—leaving instructions that his daughter's foster-father was to leave his estates for some remote spot, unknown to anyone, including himself. In Cain's place I think I should not have desired so ardently to lose all trace of the child, but no doubt he acted as he thought wisest.'

'Duc,' interposed Madame de la Roque, 'it is inconceivable that any mother could consent to such a wicked plan!'

Madame de Saint-Vire held her handkerchief to her mouth with one shaking hand.

'Al-most inconceivable,' Avon said gently. 'Probably the lady feared her husband. He was a most unpleasant person, believe me.'

'We can easily believe that,' Madame smiled. 'A villainous creature! Go on!'

From under his heavy lids Avon watched Saint-Vire tug at his cravat; his eyes travelled on to Merivale's intent countenance, and he smiled faintly.

'Cain, and his wife, and his pretended son, returned to Paris, as I have said, and greatly discomposed poor Abel. When Abel watched his nephew grow up with no trace of his family's characteristics either in face or nature, he was more than ever enraged, but although he wondered at the boy the truth never occurred to him. Why should it?' Avon shook out his ruffles.

'Having disposed of Cain for the moment, we will return to Cain's daughter. For twelve years she remained in the heart of the country, with her foster-parents, and was reared as their own child. But at the end of those years Fate once more turned her attention to Cain's affairs, and sent a plague to sweep the neighbourhood where the daughter was. This plague struck down both foster-father and mother, but my heroine escaped, as did also her foster-brother, of whom more anon. She was sent to the Curé of the village, who housed her, and cared for her. I beg you will not forget the Curé. He plays a small but important part in my story.'

'Will it serve?' Davenant muttered.

'Look at Saint-Vire!' Marling answered. 'The Curé was an inspiration! It has taken him completely by surprise.'

'We shall remember the Curé,' said Armand grimly. 'When does he play his part?'

'He plays it now, Armand, for it was into his hands that my heroine's foster-mother, before she died, placed her—written—confession.'

'Oh, she could write, then, this peasant woman?' said Condé, who had been listening with knit brows.

'I imagine, Prince, that she had once been tire-woman to some lady, for certainly she could write.' Avon saw Madame de Saint-Vire's hands grip together in her lap, and was satisfied. 'That confession lay for many years in a locked drawer in the Curé's house.'

'But he should have published it abroad!' Madame de Vauvallon said quickly.

'So I think, madame, but he was a singularly conscientious priest and he held that the seal of the confessional could never be broken.'

'What of the girl?' asked Armand.

His Grace twisted his rings.

'She, my dear Armand, was taken to Paris by her foster-brother, a youth many years her senior. His name was Jean, and he bought a tavern in one of the meanest and most noisome of your streets. And since it was inconvenient for him to have a girl of my heroine's tender years upon his hands, he dressed her as a boy.' The gentle voice grew harder. 'As a boy. I shall not discompose you by telling you of her life in this guise.'

Something like a sob broke from Madame de Saint-Vire.

'*Ah, mon Dieu!*'

Avon's lips sneered.

'It is a harrowing tale, is it not, madame?' he purred.

Saint-Vire half rose from his chair, and sank back again. People were beginning to look questioningly at one another.

'Further,' continued the Duke, 'he married a slut whose care was to illuse my heroine in every conceivable way. At this woman's hands she suffered for seven long years.' His eyes wandered round the room. 'Until she was nineteen,' he said. 'During those years she learned to know Vice, to know Fear, and to know the meaning of that ugly word Hunger. I do not know how she survived.'

'Duc, you tell us a ghastly tale!' said Condé. 'What happened then?'

'Then, Prince, Fate stepped in again, and cast my heroine across the path of a man who had never had cause to love our friend Cain. Into this man's life came my heroine. He was struck by her likeness to Cain, and of impulse he bought her from her foster-brother. He had waited for many years to pay in full a debt he owed Cain; in this child he saw a possible means to do so, for he too had remarked the plebeian manners and person of Cain's supposed son. Chance favoured him, and when he flaunted my heroine before Cain's eyes he saw Cain's consternation, and slowly pieced the tale together. Cain sent an envoy to buy his daughter from this man whom he knew to be his enemy. Thus the suspicion that this new player in the game fostered grew to be a conviction.'

'Good God, d'Anvau,' murmured de Sally, 'can it be—?'

'H'sh!' d'Anvau answered. 'Listen! This grows very interesting.'

'From Jean,' Avon continued, 'Cain's enemy learned of my heroine's old home, and of the Curé who lived there. I trust you have not forgotten the Curé?'

All eyes were on the Duke; one or two men had begun to see daylight. Condé nodded impatiently.

'No. Go on, I beg of you!'

The emerald on the Duke's finger glinted evilly.

'I am relieved. This man journeyed to the remote village, and—er— wrought with the Curé. When he returned to Paris he brought with him— that.' From his pocket Avon drew a dirty and crumpled sheet of paper. He looked mockingly at Saint-Vire, who sat as though carved in stone. 'That,' repeated his Grace, and laid the paper down on the mantelpiece behind him.

The tension could be felt. Davenant drew a deep breath.

'For a moment—I almost believed it *was* a confession!' he whispered. 'They're beginning to guess, Marling.'

His Grace studied the painting on his fan.

'You may wonder, perhaps, why he did not expose Cain at once. I admit that was his first thought. But he remembered, messieurs, the years that Cain's daughter had spent in hell, and he determined that Cain too should know hell—a little, a very little.' His voice had grown stern; the smile was gone from his lips. Madame du Deffand was watching him with horror in her face. 'And therefore, messieurs, he held his hand, and played—a waiting game. That was his way of justice.' Again he swept a glance round the room; he held his audience silent and expectant, dominated by his personality. Into the silence his words fell slowly, quite softly. 'I think he felt it,' he said. 'From one day to the next he knew not when the blow would fall; he lived in dread; he was torn this way and that by hope, and—fear, messieurs. Even he was cheated into the belief that his enemy had no proof, and for a while thought himself secure.' Avon laughed soundlessly, and saw Saint-Vire wince. 'But the old doubts came back, messieurs; he could not be sure that there was no proof. Thus he lived in an agony of uncertainty.' Avon shut his fan. 'My heroine was taken by her guardian to England, and taught to be a girl again. She was left on her guardian's estates in the care of one of his kinswomen. Little by little, messieurs, she learned to like her girlhood, and to forget, in part, the horrors that lay in the past. Then, messieurs, Cain came to England.' His Grace took snuff. 'Like a thief,' he said gently. 'He stole my heroine, he drugged her, and carried her to his yacht that awaited him at Portsmouth.'

'Good God!' gasped Madame de Vauvallon.

'He'll fail!' whispered Davenant suddenly. 'Saint-Vire has himself well in hand.'

'Watch his wife!' Marling retorted.

His Grace flicked another speck of snuff from his golden sleeve.

'I will not weary you with the tale of my heroine's escape,' he said. 'There was another player in the game who followed hot-foot to the rescue. She contrived to escape with him, but not before Cain had sent a bullet into his shoulder. Whether the shot was meant for him or for her I know not.'

Saint-Vire made a hasty movement, and was quiet again.

'That such villains live!' gasped de Châtelet.

'The wound, messieurs, was severe, and compelled the fugitives to put up at a small inn not many miles from Le Havre. Happily my heroine's guardian found her there, some two hours before the indefatigable Cain arrived.'

'He did arrive, then?' said de Sally.

'But could you doubt it?' smiled his Grace. 'He arrived, *bien sûr*, to find that Fate had foiled him once again. He said then, messieurs, that the game was not played out yet. Then he—er—retreated.'

'*Scélérat!*' snapped Condé, and cast one glance at Madame de Saint-Vire, who seemed to cower in her chair, and fixed his eyes on the Duke again.

'Exactly, Prince,' said his Grace smoothly. 'We return now to Paris, where her guardian presented my heroine to Polite Society. Be silent, Armand, I am nearing the end of my story. She made no little stir, I assure you, for she was not an ordinary débutante. She was sometimes, messieurs, just a babe, but withal she had great wisdom, and greater spirit. I might talk to you of her for hours, but I will only say that she was something of an imp, very outspoken, full of espièglerie, and very beautiful.'

'And true!' Condé interjected swiftly.

His Grace inclined his head.

'And true, Prince, as I know. To resume: Paris began presently to remark her likeness to Cain. He must have been afraid then, messieurs. But one day it came to the child's ears that the world thought her a base-born daughter of Cain.' He paused, and raised his handkerchief to his lips. 'Messieurs, she loved the man who was her guardian,' he said very levelly. 'His reputation was soiled beyond repair, but in her eyes he could do no wrong. She called him her—seigneur.'

Saint-Vire's underlip was caught between his teeth, but he sat perfectly still, apparently listening with only a casual interest. There were many shocked eyes upon him, but he made no sign. In the doorway Rupert fingered his sword-hilt lovingly.

'When the child learned what the world said of her,' Avon continued, 'she went to Cain's house and asked him if she was indeed his base-born daughter.'

'Yes? *Allons!*' Condé exclaimed.

'He conceived, messieurs, that Chance favoured him at last. He told the child that it was so.' Avon held up his hand as Armand jumped. 'He threatened, messieurs, to expose her in the eyes of the world as his bastard—and that other man's mistress. He told her—he was her father, messieurs—that he would do this that her guardian might be ruined socially for having dared to foist his base-born light-o'-love into Society.'

Madame de Saint-Vire was sitting straight in her chair now, gripping its arms with her fingers. Her lips moved soundlessly; she was very near to breaking point, and it was evident that this part of the tale was new to her.

'Ah, but what a cur!' cried Lavoulère.

'Wait, my dear Lavoulère. He was kind enough to offer the child an alternative. He promised to keep silence if she would disappear from the world she had only just entered.' Avon's eyes grew harder, his voice was like ice. 'I have said that she loved her guardian, messieurs. To leave him, to be condemned to go back to the old, sordid life, was worse than death to her.

She had just—tasted the cup of happiness.'

There were very few people in the room now who did not understand the tale; horror was in many faces; the silence was complete. Condé was leaning forward in his chair, his face grim and anxious.

'But continue!' he said harsly. 'She—went back?'

'No, Prince,' Avon answered.

'What then?' Condé had risen.

'Prince, for those who are desperate, for the unwanted, for the broken-hearted, there is always a way out.'

Madame du Deffand shuddered, and covered her eyes with her hand.

'You mean?'

Avon pointed to the window.

'Outside, Prince, not so very far away, runs the river. It has hidden many secrets, many tragedies. This child is just one more tragedy that has ended in its tide.'

A choked scream rang out, piercing and shrill. Madame de Saint-Vire came to her feet as though forced, and stumbled forward like one distraught.

'Ah no, no, no!' she gasped. 'Not that! not that! Oh, my little, little one! God, have you no mercy? She is not *dead*!' Her voice rose, and was strangled in her throat. She flung up her arm, and collapsed at Avon's feet, and lay there, sobbing wildly.

Lady Fanny sprang up.

'Oh, poor thing! No, no, madame, she is alive, I swear! Help me, someone! Madame, madame, calm yourself!'

There was a sudden uproar; Davenant wiped the sweat from his brow.

'My God!' he said huskily. 'What a night's work! Clever, clever devil!'

In the confusion a woman's voice sounded, bewildered.

'I don't understand! Why—what—is that the end of the story?'

Avon did not turn his head.

'No, mademoiselle. I am still awaiting the end.'

A sudden scuffle in the alcove drew all attention from Madame de Saint-Vire to the Comte. He had sprung up as Madame's control left her, knowing that her outburst had betrayed him completely, and now he was struggling madly with Merivale, one hand at his hip. Even as several men rushed forward he wrenched free, livid and panting, and they saw that he held a small pistol.

Condé leaped suddenly in front of the Duke, and faced that pistol.

It was over in a few seconds. They heard Saint-Vire's voice rise on a note almost of insanity:

'Devil! Devil!'

Then there was a deafening report, a woman screamed, and Rupert strode forward, and flung his handkerchief over Saint-Vire's shattered head. He and Merivale bent over the Comte's body, and his Grace came slowly up to them, and stood for a moment looking down at that which had been Saint-Vire. At the far end of the room a woman was in hysterics. His Grace met Davenant's eyes.

'I said that it should be poetic, did I not, Hugh?' he remarked, and went back to the fireplace. 'Mademoiselle'—he bowed to the frightened girl who had asked him for the story's end—'M. de Saint-Vire has provided the end to my tale.' He took the soiled paper from the mantelshelf where he had left it, and threw it into the fire, and laughed.

3 I

His Grace of Avon Wins All

Into the village of Bassincourt once again rode his Grace of Avon, upon a hired horse. He was dressed in breeches of buff cloth, and a coat of dull purple velvet, laced with gold. His high spurred boots were dusty; he carried his gloves in one hand, with his long riding crop. Into the market-place he came, from the Saumur road, and reined in as he met the uneven cobblestones. The villagers, and the farmers' wives who had come into Bassincourt for the market, gaped at him, as they gaped before, and whispered, one to the other.

The horse picked its way towards the Curé's house, and there stopped. His Grace looked round, and, seeing a small boy standing near to him, beckoned, and swung himself lightly down from the saddle.

The boy came running.

'Be so good as to take my horse to the inn, and see it safely housed and watered,' said his Grace, and tossed the boy a louis. 'You may tell the landlord that I shall come to pay the reckoning later.'

'Yes, milor'! thank you, milor'!' stammered the boy, and clutched his louis.

His Grace opened the little gate that led into the Curé's garden, and walked up the neat path to the front door. As before, the rosy-cheeked housekeeper admitted him. She recognized him, and dropped a curtsy.

'*Bonjour, m'sieur!* M. le Curé is in his room.'

'Thank you,' said his Grace. He followed her along the passage to de Beaupré's study, and stood for a moment on the threshold, point-edged hat in hand.

The Curé rose politely.

'M'sieur?' Then, as Avon smiled, he hurried forward. '*Eh, mon fils!*'

Avon took his hand.

'My ward, father?'

The Curé beamed.

'The poor little one! Yes, my son, I have her safe.'

Avon seemed to sigh.

'You have relieved my mind of a load that was—almost too great for it to bear,' he said.

The Curé smiled. 'My son, in a little while I think I should have broken my promise to her and sent a message to you. She suffers—ah, but how she suffers. And that villain—that Saint-Vire?'

'Dead, *mon père*, by his own hand.'

De Beaupré made the sign of the cross.

'By his own hand you say, my son?'

'And by contrivance,' bowed his Grace. 'I come now to fetch—Mademoiselle de Saint-Vire.'

'It is really so?' De Beaupré spoke anxiously. 'You are sure, Duc?'

'I am sure. All Paris knows. I saw to that.'

De Beaupré caught his hands and pressed them.

'M'sieur, you bring the child happiness, then. God will forgive you much for your kindness to her. She has told me.' He smiled benevolently. 'I see that I have no cause to regret my alliance with–with Satanas. You have given her life, and more than that.'

'My father, I advise you not to credit all that my infant says of me,' said Avon dryly. 'She has seen fit to place me upon a pedestal. I do not sit well there.'

De Beaupré opened the door.

'No, my son, she knows what "Monseigneur's" life has been,' he said. 'Now come to her.' He led the way to the sunny parlour at the back of the house, and, opening the door, spoke almost gleefully. '*Petite*, I bring you a visitor.' Then he stood back so that Avon might pass in, and went out quietly, and quietly shut the door.

'Of a surety God is very good,' he said wisely, and went back to his study.

In the parlour Léonie was seated by the window, with a book open on her lap. And since she had been crying she did not at once turn her head. She heard a light, firm tread, and then a beloved voice.

'*Ma fille*, what does all this mean?'

She flew up out of her chair then, and cried out in joy and astonishment.

'Monseigneur!' She was at his feet, laughing and weeping, his hand to her lips. 'You have come! You have come to me!'

He bent over her, his fingers on her curls.

'Did I not say, *ma fille*, that I should not lose you very easily. You should have trusted me, child. There was no need for your flight.'

She rose to her feet, and swallowed hard.

'Monseigneur, I–I *know*! I could not–you do not understand! It was not possible–Oh, Monseigneur, Monseigneur, why have you come?'

'To take you back, my infant. What else?'

She shook her head.

'Never, never! I c-can't! I know so well that—'

'Sit down, child. There is so much that I must tell you. Crying, *ma mie*.' He raised her hand to his lips, and his voice was very tender. 'There's naught now to distress you, *mignonne*, I swear.' He made her sit down on the couch, and placed himself beside her, still holding her hand. 'Child, you are not base-born, you are not even peasant-born. You are, as I have known from the first, Léonie de Saint-Vire, daughter of the Comte and his wife, Marie de Lespinasse.'

Léonie blinked at him.

'Mon-monseigneur?' she gasped.

'Yes, my child, just that,' said his Grace, and told her briefly what was her history. She stared at him, round-eyed and with parted lips, and when he finished could find no words for a long minute.

'Then–then I am–noble!' she said at last. 'I–Oh, is it true, Monseigneur? Is it really true?'

'I should not else have told you, *mignonne*.'

She sprang up, flushed and excited.

'I am *well*-born! I am–I am Mademoiselle de Saint-Vire! I can–I can come back to Paris! Monseigneur, I think I am going to cry!'

'I beg you will not, *ma fille*. Spare your tears for my next news.'

She paused in her dance across the room, and looked at him anxiously.

'I have to inform you, infant, that your father is dead.'

The colour returned to her cheeks.

'*Vraiment?*' she said eagerly. 'Did you kill him, Monseigneur?'

'I am very sorry, infant, but I did not actually kill him. I induced him to kill himself.'

She came back to the couch, and sat down again.

'But tell me!' she said. 'Please tell me quickly, Monseigneur! When did he kill himself?'

'On Tuesday, my child, at Madame du Deffand's soirée.'

'*Tiens!*' She was entirely unperturbed. 'Why, *enfin?*'

'I though that the earth had harboured him too long,' Avon replied.

'You did it! I know you did it!' she said exultantly. 'You meant him to die that night!'

'I did, child.'

'Was Rupert there? And Lady Fanny? *How* Rupert must have been pleased!'

'Moderately, child. He did not display any signs of the unholy ecstasy you appear to feel.'

She tucked her hand in his, and smiled trustingly up at him.

'Monseigneur, he was a pig-person. Now tell me how it happened. Who was there?'

'We were all of us there, babe, even M. Marling, and Milor' Merivale. For the rest, there was Condé, the de la Roques, the d'Aiguillons, the Saint-Vires, including Armand; Lavoulère, d'Anvau—in fact, infant, all the world.'

'Did Lady Fanny and the others know that you were going to kill the pig-person, Monseigneur?'

'Infant, pray do not go through the world saying that I killed him.'

'No, Monseigneur. But did they know?'

'They knew that I meant to strike that night. They were all very bloodthirsty.'

'*Vraiment?* Even M. Marling?'

'Even he,' nodded Avon. 'You see, *ma fille,* they all love you.'

She blushed.

'Oh. . .! What did you wear, Monseigneur?'

'Thus the female mind,' murmured his Grace. 'I wore gold, infant, and emeralds.'

'*I* know. It is a very fine dress, that one. Go on, please, Monseigneur.'

'Rupert and Hugh stood by the doors,' said his Grace, 'and Merivale engaged Saint-Vire in pleasant converse. Lady Fanny had your mother in hand. I told them your story, child. That is all.'

'*Voyons!*' she exclaimed. 'It is nothing! When you had told them, what happened?'

'Your mother collapsed. You see, my child, I let them think that you had drowned yourself. She cried out then, and Saint-Vire, since she had thus betrayed him, shot himself.'

'It must have been very exciting,' she remarked. 'I wish I had been there. I am sorry for Madame de Saint-Vire, a little, but I am glad that the pig-person is dead. What will the Vicomte do? I think it is very sad for him.'

'I believe he will not be sorry,' replied Avon. 'No doubt your uncle will make provision for him.'

Her eyes sparkled.

'*Voyons,* I have a family, it seems! How many uncles have I, Monseigneur?'

'I am not quite sure, infant. On your father's side you have one uncle, and an aunt, who is married. On your mother's side you have several uncles, I think, and probably many aunts and cousins.'

She shook her head.

'I find it very hard to understand it all, Monseigneur. And you knew? How did you know? Why did you not tell me?'

His Grace looked down at his snuff-box.

'My child, when I bought you from the estimable Jean it was because I saw your likeness to the Saint-Vire.' He paused. 'I thought to use you as a weapon to–er–punish him for something–he had once done to me.'

'Is–is that why–why you made me your ward, and gave me so many, many things?' she asked in a small voice.

He rose, and went to the window, and stood looking out.

'Not entirely,' he said, and forgot to drawl.

She looked at him wistfully.

'Was it a little because you liked me, Monseigneur?'

'Afterwards. When I came to know you, child.'

She twisted her handkerchief.

'Am I–will you–still let me be your ward?'

He was silent for a moment.

'My dear, you have a mother now, and an uncle, who will care for you.'

'Yes?' she said.

His Grace's profile was stern.

'They will be very good to you, *ma fille*,' he said evenly. 'Having them– you cannot still be my ward.'

'N-need I have them?' she asked, a pathetic catch in her voice.

His Grace did not smile.

'I am afraid so, infant. They want you, you see.'

'Do they?' She rose also, and the sparkle was gone from her eyes. 'They do not know me, Monseigneur.'

'They are your family, child.'

'I do not want them.'

At that he turned, and came to her, and took her hands.

'My dear,' he said, 'it will be best for you to go to them, believe me. One day I think you will meet a younger man than I who will make you happy.'

Two great tears welled up! Léonie's eyes looked piteously into the Duke's.

'Monseigneur–please–do not talk to me of marriage!' she whispered.

'Child—' his clasp on her hands tightened. 'I want you to forget me. I am no proper man for you. You will be wiser not to think of me.'

'Monseigneur, I never thought that you would marry me,' she said simply. 'But if–you wanted me–I thought perhaps you would–take me–until I wearied you.'

There was a moment's silence. Then his Grace spoke, so harshly that Léonie was startled.

'You are not to talk in that fashion, Léonie. You understand me?'

'I–I am sorry!' she faltered. 'I–I did not mean to make you angry, Monseigneur.'

'I am not angry,' he answered. 'Even were it possible, Léonie, I would not take you as my mistress. That is not how I think of you.'

'You do not love me?' she said, like a child.

'Too–well to marry you,' he said, and released her hands. 'It is not possible.'

She stayed quite still, looking down at the marks of his fingers about her wrists with a little wise smile.

'You will take me to this mother and uncle whom I do not know?'

'Yes,' he said curtly.

'Monseigneur, I would rather stay here,' she said. 'Since you do not want me, I will not go back. *C'est fini, tout cela.*' A sob rose in her throat. 'You bought me, Monseigneur, and I am yours till I die. I told you—once—that it was so. You do not remember?'

'I remember every word you have spoken to me.'

'Monseigneur, I—I do not want to be a burden to you. You are tired of—of having a ward, and—and I would rather leave you than stay to weary you. But I cannot go back to Paris. I *cannot!* I shall be quite—happy—here with M. de Beaupré, but I cannot bear to go back alone—to the world I have lived in with you.'

He looked across at her. She saw his hand clenched hard on his snuff-box.

'Child, you do not know me. You have created a mythical being in my likeness whom you have set up as a god. It is not I. Many times, infant, I have told you that I am no hero, but I think you have not believed me. I tell you now that I am no fit mate for you. There are twenty years between us, and those years have not been well spent by me. My reputation is damaged beyond repair, child. I come of vicious stock, and I have brought no honour to the name I bear. Do you know what men call me? I earned that nickname, child; I have been proud of it. To no women have I been faithful; behind me lies scandal upon sordid scandal. I have wealth, but I squandered one fortune in my youth, and won my present fortune at play. You have seen perhaps the best of me; you have not seen the worst. Infant, you are worthy of a better husband. I would give you a boy who might come to you with a clean heart, not one who was bred up in vice from his cradle.'

One large tear glistened on the end of her lashes.

'Ah, Monseigneur, you need not have told me this! I know—I have always known, and still I love you. I do not want a boy. I want only—Monseigneur.'

'Léonie, you will do well to consider. You are not the first woman in my life.'

She smiled through her tears.

'Monseigneur, I would so much rather be the last woman than the first,' she said.

'Infant, it's madness!'

She came to him, and put her hand on his arm.

'Monseigneur, I do not think that I can live without you. I must have you to take care of me, and to love me, and to scold me when I am *maladroite*.'

Involuntarily his hand went to hers.

'Rupert would be a more fitting bridegroom,' he said bitterly.

Her eyes flashed.

'Ah, bah!' she said scornfully. 'Rupert is a silly boy, like the Prince de Condé! If you do not marry me, Monseigneur, I will not marry anyone!'

'That would be a pity,' he said. '*Mignonne*, are you—sure?'

She nodded; a tremulous smile curved her lips.

'Oh, Monseigneur, I never thought that *you* would be so very blind!' she said.

His Grace looked deep into her eyes, and then went down on one knee, and raised her hand to his lips.

'Little one,' he said, very low, 'since you will stoop to wed me, I pledge you my word that you shall not in the future have cause to regret it.'

An insistent hand tugged at his shoulder. He rose, and opened wide his arms. Léonie flung herself into them, and they closed about her, and her lips met his.

M. de Beaupré entered softly, and, seeing, prepared to depart in haste. But they had heard the opening of the door, and they fell apart.

He beamed upon them.

'*Eh bien, mes enfants?*'

His Grace took Léonie's hand in his, and led her forward.

'*Mon père,*' he said, 'I want you to wed us.'

'Of a surety, *mon fils,*' said De Beaupré calmly, and stroked Léonie's cheek. 'I am waiting to do so.'

32

His Grace of Avon Astonishes Everyone for the Last Time

'My dear Comte,' said Fanny, in a voice of long-suffering, 'I have not seen Justin since that terrible night.'

Armand threw out his hands.

'But it is over a week ago!' he cried. 'Where is he? Where is the child?'

Lady Fanny cast up her eyes. Davenant it was who answered.

'If we knew, Armand, we should be more at ease, I assure you. The last we saw of Avon was at Madame du Deffand's.'

'Where did he go?' demanded Armand. 'Did he not return here at all?'

Marling shook his head.

'He vanished,' he said. 'We knew that he meant to set out for Anjou after the soirée, in search of Léonie, but he did not tell us exactly where he was bound. His valet is with him, and he has taken the light chaise. That is all we know.'

Armand sat down weakly.

'But—but did he set out in his ball-dress?' he said. 'He must surely have returned here first to change it for something more *convenable!*'

'He didn't,' Fanny replied positively. 'That gold dress is not in his room. We looked.'

'*Fi, donc!*' cried Armand. 'Is he travelling through France in it?'

'I should hardly think so.' Davenant was amused. 'He will have halted somewhere for the night, and if I know aught of Justin he did not set out without some baggage.'

Armand looked round helplessly.

'And not one of you in his confidence!' he said. It becomes serious! Three times have I come to see—'

'Four,' said my lady wearily.

'Is it so, madame? Four times, then, I have come to see if you have news of him, and of my niece! What can have happened, think you?'

Davenant looked at him.

'We try not to think, Armand. Believe me, our anxiety is as great as yours. We do not know whether Léonie be alive or dead.'

Lady Fanny blew her nose, and cleared her throat.

'And we can't *do* anything?' she said. 'We must just sit idle, waiting!'

Marling patted her hand.

'You at least have not been idle, my love.'

'No, indeed!' Armand turned to her. 'Madame, your kindness to my unfortunate sister overwhelms me! I can find no words! That you should have brought her here, and housed her—Madame, I can only thank—'

'Oh, fiddle!' said Fanny, reviving. 'What else could I do? She is in no fit case to be alone, I do assure you. At one time I feared she was like to die of hysterics, poor soul! She has seen a priest, and since she wrote her confession I do think she is easier. If only Justin would send us word! I cannot sleep o' nights for thinking of what may have befallen that poor, poor child!'

Davenant stirred the fire to a blaze.

'In truth,' he said, 'there can be no ease for any of us, until we know her to be safe.' His smile went awry. 'The house is like a tomb since she left it.'

No one answered him. Rupert walked in, to an uncomfortable silence.

'Hey, in the dumps again?' he said breezily. 'What, Armand here again? You'd best come and live with us, and ha' done with it!'

'I don't know how you can find the heart to laugh, Rupert!' said my lady.

'Why not?' replied the graceless Rupert, coming to the fire. 'Justin told us that he knew where Léonie had gone, and I don't see him failing now, Fan, damme, I don't! I'll lay a monkey he'll bring her back before the week's out, safe and sound.'

'If he finds her,' Marling said quietly. 'It's more than a week now, Rupert.'

'That's right, Edward,' retorted his lordship. 'Look on the cheerful side! Stap me if ever I met such a gloomy fellow! We don't know how far Justin may have had to go.'

'But he's sent us no word, Rupert!' Fanny said anxiously. 'This silence frightens me!'

Rupert regarded her in some surprise.

'Lord, and did you ever know Justin send word of what he would be at?' he demanded. 'He'll play his own game, mark my words! He's not one to take others into his confidence, and he don't need any help.' He chuckled. 'We saw that on Tuesday last, so we did! The man likes to keep us in the dark, and that's all there is to it.'

A lackey announced my Lord Merivale, and Anthony came in.

'No news?' he asked, bowing over Fanny's hand.

'No, alas!'

Rupert made room for my lord on the couch.

'Fan's in the dumps over it,' he said. 'I'm telling her she should have more faith in Justin.' He wagged his finger at her. 'He's won every trick in the game, Fan, and he wouldn't be Justin an he lost the last.'

'Faith, I believe Rupert is right,' Merivale agreed. 'I am fast coming to think Avon omnipotent.'

Marling spoke gravely.

'He is a very dangerous man,' he said. 'It will be long before I forget the happenings at that soirée.'

Rupert was disgusted.

'Y'know, Edward, you're a kill-joy,' he said.

Fanny shuddered.

'Oh, Edward, pray do not speak of it! It was horrible, horrible!'

'I do not wish to speak ill of the dead,' Davenant said, 'but it was—justice.'

'Ay, and he did it well, by Gad!' said Rupert. 'I can see him now, standing there like—damme, like an executioner! But he was devilish, oh, he was devilish! He had me fascinated, I give you my word!'

The door opened.'

'*Madame est servie*,' bowed a lackey.

Fanny rose.

'You'll dine with us, Comte? And you, Anthony?'

'I trespass upon your hospitality!' Armand protested.

'Devil a bit, man!' said Rupert. 'It's Avon's hospitality you trespass on, and our patience.'

Fanny laughed.

'Disagreeable boy! Comte, will you give me your arm? I protest I am shy amongst so many of you men!'

'What of Madame?' Marling asked, as she passed him.

'She has a tray in her room,' Fanny replied. 'I cannot induce her to join us yet, and indeed I think she is better alone.'

So they went into the dining-room, and seated themselves round the long table, Fanny at one end, and Marling at the other.

'Y'know, I scarce dare venture abroad nowadays,' remarked Rupert, shaking out his napkin. 'Wherever I go I'm pounced on for news.'

'Ay, no one seems to believe that we know no more than the rest of the world,' said Davenant.

'And the people who flock to the house to inquire if Léonie is safe!' said my lady. 'This very day I have received Condé, and de Richelieu, and the de la Roques! The child will have a great welcome when—if—if she returns.'

'Plague take your ifs, Fan!' said Rupert. 'Will you have claret, Tony?'

'Burgundy, I thank you, scamp.'

'I have ceased to answer the letters,' said Fanny. 'People have been very kind, but in truth I cannot hope to reply to all.'

'Kind?' snorted Rupert. 'Damned inquisitive, is what I say!'

'Armand, what becomes of de Valmé—I mean Bonnard?'

Armand laid down his fork.

'If you will believe me, the boy is almost glad!' he said. 'He understood not in the least what was toward at Madame du Deffand's that night, but when I explained the matter to him—what do you think he said?'

'We don't know,' said Rupert. 'We've enough mystery without you trying to start a fresh one, stap me if we've not!'

'Rupert!' My lady frowned upon him. 'Rude boy!'

'He said,' Armand went on, '"At last, at last I may have a farm!"' He looked round impressively. 'Did you ever hear the like of it?'

'Never,' said Davenant gravely. 'And so?'

'I shall buy him a farm, of course, and settle money upon him. I suggested that he might wish to remain in Paris, and assured him of my protection, but no! He hates town-life if you please!'

'Mad,' said Rupert with conviction.

Merivale started up.

'Listen!' he said sharply.

Outside in the hall was some stir, as of an arrival. Those in the dining-room sprang up, looking half shamefacedly at each other.

'A—a caller,' Fanny said. 'I'm sure it's only—'

The door was flung open, and his Grace of Avon stood upon the threshold, booted and spurred, and greatcoated. Beside him, her hand in his, was Léonie, flushed and radiant. She had shed her cloak and hat, and her bright curls were tumbled.

There was an outcry. Fanny ran forward, exclaiming incoherently; Rupert waved his napkin over his head.

'What did I tell you?' he shouted. 'Mademoiselle de Saint-Vire!'

His Grace raised one white hand, holding them in check. A curiously proud smile hovered about his mouth.

'No, Rupert,' he said, and bowed slightly. 'I have the honour to present to you all—my Duchess.'

'Thunder an' turf!' gasped Rupert, and surged forward.

Fanny reached Léonie first.

'Oh, my sweet life! I am so glad—I can hardly believe—Where did you find her, Justin? Silly, silly child! We have been in such a taking—Kiss me again, my love!'

Rupert pushed her aside.

'Hey, you little madcap!' he said, and kissed her soundly. 'What a sister you have given me, Justin! *I* knew you'd find her! But married already, egad! It beats all, so it does!'

Merivale thrust him away.

'My dear little Léonie!' he said. 'Justin, I felicitate you!'

Then Marling and Davenant in their turn pushed forward. Armand grasped Avon's hand.

'And my permission?' he asked with mock dignity.

Avon snapped his fingers.

'So much for your permission, my dear Armand,' he said, and looked across at Léonie, surrounded by the vociferous family.

'Where was she?' Armand tugged at his sleeve.

His Grace was still watching Léonie.

'Where was she? Where I had expected her to be. In Anjou with the Curé I spoke of,' he said. 'Well, Fanny? Have I your approval?'

She embraced him.

'My dear, 'tis what I planned for you months ago! But to be married thus secretly when I had dreamed of a truly magnificent wedding! It's too bad, I declare! Dear, dear child! I could weep for joy!'

A hush fell. In the doorway, shrinking, Madame de Saint-Vire stood, her eyes fixed on Léonie. There was a moment's uncomfortable silence. Then Léonie went forward, and put out her hand with pretty hesitancy.

'*Ma—mère?*' she said.

Madame gave a shattering sob, and clung to her. Léonie put an arm about her waist, and led her quietly out.

Fanny's handkerchief appeared.

'The dear, sweet child!' she said huskily.

Davenant took Avon's hand, and wrung it.

'Justin, I cannot find words to tell you how glad I am!'

'My dear, Hugh, this is most unexpected,' drawled his Grace. 'I made sure of a despondent head-shake.'

Hugh laughed.

'No, no, my friend, not this time! You have learned to love another better than yourself at last, and I believe that you will make your Duchess a good husband.'

'It is mine intention,' said his Grace, and struggled out of his coat. There was a tinge of colour in his cheeks, but he put up his glass in the old manner, and surveyed the room. 'My house seems to be remarkably full of people,' he observed. 'Is it possible we were expected?'

'Expected?' echoed Rupert. 'Stap me, but that's rich! We've done naught but expect you for the past ten days, I'll have you know! It's very well for you to go careering off to Anjou, but it's mighty poor sport for us. What with Armand hopping in and out like a jack-in-the-box, and Madame upstairs with the vapours, and half Paris forcing its way in to nose out the mystery, the house is a veritable ants' nest. I believe Merivale still sleeps with de Châtelet, for I don't see him here at breakfast, thank the Lord!'

'What I want to know,' said Merivale, ignoring his lordship, 'is this: did you journey all the way to Anjou in that preposterous gold dress?'

'Faith, he must have startled the countryside!' chuckled Rupert.

'No, my friends, no,' sighed his Grace. 'I changed it for more sober garments at the first halt. Armand, is all well?'

'Completely, Justin! My sister wrote her confession as soon as she was able, and mine erstwhile nephew is to have a farm, and retire from Society. I owe you a debt of gratitude which I can never hope to repay.'

His Grace poured himself out a glass of burgundy.

'I have taken payment, my dear, in the person of your niece,' he said, and smiled.

Then Léonie came in, and went at once to Avon's side.

'My mother desires to be left alone,' she said gravely. The sparkle came into her eyes again. 'Oh, I am so *very* pleased to see you all again!'

Rupert nudged Davenant.

'Look at Justin's face!' he whispered. 'Did you ever see aught to equal the pride of him? Léonie, I'm devilish hungry, and with your permission I'll go on with my capon.'

'I am very hungry too,' she nodded. 'Madame, you have no idea how nice it is to be a married lady!'

'Oh, have I not indeed?' cried my lady. 'How am I to take that?' She led Léonie to her own place at the foot of the table. 'Sit down, my love!'

'Madame, that is where you sit!' Léonie said.

'My sweet, I am a guest in your house now,' said Fanny, and curtsied.

Léonie looked at Avon inquiringly.

'Yes, infant. Sit down.'

'*Voyons*, I feel very important!' Léonie said, settling herself in the high-back chair. 'Rupert shall sit beside me on one side, and—and—' she debated. 'M. de Saint-Vire—I mean, my uncle, on the other.'

'Very prettily done, my dear,' nodded her ladyship, and went to a seat on Avon's right.

'And since I am now a Duchess,' said Léonie, twinkling, 'Rupert must treat me with respect, *n'est-ce pas, Monseigneur?*'

Avon smiled at her across the table.

'You have only to say the word, *mignonne*, and he shall be cast forth.'

'Respect be damned!' said Rupert. 'I'll have you remember you're my sister now, child! Lord, where are my wits!' He sprang up, wine-glass in hand. 'I give you all a toast!' he said. 'The Duchess of Avon!'

They rose as one.

'The Duchess!' Davenant bowed.

'My dearest sister!' Fanny cried.

'My wife!' said his Grace softly.

Léonie stood up, blushing, and, taking Rupert's hand, jumped on to her chair.

'Thank you very much!' she said. 'May I give a toast, please?'

'Ay, bless you!' said Rupert.

'Monseigneur!' Léonie said, and made him a quaint little bow. 'Oh, where is my glass? Rupert, hand it up to me quickly!'

The Duke's health was duly drunk.

'And now,' said Léonie, 'I think to Rupert, because he has been very good, and useful to me!'

'Here's to you, brave lad!' said his lordship gravely. 'What now, minx?'

Still perched upon the chair Léonie said gleefully:

'*Voyons*, I get higher and higher in the world!'

'You'll fall off the chair if you jump like that, silly chit!' Rupert warned her.

'Do not interrupt me,' said Léonie reprovingly. 'I am making a speech.'

'Lord save us, what next will you be at?' Rupert said, unrepentant.

'*Tais-toi, imbécile!* . . . First I was a peasant, and then I became a page. Then I was made Monseigneur's ward, and now I am a Duchess! I am become very respectable, *n'est-ce pas?*'

His Grace was at her side, and lifted her down from the chair.

'My infant,' he said, 'duchesses do not dance on chairs, nor do they call their brothers *imbécile*.'

Léonie twinkled irrepressibly.

'I do,' she said firmly.

Rupert shook his head at her.

'Justin's in the right of it,' he said. 'You'll have to mend your ways, spitfire. No more bouquets from Princes of the Blood, eh, Justin. Dignity! That's the thing! You must let your hair grow too, and speak to me politely. I'll be pinked an I'll have a sister who tells all my friends I'm an imbecile! Politeness, my lady, and some of your husband's haughtiness! That's what you must have, isn't it, Fan?'

'Ah, bah!' said the Duchess of Avon.

Sprig Muslin

Georgette Heyer

I

Mrs Wetherby was delighted to receive a morning call from her only surviving brother, but for the first half hour of his visit she was granted no opportunity to do more than exchange a few commonplaces with him over the heads of her vociferous offspring.

Sir Gareth Ludlow had arrived in Mount Street just as the schoolroom party, comprising Miss Anna, a lively damsel within a year of her début, Miss Elizabeth, and Master Philip, were returning from a promenade in the park under the aegis of their governess. No sooner did these delicately nurtured children catch sight of their uncle's tall, elegant figure than they threw to the winds every precept of gentility, so carefully instilled into their heads by Miss Felbridge, and, with piercing shrieks of: 'Uncle Gary, Uncle Gary!' raced helter-skelter down the street, to engulf Sir Gareth on their doorstep. By the time Miss Felbridge, clucking but indulgent, had overtaken them, the butler was holding open the door, and Sir Gareth was being borne into the house by his enthusiastic young relatives. He was being pelted with questions and confidences, his eldest niece hanging affectionately on one arm, and his youngest nephew trying to claim his attention by tugging violently at the other, but he disengaged himself for long enough to offer his hand to Miss Felbridge, saying with the smile which never failed to set her heart fluttering in her chaste bosom: 'How do you do? Don't scold them! It is quite my fault—though why I should have this shocking effect upon them I can't conceive! Are you quite well again? You were suffering all the discomfort of a bad attack of rheumatism when last we met.'

Miss Felbridge blushed, thanked, and disclaimed, thinking that it was just like dear Sir Gareth to remember such an unimportant thing as the governess's rheumatism. Any further interchange was cut short by the arrival on the scene of Mr Leigh Wetherby, who erupted from the library at the back of the house, exclaiming: 'Is that Uncle Gary? Oh, by Jove, sir, I'm devilish glad to see you! There's something I particularly wish to ask you!'

The whole party then swept Sir Gareth upstairs to the drawing-room, all talking at the tops of their voices, and thus deaf to a half-hearted attempt on Miss Felbridge's part to restrain her charges from bursting in upon their mama in this very irregular fashion.

It would have been useless to have persisted, of course. The young Wetherbys, from Leigh, undergoing the rigours of coaching to enable him to embark upon a University career later in the year, to Philip, wrestling with pothooks and hangers, were unanimous in giving it as their considered opinion that nowhere was there to be found a more admirable uncle than Sir Gareth. An attempt to whisk the younger members off to the schoolroom could only have resulted in failure, or, at the best, in a fit of prolonged sulks.

In the well-chosen words of Mr Leigh Wetherby, Sir Gareth was the most bang-up fellow that ever drew breath. A noted Corinthian, he was never too high in the instep to show a nephew aspiring to dandyism how to arrange his neckcloth. Master Jack Wetherby, unconcerned with such fopperies as this, spoke warmly of his openhandedness and entire comprehension of the more urgent needs of young gentlemen enduring the privations of life at Eton College. Miss Anna, by no means out yet, knew no greater source of joy and pride than to be taken up to sit beside him in his curricle for a turn or two round the Park, the envy (she was convinced) of every other, less favoured, damsel. As for Miss Elizabeth, and Master Philip, they regarded him as a fount of such dizzy delights as visits to Astley's Amphitheatre, or a Grand Display of Fireworks, and could perceive no fault in him.

They were not singular: very few people found fault with Gareth Ludlow. Watching him, as he contrived, while displaying over and over again for the edification of little Philip the magical properties of his repeating watch, to lend an ear to the particular problem exercising Leigh's mind, Mrs Wetherby thought that you would be hard put to it to find a more attractive man, and wished, as she had done a thousand times before, that she could discover some bride for him lovely enough to drive out of his heart the memory of his dead love. Heaven knew that she had spared no pains during the seven years that had elapsed since Clarissa's death to accomplish this end. She had introduced to his notice any number of eligible females, several of them as witty as they were beautiful, but she had never been able to detect in his grey eyes so much as a flicker of the look that had warmed them when they had rested on Clarissa Lincombe.

These reflections were interrupted by the entrance of Mr Wetherby, a dependable-looking man in the early forties, who grasped his brother-in-law's hand, saying briefly: 'Ha, Gary! Glad to see you!' and lost no time in dispatching his offspring about their several businesses. This done, he told his wife that she shouldn't encourage the brats to plague their uncle.

Sir Gareth, having regained possession of his watch and his quizzing-glass, slipped the one into his pocket, and hung the other round his neck by its long black riband, and said: 'They don't plague me. I think I had better take Leigh along with me to Crawley Heath next month. A good mill will give him something other to think of than the set of his coats. No, I know you don't approve of prize-fighting, Trixie, but you'll have the boy trying to join the dandy-set if you don't take care!'

'Nonsense! You don't wish to burden yourself with a scrubby schoolboy!' said Warren, imperfectly concealing his gratification at the invitation.

'Yes, I do: I like Leigh. You needn't fear I shall let him get into mischief: I won't.'

Mrs Wetherby broke in on this, giving utterance to the thought in her mind. 'Oh, my dear Gary, if you knew how much I long to see you with a son of your own to indulge!'

He smiled at her. 'Do you, Trixie? Well, as it chances, it is that subject which has brought me to see you today.' He saw the look of startled consternation in her face, and burst out laughing. 'No, no, I am not about to disclose to you the existence of a lusty love-child! Merely that I believe—or rather, that I hope—I may shortly be demanding your felicitations.'

She was for a moment incredulous, and then cried eagerly: 'Oh, Gary, is it Alice Stockwell?'

'Alice Stockwell?' he repeated, surprised. 'The pretty child you have been throwing in my way? My dear! No!'

'Told you so,' remarked Mr Wetherby, with quiet satisfaction.

She could not help feeling a little disappointed, for Miss Stockwell had seemed to be of all her protégées the most eligible. She concealed this very creditably, however, and said: 'I declare I have not the least guess, then, who it may be. Unless—oh, do, pray, tell me at once, Gary!'

'Why, yes!' he replied, amused at her eagerness. 'I have asked Brancaster's leave to address myself to Lady Hester.'

The effect of this announcement was somewhat disconcerting. Warren, in the act of taking a pinch of snuff, was surprised into sniffing far too violently, and fell into a fit of sneezing; and his lady, after staring at her brother as though she could not believe her ears, burst into tears, exclaiming: 'Oh, Gary, *no!*'

'Beatrix!' he said, between laughter and annoyance.

'Gareth, are you hoaxing me? Tell me it's a take-in! Yes, of course it is! You would never offer for Hester Theale!'

'But, Beatrix—!' he expostulated. 'Why should you hold Lady Hester in such aversion?'

'Aversion! Oh, no! But a girl—*girl*? she must be nine-and-twenty if she's a day!—a woman who has been on the shelf these nine years, and more, and never *took*, or had *countenance*, or the least degree of modishness—You must be out of your senses! You must *know* you have only to throw the handkerchief—Oh, dear, how could you do such a thing?'

At this point, her helpmate thought it time to intervene. Gareth was beginning to look vexed. A charming fellow, Gary, with as sweet a temper as any man alive, but it was not to be expected that he would bear with complaisance his sister's strictures on the lady whom he had chosen to be his bride. Why, from among all the females only too ready to receive the addresses of a handsome baronet of birth and fortune, he should have selected Hester Theale, who had retired after several unsuccessful seasons to make way for her more marriageable sisters, was certainly a baffling problem, but not one into which Warren thought it seemly to inquire. He therefore cast an admonitory look at his wife, and said: 'Lady Hester! I am not particularly acquainted with her, but I believe her to be an unexceptionable young woman. Brancaster accepted your offer, of course.'

'Accepted it?' said Beatrix, emerging from her handkerchief. 'Jumped at it, you mean! I imagine he must have swooned from the shock!'

'I wish you will be quiet!' said Warren, exasperated by this intransigent behaviour. 'Depend upon it, Gary knows what will suit him better than you can! He is not a schoolboy, but a man of five-and-thirty. No doubt Lady Hester will make him an amiable wife.'

'No doubt!' retorted Beatrix. 'Amiable, and a dead bore! No, Warren, I will not hush! When I think of all the pretty and lovely girls who have done their best to attach him, and he tells me that he has offered for an insipid female who has neither fortune nor any extraordinary degree of beauty, besides being stupidly shy and dowdy, I—oh, I could go into strong hysterics!'

'Well, if you do, Trixie, I give you fair warning that I shall empty over you the largest jug of water I can find!' responded her brother with unimpaired cordiality. 'Now, don't be such a goose, my dear! You are putting poor Warren to the blush.'

She sprang up, and grasped the lapels of his exquisitely cut coat of blue superfine, giving him a shake, and looking up into his smiling eyes with the tears still drowning her own. 'Gary, you do not love her, nor she you! I have never seen the least sign that she regards you even with partiality. Only tell me what she has to offer you!'

His hands came up to cover hers, removing them from his lapels, and holding them in a strong clasp. 'I love you dearly, Trixie, but I can't permit you to crumple this coat, you know. Weston made it for me: one of his triumphs, don't you think?' He hesitated, seeing that she was not to be diverted; and then said, slightly pressing her hands: 'Don't you understand? I had thought that you would. You have told me so many times that it is my duty to marry—and, indeed, I know it is, if the name is not to die with me, which I think would be a pity. If Arthur were alive—but since Salamanca I've known that I can't continue all my days in single bliss. So—!'

'Yes, yes, but why *this* female, Gary?' she demanded. 'She has nothing!'

'On the contrary, she has breeding, and good manners, and, as Warren has said, an amiable disposition. I hope I have as much to offer her, and I wish that I had more. But I have not.'

The tears sprang to her eyes again, and spilled over. 'Oh, my dearest brother, *still*? It is more than seven years since—'

'Yes, more than seven years,' he interrupted. 'Don't cry, Trixie! I assure you I don't grieve any longer, or even think of Clarissa, except now and then, when something occurs which perhaps brings her to my memory. But I have never fallen in love again. Not with any of the delightful girls you have been so obliging as to cast in my way! I believe I could never feel for another what I once felt for Clarissa, so it seems to me that to be making a bid for the sort of girl you would wish me to marry would be a shabby thing to do. I have a fortune large enough to make me an eligible suitor, and I daresay the Stockwells would give their consent, were I to offer for Miss Alice—'

'Indeed they would! And Alice is disposed to have a *tendre* for you, which you must have perceived. So, why—?'

'Well, for that very reason, perhaps. Such a beautiful and spirited girl is worthy of so much more than I could give her. Lady Hester, on the other hand—' He broke off, the ready laughter springing to his eyes. 'What a wretch you are, Trix! You are forcing me to say such things as must make me sound like the veriest coxcomb!'

'What you mean,' said Beatrix ruthlessly, 'is that Lady Hester is too insipid to like anyone!'

'I don't mean anything of the sort. She is shy, but I don't think her insipid. Indeed, I have sometimes suspected that if she were not for ever being snubbed by her father, and her quite odious sisters, she would show that she has a lively sense of the ridiculous. Let us say, merely, that she has not a romantic disposition! And as I must surely be considered to be beyond the age of romance, I believe that with mutual liking to help us we may be tolerably comfortable together. Her situation now is unhappy, which encourages me to hope that she may look favourably upon my proposal.'

Mrs Wetherby uttered a scornful exclamation, and even her stolid spouse blinked. That he rated his very obvious attractions low was one of the things one liked in Gary, but this was coming it a trifle too strong. 'No doubt of that,' Warren said dryly. 'May as well wish you happy at once, Gary—which I'm sure I hope you will be. Not but what—However, it is no business of mine! You know best what will suit you.'

It was not to be expected that Mrs Wetherby could bring herself to agree with this pronouncement; but she appeared to realize the futility of further argument, and beyond prophesying disaster she said no more until she was alone with her husband. She had then a great deal to say, which he bore with great patience, entering no caveat until she said bitterly: 'How any man who had been betrothed to Clarissa Lincombe could offer for Hester Theale is something I shall never understand—nor anyone else, I daresay!'

At this point, Warren's brow wrinkled, and he said in a dubious tone: 'Well, I don't know.'

'I should think not, indeed! Only consider how lovely Clarissa was, and how gay, and how spirited, and then picture to yourself Lady Hester!'

'Yes, but that ain't what I meant,' replied Warren. 'I'm not saying Clarissa wasn't a regular out-and-outer, because the lord knows she was, but, if you ask me, she had too much spirit!'

Beatrix stared at him. 'I never heard you say so before!'

'Haven't said it before. Not the sort of thing I should say when Gary was betrothed to her, and no use saying it when the poor girl was dead. But what I thought was that she was devilish headstrong, and would have led Gary a pretty dance.'

Beatrix opened her mouth to refute this heresy, and shut it again.

'The fact is, my dear,' pursued her lord, 'you were in such high gig because it was your brother who won her that you never could see a fault in her. Mind, I'm not saying that it wasn't a triumph, because it was. When I think of all the fellows she had dangling after her—lord, she could have been a duchess if she'd wanted! Yeovil begged her three times to marry him: told me so himself, at her funeral. Come to think of it, it was the only piece of good sense she ever showed, preferring Gary to Yeovil,' he added thoughtfully.

'I know she was often a little wild, but so very sweet, and with such engaging ways! I am persuaded she would have learnt to mind Gary, for she did most sincerely love him!'

'She didn't love him enough to mind him when he forbade her to drive those greys of his,' said Warren grimly. 'Flouted him the instant his back was turned, and broke her neck into the bargain. Well, I was devilish sorry for Gary, but I don't mind owning to you, Trix, that I thought he was better out of the affair than he knew.'

Upon reflection, Mrs Wetherby was obliged to acknowledge that there might be a certain amount of justice in this severe stricture. But it in no way reconciled her to her brother's approaching nuptials to a lady as sober as the dead Clarissa had been volatile.

Seldom had a betrothal met with more general approval than that of Gareth Ludlow to Clarissa Lincombe, even the disappointed mothers of other eligible damsels thinking it a perfect match. If the lady was the most courted in town, the gentleman was Society's best liked bachelor. Indeed, he had seemed to be the child of good fortune, for he was not only endowed with a handsome competence and an impeccable lineage, but possessed as well as these essentials no common degree of good looks, a graceful, well-built frame, considerable proficiency in the realm of sport, and an open, generous temper which made it impossible for even his closest rivals to grudge him his success in winning Clarissa. Sadly Mrs Wetherby looked back to that halcyon period, before the fatal carriage accident had laid Clarissa's charm and beauty in cold earth, and Gareth's heart with them.

He was thought to have made an excellent recovery from the blow; and everyone was glad that the tragedy had not led him to indulge in any extravagance of grief, such as selling all his splendid horses, or wearing mourning weeds for the rest of his life. If, behind the smile in his eyes, there was a little sadness, he could still laugh; and if he found the world empty, that was a secret he kept always to himself. Even Beatrix, who adored him, had been encouraged to hope that he had ceased to mourn Clarissa; and she had spared no pains to bring to his notice any damsel who seemed likely to captivate him. Not the mildest flirtation had rewarded her efforts, but this had not unduly depressed her. However modest he might be, he could not but know that he was regarded as a matrimonial prize of the first rank; and she knew him too well to suppose that he would raise in any maidenly breast expectations which he had no intention of fulfilling. Until this melancholy day, she had merely thought that she had not hit upon the right female, never that the right female did not exist. Her tears, on hearing his announcement, had sprung less from disappointment than from the sudden realization that more than Clarissa's loveliness had perished in that fatal accident of seven years ago. He had spoken to her as a man might who had put his youth behind him, with all its hopes and ardours, and was looking towards a placid future, comfortable, perhaps, but unenlivened by any touch of romance. Mrs Wetherby, perceiving this, and recalling a younger Gareth, who had seen life as a gay adventure, cried herself to sleep.

So, too, when the news of Sir Gareth's very flattering offer was later made known to her, did the Lady Hester Theale.

2

The Earl of Brancaster's family seat was situated not many miles from Chatteris, in the heart of the Fens. The mansion was as undistinguished as the surrounding countryside, and, since his lordship's circumstances, owing to his strong predilection for gaming, were straitened, it bore a good many signs of neglect. In theory, it was presided over by his lordship's eldest daughter, but as his son and heir, Lord Widmore, found it expedient to reside, with his wife and growing family, under his father's roof, the Lady Hester's position was, in fact, little better than that of a cipher. Upon the death of her mama, several years previously, persons who were not particularly acquainted with the Earl had thought that it was fortunate, after all, that she had been left on the shelf. She would be able, said the optimistic, to comfort her stricken parent, and to take her mama's place as the mistress of Brancaster Park, and of the house in Green Street. But as the Earl had disliked his wife he was by no means stricken by her death; and as he was looking forward to an untrammelled single existence he regarded his eldest daughter not as a comfort but as an encumbrance. Indeed, he had been heard to say, when in his cups, that he was no better off than before.

His feelings, when, recovering from a momentary stupefaction, he realized that Sir Gareth Ludlow was actually soliciting permission to marry his daughter, almost overcame him. He had given up all hope of seeing her respectably married: that she should achieve a brilliant match had never for an instant occurred to him. An unwelcome suspicion that Sir Gareth must be a trifle bosky crossed his mind, but there was nothing in Sir Gareth's manner or appearance to lend the slightest colour to it, and he banished it. He said bluntly: 'Well, I should be very well pleased to give her to you, but I'd better tell you at the outset that her portion isn't large. In fact, I shall be devilish hard put to it to raise the wind at all.'

'It is really quite immaterial,' responded Sir Gareth. 'If Lady Hester will do me the honour to accept me, I shall of course make whatever settlement upon her that our attorneys think proper.'

Greatly moved by these beautiful words, the Earl gave Sir Gareth's suit his blessing, invited him to Brancaster Park the following week, and himself cancelled three sporting engagements, leaving London on the very next day to prepare his daughter for the singular stroke of good fortune which was about to befall her.

Lady Hester was surprised by his sudden arrival, for she had supposed him to be on the point of going to Brighton. He belonged to the Prince Regent's set, and in general was to be found, during the summer months, residing in lodgings on the Steyne, or at the Pavilion itself, where it was his affable practice to share in all his royal friend's more expensive pastimes, and to play whist, for extremely high stakes, with his royal friend's brother of York. Such female companionship as he sought in Brighton had never included that of his wife, or of his daughter; so, at the end of the London Season, Lady Hester had removed, with her brother and her sister-in-law, to Cambridgeshire, whence, in due course, she would proceed on a round of yearly and very dull visits to various members of her family.

Her amiable parent, having informed her that it was a father's concern for her welfare which had brought him, at great inconvenience, to his ancestral home, said, by way of preamble to the disclosure he was about to make, that he hoped she would furbish herself up a trifle, since it would not do for her to receive guests in an old gown, and a Paisley shawl.

'Oh, dear!' said Hester. 'Are we to have visitors?' She focused her slightly myopic gaze upon the Earl, and said, with more resignation than anxiety in her voice: 'I do hope no one whom I *particularly* dislike, Papa?'

'Nothing of the sort!' he replied testily. 'Upon my soul, Hester, you are enough to try the patience of a saint! Let me tell you, my girl, that it is Sir Gareth Ludlow whom we are to entertain here next week, and if you dislike him you must be out of your senses!'

She had been somewhat aimlessly disposing the despised shawl about her shoulders, as though, by rearranging its shabby folds, she could render it less objectionable to her father, but at these words she let her hands fall, and said incredulously: '*Sir Gareth Ludlow*, sir?'

'Ay, you may well stare!' said the Earl. 'I daresay you will stare more when I tell you why he comes!'

'I should think it very likely that I should,' she agreed, in a reflective tone. 'For I cannot imagine what should bring him here, or, indeed, how he is to be entertained at this season.'

'Never mind that! He is coming, Hester, to make you an offer!'

'Oh, is he?' she said vaguely, adding, after a thoughtful moment: 'Does he want me to sell him one of Juno's pups? I wonder he should not have told me so when we met in town the other day. It is not worth his while to journey all this distance—unless, of course, he desires first to see the pup.'

'For God's sake, girl—!' exploded the Earl. 'What the devil should Ludlow want with one of your wretched dogs?'

'Indeed, it has me quite in a puzzle,' she said, looking at him inquiringly.

'Paperskull!' said his lordship scathingly. 'Damme if I know what he wants with you! He's coming to offer for your *hand*!'

She sat staring at him, rather pale at first, and then flushing, and turning away her face. 'Papa, pray—! If you are funning, it is not a kind jest!'

'Of course I'm not funning!' he answered. 'Though it don't surprise me you should think so. I don't mind owning to you, Hester, that when he broke it to me that it was my permission to address you that he was after I thought either he was foxed, or I was!'

'Perhaps you were—both of you!' she said, trying for a lighter note.

'No, no! No such thing! But for him to be taking a fancy for you, when I daresay there are a dozen females trying to fix his interest, and everyone of 'em as well-born as you, besides being younger, and devilish handsome into the bargain—well, I never was nearer to being grassed in all my life!'

'It isn't true. Sir Gareth never had a fancy for me. Not even when I was young, and, I think, quite pretty,' said Hester, with the ghost of a smile.

'Oh, lord, no! Not *then!*' said his lordship. 'You were well-enough, but you couldn't have expected him to look at you when the Lincombe chit was alive.'

'No. He didn't look at me,' she agreed.

'Well, well!' the Earl said tolerantly. 'She had 'em all beaten to flinders. By all accounts, he never cast so much as a glance at any other girl. And I've made up my mind to it that that's why he's offered for you.' He saw that she was looking bewildered, and said with some impatience: 'Now, don't be a pea-goose, girl! It's as plain as a pikestaff that what Ludlow wants is a quiet, well-bred female who won't have her head stuffed with romantic nonsense, or expect him to be thrown into a transport of passion. The more I think of it, the more it seems to me that he's acting like a man of sense. If he's still hankering after Clarissa Lincombe, it wouldn't suit him at all to offer for some out-and-outer who would expect him to be dangling after her for ever, carried away by the violence of his feelings, or some such flummery. At the same time, it's his duty to marry, and you may depend upon it he made up his mind to that when that brother of his got himself killed in Spain. Well, I don't scruple to tell you that I never thought to see such a piece of good fortune befall you, Hester! To think that you should make a better match than any of your sisters, and at your age, too! It is beyond anything great!'

'Beyond anything—oh, beyond *anything!*' she said, in a queer voice. 'And he is coming here, with your consent! Could you not have asked me first what *my* sentiments were? I do not wish for this splendid match, Papa.'

He looked as though he could hardly credit his ears. 'Don't wish for it?' he repeated, in a stupefied tone. 'You must be out of your senses!'

'Perhaps I am.' The ghostly smile that was at once nervous and mischievous again flitted across her face. 'You should have warned Sir Gareth of it, sir. I am persuaded he cannot wish to marry an idiot.'

'If,' said his lordship awfully, 'you fancy that that is a funny thing to say, let me tell you that it is not!'

'No, Papa.'

He eyed her in uncertainty, feeling that in some strange way she was eluding him. She had always been an obedient, even a meek, daughter, but he had several times suffered from the uncomfortable suspicion that behind the cloud of gentle compliance there existed a woman who was quite unknown to him. He saw that it behoved him to tread warily, so he curbed his exasperation, and said, with a very fair assumption of paternal solicitude: 'Now, what maggot has got into your head, my dear? You won't tell me you don't wish to be married, for every female must wish that!'

'Yes, indeed!' she sighed.

'Can it be that you dislike Ludlow?'

'No, Papa.'

'Well, I was sure of *that*! I daresay there isn't a better liked man in England, and as for you ladies—! The caps that have been set at him! You will be the envy of every unmarried woman in town!'

'Do you think so indeed, Papa? How delightful that would be! But perhaps I might feel strange, and unlike myself. It wouldn't be comfortable, not to be acquainted with myself.'

This baffling, and (he considered) very nonsensical observation, threw him out of his stride, but he persevered, saying with as much patience as he could command: 'Well, never mind that! To be sure, I never thought he was trying to fix your interest, but I am sure I have seen him stand up with you at balls a hundred times! Ay, and sit talking to you, when one might have supposed that he would have been making up to one of the beauties that have been hanging out lures to him for ever!'

'He is very civil,' she agreed. 'He was used to talk to me of Clarissa, because I knew her too, and no one else would ever mention her name within his hearing.'

'What, is he still doing so?' exclaimed the Earl, feeling that here must be the clue to the mystery.

'Oh, no!' she replied. 'Not for a long time now.'

'Then why the devil, if he don't want to talk of the Lincombe beauty, should he seek you out?' he demanded. 'Depend upon it, it has been to attach you!'

'He does not precisely seek me out,' she responded. 'Only, if we meet at parties, he is too kind, and, I think, too great a gentleman, to pass me by with no more than a common bow.' She paused, and sighed, blinking at her father. 'How silly! I expect you are quite right, and he has had this notion of offering for me ever since Major Ludlow was killed.'

'Of course I am right, and a fine compliment he is paying you!'

'Oh, no!' she said, and relapsed into silence, gazing thoughtfully before her.

He began to feel uneasy. It was impossible to read her countenance. It was mournful, yet tranquil; but in the tone of her voice there was an alarming note which recalled to his mind her contumacious behaviour when he had disclosed to her the only other offer he had ever received for her hand. He remembered how meekly she had borne every manifestation of his wrath, how dutifully she had begged his pardon for disobliging him. That had been five years ago, but here she was, still a spinster. After eyeing her for a moment or two, he said: 'If you let this chance of achieving a respectable alliance slip, you are a bigger fool than I take you for, Hester!'

Her eyes came round to his face, a smile quivered for an instant on her lips. 'No, how could that be, Papa?'

He decided to ignore this. 'You and he are both past the age of romantical high-flights,' he urged. 'He is a very agreeable fellow, and I don't doubt he'll make you a kind husband. Generous too! You will have enough pin-money to make your sisters stare, a position of consequence, and you will be mistress of a very pretty establishment. It is not as though your affections were engaged otherwhere: of course, if that were so, it would be another matter; but, as I told Ludlow, though I could not answer for your sentiments upon this occasion, I could assure him that you had formed no other attachment.'

'But that was not true, Papa,' she said. 'My affections were engaged many years ago.'

She said this so matter-of-factly that he thought he must have misunderstood her, and demanded a repetition of the remark. She very obligingly complied, and he exclaimed, quite thunderstruck: 'So I am to believe that you have been wearing the willow, am I? Fudge! It is the first I have ever heard of such a thing! Pray, who may this man be?'

She got up, drawing her shawl about her shoulders. 'It is of no consequence, Papa. He never thought of me, you see.'

With that, she drifted away in the indeterminate way which was peculiarly her own, leaving him baffled and furious.

He did not see her again until the family assembled for dinner; and by that time he had discussed the matter at such length with his son, his daughter-in-law, and his chaplain, and with such sublime disregard for the ears of his butler, two footmen, and his valet, all of whom at some time or another came within hearing, that there was hardly a soul in the house unaware that the Lady Hester had received, and meant to decline, a very flattering offer.

Lord Widmore, whose temper was rendered peevish by chronic dyspepsia, was quite as much vexed as his father; but his wife, a robust woman of alarmingly brusque manners, said, with the vulgarity for which she was famed: 'Oh, flim-flam! Mere flourishing! I'd lay a monkey you crammed her, sir, for that's always your way. Leave it to me!'

'She's as obstinate as a mule!' said Lord Widmore fretfully.

This made his lady laugh heartily, and beg him not to talk like a nodcock, for a more biddable female than his sister, she said, never existed.

It was perfectly true. Except in her inability to attract eligible suitors to herself, Hester was the sort of daughter with whom the most exacting parent might have been pleased. She always did as she was told, and never argued about it. She indulged neither in sulks nor in hysterics; and if she was unable to attract the right men, at least she had never been known to encourage the wrong ones. She was a good sister, too; and could always be relied upon to take charge of her young nephews and nieces in times of crisis; or to entertain, uncomplainingly, the dullest man invited (willy-nilly) to a dinner-party.

The first person to discuss Sir Gareth's proposal with her was not Lady Widmore, but the Reverend Augustus Whyteleafe, the Earl's chaplain, who seized the earliest opportunity that offered of conveying to her his own reflections upon the occasion.

'You will not object, I know, to my adverting to the topic, painful though it must be to you,' he stated. 'His lordship, I should perhaps mention, did me the honour to admit me into his confidence, feeling, I collect, that a word from a man in my position might bear weight with you.'

'Oh, dear! I am sure it ought to,' said Hester, in a conscience-stricken tone.

'But,' said Mr Whyteleafe, squaring his shoulders, 'I found myself obliged to inform his lordship that I could not take upon myself the office of Sir Gareth Ludlow's advocate.'

'How very brave of you!' Hester said, sighing. 'I am so glad, for I don't at all wish to discuss it.'

'It must indeed be repugnant to you. You will allow me, however, to tell you that I honour you for your decision, Lady Hester.'

She looked at him in mild surprise. 'Good gracious, do you? I can't think why you should.'

'You have had the courage to spurn a match of mere worldly brilliance. A match which, I daresay, would have been welcome to any lady less highminded than yourself. Let me venture to say that you have done just as you should: nothing but misery, I am persuaded, could result from an alliance between yourself and a fashionable fribble.'

'Poor Sir Gareth! I fear you are right, Mr Whyteleafe: I should make him such an odiously dull wife, should I not?'

'A man of his frivolous tastes might think so,' he agreed. 'To a man of more serious disposition, however—But on this head I must not, at present, say more.'

He then made her a bow, looking at her in a very speaking way, and withdrew, leaving her hovering between amusement and consternation.

Her sister-in-law, who had not failed to mark the exchange, from the other end of the Long Gallery, where the party had assembled after dinner, did not hesitate, later, to ask her what had been said. 'For if he had the effrontery to speak to you about this offer your papa has received, I hope you gave him a sharp set-down, Hetty! Such presumption! But there! I don't doubt your papa egged him on. I promise you I made no bones about telling him that capping hounds to a scent won't do in this case.'

'Thank you: that was kind. But Mr Whyteleafe didn't try to persuade me. Indeed, he said that he had told my father he would not, which I thought very courageous in him.'

'Ay, that was what made Lord Brancaster as sulky as a bear. I'll tell you what, Hetty: you'll do well to accept Ludlow's offer before Widmore puts it into your father's head that you mean to have a beggarly parson for your husband.'

'But I don't,' said Hester.

'Lord, I know *that*! But I have eyes in my head, and I can see that Whyteleafe is growing extremely particular in his attentions. The devil of it is that Widmore has seen it too, and you know what a slowtop he is, my dear! Your father's another. I don't doubt he said something to put you in a tweak.'

'Oh, no!' Hester said calmly.

'At all events, he told you Ludlow was still moping for that girl he was betrothed to the deuce knows how many years ago!' said Lady Widmore bluntly. 'If you take my advice, you won't heed him! I never saw a man less in the dumps than Ludlow.'

'No, indeed. Or a man less in love,' remarked Hester.

'What of it? I can tell you this, Hetty: it ain't so often that persons of our station marry for love. Look at me! You can't suppose I was ever in love with poor Widmore! But I never took, any more than you did, and when the match was proposed to me I agreed to it, because there's nothing worse for a female than to be left on the shelf.'

'One grows accustomed to it,' Hester said. 'Can you believe, Almeria, that Sir Gareth and I should—should suit?'

'Lord, yes! Why not? If the chance had been offered to me, I should have jumped out of my skin to snatch it!' responded Lady Widmore frankly. 'I know you don't love him, but what's that to the purpose? You think it over carefully, Hetty! You ain't likely to receive another offer, or, in any event, not such an advantageous one, though I daresay Whyteleafe will pop the question, as soon as he gets preferment. Take Ludlow, and you'll have a handsome fortune, a position of the first consequence, and an agreeable husband into the bargain. Send him to the rightabout, and you'll end your days an old maid, let alone be obliged to listen to your father's and Widmore's reproaches for ever, if *I* know anything of the matter!'

Hester smiled faintly. 'One grows accustomed to that too. I have sometimes thought that when Papa dies I might live in quite a little house, by myself.'

'Well, you won't,' said Lady Widmore trenchantly. 'Your sister Susan will pounce on you: I can vouch for *that*! It would suit her very well to have you with her to wait on her hand and foot, and very likely act as governess to all those plain brats of hers as well! And Widmore would think it a first-rate scheme, so you'd get no support from him, or from Gertrude or Constance either. And it's not a particle of good thinking you'd stand out against 'em, my dear, for you haven't a ha'porth of spirit! If you want a home of your own, you'll take Ludlow, and bless yourself for your good fortune, for you won't get one by any other means!'

With these encouraging words, Lady Widmore took herself off to her own bedchamber, pausing on the way to inform her lord that provided he and his father could keep still tongues in their heads she rather fancied she had done the trick.

The Lady Hester, once her maid was dismissed, the candles blown out, and the curtains drawn round her bed, buried her face in the pillow and cried herself quietly to sleep.

3

Three days later, Sir Gareth, in happy ignorance of the wretched indecision into which his proposal had thrown his chosen bride, left London, and pursued a rather leisurely progress towards Cambridgeshire. He drove his own curricle, with a pair of remarkably fine match-bays harnessed to it, and broke the journey at the house of some friends, not many miles from Baldock, where he remained for two nights, resting his horses. He took with him his head groom, but not his valet: a circumstance which disgusted that extremely skilled gentleman more than it surprised him. Sir Gareth, who belonged to the Corinthian set, was always very well dressed, but he was quite capable of achieving the effect he desired without the ministrations of the genius who had charge of his wardrobe; and the thought that alien hands were pressing his coats, or applying inferior blacking to his Hessian boots, caused him to feel no anguish at all.

He was not expected at Brancaster Park until the late afternoon, but since the month was July, and the weather sultry, he set forward for the remainder of the journey in good time, driving his pair at an easy pace, and pausing to bait, when some twenty miles had been accomplished, in the village of Caxton. The place boasted only one posting-house, and that a modest one; and when Sir Gareth strolled into the coffee-room he found the landlord engaged in what appeared to be a somewhat heated argument with a young lady in gown of sprig muslin, and a hat of chip-straw, which was tied becomingly over a mass of silken black locks.

The landlord, as soon as he perceived an obvious member of the Quality upon the threshold, abandoned the lady without ceremony, and stepped forward, bowing, and desiring to know in what way he might have the honour of serving the newcomer.

'It will be time enough to serve me when you have attended to this lady,' replied Sir Gareth, who had not failed to remark the indignant expression in the lady's big eyes.

'Oh, no, sir! No, indeed! I am quite at liberty—very happy to wait upon your honour immediately!' the landlord assured him. 'I was just telling the young person that I daresay she will find accommodation at the Rose and Crown.'

These words were added in a lowered voice, but they reached the lady's ears, and caused her to say in a tone of strong disapprobation: 'I am *not* a young person, and if I wish to stay in your horrid inn, I *shall* stay here, and it is not of the least use to tell me that you have no room, because I don't believe you!'

'I've told you before, miss, that this is a posting-house, and we don't serve your per—females—who come walking in with no more than a couple of bandboxes!' said the landlord angrily. 'I don't know what your lay is, nor I don't want to, but I haven't got any room for you, and that's my last word!'

Sir Gareth, who had retired tactfully to the window-embrasure, had been watching the stormy little face under the chip-hat. It was an enchantingly pretty face, with large, dark eyes, a lovely, wilful mouth, and a most determined chin. It was also a very youthful face, just now flushed with mortification. The landlord plainly considered its owner to be a female of no account, but neither the child's voice nor her manner, which was decidedly imperious, belonged to one of vulgar birth. A suspicion that she was a runaway from some seminary for young ladies crossed Sir Gareth's mind: he judged her to be about the same age as his niece; and in some intangible way she reminded him of Clarissa. Not that she was really like Clarissa, for Clarissa had been divinely fair. Perhaps, he thought, with a tiny pang, the resemblance lay in her wilful look, and the tilt of her obstinate chin. At all events, she was far too young and too pretty to be going about the country unattended; and no more unsuitable resting-place than the common inn to which the landlord had directed her could have been found for her. If she were an errant schoolgirl, it clearly behoved a man of honour to restore her to her family.

Sir Gareth came away from the window, saying, with his attractive smile: 'Forgive me, but can I perhaps be of some assistance?'

She eyed him uncertainly, not shyly, but with speculation in her candid gaze. Before she could answer, the landlord said that there was no need for the gentleman to trouble himself. He would have expanded the remark, but was checked. Sir Gareth said, quite pleasantly, but on a note of authority: 'It appears to me that there is considerable need. It is quite out of the question that this lady should spend the night at the Rose and Crown.' He smiled down at the lady again. 'Suppose you were to tell me where you want to go to? I don't think, you know, that your mama would wish you to stay at any inn without your maid.'

'Well, I haven't got a mama,' replied the lady, with the air of one triumphing in argument.

'I beg your pardon. Your father, then?'

'And I haven't got a father *either*!'

'Yes, I can see that you think you have now driven me against the ropes,' he said, amused. 'And, of course, if both your parents are dead we shall never know what they would have felt about it. How would it be if we discussed the matter over a little refreshment? What would you like?'

Her eyes brightened; she said cordially: 'I should be *very* much obliged to you, sir, if you would procure a glass of lemonade for me, for I am excessively thirsty, and this odious man wouldn't bring it to me!'

The landlord said explosively: 'Your honour! Miss walks in here, as you see her, wanting me to tell her when the next coach is due for Huntingdon, and when I say there won't be one, not till tomorrow, first she asks me if I'm needing a chambermaid, and when I tell her I'm not needing any such thing, she up and says she'll hire a room for the night! Now, I put it to your honour—'

'Never mind!' interrupted Sir Gareth, only the faintest tremor in his voice betraying the laughter that threatened to overcome him. 'Just be good enough to fetch the lady a glass of lemonade, and, for me, a tankard of your home-brewed, and we will see what can be done to straighten out this tangle!'

The landlord started to say something about the respectability of his house, thought better of it, and withdrew. Sir Gareth pulled a chair out from the table, and sat down, saying persuasively: 'Now that we are rid of him, do you feel that you could tell me who you are, and how you come to be wandering about the country in this rather odd way? My name, I should tell you, is Ludlow—Sir Gareth Ludlow, entirely at your service!'

'How do you do?' responded the lady politely.

'Well?' said Sir Gareth, the twinkle in his eye quizzing her. 'Am I, like the landlord, to call you miss? I really can't address you as ma'am: you put me much too strongly in mind of my eldest niece, when she's in mischief.'

She had been eyeing him rather warily, but this remark seemed to reassure her, which was what it was meant to do. She said: 'My name is Amanda, sir. Amanda S—Smith!'

'Amanda Smith, I regret to be obliged to inform you that you are a shockingly untruthful girl,' said Sir Gareth calmly.

'It is a very good name!' she said, on the defensive.

'Amanda is a charming name, and Smith is very well in its way, but it is not your surname. Come, now!'

She shook her head, the picture of pretty mulishness. 'I shan't tell you. If I did, you might know who I am, and I have a particular reason for not wishing anyone to know that.'

'Are you escaping from school?' he inquired.

She stiffened indignantly. 'Certainly not! I'm not a schoolgirl! In fact, I am very nearly seventeen, and I shall shortly be a married lady!'

He sustained this with no more than a blink, and begged pardon with suitable gravity. Fortunately, the landlord returned at that moment, with lemonade, beer, and the grudging offer of freshly baked tarts, if Miss should happen to fancy them. Judging by the hopeful gleam in Amanda's eyes that she would fancy them very much, Sir Gareth bade him bring in a dish of them, adding: 'And some fruit as well, if you please.'

Quite mollified by this openhanded behaviour, Amanda said warmly: 'Thank you! To own the truth, I am excessively hungry. Are you really an uncle?'

'Indeed I am!'

'Well, I shouldn't have thought it. Mine are the stuffiest people!'

By the time she had disposed of six tartlets, and the better part of a bowl of cherries, cordial relations with her host had been well established; and she accepted gratefully an offer to drive her to Huntingdon. She asked to be set down at the George; and when she saw a slight crease appear between Sir Gareth's brows very obligingly added: 'Or the Fountain, if you prefer it, sir.'

The crease remained. 'Is someone meeting you at one of these houses, Amanda?'

'Oh, yes!' she replied airily.

He opened his snuff-box, and took a leisurely pinch. 'Excellent! I will take you there with pleasure.'

'*Thank* you!' she said, bestowing a brilliant smile upon him.

'And hand you into the care of whoever it is who is no doubt awaiting you,' continued Sir Gareth amiably.

She looked to be a good deal daunted, and said, after a pregnant moment: 'Well, I don't think you should do that, because I daresay they will be late.'

'Then I will remain with you until they arrive.'

'They might be *very* late!'

'Or they might not come at all,' he suggested. 'Now, stop trying to hoax me with all these faradiddles, my child! I am much too old a hand to be taken in. No one is going to meet you in Huntingdon, and you may make up your mind to this: I am not going to leave you at the George, or the Fountain, or at any other inn.'

'Then I shan't go with you,' said Amanda. 'So then what will you do?'

'I'm not quite sure,' he replied. 'I must either give you into the charge of the Parish officer here, or the Vicar.'

She cried hotly: 'I won't be given into anyone's charge! I think you are the most interfering, odious person I ever met, and I wish you will go away and leave me to take care of myself, which I am very well able to do!'

'I expect you do,' he agreed. 'And, I very much fear, I am just as stuffy as your uncles, which is a very lowering reflection.'

'If you knew the circumstances, I am persuaded you wouldn't spoil everything!' she urged.

'But I don't know the circumstances,' he pointed out.

'Well—well—if I were to tell you that I am escaping from persecution—?'

'I shouldn't believe you. If you are not running away from school, you must be running away from your home, and I conjecture that you are doing that because you've fallen in love with someone of whom your relations don't approve. In fact, you are trying to elope, and if anyone is to meet you in Huntingdon it is the gentleman to whom—as you informed me—you are shortly to be married.'

'Well, you are quite out!' she declared. 'I am *not* eloping, though it would be a much better thing to do, besides being most romantic. Naturally, that was the first scheme I made.'

'What caused you to abandon it?' he inquired.

'He wouldn't go with me,' said Amanda naïvely. 'He says it is not the thing, and he won't marry me without Grandpapa's consent, on account of being a man of honour. He is a soldier, and in a *very* fine regiment, although not a cavalry regiment. Grandpapa and my papa were both Hussars. Neil is home on sick leave from the Peninsula.'

'I see. Fever, or wounds?'

'He had a ball in his shoulder, and for *months* they couldn't dig it out! That was why he was sent home.'

'And have you become acquainted with him quite lately?'

'Good gracious, no! I've known him for ever! He lives at—he lives near my home. At least, his family does. *Most* unfortunately, he is a younger son, which is a thing Grandpapa quite abominates, because Papa was one too, and so we both have very modest fortunes. Only, Neil has every intention of becoming a General, so that's nothing to the purpose. Besides, I don't want a large fortune. I don't think it would be of the least use to me, except, perhaps, to buy Neil's promotion, and even that wouldn't answer, because he prefers to rise by his own exertions.'

'Very proper,' Sir Gareth said gravely.

'Well, I think so, and when we are at war, you know, there is always a great deal of opportunity. Neil has his company already, and I must tell you that when he was obliged to come home he was a Brigade-Major!'

'That is certainly excellent. How old is he?'

'Twenty-four, but he is quite a hardened campaigner, I assure you, so that it is nonsense to suppose he can't take care of me. Why, he can take care of a whole brigade.'

He laughed. '*That*, I fancy, would be child's play, in comparison!'

She looked mischievous suddenly, but said: 'No, for I am a soldier's daughter, and I shouldn't be in the least troublesome, if only I could marry Neil, and follow the drum with him, and not have to be presented, and go to horrid balls at Almack's, and be married to an odious man with a large fortune and a title.'

'It would be very disagreeable to be married to an odious man,' he agreed, 'but that fate doesn't overtake everyone who goes to Almack's you know! Don't you think you might like to see a little more of the world before you get married to anyone?'

She shook her head so vigorously that her dusky ringlets danced under the brim of her hat. '*No!* That is what Grandpapa said, and he made my aunt take me to Bath, and I met a great many people, and went to the Assemblies, in spite of not having been presented yet, and it didn't put Neil out of my head at all. And if you think, sir, that perhaps I was not a success, I must tell you that you are quite mistaken!'

'I feel sure you were a success,' he replied, smiling.

'I was,' she said candidly. 'I had *hundreds* of compliments paid me, and I stood up for every dance. So now I know all about being fashionable, and I would liefer by far live in a tent with Neil.'

He found her at once childish and strangely mature, and was touched. He said gently: 'Perhaps you would, and perhaps you will, one day, live in a tent with Neil. But you are very young to be married, Amanda, and it would be better to wait for a year or two.'

'I have already waited for two years, for I have been betrothed to Neil since I was fifteen, secretly! And I am not too young to be married, because Neil knows an officer in the 95th who is married to a Spanish lady who is *much* younger than I am!'

There did not seem to be anything to say in reply to this. Sir Gareth, who was beginning to perceive that the task of protecting Amanda was one fraught with difficulty, shifted his ground. 'Very well, but if you are not at this moment eloping, which, I own, seems, in the absence of your Brigade-Major, to be unlikely—I wish you will tell me what you hope to gain by running away from your home, and wandering about the countryside in this very unconventional manner?'

'That,' said Amanda, with pride, 'is Strategy, sir.'

'I am afraid,' said Sir Gareth apologetically, 'that the explanation leaves me no wiser than I was before.'

'Well, it *may* be Tactics,' she said cautiously. 'Though that is when you move troops in the presence of the enemy, and, of course, the enemy isn't present. I find it very confusing to distinguish between the two things, and it is a pity Neil isn't here, for you may depend upon it he knows exactly, and he could explain it to you.'

'Yes, I begin to think it is a thousand pities he isn't here, even though he were not so obliging as to explain it to me,' agreed Sir Gareth.

Amanda, who had been frowning over the problem, said: 'I believe the properest expression is a plan of campaign! That's what it is! How stupid of me! I am not at all surprised you shouldn't have understood what I meant.'

'I still don't understand. What *is* your plan of campaign?'

'Well, I'll tell you, sir,' said Amanda, not displeased to describe what she plainly considered to be a masterpiece of generalship. 'When Neil said that on no account would he take me to Gretna Green, naturally I was obliged to think of a different scheme. And although I daresay it seems to you pretty poor-spirited of him, he is *not* poor-spirited, and I don't at all wish you to think such a thing of him.'

'Set your mind at rest on that head: I don't!' replied Sir Gareth.

'And it isn't because he doesn't wish to marry me, for he does, and he says he is going to marry me, even if we have to wait until I am of age,' she assured him earnestly. She added, after a darkling pause: 'But, I must say, it has me quite in a puzzle to understand how he comes to be a very good soldier, which everyone says he truly is, when he seems to have not the least notion of Surprise, or Attack. Do you suppose it comes from fighting under Lord Wellington's command, and being obliged to retreat so frequently?'

'Very likely,' responded Sir Gareth, his countenance admirably composed. 'Is your flight in the nature of an attack?'

'Yes, of course it is. For it was *vital* that something should be done immediately! At any moment now, Neil may be sent back to rejoin the regiment, and if he doesn't take me with him I may not see him again for years, and years, and years! And it is of no avail to argue with Grandpapa, or to coax him, because all he does is to say that I shall soon forget about it, and to give me stupid presents!'

At this point, any faint vision, which Sir Gareth might have had, of a tyrannical grandparent, left him. He said: 'I quite expected to hear that he had locked you in your room.'

'Oh, no!' she assured him. 'Aunt Adelaide did so once, when I was quite a little girl, but I climbed out of the window, into the big elm tree, and Grandpapa said I was never to be locked in again. And, in a way, I am sorry for it, because I daresay if I had been locked in Neil would have consented to an elopement. But, of course, when all Grandpapa would do was to give me things, and talk about my presentation, and send me to parties in Bath, Neil couldn't perceive that there was the least need to rescue me. He said that we must be patient. But I have seen what comes of being patient,' Amanda said, with a boding look, 'and I have no opinion of it.'

'What *does* come of it?' inquired Sir Gareth.

'Nothing!' she answered. 'I daresay you might not credit it, but Aunt Adelaide fell in love when she was quite young, like me, and *just* the same thing happened! Grandpapa said she was too young, and also that he wished her to marry a man of fortune, so she made up her mind to be patient, and *then* what do you think?'

'I haven't the remotest guess: do tell me!'

'Why, after only two years the Suitor married an odious female with ten thousand pounds, and they had seven children, and he was carried off by an inflammation of the lungs! And none of it would have happened if only Aunt Adelaide had had a grain of resolution! So I have quite made up my mind not to cultivate resignation, because although people praise one for it I don't consider that it serves any useful purpose. If Aunt Adelaide had been married to the Suitor, he wouldn't have contracted an inflammation of the lungs, because she would have taken better care of him. And if Neil is wounded again, *I* am going to nurse him, and I shall not permit *anyone*, even Lord Wellington himself, to put him on one of those dreadful spring-wagons, which was harder to bear than all the rest, he told me!'

'I'm sure it must have been. But none of this explains why you ran away from your home,' he pointed out.

'Oh, I did that to compel Grandpapa to consent to my marriage!' she said brightly. 'And also to show him that I am *not* a child, but, on the contrary, very well able to take care of myself. He thinks that because I am accustomed to be waited on I shouldn't know how to go on if I had to live in billets, or perhaps a tent, which is absurd, because I should. Only it never answers to *tell* Grandpapa anything: one is obliged to *show* him. Well, he didn't believe I should climb out of the window when I was locked into my room, though I warned him how it would be. At first, I thought I would refuse to eat anything until he gave his consent—in fact, I did refuse, one day, only I became so excessively hungry that I thought perhaps it wasn't such a famous scheme, particularly when it so happened that there were buttered lobsters for dinner, and a Floating Island pudding.'

'Naturally you couldn't forgo two such dishes,' he said sympathetically.

'Well, no,' she confessed. 'Besides, it wouldn't have shown Grandpapa that I am truly able to take care of myself, which is, I think, important.'

'Very true. One can't help feeling that it might have put just the opposite notion into his head. Now tell me why you think that running away from him will answer the purpose!'

'Well, it wouldn't: not that part of it, precisely. *That* will just give him a fright.'

'I have no doubt it will, but are you quite sure you wish to frighten him?'

'No, but it is quite his own fault for being so unkind and obstinate. Besides, it is my campaign, and you can't consider the sensibilities of the enemy when you are planning a campaign!' she said reasonably. 'You can have no notion how difficult it was to decide what was best to be done. In fact, I was *almost* at a stand when, by the luckiest chance, I saw an advertisement in the *Morning Post*. It said that a lady living at—well, living not very far from St Neots, wished for a genteel young person to be governess to her children. Of course, I saw at once that it was the very thing!' A slight choking sound made her look inquiringly at Sir Gareth. 'Sir?'

'I didn't speak. Pray continue! I collect that you thought that you might be eligible for this post?'

'Certainly I did!' she replied, with dignity. 'I am genteel, and I am young, and, I assure you, I have been *most* carefully educated. And having had several governesses myself, I know exactly what should be done in such a case. So I wrote to this lady, pretending I was my aunt, you know. I said I desired to recommend for the post my niece's governess, who had given *every* satisfaction, and was in all respects a most talented and admirable person, able to give instruction in the pianoforte, and in water-colour painting, besides the use of the globes, and needlework, and foreign languages.'

'An impressive catalogue!' he said, much struck.

'Well, I do think it sounds well,' she acknowledged, accepting this tribute with a rosy blush.

'Very well. Er—does it happen to be true?'

'Of course it's true! That is to say—Well, I am thought to play quite creditably on the pianoforte, besides being able to sing a little, and sketching is of all things my favourite occupation. And naturally I have learnt French, and, lately, some Spanish, because although Neil says we shall be over the Pyrenees in a trice, one never knows, and it might be very necessary to be able to converse in Spanish. I own, I don't know if I can *teach* these things, but that doesn't signify, because I never had the least intention of being a governess for more than a few weeks. The thing is that I haven't a great deal of money, so that if I run away I must contrive to earn my bread until Grandpapa capitulates. I have left behind me a letter, you see, explaining it all to him, and I have told him that I won't come home, or tell him where I am, until he promises to let me be married to Neil immediately.'

'Forgive me!' he interpolated. 'But if you have severed your lines of communication how is he to inform you of his surrender?'

'I have arranged for that,' she replied proudly. 'I have desired him to insert an advertisement in the *Morning Post*! I have left nothing to chance, which ought to prove to him that I am not a foolish little girl, but, on the contrary, a most responsible person, quite old enough to be married. Yes, and I didn't book a seat on the stage, which would have been a stupid thing to do, on account of making it easy, perhaps, for them to discover where I had gone. I hid myself in the carrier's cart! I had formed that intention from the outset, and that, you see, was what made it so particularly fortunate that the lady who wished for a governess lived near to St Neots.'

'Oh, she did engage you?' Sir Gareth said, unable to keep an inflexion of surprise out of his voice.

'Yes, because I recommended myself very strongly to her, and it seems that the old governess was obliged to leave her at a moment's notice, because her mother suddenly died, and so she had to go home to keep house for her papa. Nothing could have fallen out more fortunately!'

He was obliged to laugh, but he said: 'Abominable girl! What next will you say? But if you are now on your way to take up this desirable post, how come you to be trying to hire yourself as a chambermaid at this inn, and why do you wish to go to Huntingdon?'

The triumphant look in her eyes was quenched; she sighed, and said: 'Oh, it is the shabbiest thing! You would hardly believe that my scheme could miscarry, when I planned it so carefully, would you? But so it was. I am not on my way to Mrs—to That Female. In fact, quite the reverse. She is the horridest creature!'

'Ah!' said Sir Gareth. 'Did she refuse after all to employ you?'

'Yes, she did!' answered Amanda, her bosom swelling with indignation. 'She said I was by far too young, and not at all the sort of female she had had in mind. She said she had been quite deceived, which was a most unjust observation, because she said in the advertisement that she desired a *young* lady!'

'My child, you are a shameless minx!' said Sir Gareth frankly. 'From start to finish you deceived this unfortunate woman, and well you know it!'

'No, I did not!' she retorted, firing up. 'At least, only in pretending I was Aunt Adelaide, and saying I had been my own governess, and *that* she didn't know! I am truly able to do all the things I told her I could, and very likely I should be able to teach other girls to do them too. However, all was to no avail. She was very disagreeable, besides being excessively uncivil. Unreasonable, too, for in the middle of it her eldest son came in, and as soon as he heard who I was he suggested that his mama should engage me for a little while, to see how I did, which was most sensible, I thought. But it only made her crosser than ever, and she sent him out of the room, which I was sorry for, because he seemed very amiable and obliging, in spite of having spots.' She added, affronted: 'And I do not at all understand why you should laugh, sir!'

'Never mind! Tell me what happened next!'

'Well, she ordered the carriage to take me back to St Neots, and while it was being brought round she began to ask me a great many impertinent questions, and I could see she had an extremely suspicious disposition, so I thought of a splendid story to tell her. I gave myself an indigent parent, and *dozens* of brothers and sisters, all younger than I am, and instead of being sorry for me, she said she didn't believe me! She said I wasn't dressed like a poor person, and she would like to know how many guineas I had squandered on my hat! Such impudence! So I said I had stolen it, and my gown as well, and really I was a wicked adventuress. That, of course, was impolite, but it answered the purpose, for she stopped trying to discover where I had come from, and grew very red in the face, and said I was an abandoned girl, and she washed her hands of me. Then the servant came to say that the carriage was at the door, and so I made my curtsy, and we parted.'

'Abandoned you most certainly are. Were you driven to St Neots?'

'Yes, and it was then that I hit upon the notion of becoming a chambermaid for a space.'

'Let me tell you, Amanda, that a chambermaid's life would not suit you!'

'I know *that*, and if you can think of some more agreeable occupation of a gainful nature, sir, I shall be very much obliged to you,' she responded, fixing him with a pair of hopeful eyes.

'I'm afraid I can't. There is only one thing for you to do, and that is to return to your grandpapa.'

'I won't!' said Amanda, not mincing matters.

'I think you will, when you've considered a little.'

'No, I shan't. I have already considered a great deal, and I now see that it is a very good thing Mrs—That Female—wouldn't employ me. For if I were a governess in a respectable household Grandpapa would know that I was perfectly safe, and he would very likely try to—to starve me out. But I shouldn't think he would like me to be a chambermaid in an inn, would you?'

'Emphatically, no!'

'Well, there you are!' she said triumphantly. 'The instant he knows that that is what I am doing, he will capitulate. Now the only puzzle is to discover a suitable inn. I saw a very pretty one in a village, on the way to St Neots, which is why you find me in this horrid one. Because I went back to it, after the coachman had set me down, only they didn't happen to need a chambermaid there, which was a sad pity, for it had roses growing up the wall, and six of the dearest little kittens! The landlady said that I should go to Huntington, because she had heard that they needed a girl to work at the George, and she directed me to the pike-road, and that is why I am here!'

'Are you telling me,' demanded Sir Gareth incredulously, 'that you bamboozled the woman into believing that you were a maidservant? She must be out of her senses!'

'Oh, no!' said Amanda blithely. 'I thought of a splendid story, you see.'

'An indigent parent?'

'No, much better than that one. I said I had been an abigail to a young lady, who most kindly gave me her old dresses to wear, only I had been turned off, *without* a character, because her papa behaved in a very improper way towards me. He is a widower, you must know, and also there is an aunt—not like Aunt Adelaide, but more like Aunt Maria, who is a very unfeeling person—'

'Yes, you may spare me the rest of this affecting history!' interrupted Sir Gareth, between amusement and exasperation.

'Well, you *asked* me!' she said indignantly. 'And you need not be so scornful, because I took the notion from a very improving novel called—'

'–*Pamela*. And I am astonished that your grandfather should have permitted you to read it! That is to say, if you have a grandfather, which I begin to doubt!'

She showed him a shocked face. 'Of course I have a grandfather! In fact, I once had *two* grandfathers, but one of them died when I was a baby.'

'He is to be felicitated. Come, now! Was there one word of truth in the story you told *me*, or was it another of your splendid stories?'

She jumped up, very much flushed, and with tears sparkling on the ends of her long eyelashes. 'No, it was not! I thought you were kind, and a *gentleman*, and now I see I was quite mistaken, and I wish very much that I *had* told you a lie, because you are *exactly* like an uncle, only worse! And what I told those other people was just–just make-believe, and *that* is not the same thing as telling lies! And I am excessively sorry now that I drank your lemonade, and ate your tarts, and, if you please, I will pay for them *myself*! And also,' she added, as her misty gaze fell on an empty bowl, 'for the cherries!'

He too had risen, and he possessed himself of the agitated little hands that were fumbling with the strings of a reticule, and held them in a comforting clasp. 'Gently, my child! There, there, don't cry! Of course I see just how it was! Come! let us sit on this settee, and decide what is best to be done!'

Amanda, tired by the day's adventures, made only a token of resistance before subsiding on to his shoulder, and indulging in a burst of tears. Sir Gareth, who had more than once sustained the impassioned and lachrymose confidences of an ill-used niece, behaved with great competence and sangfroid, unshaken by a situation that might have cast a less experienced man into disorder. In a very few minutes, Amanda had recovered from her emotional storm, had mopped her cheeks, and blown her diminutive nose into his handkerchief, and had offered him an apology for having succumbed to a weakness which, she earnestly assured him, she heartily despised.

Then he talked to her. He talked well, and persuasively, pointing out to her the unwisdom of her present plans, the distress of mind into which a continuance of them must throw her grandfather, and all the disadvantages which must attach to a career, however temporary, as a serving-maid in a public inn. She listened to him with great docility, her large eyes fixed on his face, her hands folded in her lap, and an occasional sob catching her breath; and when he had finished she said: 'Yes, but even if it is very bad it will be better than not being allowed to marry Neil until I come of age. So will you please take me to Huntingdon, sir?'

'Amanda, have you attended to one word I've said to you?'

'Yes, I attended to all of them, and they were exactly the sort of things my own uncles would say. It is all propriety and nonsense! As for grieving Grandpapa, it is quite his own fault, because I warned him that he would be excessively sorry if he didn't give his consent to my marriage, and if he didn't believe me he deserves to be put in a pucker for being so stupid. Because I always keep my word, and when I want something very much I get it.'

'I can well believe it. You must forgive me if I tell you, Amanda, that you are a shockingly spoilt child!'

'Well, that is Grandpapa's fault too,' she said.

He tried another tack. 'Tell me this! If he knew of your exploit, do you think your Neil would approve of it?'

She replied unhesitatingly: 'Oh, no! In fact, I expect he will be very angry, and give me a tremendous scold, but he will forgive me, because he knows I would never serve *him* such a trick. Besides, he must perceive that I am doing it all for his sake. And I daresay,' she added reflectively, 'that he won't be so very much surprised, because he thinks I'm spoilt, too, and he knows *all* the bad things I've done. Indeed, he has often rescued me from a fix, when I was a little girl.' Her eyes brightened; she exclaimed: 'Why, that would be the very thing! Only I think it ought to be a dire peril this time. Then he can rescue me from it, and restore me to Grandpapa, and Grandpapa would be so grateful that he would be obliged to consent to the marriage!' She frowned in an effort of concentration. 'I shall have to think of a dire peril. I must say, it's very difficult!'

Sir Gareth, who experienced no difficulty at all in thinking of it, said in a damping voice that by the time she had contrived to advise Neil of her danger it might be too late for him to effect a rescue.

She rather regretfully acknowledged the justice of this observation, further disclosing that she was not perfectly sure of Neil's direction, since he had gone to London, for a medical inspection, after which he would report at the Horse Guards. 'And goodness knows how long that will take! And the dreadful part of it is that if the doctors think him quite well again, he may be sent back to Spain almost immediately! That is why it is *imperative* that I should lose not a moment in–in prosecuting my campaign!' She jumped up, saying with a challenging look: 'I am very much obliged to you, sir, and now, if you please, we will part, for I believe Huntingdon is almost ten miles away, and if there is no stage, and you don't wish to take me there in your carriage, I shall have to walk, so that it is high time I was setting forward.'

She then held out her hand, with all the air of a great lady taking gracious leave of an acquaintance, but upon Sir Gareth's not only taking it in his, but maintaining a firm hold on it, her grandeur abruptly deserted her, and she stamped her foot, and commanded him to let her go instantly.

Sir Gareth was in a dilemma. It was plainly useless to continue arguing with Amanda, and he had seen enough of her to be tolerably sure that an attempt to frighten her into disclosing her grandfather's name and direction would fail. If he carried into execution his threat to hand her into the charge of the Parish officer, nothing was more certain than that she would give this worthy the slip. Leave her to her own absurd devices? No: it was impossible, he decided. Headstrong and, indeed, extremely naughty she might be, but she was as innocent as a kitten, and by far too lovely to be allowed to wander unescorted about the country.

'If you don't let me go this instant, I shall bite you!' stormed Amanda, tugging fruitlessly at his long fingers.

'Then not only will you not be offered a seat in my curricle, but you will get your ears soundly boxed into the bargain,' he replied cheerfully.

'How *dare* you—' She broke off suddenly, stopped clawing at his hand, and raised a face alight with joyful expectation. 'Oh, *will* you take me up in your curricle, sir? *Thank* you!'

He would not have been in the least surprised had she flung her arms round his neck in her transport of gratitude, but she contented herself with squeezing his hand tightly between both of hers, and bestowing upon him a rapturous smile. Registering a silent vow not to let so trusting a damsel out of his sight until he could restore her to her proper guardian, he put her into a chair, and went off to inform his astonished groom that he must relinquish his seat in the curricle to a lady, and stand up behind as best he might.

Trotton thought it a strange start, but when, a few minutes later, he clapped eyes on the unexpected passenger, the disturbing suspicion that his master had run mad darted into his mind. There were plenty of gentlemen in whom such conduct would have seemed natural, but Sir Gareth, in Trotton's experience, had never been one to fall into the petticoat line. Sir Gareth had not told any member of his household what his errand was to Brancaster Park, but all his servants, from his butler down to the kitchen porter, had guessed what it must be, and it seemed to Trotton the height of insanity for him to succumb just at this moment to the lures thrown out by the pretty bit of muslin he was handing up into his curricle. A nice set-out it would be if he were to be seen driving such a prime article as that down the road! He wondered whether perhaps his master had a touch of the sun, and was trying to remember what ought to be done for sufferers from sun-stroke when Sir Gareth's voice recalled his wandering wits.

'Are you deaf, Trotton? I said, let 'em go!'

4

A couple of miles beyond the cross-road from Cambridge to St Neots the road forked. Sir Gareth took the right fork without hesitation. His youthful companion, who had (as she artlessly informed him) hitherto travelled in no more sporting vehicle than a gig, which Grandpapa sometimes permitted her to drive, was hugely enjoying herself, and was too ruthlessly intent on discovering whether her protector was a whip celebrated enough to merit the title of Nonesuch to notice a weatherbeaten signpost which bore, in faded lettering, the simple legend: *To St Ives*. It was otherwise with the faithful henchman. Standing precariously behind his master, and maintaining his balance by a firm grip on the curricle's lowered hood, he ventured to intervene. He had gathered, from Amanda's prattle, that Sir Gareth had engaged himself to drive her to Huntingdon, and he considered it his duty to point out to Sir Gareth that he had taken the wrong fork.

Restraining an impulse to curse his too-helpful retainer, Sir Gareth said calmly: 'Thank you, Trotton, I know the road.'

But the mischief was done. Bristling with suspicion, Amanda demanded: 'Is this not the road to Huntingdon?'

It had been Sir Gareth's intention to postpone for as long as possible the disclosure that he was taking Amanda not to Huntingdon but to Brancaster Park; but thus directly questioned he saw nothing for it but to tell her the truth. He replied: 'No, but I have a better plan for you.'

'You promised you would drive me to Huntingdon!' she cried hotly.

'Oh, no, I didn't! I offered you a seat in my curricle: no more than that! You cannot have forgotten that I told you I would for no persuasion leave you in a public inn.'

'Stop! Set me down at once!' she ordered. 'I won't go with you! I was never so taken in! Why—why, you are nothing but an *abductor*!'

He could not help laughing at this, which naturally made her very angry. She raged at him for several minutes, but as soon as she paused for breath he said soothingly: 'If you will be quiet for a moment, and listen to what I have to say, I'll tell you where I *am* taking you.'

'It is not of the slightest consequence, because I won't go with you *anywhere*! You are a deceiver, and a wicked person, and very likely you mean to murder me!'

'Then you are now in dire peril, and what you should do is to summon your Brigade-Major to the rescue immediately,' he returned. 'A message to the Horse Guards will undoubtedly find him. Tell me his name, and I will engage not only to bring him to you with all possible speed, but also to refrain from murdering you in the meantime.'

'I hope very much that *he* will murder *you*!' she declared through shut teeth. 'And I expect he will, when he knows how treacherously you have behaved to me!'

'But you can't expect him to murder me if you don't tell him of my treachery,' he pointed out, in a very reasonable way. 'If I were you, I would lose not a moment in summoning him to your side. Trotton shall travel post to London with a message for him. I shouldn't be astonished if I were a dead man within two days.'

From the sparkling look in her eyes, it was to be inferred that the prospect strongly attracted her. It seemed, for a moment, as though she were on the point of divulging her Brigade-Major's name, but just as Sir Gareth was silently congratulating himself on the success of his tactics, she said suddenly: 'I see what it is! It is all a trick, so that you may discover where I live, and ruin my scheme! Well, I shall *not* send a message to Neil!'

'You know, Amanda,' he said seriously, 'you may just as well tell me what I wish to know, because I am going to discover it, whether you do or whether you don't.'

'No! How can you?' she demanded.

'If you force me to do so, I shall pay a visit to the Horse Guards, and inquire of them there if they can furnish me with the direction of a captain of infantry, a Brigade-Major, sent home from the Peninsula with a ball in his shoulder, but now in hourly expectation of rejoining. I expect they will be able to help me, though I can't but feel that Neil would infinitely prefer to be discovered in a rather more private style. That is for you to decide.'

She did not speak for several moments; then she said, in a gritty little voice: 'You think you've worsted me, but you have not! I shan't tell you anything, and I promise you I—I shall come about!'

'Very well,' he replied equably.

'I believe,' said Amanda, after another seething pause, 'that kidnappers are sent to prison, or even *transported*! You would not like that, I daresay!'

'No, indeed!'

'Well! I am just warning you!' she said.

'Thank you! I am very much obliged to you.'

'And if *you*,' declared Amanda, bethinking herself of the groom, and twisting round to address him, 'had one grain of manliness, you would not permit your master to carry me off!'

Trotton, a deeply interested audience, was unprepared for this attack, and nearly lost his balance. Much discomposed, he could only stammer an unintelligible answer, and glance imploringly at Sir Gareth's back-view.

'Oh, you mustn't blame Trotton!' said Sir Gareth. 'Consider how difficult is his position! He is obliged to obey my orders, you see.'

'He is not obliged to assist you in kidnapping people!' she retorted.

'I engaged him on the strict understanding,' said Sir Gareth firmly, 'that that would form an important part of his duties.'

'I w-wish you will not be so absurd!' said Amanda, struggling to suppress a giggle.

He turned his head to smile down at her. 'That's better!'

She laid a mittened hand on his sleeve, directing a beseeching look up at him. 'Oh, will you *please* let me go? You are ruining everything!'

'I know I am, and I do beg your pardon. I must be quite the most abominable marplot imaginable.'

'Well, you are! And I thought you were so very agreeable!'

'I too have been badly deceived in myself,' he said, shaking his head. 'Would you believe it?—I had no notion that I was such a monster of inhumanity as I have proved myself to be.'

'Well, it is being a monster to betray me, and then to try to roast me!' she said, turning away her flushed countenance, and biting her lip.

'Poor Amanda! You are perfectly right: it is a great deal too bad of me, and I won't roast you any more. Let me tell you instead where I am taking you!'

'I shan't listen to a word you say,' she informed him coldly.

'That will teach me a lesson,' he observed.

'I think you are the horridest creature!' she exclaimed. 'Yes, and now I come to think of it, if you are taking me to your own home, it is most improper, and far worse than letting me go to an inn!'

'It would be,' he agreed. 'But my home isn't in this part of the country. I am taking you to Brancaster Park, where I think you will find a very kind hostess in Lady Hester Theale.'

Upon hearing these words, Trotton, who was much attached to his master, very nearly allowed a protest to escape him. If Sir Gareth meant to arrive at Brancaster Park with this dazzling young beauty on his arm, he was unquestionably out of his senses, and ought to be restrained. But it was not the business of his groom to point out to him the unwisdom of introducing his chance-met bit of muslin to the Lady Hester. Trotton dared do no more than give a warning cough, to which Sir Gareth paid no heed at all.

Sir Gareth stood in no need of a warning. Had any other solution for the safe disposal of Amanda occurred to him, he would have seized it, for he was well aware that to present himself at Brancaster Park, with the declared intention of proposing marriage to Lady Hester, accompanied by Amanda must be as prejudicial to his interests as it was ludicrous. But he believed that he could rely on Hester to receive Amanda kindly; and he hoped that she would understand that he had no other choice than to bring that headstrong damsel to the shelter of her home.

Amanda, meanwhile, was demanding to be told who lived at Brancaster Park. When she learned that she was to be the uninvited guest of Lord Brancaster, and of his daughter, she protested vehemently, saying that so far from being anxious to regain possession of her, her grandfather would in all probability be delighted to know that she was a guest in an Earl's country seat. Sir Gareth suggested helpfully that she should prevail upon Lady Hester to hire her as an abigail.

Amanda audibly ground her teeth. 'If you force me to go there with you, I shall make you very, very sorry!' she warned him.

'I expect you will and am already in a quake of terror,' he agreed.

'I *trusted* you!' she said tragically. 'Now you are going to betray my confidence, besides ruining all my schemes!'

'No, I won't betray your confidence, except, I think, to Lady Hester. When you have met her, you won't, I fancy, object to her knowing the truth.

I shall desire her not to divulge it to her father, or—if they should happen to be at Brancaster—to her brother and his wife.'

She was quick to catch a certain inflexion in his voice, and lifted her eyes to his profile, saying: 'I can tell you don't like them above half, sir. Are they horrid?'

He smiled. 'No, not horrid. I daresay very worthy people, but it so happens that they are not particular friends of mine.'

'Oh! Is Lord Brancaster a particular friend of yours, sir?'

'Well, he is considerably older than I am,' he temporized.

She digested this, inquiring presently: 'Is Lady Hester a particular friend of yours, then?'

'Why, yes! She and I have been good friends for many years now.'

He was prepared for even more searching questions, but she relapsed into silence. After several minutes, he said: 'I have been wondering what I should tell Brancaster, and the Widmores, and I am strongly of the opinion, Amanda, that you are the daughter of some acquaintances with whom I have been staying, at Baldock. You are on your way to visit relations at—Oundle, perhaps—and from some cause or another I offered to take you with me as far as to Huntingdon, where these relations had engaged themselves to meet you. Unhappily, there must have been a misunderstanding, for no carriage awaited you there. Being pledged to present myself at Brancaster Park today, what was I to do? Why, take you along with me, to be sure, with the intention of conveying you to Oundle tomorrow! How does that suit your notion of a splendid story?'

'It is quite untrue,' she said primly.

'I wonder why I should have thought that that would have recommended it to you?' he murmured.

The only reply he got to this sally was a dagger-glance. He said, over his shoulder: 'I trust you heard that, Trotton?'

'Yes, sir.'

'Well, don't forget it!'

'Pray have the goodness to inform me, sir,' said Amanda, with awful civility, 'where you have the intention of taking me tomorrow?'

'I hope, to your grandfather.'

'*No!*'

He shrugged. 'As you wish.'

Intrigued, she demanded: 'Where, then?'

'That, my child, you will see, in good time.'

'I believe you are at a stand!' she challenged him.

'Not a bit of it!'

Conversation languished after that, Amanda occupying herself for the remainder of the journey in turning over in her mind various plots for Sir Gareth's discomfiture, and returning only monosyllabic replies to his occasional remarks.

They reached Brancaster Park as the shadows were beginning to lengthen, passing through impressive lodge-gates, and driving for some way up an avenue which had been allowed to deteriorate into something akin to a cart-track. The trees, growing rather too thickly beside it, rendered it both damp and gloomy; and when the pleasure gardens came into sight these too bore unmistakable signs of neglect. Amanda looked about her with disfavour; and, when her eyes alighted on the square, grey mansion, exclaimed: 'Oh, I wish you had not brought me here! What an ugly, disagreeable house!'

'If I could have thought of any other place for you, believe me, I wouldn't have brought you here, Amanda!' he said frankly. 'For a more awkward situation I defy anyone to imagine!'

'Well, if it seems so to you, set me down now, while there is still time!' she urged.

'No, I am determined not to let you escape me,' he replied lightly. 'I can only hope to be able to pass you off with some credit—though what the household will think of a young lady who travels with her belongings contained in a couple of bandboxes heaven only knows! I trust at least that we may not find the house full of guests. No, I fancy it won't be.'

He was right, but his host, who did not scruple to exaggerate in moments of acute vexation, had been so describing it ever since the unwelcome arrival, earlier in the day, of the Honourable Fabian Theale.

Mr Theale was his lordship's brother, and if he had been born with any other object than to embarrass his family, his lordship had yet to discover it. He was a bachelor, with erratic habits, expensive tastes, and pockets permanently to let. His character was volatile, his disposition amiable; and since he had a firm belief in benevolent Providence neither duns nor impending scandals had the power to ruffle his placidity. That it was first his father, and, later, his elder brother, who enacted the rôle of Providence troubled him not at all; and whenever the Earl swore that he had rescued him for the last time he made not the slightest effort either to placate his brother or to mend his extremely reprehensible ways, because he knew that while the Earl shared many of his tastes he had also a strong prejudice against open scandals, and could always be relied upon, whatever the exigencies of his own situation, to rescue one of his name from the bailiff's clutches.

At no time was his lordship pleased to receive a visit from Mr Theale; when that florid and portly gentleman descended upon him on the very day appointed for Sir Gareth's arrival he so far forgot himself as to say, in front of the butler, a footman, and Mr Theale's own valet, that no one need trouble to carry the numerous valises upstairs, since he was not going to house his brother for as much as a night.

Mr Theale, beyond inquiring solicitously if his lordship's gout was plaguing him, paid no attention to this. He adjured the footman to handle his dressing-case carefully, and informed the Earl that he was on his way to Leicestershire.

The Earl eyed him with wrath and misgiving. Mr Theale owned a snug little hunting-box near Melton Mowbray, but if he was proposing to visit it in the middle of July this could only mean that circumstances had rendered it prudent, if not urgently necessary, for him to leave town for a space. 'What is it this time?' he demanded, leading the way into the library. 'You haven't come home for the pleasure of seeing me, so out with it! And I give you fair warning, Fabian—'

'No, no, it's no pleasure to me to see you, old fellow!' Mr Theale assured him. 'In fact, if I weren't in the basket I wouldn't have come here, because to see you fretting and fuming is enough to give one a fit of the dismals.'

'When last I saw you,' said the Earl suspiciously, 'you told me you had made a recover! Said you had had a run of luck at faro, and were as fresh as ever.'

'Dash it, that was a month ago!' expostulated Mr Theale. 'You can't expect it to be high water with me for ever! Not but what if you could trust to the form-book I ought to be able to buy an abbey by now. But there it is! First there was the Salisbury meeting—by the by, old fellow, did you lay your blunt on Corkscrew? Got a notion I told you to.'

'No, I didn't,' replied the Earl shortly.

'Good thing,' approved Mr Theale. 'Damned screw wasn't placed. Then there was Andover! Mind you, if I'd followed my own judgement, Whizgig would have carried my money, and very likely I wouldn't be here today. However, I let Jerry earwig me into backing Ticklepitcher, so here I am. I hear you was at the July meeting at Newmarket, and came off all right,' he added dispassionately.

'As to that—'

'Three winners, and a devilish long price you must have got on Trueblue, my boy! If I were half as tetchy as you are, I should take it mighty ill that you didn't pass me the word.'

'I'll grease you in the fist on one condition!' said the Earl brutally.

'Anything you please, dear boy!' said Mr Theale, impervious to insult. 'Just tip over the dibs!'

'I have Ludlow coming here today, on a visit, and I shall be glad if you will take yourself off!'

'Ludlow?' said Mr Theale, mildly surprised. 'What the devil's he coming here for?'

'He's coming to offer for Hester, and I don't want him to hedge off, which I don't doubt he will, if you try to break his shins!'

'Well, by God!' exclaimed Mr Theale. 'Damme if ever I thought Hester would contract an engagement at all, let alone catch a man like Ludlow on her hook! Well, this is famous! I wouldn't put his fortune at a penny less than twelve thousand pounds a year! Very right to warn me, dear boy: fatal to borrow any money from him until you have the knot safely tied! Shouldn't dream of making the attempt. I hope he means to come down handsome?'

'Will you,' said the Earl, controlling his spleen with a visible effort, 'take yourself off to Leicestershire?'

'Make it a monkey, old fellow, and I'll be off first thing in the morning,' said Mr Theale obligingly.

With this promise the Earl had to be content, though he made a spirited effort to improve the terms of the bargain before at last agreeing to them. Nothing, it was clear, would avail to dislodge his brother until the following day, Mr Theale pointing out very reasonably that it was rather too much to expect that he would set forth on his travels again before he had recovered from the exhaustion entailed by a journey of more than sixty miles. It had taken him two days to achieve this prodigious distance, travelling at a sedate pace in his own carriage, with his valet following behind in a hired coach with all his baggage. 'And even with my own fellow to drive me I felt queasy,' he said. 'Mind, if I had the sort of stomach that didn't turn over on me when I'm being jolted and rocked over these devilish bad roads I'd pack up and be off this instant, because I can see we're bound to spend a damned flat evening here. Wouldn't do to hook Ludlow in for a rubber or two, for though I don't doubt you and I, Giles, if we played together, which could be arranged, would physic him roundly, it would be bad policy! Besides, we should have to hook in Widmore to make a fourth, and there's no sense in winning his money, even if he could be got to sport a little blunt, which I've never known him do yet. Of course, you're his father, but you must own he's a paltry fellow!'

So the Earl was forced to resign himself, which he would have done more easily had not Mr Theale's family loyalty prompted him to lend his aid to the preparations in train for the entertainment of the expected guest. Since this took the form of an invasion of the kitchens, where he maddened the cook by freely editing the dinner to be set before Sir Gareth; and a voyage of exploration to the cellars, whence he brought to light several crusted bottles which the Earl had been jealously preserving, it was not long before his brother's little stock of patience was exhausted. Forcefully adjured to cease meddling, he was obliged to seek diversion in other fields, with the result that a young housemaid, unused to the ways of the Quality, was thrown into strong hysterics, and had to have her ears boxed before she could be induced to stop screeching that she was an honest maid, and desired instantly to return to her mother's protection.

'And very stupid it was of Mrs Farnham to send that girl of all others to make up Fabian's bed!' said Lady Widmore, in her customary forthright style. '*She* must know what your uncle is!'

By the time Sir Gareth and his protégée were ushered into the Grand Saloon the only members of the family, gathered there, whose sensibilities had not been in some way or other ruffled were Mr Theale, and Lady Widmore. The Earl was on the one hand uncertain what his daughter's answer was going to be, and on the other he had been reduced to a state of impotent fury by his brother's activities; Lord Widmore shared his parent's misgivings, and was very much put out by the discovery that five hundred pounds, urgently needed on the estate, had been bestowed upon his uncle; and Lady Hester, exhorted and commanded to the point of distraction, was looking positively hagged. A gown of lilac silk, with a demi-train, three rows of flounces, a quantity of ivory lace, and knots of violet velvet ribbons enhanced her pallor; and her abigail, in her anxiety to present her mistress at her best, had slightly over-crimped her soft brown hair. Lately, she had adopted a cap, but although this circumstance had apparently escaped the notice of her relations for several weeks it had today come in for such unmeasured censure that she had wearily removed the wisp of lace.

'And let me tell you, Hetty, that a stupid sort of indifference is by no means becoming in you!' said her father severely. 'These dawdling and languid airs are enough to give Ludlow a disgust of you.'

'Now, don't fidget the girl!' recommended Mr Theale. 'Ten to one, Ludlow won't notice she ain't in spirits, because what with you in one of your distempered freaks, and Widmore looking as sulky as a bear, he'll have enough to frighten him off without looking at Hester. In fact, it is just as well I took it into my head to visit you. You can't deny I'm a dashed sight better company than the rest of you.'

The Earl's retort was cut short on his lips by the opening of the double-doors into the saloon.

'Miss Smith!' announced the butler, in the voice of one heralding disaster. 'Sir Gareth Ludlow!'

5

'Eh?' ejaculated the Earl, in a sort of bark, wheeling round, and staring with slightly protuberant eyes at the vision on the threshold.

Amanda, colouring deliciously under the concentrated scrutiny of so many pairs of eyes, lifted her chin a little. Sir Gareth went forward, saying easily: 'How do you do? Your servant, Lady Widmore! Lady Hester!' He took the cold hand she had mechanically stretched out to him, lightly kissed it, and retained it in his. 'May I present Miss Smith to you, and solicit your kindness on her behalf? I have assured her that she may depend on *that*. The case is that she is the daughter of some old friends with whom I have been staying, and I engaged myself to conduct her to Huntingdon, where she was to be met by some relations. But either through a misunderstanding, or some mishap, no carriage had been sent to meet her there, and since I could not leave her in a public inn, there was nothing for it but to bring her here.'

Every vestige of colour had drained away from the Lady Hester's cheeks when she had looked up to perceive the lovely girl at Sir Gareth's side, but she replied with tolerable composure: 'Of course! We shall be most happy.' She drew her hand away, and went to Amanda. 'What a horrid predicament! I am so glad Sir Gareth brought you to us. I must make you known to my sister-in-law, Lady Widmore.'

Amanda raised her brilliant eyes to Lady Hester's gentle grey ones, and suddenly smiled. The effect of this upon the assembled gentlemen caused Lady Widmore's already high colour to deepen alarmingly. Mr Theale, who had been regarding the youthful beauty with the eye of a dispassionate connoisseur, sighed soulfully; the Earl's indignant stare changed to one of reluctant admiration; and Lord Widmore was moved to adjust his neckcloth, throwing out his narrow chest a little. However, as he caught his wife's fulminating eye at that moment, he was speedily recalled to a sense of his position, and altered a somewhat fatuous smile to a frown.

'An awkward situation indeed!' agreed Lady Widmore, subjecting Amanda to a critical scrutiny. 'But you have your abigail with you, I must suppose!'

'No, because she fell ill, and, besides, there was no room for her in the curricle,' replied Amanda, with aplomb.

'In the curricle?' exclaimed Lord Widmore, looking very much shocked. 'Driving with Ludlow in a curricle, without some respectable female to chaperon you? Upon my soul! I do not know what the world is coming to!'

'Now, don't talk like a nick-ninny, Cuthbert!' begged his uncle. 'Damme if I see what anyone wants with a chaperon in a curricle! If it had been a chaise, it would have been another matter, of course.'

'If Miss Smith was travelling in Sir Gareth's charge, sir, she had no need of her abigail to take care of her,' interposed Hester, her tone mildly reproving.

'No,' said Amanda gratefully. 'And I had *no* desire to go with him, either, and am very well able to take care of myself!'

'You have had your hands full, I collect!' Lady Widmore said, putting up her sandy brows at Sir Gareth.

'Not at all!' he retorted. 'I have had a charming companion, ma'am!'

'Oh, I don't doubt *that*!' she said, with a laugh. 'Well, child, I suppose I had best take you upstairs! You will wish to change your dress before dinner. I daresay they will have unpacked your trunk by now.'

'Yes,' said Amanda doubtfully. 'I mean—that is—' She stopped, blushing, and looking imploringly towards Sir Gareth.

He responded at once to this mute appeal, saying, with the flicker of a reassuring smile: 'That is the most awkward feature of the whole business, isn't it, Amanda? Her trunk, ma'am, I must suppose to be at Oundle, for it was dispatched by carrier yesterday. We could find room only for a couple of bandboxes in my curricle.'

'Dispatched yesterday?' said the Earl. 'Seems an odd circumstance, then, that these relations of hers shouldn't have kept their engagement to meet her! What the devil should she send her trunk for, if she didn't mean to follow it?'

'That, sir,' said Sir Gareth, quite unshaken, 'is what makes us fear some mischance.'

'I expect it has been delayed,' said Lady Hester. 'How vexing! But not of the least consequence.'

'Lord, Hetty, what an addle-brained creature you are!' remarked Lady Widmore, with good-natured contempt. 'If it ain't of any consequence, it ain't vexing either!'

'How silly of me!' murmured Hester, accepting this rebuke in an absentminded way. 'Will you let me take you upstairs, Miss Smith? Don't put yourself about, Almeria! I will attend to Miss Smith.'

Amanda looked rather relieved; and Sir Gareth, who had moved to the door, said, under his breath, as Hester paused beside him to let her guest pass before her out of the room: 'Thank you! I knew I might rely on you.'

She smiled a little wistfully, but said nothing. He closed the door behind her, and she paused for a moment, looking at Amanda, and blinking as though in an attempt to bring that enchanting face into focus. Amanda gave her back stare for stare, her chin well up, and she said, in her shy, soft voice: 'How *very* pretty you are! I wonder which room Mrs Farnham has prepared for you? It must be wretchedly uncomfortable for you, but pray don't heed it! We will think just what should be done presently.'

'Well,' said Amanda, following her to the staircase, 'for my part, I can see that it is most uncomfortable for you to be obliged to receive me when I haven't an evening-gown to wear, and as for Sir Gareth, it is all his fault, and he told you nothing but the most shocking untruths, besides having abducted me!'

Hester paused, with her hand on the banister-rail, and looked back, startled. 'Abducted you? Dear me, how excessively odd of him! Are you quite sure you are not making a mistake?'

'No, it is precisely as I say,' replied Amanda firmly. 'For I never set eyes on him before today, and although at first I was quite deceived in him, because he looks just like all one's favourite heroes, which all goes to show that one shouldn't set any store by appearances, I now know that he is a most odious person—though still very like Sir Lancelot and Lord Orville,' she added conscientiously.

Lady Hester looked wholly bewildered. 'How can this be? You know, I am dreadfully stupid, and I don't seem able to understand at all, Miss Smith!'

'I wish you will call me Amanda!' suddenly decided that damsel. 'I find I cannot *bear* the name of Smith! The thing is that it was the only name I could think of when nothing would do for Sir Gareth but to know who I was. I daresay you know how it is when you are obliged, on the instant, to find a name for yourself?'

'No—that is, I have never had occasion—but of course I see that one would think of something very simple,' Hester replied apologetically.

'Exactly so! Only you can have no idea how disagreeable it is to be called Miss Smith, which, as it happens, was the name of the horridest governess I ever had!'

Utterly befogged, Hester said: 'Yes, indeed, although—You know, I think

we should not stay talking here, for one never knows who may be listening!
Do, pray, come upstairs!'

She then led Amanda to the upper hall, where they were met by her
abigail, a middle-aged woman of hostile aspect, whose devotion to her
mistress's interests caused her to view Amanda with suspicion and dislike.
The news that Sir Gareth Ludlow had arrived at Brancaster with a regular
out-and-outer on his arm had rapidly spread through the house; and Miss
Povey knew just what to think of beauties who possessed no other luggage
than a couple of bandboxes, and travelled unattended by their abigails or
governesses. She informed Lady Hester that the Blue bedchamber had been
prepared for the Young Person: an announcement that brought Lady
Hester's eyes to her face, a tiny frown in them. 'What did you say, Povey?'
she asked.

The tone was as gentle as ever, but Miss Povey, permitting herself only
the indulgence of a sniff, lost no time in altering her phraseology. 'For the
young lady, I *should* say, my lady.'

'Oh, yes! The Blue bedchamber will be just the one. Thank you: I shan't
need you any longer.'

This dismissal by no means pleased the handmaiden. On the one hand,
she was extremely reluctant to wait upon Amanda, and would, indeed, have
bitterly resented a command to do so; but, on the other, she was agog with
curiosity. After a brief struggle with her feelings, she said: 'I thought, my
lady, being as how Miss hasn't brought her own abigail, she would like me
to dress her hair, and that.'

'Yes, presently,' said Hester. 'And perhaps, since Miss Smith's trunk has
gone to Oundle, you could bring that pink gown of mine to her room.' She
smiled diffidently at Amanda, adding: 'Should you object to wearing one of
my dresses? I think it would become you, for it is too young for me, and I
have not worn it more than once.'

'No, not at all. In fact, I shall be excessively obliged to you,' replied
Amanda warmly. 'For the only other gown I have with me is another morning one, and I daresay it will be odiously crumpled. And this one is very
dirty, through my having walked a great distance in it, besides being in the
carrier's cart, though I took the greatest care to wrap my cloak round me.'

'Muslin seems to pick up the dirt so *easily!*' agreed Hester, accepting the
carrier's cart as the merest commonplace. 'But Povey will wash and iron it
for you to wear again in the morning.'

With these calmly uttered words, she led Amanda into her allotted
bedchamber, firmly closing the door on her scandalized abigail.

The bandboxes had been unpacked, and Amanda's few possessions
disposed in the appropriate places. That damsel, after a comprehensive
survey of the apartment, awarded it her approval, adding candidly: 'And Sir
Gareth was quite right: I *do* like you very much, ma'am, though I quite
thought I should not!'

'I am so glad,' murmured Hester. 'Do let me untie the strings of your hat!'

'Yes,' said Amanda, submitting to this, 'but I must warn you, because I
never tell lies to people I like, that I do not at all wish to visit an Earl!'

'I expect you have been brought up on revolutionary principles,' said
Hester wisely. 'I do not, myself, know very much about it, but I believe that
many people nowadays—'

'Oh, no! But the thing is that I particularly wish to establish myself in the
sort of situation from which one's relations are bound to rescue one. And if
it had not been for Sir Gareth I daresay I might have done it. I was never so

taken-in! He said he would take me to Huntingdon, where I had every expectation of being hired as a chambermaid at the George—at least, that is what I thought he said he would do, only I soon discovered that it was all a hoax—and then, when he had lured me into his curricle, he brought me here instead!'

Lady Hester, quite bewildered by this recital, sat down a little weakly, and said: 'I don't think I *perfectly* understand, Amanda. I expect it is because I am being stupid, but if you could tell it all to me from the start I am persuaded I shall. But not, of course, if you don't wish! I don't care to ask you questions, for there is nothing more disagreeable than to be obliged to listen to questions, and scoldings, and good advice.' Her sudden smile, which betrayed a gleam of shy mischief in her eyes, swept across her face. 'You see, I have suffered from that all my life.'

'Have you?' said Amanda, surprised. 'But you are quite old! I mean,' she corrected herself hastily, 'you—you are not under age! I wonder you should not tell people who scold you to go about their business.'

'I am afraid I have not enough courage,' said Hester ruefully.

'Like my aunt,' nodded Amanda. 'She has no courage, either, and she lets Grandpapa bully her, which puts me out of all patience, because one can always get one's own way, if only one has resolution.'

'Can one?' said Hester doubtfully.

'Yes, though sometimes, I own, one is forced to take desperate measures. And it is of no use to tease oneself about propriety,' she added, with a touch of defiance, 'because it seems to me that if you never do anything that is not quite proper and decorous you will have the wretchedest life, without any adventures, or romance, or *anything*!'

'It is very true, alas!' Hester smiled at her again. 'But not for you, I think.'

'No, because I have a great deal of resolution. Also I have made a very good plan of campaign, and if you will faithfully promise not to try to overset it, I will tell you what it is.'

'I shouldn't think I could overset anyone's plans,' said Hester reflectively. 'Indeed, I promise I won't try!'

'Or tell those other people?' Amanda said anxiously.

'My family? Oh, no!'

Reassured, Amanda sat down beside her, and for the second time that day recounted the tale of her adventures. Lady Hester sat with her hands lightly clasped in her lap, and her eyes fixed wonderingly on the animated little face beside her. Several times she blinked, and once a little trill of laughter was surprised out of her; but she did not make any comment until Amanda reached the end of her recital, and then she only said: 'How very brave you are! I hope you will be able to marry your Brigade-Major, for I am sure you must have been made to be a soldier's wife. I should think, you know, that your grandfather would give his consent if only you could be content to wait for a little while longer.'

'I have waited a very long time already, and now I am determined to be married, so that I can accompany Neil to Spain,' stated Amanda, looking mulish. 'I daresay you think it is very wrong of me, and that I ought to obey Grandpapa, and so it may be—only I don't care for anything except Neil, and I won't go meekly home, whatever anyone says!'

This was uttered very challengingly, but all Hester said was: 'It is very difficult to know what would be the best thing to do. Do you think, perhaps, you should send for Neil?'

Amanda shook her head. 'No, because he would take me back to

Grandpapa, and there's no depending on Grandpapa's being grateful
enough to give his consent to our marriage. In fact, he would very likely
think I had plotted it all with Neil, which would be fatal! That is what he is
bound to think, at the outset, but when he discovers that Neil knows no
more than he does where I am, he will see that it is not so. And besides that
he will be in a much worse pucker about me, which would be a good thing.'

This ruthless speech moved Hester to make a faint protest, but it was cut
short by a tap on the door. Povey came in, with a dress of pink silk over her
arm, and an expression of long-suffering on her face; and Hester got up,
saying: 'We are very much of a height, I believe, and I am quite sure that
that gown will become you very much better than it becomes me. Will you
put it on, and then, if it needs some little adjustment, Povey will arrange it
for you?'

Amanda, whose eyes had sparkled at sight of the dress, said impulsively:
'Thank you! It is most obliging of you, and exactly the sort of gown I wish
for! I have never worn a silk one, because my aunt has the stuffiest notions,
and she will not buy anything but muslin for me, even when she took me to
the Bath Assemblies.'

'Oh, dear!' said Hester, looking conscience-stricken. 'She is perfectly
right! How shatterbrained of me! Never mind! The dress is not cut very
low, and I will lend you a lace shawl to put round your shoulders.'

She then drifted away to find the shawl, but before she had reached her
own room she heard her name spoken, and turned to see that Sir Gareth had
come out of his bedchamber.

He had changed his driving-dress for knee-breeches and silk stockings,
an elegant waistcoat of watered silk, and a swallow-tailed coat of black cloth;
and no one, observing the exquisite set of that coat across his shoulders, and
the nicety with which his starched neckcloth was arranged, could have
supposed that he had effected this transformation with extreme rapidity,
and without the assistance of his valet.

He came across the hall, saying, with his delightful smile: 'I have been
lying in wait for you, hoping to exchange a word with you before we go
downstairs again. Has that absurd child told you the truth about herself? I
warned her that I should! How good it was of you to accept her without a
murmur! But I knew you would. Thank you!'

She returned his smile, but nervously. 'Oh, no! Pray do not! there is not
the least need—I am only too happy—! She has told me how she came to
meet you. You did very right to bring her here.'

'Were you able to discover her name?' he demanded.

'No—but, then, I did not ask her to tell me. I expect she would rather not
disclose it.'

'I am well aware of that, but this grandfather of hers must be found. Good
God, she cannot be permitted to carry out her outrageous scheme!'

'It does seem very hazardous,' she agreed.

'Hazardous! Quite foolhardy! With that face, and no more worldly
wisdom than a baby, how can she escape running into danger? She is as
confiding as a kitten, too. Did she tell you I had abducted her? Well, I might
have done so, you know! She hopped up into my curricle in the most
trusting way imaginable.'

'I expect she knew she could trust you,' she replied. 'She is quite
innocent, of course, but not, I think, stupid. And so courageous!'

He said, after a tiny pause: 'Yes—a headstrong courage, an enchanting
waywardness which could so easily be her undoing. When I first saw her, I

was reminded—I hardly know by what!—the tilt of her chin, perhaps, and a certain look in her eyes—' He broke off, as though he regretted his words.

'I, too,' she said, in her quiet voice. 'I expect it was that resemblance which drew you to her.'

'Perhaps. No, I don't think it was. She was plainly a gently-bred child in difficulties: I could do no less than go to the rescue.'

'I am afraid she is not very grateful to you,' she said, with a glimmer of a smile.

'Not a bit!' he said, laughing. 'She has promised to make me very sorry, and I daresay she'll do it, for she is the naughtiest little wretch I ever encountered. My dependence is on *you*! If you can prevail upon her to disclose her grandfather's name—'

'Oh, but I can't!' she interrupted apologetically. 'You see, I promised I wouldn't try to overset her plan of campaign. So even if she were to tell me who she is I couldn't betray her confidence, could I?'

He said, between amusement and exasperation: 'In such a case as this? I hope you could, for most certainly you *should*!'

'I think she ought to be allowed to marry her soldier,' she said thoughtfully.

'What, at her age to be allowed to throw herself away on a needy young officer, and to undergo all the hardships of a life spent following the drum? My dear Lady Hester, you can have no notion of what it would be like! I am entirely at one with the unknown grandfather on that head.'

'Are you?' She looked at him in her shortsighted way, and sighed. 'Yes, perhaps. I don't know. What shall you do?'

'If she can't be persuaded to let me escort her to her home, I must find out this Brigade-Major of hers. That should not prove to be a difficult task, but it will mean my posting back to London tomorrow. I see nothing for it but to take her with me, and to place her in my sister's charge. It is really the most abominable coil!'

'Would you like to leave her in my charge?' she asked doubtfully.

'Of all things!' he replied. 'But I am reasonably certain that she would run away as soon as my back was turned! Nor do I think that your brother and his wife would welcome her as a guest here.'

'No,' she admitted. She raised her eyes to his face, and said, with an unhappy little smile: 'I beg your pardon: I am being so very unhelpful! But I could not compel Amanda to remain here, or, I am afraid, prevent Almeria's saying cutting things to her. Excuse me! I have to fetch a shawl for her to wear!'

'Must you do so immediately?' he asked, putting out his hand. 'We have spoken of nothing but Amanda, and it was not, I assure you, to talk about a troublesome schoolgirl that I came to Brancaster.'

She seemed to shrink into herself, and said quickly: 'It is almost time for dinner! I would so much rather—indeed I must not stay!'

She was gone on the words, leaving him to look after her in some little surprise. He knew her to be very shy, but it was not like her to betray agitation; and he had believed himself to be on such easy terms with her as must preclude her receiving his proposal with embarrassment. But embarrassed she undoubtedly was; and she had certainly shrunk from him. A suspicion that she was being coerced into accepting his offer crossed his mind, and brought a frown into his eyes; but that she meant to refuse it he could not believe, not deeming it possible that Lord Brancaster would have permitted him to come to Brancaster only to be rebuffed.

It was a reasonable belief, and one shared by Mr Theale; but no sooner had Sir Gareth left the saloon to change his dress than his lordship had exclaimed: 'That's knocked everything into horse-nails! What the devil made him bring that chit here? Just when I was in hope Hester meant to have him after all! Depend upon it, she'll shy off!'

'Eh?' said Mr Theale. 'Pooh! nonsense! She wouldn't be such a fool!'

'You know nothing of the matter!' snapped the Earl. 'She never had a grain of commonsense!'

'Lord, Giles, she'd enough to jump at the chance of making such a match! She won't cry off just because Ludlow has a nonpareil in his charge: not the sort of girl to take a pet, though I own I wouldn't have thought Ludlow was the man to do such a daffish thing.'

'Well, she didn't jump at the chance!' said the Earl angrily. 'Said she didn't wish for the marriage! Almeria thought she would come round to it, but I'll go bail she wasn't bargaining for this mischance!'

'Well, by God!' ejaculated Mr Theale. 'Do you mean to tell me you let the poor fellow come all this way when you ain't sure Hester means to have him? Well, damme, what a backhanded turn to serve him!'

'Oh, stuff!' said Lady Widmore, in her strident voice. 'Let him go the right way to work with her, and she'll have him! But I'll see to it that that little baggage is sent packing in the morning! Daughter of some old friends, indeed! Fine friends, to be sending their daughter about the country with no respectable female to look after her! Coming it very much too strong, I make bold to say!'

'I should not have thought it of Ludlow,' said her husband. 'Who that young female is, or what she is, I do not pretend to know, but I am very much shocked by the whole affair.'

'Don't talk like a fool!' said his father irritably. 'For anything I know, Ludlow may have half a dozen mistresses in keeping, but if you imagine he would bring some fancy-piece here you must be a bigger bottlehead than ever I guessed! *That* ain't what's worrying me!'

'Well, it ought to worry you,' observed his brother. 'I'm not a worrying man myself, but if I'd sired such a pea-goose as Widmore it would keep me awake at night, I can tell you that.'

This ill-timed facetiousness enraged the Earl so much that he looked to be in danger of bursting several blood-vessels. Before he could command his voice sufficiently to deal with Mr Theale as he deserved, his daughter-in-law, who had accorded the pleasantry a hearty laugh, intervened, saying: 'Now, you hold your tongue, Fabian, do! I know what's worrying you, sir, and small blame to you! If Hetty don't snap Ludlow up while she has the chance to do it, he'll be head over ears in love with that girl, and you may kiss your fingers to him. I don't say she's his mistress, but I'd lay you odds she's up to no good. What's more, she's a beauty—if you like those bold eyes, which, for my part, I don't, though it's easy to see they're exactly to Sir Gareth's taste! Well, what I say is that to set poor Hetty beside *that* bird of paradise is to ruin any chance she might have had!'

The truth underlying these blunt words was forcibly brought home to the company, when, just before dinner was announced, Hester led Amanda into the room.

Had Lady Widmore given way to impulse at that moment, she would have boxed her sister-in-law's ears. One glance at the radiant vision on the threshold was enough to inform her that Hester, like the hen-witted female Lady Widmore had for long considered her to be, had lent one of her own gowns to the interloper. Its rose-pink sheen had never become Hester, but it was fair to say that it might have been created especially to show Amanda off to the best advantage. The chit looked dazzlingly lovely, her great eyes sparkling with pleasure in her first silk gown, her cheeks a little flushed, and her lips just parted in a smile at once shy and triumphant. Small wonder that all the gentlemen were staring at her, like dogs at a marrowbone! thought her ladyship bitterly.

Amanda was in fine fettle, and had been peacocking in front of the mirror for several minutes, admiring herself, and playing at being a grand lady. She expected to stun all beholders by so much magnificence, and she was pleased to perceive that she had done it. A month at Bath had by no means inured her to admiration, but it had taught her a good deal about the ways of fashionable beauties. To Sir Gareth's appreciative amusement, she began to play off all the tricks she had observed, flirting with the fan Hester had given her, and making shameless use of her brilliant eyes. Nothing, he thought, could more surely have betrayed her extreme youthfulness. She was like a child, allowed to dress-up in her elder sister's clothes, and doing her best to ape the ways of her seniors. He could picture his niece, who always became alarmingly grown-up if ever he took her for a drive round the Park, play-acting in just such a style; and he knew exactly how to apply a damper to spirits mounting too high. Well, if she became too outrageous he would apply that damper; but if she kept within bounds he would let her enjoy herself: it might keep her from hatching plans of escape from him.

At that moment, she caught his eye, and threw him a look so saucy and full of challenge that he nearly laughed out. It was at this precise instant that Mr Whyteleafe entered the saloon.

Mr Whyteleafe came prepared to meet Sir Gareth, but he was by no means prepared for Sir Gareth's travelling companion, and the sight of Amanda exchanging what he afterwards described as a very Speaking Look with Sir Gareth held him transfixed for several moments. His startled eyes rolled towards Lady Hester, and she, perceiving him, kindly presented him to Amanda.

Amanda, flattered by the attentions of Mr Theale, was civil, but un-enthusiastic. Clergymen, in her view, were sober persons who almost always disapproved of her; and this one, she thought, wore an even more disapproving expression than the Rector at home. She made no effort to engage him in conversation but turned back to the practised gallantries of Mr Theale.

Mr Whyteleafe, who, to do him justice, had no desire to converse with a young female whom he had instantly perceived to be fast, made his way to Lady Widmore's side, and begged her, in an undervoice, to tell him who Amanda might be.

'Don't ask *me*!' she replied, shrugging up her shoulders. 'All I can tell you is that Sir Gareth brought her here.'

He looked very much shocked, and could not forbear to cast a glance towards Lady Hester. She did not appear to be in any way discomposed, nor did it seem as though she were offended with Sir Gareth. She was, in fact, smiling faintly at him, for he had crossed the room to her side, and had just thanked her for her kindness in providing Amanda with a dress to wear.

'Oh, no! I am so glad I had one that becomes her so well. How very beautiful she is!'

'Little monkey! You will own, however, that it would be a sin to permit her to cast herself away on her Brigade-Major before she has had a chance to

set the town ablaze! Give her a year to find her balance, and I promise you
she will.'

'Yes, I suppose she would.'

'Unconvinced?' he said quizzically.

'I don't know. She is a very unusual girl.'

'Yes, something quite out of the ordinary—but too inexperienced yet to
settle upon a husband.'

She was silent for a moment, her eyes lifted to his profile. He was
watching Amanda, but as though he was conscious of Hester's regard, he
turned his head, and smiled down at her. 'Don't you agree?'

'Perhaps you are right,' she said. 'Oh, yes, I expect you must be! She will
very likely change her mind.'

6

By the time dinner came to an end, several persons at the table were fully
persuaded that however innocent the relationship between Sir Gareth and
Amanda might be, Sir Gareth was far more interested in that lively damsel
than was at all seemly in one on the verge of proposing marriage to another
lady. He was placed between Hester and Lady Widmore, on the opposite
side of the table to Amanda, and while he conversed with easy good manners
with both of these ladies, it was noticed that his attention was seldom wholly
distracted from Amanda. What no one could have guessed from his
demeanour was that his interest was not at all pleasurable, or that this
informal dinner-party would live in his memory as the most nerve-racking
function he had ever attended.

That he must keep a watchful eye on Amanda had been decided at the
outset, when he saw her, after doubtfully considering the wine the butler
had poured into her glass, take a cautious sip. Probably one glass would do
her no harm, but if that fool of a butler tried to refill it, intervene he must.
She was behaving with perfect propriety, but she was undoubtedly flown
with pink silk and compliments, and was receiving every encouragement
from Fabian Theale to overstep the bounds of decorum. Sir Gareth was not
particularly acquainted with Mr Theale, but he knew him by reputation.
Ten minutes spent in listening with half an ear to Mr Theale's conversation
confirmed his belief in all the most scandalous stories he had heard of that
enterprising gentleman, and imbued him with a strong desire to plant him a
flush hit with a right justly famed in Corinthian circles.

But Amanda was not unacquainted with middle-aged roués who adopted
a fatherly air in their dealings with her; and Amanda, however elated, had
by no means lost her head. She was prepared to enjoy to the full a slightly
intoxicating evening undimmed by the repressive influence of a careful
aunt, but not for one moment did she forget the end she meant to achieve.
She had passed the entire company under review, and had rapidly reached
the conclusion that the only possible ally was Mr Theale. While her face
wore an expression of flattering interest in what he said to her, and her
pretty lips formed appropriate answers, her brain was busy with the
problem of how to turn him to good account.

For his part, Mr Theale was bent on discovering, before the evening was out, in what relation she stood to Sir Gareth. A worldly man, he agreed with his brother in thinking it in the highest degree unlikely that Ludlow would have brought a little barque of frailty to Brancaster; on the other hand, he could see that Ludlow was keeping a jealous eye on her, and it was entirely beyond his comprehension that he might be doing so from altruistic motives. The story of the relations at Oundle he had disbelieved from the outset; and since, in his experience, no young lady of gentle birth was ever permitted to walk abroad unattended, he was much inclined to think that Amanda was not the schoolroom miss she appeared to be, but, on the contrary, a remarkably game pullet. If that were indeed the case, he would be strongly tempted to take her off Sir Gareth's hands. She was as pretty as she could stare: just the type of ladybird he liked. Young, too, and inexperienced, which would make a pleasant change from the harpy lately living under his protection. Probably she would be grateful for little trumpery gifts, not, like the high flyers, always keeping her fingers crooked into his purse.

These ruminations were interrupted by the departure of the ladies from the dining-room. The cloth was removed, and the decanters set upon the table, but the Earl, contrary to his usual custom, did not encourage his guests to linger over the port. In his opinion, the sooner Sir Gareth was given the opportunity to pop the question to Hester the better it would be. He might not be a paragon among fathers, but he was not so improvident as to run the risk of allowing his daughter's suitor to present himself to her in a slightly bosky condition. So, at the end of half an hour, he said that they must not keep the ladies waiting, and rose from the table. He wondered whether it would be well to detach his prospective son-in-law from the rest of the party, and to thrust him and Hester into some room apart, but decided that it would probably be wiser to leave Sir Gareth to make his own opportunity for private speech with Hester. He led the way, therefore, to one of the suite of saloons ranged along the south side of the house. These opened on to a broad terrace, commanding views of the pleasure-gardens, and a small lake; and, since the evening was sultry, the long windows had not yet been closed against the night air.

Strains of Haydn greeted the gentlemen, when the Earl threw open the door into the drawing-room, and Amanda was discovered, seated at the pianoforte, and playing a sonata with considerable verve, if not with strict accuracy.

For this, Lady Widmore had been responsible. Upon first entering the room, she had supposed, with the too evident intention of discomfiting the unbidden guest, that Miss Smith was proficient upon the instrument, and had begged her to indulge her with a little music. As her ladyship was almost tone-deaf, she might have been said to have been rightly served for her malice, since Amanda, instead of being obliged to confess ignorance of an accomplishment indispensable to any female with the smallest claim to gentility, had, in the most complaisant way imaginable, instantly embarked on a very long and dull sonata.

Mr Theale, sharing her ladyship's dislike of chamber music, and prohibited by his brother's violent disapproval from indulging one of his favourite vices within the walls of Brancaster, slid unobtrusively away to enjoy a cigarillo in the moonlit garden; but the other gentlemen bravely entered the drawing-room, and disposed themselves about it, Mr Whyteleafe, to the Earl's annoyance, nimbly appropriating a chair at Lady Hester's elbow. Sir Gareth walked over to the window, and stood leaning his shoulders against the frame, his eyes on the fair performer.

'I am at a loss for words,' whispered Mr Whyteleafe, 'to convey to you my sentiments upon this occasion, Lady Hester. I can only say that if I am not surprised I am profoundly shocked. *Your* feelings I can readily imagine!'

'Oh, no, I don't think you can,' she responded, with a gleam of amusement. 'But pray hush! You must not talk just now, you know.'

He relapsed into silence, and his resolve to address such words to Lady Hester as must fortify her against the ordeal of having her hand solicited by one whom he clearly perceived to be a libertine of the most unblushing order was frustrated by Lady Widmore, who, as soon as Amanda stopped playing, began at once to make loud plans for the further entertainment of the company, and commanded him to set out a card-table. Breaking in with the rudeness for which she was famed on the compliments being paid to Amanda, she announced that a rubber of casino would be just the thing, adding, with a jolly laugh, as she caught the Earl's starting eye, that she knew better than to expect him or Fabian to take part in this amusement.

'And Hester doesn't care for cards, so if you and Fabian choose to play piquet, as I don't doubt you will, Sir Gareth must entertain her, and that will leave four of us to make up a snug game,' she said.

Even her husband, who was inured to her ways, felt that this attempt to provide Sir Gareth with an opportunity to propose to Hester was rather too blatant to be encouraged; and the Earl, mentally apostrophizing her as a cowhanded thruster, considered it enough to put up the backs of both interested parties. While her ladyship bustled about the room, directing the reluctant chaplain where to place the table, and searching for a couple of packs of cards in various chests, both he and Lord Widmore endeavoured to dissuade her from these exertions. Lady Hester, murmuring that she rather thought that the cards had last been used by the nursery party, went away to retrieve them; and Amanda, snatching the chance offered by the pre-occupation of her hosts, slipped out on to the terrace, saying in a fierce whisper as she went past Sir Gareth: 'I wish to speak to you *alone!*'

He followed her beyond the range of the window, but said, as soon as he came up with her: 'Take care, Amanda! You will set the household by the ears by such improper conduct as this. Do remember that you are the daughter of a friend of mine, who is by far too well brought-up to indulge in anything so fast as a tête-à-tête in the moonlight!'

'I am *not* the daughter of any friend of yours, and I have a very good mind to tell Lord Brancaster so!' she said crossly.

'I don't think I should, if I were you. Is that what you wished to tell me?'

'No, it is not!' She paused, and then said airily: 'In fact, I don't wish him to know the truth, because it so chances that Lady Hester has very kindly invited me to remain here for a visit, and I have made up my mind to do so.'

He laughed. 'Have you, indeed?'

'Yes, so you may be quite at your ease, and not tease yourself about me any more,' Amanda said kindly.

'Now, that,' said Sir Gareth, much moved, 'is a singularly beautiful thought! Tell me, by the way, what put the notion into your head that you had to deal with a flat?'

'I do not understand what you mean,' replied Amanda, with dignity.

'A flat, my child, is one who is easily duped.'

'Well, I don't think you that, at all events! In fact, quite the reverse, because first you duped me, and then you duped all these people! And if you try to carry me off by force tomorrow, I shall tell Lord Brancaster just how you have deceived him.'

'I hope you won't!' he said. 'I fear his lordship, whose mind is not elastic, wouldn't believe a word of your story, and then what a pickle we should be in!'

'It was abominable of you to have brought me here!'

'Yes, I fancy that opinion is shared by several other members of the party,' he observed. 'At least I won't aggravate the offence by leaving you here! No, don't begin scolding again! I know exactly what's in your foolish head: you are bent on giving me the slip, and you know you cannot do it while my eye is upon you, and so you hope to make me believe that you are willing to remain here, like the good little girl you most emphatically are not. But as soon as my back was turned you would be off—and you may make up your mind to this, Amanda: I may wish you at Jericho, but I am not going to let you escape from me! Yes, I'm well aware that I am a deceiver, an abductor, and wholly contemptible, but really you will be much better off with me than seeking menial employment, for which, believe me, you are not in the least suited! I'll let you scold tomorrow as much as you choose, but in the meantime come back into the drawing-room, and play casino!'

'I won't!' she declared, on an angry sob. 'You may tell that odious Lady Widmore that I have the headache! And though you may think you have me in your power, you will find that you have not, and at all events you can't force me to play casino, or any other horrid game.'

With these words, she retired to a stone seat at the far end of the terrace, and sat down with her face averted. Sir Gareth, well aware of the folly of arguing with damsels in a passion of fury, left her to sulk herself back to good humour, and strolled into the house again to make her apologies. He also offered to deputize for her at the card-table, but the Earl said hastily: 'Pooh! nonsense! no one wants to play a rubbishy game of casino! Come along to the library: I daresay we shall find my brother there!'

He then drew Sir Gareth out of the room, and was just wondering where the devil Hester had taken herself off to, and why the wretched girl could never be where she was wanted, when she came out of the morning-room on the opposite side of the hall, looking harassed, and saying in a distracted way that she could not imagine what the children had done with the cards.

At any other time the children's fond grandparent would have favoured her with his unexpurgated opinion of persons besotted enough to allow a pack of brats to roam at will over the house, picking up anything that chanced to take their fancy, but on this occasion he refrained, even saying benignly that it was of no consequence. 'I'll tell Almeria they can't be found!' he added, with a flash of inspiration, and went back into the drawing-room, and firmly shut the door.

Lady Hester looked after him in helpless dismay, the colour rushing to her cheeks. She glanced deprecatingly at Sir Gareth, and saw that his eyes were brimful of laughter. He said: 'Shall we see how many shifts your father and sister-in-law have in store to detach us from the rest of the company? It is extremely diverting, but, for myself, I confess I have been hoping for the opportunity to talk to you ever since I arrived at Brancaster.'

'Yes,' she said unhappily. 'I am aware—I know that it is only right that I should—Oh, dear, I am saying such foolish things, but if you knew how painful it is to me you would forgive me!'

He had taken her hand in his, and he could feel how wildly her pulse was fluttering. He drew her towards the morning-room, and gently obliged her to enter it. It was lit only by an oil-lamp, a circumstance for which Hester disjointedly apologized.

'But, Hester, what is it?' he asked, his eyes searching her face. 'Why do you tremble so? Surely you are not shy of me, such old friends as we are!'

'Oh, no! If we can but remain just that!'

'I think you must know that it is my very earnest wish to become more than your friend.'

'I do know it, and indeed I am very much obliged to you, and truly sensible of the honour you do me—'

'Hester!' he expostulated. '*Must* you talk such nonsense?'

'Not nonsense! Oh, no! You have paid me a great compliment, and journeyed all this distance, which quite sinks me with shame, for I daresay it was most inconvenient—yet how could I write to you? I am aware that it *should* have been done—it makes it so excessively disagreeable for you! But indeed I told Papa at the outset that I didn't wish for the match!'

He was perfectly silent for a moment, a tiny crease between his brows. Perceiving it, she said despairingly: 'You are very angry, and I cannot wonder at it.'

'No, I assure you! Only very much disappointed. I had hoped that you and I might have been happy together.'

'We should not suit,' she said faintly.

'If that were so, it must be my fault—and I would do my best to mend it,' he replied.

She looked startled, and exclaimed: 'Oh, no! Pray do not—I did not mean—Sir Gareth, indeed you must not press me! I am not the wife for you.'

'Of that you must let me be the judge. Are you trying to tell me civilly that I am not the husband for you? But I would do my best to make you happy.'

She slid away from the question, saying only: 'I don't think of marriage.'

He came up to her, and again possessed himself of her hand. 'Think of it now! If I don't remotely resemble the man you dreamed you would marry, how many of us marry our dreams? Not many, I think—yet we contrive to be happy.'

She said mournfully: 'So very few! Alas, my dear friend, *you* did not!'

His clasp tightened on her hand, but he did not answer her immediately. When he spoke again, it was with a little difficulty. 'Hester, if you are afraid that—if you are afraid of a ghost—you need not be! It is all so long ago! Not forgotten, but—oh, like a romantic tale, read when one was very young! Indeed, my dear, I haven't come to you, dreaming of Clarissa!'

'I know—oh, I know!' she said, in a shaking voice. 'But you don't care for me.'

'You are mistaken: I have a very great regard for you.'

'Ah, yes! And I for you,' she said, with a pitiful attempt at a smile. 'I think—I hope—that you will meet someone one day whom you will be able to love with all your heart. I beg of you, say no more!'

'I am not taking my rejection as I should, am I?' he said wryly.

'I am so very sorry! It is dreadfully mortifying for you!'

'Good God, what does that signify? But there is one thing I must say before we leave this. We are such old friends that you will let me speak frankly, I believe. Do you not think that even though we haven't tumbled into love, headlong, as we did when we were very young, we might yet be very comfortable together? If I can't give you romance, there are other things I can give you. No, I don't mean riches: I know they would not weigh with you. But your situation is not happy. Forgive me if this gives you pain! You are not valued as you should be; neither your comfort nor your sensibility is a matter of concern to any member of your family. Indeed, it has frequently seemed to me that your sisters regard you as a convenient drudge! As for your sister-in-law, the tone of her mind is such that I am tolerably convinced that to live under the same roof with her must be a severe penance! Well! I can offer you a position of the first consequence. You would be at no one's beck and call, you would be your own mistress—with a husband who, I promise you, would not make unreasonable demands of you. You may be sure that I should always attend to your wishes, and hold you in respect as well as affection. Would that not mean a happier life than the one you now lead?'

Her face was very white; she pulled her hand away, saying in a stifled voice: 'No—*anguish!*'

This seemed so strange a thing for her to have said that he thought he could not have heard her aright. 'I beg your pardon?' he said blankly.

She had moved away from him in some agitation, and said now, with her back turned to him: 'I didn't mean it—don't heed it! I say such foolish things! Pray forgive me! I am so deeply grateful to you! Your wife will be the happiest of females, unless she is a monster, and I do *hope* you won't marry a monster! If only I could find my *handkerchief!*'

He could not help smiling at this, but he said soothingly: 'Take mine!'

'Oh, thank you!' she said, clutching it gratefully, and drying her cheeks with it. 'Pray forgive me! I can't think what should possess me to behave like a watering-pot. So inconsiderate of me, when I daresay there is nothing you dislike more!'

'I dislike very much to see you in distress, and still more do I dislike the knowledge that it is my fault.'

'Indeed it is not! It is nothing but my own folly, and perhaps being a little tired tonight. I am better now. We must go back to the drawing-room.'

'We will do so, but presently, when you are more composed,' he replied, pulling forward a chair. 'Come, sit down! It won't do for you to show that face to your family, you know.' He saw that she was reluctant, and added: 'I am not going to say anything to distress you further, I promise you.'

She took the chair, murmuring: 'Thank you! Is my face quite blotched?'

'A very little: nothing to signify. Are you fixed at Brancaster for the whole summer?'

This calm, conversational gambit did much to restore her tranquillity; she replied with tolerable composure: 'No, I shall be visiting my sisters, and one of my aunts. When my brother and his wife remove to Ramsgate, with the children. My little nephew is inclined to be sickly, and it is thought that sea-bathing may be of benefit to him.'

They discussed sea-bathing, and childish ailments, until suddenly Hester laughed, and exclaimed: 'Oh, how absurd this is! I am very much obliged to you: you have made me quite comfortable again. Is my face fit to be seen? I think we should go back: Almeria is disposed to be uncivil to Amanda, I am afraid, and although I daresay Amanda is very well able to take care of herself, I do think it would be better that they should not quarrel.'

'Undoubtedly! But when I left Amanda she was indulging a fit of the sullens on the terrace, and had no intention of returning to the drawing-room.'

'Oh, dear! It will be very awkward if she won't be in the same room with Almeria,' said Hester, looking harassed. 'You see, I asked her if she would not like to remain with me, instead of seeking employment at an inn—which I *cannot* think at all suitable—and I fancy she will do so.'

'So she informed me, but I disbelieved her. Thank you: it was kind of you to invite her, but I wouldn't for the world impose so much upon your good-nature. If she remained with you, which I doubt, she would very soon have the whole house in an uproar. Indeed, I shudder to think of the battle royal which would rage between her and Lady Widmore! You would be utterly crushed between them!'

'I don't suppose I should,' she said reflectively. 'I find I don't notice things as much as perhaps I ought. I daresay it is through being pretty well accustomed to living with peevish persons. And I have my dogs, you know. Perhaps Amanda would like to have one of Juno's pups. I thought that you wished for one, but it turned out otherwise.'

'Not at all!' he responded promptly. 'I should be delighted to have one of Juno's pups!'

The fugitive smile lit her eyes. 'No, you wouldn't. You are not at all the sort of man who would wish to have a pug at his heels. Do you think that Amanda would run away from Brancaster?'

'I am perfectly sure that she would. Not, I fancy, while I am on the premises, for she's no fool, and she must know she could not hope to get more than a mile or two away before I should have overtaken her. She doesn't yet know how far it is to Chatteris, or what coaches go there, or even where to find a convenient carrier, but you may depend upon it that it would not take her long to discover these things. She would then hatch some scheme fantastic enough to baffle all conjecture, and by the time I had returned with her Brigade-Major she would have hired herself out as a washerwoman, or thrown in her lot with a band of gypsies.'

'I expect she would like to become a gypsy,' agreed Hester, apparently deeming this a reasonable ambition. 'But I believe there are none in the neighbourhood just now. Of course, no one could wonder at it if she thought this a sadly dull house, but I do think that she would be more comfortable here than at an inn, particularly if she were employed at the inn in a menial capacity.'

He laughed. 'Most certainly she would! But she won't care a button for that, you know. I'm afraid the blame is mine: I was foolish enough to tell her that I should discover the Brigade-Major's name and direction at the Horse Guards, which must scotch any hope we might otherwise have nursed of inducing her to remain under your protection. Really, I can't think how I came to be so corkbrained, but the mischief is done now, and the only thing I can do is to carry her to my sister's house.'

She got up, making an ineffectual attempt to straighten the lace shawl she wore over her shoulders. Sir Gareth took it out of her hands, and disposed it becomingly for her, which made her say, with a gleam of fun: 'Thank you! You see how unhandy I am: I should be *such* a trial to you!'

He smiled, but only said: 'You know, Hester, I am very much afraid that your father will be displeased with the outcome of this interview. Is there any way in which I can shield you?'

'Well, you *could* say that it was all a fudge, and what you really wish for is one of Juno's pups,' she offered.

'No, that I most assuredly could *not* say!'

'Never mind!' she said consolingly. 'I shall be quite in disgrace, I daresay, but it is not of the least consequence. I must find poor Amanda.'

'Very well. Unless she has recovered from the sulks, she is seated at the end of the terrace, plotting vengeance on me,' he replied, holding open the door for her.

But Amanda was no longer on the terrace. No sooner had Sir Gareth left her, than Mr Theale, an interested and shameless eavesdropper, had risen from the rustic bench immediately below the parapet, where he had been enjoying his cigarillo, and mounted the broad stone steps to the terrace. What he had heard had resolved his doubts: he was now assured that Sir Gareth had had the effrontery to introduce his particular into the chaste precincts of Brancaster Park. Mr Theale had not previously held him in much esteem, but he was obliged to own now that he had underrated the fellow: such audacity commanded his instant respect. He wondered what peculiar concatenation of circumstances had rendered it necessary for Ludlow to adopt such a desperate course, and reflected that it all went to show how unwise it was to judge a man by the face he showed to the world. One would have supposed Ludlow to be the last man alive to desire a reluctant mistress, yet here he was, plainly determined not to let this little bird of paradise escape him. Mr Theale sympathized with him, but could not forbear chuckling to himself. He rather fancied that he had the poor fellow at a disadvantage, for however infuriated he might be at having his mistress filched from him he would be obliged to accept the situation with apparent complaisance. Damn it, thought Mr Theale, he can't so much as mention the matter to me, let alone call me out! I'm poor Hetty's uncle! He may be brazen, but he won't kick up such a dust as that!

Fortified by this conviction, he threw away the butt of his cigarillo, and made his way towards the end of the terrace.

Amanda watched his advance with the light of speculation in her eye. He might be a fat old man, doddering on the brink of the grave, but he was clearly disposed to admire her, and might, with a little ingenuity, be turned to useful account. She smiled upon him, therefore, and made no objection to his seating himself beside her, and taking her hand between both of his.

'My dear little girl,' said Mr Theale, in a voice of fatherly benevolence, 'I fear you are in some trouble! Now, I wonder if I might be able to help you? I wish, my dear, that you would confide in me!'

Amanda drew a long breath of sheer ecstasy. Mr Theale mistook it for a sigh, and patted her hand, saying fondly: 'There, there! Only tell me the whole!'

'I am an orphan,' said Amanda, adding tragically: 'Cast upon the world without the means to support myself!'

'My poor child!' said Mr Theale. 'Have you no kindred to care what becomes of you?'

'No, alas!' said Amanda mournfully.

'Let us take a turn in the garden!' said Mr Theale, much heartened by this disclosure.

7

It could not have been said, when Amanda came to the end of her imaginative confidences, that Mr Theale perfectly understood all the ramifications of her story. Certain features, such as the precise nature of the circumstances which had drawn Sir Gareth into her life, remained obscure, but this did not greatly trouble him. One thing was quite plain to him: Sir

Gareth had hideously mangled a promising situation, which, reflected Mr
Theale, was a further example of the unwisdom of trusting to appearances.
One wouldn't have suspected that a fellow with such address, and such easy,
pleasant manners, would have so grossly mishandled a shy filly whom
anyone but a cod's head must have guessed would respond only to a very
light hand on the bridle. That Amanda had disliked him from the outset Mr
Theale did not for a moment believe, for the particular story Amanda had
selected for his edification was the one she owed to the pen of Mr
Richardson. Sir Gareth had recognized the provenance, and had very
unkindly said so; Mr Theale, whose reading did not embrace the works of
novelists admired by his parents, did not recognize it. Broadly speaking, he
accepted the story, but the construction he put upon it was scarcely what the
fair plagiarist would have desired. No doubt the little lovebird had
encouraged the widowed parent of her young mistress to make up to her:
probably, thought the cynical Mr Theale, she had hoped to lure him into
proposing marriage. That would account for the apparent inhumanity of
the gentleman's sister in turning her out of doors incontinent. Just how
much time had elapsed, or what had happened, between this heartless
eviction and Amanda's arrival at Brancaster under Sir Gareth's protection,
Mr Theale neither knew nor troubled to discover. She had said that she had
met Sir Gareth for the first time on the previous day, but that, naturally,
was a lie. Understandable, of course, but Mr Theale was rather too downy a
one to accept it. On his own admission, Sir Gareth had lingered on the road
from London. He had pitched them a Canterbury-story about a visit to old
friends in Hertfordshire: in Mr Theale's view, it had been a young friend
who had detained him, and had succeeded in fixing his interest so securely
that rather than lose her he had adopted the perilous course of bringing her
to Brancaster. Mr Theale considered it a bold stroke, but a trifle hare-
brained: ten to one that had been when the chit had taken fright. When all
was said and done, he thought, preening himself, an experienced man of
fifty, even though he had become a little portly, could give Ludlow points,
and beat him. A handsome face and a fine figure were very well in their way,
but what was needed in this case was delicacy.

Mr Theale, in the most delicate fashion imaginable, offered Amanda an
asylum. He did it so beautifully that even if she had been attending closely
to him she must have found it difficult to decide whether he was inviting her
to become an inmate of his hunting-box in the guise of a maidservant, or in
that of an adopted daughter. In the event, she paid very little heed to his
glibly persuasive periods, being fully occupied in considering how, and at
what stage of the journey to Melton Mowbray, to dispense with his further
escort.

On one point, Mr Theale failed to reassure her. So great was her dread of
Sir Gareth that nothing served to convince her that he would not, as soon as
her flight was discovered, pursue her relentlessly, probably springing his
horses in a very reckless way, and quite certainly, unless she had several
hours' start of him, overtaking her, and snatching her back into his power.

'No, no, he won't do that!' Mr Theale said comfortably.

'Well, I think he will,' replied Amanda. 'He is determined not to let me
escape: he said so!'

'Ay, I heard him,' said Mr Theale, chuckling to himself. 'He was
bamming you, my dear. The one thing he can't do is to get you away from
me. He's been hoaxing you more than you knew, I'll go bail he hasn't told
you what brought him here, has he?'

'No,' admitted Amanda. 'But—'

'Well, he's come to offer for my niece,' disclosed Mr Theale.

'For Lady Hester?' gasped Amanda, round-eyed with surprise.

'That's it. Sets him at a stand. A nice dust there would be if the truth of this business were to become known! Bad enough to have brought you here in the first place. The tale will be that I've taken you to those relations of yours at Oundle. Of course, he'll know I haven't done any such thing, because he knows there ain't any relations at Oundle, but he won't dare say so; and as for trying to get me to hand you over to him—well, if he's got as much effrontery as that, he's got more than any man that ever existed!'

'I think,' said Amanda firmly, 'that we should fly from this place at dawn.'

'No, we shouldn't,' replied Mr Theale, even more firmly. 'Not at dawn, my dear.'

'Well, very early in the morning, before anyone is out of bed,' she conceded.

Mr Theale, although not addicted to early rising, agreed upon reflection that it would be desirable to have left Brancaster before Sir Gareth had emerged from his bedchamber. He could not be induced to favour so ungodly an hour as that suggested by Amanda, but after some argument a compromise was reached, and they parted, Mr Theale repairing to the library, where he was later discovered, apparently sleeping off a liberal potation of brandy; and Amanda seating herself under a fine yew-tree on the lawn. Here she was found by Lady Hester, who begged her to come back into the house before she contracted a chill. Amanda, who had been pondering the astonishing intelligence conveyed to her by Mr Theale, would dearly have liked to have asked her whether she really was about to become affianced to Sir Gareth. The question was on the tip of her tongue when she reflected that if the story were untrue Lady Hester might be put out of countenance by such a question. In her youthful eyes, Hester was long past the marriageable age, but she approved of her, and was inclined to think that she would be just the wife for a gentleman also stricken in years. The unexpected streak of maturity which underlay her childish volatility made it possible for her to understand, in the light of Mr Theale's disclosure, the hitherto incomprehensible hostility of Hester's abigail; and although she was not much given to considering any other interests than her own she did feel that it would be a great shame if, through her unwitting fault, the match came to nothing. This led to the comfortable conviction that in leaving Brancaster without the formality of bidding farewell to her kind hostess she was acting almost entirely in Hester's interests. So she accompanied Hester back to the drawing-room with all the good-humour engendered by the agreeable feeling of having decided to adopt a very unselfish course of action. She was only sorry that it was impossible to guess, from either Hester's demeanour or Sir Gareth's, whether they were, in fact, betrothed, or whether the story was nothing but a hum.

An even stronger desire to know what had happened in the morning-room burned in the breasts of the other members of the party. Nothing was to be read in either of the principals' countenances, but the Earl, trying unavailingly on several occasions to catch Sir Gareth's eye, was despondent.

It was not until some time after the ladies had retired for the night that the truth was out. Mr Theale, mounting the stairs on his way to bed, reached the upper hall just as Lady Widmore, her colour considerably heightened, emerged from Hester's room, shutting the door behind her with a distinct slam. Perceiving Mr Theale, she ejaculated with all the exasperation of one whose worst fears had been realized: 'She rejected him!'

'Tell her not to make a cake of herself!' recommended Mr Theale.

'Lord, do you think I haven't? Mind, I hold him entirely to blame! What possessed the man to bring that girl here?' Mr Theale closed one eye in a vulgar wink. 'You don't say so!' her ladyship exclaimed. 'The devil take him! Upon my soul, if that ain't the biggest insult—Yes, but she don't believe it, Fabian! That's what puts me out of all patience with her. You needn't doubt I told her there was nothing in it, though from the way he kept his eyes on the little baggage—*well*! But Hester is such a zany! "Take it from me, my dear," I said, "he's no more in love with her than Cuthbert is!" And what do you think she said to that? I declare I could have boxed her ears! *You* know that way she has of answering you as though she hadn't heard above half you had said to her! "No," she said, "*not yet*!" I'm sure I don't know how I kept my temper, for if there's one thing I can't abide it's people who go off into a daze, which, let me tell you, is what Hester does! *Not yet*, indeed! "Pray, what do you mean by that?" I asked her. So then she looked at me, as if I were a hundred miles away, and said: "I think perhaps he will be." You know, Fabian, there are times when I can't but wonder whether she's queer in her attic! Depend upon it, I told her pretty roundly that if that was what she thought she'd best snap the man up before the mischief was done. All she had to say to that was that she didn't think she would, for all the world as though I had offered her a slice of cake, or some such thing. I've been talking to her for ever, but if she listened to anything I said it's more than I bargain for! Well, I've no patience with her, and so I have told her! To be whistling Ludlow down the wind at her age, and affairs here in the case they are, makes me angry enough to burst my stay-laces! He was prepared to come down devilish handsomely, you know. Well, I don't say Hester hasn't often vexed me to death, but I declare I never thought she would behave so selfishly! What his lordship will have to say about it I hope *I* don't have to listen to! I shall have enough to bear from Widmore, for this news will be bound to turn his stomach sour on him, you mark my words if it don't!'

'You know what, Almeria?' interrupted Mr Theale, a look of profound concentration on his florid countenance. 'I believe she has a *tendre* for him!'

Lady Widmore stared at him in contempt and suspicion. 'I suppose you are top-heavy,' she remarked.

Not for the first time, Mr Theale wondered what had possessed his nephew to marry this coarse-tongued and unattractive female. 'No, I'm not,' he said shortly.

'Oh, beg pardon! But what made you say such a daffish thing, if it wasn't brandy?'

'It ain't daffish, but I daresay it may seem so to you. There isn't one of you here who can see what's dashed well under your noses. It occurred to me when I saw Hester look at Ludlow.'

'I'll swear she has never given the least sign of such a thing!' she said incredulously. 'What the deuce can you possibly mean?'

'Just a certain look in her eyes,' said Mr Theale knowledgeably. 'No use asking me to explain it, because I can't, but I'd lay you odds she'd have had him if he hadn't walked in with that little ladybird on his arm.'

'I could wring her neck!' exclaimed Lady Widmore, her cheeks reddening angrily.

'No need to do that: I'm going to take her off your hands first thing in the morning. To those relations at Oundle,' he added, with another of his vulgar winks.

She regarded him with great fixity. 'Will she go with you?'

'Lord, yes! Do anything to get away from Ludlow. The silly fellow seems to have frightened her, poor little soul.'

'She! I never saw anyone less frightened in my life!'

'Well, it don't signify. The point is, I'm going to take her away. Ludlow will be obliged to put a good face on it, and I shouldn't be surprised if once Amanda is out of his eye he'll see what a cake he's been making of himself, and try Hester again.'

'If he can be persuaded to remain here,' she said. 'Does he know?'

'Of course he doesn't! Doesn't even know *I'm* leaving tomorrow. I stayed behind after he'd gone up to bed, and told my brother I meant to be off early, and would carry Miss Smith to Oundle.'

'What did he say?'

'Didn't say anything, but I could see the notion took very well with him. If you want to be helpful, you'll see to it no one hinders the child from joining me in the morning. I've ordered the carriage for seven o'clock. Breakfast in Huntingdon.'

'I'll tell Povey!' said Lady Widmore, a scheming light in her eye. 'My woman has been saying that she's as mad as fire with that chit, for coming here and spoiling Hester's chances. Would you believe Hester could be such a ninny?—She has invited the wretched wench to remain here for a week! You may lay your life Povey will take care no one stops her from going with you. I suppose there's no fear Ludlow will go after you?'

'Lord, you're as bad as Amanda!' said Mr Theale impatiently. 'Of course there's no fear of it! He'd have to tell the truth about her if he did that, and that's the last thing he's likely to do.'

'Well, I hope you may be right. At all events, it will do no harm if Povey tells Hester the girl's still abed and asleep at breakfast-time. I wouldn't put it beyond Hester to *send* Ludlow after her!'

'What the devil should she do that for?' demanded Mr Theale. 'She'll think I'm taking the girl to her relations!'

'I'll do my best to make her think that,' retorted Lady Widmore grimly, 'but ninny though she may be, she knows you, Fabian!'

He was not in the least offended by this insult, but went chuckling off to bed, where, like Amanda, he enjoyed an excellent night's repose.

They were almost the only members of the party to do so. Not until the small hours crept in did sleep put an end to Lady Hester's unhappy reflections; her father lay awake, first dwelling on her shortcomings, then blaming Sir Gareth for her undutiful conduct, and lastly arguing himself into the conviction that it formed no part of his duty to interfere with whatever plan Fabian had formed; Lady Widmore was troubled by bad dreams; and her husband, as she had prophesied, succumbed to an attack of acute dyspepsia, which caused him to remain in bed on the following day, sustaining nature with toast and thin gruel, and desiring his wife not—unless she wished to bring on his pains again—to mention his sister's name within his hearing.

Lady Widmore was the first person to put in an appearance at the breakfast-table. She, alone among the family, had attended the service Mr Whyteleafe held daily in the little private chapel. The Earl was always an infrequent worshipper, but it was rarely that Lady Hester rose too late to take part in the morning service. This morning, however, she had been an absentee. Sir Gareth, confidentially informed overnight by his host that the chaplain was employed for the edification of the servants and the ladies of the family, had not felt it to be incumbent upon him to attend either; but he was the second person to enter the breakfast-parlour.

Lady Widmore, after bidding him a bluff good morning, told him bluntly that she was sorry his suit had not prospered.

'Thank you; I too am sorry,' replied Sir Gareth calmly.

'Well, if I were you I wouldn't give up hope,' said her ladyship. 'The mischief is that Hester's the shyest thing in nature, you know.'

'I do know it,' said Sir Gareth unencouragingly.

'Give her time, and I dare swear she'll come round!' she persevered.

'Do you mean, ma'am, that she might be scolded into accepting me?' he asked. 'I trust that no one will make the attempt, for however much I must hope that her answer to me last night was not final, I most certainly don't wish for a wife who accepted me only to escape from the recriminations of her relatives.'

'Well, upon my word!' ejaculated Lady Widmore, her colour rising.

'I know that your ladyship is an advocate of plain speaking,' said Sir Gareth sweetly.

'Ay, very true!' she retorted. 'So I will make bold to tell you, sir, that it's your own fault that this business has come to nothing!'

He looked coolly at her, a hint of steel in his eyes. 'Believe me, ma'am,' he said, 'though you may be labouring under a misapprehension as little flattering to yourself as it is to me, Lady Hester is not!'

Fortunately, since her temper was hasty, the Earl came in just then, with his chaplain at his heels; and by the time he had greeted his guest, with as much cheerfulness as he could muster, and had expressed the conventional hope that he had slept well, she had recollected the unwisdom of quarrelling with Sir Gareth, and managed, though not without a severe struggle with herself, to swallow her spleen, and to call upon her father-in-law to persuade Sir Gareth not to curtail his visit to Brancaster.

The Earl, while responding with a fair assumption of enthusiasm, privately considered that it would be useless for Sir Gareth to linger under his roof. His daughter, he had decided, was destined to remain a spinster all her days; and he had formed the intention, while shaving, of putting the whole matter out of his mind, and losing no time in repairing to the more congenial locality of Brighton. He had been prepared to perform his duties as a host and a father while Hester mooned about the gardens with her affianced husband, but if this very easy way of entertaining Sir Gareth failed, as fail it assuredly must, he wondered what the devil he was to do with the fellow for a whole week in the middle of July.

'Thank you, sir, you are very good, but I fear it is not in my power to remain,' replied Sir Gareth. 'I must convey my charge to Oundle—or even, perhaps, back to her parents.'

'Oh, there is not the smallest need for you to put yourself about!' struck in Lady Widmore. 'Fabian was saying to me last night that he would be pleased to take her up in his carriage as far as to Oundle, for he goes to Melton today, you know, and it will not carry him far out of his way.'

'I am very much obliged to him, but must not trespass upon his good-nature,' replied Sir Gareth, a note of finality in his voice.

'No such thing!' said Lady Widmore robustly. 'It can make no difference to Fabian, and I am sure I know not why you should be dancing attendance upon a schoolgirl, Sir Gareth!'

There was a challenge in her eye, but before Sir Gareth could meet it, Mr Whyteleafe said with precision: 'I must venture to inform your ladyship of a circumstance which cannot but preclude Mr Theale's being able to offer his services to Miss Smith. Mr Theale's travelling carriage, closely followed by the coach containing his baggage, passed beneath my window at fourteen minutes past seven o'clock exactly. I am able, I should explain, to speak with certainty on this point because it so chanced that, being desirous of knowing the hour, I was at that instant in the act of consulting my watch.'

The Earl had never liked his chaplain, but he had not hitherto considered him actively malevolent. He now perceived that he had been cherishing a viper. Sir Gareth was of course bound to discover the truth, but it had been his lordship's intention to have taken good care that he should not do so in his presence. The more he had considered the matter, the stronger had become his conviction that the disclosure would lead to an awkward scene, and the avoidance of awkward scenes was one of the guiding principles of his life. In an attempt to gloss over the perilous moment, he said: 'Yes, yes, now you put me in mind of it, I recall that my brother said he rather thought he should make an early start. Doesn't like travelling in the heat of the day,' he added, addressing himself to Sir Gareth.

The door opened, and Lady Hester came into the room. Sir Gareth, as he rose to his feet, pushing back his chair, saw with concern that she was looking pale, and rather heavy-eyed.

'Good morning,' she said, in her soft voice. 'I am afraid I am shockingly late this morning, and as for Miss Smith, my woman tells me that she is still asleep.'

'Lady Hester, have you yourself seen Amanda?' Sir Gareth asked abruptly.

She shook her head, looking inquiringly at him. 'No, I didn't wish to disturb her. Ought I to have? Oh, dear, you don't think she can have—?'

'Yes, I do think that she can have,' said Sir Gareth. 'I have just learnt that your uncle left Brancaster two hours ago, and nothing appears to be more likely than that he took Amanda with him.'

'Well, what if he did?' demanded Lady Widmore. 'Very obliging of him, *I* should call it, and nothing to make a piece of work about! To be sure, it is excessively uncivil of her to have gone off without bidding anyone goodbye, but I, for one, am not amazed.'

'I will go up to her room immediately,' Lady Hester said, ignoring her sister-in-law.

She found Amanda's bedchamber untenanted. A note addressed to herself lay on the dressing-table. As she was reading the few lines of apology and explanation, Povey came in, checking at sight of her, and saying in some confusion: 'I beg pardon, my lady! I was just coming to see if Miss was awake!'

'You knew, Povey, when you told me that Miss Smith was asleep, that she had left the house,' said Hester quietly. 'No, do not try to answer me! You have done very wrong. I don't wish to talk to you. Indeed, I don't feel that I shall be able to forgive you.'

Povey instantly burst into tears, but to her startled dismay her tender-hearted mistress seemed quite unmoved, leaving the room without so much as another glance thrown in her direction.

Lady Hester found Sir Gareth awaiting her at the foot of the stairs. She put Amanda's note into his hand, saying remorsefully: 'It is just as you suspected. I have been dreadfully to blame!'

'You! No, indeed!' he returned, running his eye over the note. 'Well, she doesn't tell you so, but I imagine there is no doubt she went away with your uncle.' He gave the note back to her, saying, as he saw her face of distress: 'My dear, don't look so stricken! There is not so very much harm done, after all. I own, I wish I knew where Theale is taking her, but I daresay they will not be difficult to trace.'

'It is quite *shameful* of Fabian!' she said, in a tone of deep mortification.

He replied lightly: 'For anything we yet know she may have prevailed upon him to take her to Oundle, where, I don't doubt, she will try to give him the slip.'

'You say that to make me feel more comfortable, but pray don't!' she said. 'There can be no excuse for his conduct, and the dreadful thing is that there *never* is! Even if she made him think she indeed had relations at Oundle, he cannot have thought it proper to remove her from Brancaster in such a way. And I very much fear that he has not taken her to Oundle. In fact, it would be much more like him to carry her off to his hunting-box, which I should have no hesitation in saying is what he has done, only that he must know that is the first place where you would look for her.'

'Well, if we are to speak frankly of your uncle, I will own that that is precisely what I fear he may have done,' said Sir Gareth.

'Oh, yes, pray say what you like! I assure you, none of us would disagree with you, however badly you think of him, for he is almost the most severe misfortune that ever befell us. But it would be quite foolhardy of him to have taken her to Melton Mowbray!'

'I suspect that he thinks I shan't attempt to follow him,' replied Sir Gareth dryly. 'Your brother and his wife certainly believe me to have brought my mistress to Brancaster, and your uncle's conduct now leads me to suppose that they are not alone in that belief.'

'I don't know very much about such matters,' said Hester thoughtfully, 'but I shouldn't have thought you would do that.'

'You may be perfectly sure I would not!'

'Oh, yes, I am! I told Almeria so. I cannot but feel that it would be such a *silly* thing to do!'

'It would also be an extremely insulting thing to do,' he said, smiling at her tone of serious consideration. 'How Theale came to credit me with so much ill-breeding is something that perhaps he will explain to me presently.'

'Well,' said Hester, wrinkling her brow, 'I think it is just the sort of thing he would do himself, which would account for it. But what has me in a puzzle is why you should think he would not, in that event, expect you to follow him. I should have thought it quite certain you would do so—unless, of course, not pursuing people who steal your mistress is one of those rules of *gentleman's* etiquette which naturally I know nothing about.'

'No,' he answered, laughing, 'it is not! But if I had been so lost to all sense of propriety as to have brought my mistress with me, when my errand was to beg you to honour me with your hand in marriage, I must indeed have found it an awkward business—to say the least of it!—to recover Amanda from your uncle.'

'Yes, so you must!' she agreed, pleased to have the problem elucidated. 'Dear me, how excessively shabby of Fabian to try to take advantage of your position! You know, whenever he is in a scrape, one always hopes that he has gone his length, but he seems never to be at a loss to think of something worse to do. How very vexing it is for you! What shall you do?'

'Try to discover which road he took when he left this house, and go after him. What else can I do? I made myself responsible for Amanda, and although she deserves to be well spanked I can't let her run into mischief that might so easily mean her ruin. I have already desired your butler to send a message to the stables.' He held out his hand, and she put hers into it, looking fleetingly up into his face. 'I owe you an apology,' he said. 'Believe me, if I had guessed how troublesome she would be, I would not have burdened you with Amanda.' He smiled suddenly. '*One* advantage, however, must have been gained. I was obliged to tell your father the truth—or some part of it, and as he plainly considers me to be touched in the upper works I imagine he will congratulate you on your good sense in refusing to have anything to do with me!'

She flushed, and very slightly shook her head. 'Don't let us speak of that! I wish I might be of some assistance to you now, but I cannot think of anything I could usefully do. If Fabian has gone to Melton, he will have taken the road to Huntingdon, because although the more direct way is through Peterborough the road from Chatteris to Peterborough is very narrow and rough, and he will never venture on to it for fear of being made to feel ill. He is a very bad traveller.' She paused, and seemed to reflect. 'Will you feel obliged to call him out? I don't know what may be the proper thing for you to do, and I don't wish to tease you, but I can't help feeling that it would be more comfortable if you did not.'

His lips quivered, but he replied with admirable gravity: 'Just so! I shan't go to such desperate lengths as that, and although I own it would give me a good deal of pleasure to draw his cork—I beg your pardon! make his nose bleed!—I daresay I shan't even do that. He is too old, and too fat—and heaven only knows what tale Amanda may have beguiled him with! I only wish I may not figure as the villain of it.'

'Now, that,' said Hester, roused from her gentle tolerance, 'would be really *too* naughty of her, and quite beyond the line of what is excusable!'

He laughed. 'Thank you! I must go now. May I write to tell you the outcome of this nonsensical adventure?'

'Yes, indeed, I hope you will, for I shall be very anxious until I hear from you.'

He raised her hand to his lips, and kissed it, pressed it slightly, and then released it, and went away up the stairs. Lady Hester remained for a moment or two, staring absently at nothing in particular, before going slowly back into the breakfast-parlour.

8

The first check to Amanda's new plan of campaign was thrown in the way by Mr Theale, who disclosed, when midway between Brancaster Park and Huntingdon, that he had ordered his coachman to drive straight through that town to the village of Brampton, where, he said, they would pause for breakfast and a change of horses. He did not tell her that he preferred, on the whole, not to be seen in her company in a town where his was naturally a familiar figure; but was prepared, if questioned, to dilate upon the excellencies of the posting-house at Brampton: a hostelry which had never, as yet, enjoyed his patronage. But she did not question him. Successful generals did not allow their minds to be diverted by irrelevancies: they tied knots, and went on.

The set-back was not as severe as it might have been, had she been still adhering to her plan of seeking employment at one of the town's chief posting-houses. This scheme she had abandoned, knowing that the George, the Fountain, and no doubt the Crown as well, would be the first places where Sir Gareth would expect to find her. But she had ascertained from the obliging Povey that stage-coaches to various parts of the country were to be boarded in Huntingdon, and it had been her intention to have bought herself a ticket on one of these, to some town just far enough away from Huntingdon to have baffled Sir Gareth. A village situated two miles beyond Huntingdon would not suit her purpose at all: it might be hours before a coach passed through it; if she succeeded in escaping from Mr Theale there, and walked back to Huntingdon, she would run the risk of meeting Sir Gareth on the road, or find, when she reached the coach-office, that he had been there before her, and had directed the clerk to be on the watch for her. Mr Theale's society, she decided, would have to be endured for rather longer than she had hoped.

How to give Mr Theale the slip had become the most pressing of the problems confronting her, for however easy a matter it might have been in a busy country-town, it was not going to be at all easy in some small village. Artless questioning elicited the information that the next town on their road was Thrapston, which was some fifteen miles distant from Brampton. Mr Theale said that by nursing the horses a little they could very well make this their next stage, but Amanda had a lively dread that long before his leisurely carriage, with its odiously conspicuous yellow body, had reached Thrapston, it would be overtaken by Sir Gareth's sporting curricle; and she realized that as soon as she was far enough from Huntingdon she must part company with her elderly admirer.

She would do this without compunction, too, but with a good deal of relief. At Brancaster, fortified by the scarcely acknowledged protection of Sir Gareth in the background, she had thought Mr Theale merely a fat and foolish old gentleman, whom it would be easy to bring about her thumb; away from Brancaster, and (it must be owned) Sir Gareth's surveillance, although she still thought him old and fat, she found, to her surprise, that she was a little afraid of him. She had certainly met his kind before, but under her aunt's careful chaperonage no elderly and amorous beau had ever contrived to do more than give her hand a squeeze, or to ogle her in a very laughable way. She had classed Mr Theale with her grandfather's friends, who always petted her, and paid her a great many extravagant compliments; but within a very short time of having delivered herself into his power she discovered that, for all his fatherly manner, he was disquietingly unlike old Mr Swaffham, or General Riverhead, or Sir Harry Bramber, or even Major Mickleham, who was such an accomplished flirt that Grandpapa scolded him, saying that he was doing his best to turn her head. These senile persons frequently pinched her cheek, or chucked her under the chin, or even put their arms round her waist, and gave her a hug; and old Mr Swaffham invariably demanded a kiss from her; so why she should have been frightened when Mr Theale's arm slid round her was rather inexplicable. She had stiffened instinctively, and had had to subdue an impulse to thrust him away. He seemed to want to stroke and fondle her, too, and as her flesh shrank under his hand the thought flashed suddenly into her mind that not even Neil, who loved her, petted her in just such a fashion. Certain of her aunt's veiled warnings occurred to her, and she began to think that possibly Aunt was not quite as foolish and oldfashioned as she had supposed her to be. Not, of course, that she was not well able to take care of herself, or at all afraid of her aged protector: merely, he made her feel uncomfortable, and was such a dead bore that she would be glad to be rid of him.

This desire, however, carried with it no corresponding wish to see those match-bays of Sir Gareth's rapidly overtaking her; and she scarcely knew how to contain her impatience while Mr Theale, very much at his ease, selected and consumed a lavish breakfast. Her scheme for the subjugation of her grandfather had by this time become entangled with a clenched-teeth determination to outwit and wholly confound Sir Gareth. His cool assumption of authority had much incensed a damsel accustomed all her short life to being tenderly indulged. Only Neil had the right to dictate to her, and Neil never committed the heinous sin of laughing at her. Sir Gareth had treated her as though she had been an amusing child, and he must be shown the error of his high-handed ways. At the same time, he had succeeded in imbuing her with a certain respect for him, so that, although the clock in the inn's coffee-room assured her that it was in the highest degree unlikely that he had yet emerged from his bedchamber, she could not help looking anxiously out of the window every time she heard the sound of an approaching vehicle. Mr Theale, observing these signs of nervous apprehension, called her a silly little puss, and told her that she would be quite safe in his care. 'He won't chase after you, my pretty, and if he did I should tell him to go to the devil,' he said, transferring a second rasher of grilled ham from the dish to his plate, and looking wistfully at a cluster of boiled eggs. 'No, I shan't venture upon an egg,' he decided, with a sigh of regret. 'Nothing is more prone to turn me queasy, and though I am in a capital way now, we have a longish journey before us, and there's no saying that I shan't be feeling as queer as Dick's hatband before we come to the end of it.'

Amanda, who was breakfasting on raspberries and cream, paused, with her spoon halfway to her mouth, a sudden and brilliant notion taking possession of her mind. 'Do you feel unwell in carriages, sir?' she asked.

He nodded. 'Always been the same. It's a curst nuisance, but my coachman is a very careful driver, and knows he must let the horses drop into a walk if the road should be rough. Ah, that makes you think me a sad old fogey, doesn't it?'

'Oh, no!' said Amanda earnestly. 'Because it is exactly so with me!'

'God bless my soul, is it indeed? Well, we are well suited to one another, eh?' His gaze fell on her brimming plate; he said uneasily: 'Do you think you should eat raspberries, my dear? *I* should not dare!'

'Oh, yes, for I assure you I feel delightfully this morning!' she replied, pouring more cream over the mound on her plate. 'Besides, I am excessively partial to raspberries and cream.'

Mr Theale, watching with a fascinated eye, could see that this was true. He hoped very much that Amanda was not misjudging her capacity, but he felt a little anxious, and when, half an hour later, her vivacious prattle became rather forced, he was not in the least surprised. By the time they reached the village of Spaldwick, it had ceased altogether, and she was leaning back against the elegant velvet squabs with her eyes closed. Mr Theale offered her his vinaigrette, which she took with a faintly uttered word of thanks. He was relieved to see that the colour still bloomed in her cheeks, and ventured to ask her presently if she felt more the thing.

'I feel very ill, but I daresay I shall be better directly,' she replied, in brave but faltering accents. 'I expect it was the raspberries: they always make me feel like this!'

'Well, what the devil made you eat them?' demanded Mr Theale, pardonably annoyed.

'I am so *very* partial to them!' she explained tearfully. 'Pray don't be vexed with me!'

'No, no!' he made haste to assure her. 'There, don't cry, my pretty!'

'Oh, don't!' begged Amanda, as he tried to put his arm round her. 'I fear I am about to swoon!'

'Don't be afraid!' said Mr Theale, patting her hand. 'You won't do that, not while you have such lovely roses in your cheeks! Just put your head on my shoulder, and see if you don't feel better in a trice!'

'Is my face very pink?' asked Amanda, not availing herself of this invitation.

'Charmingly pink!' he asserted.

'Then I am going to be sick,' said Amanda, ever fertile of invention. 'I *always* have a pink face when I am sick. Oh, dear, I feel quite *dreadfully* sick!'

Considerably alarmed, Mr Theale sat bolt upright, and looked at her with misgiving. 'Nonsense! You can't be sick here!' he said bracingly.

'I can be sick *anywhere!*' replied Amanda, pressing her handkerchief to her lips, and achieving a realistic hiccup.

'Good God! I will stop the carriage!' exclaimed Mr Theale, groping for the check-cord.

'If only I could lie down for a little while, I should be perfectly well again!' murmured the sufferer.

'Yes, but you can't lie down by the roadside, my dear girl! Wait, I'll consult with James! Stay perfectly quiet—take another sniff at the smelling-salts!' recommended Mr Theale, letting down the window, and leaning out to confer with the coachman, who had pulled up his horses, and was craning round inquiringly from the box-seat.

After a short and somewhat agitated colloquy with James, Mr Theale brought his head and shoulders back into the carriage, and said: 'James reminds me that there is some sort of an inn a little way farther along the road, at Bythorne—only a matter of a couple of miles! It ain't a posting-house, but a decent enough place, he says, where you could rest for a while. Now, if he were to drive us there very slowly—'

'Oh, thank you, I am so much obliged to you!' said Amanda, summoning up barely enough strength to speak audibly. 'Only perhaps it would be better if he were to drive us there as fast as he can!'

Mr Theale had the greatest dislike of being hurtled over even the smoothest road, but the horrid threat contained in these sinister words impelled him to put his head out of the window again, and to order the coachman to put 'em along.

Astonished, but willing, James obeyed him, and the carriage was soon bowling briskly on its way, the body swaying and lurching in its swan-neck springs in a manner fatal to Mr Theale's delicate constitution. He began to feel far from well himself, and would have wrested his vinaigrette from Amanda's hand had he not feared that to deprive her of its support might precipitate a crisis that could not, he felt, be far off. He could only marvel that she had not long since succumbed. Every time she moaned he gave a nervous start, and rolled an anxious eye at her, but she bore up with great fortitude, even managing to smile, tremulously but gratefully, when he assured her that they only had a very little way to go.

It seemed a very long way to him, but just as he had decided, in desperation, that he could not for another instant endure the sway of the carriage, the pace slackened. A few cottages came into view; the horses dropped to a sober trot; and Mr Theale said, on a gasp of relief: 'Bythorne!'

Amanda greeted Bythorne with a low moan.

The carriage came to a gentle halt in front of a small but neat-looking inn, which stood on the village street, with its yard behind it. The coachman shouted: 'House, there!' and the landlord and the tapster both came out in a bustle of welcome.

Amanda had to be helped down from the carriage very carefully. The landlord, informed tersely by James that the lady had been taken ill, performed this office for her, uttering words of respectful encouragement, and commanding the tapster to fetch the mistress to her straight. Mr Theale, much shaken, managed to alight unassisted, but his usually florid countenance wore a pallid hue, and his legs, in their tight yellow pantaloons, tottered a little.

Amanda, supported between the landlord, and his stout helpmate, was led tenderly into the inn; and Mr Theale, recovering both his colour and his presence of mind, explained that his young relative had been overcome by the heat of the day and the rocking of the carriage. Mrs Sheet said that she had frequently been taken that way herself, and begged Amanda to come and have a nice lay down in the best bedchamber. Mr Sheet was much inclined to think that a drop of brandy would put the young lady into prime twig again; but Amanda, bearing up with great courage and nobility, said in a failing voice that she had a revivifying cordial packed in one of her boxes. 'Only I cannot remember in which,' she added prudently.

'Let both be fetched immediately!' ordered Mr Theale. 'Do you go upstairs with this good woman, my love, and I warrant you will soon feel quite the thing again!'

Amanda thanked him, and allowed herself to be led away; whereupon Mr Theale, feeling that he had done all that could be expected of him, retired to the bar-parlour to sample the rejected brandy. Mrs Sheet came surging in, some twenty minutes later, bearing comfortable tidings. In spite of the unaccountable negligence of the young lady's abigail, in having omitted to pack the special cordial in either of her bandboxes, she ventured to say that Miss was already on the high road to recovery, and, if left to lie quietly in a darkened room for half an hour or so, would presently be as right as a trivet. She had obliged Miss to drink a remedy of her own, and although Miss had been reluctant to do so, and had needed a good deal of urging, anyone could see that it had already done much to restore her.

Mr Theale, who was himself sufficiently restored to have lighted one of his cigarillos, had no objection to whiling away half an hour in a snug bar-parlour. He went out to direct James to stable his horses for a short time; and while he was jealously watching James negotiate the difficult turn into the yard behind the inn, the coach which carried his valet and his baggage drove up. Perceiving his master, the valet shouted to the coachman to halt, and at once jumped down, agog with curiosity to know what had made Mr Theale abandon the principles of a lifetime, and spring his horses on an indifferent road. Briefly explaining the cause, Mr Theale directed him to proceed on the journey, and, upon arrival at the hunting-box, to see to it that all was put in readiness there for the reception of a female guest. So the coach lumbered on its way, and Mr Theale, reflecting that the enforced delay would give his housekeeper time to prepare a very decent dinner for him, retired again to the bar-parlour, and called for another noggin of brandy.

Meanwhile, Amanda, left to recover on the smothering softness of Mrs Sheet's best feather-bed, had nipped up, scrambled herself into that sprig-muslin gown which Povey had so kindly washed and ironed for her, and which the inexorable Mrs Sheet had obliged her to put off, and had tied the hat of chip-straw over her curls again. For several hideous minutes, after swallowing Mrs Sheet's infallible remedy for a queasy stomach, she had feared that she really was going to be sick, but she had managed to overcome her nausea, and now felt ready again for any adventure. Mrs Sheet had pointed out the precipitous back-stairs to her, which reached the upper floor almost opposite to the door of the best bedchamber, and had told her that if she needed anything she had only to open her door, and call out, when she would instantly be heard in the kitchen. Amanda, having learnt from her that the kitchen was reached through the door on the right of the narrow lobby at the foot of the stairs, the other door giving only on to the yard, had thanked her, and reiterated her desire to be left quite alone for half an hour.

In seething impatience, and peeping through the drawn blinds, she watched Mr Theale's conferences with James, and with his valet. When she judged that James had had ample time in which to stable his horses, and, like his master, seek solace in the inn, she fastened her cloak round her neck, picked up her bandboxes, and emerged cautiously from the bedchamber. No one was in sight, and hastily concocting a story moving enough to command Mrs Sheet's sympathy and support, if, by ill-hap, she should encounter her on her perilous way to that door opening on to the yard, she began to creep circumspectly down the steep stairs. A clatter of crockery, and Mrs Sheet's voice upraised in admonition to some unknown person, apparently engaged in washing dishes, indicated the position of the kitchen. At the foot of the stairs a shut door promised egress to the yard. Drawing a deep breath, Amanda stole down the remaining stairs, gingerly lifted the latch of the door, and whisked herself through the aperture, softly closing the door behind her. As she had expected, she found herself in the yard. It was enclosed by a rather ramshackle collection of stables and outhouses, and paved with large cobbles. Pulled into the patch of shade thrown by a large barn, stood the yellow-bodied carriage; and, drawn up, not six feet from the backdoor of the inn, was a farm-tumbril, with a sturdy horse standing between its shafts, and a ruddy-faced youth casting empty sacks into it.

Amanda had not bargained for this bucolic character, and for a moment she hesitated, not quite knowing whether to advance, or to draw back. The youth, catching sight of her, stood staring, allowing both his jaw, and the empty crate he was holding, to drop. If Amanda had been unprepared to see him, he was even more unprepared to see, emerging from the Red Lion, such a vision of beauty as she presented to his astonished gaze.

'*Hush!*' commanded Amanda, in a hissing whisper.

The youth blinked at her, but was obediently silent.

Amanda cast a wary look towards the kitchen-window. 'Are you going to take that cart away?' she demanded.

His jaw dropped lower: he nodded.

'Well, will you let me ride in it, if you please?' She added, as she saw his eyes threaten to start from their sockets: 'I am escaping from a Deadly Peril! Oh, pray make haste, and say I may go in your cart!'

Young Mr Ninfield's head was in a whirl, but his mother had impressed upon him that he must always be civil to members of the Quality, so he uttered gruffly: 'You're welcome, miss.'

'Not so loud!' begged Amanda. 'I am very much obliged to you! How shall I climb into it?'

Young Mr Ninfield's gaze travelled slowly from her face to her gown of delicate muslin. 'It ain't fitting!' he said in a hoarse whisper. 'There's been taties in it, and a dozen pullets, and a couple o' bushels o' kindling!'

'It doesn't signify! If you could lift me into it, I can cover myself with those sacks, and no one will see me. Oh, pray be quick! The case is quite *desperate*! *Can't* you lift me?'

The feat was well within Mr Ninfield's power, but the thought of picking up this fragile beauty almost made him swoon. However, she seemed quite determined to ride in his cart, so he manfully obeyed her. She was feather-light, and smelled deliciously of violets. Mr Ninfield, handling her with all the caution he would have expended on his mother's best crockery, suffered another qualm. 'I don't like to!' he said, holding her like a baby in his muscular arms. 'You'll get your pretty dress all of a muck!'

'Joe!' suddenly called Mrs Sheet, from within the house. '*Joe!*'

'*Quickly!*' Amanded urged him.

Thus adjured, Mr Ninfield gave a gulp, and tipped her neatly into the cart, where she instantly lay down on the floor, and became screened from his bemused gaze by the sides of the cart.

'The pickled cherries for your ma, Joe!' screeched Mrs Sheet, from the kitchen-window. 'If I hadn't well-nigh forgot them! Wait, now, till I fetch the jar out to you!'

'Do not betray me!' Amanda implored him, trying to pull the empty sacks over herself.

Mr Ninfield was astonished. Mrs Sheet, besides being a lifelong crony of his mother's, was his godmother, and he had always looked upon her as a kindly and benevolent person. As she came out into the yard, he almost expected to find that she had undergone a transformation, and was relieved to see that her plump countenance was still as good-natured as ever. She handed a covered jar to him, bidding him to take care to keep it the right way up. 'And mind you give my love to your ma, and thank her for the eggs, and tell your pa Sheet would have settled for the kindling, and that, only that he's serving a gentleman,' she said. 'We've got Quality in the house: a very fine-seeming gentleman, and the prettiest young lady you ever did see! Likely she's his niece. Poor lamb, she was took ill in the carriage, and is laid down in my best chamber at this very moment.'

Mr Ninfield did not know what to reply to this, but as he was generally inarticulate his godmother set no particular store by his silence. She gave him a resounding kiss, repeated her injunction to take care of the pickled cherries, and went back into the house.

Mr Ninfield picked up the empty crate, and peeped cautiously over the side of the cart. From its floor a pair of bright, dark eyes questioned him. 'Has she gone?' whispered Amanda.

'Ay.'

'Then pray let us go too!'

'Ay,' said Mr Ninfield again. 'I'll have to put this crate in—if convenient, miss.'

'Yes, pray do so! And I will hold the jar for you,' said Amanda obligingly.

Matters being thus satisfactorily arranged, Mr Ninfield went to the horse's head, and began to lead the placid animal out of the yard, on to the road. The wheels of the cart being shod with iron, Amanda was considerably jolted, but she made no complaint. The horse plodded along the road in a westerly direction, Mr Ninfield walking beside it, pondering deeply the extraordinary adventure that had befallen him. His slow but profound cogitations caused him, at the end of several minutes, to say suddenly: 'Miss!'

'Yes?' replied Amanda.

'Where would you be wishful I should take you?' inquired Mr Ninfield.

'Well, I am not perfectly sure,' said Amanda. 'Is there anyone in sight?'

'No,' replied Mr Ninfield, having stared fixedly up and down the road for a moment or two.

Reassured on this point, Amanda knelt up, and looked down at her rescuer over the side of the cart. 'Where are you going yourself?' she asked chattily.

'Back home,' he replied. 'Leastways—'

'Where is your home? Is it on this road?'

He shook his head, jerking his thumb towards the south. 'Whitethorn Farm,' he explained laconically.

'Oh!' Amanda looked thoughtfully at him, considering a new scheme. A slow tide of bashful crimson crept up to the roots of his hair; he smiled shyly up at her, and then looked quickly away, in case she should be affronted. But the smile decided the matter. 'Do you live there with your mother?' asked Amanda.

'Ay. And me dad. It's Dad's farm, and Granfer's afore him, and me great-granfer's afore *him*,' he said, becoming loquacious.

'Would your mother let me stay there for a little while, do you think?'

This brought his head round again. He had not the smallest notion of what his mother's views might be, but he said ecstatically: 'Ay!'

'Good!' said Amanda. 'It so happens that I never thought of it before, but I now see that the thing for me to do is to become a dairymaid. I should like it of all things! I daresay you could teach me how to milk a cow, couldn't you?'

Mr Ninfield, dazzled by the very thought of teaching a fairy princess to milk a cow, gulped, and uttered once again his favourite monosyllable: 'Ay!' He then fell into a daze, from which he was recalled by the sight of an approaching vehicle. He pointed this out to Amanda, but she had seen it already, and had disappeared from view. He gave it as his opinion that she had best remain hid until they reached the lane leading, by way of the village of Keyston, to Whitethorn Farm. Fortunately, since she found it extremely uncomfortable to crouch on the floor of the cart, this was not very far distant. As soon as Mr Ninfield told her that they had left the post-road, she bobbed up again, and desired him to lift her down, so that she could ride on the shaft, as he was now doing.

'For it smells of hens on the floor,' she informed him, 'besides being very dirty. Do you think your mother would be vexed if we ate some of these pickled cherries? I am excessively hungry!'

'No,' said Mr Ninfield, for the second time recklessly committing his parent.

9

At the end of half an hour, Mr Theale consulted his watch. He thought that he would give Amanda a little longer, and took himself and his cigarillo out on to the road. There was nothing much to be seen there, and after strolling up and down for a few minutes he went back into the inn, where the landlord met him with the offer of a slice or two of home-cured ham, by way of a nuncheon. It was not yet noon, but Mr Theale had partaken of breakfast at an unwontedly early hour, and the suggestion appealed strongly to him. He disposed of several slices of ham, followed these up with a generous portion of cheese, dug from the centre of a ripe Stilton, and washed down the whole with a large tankard of beer. He then felt fortified against the rigours of travel, and, as Amanda had still not reappeared, requested Mrs Sheet to step upstairs to see how she did.

Mrs Sheet climbed laboriously up the stairs, but soon came back again, to report that the young lady was not in the best bedchamber.

'Not there?' repeated Mr Theale incredulously.

'Happen she's in the coffee-room, sir,' said Mrs Sheet placidly.

'She ain't there,' asserted the landlord. 'Stands to reason she couldn't be, because his honour's been eating a bite of ham there this half hour past. I daresay she stepped out for a breath of fresh air while you was eating your nuncheon, sir.'

Mr Theale felt that this was unlikely, but if Amanda was not in the Red Lion there seemed to be no other solution to the mystery of her disappearance, and he again stepped out on to the road, and looked up and down it. There was no sign of Amanda, but Mr Sheet, who had followed him out of the inn, thought that very likely she had been tempted to explore the spinney that lay just beyond the last straggling cottages of the village. Sir Gareth would not have wasted as much as five minutes in hunting for Amanda through a spinney, but Mr Theale, as yet unacquainted with her remarkable propensity for running away, supposed that it was just possible that she had walked out for a stroll, as he himself had done earlier. No doubt, with the sun beating down upon the road, she had not been able to resist entering the spinney. It was thoughtless of her, and, indeed, decidedly vexatious, but young persons, he believed, were irresistibly drawn by woodland, and had, besides, very little regard for the clock. He walked down the road until he came abreast of the spinney, and shouted. When he had done that several times, he swore, and himself entered the spinney through a gap in the hedge. A track wound through the trees, and he went down it for some distance, shouting Amanda's name at intervals. It was not as hot under the trees as on the sun-scorched road, but quite hot enough to make a full-bodied gentleman, clad in a tightly fitting coat, and with a voluminous neckcloth swathed in intricate folds under his chin, sweat profusely. Mr Theale mopped his face, and realized with annoyance that the high, starched points of his collar had begun to wilt. He also realized, although with some incredulity, that Amanda had given him the slip; but why she had done so, or where she could be hiding, he could not imagine. He retraced his steps, and as he plodded up the dusty road the disquieting suspicion entered his head that she was not, after all, a member of the muslin company, but in truth the innocent child she looked to be. If that were so, her desire to escape from Sir Gareth's clutches (and, indeed, his own) was very understandable. No doubt, thought Mr Theale, virtuously indignant, Sir Gareth had encountered her after her expulsion from her amorous employer's establishment, and had taken dastardly advantage of her friendless, and possibly penniless, condition. Mr Theale's morals were erratic, but he considered that such conduct was beyond the line of what was allowable. It was also ramshackle. Deceiving innocent damsels, as he could have told Sir Gareth from his own experience, invariably led to trouble. They might appear to be alone in the world, but you could depend upon it that as soon as the mischief was done some odiously respectable relative would come to light, which meant the devil to pay, and no pitch hot.

This reflection brought with it certain unwelcome memories, and made Mr Theale feel that to abandon Amanda to her fate, which had at first seemed the most sensible thing to do, would perhaps be unwise. Since she knew his name, it would be prudent to recapture her, for heaven alone knew what sort of account she might spread of the day's events if he was unable to convince her that his interest in her had all the time been purely philanthropic. That could quite easily be done, given the opportunity. The thing to do then, he decided, would be to deliver her into his housekeeper's charge, and to leave it to that capable matron to discover what family she possessed. Of course, if she really had no relations living, and seemed inclined, once her alarm had been soothed, to take a fancy to him–But that was for the future. The immediate task was to find her, and that, in so small a village, ought not to be very difficult.

Mr Theale, arrived once more at the Red Lion, proceeded to grapple with the task. It proved to be fatiguing, fruitless, and extremely embarrassing. Mrs Sheet, on thinking the matter over, had remembered the bandboxes. It was just conceivable, though very unlikely, that Amanda had wandered out to take the air, and had contrived to lose herself; that she had burdened herself with two bandboxes for a country stroll was quite inconceivable, and indicated to Mrs Sheet not a stroll but a flight. And why, demanded Mrs Sheet of her lord, should the pretty dear wish to run away from her lawful uncle?

Mr Sheet scratched his head, and admitted that it was a regular doubler.

'Mark my words, Sheet!' she said. 'He's no more her uncle than what you are!'

'He never said he was her uncle,' Mr Sheet pointed out. 'All he said was that she was a young relative of his.'

'It don't signify. It's my belief he's no relation at all. He's a wolf in sheep's clothing.'

'He don't *look* like one,' said the landlord dubiously.

'He's one of those seducing London beaux,' insisted his wife. 'He's got a wicked look in his eye: I noticed it straight off. Them bandboxes, too! I thought it was queer, a young lady not having what I'd call respectable luggage.'

'The luggage was on the other coach,' argued the landlord.

'Not hers, it wasn't,' replied Mrs Sheet positively. 'She had all her things packed into those two boxes, for I saw them with my own eyes. Lor' bless me, why ever didn't she tell me my fine gentleman was making off with her unlawful? I wish I knew where she was got to!'

But no efforts of hers, or of Mr Theale's, could discover the least trace of Amanda. She had apparently been snatched up into the clouds, for no one in the village had seen her, and no one could recall that any of the vehicles which had passed through it had halted to pick up a passenger. Mr Theale was forced, in the end, to accept the landlord's theory, which was that Amanda had slipped unperceived up the road, and had been picked up beyond the village by some carriage or stagecoach. Mrs Sheet clicked her tongue disapprovingly and shook her head; but since it would never have occurred to her that a young lady of undoubted quality, dressed, too, in the first style of elegance, would have sought refuge in a farm-tumbril, the suspicion that Joe Ninfield might be able to throw light on the mystery never so much as entered her mind. And if it had entered it, she would have dismissed it, because she knew that Joe was a shy, honest lad, who would never dream either of deceiving his godmother, or of taking up with a strange girl who was plainly a lady born.

Mr Theale was forced to continue his journey alone; and by the time he climbed into his carriage again, not only was he exhausted by his exertions, but he was as much ruffled as it was possible for a man of his temperament to be. His inquiries in Bythorne awoke a most unwelcome curiosity in its inhabitants' breasts; and although Mr Sheet continued to treat him with proper deference it was otherwise with the redoubtable mistress of the house, who made no attempt to conceal her unflattering opinion of him. Lacking the inventive genius which characterized Amanda, he was quite unable to offer Mrs Sheet an explanation which carried conviction even to his own ears; and an attempt to depress her presumption merely provoked her into favouring him with her views on so-called gentlemen who went ravening about the country, dressed up as fine as fivepence, the better to deceive the innocent maidens they sought to ruin.

It was some time before his spirits recovered their tone. The wooden countenance of his coachman did nothing to allay the irritation of his nerves. Mr Theale cherished few illusions, and he was well aware that James had not only heard every word of Mrs Sheet's homily, but would lose no time in regaling his fellow servants with the tale of his master's discomfiture. James would have to be sent packing, which was as vexatious as anything that happened during this disastrous day, since no other coachman had ever suited him half as well. Moreover, so many hours had been squandered that it was now doubtful whether he would reach Melton Mowbray that evening. The moon was at the full, but although moonlight would enable him to continue his journey far into the night, it would not save from being spoiled the excellent dinner that would certainly be prepared for his delectation, or prevent his becoming fagged to death. He was much inclined to think that if only he had not directed his valet to drive on he would have spent the night at Oakham, where, at the Crown, he was well known, and could rely upon every attention's being paid to his comfort. But his valet and his baggage were gone past reclaim, and the only piece of luggage he carried with him was his dressing-case.

He was still trying to decide, four miles beyond Thrapston, what would be best to do, when Fate intervened, and settled the question for him: the perch of the carriage broke, and the body fell forward on to the box.

Although considerably shaken, Mr Theale was not much hurt by this accident. Its worst feature was the necessity it put him under of trudging for nearly a mile to the nearest inn. This was at the village of Brigstock, and was

a small posting-house, too unpretentious to have hitherto attracted Mr
Theale's patronage. His intention was to hire a post-chaise there, but so
snug did he find its parlour, so comfortable the winged chair into which the
landlord coaxed him, so excellent the brandy with which he strove to recruit
his strength, and so tempting the dinner that was offered him, that he very
soon abandoned all idea of proceeding any farther on his journey that day.
After the cavalier treatment he had been subjected to by Mrs Sheet, the
solicitude of the host of the Brigstock Arms came as balm to his bruised
spirit. Besides, his natty boots were pinching his feet, and he was anxious to
have them pulled off. The landlord begged him to accept the loan of a pair of
slippers, promised that a night-shirt and cap should be forthcoming, and
assured him that nothing would give his good wife more pleasure than to
launder his shirt and neckcloth for him while he slept. That clinched the
matter: Mr Theale graciously consented to honour the house with his
custom, and stretched out a plump leg to have the boot hauled off. Once rid
of Hessians which were never made for country walking, he began to revive,
and was able to devote a mind undistracted by aching feet to the important
question of what dishes to select for his dinner. Encouraged and assisted by
the landlord, he ordered a delicate yet sustaining meal to be prepared, and
settled down to enjoy the healing properties of cigarillos, a comfortable
chair, and a bottle of brandy.

It was not long before a gentle sense of well-being began to creep over
him; and then, just as he was wondering whether to light another cigarillo,
or to take a nap before his dinner, his peace was shattered by the purposeful
entry into the parlour of Sir Gareth Ludlow.

Mr Theale was astonished. He had to blink his eyes several times before
he could be sure that they had not deceived him. But the newcomer was
certainly Sir Gareth, and, from the look on his face, he seemed to be in a
thundering rage. Mr Theale noticed this fleetingly, but his interest was
claimed by something of greater importance. Sir Gareth's blue coat was
protected from the dust by a driving coat of such exquisite cut that it held
Mr Theale entranced. None knew better than he how seldom a voluminous
coat with several shoulder-capes showed a man off to advantage, or how
often it made him appear to be as broad as he was long. Sir Gareth, of
course, was helped by his height, but the excellence of his figure could not
wholly account for the graceful set of the folds that fell almost to his ankles,
or for the precision with which half a dozen or more capes were graduated
over his shoulders.

'Who,' demanded Mr Theale reverently, 'made that coat for you?'

Sir Gareth had endured a wearing and an exasperating day. It had not
been difficult to trace Mr Theale to Brampton, although a good deal of time
had been wasted in seeking news of him in all the inns with which Huntingdon
was too liberally provided. It had been after Brampton that the trail had
become confused. That he had continued along the road which ran from Ely
to Kettering was established by one of the ostlers at Brampton, but at
Spaldwick, where, after studying his road-book, Sir Gareth expected to
hear that he had stopped for a change, no one seemed to have seen him. That
indicated that he had made Thrapston his first change, for there was no
other posting-house to be found on that stretch of the road. At the next pike,
the keeper rather thought that he had opened to three, or maybe four,
yellow-bodied carriages, one of which, unless he was confusing it with a
black chaise with yellow wheels, had turned northward into the lane which
bisected the post-road. Sir Gareth, after a glance at his map, decided not to

pursue this, for it led only to a string of tiny villages. A mile farther on, another, and rather wider, lane offered the traveller a short cut to Oundle, and here Sir Gareth halted to make inquiries, since it was possible, though unlikely, that Oundle was Mr Theale's destination. He could not discover that any yellow-bodied carriage had turned into the lane that morning, but a sharp-eyed urchin volunteered the information that he had seen just such a turn-out, closely followed by a coach with trunks piled on the roof, driving along towards Thrapston a couple of hours back. There could be no doubt that this was Mr Theale's cortège, and Sir Gareth, after suitably rewarding his informant, drove on, confident that he would glean certain tidings of the fugitives at one of Thrapston's two posting-houses. He swept through Bythorne, never dreaming that the carriage he was chasing was at that moment standing in the yard behind the modest little inn, with its shafts in the air.

Thrapston lay only four miles beyond Bythorne, and was soon reached, but neither at the White Hart nor at the George could Sir Gareth discover any trace of his quarry. Mr Theale was perfectly well known at both these inns, and landlords and ostlers alike stated positively that he had not been seen in the town for several months.

It seemed so incredible that Mr Theale should not have changed horses in Thrapston, that Sir Gareth had wondered if he could have bribed all these persons to cover his tracks. But those whom he questioned were so plainly honest that he dismissed the suspicion, inclining rather to the theory that just as he had chosen to stop in Brampton instead of Huntingdon, so too had Mr Theale preferred to pause for the second change of horses at some house beyond a town where his was a familiar figure. On the road which ran through Corby, Uppingham, and Oakham to Melton Mowbray there appeared to be, on the outskirts of Thrapston, a suburb, or a village, called Islip. Stringent inquiry dragged from the landlord of the George the admission that a change of horses *could* be obtained there—by such gentlemen as were not over-particular.

Meanwhile, Sir Gareth's own pair, carefully though he had nursed them, were spent, and must be stabled. It was not his practice to leave his blood-cattle in strange hands, so when Trotton heard him issuing instructions at the George on the treatment the bays were to receive, and was himself ordered to see them properly bestowed, and realized that he was not to be left in charge of them, he knew that his master's must indeed be a desperate case.

Sir Gareth, driving a pair of job horses, drew a blank at Islip, and another at Lowick. He then struck eastward, reaching, by way of an abominable lane, the road that linked Thrapston to Oundle. Here he was similarly unsuccessful, and broke back to the road that let to Kettering. Nowhere had anyone seen a yellow-bodied carriage, followed by a coach laden with baggage. He drove back to Thrapston, and, convinced in spite of all discouragement that Mr Theale was heading for the neighbourhood of Melton Mowbray, once more drove out of the town in that direction. How Mr Theale's coachman could have contrived, on such a sweltering day, to have pushed his horses beyond Islip he knew not, but that the yellow-bodied carriage had taken the road to Melton Mowbray he was certain. And he was perfectly right, as he knew, as soon as he came upon the derelict, a mile short of Brigstock.

There was considerable cause for satisfaction in this, but Sir Gareth had been driving all day, and he had eaten nothing since his interrupted breakfast at Brancaster. By the time he arrived at the Brigstock Arms he was holding his temper on a tight rein; and when he entered the parlour to find Mr Theale lounging at his ease, with a bottle at his elbow, and his slippered feet on a stool, an impulse surged up within him to pluck that conscienceless hedonist out of his chair with one hand for the simple purpose of sending him to grass with one scientifically placed punch from the other. Indeed, it had already formed itself into a fist when Mr Theale spoke.

Mr Theale's words gave Sir Gareth pause. He stood looking contemptuously down at him, his right hand unclenching as he recognized his condition. It would have been unjust to have described Mr Theale as drunk. It was his boast that no one had seen him deep-cut since the days of his youth, and certainly his capacity for brandy was prodigious. But his potations had cast a pleasant haze over the world, as he saw it, and they had induced in him a mood of immense affability. It was clearly out of the question to deal with him as he deserved. Sir Gareth said curtly: 'I see. Where is Miss Smith?'

'Schultz?' inquired Mr Theale knowledgeably.

'Where—is—Miss—Smith?' repeated Sir Gareth.

'Never heard of her,' said Mr Theale. 'Now I come to think of it, Weston makes for you, doesn't he?'

'Where is Amanda Smith?' demanded Sir Gareth, altering the wording of his question.

'Oh, her!' said Mr Theale. 'Damned if I know!'

'Doing it rather too brown!' Sir Gareth said, with a distinct rasp in his voice. 'Don't try to gammon me you didn't carry her off from Brancaster this morning!'

'Was it only this morning?' said Mr Theale, mildly surprised. 'I daresay you're right, but it seems longer.'

'Where is she?'

'I keep telling you I don't know. Yes, and now I come to think of it, a pretty cool hand you are, my boy! First you bring that fancy-piece to Brancaster, and next, damme if you don't have the effrontery to come smash up to me, trying to get me to give her up to you! If I weren't a very easy-going man I should very likely call you to account. Thought you had more delicacy of principle.'

'Rid your mind of two illusions at least! Amanda is neither my mistress nor a fancy-piece!'

'She isn't? As a matter of fact, I'd got to thinking she might not be. You take the advice of a man who's older than you, my boy, and has seen more of the world than you ever will! If she ain't Haymarket ware, hedge off! I don't say she ain't a tempting armful—well, I thought so myself!—but you may take it from me—!'

'I wish to take nothing from you but that child!' interrupted Sir Gareth. 'Stop cutting shams, and tell me what you've done with her! I warn you, Theale, I'm in no mood to listen to any more of your lies!'

'Now, don't get in a tweak!' recommended Mr Theale. 'It's no use your asking me what I've done with that chit, because I haven't done anything with her. She gave me the bag. I don't deny I wasn't best pleased at the time, but I'm not at all sure now that it ain't a good thing. Shouldn't wonder at all if she'd have put me in the basket. You too. Forget her, my boy! After all, not the thing to offer for poor Hester one moment, and to go chasing after Amanda the next.'

'When did she give you the bag, and where?' demanded Sir Gareth, ignoring this piece of advice.

'I forget the name of the place, but she'd been eating a lot of raspberries.'

'*What?*'

'I don't wonder you're surprised. You'd have been even more surprised if you'd seen the cream she kept pouring over them. I warned her how it would be, but there was no stopping her. Swore she was in high gig, and so she was, then. That didn't last, of course. She began to feel queasy—at least, that's what she said. She may have been bamboozling me, though I shouldn't think anyone could have eaten all those raspberries without becoming as sick as a horse. She sat there, moaning, and saying she must lie down. Got me to stop the carriage in some village or other. I daresay I'll remember its name in a minute: it wasn't far from Thrapston. Anyway, we went into an inn there, and Amanda went off upstairs with the landlady—a devilish woman, that! I give you my word, if I'd known what a shrew she was I wouldn't have set foot inside the place!'

'Never mind the landlady!' said Sir Gareth impatiently.

'Yes, it's all very well for you to say never mind the landlady, but you didn't have to listen to her talking as though you were a regular Queer Nabs, which I'll be damned if I am!'

'The landlady rumbled you, did she? Good! What happened when Amanda went upstairs?'

'I had a glass of bingo. I needed it, I can tell you, because what with being bounced about in the carriage, and thinking every moment Amanda was going to cast up accounts, I was feeling damned queasy myself.'

'For God's sake—!' exclaimed Sir Gareth. 'I don't wish to know what you drank, or what you felt like! What happened to Amanda?'

'How should I know? The landlady said she was going to lie down for half an hour, and that's the last I heard of her, or anyone else, for that matter.'

'Do you mean that she left the inn without anyone's seeing her?'

'That's it,' nodded Mr Theale. 'Tipped me the double, the sly little cat! Queer business: she just disappeared, though the Lord alone knows how she managed it! A pretty fix to have found myself in! Yes, and a pretty breeze she raised, too!'

'Are you telling me,' said Sir Gareth dangerously, 'that you left that child to fend for herself while you drove off at your ease?'

'There wasn't much ease about it,' objected Mr Theale. 'To start with, it's no pleasure to me to jaunter along in a carriage, and to go on with, the damned perch broke, and I had to walk a good mile in tight boots.'

'Did you make *no* effort to find Amanda?'

'Yes, I did, and how the devil I came to do anything so cork-brained—at my time of life, too!—has me lurched!'

'Where did you search for her?'

'All over the village,' replied Mr Theale bitterly. 'You wouldn't think I could be such a gudgeon, would you? Because no sooner did those gapeseeds know that Amanda had given me the bag than they began to think there was something havey-cavey going on. Naturally, I'd told 'em at the inn, when we arrived there, that Amanda was a young relative of mine. Of course, as soon as she slipped off, *that* wouldn't fadge.'

'Where, besides the village, did you search?'

'In a spinney. The landlord thought she might have gone there for a breath of air. Shouted myself hoarse, but to no purpose. That was before I guessed she'd tipped me the double.' He poured some more brandy into his glass, and drank it, and suddenly ejaculated: 'Bythorne! That was the name of the place! I thought it would very likely come back to me.'

'Bythorne! Good God! Then—When you couldn't find her in the village, where next did you go?'

Mr Theale lowered the glass, and looked at him in patient resignation. 'Well, if ever I met such a fellow for asking muttonheaded questions! I came here, of course. Where did you think I went?'

'I thought,' said Sir Gareth, in a deadly voice, 'that you must have searched any road or track that may lead from the village! Was it likely, if Amanda was trying to escape from you, that she would remain in a village which, as I recall, consists of nothing more than two rows of cottages, flanking the post-road?'

'Oh, you did, did you? You must have windmills in your head! Why the devil should I make a cake of myself, scouring the countryside for a girl I can see I'm dashed well rid of?'

'It would be useless to tell you!' Sir Gareth said, an angry pulse throbbing in his cheek. 'But if you were not fifteen years my senior, as fat as a hog, and castaway into the bargain, I would hand you such a supply of home-brewed as would send you to bed for a month!'

'Not if you want to have me for an uncle,' said Mr Theale, quite undismayed. 'Chuffy thing to do. And let me tell you, my boy, that no one's ever seen me castaway since I was up at Oxford. Never more than a trifle up in my hat: ask anyone!' He watched Sir Gareth pick up his hat and gloves, and stride towards the door, and said: '*Now* where are you off to? Ain't you stopping to dinner?'

'I am not!' replied Sir Gareth, over his shoulder. 'Surprising though it may seem to you, I am going to Bythorne!'

The door shut with a snap behind him. Mr Theale shook his head sadly, and picked up the brandy-bottle again.

'Queer in the attic,' he remarked. 'Poor fellow!'

10

Mr Sheet, summoned for the second time in one day to attend to a member of the Quality, was gratified, but a little flustered. He owned a snug property in the Red Lion, but he had never aspired to cater for carriage-people. His cellars were well stocked with beer and spirits, but he could see at a glance that if this tall exquisite in the awe-inspiring driving coat and the gleaming top-boots meant to dine in his house, he would infallibly call for a bottle of wine. Furthermore, notable cook though Mrs Sheet was, it was doubtful if the sort of fancy dishes such an out-and-outer would demand lay within the boundaries of her skill. Then Sir Gareth disclosed his errand, and Mr Sheet became still more flustered. He had naturally discussed with his wife the extraordinary affair of the young lady with the bandboxes, and at great length; and the more he had considered the matter the stronger had become his uneasy conviction that they had not heard the last of it. He did not think that blame could possibly attach to anything he had done, but still he had had a presentiment that there was trouble in store for him.

'Yes, sir,' he said, 'there *was* a young lady come here this morning, with a stout gentleman but she up and ran away, and more than that I can't tell your honour, not if I was to be hung for it!'

He found that the visitor's grey eyes were uncomfortably penetrating, but he met them squarely enough, if a trifle nervously. Sir Gareth said: 'I think I should tell you that I am that young lady's guardian. I have been looking for her all day, with what anxiety you may guess! I haven't found her, but I did find the stout gentleman, and what I learned from him made me hope with all my heart that I should find Miss Smith here.'

The landlord shook his head. 'No, sir. I'm sure, if we'd known—but she never said nothing, and being as the stout gentleman said as she was a relation of his—'

'What's all this?'

The voice came from behind Sir Gareth, and he turned quickly, to find himself confronting a buxom dame in a neat cap, tied under her plump chin in a starched bow, and with her hands folded over her ample stomach. She had a comely, good-humoured face, which yet held much determination, but there was a martial light in her eye, and she was regarding Sir Gareth, if not with hostility, certainly with suspicion.

'The gentleman was asking for that young lady, Mary,' explained Mr Sheet. 'Him being her guardian, by what he tells me.'

'That's as may be,' said Mrs Sheet cryptically.

'I beg you will tell me, ma'am, did you, as I suspect, come to her rescue?' asked Sir Gareth. 'Have you got her here, in safety?'

By this time, she had taken him in thoroughly, from his booted heels to his ordered brown locks. Her gaze came to rest on his face; and after a thoughtful moment her own face relaxed a little. 'No, sir, I have not—which isn't to say that I don't wish I had, for dear knows there was no call for her to run off like she did, if she'd only told me the trouble she was in! And who might you be, if I might make so bold, sir?'

Sir Gareth gave her his card. 'That is my name, and my direction, ma'am.'

She studied the card, and then favoured him with another long stare. 'And by what you was saying to Sheet, sir, you're the young lady's guardian?'

'I am,' replied Sir Gareth, reflecting that this at least was true, even though he was self-appointed. A sudden and rueful smile flashed in his eyes. 'For my sins! I will be perfectly frank with you, ma'am, and tell you that Miss Smith is the most wilful little monkey it has ever been my ill-fortune to have to do with. Her latest exploit is to run away from the seminary, where she was a parlour-boarder. I imagine I need not tell you that I am in considerable anxiety about her. If you can assist me to find her, I shall be very much in your debt.'

Mr Sheet, watching his wife with some misgiving, was relieved to see that she had apparently decided in the gentleman's favour. The belligerent expression had vanished, and it was with cordiality that she replied, ''Deed, and I wish I could, sir, for such a sweet, pretty young creature I never did see! But it's true, what Sheet was saying to you: she never said a word to either of us, but slipped off unbeknownst. Run away from school, had she? But however did she come to take up with that dressed-up old fidget? Sheet got the notion into his head he was her uncle, but that I'll be bound he's not!'

'No—the dancing-master!' said Sir Gareth, with a certain vicious satisfaction.

Her jaw dropped. 'What, and run off with one of the young ladies at the school? Well, I never did in all my life!'

'Miss Smith,' said Sir Gareth, rivalling Amanda in inventiveness, 'is a considerable heiress. By what means that fellow inserted himself into her good graces, I know not, but there can be little doubt that his object was to possess himself of her fortune. She is not yet seventeen, but had he succeeded in reaching Gretna Green with her, and making her his wife, what could I have done?'

Her eyes were as round as crown-pieces, but she nodded her head understandingly. 'Ay, a pretty kettle of fish that would have been, sir! Well, I never liked him, not from the start, and what has me in a puzzle is what made her take a fancy to him! Why, he's old enough to be her grandpa, and as fat as a flawn besides!'

'I am very sure she had no fancy for him at all,' said Sir Gareth. 'If I know her, she encouraged his pretensions only to win his aid in escaping from the school! Once she believed herself to be beyond the reach of–er–Miss Hitchin, she wouldn't hesitate to give him the bag. For that at least I may be thankful! But where is she?'

'Ah, that's the question!' said Mr Sheet profoundly.

'Well, surely to goodness, sir, she wouldn't run away without she had some place to go!' exclaimed Mrs Sheet. 'Hasn't she got any relations, or maybe some friends that would be glad to have her?'

'She's an orphan. She would certainly not seek refuge with any relation, for she knows very well that they would instantly tell me where she was. Nor do I know of any of her acquaintances who would do anything so improper as to conceal her whereabouts from me. What I suspect is that she means to hire herself out as an abigail, or something equally foolish.'

'Whatever for, sir?' gasped Mrs Sheet. 'A young lady like her? Good gracious, she must be fair desperate to think of such a thing! Seems to me, begging your pardon, sir, that this school you've sent her to must be a very bad sort of a place!'

'Oh, no, on the contrary!' he replied. 'Pray don't imagine, ma'am, that Miss Smith has been unkindly treated there, or, in fact, anywhere! The mischief is that she has been far too much indulged. No one but myself has ever thwarted her, and, since she is extremely highspirited, she will go to any lengths to get her own way. This exploit, I have no doubt at all, is an attempt to force me to take her away from school, and to allow her to be brought out into the world before she is seventeen.'

'Oh, what a naughty girl!' Mrs Sheet said, shocked. 'Why, she might run into all sorts of trouble, sir!'

'Exactly so! You know that, and so do I know it, but she has no more notion of it than a kitten. It's imperative I should find her before she discovers it.'

She nodded. 'Yes, indeed! Oh, dear, if I'd had only an inkling how it was—! The idea of a lovely young thing like she is, wandering about by herself, and nothing but them two bandboxes to call her own! But where she can have got to I know no more than you, sir. She didn't hide herself in the village, that's certain, for there's not a soul has seen her, and I don't see how she could have walked down the street without *someone* must have caught sight of her. We did wonder if she got taken up in someone's carriage, but I disremember that we had so much as a gig pull up here while she was in the house. And as for the stage, Mrs Bude, which keeps the chandler's shop, put a parcel on to it when it came through Bythorne at noon, and she's certain sure there was no young lady got into it.'

Sir Gareth spread open his map, and laid it on the table. 'I doubt very much whether she would have tried to escape by way of the post-road. She must have known she would be pursued, and the first thing she would do would be to get as far away from it as possible. Could she have slipped out of this house by a back way?'

'She *could*,' Mrs Sheet replied doubtfully. 'There's a door leading into the yard, but there was the coachman, and a lad, that brought some chickens and potatoes, and I should have thought they'd have been bound to see her.'

'The coachman come into the tap, soon as he'd stabled the horses,' interposed Mr Sheet.

'Yes, but Joe didn't!' she objected.

'Happen Joe did see her. He wouldn't think anything of it, not Joe! Likely he wouldn't hardly have noticed her.'

'I daresay she may have waited until his back was turned,' said Sir Gareth. 'Can the lane that crosses the post-road be reached by way of the fields behind this house?'

'Well, you could get to it that way, sir, but it's rough walking, and how would the young lady have known there was a lane?'

'She might not, but if she was on the look-out for a way of escape she would have seen that lane, just before the carriage reached Bythorne. As I remember, there is a signpost, pointing to Catworth and Kimbolton.' He laid his finger on the map. 'Catworth, I take it, is no more than a small village. Has it an inn?—No, too near the post-road: she wouldn't try to establish herself there. Kimbolton, then. Yes, I think that must be my first goal.' He folded up the map again, and straightened himself. He saw that Mrs Sheet was regarding him wonderingly, and smiled. 'I can only go by guess, you know, and this seems to me the likeliest chance.'

'But it's all of seven miles to Kimbolton, sir!' expostulated Mrs Sheet. 'Surely she wouldn't trudge all that way, carrying them handboxes?'

He thrust the map into his pocket, and picked up his hat. 'Very likely not. From my knowledge of her, I should imagine that if she saw any kind of vehicle on the road she coaxed its driver into taking her up. And I hope to God she fell into honest hands!'

He moved towards the door, but before he reached it the aperture was filled by a burly figure, in gaiters and a frieze coat, at sight of whom Mrs Sheet uttered a pleasant exclamation. 'Ned! The very person I was wishful to see! Do you wait a moment, sir, if you please! Come you in, Ned, and answer me this! When he got home, did Joe say anything to you, or Jane, about a young lady which we've got a notion he maybe saw in our yard when he was unloading the potatoes from the cart?'

The burly individual, rather bashfully pulling his forelock to Sir Gareth, replied, in a deep, slow voice: 'Ay, he did that. Leastways, in a manner of speaking, he did. Which is what brings me here, because Jane ain't by no means easy in her mind, and what she says is, if anyone knows the rights of it, it'll be Mary.'

'Sir Gareth, sir, this is Ned Ninfield, which is Joe's father, Joe being the lad I told you about,' said Mrs Sheet, performing a rapid introduction. 'And this gentleman, Ned, is the young lady's guardian, and he's looking for her all over, she having run away from school.'

Mr Ninfield's ruminative gaze travelled to Sir Gareth's face, and became fixed there, while he apparently revolved a thought in his mind.

'Did your son see the way she went?' asked Sir Gareth.

This question seemed to strike Mr Ninfield as being exquisitely humorous. A grin spread over his face, and he gave a chuckle. 'Ay! In a manner of speaking, he did. She never said nothing about any school, though.'

'Lor', Ned!' cried Mrs Sheet, in sharp suspicion. 'You're never going to tell me you've seen her too? Where is she?'

He jerked a thumb over his shoulder, saying laconically: 'Whitethorn.'

'*Whitethorn?*' she gasped. 'However did she come to get there?'

He began to chuckle again. 'In my cart! Joe brought her. Proper moonstruck, he was.'

'Ned Ninfield!' she exploded. 'You mean to tell me Joe didn't know no better than to offer a young lady like she is a ride in that dirty cart of yours?'

'Seems it was her as was set on it, not him. Told him to pick her up, and pop her into the cart where no one wouldn't see her. Which he done. And I don't know as I blame him,' added Mr Ninfield thoughtfully. 'Not altogether, I don't.'

'I don't believe it!' Mrs Sheet declared.

'Oh, yes!' Sir Gareth interposed, a good deal amused. 'Nothing, in fact, is more likely! Not so long ago, she hid herself in a carrier's cart. I expect she enjoyed the ride.'

'She did that, your honour,' corroborated Mr Ninfield. 'She and my Joe ate up the better part of a jar of pickled cherries between 'em, what's more. Sticky! Lor', you ought to have seen 'em!'

'The cherries I sent Jane special!' ejaculated Mrs Sheet.

Sir Gareth laughed. 'I offer you my apologies, ma'am: I told you she was a little monkey!' He turned, stretching out his hand to the farmer. 'Mr Ninfield, I'm very much in your debt—and more thankful than I can describe to you that my ward had the good fortune to fall in with your son. By the way, I do hope to God you didn't tell her you were coming here to make inquiries about her? If you did, she will certainly have fled from the house before I can reach it.'

'No, sir, she don't know nothing about it,' Mr Ninfield replied, rather coyly wiping his hand on his breeches before grasping Sir Gareth's. 'But the thing is—well, it's like this, sir! I'm sure I'm not wishful to give offence, but—you wouldn't be the gentleman as is father to a young lady as had Miss Amanda to wait on her, would you?'

'I would not!' said Sir Gareth, recognizing Amanda's favourite story. 'I collect you mean the gentleman who made such improper advances to her that his sister—most unjustly, one feels—turned her out of the house without a moment's warning. I haven't a daughter, and I am not even married, much less a widower. Nor has Miss Amanda ever been a waiting-woman. She got the notion out of an old novel.'

'Well, I'm bound to say you didn't look to me like you could be him,' said Mr Ninfield. 'Downright wicked, that's what I thought, but my good lady, she wouldn't have it. She says to me private that she'd go bail Miss was telling us a lot of faradiddles, because nothing wouldn't make her credit that Miss was an abigail, nor ever had been. So it was a school she ran away from, was it, sir? Well, *that* won't surprise the wife, though she did think it was p'raps her home she run away from: likely, because someone had crossed her. Powerful hot at hand, I'd say—meaning no disrespect!'

'You're very right!' Sir Gareth said. 'Under what disguise does she hope to remain in your house, by the way? Has she offered herself to your wife as a chambermaid?'

'No, sir,' grinned Mr Ninfield. 'When last I see her, she was making Joe teach her how to milk the cows, and just about as happy as a grig.'

'Ah, going to be a dairymaid, is she?' said Sir Gareth cheerfully. An idea that had peeped into his mind now began to take hopeful possession of it. He looked at Mr Ninfield consideringly, and said, after a moment: 'Is she a troublesome charge? Do you think Mrs Ninfield would be prepared to keep her as a boarder for a few days?'

'*Keep* her, sir?' repeated Mr Ninfield, staring at him.

'The case, you see, is this,' said Sir Gareth. 'Either I must take her back to school, or I must make some other arrangement for her. Well, I have been most earnestly requested *not* to take her back to the school, which puts me in something of a fix, for I can't hire a governess for her at a moment's notice. I must convey her to my sister's house in town, and, frankly, I am very sure she won't want to go with me there. Nor, I must add, am I anxious to saddle my sister with such a charge. It occurs to me that if she is happy in your wife's care it would perhaps be as well to leave her there until I am able to provide for her suitably. I daresay, if she did not know that I was aware of her direction, she would be glad to stay with you, and would no doubt enjoy herself very much, milking cows, and collecting eggs, and in general fancying herself to be very useful.'

'I'll be bound she would, the pretty dear!' said Mrs Sheet approvingly. 'A very good notion, I call it, and just what will put dancing-masters and such out of her head.'

But Mr Ninfield dashed Sir Gareth's hopes. 'Well, sir,' he said apologetically, 'I'm sure I'd be pleased to have her, and it goes against the shins with me to act disobliging, but it's Joe, you see. She's got him so as he don't know whether he's on his head or his heels. He don't take his eyes off her, and when he told his ma that Miss was like a princess out of one of them fairy stories, Mrs Ninfield she said to me, private, that we must find out quick where she comes from before Joe gets ideas into his head which is above his station. Because it wouldn't do, sir.'

'No, it wouldn't do,' agreed Sir Gareth, relinquishing his scheme with a pang. 'If that is how the land lies, of course I must take her away immediately. Where is your farm?'

'It's a matter of three miles from here, sir, but it ain't a very good road. You go up the post-road, about half a mile, and there's a lane turns off to your left. You follow that past Keyston, until you see a rough track, left again. You go down that for a mile and a half, maybe a bit more, like as if you was heading for Catworth, and just afore you come to a sharp bend you'll see Whitethorn. You can't miss it.'

'Good gracious, Ned, where have your wits gone begging?' interrupted Mrs Sheet impatiently. 'Just you get back into your gig, and lead the gentleman!'

'Thank you, I wish you will!' Sir Gareth said. 'In the direction of Catworth, is it? Tell me, can I, without too much difficulty, reach Kimbolton from Whitethorn?'

'Yes, sir, easy, you can. All you've to do is to go on down the lane till you come to the post-road—the one as runs south of this one, between Wellingborough and Cambridge. Then you swing left-handed into it, and Kimbolton's about five miles on.'

'Excellent! I'll rack up there for the night, and carry the child off to London by post-chaise tomorrow—if she doesn't contrive to give me the slip from the posting-house there! But before we set out you must join me in a glass. Ma'am, what may I have the pleasure of desiring your husband to serve you with?'

'Well, I'm sure, sir!' said Mrs Sheet, slightly overcome. 'Well, I don't hardly like to!'

However, succumbing to persuasion, she consented to drink a small glass of port. The landlord then drew three pots of his own home-brewed; and Sir Gareth, basely plotting Amanda's undoing, said thoughtfully: 'Now, I wonder what trick that abominable child will play on me next? She'll put up a spirited fight, that's certain! The last time she was in mischief she told a complete stranger that I was abducting her. I only wish I may not be in her black books for months for having disclosed that she's still a schoolgirl. Nothing enrages her more!'

Mrs Sheet said wisely that girls of her age were always wishing to be thought quite grown-up; and Mr Ninfield, hugely tickled by the thought of Sir Gareth's figuring as an abductor, confessed that he and his good lady had suspected from the start that Miss was cutting a sham.

'Ah, well, of course she didn't ought to tell such faradiddles,' said Mrs Sheet, 'but it's only play-acting, like children do, when they start in to be Dick Turpin, or Robin Hood.'

'Exactly so,' nodded Sir Gareth. 'But it is really time she grew out of it. Unfortunately, she is still at the stage when she pines for adventure. As far as I can discover, she thinks it a dead bore to be a schoolgirl, and so is for ever pretending that she is someone else. I could wish that some of her stories were less outrageous.'

Everyone agreed that it was very embarrassing for him, and the symposium presently ended on a note of great cordiality. Sir Gareth had acquired three firm friends and supporters who were as one in thinking him the finest gentleman of their acquaintance, not high in the instep, but, as Mr Sheet later expressed it, a real top-of-the-trees, slap up to the echo.

Trotton, upon hearing that the end of the hunt was in sight, was extremely thankful. It had appeared to him that his besotted master was prepared to continue driving throughout the night, and he, for one, had had enough of it. Moreover, he had been even more reluctant than Sir Gareth to leave the bays in a strange stable, having taken a dislike to the head ostler, an unfortunate circumstance which led to his becoming more and more convinced that those peerless horses would be subjected to the worst of bad treatment. He now learned that it would be his task to drive them back to London by easy stages, and grew instantly more cheerful.

'You will have to come with me to Kimbolton,' Sir Gareth said, drawing on his gloves. 'I shall be escorting the young lady to my sister's house tomorrow, and shall hire a chaise for the purpose. You may then drive the curricle back to Thrapston, settle my account there for the hire of these tits, and bring the bays up to London after me. I shan't look for you to arrive for at least two days, so take care you don't press 'em!'

'No, sir,' said Trotton, in a carefully expressionless voice. 'I wouldn't be wishful to do so—not in this hot weather!'

'Because,' said Sir Gareth, as though he had not heard, but with the glimmer of an appreciative smile in his eyes, 'I have already worked 'em far harder than I ought.'

'Just so, sir!' said his henchman, grinning at him.

It did not take long to accomplish the journey to Whitethorn Farm. Leaving Trotton with the curricle, Sir Gareth was ushered by Mr Ninfield into the rambling old house. Dusk was beginning by this time to shadow the landscape, and in the large, flagged kitchen the lamp had been kindled. Its mellow light fell on Amanda, on the floor, and playing with a litter of kittens. Seated in a windsor chair, with his hands clasped between his knees, was a stalwart youth, watching her with a rapt and slightly idiotic expression on his sunburnt countenance; and keeping a wary eye on both, while she vigorously ironed one of her husband's shirts, was a matron of formidable aspect.

Amanda glanced up casually, as the door opened, but when she saw who had entered the kitchen she stiffened, and exclaimed: '*You!* No! *No!*'

Young Mr Ninfield, although not quick-witted, took only a very few seconds to realize that here, in the person of this bang-up nonesuch, was Amanda's persecutor. He got up, clenching his fists, and glaring at Sir Gareth.

He was perfectly ready, and even anxious, to do battle, but Sir Gareth took the wind out of his sails, by first nodding at Amanda, and saying amiably: 'Good evening, Amanda!' and then coming towards him, with his hand held out. 'You must be Joe Ninfield,' he said. 'I have to thank you for taking such excellent care of my ward. You are a very good fellow!'

'It's the young lady's guardian, Jane,' Mr Ninfield informed his wife, in a penetrating aside.

'It is *not!*' Amanda declared passionately. 'He is trying to abduct me!'

Joe, who had numbly allowed Sir Gareth to grasp his hand, turned his bemused gaze upon her, seeking guidance. 'Throw him out!' ordered Amanda, a sandy kitten clasped to her breast in a very touching way.

'You'll do no such thing, Joe!' said his mother sharply. 'Now, sir! P'raps you'll be so good as to explain what this means!'

'All's right, Jane,' Mr Ninfield said, chuckling. 'It's like you thought, only that it was school Miss ran off from.'

'I didn't!' cried Amanda, her face scarlet with rage. 'And he's not my guardian! I don't even *know* him! He is an abominable person!'

'Of course I am!' said Sir Gareth soothingly. 'Though how you know that, when you are not even acquainted with me, I can't imagine!' He smiled at Mrs Ninfield, and said in his charming way: 'I do hope, ma'am, that she has not been troublesome to you? I can't thank you enough for your kindness to her!'

Under Amanda's baffled and infuriated gaze, Mrs Ninfield dropped a curtsy, stammering: 'No, no! Oh, no, indeed sir!'

Sir Gareth glanced down at Amanda. 'Come, my child, get up from the floor!' he said, in a voice of kindly authority. 'Where is your hat? I never abduct ladies without their hats, so put it on, and your cloak too!'

Amanda obeyed the first of these commands, largely because she found herself at a disadvantage when sitting at his feet. She could see that the tone he had chosen to adopt had had its inevitable effect, even upon her moon-struck admirer, but she made a desperate bid for freedom. Staring up into his amused eyes, she said: 'Very well! If you are my guardian, *who am I?*'

'An orphan, cast upon the world without a penny,' he replied promptly. 'You have lately been employed by a young lady, whose widowed father—a most reprehensible person, I fear—made such improper advances to you, that—'

'Oh, how I much hate you!' she cried, flushing with mortification, and stamping her foot. 'How dare you stand there telling such lies?'

'Well, but, missie, it's what you told us yourself!' said Mr Ninfield, hugely entertained.

'Yes, but that was because—well, that was just make-believe! *He* knows it isn't true! And it isn't true that he is my guardian, or that I ran away from school, or *anything*!'

Mrs Ninfield drew a long breath. 'Sir, *are* you her guardian, or are you not?' she demanded.

'No,' he replied, his voice grave, but his eyes dancing. 'I am an abductor. I met her only yesterday, and that by chance, snatched her up into my curricle, and bore her off in spite of all her protests to a gloomy mansion in the heart of the country. I need scarcely tell you that she contrived to make her escape from the mansion while I slept. However, it takes a good deal to daunt a thoroughgoing villain, so you won't be surprised that here I am, having hunted her down remorselessly. I am now about to carry her off to my castle. This, by the way, is perched on a precipitous rock, and, besides being in an uncomfortable state of neglect and decay, is inhabited only by ghosts and sinister retainers of mine. From this fortress, after undergoing a number of extremely alarming adventures, she will, I have little doubt, be rescued by a noble youth of handsome though poverty-stricken aspect. I expect he will kill me, after which it will be found that he is the wronged heir to a vast property—probably mine—and all will end happily.'

'Now, sir—!' protested Mrs Ninfield, trying not to laugh. 'Give over your nonsense, do!'

Joe, having listened with painstaking concentration to the programme laid down for Amanda's future entertainment, once more clenched his large fists, and uttered, slowly, but with determination: 'I won't have her put in no castle.'

'Don't be a gaby!' said his mother. 'Can't you see the gentleman's only making game of her?'

'I won't have him make game of her neither,' said Joe stubbornly.

'Please to pay no heed, sir!' begged Mrs Ninfield. 'Now, that's enough, Joseph! Do you want the gentleman to think you're no better than a knock-in-the-cradle, which I'll be bound he does?'

'Not at all! I think he's a splendid fellow,' said Sir Gareth. 'Don't worry, Joe! I was only funning.'

'I don't want you to take her anywhere,' Joe muttered. 'I'd like her to stay here, fine I would.'

'Yes, and so would I have liked to stay here!' said Amanda warmly. 'I never enjoyed anything half as much, particularly feeding all those droll little pigs, and these lovely kittens, but everything is spoilt now that Sir Gareth knows where I am, and it would be of no use staying here any more.' Her voice trembled, and a tear sparkled on the end of her long lashes. She kissed the sandy kitten, and reluctantly set it down on the floor, giving such a pathetic sniff that Mr Ninfield, a tender-hearted man, said uncomfortably: 'Don't you take on, missie! P'raps, if my missis is agreeable—' He stopped, as he caught his wife's eye, and coughed in some embarrassment.

'Cheer up, my child!' Sir Gareth said. 'This is no time for tears! You must instantly set about the task of thinking how best to revenge yourself on me.'

She cast him a darkling look, but said nothing. Inspiration came to Joe, his withers unbearably wrung by her distress. Swooping upon the sandy kitten, he picked it up by the scruff of its neck, and held it out to Amanda. 'You take him!' he said gruffly.

Nothing could have succeeded better in diverting her mind at that moment. Her face brightened; she clasped the kitten again, exclaiming: '*Oh!*

How excessively kind of you! I am *very* much obliged to you! Only—' Her eyes turned apprehensively towards her hostess, and she said prettily: 'Perhaps it is your kitten, and you would not wish me to take it away?'

'I'm sure you're very welcome to it, miss, but I'll be bound the gentleman won't want to be worried by a kitten on the journey,' Mrs Ninfield responded.

'I am going to take this dear little kitten with me,' said Amanda, addressing herself to Sir Gareth, with immense dignity, and a challenge in her eye.

'Do!' he said cordially, tickling the kitten's ear. 'What shall you call it?'

She considered the matter. 'Well, perhaps Honey, because of his colour, or—' She broke off, as her gaze alighted on the kitten's donor. 'No, I shan't!' she said, bestowing a brilliant smile upon him. 'I shall call him Joseph, after *you*, and that will remind me of feeding the pigs, and learning to milk the cow!'

At these beautiful words, Joe was so overcome that he grew beetroot-red, and lost all power of speech, merely swallowing convulsively, and grinning in a way that made his fond mother itch to box his ears. Mr Ninfield went off, in a practical spirit, to find a covered basket; and in a very short time Sir Gareth, silently invoking a powerful blessing on the head of one who had, however unwittingly, averted the threat of a disagreeable scene, was handing his charge up into the curricle, and delivering into her hands a basket in which one small kitten indignantly vociferated his disapproval of the change in his circumstances.

II

It was not to be expected that Amanda's pleasure in having acquired a new pet would for long save Sir Gareth from recrimination. She had never been wholly diverted, but had ceased from further argument because she had perceived how deftly he was cutting the ground from beneath her inexperienced feet. It made her very angry, but she could not help admiring, secretly, a strategy which she recognized to be masterly; nor, in spite of a strengthened determination to put him utterly to rout, did she think the worse of him for having got the better of her. But that she was certainly not going to tell him, far preferring to relieve her feelings by delivering herself of a comprehensive indictment of his character. To this, Trotton, perched up behind her, listened in shocked and wondering silence. What Sir Gareth could see in such a young termagant to make him fall madly in love Trotton could not imagine, but he did not for an instant doubt that his master was clean besotted.

'You are meddlesome, and tyrannical, and untruthful, and, which is worse than all, *treacherous!*' scolded Amanda.

'Not treacherous!' protested Sir Gareth. 'I promise you, I told none of those people the true story.'

'I am quite astonished that you didn't, for I daresay you don't care a button about breaking your solemn word to people!'

'I didn't think they would believe me,' explained Sir Gareth.

'And above everything you are shameless!' said Amanda indignantly.

'No, not quite, because, I assure you, I am shocked at my own mendacity.'

'You are?' she exclaimed, turning her head to study his profile.

'Profoundly! I never knew I had it in me to tell so many bouncers.'

'Well, you *did*–brazenly, too!'

'Yes, and you don't know the half of it. When I think of the Banbury story I told at the Red Lion, I know that I am sunk beyond reproach.'

This ruse succeeded. 'What was it?' Amanda demanded, much interested.

'Why, I said that you were a great heiress, and had eloped with the dancing-master, who wanted to marry you for the sake of your fortune.'

'Did you *indeed* say that?' Amanda asked, awed.

'Yes–brazenly!'

'Well, it doesn't make your conduct any better, and I am *very* angry with you, but I must say I do think it was a splendid story!' Amanda said, rather enviously. 'Particularly the bit about the dancing-master!'

'Yes, I liked that bit, too,' owned Sir Gareth. 'Did you really eat enough raspberries to make you sick?'

'Well, I ate a great many raspberries, but I wasn't sick. That was only pretending, because I couldn't think of any other way to be rid of that horrid old man. I wonder what became of him?'

'An evil fate. After searching for you in a wood until he was exhausted, he got a tremendous scold from Mrs Sheet, and then, to crown his day, the perch of his carriage broke, and he was obliged to walk a mile in tight boots to the nearest inn.'

She gave a giggle, but said: 'Have you seen him, then?'

'I have.'

'What happened!' she asked, filled with pleasurable anticipation.

'He told me where he had lost you, and I drove back to Bythorne immediately.'

'Is *that* all?' she said, disappointed. 'I quite thought that you would have challenged him to a duel!'

'Yes, I know it was very poor-spirited of me,' he agreed, 'but really I think he has perhaps been punished enough. I fancy he can't have enjoyed the drive in your company.'

'No, and I didn't enjoy it either!' said Amanda. 'He tried to make love to me!'

'I should forget about him, if I were you, for he is certainly not worth remembering. But it is not wise, my child, to let strangers make off with you, however old and respectable they may seem to you.'

'*Well!*' she cried. 'When you have been *forcing* me to go with you ever since I met you, which I wish I never had, because although you are quite old, it is very plain to me that you are not in the least respectable, but, on the contrary, a deceiving person, and quite as odious as Mr Theale!'

He laughed. 'A home thrust, Amanda!' he acknowledged. 'But at least I am not as fat as Mr Theale, however odious!'

'No,' she conceded, 'but you took much worse advantage of me!'

'Did I indeed?'

'Yes, you did! For when you told Mrs Ninfield those lies about me, you made it seem as though they were true, and then, when you did tell the truth, you made it sound like a lie! It was–it was the shabbiest trick to play on me!'

He was amused, but he said: 'I know it was. Indeed, most unhandsome of me, and I do most sincerely feel for you. It must be very disagreeable to be paid back in your own coin. And the dreadful thing is that I believe it is rapidly becoming a habit with me. I have already thought of another very truthful-sounding lie to tell about you, if you insist on denying that you are my ward.'

'I think you are abominable!' she said hotly. 'And if you do not instantly tell me where we are going I shall jump out of your horrid carriage, and very likely break my leg! *Then* you will be sorry!'

'Well, of course, if might be a little tiresome to be obliged to convey you to London with your leg in a splint, but on the other hand you wouldn't be able to run away from me again, would you?'

'London?' she ejaculated, ignoring the rest.

'Yes, London. We are going to spend the night at Kimbolton, however.'

'No! No! I won't go with you!'

He caught the note of panic, and said at once: 'I am taking you to my sister's house, so don't be a goose, Amanda!'

The panic subsided, but she reiterated her determination not to go with him, and was not in the least reconciled to her fate when he told her that she would meet his nephews and nieces there. She had a tolerably clear picture of all that would happen. Mrs Wetherby would treat her as though she were a naughty child; she would be relegated to the schoolroom, where the governess would have orders never to let her out of her sight; Sir Gareth would discover her name from Neil; and she would be taken ignominiously home, having failed either to achieve her object, or to prove to her grandfather that she was an eminently grown-up and capable woman.

The blackest depression descended upon her spirits. Sir Gareth was not going to give her the smallest opportunity to escape from him a second time; and even if he did, her experiences had taught her it was of very little avail to escape if one had no certain goal to make for. She felt defeated, tired, and very resentful; and for the remainder of the way refused even to open her lips.

There was only one posting-house in Kimbolton, and that a small and old-fashioned building. It did not hold out much promise of any extraordinary degree of comfort, but it possessed one feature which instantly recommended it to Sir Gareth. As he drew up before it, and ran a critical eye over it, he saw that its windows were all small casements. This circumstance solved for him a problem which had been exercising his mind for several miles. Sir Gareth had not forgotten the story of the elm tree.

The landlord, recognizing at a glance the quality of his unexpected guests, was all compliance and civility; and if at first he thought that it was odd conduct on the part of so grand a gentleman as Sir Gareth to carry his ward on a journey in an open carriage, and without her maid, he very soon banished any unworthy suspicions from his mind. There was little of the lover to be detected in Sir Gareth's demeanour, and as for the young lady, she seemed to be in a fit of the sullens.

Amanda made no attempt to deny that she was Sir Gareth's ward. However innocent she might be of the world's ways, she was well aware of the impropriety of her situation, having been carefully instructed in the rules governing the social conduct of young ladies. It had been permissible, though a trifle dashing, to drive with Sir Gareth in an open curricle; driving with Mr Theale in a closed carriage Aunt Adelaide would have stigmatized as fast; while putting up at an inn in the company of a gentleman totally unrelated to her was conduct reprehensible enough to put her beyond the pale. Amanda accepted this without question, but was quite unembarrassed by her predicament. None of the vague feelings of alarm which had attacked her in Mr Theale's carriage assailed her; and it did not for an instant occur to her that Sir Gareth, odious though he might be, was not entirely to be trusted. On first encountering him, she had been astonished to learn that so charming and personable a man could be an uncle; she would scarcely have been surprised now to have discovered that he was a great-uncle; and felt no more gêne in his company than if he had been her grandfather. However, she knew that her private belief that, so far from damaging her reputation, his presence was investing her adventure with a depressing respectability, would not be shared by the vulgar, so she not only held her peace when he spoke to the landlord of his ward, but seized the first opportunity that offered of pointing out to him the gross impropriety of his behaviour. Looking the picture of outraged virtue, she announced, with relish, that she was now ruined. Sir Gareth replied that she was forgetting Joseph, and recommended her, instead of talking nonsense, to restrain her chaperon from sharpening his tiny claws on the polished leg of a chair.

After such a callous piece of flippancy as this, it was only to be expected that when Amanda accompanied her protector downstairs to the coffee-room she should do so with all the air of a Christian martyr.

The landlord had been profuse in apologies for his inability to offer Sir Gareth a private parlour. The only one the White Lion possessed was occupied already by an elderly gentleman afflicted with gout, and although the landlord plainly considered Sir Gareth more worthy of it, he doubted whether the gouty gentleman would share this view.

But Sir Gareth, in spite of having thrown a judicious damper over Amanda's sudden access of maidenly modesty, was a great deal more aware of the perils of her situation than she, and he had no desire to add to the irregularity of this journey by dining with her in a private parlour. The landlord, relieved to find him so accommodating, assured him that every attention would be paid to his comfort, and added that since the only other visitor to the inn was one very quiet young gentleman he need not fear that his ward would be exposed to noisy company.

The coffee-room was a pleasant, low-pitched apartment, furnished with one long table, a quantity of chairs, and a massive sideboard. The window-embrasure was filled by a cushioned seat, and this, when Sir Gareth and Amanda entered the room, was occupied by the quiet young gentleman, who was reading a book in the fading daylight. He did not raise his eyes from this immediately, but upon Sir Gareth's desiring the waiter to bring him a glass of sherry, he looked up, and, his gaze falling upon Amanda, became apparently transfixed.

'And some lemonade for the lady,' added Sir Gareth unthinkingly.

He was speedily brought to realize that he had been guilty of gross folly. Amanda might be forced to acknowledge him as her guardian, but she was not going to submit to such arbitrary treatment as this. 'Thank you, I don't care for lemonade,' she said. 'I will take a glass of sherry.'

Sir Gareth's lips twitched. He met the waiter's understanding eye, and said briefly: 'Ratafia.'

Amanda, having by this time discovered the presence of the quiet young gentleman, thought it prudent to refrain from further argument, and relapsed into dejection. The quiet young gentleman, his book forgotten, continued to gaze at her exquisite profile, in his own face an expression of awed admiration.

Sir Gareth, already aware of his presence, was thus afforded the opportunity to study him at leisure. He would not ordinarily have felt it necessary to pay much heed to a chance-met traveller, but his short acquaintance with Amanda had taught him that that disastrously confiding damsel would not hesitate to turn any promising stranger to good account.

But what he saw satisfied him. The quiet young gentleman, whom he judged to be perhaps eighteen or nineteen years of age, was a slender youth, with a damask cheek, a sensitive mouth, and a pair of rather dreamy grey eyes. He was attired in a riding-dress whose cut, without aspiring to the heights achieved by Weston, or Schultz, or Schweitzer and Davidson, advertised the skill of a reliable provincial tailor. Tentative ambition was betrayed by a waistcoat of such bold design as might be relied upon to app al to the taste of Oxford or Cambridge collegiates; and the intricate, if not entirely felicitous, arrangement of his neckcloth exactly resembled the efforts of Mr Leigh Wetherby to copy the various styles affected by his Corinthian uncle.

As though conscious of Sir Gareth's scrutiny, he withdrew his rapt gaze from Amanda, and glanced towards him, blushing slightly as he realized that he had been under observation. Sir Gareth smiled at him, and addressed some commonplace to him. He replied with a little stammer of shyness, but in a cultured voice which confirmed Sir Gareth's estimate of his condition. An agreeable, well-mannered boy, of good breeding but little worldly experience, decided Sir Gareth. Too young to appear to Amanda in the light of a potential rescuer, but he might serve to make her forget her injuries, he thought. In any event, since he would shortly be sitting down to table with them, he could not be ignored.

Within a very few minutes, the young gentleman, his reading abandoned, had joined his fellow guests beside the empty fireplace in the middle of the room, and was chatting easily with his new acquaintance. Sir Gareth had seemed to him at first rather awe-inspiring, clearly a man of fashion, possibly (if his highly polished top-boots were anything to go by) a top-sawyer, but he soon found that he was not at all proud, but, on the contrary, very affable and encouraging. Long before the covers were set on the table, the young gentleman had disclosed that his name was Hildebrand Ross, and that his home was in Suffolk, where, Sir Gareth gathered, his father was the squire of a village not far from Stowmarket. He had got his schooling in Winchester, and was at present up at Cambridge. He had several sisters, all older than himself, but no brothers; and it was not difficult to guess that he was at once the hope and the darling of his house. He told Sir Gareth that he was on his way to Ludlow, where he expected to join a party of college friends on a walking tour of Wales. His intention had been to have spent the night at Wellingborough, but he had been attracted to the White Lion by its air of antiquity: did not Sir Gareth think that in all likelihood the inn had been standing here, just as it did today, when Queen Katherine had been imprisoned at Kimbolton?

This question could not fail to catch Amanda's attention, and she temporarily abandoned her rôle of martyred innocence to demand further information. Delighted as much to expound what appeared to be a favourite subject as to converse with the most stunningly beautiful creature he had ever beheld, Mr Ross turned eagerly towards her. Sir Gareth, thankful, at the end of a wearing day, to be relieved of the necessity of entertaining his charge, retired from the conversation, enjoying his sherry in peace, and listening, in a little amusement, to Mr Ross's earnest discourse.

Mr Ross seemed to be a romantically minded youth, with a strong liking for historic subjects. He thought that there was promising matter for a dramatic tragedy, in blank verse, in the Divorce and Death of Queen Katherine of Aragon. Only, did Amanda feel that it would be presumptuous for a lesser poet to tread in the steps of Shakespeare? Yes (blushing), his ambition was to enter the field of literature. As a matter of fact, he had written a quantity of verses already. Oh, no! not published! just fugitive fragments written when he was quite young, which he would be ashamed to see in print. He rather thought that his talent was for Drama: at least (blushing more fierily), so one or two knowledgeable persons had been kind enough to say. To own the truth, he had already written a short play, while still at Winchester, which had been performed by certain members of the Sixth. Mere schoolboy stuff, of course, but one of the situations had been considered powerful, and he fancied that there were several passages that were not wholly contemptible. But he must sound like a coxcomb!

Reassured on this point, he confided that he had for long nursed an ambition to write a Tragic Drama about Queen Katherine, but had hitherto put the project from him, fearing that until he had gained experience and knowledge of the world he might not do justice to his subject. The moment now seemed ripe; and the sight of Kimbolton, where, as Amanda was of course aware, the unfortunate queen had died, had put one or two very good notions into his head.

Amanda, who had never before met an author, much less a dramatic poet, was impressed. She begged Mr Ross to tell her more; and Mr Ross, stammering with mingled shyness and gratification, said that if she was sure she would not think him the greatest bore in nature, he would very much value her opinion of his play, as he at present conceived it.

Sir Gareth, lounging in a deep chair at his ease, with his shapely and superbly booted legs crossed at the ankles, watched them with a smile lurking at the back of his eyes. An attractive pair of children: the boy a little shy, and obviously dazzled, the girl quite free from any sort of self-consciousness, and pretty enough to turn far more seasoned heads than young Ross's. She was having much the same effect upon him as she had had upon Joe Ninfield, but she couldn't do much damage to his heart in one evening. As for the budding dramatist's play, it seemed uncertain whether it would turn out to be a chronicle, starting with Katherine's marriage to Prince Arthur (because that would make a splendid scene), and taking, according to Sir Gareth's silent estimate, at least three nights to perform, or a shorter but much gloomier production, starting with a divorce, and ending with an autopsy. The young couple, rapidly arriving at a comfortable state of intimacy, were hotly embroiled in argument by the time the covers were set on the table. Mr Ross, in thrilling accents, had told Amanda the story of Katherine's exposed heart, so indelibly blackened that not all the efforts of the chandler sufficed to wash it clean. And then the chandler had cut it in twain, and behold! it was black right to the core, with a nameless Thing clutching it so tightly that it could not be wrenched away. Amanda listened to this horrid tale with her eyes growing rounder and rounder, and was enthusiastic in her appreciation of it. Mr Ross said that it had taken strong possession of his mind also, but he doubted whether the scene would prove suitable for dramatic production. Amanda could see no difficulty. The autopsy would be performed, naturally, on a dummy, and a sponge, well soaked in pitch, would make an excellent heart. She was persuaded that no other dramatist had ever hit upon so splendid and original a final scene. But

Mr Ross, while conceding the splendour and the originality, was inclined to doubt whether it would take the public's fancy.

At this point, Sir Gareth, who had been controlling himself admirably, caught the waiter's astonished eye, and burst out laughing. As two startled faces turned towards him, he got up, saying: 'Come to dinner, you young ghouls! And I give you fair warning that anyone offering me blackened hearts as an accompaniment to roast chicken will be instantly banished from the table!'

Mr Ross, taking this in good part, grinned, but even as he rose to his feet he noticed that a distressing change had come over Amanda. A moment earlier she had been all animation and interest, her expressive eyes full of sparkle and the enchanting smile, with its hint of mischief, never far from her lips; now, as though at the waving of a wand, all the liveliness had vanished from her face, her eyes had clouded, and she looked as though she had awakened suddenly from a pleasant dream to a very disagreeable reality. For an anxious moment Mr Ross wondered whether he could possibly have said anything to offend her. Then Sir Gareth, waiting behind the chair which he had pulled out for her at the table, said, not exactly imperatively, but in a voice of authority: 'Come along, my child!'

She rose with obvious reluctance, and, as she took her place at the table, cast a look up at her guardian which considerably surprised Mr Ross, so resentful was it. He could only suppose that there had been some disagreement between them. Sir Gareth seemed to be very pleasant and good-humoured, but perhaps, under his charm of manner, he was a stricter guardian than one would guess. This conclusion was almost immediately borne out by his refusal to permit Amanda to fetch her kitten down to the coffee-room. Hardly had she seated herself than she started up again, saying that Joseph must be allowed to share the repast. She would have left the table on the words, but Sir Gareth's hand shot out, and caught her wrist. 'Oh, no!' he said.

He sounded amused, but the colour rushed up into Amanda's face, and she tried to wrench free, exclaiming in a low, shaking voice: 'I wasn't! I didn't even think of—Let me go!'

He released her wrist, but he too had risen, and he obliged her to sit down again, his hands on her shoulders. He kept them there for a minute. 'Joseph shall join us after dinner,' he said. 'I don't think we want him at table.'

He went back to his place, and, as though nothing had happened, began to talk to Hildebrand.

Had he been asked to consider the question dispassionately, Hildebrand would have given his vote against the inclusion of a kitten at the board, but confronted by Amanda's mortified face it was impossible to be dis-passionate. She was biting her pretty lip, her eyes downcast, and her cheeks still flushed, and these signs of discomfiture made Sir Gareth's conduct seem a little tyrannical. However, he had seen his sisters behave in very much the same way when thwarted, and he thought that probably she would recover from her pet if no heed were paid to her, and he resolutely turned his eyes away from her, and listened to what Sir Gareth was saying to him.

Meanwhile, Amanda, rejecting the soup, was struggling with her emotions. Mr Ross had been quite right in thinking that she had been jerked back to disagreeable reality. While she had been listening to his delightful anecdotes of Queen Katherine, she had forgotten what the future held in store for her. Sir Gareth's voice had recalled her, and all the evils of her situation came rushing in on her with such force that she almost burst into tears. A bitter sense of frustration possessed her, and the fact that Sir Gareth, who was its author, was as good-humoured as ever did nothing to soothe her. It made her very angry to be treated as though she were a child whose troubles were trivial, and would soon be forgotten; and the look Hildebrand had seen her cast at him had indeed been resentful. She had toyed with the notion of refusing to sit down to dinner, but had found herself, to her further annoyance, obeying that pleasantly spoken yet determined summons. She didn't quite know why, but it hadn't seemed possible to do anything else. Then he had refused to let her fetch her dear little kitten, because he had suspected that she was going to run away again. Since she really hadn't any such intention, this seemed to her the height of injustice, and made the cup of her wrongs flow over. And now, instead of trying to atone for the insult by coaxing her to drink her soup, and wooing her with soft words, as Grandpapa would certainly have done, he was paying no heed to her at all, but talking to Mr Ross instead. This was treatment to which she was quite unaccustomed, for although Neil had never tried to coax her out of a tantrum his methods of dealing with her had not so far included ostracism.

The sense of ill-usage grew. Not even the budding playwright, who had seemed to have a great deal of sensibility, cared a button whether she ate what was set before her, or starved. He was telling Sir Gareth all about his horse, which had been given him as a birthday present by his father. The noble animal was even now in the stable attached to the White Lion, for he was riding to Ludlow, which was far preferable to going by a stuffy coach: did not Sir Gareth agree? His mama had not liked his going off quite by himself, but Father perfectly understood that one wanted to be free to go where one chose when one was enjoying the Long Vacation. He was a great gun: not at all like some fathers one had met, who were always finding fault, or getting into a grand fuss, merely because their sons had forgotten to write home for a week or two.

How odious Sir Gareth was, thought Amanda, to encourage young Mr Ross to forget all about her! It was all of a piece: no doubt he was making himself agreeable just to spike her guns, in case she should try to enlist Mr Ross as an ally. That was what he had done at Whitethorn Farm, turning even kind Mr Ninfield against her, and inducing him to believe all the shocking lies he had uttered.

But Mr Ross had not forgotten her. He had been covertly watching her, and he now ventured to turn his face fully towards her, and to smile at her. She smiled back at him, but so pathetically that he became convinced that something must be very much amiss.

She grew rather more cheerful after dinner, for her stern guardian permitted her to bring Joseph down to the coffee-room, and after Joseph had been regaled with a portion of minced chicken he very obligingly diverted the company by engaging in a protracted form of guerrilla warfare with a ball of screwed-up paper.

In the middle of this entertainment, Trotton came in for any final orders his master might wish to give him, and while Sir Gareth was talking to him Mr Ross seized the opportunity to whisper: 'I beg pardon, but—is anything amiss?'

His fears were then confirmed. Amanda's eyes flew towards Sir Gareth in a way that clearly showed her dread of him, and she whispered in reply: '*Everything!* Hush!'

He was obediently silent, but he resolved to pursue his inquiries as soon as Sir Gareth gave him the chance to speak to her alone. Unfortunately, Sir Gareth gave him no chance, but very soon dashed all his hopes by breaking up the party at an early hour. He said that since she had had a long and tiring day, and would have another tomorrow, Amanda must go to bed in good time.

'But I don't wish to go to bed, for I am not in the *least* sleepy!' objected Amanda.

'I'm sure you're not, but I am, and you can see that Joseph is too,' returned Sir Gareth.

The very speaking look she exchanged with Mr Ross, as she reluctantly rose from her chair, was intended to convey to him her opinion of persons who ordered her to bed as though she was a baby, but he interpreted it as an appeal for aid, and his chivalry was fired.

Sir Gareth, an amused observer of this by-play, thought it time to call a halt. If this romantic and impressionable youth saw much more of Amanda, it seemed likely that his walking tour would be ruined by a severe attack of frustrated calf-love, which would be rather too bad, for he looked just the kind of over-sensitive boy to be seriously upset by it. So he bade him a kind but firm goodnight, shaking hands with him, and saying that perhaps they had better call it goodbye, since he and Amanda would be leaving Kimbolton very early in the morning.

He then swept Amanda inexorably away. Mr Ross, bent on making an assignation with this distressed damsel, conceived the happy notion of slipping a note under her bedroom door, and suddenly realized that he had no idea which room had been allotted to her. The only way of discovering this seemed to be to go upstairs himself, as though on his way to bed, and listen carefully at all the possible doors for some sound that would disclose her exact whereabouts. He was pretty sure that she would talk to Joseph while she made herself ready for bed, and in this hope he too mounted the stairs.

12

He found, when he reached the square landing at the head of the stairs, that it was going to be a simpler matter than he had feared to locate Amanda's room. The sound of her voice came to him, from the corridor that led from the landing to the end of the house, and it was evident that instead of retiring immediately to bed she had detained Sir Gareth to engage him in hot argument.

'You have no *right* to force me to go with you!'

'Very well: I have no right, but nevertheless you will go with me,' Sir Gareth replied, rather wearily. 'For Heaven's sake, stop arguing, and go to bed, Amanda!'

Hildebrand hesitated. By all the canons of his upbringing he ought either to advertise his presence, or to go away. He had almost started to tiptoe down the stairs when it occurred to him that too scrupulous a regard for his own honour in this instance might militate against his being able to rescue Amanda. He remained where he was, not, indeed, quite comfortable, but fairly well persuaded that Amanda at least would raise no objection to his eavesdropping. Her next words almost brought tears of sympathy to his eyes.

'Oh, if you had a *heart* you would let me go!' she said tragically.

From the chuckle that followed this impassioned outburst, it was to be inferred that Sir Gareth was not at all moved by it. 'That is a splendid line, and very creditably delivered,' he approved. 'Now you must ring down the curtain, for fear of falling into anticlimax! Have you everything you need for the night?'

She paid no heed to this, but said, in a voice trembling with indignation: 'I was never so deceived in anyone! No, or those others!'

'What others?'

'All of them!—that fat landlady, and the Ninfields, and now Mr Ross! You made them all l-like you, because you have ch-charming manners, and address, and they believed you when you told the w-wickedest untruths, and you make it so that it is no *use* for me to tell them that you are not a gentleman at all, but a *snake*!'

'Poor Amanda! Now, listen, you foolish child! I know I seem to you to be heartless, and detestably tyrannical, but, believe me, you'll thank me for it one day. Come, now, dry your eyes! Anyone would suppose that I really was going to carry you off to that mouldering castle of mine! Instead of that I am taking you to London. Is that so dreadful? I daresay you will enjoy it. How would it be if I took you to the play?'

'*No!*' she said passionately. 'I am not a child, and I won't be bribed like that! How dare you talk to me of going to a stupid play, when you are determined to ruin my life? You *are* detestable, and I see that it is useless to appeal to your better nature, because you haven't got a better nature!'

'Black to the core—like Queen Katherine's heart,' agreed Sir Gareth gravely. 'Go to bed, my child: the future won't look so ill in the morning. There is, however, just one thing I must tell you before I bid you goodnight. Much as I regret the necessity, I am going to lock your door.'

'No!' cried Amanda pantingly. 'You shan't, you shan't! Give me back that key! Give it back to me *instantly*!'

'No, Amanda. I warned you that you were not dealing with a flat. If I gave it to you, you would run away as soon as you thought I was asleep. You are not going to escape again.'

'You can't be so inhuman as to lock me up! I might be ill!'

'Oh, I don't think you will be!'

'I might *die*!' she urged.

'Well, if you did that, it wouldn't signify whether you were locked in, or not, would it?'

'Oh, how hateful you are! I might be burnt in my bed!'

'If the house should happen to catch fire, I will engage not only to rescue you, but Joseph as well. Goodnight—and dream of a revenge on me!'

Mr Ross heard the click of a closing door, and the grating of the key in the lock. He moved softly forward to peep round the angle of the wall, and was in time to see Sir Gareth withdraw the key from the lock of a door, and cross the corridor to a room directly opposite.

For several minutes Mr Ross remained on the landing, not knowing just what he ought to do. When he had heard Amanda beg Sir Gareth not to lock her door, his impulse had been to dash to her support. But before he could do so, all the awkwardness of his situation had been realized, and he had hesitated. Profoundly shocked though he was, and burning to perform some heroic deed for Amanda's sake, he yet could not feel that he would be justified in intervening, or even, perhaps, successful. It was cruel of Sir Gareth to lock the door on Amanda, but if he was her guardian no one could gainsay his right to do so. The things Amanda had said to him certainly indicated that he had behaved very badly to her, but what he had done, or why she was so reluctant to accompany him to Lonon, could at present be matters only for conjecture.

He decided that his first step must be to find a way of approaching Amanda, and he did not immediately perceive how this was to be accomplished. A whispered conversation through the keyhole would be a very indifferent way of communicating with her, and might well bring Sir Gareth out upon him. A little further consideration, however, put him in mind of the fact that her bedroom must, from its position, look out on to the small, walled garden at the back of the inn, and he conceived the happy idea of walking out into this, and of attracting Amanda's attention by throwing stones at her window.

Fortunately, since he might have been hard put to it to distinguish her window among several others which looked on to the garden, this expedient was found to be unnecessary. Amanda's window stood open, and Amanda was kneeling at it, clearly silhouetted by the candle behind her, her elbows on the ledge, and her face propped between her hands.

Thrust firmly into her room, and the door closed on her, the agitation from which she was suffering had found relief in a burst of tears. Without having precisely decided on a course of action, she had been turning over in her mind a plan of escaping from the White Lion as soon as it was light; and the discovery that Sir Gareth had been aware of this provoked her to quite irrational fury. Though she meant to outwit him if she could, it was insulting of him to suspect her; and his calm air of mastery made her want to hit him. Well, she would show him!

The first step towards showing him had been to run to the window, to ascertain whether it were possible to climb down from it, or even, since the upper storey of the house was at no great height from the ground, to drop down from it. She had not previously thought of this way of escape, and so had not inspected the window. It needed only the most cursory inspection now to inform her that to squeeze herself through it would be impossible. She began to cry again, and was still convulsively sobbing when Mr Ross came cautiously into the garden through a wicket-gate opening into the stable-yard, and saw her.

The moon was up, brightly illuminating the scene, so there was really no need for Mr Ross, softly treading along the flagged path until· he stood immediately beneath Amanda's window, to attract her attention by saying, thrillingly, 'Hist!' Amanda had seen him as soon as he entered the garden, and had moodily watched his approach. She could think of no way in which he could be of assistance to her.

'Miss Smith! I must have speech with you!' piercingly whispered Mr Ross. 'I heard all!'

'All what?' said Amanda crossly.

'All that you said to Sir Gareth! Only tell me what I can do to help you!'

'No one can help me,' replied Amanda, sunk in gloom.

'*I* can, and will,' promised Mr Ross recklessly.

A faint interest gleamed in her eyes. She abandoned her despairing pose, and looked down at his upturned face. 'How? He locked me in, and the window is too small for me to get out of.'

'I will think of a way. Only we cannot continue talking like this. Someone may hear us! Wait! There is bound to be a ladder in the stables! If I can contrive to do so unobserved, I'll fetch it, and climb up to you!'

Amanda began to feel more hopeful. Up till now she had not considered him in the light of a possible rescuer, for he seemed to her very young, and no match for a man of Sir Gareth's fiendish ingenuity. He now appeared to be a man of action and resource. She waited.

Time passed, and the slight hope she was cherishing dwindled. Then, just as she was thinking that there was nothing to do but to go to bed, Mr Ross came back, bearing a short ladder, which was used for climbing into the hay-loft. He set this up against the wall of the house, and mounted it. He had to climb to the topmost rung before his head rose above the window-sill, and his hands could grasp it, and the last part of the ascent was somewhat precariously accomplished.

'Oh, pray be careful!' begged Amanda, alarmed but admiring.

'It's quite safe,' he assured her. 'I beg pardon for having been such an age: I had to wait, you see, because that man—your guardian's groom—was giving the head ostler all manner of directions. Why are you locked in?'

'Because Sir Gareth is determined not to let me escape,' she replied bitterly.

'Yes, but—You see, I did not perfectly understand from what you was saying to him why you wish to escape, or what he means to do with you. Of course, I saw how much you feared him long before!'

'Saw how much I—Oh! Oh, yes!' said Amanda, swallowing with an effort her very natural indignation. 'I am wholly in his power!'

'Yes, well, I suppose—I mean, if he's your guardian, you must be. But what has he done to frighten you? Why did you say he was a snake?'

Amanda did not answer for a moment. She was feeling tired, quite unequal to the task of rapidly composing a suitable explanation. A sigh broke from her. The sadness of this sound wrought powerfully upon Mr Ross. He ventured to remove one hand from the sill, and to lay it tenderly on hers. 'Tell me!' he said.

'He is abducting me,' said Amanda.

Mr Ross was so much astonished that he nearly fell off the ladder. '*Abducting* you?' he gasped. 'You cannot be serious!'

'Yes, I am! And, what is more, it's true!' said Amanda.

'Good God! I would not have believed it to have been possible! My dear Miss Smith, you may be easy! I will instantly have you set free! There will be no difficulty. I have but to inform the parish constable, or perhaps a magistrate—I am not perfectly sure, but I shall speedily discover—'

'No, no!' she interrupted hastily. 'It would be useless! *Pray* do not do so!'

'But I am persuaded it is what I should do!' he expostulated. 'How should it be useless?'

She sought wildly for some explanation which would satisfy him. None occurred to her, until, just as she was wondering whether she dared tell him the truth, or whether (which she suspected) he would disapprove as heartily as Sir Gareth of her plan of campaign, there flashed into her brain a notion of transcendent splendour. It almost took her breath away, for not only was it an excellent story in itself: it would, properly handled, afford her the means of being exquisitely revenged on Sir Gareth. It was Sir Gareth's own story, now to prove his undoing. 'You see,' said Amanda, drawing a deep, ecstatic breath, 'I am an heiress.'

'Oh!' said Mr Ross, rather at a loss.

'I was left an orphan at an early age,' she continued, embellishing Sir

Gareth's crude handiwork. 'Alas! I am quite alone in the world, without kith or kin.'

Mr Ross, himself a great reader of romances, found nothing to object to in the style of this narrative, but cavilled at little at the matter. 'What, have you no relations at all?' he asked incredulously. 'No cousins, even?'

Amanda thought him unnecessarily captious, but obligingly presented him with a relative. 'Yes, I have an uncle,' she conceded. 'But he cannot help me, so—'

'But why not? *Surely*—'

Amanda, regretting the creation of an uncle who seemed likely to prove an embarrassment, with great presence of mind placed him beyond Mr Ross's reach. 'He is in Bedlam,' she said. 'So we need not think any more about *him*. The thing is that—'

'*Mad?*' interrupted Mr Ross, in horrified accents.

'*Raving* mad,' said Amanda firmly.

'How very dreadful!'

'Yes, isn't it? Because I have no one to turn to but Sir Gareth.'

'Is he a dangerous madman?' asked Mr Ross, apparently fascinated by the uncle.

'I do wish you would stop asking questions about my uncle, and attend to what I am saying!' said Amanda, exasperated.

'I beg pardon! It must be excessively painful for you!'

'Yes, and it is quite beside the point, too. Sir Gareth, wishing to possess himself of my fortune, is determined to force me into marriage with himself, and for this purpose is carrying me to London.'

'To London? I should have thought—'

'To London,' repeated Amanda emphatically. 'Because that is where he lives, and he means to incarcerate me in his house until I submit. And it's no use saying the parish constable would stop him, because Sir Gareth would deny every word, and say that he was taking me to live with his sister, who is a very disagreeable woman, and would do anything to oblige him. And everyone would believe him, because they always do. So you would only make a great noise, which I should very much dislike, and all to no purpose.'

Mr Ross could see that this was very likely, but he was still puzzled. 'Where have you been living?' he demanded. 'I don't perfectly understand. You said he abducted you: haven't you been residing under his roof?'

'No, no, I have hitherto resided with a very respectable woman, who—' She stopped, and decided to eliminate a possible danger. '–who is dead. I mean, she died two years ago, and Sir Gareth then placed me in a seminary, which is exactly the sort of thing he *would* do! Only now that I am old enough to be married, he came and removed me, and naturally I was pleased, because *then* I believed him to be everything that was amiable. But when he told me that I must marry him—'

'Good God, I should have thought he would have had more address!' exclaimed Mr Ross. 'Told you that you must marry him when he had only that instant removed you from the seminary?'

'Oh, no! The thing was that he supposed I should like the notion, because previously I had been excessively attached to him, on account of his being so handsome, and agreeable. Only, of course, I never thought of marrying him. Why, he's quite old! So then I was in a great fright, and I ran away from the place where we were staying last night, and he chased me all day, and found me at last, and brought me here. And I cannot think how to escape again, and oh, I am so very unhappy!'

The passionate sincerity with which these final words were uttered pierced Mr Ross to the heart. He was ashamed to think that he had for a moment doubted the story, and in some agitation implored Amanda not to cry. Amanda, between sobs, told him of her earlier adventures. These had been wholly enjoyable at the time, but regarded in retrospect, now that she was tired and defeated, the day seemed to her to have been one of unrelieved misery and discomfort.

Mr Ross had no difficulty in believing this at least. He would, indeed, have found it impossible to have believed that anything less than the direst necessity could have induced a gently-born young female to have taken so unprecedented and perilous a step as to cast herself upon the world as she had done. From the moment of her escape, the poor little thing had been mercilessly hounded. It did not surprise him to learn that the fat old gentleman who had with such false kindness offered to carry her to Oundle had tried to take advantage of her innocence. His sensitive nature made it easy for him to imagine the desperation of terror which must have had her in its grip; and the thought of so fragile and lovely a creature cowering on the floor of a farm-cart made him shudder, not the smallest suspicion entered his head that she had thoroughly enjoyed this part of her adventure. The description of the devilish cunning employed by Sir Gareth to regain possession of her lost nothing in the telling. Sir Gareth began, in Mr Ross's mind, to assume an aspect of smiling villainy. He wondered how he should have been taken-in by his pleasant manners, until he remembered certain warnings given him by his father against too readily trusting smooth-tongued and apparently creditable gentlemen of fashionable appearance. The world, said the Squire, was full of plausible banditti on the look-out for green young men of fortune. Their stock-in-trade was winning charm, and they frequently bestowed titles upon themselves, generally military. No doubt they were also on the look-out for rich wives, but naturally the Squire had not thought it necessary to tell his son this.

Had some chance brought Mr Ross face to face with Sir Gareth again, it was possible that his leaping imagination would have suffered a check. But Sir Gareth had gone to bed, and Mr Ross's last sight of him had been of him on the corridor, locking Amanda into her room. Every word he had said to Amanda bore out the truth of her story, and of his cynical heartlessness there could be no doubt. Only a hardened scoundrel, in Mr Ross's opinion, could have laughed at Amanda's anguish. Sir Gareth, not content with laughing, had mocked at her distress. He had also (now one came to think of it) tried to deceive her with promises of generous entertainment in London.

No chance brought Sir Gareth on to the scene to counteract the combined influences on an impressionable youth of Amanda and a full moon. Perched on the stable-ladder, a modern Romeo and his Juliet discussed ways and means.

It did not take them long to discard the trappings of convention. 'Oh, I wish you will not call me Miss Smith!' said Juliet. 'Amanda!' breathed Mr Ross reverently. 'And my name is Hildebrand.'

'Isn't it odd that we should both of us have the most ridiculous names?' said Amanda. 'Do you find yours a sad trial?'

Struck by her rare understanding, Mr Ross told her just how sad a trial his name had been to him, and explained to her the precise circumstances which had led to his being given a name calculated to blight his scholastic career. He had never dreamed it could sound well until he heard it on her lips.

After this digression, they became more practical, and very much more argumentative. A number of schemes for Amanda's deliverance, all of which depended upon some extremely improbable stroke of good fortune, were considered, and dismissed regretfully; and a promising new alliance was nearly ruptured by Hildebrand's rejection of a daring suggestion that he should creep into Sir Gareth's room, and steal from under his pillow (where there could be no doubt it was hidden) the key to Amanda's room. In Hildebrand, an inculcated respect for convention warred with a craving for romance. The thought of the construction Sir Gareth would inevitably place on the attempted theft of the key, should he wake (as Hildebrand rather thought he would) before the accomplishment of the design, made that young gentleman blush all over his slim body. He was naturally unable to disclose to Amanda the cause of his reluctance, and so was obliged to endure the mortification of being thought a wretchedly cowardly creature.

'Oh, well, if you are *afraid*—!' said Amanda, with a disdainful shrug of her shoulders.

Her scorn sharpened his wits. The glimmering of a plan, more daring than any that had occurred to her, flickered in his brain. 'Wait!' he commanded, his brows knit portentously. 'I have a better notion!'

She waited. After a prolonged silence, pregnant with suspense, Mr Ross said suddenly: 'Are you willing to place your honour in my hands?'

'Yes, yes, of course I am!' responded Amanda, agog with expectation.

'And do you think,' he asked anxiously, descending with disconcerting rapidity from these heights, 'that, if I were mounted on my horse, Prince, you could contrive to leap up before me?'

'I could, if you reached down your hand to me,' replied Amanda optimistically.

He considered this for a daunted moment. 'Well, I shall be holding a pistol in my right hand, and I shouldn't *think* I could contrive to hold the bridle in it as well,' he said dubiously. 'I could try, of course, but–No, I think it would be best if I tucked the reins under my knee. And even if Prince does become restive it won't signify, once I have you firmly gripped. All you will have to do is to set your foot on mine in the stirrup, and spring the moment I tell you to. Do you think you can do that?'

'Are you going to ride off with me across your saddle-bow?' demanded Amanda eagerly.

'Yes–well, no, not precisely! I mean, I thought, if you put your arms round me, you could sit before me–just until we were beyond the reach of pursuit!' he added quickly.

'Yes, that would be much more comfortable,' she agreed. 'Of course I could do it!'

'Well, when the notion first came to me, I thought you could, too, but now I come to think of it more particularly, I can see that it is a thing we ought to practise.'

'No, no, I am persuaded there can be not the least difficulty!' she urged. 'Only think how knights in olden times were for ever riding off with distressed ladies!'

'Yes, and in armour, too!' he said, forcibly struck. 'Still, we don't know but what they may have bungled it before they acquired the habit, and it won't do for us to bungle it. I think I had better dismount, and hold Prince while you get upon his back. Are you able to mount without assistance?'

'Certainly I am! But what are you going to do?'

'Hold you up on the road to Bedford!' disclosed Hildebrand.

Amanda uttered a squeak, which he correctly interpreted as an expression of admiration and approval, and gave a little jump of excitement. 'Like a highwayman? Oh, what a *splendid* scheme! *Pray* forgive me for not having thought you had any courage!'

'It's a pretty desperate thing to do, of course,' said Hildebrand, 'but I can see that only desperate measures will answer in this case and I would do *anything* to save you from your guardian! I cannot conceive why your father left you in the care of such an infamous person! It seems the oddest thing!'

'He was deceived in him, but never mind that!' said Amanda hastily. 'How do you know he means to go to Bedford?'

'I discovered it when I was waiting for an opportunity to seize this ladder! Only to think that I was wishing that groom at Jericho, when all the time I had been guided to the stables by Providence! Because the groom was arranging for the hire of a chaise for his master, and inquiring about the state of the road that runs to Bedford. It's not a pike-road, you know, but Sir Gareth means to go by it, just to Bedford, which is only one stage. And there you are to change from this chaise, which is a shabby, oldfashioned one, and go on to London in a better one, which, of course, may readily be hired in a place like Bedford. Four horses, too! By Jove, it is *another* instance of Providence! For, you know, if this weren't such a quiet place, with precious little custom, I daresay they would keep any number of fast vehicles for hire, and bang-up cattle as well, and I might have been at a stand. For I daresay I should have found it pretty hard to cover *two* postilions, as well as Sir Gareth. But only a pair of horses are hired for the first stage, which makes my task much easier. And I will own myself astonished if we do not find the road deserted, so early in the day! I mean, it can't be like the pike-roads, with mails and stages going up and down at all hours.'

Amanda agreed to this, but was shaken by doubt. 'Yes, but how will you procure a pistol?' she objected.

'Procure one! I have a pair of my own, in my saddle holsters,' said Hildebrand, unable to keep a note of pride out of his voice. 'Loaded, too.'

'Oh!' said Amanda, rather thoughtfully.

'You need not be afraid that I don't know how to handle them. My father holds that one should be accustomed to guns as soon as possible. I don't wish to boast, but I am accounted a tolerably good shot.'

'Yes, but I don't wish you to shoot Sir Gareth, or even the post-boy,' said Amanda uneasily.

'Good God, no! Of course I shall do nothing of the sort! Lord, a pretty kick-up *that* would mean! I might be obliged to fire one of the pistols over the post-boy's head, to frighten him, you know, but I promise you I shan't do more. There won't be the least need. I shall hold Sir Gareth covered, and you may depend upon it he won't dare to move, with my pistol pointing at his head. He is bound to be taken quite by surprise, but *you* will not be, and you must lose not an instant in jumping down from the chaise, and mounting Prince. Then I shall get up behind you, and we shall be off in a trice.' He paused, but Amanda said nothing. After a moment, he said, rather hurt: 'You don't care for the scheme?'

'Yes, I do!' she replied warmly. 'I like it excessively, for I have always wished to have adventures, and I can see that this would be a truly splendid adventure. Except for the pistols.'

'Oh, if that is all—! I promise you, you need not be afraid: I won't even fire in the air!'

'Oh, well then–No, it won't do. Nothing is of any use, because I have nowhere to go to,' said Amanda, plunging back into dejection.

But Hildebrand was not daunted. 'Don't be unhappy!' he begged. 'I had been thinking of where I should take you, and, if you should not dislike it, I fancy I have hit upon the very thing. Of course, if this had not chanced to fall at an awkward time, I should have taken you home, so that Mama could have looked after you, which, I assure you, she would have been delighted to do. But it so happens that my eldest sister is about to be confined, and Mama has gone away to be with her, while Father is at this very moment taking Blanche and Amabel to Scarborough, for a month. It is very vexatious, but never mind! I will take you to Hannah instead. She is the dearest creature, and I *know* you would be happy with her, for she used to be our nurse, and she will do anything in the world for me. And her husband is a very good sort of a man. He is a farmer, and they have the jolliest farm, not far from Newmarket. What I thought was that I should ride with you 'cross country, to St Neots, and there hire a chaise. I suppose I shall be obliged to stable Prince there, or perhaps I could ride him as far as to Cambridge. Yes, that would be best, for I am accustomed to keep a horse when I am up, and I shall know he will be well cared for at the livery-stables there.'

'A farm?' said Amanda, reviving as though by magic. 'With cows, and hens, and pigs? Oh, I should like that of all things! Yes, yes, *do* hold us up tomorrow!'

'Well, I will,' he said, gratified. 'Then, when I have escorted you to Nurse, I think I should post off to Scarborough, to ask Father just what ought to be done in such a case. Depend upon it, he will know exactly.'

This part of the scheme held out no appeal to Amanda, but she did not say so. There would be time enough at her disposal to dissuade Hildebrand; the immediate need was to escape from Sir Gareth. It seemed to her very unlikely that he would run her to earth at Newmarket; while a farm, as she had already decided, would be an ideal refuge in which to await the capitulation of her grandfather. Her weariness forgotten with the revival of her hopes, she discussed with Hildebrand the various ramifications of his plot; and parted from him finally with only one flaw spoiling her satisfaction. Hildebrand, although willing to engage in any dangerous enterprise for her sake, drew the line at Joseph. A kitten, he said, would place the whole enterprise in jeopardy. Moreover, he doubted very much whether Joseph would enjoy riding on a horse. He rather thought he would not. Amanda was obliged to give way on this point, and could only hope that Sir Gareth would be kind to Joseph when he found himself his sole support.

13

Mr Ross, by his own overnight request, was roused by the boots, though not without difficulty, at an unseasonably early hour on the following morning. Having consulted his watch, he was just about to turn over in bed, and sink back into slumber, when the events of the previous evening came rushing back to him. He gave a gasp, and sat up, all desire to sleep being effectually banished by a recollection which, it had to be admitted, was extremely unwelcome.

It was extraordinary what a difference daylight made. A plan which had seemed, in the moonlight, to have everything to recommend it, was no sooner inspected in the clear light of the morning than it was found to bear the hall-marks, if not of madness, at least of alarming foolhardiness. Mr Ross, thinking it over, was inclined to think he had been bewitched. It was not that he disliked the plan: given the right setting, there was nothing he had rather do than ride off with Amanda on his saddle-bow. The mischief was that the right setting was lacking. The adventure demanded an odd dragon or two in the background, and a few false knights in full armour. One could make do, at a pinch, with love-locks and a leather coat, exchanging the dragons and the knights for a contingent of Roundheads: but a nineteenth-century scene was hopelessly anachronous. It was not an encounter with a dragon which one would have to avoid, but one with a stage-coach, or a carrier's van; and instead of winning great worship by the deed one was much more likely to be sent to prison, or, at the very least, severely reprimanded for having done something that one's elders would say was not the thing.

Sitting up in bed, hugging his sheets, and staring out of the window at the promise of another hot day, Mr Ross seriously considered crying off from the engagement. But the more he thought about it, the more impossible did it appear that he could do so. For one thing, he could scarcely climb a ladder to Amanda's window in broad daylight; for another, his last words to her had been an assurance that she might trust him, and to fail her at the eleventh hour would be conduct of unforgivable baseness. She had already doubted his mettle, too. There was nothing for it but to do his best to carry the adventure through to a triumphant conclusion. Instead of wishing that he had not been quite so impulsive, he forced his mind to dwell on the wrongs Amanda had suffered at the perfidious Sir Gareth's hands; and in this way he managed to keep up his resolution. By sacrificing one of a pair of black silk evening stockings, he contrived to fashion a very tolerable mask, and when he tried it on in front of the mirror, with his frieze riding-cloak wrapped round him, and his hat pulled low on his brow, the effect was so awe-inspiring that his spirits rose considerably. But he had little appetite for his breakfast. However, he drank some coffee, and ate a slice of ham, taking care, in case Sir Gareth should later inquire for him, to talk at great length to a bored and sleepy waiter about his plans for his supposed journey into Wales. He asked searching questions about the road, and the towns he would reach, and rose at last from the table with the comfortable conviction that if Sir Gareth asked any questions he would certainly be told that Mr Ross, desirous of covering as much ground as possible before the heat of the day made travel disagreeable, had set forward on his way to Wales an hour earlier.

But Sir Gareth made no inquiries. In his experience, very young gentlemen found it much harder to wake up in the morning than did their seniors. He was frequently obliged, when he invited Mr Leigh Wetherby to visit him in the country, to employ the most ruthless methods of getting his nephew out of bed; and he had not expected to see Hildebrand at the breakfast-table.

He was glad to find that his captive was apparently resigned to her fate. She attempted no further argument, and if her expression was discontented, and the glances she cast at him repulsive, at least she was able to enjoy a pretty substantial breakfast. He refrained tactfully from addressing anything but commonplace remarks to her; and to these he received cold and generally monosyllabic answers.

The start to the journey was slightly delayed by the tardiness of the post-boy in presenting himself at the White Lion for duty. He had been granted a holiday on the previous day, and pleaded that he had not known that his services had been commanded for such an early hour. There was no post-master at the inn, since only two boys were employed there, and the landlord told Sir Gareth that all postilions were the same: dratted nuisances, always taking twice as long as they ought to lead their horses home lear, quarrelling among themselves, and for ever sneaking off into the village when they should have been at hand, ready to put off their white overalls, and jump into the saddle. He was incensed with this one for having stayed away all night; but there was one person who would have been a good deal relieved, had he known of the defection. Mr Ross, trotting along the Bedford road, on the look-out for a suitable ambush, had suddenly realized that a post-boy from the White Lion could scarcely fail to recognize the handsome chestnut which had been stabled in one of the loose-boxes there.

The chaise which Sir Gareth had been forced to hire was not one of the light, modern vehicles, nor was it very well-hung. Sir Gareth, observing the scornful and slightly affronted glance which Amanda pointedly cast at its worn squabs, gravely apologized for conveying her to Bedford in a carriage wholly unworthy of her dignity, and promised to transfer her there into the smartest and fastest chaise the best posting-house could produce. She sniffed.

She was plainly determined not to unbend; and since Sir Gareth had not the smallest wish to make civil conversation at so early an hour, he did not attempt to charm her out of her sulks, but leaned back in his own corner of the chaise, idly looking out of the window at as much of the countryside as he could see. This was not very much, for the lane, which was narrow, and appeared to be little used, was bordered by uneven and straggling hedges. It passed through no towns, and the few villages it served were none of them more than hamlets. Here and there a cluster of farm-buildings were to be seen, and several narrow lanes, no better than cart-tracks, debouched on to it. After a time, wearying of a singularly uninteresting prospect, Sir Gareth turned his head, and surveyed Amanda. It struck him immediately that her expression of sullen resignation had vanished, and, an instant later, that there was an air of suppressed excitement about her. There was a pretty colour in her cheeks, her eyes were very bright, and she was sitting bolt upright, her hands clasped tightly in her lap.

'Amanda,' said Sir Gareth, with mock severity, 'what mischief are you brewing?'

She jumped guiltily. 'I shan't tell you! But I said I should make you sorry, and I *shall*!'

He laughed, but forbore to tease her. He wondered what fantastic plot she was hatching, but not with any feeling of uneasiness. He would certainly have to keep an eye on her when they broke the journey for rest and refreshment, but he rather suspected that she would not attempt to escape again until they reached London. Well, between them, Beatrix and Miss Felbridge ought to be able to keep her under guard until he could hand her over to her grandfather.

He was lying back, with his eyes half closed, hoping that he would not find, upon inquiry at the Horse Guards, that the Brigade-Major had left town, when a loud shout smote his ears, and the chaise drew up with a jarring lurch. 'What the devil——?' he exclaimed, and sat up, looking out of the window to see what had caused the abrupt halt.

The chaise had stopped just short of a small cross-road, and the cause was instantly apparent. A sinister figure, with a mask over his face, and a voluminous cloak enveloping his frame, was covering the astonished post-boy with a silver-mounted pistol, and threatening, in alarmingly gruff accents, to blow his head off if he moved an eyelid. The apparition was bestriding a good-looking hack, and finding it a little difficult at one and the same time to keep this animal still and the pistol correctly levelled.

One comprehensive glance told Sir Gareth all he wished to know. His lips twitched, and he looked round at Amanda, saying: 'You little fiend!' and then opened the door of the chaise, and sprang lightly down on to the road.

Mr Ross became flustered. Events were not turning out quite as he had expected. He had certainly found an excellent ambush in the little cross-road, and the post-boy had not hesitated to obey at least the first part of his command to stand and deliver. Unfortunately, Prince, also bidden savagely to stand, was not as docile. For one thing, he was unaccustomed to shouts being uttered just above his head, and, for another, he could tell that his master was strangely nervous. He began to fidget, backing, sidling, trying to get his head. The harassed Mr Ross knew that Amanda would find it very hard to mount him, and became more flustered. A quick look showed him that Amanda, instead of nipping out of the chaise by the off-side door, was having difficulty in opening it. And he had not bargained for Sir Gareth's jumping down in such a reckless fashion. Everything, in fact, was going wrong. He dismounted swiftly, and ordered Sir Gareth to stand where he was, but as he dared not release Prince's bridle, and had not had the forethought to dismount on the right instead of the left, he found himself in a most awkward fix, trying to keep Sir Gareth covered by the pistol gripped in his right hand while his left was being dragged across his chest by Prince's efforts to back away.

'Don't brandish that pistol about, you young fool!' Sir Gareth said.

'Put up your hands!' retorted Hildebrand. 'If you move another step I shall fire!'

'Nonsense! Come, now, enough of this folly! Give me that pistol at once!'

Hildebrand, seeing Sir Gareth advancing in the coolest fashion, took an involuntary step backwards. Out of the corner of his eye, he saw that the post-boy had slid out of his saddle, and was preparing to attack him from the rear; he tried to shift his position so that he could keep both men covered; Prince, now thoroughly alarmed, cannoned into him; and the unexpected jolt caused his finger to tighten round the trigger of his pistol There was a loud report; Amanda screamed; the post-boy made a dive for his startled horses' heads; Prince reared up, snorting with fright; and Sir Gareth reeled back against the wheel of the chaise, a hand clapped to his left shoulder.

'How could you? Oh, how *could* you?' Amanda cried, almost tumbling out of the chaise. 'You *promised* me you would not! Now see what you've done! Are you badly hurt, sir? Oh, I am so very sorry!'

Sir Gareth could not see her very clearly. The world was spinning before his eyes, and his limbs were turning to water. His senses were slipping away too, but he knew what had happened, and he managed before he lost consciousness, to speak one word: '*Accident . . .!*'

Amanda was on her knees beside him. He had fallen on his left side, and she had seen that his hand had been pressed to that shoulder, and, exerting all her strength, she managed to pull him over on to his back. She then saw the charred rent in his coat, and, far more terrifying, the ominous stain that was rapidly spreading. She tried to pull the coat away from that shoulder, but Sir Gareth's coats were all too well cut. She cried out: 'Help me, one of you! *help* me!' and began with feverish haste to rip off Sir Gareth's neckcloth. The post-boy hesitated. His horses, no fiery steeds, had quietened, but his eyes were fixed wrathfully on the supposed highwayman, and he seemed more than half inclined to go to him rather than to Amanda. She looked round, while her hands folded and refolded Sir Gareth's neckcloth into a pad, and said furiously: '*Help* me, I said!'

'Yes, miss, but–is he to be let make off?' the post-boy said, taking a reluctant step towards her, but keeping his glowering eyes on Hildebrand.

'No, no!' Hildebrand uttered hoarsely. 'I won't–I wouldn't—!'

'Never mind, never mind, come here!' Amanda commanded, thrusting her hand, with the pad held in it, inside Sir Gareth's coat.

The post-boy went to her, but when he saw Sir Gareth's pallor, and the bloodsoaked coat, he thought he was dead, and muttered involuntarily: 'Gawd, he's snuffed it!'

'Lift him!' Amanda said, her teeth clenched to control their chattering. 'Lift him, and get his coat off! I'll help you as much as I am able, but I must keep my hand pressed to the wound!'

'It ain't no manner of use, miss!'

'Do as I bid you!' she said angrily. 'He's not dead! He is bleeding *dreadfully*, and I *know* he would not if he were dead! Oh, hurry!'

He cast her a look of compassion, but he obeyed her, raising Sir Gareth in his arms, and contriving, with a little assistance from her, to strip the coat off. She did her best to keep her determined little hand pressed hard over the wound, but the bright red blood welled up, dyeing her fingers scarlet, and dripping on to her light muslin skirt. Mr Ross, his horse at last under his control, turned to see what aid he could render, and beheld this horrid sight. With a shaking hand, he stripped off his improvised mask, and flung it down. Had either Amanda or the post-boy had leisure to look at him, they would have seen that his face was almost as white as the victim's. His lips parted stickily, he swallowed convulsively, took one wavering step forward, and sank without a sound on to the dusty road.

The post-boy glanced up quickly, and his jaw dropped. 'Well, I'll be gormed!' he ejaculated. 'Lord love me, if he ain't gone off in a swound! A fine rank-rider *he* is!'

'Take his neckcloth off!' Amanda said. 'Quick!'

The post-boy snorted. 'Let him lay!'

'Yes, yes, but bring me his neckcloth! This is not enough! Oh, hurry, hurry!'

He still thought that all her labour would be in vain, but he did as she bade him, only pausing beside Hildebrand's inanimate form for long enough to wrench the second pistol out of the saddle-holster, and to thrust it into the bosom of his own tightly fitting jacket. Prince started uneasily, and flung up his head, but the placidity of the post-horses seemed to reassure him, and he remained standing by his master's body.

Amanda had succeeded in reducing the flow of blood, but it was still welling up under the soaked pad. Panic gripped her. The post-boy was obedient, but slow to understand her orders, and he appeared to be incapable of acting on his own initiative; Hildebrand, who should have rushed to her aid, had fainted instead, and was only just beginning to show signs of recovery. Furious with both of them, frightened out of her wits, she wanted more than anything to scream. Pride and obstinacy came to her rescue: she was the daughter of a soldier, and she meant to become the wife of a soldier; and own herself beaten she would not. She overcame her rising hysteria after a struggle that made her feel weak and rather sick, and forced her shocked mind to concentrate. Sir Gareth had been hit in the hollow of his shoulder, and a much larger pad than one made by folding a neckcloth must be bound tightly in place before she dared relax the pressure of her desperate little hands. She looked round helplessly, unable for a moment to think of anything; then she remembered that Sir Gareth's portmanteaux were strapped on the back of the chaise, and she ordered the post-boy to unstrap them. 'Shirts! Yes, shirts! There must be shirts! And more neckcloths to tie it in place–get them!'

The post-boy unstrapped the portmanteaux, but hesitated, saying: 'They'll be locked, surely!'

'Break the locks, then!' she said impatiently. 'Oh, if there were only *someone* who could help me!'

By this time, Hildebrand had struggled up. He was sick, and dizzy, and his legs shook under him, but Amanda's anguished cry pulled him together. The blood rushed up into his face; he said thickly, engulfed in shame: 'I'll do it!' and went unsteadily to where the post-boy had set one of the portmanteaux down on the road.

'Ho, yes?' said that individual, bristling. 'You will, will you? *And* make off with the gentleman's goods, I daresay!'

'*Idiot!*' The word burst from Amanda. 'Can't you see he's not a highwayman? Let him get at that case! I–I *command* you!'

She sounded so fierce that the post-boy gave way instinctively. The portmanteau was not locked, and with trembling hands Hildebrand flung back the lid, and began to toss over Sir Gareth's effects. He found shirts, and many neckcloths, and a large sponge, at sight of which Amanda exclaimed: 'Oh, yes, yes! Tie that up in a shirt, tight, *tight*, and bring it to me! Oh, no, give it to the post-boy, and whatever you do, Hildebrand, don't look this way, or you will go off again in a faint, and there is no *time* to waste in fainting!'

He was much too overcome to answer her, but although he dared not let his eyes stray towards her he could do what she asked, and could even knot several of the neckcloths together. Between them, Amanda and the post-boy contrived to bind the improvised swab tightly in place; and while they worked, Amanda demanded to be told where the nearest inn, or house could be found. The post-boy at first could think of nothing nearer than Bedford, which was some eight miles distant, but upon being adjured pretty sharply to find his wits he said that there was an inn at Little Staughton, a mile down the crossroad. He added that it wasn't fit for the likes of Sir Gareth, upon which, Amanda, wrought to a dangerous pitch of exasperation, told him he was a cloth-headed gapeseed, an unladylike utterance which was culled from her grandfather's vocabulary, and which considerably startled the post-boy. She directed him to strap up the portmanteaux again; and while he was doing it, she turned her attention to Hildebrand, informing him that he must help to lift Sir Gareth into the chaise. 'It is of no avail to tell me you can't, because you *must*!' she said severely. 'And I forbid you to faint until Sir Gareth is safely bestowed! You may then do so, if you wish, but I can't stay for you, so you must take care of yourself. And I shan't have the least compunction in leaving you, for this is all your fault, and now, when we are in this fix, you become squeamish, which puts me out of all patience with you!'

The unhappy Hildebrand stammered: 'Of course I will help to lift him! I don't *wish* to faint: I can't help but do so!'

'You can do anything if only you will have a little resolution!' she told him.

The bracing treatment had its effect upon him. He could not but shudder when his eyes fell on her bloodstained gown, but he quickly averted them, choked down his nausea, and silently prayed that he might not again disgrace himself. The prayer was answered. Sir Gareth was lifted as tenderly as was possible into the chaise, where Amanda received him, and Hildebrand was still on his feet. This unlooked-for triumph put a little heart into him, and he suddenly looked very much less hang-dog, and said that he would ride on ahead to warn them at the inn to prepare to house a badly wounded man.

Amanda warmly approved this suggestion, but the post-boy who still felt that Hildebrand was a dangerous rogue, opposed it, even going to the length of pulling out the pistol from his jacket. Hildebrand, he said, would ride immediately in front of him, so that he could put a bullet through him if he tried to gallop away.

'What a detestably stupid creature you are!' exclaimed Amanda. 'It was all a jest—a wager! Oh, I can't explain it to you now, but Sir Gareth knew it was an accident! You heard him say so! Yes, and you don't suppose he would call a real highwayman a young fool, do you? Doesn't that *show* you that he knew him? And he won't try to escape, because I assure you he is excessively fond of Sir Gareth. Go *at once*, Hildebrand! And get on your horse, and follow him, and oh, pray, *pray* drive carefully!'

'Shoot me if you wish!' Hildebrand said, seizing the horse's bridle. 'I don't care! I'd rather that than be hanged or transported!'

With these reckless words, he mounted Prince, clapped his heels to the horse's flanks, and shot off down the lane.

The chaise followed at a very much more sober pace, but the lane was so narrow that the post-boy found it impossible to avoid the many pot-holes. The best he could do, whenever he saw a particular large one ahead, was to rein the horses in to a walk, lessening the jolt as much as he could. But nothing could avail to make the short journey anything but a very rough one. Amanda kept an anxious eye on her bandages, terrified that the pad might shift, and the bleeding start again. So tall a man could not be laid flat in a chaise, but Amanda had clasped her arms round Sir Gareth, supporting his head on her shoulder, and trying as best she might to ease the frequent bumps for him. Under her hand she fancied that she could feel his heart faintly beating, which brought such relief to her overcharged nerves that thankful tears sprang to her eyes, and rolled unheeded down her cheeks.

Finding that the bandages were holding, her most pressing anxiety abated, and she was able to consider all the other anxieties attached to her predicament. Chief among these was the stringent need to rescue Hildebrand from the consequences of his folly. She was not much given to self-blame, but there could be no doubt that she had been to some extent responsible for the accident. To be sure, she had extracted from Hildebrand a promise that he would not fire his pistols, but she now saw that she should have known better than to have placed the slightest reliance on his keeping his head in emergency. And although no one (or, at any rate, no one with the smallest sense of justice) could blame her for having accepted his proffered services, she did feel that she was very much to blame in having consented to any plan that could possibly put poor Sir Gareth in danger. If she had not blackened Sir Gareth's character, Hildebrand would never have dreamt of holding up the chaise; and that she had blackened his character now filled her with unaccustomed remorse. It really seemed more dreadful than all the rest, for as soon as he had sunk lifeless to the ground, her resentment had vanished, and she had seen him, not as a cruel marplot, but as her kind and endlessly patient protector. But this, she owned, Hildebrand could not have guessed, from anything she had told him; and however stupid it was of him not to have known, only by looking at Sir Gareth, that he was in every respect an admirable person, it was not just that he should suffer a hideous penalty for his folly. Sir Gareth had not wished him to suffer. With what might prove to have been his last word on earth he had exonerated Hildebrand. The thought of this noble magnanimity affected her so much, that she exclaimed aloud: 'Oh, I *wish* I had not told those lies about you! It was all my fault!'

But Sir Gareth could not hear her, so it was useless to tell him how sorry she was. And even if he had not been unconscious, she thought, her practical side reasserting itself, repentance would not mend matters. She dared not relax her arms from about him, so she could not wipe away her tears, but she stopped crying, and forced herself to think what she ought next to do. Her arms were aching almost unbearably, but that was unimportant. The important thing was to save Hildebrand from the clutches of the law. He was stupid, he lacked resolution, but she was going to need his services.

By the time the chaise reached the little village, she had herself well in hand, and knew just what must be done. Her face might be tearstained, but the landlord of the Bull Inn, horrified by the disjointed tale jerked out by a pallid young gentleman on the verge of nervous collapse, and expecting to receive a damsel in hysterics, very speedily learned that Amanda was made of sterner stuff than Hildebrand. She might look a child, but there was nothing childlike in the way in which she assumed command over the direction of affairs. Under her jealous supervision, the landlord and the post-boy bore Sir Gareth up the narrow stairs to a bedchamber under the eaves, and laid him upon the bed there; and while they were doing it she told Hildebrand, in a fierce whisper, not to say a word, but to leave all to her; and demanded from the landlord's wife the direction of the nearest doctor, and upon learning that that shocked dame knew of no doctor other than Dr Chantry, who attended the Squire, and lived at Eaton Socon, instantly ordered Hildebrand to jump on his horse again, and ride like the wind to summon this practitioner to Sir Gareth's side.

'Yes, of course!' Hildebrand said eagerly. 'But I don't know how to get there, or—or where to find the doctor, or what to do if he should not be at home!'

'Oh, do *try* not to be so helpless!' cried Amanda. 'This woman will tell you where he lives, and if he is gone out you will follow him—and do not *dare* to come back without him!' She then turned on Mrs Chicklade, and said: 'Tell him *exactly* where to go, for you can see how stupid he is!'

'I am not stupid!' retorted Hildebrand, stung to anger. 'But I was never in this part of the country before, and I don't even know in which direction I should ride!'

'No!' retorted Amanda, already halfway up the steep stairs. 'I don't know either, but I wouldn't stand there looking like a gaby, and saying *how—how—how!*'

With that, she sped on her way, leaving him seething with indignation, but considerably stiffened by a determination to prove to her his worth.

Amanda found the landlord tightening the bandages round Sir Gareth's torso, and directing the post-boy to fetch up some brandy from the tap. She was thankful to perceive that in this large, stolid man she had acquired a helper who could apparently act on his own initiative, and asked him anxiously if he thought Sir Gareth would live.

'There's no saying, miss,' he replied unencouragingly. 'He ain't slipped his wind yet, but I'd say he's lost a deal of claret. We'll see if we can get a drop of brandy down his throat.'

But when the post-boy came back with this restorative, closely followed by Mrs Chicklade, it was found to be of no avail, for it ran out of the corners of Sir Gareth's mouth. The landlord thought this a shocking waste of good liquor, and set the glass down, saying that there was nothing for it but to send for the doctor. When Amanda disclosed that Hildebrand had already sped forth on this errand, the post-boy was loud in his disapproval. He said that the young varmint would never be seen again, and at once launched into a graphic description of the hold-up.

Until that moment, the Chicklades knew no more than they had learnt from Hildebrand, which was very little. So strange a story as was now recounted immediately convinced Mrs Chicklade that she had been only too right when she had strongly counselled her husband not to have anything to do with a desperately wounded man. She had known from the moment of clapping eyes on Hildebrand that there was something havey-cavey about him; and as for Amanda, she would like to know, she said, how she came to be hand-in-glove with such a murdering young rascal.

'I wish you will stop thinking he is a highwayman!' said Amanda. 'It was all make-believe—just funning!'

'*Funning?*' gasped Mrs Chicklade.

'Yes, I tell you! He never meant to fire his pistol: indeed, he promised me he would not!'

'What did he want to take and cock it for, if he wasn't meaning to fire it, miss?' demanded the post-boy shrewdly.

'Oh, that was in case you would not pull up!' explained Amanda. 'To fire over your head, and put you in a fright. And although I didn't wish him to do so at first, I must say I am excessively sorry now that he didn't, because if only he had there would have been no harm done.'

'I never did!' exclaimed Mrs Chicklade. 'Why, you're as bad as he is! I believe the pair of you was in a plot to rob the poor gentleman, and what I want to know is how you came to wheedle yourself into his company, which it's as plain as a pikestaff you must ha' done, and very likely too, for a bolder piece I never did see, not in all my days!'

'Easy, now!' interposed the landlord, in his deep voice. 'I'll allow it's a queer-sounding business, but you've no call to speak so rough to the young lady, my dear. Who is the gentleman, missie?'

'*I* can tell you that!' said the post-boy officiously. 'He's Sir Gareth Ludlow, and a bang-up tulip, and him and her was putting-up in Kimbolton last night. He hired me for to carry them to Bedford.'

The landlord looked Amanda over thoughtfully. 'Well, now, miss, you ain't his wife, because you've got no ring on your finger, and he don't look to me old enough to be your pa, nor yet young enough to be your brother, so what's the game?'

'Ah, answer *that* if you can!' said Mrs Chicklade.

'He is my uncle,' replied Amanda calmly. 'And also he is Mr Ross's uncle. Mr Ross is the man who shot him, but quite by accident. In fact, Mr Ross and I are cousins, and it is true that we were hand-in-glove, but only to play a trick on Sir Gareth. But Sir Gareth recognized him, and I daresay he knew that he was not at all to be trusted with a pistol, because he told him not to brandish it about, and said he was a young fool. *Didn't he?*'

'Ay,' responded the post-boy reluctantly. 'But—'

'And then *you* got off your horse, and of course my cousin thought you meant to attack him, which was the cause of the accident. Because that put him in a fluster. And then his horse began to be very restive, and in the middle of it all the gun went off. He never, never meant to fire it at Sir Gareth! He wasn't even looking at him!'

'He said to the gentleman, *If you come a step nearer, I'll fire!* he said. Yes, and he threatened to blow the head off my shoulders, what's more!'

'It seems to me a great pity that he didn't do so!' said Amanda. 'I am quite *tired* of talking to anyone so stupid! If you had a particle of commonsense you would know that if he had wished to escape he might have done so when you were helping me to bind the neckcloths round Sir Gareth! And if he had meant to shoot Sir Gareth, he wouldn't have fallen down in a swoon, in that silly way, which you know very well he did!'

'Swooned off, did he?' said the landlord. 'It don't surprise me. He was looking just about as sick as a cushion when he came bursting in here. Seems to me it's likely as not it happened the way you say it did, miss, but there's no sense in argufying, whatever the rights of it may be. Martha, my dear, you take the young lady to the other bedchamber, where she can wash the blood off her hands, and put on a clean gown. When you've done that, you can pop a brick in the oven, because the gentleman's powerful cold. And as for you, young fellow, you can fetch up his baggage, and help me get the clothes off him, so as he can be laid between sheets, comfortable.'

Amanda cast a doubtful glance at Sir Gareth, but as she could think of nothing she could do to revive him, and the landlord seemed dependable, she allowed herself to be led by her disapproving hostess into the room beside the one to which Sir Gareth had been carried.

By the time Hildebrand returned to the inn, announcing that the doctor was following as fast as he could in his gig, not only had Amanda changed her gown, but she had further alienated Mrs Chicklade by demanding milk for Joseph. Mrs Chicklade said that she couldn't abide cats, and wouldn't have a pesky kitten in her kitchen, getting under her feet, but as her lord happened to come in just then, wanting to know whether the brick wasn't hot enough yet, and told her not to be disobliging, Joseph got his milk.

Chicklade reported that Sir Gareth had come out of his swoon for a brief period, when his boots were being pulled off. He had muttered something unintelligible, and had sunk back into unconsciousness before he could be got to swallow any brandy, but Chicklade considered it hopeful that he had even for no more than a minute shown a sign of life. Hildebrand came hurrying in, to be met by these joyful tidings; and so great had been his dread that he would reach the inn only to find that Sir Gareth was dead that he burst into tears. This excess of sensibility did nothing to recommend him to Amanda, but considerably relieved the unbearable tension of his nerves. He was able, in a few moments, to listen with tolerable composure to the news that, during his absence, he had acquired two new relations.

'Do you perfectly understand?' Amanda asked anxiously. 'Sir Gareth is our uncle, and you held him up because we had made a plan to play a trick on him.'

He was far from understanding, but he nodded, adding, in a hopeless tone, that when Sir Gareth came to himself he would promptly disown him.

'Of course he will not!' said Amanda. 'He wouldn't dream of doing such an unhandsome thing!'

This remark was quite incomprehensible to him, but before he could demand enlightenment the doctor had arrived, and he was left to puzzle over it in solitude.

The doctor was surprised to be received by so youthful a lady, and although he accepted without question that she was his patient's niece he was much inclined to think that Mrs Chicklade would be a more competent assistant to him in any surgery that he might have to perform. But when he saw what she had already done for Sir Gareth he changed his mind. While he unpacked his bag, and Chicklade went off to bring up a bowl of hot water, he asked her a good many questions about the affair, shooting a curious look at her every now and then from under his bushy eyebrows. He said finally that she was a very remarkable young lady, and begged pardon for having doubted her fortitude.

In the event, the operation of extracting the bullet was a sight which tried her fortitude severely, and it was only by a supreme exercise of will-power that she managed to remain at the bedside, handing Dr Chantry the various instruments, and swabs of lint which he from time to time called for.

Sir Gareth came round under the doctor's hands, and uttered a groan that made Amanda wince in sympathy. The doctor spoke to him in heartening accents, and he opened his eyes. After a bewildered moment, he seemed to realize what had happened to him, for he said, faintly, but perfectly clearly: 'I remember. Not the boy's fault!'

The doctor directed Chicklade, under his breath, to hold him, but after a few minutes of endurance he lost consciousness again.

'Ay, and just as well,' grunted Dr Chantry, when Chicklade, rather alarmed, drew his attention to this circumstance. 'It's in devilish deep, I can tell you. No sense in bringing him round, poor fellow, till I have him tied up comfortably.'

It seemed to Amanda a very long time before this last operation was performed, and she could not believe that Sir Gareth would find it comfortable. But the doctor said that by God's mercy the bullet had not touched a vital spot, which made her feel very much more cheerful, until he added that no one could say yet how it would turn out, though he hoped that with perfect quiet and good nursing all might be well.

'But he won't die, will he?' Amanda asked imploringly.

'I trust not, young lady, but it's a nasty wound, and he has lost a great deal of blood. I can tell you this: if you hadn't behaved with such presence of mind he wouldn't be alive now.'

But Amanda, who had always longed to play a heroine's part, could only see herself as little better than a murderess, and impatiently brushed this aside, saying: 'Tell me exactly what I must do to make him better! *Everything* I must do!'

He patted her shoulder. 'No, no, you're too young, my dear! Now, don't fret! I don't anticipate that there will be any complications, but what we want is an experienced woman to look after him.'

'I'll send round to Mrs Bardfield, sir,' Chicklade said.

'Oh, the midwife! Ay, an excellent notion! There's little to be done for him at present but to keep him quiet, but I shall send my boy with a cordial, and some laudanum, in case he should grow restless. I've given him something to make him sleep, but if the wound should become inflamed he may develop a little fever presently. No need to be unduly anxious, however. I shall be over to take a look at him this evening, never fear!'

I4

For a long time after the doctor's departure, Amanda remained seated beside Sir Gareth's bed. To her eye, Dr Chantry did not compare favourably with such members of the faculty as had previously come in her way, but she could see that whatever it was that he had obliged his patient to swallow had certainly been of benefit to him. He was still dreadfully pale, but he no longer lay in a death-like swoon. He seemed to be heavily asleep, but from time to time his hand, which was lying outside the blankets, twitched, or he moved his head restlessly on the pillow.

At noon, Chicklade came softly into the room, and whispered to her that Mrs Bardfield was below-stairs, having come up from her cottage at the other end of the village to take a look at her patient.

'She'll sit up with him tonight, miss. Doctor says he won't want anything for a while yet, so I don't doubt we can manage well enough till dinner-time. Will I bring her up, so as she can see how the gentleman is?'

Amanda gave ready permission. In emergency, she could act not only with courage, but with an inborn sense of what was needed; but confronted with a sick-bed she was conscious of ignorance. It was with a thankful countenance that she rose to greet a woman of experience of sick-nursing.

She suffered a severe revulsion of feeling. The lady who presently wheezed her way up the stairs, and entered the room with no light tread, was not one whose appearance invited confidence. She was extremely stout, and although she seemed from her ingratiating smile to be good-humoured Amanda thought her countenance very unprepossessing. She liked neither the expression of her curiously hazy eyes, nor their inability to remain fixed for more than a moment on any one object. The cap which she wore under a large bonnet was by no means clean, and there emanated from her person an unpleasant aroma of which the predominant elements were onions, stale sweat, and spirituous liquor. The floor shook under her heavy tread, and when she bent over Sir Gareth, she said: 'Ah, poor dear!' in an unctuous voice which filled Amanda with loathing. She then laid her hand on his brow, and said: 'Well, he ain't feverish, which is one good thing, but he looks mortal bad.' After that, she adjusted his pillows with hearty good-will, and ruthlessly straightened the blankets that covered him. He was too heavily drugged to wake, but Amanda could bear no longer to see Mrs Bardfield's rough and not over-clean hands touching him, and she said sharply: 'Don't! Leave him alone!'

Mrs Bardfield was accustomed to the nervous qualms of sick persons' relatives, and she smiled indulgently, saying: 'Lor' bless you, dearie, you don't want to worrit your head now I'm here! Many's the gentleman I've nursed, ay, and laid out too! Now, I'll stay beside him for a while, because

Mr Chicklade's got a nice bit of cold meat and pickles laid out for a nuncheon for you and the young gentleman, and a pot of tea besides. That'll do you good, and you'll know your poor uncle's in safe hands.'

Amanda managed to thank her, though in a choked voice, and fled down the stairs to find Hildebrand. He was awaiting her in the small parlour, and when he saw her face he started forward, exclaiming in horror: 'Good God, what is it? Oh, is he *worse?*'

'No, no! I wouldn't have left him if he hadn't been better! It is that detestable old woman! Hildebrand, she shan't touch him! I won't permit it! She is dirty, and rough, and she says she lays people out!'

'Yes, I know—I saw her, and I must own—But what are we to do, if you turn her off! *You* cannot nurse Sir Gareth, and Mrs Chicklade seems very unamiable, so that I shouldn't think—'

'Oh, no! I know just what I ought to do, only I cannot! I don't even know her name! His sister, I mean. So I have made up my mind that Lady Hester must come, and I think she would be willing to, because she is very kind, and she said she would like to help me if she could. And besides that, Mr Theale told me that Sir Gareth was going to offer for her, and although I don't know if it was true, perhaps it was, and she would *wish* me to send for her! So—'

'Going to offer for her?' broke in Hildebrand. 'But you said he was determined to marry you!'

'Yes, I know I did, but it wasn't true! I can't think how you came to imagine it was, for of all the *absurd* things—! I suppose I shall have to explain it all to you, but first I must know if that stupid post-boy is still here.'

'I think he's in the tap, but I've paid him off. I—I thought that would be the right thing to do.'

'Oh, yes, but I find we shall need him, *and* the chaise! Hildebrand, I do hope to goodness he doesn't still wish to inform against you?'

'No,' he replied, flushing. 'I—I told Dr Chantry, and he made all right. And I must tell you, Amanda, that even if Sir Gareth hasn't behaved well towards you, he has behaved towards me with a generosity I can *never* repay. When the doctor told me what he said when he came to himself—' He broke off, his lip quivering.

'Yes, he is the kindest creature!' she agreed. 'And though he made me very angry—and I *still* cannot feel that he had any business to interfere, and ruin my plan!—he didn't do any of the things I said he did. Never mind that now! You must go and tell the post-boy that you will be requiring him to drive you to Brancaster Park, to bring back Lady Hester. I am not perfectly sure how many miles it is to Chatteris, but I shouldn't think we can be very far from it.'

'*Chatteris?*' he interrupted. 'It must be five-and-twenty miles away, and very likely more!'

'Well, and if it is, *surely* you don't mean to say you won't go?' she demanded. 'Of all the *paltry* things!'

'Of course I don't!' he retorted, glaring at her. 'But I am not going to hire a chaise for a drive of fifty miles and more! Besides, the post-boy Sir Gareth hired wouldn't agree to it, because he was hired to go to Bedford, and nowhere else. And even if he did consent, I wouldn't have him!'

'But—'

'I'll tell you what it is, Amanda!' said Mr Ross, in a most unadmiring tone. 'You fancy no one can think of anything but yourself!'

'Well, no one has!' she said, firing up. 'And certainly not you, for you only—'

'Who thought of riding on ahead to prepare the Chicklades?'

'Oh, that!' said Amanda, hunching up one shoulder.

'Yes, that!' he said furiously. 'And, what's more, it was I who thought of holding up the chaise, not you!'

'Well, if you mean to boast of that, I suppose you will say next that you thought of shooting Sir Gareth!' cried Amanda.

Battle was now fairly joined, and for the next few minutes two overwrought young persons found relief for their shocked nerves in a right royal quarrel. Sir Gareth on his sick-bed, and the nuncheon on the table were alike forgotten in a wholesale exchange of recriminations. Chicklade, coming into the parlour with a dish of fruit, stopped on the threshold, and for several moments listened, unperceived, to a quarrel which was rapidly sinking to nursery-level. Indeed, when he presently rejoined his wife, he told her, with a chuckle, that there could be no doubt that the young lady and gentleman were related: to hear them, you'd have thought them brother and sister.

As soon as they became aware of his presence, their quarrel ceased abruptly. In cold and haughty silence, they took their places at the table. Neither had any appetite, but each drank a cup of tea, and felt better. Amanda stole a surreptitious look at Hildebrand, found that he was stealing one at her, and giggled. This broke the ice; they both fell into laughter; after which Hildebrand begged pardon, if he had been uncivil; and Amanda said that she hadn't really meant to say that she was sure he couldn't write a play.

Friendly relations were thus re-established, but Hildebrand's brief period of enchantment was over. It had not, in fact, survived the impatience she had shown when he had recovered from his swoon. She was still a very pretty girl, though not (when one studied her dispassionately) as beautiful as he had at first thought her; and she certainly had a great deal of spirit, but he preferred girls with gentler manners. He was inclined to think that, in addition to being much too masterful, she was unbecomingly bold. By the time she had confided to him, under the seal of secrecy, the exact circumstances which had led up to her encounter with Sir Gareth, he was sure of this. His shocked face, and unhesitating condemnation of her plan of campaign, very nearly resulted in the resumption of hostilities. To disapproval of her outrageous scheme was added indignation that she should have enlisted his support by painting Sir Gareth in false colours. He exclaimed that it was the shabbiest thing; and as she secretly agreed with him her defence lacked conviction.

'But it *is* true that he abducted me,' she argued.

'I consider that his behaviour has throughout been chivalrous and gentlemanly,' replied Hildebrand.

'I thought you looked to be stuffy as soon as I saw you,' said Amanda. 'That is why I didn't tell you how it really was. And I was quite right.'

'It is not a question of being stuffy,' said Hildebrand loftily, 'but of having worldly sense, and proper notions of conduct. And now that I know the truth I can't suppose that this Lady Hester would dream of coming here. How very much shocked she must have been!'

'Well, she was not!' said Amanda. 'She was most truly sympathetic, so you know nothing of the matter! And also she told me that she has had a very dull life, besides being obliged to live with the most disagreeable set of people I ever saw, so I daresay she will be very glad to come here.' She paused, eyeing him. He still looked dubious, so she said in another, and much more earnest voice: '*Pray*, Hildebrand, go and fetch her! That dreadful old woman upstairs will very likely kill poor Sir Gareth, because she is rough, and dirty, and I can see she means to lay him out! I won't permit her to nurse him! I will nurse him myself, only—only that doctor said that he might grow feverish, and if, perhaps, I didn't do the things I should for him, and he didn't get better, but *worse*, and there was only you and me to take care of him—Hildebrand, I *can't*!'

She ended on a note of suppressed panic, but Hildebrand was already convinced. The picture her words had conjured up made him blench. In his relief at finding that he had not killed Sir Gareth outright, optimism, which he now saw to have been unjustified, had sprung up in his breast. The thought that Sir Gareth might still die, here, in this tiny inn, far from his own kith and kin, attended only by a schoolroom miss and his murderer, made him shudder. Before his mind's eye flitted a horrifying vision of himself seeking out Sir Gareth's sister, and breaking to her the news that her brother was dead, and by his hand. He set his teacup down with a jar, exclaiming: 'Good God, no! I hadn't considered—Of course I will go to Chatteris! I never meant that I would not—and even if this Lady Hester should refuse to come back with me she will be at least able to tell me where I may find Sir Gareth's sister!'

'She *will* come!' Amanda averred. 'So will you go at once to tell the post-boy he must drive you to Brancaster Park?'

'No,' replied Hildebrand, setting his jaw. 'I'll have nothing to do with the fellow! Besides, what a shocking waste of money it would be to be hiring a chaise to carry me to Brancaster Park, when I shall reach it very much more quickly if I ride there—or, at any rate, to Huntingdon, where I may hire a chaise for Lady Hester's conveyance—that is, if you think she won't prefer to travel in her own carriage?'

Amanda, thankful to find him suddenly so amenable, said approvingly: 'That is an excellent notion, and *much* better than mine! I see you have learnt habits of economy, which is something I must do too, for an expensive wife would not suit Neil at all, I daresay. But I have a strong feeling that that odious Lady Widmore would cast a rub in the way of Lady Hester's coming to my aid, if she could, and she would be bound to discover what she meant to do, if Lady Hester ordered her carriage. In fact, the more I think of it, the more I am persuaded that Lady Hester must slip away secretly. So when you reach Brancaster Park, you must insist on seeing her *alone*, and on no account must you disclose your errand to anyone else.'

Hildebrand was in full agreement with her on this point, having the greatest reluctance to spread further than was strictly necessary the story of the day's dreadful events, but an unwelcome consideration had occurred to him, and he said uneasily: 'Will it not make Mrs Chicklade even more unamiable, if we bring Lady Hester here to stay? You know, I don't like to mention it to you, but she has been saying *such* things! I don't think Chicklade will attend to her, because he seems to be a good sort of a fellow, but she wants him to tell Dr Chantry he won't have Sir Gareth here, or any of us, because nothing will persuade her we are respectable persons—which, when one comes to think of it, we are not,' he added gloomily. 'Depend upon it, she doesn't believe the hum you told her, about Sir Gareth's being our uncle.'

'We must remember always to say "my uncle" when we have occasion to mention him,' nodded Amanda. 'In fact, we had better call him Uncle Gareth even between ourselves, so that we get into the habit of it.'

'Yes, but she is so horridly suspicious that I daresay that won't answer. And, in any event, it wouldn't explain Lady Hester. I don't think we ought to say that she is betrothed to Sir–to Uncle Gareth–if you are not perfectly sure of it. Ten to one, it would make her feel very awkward, if it turned out to be no such thing.'

'Yes, very true,' she replied, frowning over this difficulty. 'I don't at all wish to put her in an uncomfortable situation, so we must think of some tale which that disagreeable woman *will* believe.'

'He watched her doubtfully, but after a moment her brow cleared, and she said: 'Of course I know the very thing to make all right! Lady Hester must be my aunt! Because it is the circumstance of my having no chaperon that makes Mrs Chicklade so disobliging. While I was putting off my stained gown, she kept on asking me the most impertinent questions, and saying that she wondered that my mother should let me travel in such a way, just as if she were sure I had no mother, which, indeed, I haven't, as I told her. And also I told her that I had an aunt instead, and I could see that she didn't believe me, though it is quite true. So, I think, Hildebrand, that the thing for you to do is to inform Chicklade that you feel it to be your duty to fetch my aunt, and that will convince Mrs Chicklade that I *was* speaking the truth!'

Thus it was arranged, Chicklade greeting the suggestion with instant approval, and a good deal of relief. Hildebrand saddled Prince, and rode off, leaving Amanda preparing to banish Mrs Bardfield irrevocably from the sick-room. It seemed likely that she would enjoy this task very much more than he expected to enjoy his.

He managed to reach Huntingdon in good time, by riding wherever possible across country. He learned there that his goal was situated very much nearer to St Ives, and so rode on to that town. At the Crown, he was able to hire a post-chaise and pair, and to stable Prince; and midway through the afternoon he arrived at Brancaster Park.

Amanda, having strictly enjoined him to disclose his errand to none but Lady Hester, had seemed to think there could be no difficulty about doing this, but when he was admitted into the house by a servant, who civilly inquired what his name was, he saw that it was only too probably that Lady Hester would refuse to receive a gentleman quite unknown to her. He explained, stammering a little, that his name would not be familiar to her ladyship; and then, as he thought the servant was looking suspiciously at him, he added that he was the bearer of an urgent message. The man bowed, and went away, leaving him in the large saloon, where he instantly fell a prey to all sorts of forebodings. Perhaps the Earl would come in, and demand to know his business; perhaps Lady Widmore would intercept the message to her sister-in-law; or, worse than all, perhaps Lady Hester was not at home.

The minutes ticked by, and he became more and more apprehensive. He hoped that his neckcloth was straight, and his hair tidy, and, seeing that a mirror hung at one end of the room, he went to it, to reassure himself on these points. He was engaged in smoothing his rather creased coat when he heard the door open behind him, and turned quickly to find that he was being regarded by a lady in a pomona green half-dress and a lace cap tied over her softly waving brown hair. Much discomposed to have been surprised preening himself in front of a mirror, he blushed scarlet, and became tongue-tied.

After thoughtfully observing these signs of embarrassment, the lady smiled, and stepped forward, saying: 'Pray do not mind! I know *exactly* how one is always quite positive that one's hat is crooked, or that there is a smut on one's face. How do you do? I am Hester Theale, you know.'

'How do you do?' he returned, still much flushed. 'My name is Ross—Hildebrand Ross, but—but you don't know me, ma'am!'

'No,' she agreed, sitting down on the sofa. 'But Cliffe said that you have a message for me. Won't you be seated?'

He thanked her, and sat down on the edge of a chair, and swallowed once or twice, trying to think how best to explain himself to her. She waited patiently, her hands folded in her lap, and smiled encouragingly at him.

'It is Amanda!' he blurted out. 'I mean, it was she who made me come, because she said she knew you would help her, but I didn't above half like to do it, ma'am, only—only the case is so desperate, you see!'

She looked startled, and exclaimed: 'Oh, *dear*! Didn't Sir Gareth find her, then? Of course I will do anything I can to help her, and if my uncle is the cause of her sending you to me, it is quite too dreadfully mortifying—though only to be expected, I am ashamed to say.'

'No, no! I mean, Sir Gareth did find her, but—well, it isn't for herself that Amanda wishes you to go to her, but for him!'

She blinked at him. 'I beg your pardon?' she said, bewildered.

He got up jerkily, squaring his shoulders. 'The thing is—I don't know how to tell you—but I—but he is very ill, ma'am!'

'Sir Gareth very ill?' she repeated, still looking bewildered. 'Surely you must be mistaken? He was perfectly stout when I saw him yesterday!'

'Yes, but the thing is that I have shot him!' said Hildebrand, rushing his fence.

He hoped very much that she would not swoon away, or fall into hysterics, and was at first relieved that she neither moved nor spoke. Then he saw that not only was she alarmingly pale, but her eyes were staring at him blindly, and he had a horrid fear that perhaps she was about to have a spasm. But when she spoke, it was in a strangely calm voice that seemed to come from a long way away. 'You said—very ill. Did you mean—dead?'

'No, upon my honour!' he answered eagerly. 'And the doctor assured us that the bullet didn't touch a vital spot, but he lost so much blood, in spite of Amanda's doing all she could to stanch it—which, I must say, she did—and it was in so deep, that he may become feverish, and there is only Amanda to nurse him—though I am ready to do *anything* in my power—because she won't let the midwife touch him. She says she is dirty and rough, and for my part I think she's an elbow-crooker, because she reeks of spirits.'

She listened to this not very lucid speech intently, but it was apparently beyond her comprehension, for when he stopped she got up, and went to him, laying her hand on his sleeve, and saying: 'I beg your pardon, but I don't understand what you are trying to tell me. I think there has been an accident, has there not? And Sir Gareth was hurt, but not fatally?'

'Yes—that is, I never meant to shoot him, I swear!'

'Oh, no, I am sure you could not have meant to!'

These soothing words, and the smile that went with them, made him say impulsively: 'I was afraid you would be very angry. But Amanda said you would not, ma'am—though when you learn the whole—'

'I don't think I shall be *angry*. But I should be very much obliged to you if you would sit down beside me here, on the sofa, and tell me just how it happened, because at present it does seem very odd to me that Sir Gareth should have been shot. Unless, of course, you had taken your gun out after wood-pigeons, and shot him by accident?'

'Worse!' uttered Hildebrand, with a groan. 'I held up his chaise!'

'But he wasn't travelling in a chaise,' said Lady Hester.

'Yes, he was, ma'am. A hired chaise, to carry him and Amanda to Bedford.'

'Is that where she lives?' Lady Hester asked hopefully.

'Oh, no! At least, I don't know, but I shouldn't think so. He was meaning to hire a better chaise there, for they only had one at Kimbolton, and the shabbiest old thing! That is where I fell in with them. I am on my way to Wales.'

'Now I begin to understand!' she said, pleased to find that he was not, as she had begun to fear, suffering from sun-stroke. 'I daresay you fell into conversation with Amanda, and that is how it all came about. What a resourceful girl she is, to be sure!'

'Yes, I suppose she is,' he said reluctantly. 'Though it wasn't she who thought of holding up the chaise. *I* thought of it!'

'I expect you are very resourceful too,' she said kindly.

'Well, I did think of that—not that I wish to boast, and of course I see *now* that it was very wrong—but from the way Amanda talks, you would imagine—You see, ma'am, this is how it was!'

He then poured into her ears an account of the whole affair. He discovered her to be a good listener, and since she did not put him out by uttering exclamations of horror or condemnation, he was encouraged to confide everything to her, even his own unfortunate weakness, which he could not mention without severe mortification. Indeed, he found it difficult to describe the scene in the lane without turning squeamish, and he was not at all surprised that his words drove the colour out of Lady Hester's cheeks again. 'It was horrible!' he muttered, covering his face with his hands, and shuddering. '*Horrible!*'

'Yes,' she agreed faintly. 'But you said—surely you said!—not fatal?'

'Dr Chantry told us that he did not anticipate that it would be so, but he says he must be most carefully nursed, and that is why Amanda made me come to fetch you, because she doesn't know where his sister lives, or even what her name is.'

'To fetch me?' she said, startled. 'But—' She stopped, looking at him blankly.

'Of, if you please, *won't* you come?' Hildebrand begged. 'I told Amanda I was sure you would not, but the case is desperate, and even if you tell me where to find Sir Gareth's sister it must be at least two days before she could reach him, and it might be too late! And, what is more,' he added, bethinking himself of a fresh difficulty, 'I don't think I have enough money left to pay for such an expensive journey.'

'Oh, if only I *could* come!' she said, in an anguished tone. She got up quickly, and began to walk about the room. 'You see, it isn't possible! My father has gone to Brighton, but there is still my brother, and his wife, and the servants—' Again she stopped, but this time it was as though an idea had occurred to her. Hildebrand watched her anxiously. Suddenly her myopic gaze focused on his face, and she smiled. 'Dear me, what a very poor creature I must seem to you! You see, I have never been in the habit of doing anything at all out of the way, so you must forgive me for not immediately thinking that I could. I daresay nothing could be easier. After all, Amanda contrived to escape from her home without the least difficulty, and I expect she was much more closely watched than I am. Let me consider a little!'

He waited in pent-up silence, venturing after a few moments to say: 'I have a chaise waiting outside, if—if you feel that you could come with me, ma'am.'

'Have you? Oh, well, that makes everything perfectly simple!' she said, her worried frown lightening. 'I shall tell the servants that you have come to me from my sister, Lady Ennerdale. I wonder what can have happened at Ancaster? The children, of course—they must be ill! Now, was it the Ennerdale children who had measles two years ago, or was it my sister Milford's children? No, the Ennerdales have *not* had the measles: it was whooping-cough, now I come to think of it. Very well, they shall have the measles—all five of them, which would quite account for my sister's desiring me to go to her.' She smiled vaguely upon Hildebrand, and said, gathering her half-train up: 'Will you wait while I direct my woman to pack for me? My sister-in-law has driven to Ely, and I do not expect her to return until dinner-time. My brother is somewhere on the estate, but even if he were to come in, I daresay we may fob him off very easily. Do you think, in case you found yourself obliged to answer any awkward questions, you could decide how it comes about that my sister sent you to fetch me rather than one of her servants? It seems an odd thing for her to have done, but I am sure you will think of a very good reason. Sir Matthew Ennerdale-Ancaster—three boys and two girls, and poor little Giles is very sickly, and my sister sadly nervous!'

With these cryptic words, she went away, leaving Hildebrand quite as nervous as Lady Ennerdale. He hoped devoutly that Lord Widmore would not come in: the information conveyed to him by Lady Hester seemed to him meagre.

Upstairs, Lady Hester overcame the difficulty of answering Povey's surprised questions by ignoring them. This, since she knew herself to be in disgrace, did not astonish Povey, but when she learned that she was not to accompany her mistress to the stricken household she was moved to the heart, and burst into tears. Lady Hester was sorry for her distress, but since some explanation would have to be forthcoming for her unprecedented conduct in going away unattended by her maid, she thought the best thing to do would be to pretend that she was still too angry with Povey to wish for her company. So she said, with gentle coldness: 'No, Povey, I do not want you. Lady Ennerdale's woman will do all I require. Do not pack any evening gowns, if you please: they will not be needed.'

At any other time, Povey would have expostulated, for however ill Lady Ennerdale's offspring might be it was in the highest degree unlikely that her ladyship would collapse into a state of what she, as well as Povey, would certainly consider to be squalor. But the awful punishment that had been meted out to her possessed her mind so wholly that it was not until much later that the strange nature of the packing she had mechanically performed occurred to her. It was conceivable that Lady Hester might discover a need for hartshorn, but what she wanted with a roll of flannel, or why she insisted on taking her own pillow to her sister's well-appointed house, were matters that presently puzzled Povey very much indeed.

When she came downstairs again, a plain pelisse worn over a sad-coloured morning-dress which she commonly wore when engaged in gardening, or attending to her dogs, Hester found the butler awaiting her in the hall, and she knew at once, from the look on his face, that he was not going to be as easy to deceive as the lachrymose Povey.

She paused at the foot of the stairs, drawing on her gloves, and looking at Cliffe with a little challenge in her eyes.

'My lady, where are you going to?' he asked her bluntly. 'That chaise never came from Ancaster! It's from the Crown at St Ives, and the post-boy with it!'

'Oh, dear, how vexatious of you to recognize it!' sighed Hester. 'And now I suppose you have told all the other servants!'

'No, my lady, I have not, and well you know I would not!'

She smiled at him, a gleam of mischief in her face. 'Don't! I *rely* on you to tell my brother, and her ladyship, that I have gone to Lady Ennerdale–because the children *all* have the measles.'

'But where *are* you going, my lady?' Cliffe asked, perturbed.

'Well, I don't precisely know, but it really doesn't signify! I shall be quite safe, and not very far from here, and I shall return–oh, very soon, alas! Don't try to detain me, *pray*! I have written a very untruthful letter to her ladyship: will you give it to her, if you please?'

He took it from her, and after staring very hard at her for a moment, he bowed, and said: 'Yes, my lady.'

'You have always been such a kind friend to me: thank you!'

'There is no one in this house, my lady, barring those it wouldn't be seemly for me to name, who wouldn't be happy to serve you–but I wish I could be sure I was doing right!'

'Oh, yes! For I am going upon an errand of mercy, you might say. Now I must not waste any more time: will you tell Mr Ross I am quite ready to start?'

'Yes, my lady. I should perhaps mention that Mr Whyteleafe has been with him for the past twenty minutes, however.'

'Dear me, how very unfortunate! I wish I knew what Mr Ross may have told him!' she murmured. 'Perhaps I had better go to the Red Saloon myself.'

She entered this apartment in time to hear Mr Ross's firm assertion that *all* the children had the measles, though none was so alarmingly full of them as little Giles. Lady Ennerdale, he added, was prostrate with anxiety.

'You astonish me!' exclaimed the chaplain, rather narrowly observing him. 'I had not thought her ladyship—'

'Because,' said Mr Ross hurriedly, 'the nurse had the misfortune to fall down the stairs, and break her leg, and so everything falls upon her shoulders!'

'Yes, is it not dreadful?' interposed Lady Hester. 'Poor Susan! no wonder she should be distracted! I am quite ready to set forward, Mr Ross, and indeed I feel that we should lose no time!'

'All the way to Ancaster!' Mr Whyteleafe said, looking thunderstruck. 'You will never reach it tonight, Lady Hester! Surely it would be wiser to wait until tomorrow?'

'No, no, for that would mean that I should not arrive until quite late, and knocked up by the journey, I daresay. We shall spend the night somewhere on the road. And then I shan't be extraordinarily fatigued, and shall be able to render my sister all the assistance possible.'

'If you *must* go, Lady Hester, I wonder at it that Sir Matthew should not have had the courtesy to fetch you himself! I make no apology for speaking plainly on this head! There is a lack of consideration in such behaviour, a—'

'Sir Matthew,' said Mr Ross, 'is away from home, sir. That is why I offered to be his deputy.'

'Yes, and how very much obliged to you I am!' said Hester. 'But do not let us be dawdling any longer, I beg!'

Mr Whyteleafe said no more, but he was evidently very much shocked by this renewed instance of the shameless demands made upon Hester by her sisters, and it was with tightly folded lips that he accompanied her to where the chaise waited. She was afraid that he too would recognize the post-boy, but he did not bestow more than a cursory glance on him, the circumstance of Lady Ennerdale's having been shabby enough to have sent a hired vehicle, with only two horses, for the conveyance of her sister, ousting all else from his head. Lady Hester was handed up into the chaise, Mr Ross jumped in after her, the steps were let up, and in another minute they were drawing away from the house.

'Phew!' Hildebrand said involuntarily, pulling out his handkerchief, and mopping his brow. 'I can't tell you how thankful I was that you came in just then, ma'am, for he was asking me all manner of questions! He would know who I was, and I was obliged to tell him that I was employed by Sir Matthew as a secretary.'

'How very clever of you! I daresay he was very much surprised, for Sir Matthew is interested in nothing but sport.'

'Yes, he was—in fact, he said he could not imagine what I should find to do for Sir Matthew. So I said Sir Matthew had formed the intention of going into politics.'

This made her laugh so much that he lost any lingering shyness, and ventured to break to her the news that she had become, without her knowledge, Amanda's aunt. He was a little afraid that she might be affronted, for she was much younger than Amanda had led him to suppose; but she accepted the relationship with approval, and said that perhaps she had better become his aunt too.

By the time the chaise arrived at Little Staughton, they were fast friends. Dusk was falling when it drew up before the Bull Inn, and lamplight shone through several of the windows. As Hildebrand jumped down, and turned to Lady Hester, Amanda leaned out of one of the casements set under the eaves, and called, in a voice sharpened by anxiety: 'Hildebrand? Oh, Hildebrand, have you brought her?'

He looked up. 'Yes, here she is! Take care you don't fall out of the window!'

She disappeared abruptly. The hand in Hildebrand's trembled convulsively, but Lady Hester's voice, when she spoke, was quite quiet. 'I must leave you to settle with the post-boy, Hildebrand. I am afraid—'

She did not say what she was afraid of, but went swiftly into the inn. As she crossed the threshold, Amanda reached the foot of the steep stairs, and fairly pounced on her, dryly sobbing from mingled fright and relief. 'Oh, thank God you are come at last! He is very, very ill, and I cannot make him lie still, or even hear me! Oh, La—Aunt Hester, *come*!'

'Ah, I thought Miss would be sorry she turned off Mrs Bardfield so hasty!' remarked Mrs Chicklade, in the background, and speaking with a morbid satisfaction which made Amanda round on her like a young tigress.

'Go away, you odious, impertinent creature! You said you washed your hands of it, and so you may, for I don't want help from such a *heathen* as you are!'

Mrs Chicklade's colour rose alarmingly. 'Oh, so I'm a heathen, am I? Me as has been a churchgoer all my life, and kept my house respectable—till this day!'

'Good evening.'

The gentle, aloof voice acted on the incensed landlady like a charm. Cut short in mid-career, she stared at Lady Hester, her rich colour slowly fading.

'I am afraid,' said Hester, with cool courtesy, 'that you are being put to a great deal of trouble. It is perhaps a pity I did not, after all, bring my maid with me. My nephew thought, however, that there would be no room for her in so small a house.'

Mrs Chicklade felt herself impelled to abandon her martial attitude, and to drop an unwilling curtsy. 'I'm sure, ma'am, I'm not one to grudge a bit of trouble. All I say is—'

'Thank you,' Hester said, turning away from her. 'Take me up to your uncle's room, Amanda!'

Amanda was only too glad to do so. Chicklade, an expression of considerable concern on his face, was bending over the bed on which Sir Gareth tossed and muttered. He looked round as the ladies entered the room, and said: 'I don't like the looks of him—not at all, I don't! Mortal bad, he is, ma'am, but I don't doubt he'll be better now he has his good lady to tend him.'

Hester, casting off her bonnet and pelisse, hardly heard this speech, her attention being fixed on Sir Gareth, She went to the bed, and laid her hand fleetingly on his brow. It was burningly hot, and the eyes that glanced unrecognizingly at her were blurred with fever. She said: 'Has the doctor seen him since this morning?'

'No!' answered Amanda, in a choked voice. 'I have been waiting and waiting for him, for he promised he would come again!'

'Then I think someone should ride over to desire him to come as soon as he may. Meanwhile, if Hildebrand will bring up the smaller of my two valises, and you, landlord, will desire your wife to set a kettle on to boil, I hope we may make him more comfortable.'

'Is he going to die?' whispered Amanda, her eyes dark with dread.

'No!' Hester replied calmly. 'He is not going to die, but he has a great deal of fever, and I fancy his wound is much inflamed. The arm is swollen, and these tight bandages are making it worse. Pray go down, my dear, and send Hildebrand up to me!'

Amanda sped away on this errand, and returned very speedily, followed by Hildebrand, bearing a valise. He was looking scared, and cast one shrinking glance at Sir Gareth, and then quickly averted his eyes. Lady Hester had stripped the blankets off the bed, so that Sir Gareth was now covered only by the sheet. Without seeming to notice Hildebrand's sickly pallor, she directed him, in her quiet way, to open the valise. 'You will find a roll of flannel in it, and some scissors. I am going to apply fomentations to the wound. Will you help me, if you please?'

'*I* will!' Amanda said. 'Hildebrand faints if he sees blood.'

'He won't see any blood, and I am quite sure he will not faint.'

'No, I—I swear I won't!' Hildebrand said, through his clenched teeth.

'Of course not. You could not, when we depend so entirely upon you, could you? For, you know, I am not strong enough to lift Sir Gareth. It is a great comfort to know that you are here to share the nursing with me. Amanda, while I am busy with the fomentation, do you go down and try whether there is any wine to be obtained. A little hot wine will often relieve a fever.'

Amanda seemed for a moment as though she would have rebelled against what she suspected to be an attempt to exclude her from the sickroom, but after throwing a rather jealous glance at Hildebrand, she went away.

By the time she came back, carefully carrying, wrapped in a cloth, a glass of hot claret, Lady Hester had tied the last bandage, and was exchanging the very lumpy pillow on the bed for her own one of down. Hildebrand, who was supporting Sir Gareth in his arms, had not only recovered his colour, but looked to be in much better spirits. He had been able to look upon his handiwork without fainting; and Lady Hester, so far from reviling or despising him, had said that she did not know how she would go on without him.

Amanda reported that Chicklade had sent off the boy who helped him in the tap, and the small stable, to hasten the doctor, so Lady Hester said that since Sir Gareth seemed a little easier they would not try to get any of the mulled claret down his throat just at present. Hildebrand lowered him on to the pillow again, and although he was still very restless it was plain that the fomentation was already bringing him a certain measure of relief. Lady Hester sat down at the head of the bed, and began to bathe his face with lavender-water, softly directing her youthful helpers to go downstairs to await the doctor's arrival. They tiptoed away. Left alone with Sir Gareth, Lady Hester smoothed back the tumbled curls from his brow with a loving hand. He stared up at her, and said in a hurried, fretting tone: 'I must find her. I must find her.'

'Yes, Gareth, you shall,' she answered soothingly. 'Only be still, my dearest.'

For a moment she thought there was a gleam of recognition in his eyes; then he turned his head away, and resumed his incoherent muttering. His hand, aimlessly brushing the sheet, found her wrist, and grasped it strongly; he said, quite audibly: 'You won't escape me again!'

When, presently, the doctor was brought into the room by Amanda, he thought that the lady who rose to meet him had been crying a little. He was not surprised; and he said, with rough kindness: 'Well, now, what is all this I am hearing about my patient? Some fever was to be expected, you know, but you may depend upon it that a man with a good constitution will recover from worse hurts than a mere hole in his shoulder. You need not tell me that he has *that*, ma'am! I have seldom attended a more splendid specimen than your husband, and I don't doubt that between us we shall have him going on prosperously in a very short time.'

'But he is not my husband!' said Hester involuntarily.

'Not your husband?' he said, looking at her very hard. 'I beg your pardon, but I understood from Chicklade that Mr Ross had fetched Sir Gareth's wife to him!'

'No,' said Hester helplessly. 'Oh, no!'

'Then who may you be, ma'am?' he demanded bluntly.

'She is his sister, of course!' said Amanda with great promptness. 'I suppose that when my cousin said he would fetch our aunt, Chicklade thought she must be Uncle Gareth's *wife*, but she isn't.'

'Oh!' said the doctor. 'So *that's* how it is!'

'Yes, that's how it is,' agreed Hester, accepting the situation.

15

Sir Gareth, opening his eyes on unfamiliar surroundings, wondered where he was. He appeared to be lying in an attic, which seemed very odd, though not of any great importance. He considered the matter idly, and next discovered that something was wrong with his left shoulder. He tried to bring his other hand to feel it, but found that the effort was too much for his strength. Also, which was strange, he was very tired. Decidedly something must be wrong, he thought, unperturbed, but puzzled. He turned his head on the pillow, and his eyes fell upon a slim youth, who was watching him intently from a chair by the window. The wreaths of sleep which were clinging to his brain began to drift away. He frowned. A boy in a coffee-room, talking some nonsense about a blackened heart, and Amanda– *Amanda*? 'Good God!' said Sir Gareth faintly, as memory came rushing back.

Hildebrand, uncertain whether he was himself, or still light-headed, said tentatively: 'Are you better, sir?'

'Hildebrand Ross,' stated Sir Gareth. 'Where the devil am I?'

'Well, I don't suppose you would know the place, sir, but pray do not be uneasy! You are quite safe.'

'Did you put a bullet into me?' inquired Sir Gareth, dreamily interested.

'Yes, I did, sir, but *indeed* I never meant to! Pray do not let yourself be angry with me! I mean, not *yet*, while you are so weak!'

'I remember telling you not to wave that pistol about,' remarked Sir Gareth, in a reminiscent voice. 'What happened after that?'

'Well, I–I shot you, sir, but don't talk about it now! The doctor says you must be perfectly quiet.'

'How long have I been here?'

'Four days, sir–and I think I had better fetch Aunt Hester!' said Hildebrand nervously.

Sir Gareth, left to make what he could of this, found it beyond his comprehension, and closed his eyes again.

When he awoke for the second time, he remembered that he had been talking to Hildebrand, and looked towards the window. But Hildebrand was no longer there. Lady Hester was seated in the windsor chair, reading a book. Sir Gareth had thought that he was better, but he now suspected that he was delirious. There was a sandy kitten curled up in her lap, too, and he knew that kitten. Hester had nothing to do with Joseph, so probably he was still floating in a muddled dream. 'Besides,' he said aloud, 'she doesn't wear a cap. How absurd!'

She looked up quickly, and rose, setting Joseph down. 'Hildebrand came running to tell me that you had waked up, quite yourself again, but when I reached you, you were so soundly asleep that I almost doubted him,' she said, taking his hand, and feeling his pulse. 'Oh, that is so much better! Do you feel more the thing?'

His fingers closed weakly round her hand. 'But this is fantastic!' he said.

'Are you sure I am not dreaming?'

'Quite sure,' she replied, smiling mistily down at him. 'I daresay you may be wondering how I come to be here, but it is not at all important, and there is no need for you to tease yourself about it just now.'

He studied the offending cap frowningly, 'Why do you wear that thing?'

'Well, I think I have reached the age when perhaps I should.'

'Nonsense! I wish you will take if off.'

'Should you mind very much if I don't?' she said apologetically. 'There is something so very respectable about a cap, you know.'

That made him smile. 'Must you look respectable?'

'Yes, indeed I must. Now, my dear friend, I am going to call Chicklade that he may bring up the broth Mrs Chicklade has been keeping hot for you, the instant you should wake up.'

'Who is Chicklade?'

'How stupid of me! He is the landlord, an excellent man, *quite* unlike his wife, who is really the most tiresome creature. I shall let him come into the room, because he has been so very obliging, and, besides that, I want him to raise you while I slip another pillow behind you. I shall warn him he must not encourage you to talk, but, in case you should say something to undo us all, will you remember that Hildebrand is your nephew?'

'Either I *am* dreaming, or you must have run mad suddenly,' said Sir Gareth. 'Hildebrand was the name of the young idiot who shot me. That I *do* remember!'

'Yes, so *careless* of him! I daresay you will feel that you ought to give him a scold, and perhaps I should have done so, when he told me about it. But he was in such distress, and so truly repentant, that I could see it was not at all necessary. I don't mean to dictate to you, but if you *should* be meaning to give him up to justice, which he quite expects, poor boy, I wish you won't! He has been helping me to nurse you, and running all the errands with such readiness that it would be quite dreadfully ungrateful to send him to prison. Besides, it would appear very odd if you were to do so, when everyone thinks he is your nephew.'

'Is that why he became my nephew?' he asked, looking amused.

'Yes, and I need scarcely tell you that it was Amanda's notion. She said that Hildebrand held you up for a jest, and had never meant to shoot you, which, indeed, was perfectly true. I own, Amanda is very naughty, but one cannot help admiring her! She is never at a loss!'

'Where is Amanda?' he interrupted.

'She has walked over to Great Staughton with Hildebrand, to purchase some things for me there.'

'Do you mean to tell me she hasn't run away?' he said incredulously.

'Oh, no!'

'How in the world did you contrive to keep her here?'

'Oh, I didn't! I am sure I could not. She would not think of running away *now*. Besides, she is very well satisfied to be here, for it is the tiniest village, where I shouldn't think her grandfather would ever find her. You shall see her when you are a little stronger. Oh, I forgot to mention that she is your niece! She and Hildebrand are cousins.'

'I seem to have been acquiring an alarming number of new relatives,' he remarked.

'Yes,' she agreed. She hesitated, colouring faintly. 'Which puts me in mind that I should warn you that I shall be obliged to call you Gareth while we remain in this inn. I am afraid you may not quite like it, but—'

'On the contrary!' he said, smiling. 'Are you also related to me?'

'Well, yes!' she confessed. 'We—we thought it best that I should be your sister. You see, I didn't feel I *could* be your wife!'

'That also I remember,' he said.

Her colour deepened; she looked away, and said in a little confusion: 'The thing was that when Amanda sent Hildebrand to fetch me, she told the Chicklades that I was her aunt, which, I must say, was most sensible of her. But they supposed from that that I must be your wife, and they told the doctor so. Which nearly led to our undoing, because you know how foolish I am! I blurted out that I was no such thing, and the doctor stared at me in such a way! However, Amanda instantly said that I was not your wife, but your sister, which perfectly satisfied him. I hope you are not vexed! Now I must go and call to Chicklade.'

She went away, and when she returned, a few minutes later, she was accompanied by Chicklade, who bore a small tray into the room, which he set down on the table by the bed. He then said that he was glad to see Sir Gareth looking more stout, speaking in a painstakingly lowered voice.

Sir Gareth roused himself to play the part expected of him. He said: 'Thank you, I'm as weak as a cat, but you will see how quickly I shall be on my feet again. I am afraid I have been a shocking charge upon you. My sister has been telling me how you have helped to nurse me.' He held out his hand. 'Thank you: I am very much obliged to you! You must be heartily sick of such a troublesome guest, but really I am not to be blamed! My young fool of a nephew is the culprit.'

'Ay, sir, he is that!' Chicklade said, cautiously taking the hand in his. 'Properly speaking, he ought to be given a rare dressing, but I don't doubt it was Miss who set him on, and I'm bound to say he's had the fright of his life. Nor I don't grudge the trouble. If there's aught I can do, your honour has only to mention it.'

'Then I beg you will shave me!' said Sir Gareth, passing his hand ruefully over his chin.

'Tomorrow, perhaps,' said Hester, waiting to place another pillow behind his head. 'Will you lift him now, if you please? Don't try to help yourself, Gareth; Chicklade is very strong, you will find.'

'What was your fighting weight?' asked Sir Gareth, as the landlord lowered him tenderly on to the pillows.

A slow smile spread over the broad face. 'Ah, I was never reduced beyond thirteen stone eight, sir, and, of course, nowadays—well! If I might make so bold, I'd say your honour displays to advantage.'

'You will be able to enjoy many delightful talks about prize-fighting with Sir Gareth when he is a little stronger,' said Lady Hester gently.

The landlord, thus recalled to a sense of Sir Gareth's weakness, cast an apologetic glance at her, and beat a retreat. She sat down by the bed, and offered her patient a spoonful of broth. 'I hope it is good,' she said, smiling at him. 'As soon as your fever began to abate, Chicklade killed one of his cockerels, so that we might have a sustaining broth ready for you. Hildebrand was disgusted, because Amanda saw its neck wrung, but I daresay she was quite right to do so. She seems to think that if she goes to the Peninsula she might be obliged to kill chickens, though I myself should rather suppose that the batman would do it for her. Poor Hildebrand is very squeamish, so naturally he was much shocked at Amanda's wishing to learn how to wring a chicken's neck. Do you think you could eat a morsel of toast, if I dipped it in the broth?'

'Thank you, I had liefer eat it undipped. I detest sops! Hester, I wish you will explain to me how you come to be here! Amanda had no business to ask it of you, and how you can have prevailed upon your family to consent to such a thing I can't conceive.'

'Oh, I didn't! They think I have gone to be with my sister Susan, because her children have the measles. Don't look so dismayed! I never enjoyed anything half as much, I assure you. You cannot think what a relief it is to have shaken off every one of my relations! I don't feel like myself at all, and that is a relief, too.'

'But, my dear, it is the craziest thing to have done!' he expostulated, half-laughing.

'Yes, isn't it?' she agreed cordially. 'That is what makes it so delightful, for I have never done anything crazy before. Just a little more of this broth! How pleased Amanda and Hildebrand will be when they learn that you have drunk it all up! I wonder whether they have been able to purchase any playing-cards in Great Staughton?'

Her inconsequence made him smile. 'Do you wish for some?'

'Oh, no! Only that it is very dull for those children, and I thought if only they had some cards they could play games together in the evening, instead of quarrelling. Hildebrand was much inclined to think that it would be very wrong to buy cards, but I assured him you would have not the least objection.'

'I?' he said. 'What made the boy think me so straight-laced?'

'Oh, he didn't! The thing is that although he owns that we may purchase what *you* need with perfect propriety, he says that anything else is most improper: in fact, quite dishonest. We were obliged to steal your money, you see.'

'How very dreadful!' he murmured. 'Am I left destitute?'

'No, indeed! And Hildebrand is keeping strict account of every penny we spend. What a huge sum of money you carry on your person, Gareth! When we found that roll of bills in your pocket I thought we need have no scruples. You see, we were at a stand, because what with paying for the post-chaises, and stabling his horse, and buying the drugs we needed for you, Hildebrand was soon ruined. Amanda had a little money, but not nearly enough to pay our shot here, or the doctor; and I had nothing but what was in my purse. I do wish I were not so shatterbrained! I ought to have broken open Widmore's strong-box, of course, but in the agitation of the moment I never thought of it.'

The tone of self-censure which she used proved too much for Sir Gareth's gravity. He began to laugh, which caused him to feel a twinge in his shoulder sharp enough to make him wince. Lady Hester apologized, but said that she thought it did people no harm to laugh, even if it did hurt them a trifle.

It certainly seemed to do Sir Gareth no harm. The doctor, visiting him that evening, called upon Lady Hester to observe how famously he had responded to his treatment, and said that in less than no time he would be as right as a trivet; and although it was evident that it would, in fact, be some considerable while before he regained his strength, he began to improve so rapidly that on the following day Lady Hester permitted Amanda to visit him. She could only hope that he would not find her, in his present state, rather overpowering: perhaps, even, a little agitating. How great his interest in this turbulent beauty might be, she could not decide. Such intelligible utterances as he had made during his delirium had all concerned Amanda;

she had been vaguely surprised that never once had she caught Clarissa's name in his incoherent mutterings. That seemed to indicate that his mind, if not his heart, was obsessed by Amanda. The fever past, the only sign he had given of any extraordinary interest in her had been his immediate anxiety to know where she was. But Lady Hester knew that he was not the man to betray himself; and she feared that he was going to be hurt. Amazing though it might be (and to Hester it appeared incomprehensible), he had not made the smallest impression on Amanda's heart. She liked him very well; she said he resembled all her favourite heroes of romance; and she remained unshaken in her devotion to her Brigade-Major. If Sir Gareth cherished hopes of winning her, he was doomed to disappointment; and although this would not be the tragedy that Clarissa's death had been, it would be a hurt, and Hester would have happily immolated herself to have averted it. But there was nothing she could do. She allowed Amanda twenty minutes, and then since, Amanda had not emerged, she went up to the sickroom, to bring the session to an end.

The sight which met her eyes held her frozen on the threshold, and the thought flashed across her mind that she knew now how it felt to die. If it had lain within her power to have given Sir Gareth his heart's desire, she would have done it; but she had not known how sharp a pain she would suffer when she saw Amanda's face buried in his sound shoulder, and his arm about her.

He looked up, and the short agony was at an end. Never did a man more clearly signal an appeal for help than Sir Gareth at that moment. He did not look at all like a man in love; he looked extremely harassed. Then Hester perceived that Amanda was indulging in a hearty burst of tears, and the smile which held so much unexpected mischief suddenly danced in her eyes. 'Good heavens, what is the matter?' she said, advancing into the room, and gently removing Amanda's hand from about Sir Gareth's neck. 'Dear child, this is not at all the way to behave! Do, pray, stop crying!'

She raised her brows at Sir Gareth, in mute inquiry, and he said ruefully: 'She is enjoying an orgy of remorse. I never dreamed that there could be anything more exhausting than Amanda in high gig, but I have discovered my error. Now, do cheer up, you little goose! It served me right for not heeding your warning that you would make me sorry.'

'Besides, she saved your life,' said Hester. 'We have not liked to talk very much about the accident, but I do think you should know that if Amanda hadn't acted with the greatest presence of mind, you would have bled to death, Gareth. And she had no one to turn to, either, because poor Hildebrand swooned from the shock, and the sight of the blood. Indeed, you are very much obliged to her.'

He was surprised, and a good deal touched, but Amanda would have none of his gratitude. She stopped crying, however, and raised her head from his shoulder. 'Well, I *had* to do something, and, besides, it was very good practice, in case Neil should be wounded again. I didn't mean to cry, and if only you had looked vexed when I came into the room, instead of smiling at me, and holding out your hand, I shouldn't have.'

'It was most inconsiderate of me, and I can only beg your pardon,' he responded gravely. He watched her dry her cheeks, and then said: 'Will you do something to oblige me?'

'Yes, to be sure I—at least, I *might*!' she said suspiciously. 'What is it?'

'Write immediately to your grandfather, telling him that you are here, and in Lady Hester's care!'

'I thought you were trying to trick me!' she exclaimed.

'My child, it must be a week since you ran away, and all that time he has been in the greatest anxiety about you! Think! You cannot wish him—'

'You are perfectly right!' she interrupted. 'What a fortunate thing it is that you should have put me in mind of it, for so many things have happened that it went out of my head! Good gracious, he may have put the advertisement in the *Morning Post* days ago! I must find Hildebrand!'

She jumped up from her knees, and sped forth, leaving the door opened. Lady Hester went to shut it, saying, with mild curiosity: 'I wonder what she wants Hildebrand to do?'

'Of all the heartless little wretches!' Sir Gareth said.

She looked rather surprised. 'Oh, no, not heartless! Only she is so passionately devoted to Neil, you see, that she doesn't care a button for anyone else.'

'Ruthless, then. Hester, can't you prevail upon her to put that unfortunate old man out of his suspense?'

'I am afraid I can't,' she said. 'Of course, one can't help feeling very sorry for him, but I do think she should be allowed to marry Neil. Don't tease yourself about her, Gareth! After all, she is quite safe while she remains with us.'

'You are as bad as she is,' said Sir Gareth severely.

'Yes, but not so resourceful,' she agreed. 'And you are very tired, so you will have a sleep now, and no more visitors.'

There did not seem to be any more to be said. Until he was on his feet again, Sir Gareth knew that he was powerless to restore Amanda to her family; and since he was too weak to exert himself even in argument, he abandoned the struggle, and gave himself up to lazy convalescence, accepting the fantastic situation in which he found himself, and deriving a good deal of amusement from it. His adopted family cosseted him jealously, appealed to him to settle disputes, or decide knotty problems, and made his room, as he grew stronger, their headquarters. Amanda had from the outset regarded him much in the light of an uncle. Hildebrand had thought that, so far from doing the same, he would never be able to confront him without being crushed by a sense of guilt. Once Sir Gareth was himself again, it had taken much courage to enter his room. But as Hildebrand was his chief attendant, the awful moment had to be faced. He had gone in, braced to endure whatever might be in store for him. 'Well, nephew?' had said Sir Gareth. 'And what have you to say for yourself?' He had had an abject apology all prepared, but it had been cut short. 'Only wait until I am on my feet again!' had said Sir Gareth. '*I'll* teach you to brandish loaded pistols!'

After that, there had been no difficulty at all in looking upon Sir Gareth as an uncle. Indeed, it very soon seemed to Sir Gareth that neither Amanda nor Hildebrand remembered that he was not their uncle.

Hildebrand's chief preoccupation was how to regain possession of his horse, but since he could not bring himself to let some heavy-handed post-boy or ostler ride Prince, and spurned indignantly a suggestion that he should hire a chaise to carry him to St Ives, so that he could himself bring Prince to Little Staughton, there seemed to be no solution to the problem. 'As though I should think of leaving you for all those hours!' he said. 'Besides, only consider what it would cost, sir!'

'What, is it low tide with us?'

'Good God, no! But you *can't* think I would first shoot you, Uncle Gary, and then make you pay for me to get my horse back! And in any event, I don't think I should go, because if I don't keep an eye on Amanda, the lord only knows what she'll do next!'

'Then for God's sake do keep your eye on her!' said Sir Gareth. 'What fiendish plot is she hatching now?'

'Well, you know how she disappeared yesterday, and was gone for hours?—Oh, no, Aunt Hester thought we shouldn't tell you! I beg your pardon, Aunt Hester, but it don't signify, because she hadn't run away after all! Well, do you know what she did? She went to Eaton Socon in Farmer Upwood's gig, just to discover where she could get her hands on the *Morning Post!*'

'But I think that was such a sensible thing to do!' said Lady Hester. 'And she did discover it, too, which I'm sure I should never have done.'

'Yes, you would, ma'am! She discovered it at the receiving-office, and anyone would have known that was the place to go to!'

'Not Aunt Hester,' said Sir Gareth, his eyes quizzing her. 'Who does take the *Morning Post* in these rural parts?'

'Oh, some old fellow, who lives near Colmworth, which is about four miles from here! He is an invalid, and never stirs out of his house, so Chicklade says. The thing is that if I don't go for her, Amanda swears she will go herself, to ask the old man to let her look at every *Morning Post* he has received this week!'

'You know, I have suddenly thought of something very discouraging!' said Hester. 'I shouldn't wonder at it if they had been used for lighting the kitchen-fire! Now, that would be too bad, but exactly the sort of thing that is bound to happen!'

'If you think there is any chance that Amanda's grandfather may have yielded, we had better send to the office of the *Morning Post* immediately,' said Sir Gareth. 'In his place, I had rather have gone to Bow Street, but one never knows.'

'Well, do you think I should try first at this old fellow's house, sir?' Hildebrand asked.

'By all means—if you can think of a sufficiently plausible excuse for wishing to see so many copies of his newspaper. I daresay you will be thought insane, but if you don't regard that, why should I?'

'No, why? I shall say that I want them for you, because you are laid by the heels here, and have nothing to read.'

'I wonder why I shouldn't have guessed that you would drag me into it?' observed Sir Gareth, in a musing tone.

Hildebrand grinned, but assured him that he need have no fear.

'I must own, Gareth,' said Hester thoughtfully, after Hildebrand had departed, 'that I can't help hoping you may be wrong about Bow Street. What shall we do, if we have Runners after us?'

'Emigrate!' he replied promptly.

She smiled, but said: 'You know, it would be very exciting, but not, I think, quite comfortable, because, although we have done nothing wrong, the Runners might not perfectly understand just how it all came about. Unless, of course, Amanda is able to think of another splendid story.'

'Any story of Amanda's will infallibly land us all in Newgate. I see nothing for it but emigration.'

'Not *all* of us, Gareth: only you!' she said, with a gleam of humour. 'She will certainly tell them that you abducted her, because nothing will persuade her that an abduction is something quite different. Oh, well, we must just hope that there may be a notice in one of the papers! And I should think that there would be, for the grandfather *must* wish to get Amanda back as soon as ever he may.'

But when Hildebrand returned, later in the day, from his errand, she was found to have been wrong. Hildebrand came into Sir Gareth's room, laden with periodicals, which he dumped on the floor, saying breathlessly: 'All for you, Uncle Gary! He *would* have me bring them, because he says he *knows* you! Lord, I thought we were in a fix then, but I don't fancy any harm will come of it.'

'Oh, my God!' exclaimed Sir Gareth. 'I suppose you *had* to tell him my name? Who is he?'

'Well, I never thought it would signify. And, in any event, everyone knows who you are, because the post-boy told Chicklade what your name was, when you were carried in, that day.'

Amanda, who was seated on the floor, scanning, and discarding, copy after copy of the *Morning Post,* looked up to say: 'I *told* you you would only make a muff of it! If I had gone myself, I should have made up a very good name for Uncle Gary, only you have no ingenuity, and can think of nothing!'

'Yes!' retorted Hildebrand. 'You would have said he was Lancelot du Lake, or something so silly that no one would have believed it!'

'Don't imagine you are going to quarrel over me!' interposed Sir Gareth. 'What I want to know is not what name of unequalled splendour Amanda would have bestowed on me, but what is the name of this recluse, who says he knows me?'

Amanda, uninterested, retired again into the advertisement columns of the *Morning Post.* Hildebrand said: 'Vinehall, sir: Barnabas Vinehall.'

'Well, I should never have made up as silly a name as that!' interpolated Amanda scornfully.

'Good God!' ejaculated Sir Gareth. 'I thought he was dead! You don't mean to say he lives *here?*'

'Yes, but there's no need for any of us to be in a quake, because he never goes out now: he told me so!' said Hildebrand reassuringly. 'He is the fattest man I ever laid eyes on!'

'I fail to see—'

'No, but only listen, Uncle Gary! It's dropsy!'

'Poor man!' said Hester sympathetically. 'Who is he, Gareth?'

'He was a crony of my father's. I haven't seen him for years. Dropsy, eh? Poor old Vinehall! What did you tell him, Hildebrand?'

'Well, only that you had had an accident, and were laid up here. The mischief was that I had previously said I was your nephew, because as soon as he knew your name he said I must be Trixie's eldest son. I didn't know who Trixie was—'

'—so, of *course*, you said you were not!' put in Amanda.

'No, I did not! You are not the only person who can tell untruths!' retorted Hildebrand. 'I said I was!'

'Who did you say I was?' demanded Amanda.

'Nobody. You were not mentioned,' replied Hildebrand, depressing pretension. 'The only thing that put me in a fright, sir, was Mr Vinehall's supposing that Aunt Hester must be this Trixie. Because I had said that your sister was nursing you, and I collect that Trixie *is* your sister.'

'My only sister!' said Sir Gareth, covering his eyes with his hand. 'What I have ever done to deserve being saddled with such a nephew as you—! Go on! Let me know the worst!'

'There *is* no worst! He did say that he hoped Trixie–your sister, I mean, sir–would visit him, but I made that right immediately, by saying that she might not leave you while you were ill, and that as soon as you were better she would be obliged to hurry back to her own home. Then I said that I was sure you would wait on him, as soon as you were able, which seemed to please him very much. Then he talked about your father, and at last he made his butler tie up a great bundle of papers and periodicals for you to read, and so I made my escape. *Now* tell me if I did wrong, sir?'

'*Well!*' The word burst from Amanda, sitting back on her heels in a welter of newspapers, her eyes flashing. 'Would you have *believed* it? He has not done it! Why–why–one would almost think he did not wish to have me back!'

'Impossible!' murmured Sir Gareth.

'Of course it is impossible!' said Hester, casting a reproving glance at him. 'I daresay there has not been yet time for the advertisement to be inserted. Wait a few days longer!'

'Is Hildebrand to visit Vinehall every day?' inquired Sir Gareth, 'courting disaster–but far be it from me to complain!'

'No, for he said he would send his groom over with the newspapers,' said Hildebrand. 'No harm can come of that, surely, sir?'

'None at all–provided he doesn't take it into his head to come himself.'

'Oh, no fear of that!' Hildebrand said cheerfully. 'He told me that he finds it hard to get about, and was only sorry that he was unable to drive over to see you.'

He had underrated Mr Vinehall's spirit. On the following afternoon, when both the ladies of the party were in the parlour, Amanda standing in the middle of the room, and Lady Hester kneeling at her feet to stitch up a torn flounce on her dress, a vehicle was heard to drive up. Neither paid much heed, since this was no unusual circumstance; but after a minute, Amanda, craning her neck, managed to catch a glimpse of it, and exclaimed: 'Good gracious, it's a carriage! The most oldfashioned thing! Whoever can it be?'

They were not left above a couple of minutes in suspense. Whoever it was had already entered the inn, and the arrival seemed to have thrown the Chicklades into strange confusion. A babel of voices sounded, Chicklade's deep one sharpened by surprise, and a still deeper one wheezing an answer.

'Good God!' uttered Hester, in a panic. 'Could it be Mr Vinehall? Amanda, what are we to do? If he sees me—'

The words died on her lips, for the door had been flung open, and she heard Chicklade say: 'If your honour will be pleased to step into the parlour! You'll find Sir Gareth's sister and niece, and very glad to see you, sir, I'll be bound.'

Gladness was not the predominant expression in either lady's face. Hester, hurriedly breaking off her thread, and getting up, was looking perfectly distracted; and Amanda's eyes, fixed on the doorway, were growing rounder and rounder in astonishment.

Hildebrand was not exaggerated in his description of Mr Vinehall. His bulk filled the aperture. He was a man in the late sixties, dressed in clothes as oldfashioned as his carriage. A stalwart footman hovered watchfully behind him, and, as soon as he was clear of the doorway, hastened to lend him the support of his arm, and to lower him on to a chair, where he sat, breathing heavily, and staring at Amanda. An appreciative smile gradually spread over his very red face, and he said: 'So you are little Trixie's girl, my dear? Well, well, you don't resemble her greatly, but *I've* no complaint to make! I'll wager you'll break as many hearts as she did!' His mountainous form shook alarmingly, and a rumbling laugh appeared to convulse him. The footman patted him on the back, and after wheezing a good deal, he gasped: 'You don't know who the devil I am, eh? Well, my name's Vinehall, and I knew your mama when she was in a cradle. Gary, too. To think of his being within five miles of my place, and me having not a suspicion of it! If it hadn't been for your brother's coming to call on me yesterday, I daresay I should never have been a penny the wiser, for the only news I get is from the doctor, and he hasn't been next or nigh me for ten days. Damme, I thought, when the lad was gone off, why don't I heave myself into my carriage, and go to see Gary, since he can't come to see me? So here I am, and not a penny the worse for it. Now, where's your mama, my dear? I'll warrant she'll bless herself when she hears who's come to wait on her!'

'She—she isn't here, sir,' said Amanda.

'Not here? Where's she gone off to, then? The boy told me she couldn't leave Gary!'

'I don't know. I mean, she never was here! It is my Aunt Hester who is nursing Uncle Gary!'

'But your brother said—'

'Oh, I expect he did not hear just what you were asking him!' said Amanda glibly. 'He is very deaf, you know!'

'God bless my soul! Didn't seem to be deaf to me!'

'No, because he very much dislikes to have it known, and so he pretends that he can hear quite well.'

'You don't mean it! I should never have suspected it. So Trixie ain't here after all! Who is this Aunt Hester you spoke of? One of your papa's sisters?' He seemed to become aware of Hester, standing frozen behind Amanda, and bowed. 'How de do, ma'am? You'll excuse my getting up!'

'Yes, indeed!' Hester said faintly. 'How do you do?'

He frowned suddenly. 'Ay, but you can't be Gary's sister, if you're a Wetherby!'

'No, no! I mean, I'm not a Wetherby! That is—'

Amanda, observing her flounderings, rose nobly, but disastrously to the rescue. 'She is Uncle Gary's *other* sister,' she explained.

'Other sister? He ain't got another!' said Mr Vinehall. 'Never more than three of them: Gary, poor Arthur, and Trixie! What's the game, you little puss? Trying to humbug an old man? No, no, you'll catch cold at that!'

'Excuse me!' Hester said, unable to bear another moment of what was fast developing into an inquisition. 'I will see if Sir Gareth can receive you, sir!'

With these hastily uttered words, she slipped from the room, and fled upstairs, tripping on her dress, and arriving in Sir Gareth's room out of breath, and with her cap crooked. 'Gareth!' she gasped. 'The most dreadful thing! We are quite undone!'

He lowered the copy of the *Quarterly*, which he had been reading. 'Good God, what is it?'

'Mr Vinehall!' she said, sinking limply into a chair.

'What, here?' he demanded.

'In the parlour, talking to Amanda. He has come to see you!'

'Now we *are* in the basket!' said Sir Gareth, accepting the situation with maddening calm. 'Has he seen you?'

'Yes, of course he has, and of course he knew I wasn't Mrs Wetherby! I was ready to sink, for I could think of nothing to say, and Amanda made a fatal mistake! Gareth, how *can* you lie there laughing?'

'My dear, I can't help but laugh when you burst in upon me looking perfectly demented, and with that ridiculous cap over one eye! I do wish you will throw it away!'

'This is *no* moment to be discussing my cap!' she scolded. 'Amanda told him I was your *other* sister!'

'Now, that is not worthy of Amanda,' he said, shaking his head. 'He won't swallow it. She must think of something better.'

'I don't see how she *can*! And, depend upon it, Hildebrand will come in, having no notion that he's very deaf, just to make matters worse?'

'Oh, is Hildebrand deaf?' he asked, interested.

'Yes—that is, no, you know well he isn't! Oh, dear, I ought to have said I *was* a Wetherby! What's to be done now? *One* thing I am determined on! I won't meet him again! What shall you tell him?'

'I can't imagine,' he said frankly. 'It will depend on what Amanda may have told him.'

'You may be obliged to tell the truth.'

'I may, but I shall do my best to avoid the necessity.'

'Yes, pray do! It is such a very complicated story, and I daresay it would quite exhaust you to have to explain it all to him.'

His lips quivered, but he replied gravely: 'And then we might discover that he hadn't believed a word of it.'

'Yes, very true! Good God, he is coming!' she cried, springing out of her chair. 'I can't and I won't face him! I should be bound to ruin everything by saying something bird-witted—you must know I should!'

'Yes, but I own I should dearly love to hear you!' Sir Gareth said, his eyes warm with amusement.

'How can you be so unfeeling? Where can I hide?' she said, looking wildly round.

'Slip away to your own room until he has gone!' he advised.

'I can't! The stairs are directly opposite this door! Oh, heavens, Gareth, only listen to him! How dreadful if he were to expire on the stairs! Though it would be a great stroke of good fortune for us, of course. But one cannot wish it to happen—unless, perhaps, it would be a merciful release for him, poor man! I shall have to get behind the curtain. For heaven's sake, Gareth, think of something to say that will satisfy him!'

The little bedchamber did not boast a wardrobe, but a chintz curtain had been hung across one corner of the room. To Sir Gareth's deep delight, Lady Hester plunged behind it, among his coats, just as Chicklade, who had aided the footman to push and haul Mr Vinehall up the narrow stairs, opened the door, and announced the visitor.

Sir Gareth composed his countenance admirably, and greeted his father's old friend with every proper expression of gratitude and pleasure. It was some moments before Mr Vinehall, deposited in a chair beside the bed, could recover his breath. His exertions had turned the red in his cheeks to purple, but this gradually abated. He waved his solicitous attendants out of the room, and said: 'Gary! Well, by Jupiter! It must be a dozen years since I saw you last! How are you, my dear boy? Not in good point, I hear. How came you to break your arm? Lord, I should have recognized you anywhere!' He barely gave Sir Gareth time to answer suitably before he was off again, dropping his voice confidentially, and saying: 'I'm glad I don't find that young lady with you, for I shouldn't know what to say to her, upon my word I should not! I wouldn't have put her out of countenance for the world, as I hope you know!'

'I am quite sure you would not, sir,' said Sir Gareth, feeling his way.

'Ay, but it was not a very gallant way to behave, and I could see she was put out. Well, no wonder, for there was I blundering along, and Trixie's girl tells me she is devilish sensitive!'

'She has a great deal of sensibility,' admitted Sir Gareth cautiously.

'Ay, I daresay, and there I was, bringing home the evils of her situation to her, like a regular blubberhead! I should have known how it was as soon as that pretty chit said she was your other sister, but it never so much as crossed my mind. As soon as she was gone, Trixie's girl told me, and, I give you my word, Gary, I was never more thunderstruck in my life! God bless my soul, I should have said your dear father was the last man on earth—why, even when he was cutting a dash in his salad days I never knew him to be in the petticoat-line! Ay, and I was as well acquainted with him as any man. I declare I can't get over it! You acknowledge her, I see?'

'Quite—quite privately!' said Sir Gareth, only the faintest tremor in his voice.

'Ay, very proper,' nodded Mr Vinehall. 'Was your mother aware of her existence?'

'Happily, no!'

'Just as well. She wouldn't have liked it. Nasty shock for her, for she doted on your father. Well, well, poor George, he managed to keep it dark, and you needn't fear I shall spread the tale about. Couldn't, if I wanted to, for it's seldom I see anyone these days. You'll know how to tell the poor girl she don't have to fear me. It's a sad business. Taking little thing, too: got a sweet face! What you should do, Gary, is to find her a respectable husband.'

'I shall do my best to, sir.'

'That's right: you're too like your father not to do just as you ought! But tell me, my boy, how do you go on? How is Trixie? That was a tragic thing, Arthur's getting himself killed.'

He remained for some twenty minutes, chatting in a rambling way about old times and old acquaintances; but he had evidently been warned by Amanda that he must not stay for long with the invalid, for he soon pulled out his watch, and said that he must be off. He could not rise unassisted from his chair, but his attendant was waiting outside the door, and came in answer to his husky bellow. After grasping Sir Gareth's hand, and adjuring him not to leave the district without coming over to see him, he went ponderously away, and was soon heard cursing Chicklade genially for some piece of clumsiness.

Lady Hester emerged from her hiding-place, her cap now wildly askew. Sir Gareth lay back against his pillows, watching her, a question behind the brimming laughter in his eyes.

'Gareth!' said Hester, in an awed voice: 'You *must* own that Amanda is wonderful! I should *never* have thought of saying I was your natural sister!'

He was shaking with laughter, his hand pressed instinctively to his hurt shoulder. 'No? Nor I, my dear!'

Suddenly she began to laugh too. 'Oh, dear, of all the absurd situations—! I was just thinking how W-Widmore would l-look if he knew!'

The thought was too much for her. She sat down in the windsor chair, and laughed till she cried. Mopping her streaming eyes at last, she said: 'I don't think I have ever laughed so much in all my life. But I must say, Gareth, there is one thing about this story of Amanda's which I cannot like!'

'Oh, no, is there?' he said unsteadily.

'Yes,' she said, sober again. 'It was *not* well done of Amanda to make up such a tale about your father. For he was a most excellent person, and it seems quite dreadful to be slandering him! Really, Gareth, you should have denied it!'

'I assure you, he would have delighted in the story, for he was blessed with a lively sense of humour,' Sir Gareth replied. He looked at her, a glimmer in his eyes, and a smile quivering on his lips. 'Do you know, Hester, in all these years I have held you in esteem and regard, yet I never knew you until we were pitchforked into this fantastic imbroglio? Certainly Amanda is wonderful! I must be eternally grateful to her!'

16

Sir Gareth, slowly winning back to strength, knew very well that it behoved him to send word to his household that he had not been kidnapped, or snatched up into thin air, but he preferred to let the world slide for just a little longer. It would never do, he told himself, to let his servants get wind of his whereabouts, for ten to one they would allow their tongues to wag; or, worse, Trotton, already strongly suspecting him of having taken leave of his senses, might arrive at the Bull, in an excess of zeal, and the unshakeable belief that his services could not be dispensed with. It was really quite impossible to explain to them what had happened; to tell them not to mention his whereabouts to anyone would be to invite an extremely undesirable curiosity. After all, he was known to have gone into the country for several days, and it would probably be thought that he had prolonged his visit, or perhaps formed the sudden resolve to go from Brancaster to stay with one of his numerous friends. Trotton, of course, would expect to find his master in Berkeley Square when he reached town, and would undoubtedly suppose that Amanda had again given him the slip. Well, that couldn't be helped, and at least Trotton wouldn't be anxious. He did toy with the idea of writing to his brother-in-law, to enlist his aid in running a nameless Brigade-Major to earth, and even got as far as starting a letter to him. But it proved to be rather too exhausting a task. One sheet of literary composition was enough to make his head swim; and when he read over what he had written, he tore it up. Warren would undoubtedly think he had run mad. So he told himself that in all likelihood no one was worrying about him at all, and gave himself up to lazy enjoyment.

Hester was similarly unconcerned. The Widmores must believe her to be with her sister Susan; and even if some chance presently revealed to them that she was not at Ancaster she did not flatter herself that they would feel any particular concern. They might wonder, and conjecture, and they would certainly think it odd of her; but the chances were that Almeria at least would assume that having rejected Sir Gareth's offer she had left Brancaster to escape the recriminations of her family.

But Sir Gareth and Lady Hester underrated their relations. By ill-luck, Lady Ennerdale had occasion to write to her brother, and the contents of her letter made it abundantly plain that her children were all in health and spirits, and that so far from enjoying Hester's companionship she supposed her to be at Brancaster. Exactly as Hester had foreseen, Lady Widmore instantly informed her lord that Hester had taken a crackbrained notion into her head of setting up house on her own. Not a doubt but that was what she was meaning to do: idiotish, of course, but just like her. All this upset over Ludlow's offer had irritated her nerves: my lady had thought her manner very strange. But then she was always totty-headed!

Lady Hester had been right, too, in thinking that her brother would not succumb to anxiety; but she had underestimated his dislike of scandal. Lord Widmore, had she gone to live with one of her sisters, would have raised not the smallest objection, for no one would have wondered at it. But people would wonder very much at it if an unattached lady left the shelter of her father's roof to live alone. To make it worse, she was not yet thirty. What, he asked his wife, would people think, if ever it leaked out that Hetty had tried to escape from her family? She must be found, and brought to her senses—unless she was all the time with Gertrude, or Constance. It would be excessively like her to have said Susan, when she meant Gertrude: he would write immediately to both his other sisters.

In London, a far greater degree of anxiety was felt than Sir Gareth had anticipated. Trotton did indeed assume that he was still chasing Amanda; but he was very far from accepting this solution to the mystery with equanimity. Devotion to the master he had served since his boyhood, coupled with jealousy of Sir Gareth's butler and his valet, prevented him from taking them one inch into his confidence; he told them that Sir Gareth had said he might break his journey at a friend's house; but he was deeply perturbed. Sir Gareth was behaving in a way so utterly at variance with his usual calm and well-bred self-possession that Trotton seriously supposed him either to be going out of his mind, or to have fallen desperately in love with a chit of a girl who would make him the worst wife in the world. Trotton had no opinion of Amanda. A bit of muslin, that's what he had thought she was at first. Then it had seemed that he had been wrong; and although he didn't believe more than half of the things he had heard her say to Sir Gareth, there was no denying she hadn't gone with him willingly. Dicked in the nob, Sir Gareth must be, to make off with a girl who was trying all the time to escape from him! High-handed too: he'd never known him act like it before. A nice kick-up there would be, if her father, or maybe her brother, got to know about all this bobbery! It behoved anyone who held Sir Gareth in affection to make a push to rescue him from the consequences of his folly, and Trotton held him in considerable affection.

So, too, did his sister. Mrs Wetherby saw her adored brother set off for Brancaster, and had very little hope that he would meet with a rebuff there. When, at the end of a week, he had not returned to his house in Berkeley Square, that little died: he would scarcely have remained so long at Brancaster if his suit had not prospered. She expected every day to receive a letter from him, announcing his betrothal, but no letter came. She could scarcely believe that he would not have informed her of it before admitting the rest of the world into his confidence, but she, like Amanda, began to study the columns of the *Morning Post*, and the *Gazette*. She found no mention of Sir Gareth's name; and it was at this point that the conviction that something had happened to him took strong possession of her mind. Mr Wetherby kindly and patiently proved to her how unlikely it was that any disaster could have befallen Gary of which she would not have been apprized long since, but he might as well have spared his breath. No, she said, she had not the remotest conjecture of the nature of the accident which she supposed to have occurred: she just had a Feeling that all was not well with Gary. Mr Wetherby, well acquainted with her Feelings, recommended her not to be on the fidgets, and dismissed the matter from his mind.

But not for long. It was recalled by a chance meeting at his club with an acquaintance who let fall a scrap of information which, the more he considered it, seemed to him of sufficient interest to recount to his wife. It was curious: not alarming—in fact, the inference to be drawn from it would probably do much to banish Trixie's blue devils—but it did make one wonder a trifle. It was not important enough to occupy a prominent place in his memory: he remembered it when he was in the middle of telling Trixie about young Kendal, whom he had run smash into as he was coming away from White's.

'Not that I knew who he was, for although I daresay I may have seen him when he was a child I don't recall it,' he said reflectively. 'However, Willingdon was with me, and at once introduced him. You remember Jack Kendal, Trixie? Fellow that was up at Cambridge with me—came in for a neat little place in Northamptonshire, and married some Scotch girl or other. I went to his funeral about five years ago,' he added helpfully, perceiving a slight lack of interest in his wife's face. 'Poor fellow! I didn't see much of him after he got married, but he used to be a close friend of mine. Well, this boy I was telling you about is his second son. Well set-up young fellow, though he don't favour Jack much: got sandy hair, like his mother. Queer dance, my meeting him like that. Which reminds me!' he said, digressing suddenly. 'Knew I had something to tell you! Cleeve was in the club today, and he happened to mention Brancaster.'

'Brancaster?' said Beatrix quickly, her interest immediately roused. 'Did Lord Cleeve know—did he give you any news of Gareth?'

'No, no, nothing like that! But from what he said it seems Brancaster is down at Brighton. He spoke of having dined with him in town the day he came up from Brancaster Park. He went off to join the Regent the next morning. What struck me as odd was that, by what I was able to make out, he must have left Brancaster the day after Gary arrived there. That is, if Gary held by his intention of going first to Rydes. Said he meant to spend a couple of days with them, didn't he?'

'Yes, certainly he did, and Gary would never break an engagement of that nature! Then Gary cannot be at Brancaster! Warren, it must surely mean—though I find it hard to credit it!—that Lady Hester rejected him!'

'Looks like it,' agreed Warren. 'Brancaster's a ramshackle fellow, but he wouldn't go off to Brighton if he had Gary staying with him in Cambridgeshire. I thought you'd be interested.'

'*Thankful!*' she declared. Her brow creased. 'Yes, but—Warren, if Gary left Brancaster over a fortnight ago, what can have become of him?'

'Lord, I don't know! Daresay he went on to visit some of his friends. To get back to what I was saying to you about young Kendal—'

'He would not have done so without writing to me! He must have known how anxious I should be!'

'Anxious! Why should you be anxious? Gary ain't a schoolboy, my dear! I own it ain't like him to go off without telling anyone where he was bound for, or how long he meant to be away—but for anything we know he may have sent word to Berkeley Square.'

'I shall call there tomorrow morning, and ask Sheen whether he has had any news of his master,' said Beatrix in a determined voice.

'No harm in doing that, but mind, now, Trixie!—if he hasn't written to

Sheen, Gary won't thank you for kicking up a dust, so take care what you say to Sheen! Well, about young Kendal! I invited him to come and take his pot-luck with us tomorrow. Jack's boy, you know!'

She was frowning over the mystery of her brother's continued absence from town, but these words successfully diverted her mind. 'Invited him to dine with us tomorrow?' she exclaimed. 'Good gracious, Warren, could you not have invited him to White's? Pray, how, at such short notice, am I to arrange a suitable party for his entertainment, with London so thin of company? And Leigh gone off to stay with the Maresfields, too!'

'Leigh? Lord, Kendal ain't a scrubby schoolboy! He's four or five-and-twenty, and has seen eight years' service besides! What should he have to say to a whipper-snapper like Leigh? As for company, you need not put yourself about, for I told him he would meet none but ourselves.'

'Oh, very well!' she said. 'I must say, though, that I should think he would be heartily bored!'

'Nonsense! He will be mighty glad to sit down to one of your dinners, my love. He has been putting up at an hotel these past few weeks, and I'll be bound he'll welcome a change from chops and steaks. He told me that he's been kept kicking his heels in town by those fellows at the Horse Guards, while the military doctors made up their minds whether he was fit to go back to his duties or not. Got a ball in his shoulder, and was sent home on sick furlough some months ago. He's a Light Bob: 43rd Regiment.'

The vexed look vanished from her face. It was tiresome to be obliged to entertain a stranger at this season, when she was on the point of shutting up the London house for a couple of months, but no officer from the Peninsula need doubt his welcome in Mount Street. 'Oh, was he in Spain? I wonder if he ever met Arthur? Of course he must dine with us!' she said cordially.

Nothing could have been kinder than her greeting, when Captain Kendal was ushered into her drawing-room on the following evening; but what she had learnt at Sir Gareth's house that morning had destroyed all desire to entertain even a Peninsular veteran who might have been acquainted with her brother Arthur.

Sheen had received no commands from his master, since Trotton, more than a fortnight ago, had delivered a message that Sir Gareth expected to be at home again on the following evening. He had not come, and Trotton had disclosed that when he had parted from him, Sir Gareth had said that he might, perhaps, visit my Lord and Lady Stowmarket, which was no doubt what he had done.

Two pieces of disquieting intelligence were conveyed to Mrs Wetherby in this speech. The first was that Sir Gareth should have sent Trotton home; the second, that he should have said he was going to stay with the Stowmarkets. It was very unlike him to prefer post-chaise travel to driving his own horses; and none knew better than he that the Stowmarkets were away from home. There was some mystery attached to his movements, and the more Beatrix thought about it the uneasier did she become. She betrayed nothing to Sheen, however, merely desiring him to tell Trotton, when he should see him, that she wished him to wait on her in Mount Street.

Nor would anyone have guessed, watching her as she sat chatting to Captain Kendal, that at least half her mind was occupied in turning over and over the problem of Sir Gareth's disappearance.

Captain Kendal was a rather stocky young man, with sandy hair and brows, a square, purposeful countenance, and a pair of very direct blue eyes. His varied career—for he had seen service in South America, before joining Sir John Moore's expedition to Spain—had given him an assurance which made him appear older than his twenty-four years; and his manner, which, although perfectly unassuming, was very decided, indicated that he was accustomed to command. His private fortune was small, but there seemed to be little doubt that he would succeed in his profession. Young as he was, when he had been wounded he had been Acting Brigade-Major. He was not very talkative, but this seemed to arise from a natural taciturnity rather than from shyness; and from having been with the army abroad ever since he had left school, he had none of the social graces that characterized the young man of fashion. He had not been acquainted with Major Ludlow, but in spite of this Beatrix liked him. The only fault she had to find with him was that his mind was cast in rather too serious a mould for her taste.

It was not easy to draw him out on his personal affairs, but he was ready enough to talk of military matters, or of any interesting things he had seen on his travels. Beatrix, inquiring about billeting arrangements in Spain, won far more from him than Warren, asking questions about his family, or his ambitions.

'It's several years since I had the pleasure of meeting your mother,' said Warren. 'I hope she's well?'

'Very well, thank you, sir,' responded Captain Kendal.

'Does she still live in Northamptonshire?'

'Yes, sir.'

'And—now let me see! How many brothers is it that you have?'

'Only one, sir.'

'Only one, eh? But you have several sisters, I fancy.'

'I have three sisters.'

'Three, is it?' said Warren, persevering. 'And your brother—he was married not so long ago, wasn't he?'

'Two years ago,' said Captain Kendal.

'Is it as much as that? I remember seeing the notice of it. Well, well! I suppose he must have been a schoolboy when I saw him last. I was used frequently to visit your father, you know, and was once pretty familiar with your part of the country. Lately, I don't know how it may be, but I have very seldom been in Northamptonshire. I daresay, however, that we have several acquaintances in common. The Birchingtons, for instance, and Sir Harry Bramber?' Captain Kendal bowed. 'Yes, I was sure you must know them. Yes, and I'll tell you who is in town, who is quite a near neighbour of yours! Old Summercourt! But I daresay you knew that.'

'I didn't know it, sir. I am, of course, acquainted with General Summercourt.'

'Friend of my father's,' said Warren. 'I met him today, at White's. Breaking up a trifle, I thought. Not like himself. But I only had a couple of words or so with him: he was in the devil of a hurry—only dropped into the club to see if there were any letters for him. Said he couldn't stay, because he must call at Bow Street. Seemed an odd start to me. Not getting to be a trifle queer in his attic, is he?'

'Not to my knowledge,' said Captain Kendal, staring rather fixedly at him. '*Bow Street*, did you say?'

'Yes: I couldn't help wondering what took him there. He was looking a trifle hagged, too. Nothing wrong, is there?'

'To my knowledge, nothing whatsoever,' replied Captain Kendal, a crease between his brows.

Warren began to talk of something else, but after a few minutes the Captain said abruptly: 'I beg pardon, sir, but can you furnish me with General Summercourt's direction?'

'I didn't ask where he was staying, but I fancy he usually puts up at Grillon's when he's in town,' replied Warren, looking an inquiry.

The Captain coloured slightly. 'Thank you. If he is in some trouble—I am pretty well acquainted with him—it would be civil to call upon him!'

Nothing more was said on the subject, but Beatrix received the impression that the casual pieces of information let fall by her husband had arrested Captain Kendal's attention more than had anything else that had been said to him.

Not long after dinner, when the gentlemen had joined Beatrix in the drawing-room, the butler came in, and, after hesitating for a moment, went to where his master was sitting, and bent to say, in an apologetic and lowered tone: 'I beg your pardon, sir, but Sir Gareth's head groom is below. I said you was engaged, but he seems very anxious to speak to you.'

The words were intended only for Mr Wetherby's ears, but Beatrix's hearing was sharp, and she heard them. She broke off in the middle of what she was saying to her guest, and demanded: 'Did you say Sir Gareth's head groom? I will come at once.' She nodded to her husband, and got up. 'I left a message in Berkeley Square that I wished Trotton to come here. Captain Kendal will excuse me, I am sure, if I run away for a few minutes.'

'I beg pardon, ma'am, but it is the *master* Trotton has come to see,' interposed the butler, catching Mr Wetherby's eye, and exchanging with him a meaning look.

'Nonsense! It is I who want to see Trotton, not your master!' said Beatrix, not blind to this by-play.

'Stay where you are, my dear,' said Warren, going to the door. 'I'll find out what Trotton wants. There's no occasion for you to put yourself out.'

She was vexed, but to engage in a dispute with him in the presence of a guest did not suit her notions of propriety. She resumed her seat, and said, with rather a forced smile: 'Pray forgive us! The thing is that I am in some anxiety about my brother, whose groom it is who has just come here.'

'I am excessively sorry!' he said. 'I collect he is ill? Would you like me to go away? You must be wishing me at the devil!'

'Indeed I am not! I beg you won't think of running away! My brother is not ill—at least, I don't think so.' She stopped, and then said, with a little laugh: 'It is very likely nothing at all, and I am refining too much upon the event. The fact is that my brother went into the country on a visit more than a fortnight ago, and although his servants were in the expectation of his returning four days later, he *didn't* return, or send any word, so that I cannot help indulging a great many foolish fancies. But you were telling me about the *fiestas* in Madrid: do continue! How pretty the candles set on all the windowsills must have looked! Were you quartered in the town, Captain Kendal?'

He answered her, and she led him on to describe such features of the Spanish scene as he had thought memorable, an expression on her face of absorbed interest, suitable comments rising mechanically to her lips, and her mind almost wholly divorced from anything he was saying.

The circumstance of Trotton's asking particularly to speak with Warren rather than with herself was not reassuring; a chilling fear that some dreadful news was presently to be broken gently to her by her husband began to creep into her heart; and only her good breeding kept her from jumping up, and following Warren.

He was gone for what seemed to her to be an ominously long time, and when he at last came back into the room he was wearing the expression of a man who did not wish his wife to suspect that anything was wrong. It was too much; she exclaimed sharply: 'What is it? Has some accident befallen Gary?'

'No, no, nothing of the sort! I'll tell you about it presently, but there's no need for you to worry your head over it.'

'Where is Gary?' she demanded.

'Well, I can't tell you that, but you may depend upon it he's perfectly well and safe wherever he is. Trotton parted from him at Kimbolton, so I daresay he may have gone off to stay with Staplehurst.'

'*Kimbolton?*' she repeated, astonished. 'What in the world took him there, pray?'

'Oh, well, that's a long story, and of no interest to Kendal, my love!'

'If you'll allow me, sir, I'll take my leave,' said the Captain. 'Mrs Wetherby must be very anxious to learn more. I would have gone before, only that she wouldn't suffer me to!'

'I should rather think not, and nor will I! Sit down, my boy!'

'Oh, yes, pray do!' Beatrix said. 'Is Trotton still in the house, Warren?'

'Having a heavy-wet in the pantry, I expect.'

'Then, if Captain Kendal will excuse me, I will go down and speak to him myself!' she said. 'I don't stand on ceremony with you, sir, but I am persuaded you will not care for that.'

'I should rather think not, ma'am!'

She smiled, and hurried out of the room. The Captain looked at his host, and said bluntly: 'Bad news, sir?'

'Lord, no!' said Warren, with a chuckle. 'But it ain't the sort of news to blab to his sister! The groom's a silly clutch, but he had that much sense! From what I can make out, my brother-in-law has picked up a very prime article, and has made off with her the lord knows where! He's never been much in the petticoat-line, so his groom don't know what to make of it. Told me he was sure Ludlow had gone out of his mind!'

'Oh, I see!' said the Captain, with a laugh. 'No, that's not a story for Mrs Wetherby, certainly!'

'Trust Trotton to turn her up sweet!' said Warren confidently. 'Catch him giving his master's secrets away! Devoted to him, you know: been with him since Gareth was a lad. The only wonder is he told me. Don't suppose he would have, if my wife hadn't summoned him to come here. The silly fellow's in the deuce of a pucker: thinks his master's heading for trouble! Funny thing about these old servants: never can be brought to believe one ain't still in short coats!'

'No, by Jupiter!' agreed the Captain. 'Like my old nurse, who is persuaded I got hit because she wasn't there to tell me not to get in the way of the nasty guns!'

'Exactly so!' said Warren, laughing heartily. 'I told Trotton I never knew a man more able to take care of himself than Ludlow, but I might as well have spared my breath. I shall have to discover what tale he's fobbed my wife off with, or I shall be bowled out.'

But when Mrs Wetherby came back into the room he soon found that this would be unnecessary. She was looking so much amused that he was surprised into exclaiming: 'What the deuce did Trotton tell you to set you off laughing?'

She threw him a saucy look. 'The truth, of course! Did you think I couldn't get him to tell me the whole? Pooh! How could you be so non-sensical as to suppose I should be shocked, as though I were a school-room miss? I was never more enchanted! When I had despaired of ever seeing the *old* Gary again, doing such daring things, and being so gay, and adventurous! *How* I wish I could have seen him snatching up this beautiful girl in his curricle, and driving off with her! Of all the absurd starts! Depend upon it, he sent Trotton home because he was off to the Border with his Amanda! Did Trotton tell you what was her name? Isn't it pretty?'

'*What?*' ejaculated Captain Kendal.

She was surprised, for he had fairly shot the word at her, but before she could answer Warren intervened, saying in a displeased voice: 'You are talking nonsense, my dear, and allowing your romantic notions to run away with you. The Border, indeed! You may be sure there is no question of *that*!'

'Oh, you are thinking of her trying to escape from him, and his chasing after her, and finding her in a cow-byre, or some such thing!' she said, laughing. 'My dear Warren, how can you be so green? No female in her senses would wish to escape from Gary, least of all a girl who was found in a common inn, entirely unattended!'

'You will be giving Kendal a very odd idea of your brother if you lead him to suppose that Gary would for a moment contemplate marriage with such a girl,' Warren said repressively.

She was aware that her natural liveliness, exaggerated as it was by relief, had betrayed her into raillery that was beyond the line of being pleasing, and coloured, saying: 'I was only funning, of course! It cannot be more than a—well, a charmingly romantic interlude!—but it will do Gary a great deal of good, so you must not expect me to pull down my mouth, and preach propriety, if you please!'

After his one startled exclamation, Captain Kendal had not again un-closed his lips. They were indeed tightly gripped together, in a way that suggested to his hostess that he was tiresomely prudish. There was a stern look in his face, and an expression in his eyes which quite startled her. He might disapprove of her vivacity, but why he should look murderous she was at a loss to understand. She stared at him; he lowered his eyes; seemed to make an effort to suppress whatever emotion it was that had him in its clutch; and said curtly that it was time he took his leave. He would not stay for tea, but he said everything that was proper before shaking hands briefly with his hostess. Warren accompanied him to the front-door. 'My wife, when she is in funning humour, talks a great deal of flummery,' he said. 'I need not ask you not to repeat her nonsense, I know.'

'You need have no fear of that, sir!' said Captain Kendal emphatically. 'Goodnight! And thank you for a—very pleasant evening!'

A bow, and he was gone. Warren went upstairs again to scold his wife for having shocked her guest, and to read her a homily on the evils of a long tongue; but he was himself a little puzzled by the Captain's behaviour.

Captain Kendal, meanwhile, hailed the first hackney he saw, and bade the jarvey drive him to Grillon's Hotel. While this aged vehicle lumbered on its way to Albemarle Street, he sat rather rigidly upright, clenching and unclenching one fist, and frowning straight ahead. Arrived at Grillon's, he demanded General Summercourt in a voice grim enough to make the porter look rather narrowly at him.

The General was discovered, seated at a desk in a small writing-room. There was no one else in the room. The General looked up, and when he saw who had come in, his face hardened, and he said: 'You, eh? And just what do you want, young man?'

'I want to know what took you to Bow Street today, sir!' the Captain replied.

'Oh, you do, do you?' snapped the General, exploding into the wrath of a much harassed man. 'Then I will tell you, you damned, encroaching jackanapes! Thanks to you my grand-daughter has been missing from her home for more than a fortnight. Read that!'

Captain Kendal almost snatched the sheet of writing-paper that was being thrust at him, and rapidly read the lines written in Amanda's childish hand. When he came to the end, he looked up, and said fiercely: 'Thanks to *me*? Do you imagine, sir, that Amanda took this step with my knowledge? That I would permit her—By God, if that is the opinion you hold of my character I do not wonder at your refusing your consent to our marriage!'

The General glared at him for a moment. 'No, I don't,' he said shortly. 'If I had, I should have come to you and *choked* her whereabouts out of you! But if you hadn't come making up to her, putting ideas into her head, egging her on to defy me—'

'So far from egging her on to defy you, I have told her that I will not, while she is so young, marry her without your consent, sir! And she knows I mean what I say!'

'Yes! And this is the outcome! I am to be forced to consent! Well, you may be sure of this, Neil Kendal!—I will not! *Damme*, I will not!'

'I collect, then, that you haven't put a notice in the *Morning Post*, sir?'

'No! I have put the matter in the hands of the Runners. They have been searching for her now for a se'enight!'

'And she has been missing above a fortnight!' the Captain flung at him. 'Taking it mighty coolly, are you not, sir?'

'Damn your impudence, I made sure she was hiding in the woods! She did so once before, when she couldn't get her own way, the little puss!'

'Call off the Runners!' said the Captain. '*I* can tell you more than they appear to have discovered, and pretty hearing it is! *Where* Amanda is I don't know, but *whom* she is with I do know!'

'For God's sake, Neil, what do you mean?' demanded the General, turning pale. 'Out with it!'

'She is with a fellow called Ludlow—Gareth Ludlow—who came upon her in a common inn, where, I know not, and bore her off to Kimbolton. I have been dining tonight with Ludlow's sister, a Mrs Wetherby, and what I heard in that house—My God, I don't know how I contrived to keep my tongue still!'

'Ludlow?' the General said numbly. 'Bore her off? My little Amanda? No, no, it isn't possible! Tell me the whole, damn you!'

He listened in silence to Captain Kendal's succinct recital, but it seemed as though he had hardly taken it in, for he sat looking blankly at the Captain, repeating uncomprehendingly: 'Abducted her—trying to escape from him—found in a *cow-byre*?' He managed to pull himself together, and said in a firmer voice: 'It isn't possible! She's nothing but a child! Did you discover from these Wetherbys—'

'Exactly what I have told you! They knew no more, and you may be sure I asked no questions! They suppose Amanda to belong to the muslin company: a *very prime article* was the term used by Wetherby! Upon no account would I have said one word that might lead them to the truth!'

'It isn't possible!' the General said again. 'A man of Ludlow's quality—Good God, in whatever case he met her he must have recognized at a glance that she was a child—a gently-bred child, and as innocent—Why the devil didn't he restore her to me? Or, if she wouldn't tell him what her name was, place her in the care of a respectable woman?'

'Yes, *why*?' said the Captain harshly. 'That is a question he will answer to me before he is much older! What kind of a man is he?'

The General made a hopeless gesture. 'How should I know? I'm not acquainted with him. A man of fashion: he belongs to the Corinthian set. Handsome fellow, with a fine figure, rich enough to be able to buy an abbey. He's not married—I fancy there was some sort of a tragedy, years ago. I've never heard any ill of him: on the contrary, I believe him to be very well liked. But what's that to the purpose? If she has been all this time with him—By God, he shall marry her! He has compromised her—my grand-daughter!—and if he thinks—'

'*He* marry her—! We'll see that!' interrupted the Captain grimly. 'Now, sir! The first thing you must do is to call off the Runners, so that we may get through this damnable business with as little noise as possible. I'm off to Kimbolton in the morning, and if I can get no news of Ludlow there I'll try a cast or two. But something I must learn: he cannot have passed unnoticed in so small a place. If you like to leave it in my hands, very well! If you prefer to accompany me, better!'

'*Accompany* you, you insubordinate, insolent young dog?' exploded the General. 'What right have you to meddle in my affairs? Don't think I'll consent to let you marry Amanda, for I won't! *My* granddaughter to throw herself away on a penniless cub in a Line Regiment? No, by God! *I* am going to Kimbolton, and I desire neither your aid nor your company!'

'As you please!' shrugged Captain Kendal. 'I shall be leaving at first light, and no doubt that would not suit you. I beg you will not neglect to send a letter to Bow Street. We shall meet in Kimbolton! Goodnight!'

17

At very much the same time as these stirring events were taking place in London, Lord Widmore received letters from his two younger sisters, and learned from them that with neither had Lady Hester sought shelter. As he had by then argued himself into a belief that she could have gone nowhere else, the tidings came as a severe shock to him, and caused him to exclaim unguardedly: 'Gertrude and Constance have not seen Hester since we left London!'

Until that moment, Mr Whyteleafe had been left in ignorance of the true state of affairs, Lord Widmore being very much more circumspect than his sire. But Mr Whyteleafe was present when the letters were brought up from the receiving-office, and this involuntary outburst not only arrested his attention, but caused him to demand from his lordship an explanation. He got the explanation from Lady Widmore. Her ladyship's disregard for appearances made her much inclined to treat the escapade as a very good joke, an attitude of mind which so much revolted her lord that it was with relief that he unburdened himself to the chaplain. Mr Whyteleafe's reactions were all that they should have been. He changed colour, and uttered: 'Not at Lady Ennerdale's! Not with Mrs Nutley, or Lady Cookham! Good God, sir, this is terrible!'

Lord Widmore, looking upon him with approval, decided to admit him into his confidence. As a result, he learned for the first time of the existence of Hildebrand Ross. Until that moment no one had told him that the person supposedly sent by Lady Ennerdale to escort her sister on the journey had been other than a servant. He now discovered that Hester had gone away with an unknown young gentleman of undoubted gentility but suspicious aspect, and exclaimed: 'She has eloped!'

But Mr Whyteleafe did not think that Hester had eloped. Mr Ross, although sufficiently depraved to utter unblushing lies to a man whose cloth should have commanded his respect, was scarcely of an age to contemplate marriage with a lady approaching her thirtieth year. Mr Ross, he feared, was no more than a go-between.

Lady Widmore, laughing in a very vulgar way, asked who the deuce was there for Mr Ross to go between, but she was not attended to. By rapid stages Mr Ross became an infernal agent, employed either by a secret and obviously ineligible lover, or by a daring kidnapper. Lady Widmore, declaring that she was in stitches, said that any kidnapper who thought to wring a groat out of a family that had not a feather to fly with must be so bottleheaded that even such a goosecap as Hester would be able to escape from his clutches. In her opinion, Hester herself, more sly than any of them had suspected, had employed Mr Ross to assist her to slip away from Brancaster without exciting surprise or opposition. She recommended her husband to subject his butler to a rigorous inquisition. If anyone knew what kind of an undergame Hester was engaged in, she said, he might lay his life that one was Cliffe, whose maudlin affection for Hester had often put her ladyship out of all patience.

Lord Widmore failed to elicit any information from Cliffe, but Mr Whyteleafe was more successful. Cliffe, already anxious and more than a little doubtful of the wisdom of his having abetted Hester, crumbled under the powerful exhortations of the chaplain. He was brought to realize that his mistress's reputation, nay, even her life, perhaps, was at stake, and, weeping, he gave up the only piece of information he had. He told Mr Whyteleafe that he had recognized the post-boy in charge of the chaise that had borne Lady Hester away as one of the lads employed at the Crown Inn at St Ives.

From then onward Mr Whyteleafe assumed command. In a manner calculated to convince the trembling butler that he had aided Lady Hester to commit an indiscretion which must plunge her entire family into a ruinous scandal, he laid a strict charge of silence upon Cliffe. Almost as impressively he pointed out to Lord Widmore that no whisper of the affair must be allowed to reach the ears of any but themselves. Together he and his lordship would discover, at St Ives, the destination of that post-chaise; together they would track down the fugitive. No coachman or postilion should go with them: they would set forth alone, and in the curricle which the Earl kept at Brancaster for his use when in Cambridgeshire. 'And I,' added Mr Whyteleafe, recollecting that Lord Widmore was a very indifferent whip, 'will drive it!'

Meanwhile, in happy ignorance of the hostile forces converging upon him, Sir Gareth was making a recovery upon which his medical attendant never ceased to congratulate himself. It would be some time before his wound would cease to trouble him (a circumstance due, Lady Hester had no hesitation in asserting, to the shockingly rough and ready methods employed in the extraction of the bullet), and still longer before he could hope to regain his full strength; but the progress he made was steady; and it was not long before he was able to persuade his several nurses to let him leave his bed, and try what the beneficial effects of fresh air would do for him. A small orchard lay behind the inn, and, as the weather continued to be sultry, one golden day succeeding another, it was here that he spent his days, in an idyllic existence which not even the ill-humour of Mrs Chicklade could mar. That stern moralist had never been convinced of the respectability of the party she was called upon to serve; and when she saw the parlour chairs carried into the orchard, together with a table, and all the cushions the inn could yield, and further discovered that her misguided spouse had consented to carry meals there, she knew that her worst suspicions had fallen short of the truth. A set of heathen gypsies, that's what Chicklade's precious ladies and gentleman of quality were, and let no one dare to tell her different! But Chicklade said that he knew the Quality when he saw it, and while the dibs were in tune the visitors might eat their dinner on the roof, if that was their fancy. As for the morals of the party, it was not for him to criticize an out-and-outer who dropped his blunt as freely as did Sir Gareth.

So Mrs Chicklade, appeased by the thought of the gold that was flowing into her husband's coffers, continued to cook three handsome meals a day for her disreputable guests, and startled her neighbours by appearing suddenly in a new and impressive bonnet, and a gown of rich purple hue.

As for the disreputable guests, only Amanda was not entirely content to remain at Little Staughton. Sir Gareth had his own reasons for not wishing to bring his stay to an end; Lady Hester, tending him, sitting in comfortable companionship beside him under the laden fruit trees, valued as she had never been before, was putting on a new bloom; and Hildebrand, inspired by the rural solitude, had made a promising start to his tragic drama, and was not at all anxious to return to a more exacting world. He had got his horse back, too, yielding at last to a command from his adopted uncle to stop being a gudgeon, and to retrieve the noble animal without more ado. He still slept on a camp-bed set up in Sir Gareth's room: not because his services were any longer needed during the night-watches, but because there were only two guest-chambers in the inn. Sir Gareth was thus kept fully abreast of the drama's progress, the day's literary output being read to him each night, and his criticisms and suggestions invited. No qualms were suffered by Hildebrand: he blithely assured Sir Gareth that his parents, believing him to be on a walking-tour of Wales, would not expect to receive any letters from him; and as for the friends he should have joined, they would think only that he had changed his plans, or had been delayed, and would doubtless overtake them.

'Well, wouldn't you like to?' Sir Gareth asked him. 'You know, I am really very well able to manage for myself now, and I don't want you to feel yourself obliged to remain here on my account. Chicklade can do all I need.'

'Chicklade?' said Hildebrand, revolted. 'What, let him tie your cravats with his great clumsy hands? I should rather think not! Just as you have taught me how to tie a Waterfall, too! Besides, Aunt Hester and I have decided that when you are well enough to travel to London I am to go with you, to take care of you on the journey. What's more, if Amanda should take it into her head to run away again *you* cannot chase after her, Uncle Gary! And while I am in the vein, I do think that it would be a pity to break the thread of my play. Should you object to it if I just read you the second scene again, now that I have rewritten it?'

So Hildebrand was allowed to remain, although Sir Gareth did not think that Amanda had any intention of running away. Amanda, for once, was at a stand. It had never occurred to her that her grandfather would fail to obey her directions, and how to bring added pressure to bear on him was a problem to which there seemed to be no solution. Time was slipping by, and it might well be that already Neil was under orders to rejoin his brigade. She had not quite reached the stage of capitulation, and still exhaustively scanned the *Morning Post*, which Mr Vinehall obligingly sent to the Bull each day; but Sir Gareth was hopeful that by the time he was adjudged to be well enough to travel he would have little difficulty in persuading her to accompany him to London. Nothing would prevail upon her to disclose her grandfather's identity, but she had begun to toy with a scheme whereby not her grandfather's hand, but Neil's, might be forced. Did not Uncle Gary think that if he believed her reputation to be lost, Neil would marry her out of hand?

'It seems most unlikely,' he replied. 'Why should he?'

She was sitting on the ground, a half-made cowslip ball in her hands, looking so absurdly youthful as she propounded her outrageous scheme, that he was hard put to it to maintain his gravity. 'To save my good name,' she said glibly.

'But he wouldn't be doing anything of the sort,' he objected. 'He would be giving you quite a different name.'

'Yes, but if you lose your reputation, you have to be married in a hurry,' she argued. 'I know that, because when Theresa—when *someone* I know lost hers, which she did, though I am not perfectly sure how, someone *else* I know said to my aunt that there was nothing for it but to get her married immediately, to save her good name. Well, if you stay all alone with a gentleman you lose your reputation *at once*, so if I pretended Aunt Hester and Hildebrand weren't here, wouldn't Neil feel that it was his duty to marry me, whatever Grandpapa says?'

'No, he would be more likely to feel that *I* must marry you, and you wouldn't like that, you know.'

'No, of course I shouldn't, but you could refuse to marry me, couldn't you? That would put Neil in a fix!'

'Yes, indeed!' agreed Hester, with unruffled calm. 'But I believe that he would think it his duty to challenge Uncle Gary to a duel, and although Uncle is much better, he isn't strong enough to fight a duel. You wouldn't wish him to overtax himself.'

'No,' Amanda said reluctantly. 'Well, Hildebrand must be the one to do it. Hildebrand! *Hildebrand!*'

Hildebrand, lying on his stomach at some little distance from them, his fingers writhing among his disordered locks as he wrestled with literary composition, vouchsafed only an absent grunt.

'Hildebrand, would you be so obliging as to pretend to compromise me, and then refuse to marry me?' said Amanda cajolingly.

'No, can't you see I'm busy? Ask Uncle Gary!' said Hildebrand.

This was not encouraging, nor, when he was brought to attend to what was being said to him, did he return any more satisfactory answer. He recommended her not to be silly, and added that she didn't know what she was talking about.

'I think you are uncivil and disobliging!' said Amanda roundly.

'Oh, no, I'm sure he doesn't mean to be!' said Hester, looking round for her scissors. 'I expect—oh, there they are! however did they come to get over there?—I expect he did not quite understand. Really, Hildebrand, you will only have to refuse to marry Amanda, and surely that is not much to ask?'

'Oh, I don't mind doing *that*!' he said, grinning.

'You are an unprincipled woman, Hester,' Sir Gareth told her, at the earliest opportunity.

'Yes, I think I am,' she agreed reflectively.

'There can be no doubt of it. Are you really proposing to allow Amanda to regale her Brigade-Major with this abominable story she has concocted?'

'But I can see no harm in *that*, Gareth!' she said, vaguely surprised. 'It will make her wish to go to London, besides giving her something to do in planning it all, which she *needs*, you know, because since the calf at the farm was sent off to the market it is really very dull for her here. And the Brigade-Major cannot possibly be foolish enough to believe the story. Anyone must see that she hasn't the least notion of what it means to be compromised.'

'And having said that, do you still maintain that she should be permitted to marry the fellow?' he asked.

'It depends on what he is like,' she replied thoughtfully. 'I should wish to see him before I made up my mind.'

Her wish was granted on the following afternoon. Sir Gareth, half asleep under a big apple-tree, with Joseph wholly asleep on his knee, became drowsily aware of a menacing presence, and opened his eyes. They fell upon a sandy-haired, stockily built young gentleman who was standing a few feet away, grimly surveying him. Contempt and wrath flamed in his blue eyes as they took in the splendour of the frogged dressing-gown, which, since his coats fitted him far too well to be eased on over his heavily bandaged shoulder, Sir Gareth was obliged to wear. Interested, and mildly surprised, Sir Gareth sought his quizzing-glass, and through it inspected his unknown visitor.

Captain Kendal drew an audible breath, and pronounced in a voice of awful and resolute civility: 'Am I correct, sir, in thinking that I address Sir Gareth Ludlow?'

'Sir,' responded Sir Gareth gravely, but with a twitching lip, 'you are!'

Captain Kendal appeared to struggle with himself. His fists clenched, and his teeth ground together; he drew another painful breath, and said in measured accents: 'I am sorry, sir—*damned* sorry!—to see that you have your arm in a sling!'

'Your solicitude, sir,' said Sir Gareth, entering into the spirit of this, 'moves me deeply! To own the truth, I am sorry to see it there myself.'

'Because,' said Captain Kendal, through his shut teeth, 'your disabled condition renders it impossible for me to deal with you as you deserve! My heartfelt wish is that you may recover the use of your arm before I am obliged to leave England!'

'Good God!' exclaimed Sir Gareth, enlightenment dawning on him. He lifted his quizzing-glass again. 'Do you know, I had quite a different picture in my mind? I wish you will tell me what your name is!'

'That, sir, you will know in good time! You will allow me to tell you that what I learned at Kimbolton brought me here with two overmastering desires: the first to bring you to book, and the second to shake the hand of the boy who tried to rescue from your clutches a girl whose youth and innocence must have protected her from any but an unprincipled villain!'

'Well, I am afraid you can't realize the first of these very proper ambitions,' said Sir Gareth apologetically, 'but there's nothing easier to accomplish than the second.' He sat up, and looked round, disturbing Joseph, who stood up, sneezed, and sprang off his knee. 'When I last saw him he was in the throes of dramatic composition, over there. Yes, there he is, but not, I perceive, still wrestling with his Muse.'

'*What?*' said Captain Kendal, taken aback. 'Are you trying to hoax me, sir?'

'Not at all! Wake up, Hildebrand! We have a visitor!'

'Do you imagine,' demanded the Captain, 'that I am the man to be taken in by your shams?'

'I am sure you are not,' replied Sir Gareth soothingly. 'You do seem to leap a little hurriedly to conclusions—but, then, I don't know yet precisely what it was you learned at Kimbolton.'

'Why,' the Captain shot at him, 'did the chambermaid find your *ward's* door locked? Why did your *ward* think it necessary to lock her door?'

'She didn't. I locked the door, so that she shouldn't escape a second time. Yes, come over here, Hildebrand! Our visitor wishes to shake you by the hand. Let me present Mr Ross to you, sir! This, Hildebrand, unless I much mistake the matter, is the Brigade-Major.'

'What, Amanda's Brigade-Major?' exclaimed Hildebrand. 'Well, of all things! However did you find us out, sir?'

'For God's sake, have I strayed into a *madhouse*?' thundered the Captain. '*Where is Amanda?*'

'Well, I don't know,' said Hildebrand, looking startled. 'I daresay she has gone down the road to the farm, though. Shall I go and see if I can find her? Oh, I say, sir, I wish you will tell me!—*will* she be obliged to wring chickens' necks if she goes to Spain?'

'Wring—No!' said the Captain, thrown by this time quite off his balance.

'I *knew* it was all nonsense!' said Hildebrand triumphantly. 'I told her it was, but she always thinks she knows everything!'

'*Neil!*'

The Captain spun round. Amanda had just entered the orchard, bearing a glass of milk and a plate of fruit on a small tray. As the shriek broke from her, she dropped the tray, and came flying across the grass, to hurl herself on to the Captain's broad chest. 'Neil, Neil!' she cried, both arms flung round his neck. 'Oh, Neil, have you come to rescue me? Oh, how *splendid*! I didn't know *what* to do, and I was almost in despair, but now everything will be right!'

The Captain, holding her in a crushing hug, said thickly: 'Yes, everything. I'll see to that!' He disengaged himself, and held her off, his hands gripping her shoulders. 'Amanda, what has happened to you? The truth, now, and no playing off any tricks!'

'Oh, you wouldn't *believe* the adventures I have had!' she said earnestly. 'First there was a horrid woman, who wouldn't have me for a governess, and then there was Sir Gareth Ludlow, who abducted me, and next there was Mr Theale, who said he would rescue me from Sir Gareth, only he was so odious that I was obliged to escape from *him*, and after that there was Joe, who was *most* kind, and gave me my dear little kitten. I wanted to stay with Joe, though his mother didn't seem to wish me to, but Sir Gareth found me, and told the most shocking untruths which the Ninfields believed, and went *on* abducting me, and locking me in my room, and behaving in the most *abominable* way, in spite of my *begging* him to let me go, so that though I *truthfully* never meant Hildebrand to shoot him, it quite served him

right–Oh, Neil, this *is* Sir Gareth! Uncle Gary, *this* is Neil!–Captain
Kendal! And that's Hildebrand Ross, Neil. Oh, Uncle Gary, I am
excessively sorry, but I threw your glass of milk away! Hildebrand, would
you be so obliging as to fetch another one?'

'Yes, very well, but you needn't think I'm going to let you stand there
telling bouncers about Uncle Gary!' said Hildebrand indignantly. 'He did
not abduct you, and as for telling lies about you–well, yes, but you told
much worse ones about him! Why, you told *me* he was forcing you to marry
him because you were a great heiress!'

'Yes, but I had to do that, or you wouldn't have helped me to escape from
him!'

The Captain, a trifle stunned, released his betrothed, and turned to Sir
Gareth. 'I don't understand yet what happened, sir, but I believe I have
been doing you an injustice. If that's so, I beg your pardon! But why you
should not have restored Amanda immediately to General Summercourt, or
at the very least have written to inform him—'

'He couldn't!' said Amanda proudly. 'He spoiled *all* my plan of campaign, and he carried me off by force, but he couldn't make me tell him
who I was, or Grandpapa, or you, Neil! I *did* think he would win even over
that, because he meant to carry me off to his sister, in London, and discover
your name at the Horse Guards, only he wasn't able to, because, by the
greatest stroke of good fortune, we met Hildebrand, and Hildebrand shot
him–though that wasn't what he meant to do, of course.'

'There is a great deal about this business I don't understand, but one
thing is plain!' said the Captain, sternly eyeing his beloved. 'You have been
behaving very badly, Amanda!'

'Yes, but I *had* to, Neil!' she pleaded, hanging her head, 'I was afraid you
would be a little vexed, but—'

'You knew that I should be very angry indeed. Don't think you can cajole
me, my girl! You may reserve that for your grandfather! He will be here at
any moment now, let me tell you, for he was following me from London,
and I left a message for him at Kimbolton. Do you know that he has had to
call in the Bow Street Runners to find you?'

'No!' cried Amanda, reviving as if by magic. 'Uncle Gary, did you hear
that? The Runners are after me!'

'I did, and it confirms my worst fears,' said Sir Gareth. 'What a pity,
though, that you have only just learnt that you are being hunted! You could
have made up an even more splendid story, if only you had thought of it.'

'Yes, I could,' she said regretfully. 'Still, it would have been much better
if Grandpapa had done what I told him to.'

'No, by God, it would not!' said the Captain forcefully. 'And if you
imagine, Amanda, that I would have married you, had the General been
weak enough to have yielded to such a disgraceful trick, you much mistake
the matter!'

'Neil!' she cried, her eyes flying to his face, and widening in dismay.
'Don't–don't you *wish* to marry me?'

'That,' said the Captain, 'is another matter! Now, you come into the
house, and make a clean breast of the whole, without any more excuses, or
any of your make-believe nonsense!'

'I wouldn't! you know I wouldn't!' Amanda stammered, flushing. 'Not to
you! Neil, you *know* I wouldn't!'

'It will be as well for you if you don't,' said the Captain, inexorably
marching her off.

Hildebrand, watching with dropped jaw, turned his eyes towards Sir Gareth. '*Well!*' he gasped. 'She—went with him as meek as a nun's hen! *Amanda!*'

It was some time before Captain Kendal emerged again from the house, and when at last he came striding through the orchard he was alone. Lady Hester, who had been sitting with Sir Gareth for some little while, blinked at him, and said: 'Good gracious, Gareth, how *very* odd of Amanda! I quite thought he would be a *heroic*-looking young man, did not you?'

Captain Kendal, reaching them, bowed slightly to Hester, but addressed himself to Sir Gareth. 'I hope you will accept my apologies, sir. I don't know how to thank you enough. I got the whole story out of her, and you may be sure I've given her a rare dressing. You must have had the devil of a time with her!'

'Nonsense!' Sir Gareth said, holding out his hand.

The Captain gripped it painfully. 'You didn't handle her right, you know,' he said. 'She's as good as gold, if you don't give her her head. The mischief is that the General and Miss Summercourt have spoilt her to death, and as though that wasn't enough, she's been allowed to stuff her head with a lot of trashy novels. I can tell you, it fairly made my hair stand on end when I heard the stories she's been making up! But the thing is that she hasn't the ghost of a notion what they really mean. I daresay you know that. I hope you do!'

'Of course I know it! My favourite is the one about the amorous widower—though I must own that the latest gem, in which Hildebrand is to play the leading rôle, has rare charm. Now you must let me introduce you to my natural sister, Lady Hester Theale!'

The Captain shook hands with Hester, saying seriously: 'I am excessively sorry, ma'am, and I beg you will forgive her! I was never more shocked! I shall break her of these tricks, you may be sure, but in some ways she's no more than a baby, which makes it devilish hard to explain to her why she mustn't make up faradiddles about being compromised and the rest of it.'

Lady Hester, casting a look of mild triumph at Sir Gareth, said: 'I told you it would depend on what he was like, and I could see you didn't believe me, only you perceive that I was right! Captain Kendal, don't listen to *anything* that *anybody* may say to you, but just marry Amanda, and take her to Spain with you. It would be too bad if you did not, because she has been to a great deal of trouble over it, besides learning to wring chickens' necks, and being exactly the sort of wife you ought to have, if you should happen to be wounded again.'

'Well, I don't want her to wring chickens' necks—in fact, I won't have her doing such things!—and I'd as lief not have her by, if I were to be hit again—thought I'm glad she'd the sense to stop you bleeding to death, sir!—but, by Jupiter, ma'am, if *you* think that's what I should do, I will do it!' said the Captain, once more shaking her by the hand. 'I'm very much obliged to you. It isn't that I don't know she'd do much better with me than with her grandfather, but she *is* very young, and I don't want to take advantage of her. However, if you think it right, the General may go hang! Hallo! That sounds like his voice! Ay, here he comes—but who the devil has he got with him?'

Lady Hester, gazing in a petrified way at the three figures advancing towards her, said faintly: 'Widmore and Mr Whyteleafe! *Just* when we were so comfortable!'

18

It was immediately apparent that although the three gentlemen bearing down upon the group under the apple-tree had arrived together at the Bull, this had not been through any choice of theirs. All were looking heated, and Lord Widmore was glaring so hard at Summercourt that it was not until Mr Whyteleafe ejaculated: '*Sir Gareth Ludlow*! Here—and with Lady Hester?' that he became aware of the identity of the figure in the brocade dressing-gown. Since not even his wildest imaginings had pictured Hester in Sir Gareth's company, he was so dumbfounded that he could only goggle at him. This gave the General an opportunity to step into the lead, and he was quick to pounce on it. Brushing past his lordship, and annihilating Mr Whyteleafe with the stare which had in earlier days turned the bones of his subordinates to water, he strode up to Sir Gareth's chair, and said, in a sort of bark: 'You will be good enough, sir, to grant me the favour of a private interview with you! When I tell you that my name is Summercourt—yes, *Summercourt*, sir!—I rather fancy that you will not think it marvellous that I have come all the way from London for the express purpose of seeking you out! I do not know—nor, I may add, do I *wish* to know, who these persons may be,' he said, casting an eye of loathing over Lord Widmore and the chaplain, 'but I might have supposed that upon my informing them that I had urgent business to discuss here, common civility would have prompted them to postpone whatever may be their errand to you until my business was dispatched! Let me say that these modern manners do not commend themselves to me—though I should have known how it would be, from a couple of cowhanded whipsters as little able to control a worn-out donkey as a pair of carriage-horses!'

'It was not my chaplain, sir, who was driving down a narrow lane at what I do not scruple to call a shocking pace!' said Widmore, firing up.

'The place for a parson, I shall take leave to tell you, sir, is not on the box of a curricle, but in his pulpit!' retorted the General. 'And now, if you will be good enough to retire, I may perhaps be allowed to transact the business which has brought me here!'

Mr Whyteleafe, who had been staring at Hester with an expression on his face clearly indicative of the feelings of shock, dismay, and horror which had assailed him on seeing her thus, living, apparently, with her rejected suitor in a discreetly secluded spot, withdrew his gaze to direct an austere look at the General. The aspersion cast on his driving skill he disdained to notice, but he said, in a severe tone: 'I venture to assert, sir, that the business which brings Lord Widmore and myself to call upon Sir Gareth Ludlow is sufficiently urgent to claim his instant attention. Moreover, I must remind you that *our* vehicle was the first to draw up at this hostelry!'

The General's eyes started at him fiercely. 'Ay! So it was, indeed! I am not very likely to forget it, Master Parson! Upon my soul such effrontery I never before encountered!'

Lord Widmore, whose fretful nerves had by no means recovered from the shock of finding his curricle involved at the cross-road in a very minor collision with a post-chaise and four, began at once to prove to the General that no blame attached to his chaplain. As irritation always rendered him shrill, and the General's voice retained much of its fine carrying quality, the ensuing altercation became noisy enough to cause Lady Hester to stiffen imperceptibly, and to lay one hand on the arm of Sir Gareth's chair, as though for support. He was aware of her sudden tension, and covered her hand with his own, closing his fingers reassuringly round her wrist. 'Don't be afraid! This is all sound and fury,' he said quietly.

She looked down at him, a smile wavering for a moment on her lips. 'Oh, no! I am not afraid. It is only that I have a foolish dislike of loud, angry voices.'

'Yes, very disagreeable,' he agreed. 'I must own, however, that I find this encounter excessively diverting. Kendal, do you care to wager any blunt on which of my engaging visitors first has private speech with me?'

The Captain, who had bent to catch these words, grinned, and said: 'Oh, old Summercourt will bluster himself out, never fear! But who is the other fellow?'

'Lady Hester's brother,' replied Sir Gareth. He added, his eyes on Lord Widmore: 'Bent, if I know him, on queering my game and his own!'

'I beg pardon?' the Captain said, bending again to hear what had been uttered in an undertone.

'Nothing: I was talking to myself.'

Hester murmured: 'Isn't it *odd* that they should forget everything else, and quarrel about such a trifle?' She seemed to become aware of the clasp on her wrist, and tried to draw her hand away. The clasp tightened, and she abandoned the attempt, colouring faintly.

Mr Whyteleafe, whose jealous eyes had not failed to mark the interlude, took a quick step forward, and commanded in a voice swelling with stern wrath: 'Unhand her ladyship, sir!'

Hester blinked at him in surprise. Sir Gareth said, quite amiably: 'Go to the devil!'

The chaplain's words, which had been spoken in a sharpened voice, recalled the heated disputants to matters of more moment than a grazed panel. The quarrel ceased abruptly; and the General, turning to glare at Sir Gareth, seemed suddenly to become aware of the lady standing beside his chair. His brows twitched together in a quelling frown; he demanded: 'Who is this lady?'

'Never mind that!' said Lord Widmore, directing at Sir Gareth a look of mingled prohibition and entreaty.

Sir Gareth met it blandly, and turned his head towards the General. 'This lady, sir, is the Lady Hester Theale. She has the misfortune to be Lord Widmore's sister, and also to dislike heated altercations.'

His lordship's angry but incoherent protest was overborne by the General's more powerful voice. 'Have I been led here on a fool's errand?' he thundered. He rounded on Captain Kendal. 'You young jackass, I told you to keep out of my affairs! I might have known you would lead me on a wild goose chase!'

Captain Kendal, quite undismayed by this ferocious attack, replied: 'Yes, sir, in a way that's what I have done. But all's right, as I will explain to you, if you care to come into the house for a few minutes.'

A look of relief shot into the General's eyes; in a far milder tone, he asked; 'Neil, where is she?'

'Here, sir. I sent her upstairs to wash her face,' said the Captain.'

'Here? With this—this—And you tell me all's *right*?'

'I do, sir. You are very much obliged to Sir Gareth, as I shall show you.'

Before the General could reply, an interruption occurred. Amanda and Hildebrand, attracted by the sounds of the late altercation, had come out of the house, and had paused, surprised to find so many persons gathered around Sir Gareth. Amanda had washed away her tear stains, but she was looking unwontedly subdued. Hildebrand was carefully carrying a brimming glass of milk.

The General saw his granddaughter, and abandoned the rest of the company, going towards her with his hands held out. 'Amanda! Oh, my pet, how *could* you do such a thing?'

She flew into his arms, crying that she was sorry, and would never, never do it again. The Captain, observing with satisfaction that his stern instructions were being obeyed, transferred his dispassionate gaze to the chaplain, who, upon recognizing Hildebrand, had flung out his arm, pointing a finger of doom at that astonished young gentleman, and ejaculating: '*That* is the rascal who lured Lady Hester to this place, my lord! Unhappy boy, you are found out! Do not seek to excuse yourself with lies, for they will not serve you!'

Hildebrand, who had been gazing at him with his mouth at half-cock, looked for guidance towards Sir Gareth, but before Sir Gareth could speak Mr Whyteleafe warned him that it was useless to try to shelter behind his employer.

'Oh, Hildebrand, is that Uncle Gary's milk?' said Hester. 'What a good, *remembering* boy you are! But I quite thought I had given the glass to Amanda, which just shows what a dreadful memory I have!'

'Oh, you did, but she threw it away!' replied Hildebrand. 'Here you are, sir: I'm sorry I have been such an age, but it went out of my head.'

'The only fault I have to find is that it ever re-entered your head,' said Sir Gareth. '*Is* this a moment for glasses of milk? Take it away!'

'No, pray don't! Gareth, Dr Chantry said that you were to drink a great deal of milk, and I won't have you throw it away merely because all these absurd people are teasing you!' said Hester, taking the glass from Hildebrand. 'And Sir Gareth is *not* Mr Ross's employer!' she informed the chaplain. 'Of course, my brother-in-law isn't his employer either, but never mind! It was quite my fault that he was obliged to be not perfectly truthful to you.'

'Lady Hester, I am appalled! I know not by what means you were brought to this place—'

'Hildebrand fetched me in a post-chaise. Now, Gareth!'

'You misunderstand me! Aware as I am, that Sir Gareth's offer was repugnant to you, I cannot doubt that you were lured from Brancaster by some artifice. What arts—I shall not say threats!—have been used to compel your apparent complaisance today I may perhaps guess! But let me assure you—'

'That will do!' interrupted Sir Gareth, with an edge to his voice.

'Yes, but this is nothing but humdudgeon!' said Hildebrand. 'I didn't lure her! I just brought her here because Uncle Gary—Sir Gareth, I mean—needed her! She came to look after him, and we pretended she was his sister, so you may stop looking censoriously, which, though I don't mean to be uncivil to a clergyman, is a great piece of impertinence! And as for *threatening* her, I should just like to see anyone try it, that's all!'

'Oh, Hildebrand!' sighed Hester, overcome. 'How *very* kind you are!'

'Good boy!' Sir Gareth said approvingly, handing him the empty glass. 'Widmore, if you can contrive to come out of a state of what would appear to be a catalepsy, assemble the few wits God gave you, and attend to me, I trust I may be able to allay your brotherly anxiety!'

Lord Widmore, who, from the moment of Amanda's arrival on the scene, had been standing in a spellbound condition, gave a start, and stammered: 'How is this? Upon my soul! I do not know what to think! This goes beyond all bounds! That is the girl you had the effrontery to bring to Brancaster! So it was to take her to those relations of hers at Oundle, was it, that you went chasing after my uncle? Not that I believed it! I hope I am not such a gull!'

'That girl, sir,' said Captain Kendal, dropping a restraining hand on Sir Gareth's shoulder, and keeping his penetrating eyes on Lord Widmore's face, 'is Miss Summercourt. She is shortly to become my wife, so if you have any further observations to make on this head, you may address them to me!'

'Widmore, do *try* not to be so silly!' begged Hester. 'I can't think how you can have so little commonsense! It is quite true that I came here to nurse Gareth, for he had had a very serious accident, and nearly died; but also I came to be a chaperon for Amanda—not that there was the least need of such a thing, when she was in Gareth's charge, but although I have not a great deal of sense myself I do know that persons like you would think so. And I must say, Widmore, that it is very lowering to be so closely related to anyone with such a dreadfully *commonplace* mind as you have!'

He was so much taken aback by this unprecedented assault that he could find nothing to say. Amanda, who had poured the tale of her odyssey into her grandsire's ears, seized the opportunity to address him. 'Oh, Lord Widmore, pray excuse me for having been so uncivil as to run away with your uncle without taking leave of you and Lady Widmore and Lord Brancaster, or saying thank you for a very pleasant visit! And, please, Uncle Gary, forgive me for having been troublesome, and uncivil, and telling people you were abducting me, which Neil says you didn't, though I must say it *is* abducting, when you force people to go with you. However, I am truly grateful to you for having been so kind, and letting me have Joseph. And Aunt Hester too. And now I have begged *everybody's* pardon, except Hildebrand's,' she continued, without the smallest pause, 'so, *please*, Neil, don't be vexed with me any more!'

'That's a good girl,' said her betrothed, putting his arm round her, and giving her a slight hug.

'Amanda!' said the General sharply, as she rubbed her cheek against Captain Kendal's arm. 'Come here, child!'

The Captain released her, and her grandfather bade her run away and pack her boxes. She looked mutinous, but Captain Kendal endorsed the command, upon which she sighed, and went with lagging steps into the house.

'Now, sir!' said the General, turning to Sir Gareth. 'I am satisfied that you have behaved like a man of honour to my granddaughter, and I will add that I am grateful to you for your care of her. But although I do not say that you are to blame for it, this has been a bad business—a very bad business! Should it become known that my granddaughter has been for nearly three weeks living under your protection, as I cannot doubt it will, since so many persons are aware of this circumstance, the damage to her reputation would be such as to—'

'Dear me, didn't she tell you that I have been here all the time?' inquired Lady Hester.

'Ma'am,' said the General, 'you were not with her at Kimbolton!'

'I beg pardon, sir,' put in Hildebrand diffidently, 'but nobody saw her there but me, except the servants, of course, and *they* didn't think anything but that she was Uncle Gary's ward. Well, I thought she was, too!'

'What you thought, young man,' said the General crushingly, 'is of no value! Be good enough not to interrupt me again! Ludlow, I am persuaded that I shall not find it necessary to urge you to adopt the only course open to a man of honour! You know the world: it has been impossible to keep my granddaughter's disappearance from her home a secret from my neigh- bours. I am not so simple as to suppose that conjecture is not rife among them! Or, let me add, that your zeal in pursuing her sprang merely from altruistic motives! She is young, and I do not deny that she has some foolish fancies in her head, but I don't doubt that a man of your address would very speedily succeed in engaging her affections.'

'Believe me, sir, you flatter me!' said Sir Gareth dryly.

'Ludlow, am I to *demand* that you should do the only thing that lies in your power to protect my granddaughter's reputation.'

'I begin to see that in blaming the circulating libraries for the extremely lurid nature of Amanda's imagination I have been unjust,' remarked Sir Gareth. 'You will permit me to tell you, sir, that you are being absurd.'

'Not absurd!' struck in Captain Kendal. 'Ambitious!'

Lord Widmore, who had been standing wrapped in hurried and constructive thought, suddenly made his presence felt. 'Quite absurd! Laughable, indeed! Miss Summercourt—pooh, a schoolgirl! I venture to say that her youth is protection enough! You may be easy, General: I give you leave to inform your acquaintance that she has been visiting Lady Widmore at Brancaster, should you think it necessary to put out some story to satisfy the curiosity of the vulgar. But my unfortunate sister's predicament is a different matter! *She* is not a child! I do not say that the blame for her having been mad enough to come here is to be laid at your door, Ludlow, but I must deem you grossly to blame for her continued presence here! I would not have believed that you could have been so careless of her reputation had I not been aware of what passed between you at Brancaster. I cannot do other than censure the means you have thought proper to employ to induce my sister to give you another answer than the one you received from her not so long since, but no other course is open to me than to tell her that she has no choice but to become your wife!'

'Kendal!' said Sir Gareth. 'Be so good as to act as my deputy, and kick Widmore out! Try if you can find a midden!'

'Yes, pray do!' said Lady Hester cordially.

'With all the pleasure on earth!' said the Captain, stepping forward in a purposeful fashion.

'Hold!' commanded Mr Whyteleafe, in such throbbing and portentous accents that every eye turned towards him. 'His lordship is mistaken! *One* other choice lies open to Lady Hester, which I dare to think must be preferable to her than to be linked to a fashionable fribble! Lady Hester, I offer you the protection of *my* name!'

'*Two* middens!' said Sir Gareth savagely.

'No, because I am persuaded he means it very kindly,' intervened Hester. 'I am so much obliged to you, Mr Whyteleafe, but it is quite unnecessary for anyone to offer me the protection of their names, because Widmore is talking nonsense, as he very well knows. And I shall be still more obliged to you if you will take him away!'

'You do not mean to *remain* here?' exclaimed the chaplain, in horror.

She did not answer, for she was a little agitated. It was Hildebrand who said hotly: 'She needn't scruple to do so, because *I* shan't leave Uncle Gary, and I will take very good care of her, I assure you! That is to say, I should, if he was the sort of person you think, but he is not! Uncle Gary, let *me* throw him out!'

'No,' said Sir Gareth. 'You may indeed help me out of this chair! Thank you! No, I don't need any further support. Now! You have all talked yourselves out, I trust, for *I* am going to say a few words! First, let me make it plain to you that I have not the slightest intention of allowing myself to be coerced into offering marriage to either of the ladies whose reputations I am alleged to have damaged! Second, I have not, in fact, damaged anyone's reputation. It would be hard to imagine how I could have done so during the time I have been in this inn, and as for the one night at Kimbolton, your granddaughter, General, passed as my ward, as Hildebrand has already told you. Let me add that in no other light have I at any time during my acquaintance with her regarded her. So far from having, as you seem to think, a *tendre* for her, I can think of few worse fates than to be married to a girl who is not only young enough to be my daughter, but who has what I suspect to be an ineradicable habit of flinging herself into the arms of the military. I suggest, if you feel her fair name to have been smirched in the eyes of your neighbours, that you lose no time in getting her out of the country. No doubt Captain Kendal will be happy to assist you in achieving this object!'

'Thank you: I will!' said the Captain briskly.

'Nothing will induce me—' began the General.

'Just let me say what I have to, sir, if you please!' interposed Captain Kendal. 'I have hitherto acquiesced in your resolve not to allow Amanda to become my wife while she is still so young. Our attachment is of pretty long standing, but the force of your objections was fully realized by me. I shall not expatiate on that head, because this prank she has played has made me change my mind. It is quite obvious to me, sir, that neither you nor Miss Summercourt has the smallest control over her, and if I don't take her in hand now she will be utterly ruined! She doesn't play these tricks on me, so you needn't be afraid she'll get into mischief when I have her in Spain: I'll see to that! And you needn't be afraid, either, that she won't be happy, because I'll see to that, too! I should wish to marry her by special licence, with your consent. If you continue to withold your consent, I shall be obliged to postpone the ceremony until we reach Lisbon. That's all I have to say, sir.' He perceived his betrothed coming through the trees, and called: 'Here, Amanda, I want you!'

'You know, General, I am quite, quite sure that Captain Kendal is just the man for her,' said Hester persuasively.

He groaned. 'To be throwing herself away on Neil Kendal! It is not what I wish for her!'

'Throwing herself away?' said Sir Gareth. 'My dear sir, that young man is clearly destined to become a Marshal!'

'Young Neil?' said the General, as though such a notion was new to him.

'Certainly! If I were you, I would give in with a good grace. If you could incarcerate her until Kendal has left the country, I should be astonished if I did not hear next that she had stowed away on a vessel bound for Spain.'

The General shuddered. His granddaughter, having been informed, very kindly, by her strongminded lover, that if she was a good girl, and did as she was told, he would marry her after all, and take her to Spain, first embraced him fervently, then flung her arms round the General's neck, and ended by hugging both Lady Hester and Sir Gareth for good measure.

It was fully an hour before the Bull Inn sank back into its accustomed quiet. The General's party was the first to leave, and if he was by no means reconciled to his granddaughter's engagement a suggestion made by his prospective son-in-law that he should accompany the bridal pair to Lisbon had undoubtedly found favour with him.

Lord Widmore lingered, alternately commanding and beseeching his sister to return immediately to her home. In these exhortations he was joined by the chaplain. Lady Hester listened to them with patience, but although she said she was sorry to vex her brother, she remained gently determined not to desert her patient. Lord Widmore then declared that since she was of age she might please herself, but that for his part he washed his hands of her.

'Oh, do you?' she said. 'I am so glad, for it is what I have longed for you to do *such* a time! Pray give my love to Almeria! I must take Gareth his medicine now: excuse me, please!'

Sir Gareth, left alone in the orchard to recover from the exhausting effect of his guests, watched her come towards him, carrying his medicine. 'I am glad you haven't left me to my fate,' he remarked.

'Oh, no! Such nonsense! Here is this *evil*-smelling dose which Dr Chantry says is what you should take.'

'Thank you,' he said, receiving the glass from her, and pouring its contents on to the grass.

'Gareth!'

'I have had enough of Dr Chantry's potions. Believe me, they taste worse than they smell! Hester, that brother of yours is a sapskull.'

'Oh, yes, I know he is!' she agreed.

'I meant what I said, you know. I don't think myself bound to offer you the protection of my name—did you ever listen to so much fustian? I'll swear I never did!—because the suggestion that I have compromised you is as ludicrous as it is nauseating.'

'Of course it is. Don't let us talk about it! It was so stupid!'

'We will never mention it again, if you will give me your assurance that you have no qualms. Look at me!'

She obeyed, with a tiny smile. 'Gareth, it is *too* foolish! How can you ask me such a question?'

'I couldn't bear to think, love, that you might consent to marry me for such a reason as that,' he said quietly.

'No,' she answered. 'Or I that you might ask me for such a reason as that.'

'You may be very sure I would not. This is not the first time I have asked you to marry me, Hester.'

'Not the first time, but this is different—I think?' she said shyly.

'Quite different. When I asked you at Brancaster I held you in affection and esteem, but I believed I could never be in love again. I was wrong. Will you marry me, my dear and last love?'

She took his face between her hands, and looked into his eyes. A sigh, as though she were rid of a burden, escaped her. 'Yes, Gareth,' she said. 'Oh, yes, *indeed* I will!'

Sylvester

Georgette Heyer

SYLVESTER

or
The Wicked Uncle

I

Sylvester stood in the window of his breakfast-parlour, leaning his hands on the ledge, and gazing out upon a fair prospect. No view of the ornamental water could be obtained from this, the east front of Chance, but the undulations of a lawn shaved all summer by scythemen were broken by a cedar, and beyond the lawn the stems of beech-trees, outliers of the Home Wood, shimmered in wintry sunlight. They still held their lure for Sylvester, though they beckoned him now to his coverts rather than to a land where every thicket concealed a dragon, and false knights came pricking down the rides. He and Harry, his twin, had slain the dragons, and ridden great wallops at the knights. There were none left now, and Harry had been dead for almost four years; but there were pheasants to tempt Sylvester forth, and they did tempt him, for a succession of black frosts had made the ground iron-hard, robbing him of two hunting days; and a blusterous north wind would not have invited the most ardent of sportsmen to take a gun out. It was still very cold, but the wind had dropped, and the sun shone, and what a bore it was that he should have decided that this day, out of all the inclement ones that had preceded it, should be devoted to business. He could change his mind, of course, telling his butler to inform the various persons now awaiting his pleasure that he would see them on the following day. His agent-in-chief and his man of business had come all the way from London to attend upon him, but it did not occur to Sylvester that they could find any cause for complaint in being kept kicking their heels. They were in his employ, and had no other concern than to serve his interests; they would accept his change of mind as the caprice to be expected from a noble and wealthy master.

But Sylvester was not capricious, and he had no intention of succumbing to temptation. Caprice bred bad servants, and where the management of vast estates was concerned good service was essential. Sylvester had only just entered his twenty-eighth year, but he had succeeded to his huge inheritance when he was nineteen, and whatever follies and extravagances he had committed they had never led him to treat that inheritance as his plaything, or to evade the least one of its responsibilities. He had been born to a great position, reared to fill it in a manner worthy of a long line of distinguished forebears, and as little as he questioned his right to command the obedience of all the persons whose names were inscribed on his staggering payroll did he question the inescapability of the duties which had been laid on his shoulders. Had he been asked if he enjoyed his consequence he would have replied truthfully that he never thought of it; but he would certainly have disliked very much to have had it suddenly removed.

No one was in the least likely to ask him such a question, of course. He was generally considered to be a singularly fortunate young man, endowed with rank, wealth, and elegance. No bad fairy had attended his christening to leaven his luck with the gift of a hunchback or a harelip; though not above medium height he was well proportioned, with good shoulders, a pair of shapely legs, and a countenance sufficiently pleasing to make the epithet *handsome*, frequently bestowed on it, not altogether ridiculous. In a lesser man the oddity of eyes set with the suspicion of a slant under flying black brows might have been accounted a blemish; in the Duke of Salford they were naturally held to lend distinction; and those who had admired his mother in her heyday remembered that she too had that thin, soaring line of eyebrow. It was just as though the brows had been added with a paintbrush, drawn in a sleek line upwards towards the temples. In the Duchess this peculiarity was charming; in Sylvester it was less attractive. It gave him, when he was vexed, and the upward trend was exaggerated by a frown, a slight look of a satyr.

He was about to turn away from the window when his attention was caught by a small, scampering figure. Emerging from the shelter of a yew hedge, a little boy with a cluster of golden curls set off across the lawn in the direction of the Home Wood, his nankeen-covered legs twinkling over the grass, and the freshly laundered frill of his shirt rucked up under one ear by a duffle coat, dragged over his little blue jacket by hurried and inexpert hands.

Sylvester laughed, throwing up the window. His impulse was to wish Edmund success in his adventure, but even as he leaned out he checked it. Though Edmund would not stop for his nurse or his tutor he would do so if his uncle called to him, and since he seemed to have made good his escape from these persons it would be unsportsmanlike to check him when his goal was within sight. To keep him dallying under the window would put him in grave danger of being captured, and that, reflected Sylvester, would lead to one of those scenes which bored him to death. Edmund would beg his leave to go off to the woods, and whether he gave it or withheld it he would be obliged to endure the reproaches of his widowed sister-in-law. He would be accused of treating poor little Edmund either with brutal severity, or with a heartless unconcern for his welfare; for Lady Henry Rayne could never bring herself to forgive him for having persuaded his brother (as she obstinately affirmed) to leave Edmund to his sole guardianship. It was of no use for anyone to tell Lady Henry that Harry's will had been drawn up on the occasion of his marriage, merely to ensure, in the event of accident, which no one had thought more unlikely than Harry himself, that any offspring of the match would be safe under the protection of the head of his house. However stupid Sylvester might think her she hoped she was not so green as to imagine that his attorney would have dared to insert so infamous a clause except at his express command. Sylvester, with the wound of Harry's death still raw, had allowed himself to be goaded into bitter retort: 'If you imagine that I wished to have the brat thrust on to me you are even greener than I had supposed!'

He was to regret those hasty words, for although he had immediately retracted them he had never been allowed to forget them; and they formed today, when the custody of Edmund had become a matter of acute importance, the foundation-stone of Lady Henry's arguments. 'You never wanted him,' she reminded him. 'You said so yourself!'

It had been partly true, of course: except as Harry's son he had had very little interest in a two-year-old infant, and had paid no more heed to him than might have been expected of a young man. When Edmund began to grow out of babyhood, however, he saw rather more of him, for Edmund's first object, whenever his magnificent uncle was at Chance, was to attach himself as firmly as possible to him. He had qualities wholly lacking in

Button, Edmund's nurse (and his father's and uncle's before him), or in Mama. He showed no disposition to fondle his nephew; he was indifferent to torn clothes; such conversation as he addressed to Edmund was brief and to the point; and while he might, in an unpropitious mood, send him somewhat peremptorily about his business, it was always possible that he would hoist him up on to his saddle before him, and canter off with him through the park. These attributes were accompanied by a less agreeable but equally godlike idiosyncrasy: he exacted instant obedience to his commands, and he had a short way of dealing with recalcitrants.

Sylvester thought that Ianthe and Button were doing their best to spoil Edmund, but while he did not hesitate to make plain to that astute young gentleman the unwisdom of employing with him the tactics that succeeded so well in the nursery it was rarely that he interfered with his upbringing. He saw no faults in Edmund that could not speedily be cured when he was rather older; and by the time he was six had grown to like him as much for his own sake as for his father's.

Edmund had disappeared from view. Sylvester pulled the window down again, thinking that he really ought to provide the brat with a livelier tutor than the Reverend Loftus Leyburn, the elderly and rather infirm cleric who was his—or, more accurately, his mother's—chaplain. He had thought it a poor arrangement when Ianthe had begged Mr Loftus to teach Edmund his first lessons, but not a matter of sufficient moment to make it necessary for him to provoke her by refusing to agree to the scheme. Now she was complaining that Edmund haunted the stables, and learned the most vulgar language there. What the devil did she expect? wondered Sylvester.

He turned from the window as the door opened, and his butler came in, followed by a young footman, who began to clear away the remains of a substantial breakfast.

'I'll see Mr Ossett and Pewsey at noon, Reeth,' Sylvester said. 'Chale and Brough may bring their books in to me at the same time. I am going up to sit with her grace now. You might send down a message to Trent, warning him that I may want—' He paused, glancing towards the window. 'No, never mind that! The light will be gone by four o'clock.'

'It seems a pity your grace should be cooped up in the office on such a fine day,' said Reeth suggestively.

'A great pity, but it can't be helped.' He found that he had dropped his handkerchief, and that the footman had hurried to pick it up for him. He said, 'Thank you', as he took it, and accompanied the words with a slight smile. He had a singularly charming smile, and it ensured for him, no matter how exacting might be his demands, the uncomplaining exertions of his servants. He was perfectly well aware of that, just as he was aware of the value of the word of praise dropped at exactly the right moment; and he would have thought himself extremely stupid to withhold what cost him so little and was productive of such desirable results.

Leaving the breakfast-parlour, he made his way to the main hall, and (it might have been thought) to another century, since this central portion of a pile that sprawled over several acres was all that remained of the original structure. Rugged beams, plastered walls, and a floor of uneven flagstones lingered on here in odd but not infelicitous contrast to the suave elegance of the more modern parts of the great house. The winged staircase of Tudor origin that led up from the hall to a surrounding gallery was guarded by two figures in full armour; the walls were embellished with clusters of antique weapons; the windows were of armorial glass; and under an enormous hood a pile of hot ashes supported several blazing logs. Before this fire a liver-and-white spaniel lay in an attitude of watchful expectancy. She raised her head when she heard Sylvester's step, and began to wag her tail; but when he came into the hall her tail sank, and although she bundled across the floor to meet him, and looked adoringly up at him when he stooped to pat her, she neither frisked about him nor uttered barks of joyful anticipation. His valet was hardly more familiar with his wardrobe than she, and she knew well that pantaloons and Hessian boots meant that the most she could hope for was to be permitted to lie at his feet in the library.

The Duchess's apartments comprised, besides her bedchamber, and the dressing-room occupied by her maid, an ante-chamber which led into a large, sunny apartment, known to the household as the Duchess's Drawing-room. She rarely went beyond it, for she had been for many years the victim of an arthritic complaint which none of the eminent physicians who had attended her, or any of the cures she had undergone, had been able to arrest. She could still manage, supported by her attendants, to drag herself from her bedchamber to her drawing-room, but once lowered into her chair she could not rise from it without assistance. What degree of pain she suffered no one knew, for she never complained, or asked for sympathy. 'Very well' was her invariable reply to solicitous enquiries; and if anyone deplored the monotony of her existence she laughed, and said that pity was wasted on her, and would be better bestowed on those who danced attendance on her. As for herself, with her son to bring her all the London on-dits, her grandson to amuse her with his pranks, her daughter-in-law to discuss the latest fashions with her, her patient cousin to bear with her crotchets, her devoted maid to cosset her, and her old friend, Mr Leyburn, to browse with her amongst her books she thought she was rather to be envied than pitied. Except to her intimates she did not mention her poems, but the fact was that the Duchess was an author. Mr Blackwell had published two volumes of her verses, and these had enjoyed quite a vogue amongst members of the ton; for although they were, of course, published anonymously the secret of their authorship soon leaked out, and was thought to lend considerable interest to them.

She was engaged in writing when Sylvester entered the room, on the table so cleverly made by the estate carpenter to fit across the arms of her wing-chair; but as soon as she saw who had come in she laid down her pen, and welcomed Sylvester with a smile more charming than his own because so much warmer, and exclaimed: 'Ah, how delightful! But so vexatious for you, love, to be obliged to stay at home on the first good shooting-day we have had in a se'enight!'

'A dead bore, isn't it?' he responded, bending over her to kiss her cheek. She put up her hand to lay it on his shoulder, and he stayed for a moment, scanning her face. Apparently he was satisfied with what he saw there, for he let his eyes travel to the delicate lace confection set on her silvered black hair, and said: 'A new touch, Mama? That's a very fetching cap!'

The ready laughter sprang to her eyes. 'Confess that Anna warned you to take notice of my finery!'

'Certainly not! Do you think I must be told by your maid when you are looking in great beauty?'

'Sylvester, you make love so charmingly that I fear you must be the most outrageous flirt!'

'Oh, not *outrageous*, Mama! Are you busy with a new poem?'

'Merely a letter. Dearest, if you will push the table away, you may draw up that chair a little, and we can enjoy a comfortable prose.'

This he was prevented from doing by the hurried entrance from the adjoining bedchamber of Miss Augusta Penistone, who begged him, somewhat incoherently, not to trouble himself, since she considered the task peculiarly her own. She then pushed the table to the side of the room, and instead of effacing herself, as he always wished she would, lingered, amiably smiling at him. She was an angular, rather awkward lady, as kind as she was plain, and she served the Duchess, whose kinswoman she was, in the capacity of a companion. Her good-nature was inexhaustible, but she was unfortunately quite unintelligent, and rarely failed to irritate Sylvester by asking questions to which the answers were patent, or commenting upon the obvious. He bore it very well, for his manners were extremely good, but when, after stating that she saw he had not gone out hunting, she recollected that one didn't hunt after severe frost and said, with a merry laugh at her mistake: 'Well, that *was* a stupid thing for me to have said, wasn't it?' he was provoked into replying, though with perfect suavity: 'It was, wasn't it?'

The Duchess intervened at this stage of the dialogue, urging her cousin to go out into the sunshine while it lasted; and after saying that, to be sure, she might venture to do so if dear Sylvester meant to sit with his mama, which she had no doubt of, and pointing out that Anna would come if the Duchess rang the bell, she got herself to the door, which Sylvester was holding open. She was obliged to pause there to tell him that she was now going to leave him to chat with his mama, adding: 'For I am sure you wish to be private with her, don't you?'

'I do, but how you guessed it, cousin, I can't imagine!' he replied.

'Oh!' declared Miss Penistone gaily, 'a pretty thing it would be if I didn't know, after all these years, just what you like! Well, I will run away, then—but you should not trouble to open the door for me! That is to treat me like a stranger! I am for ever telling you so, am I not? But you are always so obliging!'

He bowed, and shut the door behind her. The Duchess said: 'An undeserved compliment, Sylvester. My dear, how came you to speak as you did? It was not kind.'

'Her folly is intolerable!' he said impatiently. 'Why do you keep such a hubble-bubble woman about you? She must vex you past bearing!'

'She is not very wise, certainly,' admitted the Duchess. 'But I couldn't send her away, you know!'

'Shall I do so for you?'

She was startled, but, supposing that he was speaking out of an unthinking exasperation, only said: 'Nonsensical boy! You know you could no more do so than I could!'

He raised his brows. 'Of course I could do it, Mama! What should stop me?'

'You cannot be serious!' she exclaimed, half inclined still to laugh at him.

'But I'm perfectly serious, my dear! Be frank with me! Don't you wish her at Jericho?'

She said, with a rueful twinkle: 'Well, yes—sometimes I do! Don't repeat that, will you? I have at least the grace to be ashamed of myself!' She perceived that his expression was one of surprise, and said in a serious tone: 'Of course it vexes you, and me too, when she says silly things, and hasn't the tact to go away when you come to visit me, but I promise you I think myself fortunate to have her. It can't be very amusing to be tied to an invalid, you know, but she is never hipped or out of temper, and whatever I ask her to do for me she does willingly, and so cheerfully that she puts me in danger of believing that she enjoys being at my beck and call.'

'So I should hope!'

'Now, Sylvester—'

'My dear Mama, she has hung on your sleeve ever since I can remember, and a pretty generous sleeve it has been! You have always made her an allowance far beyond what you would have paid a stranger hired to bear you company, haven't you?'

'You speak as though you grudged it!'

'No more than I grudge the wages of my valet, if you think her worth it. I pay large wages to my servants, but I keep none in my employment who doesn't earn his wage.'

There was a troubled look in the eyes that searched his face, but the Duchess only said: 'The cases are not the same, but don't let us brangle about it! You may believe that it would make me very unhappy to lose Augusta. Indeed, I don't know how I should go on.'

'If that's the truth, Mama, you need say no more. Do you suppose I wouldn't pay anyone who wished to keep about you double—treble—what you pay Augusta?' He saw her stretch out her hand to him, and went to her immediately. 'You know I wouldn't do anything you don't like! Don't look so distressed, dearest!'

She pressed his hand. 'I know you wouldn't. Don't heed me! It is only that it shocked me a little to hear you speak so hardly. But no one has less cause to complain of hardness in you than I, my darling.'

'Nonsense!' he said, smiling down at her. 'Keep your tedious cousin, love—but allow me to wish that you had with you someone who could entertain you better—enter into what interests you!'

'Well, I have Ianthe,' she reminded him. 'She doesn't precisely enter into my interests, but we go on very comfortably together.'

'I am happy to hear it. But it begins to seem as if you won't have the doubtful comfort of her society for much longer.'

'My dear, if you are going to suggest that I should employ a second lady to keep me company, I do beg of you to spare your breath!'

'No, that wouldn't answer.' He paused, and then said quite coolly: 'I am thinking of getting married, Mama.'

She was taken so much by surprise that she could only stare at him. He had the reputation of being a dangerous flirt, but she had almost given up hope of his coming to the point of offering for any lady's hand in matrimony. She had reason to think that he had had more than one mistress in keeping—very expensive Cythereans some of them had been if her sister were to be believed!—and it had begun to seem as if he preferred that way of life to a more ordered existence. Recovering from her stupefaction, she said: 'My dear, this is very sudden!'

'Not so sudden as you think, Mama. I have been meaning for some time to speak to you about it.'

'Good gracious! And I never suspected it! Do, pray, sit down and tell me all about it!'

He looked at her keenly. 'Would you be glad, Mama?'

'Of course I should!'

'Then I think that settles it.'

That made her laugh. 'Of all the absurd things to say! Very well! having won my approval, tell me everything!'

He said, gazing frowningly into the fire: 'I don't know that there's so much to tell you. I fancy you guessed I haven't much cared for the notion of becoming riveted. I never met the female to whom I wished to be leg-shackled. Harry did, and if anything had been needed to confirm me in—'

'My dear, leave that!' she interposed. 'Harry was happy in his marriage, remember! I believe, too, that although Ianthe's feelings are not profound she was most sincerely attached to him.'

'So much attached to him that within a year of his death she was pining for the sight of a ballroom, and within four is planning to marry a worthless fribble! It will not do, Mama!'

'Very well, my dear, but we are talking of your marriage, not Harry's, are we not?'

'True! Well, I realized—oh, above a year ago!—that it was my duty to marry. Not so much for the sake of an heir, because I have one already, but—'

'Sylvester, don't put that thought into Edmund's head!'

He laughed. 'Much he would care! His ambition is to become a mail-coachman—or it was until Keighley let him have the yard of tin for a plaything! Now he cannot decide whether to be a coachman or a guard. Pretty flat he would think it to be told that he would be obliged instead to step into my shoes!'

She smiled. 'Yes, *now* he would, but later—'

'Well, that's one of my reasons, Mama. If I mean to marry I ought, I think, to do so before Edmund is old enough to think his nose has been put out of joint. So I began some months ago to look about me.'

'You are the oddest creature! Next you will tell me you made out a list of the qualities your wife must possess!'

'More or less,' he admitted. 'You may laugh, Mama, but you'll agree that certain qualities are indispensable! She must be well born, for instance. I don't mean necessarily a great match, but a girl of my own order.'

'Ah, yes, I agree with *that!* And next?'

'Well, a year ago I should have said she must be beautiful,' he replied meditatively. (She is not a beauty, thought the Duchess.) 'But I'm inclined to think now that it is more important that she should be intelligent. I don't think I could tolerate a hen-witted wife. Besides, I don't mean to foist another fool on to you.'

'I am very much obliged to you!' she said, a good deal entertained. 'Clever, but not beautiful: very well! continue!'

'No, some degree of beauty I do demand. She must have countenance, at least, and the sort of elegance which you have, Mama.'

'Don't try to turn my head, you flatterer! Have you discovered amongst the débutantes one who is endowed with all these qualities?'

'At first glance, I suppose a dozen, but in the end only five.'

'Five!'

'Well, only five with whom I could perhaps bear to spend a large part of my life. There is Lady Jane Saxby: she's pretty, and good-natured. Then there's Barningham's daughter: she has a great deal of vivacity. Miss Bellerby is a handsome girl, with a little reserve, which I don't dislike. Lady Mary Torrington—oh, a diamond of the first water! And lastly Miss Orton: not beautiful, but quite taking, and has agreeable manners.' He paused, his gaze still fixed on the smouldering logs. The Duchess waited expectantly. He looked up presently, and smiled at her. 'Well, Mama?' he said affably. 'Which of them shall it be?'

2

After an astonished moment the Duchess said: 'Dearest, are you roasting me? You can't in all seriousness be asking me to choose for you!'

'No, not choose precisely. I wish you will advise me, though. You're not acquainted with any of them, but you know their families, and if you should have a decided preference—'

'But, Sylvester, have *you* no preference?'

'No, that's the devil of it: I haven't. Whenever I think one more eligible than any of the others as sure as check I find she has some fault or trick which I don't like. Lady Jane's laugh, for instance; or Miss Orton's infernal harp! I've no turn for music, and to be obliged to endure a harp's being eternally twanged in my own house—no, I think that's coming it a trifle too strong, don't you, Mama? Then Lady Mary—'

'Thank you, I have heard enough to be able to give you my advice!' interrupted his mother. 'Don't make an offer for any one of them! You are not in love!'

'In love! No, of course I am not. Is that so necessary?'

'Most necessary, my dear! Don't, I beg you, offer marriage where you can't offer love as well!'

He smiled at her. 'You are too romantic, Mama.'

'Am I? But you seem to have no romance in you at all!'

'Well, I don't look for it in marriage, at any rate.'

'Only in the muslin company?'

He laughed. 'You shock me, Mama! That's a different matter. I shouldn't call it romance either—or only one's first adventure, perhaps. And even when I was a greenhead, and fell in love with the most dazzling little bird of Paradise you ever saw, I don't think I really fancied myself to have formed a lasting passion! I daresay I'm too volatile, in which case—'

'No such thing! You have not yet been fortunate enough to meet the girl for whom you *will* form a lasting passion.'

'Very true: I haven't! And since I've been on the town for nearly ten years, and may be said to have had my pick of all the eligible débutantes that appear yearly on the Marriage Mart, we must conclude that if I'm not too volatile I must be too nice in my requirements. To be frank with you, Mama, you are the only lady of my acquaintance with whom I don't soon become heartily bored!'

A tiny frown appeared between her winged brows as she listened to this speech. It was spoken in a bantering tone, but she found it disturbing. 'Your *pick* of them, Sylvester?'

'Yes, I think so. I must have seen all the eligibles, I fancy.'

'And have made quite a number of them the objects of your gallantry—if the things I hear are to be believed!'

'My aunt Louisa,' said Sylvester unerringly. 'What an incorrigible gossip your sister is, my dear! Well, if I have now and then shown a preference at least she can't accuse me of having been so particular in my attentions as to have raised false hopes in any maiden's bosom!'

The hint of laughter had quite vanished from her eyes. The image she cherished of this beloved son was all at once blurred; and a feeling of disquiet made it difficult for her to know what she should say to him. As she hesitated, an interruption occurred. The door was opened; a pretty, plaintive voice said: 'May I come in, Mama-Duchess?' and there appeared on the threshold a vision of beauty dressed in a blue velvet pelisse, and a hat with a high poke-front which made a frame for a ravishing countenance. Ringlets of bright gold fell beside damask cheeks; large blue eyes were set beneath delicately arched brows; the little nose was perfectly straight; and the red mouth deliciously curved.

'Good-morning, my love. Of course you may come in!' said the Duchess.

The vision had by this time perceived her brother-in-law, and although she did come in she said with a marked diminution of cordiality: 'Oh! I didn't know you had Sylvester with you, ma'am. I beg your pardon, but I only came to discover if Edmund was here.'

'I haven't seen him this morning,' replied the Duchess. 'Is he not with Mr Leyburn?'

'No, and it is particularly vexatious because I wish to take him with me to visit the Arkholmes! You know I have been meaning for days to drive over to the Grange, ma'am, and now, on the first fine morning we have had for an age, no one can tell me where he is!'

'Perhaps he has slipped off to the stables, little rogue!'

'No, though, to be sure, that was what I expected too, for ever since Sylvester took to *encouraging* him to haunt the stables—'

'My dear, they all do so, and without the least encouragement!' interposed the Duchess. 'Mine certainly did—they were the most deplorable urchins! Tell me, did you have that charming pelisse made from the velvets we chose from the patterns sent down last month? How well it has made-up!'

The effect of this attempt to divert the beauty's thoughts was unfortunate. 'Yes, but only think, ma'am!' exclaimed Ianthe. 'I had a suit made from it for Edmund to wear when he goes out with me—quite simple, but after the style of that red dress the boy has on in the picture of Reynolds. I forget where I saw it, but I thought at once how well Edmund would look in it if only it were not red but blue!'

'Wouldn't he just!' muttered Sylvester.

'What did you say?' demanded Ianthe suspiciously.

'Nothing.'

'I suppose it was something ill-natured. To be sure, I never hoped that *you* would think it pretty!'

'You are mistaken. The picture you would both present would be pretty enough to take one's breath away. Assuming, of course, that Edmund could be persuaded to behave conformably. Standing within your arm, with that soulful look on his face—no, that won't do! He only wears that when he's plotting mischief. Well—'

'Sylvester, *will* you be silent?' begged the Duchess, trying not to laugh. 'Don't heed him, my dear child! He's only quizzing you!'

'Oh, I know that, ma'am!' said Ianthe, her colour considerably heightened. 'I know, too, who it is who teaches poor little Edmund not to mind me!'

'Oh, good God, what next?' Sylvester exclaimed.

'You do!' she insisted. 'And it shows how little affection you have for him!

If you cared a rap for him you wouldn't encourage him to run into heaven knows what danger!'

'*What* danger?'

'Anything might happen to him!' she declared. 'At this very moment he may be at the bottom of the lake!'

'He is nowhere near the lake. If you must have it, I saw him making off to the Home Wood!'

'And you made not the smallest effort to call him back, I collect!'

'No. The last time I interfered in Edmund's illicit amusements I figured in your conversation as a monster of inhumanity for three days.'

'I never said any such thing, but only that—besides, he may change his mind, and go to the lake after all!'

'Make yourself easy: he won't! Not while he knows I'm at home, at all events.'

She said fretfully: 'I might have known how it would be! I would as lief not to go to the Grange at all now, and I wouldn't, only that I have had the horses put to. But I shan't know a moment's peace of mind for wondering if my poor, orphaned child is safe, or at the bottom of the lake!'

'If he should fail to appear in time for his dinner, I will have the lake dragged,' promised Sylvester, walking to the door, and opening it. 'Meanwhile, however careless I may be of my nephew I am not careless of my horses, and I do beg of you, if you have had a pair put to, not to keep them standing in this weather!'

This request incensed Ianthe so much that she flounced out of the room in high dudgeon.

'Edifying!' remarked Sylvester. 'Believing her orphaned son to be at the bottom of the lake this devoted parent departs on an expedition of pleasure!'

'My dear, she knows very well he isn't at the bottom of the lake! Can you *never* meet without rubbing against one another? You are quite as unjust to her as she is to you, I must tell you!'

He shrugged. 'I daresay. If I had ever seen a trace of her vaunted devotion to Edmund I could bear with her patiently, but I never have! If he will be so obliging as to submit to her caresses she is pleased to think she dotes on him, but when he becomes noisy it is quite a comedy to see how quickly she can develop the headache, so that Button must be sent for to remove her darling! She never went near him when he had the measles, and when she made his toothache an excuse to carry him off to London, and then was ready to let the brat's tooth rot in his head rather than put herself to the trouble of compelling him to submit to its extraction—'

'I knew we should come to it!' interrupted the Duchess, throwing up her hands. 'Let me tell you, my son, that it takes a great deal of resolution to drag a reluctant child to the dentist! I never had enough! It fell to Button to perform the dreadful duty—and so it would have done in Edmund's case, only that she was ill at the time!'

'I shan't let you tell me, Mama,' he said, laughing. 'For I *have* performed the dreadful duty, remember!'

'So you have! Poor Edmund! Swooped upon in the Park, snatched up into your curricle, and whisked off to the torture-chamber in such a ruthless style! I promise you my heart bled for him!'

'It might well have done so had you seen his face as *I* saw it! I suppose the witless abigail who had him in charge told you I *swooped* upon him? All I did was to drive him to Tilton's immediately, and what was needed was not resolution but firmness! No, Mama: don't ask me to credit Ianthe with devotion to her brat, for it sickens me! I only wish I knew who was the sapskull who told her how lovely she appeared with her child in her arms. Also that I hadn't been fool enough to allow myself to be persuaded to commission Lawrence to paint her in that affecting pose!'

'You did so to give Harry pleasure,' said the Duchess gently. 'I have always been glad to think it was finished in time for him to see it.'

Sylvester strode over the window, and stood looking out. After a few minutes he said: 'I'm sorry, Mama. I should not have said that.'

'No, of course you should not, dearest. I wish you will try not to be so hard on Ianthe, for she is very much to be pitied, you know. You didn't like it when she began to go into society again with her mama, at the end of that first year of mourning. Well, I didn't like it either, but how could one expect such a pleasure-loving little creature to say moping here, after all? It was not improper to her to put off her blacks.' She hesitated, and then added: 'It is not improper to her to be wishing to marry again now, Sylvester.'

'I haven't accused her of impropriety.'

'No, but you are making it dreadfully hard for her, my love! She may not be devoted to Edmund, but to take him from her entirely—'

'If that should happen, it will be her doing, not mine! She may make her home here for as long as she chooses, or she may take Edmund to live with her at the Dower House. All I have ever said is that Harry's son will be reared at Chance, and under my eye! If Ianthe marries again she is welcome to visit Edmund whenever she pleases. I have even told her she may have him to stay with her at reasonable intervals. But one thing I will never do, and that is to permit him to grow up under Nugent Fotherby's aegis! Good God, Mama, how can you think it possible I would so abuse my twin's trust?'

'Ah, no, no! But is Sir Nugent so very bad? I was a little acquainted with his father—he was so amiable that he said yes and amen to everything!—but I think I never met the son.'

'You needn't repine! A wealthy fribble, three parts idiot, and the fourth—never mind! A pretty guardian I should be to abandon Edmund to his and Ianthe's upbringing! Do you know what Harry said to me, Mama? They were almost the last words he spoke to me. He said: "You'll look after the boy, Dook."'' He stopped, his voice cracking on that last word. After a moment he said, not very easily: 'You know how he used to call me that—with that twinkle in his eye. It wasn't a question, or a request. He *knew* I should, and he said it, not to remind me, but because it was a comfortable thought that came into his head, and he always told me what he was thinking.' He saw that his mother had shaded her eyes with one hand, and crossed the room to her side, taking her other hand, and holding it closely. 'Forgive me! I must make you understand, Mama!'

'I do understand, Sylvester, but how can I think it right to keep the child here with no one but old Button to look after him, or some tutor for whom he's far too young? If I were not useless—' She clipped the words off short.

Knowing her as he did, he made no attempt to answer what had been left unspoken, but said calmly: 'Yes, I too have considered that, and it forms a strong reason for my marriage. I fancy Ianthe would soon grow reconciled to the thought of parting with Edmund, could she but leave him in his *aunt's* charge. She wouldn't then incur the stigma of heartlessness, would she? She cares a great deal for what people may say of her—and I must own that after presenting a portrait of herself to the world in the rôle of devoted parent, I don't perceive how she *can* abandon Edmund to the mercy of his wicked uncle. My wife, you know, could very well be held to have softened my disposition!'

'Now, Sylvester—! She can never have said you were wicked!'

He smiled. 'She may not have used that precise term, but she has regaled everyone with the tale of my disregard for Edmund's welfare, and frequent brutality to him. They may not believe the whole, but I've reason to suppose that even a man of such good sense as Elvaston thinks I treat the boy with unmerited severity.'

'Well, if Lord Elvaston doesn't know his daughter better than to believe the farradiddles she utters I have a poor opinion of his sense!' said the Duchess, quite tartly. 'Do let us stop talking about Ianthe, my love!'

'Willingly! I had rather talk of my own affairs. Mama, what sort of female would you wish me to marry?'

'In your present state, I don't wish you to marry *any* sort of a female. When you come out of it, the sort *you* wish to marry, of course!'

'You are not being in the least helpful!' he complained. 'I thought mothers always made marriage plans for their sons!'

'And consequently suffered some severe disappointments! I am afraid the only marriage I ever planned for you was with a three-day infant, when you were eight years old!'

'Come! this is better!' he said encouragingly. 'Who was she? Do I know her?'

'You haven't mentioned her, but I should think you must at least have seen her, for she was presented this year, and had her first season. Her grandmother wrote to tell me of it, and I almost asked you—' She broke off, vexed with herself, and altered the sentence she had been about to utter. '—to give her a kind message from me, only did not, for she could hardly be expected to remember me. She's Lady Ingham's granddaughter.'

'What, my respected godmama? One of the Ingham girls? Oh, no, my dear! I regret infinitely, but—*no*!'

'No, no, Lord Marlow's daughter!' she replied, laughing. 'He married Verena Ingham, who was my dearest friend, and the most captivating creature!'

'Better and better!' he approved. 'Why have I never encountered the captivating Lady Marlow?' He stopped, frowning. 'But I have! I'm not acquainted with her—in fact, I don't remember that I've ever so much as spoken to her, but I must tell you, Mama, that whatever she may have been in her youth—'

'Good heavens, *that* odious woman is Marlow's second! Verena died when her baby was not a fortnight old.'

'Very sad. Tell me about her!'

'I don't think you would be much the wiser if I did,' she answered, wondering if he was trying to divert her mind from the memories he had himself evoked. 'She wasn't beautiful, or accomplished, or even modish, I fear! She defeated every effort to turn her into a fashionable young lady, and never appeared elegant except in her riding-dress. She did the most outrageous things, and nobody cared a bit—not even Lady Cork! We came out in the same season, and were the greatest of friends; but while I was so fortunate as to meet Papa—and to fall in love with him at sight, let me tell you!—she refused every offer that was made her—scores of them, for she never lacked for suitors!—and declared she preferred her horses to any man she had met. Poor Lady Ingham was in despair! And in the end she married Marlow, of all people! I believe she must have liked him for his horsemanship, for I am sure there was nothing else to like in him. Not a very exciting story, I'm afraid! Why did you wish to hear it?'

'Oh, I wished to know what sort of a woman she was! Marlow I do know, and I should suppose that any daughter of his must be an intolerable bore. But your Verena's child might be the very wife for me, don't you think? *You* would be disposed to like her, which must be an object with me; and although I don't mean to burden myself with a wife who wants conduct, I should imagine that there must be enough of Marlow's blood in this girl to leaven whatever wildness she may have inherited from her mother. Eccentricity may be diverting, Mama, but it is out of place in a wife: certainly in my wife!'

'My dear, what nonsense you are talking! If I believed you meant it I should be most seriously disturbed!'

'But I do mean it! I thought you would have been pleased, too! What could be more romantic than to marry the girl who was betrothed to me in her cradle?'

She smiled, but she did not look to be much amused. His eyes searched her face; he said in the caressing tone he used only to her: 'What is it, my dear? Tell me!'

She said: 'Sylvester, you have talked of five girls who might perhaps *suit* you; and now you are talking of a girl of whose existence you were unaware not ten minutes ago—and as though you had only to decide between them! My dear, has it not occurred to you that you might find yourself rebuffed?'

His brow cleared. 'Is *that* all? No, no, Mama, I shan't be rebuffed!'

'So sure, Sylvester?'

'Of course I'm sure, Mama! Oh, not of Miss Marlow! For anything I know, her affections may be engaged already.'

'Or she might take you in dislike,' suggested the Duchess.

'Take me in dislike? Why should she?' he asked, surprised.

'How can I tell? These things do happen, you know.'

'If you mean she might not *fall in love* with me, I daresay she might not, though I know of no reason, if she doesn't love another man, why she shouldn't come to do so—or, at any rate, to like me very tolerably! Do you suppose me to be so lacking in address that I can't make myself agreeable when I wish to? Fie on you, Mama!'

'No,' she said. 'But I didn't know you had so much address that you could beguile no fewer than five girls of rank and fashion to be ready to accept an offer from you.'

He could not resist. 'Well, Mama, you said yourself that I make love charmingly!' he murmured.

It drew a smile from her, because she could never withstand that gleaming look, but she shook her head as well, and said: 'For shame, Sylvester! Do you mean to sound like a coxcomb?'

He laughed. 'Of course I don't! To be frank with you, there are not five but a dozen young woman of rank and fashion who are perfectly ready to receive an offer from me. I'm not hard to swallow, you know, though I don't doubt I have as many faults as a Mr Smith or a Mr Jones. Mine are more palatable, however: scarcely noticeable for the rich marchpane that covers them!'

'Do you wish for a wife who marries you for the sake of your possessions?' the Duchess asked, arching her brows.

'I don't think I mind very much, provided we were mutually agreeable. Such a wife would be unlikely to enact me any tragedies, and anything of that nature, Mama, would lead to our being regularly parted within a twelvemonth. I couldn't endure it!'

'The enacting of tragedies, my son, is not an invariable concomitant of love-matches,' she said dryly.

'Who should know that better than I?' he retorted, his smile embracing her. 'But where am I to look for your counterpart, my dear? Show her to me, and I will engage to fall desperately in love with her, and marry her, fearing no after-ills!'

'Sylvester, you are too absurd!'

'Not as absurd as you think! Seriously, Mama, although I have seen some love-matches that have prospered, I have seen a great many that most certainly have not! Oh! no doubt some husbands and wives of my acquaintance would stare to hear me say I thought them anything but happy! Perhaps they enjoy jealousies, tantrums, quarrels, and stupid misunderstandings: I should not! The well-bred woman who marries me because she has a fancy to be a duchess will suit me very well, and will probably fill her position admirably.' His eyes quizzed her. 'Or would you like me to turn my coat inside out, and sally forth in humble disguise, like the prince in a fairy-tale? I never thought much of that prince, you know! A chuckle-headed fellow, for how could he hope, masquerading as a mean person, to come near any but quite ineligible females whom it would have been impossible for him to marry?'

'Very true!' she replied.

He was always watchful where she was concerned. It struck him now that she was suddenly looking tired; and he said with quick compunction: 'I've fagged you to death with my nonsense! Now, why did you let me talk you into a head-ache? Shall I send Anna to you?'

'No, indeed! My head doesn't ache, I promise you,' she said, smiling tenderly up at him.

'I wish I might believe you!' he said, bending over her to kiss her cheek. 'I'll leave you to rest before you are assailed by Augusta again: don't let her plague you!'

He went away, and she remained lost in her reflections until roused from them by her cousin's return.

'All alone, dear Elizabeth?' Miss Penistone exclaimed. 'Now, if I had but known–but in general I do believe Sylvester would stay with you for ever, if I were not obliged at last to come in! I am sure I have said a hundred times that I never knew such an attentive son. So considerate, too! There was never anything like it!'

'Ah, yes!' the Duchess said. 'To me so considerate, so endlessly kind!'

She sounded a little mournful, which was unusual in her. Miss Penistone, speaking much in the heartening tone Button used to divert Edmund when he was cross, said: 'He was looking particularly handsome today, wasn't he? Such an excellent figure, and his air so distinguished! What heart-burnings there will be when at last he throws the handkerchief!'

She laughed amiably at this thought, but the Duchess did not seem to be amused. She said nothing, but Miss Penistone saw her hands clasp and unclasp on the arm of the chair, and at once realized that no doubt she must be afraid that so rich a prize as Sylvester might be caught by some wretchedly designing creature quite unworthy of his attention. 'And *no* fear of his marrying to disoblige you, as the saying goes,' said Miss Penistone brightly, but with an anxious eye on the Duchess. 'With so many girls on the catch for him I daresay you would be quite in a worry if he were not so sensible. That thought came into *my* head once—so absurd!—and I mentioned it to Louisa, when she was staying here in the summer. "Not he!" she said—you know her abrupt way! "He knows his worth too well!" Which set my mind quite at rest, as you may suppose.'

It did not seem to have exercised the same beneficial effect on the Duchess's mind, for she put up a hand to shade her eyes. Miss Penistone knew then what was amiss: she had had one of her bad nights, poor Elizabeth!

3

Sylvester made no further mention of his matrimonial plans; nor, since she could not fail to be cheerful whenever he came to visit her, did he suspect that his mother was troubled for him. Had he known it he would have supposed her merely to dislike the thought of his marriage, and would not have found it difficult to put any such scheme aside; if she had told him that she was more disturbed by the fear, which was taking uncomfortably strong possession of her mind, that he had become arrogant he would have been distressed to think that he could have said anything to put such a notion into her head, and would have done his best to joke her out of it. He knew it to be false: he was acquainted with several persons to whom the epithet might well apply, and he thought them intolerable. Few men were more petted and courted than he; there were not many hostesses who would not have forgiven him such slights as were not uncommonly dealt them by spoiled men of rank and fashion. But no hostess would ever be given cause to complain of Sylvester's courtesy; and no insignificant person who perhaps rendered him a trifling service, or even did no more than touch his hat to him, would have reason to think himself despised. To reserve one's civility for people of consequence was a piece of ill-breeding, dishonourable to oneself, as disgusting as to make a parade of greatness, or to curse a servant for clumsiness. Sylvester, who did not arrive at parties very late, refuse to stand up for country-dances, take his bored leave within half an hour of his arrival, leave invitations unanswered, stare unrecognizingly at one of his tenants, or fail to exchange a few words with every one of his guests on Public Days at Chance, was not very likely to believe that a charge of arrogance levelled against him was anything but a calumny, emanating probably from a tuft-hunter whom he had snubbed, or some pert mushroom of society whose pretensions he had been obliged to depress.

The Duchess knew this, and felt herself to be at a loss. She would have liked to have been able to consult with someone who had his interests as much to heart as herself, and must know better than she (since she never saw Sylvester but in her own apartments) how he conducted himself in society. There was only one such person; but although she felt both respect and affection for Lord William Rayne, Sylvester's uncle, and for two years his guardian, very little reflection was needed to convince her that any attempt to get him to enter into her rather vague apprehensions would only make him think her the victim of such crotchets as might be expected to attack an invalid. Lord William was old-fashioned, very bluff and kind, but very full of starch as well. He had some influence over Sylvester, of whom he was as fond as he was proud: a word from him would carry weight, but unfortunately one of his terse reproofs would be more easily drawn from him by what he thought a failure on his nephew's part to remember his exalted station, than by his placing himself on too high a form.

He stayed at Chance at Christmas, and so far from affording the Duchess reassurance considerably depressed her, though this was far from being his intention. He had nothing but praise to bestow on Sylvester. He told the Duchess that the boy did just as he ought, his manners being particularly correct. 'Very affable and civil, you know, but knows how to keep a proper distance,' said Lord William. 'No need to fear he'll forget what he owes to his position, my dear sister! He tells me he's thinking of getting married. Very proper. High time he was setting up his nursery! He seems to be going about the business exactly as he should, but I dropped him a hint. Don't think it was necessary, mind, but I shouldn't like to see him make a fool of himself for want of a word of advice. But thank the lord he's got no rubbishing romantical notions in his head!'

It was the immutable custom of the House of Rayne for as many members of it as could possibly do so to gather together at Christmas under the roof of the head of the family. As the family was enormous, and most of those who congregated at Chance remained for a month, Sylvester had little leisure, and saw less of his mother than he liked. He was an excellent host, and he had an excellent supporter in his sister-in-law, who, besides having a turn for entertaining, very much enjoyed acting as deputy for the Duchess, and consequently became more cheerful as soon as the first of the visitors crossed the threshold. Her pleasure was only marred by Sylvester's refusal to invite Sir Nugent Fotherby to join the party. She argued that if he could invite her father and mother he could with equal propriety invite her affianced husband, but any intention she might have had of developing this grievance was checked by the intervention of both parents. Lord Elvaston, to whom Sir Nugent was objectionable, informed her that if he had found the fellow at Chance he would have gone home instantly, and Lady Elvaston, though willing to tolerate Sir Nugent for the sake of his vast wealth, told her that if she thought to win Sylvester round by affording him the opportunity of studying that amiable dandy at close quarters she was no better than a ninnyhammer.

Sylvester left Chance towards the end of January, a day later than his last, lingering guest. He was bound for Blandford Park, whither his hunters were sent by the direct route from Leicestershire; but he went first to London, a deviation that caused no surprise, since he told his mother he had business there. As it was hunting, not matrimony, that took him to Blandford Park she was able to see him off without any immediate apprehension of his proposing to one of the five eligible candidates for his hand. None of these ladies would be at Blandford Park; and it was in the highest degree unlikely that they were to be found in London either, at the end of January. The Duchess believed he would be granted little opportunity to commit his contemplated imprudence until the beginning of the season. But he had omitted to tell her what was his chief business in town. He went to pay a morning visit to his godmother.

The Dowager Lady Ingham lived in Green Street, in a house bursting with all the furniture and ornaments she had insisted on removing from Ingham House on the occasion of her son's marriage, and her own retirement to Green Street. Any piece for which she had a fancy she insisted was her personal property; and since neither Ingham nor his gentle bride was a match for her she bore off several heirlooms, handsomely promising, however, to bequeathe them to their rightful owner. She also removed the butler, but as he was growing old and was obstinate in his adherence to customs Lord Ingham thought obsolete, this was not felt to be a loss. He was now considerably stricken in years, went about his duties in a slow and stately manner, and discouraged the Dowager from holding any entertainments more arduous than a small soirée, or a card-party. Fortunately she had no wish to give dinner-parties, or breakfasts, excusing herself on the score of age and infirmity. She was not, in fact, much above five-and-sixty; and beyond a tendency to gout no one had any very clear idea of what her infirmities might be. She certainly walked with the aid of an ebony cane; and whenever she was confronted with any disagreeable form of exertion she was threatened with palpitations, and was obliged to send for Sir Henry Halford, who understood her constitution so well that he could always be depended on to recommend her to do precisely what she wished.

When Sylvester was ushered into her crowded drawing-room she greeted him with a snort; but she was pleased to receive a visit from him nevertheless; and after telling him acidly that she had well-nigh forgotten what he looked like she unbent sufficiently to give him her hand, and allow him to kiss it. Mollified by the grace with which he performed this courtesy she waved him to a chair on the opposite side of the fireplace and bade him tell her how his mother did.

'I left her pretty well, I think,' he answered. 'But tell me, ma'am, how *you* do?'

She told him. The recital lasted for twenty minutes, and might have lasted longer had she not suddenly bethought herself of something she wanted to know. She broke off her account of her aches and ails abruptly, saying: 'Never mind that! What's this I'm hearing about your brother's widow? The on-dit is that she's going to marry a man-milliner. I knew his father: a namby-pamby creature *he* was, though he passed for an amiable man. They tell me the son is a Pink of the Ton. I suppose he has a genteel fortune? Old Fotherby should have cut up warm.'

'Oh, as rich as Golden Ball!' Sylvester replied.

'Is he indeed? H'm!' She was evidently impressed by this, but said after a reflective moment: 'In a vast hurry to be married again, ain't she? What happens to the boy?'

'He will remain at Chance, of course.'

She stared at him. 'What, is your poor mother to be charged with the care of him?'

'No, certainly not.' He held up his quizzing-glass, twisting it between finger and thumb, and watching the flash of firelight on its magnifying lens. 'I am thinking of getting married myself, ma'am.'

'Well, it's high time,' she responded snappishly. 'The Torrington girl, I collect?'

'I suppose she might answer the purpose—if I could be sure she would not be hipped at Chance. It is an object with me, you know, ma'am, to choose a wife who will be acceptable to my mother.'

If she thought this an odd reason for matrimony she did not say so. 'Is your heart engaged?' she demanded.

'Not in the least,' he replied. 'You see what a quandary I am in! Do advise me!'

She did not speak for a minute, but he knew that she was on the alert, and was content to wait, idly swinging his quizzing-glass.

'You can pour yourself out a glass of wine!' she said suddenly. 'I'll take one too—though I don't doubt I shall suffer for it.'

He rose, and crossed the room to where Horwich had set a silver tray on a side-table. When he came back to the fire, and put a glass of sherry into the Dowager's hand, he said lightly: 'Now, if you were only a fairy godmother, ma'am, you would wave your wand, and so conjure up exactly the bride I want!'

He returned to his chair as he spoke, and had embarked on a change of subject when she interrupted him, saying: 'I may not be able to wave a wand, but I daresay I could produce an eligible bride for you.' She set her glass down. 'What you want, Sylvester, is a pretty-behaved girl of good birth, good upbringing, and an amiable disposition. If your Uncle William were not a zany he would have arranged just such an alliance for you years ago, and you may depend upon it you would have been very comfortable in it. Well, *I* haven't meddled, though I own I've been tempted, when I've heard how you were making up to first this female and then that. However, you've now applied to me, and it's my belief that if you wish for a wife who will know what her duty is and be more acceptable than any other to your mother, you could do no better for yourself than to offer for my grand-daughter. I don't mean one of Ingham's girls, but Phoebe: my Verena's child.'

He was extremely annoyed. His godmother was not playing the game as he had planned it. Those carefully casual words of his should have prompted her not to hold him up at the sword's point, but to have produced her granddaughter presently (at the start of the season, perhaps) for his inspection. There was a lack of finesse about her conduct of the affair which vexed and alarmed him; for while the notion of marrying the daughter of his mother's dear friend had taken possession of his mind its hold was not so strong that it could not speedily be broken by the discovery that Miss Marlowe was lacking in the qualities he considered indispensable in his wife. In Lady Ingham's bluntness he saw an attempt to force his hand, and nothing could more surely set up the back of a young man who had been, virtually, his own master from the time he was nineteen, and the master of a great many other persons as well. He said in a cool tone: 'Indeed? Have I met your granddaughter, ma'am? I think I have not.'

'I don't know. She was brought out last season—it should have been done before, but she contracted scarlet fever, and so it was put off for a year. She will be twenty in October: I'm not offering you a schoolroom miss. As for the rest—I imagine you must several times have been in company with her, for she was taken to all the *ton* parties. *I* saw to that! If I had left it to that woman Marlow married as his second the poor child would have spent her time at museums, and the Concerts of Ancient Music, for that's Constance Marlow's notion of disporting herself in town! Marlow married her before Phoebe was out of leading-strings, the more fool he! Not but what I give the woman credit for having done her duty by the child. She has been well brought-up—no question about that!' Glancing across at Sylvester she saw that he was wearing his satyr-look, and she said with the sharpness of defiance: '*I* couldn't take charge of the girl! At my age, and with my indifferent health it wasn't to be thought of!'

He said nothing, nor did the satyr-look abate. Since Lady Ingham had made no attempt during the previous season to bring her granddaughter to his notice he concluded that Miss Marlow was probably a plain girl, unlikely to attract him. He tried to remember whether he had seen a girl with Lady Marlow on the few occasions when he had found himself in company with that forbidding lady. If he had, she held no place in his memory.

'Phoebe's not one of your beauties,' said the Dowager, almost as if she had read his mind. 'She don't show to advantage with her mother-in-law, but to my way of thinking she's not just in the ordinary style. If pink-and-white's your fancy, she wouldn't do for you. If you want quality, and a girl with a quick understanding, you'd like her. As for her fortune, she won't inherit much from Marlow, but her mother's dowry was tied up in her, so she'll have that, besides what I shall leave her.' She was silent for a minute, but said presently: 'It would please your mother, and I don't deny it would please me too. I want to see Verena's child comfortably established. She's not an heiress, but her fortune won't be contemptible; and as for her birth, Marlow's a fool, but his blood's well enough; and the Inghams may look as high as they please when it comes to matchmaking. But if an alliance with my granddaughter isn't to your taste, pray don't hesitate to tell me so!'

This set the seal on his resentment. She was apparently trying to fluster him into committing himself. A stupid move: she ought to know that hers was not the first trap set for him. He rose, smiling at her with apparently unruffled serenity, and said, as he lifted her hand to his lips: 'I can't suppose, my dear ma'am, that you need my assurance that on the score of eligibility I could have no possible objection to the match. I shall only say, therefore, that I hope to have the pleasure of meeting Miss Marlow—this season, perhaps? Ah, that will be delightful!'

He left her with no clue to his sentiments, but in an angry mood that was not soothed by the reflection that he had laid himself open to her attack. She had proposed to him only what he had had in mind when he visited her, but the alacrity with which she had snapped at the chance offered her was almost as offensive as her attempt to force his hand. It was also stupid, for it inspired him with nothing more than a desire to cross Miss Marlow off the list of his eligibles, and propose without much waste of time to one of the remaining five. Unfortunately, the impropriety of such conduct made it impossible for him to administer this salutary lesson to the Dowager. She must regard it as a studied insult (which, indeed, it would be), and so wholly beneath him was it to insult her that he could only shrug, and resign himself. There was nothing to be done now until he had met Miss Marlow.

He put the matter aside, only to be confronted with it again the following week, when, upon arrival at Blandford Park, he found Lord Marlow to be one of his fellow guests.

In itself this circumstance was not suspicious. Marlow and the Duke of Beaufort were old friends; and since Austerby, Marlow's seat, was situated in the rather indifferent country south of Calne he was a frequent visitor to Badminton during the hunting-season. The Heythrop country, which was hunted by the Duke alternately with the Badminton district, was farther from Austerby and saw his lordship less often, but he was not a stranger to the hunt. Sylvester could have believed that his presence at Blandford Park was due to the workings of chance had it not soon been borne in upon him that Marlow was there by design.

Lord Marlow was always bluff and good-natured, but he had never been on anything more than common civility terms with Sylvester, twenty-five years his junior. On this occasion, however, his object was to stand well with him, and nothing could have exceeded his affability. Sylvester saw that Lady Ingham had been busy, and had the encounter taken place anywhere but at a hunting-party he might have rebuffed his lordship's overtures with the chilling formality he was quite capable of adopting whenever it seemed expedient to him to do so. But Lord Marlow blundering joviaily through the London scene and Lord Marlow bestriding one of his high-bred hunters were two very different persons. The one could be held in contempt; the other commanded the respect of every hunting-man. Whether over the black fences of Leicestershire or the stone walls of the Cotswold uplands he had few equals, and not even Lord Alvanley could match him for intrepidity. Every available penny from the yield of a fortune long since found to be inadequate was spent on his slapping hunters, of which he never had fewer than fourteen in his stables; and to be singled out by him on the field for a word of advice or approval was the ambition of every young blood seeking to emulate his prowess. Sylvester might know very well why he had suddenly become the recipient of his lordship's favours, but he could not be indifferent to the bluff word of praise, or ungrateful for the advice which taught him the trick of the stone walls. One thing leading to another, before the end of the week he was fairly caught, and had accepted an invitation to stay for a few days at Austerby when he left Blandford Park. Lord Marlow was generally thought to be a stupid man, but he was not so stupid as to let it appear that he had any other object in mind than to show Sylvester what sport was to be had in admittedly humbug country; and possibly (if it should suit him) to sell him a promising five-year-old that was not quite up to his own weight. There was to be no ceremony about this visit; they would leave Blandford Park together, and Salford would take his pot-luck at Austerby. Lord Marlow made no mention of his daughter; and in these circumstances Sylvester allowed himself to be persuaded. On the whole he was not displeased. Under his host's unexpectedly tactful handling of the affair he could make the acquaintance of Miss Marlow without in any way committing himself: a better arrangement, he was disposed to think, than a formal London party to which he would be invited for the express purpose of meeting the young lady.

4

The schoolroom of Austerby was presided over by a lady of quelling aspect whose rawbone frame was invariably clad in sober-hued dresses made high to the neck and unadorned by flounces. Her sandy hair was smoothly banded under a cap; her complexion was weatherbeaten; her eyes of a pale blue; and her nose, the most salient feature of her countenance, jutted out intimidatingly. She had a gruff way of talking, and as her voice was a deep one this helped to make her seem a veritable dragon.

Appearances, however, were deceptive. Under Miss Sibylla Battery's formidable front beat a warmly affectionate heart. With the possible exception of Eliza, Lady Marlow's third and best-loved daughter, her young charges all adored her; and Phoebe, Susan, Mary, and even little Kitty confided their hopes and their griefs to her, and loyally shielded her from blame in their peccadilloes.

It might have been supposed that Miss Phoebe Marlow, nineteen years of age, and a débutante of a season's standing, would have been emancipated from the schoolroom; but as she feared and disliked her stepmother, and was cordially disliked by Lady Marlow, she was glad to make Italian lessons with Miss Battery an excuse to spend what time she could spare from the stables in the schoolroom. This arrangement suited Lady Marlow equally well, for although she had striven her utmost to rear her stepdaughter in the image of a genteel young female, none of the whippings Phoebe had received and no weight of hours spent in solitary confinement had availed to purge her of what her ladyship called her hoydenish tricks. She careered all over the country-side, mounted either on her own cover-hack, or on one of her father's big hunters; tore her clothes; hobnobbed with grooms; stitched abominably; and was (in Lady Marlow's opinion) on far too easy terms with Mr Thomas Orde, her life-long friend and the son of the Squire. Had she had her way Lady Marlow would have very speedily put a stop to any but the mildest form of equestrian exercise; but to every representation made to him on this sore subject Lord Marlow turned a deaf ear. He was in general the most compliant of husbands, but horses were his passion, and her ladyship had learnt long ago that any attempt to interfere in what concerned the stables would fail. Like many weak men, Lord Marlow could be mulish in obstinacy. He was proud of Phoebe's horsemanship, liked to take her out with him on hunting-days, and could ill have spared her from his stables, which she managed, in theory, during his frequent absences from home, and, in practice, at all times.

Summoned peremptorily to London by Lady Ingram, Lord Marlow, an indolent man, left Austerby grumbling. He returned two days later in the best of spirits, and in unaccustomed charity with his one-time mother-in-law. Such a brilliant match as she seemed to have arranged for Phoebe he had never hoped to achieve, for Phoebe had not taken very well during her London season. Lady Marlow had drilled her into propriety; it was Lord Marlow's unexpressed opinion that she had overdone it. A little more vivacity, of which he knew Phoebe to have plenty, was needed to overcome the disadvantages of a thin, wiry figure, a brown complexion, and no more beauty than could be found in a pair of clear gray eyes, which could certainly twinkle with mischief, but which more frequently held a look of scared apprehension.

Lady Marlow was a Christian woman, and she did not grudge Phoebe her astonishing good fortune, however unworthy of it she might be. Indeed, she determined to see to it that Phoebe did nothing to alienate such an eligible suitor during his stay at Austerby. 'For, you may depend upon it,' she said, 'that whatever whimsical notion Salford may have taken into his head of offering for the daughter of his mama's friend he will marry none but a female who conducts herself with propriety. For my part, I am persuaded this marriage has been proposed to him by Lady Ingham. Phoebe has yet to establish herself in his eyes. He met her in London in the spring–indeed, he stood up with her at Lady Sefton's ball–but if he would recognize her again it is more than I bargain for.'

'You don't think, my love,' his lordship ventured to suggest, 'that it might be wiser not to inform her why he comes to visit us–that is, if he does come, which, you know, is not certain?'

No, her ladyship did not think so at all, unless it was my lord's wish that his daughter should instantly disgust the Duke by coming in spattered all over with mud, blurting out one of her ill-considered remarks, or giving him a very odd notion of her character by encouraging the familiarities of young Orde.

Lord Marlow wished for none of these things, and although he saw no harm in her alliance with young Orde, and knew their relationship to be that of brother and sister, he was easily brought to believe that it might be misunderstood by Salford, a pretty high stickler. He agreed that Tom's visits to Austerby, and Phoebe's to the Manor, should be discouraged, and kept to himself his earnest hope that his helpmate might not offend the Squire and his lady. Lord Marlow did not like to be on bad terms with his neighbours; besides, the Squire was the Master of the hunt, and although his lordship did most of his hunting in the shires it still would by no means suit him to fall out with the local Master. But Lady Marlow said commandingly: 'Leave it to me!' and, on the whole, he was only too glad to do so.

It was agreed that nothing should be said to Phoebe until he had secured the Duke's promise to visit Austerby; but when his second groom came over from Blandford Park with a letter from him to her ladyship, warning her that when he returned at the end of the week Salford would be accompanying him, she instantly sent for Phoebe to her dressing-room.

Phoebe obeyed the summons in considerable trepidation; but when she entered the dressing-room she was greeted, if not with cordiality, at least not with the bleak look that still had the power to make her heart knock against her ribs. Lady Marlow told her to shut the door and sit down. She then noticed that one of the flounces of Phoebe's gown had come unstitched, and drew her attention to it, reading her a homily on the evils of slovenliness, and expressing the hope that she would have no occasion, in the near future, to blush for her.

'No, Mama,' Phoebe said, wondering why the near future was of particular importance.

'I have sent for you,' pursued her ladyship, 'to inform you of a very gratifying circumstance. I do not scruple to say that the good fortune which is coming to you is a great deal more than you have done anything to deserve, and I can only trust that you may be found to be worthy of it.' She paused, but Phoebe only looked rather bewildered. 'I daresay,' she continued, 'that you may have wondered what it was that took your papa to London at this season.'

Since she had not given the matter a thought Phoebe was a good deal astonished. It was not Lady Marlow's custom to encourage the girls to indulge in curiosity, and an enquiry into the nature of Papa's business in town would certainly have met with a heavy snub.

'You are surprised that I should mention the matter to you,' said her ladyship, observing Phoebe's expression. 'I do so because it was on your behalf that he undertook the fatigue of a journey to London. You should be very much obliged to him, which I am persuaded you must be when I tell you that he is about to arrange a very advantageous marriage for you.'

Phoebe was well aware that in failing to secure at least one respectable offer during her London season she had fallen lamentably short of expectation, and this announcement made her look more astonished than ever. 'Good gracious!' she exclaimed involuntarily. 'But I don't think—I mean, no one made up to me, except old Mr Hardwick, and that was only because of my mother!'

She then quailed, flushing to the roots of her hair as she came under a basilisk stare from Lady Marlow's cold eyes.

'*Made up to you*—!' repeated Lady Marlow ominously. 'I need not ask from whom you learned such a vulgarism, but perhaps you will inform me how you dared permit me to hear it on your lips?'

'I beg your pardon, ma'am!' faltered Phoebe.

'Such language may do very well for young Orde,' said her ladyship bitingly. 'No female with the smallest claim to refinement would use it. And if you were to express yourself in such a manner to the Duke of Salford I tremble to think what the consequences might be!'

Phoebe blinked at her. 'To the Duke of Salford, ma'am? But how should I? I mean, I am sure there can be no danger, for I am barely acquainted with him. I shouldn't think,' she added reflectively, 'that he even remembers me.'

'You are mistaken,' replied Lady Marlow. 'He is to visit us next week, with what object I imagine you may guess.'

'Well, I haven't the least notion what it may be,' said Phoebe in a puzzled voice.

'He is coming with the intention of making you an offer—and you will oblige me, Phoebe, by not sitting there in a stare, and with your mouth open!'

'M-me?' stammered Phoebe. '*The Duke of Salford?*'

Not displeased to find her daughter incredulous, Lady Marlow bestowed a thin smile upon her. 'I do not wonder that you should be surprised, for it is far more than *I* ever hoped for you, I can tell you. I shall expect to hear you express your gratitude to Papa for his kindness in arranging so splendid a match for you.'

'I don't believe it!' Phoebe cried vehemently. 'Besides, I don't want to marry the Duke of Salford!'

No sooner had the words been uttered than she trembled at her boldness, and for several moments dared not raise her eyes to the austere countenance confronting her. An awful silence greeted her rash speech, which was broken at last by Lady Marlow's demanding to know whether her ears had deceived her. Judging this question to be rhetorical Phoebe made no attempt to answer it, but only hung her head.

'A marriage of the first consequence is offered to you: a marriage that must make you the envy of a score of young females, all of them by far more handsome than you will ever be, and you have the audacity to tell me you do not want it! Upon my word, Phoebe—'

'But, ma'am, I am persuaded it is all a mistake! Why, I only spoke to him once in my life, and that was at the Seftons' ball, when he stood up with me for one dance. He thought it a great bore, and when I saw him not three days after, at Almack's, he *cut* me!'

'Pray do not talk in that nonsensical style!' said her ladyship sharply. 'Your situation in life renders you an eligible wife for a man of rank, however unsuited to a great position I may consider you to be; and I don't doubt the Duke must be aware that your upbringing has been in accordance with the highest principles.'

'But there are others j-just as well brought up, and m-much prettier!' Phoebe said, twisting her fingers together.

'You have over them what his grace apparently believes to be an advantage,' responded Lady Marlow repressively. 'Whether he may be right is not for me to say, though I should rather have supposed— however, on *that* subject I prefer to be silent. Your mother was a close friend of the Duke's mother, which is why you have been singled out. I tell you this so that you shall not become puffed up in your own conceit, my dear Phoebe. Nothing is more unbecoming in a young woman, I can assure you.'

'Puffed up! I should rather think not!' Phoebe said hastily. 'Offer for me because his mother knew mine? I–I never heard of anything so–so monstrous! When he is barely acquainted with me, and has never made the least push to engage my interest!'

'It is for that precise reason that he is coming to visit us,' said Lady Marlow, with the patience of one addressing an idiot. 'He desires to become better acquainted with you, and I trust you are neither so foolish nor so undutiful as to conduct yourself in a way that must make him think better of offering for your hand.' She paused, scanning Phoebe's face. What she read in it caused her to change her tactics. The girl, though in general biddable enough, showed occasionally a streak of obstinacy. Lady Marlow did not doubt her ability to command her ultimate obedience, but she knew that if Phoebe were to take one of her odd notions into her head she was quite capable of repulsing the Duke before there was time to bring her back to a state of proper submission. So she began to point out the advantages of the match, even going so far as to say that Phoebe would like to be mistress of her own establishment. Winning no other response than a blank stare, she lost no time in drawing, with vigour and fluency, a grim picture of the alternative to becoming the Duchess of Salford. As this seemed to include a life of unending disgrace at Austerby (for it was not to be expected that Lord Marlow, with four more daughters to establish, would waste any more money on his ungrateful eldest-born); the reproaches of her sisters, of whose advancement she would have shown herself to be wickedly careless; and various other penalties, a number of which were not rendered less terrible for being left unnamed, it should have been enough to have brought a far more recalcitrant girl than Phoebe to her senses. She did indeed look very white and frightened, so Lady Marlow dismissed her to think it over.

Phoebe fled back to the schoolroom. Here she found not only Susan, but her two next sisters as well: thirteen-year-old Mary, and the saintly Eliza. Susan, perceiving that Phoebe was big with news, instantly banished Eliza to the nursery, and, when that affronted damsel showed signs of re-calcitrance, forcibly ejected her from the room, recommending her to go and tell Mama, and to be careful how she got into bed later. This sinister warning quelled Eliza, the horrid memory of a slug found between her sheets still lively in her mind, and she prepared to join the youngest of the family in the nursery, merely apostrophizing Susan, through the keyhole, as the greatest beast in nature before taking herself off. Unfortunately, Miss Battery came along the passage at that moment and very properly consigned her to her bedroom for using language unbecoming to a young lady of quality. Eliza complained in a whining voice that Phoebe and Sukey were very unkind and would not tell her any of their secrets, but this only drew down on her a reprimand for indulging the sin of curiosity. Miss Battery led her inexorably to her bedchamber before repairing to the schoolroom.

She reached the room just as Mary, a humble-minded girl, gathered her books together, asking her sister whether she too must go away.

'Not unless Phoebe wishes it,' replied Susan. '*You* don't carry tales to Mama!'

'Oh, no!' Phoebe said. 'Of course I don't wish you to go, Mary! Besides, it isn't a secret.' She looked round quickly as the door opened, and exclaimed: 'Oh, Sibby, did *you* know? Did Mama tell you?'

'No,' said Miss Battery. 'I overheard something your papa said to her, though. Couldn't help but do so. I thought it not right to say anything to you, but when I heard you had been sent for to the dressing-room I guessed what it must be. Your papa has received an offer for your hand.'

'No!' cried Susan. 'Phoebe, has he indeed?'

'Yes—at least, I think—Oh, I don't know, but Mama seems to think he *will*, if only I will conduct myself *conformably*!'

'Oh, famous!' Susan declared, clapping her hands. 'Who is he? How could you be so sly as never to breathe a word about it? Did you meet him in London? Is he passionately in love with you?'

'No,' replied Phoebe baldly.

This damping monosyllable checked Susan's raptures. Miss Battery looked rather anxiously at Phoebe; and Mary said diffidently that she rather supposed that persons of quality did not fall in love.

'That's only what Mama says, and *I* know it isn't true!' said Susan scornfully. '*Is* it, ma'am?'

'Can't say,' responded Miss Battery briefly. 'Nor can you. Shouldn't be thinking of such things at your age.'

'Pooh, I am nearly sixteen, and I can tell you I mean to get a husband as soon as I can! Phoebe, do stop being missish, and tell us who he is!'

'I'm not being missish!' said Phoebe indignantly. 'I am in flat despair, and he is the Duke of Salford!'

'W-what?' gasped Susan. 'Phoebe, you wretch, you're hoaxing us! Only fancy you as a duchess!'

Phoebe was not in the least offended by her burst of hearty laughter, but Mary said stoutly: 'I think Phoebe would make a very *nice* duchess.'

That made Phoebe laugh too, but Miss Battery nodded, and said: 'So she would!'

'How can you say so?' expostulated Phoebe. 'When I haven't the smallest turn for fashion, and never know what to say to strangers, or—'

'Is he fashionable?' interrupted Susan eagerly.

'Oh, excessively! That is, I don't know, but I should think he would be. He is always very well dressed, and he goes to all the ton parties, and drives a splendid pair of dapple-grays in the Park. I shouldn't wonder at it if he spent as much as a hundred pounds a year on soap in his stables.'

'Well, that ought to make him acceptable to you!' observed Susan. 'But what is he like? Is he young? Handsome?'

'I don't know what his age may be. He is not *old*, I suppose. As for handsome, people say he is, but *I* do not think so. In fact—' She stopped suddenly, aware of Mary's innocently enquiring gaze, and ended her description of Sylvester by saying only that she judged him to ride about twelve stone.

Mary, who had a retentive memory, said hopefully: 'Papa used to ride twelve stone when he was a young man. He said so once, and also that it is the best weight for hunting over strong country. Does the Duke hunt over strong country, Phoebe?'

Susan broke in on this with pardonable impatience. 'Who cares a fig for that? I wish you won't be so provoking, Phoebe! Why don't you want him to offer for you? Is he disagreeable? For my part, if he were rich and reasonably civil I shouldn't care for anything else. Only fancy! You would have a house of your own, and as many new dresses as you wished, and very likely splendid jewels as well, besides being able to do just as you chose!'

Miss Battery eyed her with disfavour. 'If you can't refrain from expressing yourself with what I can't call anything but vulgarity, Susan, I must impose silence upon you. In any event, it is past the hour, and you should be practising that sonatina.'

Having in this masterly fashion disposed of Susan, Miss Battery recommended Mary to occupy herself for half an hour with the sampler she was embroidering for her Mama's birthday, and left the room, taking Phoebe with her. Firmly shutting the schoolroom door she said in a lowered voice: 'Thought it best you should say no more to Susan. Good girl, but wants discretion. You're all of a twitter: why?'

'It is the most shocking thing!' Phoebe declared, looking quite distracted. 'If it were anyone but Mama I should think it a take-in! But *Mama*—! Oh dear, I am utterly confounded! I feel as though my senses won't be straight again for a twelvemonth!'

'Not so loud!' said Miss Battery. 'Tell me in your bedchamber! Try to recover your composure, my dear.'

Thus adjured, Phoebe followed her meekly along the corridor to her bedchamber. Since one of Lady Marlow's favourite economies was to allow no fires to be kindled in any bedchamber but her own, her lord's, and those occupied by such guests as were hardy enough to visit Austerby during the winter months, this apartment might have been considered singularly unsuitable for a *tête-à-tête*. Phoebe, however, was inured to its rigours. Miss Battery, stalking over to the wardrobe, and unearthing from it a large shawl, wrapped this round her pupil's thin shoulders, saying as she did so: 'I collect you don't wish for this match. Can't deny that it's a flattering one, or that I should like to see you so well established. Now, tell me this, child: have you got some silly notion in your head about that scheme of yours to set up for yourself with me to bear you company? Because if so don't give it a thought! *I* shant.' Never supposed it would come to pass—or wished for it, if you received an agreeable offer.'

'No, no, it's not that!' Phoebe said. 'For if I were to be married who but you should I want to instruct my children? Sibby, do you know who Salford is?'

Miss Battery frowned at her in a puzzled way. 'Who he is?' she repeated. 'You said he was a duke.'

Phoebe began to laugh a little hysterically. 'He is Count Ugolino!' she said.

It might have been expected that this extraordinary announcement would have still further bewildered Miss Battery, but although she was certainly startled by it, she found it perfectly intelligible. Ejaculating: 'Merciful heavens!' she sat down limply, and stared at Phoebe in great perturbation. She was well acquainted with the Count: indeed, she might have been said to have been present at his birth, an event for which she was, in some measure, responsible, since she had for several years shared with Phoebe the romantic novels which were the solace of her own leisure hours. Her only extravagance was a subscription to a Bath lending library; her only conscious sin was that she encouraged Lady Marlow to suppose that the package delivered weekly by the carrier contained only works of an erudite or an elevating character. So strong was Lady Marlow's disapproval of fiction that even Miss Edgeworth's moral tales were forbidden to her daughters. Her rule was so absolute that it never occurred to her to doubt that she was obeyed to the letter; and as she was as imperceptive as she was despotic no suspicion had ever crossed her mind that Miss Battery was by no means the rigid disciplinarian she appeared.

In none of Lady Marlow's own daughters did Miss Battery discover the imaginative turn of mind so much deprecated by her ladyship; in Phoebe it was pronounced, and Miss Battery, loving her and deeply pitying her, fostered it, knowing how much her own joyless existence was lightened by excursions into a world of pure make-believe. From the little girl who scribbled fairy stories for the rapt delectation of Susan and Mary, Phoebe had developed into a real authoress, and one, moreover, who had written a stirring romance worthy of being published.

She had written it after her London season. It had come white-hot from her ready pen, and Miss Battery had been quick to see that it was far in advance of her earlier attempts at novel-writing. Its plot was as extravagant as anything that came from the Minerva Press; the behaviour of its characters was for the most part wildly improbable; the scene was laid in an unidentifiable country; and the entire story was rich in absurdity. But Phoebe's pen had always been persuasive, and so enthralling did she contrive to make the adventures of her heroine that it was not until he had reached the end of the book that even so stern a critic as young Mr Orde bethought him of the various incidents which he saw, in retrospect, to be impossible. Miss Battery, a more discerning critic, recognized not only the popular nature of the tale, but also the flowering in it of a latent talent. Phoebe had discovered in herself a gift for humorous portraiture, and she had not wasted her time in London. Tom Orde might complain that a score of minor characters were irrelevant, but Miss Battery knew that it was these swift, unerring sketches that raised *The Lost Heir* above the commonplace. She would not allow Phoebe to expunge one of them, or a line of their wickedly diverting dialogues, but persuaded her instead to write it all out in fairest copperplate. Phoebe groaned at this tedious labour, but since neither she nor Miss Battery knew of a professional copyist, and would have been hard put to it to have paid for such a person's services, she submitted to the drudgery. After that the book was packed up, and despatched by the mail to Miss Battery's cousin, Mr Gilbert Otley, junior partner in the small but aspiring firm of Newsham & Otley, Publishers.

Mr Otley, receiving the manuscript and perusing the accompanying letter from Miss Battery, was unimpressed. At first glance he did not think *The Lost Heir* the sort of book he wished to handle; and the intelligence that it was the work of a Lady of Quality drew from him only a heavy sigh. However, he took *The Lost Heir* home with him, and read it at a sitting. It did not take him long to perceive that it was to some extent a *roman à clef*, for although he was unacquainted with the members of the *haut ton* he was shrewd enough to realize that the authoress in depicting many of her characters was drawing from the life. The success of *Glenarvon*, published some eighteen months previously, was still fresh in his mind; and it was this circumstance which led him, rather doubtfully, to hand *The Lost Heir* to his partner.

Mr Harvey Newsham was unexpectedly enthusiastic; and when Mr Otley pointed out to him that it was not such a book as they had been used to produce he replied caustically that if it enjoyed better sales than had the last three of these works he for one should not complain.

'But will it?' said Mr Otley. 'The story is no great thing, after all—in fact it's nonsensical!'

'No one will care for that.'

'Well, I don't know. I should have thought it too fantastical myself. In fact, it still has me in a puzzle. How the devil did that Ugolino-fellow get hold of his nephew in the first place? And why didn't he smother him, or something, when he *had* got hold of him, instead of keeping him prisoner in that castle of his? And as for the boy's sister managing to get into the place, let alone that corkbrained hero, and then the pair of them setting sail with the boy—well, they couldn't have done it!'

Mr Newsham dismissed such trivialities with a wave of his hand. 'It doesn't signify. This female—' he jabbed a finger at Phoebe's manu-script—'knows how to do the trick! What's more, the book's stuffed with people she's met, and *that's* what will make the nobs buy it.' He glanced down at the manuscript appraisingly. 'In three volumes, handsomely bound,' he said thoughtfully. 'At the start of next season. Say April—skilfully puffed-off, of course. I think it will do, Otley!'

'It will be pretty expensive,' objected Mr Otley.

'I mean this book to be in every fashionable drawing-room, and it won't do to get it up shoddy. Colburn issued Lady Caroline Lamb's tale in tooled leather. It looked very well.'

'Ay, but you may depend upon it Lady Caroline paid for it,' retorted Mr Otley.'

'No reason to suppose this author won't do the same,' said the optimistic Mr Newsham. 'Offer her profit-sharing terms, she to pay all losses. You know, my boy, if the book were to take, Colburn will be as surly as a butcher's dog to think it wasn't offered him!'

'So he will!' agreed Mr Otley, cheered by this reflection. 'I'll write off to my cousin next week: we don't wish to appear over-anxious to come to terms. I shall tell her it ain't just in our line, besides having a good many faults.'

This programme, being approved by the senior partner, was carried out; but from then on the negotiations proceeded on quite different lines from those envisaged by Mr Otley. Miss Battery's prompt reply afforded him a new insight into that lady's character. Begging his pardon for having put him to the trouble of reading a work which she now realized to be unsuitable matter for the firm of Newsham & Otley she requested him to return it to her by the mail, care of the receiving office in Bath. Further enquires had given her to think that the manuscript ought to be offered to Colburn, or perhaps to Egerton. She would be much obliged to him for his advice on this point, and remained his affectionate cousin, Sibylla Battery.

Recovering from this setback, Mr Otley then entered upon some spirited bargaining, agreement being finally reached at the sum of £150, to be received by Miss Battery on behalf of the author upon receipt by the publisher of the bookseller's accounts. Left to himself Mr Otley would have done his possible to have reduced this figure by £50, but at this stage of the negotiations Mr Newsham intervened, giving it as his opinion that to behave scaly to a promising new author could result only in her offering her second book to a rival publisher. He would have been gratified could he but have known to what dizzy heights his generosity raised Miss Marlow's spirits. The sum seemed enormous to her; and then and there was born her determination to leave Austerby as soon as she came of age, and with Miss Battery for chaperon to set up a modest establishment of her own in which she would be able without interference to pursue her lucrative vocation.

Besides Miss Battery only Mr Orde shared the secret of her authorship, and it was not until he had been permitted to see the proof-sheets that Mr Orde was relieved of his suspicion that the whole affair was an attempt to hoax him. He was much more impressed by the sight of the story in actual print than he thought it proper to admit; but he very handsomely acknowledged to the proud author that he had not believed it could read half as well.

5

Miss Battery, a strong-minded female, did not for many minutes allow her consternation to overpower her. Squaring her shoulders, she said: 'Unfortunate! That you should have taken him in dislike, I mean. No more to be said, if that's the case. Though I don't suppose he can be as villainous as Count Ugolino. No one could be.'

'Oh, no! He isn't villainous at all—at least, I shouldn't think he would be, but I'm not even acquainted with him! I only chose him for Ugolino because of the way his eyebrows slant, which makes him look just like a villain. And also, of course, because of his—his *crested* air, which made me long to give him a set-down!'

'Self-consequence?' said Miss Battery, a little at sea. 'Thinks too much of his rank?'

Phoebe shook her head, frowning. 'No, it isn't that. It is—yes, it is worse than that! I think it is so natural to him to have all that consequence that he doesn't give it a thought. Do you understand, Sibby?'

'No. Oughtn't to give it a thought.'

'It is very difficult to explain, but I am persuaded you *will* understand, when you see him. It is as though being a duke is so much a part of him that he takes it perfectly for granted, and quite unconsciously expects to be treated everywhere with distinction. I don't mean to say that his manner are not what they ought to be, for he has a great deal of well-bred ease—a sort of cool civility, you know, towards persons who don't interest him. I believe he is very amiable to those whom he likes, but the thing is—or so I fancy—that he doesn't care a button for what anyone may think of him. To be sure, *that* isn't wonderful,' she added reflectively, 'for the way he is courted and toad-eaten is quite repulsive! Why, when Lady Sefton brought him up to me—she is the Baroness Josceline in my story, you know: the affected, fidgety one!—she introduced him as though she were conferring the greatest favour on me!'

'That doesn't signify,' interrupted Miss Battery. 'Did *he* behave as though he thought it so?'

'Oh, no! He is so much accustomed to such flattery that he doesn't appear even to heed it. Being civil to poor little dabs of females who have neither beauty nor conversation is one of the tiresome duties his exalted situation obliges him to perform.'

'Well, if I were you, my dear, I wouldn't fly into a pucker yet awhile,' said Miss Battery with strong commonsense. 'Seems to me you don't know anything about him. One thing you can depend on: if he's coming here to make you an offer he won't treat you with cool civility!'

'Even if he did not—oh, he must have changed indeed if I were to like him well enough to marry him!' declared Phoebe. 'I *could* not, Sibby!'

'Then you will decline his offer,' said Miss Battery, with a conviction she was far from feeling.

Phoebe looked at her rather hopelessly, but said nothing. She knew it to be unnecessary. No one understood more thoroughly the difficulties of her situation than her governess; and no one was better acquainted with the ruthlessness of Lady Marlow's imperious temper. After a few moments' reflection Miss Battery said: 'Speak to your father. He wouldn't wish you to be forced into a marriage you disliked.'

This advice was repeated, in substance, by young Mr Orde, upon the following day, when Phoebe, knowing her mama to be out of the way, rode over to the Manor House to confer with him.

Thomas was the only child of the Squire of the district, a very respectable man, who contrived to maintain thirty or more couples of hounds, a score of hunters for himself, his son, and his huntsmen, several coach-horses and cover-hacks, half a dozen spaniels, and upwards of a hundred gamecocks at walk, on an income of no more than eight thousand pounds a year, and that without being obliged to stint his lady of the elegancies of life, or to allow to fall into disrepair the dwellings of his numerous tenants. His family had been established in the county for many generations, most of its members having been distinguished for their sporting proclivities, and none of them having made any particular mark in the world. The Squire was a man of excellent plain sense, much looked up to as a personage of the first consequence within his circle. While perfectly aware of his own worth, his way of life was unpretentious; although he employed, besides his huntsman, several grooms, a coachman, a gamekeeper, an experienced kennelman, and a cocker, he was content, when he travelled any distance from Somerset, to hire postilions; and his household boasted no more than three indoor men-servants.

He was a fond as well as a judicious parent, and had his son shown the least leaning towards academic pursuits he would have sent him to Oxford upon his leaving Rugby, whatever retrenchments this might have entailed. That they must have been heavy he knew, for it was impossible for such a thoroughgoing sportsman as Tom to maintain a creditable appearance at Oxford on a penny less than six hundred pounds a year, setting aside such debts as the squire thought him bound to incur. A sense of what was due to his heir enabled him to face the necessity of reducing his stable and disposing of his cocks without grumbling or trying to impress Tom with the notion that he was fortunate to possess so generous a father; but he was not at all displeased when Tom said that he thought it would be a great waste of time for him to go up to Oxford, since he was not bookish, and would very likely be ploughed there. What with cocking and coursing, fishing and flapper-shooting in the summer, hunting and pheasant-shooting through the winter, acquiring a knowledge of farming from the bailiff, and learning how to manage the estate, he thought he would be much better employed at home. He was allowed to have his way, the Squire resolving to arrange for him to be given a little town polish when he should be rather older.

Except for one or two visits to friends living in a different part of the country he had been at home for a year now, enjoying himself very much, and justifying his father's secret pride in him by taking as much interest in crops as in hounds, and rapidly becoming as popular with the villagers as he was with the neighbouring gentry.

He was a pleasant youth, sturdy rather than tall, with a fresh, open countenance, unaffected manners, and as much of the good sense which characterized his father as was to be expected of a young gentleman of nineteen summers. From the circumstances of his being an only child he had from his earliest youth looked upon Phoebe, just his own age, as a sister; and since she had been, as a child, perfectly ready to engage with him on whatever dangerous pursuit he might suggest to her, besides very rapidly becoming a first-rate horsewoman, and a devil to go, not even his first terms at Rugby had led him to despise her company.

When Phoebe divulged to him her astonishing tidings, he was as incredulous as Susan had been, for, as he pointed out with brotherly candour, she was not at all the sort of girl to achieve a brilliant marriage. She agreed to this, and he added kindly: 'I don't mean to say that I wouldn't as lief be married to you as to some high flyer, for if I was obliged to marry anyone I think I'd offer for you rather than any other girl I know.'

She thanked him.

'Yes, but I'm not a fashionable duke,' he pointed out. 'Besides, I've known you all my life. I'm dashed if I understand why this duke should have taken a fancy to you! It isn't as though you was a beauty, and whenever your mother-in-law is near you behave like a regular pea-goose, so how he could have guessed you ain't a ninnyhammer I can't make out!'

'Oh, he didn't! He wishes to marry me because his mama was a friend of mine.'

'That *must* be a bag of moonshine!' said Tom scornfully. 'As though anyone would offer for a girl for such a reason as that!'

'I think,' said Phoebe, 'it is on account of his being a person of great consequence, and wishing to make a suitable alliance, and not caring whether I am pretty, or conversible.'

'He can't think you suitable!' objected Tom. 'He sounds to me a regular knock-in-the-cradle! It may be a fine thing to become a duchess, but I should think you had much better not!'

'No, no, but what am I to do, Tom? For heaven's sake don't tell me I have only to decline the Duke's offer, for you at least know what Mama is like! Even if I had the courage to disobey her only think what misery I should be obliged to endure! And don't tell me not to regard it, because to be in disgrace for weeks and weeks, as I would be, so sinks my spirits that I can't even *write*! I know it's idiotish of me, but I can't overcome my dread of being in her black books! I feel as if I were withering!'

He had too often seen her made ill by unkindness to think her words over-fanciful. It was strange that a girl so physically intrepid should have so much sensibility. In his own phrase, he knew her for a right one; but he knew also that in a censorious atmosphere her spirits were swiftly overpowered, none of her struggles to support them alleviating the oppression which transformed her from the neck-or-nothing girl whom no oxer could daunt to the shrinking miss whose demeanour was as meek as her conversation was insipid. He said, rather doubtfully: 'You don't think, if you were to write to him, Lord Marlow would put the Duke off?'

'You know what Papa is!' she said simply. 'He will always allow himself to be ruled by Mama, because he can't bear to be made uncomfortable. Besides, how could I get a letter to him without Mama's knowing of it?'

He considered for a few moments, frowning. 'No. Well–You are quite *sure* you can't like the Duke? I mean, I should have supposed anything to be better than to continue living at Austerby. Besides, you said yourself you only once talked to him. You don't really know anything about him. I daresay he may be rather shy, and that, you know, might easily make him appear stiff.'

'He is not shy and he is not stiff,' stated Phoebe. 'His manners are assured; he says everything that is civil because he places himself on so high a form that he would think it unworthy of himself to treat anyone with anything but cool courtesy; and because he knows his consequence to be so great he cares nothing for what anyone may think of him.'

'You *did* take him in dislike, didn't you?' said Tom, grinning at her.

'Yes, I did! But even if I had not, how could I accept an offer from him when I made him the villain in my story?'

That made Tom laugh. 'Well, you needn't tell him that, you goose!'

'Tell him! He won't need telling! I described him *exactly*!'

'But, Phoebe, you don't suppose he will *read* your book, do you?' said Tom.

Phoebe could support with equanimity disparagement of her person, but this slight cast on her first novel made her exclaim indignantly: 'Pray, why should he not read it? It is going to be *published*!'

'Yes, I know, but you can't suppose that people like Salford will buy it.'

'Then who will?' demanded Phoebe, rather flushed.

'Oh, I don't know! Girls, I daresay, who like that sort of thing.'

'You liked it well enough!' she reminded him.

'Yes, but that was because it was so odd to think of your having written it,' explained Tom. He saw that she was looking mortified, and added consolingly: 'But I'm not bookish, you know, so I daresay it's very fine, and will sell a great many copies. The thing is that no one will know who wrote it, so there's no need to tease yourself over *that*. When does the Duke come to Austerby?'

'Next week. It is given out that he is coming to try the young chestnut. He is going to hunt too, and now Mama is trying to decide whether to dish up all our friends to entertain him at a dinner-party, or to leave it to Papa to invite Sir Gregory Standish and old Mr Hayle for a game of whist.'

'Lord!' said Tom, in an awed tone.

Phoebe gave a giggle. '*That* will teach him to come to Austerby in this odious, condescending way!' she observed, with satisfaction. 'What is more, Mama does not approve of newfangled fashions, so his grace will find himself sitting down to dinner at six o'clock, which is not at all the style of thing he is accustomed to. And when he comes into the drawing-room after dinner he will discover that Miss Battery has brought Susan and Mary down. And then Mama will call upon me to go to the pianoforte—she has told Sibby already to be sure I know my new piece thoroughly!—and at nine o'clock Firbank will bring in the tea-tray; and at half past nine she will tell the Duke, in that complacent voice of hers, that we keep early hours in the country; and so he will be left to Papa and piquet, or some such thing. I wish he may be heartily bored!'

'I should think he would be. Perhaps he won't offer for you after all!' said Tom.

'How can I dare to indulge that hope, when all his reason for visiting us is to do so?' demanded Phoebe, sinking back into gloom. 'His mind must be perfectly made up, for he knows already that I am a dead bore! Oh, Tom, I am *trying* to take it with composure, but the more I think of it the more clearly do I see that I shall be forced into this dreadful marriage, and I feel sick with apprehension already, and there is no one to take my part, no one!'

'Stubble it!' ordered Tom, giving her a shake. 'Talking such slum to me! Let me tell you, my girl, that there's not only me to take your part, but my father and mother as well!'

She squeezed his hand gratefully. 'I know you would, Tom, and Mrs

Orde has always been so kind, but—it wouldn't answer! You know Mama!'

He did, but said, looking pugnacious: 'If she tries to bully you into this, and your father don't prevent her, you needn't think I shall stand by like a gapeseed! If the worst comes to the worst, Phoebe, you'd best marry me. I daresay we shouldn't think it so very bad, once we had grown accustomed to it. At all events, I'd rather marry you than leave you in the suds! What the devil are you laughing at?'

'You, of course! Now, Tom, don't be gooseish! When Mama is so afraid we might fall in love that she has almost forbidden you to come within our gates! She wouldn't hear of it, or Mr Orde either, I daresay!'

'I know that. It would have to be a Gretna Green marriage, of course.'

She gave a gasp. 'Gretna Green? Of all the hare-brained—No, really, Tom, how can you be so tottyheaded? I may be a hoyden, but I'm not abandoned! Why, I wouldn t do such a shocking thing even if I were in love with you!'

'Oh, very well!' he said, a trifle sulkily. '*I* don't want to do it, and if you prefer to marry Salford there's no more to be said.'

She rubbed her cheek against his shoulder. 'Indeed, I am very much obliged to you!' she said contritely. 'Don't be vexed with me!'

He was secretly so much relieved by her refusal to accept his offer that after telling her severely that it would be well if she learned to reject such offers with more civility he relented, owned that a runaway marriage was not quite the thing, and ended by promising to lend his aid in any scheme she might hit on for her deliverance.

None occurred to her. Lady Marlow took her to Bath to have her hair cut in a smarter crop, and to buy a new dress, in which, presumably, she was to captivate the Duke. But as Lady Marlow considered white, or the palest of blues and pinks, the only colours seemly for a débutante, and nothing showed her to worse advantage, it was hard to perceive how this staggering generosity was to achieve its end.

Two days before the arrival of Lord Marlow and the Duke it began to seem as if one at least of the schemes for his entertainment was to be frustrated. Lord Marlow's coachman, a weather-wise person, prophesied that snow was on the way; and an item in the *Morning Chronicle* carried the information that there had been heavy falls already in the north and east. A hope, never very strong, that the Duke would postpone his visit wilted when no message was brought to Austerby from its master, and was speedily followed by something very like panic. If the Duke, who was coming ostensibly to see how he liked the young chestnut's performance in the hunting-field, was undeterred by the threat of snow he must be determined indeed to prosecute his suit; and if there were no hunting to remove him during the hours of daylight from the house he would have plenty of opportunity to do it. Try as she would Phoebe could not persuade herself that the weather, which had been growing steadily colder, showed any sign of improvement; and when the Squire cancelled the first meeting of the week, and followed that up by going away to Bristol, where some business had been for some time awaiting his attention, it was easy to see that he, the best weather-prophet in the district, had no expectation of being able to take his hounds out for several days at least.

It was very cold, but no snow had fallen when Lord Marlow, pardonably pleased with himself, arrived at Austerby, bringing Sylvester with him. He whispered in his wife's ear: 'You see that I have brought him!' but it would have been more accurate to have said that he had been brought by Sylvester, since he had accomplished the short journey in Sylvester's curricle, his own and Sylvester's chaise following with their valets, and all their baggage. The rear of this cavalcade was brought up, some time later, by his lordship's hunters, in charge of his head groom, and several underlings. Sylvester, it appeared, had sent his own horses back to Chance from Blandford Park. Keighley, the middle-aged groom who had taught him to ride his first pony, was perched up behind him in the curricle; but although the postilions in charge of his chaise wore his livery the younger Misses Marlow, watching the arrivals from an upper window, were sadly disappointed in the size of his entourage. It was rather less impressive than Papa's, except that Papa had not taken his curricle to Blandford Park, which, after all, he might well have done. However, his chaise was drawn by a team of splendid match-bays; the pair of beautiful gray steppers harnessed to the curricle were undoubtedly what Papa would call complete to a shade; and to judge from the way this vehicle swept into view round a bend in the avenue the Duke was no mere whipster. Mary said hopefully that perhaps this would make Phoebe like him better.

Phoebe, in fact, was not privileged to observe Sylvester's arrival, but since she had frequently seen him driving his high-perch phaeton in Hyde Park, and already knew him to be at home to a peg, her sentiments would scarcely have undergone a change if she had seen how stylishly he took the awkward turn in the avenue. She was with Lady Marlow in one of the saloons, setting reluctant stitches in a piece of embroidery stretched on a tambour-frame. She wore the white gown purchased in Bath; and as this had tiny puff sleeves, and the atmosphere in the saloon, in spite of quite a large fire, was chilly, her thin, bare arms showed an unattractive expanse of gooseflesh. To Lady Marlow's eye, however, she presented as good an appearance as could have been hoped for. Dress, occupation, and pose befitted the maiden of impeccable birth and upbringing: Lady Marlow was able to congratulate herself on her excellent management: if the projected match fell through it would not, she knew, be through any fault of hers.

The gentlemen entered the room, Lord Marlow ushering Sylvester in with a jovial word, and exclaiming: 'Ah, I thought we should find you here, my love! I do not have to present the Duke, for I fancy you are already acquainted. And Phoebe, too! you know my daughter, Salford—my little Phoebe! Well, now what could be more comfortable? Just a quiet family party, as I promised you: no ceremony—you take your pot-luck with us!'

Sylvester, uttering his practised civilities as he shook hands with his hostess, was out of humour. He had had time enough in which to regret having accepted Marlow's invitation, and he had been wishing himself otherwhere ever since leaving Blandford Park. His lordship's prowess in the hunting-field was forgotten, and the tedium of his conversation re-membered; and long before Austerby was reached he had contrived not only to bore Sylvester, but to set up his back as well. Naturally expansive, he had not deemed it necessary, once he was sure of his noble guest, to maintain the discretion imposed on him by Lady Ingham. He had let several broad hints drop. They had fallen on infertile soil, their only effect having been to ruffle Sylvester's temper. He had told Sylvester, too, that he would find himself the only guest at Austerby, which was by no means what Sylvester had bargained for, since such an arrangement lent to his visit a particularity he had been anxious to avoid. Whatever his lordship might have said about not standing on ceremony with him he had supposed that he would find several other persons gathered at Austerby, for form's sake, if not in an endeavour to render his chief guest's stay agreeable. His lordship, concluded Sylvester, was devilish anxious to get his daughter off; but if he imagined that the head of the great house of Rayne could be jockeyed into taking one step not of his own choosing he would very soon learn his mistake. It had then occurred to Sylvester that he might be said to have taken one such step already, in coming to Austerby: a reflection which piqued him so much that he decided, a little viciously, that unless Miss Marlow proved to be something quite out of the common way he would have nothing to say to the proposed connection.

This unamiable resolve was strengthened by his first impression of Austerby. One swift glance round the entrance hall was enough to convince him that it was not at all the sort of household he liked. The furniture was arranged with rigid formality; the small fire smouldering on the hearth was inadequate to overcome the icy nature of several draughts; and although there was really no fault to be found with the butler, or with the two London-bred footmen, who relieved the gentlemen of their coats and hats, Sylvester was sure that the establishment would be found to be under-staffed. It would not surprise him to learn that a female presided over the kitchen; and he had little doubt that there was no groom of the chambers to attend to the comfort of visitors. The fact that he frequently stayed in houses by far less magnificent than his own and never gave the size and style of their domestic arrangement a thought did not, in his present mood, occur to him; and the knowledge that he was so severely critical of Lord Marlow's house would have greatly astonished a number of his less affluent friends and relations. One of his favourite cousins, a lively young woman married to an impecunious Major of Dragoon Guards, would, indeed, have been incredulous, since none of the visitors to her modest establishment was more adaptable than he, or more ready to be pleased with his entertainment. But Sylvester liked Major and Mrs Newbury; Lord Marlow he was in a fair way to disliking cordially.

He was received by Lady Marlow in what her lord recognized as her most gracious manner. It struck Sylvester as condescending, and he was taken aback by it.

He turned from her to meet Miss Marlow, and his gloomiest forebodings were realized. She had neither beauty nor countenance, her complexion was poor and her figure worse, her dress was tasteless, and the colourless voice in which she murmured how-do-you-do confirmed him in his instant belief that she was insipid. He wondered how soon he would be able to bring his visit to an end.

'You will remember my little Phoebe, Salford,' persevered Lord Marlow optimistically. 'You have danced with her in London, haven't you?'

'Of course—yes!' said Sylvester. He perceived that more was required of him, and fired a shot at a fairly safe venture. 'At Almack's was it not?'

'No,' said Phoebe. 'At the Seftons' ball. When you saw me at Almack's I don't think you recognized me.'

This girl, thought Sylvester indignantly, wants conduct as well as countenance! Is she trying to put me to the blush? Very well, Miss Marlow! Aloud, he said lightly: 'How rude of me! But perhaps I *didn't* see you.' Then he perceived that she had flushed up to the roots of her hair, her eyes flying to her mother-in-law's face, and he remembered that Lady Ingham had said she did not show to advantage in Lady Marlow's presence. A glance at this lady surprised a quelling stare directed at Phoebe, and he was a little sorry: enough to make him add: 'I have frequently been accused of cutting people at Almack's. But the Assemblies have becomes such shocking squeezes that it is wonderful if one can discover one's oldest friends amongst such a press of persons.'

'Yes, it—it is—isn't it?' stammered Phoebe.

'Pray be seated, Duke!' commanded Lady Marlow. 'You have been staying with the Beauforts. You are a hunting-man, I collect. I am not myself a friend to the sport, but Marlow is greatly addicted to it.'

'Oh, you must not talk so to Salford!' said Lord Marlow. 'He is a clipping rider, you know: showed us all the way!'

Beyond directing an enigmatical look at his host Sylvester made no response to this piece of flattery. Lady Marlow said that she believed the Duke of Beaufort to be a very worthy man, but as she followed up this encomium by deploring the dandyism of his heir the conversation did not prosper. Lord Marlow struck in with a sporting anecdote, and Phoebe, picking up her tambour-frame and setting another crooked stitch, sat listening for the next twenty minutes to a three-cornered dialogue that would have diverted her had it not vexed her too much to seem amusing. Lady Marlow's part in it took the form of a series of statements, which, according to her custom, she announced in a fashion that admitted of no argument; Lord Marlow, in an effort to check her, broke in whenever he could with a flow of jovial remarks and reminiscences, all of which were extremely trivial; and Sylvester, civil, and cool, and unhelpful, replied to each of his hosts in turn, and encouraged neither.

To hear her father striving with such eager anxiety to engage Sylvester's interest very soon made Phoebe angry. He was an inveterate talker, and his most fervent admirers could scarcely have called him a sensible man, but he was a much older man than Sylvester, he was doing his best to please, and she thought it detestable of Sylvester to accord him nothing but polite tolerance. Her dislike of him grew to such large proportions that when Lady Marlow announced that they dined at six o'clock she was almost disappointed to see that he bore the announcement with fortitude. Fuel for her rancour would have been supplied by the knowledge, could she but have come by it, that it was just what he had expected.

When she entered her chilly bedchamber to change her dress for dinner Phoebe found a screw of paper stuck into the frame of the looking-glass, and realized, as she drew it out and unfolded it, that it must have been put there by Firbank, the butler, whose extraordinary grimaces, as she had passed him in the hall in the wake of Lady Marlow, she had been quite unable to interpret. She saw that it was from Tom, but its message was slightly disappointing. After informing her that he was on his way to dine with friends he added that he should leave betimes, and drop in at Austerby on his way home to learn how she had gone on. *'I have greased Firbank in the fist, and he will let me in the side-door, and says we shall be safe in the morning-room, so come there before you retire to bed. By the bye, the Mail was four hours late reaching Bath today on account of snow as far as Reading. I shouldn't wonder at it if you had this Duke of yours quartered on you for a se'enight.'*

At Austerby Phoebe did not enjoy the luxury of an abigail, so there was no one to compel her to spend more time than was strictly necessary over the changing of her dress. She made haste out of her muslin frock and arrayed herself in a somewhat scrambling way in the evening-gown prescribed by Lady Marlow. It was as unbecoming to her as the muslin, but beyond combing out her ringlets and clasping a string of pearls round her throat she made no attempt to render herself more presentable. Her ears were on the prick to catch the sounds of male voices. When she heard these, and knew that her father was escorting the Duke to his bedchamber, her toilet was done. Wrapping a shawl round her shoulders she slipped out of her room, and across the hall to Lord Marlow's dressing-room.

'Papa, may I speak to you?'

His valet was with him, and he had already put off his coat, but being naturally affable he was about to welcome his daughter, when he saw that she was labouring under barely repressed agitation, and he at once felt uneasy. He said in a bluff voice: 'Well, unless it is of immediate importance, my dear—'

'It is of most immediate importance, Papa!'

His uneasiness grew. 'Oh, well, then—! Well, I can spare you five minutes, I daresay!'

His valet went out of the room. Hardly had he shut the door than Phoebe said breathlessly: 'Papa, I wish to tell you–I cannot like the Duke of Salford!'

He stood there staring at her, at first aghast, and then, as a sense of ill-usage crept over him, with gathering choler. He said explosively: 'Well, upon my word, Phoebe! A fine moment you have chosen to break this news to me!'

'How could I break it to you earlier? If you had but told me before you went to Blandford Park what you intended! Papa, you know Mama would never have permitted me to send a servant there with a letter from me, begging you to go no further in the business! Oh, pray, Papa, don't be angry! Indeed, it is not my fault you were kept in ignorance of–of my sentiments upon this occasion!'

The colour in his florid cheeks darkened; he really did feel that he had been abominably used. His pride in having contrived to draw the Duke into Lady Ingham's net had been great; already he was three parts persuaded that the scheme had been all his own, and that he had been put to considerable trouble on his daughter's behalf. Now it seemed that his care was to be thrown away. That was bad; and still worse would be the awkwardness of his situation, if he were obliged to inform Sylvester that Phoebe would have none of him. In an attempt to turn aside her protests, he said: 'Pooh, nonsense! The merest irritation of nerves, my dear! You are shy–yes, yes, you are shy, I say, and who should know better than your father? You have a great deal of sensibility–I always thought it had been wiser not to have told you what Salford's purpose was in visiting us, but your mama–however, that's nothing to the purpose now the mischief has been done! Your senses are in disorder! I don't deny that your situation is embarrassing. I declare I am vexed to death that your mama should have–But you will not regard it! I assure you, I have given a great deal of thought to this matter, and am satisfied that Salford will make you an amiable husband. You will allow that I am more fitted to be the judge of a man's character than you! Well, I am satisfied with Salford: he is as sound as a roast!' He gave his hearty laugh, and added: 'I am prepared to wager the day is not far distant when you will wonder how you can have been such a goose! How I shall joke you about it!'

'Papa, I cannot like him!' she repeated.

'For God's sake, girl, don't talk such fustian!' he said irascibly. 'You are barely acquainted with him! A pretty pass we have come to when a chit of a girl holds up her nose at a man of Salford's estate! Let me tell you that you should rather be blessing yourself for your good fortune!'

She said imploringly: 'Papa, you know I would not willingly displease you, but—'

'Very fine talking!' he interrupted. 'You haven't a penny-worth's consideration for me! What a fix you would put me in! Good God, it is beyond anything! So I am to inform Salford you cannot like him! Upon my word, it puts me out of all heart, I declare to heaven it does! Here am I, putting myself to all this trouble—ay, and expense! for if Salford should take a fancy to the young chestnut I must let him have the horse at a price that will put me sadly out of pocket, of course. Not to mention the new dress that was purchased for you, and I dare not say how many bottles of the good claret! A hundred pounds I paid for one hogshead, and no more than fifty bottles left, by what Firbank tells me. Carbonnell's Best!'

'Papa—'

'Don't talk to me!' he said, lashing himself into a weak man's rage. 'I have no patience left to speak to you! And what your mama will say—!'

'Oh, you won't tell her! *Surely* you won't?' she cried. 'You could tell the Duke—that you find you were mistaken in my sentiments, so that he won't propose to me! Papa—!'

'If I am to be put into such a position she must know the whole!' he said, taking instant advantage of her fright. 'I should be sorry indeed if I were obliged to divulge to her what has passed between us, but if you continue in this obstinacy I must do so. Now, my dear child, consider! Salford has had no opportunity to fix his interest with you: at least grant him that opportunity! If you find you are still unable to like him when he has been staying with us some few days, we will talk of this again. Meanwhile I shall say nothing of this interview to Mama, and you need not either. There, I fancy your senses are in a way to being straight again, are they not?' He gave her shoulder a pat. 'Now I must send you away, or Salford will be down before me. I am not vexed with you: you have sometimes an odd kick in your gallop, but you are a good girl at heart, and you know you may trust your father!'

She went away without another word. The optimistic trend of his mind made it easy for him to believe that he had talked her into submission, but the truth was she knew him too well to persevere. His dislike of finding himself in an uncomfortable predicament was stronger than his love for his children; so far from trusting him she felt sure that before he slept that night he would have told his wife the whole. He would not bring pressure to bear upon his daughter, for that would be uncomfortable too; but he would look the other way while his wife did so.

Until the morning Phoebe thought she must be safe from attack. There was not much time left to her to think of some means of escape from a fate that had begun to seem inevitable; and she could look for no help from any inmate of Austerby. To ask it of Miss Battery would be not only to place the governess in a position of great difficulty, but to ensure her being dismissed from her post under such conditions as must make it hard indeed for her to establish herself in another household. Tom could be relied on to do whatever was required of him, but it was hard to see how his support could be of assistance. She could think of no one but her grandmother who might be able to lend her effective aid. She was not intimately acquainted with Lady Ingham, but she knew her to be well disposed towards her, and she knew too that she held Lady Marlow in contempt and dislike. If Austerby had been within reach of London, Phoebe would have had no hesitation in claiming her protection. But Austerby was ninety miles from London. It would be useless to write a letter, for it was not to be supposed that an invalid would come posting into Somerset to rescue her in the middle of a hard winter, and although Grandmama had several times shown herself to be more than a match for Mama when they had met face to face, at a distance Mama would have everything all her own way.

Even as her spirits sank under these reflections Phoebe remembered Tom, who was coming to see her this evening. Hope began to flower; she began to weave plans; and became so absorbed in these that she forgot she had been ordered to attend Lady Marlow in her room as soon as she was dressed, and instead made her way to the gallery in which it was the bleak custom of the family to assemble before dinner.

6

Sylvester was in the gallery, alone, and glancing through the pages of a periodical. He was standing in front of the fire, which was burning sluggishly, and every now and then gave forth a plume of smoke. He was dressed with his usual quiet elegance in a black coat and pantaloons, and a plain white waistcoat. A single fob hung at his waist, a single diamond glinted from between the folds of his neckcloth, and one ring, his heavy signet, adorned his hand. He adopted none of the extravagances of the dandy-set, but his air was one of decided fashion, and the exquisite cut of his coat made Phoebe feel more than ordinarily dowdy.

She was startled to find him in the gallery, and checked on the threshold, exclaiming involuntarily: 'Oh—!'

He looked up in faint surprise. After a moment he put the periodical down, and said pleasantly: 'It's a bad guest, is it not, who comes down before his host? Let me draw a chair to the fire for you! It is smoking a trifle, but not enough, I am sure, to signify.'

The acid note was faint, but it did not escape her. She came reluctantly down the gallery, saying as she seated herself in the chair he had pulled forward: 'All the chimneys smoke at Austerby when the wind is in the north-east.'

Having received abundant evidence of the truth of this statement in the bedchamber allotted to him, he did not question it, merely replying: 'Indeed? Every house has its peculiarities, I fancy.'

'Do none of the chimneys smoke in your house?' she asked.

'I believe they were used to, but it was found possible to remedy the fault,' he said, conveniently forgetting how often in exasperation at finding the hall at Chance dense with smoke, he had sworn to replace its mediaeval fireplace with a modern grate.

'How fortunate!' remarked Phoebe.

Silence fell. Miss Marlow sat gazing abstractedly at a Buhl cabinet; and his grace of Salford, unaccustomed to such treatment, eyed her in gathering resentment. He was much inclined to pick up the newspaper again, and was only deterred from doing so by the reflection that disgust at her want of conduct was no excuse for lowering his own standard of good manners. He said in the voice of one trying to set a bashful schoolgirl at her ease: 'Your father tells me, Miss Marlow, that you are a notable horsewoman.'

'Does he?' she responded. 'Well, he told us that you showed him the way with the Heythrop.'

He glanced quickly down at her, but decided, after an instant, that this remark sprang from inanity. 'I imagine I need not tell you that I did no such thing!'

'Oh, no! I am very sure you did not,' she said.

He almost jumped; and being now convinced that this seeming *gaucherie* was deliberate began to feel as much interested as he was ruffled. Perhaps there was rather more to this little provincial that he had supposed, though why she should utter malicious remarks he was at a loss to understand. It was coming it too strong if she was piqued by his failure to recall on what occasion he had danced with her: did she think he could remember every insignificant girl with whom he had been obliged to stand up for one country dance? And what the devil did she mean by relapsing again into indifferent silence? He tried a new tack: 'It is now your turn, Miss Marlow, to start a topic for conversation!'

She withdrew her gaze from the cabinet, and directed it at him for a dispassionate moment. 'I haven't any conversation,' she said.

He hardly knew whether to be diverted or vexed; he was certainly intrigued, and had just decided that although he had not the remotest intention of offering for this outrageous girl, it might not be unamusing to discover what (if anything) lay behind her odd manners when Lady Marlow came into the gallery. Finding her guest there before her she pointed out to him that he was in advance of the hour, which nettled him into replying: 'You must blame the wind for being in the north-east, ma'am.'

The shaft went wide. 'You mistake, Duke: no blame attaches to your being so early. Indeed, I consider it a good fault! My daughter has been entertaining you, I see. What have you been talking of together, I wonder?'

'We can scarcely be said to have talked of anything,' replied Sylvester. 'Miss Marlow informs me that she has no conversation.'

He glanced at Phoebe as he spoke, and encountered such a burning look of reproach that he repented, and tried to mend matters by adding with a laugh: 'In point of fact, ma'am, Miss Marlow entered the room a bare minute before yourself, so we have had little opportunity to converse.'

'My daughter-in-law is shy,' said Lady Marlow, with a look at Phoebe which promised signal vengeance presently.

It occurred to Sylvester that after her first start of surprise Phoebe had not appeared to be at all shy. He remembered that Lady Ingham had said she was not just in the ordinary style, and wondered if there might be something more in her than he had as yet detected. Since she was making no effort to engage his interest he concluded that she did not know that he had come to Austerby to look her over. That made it fairly safe to try whether he could charm her out of her farouche behaviour. He smiled at her, and said: 'I must hope, then, that she will not be too shy to converse with me when we are a little better acquainted.'

But by the time he rose from the dinner-table all desire to become better acquainted with Phoebe had left him, and the only thing he did desire was an excuse to leave Austerby not later than the following morning. As he sat through an interminable dinner, enduring on one side a monologue delivered by his hostess, at her most consequential, on such topics of interest as the defections of the latest incumbent of the Parish, the excellence of the Bishop, the decay of modern manners, and the customs obtaining in her dear father's household; and on the other a series of sporting recollections from his host, the look of the satyr became ever more strongly marked on his countenance. Never had he been subjected to such treatment as he was meeting with at Austerby! When he accepted invitations to stay with friends he knew that he would find himself one of a party composed of agreeable persons, with whom he was well acquainted; and that every form of sport or amusement would be provided for their entertainment. One hunted, or one shot; and if the weather became inclement one played at whist, and billiards, took part in theatricals, danced at impromptu balls, and flirted desperately with the prettiest of the ladies. That was how he entertained his own guests: so much the way of his world that it never occurred to him that quite a number of the hostesses who secured him for their parties put forth their best efforts to entertain him royally. But when he found himself the sole guest at Austerby, had been promised by his host an evening's whist with two obscure country gentlemen; and, by his hostess, the felicity of meeting the Bishop of Bath and Wells, it occurred to him forcibly that in making no proper provision for his entertainment Lord Marlow had been guilty of a social solecism.

He had been received by a hostess who seemed to think she was conferring a high treat upon him. He was contemptuous of flattery, he disliked toad-eaters, he did not consciously expect to be welcomed with distinction, but to be met with condescension was a new experience which set him instantly on his high ropes.

His bedchamber was rendered untenable by the smoke which gushed from the chimney; the water in the brass ewer had been tepid, so that his valet had had to fetch a fresh supply from the kitchens; the eldest daughter of the house had uttered no more than half a dozen sentences since they had entered the dining-room; and although Lord Marlow's wines were good, the dinner set before the company was as commonplace as it was long drawn out.

By the time Lord Marlow, promising some rubbers of piquet later in the evening, took him to join the ladies in the drawing-room, he had resigned himself to boredom; but when the first object to meet his gaze, upon entering the room, was a grim female, dressed in black bombazine and seated bolt upright in a chair slightly drawn back from the circle round the fire, he realized that he had grossly underestimated the horrors that lay before him. Besides the grim female two schoolgirls had joined the party, the elder a bouncing young woman with a high complexion, and her father's rather protuberant blue eyes; the younger a sallow girl too bashful to speak above a whisper or without blushing fierily from neck to brow. Lady Marlow made them both known to him, but ignored the claims of the grim lady to a share of his civility. He concluded that she must be the governess; and instantly determined to show his hostess what he thought of her insufferable manners. He favoured Miss Battery with a slight bow, and his most pleasant smile, and directed at Lady Marlow an enquiring look she was unable to ignore.

'Oh—! My daughters' governess,' she said shortly. 'Pray come to the fire, Duke!'

Sylvester, choosing instead a chair rather nearer to Miss Battéry than to the fireside party, addressed a civil remark to her. She answered it with composure, but gruffly, looking at him with unnerving fixity.

Lord Marlow, always very easy and good-natured with his dependants, then added to his wife's displeasure by saying: 'Ah, Miss Battery! I have not seen you since I came home! How do you go on? But I need not ask: you are always well!'

That gave Sylvester the opportunity to ask her if she were related to a family of the same name living in Norfolk. She replied: 'Shouldn't think so, sir. Never heard of them until your grace mentioned them.'

As the family had no existence outside his imagination this was not surprising; but his question seemed to have broken the ice: Miss Battery, appearing slightly mollified, disclosed that she came from Hertfordshire.

Lady Marlow, breaking rudely in on this, said loudly that she had no doubt the Duke would enjoy a little music, and waved Phoebe towards the pianoforte.

Phoebe was an indifferent performer, but as neither her father nor Lady Marlow was at all musical they were perfectly satisfied, as long as she did not falter, or play any unmistakably wrong notes. Sylvester was not musical either, but he had been used to listen to the first musicians of the day, and thought he had never heard anyone play with less taste or feeling. He could only be thankful that she did not play the harp; but when, in response to some affectionate urging from her father, she sang an old ballad in a small, wooden voice he was much inclined to think that even a harp might have been preferable.

At half past eight the schoolroom party withdrew, and after half an hour's desultory conversation the tea-tray was brought in. Sylvester saw the end of his purgatory, and so it was. Punctually at half past nine Lady Marlow informed him that they kept early hours at Austerby, bade him a formal good-night, and went away, with Phoebe following in her wake. As they mounted the stairs she said complacently that the evening had gone off very well. She added that although she feared the Duke was a man of fashion, she was on the whole pleased with him. 'Your father informs me that hunting will be out of the question tomorrow,' she observed. 'If it should not be snowing I shall suggest to Salford that he might like to walk with you and your sisters. Miss Battery will accompany you, of course, but I shall tell her she may fall behind, with the girls, and give her a hint at the same time not to be putting herself forward, as I was excessively surprised to see her doing this evening.'

This programme, which, a few hours earlier, would have appalled her, Phoebe listened to with a calm born of her fixed resolve to be gone from Austerby long before it could be put into execution. Parting from Lady Marlow at the head of the stairs she went away to her bedchamber, knowing that both Susan and Miss Battery would come to her there, and that it would consequently be dangerous to repair to the morning-room before she had received these visitors.

Susan was soon got rid of; but Miss Battery, who followed her, showed a disposition to linger. Seating herself at the foot of the bed, and tucking her hands into the sleeves of her thick woollen dressing-gown, she told Phoebe that she thought she had done Sylvester less than justice.

'Sibby! You did not *like* him?' cried Phoebe.

'Don't know him well enough to like him. I didn't *dis*like him, at all events. No reason why I should: very civil to me!'

'Yes, to vex Mama!' Phoebe said shrewdly. 'He was wanting to give her a set-down all through dinner!'

'Well,' said Miss Battery, 'can't blame him for that! Shouldn't say so, of course, but there it is! Got a charming smile too.'

'I haven't observed it.'

'You wouldn't have taken him in such aversion if you had. *I* observed it.'

What's more,' added Miss Battery candidly, 'he bore your playing very well, you know. Most truly the gentleman! He must be bent on making you an offer to have solicited you for another song.'

She remained for several more minutes, but finding Phoebe deaf to whatever she chose to advance in Sylvester's favour she presently went away; and Phoebe, after a discreet interval, slipped out of her room, and along the corridor to the west wing of the house. Here, besides the schoolroom, the nurseries, and various bedchambers, the morning-room was situated, a shabby apartment which, while still dignified by its original title, had dwindled into a mere sewing-room. It was lit by an oil lamp set in the middle of a bare table; and by this indifferent light young Mr Orde, his overcoat buttoned up to his throat, sat reading a book of Household Hints, which was all the literature the room afforded. He seemed to have found it rewarding, for upon Phoebe's entrance he looked up, and said with a grin: 'I say, Phoebe, this is a famous good book! It tells you how to preserve tripe to go to the East Indies–which is just the sort of thing one might want to know any day of the week. All you need do is to *Get a fine Belly of Tripe, quite fresh—*'

'Ugh!' shuddered Phoebe, carefully shutting the door. 'How horrid! Do put the book away!'

'All in good time! If you don't want to know how to preserve tripe, what about an *Excellent Dish for six or seven Persons for the Expense of Sixpence*? Just the thing for the ducal kitchens, *I* think! It's made with calf's lights, and bread, and fat, and some sheeps' guts, and—'

'How can you be so absurd? Stop reading that nonsense!' scolded Phoebe.

'*Nicely cleaned*,' pursued Tom. 'And if you don't fancy sheeps' guts you may take hogs', or—'

But at this point Phoebe seized the book, and after a slight struggle for possession he let her have it.

'For heaven's sake don't laugh so loud!' she begged him. 'The children's bedchamber is almost opposite this room! Oh, Tom, you can't conceive what a shocking evening I've spent! I begged Papa to send the Duke away, but he wouldn't, so I have made up my mind to go away myself.'

He was conscious of a sinking feeling at the pit of his stomach, but replied staunchly: 'Well, I told you I was game. I only hope we don't find the roads snow-bound in the north. Gretna Green it shall be!'

'Not so loud! Of course I'm not going to Gretna Green!' she said in an indignant under-voice. 'Keep your voice low, Tom! If Eliza were to wake and hear us talking she would tell Mama, as sure as check! Now listen! I thought it all out at dinner! I must go to London, to my grandmother. She told me once that I might depend on her to do all she could for me, and I think–oh, I am sure she would support me in this, if only she knew what was happening! The only thing is–Tom, you know Mama buys all my dresses, and lets me have very little pin-money! Could you–would you lend me the money for the coach-fare? I think it costs about five-and-thirty shillings for the ticket. And then there is the tip to the guard, and—'

'Yes, of course I'll lend you as much rhino as you want!' Tom interrupted. 'But you can't mean to travel to London on the stage!'

'Yes, I do. How could I go post, even I could afford to do so? There would be the hiring of the chaise, and then all the business of the changes–oh, no, it would be impossible! I haven't an abigail to go with me, remember! I shall be much safer in the common stage. And if I could contrive to get a seat in one of the fast day coaches—'

'Well, you couldn't. They are always booked up as full as they can hold in Bath, and if you aren't on the way-bill— Besides, if the snow is as deep beyond Reading as they say it is those coaches won't run.'

'Well, never mind! Any coach will serve, and I don't doubt I shall be able to get a place, because people won't care to travel in this weather, unless they are obliged. I have made up my mind to it that I must be gone from here before anyone can prevent me, very early in the morning. If I could reach Devizes–it is nearer than Calne, and I know some of the London coaches do take that road–only I shall have a portmanteau to carry, and perhaps a bandbox as well, so— Oh, Tom, could you, do you think, take me to Devizes in your gig?'

'Will you *stop* fretting and fuming?' he said severely. 'I'll take you anywhere you wish, but this scheme of yours— You know, I don't wish to throw a rub in the way, but I'm afraid it may not hold. This curst weather! A pretty piece of business it would be if you were to get no farther than Reading! It might well turn out so, and then it would be all holiday with you.'

'No, no, I have thought of that already! If the coach goes on, I shall stay with it, but if the snow is very bad I know just what I must do. Do you remember Jane, that used to be the maid who waited on the nursery? Well, she married a corn-chandler, in a very good way of business, I believe, and lives at Reading. So, you see, if I can't travel beyond Reading I may go to her, and stay with her until the snow has melted!'

'Stay in a corn-chandler's house?' he repeated, in accents of incredulity.

'Good God, why should I not? He is a very respectable man, and as for Jane, she will take excellent care of me, I can assure you! I suppose you had rather I stayed in a public inn?'

'No, that I wouldn't! But—' He paused, not liking the scheme, yet unable to think of a better.

She began to coax him, representing to him the advantages of her plan, and all the hopelessness of her situation if she were forced to remain at Austerby. He was easily convinced of this, for it did indeed seem to him that without her father's support her case was desperate. Nor could he deny that her grandmother was the very person to shield her; but it took a little time to persuade him that neither danger nor impropriety would attend her journey to London in a stage-coach. It was not until she told him that if he would not lend her his aid she meant to trudge to Devizes alone that he at last capitulated. Nothing remained, after that, but to arrange the details of her escape, and this was soon accomplished. Tom promised to have his gig waiting in the lane outside one of the farm gates of Austerby at seven o'clock on the following morning; Phoebe pledged herself not to keep him waiting there; and they parted, one of them full of confidence, the other trying to smother his uneasiness.

She was punctual at the rendezvous; he was not; and for twenty nerve-racking minutes she paced up and down the lane, in the lee of the hedge, her imagination running riot amongst the various disasters which might have overtaken him. The most likely of these was that he had overslept, a probability which added rage to her anxiety. It had been dark when she herself had dressed, and packed her night gear into the already bulging portmanteau, but by seven o'clock it was daylight, and at any moment, she felt, she might be discovered by some villager or farm-hand to whom she must be well known. The day was cheerless, the wind blowing from the north, and the clouds ominously thick. Anger and apprehension steadily mounted, but both were forgotten in surprise when Tom arrived on the scene, driving, instead of his gig, his father's curricle, with those two tidy brown steppers, Trusty and True, harnessed to it.

He pulled up beside her and commanded her, without preamble, to go to the horses' heads. She obeyed, but said, as he cast off the rug wrapped about his legs and jumped down into the road: 'But, Tom, how is this? Why have you brought the curricle? I am persuaded you ought not!'

He had picked up her portmanteau, and was lashing it quickly in place. 'Yes, I ought. Did you think I was never coming? I'm sorry to be so late, but, you see, I had to go back. We must put this bandbox under the seat.' He stowed it away as he spoke, and came striding up to her. 'I'll take 'em. Do you jump up, and take the ribbons! Take care! they haven't been out since my father went away, and they're as lively as be-damned! You will find my father's old driving-coat: put it on, and wrap that fur rug well round you! And don't waste time disputing!' he added.

She did as he bade her, but she was considerably astonished, and demanded, as soon as he had climbed up beside her, and taken the reins from her competent hands. 'Have you run mad, Tom? What in the world—'

'No, of course I haven't. The thing is I was the most complete gudgeon last night, not to have seen what I ought to do. Plain as a pikestaff, but it never occurred to me till I had actually set out to come to you. Mind you, I wasn't easy in my mind! Kept on waking up all night, wondering what I should do. It only came to me when I was on my way here, driving the gig. So I turned sharp about, scribbled a note for my mother, got Jem to fig out Trusty and True—'

'But *why*?' she interrupted.

'Going to take you to London myself,' he replied briefly.

Her first feeling was one of gratitude, but she was instantly assailed by qualms, and said: 'No, no, you can't do so, Tom!'

'Nonsense, what could be easier? Trusty and True are good for two full stages, and very likely more, if I don't press them. After that, of course, I must hire job-horses, but unless we learn at Reading that the road from there is too deep to make the attempt we shall be in London by tonight. I shan't try it, mind, if we get bad news at Reading! If that should be the case, I'll take you to this corn-chandler of yours, and put up myself at the Crown. The only thing is that you may find it pretty cold.'

'Oh, *that* doesn't signify! But indeed, Tom, I think you ought not! Perhaps—'

'Well, it makes no odds what you think,' he returned. 'I'm going to do it.'

'But Mrs Orde—your father—'

'I *know* my father would say I shouldn't let you go alone; and as for Mama, she won't be thrown into a pucker, because I dashed off a note to her, telling her she need not be. And don't you fly into one of your fusses either! I didn't say where I was taking you, but only that I was obliged to rescue you from that Duke, and very likely should be away from home for a little while. So that's all right and tight.'

She could not be perfectly satisfied, but since there was plainly no hope of turning Tom from his purpose, and she was besides thankful not to be obliged to journey alone to London, she said no more to dissuade him.

'That's a good girl!' he said, correctly interpreting her silence. 'Lord, I call it a famous lark, don't you? If only we don't run into snow, and I must own I don't like the look of the sky above half.'

'No, nor I, but if we can reach Reading I shan't care for anything else, for even if it was discovered which way we were gone I don't think I should be looked for there.'

'Oh, we shall reach Reading!' Tom said cheerfully.

She drew a long breath, and said in a thankful tone: 'Tom, I can't *tell* you how much I'm obliged to you! To own the truth, I didn't at all want to go all by myself, but now—oh, now I can be easy!'

7

Breakfast was served at Austerby, on all but hunting-days, at ten o'clock, which, in Sylvester's opinion, was at least an hour too early. In general, the custom obtaining at country-house parties was for guests to breakfast at eleven, or even twelve o'clock. Lady Marlow knew it, but she told Sylvester that she disapproved of such hours. Sylvester, to whom the imperative summons of the bell had been an offence, received this information with a slight smile, and a polite inclination of the head, but offered no comment.

It was not long before Lord Marlow, noticing the absence of his daughter, wondered aloud where she could be. Her ladyship, speaking with careful restraint, replied that she fancied she must have gone out for a walk.

'Gone out for a walk!' repeated Lord Marlow, chuckling. 'Not she! Gone down to the stables, more like. You must know, Salford, that there is no keeping that girl of mine away from the horses. I wish you might have seen her in the field. A capital seat, good, even hands, and the most bruising little rider you ever saw! Never any need to tell her to throw *her* heart over! Anything her horse can take she will too: stake-and-bound, a double, an in-and-out, a ridge and furrow—all one to Phoebe! I've seen her laid on her back in a ditch, but much she cared!'

Oblivious to his wife's attempts to catch his eye, he would have continued talking in this strain had Firbank not come into the parlour just then, with the intelligence that Mrs Orde wished to speak to him.

He was surprised, and Lady Marlow still more so. She thought it an extraordinary circumstance, and said: 'Depend upon it, she wishes to see *me*, Marlow. I do not know why she should disturb us at such an hour. It is not at all the thing. Inform Mrs Orde, Firbank, that I am at breakfast, but will come to her presently.'

He withdrew, but came back again almost immediately, looking harassed, and with a plump, bright-eyed lady hard on his heels.

'I regret, ma'am, to be obliged to break in on you with so little ceremony,' announced Mrs Orde, who appeared to be labouring under strong emotion, 'but my business will not await your pleasure!'

'Not at all! Delighted to welcome you, ma'am!' said Lord Marlow hastily. 'Always happy to be of service! You wish to see me—precisely, yes!'

'On a matter of the utmost urgency!' she said. 'Your daughter, sir, has run away with my son!'

The company was not unnaturally startled into silence by this announcement. Without giving her hosts time to recover from the shock Mrs Orde loosed the vials of her pent-up wrath upon them. 'I don't know why you should look amazed!' she declared, her eyes snapping at Lady Marlow. 'You have left no stone unturned to achieve this result! *I* guessed how it would be from the instant my son told me what his reception has been in this house for the past ten days! I pass over the insulting nature of your conduct, ma'am, but I shall take leave to inform you that nothing is further from the wishes of his parents than an alliance between Tom and your family! I am excessively attached to Phoebe, poor child, but his father and I have other plans for Tom, and they don't, let me assure you, include his marriage at the age of nineteen!'

'Nonsense! Such a thought was never in either of their heads!' exclaimed Lord Marlow, in an attempt to stem this blistering eloquence.

He was promptly demolished. 'No! Never until her ladyship planted it there!' Mrs Orde said fiercely. 'If *I* had viewed their friendship with apprehension I should have thought myself a ninnyhammer to have acted as she has! And what has been the result? Exactly what might have been foreseen!'

'Upon my word!' broke in Lady Marlow. 'I could almost believe you to have taken leave of your senses, ma'am! A very odd rage you have flown into, and all because my daughter-in-law (as I do not doubt!) has gone out riding with Mr Thomas Orde!'

'Gone out riding!' Mrs Orde exclaimed contemptuously. 'She has run away from this house, and for that, Lady Marlow, *you* are to blame, with your Turkish treatment of her, poor little soul! Oh, I have no patience to talk to you! My errand is not to you, but to Phoebe's father! Read *that*, my lord!'

With these peremptory words she thrust a single sheet of paper into Lord Marlow's hand. While he perused the few lines Tom had scrawled to allay any anxiety his mother might feel, Lady Marlow commanded him to show her the note, and Sylvester retired discreetly into the window embrasure. A man of delicacy, he knew, would seize this opportunity to withdraw from the parlour. He accepted with fortitude the realization that he was lacking in delicacy, and wondered whether there was any chance of his being allowed a glimpse of a missive which was exercising so powerful an effect upon his host.

> My dear Mama, *Tom had scribbled*, I am obliged to go away without taking leave of you, but do not be in a worry. I have taken my father's curricle, and may be absent for some few days, I cannot say precisely how many. Things have come to such a pass at Austerby that there is no bearing it. I must rescue Phoebe, and am persuaded you and my father will understand how it is when you know the whole, and think I did right, for you have always held her in affection.

As he read these lines Lord Marlow's cheeks lost some of their ruddy colour. He allowed his wife to twitch the paper out of his hand, stammering: 'Impossible! I do not credit it! P-pray, where could they have gone?'

'Exactly! *Where?*' demanded Mrs Orde. 'That question is what brings me here! If my husband were not in Bristol at this moment—but so it is always! Whenever a man is most needed he is never to be found!'

'I do not know what this message means,' announced Lady Marlow. 'I do not pretend to understand it. For my part I strongly suspect Mr Thomas Orde to have been inebriated when he wrote it.'

'How dare you?' flashed Mrs Orde, her eyes sparkling dangerously.

'No, no, of course he was not!' interposed Lord Marlow hurriedly. 'My love, let me beg of you—Not but what it is so extraordinary that—Though far be it from me to suggest—'

'Oh!' cried Mrs Orde, stamping her foot, 'don't stand there in that addle-brained fashion, saying nothing to the purpose, my lord! Is it *nothing* to you that your daughter is at this very moment *eloping*? You must go after her! Discover where she meant to go! Surely Susan might know! Or Miss Battery! She may have let fall a hint—or one of them, better acquainted with her than you, might guess!'

Lady Marlow was inclined to brush this suggestion aside, but her lord, the memory of his overnight interview with Phoebe lively in his mind, was by this time seriously alarmed. He said at once that Susan and Miss Battery should be sent for, and hastened to the door, shouting to Firbank. While a message was carried up to the schoolroom, Mrs Orde at once relieved her overcharged nerves and paid off every arrear of a debt of rancour that had been mounting in her bosom for years by telling Lady Marlow exactly what she thought of her manners, conduct, insensibility, and gross stupidity. Lord Marlow was inevitably drawn into the altercation; and in the heat of battle Sylvester's presence was forgotten. He did nothing to attract attention to himself. The moment for that had not yet come, though he had every hope that it was not far distant. Meanwhile he listened to Mrs Orde's masterly indictment of his hostess, gratefully storing up in his memory the several anecdotes illustrative of Lady Marlow's depravity, every detail of which Mrs Orde had faithfully carried in her mind for years past.

She was silenced at last by the entrance into the room of Miss Battery, accompanied not only by Susan but by Eliza as well. To this circumstance Lady Marlow took instant and pardonable exception; but when she would have dismissed her Miss Battery said grimly: 'I thought it my duty to bring her to your ladyship. She says she knows where her sister has gone. Don't think it, myself.'

'Phoebe would never tell *Eliza*!' asserted Susan. 'And particularly when she never breathed a word to *me*!'

'I *do* know where she has gone!' said Eliza. 'And I was going to tell Mama, because it is my duty to do so.'

'Yes, well, never mind that!' said Lord Marlow testily. 'If you know, tell me at once!'

'She has gone to Gretna Green with Tom Orde, Papa,' said Eliza.

The tone in which she uttered this staggering information was so smug that it goaded Susan into exclaiming impetuously: '*I* know that's a rapper, you odious little mischief-maker, you!'

'Susan, you will go to my dressing-room and remain there until I come to you!' said Lady Marlow.

But greatly to her surprise Lord Marlow came to Susan's rescue. 'No, no, this matter must be sifted! It's my belief Sukey is in the right of it.'

'Mine too,' interpolated Miss Battery.

'Eliza is a very truthful child,' stated Lady Marlow.

'How do you know she is gone to Gretna Green?' demanded Mrs Orde. 'Did she tell you so?'

'Oh, no, ma'am!' said Eliza, looking so innocent that Susan's hand itched to slap her. 'I think it was a secret between her and Tom, and it has made me very unhappy, because it is wrong to have secrets from Mama and Papa, isn't it, Mama?'

'Very wrong indeed, my dear,' corroborated Lady Marlow graciously. 'I am glad to know that *one* at least of my daughters feels as she ought.'

'Yes, very likely,' said Lord Marlow without any marked display of enthusiasm, 'but how do you come to know this, girl?'

'Well, Papa, I don't like to tell tales of my sister, but Tom came to see her last night.'

'Came to see her last night? When?'

'I don't know, Papa. It was very late, I think, because I was fast asleep.'

'Then you couldn't have known anything about it!' interrupted Susan.

'Be silent, Susan!' commanded Lady Marlow.

'I woke up,' explained Eliza. 'I heard people talking in the morning-room, and I thought it was robbers, so I got up, because it was my duty to tell Papa, so that he could—'

'Oh, you wicked, untruthful brat!' gasped Susan. 'If you had thought that you would have put your head under the blankets in a quake of fright!'

'Am I to speak to you again, Susan?' demanded Lady Marlow.

'Perfectly true,' said Miss Battery. 'Never had such an idea in her head. Not at all courageous. Got up out of curiosity.'

'Oh, what does it signify?' cried Mrs Orde. 'Tom must have come to see Phoebe on his way home last night, that much is certain! You heard them talking in the morning-room, did you, Lizzy? What did they say?'

'I don't know, ma'am. Only that just as I was about to run to find Papa I heard Tom speak, quite loud, so I knew it wasn't house-breakers. He said he hoped there wouldn't be snow in the north, because it must be Gretna Green.'

'Good God!' ejaculated Lord Marlow. 'The young— And what had Phoebe to say that, pray?'

'She told him not to speak so loud, papa, and then I heard no more, for I went back to bed.'

'Yes, because try as you might you *couldn't* hear any more!' said Susan.

'You behaved very properly,' said Lady Marlow. 'If your sister is saved from the dreadful consequences of her conduct she will owe it to your sense of duty. I am excessively pleased with you, Eliza.'

'Begging your pardon,' ma'am,' said Miss Battery, '*I* should like to know why Eliza's sense of duty didn't prompt her to come immediately to my bedchamber to inform me of what was going forward! Don't scruple to tell you, ma'am, that I don't think there's a word of truth in the story.'

'Yes, by God!' said Lord Marlow, kindling. 'So should I like to know that! *Why* didn't you rouse Miss Battery immediately, Eliza? Susan's right! You made up the whole story, didn't you? Eh? Answer me!'

'I didn't! Oh, Mama, I didn't!' declared Eliza, beginning to cry.

'Good gracious, my lord!' cried Mrs Orde. 'I should hope that it would be beyond the power of a child of her age to *imagine* such a tale! Pray, what should she know of Gretna Green? I do not doubt her: indeed, the terrible suspicion had already crossed my mind! What else can we think, in face of what my son wrote? If he felt himself obliged to *rescue her*, how could he do so except by marrying her? And where could he do *that*, being under age, except across the Border? I beg of you—I *implore* you, sir!—to go after them!'

'Go after them!' ejaculated his lordship, his face alarmingly suffused with colour. 'I should rather think so, ma'am! Implore me, indeed! Let me tell you you have no need to do *that*! My daughter to be running off to Gretna Green like any— Oh, let the pair of them but wait until I catch up with them!'

'Well, they won't do that!' said Mrs Orde, with some asperity. 'And if you *do* catch them (which I don't consider certain, for you may depend on it they have several hours' start of you, and will stay away from the post roads for as far as they may) you will be so good as to remember, sir, that my son is little more than a schoolboy, and has acted, I don't question, from motives of the purest chivalry!'

At this point, perceiving that his host, having forgotten all about him, was preparing to storm out of the room, Sylvester judged it to be time to make his presence felt. Coming back into the centre of the room, he said soothingly: 'Oh, I should think he would catch them quite easily, ma'am! The strongest probability is that they will run into a snow-drift. I believe it has been snowing for several days in the north. My dear Lord Marlow, before you set out in pursuit of the runaways you must allow me to take my leave of you. In such circumstances I daresay you and her ladyship must be wishing me at Jericho. Accept my thanks for your agreeable hospitality, my regret for its unavoidable curtailment, and my assurance–I trust unnecessary!–that you may rely upon my discretion. It remains only for me to wish you speedy success in your mission, and to beg that you will not delay your departure on my account.'

With these words, delivered very much in the grand manner, he shook hands with Lady Marlow, executed two slight bows to Mrs Orde and Miss Battery, and was gone from the room before his host had collected his wits enough to do more than utter a half-hearted protest.

His valet, a very correct gentleman's gentleman, received the news of his immediate departure from Austerby with a deferential bow and an impassive countenance; John Keighley, suffering all the discomfort of a severe cold in his head, bluntly protested. 'We'll never reach London, your grace, not with the roads in the state they're in, by all accounts.'

'I daresay we shan't,' replied Sylvester. 'But do you think I can't reach Speenhamland? I'll prove you wrong!'

Swale, already folding one of Sylvester's coats, heard this magical word with relief. Speenhamland meant the Pelican, a hostelry as famous for the excellence of its accommodation as for the extortionate nature of its charges. Far better entertainment would be found there than at Austerby, as well for his grace's servants as for his grace himself.

Unmoved by this reflection, Keighley objected: 'It's more than thirty miles from here, your grace! You'll have to change horses, and postilions too, because the boys couldn't do it, not if we run into snow.'

'Oh, I'm not travelling in the chaise!' said Sylvester. 'I'll take the curricle, of course, and drive myself. You will come with me, and Swale can follow in the chaise. Tell the boys they must go as far as they can without a change. They are to bring my own team on by easy stages to the Pelican, and if I'm not there, to town. Swale, put up all I might need for several days in one of my portmanteaux!'

'If your grace should wish me to travel in the curricle I shall be happy to do so,' said Swale, with less truth than heroism.

'No, Keighley will be of far more use to me,' replied Sylvester.

His devoted retainer grunted, and went off to the stables. Within half an hour, resigned to his fate, he was seated beside his master in the curricle, gloomily surveying the prospect, which had by this time become extremely threatening. He had added a large muffler to his attire, and from time to time blew his nose on a handkerchief drenched with camphor. Upon Sylvester's addressing a chatty remark to him, he said primly: 'Yes, your grace.' To a second effort to engage him in conversation he replied: 'I couldn't say, your grace.'

'Oh, couldn't you?' Sylvester retorted. 'Very well! Say what you wish to: that it's devilish cold, and I'm mad to make the attempt to get to the Pelican!

It's all one to me, and will very likely make you feel more amiable.'

'I wouldn't so demean myself, your grace,' replied Keighley, with dignity.

'Well, that's a new come-out,' commented Sylvester. 'I thought I was in for one of your scolds.' Receiving no response to this, he said cajolingly: 'Come out of the sullens, John, for God's sake!'

Never, from the day when a very small Sylvester had first coaxed him to do his imperious will, had Keighley been able to resist that note. He said severely: 'Well, if ever there was a crack-brained start, your grace! Driving right into a snowstorm, like you are! All I say is, don't you go blaming me if we end up in a drift!'

'No, I won't,' Sylvester promised. 'The thing was, you see, it was now or never—or at least for a week. You may have been enjoying yourself: I wasn't! In fact, I'd sooner put up at a hedge tavern.'

Keighley chuckled. 'I suspicioned that was the way of it. I didn't think we should be there long: not when I heard about the smoke in your grace's bedchamber. Nor Swale didn't like it, being very niffy-naffy in his ways.'

'Like me,' remarked Sylvester. 'In any event, I could hardly have remained, when his lordship was suddenly called away, could I?'

'No, your grace. Particularly seeing as how you wasn't wishful to.'

Sylvester laughed; and good relations being restored between them they proceeded on their way in perfect amity. It was snowing in Devizes, but they reached Marlborough in good time, and at the Castle Inn stopped to rest the horses, and to partake of a second breakfast. Roaring fires and excellent food strongly tempted Sylvester to remain there, and he might have done so had it not occurred to him that it was situated rather too near to Austerby for safety. The arrival of the Bath Mail clinched the matter. It was several hours late, but Sylvester learned from the coachman that although the road was bad in parts, it was nowhere impassable. He decided to push on. Keighley, fortified by a potation of gin, beer, nutmeg, and sugar, which he referred to as hot flannel, raised no objection; so the horses were put to again.

It was heavier going over the next ten miles, and once beyond the Forest of Savernake Sylvester was obliged, once or twice, to pull up, while Keighley got down from the curricle to discover the line of the road. Hungerford was reached, however, without mishap. Sylvester's famous dapple-grays, with a light vehicle behind them, were tired, but not distressed. If rested for a space, he judged them to be perfectly capable of accomplishing the next stage, which would bring them to Speenhamland, and the Pelican.

By the time they set forward again on their journey it was past four o'clock, and to the hazards of the weather were added those of failing daylight. With the sky so uniformly overcast Keighley was of the opinion that it would be dark before they reached Newbury, but he knew his master too well to waste his breath in remonstrance. Sylvester, who could have numbered on one hand the occasions when he had been ill enough to coddle himself, was neither disconcerted by the blinding snow, nor troubled by its discomforts. Keighley, his cold at its zenith, wondered whether he could be persuaded to draw rein at the Halfway House, and would not have been altogether sorry had they foundered within reach of this or any other hostelry. Neither he nor Sylvester was familiar with the road, but fortune favoured them, just when it became most difficult. They met a stage-coach making its slow and perilous progress towards Bath, and were able to follow its deep tracks for several miles, before these became obliterated by the falling snow-flakes. They were still discernible when Keighley's sharp eyes saw the wreck of a curricle lying in the ditch, and remarked that someone had had a nasty spill. The curricle was covered with snow, but it was plainly a sporting vehicle, and had just as plainly been travelling eastward. Sylvester was assailed suddenly by a suspicion. He pulled up, the better to scrutinize the derelict. 'It's a curricle, John.'

'Yes, your grace,' agreed Keighley. 'Broken shaft, let alone the near-side wheels, which I dare say are smashed. Now, for goodness' sake, do you take care how you go! Nice bobbery if we was to end up the same way!'

'I wonder?' said Sylvester, unholy amusement in his voice. 'I shouldn't suppose there could be many desperate enough to take a curricle out in this weather. I *wonder?*'

'But they was making for the Border, your grace!' said Keighley, betraying a knowledge he had hitherto discreetly concealed.

'That was only what Miss Eliza said. I thought young Orde must be a regular greenhead to have supposed there was the least chance of his getting within two hundred miles of the Border. Perhaps he isn't a greenhead, John! I think we are going to make his acquaintance. I *am* glad we decided to push on to the Pelican!'

'Begging your grace's pardon,' said Keighley grimly, '*we* didn't decide no such thing! What's more, if I may make so bold as to say so, you don't want to make his acquaintance. Nor you don't want to meet Miss again—not if *I* know anything about it!'

'I daresay you know all about it,' retorted Sylvester, setting his horses in motion again. 'You usually do. What happened when they ran into the ditch?'

'I don't know, your grace,' replied Keighley irascibly. 'Maybe there was a coach passed, and they got into it.'

'Don't be a clunch! What became of the horses? They don't belong to Master Tom, but to his father. He'd take precious good care of 'em, wouldn't he?'

'He would, if his father's the cut of your grace's honoured father,' acknowledged Keighley, with mordant humour. 'Lord, what a set-out we did have, that time your grace took the young bay out, and—'

'Thank you, I haven't forgotten it! Master Tom, John, got his horses disentangled from that wreck, and led them to the nearest shelter. There can't have been any broken legs, but I fancy they didn't come off entirely scatheless. Keep your eyes open for a likely farm, or inn!'

Keighley sighed, but refrained from comment. In the event no great strain was imposed upon his visionary powers, for within half a mile, hard by a narrow lane which crossed the post road, a small wayside inn stood, set back a few yards from the road, with its yard and several outbuildings in its rear.

'Aha!' said Sylvester. 'Now we shall see, shan't we, John? Hold 'em for me!'

Keighley, receiving the reins, was so much incensed by this wayward conduct that he said with awful sarcasm: 'Yes, your grace. And if you was to be above an hour, should I walk them, just in case they *might* happen to take cold?'

But Sylvester, springing down from the curricle, was already entering the Blue Boar, and paid no heed to this sally.

The door opened on to a passage, on one side of which lay the tap, and on the other a small coffee-room. Opposite, a narrow staircase led to the upper floor, and at the head of it, looking anxiously down, stood Miss Phoebe Marlow.

8

The startled exclamation which broke from her, and the look of dismay which came into her face, afforded Sylvester malicious satisfaction. 'Ah, how do you do?' he said affably.

One hand gripping the banister-rail, a painful question in her eyes, she uttered: 'Mama—?'

'But of course! Outside, in my curricle.' Then he saw that she had turned perfectly white, and said: 'Don't be such a goose-cap! You can't suppose I would drive your mother-in-law thirty yards, let alone thirty miles!'

Her colour came rushing back; she said: 'No—or she consent to drive in a curricle! What—what brings you here, sir?'

'Curiosity, ma'am. I saw the wreck on the road, and guessed it to be Mr Orde's curricle.'

'Oh! You didn't—you were not—' She stopped in some confusion; and then, as he looked up at her in bland enquiry, blurted out: 'You didn't come to find me?'

'Well, no!' he answered apologetically. 'I am merely on my way to London. I am afraid, Miss Marlow, that you have been labouring under a misapprehension.'

'Do you mean you were not going to make me an offer?' she demanded.

'You *do* favour the blunt style, don't you? Bluntly, then, ma'am, I was not.'

She was not at all offended, but said, with a sigh of relief: 'Thank goodness! Not but what it is still excessively awkward. However, you are better than *nobody*, I suppose!'

'Thank you!'

'Well, when I heard you come in I hoped you had been that odious ostler.'

'What odious ostler?'

'The one who is employed here. Mrs Scaling—she's the landlady—sent him off to Newbury to purchase provisions when she feared they might be snowed up here for weeks, perhaps, and he has not come back. His home is there, and Mrs Scaling thinks he will make the snow an excuse for remaining there until it stops. And the thing is that he has taken the only horse she keeps! Tom—Mr Orde—won't hear of my trying if I can ride Trusty—and I own it *would* be a little difficult, when there's no saddle, and I am not wearing my riding-dress. And no one ever *has* ridden Trusty. True would carry me, but that's impossible: his left hock is badly strained. But that leg is certainly broken, and it *must* be set!'

'Whose leg?' interrupted Sylvester. 'Not the horse's?'

'Oh, no! It's not as bad as *that*!' she assured him. 'Mr Orde's leg.'

'Are you sure it's broken?' he asked incredulously. 'How the deuce did he get here, if that's the case? Who got the horses out of their traces?'

'There was a farm-hand, leading a donkey and cart. It was that which caused the accident: Trusty holds donkeys in the greatest aversion, and the wretched creature brayed at him, just as Tom had him in hand, as I thought. Tom caught his heel in the rug, I think, and that's how it happened. The farm-hand helped me to free Trusty and True; and then he lifted Tom into his cart, and brought him here, while I led the horses. Mrs Scaling and I contrived to cut off Tom's boot, but I am afraid we hurt him a good deal, because he fainted away in the middle of it. And here we have been ever since, with poor Tom's leg not set, and no means of fetching a surgeon, all because of that abominable ostler!'

'Good God!' said Sylvester, struggling with a strong desire to laugh. 'Wait a minute!'

With these words, he went out into the road again, to where Keighley waited him. 'Stable 'em, John!' he ordered. 'We are putting up here for the night. There is only one ostler, and he has gone off to Newbury, so if you see no one in the yard, do as seems best to you!'

'Putting up *here*, your grace?' demanded Keighley, thunderstruck.

'I should think so: it will be too dark to go farther in another couple of hours,' replied Sylvester, vanishing into the house again.

He found that Phoebe had been joined by a stout woman with iron-gray curls falling from under a mob cap, and a comely countenance just now wearing a harassed expression. She dropped a curtsey to him; and Phoebe said, with careful emphasis: 'This is Mrs Scaling, sir, who has been so very helpful to *my brother* and to me!'

'How kind of her!' said Sylvester, bestowing upon the landlady the smile which won for him so much willing service. 'Their parents would be glad to know that my imprudent young friends fell into such good hands. I have told my groom to stable the horses, but I daresay you will tell him just where he may do so. Can you accommodate the pair of us?'

'Well, I'm sure, sir, I should be very happy—only this is quite a simple house, such as your honour— And I've took and put the poor young gentleman in my best room!' said Mrs Scaling, considerably flustered.

'Oh, that makes no odds!' said Sylvester, stripping off his gloves. 'I think, ma'am, it would be as well if you took me up to see your brother.'

Phoebe hesitated, and when Mrs Scaling bustled off to the back premises, said suspiciously: 'Why do you wish to see Tom? Why do you wish to remain here?'

'Oh, it's not a question of wishing!' he returned, a laugh in his eyes. 'Pure fellow-feeling, ma'am! What a dog I should be to leave the poor devil in the hands of two females! Take me up! I promise you, he will be very glad to see me!'

'Well, I don't think he will,' said Phoebe, regarding him in a darkling way. 'And *I* should like to know why you talked of us to Mrs Scaling as though you had been our grandfather!'

'I feel like your grandfather,' he replied. 'Take me up to the sufferer, and let us see what can be done for him!'

She still seemed to be doubtful, but after a moment's indecision she said ungraciously: 'Oh, very well! But I won't have him ranted at, or reproached, mind!'

'Good God, who am I to give him a trimming?' Sylvester said, following her up the narrow stair.

Mrs Scaling's best bedchamber was a low-pitched room in the front of the house. A fire had been lit in the grate, and the blinds drawn across the dormer window to shut out the bleak dusk. An oil lamp had been set on the dressing-table, and a couple of candles on the mantelshelf, and as the window-blinds and the curtains round the bed were of crimson the room presented a pleasantly cosy appearance. Tom, fully dressed except for his boots and stockings, was lying on the bed, with a patchwork quilt spread lightly over his legs, and his shoulders propped up by several bulky pillows. There was a haggard look on his face, and the eyes which he turned towards the door were heavy with strain.

'Tom, this—this is the Duke of Salford!' said Phoebe. 'He *would* have me bring him up, so—so here he is!'

This startling intelligence made Tom wrench himself up on to his elbow, wincing, but full of determination to protect Phoebe from any attempt to drag her back to Austerby. '*Salford?*' he ejaculated. 'You mean to tell me— Come over here, Phoebe, and don't you be afraid! He has no authority over you, and so he knows!'

'Now, don't you enact me a high tragedy!' said Sylvester, walking up to the bed. 'I haven't any authority over either of you, and I'm not the villain of this or any other piece. How do you do?'

Finding that a hand was being held out to him Tom, much disconcerted, took it, and stammered: 'Oh, how—how do you do, sir? I mean—'

'Better than you, I fear,' said Sylvester. 'In the devil of a hobble, aren't you? May I look?' Without waiting for an answer he twitched the quilt back. As Tom instinctively braced himself, he glanced up with a smile, and said: 'I won't touch it. Have you been much mauled?'

Tom grinned back at him rather wanly. 'Oh, by Jove, haven't I just!'

'Well, I am very sorry, but we had to get your boot off, and we did *try* not to hurt you,' said Phoebe.

'Yes, I know. It wasn't so much that as that booberkin thinking he knew how to set a bone, and Mrs Scaling believing him!'

'It sounds appalling,' remarked Sylvester, his eyes on the injured leg, which was considerably inflamed, and bore the marks of inexpert handling.

'It was,' asseverated Tom. 'He is Mrs Scaling's son, touched in his upper works, *I* think!'

'Well, he is a natural,' amended Phoebe. 'Indeed I wish I hadn't allowed him to try what he could do, but he was not at all unhandy with poor True, which made me think he would very likely know how to set your leg, for such persons, you know, frequently have that kind of knowledge.' She saw that Sylvester was regarding her with mockery, and added defensively: 'It *is* so! There is a natural in our village who is better than any horse-doctor!'

'You should have been a horse, Orde,' said Sylvester. 'How many hours is it since this happened?'

'I don't know, sir. A great many, I daresay: it seems like an age,' replied poor Tom.

'I am not a doctor—even a horse-doctor—but I fancy the bone should be set as soon as possible. We shall have to see what we can do. Oh, don't look so aghast! *I'm* not going to make the attempt! We need Keighley—my groom. I shouldn't be at all surprised if he knows how to do the trick.'

'Your groom?' said Phoebe sceptically. 'How should he know anything of the sort, pray?'

'Perhaps he doesn't, in which case he will tell us so. He put my shoulder back once, when I was a boy and dislocated it, and I recall that when the surgeon came he said he could not have done it better himself. I'll call him,' said Sylvester, walking to the door.

He went out, and Tom turned wondering eyes towards Phoebe. 'What the deuce brought him here?' he asked. 'I thought he had been chasing us, but if that was the way of it what makes him care a button for my leg?'

'I can't think!' said Phoebe. 'But he didn't come in search of me, that I *do* know! In fact, he says he didn't come to Austerby to offer for me at all. I was never more relieved in my life!'

Tom looked at her in a puzzled way, but since he was a good deal exhausted by all he had undergone, and his leg was paining him very much, he felt unequal to further discussion, and relapsed into silence.

In a short space of time Sylvester came back, bringing Keighley with him, and carrying a glass half full of a rich brown liquid, which he set down on a small table beside the bed. 'Well, Keighley says that if it is a simple fracture he can set it for you,' he remarked cheerfully. 'Let us hope it is, therefore! But I can't help feeling that the first thing to do is to get you out of your clothes, and into your nightshirt. You must be excessively uncomfortable!'

'Oh, I do *wish* you will persuade him to be undressed!' exclaimed Phoebe, regarding Sylvester for the first time with approval. 'It is precisely what Mrs Scaling and I wanted to do for him at the outset, but nothing would prevail upon him to agree to it!'

'You amaze me!' said Sylvester. 'If I find him similarly obstinate Keighley and I will strip him forcibly. Meanwhile, Miss Marlow, *you* may go downstairs—if you will be so obliging!—and assist Mrs Scaling to tear up a sheet for bandages. No, I know you don't wish to leave him to our mercy, but, believe me, you are shockingly in the way here! Go and brew him a posset, or some broth, or whatever you think suitable to this occasion!'

She looked a trifle mulish, but a chuckle from Tom clinched the matter. 'Oh, do go away, Phoebe!' he begged.

She went, but the incident did nothing to put her in charity with Sylvester, politely holding the door for her, and saying with odious kindness, as she passed him: 'You shall come back presently!'

Tom, however, was so grateful that he began to think Sylvester a very tolerable sort of a man; and when Sylvester, turning away from the door, winked at him, he grinned, and said shyly: 'I'm much obliged to you, sir! She's a good girl—as good as ever twanged, in fact—but—but—'

'I know,' said Sylvester sympathetically. 'They *will* be ministering angels!'

'Yes,' agreed Tom, somewhat uneasily eyeing Keighley, who, having shed his coat, was now rolling up his shirtsleeves in an ominous manner.

'You want to bite on the bullet, sir,' recommended Keighley. 'Because I'll have to find out just what you have broke in your leg, if you've broken anything, which I've only got your word for, when all's said.'

Tom assented to this, clenched his teeth and his fists, and enduring in sweating silence while Keighley discovered the exact nature of his injury. The rough cart-journey, and the inexpert attempts of Will Scaling to set the broken bone, had caused considerable inflammation. Keighley said, as he straightened himself: 'Properly mauled you they did, sir! True enough, you've broken your fibula—which is what you might call Dutch comfort, because it might have been worse. Now, if that jobbernoll below stairs has sawn me off a nice splint, like I told him to do, we'll have you going along like winking in a pig's whisper, sir!'

'Are you sure of that, John?' Sylvester asked. 'It won't do to be making a mull of it!'

'I shan't do that, your grace. But I'm thinking it would be as well if the young gentleman was put to bed. I'll have to slit his breeches up the left side, but I can get 'em off easier without his leg being splinted.'

Sylvester nodded; Tom said faintly: 'My razor is on the dressing-table. You may as well use it. It's ruined already, cutting my boot.'

'Don't let that vex you!' said Sylvester. 'You can borrow one of mine.'

Tom thanked him. He submitted to being stripped, and put into his nightshirt, and owned, upon being lowered again on to the pillows, that he felt a degree more comfortable. Keighley then went away to collect splints and bandages; and Tom, a little white about the gills, said with what jauntiness he could muster that he would be devilish glad when it was over.

'I should think you would be,' agreed Sylvester. He picked up the glass he had brought into the room, and held it out. 'Meanwhile, here's a drink to fortify you. No daylights, mind!'

Tom looked rather dubiously at the dark potion, but took the glass, and raised it to his lips. Then he lowered it again. 'Yes, but it's rum, isn't it, sir?'

'Yes. Don't you like it?'

'Well, not above half. But the thing is I should be as drunk as a wheelbarrow if I drank all this!'

'That isn't of the slightest consequence. Oh, are you thinking of what Miss Marlow might say? You need not: I shan't let her come back until you've slept it off. Don't argue with me! Just drink it, and be thankful.'

Keighley, returning to find his patient happily, if somewhat muzzily, smiling, said with approval: 'That's the dandy! Properly shot in the neck, ain't you sir? It won't make any odds to you *what's* done to you. Now, if your grace will lend a hand—?'

If Tom was not quite as insensible as Keighley optimistically prophesied, the rum undoubtedly made it much easier for him to bear the exquisite anguish of the next minute or two. He behaved with great fortitude, encouraged by Keighley, who told him he was pluck to the backbone. The ordeal was soon at an end. It left him feeling limp and rather sick. His leg ached; and he found that everything he tried to look at swam so giddily before him that he was obliged to close his eyes, yielding to the powerful effect of rum. Keighley, observing with satisfaction that he was sinking into stertorous sleep, nodded at Sylvester, and said briefly: 'He'll do now, your grace.'

'I hope he may, but it will be as well if we get a surgeon to him,' replied Sylvester, frowning down at Tom. 'If anything were to go amiss, I've no mind to be responsible. He's under age, you know. I wonder why the devil I embroiled myself in this affair?'

'Ah!' said Keighley, snuffing the candles. 'Just what I've been asking myself, your grace!'

They left the room together, and descended the stairs to the coffee-room. Here they found Phoebe, sitting before a brisk fire, and looking anxious. Sylvester said: 'Well, Keighley has set the bone, and Orde is now asleep. For anything I know, there's nothing more to be done, but at the same time—What's the weather like?' He stepped up to the window, and drew the blind aside. 'Still snowing, but not dark yet. What do you wish, Miss Marlow?'

She had smiled at Keighley, and thanked him; but at these words she cast him an apologetic glance, and said: 'I should *wish* to bring a doctor to see him, because if it hadn't been for me it would never have happened, and I know Mrs Orde would do so. It is the most vexatious thing! Mrs Scaling only spoke to me of a doctor at Newbury, and now I've discovered that there is a Dr Upsall, living at Hungerford! If I had known of him earlier I might have walked there, for I don't think it's much above four miles. Mrs Scaling didn't think to tell me of him, because from what she says I collect he is above her touch.'

'Let us hope he doesn't consider himself above mine. Do you suppose the half-wit capable of guiding one to his house?'

'I should think he would be. He says so, at all events. But it is growing dark, and perhaps the doctor might not choose to venture out, for a stranger?'

'Nonsense!' Sylvester said. 'It is his business to venture out. He will be well paid for his trouble. You had better put the horses to immediately, John—and tell young Scaling he is to go with you! You may present my card to this Dr Upsall, and say that I shall be obliged to him if he will come here at once.'

'Very good, your grace,' Keighley said.

Phoebe, who had listened to Sylvester's orders in gathering indignation, waited only until Keighley had left the room before exclaiming in accents of strong censure: 'You cannot mean to send that unfortunate man out in this weather!'

He looked surprised. 'You said you wished a doctor to see Orde, didn't you? I own, I wish it too, and though he might take no particular harm through waiting until the morning it is quite possible, you know, that the road may be impassable by then.'

'Indeed, I wish him to see a doctor!' she said. 'And if you will trust your horses to me I'll fetch him myself—since *you* do not care to go!'

'*I?*' he demanded. 'Why should I do any such thing?'

'Can't you see that your groom has the most shocking cold?' she said fiercely. 'He is looking worn to a bone already, and here you are, sending him out again without a thought to what may come of it! I suppose it is of no consequence if he contracts an inflammation of the lungs, or falls into a confirmed consumption!'

He flushed angrily. 'On the contrary! I should find it excessively inconvenient!'

'Oh, surely you have other grooms? I am persuaded there could never be a want of servants to spare you the least exertion!'

'Many other grooms! But only one Keighley! It may interest you to know, Miss Marlow, that I have a considerable regard for him!'

'Well, it doesn't interest me, because I don't believe it!' she said warmly. 'You couldn't have brought him thirty miles in an open carriage on such a day if you had a *regard* for him! Would *you* have set out from Austerby if you had had a bad cold? No such thing!'

'You are mistaken! I should! I never pay the least heed to such trifling ailments!'

'*You* are not fifty years old, or more!'

'Nor is Keighley! Fifty years old indeed! He is not much above forty!' said Sylvester furiously. 'What's more, if he had thought himself too unwell to travel he would have told me so!'

Her lips curled derisively. 'Would he?'

'Yes, he—' Sylvester stopped suddenly, staring at her with very hard, frowning eyes. A dull colour crept into his cheeks; he said stiffly: 'He should have done so, at all events. He knows very well I wouldn't—Good God, you seem to think me an inhuman taskmaster!'

'No, only *selfish*!' she said. 'I daresay you never so much as noticed that the poor man had caught cold.'   A retort sprang to his lips, but he checked it, his colour deepening as he recollected feeling vexed with Keighley for contracting an epidemic cold, and hoping that he would not take it from him.

But no sooner had Phoebe uttered her last stricture than she too suffered an uncomfortable recollection. Flushing far more vividly than Sylvester, she said in a conscience-stricken voice: 'I beg your pardon! It was very bad of me to have said that, when—when I am so much obliged to you! Pray forgive me, sir!'

'It is of no consequence at all, Miss Marlow,' he replied coldly. 'I should be grateful to you for calling my attention to Keighley's state. Let me assure you that you need feel no further anxiety! I am far too selfish to wish to have him laid up, and shall certainly not send him to Hungerford.'

Before she could reply to this Keighley came back into the room, muffled in his heavy driving-coat. 'Beg pardon, your grace, but I went off without the card.'

'I've changed my mind, John,' Sylvester said. 'I'll go myself.'

'*Go yourself*, your grace?' repeated Keighley. 'And may I make so bold as to ask why? If your grace don't care to have me driving the grays, I hope your grace will pardon me if I was to say that it won't be *quite* the first time I've done so! P'raps your grace would as lief drive them without me in the curricle at all?'

This withering sarcasm had the effect of clearing the frown from Sylvester's brow. 'Exactly so!' he said, his eyes quizzing his offended henchman. 'I am going alone! Oh, no I'm not! I shall have the half-wit with me, shall I not? I hope he may not murder me, or anything of that nature! No, don't argue with me! Miss Marlow believes you to be sinking into a confirmed consumption, and I will *not* have your death upon my conscience! Besides, what *should* I do without you? Where is my greatcoat?'

Keighley turned an amazed and slightly reproachful gaze upon Phoebe. '*Me*? Lor', ma'am, there's nothing amiss with me barring a bit of a cold in my head! Now, if your grace will give me your card, I'll be off! And no more funning, *if* you please, because if I don't get started quick there's no saying but what *I'll* end in the ditch, and a nice set-out that would be!'

'No, I am quite determined you shan't go,' Sylvester said. 'Did you put my coat in my bedchamber? Where *is* my bedchamber? Direct me to it instantly, and be off to put the horses to! Good God! Ought I, perhaps, to do that too? Miss Marlow, do you think—?'

Keighley intervened before Phoebe was obliged to answer a question she suspected to be deliberately provocative. Reiterating his request to Sylvester to stop funning, he added a strongly worded protest against the impropriety of his chasing all over the country after a mere sawbones. Such unbecoming conduct, he said severely, would not do.

'I'm the best judge of that,' returned Sylvester. 'Put the horses to, at once, if you please!'

He strode to the door, but was arrested by Phoebe, who said suddenly: 'Oh, pray—! I don't wish to charge you with an office you might think troublesome, but—but if you *are* going to Hungerford, would you be so very obliging as to try if you can procure for me a few ounces of muriate of ammonia, a pint of spirit of wine, and some spermacetti ointment?'

Sylvester's lip twitched, and he burst out laughing. 'Oh, certainly, Miss Marlow! Are you sure there is nothing else you would wish me to purchase for you?'

'No,' she replied seriously. 'Mrs Scaling has plenty of vinegar. And if you can't come by the ointment, she will let me have some lard instead—only I can't be sure it is perfectly free from salt. It is to put on Trusty's foreleg,' she explained, seeing that he was still much inclined to laugh. 'It is badly grazed: I fancy poor True may have kicked him, when he was struggling to get out of the ditch.'

'I'll come and take a look at that, miss,' said Keighley, his professional interest aroused. 'Showing red, is it? It'll have to be fomented before the ointment's put on it.'

'Oh, yes, I have been doing so, every hour, and True's hock as well! I should be very much obliged to you, if you will look at it, Keighley, and tell me if you think I should apply a bran poultice tonight.'

'Render Miss Marlow all the assistance you can, John, but first put the grays to!' interrupted Sylvester. 'See to it that fires are lit in our rooms, bespeak dinner, and a private parlour—no, I expect there isn't one in so small a house: you had better tell the landlady I'll hire this room—don't disturb Mr Orde, and have everything ready for a bowl of punch as soon as I return. And don't let Miss Marlow keep you out in the draughty stable too long!'

On this Parthian shot he departed, closely followed by Keighley, who did not cease to expostulate with him until he was actually preparing to mount into the curricle.

'Be damned to you, John, *no!*' he said. 'You will stay here, and nurse your cold. Why didn't you tell me you were out of sorts, you stupid fellow? I could have taken Swale with me, and left you to follow in the chaise.'

He sounded a little contrite, which would have surprised Keighley had he not been so much revolted by the thought of relinquishing his post to Swale that he never noticed Sylvester's unusual solicitude. By the time he could trust himself to repudiate the disgraceful suggestion in anything but terms quite unsuited to his position, Sylvester had swung himself up into the curricle, and set his pair in motion. Beside him, Will Scaling, a shambling and overgrown youth of somewhat vacuous amiability, grinned hugely, and sat back with all the air of one prepared to enjoy a high treat.

9

It was nearly eight o'clock before Sylvester returned to the Blue Boar, and for a full hour Phoebe had been picturing just such an accident as had befallen Tom, and wishing that she had not sent him forth on his errand. When he did at last arrive he took her by surprise, for the snow muffled the sound of the horses' hooves, and he drove his curricle straight into the yard, and came into the house through the back-door. She heard a quick stride in the passage, and looked up to see him standing in the doorway of the coffee-room. He had not stayed to put off his long driving-coat, which was very wet, and had snow still clinging to its many shoulder-capes. She started up, exclaiming: 'Oh, you are safely back! I have been in such a fidget, fearing you had met with an accident! Have you brought the doctor, sir?'

'Oh, yes, he is here—or will be in, a few minutes. I came ahead. Is there a fire in your bedchamber, Miss Marlow?'

'Yes, but—'

'Then may I suggest that you retire there until the surgeon has departed? I haven't mentioned your presence here to him, for although your brother and sister story may do well enough for the landlady, it is quite possible, you know, that a doctor living at Hungerford might recognize one or other of you. You will agree that the fewer people to get wind of this escapade of yours the better.'

'I shouldn't think he would know either of us,' she replied, with what he considered to be quite unbecoming *sangfroid*. 'However, I daresay you are right, sir. Only, if I am not to see the doctor, will you take him up to Tom, if you please, and hear what he thinks we should do for him?'

'I've told Keighley to do so. He knows much more about such matters than I do. Moreover, I want to put off these wet clothes. Have you dined?'

'Well, no,' she owned. 'Thought I ate a slice of bread-and-butter just after you went away.'

'Good God! Why didn't you order dinner when you wished for it?' he said, rather impatiently.

'Because *you* bespoke it for when you should return. Mrs Scaling has only one daughter to help her, you know, and she couldn't dress *two* dinners. In fact, she has been in a grand fuss ever since she discovered who you are, because, of course, she is not at all in the habit of entertaining dukes.'

'I hope that doesn't mean that we shall get a bad dinner.'

'Oh, no on the contrary! She means to feed you in the most *lavish* way!' Phoebe assured him.

He smiled. 'I'm happy to know it: I could eat an ox whole! Stay in this room until you hear Keighley take the surgeon upstairs, and then slip away to your own. I suppose I must, in common charity, give the man a glass of punch before he sets out for Hungerford again, but I'll get rid of him as soon as I can.' He nodded to her, and went away, leaving her with her mind divided between resentment at his cool assumption of authority and relief that some at least of her burden of responsibility had been lifted from her shoulders.

When the surgeon presently left Tom, she ventured to go and tap on the door of the best bedroom. Tom bade her come in, and she entered to find him sitting up in bed, much restored by his long sleep, but fretting a good deal over her predicament, his own helplessness, and the condition of his father's horses. She was able to give him a comfortable account of the horses; as for herself, she said that since they could scarcely have hoped to reach Reading she was quite as well off at the Blue Boar as she would have been at an inn in Newbury.'

'Yes, but the Duke!' Tom objected. 'I must say, there was never anything more awkward! Not but what I'm devilish obliged to him. Still—!'

'Oh, well!' said Phoebe. 'We must just make the best of him! And his groom, you know, is a most excellent person. He put the poultice on Trusty's fore, and he says if we keep the wound pliant with spermacetti ointment until it is perfectly healed, and then dress it with James's blister, he thinks there will be no blemish at all.'

'Lord, I hope he may be right!' Tom said devoutly.

'Oh, yes, I am persuaded he is!' She then bethought her that the horses had not been the only sufferers in the spill, and conscientiously enquired after Tom's broken fibula.

He grinned his appreciation of this palpable afterthought, but replied that the surgeon had not meddled with Keighley's handiwork, beyond applying a lotion to the inflamed surface, and bandaging the leg to a fresh and less makeshift splint. 'But the devil of it is that he says I must be abed for at least a week. And even then I shall be in no case to drive you to London. Lord, I hadn't thought I was such a clunch as to overturn like that! I am as sorry as could be, but that's no use! What are we to do?'

'Well, we can't do anything at present,' she answered. 'It is still snowing, you know, and I shouldn't wonder at it if we were to find ourselves beleaguered by the morning.'

'But what about the Duke?'

She considered the Duke. 'Oh, well, at least I'm not afraid of him! And I must own that although I cannot approve of his conduct—he seems to think he can have anything he wants, you know!—he *has* made us excessively comfortable. Only fancy, Tom! I have a fire in my bedchamber! A thing Mama never allowed at home, except when I have been ill! Then he said he must have a private parlour, and would hire the coffee-room, I daresay not so much as considering whether it might not be inconvenient for Mrs Scaling to give it to him—and of course she didn't dare say a word, because she is so much dazzled by his being a duke that she would give up the whole house to him if he should take it into his head to wish for it.'

'I expect he will pay her handsomely—and who would be coming here on such a night?' said Tom. 'Are you going to sit down to dinner with him? Shall you find it awkward?'

'Well, I daresay it may be a trifle awkward,' she acknowledged. 'Particularly if he should ask me why I am on my way to London. However, he may not do so, because he will very likely still be in a miff with me.'

'In a miff with you? Why?' demanded Tom. 'He didn't seem to me as though he cared a groat for your having run away!'

'Oh, no! Only we quarrelled, you see. Would you believe it? He had the intention of sending poor Keighley to fetch the surgeon! It put me in such a passion that there was no bearing it, and—well, we came to cuffs! But he *did* go himself, in the end, so I don't regret it. In fact,' she added reflectively, 'I am glad of it, because I was feeling miserably shy before I quarrelled with him, and there is *nothing* like quarrelling with a person to set one at one's ease!'

Unable to take this philosophic view of the matter, Tom said, in a shocked voice: 'Do you mean to tell me you sent him out just to fetch the surgeon for me?'

'Yes, why not?' said Phoebe.

'Well, my God, if that's not the outside of enough! as though he had been *anybody*! You are the most outrageous girl, Phoebe! I shouldn't think he would ever wish to offer for you after such treatment as that!'

'Well, what a good thing that would be! Not that I think he ever did wish to offer for me. It is the strangest business! I wonder why he came to Austerby?'

Speculation on this point was interrupted by the entrance of Keighley, bearing a heavily laden tray. Neither his injury nor his subsequent potations having impaired Tom's appetite, he temporarily lost interest in any other problem than what might be concealed beneath the several covers on the tray. Keighley, setting the whole down on the table by the bed, asked him in a fatherly way if he was feeling peckish; and upon being assured by Tom that he was, smiled benevolently at him, and said: 'That's the barber! Now, you keep still, sir, and leave me to fix you up so as you can manage! As for you, miss, the covers are set downstairs, and his grace is waiting for you.'

Dismissed in this kind but firm manner Phoebe withdrew, promising in response to a somewhat peremptory command from Tom to return to him as soon as she should have dined. Tom had suddenly been attacked by qualms. Phoebe was at once too innocent and too intimate with him to see anything equivocal in her position; he was fully alive to its impropriety, and he felt that he ought to keep her under his eye. Sylvester had certainly seemed to him to be a very good sort of a man, but he did not know him, after all: he might be a hardened rake, and if that were so a very uncomfortable time Phoebe would have of it, alone with him in the coffee-room, while her supposed protector lay tied by the leg in the best bedroom.

Had he but known it, Sylvester was not feeling at all amorous. He was tired, hungry, and in a fair way to regretting the impulse which had made him stop at the Blue Boar. To assist in an elopement was conduct quite unbecoming his position; moreover, it would lay him open to censure, which would not be easier to bear because it was justified. He was frowning down into the fire when Phoebe came into the room, and although he looked up at her entrance the frown did not immediately leave his brow.

She read in it condemnation of her attire, for she was still wearing her stuff travelling dress. He, on the other hand, had changed his buckskins and frockcoat for pantaloons and a longtailed coat of fine blue cloth, and had arranged a fresh necktie in intricate folds about his throat. It was morning dress, but it made her feel dowdy. To her vexation she found herself explaining that she had not changed her own dress because she would be obliged to go out again to the stable.

He had not noticed what she was wearing, and he replied in the light, indifferent tone which always set up her back: 'My dear Miss Marlow, there is no occasion to change your dress that I know of—and none for you to visit the stable again tonight, let me add!'

'I must be satisfied that Trusty has not contrived to rid himself of his poultice,' she said firmly. 'I have very little faith in Will Scaling.'

'You may have complete faith in Keighley.'

She made no reply to this, for while she felt that Keighley, who was developing a cough, ought not to leave the house, she was reluctant to reopen a quarrel just as she was about to sit down to dinner with Sylvester. She glanced uncertainly at him, and saw that the frown had yielded to a look of slight amusement. Having no idea that her countenance was a tolerably exact mirror for her thoughts, or that he had correctly interpreted the changes of expression that flitted across it, she was surprised, and looked enquiringly at him, her head a little tilted to one side.

She put him in mind of some small, brown bird. He laughed, and said: 'You look like—a sparrow! Yes, I know just what you are wondering whether or not to say. As you wish, Miss Marlow: I will cast an eye over the horses before I go to bed, and if I find that that singularly inappropriately named horse has eaten his poultice I will engage to supply him with a fresh one!'

'Do you know how to mix a bran poultice?' she asked sceptically.

'Better than you, I daresay. No, I don't, in general, apply them myself, but I hold it to be an excellent maxim that every man should know more than his grooms, and be as well able to deal with whatever need may arise in his stables. When I was a boy the farrier was one of my closest friends!'

'Do you have your own farrier?' she asked, diverted. 'My father does not, and it is something I have always wished for! But you will not mix a poultice in those clothes!'

'Rather than incur your displeasure I will even do that!' he assured her. 'It will expose me to Keighley's displeasure, of course, but I shan't regard that. Which puts me in mind of something I have to tell you. I find that the grooms' quarters here are not at all what Keighley is accustomed to: there is, in fact, only the room in which the ostler sleeps and that, being above that very ill-built stable, is extremely cold. I know you will agree that that will not do, and I hope you won't dislike the arrangement I have made, which is that the daughter of the house is to give up her chamber to Keighley, and herself sleep on a trestle-bed in your room.'

'Why shouldn't she sleep in her mother's room?' objected Phoebe, by no means pleased with this further example of Sylvester's high-handed ways.

'There is not space enough,' said Sylvester.

'Or Keighley might share Will Scaling's room?'

'He would be afraid to.'

'Nonsense! the poor boy is perfectly harmless!'

'Keighley has the greatest dislike of half-wits.'

'Then why don't you let him set up a trestle-bed in *your* room?' she demanded.

'Because I should be very likely to catch his cold,' explained Sylvester.

She sniffed, but appeared to find this answer reasonable, for she said no more. A welcome interruption was provided by the arrival upon the scene of Miss Alice Scaling, panting under the load of a tray piled high with covered dishes. She was a strapping girl, with apple-red cheeks, and a wide grin, and when she had dumped the tray down on the sideboard she paused a moment to fetch her breath before bobbing a curtsey to Sylvester, and reciting: 'Mother's compliments, and there's chickens, and rabbit-stew, and a casserole of rice with the giblets, and curd pudding, and apple fritters, and please to say if your honour would fancy the end of the mutton-pie Mother and me and Will had to our dinner.' A hissing admonition from the passage caused her to amend this speech. 'Please to say if *your grace* would fancy it! There's a tidy bit of it left, and it's good,' she added confidentially.

'Thank you, I am sure it is,' he replied. 'I hardly think we shall need it, however.'

'You're welcome if you do,' said Miss Scaling, setting out the dishes on the table with hearty good-will. 'And no need to fear going short tomorrow, because you're going to have a boiled turkey. I shall wring his neck first thing in the morning, and into the pot he'll go the instant he's plucked and drawed. That way he won't eat tough,' she explained. 'We hadn't meant to have killed him, but Mother says dukes is more important than a gobble-cock, even if he *is* a prime young 'un. And after that we'll have Mr Shap's pig off of him, and there'll be the legs and the cheeks, and the loin, and the chitterlings and all, your honour! No, your *grace*! I do be forgetting!' she said, beaming apologetically.

'It makes no matter what you call me, but pray don't wring your turkey's neck on my account!' he said, with a quelling glance at Phoebe, who showed every sign of succumbing to an unseemly fit of giggling.

'What's a turkey?' said Miss Scaling, in a large-minded spirit. 'Happen we can come by another of *them*, but dukes ain't found under every bush, that's what Mother says.'

On this piece of worldly wisdom she withdrew, pulling the door shut behind her with enough vigour to drown Phoebe's sudden peal of laughter.

'What an atrocious girl you are!' remarked Sylvester. 'Don't you know better than to laugh at yokels?'

'It was your face, when she said you were more important than a gobble-cock!' explained Phoebe, wiping her eyes. 'Has anyone ever told you that before?'

'No, never. I take it to be a handsome compliment. But she mustn't slay that turkey.'

'Oh, you have only to give her the price of another bird and she will be perfectly satisfied!'

'But nothing would prevail upon me to eat a bird that had been thrust warm into the pot!' he objected. 'And what are chitterlings?'

'Well, they are the *inside* parts of the pig,' said Phoebe, bubbling over again.

'Good God! Heaven send it may stop snowing before we come to *that*! In the meantime, shall I carve these chickens, or will you?'

'Oh, no! You do it, if you please!' she replied, seating herself at the table. 'You cannot imagine how hungry I am!'

'I can, for I am very hungry myself. I wonder why quite half this bird has been removed? Oh, I suppose it was for Orde! How is he, by the by?'

'Well, he seems to be going on quite prosperously, but the doctor said he must not get up for a week. I don't know how I shall contrive to keep him in bed, for he will find it a dead bore, you know.'

He agreed to this, reflecting, however, that Tom would not be the only one to find a prolonged sojourn at the inn a dead bore.

Conversation during the meal was desultory, Sylvester being tired and Phoebe careful to inaugurate no topic for discussion that might lead him to ask embarrassing questions. He asked her none, but his mind was not so much divorced from interest in her adventure as she supposed. Between the snow and Tom's broken leg it seemed probable that they would all of them be chained to the Blue Boar for some appreciable time. Sylvester had taken his own measures to invest Phoebe's situation with a certain measure of propriety, but very little doubt existed in his brain that it was the part of a man of the world at least to do what lay within his power to frustrate an elopement. The evils of so clandestine an adventure might not be apparent to a country-bred boy of nineteen, but Sylvester, older than Tom by far more than the eight years that lay between them, was fully alive to them. He supposed he could do no less than bring them to Tom's notice. He had not the smallest intention of discussing the affair with Phoebe: an awkward task in any circumstances, and in her case likely to prove fruitless, since her entire freedom from the confusion natural to a girl discovered in an escapade she must know to be grossly improper argued a singularly brazen disposition.

As soon as dinner was over she withdrew to Tom's room, to find that he had been devoting considerable thought to her predicament. One aspect of it had struck him forcibly, and he lost no time in presenting it to her.

'You know what we were saying, when Keighley brought in my dinner? About the Duke's not wishing to offer for you? Well, if that's the case, Phoebe, you need not go to London after all! What a pair of gudgeons we were not to have thought of that before! I have been racking my brains to hit upon a way of getting you there, too!'

'I did think of it,' replied Phoebe. 'But even though the Duke won't be a danger I am quite determined to go to my grandmother. It isn't only being afraid of Mama, Tom—though when I consider how angry she will be with me for running away, I own I feel *sick* with terror!—it is—oh, having once escaped I cannot—*will* not—go back! You see, even Papa doesn't love me very much. Not enough to support me, when I implored him to do so. When he held it over my head that if I wouldn't accept an offer from Salford he would tell Mama I felt myself free from *every* bond.'

'But you aren't, Phoebe,' Tom pointed out. 'You are under age, and he is your father, you know. Your grandmother has no power to keep you against his will.'

'Oh, no! And perhaps, if he truly wished for my return, I should go back willingly. But he won't. If I can prevail upon Grandmama to keep me with her I think Papa will be as glad as Mama to be rid of me. At any rate, he won't care whether I am at Austerby or not, except that he will miss me a little when he discovers how unreliable Sawley is when there is no one to watch over the stables.'

Tom did not know what to say to this. He had thought it reasonable enough that she should have fled from her home when faced (as she had believed) with a distasteful marriage; but that she should do so for no other reason than that she was not happy there shocked him a little. He could not approve; on the other hand he was well aware of the misery she would be made to suffer if she were forced to return to Austerby after such an exploit, and he was much too fond of her to withhold whatever help he could render. So he said presently: 'What can I do, Phoebe? I've made a mull of it, but if there *is* anything I can do I promise you I will.'

She smiled warmly at him. 'You didn't make a mull of it: it was all that wretched donkey! Perhaps, if we are not discovered before you are able to help yourself, I might still go to London on the stage-coach, and you will buy my ticket for me. But there is no question of that yet.'

'No, not while the snow lasts. And in any event—'

'In any event I hope you don't think I would leave you in this case! I'm not so shabby! No, don't tease yourself, Tom! I shall come about, see if I don't! Perhaps, when the Duke goes away–I should think he would do so as soon as it may be possible, wouldn't you?–he will carry a letter to Grandmama for me.'

'Phoebe, has he said anything? About your having run away, I mean?' Tom asked abruptly.

'No, not a word! Isn't it fortunate?' she replied.

'I don't know that. Seems to me–Well, he must think it excessively odd! What happened at Austerby, when it was discovered that you had gone away? Hasn't he even told you that?'

'No, but I didn't ask him.'

'Good God! I hope he does not think–Phoebe, did he say if he meant to come up to visit me presently?'

'No, do you wish him to?' she asked. 'Shall I send him to you? That is, if he has not already gone to look at Trusty for me. He promised he would do so, and put on a fresh poultice if it should be needed.'

'Phoebe!' uttered Tom explosively. 'If you made him do so it was perfectly outrageous! You are treating him as though he were a lackey!'

She gave an involuntary chuckle. 'No, am I? I daresay it would do him a great deal of good, but I didn't make him go out to attend to the horses. He offered to do so, and I own I was surprised. Why do you wish him to visit you?'

'That's my concern. Keighley will be coming in before he goes to bed, and I'll ask him to convey a civil message to the Duke. You are not to go downstairs again, Phoebe. Understand?'

'No, I am going to bed,' she replied. 'I am so sleepy I can hardly keep my eyes open. But what do you think? That odious man has had Alice Scaling give up her bedchamber to Keighley and set up a trestle for herself in mine! Without so much as asking my leave, and all because he is too proud to let

Keighley have a trestle-bed in *his* room! He said it was because he feared to catch his cold, but I know better!'

'So do I—much better!' said Tom. 'Lord, what a goose you are! You go to bed! And mind, Phoebe! be civil to the Duke when you meet him again!'

She was granted the opportunity to obey this order sooner than he had expected, for at that moment Sylvester walked in, saying: 'May I come in? How do you go on, Orde? You look a degree better, I think.'

'Yes, pray do come in!' said Phoebe, before Tom could speak. 'He was wishing you would come to visit him. Have you been out to the stable yet?'

'I have, ma'am, and you may go to bed with a quiet mind. Trusty shows no disposition to rid himself of his poultice. There is some heat still in his companion's hock, but nothing to cause uneasiness.'

'Thank you! I am truly obliged to you!' she said.

'So am I, sir—*most* truly obliged to you!' said Tom. 'It is devilish kind of you to put yourself to all this trouble! I don't know how to thank you.'

'Well, I *have* thanked him,' said Phoebe, apparently feeling that any further display of gratitude would be excessive.

'Yes, well, it's time you went to bed!' said Tom, directing a speaking look at her. 'His grace will excuse you, so you may say good-night, and be off!'

'Yes, Grandpapa!' said Phoebe incorrigibly. 'Good-night, my lord Duke!'

'Sleep well, Sparrow!' retorted Sylvester, holding the door for her.

To Tom's relief she went away without committing any more solecisms. He drew a long breath, as Sylvester shut the door, and said: 'I am very conscious, my lord Duke, that an explanation—'

'Call me Salford,' interrupted Sylvester. 'Did the sawbones subject you to further tortures? I trust not: he told me that Keighley had done all he should.'

'No, no, he only bound it up again when he had put some lotion on it!' Tom assured him. 'And that puts me in mind of something else! I wish you had not gone out in such weather to fetch him, sir! I was excessively shocked when I heard of it! Oh, and you must have paid him his fee, for I did not! If you will tell me what it was—'

'I will render a strict account to you,' promised Sylvester, pulling up a chair to the bedside, and sitting down. 'That hock, by the by, will have to be fomented for a day or two, but there should be no lasting injury. A tidy pair, so far as I could judge by lantern-light.'

'My father bought them last year—proper high-bred 'uns!' Tom said. 'I wouldn't have had this happen to them for a thousand pounds!'

'I'll go bail you wouldn't! A harsh parent?'

'No, no, he's a prime gun, but—!'

'I know,' said Sylvester sympathetically. 'So was mine, *but*—!'

Tom grinned at him. 'You must think me a cowhanded whipster! But if only that curst donkey hadn't brayed—However, it's no use saying that: my father will say I made wretched work of it, and the worst of it is I think I did! And what sort of a case I should have been if you hadn't come to the rescue, sir, I don't know!'

'If you must thank anybody, thank Keighley!' recommended Sylvester. 'I couldn't have set the broken bone, you know.'

'No, but it was you who fetched Upsall, which was a great deal too kind of you. There's another thing, too.' He hesitated, looking rather shyly at Sylvester, and colouring a little. 'Phoebe didn't understand—she isn't by any means fly to the time of day, you know!—but I did, and—and I'm very much obliged to you for what you've done for her. Sending that girl to sleep with her, I mean. I don't know if it will answer, or if—Well, the thing is, sir—now that we are in such a rare mess do you think I ought to marry her?'

Sylvester had been regarding him with friendly amusement, but the naïve question brought a startled frown to his face. 'But isn't that your intention?' he asked.

'No—oh, lord, no! I mean, it *wasn't* my intention (though I did offer to!) until we were grassed by that overturn. But now that we're cooped up here perhaps I ought, as man of honour—Only ten to one she'll refuse to marry me, and then were shall we be?'

'If you are not eloping, what *are* you doing?' demanded Sylvester.

'I guessed that was what you must be thinking, sir,' said Tom.

'I imagine you might. Nor am I the only one who thinks it!' said Sylvester. 'When I left Austerby I did so because Marlow had already set out for the Border in pursuit of you!'

'No!' exclaimed Tom. 'Well, what a gudgeon! If he thought Phoebe had run off with me why the deuce hadn't he the wit to enquire for me at the Manor? My mother could have told him all was well!'

'I can only say that she did not appear to me to have perfectly understood that,' responded Sylvester dryly. 'As it chanced it was she who came to Austerby, bringing with her the letter you had written to her. You young idiot, I don't know precisely what you told her, but it certainly didn't persuade her that all was well! It threw her into a state of great affliction—and what she said to Lady Marlow I shall always be happy to think I was privileged to hear!'

'Did she give her snuff?' asked Tom appreciatively. 'But she *can't* have thought I had eloped with Phoebe! Why, I particularly told her there was no need for her to be in a fidget! Lord Marlow might, I daresay, but not Mama!'

'On the contrary! Lord Marlow pooh-poohed the suggestion. He was only brought to believe it on the testimony of one of his younger daughters. I forget what her name is: a sanctimonious schoolgirl whose piety I found nauseating.'

'Eliza,' said Tom instantly. 'But she knew nothing about it! Unless she was listening at the keyhole, and if that was the case she must have known we hadn't gone to the Border.'

'She was, but she insisted that she had heard you say you were going to Gretna Green.'

Tom frowned in an effort of memory. 'I suppose I might have said so: I know I couldn't see any other way out of the fix. But Phoebe had a much better scheme, as it happened, which I own I was devilish glad to hear! I'm as fond of her as I could be—well, I've run tame at Austerby ever since I was breeched, you know, and she's like my sister!—but I'm damned if I want to marry her! The thing was I promised I'd help her, and the only way I could think of to do it was by doing so.'

'Help her to do what?' interrupted Sylvester, considerably mystified.

'To escape from Austerby. So—'

'Well, I blame no one for wishing to do that, but what the devil made you choose such a moment? Didn't you know there was snow in the air?'

'Yes, of course I did, sir, but I *had* no choice! The need was urgent—or, at least, Phoebe thought it was. If I hadn't taken her she meant to go to London by herself, on the common stage!'

'Why?'

Tom hesitated, glancing speculatively at Sylvester. Sylvester said encouragingly: 'I won't cry rope on you!'

The smile won Tom; he said in a burst of confidence: 'Well, the truth is the whole thing was a fudge, but Lady Marlow told Phoebe you were going to Austerby to make her an offer! I must say it sounded like a hum to me, but it seems Lord Marlow thought so too, so one can't blame Phoebe for being taken in, and cast into flat despair because of it.'

'In fact,' said Sylvester, 'an offer from me would not have been welcome to her?'

'Oh, lord, no!' said Tom. 'She said nothing would induce her to marry you! But I daresay you may have seen how it is in that house: if you had meant to offer for her Lady Marlow would have bullied her into submitting. The only thing was for her to run away.' He stopped, uneasily aware of having said more than was discreet. There was an odd expression in Sylvester's eyes, hard to interpret but rather disquieting. 'You know what females are, sir!' he added, trying to mend matters. 'It was all nonsense, of course, for she scarcely knew you. I hope—I mean—perhaps I shouldn't have told you!'

'Oh, why not?' Sylvester said lightly, smiling again.

10

Tom was relieved to see the smile, but he was not wholly reassured. 'I beg pardon!' he said. 'I thought it wouldn't signify, telling you how it was, if you *didn't* wish to offer for her—and you don't, do you?'

'No, certainly not! What did I do to inspire Miss Marlow with this violent dislike of me?'

'Oh, I don't know! Nothing, I daresay,' said Tom uncomfortably. 'I expect you are not just her style, that's all.'

'Not timbered up to her weight, in fact. Where, by the way, are you meaning to take her?'

'To her grandmother. She lives in London, and Phoebe is persuaded she will take her part—or that she *would* have done so, if it had been necessary.'

Sylvester's eyes lifted suddenly to Tom's. 'Do you mean Lady Ingham?' he asked.

'Yes,' Tom nodded. 'The other one died years ago. Are you acquainted with Lady Ingham, sir?'

'Oh, yes!' replied Sylvester, a laugh in his voice. 'She is my godmother.'

'Is she, though? Then you must know her pretty well. Do you think she will let Phoebe stay with her? Phoebe seems to think there can be no doubt, but *I* can't help wondering whether she won't think it pretty shocking of her to have run off from home, and perhaps send her back again. What do *you* think, sir?'

'How can I say?' countered Sylvester. 'Miss Marlow, I collect, still holds by her scheme, even though the menace of an offer from me doesn't exist?'

'Oh, yes! I did suggest to her that she need not go to London after all, but she says she will do so, and I must say I think she should—if only the old lady will receive her kindly! You know, sir, Lady Marlow is a regular brute, and it's not a particle of use thinking Marlow will protect Phoebe, because he won't! Phoebe knows there's no help to be got from him—well, he told her so, when she begged him to stand by her!—and now she says she shan't go back on any account. Only what's to be done? Even if the snow melted tomorrow I can't escort her, and I *know* I ought not to let her go alone. But if that detestable woman catches her here the trap will be down!'

'Not so much fretting and fussing, Galahad!' said Sylvester. 'There's no immediate danger, and before it becomes imminent I don't doubt you will have hit upon an answer to the problem. Or I might do so for you.'

'How?' asked Tom quickly.

'Well,' replied Sylvester, getting on, 'somewhere between this place and Austerby I have a chaise. I have left orders at the Bear, in Hungerford, that when it arrives there my servants are to be directed to this inn. In the circumstances, I shall be delighted to convey Miss Marlow to her grandmother!'

Tom's face lightened; he exclaimed: 'Oh, by Jove, would you do that, sir? It would be the very thing—if she will go with you!'

'Let me beg you not to fidget yourself into a fever on the chance that she won't! You had much better try if you can go to sleep. I only hope you may not be too uncomfortable to do so.'

'Oh, no! That is, Dr Upsall left some stuff he said I should drink: syrup of poppies, or some such thing. I daresay I shall sleep like a log.'

'Well, if you should wake, and wish for anything, knock on the wall behind you,' said Sylvester. 'I shall hear you: I am a tolerably light sleeper. I'll send Keighley to you now. Good-night!'

He went away with a nod and a smile, leaving Tom to his various reflections. Prominent amongst these was a determination to endure hours of wakefulness rather than to drag his noble acquaintance from his bed. Thanks, however, to Keighley, interpreting the surgeon's instructions liberally, he very soon succumbed to a large dose of the narcotic prescribed for him, and slept the night through. His dreams were untroubled, for although, when Sylvester left him, he thought over all that he had disclosed, and wished the greater part of it unsaid, he was soon able to persuade himself that he had been grossly indulging his imagination when he had read danger in that queer look of Sylvester's. When he came to consider the matter he could not remember that he had said anything to arouse anger in Sylvester. It was not given to Tom, rating himself modestly, to understand the emotions of one who had been encouraged all the years of his adult life to set his value high.

But the discovery that Phoebe had decided he was not at all the sort of man she wished to marry had made Sylvester furious. While he believed her to be eloping with her true love he bore her no ill-will; but the case was now altered, and the more he thought of it the more did the wound to his self-esteem smart. He had chosen to single out from amongst the débutantes a little dab of a country girl, without style or countenance, and she had had the impertinence to snub him. She had done it in such a way, too, as to make a fool of him, and that was not an injury he could easily forgive. It was possible to forgive it when he supposed her to be in love with another man; but when he learned that her flight from her home—an outrageous action which only a passionate attachment to Tom could in some measure excuse—was due to a dread of being compelled to receive his addresses he was not only unable to forgive it, but became possessed of a strong desire to teach Miss Marlow a lesson. To be sure, her crest would very soon be lowered if she thought any match half as brilliant would be offered her, but that was not quite what Sylvester wanted. Something of greater importance than his consequence had been hurt. That he could shrug away; he could not shrug off the knowledge that she apparently found him repulsive. She had had the insolence to criticize him, too; and she did not scruple to show him that she held him cheap. What was it Tom had said? *Nothing would induce her to marry you!* A little too cock-sure, Miss Marlow! The opportunity will not be granted you—but let us see if you can be made to feel sorry!

Sylvester dropped asleep on this vengeful thought; and since no summons was rapped on the wall dividing his room from Tom's, he did not wake until Keighley brought his breakfast to him at ten o'clock next morning. He then discovered that his faithful henchman was not only looking heavy-eyed, but had lost his voice as well. He said: 'Go back to bed at once, John! Good God, I *have* knocked you up! you ought to have a mustard-plaster on your chest. Tell Mrs Scaling to fetch one up to you—and go away!'

Keighley started to whisper reassurance, but was stopped by a paroxysm of coughing.

'John, don't be a nodcock! Do you think I want your death at my door! Go to bed! And tell them to kindle a fire in your room—*my* orders!'

'How *can* I lay up, your grace?' whispered Keighley. 'Who's to look after Mr Orde if I do?'

'To hell with Mr Orde! Can't the half-wit attend to him? Well, if he can't, I must. What has to be done for him?'

'I've done all that's needful for the moment, your grace, and seen to the grays, but—'

'Then you have nothing further to worry about, and may go to bed without more ado. Now, don't be a gudgeon, John! You will only give him your cold if you hang about him!'

'He's got it,' croaked Keighley.

'No, has he? Well, *I* have no wish to catch it, so don't let me see you again until you're rid of it!' He saw that Keighley was torn by a longing for his bed and a determination not to leave his post, and said threateningly: 'If I have to get up to you, John, you'll be sorry!'

That made Keighley laugh, which brought on another paroxysm. This left him feeling so exhausted that he was very glad to obey his master.

An hour later, Sylvester, beautiful to behold in a frogged dressing-gown of crimson and gold brocade, strolled into Tom's room, saying cheerfully: 'Good-morning, Galahad! So you've taken Keighley's cold, have you? What a mutton-headed thing to do! Did you sleep well?'.

'Oh, like a top, thank you, sir! As for the cold, if I *must* stay in bed I might as well have a cold as not. But I'm devilish sorry for Keighley: he's as sick as a horse!'

'You will soon be devilish sorry for yourself, for I've sent him to bed, and you will be obliged to endure my ministrations in place of his. What, as a start, can I do for you?'

'Good God, nothing!' replied Tom, looking horrified. 'As though I would let you wait on me!'

'You won't have any choice in the matter.'

'Yes, yes, I will! The boy can do all I want, sir!'

'What, the half-wit? If you think that a choice I'll thank you not to be so insulting, Thomas!'

Tom laughed at that, but insisted that for the moment at least he needed nothing, except (with a sigh) something to do.

'That's what we shall all of us be pining for, if the snow lasts,' said Sylvester. 'If Mrs Scaling cannot supply us with a pack of cards we shall be obliged to make up charades, or something of that nature. Do you care to read *The Knight of St John*? It came out last year, and is by the author of *The Hungarian Brothers*. I'll fetch it for you.'

Tom was no great reader, but when Sylvester, handing him the first volume of Miss Porter's lastest romance, said: 'I don't like it as well as *The Hungarian Brothers*, but it's quite a lively tale,' he realized that the work was not, as he had feared, a history, but a novel, and was much relieved. He accepted it with thanks, and then, after a thoughtful moment, asked Sylvester if he read many novels.

'Any that come in my way. Why?'

'Oh, I don't know!' Tom said. 'I thought perhaps you might not.'

Sylvester looked a little surprised, but said after a moment: 'Oh, did you think that because my mother is a poetess I might have a turn for verse? No: nothing of the sort!'

'*Is* she?' said Tom, awed.

'Yes, indeed she is. And I assure you she does not despise novels! I fancy she buys almost all that are published. She is an invalid, you see, and reading is her greatest solace.'

'Oh!' said Tom.

'I must go and look to my horses,' said Sylvester. 'I collect that Miss Marlow is in the stables already, probably fomenting that hock. I only hope I may not fall under her displeasure for making so belated an appearance!'

He went away to finish dressing; and then, after consigning Keighley to Mrs Scaling's care, went out to join Phoebe. It was still snowing hard, but a brazier was burning in the stable, Phoebe, having turned True in his stall, and removed his quarterpiece, was vigorously brushing him.

'Good-morning!' said Sylvester, removing his coat, and rolling up his sleeves. 'I'll do that for you, Miss Marlow. How is the hock?'

'Better, I think. I have just been fomenting it again. I don't think Tom would like it if I let you dress the horses, Duke.'

'Then don't tell him,' said Sylvester, taking the brush away from her. 'Doesn't he think me capable of the task?'

'Oh, it isn't that! He has a great respect for your consequence, you see, and perhaps wouldn't think it proper for you to do it! But in general he is not at all stupid, I assure you!'

The smile that went with this remark was so ingenuous that Sylvester was obliged to laugh. Phoebe would have set to work on Trusty with the currycomb, but was deterred by Sylvester's pointing out to her that her skirt was already covered with True's hairs. He recommended her to change her dress, giving the one she had on to Alice to brush, but she replied that as the only other dress she had with her was of muslin, she rather thought she might freeze to death in it. 'Besides, Alice has gone to tell old Mr Shap that we must have his pig. It isn't full-grown, so perhaps he won't sell it.'

'Why not?'

'Because he would get more for it later, of course. And also he may be in a bad skin.'

'In a *what*?'

She looked up, twinkling, from the task of picking the short hairs out of her skirt. 'I think it means he had a sullen disposition! But I expect Alice will get the pig: she is a most redoubtable girl!'

'You and she should deal extremely,' he commented, turning True about, and stripping off the rest of his clothing.

At that she raised her head again, tilting it enquiringly. 'Do you mean that I am redoubtable? Oh, you are quite mistaken!'

'Am I? Then let us say intrepid!'

She sighed. 'I wish I were! The case is that I am a wretched coward.'

'Your father gives you quite another character.'

'I don't fear fences.'

'What, then?'

'People—some people! To—to be slain by unkindness.'

He looked at her with a slight frown; but before he could ask her to explain what she meant they were interrupted by Alice, who came in, stamping her feet to rid her pattens of the clogged snow, and followed by an ancient with very few teeth but a crafty eye. This individual she introduced as a nasty, twitty old maw-worm, disclosing that he wouldn't sell his pig until convinced that it would be eaten by a duke, and not by a Captain Sharp, masquerading as such.

Considerably taken aback, for he had never before had his credentials doubted, much less taken for a Captain Sharp, Sylvester said: 'Well, I don't know how I should be able to convince him! Unless he'd like one of my visiting-cards?'

But this Mr Shap rejected, informing the company that he wasn't a lettered man. He apparently felt this to be a triumph, for he then fell into a fit of cackling mirth. Assured by Phoebe that Sylvester was a duke, he told her, but kindly, that she had been took in by a lot of slum. 'You don't want to listen to this great fussock here, missie!' he said, jerking his thumb at Alice. 'She's got a brother what's dicked in the nob, and a proper jobbernoll *she* is! Ah!'

He then nodded his head cunningly several times, and demanded to be told who had ever heard of a duke dressing his horses. But by this time Sylvester had taken the purse from his coat-pocket, and said briefly: 'What's the figure?'

Mr Shap, with great promptness, named a price which drew a shriek of scandalized wrath from Alice. She begged Sylvester not to be choused out of his money by a wicked old lick-penny; but Sylvester, who was tired of Mr Shap, dropped three sovereigns into his gnarled hand, and told him to be off. Such openhanded conduct caused Mr Shap to dang himself if it weren't a duke after all; and after giving Sylvester a fatherly admonition not to allow himself to be clerked by Widow Scaling, he hobbled off, calling, in a cracked, senile voice, to Will to come and fetch away the pig.

'Well,' said Alice, preparing to follow him, 'I'm proper set about he should have behaved like a smidge, but one thing's sure, your honour! with you paying him so handsome he knows you are a duke, and so he'll tell everyone.' She nodded, her eyes sparkling with joyful anticipation. 'Happen we'll have 'em all up to the tap today, wishful for to see you with their own eyes!' she told Sylvester. 'Why, there's been nothing like it, not since we had the girl with two heads putting up here! Her dad was taking of her to London, being wishful to put her into a big fair they do be having there. We had half Hungerford here, as well as Kintbury, and not a drop of liquor left in the house by ten o'clock.'

The fascinated horror with which Sylvester listened to these artless confidences had long since proved to be too much for Phoebe's gravity. Alice, grinning sympathetically upon her mirth, went off to supervise the transport of Mr Shap's pig; and Sylvester demanded, with some asperity, whether his attractions were rated above or below those of a freak.

'Oh, below!' Phoebe answered, wiping her streaming eyes. 'For you are not in yourself remarkable, you know! Your oddity is in being out of place. I daresay, had you been putting up at the Pelican, your presence in the district wouldn't have aroused the least interest.'

'How much I wish we were all of us at the Pelican!' he exclaimed. 'Only think how different our lot would be! No, *don't* let us think of it!'

'I don't mean to,' responded Phoebe cheerfully. 'The Pelican would not do for me at all, in such a situation. But if Keighley is better tomorrow, I shouldn't wonder at it if you were able to reach Speenhamland. It can't be many miles ahead, after all!'

'And abandon you and Thomas to your fates? If that's the opinion you hold of me I am able to understand your reluctance to receive my addresses, Miss Marlow!'

She blushed fierily, for although Tom had warned her of his indiscretion she had been encouraged by Sylvester's previous manner to believe that he would not refer to it. 'I beg pardon! Of course I did not—it wasn't—I mean, it was all a stupid mistake, wasn't it?' she stammered.

Venturing to look up into his face she saw that his eyes were gleaming with mockery; and she could not doubt that he was enjoying her discomfiture. But as resentment rose in her breast the malice vanished from his expression; and she perceived that he really had got an enchanting smile. This was surprising. She had not before encountered that engaging look; and a moment earlier there had been no trace of it. She was suspicious of it, and yet could not help responding to it.

'Yes, just a stupid mistake!' he said reassuringly. 'Shall I promise not to pay my addresses to you? I am perfectly ready to do so, if it will make you more comfortable.'

But she only laughed at this, and got up, saying that she had no longer any fears on that head. She went away then, and when he saw her next it was an hour later, in Tom's room, polishing with a scrap of sandpaper the spillikins Tom was cleverly whittling from some wood begged from Mrs Scaling. Tom looked up, smiling, and said: 'Can you play spillikins, sir? I was used to be a dab at the game, and am issuing a challenge to all comers!'

'I don't fear you,' responded Sylvester, handing him a large pewter tankard. 'Home-brewed, Thomas—the best thing we've yet had here!—Your skill may be superior, but I'll swear I'm the more in practice! Unless you have young brothers and sisters, in which case I may hedge off a trifle.'

'No, I haven't,' grinned Tom. 'Have you?'

'No, but I have frequently played with my nephew,' Sylvester replied.

His attention was just then diverted by a kick on the door, followed by a demand from Will Scaling to be admitted. He turned to open the door, and so did not see the looks of consternation which his words brought to his young friends' faces. By the time he had foiled an attempt by Will to dump a heavy nuncheon-tray down on Tom's legs they had revived sufficiently from the shock of discovering that he had a nephew to be able to meet his casual glance with the appearance at least of composure. They were granted no opportunity for an exchange of more than looks until later in the day, for Sylvester returned with Phoebe to Tom's room after their nuncheon, and only left it when it became time to attend again to the horses. Mrs Scaling having unearthed from the recesses of a cupboard a pack of somewhat greasy playing-cards the beleaguered travellers were not restricted to spillikins or paper games, but embarked on several desperate gambling ventures, using dried peas for counters, and managing the cards and the bets of all the imaginary persons created by them to make up the correct number of gamesters. This was the sort of fooling that might have amused them for a few minutes, but Phoebe's talent for endowing her creations with names and characteristics invested the nonsense with wit; and when Sylvester, not slow to follow her lead, invented two eccentrics on his own account the game rapidly became a sort of charade, exercising the histrionic ability of the two players, and keeping Tom, who did not aspire to such heights, in a continuous chuckle. But although Tom laughed he thought it a dangerous diversion, for every now and then Phoebe could not resist indulging her genius for mimicry. Tom recognized several characters from *The Lost Heir*; he was unacquainted with the originals, but to judge by Sylvester's swift response Phoebe hit them off very recognizably.

'For the lord's sake take care what you're about!' Tom warned her, as soon as Sylvester had left the room. 'If he *should* read your book I wouldn't wager a groat against the chance of his recalling all this mummery of yours, and then putting two and two together, for he's no fool! You know, Phoebe, I do think you should make a push to alter that book! I mean, after the way he has behaved to us it seems the shabbiest thing to make him out a villain! I can't think why you should have done so, either, or have supposed him to be insufferably proud. Why, he hasn't the least height in his manner!'

'I must own I never expected him to be so amiable,' she acknowledged. 'Not but what to be assuming the airs of a great man in such a place as this would be quite absurd, and I give him credit for knowing it.'

'Phoebe, you must change the book!' he urged. 'First, we know that he reads novels, and now he says he has a nephew! Lord, I didn't know where to look!'

'No, I was ready to sink myself,' she agreed. 'However, I don't think it signifies so very much. Everyone has nephews, after all! I daresay he may have several of them, but the thing is, remember, that Maximilian was wholly in Count Ugolino's power, being an orphan. There can be no resemblance!'

'What *is* Salford's family?' Tom asked.

'Well, I don't know precisely. There are quite a number of Raynes, but how nearly they may be related to him I haven't a notion.'

'I must say, Phoebe, I think you should have discovered just how it was before you put him into your book!' said Tom, in accents of strong censure. 'Surely your father must have a *Peerage*?'

'I don't know if he has,' she said guiltily. 'I never thought—I mean, when I wrote the book I didn't imagine it would be published! I own, I wish now that I hadn't made Salford the villain, but, after all, Tom, if I can but change his *appearance* no one will ever guess who Ugolino is! It is all the fault of his wretched eyebrows: if Salford had not had that *tigerish* look I should never have thought of making him a villain!'

'What a bag of moonshine!' Tom exclaimed. 'Tigerish look, indeed! He has a most agreeable countenance!'

'Now that is coming it *too* strong!' interrupted Phoebe, roused to indignation. 'His *smile* is agreeable, but in general his expression is one of haughty indifference! I had nearly said *disdain*, but he is not disdainful of his fellows because he scarcely notices them.'

'I suppose you think he has scarcely noticed me?' said Tom, with heavy sarcasm.

'No, because he took a fancy to you, and so it pleases him to treat you with flattering distinction. And also,' Phoebe pursued, her eyes narrowing as though to bring Sylvester's image into perspective, 'I believe it piqued him to be told that I disliked him.'

'I wish I had not said anything about that!'

'Oh, don't tease yourself over it! I am persuaded it has done him a great deal of good!' she said blithely. 'I assure you, Tom, when I met him previously, in London, his manners were very different. *Then* he had no thought of engaging the good opinion of such a poor little dab as I am; *now* he bestows every degree of attention on me, until I daresay I shall soon find myself obliged to be in raptures about him.'

'You may well!' returned Tom. 'Let me tell you, Phoebe, that if you do contrive to reach London it will be thanks to his good offices, not to mine! He says he will escort you there in his chaise, so for the lord's sake be civil to him!'

'No!' she exclaimed. 'Did he say so indeed? Well, I must own that that's excessively handsome of him, but it won't answer, of course: I can't leave you here alone, and in such a case! Why, what a monster I should be to think of doing anything so inhuman!' She added naughtily: 'So I need not be civil after all, need I?'

I I

Sylvester, when presently applied to, gave his support to both contestants. He said that Tom must certainly not be abandoned to his fate; but he also said that Phoebe had no need to delay her journey on that account, since he himself would remain at the Blue Boar, delegating to Keighley the task of conveying her to her grandmother. She could not but be grateful to him for so practical a solution to her difficulty, her only remaining anxiety being the fear that she would be overtaken by her father before the arrival of Sylvester's chaise at the Blue Boar.

'I can only say, Miss Marlow,' responded Sylvester to this confidence, 'that if the first vehicle to reach us from the west is not my chaise two Hounslow-bred postilions will shortly be seeking situations in some other household than mine!'

In fact, his chaise arrived two days later, within a very short time of the snow's ceasing to fall. Since it had taken the postilions more than two hours to accomplish the stage between Marlborough and Hungerford, Swale's graphic description of the perils overcome in the cause of duty were not needed to convince Phoebe that the condition of the roads was still too bad to make her father's appearance on the scene anything but a remote contingency.

Sylvester sent his chaise on to the Halfway House, a couple of miles up the road, but kept Swale at the Blue Boar. Swale, discovering that he must share a bedchamber with Keighley, and eat all his meals in the kitchen, was so much affronted that he hovered for as much as thirty seconds on the brink of tendering his resignation to his noble employer. He bowed stiffly when commanded to wait upon Mr Orde, and sought solace for his lacerated sensibilities in treating that hapless young gentleman with such meticulous politeness that Tom was very soon begging Sylvester to leave him to the less expert but less intimidating ministrations of Will Scaling. Tom's shyness of Sylvester had not survived forty-eight hours of depending upon him for his every need; and within an hour of having lodged this laughing complaint with him he was taking him roundly to task for having acted upon it in an ill-judged manner. 'The lord knows what you said to the poor fellow, but if I'd guessed you would say anything at all I never would have told you about it!' he said. 'It was worse than anything! He has been in here, begging my pardon, and telling me a bamboozling tale of having been feeling out of sorts, and hoping I shan't have cause to complain to you *again*! Lord! I promise you I was never more mortified in my life! A pretty sneaksby you made me, Salford! Did you threaten to turn him off, just because he don't care to wait on me?'

'I'm not so high-handed, Thomas. I only asked him to tell me if he was quite happy in my service.'

'Oh, was *that* all?' exclaimed Tom. 'No wonder he was looking so Tyburn-faced! And you say you're not high-handed! Well, *I* think you're *mediaeval*!'

That made Sylvester laugh. 'But in what way am I mediaeval? I pay him a handsome wage, you know.'

'But you didn't hire him to take care of me!'

'My dear Thomas, what in the world has he to do besides?' Sylvester interrupted, a little impatiently. 'All the work he has to do for *me* in this hedge-tavern could not occupy him for as much as a couple of hours out of the twenty-four!'

'No, but he is *your* valet, not mine! You might as well have ordered him to groom your horses, or sweep the floor. And beyond all else you told him he must share Keighley's room! Now, Salford, you *must* know that your valet is much above your groom's touch!'

'Not in my esteem.'

'Very likely not, but—'

'But nothing, Thomas! In my own household my esteem is all that signifies. Does that seem mediaeval to you? If it seems so to Swale he may leave me: he's not my slave!' He smiled suddenly. 'Keighley is more my slave, I assure you—and I never engaged him, and could never dismiss him. Now, what is there in that to make you frown at me?'

'I wasn't—I mean, I can't explain it, only my father always says one should take care not to offend the sensibilities of inferior persons, and though I daresay you didn't intend to do so, it does seem to me as if— But I should not say so!' Tom ended, rather hurriedly.

'Well, you have said so, haven't you?' said Sylvester, quite gently, but with the smile hardening on his lips.

'I beg your pardon, sir!'

Sylvester made no reply to this, but remarked in a thoughtful tone: 'To have become acquainted with you and with Miss Marlow ought to do me a great deal of good, I hope. What a number of faults I have of which I was never previously made aware!'

'I don't know what more I can do than beg your pardon,' Tom said stiffly.

'Why, nothing! Unless you like to instruct me how I should treat my servants?' He paused, as Tom looked at him with belligerence in his eyes, and his lips very resolutely closed, and said quickly: 'Oh, no! What an unhandsome thing to say to you! Forgive me: I didn't mean it!'

There could be no resisting that coaxing note, or the softened expression, half contrite, half quizzical, that put to rout the satyr-look. Tom had been conscious of a thin film of ice behind which Sylvester had seemed to withdraw; he had resented it; but it had melted, and he found himself no longer angry, but stammering: 'Oh, stuff! Besides, I had no business to be criticizing you! Particularly,' he added rather naïvely, 'when you have been so devilish kind to me!'

'Humdudgeon!'

'No, it ain't. What's more—'

'If you mean to be a dead bore, Thomas, I'm off!' Sylvester interrupted. 'And let me tell you that if you are trying to turn me up sweet you will be speedily bowled out! *Kind* was not the epithet you chose to describe my charitable attempt to make your bed more comfortable this morning!'

'Oh, well, I see I can't please you!' Tom said, grinning. 'First, I'm ungrateful, and now I'm a dead bore! But I'm not ungrateful, you know. I thought the trap was down when you arrived here, and so it was, for I'm in no case to help Phoebe. But you mean to do so, don't you?'

'Do I? Oh, convey her to London! Yes, I'll do that,' Sylvester replied. 'If she still wishes it—though what she now hopes to achieve by it I don't immediately perceive.'

Tom was unable to enlighten him, but Phoebe told him frankly that she hoped never to return to Austerby. This was sufficiently startling to make him put up his brows. She said, her eyes searching his face: 'My grandmother told me once that she wished she might have me to live with her—had always wished it! Only when my mother died it was not possible, from some cause or another, for her to make that offer to Papa. And then, you know, he married Mama, which made it, she thought, unnecessary, as well as grossly uncivil, to remove me from Austerby.'

A slightly sardonic gleam of amusement flickered in his eyes. 'But she did not, last year, invite you to remain with her?' he suggested.

A look of anxiety came into her face; her eyes, still fixed on his, seemed to question him. She said: 'No. But she thought—Sir Henry Halford warning her against my unusual exertion—well, she thought it not right to ask Papa to leave me in her charge, since she is unequal to the task of taking me to balls, and— But I think—I am sure—she didn't perfectly enter into my sentiments upon that head! I don't care for balls, or fashionable life. At least, it was very agreeable when I went out with my aunt Ingham, for she is excessively good-natured, and doesn't scold, or watch one all the time, or— But indeed I don't hanker after gaiety, and although, at that time, it didn't occur to me to ask her if I might live with her, when—' She paused, feeling the ice thin under her feet, and coloured.

'When you feared to be forced into a distasteful marriage?' he supplied helpfully.

Her colour deepened, but his words brought her engaging twinkle into her eyes. 'Well, yes!' she acknowledged. 'When *that* happened, I thought suddenly that if Grandmama would let me reside with her I need not be a trouble, but, on the contrary, *useful*, perhaps. And, in any event, it won't be so very long now before I come of age, and then I hope—I believe—the case will be quite altered, and I need be a charge on no one.'

He instantly suspected her of having formed an attachment for some hopeless ineligible, and asked her bluntly if she had matrimony in view.

'Matrimony! Oh, no!' she responded. 'I daresay I shall never be married. I have another scheme—quite different!' She added, in some confusion: 'Excuse me on that head, if you please: I had not meant to speak of it, and must not! Pray do not regard it! Only tell me if you think—for perhaps you are better acquainted with her than I—that my grandmother will like to have me to live with her?'

He believed that there was nothing Lady Ingham would like less; but he believed also, and maliciously, that she would find it impossible to repulse her granddaughter; and he replied, smiling: 'Why not?'

She looked relieved, but said very earnestly: 'Every day I spend away from Austerby strengthens my resolve never to go back there! I was never so happy in my life before! You can't understand how that should be so, I daresay, but I have felt, these last few days, as though I had escaped from a cage!' Her solemnity vanished. 'Oh! what a trite simile! Never mind!'

'Very well,' he said. 'Keighley shall escort you to London as soon as the roads are passable.'

She thanked him, but said doubtedly: 'And Tom?'

'I shall send a message to his parents, when you are gone. Don't you trust me? I shan't leave him until I have handed him over to his father.'

'Yes, indeed I trust you. I was wondering only whether I ought to accept so much help from you—using your chaise—depriving you of your groom!' She added naïvely: 'When I was not, at first, very civil to you!'

'But you are never civil to me!' he complained. 'You began by giving me a heavy set-down, and you followed that with a handsome trimming! And now you threaten to deny me a chance to retrieve my character!' He laughed, seeing her at a loss for words, and took her hand, and lightly kissed it. 'Cry friends, Sparrow! Am I so *very* bad?'

'No! I never said that, or thought it!' she stammered. 'How could I, when I scarcely knew you?'

'Oh, this is worse than anything!' he declared. 'No sooner seen than disliked! I understand you perfectly: I have frequently met such persons—only I had not thought myself to have been one of them!'

Goaded, she retorted: 'One does not, I believe!' Then she immediately looked stricken, and faltered: 'Oh, dear, my *wretched* tongue! I beg your pardon!'

The retort had made his eyes flash, but the look of dismay which so swiftly succeeded it disarmed him. 'If ever I met such a chastening pair as you and Orde! What next will you find to say to me, I wonder? Unnecessary, I'm persuaded, to tell you not to spare me!'

'Now *that* is the most shocking injustice!' she exclaimed. 'When Tom positively toad-eats you!'

'*Toad-eats* me? You can know nothing of toad-eaters if that is what you think!' He directed a suddenly penetrating look at her, and asked abruptly: 'Do you suppose that that is what I like? to be toad-eaten?'

She thought for a moment, and then said: 'No, not precisely. It is, rather, what you *expect*, perhaps, without liking or disliking.'

'You are mistaken! I neither expect it nor like it!'

She bowed her head, it might have been in acquiescence, but the ghost of a smile on her lips nettled him.

'Upon my word, ma'am—!' he said angrily, and there stopped, as she looked an enquiry. A reluctant laugh was dragged out of him. 'I recall now that I was told that you were not just in the common way, Miss Marlow!'

'Oh no! Did someone *indeed* say that of me!' she demanded, turning quite pink with pleasure. 'Who was it? Oh, do pray, tell me!'

He shook his head, amused by her eagerness. It was such a mild compliment, yet here she was, all agog to learn its source, looking like a child tantalized by a toy held out of her reach. 'Not I!'

She sighed. 'How infamous of you! Were you hoaxing me?'

'Not at all! Why should I?'

'I don't know, but it seems as though you might do so. People don't say pretty things of me–or, if they do, I never heard of it.' She pondered it. 'Of course, it might mean that I was merely *odd*–in a gothic way,' she said doubtfully.

'Yes–or outrageous!'

'No,' she decided. 'It couldn't have meant that, because I wasn't outrageous when I went to London. I behaved with perfect propriety–and insipidity.'

'You may have behaved with propriety, but insipidity I cannot allow!'

'Well, you thought so at the time!' she said tartly. 'And, to own the truth, I *was* insipid. Mama was watching me, you see.'

He remembered now how silent and stupid she had appeared at Austerby, and said: 'Yes, you must certainly escape from her. But not on the common stage, and not unescorted! Is that agreed?'

'Thank you,' she replied meekly. 'I own it will be more comfortable to travel post. When shall I be able to set forward, do you think?'

'I can't tell that. No London vehicles have gone by yet, which leads me to suppose that the drifts must be lying pretty thick beyond Speenhamland. Wait until we have seen the Bristol Mail go past!'

'I have a lowering presentiment that we shall see Mama's travelling-carriage instead–and it will *not* go past,' stated Phoebe, in a hollow tone.

'I pledge you my word you shan't be dragged back to Austerby–and *that* you may depend on!'

'What a very rash promise to make!' she observed.

'Yes, isn't it? I am fully conscious of it, I assure you, but having given my word I am now hopelessly committed, and can only pray to heaven I may not find myself involved in any *serious* crime. You think I'm funning, don't you? I'm not, and will immediately prove my good faith by engaging Alice's services.'

'Why, what can she do?' demanded Phoebe.

'Go with you as your maid, of course. Come, come, ma'am! After such a strict upbringing as you have endured is it for me to tell you that a young female of your quality may not travel without her abigail?'

'Oh, what fustian!' she exclaimed. 'As though I cared for that!'

'Very likely you do not, but Lady Ingham will, I promise you. Moreover, if the road should be worse than we expect you might be obliged to spend a night at some posting-house, you know.'

This was unanswerable, but she said mutinously: 'Well, if Alice doesn't choose to go I shan't regard such nonsensical stuff!'

'Oh, now you are glaringly abroad! Alice will do precisely what I tell her to do,' he replied, smiling.

The easy confidence with which he uttered these words made her hope very much that he would meet with a rebuff from Alice, but nothing so salutary happened. Learning that she was to accompany Miss to the Metropolis, Alice fell into blissful ecstasy, gazing upon Sylvester with incredulous wonder, and breathing reverently: '*Lunnon!*' When it was disclosed to her that she should be given five pounds to spend, and her ticket on the stage for her return-journey, she became incapable of speech for several minutes, being afeared, as she presently informed her awed parent, to bust her stay-laces.

The thaw set in, and with it arrived the errant ostler, full of hair-raising accounts of the state of the road. Mrs Scaling told him darkly that he would be sorry presently that he had not made a push to return immediately to the Blue Boar; and when he learned what noble guests she was entertaining he was indeed sorry. But when he discovered that the stables had fallen under the governance of an autocrat who showed no disposition to abdicate in his favour, but, on the contrary, every disposition to set him to work harder than he had ever done, he was not so sorry. He might have missed handsome largesse, but he had also missed several days of being addressed as 'my lad', and having his failings crisply pointed out to him, and being commanded to perform all over again such tasks as Keighley considered him to have scamped. Nor were his affronted sensibilities soothed by the treatment he received at Swale's hands. Swale was forced to eat his dinner in the kitchen amongst the vulgar, but no power known to man could force him to notice the existence of a common ostler. So aloof was his demeanour, so disdainful his glance, that the osler at first mistook him for his master. He discovered later that the Duke was more approachable.

The first vehicles to pass the inn came from the west, a circumstance which made Phoebe very uneasy; but a day later the Bristol Mail went by, at so unusual an hour that Mrs Scaling said they might depend upon it the road was still mortal bad to the eastward. 'Likely as not they've been two days or more getting here,' she said. 'They do be saying in the tap that there's been nothing like it since four years ago, when the river froze over in London-town, and they had bonfires on it, and a great fair, and I don't know what-all. I shouldn't wonder at it, miss, if you was to be here for another se'enight,' she added hopefully.

'Nonsense!' said Sylvester, when this was reported to him. 'What they say in the tap need not cast you into despair. Tomorrow I'll drive to Speenhamland, and discover what the mail-coachmen are saying.'

'If it doesn't freeze again tonight,' amended Phoebe, a worried frown between her brows. 'It was shockingly slippery this morning, and you will have enough to do in holding those grays of yours without having that added to it! I *could* not reconcile it with my conscience to let you set forth in such circumstances!'

'Never,' declared Sylvester, much moved, 'did I think to hear you express so much solicitude on my behalf, ma'am!'

'Well, I can't but see what a fix we should be in if anything should happen to you,' she replied candidly.

The appreciative gleam in his eyes acknowledged a hit, but he said gravely: 'The charm of your society, my Sparrow, lies in not knowing what you will say next—though one rapidly learns to expect the worst!'

It did not freeze again that night; and the first news that greeted Phoebe, when she peeped into Tom's room on her way downstairs to breakfast, was that he had heard a number of vehicles pass the inn, several of which he was sure came from the east. This was presently confirmed by Mrs Scaling, who said, however, that there was no telling whether they had come from London, or from no farther afield than Newbury. She was of the opinion that it would be unwise to venture on such a hazardous journey until the snow had entirely gone from the road; and was regaling Phoebe with a horrid story of three outside passengers on the stage-coach who had died of the cold in just such weather, when Sylvester arrived on the scene, and put an end to this daunting history by observing that since Miss Phoebe was not proposing to travel to London on the roof of a stage-coach there was no need for anyone to feel apprehensive on her account. Mrs Scaling reluctantly conceded this point, but warned his grace that there was a dangerous gravel-pit between Newbury and Reading, very hard to see when there had been heavy falls of snow.

'Like the coffee-pot,' said Sylvester acidly. 'I don't see that at all–and I should wish to do so immediately, if you please!'

This had the effect of sending Mrs Scaling scuttling off to the kitchen 'Do you suppose there really is any danger of driving into a gravel-pit, sir?' asked Phoebe.

'No.'

'I must say, it sounds very unlikely to me. But Mrs Scaling seems to think—'

'Mrs Scaling merely thinks that the longer she can keep us here the better it will be for her,' he interrupted.

'Well, you need not snap *my* nose off!' countered Phoebe. 'Merely because you have come down hours before you are used to do!'

'I beg your pardon, ma'am!' he said frigidly.

'It's of no consequence at all,' she assured him, smiling kindly at him. 'I daresay you are always disagreeable before breakfast. Many people are, I believe, and cannot help themselves, try as they will. I don't mean to say that you do try, of course: why should you, when you are not obliged to be conciliating?'

It was perhaps fortunate that the entrance of Alice at this moment obliged Sylvester to swallow the retort that sprang to his lips. By the time she had withdrawn again he had realized (with far less incredulity than he would have felt a week earlier) that Miss Marlow was being deliberately provoking; and he merely said: 'Though *I* may not be obliged to conciliate, you should reflect, ma'am, that it is otherwise with *you*! I rose at this unseasonable hour wholly on your behalf, but I might yet decide not to go to Newbury after all.'

'Oh, are you capricious as well?' asked Phoebe, raising eyes of innocent enquiry to his face.

'As well as what?' demanded Sylvester. He saw her lips part, and added hastily: 'No, don't tell me! I can hazard a tolerably accurate conjecture, I imagine!'

She laughed, and began to pour out the coffee. 'I won't say another word till you've come out of the sullens,' she promised.

Though strongly tempted to reply in kind, Sylvester decided, upon reflection, to hold his peace. Silence prevailed until, looking up from his plate a few minutes later, he found that she was watching him, with so much the air of a bird hopeful of crumbs that he burst out laughing, and exclaimed: 'Oh, you–*Sparrow*! What an abominable girl you are!'

'Yes, I am afraid I am,' she said, quite seriously. 'And nothing seems to cure me of saying things I ought not!'

'Perhaps you don't *try* to overcome the fault?' he suggested, quizzing her.

'But, in general, I *do* try!' she assured him. 'It is only when I am with persons such as you and Tom–I mean—'

'Ah, just so!' he interrupted. 'When you are with persons whose opinions are of no particular consequence to you, you allow rein to your tongue?'

'Yes,' she agreed, pleased to find him of so ready an understanding. 'That is the matter in a nutshell! Will you have some more bread-and-butter, sir?'

'No, thank you,' he responded. 'I find I have quite lost my appetite.'

'It would be wonderful if you had not,' she said cheerfully. 'Cooped up in the house as you have been all this while! Will you set out for Newbury *soon*? I daresay it is foolish of me, but I can't be easy! Whatever should I do if Mama were to arrive while you are gone?'

'Hide in the hay-loft!' he recommended. 'But if she has a particle of commonsense she won't make the smallest push to recover you!'

12

Having watched Sylvester depart, Phoebe sat down to play piquet with Tom. The sound of wheels outside made her once or twice look up apprehensively, but the approach of a ridden horse along the road caused her no alarm. She heard, but paid no heed; and so it was that Mr Orde, walking into the room without ceremony, took her entirely by surprise. She gave a gasp, and dropped the cards she was holding. Tom turned his head, and exclaimed in dismay: '*Father!*'

The Squire, having surveyed the truants with the air of one who had known all along how it would be, shut the door, and said: 'Ay! Now, what the devil do you mean by this, either of you?'

'It was my fault! Oh, pray don't be vexed with Tom!' begged Phoebe.

'No, it was not!' asserted Tom. 'It was mine, and I made a mull of it, and broke my leg!'

'Ay, so I know!' said his fond parent. 'I may think myself fortunate you didn't break your neck, I suppose. Young cawker! And what did my horses break?'

'No, no, only a strained hock!' Phoebe assured him. 'And I have taken the greatest care—Oh, pray let me help you out of your coat, dear sir!'

'It's no use trying to flummery me, girl!' said the Squire severely, but accepting her aid. 'A pretty riot and rumpus you've caused, the pair of you! Let alone being the death of your father!'

'Oh, *no!*' cried Phoebe, blenching.

He relented, seeing that he had really frightened her, and patted her whitened cheek. 'No, it ain't as bad as that, but you know what he is when anything ails him!'

'Father, we were *not* eloping!' Tom interrupted.

The Squire threw him a glance of affectionate scorn. 'A tinker's budget, Tom: I never supposed you was. Perhaps you'll tell me what the devil you *were* doing—besides driving my new curricle into the ditch, and smashing two of its wheels?'

'I was taking Phoebe to London, to her grandmother. She would have gone on the common stage if I had not, sir!'

'And indeed it wasn't Tom's fault that we ended in a ditch, sir!' interpolated Phoebe. 'He was driving to an inch until we met that evil donkey!'

'Met a donkey, did you? Oh!' said the Squire. 'Well, there was *some* excuse for you, if that was the case.'

'No, there wasn't,' said Tom frankly. 'I ought to have managed better, and I had rather I had broke both my legs than have let True strain his hock!'

'Well, well!' said his father, visibly mollified. 'Thank the lord you didn't!

I'll take a look at that hock presently. I was afraid I should find it to be a case of broken knees.'

'Mr Orde,' Phoebe said anxiously, 'pray tell me!—Does Papa know where I am?'

'Well, of course he does!' replied the Squire. 'You couldn't expect I wouldn't tell him, now, could you?'

'Who told you, Father?' Tom demanded. 'I collect it must have been Upsall, but I never saw him before in my life, and none of us disclosed my name to him! And Phoebe he didn't set eyes on!'

But the news had come from the doctor, of course. He had not discovered the identity of his patient, but he knew who was the elegant young man who had commanded his attendance at the Blue Boar; and it was rather too much to expect of a humble country practitioner that he would refrain from letting it be known as widely as possible that he had lately been called by His Grace of Salford. The news had spread, in the mysterious country-fashion; and if, by the time it reached the Squire's ears, it had become garbled almost out of recognition it still retained enough of the truth to convince that shrewd gentleman that the supposed scion of the house of Rayne, who had overturned some vehicle on the Bath Road, was none other than his own son.

No, he had not been much surprised. Reaching the Manor not many hours after Tom had left it, he had been met by a distracted helpmate, who poured horrifying tidings into his incredulous ears. But he hoped he knew Tom well enough to be sure he had not eloped. A pretty gudgeon he had thought Marlow, to be hoaxed by such a tale! He had assumed his heir to be well able to take care of himself, as the lord knew (with an ironical eyebrow cocked at Tom) he ought to have been! He had awaited events. The first of these had been the return of Marlow to Austerby with a bad chill, and no news of the fugitives. If her ladyship were to be believed, the chill had developed into a congestion of the lung: at all events, his lordship was feeling devilish sorry for himself, and no wonder, lying in a room so hot as to make him sweat like a gamecock. So far as the Squire had been able to discover, Phoebe had run away to escape a proposal from the Duke of Salford. Well, he had thought that an unlikely tale at the outset; and since he had ascertained that he had been right in thinking that it was on Tom's behalf Salford had called in the sawbones he knew it for a Banbury story. And now he would be obliged to them if they would explain to him what the devil *had* made them go off in such a crackbrained style.

It was really very difficult to explain it to him; and not surprising that he should presently declare himself unable to make head or tail of the story. First, this Duke of Phoebe's was a monster from whose advances she had been obliged to fly; next, he was transformed without cause into a charming fellow with whom she had been consorting on terms of amity for the best part of a se'enight.

'*I* never said he was charming,' objected Phoebe. 'That was Tom. He toad-eats him!'

'No such thing!' said Tom indignantly. '*You* don't treat him with common civility!'

'Now, that's enough!' interposed the Squire, inured to sudden squabbles between his heir and his heir's lifelong friend. 'All I know is that I'm very much obliged to the Duke for taking care of as silly a pair of children as ever I knew! Well, I told her ladyship we should find it to be much ado about nothing, and so it is! It's not my business to be giving you a scold, my dear, but there's no denying you deserve one! However, I shall say no more to either of you. A broken leg is punishment enough for Tom; and as for you—well, there's no sense in saying her ladyship ain't vexed with you, because she is—very!'

'I'm not going back to Austerby, sir,' said Phoebe, with the calm of desperation.

The Squire was very fond of her, but he was a parent himself, and he knew what he would think of any man who aided a child of his to flout his authority. He said kindly, but with a firm note in his voice which Tom at least knew well, that she was certainly going back to Austerby, and under his escort. He had promised Marlow that he would bring his daughter safely back to him, and that was all there was to be said about it.

In this he erred: both Phoebe and Tom found much more to say; but nothing they could say availed to turn the Squire from what he conceived to be his duty. He listened with great patience to every argument advanced, but at the end of an impassioned hour he patted Phoebe's shoulder, and said: 'Yes, yes, my dear, but you must be reasonable! If you wish to reside with your grandmother you should write to her, and ask her if she will take you, which I'm sure I hope she may. But it won't do to go careering over the country in this way, and so she would tell you. As for expecting me to abet you—now, you don't want for sense, and you know I can't do it!'

She said despairingly: 'You don't understand!'

'*Won't* understand!' muttered Tom savagely.

'Don't Tom! Perhaps, if I write to her, Grandmama might—Only they will be so dreadfully angry with me!' A tear trickled down her cheek; she wiped it away, saying as valiantly as she could: 'Well, at least I have had one very happy week. When must I go, sir?'

The Squire said gruffly: 'Best to do so as soon as possible, my dear. I shall hire a chaise to convey you, but Tom's situation makes it a trifle awkward. Seems to me I ought first to consult with this doctor of his.'

She agreed to this; and then, as another tear spilled over, ran out of the room. The Squire cleared his throat, and said: 'She will feel better when she's had her cry, you know.'

It was Phoebe's intention to do just this, in the privacy of her bedchamber; but she found Alice there, sweeping the floor, and retreated to the stairs, just as the door leading to the back of the inn opened, and Sylvester came into the narrow passage. She stopped, halfway down the stairs, and he looked up. He saw the tear-stains on her cheeks, and said: 'What's the matter?'

'Tom's papa,' she managed to reply. 'Mr Orde . . .'

He was frowning now, the slant of his brows accentuated. 'Here?'

'In Tom's room. He—he says—'

'Come down to the coffee-room!' he commanded.

She obeyed, blowing her nose, and saying in a muffled voice: 'I beg your pardon: I am *trying* to compose myself!'

He shut the door. 'Yes, don't cry! What is it that Orde says?'

'That I must go home. He promised Papa, you see, and although he is very kind he doesn't understand. He is going to take me home as soon as he can.'

'Then you haven't much time to waste,' he said coolly. 'How long will it take you to make ready?'

'It doesn't signify. He has to go to Hungerford first to see Dr Upsall, as well as to hire a chaise.'

'I am not talking of a journey to Austerby, but of one to London. Isn't that what you want?'

'Oh, yes, yes, indeed it is! Do you mean—But he won't permit me!'

'Must you ask his leave? If you choose to go, my chaise is at the Halfway House, and I will drive you there immediately. Well?'

A faint smile touched his lips, for these words had acted on her magically. She was suddenly a creature transformed. '*Thank you!* Oh, how good you are!'

'I'll tell Keighley not to stable the grays. Where's Alice?'

'In my bedchamber. But will she—'

'Tell her she may have precisely fifteen minutes in which to pack up what she may need, and warn her that we shan't stay for her,' he said, striding to the door.

'Mrs Scaling—?'

'I'll make all right with her,' he said, over his shoulder, and was gone.

Alice, at first bemused, no sooner learned that she would not be waited for than she cast her duster from her with the air of one who had burnt her boats, and said tersely: 'I'll go if I bust!' and rushed from the room.

Fearing that at any moment the Squire might come to find her, Phoebe dragged her portmanteau from under the bed and began feverishly to cram her clothes into it. Rather less than fifteen minutes later both damsels crept down the stairs, one clutching a portmanteau and a bandbox from under whose lid a scrap of muslin flounce protruded, the other clasping in both arms a bulky receptacle made of plaited straw.

The curricle was waiting in the yard, with Keighley at the grays' heads and Sylvester standing beside him. Sylvester laughed when he saw the two dishevelled travellers, and came to relieve Phoebe of her burdens, saying: 'My compliments! I never thought you would contrive to be ready under half an hour!'

'Well, I'm not,' she confessed. 'I was obliged to leave several things behind, and—oh, dear! part of my other dress is sticking out of the bandbox!'

'You may pack it again at the Halfway House,' he said. 'But straighten your hat! I will not be seen driving a lady who looks perfectly demented!'

By the time she had achieved a more respectable appearance the luggage had been stowed under the seat, and Sylvester was ready to hand her up. Alice followed her, and in another minute they were away. Keighley swinging himself up behind as the curricle moved forward.

'Shall I reach London tonight, do you think, sir?' Phoebe asked, as soon as Sylvester had negotiated the narrow entrance to the yard.

'I hope you may, but it's more likely you will be obliged to rack up for the night somewhere. There's no danger of running into drifts now, but it will be heavy going, with the snow turning everywhere into slush. You must leave it to Keighley to decide what is best to do.'

'The thing is, you see, that I haven't a great deal of money with me,' she confided shyly. 'In fact, very little! So if we *could* reach London—'

'No need to tease yourself over money. Keighley will attend to all such matters as inn charges, tolls, and changes. You will take my own team over the first few stages, but after that it must be hired cattle, I'm afraid.'

'Thank you! you are very good,' she said, rather overwhelmed. 'Pray desire him to keep account of the money he may have to lay out!'

'He will naturally do so, Miss Marlow.'

'Yes, but I mean—'

'Oh, I know what you mean!' he interrupted. 'You would like me to present you with a bill, and no doubt I should do so–if I were a job-master.'

'I may be very much beholden to you, Duke,' said Phoebe coldly, 'but if you speak to me in that odiously snubbing way I shall–I shall—'

He laughed. 'You will what?'

'Well, I don't know yet, but I shall think of something, I promise you! Because you are quite at fault! I fancy it may be proper for you to pay the post charges, but it would be most improper for you to pay my bill at an inn!'

'Very well. If there should be such a bill I will hand it to you when next we meet.'

She inclined her head graciously. 'I am obliged to you, sir.'

'Is that the way I speak when I am being odiously snubbing?' enquired Sylvester.

She gave a tiny chuckle, and said handsomely: 'I must own that you are not at all stupid!'

'Oh, no, I'm not stupid! I have a good memory, too. I haven't forgotten how well you contrived to hit off a number of our acquaintances, and I make no secret of my uneasiness. You have an uncomfortable knack of hitting off just what is most ridiculous in your victims!'

She did not reply. Glancing down at her he saw a very grave look in her face. He wondered what she had found to disturb her in his bantering speech, but he did not ask, because they had by this time reached the Halfway House, and he was obliged to give his attention to the ostler, who came running to hold the grays.

It was not long before the chaise stood waiting to convey the travellers to London. Alice, who had sat lost in a beatific dream in the curricle, was quite overcome by the sight of the elegant equipage in which she was now to travel, with the crest upon its panel, its four magnificent horses stamping and fretting and tossing up their heads, its smart postilions, the deep squabs of the seats, and the sheepskin that covered the floor. To Phoebe's dismay she burst into tears. However, when anxiously begged to say what was distressing her she replied, between snorting sobs, that she was thinking of her neighbours, denied the privilege of watching her drive off like a queen.

Relieved, Phoebe said: 'Well, never mind! you will be able to tell them all about it when you go home again! Jump up, and don't cry any more!'

'Oh, no, miss! But I do be so happy!' said Alice, preparing to clamber into the chaise.

Phoebe turned, and looked at Sylvester, waiting to hand her up the steps. Her colour rose; she put out her hand, and as he took it in his, said haltingly: 'I have been trying to think how to tell you how–how *very* grateful I am, but I can't find the words. But, oh, I *thank* you!'

'Believe me, Sparrow, you make too much of a very trifling service. Convey my compliments to Lady Ingham, and tell her that I shall do myself the honour of calling on her when I come to town. In my turn, I will convey yours to Thomas and his father!'

'Yes, pray do! I mean, you will tell Tom how it was, won't you? And perhaps you could convey my *apologies* to the Squire, rather than my compliments?'

'Certainly, if that is your wish.'

'Well, I think it would be more civil. I only hope he won't be out of reason vexed!'

'Don't tease yourself on that head!'

'Yes, but if he should be I know you will give him one of your freezing set-downs, and *that* I couldn't bear!' she said.

'I thought it would not be long before you came to the end of your unnatural civility,' he observed. 'Let me assure you that I have no intention of conducting myself with anything less than propriety!'

'That's *exactly* what I dread!' she said.

'Good God, what an abominable girl you are! Get into the chaise before I catch the infection!' he exclaimed, between amusement and annoyance.

She laughed, but said, apologetically, as he handed her up: 'I wasn't thinking! *Truly* I meant not to say one uncivil thing to you!'

'You are certainly incorrigible. *I*, on the other hand, am so magnanimous as to wish you a safe and speedy journey!'

'Magnanimous indeed! Thank you!'

The steps were let up; Alice's voice was the last to be heard before the door was shut. 'Hot bricks, and a fur rug, miss!' disclosed Alice. '*Spanking*, I call it!'

Phoebe leaned forward to wave farewell, the ostlers let go the wheelers' heads, and the chaise started to move, swaying on its excellent springs. Sylvester stood watching it until it disappeared round a bend in the road, and then turned to Keighley, waiting beside him, the bridle of a hired riding-hack in his hand. 'Get them to London tonight if you can, John, but run no risks,' he said. 'Money, pistols—I think you have everything.'

'Yes, your grace, but I wish you'd let me come back!'

'No, wait for me at Salford House. I can't take both you and Swale. Or, at any rate, I won't! Curricles were never meant to carry three persons.'

Keighley smiled grimly, as he hoisted himself into the saddle. 'I thought your grace was being a trifle crowded,' he remarked, with a certain amount of satisfaction.

'And hope it may be a lesson to me! Be damned to you!' retorted Sylvester.

He accomplished the short journey back to the Blue Boar at a leisurely trot, his mind occupied, not altogether pleasurably, with the events of the past week. He ought never to have stopped at the Blue Boar. He wondered what could have possessed him, and was much inclined to think it had been perversity: John had tried to dissuade him—*damn* John for being in the right of it, as usual!—and he had done it as much to tease him as for any other reason. Well, he had been well served for that piece of mischief! Once he had found young Orde in such a fix he had been fairly caught: only a monster could have abandoned the boy to his fate. Besides, he liked Thomas, and had not foreseen that his act of charity would precipitate him into the sort of imbroglio he particularly disliked. He could only be thankful that he was not a frequent traveller on the Bath road: he had given them plenty to talk about at the Halfway House, and to afford the vulgar food for gossip was no part of his ambition. That hurly-burly girl! She wanted both manners and conduct; she was disagreeably pert, and had no beauty: he cordially disliked her. What the devil had made him come to her rescue, when all his saner self desired was to see her thoroughly set-down? There had not been the least necessity—except that he had pledged his word. But when he had seen her on the stairs, so absurdly woebegone but trying rather pathetically to smile, he hadn't recollected that foolish promise: he had acted on impulse, and had only himself to thank for the outcome. Here he was, tied still to a primitive inn, and a young man whose welfare was no concern of his; deprived of his groom; open to the justifiable censure of some unknown country squire—the sort of worthy person, in all probability, whom he entertained at Chance on Public Days; and the subject (if he knew his world) of scandalous conjecture. In some form or another the story would be bound to leak out. The best he could hope for was to be thought to have taken leave of his senses; the worst, that for all his famed fastidiousness he had fallen laughably in love with a dab of a female without style or countenance, who scorned his supposed advances.

No, decided Sylvester, turning neatly into the yard of the Blue Boar: that was rather too much to expect him to bear! Miss Marlow should *not* exhibit her poor opinion of him to the interested ton. Miss Marlow, in fact, should exhibit something very different from contempt: he was damned if he was going to be the only one to learn a salutary lesson!

His expression, when he alighted from the curricle, and stood watching, with a merciless eye, the exact carrying out of his curt orders, was un-amiable enough to make the ostler break into a sweat of anxiety; but when he presently strolled into Tom's room all traces of ill-humour had vanished from his countenance.

He entered upon a scene of constraint. The Squire, peckish after his ride, had just disposed of a substantial nuncheon, and Tom, having talked himself out of arguments, had been preserving for the past ten minutes a silence pregnant with resentment. He looked round at the opening of the door, his eyes still smouldering, and as soon as he saw that it was Sylvester who had come in, burst out: 'Salford! The—the most *damnable* thing! Perhaps you can prevail upon my father to listen to reason! I never would have believed it possible he could—oh, this *is* my father!'

'I don't know what you would never have believed possible,' said the Squire, getting up from his chair, and bowing to Sylvester, 'but let me tell you, my boy, *I* wouldn't have believed you had only to be away from home for a week to lose your manners! I should think your grace must be wondering if he was reared in a cow-byre, and I'm sure I don't blame you. He wasn't, however—and a thundering scold he'd get from his mother if *she* were here!' He saw that Sylvester, advancing into the room, was holding out his hand, and shook it warmly. 'I'm honoured to make your grace's acquaintance—and feel myself to be devilish obliged to you, as you may guess! You've been a great deal too kind to Tom, and how to thank you I don't know!'

'But there's no need to thank me at all, I assure you, sir,' Sylvester said, at his most charming. 'I've spent a most entertaining week—and made a new friend, whom I can't allow you to scold! It would be most unjust, you know, for he abandoned his really oppressive civility only at my request. Besides, he has endured six days of boredom without a murmur of complaint!'

'Ay, and serve him right!' said the Squire. 'A bad business this, my lord Duke! I left Marlow in a rare taking, I can tell you. Well, well! he's the best man to hounds I ever saw, but I never thought his understanding more than moderate. Gretna Green, indeed! Of all the hare-brained notions to have taken into his head!'

'I wish to God I *had* taken her to Gretna Green!' said Tom savagely. 'Salford, my father is determined to carry her back to Austerby! I can't make him understand that only a regular brute would do so, after such an escapade as this!'

'Now, now!' said the Squire. 'There's been no harm done, and no one but ourselves any the wiser—thanks to his grace!—and so I shall tell her ladyship.'

'As though she would pay the least heed! And what a figure *I* must cut! I wouldn't let her go on the stage, and if I had she would have been with Lady Ingham days ago! I promised to take her there myself, and all I've done is to land her in a worse case than ever! *Father—*'

'Calm yourself, Galahad!' interposed Sylvester. 'There is really no occasion to be cast into despair. Miss Marlow left for London an hour ago.'

An astonished silence succeeded these words. Tom broke it with a shout of triumph. 'Oh, you *Trojan*, Salford!'

This made Sylvester laugh; but an instant later he was putting up his brows, for the Squire, after staring at him fixedly, said bluntly: 'If that was your grace's doing, as I collect it must have been, I shall take leave to tell you it was wrong of you, my lord Duke–very wrong!'

Tom, recognizing that look of withdrawal, intervened quickly. 'You mustn't say that, Father–indeed you must not! Pray—!'

'I shall say just what I think, Tom,' said the Squire, still looking at Sylvester from under his brows. 'If his grace don't like it, why, I'm sorry for it, but I've said it, and I stand by it!'

Tom glanced apprehensively at Sylvester, but his intervention had been more successful than he knew. Meeting his eyes Sylvester realized, with a slight shock, that he was trying to prevent the Squire's being wounded by a snub. He had been unaware of his own stiffening; for an instant he remembered Phoebe's words. He had dismissed them as an impertinent attempt to vex him; he wondered now if it could be true that he, who prided himself on his good manners, appeared to others to be insufferably high in the instep. He said, smiling: 'Well I *don't* like it, for you are doing me an injustice, sir! *You* may have pledged your word to Marlow, but *I* pledged mine to his daughter!'

'Ay, that's very pretty talking!' retorted the Squire. 'But what the devil am I to tell him, Duke?'

'If I were you,' replied Sylvester, 'I rather think I should merely tell him that I had been unable to bring Miss Marlow back with me because she had already left for town–on a visit to her grandmother.'

The Squire, having thought this over, said slowly: 'I could say that, of course. To be sure, they don't know Phoebe has been here all along–and it would be as well, I daresay, if they never did get to know of it. At the same time, I don't like hoaxing Marlow, for that's what I should be doing, no question about it!'

'But, Father, what good would it do to tell them you found Phoebe here?' asked Tom. 'Now that she's gone, it could only do harm!'

'Well, that's true enough,' admitted the Squire. 'What *am* I going to tell them?'

'That Miss Marlow travelled to town in my chaise, escorted by my head groom, and attended by a respectable abigail,' replied Sylvester fluently. 'Not even Lady Marlow could demand a greater degree of propriety, surely?'

'Not if she don't set eyes on the respectable abigail!' murmured Tom.

'Don't put mistaken notions into your father's head, Thomas! Let me reassure you, sir! The landlady's daughter has gone with Miss Marlow. She is unquestionably respectable!'

'Yes, but such a toad-eater!' said Tom wickedly. 'Saying you were more important than a gobble-cock—!'

13

Contrary to Sylvester's expectation Phoebe reached her grandmother's house at half past ten that evening. She had been travelling for nearly eight hours, for the state of the roads had compelled the postilions to proceed at a very sober pace, and she was as weary as she was anxious. Her initial reception in Green Street was not encouraging. While she waited in the chaise, with the window let down, watching him, Keighley trod up the steps to the front door and plied the heavy knocker resoundingly. A long, long pause followed, and a nerve-racking fear that Lady Ingham was out of town assailed Phoebe. But just as Keighley raised his hand to repeat his summons she saw him check, and lower his arm again. The quelling noise of bolts being drawn back was next heard, and Phoebe, craning eagerly forward, saw her grandmother's butler standing on the threshold, with a lamp in his hand, and heaved a sigh of relief.

But if she expected to receive a welcome from Horwich she was the more deceived. Persons who demanded admittance at unseasonable hours were never welcome to him, even when they arrived in chaise-and-four and escorted by a liveried servant. A street lamp illumined the chaise, and he perceived that for all the dirt that clung to the wheels and panels it was an extremely elegant vehicle: none of your job-chaises, but a carriage built for a gentleman of means and taste. A glimpse of a crest, half concealed by mud, caused him to unbend a trifle, but he replied coldly to Keighley's enquiry that her ladyship was not at home to visitors.

He was obliged to admit Phoebe, of course. He did it with obvious reluctance, and stood, rigid with disapproval, while she thanked Keighley for his services, and bade him good-bye with what he considered most unbecoming friendliness.

'I will ascertain whether her ladyship will receive you, miss,' he said, shutting the door at last upon Keighley. 'I should inform you, however, that her ladyship retired to rest above an hour ago.'

She tried not to feel daunted, and said as confidently as she could that she was sure her grandmother would receive her. 'And will you, if you please, look after my maid, Horwich?' she said. 'We have been travelling for a great many hours, and I expect she will be glad of some supper.'

'I will that, and no mistake!' corroborated Alice, grinning cordially at Horwich. 'Don't you go putting yourself out, though! A bit of cold meat and a mug of porter will do me fine.'

Phoebe could not feel, observing the expression on Horwich's face, that Sylvester had acted wisely in sending Alice to town with her. Horwich said in arctic accents that he would desire the housekeeper—if she had not gone to bed—to attend to the Young Person presently. He added that if Miss would be pleased to step into the morning-room he would send her ladyship's maid up to apprise my lady of Miss's unexpected arrival.

But by this time Phoebe's temper had begun to mount, and she surprised the venerable tyrant by saying tartly that she would do no such thing. 'You need not put yourself to the trouble of escorting me, for I know my way very well! If her ladyship is asleep I shall not wake her, and if she is not I don't need Muker to announce me!' she declared.

Her ladyship was not asleep. Phoebe's soft knock on her door was answered by a command to come in; and she entered to find her grandmother sitting up in her curtained bed, with a number of pillows to support her, and an open book in her hands. Two branches of candles and the flames of a large fire lit the scene, and cast into strong relief her lady-ship's aquiline profile. 'Well, what is it?' she said testily, and looked round. '*Phoebe*! Good God, what in the world—? My dear, dear child, come in!'

A weight slid from Phoebe's shoulders; her face puckered, and with a thankful cry of: 'Oh, *Grandmama*!' she ran forward.

The Dowager embraced her warmly, but she was not unnaturally alarmed by so sudden an arrival. 'Yes, yes, of course I am glad to see you, my love! But tell me at once what has happened! Don't try to break it to me gently! Not, I do trust, a fatal accident to your papa?'

'No–oh, no! nothing of *that* nature, ma'am!' Phoebe assured her. 'Grandmama, you told me once that I might depend on you if–if ever I needed help!'

'That Woman!' uttered the Dowager, sitting bolt upright.

'Yes, and–and Papa too,' said Phoebe sadly. 'That was what made it so desperate! Something happened–at last, I believed it was going to happen–and I couldn't *bear* it, and so–and so I ran away!'

'Merciful heavens!' exclaimed Lady Ingham. 'My poor child, what have they been doing to you? Tell me the whole!'

'Mama told me that Papa had arranged a–a very advantageous marriage for me with the Duke of Salford,' began Phoebe haltingly. She was conscious that her grandmother had stiffened, and paused nervously. But the Dowager merely adjured her to continue, so she drew a breath, and said earnestly: 'I *couldn't* marry him, ma'am! You see, I had only met him once in my life, and I disliked him excessively. Besides, I knew very well that he didn't so much as remember me! Even if I had liked him I couldn't have borne to marry a man who only offered for me because his mother wished him to!'

The Dowager, controlling herself with a strong effort, said: 'Is that what That Woman told you?'

'Yes, and also that it was because I had been brought up as I should be, which made him think I should be *suitable*!'

'Good God!' said the Dowager bitterly.

'You–you do understand, don't you, ma'am?'

'Oh, yes! I understand only too well!' was the somewhat grim response.

'I was persuaded you would! And the dreadful thing was that Papa was bringing him to Austerby to propose to me. At least, so Mama said, for Papa had told her so.'

'When I see Marlow–*Did* he bring Salford to Austerby?'

'Yes, he did, but how he came to make such a mistake–unless, of course, Salford did mean to offer for me, but changed his mind as soon as he saw me again, which, I must say, no one could wonder at. I don't know precisely how it may have been, but Papa was sure he meant to make me an offer, and when I told him what my sentiments were, and begged him to tell the Duke–he would not,' said Phoebe, her voice petering out unhappily. 'So I knew then that there wasn't anybody, except you, Grandmama, who could help me. And I ran away.'

'*Alone?*' demanded the Dowager, horrified. 'Never tell me you've come all that distance on the common stage and by yourself!'

'No, indeed I haven't!' Phoebe hastened to reassure her. 'I came in Salford's chaise, and he made me bring a–a maid with me, besides sending his groom to look after *everything* for me!'

'*What?*' said the Dowager incredulously. 'Came in *Salford's* chaise?'

'I–I must explain it to you, ma'am,' said Phoebe, looking guilty.

'You must indeed!' said the Dowager, staring at her in the liveliest astonishment.

'Yes. Only, it–it is rather a long story!'

'In that case, my love, be good enough to pull the bell!' said the Dowager. 'You will like a glass of hot milk after your journey. And I think,' she added, in fainter accents, 'that I will take some myself, to sustain me.'

She then (to Phoebe's alarm) sank back against her disordered pillows, and closed her eyes. However, upon the entrance of Miss Muker presently, she opened them again, and said with surprising vigour: 'You make take that sour look off your face, Muker, and fetch up two glasses of hot milk directly! My granddaughter, who has come to pay me a visit, has endured a most fatiguing journey. And when you have done that, you will see that a warming-pan is slipped between the sheets of her bed, and a fire lit, and everything made ready for her. In the best spare bedchamber!'

When my lady spoke in that voice is was unwise to argue with her. Muker, who had responded to Phoebe's greeting in a repressive voice, and with the slightest of curtsies, received her orders without comment, but said with horrid restraint: 'And would Miss wish to have the Female which I understand to be her maid attend her here, my lady?'

'No, pray send her to bed!' said Phoebe quickly. 'She–she is not precisely my maid!'

'So, if I may say so, miss, I apprehend!' said Muker glacially.

'Disagreeable creature!' said the Dowager, as the door closed behind her devoted abigail. 'Who is this Female, if she is not your maid?'

'Well, she's the landlady's daughter,' Phoebe answered. 'Salford *would* have me bring her!'

'*Landlady's daughter?* No, don't explain it to me yet, child! Muker will come back with the hot milk directly, and something seems to tell me that if we suffer an interruption I shall become perfectly bewildered. Take that ugly pelisse off, my love–good gracious, where did you have that dreadful gown made? Has That Woman *no* taste? Well, never mind! Whatever happens I'll set *that* to rights! Draw that chair to the fire, and then we can be comfortable. And perhaps if you were to give me my smelling-salts–yes, on that table, child!–it would be a good thing!'

But although the story presently unfolded to her might have been thought by some to have been expressly designed to cast into palpitations any elderly lady in failing health, the Dowager had no recourse to her vinaigrette. The tale was so ravelled as to make it necessary for her to interpolate a number of questions, and there was nothing in her incisive delivery of these to suggest frailty either of body or intellect.

The most searching of her enquiries were drawn from her by the intrusion into the recital of Mr Thomas Orde. She appeared to be much interested in him; and while Phoebe readily told her all about her oldest friend she kept her eyes fixed piercingly upon her face. But when she learned of Tom's nobility in offering a clandestine marriage to her granddaughter ('which threw me into whoops, because he isn't *nearly* old enough to be married, besides being just like my brother!') she lost interest in him, merely requesting Phoebe, in a much milder tone, to continue her story. There was nothing to be feared, decided her ladyship, from young Mr Orde.

The last of her questions were posed almost casually. 'And did Salford chance to mention me?' she asked.

'Oh, yes!' replied Phoebe blithely. 'He told me that he was particularly acquainted with you, because you were his godmother. So I ventured to ask him if he thought you might—might *like* to let me reside with you, and he seemed to think you *would*, Grandmama!'

'Did he indeed!' said the Dowager, her countenance inscrutable. 'Well, my love—' with sudden energy–'he was perfectly right! I shall like it excessively!'

It was long before her ladyship fell asleep that night. She had been provided by her innocent granddaughter with food for much thought, and still more conjecture. Lord and Lady Marlow were soon dismissed from her mind (but a large part of the following morning was going to be pleasurably spent in the composition of a letter calculated to bring about a dangerous relapse in his lordship's state of health); and so too was young Mr Orde. What intrigued Lady Ingham was the position occupied by Sylvester in the stirring drama disclosed to her. The rôle of *deus ex machina*, which he appeared to have undertaken, sounded most unlike him; nor could she picture him living in what she judged to be the depths of squalor, and spending his time between the stables and a sickroom. In fact, the only recognizable thing he seemed to have done was to encourage Phoebe to seek refuge in Green Street. That, thought the Dowager indignantly, rang very true! She had no doubt, either, that he had done it out of pure malice. Well! he would shortly discover that he had shot wide of the mark. She was delighted to welcome Phoebe. She wondered that it should not have occurred to her that the very thing needed to relieve the intolerable boredom she had been suffering during the past few months, when the better part of her acquaintance had retired into the country, was the presence in her house of a lively granddaughter. She now perceived that to keep Phoebe with her would be in every way preferable to the fatigue of a journey to Paris, a project which she had had in doubtful contemplation ever since one of her chief cronies had written thence to urge her to join the throng of well-born English who were disporting themselves so agreeably in that most delightful of capitals. She had been tempted, but there were grave drawbacks to the scheme. It would mean putting oneself beyond the reach of dear Sir Henry; Muker would be certain to dislike it; and whatever poor Mary Berry might allege to the contrary it was the Dowager's unalterable conviction that the escort of a gentleman was indispensable to any lady bent on foreign travel. One could admittedly engage a courier, but to do so merely added to one's expenditure, since the gentleman was still necessary, to keep a watchful eye on the activities of this hireling. No: on every account it would be better to adopt Phoebe, and try what *she* could achieve for the child. Once she had rigged her out becomingly she would positively enjoy taking her, whenever her health permitted, into society.

Here her ladyship's thoughts suffered a check. She had no intention of allowing Phoebe to abjure the world (as Phoebe had suggested), but although her health might benefit by chaperoning the child to one or two private balls, nothing could be more prejudicial to it than interminable evenings spent at Almack's Assembly Rooms, or at parties given by hostesses with whom she was barely acquainted. But the check was only momentary: the Dowager remembered the existence of her meek daughter-in-law, Rosina, with two girls of her own to chaperon, could very well take her niece under her wing: such an arrangement could make no possible difference to her.

This was a small matter, and soon disposed of; far more important, and far more difficult to solve, was the riddle of Sylvester's behaviour.

He was coming to visit her. She had received this message with every appearance of indifference, but she had pricked up her ears at it. He was, was he? Well, it would go against the grain to do it, but if he did come she would receive him affably. Perhaps, if she saw him, she might be able to discover just what game he was playing. His actions invited her to suppose that he had fallen in love with Phoebe, and was bent on displaying himself to her in most pleasing colours. But if Phoebe's account of what had passed during his stay at Austerby were to be believed it was hard to detect what he had seen in her to captivate him. The Dowager did not think he had gone to Austerby with the intention of liking what he found there, for she was well aware that she had erred a trifle in her handling of him, and set up his back. It had been quite a question, when she had seen that sparkle of anger in his eyes, whether she should push the matter farther, or let it rest. She had decided on the bolder course because he had told her that it was his intention to marry; and once he had made up his mind to it there was clearly not a day to be wasted in presenting Phoebe to his notice.

Recollecting in what stringent terms she had commanded Marlow not to breathe a word to a soul, her thin fingers crooked into claws. She might have known that That Woman would speedily drag the whole business out of such a prattle-box; but could anyone have foreseen that she was such a fool as to tell Phoebe everything that was most certain to set her against Sylvester?

Well, it was useless to rage over the irrevocable past. The future, she thought, was not hopeless. Too often men fell in love with the unlikeliest girls; it was possible that Sylvester, indifferent to the charms of the many Beauties who had flung out lures to him season after season, had been attracted to Phoebe because she was (to say the least of it) an unusual girl, and, far from encouraging his addresses, had repulsed them.

Possible, but not probable, thought Lady Ingham, considering Sylvester. He might have been piqued; she found it hard to believe that he had been fascinated. A high stickler, Sylvester: never, even in his callow youth, a Blood who sought fame in eccentricity. Indeed, the scandalous exploits of this fraternity won from him no other comment than was conveyed by a slight, contemptuous shrug of his shoulders; so how could one suppose that he would see anything to admire in a girl who outraged convention? Such conduct as Phoebe's was much more likely to have disgusted him. Angered him, too, reflected the Dowager, as well it might! A mortifying experience for any man to know that the prospect of receiving a proposal of marriage from him had driven a gently nurtured girl into headlong flight, and, for one of Sylvester's pride, intolerable.

Suddenly the Dowager wondered whether it had been with the intention of punishing Phoebe rather than her grandmother that Sylvester had sent her up to London. He might certainly have supposed that a grandmother, learning of her outrageous behaviour, would have dealt her very short shrift. He could not have guessed that when the child had poured out to her the story of her adventure she had seen not Phoebe but Verena, for

Sylvester

Sylvester had never known Verena.

An excess of sensibility was not one of Lady Ingham's failings. There had been a moment of aching memory, awakened by some fleeting expression on Phoebe's face, but her ladyship was not going to think of that. She was not concerned with Verena now, but with Verena's daughter. If Sylvester hoped to find Phoebe in her black books he was going to suffer a disappointment, and would be well served for his malice.

It was not until she was slipping over the edge of wakefulness that Lady Ingham remembered the landlady's daughter. It was Sylvester who had insisted on her accompanying Phoebe to London, and whatever motive it was that had prompted him it was not malice. It would be unwise to hope, she thought drowsily, but there was no need yet to despair.

14

On the following morning Phoebe found her grandmother in brisk spirits, and very full of plans for the day. Foremost amongst these was a visit to a silk-warehouse and another to her ladyship's own modiste. 'To dress you becomingly is the first necessity, child,' said the Dowager. 'The sight of you in that shabby gown makes me nervous!'

The prospect of choosing fashionable raiment was enticing, but Phoebe was obliged to beg her grandmother to postpone this programme. She had promised to show Alice all the most notable sights of London and, in particular, to take her to the Pantheon Bazaar.

She had a little difficulty in persuading the Dowager to consent to any part of this scheme, for it did not at all suit that lady's sense of propriety to permit her granddaughter to wander about, seeing the lions, with no other escort than a raw country-girl. She told Phoebe that Alice would enjoy herself more in the company of one of the maidservants, but was persuaded finally to sanction an expedition to the Pantheon Bazaar, having recollected that before herself could prosecute her various designs she must write a letter to Lord Marlow, and another to her daughter-in-law. Phoebe's own letter to her papa was already written; and she was able to frustrate the Dowager's intention to send her forth in her town carriage by reminding her how much her coachman was likely to object to having his horses kept standing in inclement weather. Phoebe had a piece of very secret business to transact, and she by no means wished Lady Ingham's coachman to report to his mistress that her first port of call had been the offices of Messrs Newsham & Otley, Publishers.

She entered these premises with high hopes, and left them in a mood of such black foreboding as made it hard for her to enter into Alice's raptures at all that met her eyes. If had not occurred to Phoebe that it might be too late for her to delete from her forthcoming romance every mention of Count Ugolino's distinctive eyebrows.

But so it was. Mr Otley, confronted by a nameless lady in an ugly stuff gown who announced herself to be the authoress of *The Lost Heir*, almost burst with curiosity. He and his senior partner had often speculated on the identity of that daring authoress, but neither of them had supposed that she would prove to be nothing more than a dowdy schoolgirl. His manner underwent a change, and a note of patronage crept into his voice. Phoebe's disposition was friendly to a fault, but she was quite unused to being addressed in such a way by a person of Mr Otley's order. Mr Otley, encountering an amazed stare, hastily revised his first impression, and decided that it might be wise to call in the senior partner.

Mr Newsham's manner was perfect: a nice blend of the respectful and the fatherly. Had it been possible he would have delayed publication gladly, and as gladly have incurred the expense of having the book entirely reset. But, alas! The date of issue was fixed, a bare month ahead, the edition fully prepared. Nothing could have been more unfortunate, but he ventured to think that she must still be pleased by the result of his labours.

Well, she was pleased. So handsome were they, those three slim volumes, elegantly attired in blue leather, the fore-edges of the pages gilded, and the title enclosed in a scroll! It didn't seem possible that between those opulent covers reposed a story of her weaving. When the volumes were put into her hands she gave an involuntary gasp of delight; but when she opened the first volume at random her eyes fell upon a fatal paragraph.

> Count Ugolino's appearance was extraordinary. His figure was elegant, his bearing graceful, his air that of a well-bred man, and his lineaments very handsome; but the classical regularity of his countenance was marred by a pair of feline orbs, which were sinister in expression. Matilda could not repress a shudder of revulsion.

Nor could Matilda's creator, hurriedly shutting the volume, and looking imploringly up at Mr Newsham. 'I *cannot* allow it to be published!'

It took patience and time to convince Phoebe that it was not in her power to arrest publication, but Mr Newsham grudged neither. His tongue was persuasive, and since he was astute enough to perceive that an optimistic forecast of the book's chances of success would only dismay her he explained to her how rarely it was that a first novel enjoyed more than a modest sale, and how improbable it was that it would come under the notice of persons of ton.

She was a little reassured, but when she parted from him it was with the resolve to write immediately to Miss Battery, imploring her to use her influence with her cousin to arrest publication. For his part, having bowed her off the premises, Mr Newsham instantly sought out the junior partner, demanding: 'Didn't you tell me that that cousin of yours is governess in a nobleman's household? Who is he? Mark my words, that chit's his daughter, and we've got a hit!'

'Who is the fellow—I mean the real fellow—she wants to alter?' asked Mr Otley uneasily.

'I don't know. Only one of the nobs,' replied his partner cheerfully. '*They* don't bring actions for libel!'

It was nearly a week later when Miss Battery's letter reached her one-time pupil, and by then Phoebe, caught up in what seemed to her a whirl of fashionable activity, had little time to spare for her literary troubles. It was impossible to be apprehensive for very long at a time when her life had been miraculously transformed. Lady Marlow's unsatisfactory daughter-in-law had become her grandmother's pet, and it was wonderful what a change it wrought in her. Lady Ingham was well-satisfied. Phoebe would never be a beauty, but when she was prettily dressed, and not afraid of incurring censure every time she unclosed her lips, she was quite a taking little thing. A touch of town-bronze was needed, but she would soon acquire that.

Miss Battery wrote affectionately but not helpfully. More conversant than Phoebe with the difficulties of publishing, she could only recommend her not to tease herself too much over the remote possibility of the Duke's reading her book. Very likely he would not; and if he did Phoebe must remember that no one need know she was the authoress.

That was consoling, but Phoebe knew she would feel guilty every time she met Sylvester, and almost wished the book unwritten. After his kindness to have portrayed him as a villain was an act of treachery; and it was no use, she told herself sternly, to say that she had done this before she became indebted to him, for that was mere quibbling.

The season had not begun, but the unusually hard weather was driving a number of people back to town. Several small parties were being given; Grandmama prophesied that long before Almack's opening night the season would be in full swing, and she wish to lose no time in making it known that she now had her granddaughter living with her. In vain did Phoebe assure her that she did not care for balls. 'Nonsense!' said her ladyship.

'But it's true, ma'am! I am always so stupid at big parties!'

'Not when you know yourself to be as elegantly dressed as any girl in the room—and very much more elegantly than most of 'em!' retorted the Dowager.

'But, Grandmama!' said Phoebe reproachfully. 'I meant to be a comfort to you: not to go out raking every night!'

The Dowager glanced sharply at her, saw that the saintly tone was belied by eyes brimming with mischief, and thought: If Sylvester has seen *that* look—! But why the deuce hasn't he paid us a visit yet?

Phoebe wondered why he had not, too. She knew of no reason why he should wish to see her again, but he had asked her to tell Grandmama that he would call on her when he came to town, and surely he must have reached town days ago? Tom, she knew, was at home; so the Duke could not still be at the Blue Boar. She was not in the least affronted, but she found herself wishing several times that he would call in Green Street. She had such a lot to tell him! Nothing of importance, of course: just funny things, such as Alice's various remarks, which Grandmama had not thought very funny (Grandmama had not taken kindly to Alice), and how Papa had written her a thundering scold, not for having run away from Austerby, but for having done so without first telling him where she kept the key to the chest containing the horse-medicines. Grandmama had not thought that funny either; and a joke lost some of its savour when there was no one with whom one could share it. It was a pity the Duke had not come to London after all.

In point of fact he had come, but he had left again almost immediately for Chance, one of the first scraps of news that had greeted him on arrival at Salford House being that Lady Henry was also in town, with her child, staying with Lord and Lady Elvaston. Since she had not mentioned to him that she had formed any such intention this made him very angry. Her comings and goings were no concern of his (though she had no right to remove Edmund without his permission), but he thought it unpardonable that she should have left the Duchess during his absence, and without a word of warning to him. He posted back to Leicestershire; but as he found his mother not only in good spirits but looking forward to a visit from her sister he did not remain for more than a few days at Chance. During his stay he made no mention of his visit to Austerby. The Duchess was left with the impression that he had been all the time at Blandford Park; and since he had straitly charged Swale and Keighley to preserve discreet silence he was reasonably sure that no account of his adventures would filter through the household channels to her ears.

Just why he was reluctant to divulge to her an episode which would certainly amuse her was a question he found difficult to answer; and since a fleeting apprehension of this occurred to him he did not tax his brain with it. After all, it could afford her no pleasure to know that he had passed the daughter of her dearest friend under review and found her to be unworthy to become his wife.

In London he found quite a pile of invitations awaiting him, including a graceful note from Lady Barningham, bidding him (if he did not disdain a small, informal party) to a little dance at her house that very evening. Now, Lady Barningham's daughter was the vivacious girl who came second on the list of the five candidates for his hand. Having formed no other plan than to look in at one or other of his clubs, he decided to present himself at the Barninghams' house, where he could be sure of meeting several friends, and sure also that his hostess would accept his excuses for having left her invitation unanswered.

He was right on both counts. His arrival coincided with that of Lord Yarrow, who hailed him on the doorstep, and demanded where the devil he had been hiding himself; he found two more of his intimates in the drawing-room; and was received by a hostess who told him that his apologies were unnecessary—indeed, absurd, for he must know that this dance was the merest impromptu. What *was* one to do, Duke, in March, of all impossible months, and with London still so thin of company?

'You have hit on the very thing, of course,' he replied. 'I have nothing to do but be glad I reached London in time to present myself, and was so fortunate as to escape a deserved scold!'

'As though we were not well enough acquainted to dispense with ceremony! I warn you, you will find none here tonight! I perform no introductions, but leave you to choose whom you will for your partner, since I fancy all are known to you.'

In high good-humour was her ladyship, but careful not to betray her triumph to jealous eyes. With Salford one never knew, and a hint of complacence now would be remembered by the dear friends who were present, if he let another season go without making Caroline an offer, or offered instead for Sophia Bellerby, or the lovely Lady Mary Torrington. It would not do to indulge optimism too far. She had done that last year, and his grace had not come up to the scratch; and however pleased he seemed to be in Caroline's company no one could accuse him of making her his sole object. Not one of the twelve young ladies present would go home feeling that he had slighted her; three of them at least had enjoyed charming flirtations with him.

She would have been dismayed had she known that Sylvester had discovered a sad fault in Miss Barningham. She was too compliant. He had only to lift his brows, to say: 'You cannot be serious!' and she was ready in an instant to allow herself to be converted. She was not going to argue with him, she knew his intellect to be superior. Well! if people (unspecified) supposed him to like that sort of flattery they were mistaken: it was a dead bore. Not that he had not enjoyed the party: he had spent an agreeable evening amongst friends; and it had been pleasant, after his experience in Somerset, to be welcomed with such cordiality. He wondered how he would

be received in Green Street, and smiled wryly as he recollected what cause
he had given his godmother to regard him with a hostile eye.

But there was no trace of hostility in Lady Ingham's face or manner when
he was ushered into her drawing-room; indeed, she greeted him with more
enthusiasm than her granddaughter. He found both ladies at home, but
Phoebe was engaged in writing a note for the Dowager, and although she
rose to shake hands, and smiled at Sylvester in a friendly way, she asked him
to excuse her while she finished her task.

'Come and sit down, Sylvester!' commanded Lady Ingham. 'I have been
wishing to thank you for taking care of Phoebe. You may guess how very
much obliged to you I am. According to what she tells me she wouldn't be
with me today if it hadn't been for your kind offices.'

'Now, how, without disrespect, does one tell one's godmother that she is
talking nonsense?' countered Sylvester, kissing her fingers. 'Does Miss
Marlow make a long stay, ma'am?'

'She is going to make her home with me,' replied the Dowager, smiling
blandly at him.

'But how delightful!' he said.

'What a hoaxing thing to say!' remarked Phoebe, hunting in the writing-
table for a wafer. 'You can't pretend *you* thought it delightful to endure my
company!'

'I have no need to pretend. Do you think we didn't miss you abominably?
I promise you we did!'

'To make a fourth at whist?' she said, pushing back her chair.

He rose as she came to the fire, retorting: 'No such thing! Whist was never
in question. Mr Orde remained with us only one night.'

'What, did he take Tom home immediately?'

'No, he left him with me while he himself went home to allay the anxieties
of Mrs Orde and your father. He came back three days later, and bore
Thomas off most regally, in an enormous carriage, furnished by Mrs Orde
with every imaginable comfort, from pillows to smelling-salts.'

'Smelling-salts! Oh, no!'

'I assure you. Ask Thomas if he didn't try to throw them out of the
window! Tell me how you fared! I know from Keighley that you did reach
town that night: were you very tired?'

'Yes, but I didn't care for that. And as for Alice, I think she would have
driven on for hours, and still enjoyed it! Oh, I must tell you that you have
been eclipsed in her eyes, Duke!'

'Ah, have I?' he said, eyeing her suspiciously. 'By a freak?'

She laughed. 'No, no, by *Horwich*!'

'Come, that's most encouraging! What did he do to earn her admiration?'

'He behaved to her in the most odious way imaginable! As though she had
been a cockroach, she told me! I was afraid she must be wretchedly
unhappy, but I don't think anything she saw in London impressed her half
as much! She confided to me that he was much more her notion of a duke
than you are!'

He burst out laughing, and demanded further news of Alice. But the
Dowager said that rustics didn't amuse her, so, instead, Phoebe told him
about her father's letter, and he incensed the Dowager by enjoying that
hugely. Even less than by rustics was she amused by Lord Marlow's fatuity.

Sylvester did not remain for long, nor was he offered the chance of a *tête-
à-tête* with Phoebe. The only *tête-à-tête* granted him was a brief one with the
Dowager, who found an excuse to send Phoebe out of the room for a few

minutes, so that she could say to him: 'I'm glad you didn't tell the child she had me to thank for your visit to Austerby. I'm sorry for that, Sylvester, and think the better of you for having sent her to me, when I don't doubt you were feeling vexed with me. Mind, if I'd known she'd met you already, and not fancied you, I would never have done it! However, there's no harm done, and no need to think of it again. *She* won't, and you may depend on it I shan't either. Now that I know her better I see you wouldn't suit at all. I shouldn't wonder at it if she's going to prove as hard to please as her mother was.'

He was spared having to answer this speech by Phoebe's coming back into the room. He rose to take his leave, and, as he shook hands with Phoebe, said: 'I hope we may meet again soon. You will be attending all the balls, I expect. I hardly dare ask you–if I really did cut you at Almack's!–if you will stand up with me?'

'Yes, of course,' she responded. 'It wouldn't be very civil in me to refuse, would it?'

'I might have known it!' he exclaimed. 'How *could* I be such a flat as to offer you the chance to give me one of your set-downs?'

'I didn't!' she protested.

'Then heaven help me when you do!' he said. 'Goodbye! Don't grow *too* civil, will you? But I need not ask that: you won't!'

15

Before Phoebe saw Sylvester again she had encountered another member of his family: accompanying her grandmother on a morning visit she met Lady Henry Rayne.

Several ladies had elected to call on old Mrs Stour that day, but the younger generation was represented only by Lady Henry and Miss Marlow. Lady Henry, brought by her mama, was so heartily bored that even the entrance of an unknown girl came to her as an alleviation. She seized the first opportunity that offered of changing her seat for one beside Phoebe's, saying, with her pretty smile: 'I think we have met before, haven't we? Only I am so stupid at remembering names!'

'Well, not precisely,' replied Phoebe, with her usual candour. 'I never saw you but twice in my life, and I wasn't introduced to you. Once was at the Opera House, but the first occasion was at Lady Jersey's ball last year. I am afraid it was the circumstance of my staring at you so rudely which makes you think we have met! But you looked so beautiful I couldn't drag my eyes away! I beg your pardon! you must think me very impertinent!'

Not unnaturally Ianthe found nothing impertinent in this speech. Her own words had been a mere conversational gambit; she had no recollection of having seen Phoebe before, but she said: 'Indeed I didn't! I am sorry we were never introduced until today. I am not often in London.' She added, with a wistful smile: 'I am a widow, you know.'

'Oh—!' Phoebe was genuinely shocked. It seemed incredible, for she had supposed Ianthe to be little older than herself.

'I was hardly more than a child when I was married,' explained Ianthe. 'I am not so very old now, though I have been a widow for several years!'

'I thought you were my own age!' said Phoebe frankly.

No more was needed to seal the friendship. Ianthe, laughing at this misapprehension, disclosed that her only child was six years of age; Phoebe exclaimed: 'Oh, no! impossible!' and stepped, all unknown to herself, into the rôle of Chief Confidante. She learned within the space of twenty minutes that the life of a recluse had been imposed on Ianthe by her husband's family, who expected her to wear out the rest of her widowhood in bucolic seclusion.

'I wonder you should yield to such barbarous notions!' said Phoebe, quite appalled.

'Alas, there is *one* person who holds a weapon I am powerless to withstand!' said Ianthe in a melancholy tone. 'He is the sole arbiter of my poor child's destiny. Things were so left that I found myself bereft at one stroke of both husband and son!' She perceived a startled look on Phoebe's face, and added: 'Edmund was not left to my guardianship. I must not say more, and should not have said as much, only that I knew, as soon as we met, that you would understand! I am persuaded I can trust you! You cannot conceive the relief of being able to speak openly: in general I am obliged to be reserved. But I mustn't talk any more about my troubles!'

She was certainly unable to do so, for at that moment her attention was drawn to Lady Elvaston, who had risen to take leave of her hostess. She too got up, and put out her hand to Phoebe, saying in her soft voice: 'I see Mama is ready to go, and so I must say goodbye. Do you make a long stay in town? It would be so agreeable to meet again! Perhaps you would give me the pleasure of coming to see me one day? I should like you to see my little boy.'

'Oh, is he with you?' exclaimed Phoebe, a good deal surprised. 'I had recollected—I mean, I should like very much to visit you, ma'am!'

'My bringing him to town was not at all approved of, I can assure you,' responded Ianthe plaintively. 'But even his guardian can scarcely forbid me to take him to stay with my parents! Mama quite dotes on him, and would have been so grieved if I hadn't brought him with me!'

She pressed Phoebe's hand, and floated away, leaving Phoebe a prey to doubt and curiosity.

From the outset Phoebe had been fascinated by her beauty; within a minute of making her acquaintance she had been captivated by her appealing manners, and the charm of a smile that hinted at troubles bravely borne. But Phoebe was a shrewd observer; she was also possessed of strong commonsense; and while the romantic side of her nature responded to the air of tragic mystery which clung about Ianthe the matter-of-fact streak which ran through it relentlessly pointed out to her certain anomalies in what had been disclosed, and compelled her to acknowledge that confidences uttered upon so short an acquaintance were not, perhaps, to be wholly credited.

She was anxious to discover Ianthe's identity. She now knew her to be a member of the Rayne family, but the family was a large one, and in what degree of relationship to Sylvester Ianthe stood she had no idea. Her grandmother would no doubt be able to enlighten her.

Lady Ingham was well able to enlighten her. 'Ianthe Rayne?' she said, as they drove away from Mrs Stour's house. 'A pretty creature, isn't she? Gooseish, of course, but one can't but pity her. She's Elvaston's daughter, and married poor Harry Rayne the year she was brought out. He died before their son was out of short coats. A dreadful business! I fancy they never discovered what ailed him: you would have said there was not a healthier young man alive! Something internal: that's all I ever heard. Ah, if they had but called in dear Sir Henry Halford!'

'I knew she had been married to a member of that family, ma'am, but–who *was* her husband?'

'Who was he?' repeated the Dowager. 'Why, Sylvester's younger brother, to be sure! His twin-brother, too, which made it worse.'

'Then the child–Lady Henry's little boy—?' Phoebe faltered.

'Oh, there's nothing amiss with him that ever I heard!' replied the Dowager, leaning forward to obtain a clearer view of a milliner's shop-window as she spoke. 'My love, I wonder if that chip-straw–no, those pink flowers wouldn't become you! What were you saying? Oh, Harry's son! A splendid little fellow, I'm told. I've never seen him myself: he lives at Chance.'

'And he is–I understand Lady Henry to say–the Duke's ward?'

'Yes, and his heir as well–not that that is likely to signify! Was Ianthe complaining to you about that business?' She glanced at Phoebe, and said bluntly: 'You would be ill-advised to refine too much on what she may have said to you, my love. The truth is that she and Sylvester can never deal together. *She* fell into a pelter as soon as she found how things were left–well, I must own I think she should have been joined with Sylvester in the guardianship!–and *he* don't take the trouble to handle her tactfully.'

'I can readily believe that!' Phoebe interjected. 'Is he fond of the little boy, ma'am?'

'I daresay he may be, for Harry's sake–though they say the boy is the image of his mother–but the fact is, my dear, young men don't commonly dote on nursery brats! He will certainly do his duty by the boy.'

'Mama did her duty by me,' said Phoebe. 'I think I understand what Lady Henry's feelings must be.'

'Fiddle!' said the Dowager. 'I don't scruple to tell you, my love–for you are bound to hear it–that they are at odds *now* because the little ninny has got a second marriage in her eye, and knows Sylvester won't let her take the boy away from Chance.'

'Oh!' Phoebe exclaimed, her eyes flashing. 'How could he be so inhuman? Does he expect her to remain a widow all her life? Ah, I suppose it should be enough for her to have been married to a Rayne! I don't believe there was ever anyone more arrogant!'

'Before you put yourself in a taking,' said the Dowager dryly, 'let me tell you that if it is arrogance which prompts Sylvester to say he won't have his heir brought up by a Nugent Fotherby it is a fortunate circumstance for the boy that he *is* arrogant!'

'Nugent Fotherby?' gasped Phoebe, her righteous wrath suddenly and ludicrously arrested. 'Grandmama, you can't mean it? That absurd creature who can't turn his head because his shirt points are too high, and who let Papa chouse him out of three hundred guineas for a showy chestnut anyone but a flat must have seen was short of bone?'

Somewhat taken aback, the Dowager said: 'I don't know anything about horses. And as for your father, if he persuaded Fotherby to buy one that was unsound I call it very shabby dealing!'

'Oh, *no*, ma'am!' Phoebe said earnestly. 'I assure you there is nothing wrong in *that*! If a man who can't tell when a horse isn't fit to go chooses to set up as a knowing one he must expect to be burnt!'

'Indeed!' said the Dowager.

Phoebe was silent for a minute or two; but presently she said thoughtfully: 'Well, ma'am, I don't think one can precisely blame Salford for not wishing to let his nephew grow up under such a man!'

'I should think not indeed! What's more, I fancy that on that head Sylvester and Elvaston are at one. Of course Elvaston don't like the match, but I daresay he'll swallow it.'

'Well, Papa wouldn't!' said Phoebe frankly. 'In fact, he told me once that if ever I took it into my head to marry a bleater who, besides being a man-milliner and a cawker who don't know a blood-horse from a commoner, encourages every barnacle on the town to hang on him, he would wash his hands of me!'

'And if that is the language he sees fit to teach you, the sooner he does so the better!' said her ladyship tartly.

Much abashed, Phoebe begged her pardon; and continued to meditate in silence for the rest of the drive.

Her thoughts were not happy, but it was not Lady Henry's lapse of taste which cast a damper over her spirits. It was the existence of Lady Henry's fatherless child.

Dismay had been her first reaction to the evil tidings; it was succeeded by a strong conviction that Fate and Sylvester between them had contrived the whole miserable business for no other purpose than to undo her. She had long known Fate for her enemy, and Fate was clearly responsible for Coincidence. As for Sylvester, however much it might seem to the casual observer that he was hardly to be blamed for possessing a nephew who was also his ward, anyone with the smallest knowledge of his character must recognize at a glance that it was conduct entirely typical of him. And if he had not wished to figure as the villain in a romance he should not have had satanic eyebrows—or, at any rate, amended the ill-used authoress, he should have exerted himself to be more agreeable to her at Lady Sefton's ball, instead of uttering formal civilities, and looking at her with eyes so coldly indifferent that they seemed scarcely to see her. It would never then have occurred to her to think him satanic, for when he smiled he did not look in the least satanic. Far otherwise, in fact, she decided, realizing with faint surprise that although he had frequently enraged her during their sojourn at the Blue Boar she had never, from his first entering that hostelry, perceived anything villainous in his aspect.

This reflection led her to recall how much she stood in his debt, which resulted in a fit of dejection hard to shake off. Only one alleviating circumstance presented itself to her: he need never know who had written *The Lost Heir*. But that was a very small grain of comfort, since his ignorance would not make her feel less treacherous.

It was probable that if they had not chanced to meet again only two days later nothing further would have come of Ianthe's desire to know Phoebe better; but Fate once more took a hand in Phoebe's affairs. Sent out under the escort of Muker to execute some commissions for her grandmother in Bond Street, she came abreast of a barouche, drawn up beside the flagway, just as Ianthe, a picture of lovely maternity, was helping her child to climb into it. When she saw Phoebe she exclaimed, and at once shook hands. 'How charming this is! Are you bent on any very important errand? Do come home with me! Mama has driven out to Wimbledon to visit one of my sisters, so we will be quite alone, and can enjoy such a comfortable chat!' She hardly waited for Phoebe to accept the invitation, but nodded to Muker, saying that Miss Marlow should be sent home in the carriage later in the day, and made Phoebe get into the carriage, calling on Master Rayne to say how do you do politely.

Master Rayne pulled off his tasselled cap, exposing his sunny curls to the breeze. His resemblance to his mother was pronounced. His complexion was as delicately fair, his eyes as large and as deeply blue, and his locks as silken as hers; but a sturdy frame and a look of determination about his mouth and chin saved him from appearing girlish. Having subjected Phoebe to a dispassionate scrutiny he decided to make her the recipient of an interesting confidence. 'I am wearing gloves,' he said.

'So you are! Very smart ones too!' she replied admiringly.

'If I was at home,' said Master Rayne, with a darkling glance at his parent, 'I wouldn't have to wear them.'

'Now, Edmund—'

'But I expect you are enjoying your visit to London, are you not?' asked Phoebe, diplomatically changing the subject.

'Indeed he is!' said Ianthe. 'Only fancy! his grandpapa promises to take him riding in the Park one morning, doesn't he, my love?'

'If I'm good,' said Edmund, with unmistakable pessimism. 'But I won't have my tooth pulled out again!'

Ianthe laughed. 'Edmund, you know Mama said you should not go to Mr Tilton this time!'

'You said I shouldn't go when we came to London afore,' he reminded her inexorably. 'But Uncle Vester said I should. And I did. I do not like to have my tooth pulled out, *even* if I am let keep it in a little box, and people do *not* throw it away,' said Edmund bitterly.

'No one does,' intervened Phoebe. 'I expect, however, that you were very brave.'

'Yes,' acknowledged Edmund. 'Acos Uncle Vester said he would make me sorry if I wasn't, and I don't like Uncle Vester's way of making people sorry. It hurts!'

'You see!' said Ianthe in a low voice, and with a speaking look at Phoebe.

'Keighley said I was brave when I fell off my pony,' disclosed Edmund. 'Not one squeak out o' me! Full o' proper spunk I was!'

'*Edmund*!' exclaimed Ianthe angrily. 'If I have told you once I won't have you repeating the vulgar things Keighley says to you I have told you a hundred times! Beg Miss Marlow's pardon this instant! I don't know what she must think of you!'

'Oh, no, pray do not bid him do so!' begged Phoebe, perceiving the mulish set to Master Rayne's jaw.

'Keighley!' stated Edmund, the light of battle in his eyes, 'is a prime gun! He is my *partickler* friend.'

'I don't wonder at it,' returned Phoebe, before Ianthe could pick up this gage. 'I am a little acquainted with him myself, you know, and I am sure he is a splendid person. Did he teach you to ride your pony? I wish you will tell me about your pony!'

Nothing loth, Edmund embarked on a catalogue of this animal's points. By the time Lord Elvaston's house in Albemarle Street was reached an excellent understanding flourished between him and Miss Marlow, and it was with considerable reluctance that he parted from her. But his mother had had enough of his company, and she sent him away to the nursery, explaining to Phoebe that if she allowed him to remain with her once he would expect to do so always, which would vex Lady Elvaston. 'Mama doesn't like him to play in the drawing-room, except for half an hour before he is put to bed.'

'I thought you said that she doted on him!' said Phoebe, forgetting to check her unruly tongue.

'Oh, yes! Only she thinks that it isn't good for him to be put forward too much!' said Ianthe, with commendable aplomb. 'Now I am going to take you upstairs to my bedchamber, so that you may put off your hat and pelisse, for I don't mean to let you run away in a hurry, I can tell you!'

It was indeed several hours later when the carriage was sent for to convey Phoebe to Green Street; and she was by that time pretty fully informed of all the circumstances of Ianthe's marriage, widowhood, and proposed remarriage. Before they had risen from the table upon which a light nuncheon had been spread she knew that Sylvester had never wanted to be saddled with his brother's child; and she had been regaled with a number of stories illustrative of his harsh treatment of Edmund, and the malice which prompted him to encourage Edmund to defy his mother's authority. Count Ugolino was scarcely more repulsive than the callous individual depicted by Ianthe. Had he not been attached to his twin-brother? Oh, well, yes, in his cold way, perhaps! But never would dearest Harry's widow forget his unfeeling conduct when Harry, after days of dreadful suffering, had breathed his last. 'Held up in his arms, too! You would have supposed him to be made of marble, my dear Miss Marlow! Not a tear, not a word to *me!* You may imagine how wholly I was overset, too—almost out of my senses! Indeed, when I saw Sylvester lay my beloved husband down, and heard his voice saying that he was dead—in the most *brutal* way!—I was cast into such an agony of grief that the doctors were alarmed for my reason. I was in hysterics for three days, but he cared nothing for that, of course. I daresay he never even knew it, for he walked straight out of the room without one look towards me, and I didn't set eyes on him again for weeks!'

'Some people, I believe,' Phoebe said, rendered acutely uncomfortable by these reminiscences, 'cannot bring themselves to permit others to enter into their deepest feelings. It would not be right—excuse me!—to suppose that they have none.'

'Oh, no! But reserve is repugnant to me!' said Ianthe, rather unnecessarily. 'Not that I believe Sylvester to have feelings of that nature, for I am sure I never knew anyone with less sensibility. The only person he holds in affection is his mama. I own him to be quite devoted to *her*—*absurdly* so, in my opinion!'

'But you are fond of the Duchess, I collect?' Phoebe asked, in the hope of giving Ianthe's thoughts a happier direction. 'She is kind to you?'

'Oh, yes, but even *she* does not perfectly understand the misery of my situation! And I dare not hope that she will even try to prevail upon Sylvester not to tear my child from my arms, because she quite idolizes him. I pity his wife! She will find herself expected to defer in everything to Mama-Duchess!'

'Well, perhaps he won't have a wife,' suggested Phoebe soothingly.

'You may depend upon it he will, just to keep poor little Edmund out of the succession. Mama is persuaded that he is hanging out for one, and may throw the handkerchief at any moment.'

'I daresay! It takes two to make a marriage, however!'

'Do you mean he might meet with a *refusal?*'

'Why not?' said Phoebe.

'*Sylvester?* With all that he has to offer? Of course he won't! I wish he might, for it would do him good to be rebuffed. Only ten to one if it did happen he would set to work to make the girl fall in love with him, and then offer for another!'

'I see no reason for anyone to fall in love with him,' declared Phoebe, a spark in her eye.

'No, nor do I, but you would be astonished if you knew how many girls have positively *languished* over him!'

'I should!' said Phoebe fervently. 'For my part I should suppose them rather to have fallen in love with his rank!'

'Yes, but it isn't so. He can make girls form a tendre for him even when they have started by not liking him in the least. He knows it, too. He bet Harry once that he would succeed in attaching Miss Wharfe, and he *did*!'

'*Bet*—' gasped Phoebe. 'How–how infamous! How could any gentleman do such a thing?'

'Oh, well, you know what they are!' said Ianthe erroneously. 'I must own, too, that Miss Wharfe's coldness was one of the on-dits that year: she was a very handsome girl, and a great heiress as well, so of course she had *dozens* of suitors. She snubbed them all, so that it got to be a famous jest. They used to call her the Impregnable Citadel. Harry told Sylvester–funning, you know: they were always funning!–that even he would not be able to make a breach in the walls, and Sylvester instantly asked him what odds he was offering against it. I believe they were betting heavily on it in the clubs, as soon as it was seen that Sylvester was *laying siege* to the Citadel. Men are so odious!'

With this pronouncement Phoebe was in full agreement. She left Albemarle Street, amply provided with food for thought. She was shrewd enough to discount much that had been told her of Sylvester's treatment of his nephew: Master Rayne did not present to the world the portrait of an ill-used child. On the other hand, his mama had unconsciously painted herself in unflattering colours, and emerged from her various stories as a singularly foolish parent. Probably, Phoebe decided, Sylvester was indifferent to Edmund, but determined, in his proud way, to do his duty to the boy. That word had no very pleasant connotation to one who had had it ceaselessly dinned in her ears by an unloving stepmother, but it did not include injustice. Lady Marlow had always been rigidly just.

It was Ianthe's last disclosure that gave Phoebe so furiously to think. She found nothing in it to discount, for the suspicion had already crossed her mind that Sylvester's kindness had been part of a deliberate attempt to make her sorry she had so rudely repulsed him. His manners, too, when he had called in Green Street, even the lurking smile in his eyes when he had looked at her, were calculated to please. Yes, Phoebe admitted, he *did* know how to fix his interest with unwary females. The question was whether to repulse him, or whether, safe in the knowledge that he was laying a trap for her, to encourage his attentions.

The question remained unanswered until the following day, when she met him again. She was riding with her Ingham cousins in the Park in a sedate party composed of herself, Miss Mary and Miss Amabel, young Mr Dudley Ingham, and two grooms following at a discreet distance; and she was heartily bored. The Misses Ingham were very plain, and very good, and very dull; and their brother, Lord Ingham's promising second son, was already bidding fair to become a solid member of some future government; and the hack provided for her use was an animal with no paces and a placid disposition.

Sylvester, himself mounted on a neatish bay, and accompanied by two of his friends, took in the situation in one amused glance, and dealt with it in a way that showed considerable dexterity and an utter want of consideration for Lord Yarrow and Mr Ashford. Without anyone knowing (except himself) how it had come about, the two parties had become one; and while his hapless friends found themselves making polite conversation to the Misses Ingham, Sylvester was riding with Phoebe, a little way behind.

'Oh, my poor Sparrow!' he said, mocking her. 'Never have I encountered so heartrending a sight! A job-horse?'

'No,' replied Phoebe. 'My cousin Anne's *favourite* mount. A very safe, comfortable ride for a lady, Duke.'

'I *beg* your pardon! I have not seen him show his paces, of course.'

She cast him a glance of lofty scorn. 'He has none. He has a very elegant shuffle, being just a trifle tied in below the knee.'

'But such shoulders!'

Gravity deserted her; she burst into laughter, which made Miss Mary Ingham turn her head to look at her in wondering reproof, and said: 'Oh, dear, did you ever set eyes on such a flat-sided screw?'

'No–or on a lady with a better seat. The combination is quite shocking! Will you let me mount you while you are in town?'

She was so astonished she could only stare at him. He smiled, and said: 'I keep several horses at Chance for my sister-in-law's convenience. She was used to ride a great deal. There would be nothing easier than for me to send for a couple to be brought up to London.'

'Ride Lady Henry's horses?' she exclaimed. 'You must be mad! I shouldn't dream of doing such a thing!'

'They are not her horses. They are mine.'

'You said yourself you kept them for her use: she must consider them as good as her own! Besides, you must know I couldn't permit you to mount me!'

'I suppose you couldn't,' he admitted. 'I hate to see you so unworthily mounted, though.'

'Thank you–you are very good!' she stammered.

'I am *what*? Sparrow, I do implore you not to let Lady Ingham teach you to utter civil whiskers! You know I am no such thing, but, on the contrary, the villain whose evil designs drove you from home!' He stopped, as her eyes flew involuntarily to meet his. The look held for no more than an instant, but the expression in her eyes drove the laughter from his own. He waited for a moment, and then asked quietly: 'What is it? What did I say to make you look at me like that?'

Scarlet-cheeked, she said: 'Nothing! I don't know how I looked.'

'Very much as I saw you look once at your mother-in-law: stricken!'

She managed to laugh. 'How absurd! I am afraid you have too lively an imagination, Duke!'

'Well, I *hope* I may have,' he returned.

'There can be no doubt. I was–oh, shocked to think that after all that has passed you could suppose me to regard you in the light–in the light of a villain. But you were only funning, of course.'

'I was, but I'm not funning when I tell you that I was not *maliciously* funning–to distress you.'

She turned her head to look at him again, this time in candid appraisal. 'No. Although it is a thing you *could* do, I fancy.'

'You may believe that I did not.'

'And *you* may believe I don't think you villainous!'

'Oh, that is a much harder task!' he protested, rallying her. 'When I think of the reception I was accorded at that appalling inn I have the gravest misgivings!'

She laughed, but tacitly refused the challenge. He did not pursue the subject; and after riding beside him in silence for a few minutes she introduced another, saying: 'I had almost forgotten to tell you that I had the pleasure of meeting your nephew yesterday, Duke! You must be very proud of him: he is a most beautiful child!'

'He is a very spoilt one. Are you acquainted with my sister-in-law?'

'I made her acquaintance a few days ago, and she was so kind as to invite me to spend the afternoon with her yesterday.'

'Ah, *now* I understand the meaning of that stricken look!' he remarked. 'Did I figure as the Unfeeling Brother-in-law, or as the Wicked Uncle?'

She was not obliged to answer him, for as the words left his tongue his attention was diverted. A lady who was walking beside the carriage-way just then waved to him. He recognized his cousin, Mrs Newbury, and at once desired Phoebe to rein in. 'If you are not already known to one another I should like to introduce you to Mrs Newbury, Miss Marlow. She is quite the most entertaining of my cousins: I am persuaded you would deal extremely!–Georgie, what a stunning sight! How comes it about that you are walking in this demure style? No faithful husband to ride with you? Not *one* cicisbeo left to you?'

She laughed, stretching up her hand to clasp his. 'No, isn't it infamous? Lion has a spell of duty, and *all* my cicisbeos have failed me! Those who are not still buried in the country have their feet in mustard-baths, so that I've sunk to walking with a mere female. No, you can't see her, because we have parted company.'

He had leaned down to take her hand, and now, just before he released it, he pressed it meaningly, saying: 'Sunk indeed! Are you acquainted with Miss Marlow, or may I introduce her to you?'

'So that is who you are!' she said, smiling up at Phoebe. 'To be sure, I should have guessed it, for I have just been exchanging bows with your cousins. You are Lady Ingham's granddaughter, and–you are riding Anne Ingham's deplorable slug! But you should not be: it is quite shocking! Even under that handicap you take the shine out of us all.'

'I have been trying to persuade her to let me have the privilege of mounting her, but she insists it will not do,' Sylvester said. 'I have now a better notion, however. I fancy your *second* hack would be just the thing for her.'

Mrs Newbury owned only one hack, but she had been on the alert from the moment of having her hand significantly squeezed, and she took this without a blink, interrupting Phoebe's embarrassed protests to say warmly: 'Oh, don't say you won't, Miss Marlow! You can't think how much obliged to you I shall be if you will but ride with me sometimes! I detest walking, but to ride alone, with only one's groom following primly behind, is intolerable! I am pining for a good gallop, too, and that can't be had in Hyde Park. Sylvester, if I can prevail upon Miss Marlow to go, will you escort the pair of us to Richmond Park upon the first real spring day?'

'But with the greatest pleasure, my dear cousin!' he responded.

'Do say you would like it!' Mrs Newbury begged Phoebe.

'I should like it of all things, ma'am, but it is quite dreadful that you should be obliged to invite me!'

'But I promise you I'm not! Sylvester knew I should be charmed to have a companion—and, you know, I could have said my other horse was lame, or sold, if I had wished to! I shall come to pay Lady Ingham a morning-visit, and coax her into giving her consent.'

She stepped back then, and as they parted from her cast a quizzing look up at Sylvester. He met it with a smile, so she concluded that he was pleased, and went on her way, wondering whether he was indulging a fit of gallantry, or if it was possible that he was really trying to fix his interest with Miss Marlow. It seemed unlikely, but no more unlikely than his having singled her out for his latest flirt. Or was he merely being kind to Lady Ingham's countrified little granddaughter? Oh, no! not Sylvester! decided Mrs Newbury. He could be kind, but only where he liked. Well, it was all very intriguing, and for her part she was perfectly ready to lend him whatever aid he wanted. One did not look gift-horses in the mouth, certainly not a gift-horse of Sylvester's providing.

16

The encounter in the Park decided the matter: Sylvester was not to be immediately rebuffed. He had certainly made it almost impossible for Phoebe to do so, but this was a consideration that only occurred to her after she had made her decision. Without standing the smallest danger of losing her heart to him, she found his company agreeable, and would be sorry to lose it. If he was trying to serve her as he had served the unknown Miss Wharfe there could be no better way of discomfiting him than by receiving his advances in a spirit of cool friendliness. This was an excellent reason for tolerating Sylvester; within a very short time Phoebe had found another. With the return to London of so many members of the ton quite a number of invitations arrived in Green Street; and Phoebe, attending parties in some trepidation, rapidly discovered the advantages attached to her friendship with him. Very different was her second season from the first! Then she had possessed no acquaintance in town; she had endured agonies of shyness; and she had attracted no attention. Now, though the list of her acquaintances was not large, she attracted a great deal of attention, for she was Salford's latest flirt. People who had previously condemned Phoebe as a dowd with neither beauty nor style to recommend her now discovered that her countenance was expressive, her blunt utterances diverting, and her simplicity refreshing. Unusual: that was the epithet affixed to Miss Marlow. It emanated from Lady Ingham, but no one remembered that: a quiet girl with no pretension to beauty must be unusual to have captured Sylvester's fancy. There were many, of course, who could not imagine what he saw in her; she would never rival the accredited Toasts, or enjoy more than a moderate success. Happily she was satisfied merely to feel at home in society, to have made a few agreeable friends, and never to lack a partner at a ball. No lady whose hand was claimed twice in one evening by Sylvester need fear that fate. Nor did Sylvester stand in danger of being rebuffed while he continued to treat her with just the right degree of flattering attention. His motive might be perfidious, but it could not be denied that he was a delightful companion; and one, moreover, with whom it was not necessary to mind one's tongue. His sense of humour, too, was lively: often, if a fatuous remark were uttered, or someone behaved in a fashion so typical as to be ludicrous, Phoebe would look instinctively towards him, knowing that he must be sharing her amusement. It was strange how the dullest party could be enjoyed because there was one person present whose eyes could be met for the fraction of a second, in wordless appreciation of a joke unshared by others: almost as strange as the insipidity of parties at which that person was not present. Oh, no! Miss Marlow, though fully alive to his arrogance, his selfishness, and his detestable vanity had no intention—no *immediate* intention—of repulsing Sylvester.

Besides, he had provided for her use a little spiriting mare with a silken mouth, perfect in all her paces, and as full of playfulness as she could hold. Phoebe had cried out involuntarily when first she had seen the Firefly: how could Mrs Newbury bear to let another ride her beautiful mare? Mrs Newbury did not know how it was, but she preferred her dear old Jupiter. Phoebe understood at once: she herself owned a cover-hack long past his prime but still, and always, her favourite hack.

It was not long before she had discovered the truth about the Firefly. Major Newbury, very smart in his scarlet regimentals, had seen his wife and her new friend off on their almost daily ride one day. He had come out on to the step leading up to the door of his narrow little house, and no sooner had he set eyes on the Firefly than he had exclaimed: 'Is that the mare Sylvester gave you, Georgie? Well, by Jove—!'

Phoebe had been standing just far enough away to make it possible that she had not heard either this remark or the Major's subsequent, and conscience-stricken: 'Eh? Oh—! Just so, my love! Forgot!' For a rather dreadful moment she had wondered what she ought to do; then she had made up her mind to pretend she had not heard, prompted as much by consideration for Georgiana as by reluctance to forgo her rides.

Sylvester had been right when he had prophesied that she and Georgiana would deal extremely: each took an instant liking to the other; and since the Dowager raised no objection Phoebe became a frequent guest in the Newburys' haphazard house. Lady Ingham said they were a ramshackle pair; Phoebe, who had hitherto attended only large, formal parties in London, thought them delightful, and enjoyed nothing so much as the evenings she spent in their very ill-run house. One never knew what might happen at one of Georgie's parties, said Lord Yarrow, declaring that he had once arrived five minutes after the crystal chandelier in the drawing-room had crashed to the floor, and had found Georgie standing like Dido amongst the ruins of Carthage, only rather more composed. Sylvester agreed that this had been a remarkably good party, but contended that by far the best evening he had yet spent in the establishment was that on which the new butler, having admitted him into the ball, had fallen flat on his face in a drunken stupor. Phoebe had never dreamed that people could be as gay and as unceremonious as they were in Georgie's house. Nor had she ever liked Sylvester as well as when she saw him there, amongst his intimates. It might be another instance of his pride that he should show his most agreeable side only to his relations and his closest friends, but it was impossible to deny that that side was endearing.

He was just as charming when the projected expedition to Richmond Park took place, and even more surprisingly, since the original party was augmented by three persons, one of whom was not very acceptable to him. He welcomed the news that Major Newbury was to join it; when his sister-in-law, hearing of the scheme, announced that she would come too, with her brother Charles, he bore it with equanimity; but when the day dawned, and it was discovered that Ianthe, instead of by her brother, was escorted by Sir Nugent Fotherby, even the Major, not famed for perspicacity, informed his wife, in a penetrating whisper, that he had a very good mind to tip the double, since he clearly saw that this expedition of pleasure was bitched at the outset.

For an anxious minute it did indeed seem that it was doomed to failure. It had been arranged that Ianthe and her brother would meet the rest of the party at Roehampton Gate, having sent their horses on in charge of a groom: a last-minute alteration in plan which was only made known to Sylvester when he arrived at the Newburys' house to escort the party. He looked vexed when the message was repeated to him, and exclaimed: 'Good God, Georgie, why didn't you tell Ianthe that if she didn't choose to go with us she might remain at home? She'll keep us waiting an hour, and very likely more!'

'I daresay she will, but it's of no use to fly into a pet with me,' responded Georgiana calmly. 'I received her note not twenty minutes ago, and all I could do was to send the footman back to her with a reminder that since you held the tickets of admission she must take care not to be late.'

'Much good that will do!' he observed.

But when they reached the Roehampton Gate he was agreeably surprised to find his sister-in-law already there, and was beginning to feel quite in charity with her when he suddenly perceived that the sprig of fashion with her was not her brother but Sir Nugent Fotherby. He stiffened, the expression of easy good-humour on his face changing on a flash to one of haughty astonishment. Phoebe, obliged to repress a strong desire to tell him precisely what she thought of such odious self-consequence, could only be sorry for Sir Nugent.

Her pity was wasted. Sir Nugent knew that Sylvester did not like him, but it never crossed his mind that Sylvester, or anyone else, held him in contempt. If he could have been brought to believe it, he would have known that Sylvester was queer in his attic, and he would have been very much shocked. When Sylvester raised his quizzing-glass he was not at all unnerved, because it was plain that Sylvester was studying the exquisite folds of his neck-cloth. He was not surprised; he would have been disappointed if what had cost him so much time and skill to arrange had attracted no attention. It was not everyone who could tie an Oriental: he was pretty sure Sylvester couldn't; and if Sylvester were to ask him how it was done he would be obliged to tell him that it took years to learn the art, and often several hours of concentrated effort to achieve a respectable result when one had learnt it. Other men might envy Sir Nugent; they could not despise him, for his pedigree was impeccable, his fortune exceeded sixty thousand pounds a year, and he had it on the authority of those boon-companions whom Lord Marlow rudely stigmatized as barnacles that, just as in all matters of fashion he was the finest Pink of the Ton, in the world of sport he figured as a Nonpareil, a regular Top-of-the-Trees, a Sure Card, up to all kinds of slums, never to be beaten on any suit.

His imperviousness to insult saved the day's pleasure from wreck. He seized the earliest opportunity that offered of edging his showy chestnut alongside Sylvester's hack for the purpose of drawing his attention to the circumstance of his having, as he phrased it, brought Lady Henry bang up to the mark on time.

'You are to be congratulated,' said Sylvester, in a discouraging tone.

'Devilish good of you to say so, Duke!' responded Sir Nugent, acknowledging the tribute with a slight bow. 'Don't mind owning it wasn't easy. Took a devilish deal of address. If there *is* a thing I pride myself on it's that. "Lady Henry," I said—well, not to cut a wheedle with you, Duke, I put it a devilish sight stronger than that! "My love," I said, "we shan't turn his grace up sweet if we keep him kicking his heels at the rendezvous. Take my word for it!" She did.'

In spite of himself Sylvester's face relaxed. 'She did?'

'She did,' asseverated Sir Nugent gravely. '"My sweet life," I said—you've no objection to that, Duke?'

'Not the least in the world.'

'You haven't?' exclaimed Sir Nugent, slewing his body round to stare at Sylvester, an exertion which the stiff points of his collar and the height of that Oriental Tie made necessary.

'Why should I?'

'You've put your finger on the nub, Duke!' said Sir Nugent. 'Why should you? *I* can't tell, and I believe I've cut my wisdoms. "My love," I said (if you've no objection) "you've got a maggot in your Idea-pot."'

'And what had she to say to that?' enquired Sylvester, conscious of a wish that Phoebe had not cantered ahead.

'She denied it,' said Sir Nugent. 'Said you were bent on throwing a rub in our way.'

'Oh?'

'Just what I said myself! "Oh!" I said.'

'Not "my love"?'

'Not then. Because I was surprised. You might say I was betwattled.'

'Like a duck in a thunderstorm.'

'No,' said Sir Nugent, giving this his consideration. 'I fancy, Duke, that if you were to ask all round the ton if Nugent Fotherby had ever looked like any species of fowl in such a situation the answer would be, in a word, No!'

'Well, I haven't the least desire to throw a rub in the way of your marriage to my sister-in-law. You may marry her with my good-will, but you will not prevail upon me to relinquish my nephew into your care.'

'But that's another nub!' objected Sir Nugent. 'You may say it's the primest nub of all! Her la'ship won't give him up!'

'A man of your address must surely be able to persuade her to do so.'

'Well, that's what I thought myself,' said Sir Nugent. 'Queer creatures, females! Devilish attached to the infantry. Let us discuss the matter!'

'No. Let us do no such thing!' interrupted Sylvester. 'Talking to me will pay no toll. I have only this to say: I have neither the power nor the desire to scotch your marriage to Ianthe, but there is no argument you can advance that will induce me to delegate the least part of my authority over Edmund to you or to anyone! Try if you can twist Ianthe round your thumb: don't waste your time on me!'

He spurred his horse forward as he spoke, and cantered on to overtake the rest of the party.

Phoebe, meanwhile, after enjoying an all too brief gallop, had been forced to pull up, and to continue at a walking-pace beside Ianthe, who wanted to talk about herself, and had found Georgiana an unresponsive audience. She disclosed that she had brought Sir Nugent in place of her brother because she was convinced that Sylvester's dislike of him arose from mere prejudice. He was barely acquainted with Sir Nugent: did not Phoebe think that if he were given this opportunity of getting to know him better he might well reconsider his cruel decision to part a mother from her child?

Phoebe found it impossible to answer this question, since a flat negative was clearly ineligible. Fortunately Ianthe was more interested in her own opinion than in Phoebe's, and had posed the question in a rhetorical spirit. Without waiting for an answer, she continued: 'For my part, I am persuaded that Sylvester must be agreeably surprised in him. I don't mean to say that his understanding is superior, for it is not–in fact, he has a great deal less than commonsense, and is sometimes quite addle-brained–but if I don't care for that I'm sure I don't know why Sylvester should! His disposition is amiable, and his manners excessively polished and civil. He is a man of rank, and of the first stare of fashion; and if he does associate with inferior persons, and fritter a fortune away in gaming-halls, *that* will cease when he is married. And as for his racehorses, he is so wealthy that losses on the Turf can't signify. In any event, it is nonsensical to suppose that it would do Edmund the least harm. Besides, even Sylvester must own that there can be no one better able to teach Edmund just how he should go on in all matters of taste and ton! He is always in the high kick of fashion, and makes the other men appear positively *shabby*! You have only to look at him!'

Phoebe looked instead at her, and in wonder. Beside Sylvester's quiet elegance and Major Newbury's military cut she had been thinking that Sir Nugent presented all the appearance of a coxcomb. He was a tall man, rather willowy in build, by no means unhandsome, but so tightly laced-in at the waist, so exaggeratedly padded at the shoulders, that he looked a little ridiculous. From the striking hat set rakishly on his Corinthian crop (he had already divulged that it was the New Dash, and the latest hit of fashion) to his gleaming boots, everything he wore seemed to have been chosen for the purpose of making him conspicuous. His extravagantly cut coat was embellished with very large and bright buttons; a glimpse of exotic colour hinted at a splendid waistcoat beneath it; his breeches were of white corduroy; a diamond pin was stuck in the folds of his preposterous neckcloth; and he wore so many rings on his fingers, and so many fobs and seals dangling at his waist, that he might have been taken for a jeweller advertising his wares.

Phoebe was not obliged to make any comment on Ianthe's last obser-vation, for Sylvester overtook them just then, and a minute later Sir Nugent ranged alongside, trying to convey to Ianthe by a series of shrugs and grimaces, which nearly overset Phoebe's gravity, that his mission had not prospered. She stole an apprehensive glance at Sylvester, fearing that Sir Nugent had put him out of temper, and was relieved to see no trace of the cold look of indifference she so much disliked. He looked rather amused, and when he addressed Sir Nugent it was in a light, good-humoured tone. Encouraged by this, Sir Nugent, who had been looking dejected, bright-ened, and asked him for his opinion of the horse he was riding. He won so courteous a reply that Phoebe took her underlip firmly between her teeth, and stared resolutely ahead. Sir Nugent, gratified by Sylvester's praise, drew his attention to the chestnut's manifold excellences, and confided that he had bought the animal at a devilish long price. A stifled sound from Phoebe, who knew just how long a price he had paid, made Sylvester's lips quiver, but he said, without a tremor: 'Did you indeed?'

It might have been thought odd conduct in a sporting man to use his hunters for hacking at the end of the hunting season, but his idiosyncrasy was not as inhumane as it seemed to the uninitiated. Sir Nugent was a member of several hunts, and he owned an astonishing number of horses, which he stabled all over the country, and seldom rode. When he did turn out it was rarely that he went beyond the first few fields, for, like Mr Brummell when he led the ton, he wore white tops to his boots, and feared to get them splashed. Lord Marlow's showy chestnut certainly looked to be more in need of exercise than of rest, and succeeded, by sidlings, plungings, and head-tossing, in giving Sir Nugent an uncomfortable ride.

As soon as he could contrive to do it without the appearance of incivility, Sylvester suggested to Phoebe that they should shake the fidgets out of the horses. She agreed to it in a strangled voice; the Firefly broke into a canter, lengthened her stride to a gallop; and in a few moments carried Phoebe far beyond earshot of Ianthe and Sir Nugent. Beside her thundered Sylvester's black, but neither she nor Sylvester spoke until they presently reined in at the end of the stretch of greensward. Then, as Phoebe bent forward to pat the Firefly's neck, Sylvester said in a voice of mock censure: 'Miss Marlow, I had occasion once to reprove you for laughing at rustics! *Now* I find you laughing at the very finest Pink that blooms in the Ton! You are incorrigible!'

'Oh, I didn't!' she protested, gurgling irrepressibly. 'You know I didn't!'

'Do I, indeed? I promise you I was in the liveliest dread that you would start at any moment to giggle. If you had seen your own face—'

'Well, I own it was a very close-run thing with me,' she admitted. 'How you were able to answer him so gravely I can't imagine!'

'Oh, he has been on the town for as long as I have, so that I have grown inured to him! I can understand, of course, that the first sight of his magnificence must come as a severe shock.'

She laughed. 'Yes, but I can't plead that excuse. I was for ever seeing him last year. In fact, I—'

'In fact you—?' he prompted, after waiting for a moment for her to finish the sentence.

She had broken off in confusion, the words: *I put him into my book* only just bitten back in time. She said now, with a tiny gasp: 'Grew so accustomed to him that I began not to notice him! Except when he came to a ball in a green velvet coat, and a waistcoat embroidered all over with pink roses!'

He did not immediately reply, and glancing a little nervously at him she saw that the flying line of his brows was accentuated by a slight frown which drew down their inner corners. He looked steadily at her, and said: 'Yes? But that isn't what you were going to say, is it?'

She hoped her countenance did not betray her, and said, with a fair assumption of ease: 'No, but I daresay I ought not to tell you what *that* was. You won't repeat it? It was not his appearance which nearly had me in whoops, but that peacocky chestnut of his, and the things he said of him! He bought him from Papa, and paid three hundred guineas for him! And thinks himself a *downy one!*'

He burst out laughing, and she hoped the dangerous moment had passed. But although he laughed at Marlow's successful essay in flat-catching, he said: 'I am still wondering what it was that you really meant to say, Sparrow.'

She was thankful to see Major and Mrs Newbury cantering towards them. There was time only to return a light rejoinder before Georgie called out to them, with news of a charming glade to be visited. They waited for

Ianthe and Sir Nugent to come up with them and there was no further opportunity for private talk.

The incident cast a cloud over Phoebe's pleasure. She could not be comfortable. To uneasiness was added a strong sense of guilt, which was not rendered less by the flattering distinction with which Sylvester was treating her. It was scarcely to be called gallantry, though he showed her wishes to be his first object; he quizzed rather than flirted; but there was a smiling look in his eyes when they met hers, and an informality in his manners that made her feel as if she had known him for a very long time. There had been a moment, before the Newburys had joined them, when she had hovered on the brink of telling him just what she had done. She had been strongly tempted, and the temptation recurred several times, only to be driven back by fear of what the consequences might be. When Sylvester looked at her with warmth in his eyes she felt that she could tell him anything, but she had seen him wear quite another expression; and she knew just how swiftly and with what perfect civility he could retire behind a film of ice.

She was still in a state of wretched indecision when she parted from him at the end of the day; but as she trod up the steps of Lady Ingham's house she thought suddenly that if anyone could advise her it must be her grandmother; and she determined, if her mood was propitious, to tell her the whole.

She found the Dowager in perfect good-humour, but a trifle preoccupied. She had received a visit from an old friend, just returned from a protracted sojourn in Paris, and Mrs Irthing's account of the delightful time she had spent there, the charming nature of the parties given by dear Sir Charles Stuart and Lady Elizabeth at the Embassy—just as it was used to be before that horrid Bonaparte spoilt everything with his vulgar ways!—the exclusiveness of society—so different from London, where one was increasingly at the mercy of mushrooms and tuft-hunters!—the comfort of the hôtels, and the amazing quality and style of the goods in all the shops had reawakened her desire to remove to Paris for a few months herself. It was just the right time of year for such a visit; the Ambassador and his wife were old friends of hers; and Mrs Irthing had been charged with messages for her from quite a number of French acquaintances whom she had not met for years but who all remembered her and wished that they might have the felicity of seeing her again. Well, she wished it too, and was much inclined to think it would do her a great deal of good to go abroad for a spell. She did not regret having assumed the charge of her granddaughter, of course, but it did just cross her mind that Phoebe might very well reside with Ingham and Rosina while she was away. A moment's reflection, however, caused her to abandon this scheme: Rosina was a fool, in no way to be trusted with the delicate task of promoting a marriage between Phoebe and Sylvester. The Dowager was feeling very hopeful about this affair, but there was no doubt that it needed skilful handling. Rosina would be bound to blunder; moreover, nothing was more likely to cause Sylvester to shy off than to find Phoebe always in company with her good, dull cousins. No, it would not do, the Dowager decided. It would not do to take Phoebe to Paris either: the Dowager was no believer in the power of absence over the heart, particularly when the heart in question belonged to Sylvester, who had so many girls on the catch for him.

The project had to be abandoned, but Mrs Irthing's visit had roused many memories. The Dowager fell into a reminiscent vein, and it was not until she and Phoebe removed to the drawing-room after dinner that she emerged from it, and bade Phoebe tell her about her own day. Phoebe said that she had enjoyed herself very much, and then, drawing a resolute breath, took the plunge. 'Grandmama, there is something I must tell you!'

She would not have been surprised if her confession of having commenced author had met with censure; but the Dowager, once assured that a strict anonymity had been preserved, was rather amused. She even said that she had always known Phoebe to be a clever little puss.

Possibly she considered it unlikely that her granddaughter's book would be read by any member of the ton; possibly she thought it even more unlikely that a portrait drawn by so inexperienced a hand would be recognizable. She only laughed when Phoebe told her the dreadful truth. But when Phoebe asked her if she thought Sylvester ought to be warned of what was hanging over his head she said quickly: 'On no account in the world! Good God, you must be mad to think of such a thing!'

'Yes, ma'am. Only—I can't be comfortable!' Phoebe said.

'Nonsense! He will know nothing about it!' replied the Dowager.

17

Unlike Lord Byron, Phoebe could not say that she awoke one morning to find herself famous, for clever Mr Newsham had allowed no clue to her identity to escape him. He saw no profit in allowing it to be known that a schoolroom chit had written *The Lost Heir*: far better, he told his partner, to set the ton wondering. Poor Mr Otley, protesting in vain that none but sapskulls would sport the blunt to the tune of eighteen shillings for a romance by an unknown author, resigned himself to ruin, and watched with a jaundiced eye the efforts of the senior partner to puff off the book to the ton.

But Mr Newsham had been right all along. The skilful letters he had written to influential persons, the flattery he had expended, the mysterious hints he had dropped, bore abundant fruit. The list of private subscribers presently caused Mr Otley's eyes to start in his head. 'Ay! and that's only the beginning!' said Mr Newsham. 'These are the nobs who would melt a fortune not to be behindhand in the mode. All females, of course: *I* knew they wouldn't risk the chance that a *roman à clef* might not take! By the by, I've discovered who that fellow with the eyebrows is: none other than his grace of Salford, my boy! If that ain't enough to make the nobs mad after the book, tell me what is!'

Since Mr Newsham continued to correspond only with Miss Battery, Phoebe never knew that her book had been launched until she saw the three handsome volumes in Lady Sefton's drawing-room. 'Dear Lady Ingham, has this audacious book come in your way? But I need not ask? Is it not the wickedest thing imaginable?' cried her ladyship, with much fluttering of her fan and her eyelids. 'Odious creature, whoever she is!—and it is *not* Caro Lamb, or that Irish woman: that I know for a fact! Setting us all in the pillory! I forgive her only for her sketch of poor dear Emily Cowper! I own I laughed myself into stitches! She has not the least notion of it, of course—thinks it meant for the likeness of Mrs Burrell! But Ugolino—oh, dear, dear, *what* must be his feelings if ever the book should come in his way? And that it must, you know, because everyone is talking about it!'

Too soon for her peace of mind did Phoebe prove the truth of this statement. Some, like the haughty Countess Lieven, shrugged it off, calling it an almond for a parrot; some delighted in it; some were shocked by it; but all were eager to discover its authorship. Never, thought Phoebe, could an author have watched the success of her first venture with more consternation! All her pride and pleasure in it were destroyed, and by one tiny thing that might so easily have been changed! Could she but have removed from the book every mention of a pair of eyebrows the rest would have been forgiven her, for only in that one portrait had she been blind to the virtues of her victims.

Lady Ingham, startled to find that the whole town (or as much of it as signified) was discussing her granddaughter's novel, demanded a copy of it from the reluctant author. Phoebe, who had received a set, forwarded to her by Miss Battery, shrinkingly presented her ladyship with the three elegant volumes.

The Dowager read it through, for some time anxiously watched by her trembling granddaughter, whose nerves suffered severely from the rapid transitions from hope to despair engendered by the Dowager's frequent utterances. A chuckle sent her spirits up; an ejaculated 'Good God!' brought them down with a rush; and she was obliged many times to slip out of the room, unable to bear the suspense.

'Recognize himself?' said the Dowager, when she had come to the end. 'Of course he will! Lord, child, how came you to commit such an imprudence? What a mercy that the whole thing is such a farrago of nonsense! I shouldn't wonder at it if Sylvester treats it as beneath his notice. We must hope he will, and at all events it need never be known that you wrote it. Who knows the truth besides your governess?–I collect she is to be trusted?'

'Indeed, she is, ma'am! The only other is Tom Orde.'

The Dowager clicked her tongue. 'I don't like that! Who's to say that a young rattle won't boast of being acquainted with the author when he finds you've become famous? You must write to him instantly, Phoebe, and warn him!'

Phoebe was hot in defence of her old playfellow, but it was not her championship that allayed the Dowager's alarm: it was the appearance on the scene of Tom himself, accompanied by his father, and managing to walk very creditably with the aid of a stick.

No sooner were the guests announced than Phoebe flew across the room to hug first one and then the other. The Squire, kissing her in a fatherly way, said: 'Well, puss, and what have you to say for yourself, eh?' and nothing could have been more brotherly than Tom's greeting. 'Hallo, Phoebe!' said Tom. 'Take care what you're about, now! Don't you go rumpling my neckcloth, for the lord's sake! Well, by Jove!' (surveying her) 'I'm dashed if you don't look quite modish! Won't Susan stare when I tell her!'

Nothing lover-like about Tom, decided the Dowager, turning her attention to the Squire.

It could not have been said that Lady Ingham and Mr Orde had much in common, but her ladyship, welcoming the Squire kindly for Phoebe's sake, soon found him to be a blunt, sensible man, who seemed to feel just as he ought on a number of important subjects, notably the folly of Lord Marlow, and the pretentiousness, sanctimonious hypocrisy, and cruelty of his spouse. They soon had their heads together, leaving Tom and Phoebe to talk undisturbed in the window-bay.

Knowing his Phoebe, Tom had come in the expectation of being pelted with questions about everyone at Austerby and at the Manor, but except for a polite enquiry after Mrs Orde's health, and an anxious one about Trusty and True, Phoebe asked him none. She was in regular communication with Miss Battery, an excellent correspondent, had received several letters from Susan, and even one or two scribbled notes from Lord Marlow, his lordship's happy disposition having led him to believe, within a very short time, that if he had not actually connived at his daughter's flight to her grandmother, at least this adventure had had his approval. Phoebe was more interested to learn what had brought Tom to town, and for how long he meant to remain.

Well, the Squire had had business to transact, and it was so abominably slow at home, when one couldn't yet ride, or fish, or even walk very far, that there was no bearing it, so Tom had come to London with his father. They were putting up at Reddish's Hotel, and meant to stay for at least a se'enight. The Squire had promised to take his son to visit one or two places he had long wanted to see. No, no, not *edifices*! He had seen them years ago! *Interesting* places, such as the Fives Court, and Jackson's Saloon, and Cribb's Parlour, and the Castle Tavern. Not in Phoebe's line, of course. And he was going to call on Salford.

'He told me to be sure and do so if ever I was in town, so I shall. He wouldn't have said it if he hadn't meant it, do you think?'

'Oh, no, but he has gone out of town,' Phoebe replied. 'I am not perfectly sure when he means to return, but I daresay it will be before you go away: he spoke of it as if he meant only to be gone a short while. He is at Chance, visiting his mother.'

'Do you see him, then?' Tom asked, surprised.

'Yes, frequently,' Phoebe answered, blushing faintly. 'I have come to know one of his cousins, you see, and—and so we often meet. But, oh, Tom, the most terrible thing has happened, and if you do see Salford you must take the greatest care not to betray me! I *dread* his return, for how to look him in the face I don't know!'

'Betray you!' demanded Tom, astonished. 'What the deuce are you talking about?'

'My wretched, wretched book!'

'Your—Oh, that! Well, what of it?'

'It is a success!' said Phoebe, in a voice of tragedy.

'Good God, you don't mean it? I wouldn't have believed it!' exclaimed Tom, adding still more infelicitously. 'Though I must say it has a devilish handsome binding: Sibby showed it to me, you know.'

'It isn't the binding people are talking about!' said Phoebe, with asperity. 'They are talking about the characters in it, and the author! Everyone wants to know who wrote it! *Now* do you understand?'

Tom did understand. He pursed his lips in a silent whistle, and after a minute said: 'Has Salford read it?'

'No—at least—no, he can't have done so yet, surely! He went away almost immediately after it was published.'

'I wonder if he'll guess?' said Tom slowly. 'You needn't be afraid I shall let it out, but it wouldn't surprise me if— You know what I should do if I were you?' She shook her head, her eyes fixed on his face. 'I'd make a clean breast of it,' said Tom.

'I did think of doing so, but when I remember what I wrote—' She broke off with a shudder.

'Devilish difficult thing to do,' he agreed. 'All the same—'

'I don't think I could,' she confessed. 'If he were to be angry—! It makes me sick only to imagine it! And my grandmother says on no account must I tell him.'

'Well, I daresay she knows best,' responded Tom somewhat dubiously. 'What will you do if he charges you with it? Deny it?'

'Oh, don't, Tom!' begged Phoebe.

'Yes, but you'd best make up your mind,' he insisted. 'I shouldn't think, myself, that he'll believe you: you never could tell a bouncer without looking guilty!'

'If he asks me,' said Phoebe despairingly, 'I must tell the truth.'

'Well, perhaps he won't ask you,' said Tom, perceiving that she was looking rather sickly already. 'But take care you don't mention it to anyone else, that's all! Ten to one you'll blurt it out to somebody! *I* know you!'

'Blurt it out! No, indeed!' she assured him.

She thought there could be little fear of it, but some severe trials had to be undergone, when she found herself obliged to endure in silence such discussions about her book as made her long to cry out: *No! I never meant it so!* For the one feature of *The Lost Heir* which aroused the curiosity of society was the character of Count Ugolino. The levelheaded might dismiss it as a piece of impertinence; Sylvester's friends might be up in arms; but it seemed to Phoebe that the idiots who asserted there was never smoke without a fire were legion. She was speedily made to realize that she had not been Ianthe's only confidante. Before ever *The Lost Heir* was written Ianthe had apparently blackened Sylvester's character to as many persons as would listen to her grievances. 'Oh, the *circumstances* have been changed, of course!' some avid-eyed female would say. 'I don't mean to say that Salford has done the same as Ugolino—well, he *couldn't*, nowadays! But as soon as I read the book I remembered how poor Lady Henry told me once. . .'

'*Could* it be true that Lady Henry's son is the real Duke of Salford?' breathed the credulous. 'They were twins, were they not, Salford and Lord Henry?'

That lurid fancy had almost proved to be Phoebe's breaking-point. But for her grandmother's quelling eye she believed she must have spoken. It caught hers in the very nick of time, and she remained silent. That eye was absent when she heard the same lurid fancy on Ianthe's lips.

'Whoever it was who wrote the book,' said Ianthe impressively, 'knows a great deal about the Raynes! That much is certain! Everyone says it is a female: do *you* think so, Miss Marlow?'

'Yes—and a shockingly silly female!' said Phoebe. 'It is the most absurd thing I ever read!'

'But it isn't!' insisted Ianthe. 'Chance is not a castle, of course, and Sylvester couldn't possibly keep poor little Edmund *hidden*, and Edmund hasn't got a sister, but that's nothing! I have read the book twice now, and I believe there is a warning in it!'

'A warning?' echoed Phoebe blankly.

'To me,' nodded Ianthe. 'A warning that danger threatens my child. There can be no doubt that Matilda is meant to be me, after all.'

These naïve words struck Phoebe dumb for several moments. It had not previously occurred to her that Ianthe might identify herself with *The Lost Heir's* golden-haired sister. Having very little interest in mere heroes and heroines she had done no more than depict two staggeringly beautiful puppets, endow them with every known virtue, and cast them into a series of hair-raising adventures from which, she privately considered, it was extremely improbable they would ever have extricated themselves.

'Though Florian is not Fotherby, of course,' added Ianthe, unconsciously answering the startled question in Phoebe's mind. 'I think he is just a made-up character. Poor Nugent wouldn't *do* for a hero. Besides, he is Baron Macaronio: everyone knows *that!*'

The unruffled complaisance in her face and voice provided Phoebe with the second shock of the day. This one was not of long duration, however, a bare minute's reflection sufficing to inform her that the grossest of libels could be pardoned in an author who painted Lady Henry herself in roseate hues.

'And Harry was Sylvester's twin-brother,' pursued Ianthe.

'Count Ugolino's brother was not his twin!' Phoebe managed to say.

'No, but I daresay the author was afraid to make it all precisely the same. The thing is, Ugolini was a usurper.'

'Lady Henry!' said Phoebe, speaking in a voice of careful control. 'You cannot seriously suppose that Salford is a usurper!'

'No, except that there *have* been such things, and he was a twin, and I have often thought, when he has encouraged Edmund to do dangerous things, like riding his pony all over the park, all by himself, and climbing trees, that he would be positively glad if the poor little fellow were to fall and break his neck!'

'Oh, hush!' Phoebe exclaimed. 'Pray, pray do not say so, Lady Henry! You are funning, I know, but indeed you should not!'

An obstinate look came into Ianthe's lovely face. 'No, I am not. I don't say it *is* so, for I can't think Mama-Duchess would have changed the twins—for why should she? But Sylvester has never liked Edmund! He said himself he didn't want him, and although he pretended afterwards that he hadn't meant it I have always known it was the truth! Well, *why* does he hate Edmund?'

'Lady Henry, you must not indulge your fancy in this way!' Phoebe cried, quite appalled. 'How can you suppose that a foolish romance bears the least relation to real life?'

'*The Lost Heir* is no more foolish than *Glenarvon,* and you can't say that bore no relation to real life!' countered Ianthe instantly.

Phoebe said: 'I know—I have reason to know—that the author of the book was wholly ignorant of any of the circumstances attaching to Salford, or to any member of his family!'

'Nonsense! How can you know anything of the sort?'

Phoebe moistened her lips, and said in a shaking voice: 'It so happens that I am acquainted with the author. I mustn't tell you, and you won't ask me, I am persuaded, or—or mention it!'

'Acquainted with the author?' Ianthe gasped. 'Oh, *who* is she? You can't be so cruel as not to tell me! I won't breathe a *word*, dear Miss Marlow!'

'No, I must not. I should not have spoken at all, only that I felt myself obliged, when I found you had taken such a fantastic notion into your head! Lady Henry, my friend had never seen Salford but once in her life: knew nothing more of him than his name! She was struck by his strange eyebrows, and when she came to write that tale she remembered them, and thought she would give Ugolino brows like that, never dreaming that anyone would think—'

'But she must have known more!' objected Ianthe, staring rather hard at Phoebe. 'She knew he was Edmund's guardian!'

'She did not. It was—she told me—nothing but the unhappiest of coincidences!'

'I don't believe it! It could not have been so!'

'But it was, it *was*!' Phoebe said vehemently. 'I know it for a fact!'

There was a momentary silence. As she stared, a look of comprehension stole into Ianthe's eyes. 'Miss Marlow! *You* are the author!'

'No!'

'You are! I know you are! Oh, you sly thing!' cried Ianthe.

'I tell you, *no*!'

'Oh, you won't take me in, I promise you! I see it all now! What a rage Sylvester would be in if he knew—when he has been so condescending as to make you the latest object of his gallantry, too! I only wish he may discover it.' She saw the widening look of horror in Phoebe's eyes, and said: '*I* shan't tell him, of course: you may be easy on that head!'

'Indeed, I hope you won't tell anyone, for it is untrue, and absurd as well!' replied Phoebe, trying to speak as though she were amused. 'And pray don't mention either that I am acquainted with the real author! I need not ask you: you must perceive how very disagreeable it would be for me—bound not to divulge the secret, and—and besieged with questions, as I should be!'

'Oh, no, of course I shall not! Only fancy being able to write books! I am sure I could never do so. How clever you must be! But were you really ignorant of the circumstances? It is the oddest thing! How in the world do you contrive to think of such exciting adventures? I hadn't the least guess how Matilida and Florian would contrive to rescue poor Maximilian, and know. I could not put the last volume down until they ran the boat ashore, and Florian cried: "*Safe! Safe, Matilda! At last we stand where Ugolino holds no sway!*" I almost shed tears, it was so affecting!'

She rattled on in this way for some minutes. Phoebe was powerless to stop her. She could only repeat that she was not the book's author, which made Ianthe laugh; and derive a little doubtful comfort from Ianthe's assurance that she would not breathe a syllable to a soul.

18

The first repercussions of this interlude began to be felt by Phoebe almost at once. She saw one or two covert glances directed at her, and guessed several times that she was the subject of a whispered confidence. She was rendered acutely uncomfortable; and when, in a few days, she received the coldest and most infinitesimal of bows from two of the Patronesses of Almack's, and the cut direct from Lady Ribbleton, only and formidable sister of the Duchess of Salford, she could no longer attempt to persuade herself that she was imagining the whole. She did her best to maintain an air of cheerful unconcern, but she quaked inwardly. Only one person ventured to ask her if it were true that she had written *The Lost Heir*, and that an ingenuous young lady embarking on her first season, who was at once frowned down by her mama. Phoebe exclaimed with a tolerable assumption of amazement: '*I?*' and at least had the satisfaction of knowing that she had lulled one person's suspicions. Mrs Newbury, the only other who might, perhaps, have openly taxed her with what she was fast coming to consider her crime, had been confined to the house by some indisposition, and might be presumed to know nothing about the gathering rumours.

The Dowager learned of the turn affairs had taken from her daughter-in-law, to whom had been entrusted the task of chaperoning Phoebe. It was with great diffidence that Rosina approached her, for it seemed very shocking to her that such a suspicion should attach to Phoebe, and she sometimes wondered if she had misunderstood certain remarks that had been made to her. No one had asked her any questions, or said anything to which exception could have been taken. Only there had been hints.

The Dowager, demanding the truth from Phoebe, heard what had passed between her and Ianthe, and was pardonably angry. If she understood the feelings which had compelled Phoebe to come so close to disclosing her secret she did not betray this, saying impatiently that no one whose opinion was worth a groat would be likely to set any store by the silly things Ianthe said of Sylvester. As for placing the smallest reliance on Ianthe's ability to keep such a tit-bit of news to herself, she wondered that Phoebe could be such a greenhead. She forgave her only because she had had at least enough sense to remain constant in denial.

'She cannot say that you told her you were the author, and as for the rest, the only thing to be done is to say that you *think* you know who the author is. That may readily be believed! I am sure there must be a score of persons who are saying the same. If people can be made to believe that Ianthe, after her usual fashion, added straws of her own providing to a single one dropped by you, until she had furnished herself with a nest, so much the better! If they don't think that, they may well think that it was you who exaggerated, pretending to know more than others, to be interesting. Yes, my love, I've no doubt you had rather not appear in such a light, but that you should have thought of before. Don't fall into flat despair! The case is not desperate, if only you will do as I bid you.' She tapped her fan on her knee with a gesture of exasperation. 'I might have known what would come of it if I let Rosina take care of you! Idiotish woman! *I* could have scotched the business days ago! Well, never mind that now! When is the Castlereaghs' ball? Tomorrow? Good! It will be the first crush of the season, and nothing could be better! I shall take you to it myself, child, and see what I can achieve!'

'Grandmama—must I go to it?' Phoebe faltered. 'I had so much rather not!'

'Not go to it? Good God, do you want to *confirm* suspicion? You will wear your new dress—the pretty green one, with the pearl embroidery!—and you will—you *must!*—appear perfectly unconscious. I, on the other hand, am going to be very conscious—and never so much diverted in my life! That ought to take the trick! And it will be well if it does,' she added, a trifle grimly. 'I don't scruple to tell you, my love, that if this scandal is not put an end to I have grave fears that even my influence may not avail to procure you vouchers for Almack's. I imagine you must know what *that* would mean!' She saw that Phoebe was looking crushed, and relented, leaning forward to pat her hand, and saying: 'There! No more scolding! Dear me, what a pity Tom cannot dance, with that leg of his! I declare, I would invite him to go with us to the Castlereaghs', just to put some heart into you, silly child!'

The Dowager had taken a great fancy to young Mr Orde, but she would have found it difficult under any circumstances to have persuaded him to attend a dress-party at which he would have been obliged, as he phrased it, to do the pretty to a lot of fashionable strangers. Such affairs, he told Phoebe firmly, were not in his line: he was never more glad of a lame leg.

So Tom went off on the fateful night to be choked by the new gas-lighting at Drury Lane; and Phoebe was escorted by the Dowager, shortly after ten o'clock, to the Castlereagh mansion.

The Dowager saw immediately how close to the brink of social disaster Phoebe had approached, and her keen eyes snapped dangerously as they marked the various dames who dared to look coldly at her granddaughter. These ladies should shortly be made to regret their insolence: one might have chosen to retire a little from the world of fashion, but one was not yet quite without power in that world! She saw, with satisfaction, that Phoebe's chin was up; and, with relief, that her hand was soon solicited for the country-dance that was then forming.

Phoebe's partner, a young gentleman very conscious of his first longtailed coat and satin knee-breeches, was shy, and in striving to set him at his ease Phoebe forgot her own nervousness, and smiled, and chatted with all the unconcern that her grandmother could have wished her to show. It was when she was halfway down the second set that she saw Sylvester, and felt her heart bump against her ribs.

He was talking to his hostess, in a knot of persons by the door. He was laughing, tossing a retort over his shoulder to some friend, shaking hands with another: in spirits, she thought hopefully. He glanced round the ballroom, but cursorily; their eyes did not meet. She wondered if he would presently look for her, and hardly knew which would be the sterner trial: to be ignored by him, or to be obliged to face him.

The next dance was a waltz. She did not think that Sylvester had yet seen her, but as the fiddlers struck up he came across the floor to where she sat beside the Dowager, and said: 'How do you do, ma'am? I am charged with all kinds of messages for you from my mother. You will like to know that I left her well—wonderfully well! Miss Marlow, may I have the honour?'

As she rose to her feet she looked fleetingly up at him, and again felt that sickening thud of the heart. His lips smiled, but there was a glitter in his eyes that was strange to her, and frightening, and the suggestion of a quiver about his up-cut nostrils.

He led her on to the floor, and into the dance. She hoped he could not feel the flurry of her pulses, and forced herself to speak. 'I did not know you had returned to town, Duke.'

'Didn't you? I came back from Chance yesterday, on purpose to attend this party. I am glad you are here—and admire your courage.'

She knew that her hand was trembling in his light clasp, but she tried to rally herself. 'Oh, I am not now so shy as I was used to be!'

'Obviously you are not. You must allow me to offer you my compliments, and to felicitate you on having made so notable a hit.'

'I cannot imagine what you mean!'

'Oh, I think you can! You have written a romance that has set the ton by the ears: a feat indeed! Very clever, Miss Marlow, but could you find no better name for me than Ugolino?'

'You are mistaken—quite mistaken!' she stammered.

'Don't lie to me! Believe me, your face betrays you! Did you suppose I should not guess the truth? I am not a fool, and I have a tolerably good memory. Or did you think I should not read your book? If that was so you have been unfortunate. I might not have read it had my mother not desired me to do so. She wished—not unnaturally—to know what I had done to arouse such enmity, whom it was I had so bitterly offended. I was quite unable to answer the first of her questions. The second, I must confess, found me equally at a loss until I had read your book. I could have answered it then, of course, had I chosen to do so.'

'Oh, I am sorry, I am sorry!' she whispered, in an anguished tone.

'Don't hang your head! Do you wish the whole room to know what I am saying to you?'

She raised it. 'I tried to alter it. It was too late. I ought never to have done it. I didn't know—never dreamed— Oh, how can I explain to you? What can I say?'

'Oh, there is a great deal you might say, but it is quite unnecessary to do so! There is only one thing I am curious to know, for tax my memory as I may I cannot find the answer. What *did* I do, Miss Marlow, to deserve to be set in the pillory?'

'Nothing, nothing!'

'*Nothing?* I am aware that you took me in dislike at our first meeting; you have told me that I did not recognize you when we met for the second time. Was that all your reason for making me the model for your villain? Did you, for such small cause, put yourself to the labour of discovering the affairs of my family so that you might publish a spiteful travesty of them to the world?'

'No! Had I known—oh, how can you think I would have written it if I had known you had a nephew—were his guardian? I had not the least suspicion of it! It was coincidence: I chose you for Ugolino because—because of the way your eyebrows slant, and because I thought you arrogant! I never dreamed then the book would be published!'

'Doing it rather too brown, are you not? You can't really suppose I shall swallow *quite* so unlikely a story!'

She looked up, and saw that while he talked to her, between his teeth, he was smiling still. The sensation of moving through a nightmare threatened to overpower her. She said faintly: 'It's true, whatever you believe. When I found out—about Edmund—I was ready to sink!'

'But not ready to stop the publication of this sad coincidence.'

'I couldn't do so! They would not even let me alter it! the book was already bound, Duke! When I reached London it was the first thing I did. I went immediately to the publishers—indeed, indeed, I did!'

'And, of course, it never occurred to you that if I were warned I might prove more successful than you in arresting publication,' he said affably.

'No. *Could* you have done so?' she asked wonderingly.

'Oh, that is much better!' he approved, his eyes glinting down at her. 'That innocent stare is excellent: you should cultivate it!'

She flushed vividly. 'Please say no more! Not here—not now! I can't answer you. It was wrong of me—inexcusable! I—I *bitterly* regret it!'

'Why, yes, I imagine you might well! How many people have cut you tonight?'

'Not for that reason!' she answered hotly. 'You know I didn't mean that! Do you think I am not fully sensible of your kindness, when you found us—Tom and me—and did so much for us?'

'Oh, don't give that a thought!' he replied. 'What a stupid thing to say!—you didn't, of course.'

She winced. 'Oh, stop, stop! I never meant to do you an injury! I might as easily have made you the model for my hero!'

'Ought I to be grateful? Is it beyond your comprehension that to discover myself figuring in a novel—and, if you will forgive me, *such* a novel!—in *any* guise is an experience I find nauseating? You might have endowed me with every virtue imaginable, but I should still have considered it a piece of intolerable impertinence!'

She was beginning to feel as physically sick as she had so often felt when rated by her stepmother. 'Take me back to my grandmother!' she begged. 'I don't know why you asked me to dance with you! Could you not have chosen another occasion to say what you wished to me?'

'Easily, but why should I? I shall restore you to Lady Ingham when the music ceases: not before! You are ungrateful, Sparrow: you shouldn't be, you know!'

'Don't call me that!' she said sharply, stung by his tone.

'No, it doesn't suit you,' he agreed. 'What will you have me call you? Jay?'

'Let me go! You may ignore me—you need not insult me!'

His clasp on her hand tightened unkindly. 'You may be thankful I haven't ignored you. Do you know what would have happened had I done so? Do you know how many pairs of eyes were watching to see just what I should do? I asked you to dance because if I had not, every suspicion that you are indeed the author of that book would have been confirmed, and you would have found yourself, by tomorrow, a social outcast. You would have been well served, and I own I was strongly tempted. But I should think myself as contemptible as your villainous Count if I stooped to such a paltry revenge! You may be sure of my support, Miss Marlow. What I may choose to say to you you will have to learn to accept with a good grace. I'll call in Green Street tomorrow to take you driving in the Park: that ought to convince the doubters!'

It was too much. She wrenched herself out of his hold, heedless alike of her surroundings and the consequences, and hurried off the floor to her grandmother's side, so blinded by the tears she was unable to keep back that she blundered into several couples, and did not see how everyone was staring, first at her, and then at Sylvester, left ridiculously alone in the middle of the ballroom floor, his face white with fury.

19

Lady Ingham was indisposed; Sir Henry Halford had said that on no account must her ladyship be agitated; her ladyship was not receiving visitors today. Miss Marlow was indisposed too and was laid down on the sofa in the Small Parlour; Miss Marlow was not receiving visitors today.

These melancholy tidings, delivered by Horwich in a voice of sepulchral gloom, daunted one of the two callers standing on the steps of the house in Green Street, but left the other unmoved. 'Her ladyship will receive me,' said Mrs Newbury briskly. 'Very proper of you to warn me, however, Horwich! I shall take care not to agitate her.'

'I could not take it on myself to answer for her ladyship, madam. I will enquire.'

'Quite unnecessary! Is her ladyship in her dressing-room? I will go up, then.'

Emboldened by the success achieved by this bright-eyed lady the second caller said firmly: 'Miss Marlow will receive me! Be so good as to take my card up to her!'

Mrs Newbury ran up the stairs, and having tapped on the dressing-room door peeped in, saying softly: 'Dear Lady Ingham, may I come in? I am persuaded you won't be vexed with me—say you are not!'

The blinds had been drawn halfway across the two windows; a strong aroma of aromatic vinegar pervaded the air; and a gaunt figure advanced, hissing that her ladyship must not be disturbed.

'Is that you, Georgiana?' faintly demanded the Dowager from the sofa. 'I am too unwell to see anyone, but I suppose you mean to come in whatever I say. No one cares how soon I am driven into my grave! Set a chair for Mrs Newbury, Muker, and go away!'

The grim handmaid disapprovingly obeyed this order; and Georgiana, her eyes becoming accustomed to the gloom, trod over to the sofa, and sat down by it, saying coaxingly: 'I have not come to tease you, ma'am—only to help you, if I can!'

'No one can help me,' said the sufferer, with awful resignation. 'I need not ask if it is all over town!'

'Well, I should think it would be,' said Georgiana candidly. 'Charlotte Retford came to see me this morning, and I must own she said that people *are* talking. She described to me what happened last night, and—oh, I thought I must come to see you, because even if Phoebe did write that book I can't but like her still, and, whatever Lion may say about not meddling, if I can help her I will!'

'I imagine no one can now doubt that she wrote it,' said the Dowager. 'When I think of all I did for her last night, even convincing Sally Jersey that the whole thing was a hum, set about by that pea-goose, Ianthe Rayne—Where are my salts?'

'Why did she write it, ma'am?' asked Georgiana. 'One would say she must detest Sylvester, but *that* she doesn't!'

The Dowager, between sniffs at her vinaigrette, enlightened her. After that she took a sip of hartshorn and water, and lay back with closed eyes. Mrs Newbury sat wrapped in meditation for a few minutes, but presently said: 'I shouldn't think that Sylvester will betray her, whatever she may have said to him.'

'She betrayed herself! Leaving him in the middle of the floor as she did! I did my best, Georgiana, but what was the use of saying she was faint when there was Sylvester, looking like a devil? I will never forgive him, never! To overset her *there*! Heaven knows I don't excuse the child, but what *he* did was wicked! And I can't even take comfort from the reflection that she made a laughing-stock of him, because she ruined herself in doing it!' said the Dowager.

'He must have been very angry,' said Georgiana, frowning. 'Too angry to consider what might be the consequence of dashing her down in public. For it was not at all like him, you know, ma'am. Nothing disgusts him more than a want of conduct! I wonder if Lion was right after all?'

'Very unlikely!' snapped the Dowager.

'Well, that's what I thought,' agreed the Major's fond spouse. 'He said it was a case between them. In fact, he laid me a bet, because I wouldn't allow it to be so. I know just how Sylvester behaves when he starts one of his *à suivie* flirtations, and it was not at all like that. Can it be that he had formed a serious attachment?'

The Dowager blew her nose. 'I thought it as good as settled!' she disclosed. 'The wish of my heart, Georgie! Everything in such excellent train, and all shattered at a blow! Dare I suppose that his affections will reanimate towards her? No! They will not!'

Georgiana, with the sapient Lion's comments in mind, was glad that Lady Ingham had supplied the answer to her own question. 'Dished!' had said the Major. 'Pity! Nice little gal, I thought. Won't pop the question to her now, of course. Couldn't have found a surer way to drive him off than by making him ridiculous.'

'What to do I don't know!' said the Dowager. 'It is of no use to tell me she should brave it out: she ain't the sort of girl who could carry it off. Besides, she'll be refused vouchers for Almack's. I shan't even try for them: nothing would delight that odious Burrell creature more than to be able to give me a set-down!'

'No, that won't do,' said Georgiana. 'I have a better scheme, ma'am: that's why I came! Take her to Paris!'

'Take her to Paris?' repeated the Dowager.

'Yes, ma'am, to Paris!' said Georgiana. 'Do but consider! Phoebe can't remain mewed up within doors, and to send her home would be worse than anything, because it would be to abandon every hope of re-establishing her presently. Paris would be the very thing! Everyone knows that you have had some thought of removing there. Why, I heard you talking of it myself, to Lady Sefton!'

'Everyone may know it, but everyone would also know why I had gone there.'

'That can't be helped, dear ma'am. At least they will know that *you* have not cast Phoebe off. And you know how quickly the most shocking scandals are forgotten!'

'This one won't be.'

'Yes, it will. I promise you I shall be busy while you are away, and you know that no one can be more valuable than I in this affair, because I am Sylvester's cousin, and what I say of him will be believed rather than what Ianthe says. I shall set it about that the scene last night was the outcome of a quarrel which began before Sylvester went away to Chance, and had nothing to do with *The Lost Heir*. I shall say that that was why he went to Chance: what could be more likely? *And*,' said Georgiana, in a voice of profound wisdom, 'I shall tell it all in the *strictest* confidence! To one person, or perhaps two, just to make sure of the story's spreading.'

There was a short silence. The Dowager broke it. 'Pull the blinds back!' she commanded. 'What does Muker mean by leaving us to sit in the dark, stupid woman? You're a flighty, ramshackle creature, Georgie, but one thing I'll allow! You have a good heart! But will anyone believe Phoebe didn't write that book?'

'They must be *made* to, even if I have to say I too know who is the real author! If Sylvester had taken it in good part—made a joke of it, as though he didn't care a button, and had been in the secret the whole time—it wouldn't have signified a scrap, because he was the only person unkindly used in the book, and if he hadn't taken it in snuff all the others whom Phoebe dug her quill into must have followed his example.'

'Don't talk to me of Sylvester!' said the Dowager, with loathing. 'If I hadn't set my heart on his marrying Phoebe I should be in transports over her book! For she hit him off to the life, Georgie! If he ain't smarting still I don't know him! Oh, drat the boy! He might have spared a thought for me before he provoked my granddaughter to enact a Cheltenham tragedy in the middle of a ballroom!'

Perceiving that slow, unaccustomed tears were trickling down her ladyship's cheeks, Georgiana overcame a desire to retort in defence of Sylvester, and made haste to soothe her, and to turn her thoughts towards Paris.

'Yes, but it's useless to think of it,' said the Dowager, dabbing at her eyes. 'I cannot go without some gentleman to escort me! Poor Ingham would turn in his grave! Don't talk to me of couriers! I won't have strangers about me. And I am a wretched traveller, always seasick, and as for depending on Muker, she, you may lay your life, will be in the sullens, because she don't want to go to France!'

Georgiana was rather daunted by this. After having her suggestion that the present Lord Ingham might escort his parent spurned she was at a loss, and could only say that it seemed a pity if the scheme must fail after all.

'Of course it is a pity!' said the Dowager irascibly. 'But with my constitution it would be madness for me to attempt the journey without support! Sir Henry wouldn't hear of it! If Phoebe had a brother—' She broke off, and startled Georgiana by exclaiming: 'Young Orde!'

'I beg your pardon, ma'am?'

The Dowager sat up with surprising energy. 'The very person! I will write at once to Mr Orde! Where are they putting up? Reddish's! Georgie, my love, the ink, my pen, paper, wafers! In that desk! No! I will get up! Here, take all this away, child!'

'But who *is* he?' asked Georgiana, receiving from the Dowager a fan, a vinaigrette, a bottle of eau-de-Cologne, another of sal volatile, and three clean handkerchiefs.

'He's as good as a brother. Phoebe's known him all her life!' replied the Dowager, beginning to divest herself of various scarves, shawls, and rugs. 'A very pretty-behaved boy! Wants town-polish, but most gentlemanly!'

Georgiana put up her brows. 'A fresh-faced young man, with a shy smile? Does he walk with a limp?'

'Yes, that's he. Just give me your hand—or no! Where has Muker put my slippers?'

'Then I fancy he is with Phoebe at this very moment,' said Georgiana. 'We met on the doorstep: I wondered who it could be!'

The Dowager sank back again. 'Why didn't you tell me so before?' she demanded. 'Ring the bell, Georgie! I'll have him up here at once!'

Georgiana obeyed, but said, as she did so: 'To be sure, ma'am—if you think it right to take him?'

'Right? Why shouldn't it be? It will do him good to see something of the world! Oh, are you thinking they might fall in love? No fear of that, I assure you—though why I should say *fear* I don't know,' added her ladyship bitterly. 'After last night I should be thankful to see her married to anyone!'

Tom, entering the dressing-room a few minutes later, was looking grave. He cast an awed glance at the battery of medicines and restoratives set out on the table beside the Dowager's sofa, but was relieved to hear himself hailed in robust accents. When asked abruptly, however, if he would escort her ladyship and Miss Marlow to Paris he looked to be more appalled than pleased; and although, when the inducement of a week in Paris as her ladyship's guest was held out to him, he stammered that he was much obliged, it was plain that this was a mere expression of civility.

'Let me tell you, Tom, that foreign travel is a necessary part of every young man's education!' said the Dowager severely.

'Yes, ma'am,' said Tom. He added more hopefully: 'Only I daresay my father would not wish me to go!'

'Nonsense! Your father is a sensible man, and he told me he thought it time you got a little town bronze. Depend upon it, he can very well spare you for a week or two. I shall write him a letter, and you may take it to him. Now, boy, don't be tiresome! If you don't care to go on your own account you may do so on Phoebe's.'

The matter being put thus to him Tom said that of course he was ready to do anything for Phoebe. Then he thought that this was not quite polite, so he added, blushing to the roots of his hair, that it was excessively kind of her la'ship, he was persuaded he would enjoy himself excessively, and his father would be excessively obliged to her. Only perhaps he ought to mention that he knew very little French, and had not before been out of England.

These trifling objections waved aside, the Dowager explained why she was so suddenly leaving London. She asked him if Phoebe had told him of the previous night's happenings. That brought the grave look back into his face. He said: 'Yes, she has, ma'am. It's the very deuce of a business, I know, and I don't mean to say that it wasn't wrong of her to have written all that stuff about Salford, but it was just as wrong of him to have given her a trimming in public! I—I call it a dashed ungentlemanly thing to have done, because he must have *meant* to sink her to the ground! What's more, I wouldn't have thought it of him! I thought he was a first-rate sort of a man—a regular Trojan! Oh lord, if only she had told him! I had meant to have visited him, too! I shan't now, of course, for whatever she did I'm on Phoebe's side, and so I should tell him!'

'No, I shouldn't visit him just yet,' said Georgiana, regarding him with warm approval. 'He *is* a Trojan, but I am afraid he may be in a black rage. He wouldn't otherwise have behaved so improperly last night, you know. Poor Phoebe! Is she very much afflicted?'

'Well, she was in the deuce of a way when I came,' replied Tom. 'Shaking like a blancmange! She does, you see, when she's been overset, but she's better now, though pretty worn down. The thing is, Lady Ingham, she wants me to take her home!'

'Wants you to take her *home*?' exclaimed the Dowager. 'Impossible! She cannot want that!'

'Yes, but she does,' Tom insisted. 'She will have it she has disgraced you as well as herself. And she says she had rather face Lady Marlow than anyone in London, and at all events she won't have to endure Austerby for long, because as soon as those publisher-fellows hand over the blunt—I mean, as soon as they pay her!—she and Sibby will live together in a cottage somewhere. She means to write another novel immediately, because she has been offered a great deal of money for it already!'

The disclosure of this fell project acted alarmingly on the Dowager. To Tom's dismay she uttered a moan, and fell back against her cushions with her eyes shut. Resuscitated by smelling-salts waved under her nose, and eau-de-Cologne dabbed on her brow, she regained enough strength to tell Tom to fetch Phoebe to her instantly. Georgiana, catching the doubtful glance he cast at her, picked up her gloves and her reticule, and announced that she would take her leave. 'I expect she feels she had rather not meet me, doesn't she? I perfectly understand, but pray give her my love, Mr Orde, and assure her that I am still her friend!'

The task of persuading Phoebe to view with anything less than revulsion the prospect of being transported from the fashionable world of London to that of Paris was no easy one. In vain did the Dowager assure her that if some ill-natured gossip should have written the story of her downfall to a friend in Paris it could be denied; in vain did she promise to present her to King Louis; in vain did she describe in the most glowing terms the charm and gaiety of French society: Phoebe shuddered at every treat held out to her. Tom, besought by the Dowager to try what he could achieve, was even less successful. Adopting a bracing note, he told Phoebe that she must shake off her blue devils, and try to come about again.

'If only I might go home!' she said wretchedly.

That, said Tom, was addle-brained, for she would only mope herself to death at Austerby. What she must do was to put the affair out of her head—though he thought she would perhaps write a civil letter of apology to Salford from Paris. After that she could be comfortable, for she would not be obliged to meet him again for months, if Lady Ingham hired a house in Paris, as she had some notion of doing.

But the only effect of this heartening speech was to send Phoebe out of the room in floods of tears.

It was left to the Squire to bring her to a more submissive frame of mind, which he did very simply, by telling her that she owed it to her grandmother, after causing her so much trouble, to cheer up and do as she wished. 'For it's my belief,' said the Square shrewdly, 'that she wants to go as much for her own sake as yours. I must say I should like Tom to get a glimpse of foreign parts, too.'

That settled it: Phoebe would go to Paris for Grandmama's sake, and try very hard to enjoy it. Her subsequent efforts to appear cheerful were heroic, and quite enough (said Tom) to throw the whole party into the dismals.

Between Phoebe's brave front and Muker's undisguised gloom the Dowager might well have abandoned the scheme had it not been for the support afforded her by young Mr Orde. Having consented to go with her, Tom resigned himself with a good grace, and threw himself into all the business of departure with so much energy and good-humour that he soon began to rival Phoebe in the Dowager's esteem. With a little assistance from the Squire, before that excellent man returned to Somerset, he grappled with passports, customs, and intineraries; ascertained on which days the mails were made up for France, and on which days the packets sailed; calculated how much money would be needed for the journey; and got by heart such French phrases as he thought would be most useful. A Road Book was his constant companion; and whenever he had occasion to pull out his pocket-book a shower of leaflets accompanied it.

It did not take him long to discover that the task of conveying Lady Ingham on a journey was no sinecure. She was exacting, and she changed her mind almost hourly. No sooner had he gone off with her old coachman to inspect her travelling-carriage (kept by her longsuffering son in his coach-house and occupying a great deal of space which he could ill-spare) than she decided that it would be better to travel post. Off went Tom in a hack to arrange for the hire of a chaise, only to find on his return to Green Street that she had remembered that since Muker would occupy the forward seat they would be obliged to sit three behind her, which would be intolerable.

'I am afraid,' said Lord Ingham apologetically, 'that you have taken a troublesome office upon yourself, my boy. My mother is rather capricious. You mustn't allow her to wear you to death. I see you are lame, too.'

'Oh, that's nothing, sir!' said Tom cheerfully. 'I just take a hack, you know, and rub on very well!'

'If I can be of assistance,' said Lord Ingham, in a dubious tone, 'you—er—you must not hesitate to apply to me.'

Tom thanked him, but assured him that all was in a way to be done. He could not feel that Lord Ingham's assistance would expedite matters, since he knew by now that the Dowager invariably ran counter to his advice, and was exasperated by his rather hesitant manners. Lord Ingham looked relieved, but thought it only fair to warn Tom that there was a strong probability that the start would be delayed for several days, owing to the Dowager's having decided at the last minute that she could not leave town without a gown that had not yet been sent home by her dress-maker, or some article that had been put away years before and could not now be found.

'Well, sir,' said Tom, grinning, 'she had the whole set of 'em turning the house out of the windows to find some cloak or other when I left, but I'll bring her up to scratch: see if I don't!'

Lord Ingham shook his head, and when he repaired to Green Street on the appointed day to bid his parent a dutiful farewell it was in the expectation of finding the plans changed again, and everything at odds. But Tom had made his word good. The old-fashioned coach stood waiting, piled high with baggage; and Lord Ingham entered the house to find the travellers fully equipped for the adventure, and delayed only by the Dowager's sudden conviction that her curling-tongs had been forgotten, which entailed the removal of everything from her dressing-case, Muker having packed them at the bottom of it.

Lord Ingham, eyeing young Mr Orde with respect, was moved to congratulate him. Young Mr Orde then confided to him that it had been a near-run thing, her la'ship having been within ames-ace of crying off as late as yesterday, when the weather took a turn for the worse. 'But I managed to persuade her, sir, and I think I shall be able to get her aboard Thursday's packet all right and tight,' said optimistic Tom.

Lord Ingham, casting an apprehensive glance at the hurrying clouds, thought otherwise, but refrained from saying so.

20

Lord Ingham was right. The first glimpse caught of the sea afforded the Dowager a view of tossing gray waters, flecked with foam; and long before she was handed down from the coach at the Ship Inn she had informed Tom that a regiment of Guards would not suffice to drag her on board the packet until the wind had abated. Two days of road travel (for to avoid fatigue she had elected to spend one night at Canterbury) had given her the headache; and during the rest of the journey she became steadily more snappish. Her temper was not improved, on alighting at Dover, by having the hat nearly snatched from her head by a gust of wind; and it seemed for several minutes as though she might re-enter the coach then and there, and return to London. Fortunately Tom had written to bespeak accommodation for the party; and the discovery that the best bedchamber had been reserved for her, and the best parlour, with fires kindled in both, mollified her. A dose of the paregoric prescribed by Sir Henry Halford, followed by an hour's rest, and an excellent dinner did much to restore her, but when Tom told her that the packet had sailed for Calais that day as usual, from which circumstance it might be inferred that no danger of shipwreck attended the passage, she replied discouragingly: 'Exactly what I am afraid of!'

On the following morning, in conditions described by knowledgeable persons as fair sailing weather, Tom made the discovery that fair sailing weather, in Lady Ingham's opinion, was flat calm. April sunshine lit the scene, but Lady Ingham could see white crests on the sea, and that was enough for her, she thanked Tom. An attempt to convince her that a passage of perhaps only four hours with a little pitching would be preferable to being cooped up in a stuffy packet for twice as long succeeded only in making her pick up her vinaigrette. She begged Tom not to mention that horrid word *pitching* again. If he and Phoebe had set their hearts on the Paris scheme she would not deny them the treat, but they must wait for calm weather.

They waited for five days. Other travellers came and went; Lady Ingham and Party remained at the Ship; and Tom, forewarned that the length of the bills presented at this busy hostelry was proverbial, began to entertain visions of finding himself without a feather to fly with before he had got his ladies to Amiens.

Squally weather continued; the Dowager's temper worsened; Muker triumphed; and Tom, making the best of it, sought diversion on the waterfront. Being a youth of an enquiring turn of mind and a friendly disposition he found much to interest him, and was soon able to point out to Phoebe the various craft lying in the basins, correctly identifying brigantines, hoys, sloops, and Revenue cutters for her edification.

The Dowager, convinced that every haunt of seafaring persons teemed with desperate characters lying in wait to rob the unwary, was strongly opposed to Tom's prowling about the yard and basins, but was appeased by his depositing in her care the packet of bills she had entrusted to him. It would have been better, in her opinion, had he and Phoebe climbed the Western Heights (for that might have blown Phoebe's crotchets away), but she was forced to admit that for a man with a lame leg this form of exercise was ineligible.

It seemed a little hard to Phoebe that she should be accused of having crotchets when she was taking such pains to appear cheerful. She only once begged to be allowed to go back to Austerby; and since this lapse was the outcome of her grandmother's complaining that she had allowed Mrs Newbury to over-persuade her, it was surely pardonable. 'Pray, pray, ma'am don't let us go to Paris on my account!' she had said imploringly. 'I only said I would go because I thought you wished it! And I don't think Tom cares for it either, in his heart. Let him take me home instead!'

But the Dowager had been pulled up short by this speech. She was not much given to considering anyone but herself, but she was fond of Phoebe. Her conscience gave her a twinge, and she said briskly: 'Fiddle-de-dee, my love! Of course I wish to go, and so I shall as soon as the weather improves!'

It began to seem, on the fifth day, that they were doomed to remain indefinitely at Dover, for the wind, instead of abating, had stiffened, and was blowing strongly off-shore. Tom's waterfront acquaintances assured him that he couldn't hope for a better to carry him swiftly across the Channel, but Tom knew that it would be useless to repeat this to the Dowager, even if she had not been keeping her bed that day. She was bilious. Sea-air, said Muker, always made my lady bilious, as those who had waited on her for years could have told others, had they seen fit to ask.

So Phoebe, having the parlour to herself, tried for the fourth time to compose a letter to Sylvester that should combine contrition with dignity, and convey her gratitude for past kindness without giving the least hint that she wished ever to see him again. This fourth effort went the way of its predecessors, and as she watched the spoiled sheets of paper blacken and burst into flame she sank into very low spirits. It was foolish to fall into a reminiscent mood when every memory that obtruded itself (and most of all the happy ones) was painful, but try as she would to look forward no sooner was she idle than back went her thoughts, and the most cheerful view of the future which presented itself to her was a rapid decline into the grave. And the author of all her misfortunes, whose marble heart and evil disposition she had detected at the outset, would do no more than raise his fatal eyebrows, and give his shoulders the slight, characteristic shrug she knew so well, neither glad nor sorry, but merely indifferent.

She was roused from the contemplation of this dismal picture by Tom's voice, hailing her from the street. She hastily blew her nose, and went to the window, thrusting it open, and looking down at Tom, who was standing beneath it, most improperly hallooing to her.

'Oh, there you are!' he observed. 'Be quick and come out, Phoebe! Such doings in the harbour! I wouldn't have you miss it for a hundred pounds!'

'Why, what?'

'Never mind what! Do make haste, and come down! I promise you it's as funny as any farce *I* ever saw!'

'Well, I must put on my hat and pelisse,' she said, not wanting very much to go.'

'Lord, you'd never keep a hat on in this wind! Tie a shawl over your head!' he said. 'And don't dawdle, or it will all be over before we get there!'

Reflecting that even being buffeted by a cold wind would be preferable to further reverie, she said that she would be down in a trice, shut the window again, and ran away to her bedchamber. The idea of tieing a shawl round her head did not commend itself to her, but the Dowager had bought a thick travelling cloak with a hood attached for her to wear on board the packet, so she fastened that round her throat instead, and was hastily turning over the contents of a drawer in search of gloves when she was made to jump almost out of her skin by hearing herself unexpectedly addressed.

'May I make so bold as to enquire, miss, if you was meaning to go out?'

Phoebe looked quickly round, exclaiming: 'Good gracious, what a start you gave me, Muker! I never heard you come in!'

'No, miss?' said Muker, standing with primly folded arms on the threshold. 'And was you meaning to go out, miss?'

Her tone was very much that of a gaoler. It nettled Phoebe, but although she flushed a little she said only: 'Yes, I am going for a walk,' because she knew that Muker's dislike of her arose from jealousy, for which she was more to be pitied than blamed.

'May I ask, miss, if her ladyship is aware of your intention?'

'You may ask, but I don't know why you should, or why I should answer you,' replied Phoebe, her temper rising.

'I shouldn't consider it consistent with my duty, miss, to permit you to go out without her ladyship was aware of it.'

'Oh, *wouldn't* you?' retorted Phoebe, by this time roused to real wrath. 'Try if you can stop me!'

Muker, thrust with some violence out of the way, followed her from the room, two spots of colour flaming on her cheekbones. 'Very well, miss! Very well! Her ladyship shall hear of this! I should have thought she had had enough to worrit her, poor dear, without—'

'How dare you speak to me in that insolent way?' Phoebe interrupted, pausing at the head of the stairs to look back. 'If my grandmother should wish to know where I am gone, you will please tell her that she need have no anxiety, since I am with Mr Orde!'

'Hurry, Phoebe!' said Tom, from the hall below. 'It will be too late soon!'

'I'm coming!' she answered, running down to join him.

'What an age you've been!' he said, pushing her through the doorway into the street. 'You had better hold that cloak tightly round you, or you'll be blown away. What's the matter?'

'That odious Muker!' she fumed. 'Daring to tell me *she* would not permit me to go out!'

'Oh, never mind her!' said Tom, limping along as fast as he could. 'Sour old squeeze-crab! You wait till you see the pantomime in the harbour! I shouldn't wonder at it if we find the whole town's turned out to watch it by the time we get there. Lord, I hope they haven't got the thing aboard yet!'

'*What* thing?' demanded Phoebe.

'Some sort of a travelling carriage,' replied Tom, with a chuckle.

'Oh, Tom, you wretch, is *that* all?'

'All! It's no ordinary carriage, I can tell you. It belongs to some fellow who has chartered a schooner to take his coach and his family to Calais, and there's him, and a little chitty-faced fellow that looks like a valet, and— but you'll see! When I left they were all arguing whether it oughtn't to be got aboard in slings, and there was a string of porters carrying enough champagne and hampers of food for a voyage to India! There! what did I tell you? Half the town at least!'

If this was an exaggeration there was certainly a crowd of people watching with deep interest the activities of those preparing to get a large travelling carriage aboard the *Betsy Anne*. The little man described by Tom as a valet was keeping a vigilant eye on this astonishing vehicle, every now and then darting forward to ward off the urchins who wanted to look inside it, and saying in a tearful falsetto: 'I forbid you to lay your greasy hands on it! Go away! Go away, I say!'

His agitation was pardonable, for never was there so glossy and so exquisite a chariot, double-perched, slung high between high wheels, fitted with patent axles, and embellished with a gilded iron scroll-work all round the roof. The body was painted a bright tan, with the wheels and the panels of sky-blue; and the interior, which, besides a deeply cushioned seat, included a let-down table, appeared to be entirely lined with pale blue velvet.

'Cinderella's coach!' said Phoebe promptly. 'Who in the world can have ordered such a ridiculous thing?'

On board the schooner all was bustle and noise, the crew being much impeded in their tasks by the number of porters who got in their way, and voicing their disapproval in loud and frank terms.

'Getting ready to set sail,' said Tom. 'I should laugh if they were to miss the tide!'

As Phoebe's amused eyes ran over the crowded deck they alighted on the figure of a small boy, who was critically observing the various activities in progress. For an instant she stared unbelievingly, and then she clutched Tom's arm, exclaiming: *"Edmund!"*

'Eh?' said Tom. He saw that she was looking at the small boy as though she saw a ghost. '*Now* what's the matter?' he demanded.

'Edmund Rayne! Salford's nephew!' she stammered. 'There—on the boat!'

'Is it?' said Tom, glancing at the child. 'Are you poz?'

'Yes, yes, how could I mistake? Oh, Tom, I have the most dreadful fear—What was he like, the man who owns the coach?'

'Like a counter-coxcomb!' replied Tom. 'I never saw such a quiz!'

She turned pale. 'Fotherby! Then Lady Henry must be aboard. Did you see her? Very fair—very beautiful?'

'No, I only saw the dandy, and the valet, and that fellow over there, whom I take to be the courier. Why, you don't mean to say you think they're eloping?'

'I don't know that, and I don't care! They are kidnapping Edmund, and—oh, Tom, it is *my* fault! I am going aboard!'

He detained her. 'No, you don't! How could it be your fault, pray? I wish you won't fall into such distempered freaks, Phoebe!'

'Don't you *see*, Tom? I told you what it was that made my book so particularly abominable!'

'I haven't forgotten. But your book ain't to be blamed for Lady Henry's running off with that Jack-a-dandy. If you've got some notion of trying to interfere, let me tell you, I shan't let you make such a cake of yourself! It's none of your business.'

She said with determined calm: 'Tom, if it is as I believe, and Lady Henry is taking that child out of England, I am so much to blame that I think I shall never hold up my head again. *I* put the scheme into her head! It was never there before she read my book. Oh, she told me herself how much struck she was by the end of it, and I never guessed, never suspected—!'

'Took the scheme out of a trumpery novel? She couldn't be such a greenhead!'

'She is just such a greenhead! I don't know how it will be, if they get Edmund to France, whether it will be possible for Salford to recover him, or even to find him, but only think what it must mean! More trouble, more scandal, and all to be laid at my door! I can't bear it, Tom! You must let me go aboard that boat! Perhaps, if I could prevent this, he—people—might not think so badly of me. Tom, I've wished the book had never been written over and over again, but I can't unwrite it, and don't you think that this—if I could stop it—would be a sort of—of atonement?'

He was struck by her earnest manner, and even more by the expression in her eyes, which was almost tragic. After a moment he said: 'Well—if you think you should, I suppose—Come to think of it, if the boy is being taken out of the country without his guardian's leave it's against the law! So we have got *some* right to meddle. I only hope we don't catch cold at it, that's all!'

But Phoebe had already stepped on to the gangway. As she reached the deck Sir Nugent Fotherby emerged from a doorway behind the ladder leading to the quarterdeck, and at once perceived her.

After looking at her through his quizzing-glass for a minute he came forward, bowing, and saying in a pleased voice: 'Miss Marlow! How-de-do? 'Pon my soul, I take it very kind in you to have called, and so, I venture to say, will her la'ship! Happy to welcome you aboard! Tidy little craft, ain't she? Chartered her, you know: couldn't take her la'ship on the common packet!'

'Sir Nugent, will you have the goodness to lead me to Lady Henry?' said Phoebe, ignoring these civilities.

'Greatest pleasure on earth, ma'am! But—you won't take it amiss if I give you a hint?—*not* Lady Henry!'

'I see. I should have said Lady Fotherby, perhaps?'

'No,' replied Sir Nugent regretfully. '*Not* Lady Fotherby. Lady Ianthe Fotherby. *I* don't like it as well, but her la'ship informs me that to be called Lady Ianthe again makes her feel ten years younger, which is a gratifying circumstance, don't you think?'

At this point they were interrupted. Master Rayne had approached, and he planted himself squarely before Sir Nugent, demanding: 'When are we going to see the circus?'

Master Rayne had to look a long way up to Sir Nugent's face, but his gaze was stern and unwavering, and under it Sir Nugent was visibly embarrassed. 'Oh—ah—the circus!' he said. 'Precisely so! The circus!'

'You said we were going to the circus,' said Edmund accusingly. 'You said if I didn't kick up riot and rumpus I should go to the circus.'

'Did I?' said Sir Nugent, eyeing him uneasily. 'Said that, did I?'

'Yes, you did,' asserted Edmund. 'Turnin' me up sweet!' he added bitterly.

'Well, there you have the matter in a nutshell,' responded Sir Nugent confidentially. 'Must realize it was a devilish awkward situation, my dear boy!'

'You told me a whisker,' stated Edmund. 'You are a Bad Man, and I won't have you for a new papa. *My* papa didn't tell whiskers.'

'Be reasonable!' begged Sir Nugent. 'You must own it was the only thing to be done, with you saying you didn't wish to go driving with us, and threatening to raise a dust! Why, you'd have had the whole household out on us!'

'I want to go home,' said Edmund.

'Do you, my dear?' interpolated Phoebe. 'Then I will ask your mama to let me take you home! Do you remember me? You told me all about your pony!'

Edmund considered her. Apparently he remembered her with kindness, for his severity relaxed, and he politely held out his hand. 'You are the lady which knows Keighley. I will let you take me home. An' p'raps if you tell me some more about *your* pony I won't feel sick,' he added.

'Very bad traveller,' said Sir Nugent in an audible aside. 'Seems to turn queasy every time he goes in a chaise. Dashed unfortunate, because it fidgets her la'ship. Pity we couldn't have brought his nurse, but her la'ship said no. No use trying to bribe her: had to bamboozle her instead. Meant he should travel with her la'ship's maid, but at the last moment we were queered upon that suit too. Maggoty female couldn't be brought up to the scratch! Said she was scared to go on a ship. "What would have happened if Nelson had been scared to go on a ship?" I said. She said she didn't know. "The Frogs would have landed," I said. "No one to stop 'em," I said. No use. Said she couldn't stop 'em even if she did go to sea. Bit of a doubler, that, because I don't suppose she could. So there we were, floored at all points.'

'Who is this gentleman?' suddenly demanded Edmund.

'That is Mr Orde, Edmund. Sir Nugent, will you—'

'I'm glad he asked that,' said Sir Nugent. 'Didn't quite like to do it myself. Happy to make your acquaintance, sir! Daresay her la'ship would say the same, but she's rather fagged. Gone to lie down in her cabin. Allow me to escort you, ma'am!'

'I'll wait for you here, Phoebe,' Tom said. 'Come on, Master Poll Parrot, you may bear me company!'

Sir Nugent, handing Phoebe down the short companion-way, told her that Ianthe found her quarters rather constricted but was bearing every inconvenience with the fortitude of an angel. He then opened one of the two doors at the bottom of the companion-way and announced: 'A visitor, my love!'

Ianthe had been lying on one of the two berths in what seemed to Phoebe quite a spacious cabin, but upon hearing these words she uttered a shriek, and sat up, her hands clasped at her bosom. But as soon as she saw who it was who had entered, her fright vanished, and she exclaimed: 'Miss Marlow! Good God, how comes this about? Oh, my dear Miss Marlow, how glad I am to see you! To think that you should be the first to felicitate me! For you must know that Nugent and I were married by special licence yesterday! We fled immediately from the church door, in the travelling chariot Nugent has had built for me. Was it not particularly touching of him? It is lined with blue, to match my eyes! Nugent, do go and tell them to make less noise! I shall be driven distracted by it! Shouting, and tramping, and clanking, and creaking till I could scream! You must tell the sailors that I have the headache, and cannot endure such a racket. Dear Miss Marlow, I thought you had gone to Paris a week ago!'

'We have been delayed. Lady Ianthe, I wish you very happy, but—excuse me—!—that was not my purpose in coming aboard. I saw Edmund, and realized what must be the reason for his being here. You will think me impertinent, but you must not steal him out of England! Indeed, indeed you must not!'

'Not steal him out of England? Why, how *can* you say so when it was you who showed me what I must do?'

'Oh, don't say so!' Phoebe cried sharply.

Ianthe laughed. 'But of course it was you! As soon as I read how Florian and Matilda smugged Maximilian on to that boat—'

'I implore you, stop!' begged Phoebe. 'You cannot think that I meant that nonsense to be taken seriously! Lady Henry, you must let me take Edmund back to London! When I wrote that Ugolini couldn't pursue Maximilian out of his own country it was make-believe! But this is real life, and I assure you Salford can pursue you—perhaps even have you punished by the law!'

'He won't know where we are,' replied Ianthe confidently. 'Besides, Sylvester hates scandal. I am persuaded he would endure anything rather than let the world know the least one of the family secrets!'

'Then how could you serve him such a trick?' demanded Phoebe hotly. 'The Duchess too! You cannot have considered what distress you will cause her if you hold by this scheme!'

Ianthe began to pout. 'She is not Edmund's mama! I think you are being very unjust! You don't care for my distress! You cannot enter into the feelings of a mother, I daresay, but I should have thought you must have known I could never abandon my child to Sylvester. And don't tell me you didn't mean Maximilian for Edmund, because everyone knows you did!'

'Yes!' flashed Phoebe. 'Because you told everyone so! Oh, haven't you harmed me enough? You promised me you wouldn't repeat what passed between us—'

'I didn't repeat it! The only person I told was Sally Derwent, and I particularly warned her not to mention it to a soul!' interrupted Ianthe, much aggrieved. 'How can you be so unkind to me? As though my nerves were not worn down enough! I have had to bring Edmund without Button, and I am obliged to do everything for him, because he is so cross and naughty with poor Nugent, and I scarcely closed my eyes all night, because we were travelling, and I had to hold Edmund in my lap, and he kept waking up and crying, and saying he wanted to be sick, till I was fagged to death! If I told him one fairy-tale I told him fifty, but he would do nothing but say he wished to go home, till I could have slapped him! And that odious abigail refusing at the last minute to go with me, and now you reproaching me–oh, it is too bad! I don't know how I shall manage, for I am feeling very unwell already! Why can't those horrid sailors keep the boat *still*? Why does it rock up and down when it isn't even moving yet? I know I shall be prostrate the instant we set sail, and then who is to take care of Edmund?'

This impassioned speech ended in a burst of tears, but when Phoebe, seizing on the final woe, represented to the injured beauty how imprudent it would be to embark with Edmund upon a rough sea passage without providing him with an attendant, Ianthe declared herself already to sacrifice her health, comfort, and even her sanity rather than give up her child; adding, however, with a slight lapse from nobility: 'People would say I cared more for riches than Edmund!'

Since this seemed more than likely Phoebe found it difficult to reassure her; but before she had uttered more than a dozen words Ianthe was struck by a brilliant notion, and started up from her berth, her face transfigured. 'Oh, Miss Marlow, I have hit on the very thing! We will take you with us! Just as far as to Paris, I mean. There can be no objection: you mean to go there, and I am sure there is no occasion for you to travel with Lady Ingham if you don't choose to do so! She may join you in Paris–you can stay at the Embassy until she comes: that may easily be arranged!–and she must surely be able to undertake the journey without you. She has her abigail to go with her, remember! I am persuaded she would be the first to say I ought not to be obliged to travel without a female to support me. Oh, Miss Marlow, do, pray, say you will stay with me!'

Miss Marlow was still saying that she would do no such thing when Sir Nugent once more begged his bride's permission to come in.

He was followed by Tom, whom he at once presented, with great punctilio. Tom said that he begged her ladyship's pardon for intruding upon her, but had come to tell Phoebe it was time to be going ashore again. A speaking look directed at his childhood's friend conveyed to her the information that his attempts to bring Sir Nugent to a sense of his wrongdoing had met with failure.

Beyond bestowing a mechanical smile upon him, Ianthe paid him little heed, addressing herself instead to Sir Nugent, and eagerly explaining to him her brilliant notion. In him she found her only supporter: not only did he think it a stroke of genius, but he called upon Phoebe and Tom to applaud it. He won no response. Politely at first, and later with distressing frankness, Tom explained to him why he thought it rather the hall-mark of folly. He said that he would neither accompany the party to France nor remain behind to tell Lady Ingham why her granddaughter had abandoned her, and from this standpoint nothing would move him.

He had entered the cabin with the intention only of taking Phoebe ashore. In his view, there was nothing more to be done, and she might wash her hands of the affair with a clear conscience. But as Ianthe reiterated her former arguments, several times asserting that it was absurd of Phoebe to have scruples now, when everyone knew she had instigated the plot, his sentiments soon underwent a change. He saw all the force of what Phoebe had previously urged, and ranged himself on her side, even going so far as to talk of laying information with the nearest magistrate.

'Very ungentlemanly thing to do,' said Sir Nugent, shaking his head. 'Don't think you should. Besides, there's no sense in it: *you* go to the magistrate, *we* set sail, and then where are you?'

Tom, who was becoming heated, retorted: 'Not if I don't go ashore till you've lost the tide! What's more I'll take the boy with me, because I've a strong notion it would be perfectly lawful to do so, and if you try to stop me it will very likely be a felony!'

'You rude, odious— Nugent! Where *is* Edmund?' cried Ianthe. 'How could you leave him alone? Good God, he may have fallen overboard! Bring him to me this instant, unless you want me to run mad with anxiety!'

'No, no, don't do that, my love! Plenty of sailors to fish him out again, you know,' Sir Nugent assured her. 'Not but what I'll fetch him to you, if you *want* him!'

'*He* won't fall overboard,' said Tom, as Sir Nugent departed on his errand.

'You know nothing about it!' snapped Ianthe. '*I* am his mother, and I shan't know one moment's peace until he is safe in my arms.'

She repeated this statement with even more emphasis when Sir Nugent presently reappeared with the comforting intelligence that Edmund, safe in the valet's charge, was watching the men bring the carriage aboard; but when she learned that an attempt to pick him up had led him to kick his new papa severely before assuming an alarming rigidity, she seemed to feel that his presence in the cabin would not be conducive to peace, for she said only that if he began to scream it would be more than her nerves could endure without breaking under the strain.

Harping on this string, Phoebe then did her best to convince her that this sad accident would inevitably befall her if she were obliged to look after Edmund during the passage. She received unexpected support from Sir Nugent, who said that the more he considered the matter the more he thought it would be a devilish good notion to let Miss Marlow take Edmund home. 'What I mean is,' he explained, 'it's a notion that took very well with him. He seems set against going to France. I daresay he don't like foreigners. Very understandable: I don't know that I like 'em myself.'

This treachery naturally incensed Ianthe beyond measure. Having poured forth the vials of her wrath upon him, she said tragically that everyone was against her, and burst into a fit of hysterical tears. Feeling the battle to be almost won, Phoebe redoubled her efforts to persuade her, while Tom applied himself to the task of bringing over the waverer. With four people engaged in hot argument the sounds of increased activity on deck passed unheeded. The swell that had all the time been gently rocking the schooner had for several minutes been growing heavier, but it was not until the *Betsy Anne* took a plunge which made him stagger that Tom realized what must be happening.

'My God!' he gasped. 'We're *moving*!'

Sir Nugent gave a chuckle. 'Told 'em to cast off when I went up to fetch Edmund,' he explained. 'Told *you* he was watching the carriage got aboard! Diddled the dupes, my lady! Ah, I fancy Nugent Fotherby has rather more of quickness than most, eh?'

'Then you *didn't* mean to let Miss Marlow take Edmund away? Oh, Nugent!' said Ianthe admiringly.

'Did it pretty neatly, didn't I? Wouldn't you say I did it neatly, Orde?'

Tom, who had managed to reach the porthole without losing his balance, saw gray seas tumbling past, and turned a face pale with anger towards Sir Nugent. 'I'd say you're a damned nail!' he replied fiercely.

'Not in front of ladies!' protested Sir Nugent.

'You must be mad!' Phoebe cried. 'Turn back! Good God, you can't carry us off like this! Grandmama—all our baggage—! Do you realize that my grandmother has no notion where I am, and neither Tom nor I has a stitch to wear but what we have on our backs? Tell the captain he must turn about!'

'He won't do it,' said Sir Nugent.

'Oh, won't he?' said Tom, making his precarious way to the door. 'We'll see to that!'

Sir Nugent obligingly opened the door for him, saying amiably: 'No sense in stopping him. Let us discuss the matter while he's gone!'

Tom, reaching the deck, found that the *Betsy Anne* was clear of the mouth of the Tidal Harbour, with the wind filling the sails. He had negotiated the companion-way, but the ladder leading to the quarterdeck presented a worse problem to a man with a stiff leg. He was obliged to shout at the stalwart individual above him, which set him, he felt, at a disadvantage. Certainly the ensuing dialogue was not a success. Admitting that he was the skipper, the stalwart individual seemed to be amused by Tom's demand to be set ashore. He asked if Tom had chartered the *Betsy Anne*, and upon being reassured said that that had removed a weight from his mind.

'Now, listen!' said Tom, keeping his temper. 'You'll find yourself in trouble if you don't put back!'

'I'll find myself in trouble if I do!' responded the skipper.

'No, you won't. If you take me, and the lady who is with me, to France against our will, it's kidnapping!'

'Is it, now?' said the skipper, impressed. 'That's bad, that is.'

'As bad as it could be!'

The skipper shook his head. 'It don't bear thinking on. And yet I don't seem to recall as you was forced to come aboard. Nor yet I never see anyone a-luring of you. Dang me if I see anyone *arsting* you! All I see was you and the young lady coming aboard without so much as a by-your-leave! Maybe I'm mistook, though.'

'No, damn you, you aren't!' said Tom, incurably honest. 'Now, be a good

fellow, and put back! You wouldn't wish to upset the lady, and if she's taken
off to France she'll be in the devil of a fix!'

'I'll tell you what!' offered the skipper handsomely. 'You come up here,
sir, and I'll hand the ship over to you! I ain't seaman enough to put into
Dover with the wind in this quarter, but then I've only *been* at sea a matter
of forty years.'

Aware of several grinning faces turned his way Tom flushed. 'Do you
mean you can't put back?'

'*I* can't!' said the skipper.

'Hell and the devil!' ejaculated Tom. 'Now we are in the suds!' He burst
out laughing. 'Lord, what a mess! Hi, skipper! I'd like to come up there
presently to watch how you do the trick!'

'You're welcome,' responded the skipper.

Returning to the cabin, Tom found Ianthe reclining once more on her
berth, a bottle of smelling-salts clutched in her hand. This had apparently
been abstracted from a large dressing-case, which was standing open on the
deck with a number of its expensive contents spilled round it. A dazzling
array of gold-topped bottles, initialled with sapphires, met Tom's awed
gaze, and he blinked. Sir Nugent, observing this, said with simple pride:
'Something like, eh? My own design. I daresay they showed me fifty cases,
but, "No," I said. "Not up to the rig! Trumpery," I said. "Nothing for it
but to design a case myself," I said. *This* is the result. Same thing happened
when I wanted a carriage for her la'ship. "Windus," I said, "it must be of
the first stare. None of these will do," I said. "Build me one to my design!"
Which he did. I am very fond of designing things.'

'Well, I wish you will design us out of this rare mess you've pitched us
into!' said Tom. 'It's no go, Phoebe: the skipper says he can't put back:
wind's in the wrong quarter.'

'Then what in heaven's name are we to do?' she cried.

'Make the best of it. Nothing else we can do,' he answered ruefully.

He was mistaken. The door was just then rudely thrust open, and the
valet appeared on the threshold, his aspect alarming, his eyes glazed. He
clung with one hand to the door, and over his shoulder drooped a small,
wilted figure. 'Sir—my lady—the young gentleman!' he said, in a strange
voice. 'Must request you—*take him quick!*'

'My child!' shrieked Ianthe, struggling up. 'Is he *dead*?'

'No, of course he is not!' said Phoebe hurriedly relieving the valet of his
burden.

'I regret, sir—shall not be available—rest of the passage!' gasped the valet,
clinging now with both hands to the door.

'Well, of all things!' exclaimed Sir Nugent. 'No, dash it, Pett, you *can't* be
ill!'

'Sir,' said Pett, 'I *must!*'

With these tortured words, he disappeared with great precipitancy from
the cabin, his exit being accelerated by the deck's rising suddenly at a steep
angle as the *Betsy Anne* triumphantly lifted her bows over the trough of the
waves.

'Edmund!' cried his anguished parent. 'Speak to me!'

'Don't be so ridiculous!' said Phoebe, out of all patience. 'Can't you *see*
what's the matter with him, poor child?'

Master Rayne, game to the last, raised his head from Phoebe's shoulder,
and spoke gallant words. 'I'm not dead, Mama. J-just cast up me accounts!'

Tom, who had no sooner set eyes on him than he had started, with great presence of mind, to search for a basin, now handed this homely article to Phoebe, saying, with a grin: 'That's the dandy, old chap! You're a prime gun!'

But Master Rayne had shot his bolt. His lip trembled. 'I want to go home!' he said tearfully. 'I don't *like* it!'

'Dearest, *try* not to be ill!' begged his mother. 'Think of something else!'

'I *can't* think of anything else!' wept Edmund, once more in the throes.

Ianthe, who was growing steadily paler, shuddered, and sank back with the smelling-salts to her nose, and her eyes shut.

'You feeling queasy too, my love?' asked Sir Nugent, concerned. 'Now, I'll tell you what: I'll get you a drop of brandy, and you'll be as right as a ram's horn! Nothing like it!'

'No!' faintly moaned his love.

'Extraordinary thing, ain't it?' said Sir Nugent, addressing himself to Tom. 'Some people only have to look at a ship for their stomachs to start turning over; other people wouldn't be sick in a hurricane. Runs in families, I daresay. Take my father: excellent sailor! Take me: the same! Famous for it! Made the crossing two years ago with George Retford. Now, that *was* a rough passage! People hanging over the rails all the way: most diverting spectacle! "Nugent," George said to me—and as game a man as ever lived, mind you! "Take your choice!" he said. "Either that cigar of yours goes overboard, or I do!" Curious, wasn't it? Nothing else turned him queasy, never blenched at his dinner: in fact—'

But as this point his bride brought his reminiscences to a close by requesting him, in a voice of loathing, to go away.

'Well, if there ain't anything I can do, I was thinking Orde and I might crack a bottle,' he said. 'Very willing to remain, however. Swore I'd cherish you, didn't I? Nugent Fotherby is not the man to go back on his word. Ask anyone!'

'Go away, go *away*!' screamed Ianthe. 'Do you wish to *kill* me?'

Seeing that Sir Nugent was about to assure her that he had no such desire, Tom thrust him out of the cabin. 'I'd better go too,' he said, with an uneasy glance at Ianthe. 'Unless you'd like me to stay, Phoebe?'

'No, no, there's nothing for you to do here. There, there, Edmund! Let Phoebe tuck you up warmly, and you'll soon be better!'

'Well, call, if you need me,' said Tom. 'I won't go out of earshot.'

He then withdrew, in the comfortable conviction that both sufferers would probably fall asleep, leaving Phoebe nothing to do but to watch over their slumbers. He was astonished, and considerably concerned, when he heard her calling to him from the foot of the companion-way less than an hour later, and learned that Edmund was very much worse. He saw that Phoebe was looking pale herself, and exclaimed: 'I say, Phoebe, you aren't feeling seasick, are you?'

'I? No, indeed! I have no time to be seasick!' she replied acidly. 'Don't come down! I want you to ask that wretched man if I may carry Edmund into the other cabin. I believe it is his, but he can't want it, after all. And, Tom, try if you can come by a hot brick! Edmund shivers all the time, and do what I will I can't get him warm.'

'Good God, he must be pretty bad! You don't mean to say he's still sick?'

'Not actually sick, no, but those dreadful paroxysms go on, and it hurts him so, poor little man, that he can't help but cry. I've never seen a child so utterly knocked-up, and I've helped to nurse my sisters often and often. It was *wicked* to have brought him on such a journey! She must have known how it would be! She *did* know, and all she will say is that he could be well if he would but make an effort! *She* makes no effort! She is feeling far too ill herself, and her sensibility is so exquisite that she can never bear to be near him when he is ailing! It gives her palpitations. She has them now, so he must be removed from her cabin. Tom, if I could be taken back to Dover on a magic carpet I would not go! No! Or leave that child until I see him safe in Salford's charge! Whatever his sentiments may be towards Edmund he *cannot* be more unfeeling than that *creature*!'

'Steady, steady!' said Tom. 'Throwing your tongue too much, my girl!'

She gave an unsteady laugh, brushing her hand across her brow. 'I know. But only to you, Tom! I've been running mute enough, I promise you.' She raised her finger suddenly, listening, and called: 'I'm coming, darling!'

Not his greatest enemy could have denied that Sir Nugent was as compliant as he was amiable. Upon hearing what was required, he instantly went below, to beg Phoebe to consider his cabin her own. He was very much shocked by Edmund's appearance, and said: 'Poor little fellow! Burned to the socket!' so many times that it irritated Ianthe's nerves. Informed of this, he withdrew his attention from Edmund, and said solicitously: 'Still a trifle out of sorts, my love? Now, see if I don't tell you something that'll do you good! With this wind we shall be in Calais in only four hours!'

'Four hours!' Ianthe said, in a hollow voice. 'Oh, how could you be so brutal as to tell me? Four more hours of this! I shall never survive it. My head! oh, my head!'

'What's to be done?' whispered Sir Nugent in Phoebe's ear. 'Seems to be bellows to mend with her. Devilish distressing: wouldn't have had it happen for the world!'

'I expect,' said Phoebe, somewhat woodenly, 'that she will feel better when she is alone. Lady Ianthe, will you tell me where I may find a nightshirt for Edmund? Were they packed in your trunk? May I look for them there?'

But Ianthe had been unable to bring away any of Edmund's raiment without arousing suspicion in her parent's household.

Phoebe looked wonderingly at the smart new trunk, at a pile of bandboxes, and dress-boxes. 'But—'

'I had to purchase *everything* new! And in such haste that I was quite distracted,' said Ianthe, in failing accents.

'Told her la'ship to rig herself out in the first style of elegance, and have everything sent to my house,' explained Sir Nugent. 'Good notion, don't you agree?'

Her ladyship, in fact, had forgotten, in an orgy of expensive shopping, to provide for her son's needs.

Removed to the smaller cabin, tucked up in its berth, with a champagne bottle full of hot water produced by Tom, Edmund seemed to grow easier. Phoebe had the satisfaction presently of seeing him drop asleep, and was about to snatch a little rest herself when Sir Nugent came to beg the favour of her attendance on Ianthe. Her la'ship, he whispered, was in devilish queer stirrups, and wished for assistance in an affair of too much delicacy to be mentioned.

Mystified, Phoebe went back to the larger cabin, leaving Sir Nugent to maintain a watch over his stepson. The affair of delicacy proved merely to be a matter of untieing Ianthe's stay-laces, but one glance at her was enough to inform Phoebe that Sir Nugent had not exaggerated her condition. She looked to be in extremely queer stirrups, and when Phoebe felt her pulse she discovered it to be tumultuous.

Phoebe was absent from Edmund's side for a considerable period. Unfortunately he woke up while she was away, and no sooner saw Sir Nugent than he repudiated him. Sir Nugent remonstrated with him, pointing out that for Edmund to order him out of his own cabin was coming it a trifle too strong. However, when he heard himself apostrophized as a Bad Man he realized that Edmund was lightheaded, and strove to reassure him. His efforts failed. During his late agony Edmund had had no leisure to consider anything but his body's ills. It was otherwise now. No longer racked by paroxysms, but only a very small boy pitchforked into nightmare, a pressing need presented itself to him. His face puckered. 'I want my Button!' he sobbed.

'Eh?' said Sir Nugent.

Edmund, turning his face into the pillow, repeated his desire in muffled but passionate accents.

'Want a button, do you?' said Sir Nugent. 'Now, don't cry, dear boy! Seems a devilish queer thing to want, but–*which* button?'

'*My* Button!' said Edmund, in a perfect storm of sobs.

'Yes, yes, precisely so!' said Sir Nugent hastily. 'Be calm, dear boy! I assure you there's no need to put yourself in a taking! If you would but tell me—'

'Button, Button, Button!' wept Edmund.

Tom, looking into the cabin five minutes later to ask Phoebe if all was well, found a distressing scene in progress, bitter sounds of grief issuing from the blankets under which Edmund had wholly retired, and his harassed stepfather feverishly turning out the pockets of a small pair of nankeen pantaloons.

'Good God, what's the matter?' Tom demanded, coming into the cabin, and shutting the door. 'Where's Miss Marlow?'

'With her la'ship. Don't care to fetch her away!' said Sir Nugent distractedly. 'Left me to mind Edmund! Extraordinary boy! Took me for a bad man: doesn't seem to know me at all! Now he wants a button.'

'Well, give him a button!' said Tom, limping to the berth, and trying to draw the blanket back. 'Hi, Edmund, what's all this?'

'I–want–my–Button!' wailed Edmund, diving deeper into the blankets.

'Never knew such a corkbrained boy!' fumed Sir Nugent. 'Can't get another word out of him. It's my belief he hasn't brought it with him. What's more, I don't see that it would be a bit of use to him if I *could* find it. Well, I put it to you, Orde, would *you* want a button in such a case?'

'Oh, children often have a liking for odd toys!' said Tom. 'I did myself. Give him one of your own buttons!'

'Dash it, I haven't got any!' A dreadful possibility reared its head. 'You don't mean *cut one off?*'

'Lord, why not?' said Tom impatietly.

Sir Nugent reeled under the shock, but rallied. '*You* cut one off!' he countered.

'Not me!' replied Tom crudely. 'This is the only suit of clothes I have, thanks to you! Besides, *I'm* not the boy's papa-in-law!'

'Well, he won't have it if I am either, so that doesn't signify. To own the truth, I'd as lief I wasn't. Dashed embarrassing, you must agree, to have a son-in-law telling everyone I'm a bad man.'

Tom, not thinking it worth while to reply to this, merely adjured him to find a suitable button. Sighing heavily, Sir Nugent unstrapped one of his numerous portmanteaux. It took him a little time to decide which of his coats he would be least likely to need in the immediate future, and when he made up his mind to the sacrifice of an elegant riding-coat, and started to saw off one of its buttons with his pocket-knife it was easy to see that the operation cost him considerable pain. He was slightly cheered by the reflection that the presentation of so large and handsome a button must raise him in Edmund's esteem. Advancing to the berth, he said winningly: 'No need to cry any more, dear boy! Here's your button!'

The sobs ceased abruptly; Edmund emerged from the blankets, tear-stained but joyful. 'Button, Button!' he cried, stretching out his arms. Sir Nugent put the button into his hand.

There was a moment's silence, while Edmund, staring at this trophy, realized to the full Sir Nugent's perfidy. To blinding disappointment was added just rage. His eyes blazing through his tears he hurled the button from him, and casting himself face downward gave way to his emotions.

'For the lord's sake—!' expostulated Tom. 'What *do* you want, you silly little lobcock?'

'My *own* Button!' wailed Edmund.

Fortunately, the noise of his lamentations reached Phoebe's ears. She came quickly into the cabin, and upon being assured by Sir Nugent that so far from bullying his son-in-law he had ruined one of his coats to provide him with the button he so insistently demanded said contemptuously: 'I should have thought you must have known better! He means his nurse, of course! For heaven's sake, go away, both of you! There, my dear, come to Phoebe, then! *Poor* little man!'

'He s-said it was my Button!' sobbed Edmund into her shoulder. 'He is *bad*! I won't have him, I won't, I won't!'

22

The Lion d'Argent was Calais' most fashionable inn. A parlour and its two best bedchambers had been engaged by Sinderby, the courier hired by Sir Nugent to smooth the furrows from the path of what promised to be a protracted honeymoon. Sinderby had crossed to Calais to be sure of securing accommodation worthy of his wealthy patron, both at the Lion d'Argent and at Abbeville's best hôtel. He had also hired a *bonne* to wait on Master Edmund; and he returned to Dover to superintend the embarkation of the party, feeling that he had provided for every eventuality.

He could not like the chariot of Sir Nugent's design but he accepted it; the arrival of my lady without her maid was harder to accept, for he foresaw that he would be expected to produce a first-rate abigail as soon as he landed again in France, which would be impossible. Her ladyship would have to be content with the services of some quite inferior person until she came to Paris, and she did not bear the appearance of a lady easily contented. With the arrival on board the *Betsy Anne* of Miss Marlow and Mr Orde his spirits sank. Not only did the addition of two more people to the party overset his careful plans, but he could not approve of these unexpected travellers. He speedily came to the conclusion that there was something smoky about them. They had no baggage; and when, on arrival at Calais, he had requested Mr Orde to give into his charge his and Miss Marlow's passports Mr Orde, clapping a hand to his pocket, had uttered an exclamation of dismay. 'Don't say you haven't got the passports!' had cried Miss Marlow. 'Oh, no!' had been Mr Orde's grim response. 'I've got 'em all right and tight! *All* of 'em!' Upon which Miss Marlow had looked ready to faint. Something very havey-cavey about Miss Marlow and Mr Orde, decided Sinderby.

He had foreseen that a wearing time awaited him in Calais, but he had not bargained for a search amongst the haberdashers' shops for a nightshirt to fit a six-year-old child. Furthermore, neither Sir Nugent's wealth nor his own address could procure two extra bedchambers at the Lion d'Argent, as full as it could hold. He was obliged to accept for Miss Marlow the apartment hired for my lady's abigail, and to put Mr Orde in with Sir Nugent, an arrangement which was agreeable to neither of these gentlemen. The Young Person he had found to wait on my lady clearly would not do: she lacked quality. There would be complaints from my lady.

When he returned from scouring the town for a nightshirt it was to discover that another of his arrangements had been overset. Master Rayne had flatly refused to have anything to do with the excellent *bonne* provided for him. 'Had to send her off,' said Sir Nugent. 'Silly wench started gabbling French to him! He wouldn't stand that, of course. Took it in snuff immediately. I knew he would, the moment she said bong-jaw. "Mark me," I said to Miss Marlow, "if *her* tale ain't told!" Which it was. However, it don't signify: Miss Marlow means to look after him. Devilish good thing we brought her with us!'

Lady Ianthe having retired to bed as soon as she had arrived at the Lion d'Argent, only three of the party sat down to dinner in the private parlour. Edmund, who had revived the instant he had set foot on land, had providentially dropped asleep in the little bed set up for him in Phoebe's attic, and Pett was mounting guard over him. He was also washing and ironing his only day-shirt, an office which he promised to perform every evening until the young gentleman's wardrobe could be replenished.

Phoebe was too tired to talk, and Tom too much preoccupied with the problems besetting them, so the burden of conversation fell on Sir Nugent, who maintained throughout the meal a stream of amiable reminiscences. However, when the covers were removed he excused himself, and went off to enjoy one of his cigars downstairs.

'Thank the lord!' said Tom. 'Phoebe, we must discuss what's to be done. I don't want to croak, but the fact is we're in the devil of a fix.'

'I suppose we are,' she agreed, with remarkable calm. 'But at least I know what *I* must do. Should you mind, Tom, if I write two letters before we discuss anything? I have spoken to the courier, and he engages to have them conveyed to England by the next packet, by a private hand. My letter to Grandmama, and the passports, will be taken directly to the Ship, but the courier warns me that if this wind continues the packet may not sail tomorrow.' She sighed, and said resignedly: 'I hope it may, but if it doesn't there's no other way of reaching poor Grandmama, so it's no use fretting.'

'Who is the other letter for? Salford?' asked Tom shrewdly.

'Yes, of course. If he is unable to discover in which direction Ianthe fled—'

'I shouldn't think that likely,' interrupted Tom. 'Not if he gets wind of that carriage!'

'No, that's what I hope,' she agreed. 'But he might not, you know. So I shall send him word, and tell him also that I don't mean to leave Edmund, and will contrive somehow to leave word for him wherever we stop on the road.'

'Oh!' said Tom. 'So that's it, is it? Never mind the letters yet! We'll discuss this business first. How much money have you?' She shook her head. 'None, eh? I thought not. Well, all I have is the ready in my pockets, and it don't amount to more than a couple of Yellow Boys, fifteen shillings in coachwheels, and a few ha'pence. The roll of soft Father gave me is locked in my portmanteau. I daresay I could borrow from Fotherby, but I don't mind telling you it'll go against the shins with me to do it! I've had to borrow one of his shirts already, and a few neckcloths and handkerchiefs, you know. What about you?'

'Oh, isn't it *horrid?*' she exclaimed. 'I've had to borrow from Lady Ianthe, and one would so much prefer not to be beholden to either of them! But perhaps we may be able to set it right again, if things go as I hope they may. Grandmama will receive those passports with my letter, and *surely* she must set out at once, whatever the weather?'

'I should think so,' he agreed. 'And a rare tweak she'll be in! Phew!'

'Yes, and how could one blame her? And if I were obliged to go beyond Paris—No, I think Salford must have overtaken us before that could happen, even if he doesn't start until he has read my letter. I know that Sir Nugent means to take four days on the road to Paris, and I fancy he will find he must take more, with Edmund on his hands. If he leaves Calais at all!'

'Leaving tomorrow, aren't they?'

'Yes, that's what they mean to do, but I shouldn't wonder at it if they find themselves fixed here for several days. Tom, I think Lady Ianthe really is ill!'

'Well, I own that would be nuts for us, but what if she ain't?'

'Then I am going with them,' said Phoebe. 'I won't leave Edmund. Oh, Tom, for all his quaint ways he's the merest baby! When I kissed him good-night he put his arms round my neck, and made me promise not to go away! I nearly cried myself, for it was so very affecting. He can't understand what is happening to him, and he was afraid I might slip away if he let me out of his sight. But when I said I would stay until he has Button again he was quite satisfied. I don't mean to break faith with him, I assure you.'

'I see,' Tom said.

She looked gratefully at him. 'I knew you would. But I have been thinking whether it might not be best, perhaps, if you borrowed enough money from Sir Nugent to buy your passage back to Dover, to escort Grandmama?'

'You needn't say any more!' he interrupted. 'If you think I'll leave you to career across France with this ramshackle pair you were never more mistaken in your life!'

'Well, to own the truth I didn't think you would,' she said candidly. 'And I must say I am thankful for it! Not but what Sir Nugent is very good-natured.'

'Oh, he's good-natured enough!' Tom said. 'But don't you get it into your head that he's a man of character, because he ain't! He's a pretty loose fish, if you want the truth! He was talking to me for ever aboard the schooner, and it's as plain as a pack-saddle he hobnobs with a set of dashed Queer Nabs: all sorts upon the lark! In fact, he's what my father calls half flash and half foolish. Well, good God, if he had any principles he wouldn't have kidnapped Edmund!'

She smiled. 'A Bad Man!'

'Ah, there's a deal of sense in young Edmund's cock-loft!' he said, grinning.

On the following morning Phoebe led Edmund down to breakfast to find that Ianthe was still keeping her bed; but her hopes of delay were dashed when Sir Nugent informed her with an air of grave concern that although her la'ship was feeling devilish poorly she was determined to leave Calais that morning. She had not closed her eyes all night. People had tramped past her door; boots had been flung about in the room above hers; doors had been slammed; and the rumble of vehicles over the *pavé* had brought on her nervous tic. Though it killed her she would drive to Abbeville that day.

Edmund, who was seated beside Phoebe at the table, a napkin knotted round his neck, looked up at this. 'You wish to kill Mama,' he stated.

'Eh?' ejaculated Sir Nugent. 'No, dash it—' You can't say things like that!'

'Mama said it,' replied Edmund. 'On that boat she said it.'

'Did she? Well, but—well, what I mean is it's a bag of moonshine! Devoted to her! Ask anyone!'

'And you told lies, and—'

'You eat your egg and don't talk so much!' intervened Tom, adding in an undervoice to his perturbed host: 'I shouldn't argue with him, if I were you.'

'Yes, that's all very well,' objected Sir Nugent. 'He don't go about telling people *you* are a regular hedge-bird! Where will he draw the line, that's what I should like to know?'

'When Uncle Vester knows what you did to me he will punish you in a terrible way!' said Edmund ghoulishly.

'You see?' exclaimed Sir Nugent. 'Now we shall have him setting it about I've been ill-using him!'

'Uncle Vester,' pursued his small tormentor, 'is the terriblest person in the world!'

'You know, you shouldn't talk like that about your uncle,' Sir Nugent said earnestly. 'I don't say I like him myself, but I don't go about saying he's terrible! Top-lofty, yes, but—'

'Uncle Vester doesn't *wish* you to like him!' declared Edmund very much flushed.

'I daresay he don't, but if you mean he'll call me out—well, I don't think he will. Mind, if he chooses to do so—'

'Lord, Fotherby, don't encourage him!' said Tom, exasperated.

'Uncle Vester will grind your bones!' said Edmund.

'Grind my bones?' repeated Sir Nugent, astonished. 'You've got windmills in your head, boy! What the deuce should he do that for?'

'To make him bread,' responded Edmund promptly.

'But you don't make bread with bones!'

'Uncle Vester does,' said Edmund.'

'That's enough!' said Tom, trying not to laugh. 'It's you that's telling whiskers now! You know very well your uncle doesn't do any such thing, so just you stop pitching it rum!'

Edmund, apparently recognizing Tom as a force to be reckoned with, subsided, and applied himself to his egg again. But when he had finished it he shot a speculative glance at Tom under his curling lashes, and said: 'P'raps Uncle Vester will nap him a rum 'un.'

Tom gave a shout of laughter, but Phoebe scooped Edmund up and bore him off. Edmund, pleased by the success of his audacious sally, twinkled engagingly at Tom over her shoulder, but was heard to say before the door closed 'We Raynes do not like to be carried!'

The party left for Abbeville an hour later, in impressive style. Sir Nugent having loftily rejected a suggestion that the heavy baggage should be sent to Paris by the *roulier*, no fewer than four vehicles set out from the Lion d'Argent. The velvet-lined chariot bearing Sir Nugent and his bride headed the cavalcade; Phoebe, Tom, and Edmund followed in a hired post-chaise; and the rear was brought up by two cabriolets, one occupied by Pett and the Young Person hired to wait on my lady, and the other crammed with baggage. Quite a number of people gathered to watch this departure, a circumstance that seemed to afford Sir Nugent great satisfaction until a jarring note was introduced by Edmund, who strenuously resisted all efforts to make him enter the chaise, and was finally picked up, kicking and screaming, by Tom, and unceremoniously tossed on to the seat. As he saw fit to reiterate at the top of his voice that his father-in-law was a Bad Man, Sir Nugent fell into acute embarrassment, which was only alleviated when Tom reminded him that the interested onlookers were probably unable to understand anything Edmund said.

Once inside the chaise Edmund stopped screaming. He bore up well for the first stages, beguiled by a game of Travelling Piquet. But as the number of flocks of geese, parsons riding gray horses, or old women sitting under hedges was limited on the post-road from Calais to Boulogne, this entertainment soon palled, and he began to be restive. By the time Boulogne was reached Phoebe's repertoire of stories had been exhausted, and Edmund, who had been growing steadily more silent, said in a very tight voice that he felt as sick as a horse. He was granted a respite at Boulogne, where the travellers stopped for half an hour to refresh, but the look of despair on his face when he was lifted again into the chaise moved Tom to say, over his head: 'I call it downright cruel to drag the poor little devil along on a journey like this!'

At Abbeville, which they reached at a late hour, Sinderby was awaiting them at the best hôtel with tidings which caused Sir Nugent to suffer almost as much incredulity as vexation. Sinderby had to report failure. He had been unable to persuade the best hôtel's proprietor either to eject his other clients from the premises, or to sell the place outright to Sir Nugent. 'As I ventured, sir, to warn you would be the case,' added Sinderby, in a voice wholly devoid of expression.

'Won't sell it?' said Sir Nugent. 'You stupid fellow, did you tell him who I am?'

'The information did not appear to interest him, sir.'

'Did you tell him my fortune is the largest in England?' demanded Sir Nugent.

'Certainly, sir. He desired me to offer you his felicitations.'

'He must be mad!' ejaculated Sir Nugent, stunned.

'It is curious that you should say so, sir,' replied Sinderby. 'Precisely what *he* said—expressing himself in French, of course.'

'Well, upon my soul!' said Sir Nugent, his face reddening with anger. 'That to *me?* I'll have the damned ale-draper to know I ain't in the habit of being denied! Go and tell him that when Nugent Fotherby wants a thing he buys it, cost what it may!'

'I never listened to such nonsense in my life!' said Phoebe, unable any longer to restrain her impatience. 'I wish you will stop brangling, Sir

Nugent, and inform me whether we are to put up here, or not! It may be nothing to you, but here is this unfortunate child nearly dead with fatigue, while you stand there puffing off your consequence!'

Sir Nugent was too much taken aback by this sudden attack to be able to think of anything to say; Sinderby, regarding Miss Marlow with a faint glimmer of approval in his cold eyes, said: 'Bearing in mind, sir, your instructions to me to provide for her ladyship the strictest quiet, I have arranged what I trust will be found to be satisfactory accommodation in a much smaller establishment. It is not a resort of fashion, but its situation, which is removed from the centre of the town, may render it agreeable to her ladyship. I am happy to say that I was able to persuade Madame to place the entire inn at your disposal, sir, for as many days as you may desire it, on condition that the three persons she was already entertaining were willing to remove from the house.'

'You aren't going to tell us that they *were* willing, are you?' demanded Tom.

'At first, sir, no. When, however, they understood that the remainder of their stay in Abbeville—I trust not a protracted one—would be spent by them in the apartments I had engaged at this hôtel for Sir Nugent, and at his expense, they expressed themselves as being enchanted to fall in with his wishes. Now, sir, if you will rejoin her ladyship in the travelling chariot, I will escort you to the Poisson Rouge.'

Sir Nugent stood scowling for a moment, and pulling at his underlip. It was left to Edmund to apply the goad: 'I want to go home!' announced Edmund fretfully. 'I want my Button! I'm not *happy!*'

Sir Nugent started, and without further argument climbed back into the chariot.

When he saw the size and style of the Poisson Rouge he was so indignant that had it not been for Ianthe, who said crossly that rather than go another yard she would sleep the night in a cow-byre, another altercation might have taken place. As she was handed tenderly down the steps, Madame Bonnet came out to welcome her eccentric English guests, and fell into such instant raptures over the beauty of miladi and her enchanting little son that Ianthe was at once disposed to be very well pleased with the inn. Edmund, glowering upon Madame, showed a tendency to hide behind Phoebe, but when a puppy came frisking out of the inn his brow cleared magically, and he said: 'I like this place!'

Everyone but Sir Nugent liked the place. It was by no means luxurious, but it was clean, and had a homelike air. The coffee-room might be furnished only with benches and several very hard chairs, but Ianthe's bedchamber looked out on to a small garden and was perfectly quiet, which, as she naïvely said, was all that signified. Moreover, Madame, learning of her indisposition, not only gave up her own featherbed to her, but made her a tisane, and showed herself to be in general so full of sympathy that the ill-used beauty, in spite of aching head and limbs, began to feel very much more cheerful, and even expressed a desire to have her child brought to kiss her before he went to bed. Madame said she had a great envy to witness this spectacle, having been forcibly reminded of the *Sainte Vierge* as soon as she had set eyes on the angelic visages of miladi and her lovely child.

A discordant note was struck by Phoebe, who entered upon this scene of ecstasy only to tell Ianthe bluntly that she had not brought Edmund with her because she had a suspicion that what ailed his doting mother was nothing less than a severe attack of influenza. 'And if he were to take it from

you, after all he has been made to undergo, it would be beyond everything!'
said Phoebe.

Ianthe achieved a wan, angelic smile, and said: 'You are very right, dear
Miss Marlow. Poor little man! Kiss him for me, and tell him that Mama is
thinking of him all the time!'

Phoebe, who had left Edmund playing with the puppy, said: 'Oh yes! I
will certainly do so, if he should ask for you!' and withdrew, leaving Ianthe
to the more agreeable companionship of her new admirer.

Upon the following day a physician was summoned to Ianthe's sick-bed.
He confirmed Phoebe's diagnosis, and with very little prompting said that
with persons of miladi's delicate constitution the greatest care must be
exercised: miladi should beware of over-exertion.

'So I fancy we may consider ourselves as fixed here for at least a week,'
Phoebe said, setting out with Tom and Edmund to buy linen for Edmund.
'Tom, did you contrive to leave word at that hôtel where we were to be
found? For Salford, you know!'

'Leave word!' echoed Tom scornfully. 'Of course I didn't! You don't
suppose they will forget Fotherby there in a hurry, do you? Trying to
purchase the place! Well, of all the gudgeons!'

'Gudgeon,' repeated Edmund, committing this pleasing word to
memory.

'Oh, lord!' said Tom. 'Now, don't you repeat that, young Edmund! And
another thing! You are not to call Sir Nugent a moulder!' He waited until
Edmund had run ahead again, and then said severely to Phoebe: 'You know,
Phoebe, you've no business to encourage him to be rude to Fotherby!'

'I don't *encourage* him,' she said, looking a little guilty. 'Only I can't help
feeling that it would be foolish to stop him, because that might make Sir
Nugent wish to keep him. And you can't deny, Tom, that if he were to take
him in dislike it would make it much easier for—it would make it much easier
to persuade Lady Ianthe to give him up!'

'Well, of all the unprincipled females!' gasped Tom. 'Take care Fotherby
ain't goaded into murdering him, that's all! He ain't in the humour to stand
the roast much longer, and the way that young demon keeps on asking him
if he can take a fly off a horse's ear, or some such thing, and then saying that
his Uncle Vester can, is enough to drive the silly chuckle-head into a
madhouse!'

Phoebe giggled, but said: 'I must say, one can't wonder at his being out of
humour! With an ailing bride and a son-in-law who detests him I do think
he is having a *horrid* honeymoon, don't you?'

But neither of these disagreeable circumstances was, in fact at the root of
Sir Nugent's loss of equanimity, as Phoebe was soon to discover. Finding
her alone in the coffee-room that afternoon it was not long before he was
confiding to her the true cause of his dissatisfaction. He disliked the Poisson
Rouge. Phoebe was rather surprised at first, because Madame Bonnet,
besides being a notable cook, treated him with all the deference and anxiety
to please that the most exacting guest could have demanded; and everyone
else, from the waiter to the boots, scurried to obey his lightest commands.
After listening to his discourse for a few minutes she understood the matter
better. Sir Nugent had never before so lowered himself as to put up at any
but the most fashionable and expensive hostelries. Both his consequence
and his love of display had suffered severe wounds. More sensitive souls
might shrink from attracting public notice; to Sir Nugent Fotherby, the
wealthiest man in England, it was the breath of life. He had hugely enjoyed

the sensation caused by Ianthe's opulent chariot; it afforded him intense pleasure to be ushered by landlords, bent nearly double in obsequiousness, into the best apartments, and to know that his sauntering progress was watched by envious eyes. No such eyes were to be found at the Poisson Rouge. To be sure, had he been able to purchase the Hôtel d'Angleterre, and to eject from it all other guests, he would have found himself similarly bereft; but what a gesture it would have been! how swiftly would the news of his eccentricity have spread over the town! with what awe would the citizens have pointed him out whenever he had sallied forth into the street! To have commandeered an unfashionable inn in a quiet road might be eccentric, but conveyed no sense of his fabulous wealth to the inhabitants of Abbeville. It was even doubtful if anyone beyond Madame Bonnet's immediate circle knew anything about it.

Naturally, he did not phrase his grievance so plainly: it rather crept through his other complaints. Acquainted as Phoebe was with another kind of pride, she listened to him with as much amazement as enjoyment. It would have been idle to have denied enjoyment, which was tempered only by regret that the rich mine of absurdity underlying his foppish appearance had been unknown to her when she had caused his image to flit through the pages of *The Lost Heir*. She found herself weaving a new story round him, and greeted with relief (since the outcome of her first literary adventure had been so appalling) the entrance into the room of Master Rayne, his new friend prancing at his heels.

Madame had bestowed the name of Toto upon the puppy, but he was known to her guests as Chien, a slight misunderstanding having arisen between Madame and Master Rayne. Edmund, overcoming his dislike of foreigners in his desire to pursue his acquaintanceship with Toto, had nerved himself to seek him in the kitchen, and even to demand his name of Madame. Chien was what Madame had said, and when he had repeated it she had nodded and clapped her hands. So Chien the puppy had to be.

Sir Nugent eyed his stepson with apprehension, but Edmund addressed himself to Phoebe. He wanted the coloured chalks Tom had bought for him, Chien having expressed a desire of having his likeness drawn. Having been supplied with the chalks and some paper he disposed himself on the floor and abandoned himself to art. The amiable Chien sat beside him, thumping his tail on the floor, and gently panting.

Seeing that Edmund was absorbed in his own affairs Sir Nugent resumed his discourse, walking up and down the room while he enumerated his grievances.

He had arrayed himself that morning in the nattiest of town-wear. His costume, besides such novel features as white pantaloons, and the Fotherby Tie, included a pair of Hessian boots, never before worn, and decorated with extra-large gold tassels. Hoby had made them to his design, and not Lord Petersham himself had ever been seen in more striking footwear. As Sir Nugent strode about the coffee-room the tassels swung with his every step, just as he had hoped they would. No one could fail to notice them: not even a puppy of dubious lineage.

Chien was fascinated by them. He watched them with his head on one side for several minutes before succumbing to temptation, but they beckoned too alluringly to be withstood. He rose to investigate them more nearly, and snapped at the one bobbing closest to his nose.

An exclamation of horror broke from Sir Nugent, followed by a stentorian command to Chien to drop it. Chien responded by growling as he tugged at the bauble, and wagging his tail. Edmund burst into a peal of joyous laughter, and clapped his hands. This outburst of innocent merriment drew from Sir Nugent so fierce an expletive that Phoebe thought it prudent to go to his rescue.

Tom entered on a scene of turmoil. Chien was barking excitedly in Phoebe's arms; Edmund was still laughing; Pett, attracted by his master's anguished cries, was kneeling before him, tenderly smoothing the tassel; and Sir Nugent, red with fury, was describing in intemperate language the various forms of execution of which Chien was deserving.

Tom acted with great presence of mind, commanding Edmund so peremptorily to take Chien away that Edmund obeyed him without venturing on argument. He then frowned down Phoebe's giggles, and mollified Sir Nugent by promising that Chien should not be allowed in the coffee-room again.

Informed of this ban Edmund was indignant, and had to be called to order for begging Tom to give Sir Nugent a pelt in the smeller. He retired in high dudgeon with Chien to the kitchen, where he spent the rest of the afternoon, playing with a lump of dough, and being regaled with raisins, marchpane and candied peel.

On the following day Sir Nugent wisely forbore to wear his beautiful new boots; and Edmund surprised his protectors by behaving in such a saintly fashion that Sir Nugent began to look upon him with reluctant favour.

It came on to rain in the afternoon, and after drawing several unconvincing portraits, which he kindly bestowed on Phoebe, Edmund became a trifle disconsolate, but was diverted by rain-drop races on the window-pane. He was kneeling on a chair, reporting the dilatory progress of her allotted drop to Phoebe, when a post-chaise and four came along the street, and drew up outside the Poisson Rouge.

Edmund was interested, but not more so than Phoebe, who no sooner heard the clatter of the approaching equipage than she came over to the window. It was the sound she had been hoping to hear, and as the chaise drew to a standstill her heart began to beat fast with hope.

The door was opened, and a figure in a caped overcoat of white drab sprang lightly down, turned to give some order to the postilions, and strode into the inn.

A long sigh escaped Phoebe; Master Rayne uttered a piercing scream, scrambled down from his chair, and tore across the room, shrieking. 'Uncle Vester, Uncle *Vester!*'

23

Edmund succeeded in opening the door, still shrieking *Uncle Vester!* at the top of his voice, just as Sylvester reached the coffee-room. He was halted on the threshold by having his legs embraced, and said, as he bent to detach himself from his nephew's frenzied grip: 'Well, you noisy brat?'

'Uncle Vester, Uncle Vester!' cried Edmund.

Sylvester laughed, and swung him up. 'Edmund, Edmund!' he mocked. 'No, don't strangle me! Oh, you rough nephew!'

As yet unperceived, Phoebe remained by the window, watching with

some amusement Edmund's ecstatic welcome to his wicked uncle. She was
not so very much surprised, though she had not expected him to be cast into
quite such transports of delight. If anything surprised her it was Sylvester's
amused acceptance of Edmund's violent hug. He did not look at all like a
man who disliked children; and he did not look at all like the man who had
said such terrible things to her at Lady Castlereagh's ball. That image,
which had so painfully obsessed her, faded, and with it the embarrassment
which had made her dread his arrival almost as much as she had hoped for
it.

'Tell that Bad Man I am *not* his little boy!' begged Edmund. 'Mama says
I don't belong to you, Uncle Vester, but I *do*, don't I?'

This was uttered so passionately that Phoebe could not help laughing.
Sylvester looked round quickly, and saw her. Something leaped in his eyes;
she had the impression that he was going to start towards her. But the look
vanished in a flash, and he did not move. The memory of their last meeting
surged back, and she knew herself to be unforgiven.

He did not speak immediately, but set Edmund on his feet. Then he said:
'A surprise, Miss Marlow—though I daresay I should have guessed, had I
put myself to the trouble of considering the matter, that I should be very
likely to find you here.'

His voice was level, concealing all trace of the emotions seething in his
breast. They were varied, but uppermost was anger: with her for having, as
he supposed, assisted in the abduction of Edmund; with himself for having,
for an unthinking moment, been so overjoyed to see her. That made him so
furious that he would not open his lips until he could command himself. He
had been trying, ever since the night of the ball, to banish all thought of her
from his mind. This had not been possible, but by dint of dwelling on the
injury she had done him he had supposed he had at least cured himself of his
most foolish tendre for her. It had been an easy task to remember only her
shameful conduct, for the wound she had inflicted on him could not be
forgotten. She had held him up as a mockery to the world: that in itself was
an offence, but if the portrait she had drawn of him had been unrecognizable
he could have forgiven her. He had thought it so, but when he had turned to
his mother, who had given the book to him to read, prepared to shrug it off,
to tell her that it was too absurd to be worth a moment's indignation, he had
seen in her face not indignation but trouble. He had been so much shocked
that he had exclaimed: 'This is not a portrait of me! Oh, I grant the
eyebrows, but nothing else!' She had replied: 'It is overdrawn, of course.' It
had been a full minute before he could bring himself to say: 'Am I like this
contemptible fellow, then? Insufferably proud, so indifferent—so puffed up
in my own esteem that—Mama!' She had said quickly, stretching out her
hand to him: 'Never to me, Sylvester! But I have sometimes wondered—if
you had grown to be a little—uncaring—towards others, perhaps.'

He had been stricken to silence, and she had said no more. There had
been no need: Ugolino was a caricature, but a recognizable one; and because
he was forced to believe this, his resentment, irrationally but inevitably in
one of his temperament, blazed into such rage as he had never known
before.

As he looked at Phoebe across the coffee-room he knew her for his evil
genius. She had embroiled him in her ridiculous flight from her home; she
had led him to pay her such attentions as had brought them both under the
gaze of the interested ton. He forgot that his original intention had been to
win her regard only to make her regret her rejection of his suit: he had

forgotten it long ago. He knew that her book must have been written before she had become so well acquainted with him, but she had neither stopped its publication nor warned him of it. She had been the cause of his having behaved, at that accursed ball, in a manner as unworthy of a man of breeding as anything could well have been. What had made him do it he would never know. It had been his intention to treat her with unswerving civility. He had meant to make no mention, then or thereafter, of her book, but to have conducted himself towards her in such a way as must have shown her how grossly she had misjudged him. He had been sure that he had had himself well in hand; and yet, no sooner was his arm round her waist and his hand clasping hers than his anger and a sense of bitter hurt had mastered him. She had broken from his hold in tears, and he had been furious with her for doing it, because he knew he had brought that scene on himself. And now he found her in Abbeville, laughing at him. He had never doubted that it was she who had put the notion of a flight from England into Ianthe's head, but he had believed she had not meant to do so. It was now borne in upon him that she must have been throughout in Ianthe's confidence.

Knowing nothing of what was in his mind Phoebe watched him in perplexity. After a long pause she said, in a constricted tone: 'I collect you have not received my letter, Duke?'

'I have not had that pleasure. How obliging of you to have written to me! To inform me of this affair, no doubt?'

'I could have no other reason for writing to you.'

'You should have spared yourself the trouble. Having read your book, Miss Marlow, it was not difficult to guess what had happened. I own it did not occur to me that you were actually aiding my sister-in-law, but of course it should have. When I discovered that she had taken Edmund away without his nurse I ought certainly to have guessed how it must be. Are you filling that position out of malice, or did you feel, having made London too hot to hold you, that it offered you a chance of escape?'

As she listened to these incredible words Phoebe passed from shock to an anger as great as his, and not as well concealed. He had spoken in a light, contemptuous voice; she could not keep hers from shaking when she retorted: 'From malice!'

Before he could speak again Edmund said, in an uneasy tone: 'Phoebe is my *friend*, Uncle Vester! Are—are you vexed with her? Please don't be! I love her next to Keighley!'

'Do you, my dear?' said Phoebe. 'That is praise indeed! No one is vexed: your uncle was funning, that's all!' She looked at Sylvester, and said as naturally as she could: 'You must wish to see Lady Ianthe, I daresay. I regret that she is indisposed—is confined to her bed, in fact, with an attack of influenza.'

His colour was rather heightened; for he had forgotten that Edmund was still clinging to his hand, and was annoyed with himself for having been betrayed into impropriety. He said only: 'I trust Fotherby is not similarly indisposed?'

'No, I believe he is sitting with Lady Ianthe. I will inform him of your arrival directly.' She smiled at Edmund. 'Shall we go and see if that cake Madame said she would bake for your supper is done yet?'

'I think I will stay with Uncle Vester,' Edmund decided.

'No, go with Miss Marlow. I am going to talk to Sir Nugent,' said Sylvester.

'Will you grind his bones?' asked Edmund hopefully.

'No, how should I be able to do that? I'm not a giant, and I don't live at the top of a beanstalk. Go, now.'

Edmund looked regretful, but obeyed. Sylvester cast his driving-coat over a chair, and walked over to the fire.

He had not long to wait for Sir Nugent. That exquisite came into the room a very few minutes later, exclaiming: 'Well, upon my soul! I declare I was never more surprised in my life! How do you do? I'm devilish glad to see your grace!'

This entirely unexpected greeting threw Sylvester off his balance. '*Glad to see me?*' he repeated.

'*Devilish* glad to see you!' corrected Sir Nugent. 'Ianthe was persuaded you wouldn't follow us. Thought you wouldn't wish to kick up a dust. I wouldn't have betted on it, though I own I didn't expect you to come up with us so quickly. Damme, I congratulate you, Duke! No flourishing, no casting, and how you picked up the scent the lord only knows!'

'What I want, Fotherby, is not your congratulation, but my ward!' said Sylvester. 'You will also be so obliging as to explain to me what the devil you meant by bringing him to France!'

'Now, there,' said Sir Nugent frankly, 'you have me at Point Non-Plus, Duke! I fancy Nugent Fotherby ain't often at a loss. I fancy you'd be told, if you was to ask anyone, that Nugent Fotherby is as shrewd as he can hold together. But that question is a doubler. I don't mind telling you that every time I ask myself why the devil I brought that boy to France I'm floored. It's a great relief to me to hear you say you want him—you *did* say so, didn't you?'

'I did, and I will add that I am going to have him!'

'I take your word for that,' Sir Nugent said. 'Nugent Fotherby ain't the man to doubt a gentleman's honour. Let us discuss the matter!'

'There is nothing whatsoever to discuss!' said Sylvester, almost grinding his teeth.

'I assure your grace discussion is most necessary,' said Sir Nugent earnestly. 'The boy has a mother! She is not at the moment in plump currant, you know. She must be cherished!'

'Not by me!' snapped Sylvester.

'Certainly not! If I may say so—without offence, you understand—it's not your business to cherish her: never said you would! I daresay, being a bachelor, you may not know it, but *I* did. I'm not at all sure I didn't swear it: it sounded devilish like an oath to me.'

'If all this is designed to make me relinquish my claim on Edmund—'

'Good God, no!' exclaimed Sir Nugent, blenching. 'You mistake, Duke! Only too happy to restore him to you! You know what I think?'

'No! Nor do I wish to!'

'He's like some fellow in the Bible,' said Sir Nugent, ignoring this savage interpolation. 'Or was it a pig? Well, it don't signify. What I mean is, he's possessed of a devil.' He added rather hastily: 'No need to take a pet: you can rely on my discretion: shouldn't dream of spreading it about! Well, by Jove, now I know why you're so anxious to get him back, and, what's more, I don't blame you. He's your heir too, ain't he. Tut, tut, tut, it's a nasty business! Very understandable you should wish to keep him hidden away. Shouldn't be surprised if he got to be dangerous when he grows up.'

Sylvester said with ominous calm: 'Will you have the goodness, sir, first to stop talking nonsense, and second to ask Lady Ianthe, without more ado, if she will receive me—for five minutes! No longer!'

'Five minutes! Why, she can be cast down in five seconds!' exclaimed Sir Nugent. 'In fact, she would be cast down by the very sight of you, Duke. This business must be handled with delicacy. Her la'ship hasn't a suspicion in her noddle that you are here. It was a near-run thing, though. I came out of her room just as Miss Marlow was about to knock on the door. I instantly charged her not to breathe a word to her la'ship. "Miss Marlow," I said—Good God!' he ejaculated, with a sudden change of tone. 'The abigail! the landlady! Must crave your grace's indulgence—not a moment to be lost! They must be warned! Obliged to leave you!'

He hurried over to the door as he spoke, and collided with Tom on the threshold. 'The very person!' he said. 'Allow me to present Mr Orde to your grace! It's Salford, Orde: beg you will entertain him while I'm gone! Feel sure you'll be pleased with one another!'

'No need to put yourself about,' Tom said. 'I want a few words with his grace myself.'

'You do? Well, that's a devilish fortunate circumstance because I think I should take a look in at her la'ship, in case she's got wind of Salford.'

Tom shut the door upon him, and turned to confront Sylvester, standing by the table, his eyes as hard as agates, and as glittering. Tom met their challenge unwaveringly, and limped forward.

'If there was one person whom I never expected to have lent himself to this damnable affair it was you,' said Sylvester very evenly. 'What, if you please, am I to understand by it?'

'From all I've been able to make out,' said Tom, continuing to look him in the eye, 'you're riding too damned rusty to understand anything, my lord Duke! What the devil do you think I'm doing here? Trying to serve you a backhanded turn?'

Sylvester shrugged, and turned away to lean his arm along the mantelshelf. 'I suppose you to be here in support of Miss Marlow. The distinction between that and serving me a backhanded turn may be plain to you: it is not so to me.'

'The only persons who have been trying to serve you a backhanded turn, my lord Duke, are Lady Ianthe and the court-card she's married!' said Tom. 'As for Phoebe, the lord knows I didn't wish her to meddle in this business, but when I think of all she's done for you, and the thanks she's had for it, damme, I'd like to call you out! Oh, I know you wouldn't meet me! You needn't tell me I'm not of your rank!'

Sylvester turned his head, and looked at him, a puzzled frown in his eyes. 'Don't talk to me like that, Thomas!' he said, in a quieter tone. 'You had better sit down: how is that leg of yours?'

'Never mind my leg! It may interest you to know, my lord Duke—'

'For God's sake, will you stop calling me my lord Duke every time you open your mouth?' interrupted Sylvester irascibly. 'Sit down, and tell me what Miss Marlow has done for me to earn my gratitude!'

'Well, that's what I meant to do at the start, but you made me lose my temper, which was the one thing I meant *not* to do,' said Tom. 'And what with you fit to murder the lot of us, and Phoebe swearing she'll starve in a ditch before she travels a yard in your company it'll be as well if I don't do it again!'

'She will not be asked to travel an inch in my company!'

'We'll see that presently. If *you* will sit down I'll tell you just how we both come to be here. But first I'd be glad to know if Lady Ingham's still at

Dover. Or didn't you come by way of Dover?'

'I did, but I have no idea where Lady Ingham may be.'

'I hoped you might have passed her on the road. Looks as though she couldn't face the jump. I take it you didn't put up at the Ship?'

'I didn't put up anywhere. I came down by the night-mail,' said Sylvester.

'Oh! Well, I daresay the old lady is still there. Now, the long and the short of it is, Salford, that Phoebe and I were dashed well kidnapped! I'll tell you how it was.'

Sylvester heard him in unresponsive silence, and at the end of the recital said coldly: 'I regret having done Miss Marlow an injustice, but I should feel myself obliged to her if she would confine her love of romantic adventure to her novels. If she felt she owed me some form of reparation she might, with more propriety and better effect, have written to me from Dover to tell me that Edmund had been taken to France.'

'If Fotherby hadn't told the skipper to set sail I expect that's what she would have done,' replied Tom equably.

'She had no business to go aboard the schooner at all. My nephew's movements are not her concern,' said Sylvester, so haughtily that Tom had much ado not to lose his temper again.

'So I told her,' he said. 'But she thought them very much her concern, and you know why! I don't blame you for being angry with her for having written that dashed silly book. I didn't even blame you for having given her a trimming–though I did think that it was ungentlemanly of you to have done so in public. You may be a duke, but—'

'That will do!' Sylvester said, flushing. 'That episode also–I regret!–deeply regret! But if you imagine that I think my rank entitles me to behave–*ungentlemanly* you are doing me as great an injustice as any that I have done Miss Marlow! You appear to believe that I set inordinate store by my dukedom: I do not! If I have pride it is in my lineage! You should understand that: your father has the same pride! *We Ordes* was what he said to me, when we sat at dinner together: not *I am the Squire!*'

'Beg pardon!' Tom said, smiling a little.

'Yes, very well! but don't throw my rank in my face again! Good God, am I some money-grabbing Cit, sprung from obscurity, decorated with a title for political ends, and crowing like a cock on its own dunghill?' He broke off, as Tom shouted with laughter, and regarded him almost with hostility. 'It was not my intention to divert you!'

'I know it wasn't,' said Tom, wiping his eyes. 'Oh, don't fall into a miff! I see precisely how it is! You are *very* like my father, Salford! It's as natural for you to be a duke as it is for him to be the Squire, and the only time when either of you remembers what you are is when some impudent fellow don't treat you with respect! Oh, lord, and I shall be just the same myself!' He began to laugh again, but gasped: 'Never mind! The thing is that you take it in snuff that Phoebe meddled in your affairs, as though she were encroaching! Well, she wasn't. The only idea she had in her head was how to undo the harm she never meant to bring on you!'

Sylvester got up, and went back to the fire, and said, as he stirred a log with one booted foot: 'You think I should be grateful to her, do you? No doubt her intentions were admirable, but when I think how easily I might but for her interference have recovered Edmund without creating the smallest noise, I am not at all grateful.'

'Yes, I *do* think you should be grateful!' retorted Tom. 'If it hadn't been for her looking after him on board the *Betsy Anne* he might have stuck his spoon in the wall! I never saw anyone in worse case, and there was no one else to care what became of him, let me tell you!'

'Then I am grateful to her for that at least. If my gratitude is tempered by the reflection that Edmund would never have been taken to sea if *she* had not put the notion into his mother's head—'

'Salford, can't you forget that trumpery novel?' begged Tom. 'If you mean to brood over it all the way home, a merry journey we shall have!'

Sylvester had been looking down at the fire, but he raised his head at that. '*What?*'

'How do you imagine I'm to get Phoebe home?' asked Tom. 'Was you meaning to leave us stranded here?'

'Stranded! I can't conceive what need you can possibly have of my services when you appear to be on excellent terms with a man of far greater substance! I suggest you apply to Fotherby for a loan.'

'Yes, that's what I shall be forced to do, if you're set on a paltry revenge,' said Tom, with deliberation.

'Take care!' said Sylvester. 'I've borne a good deal from you, Thomas, but that is a trifle too much! If I had a banking correspondent in France you might draw on me to any time you pleased, but I have not! As for travelling Tab with Miss Marlow—no, by God, I won't! Ask Fotherby to accommodate you. You may as well be indebted to him as to me!'

'No, I may not,' returned Tom. 'You may not care for the mess Phoebe's in, but I do! You know Lady Ingham! That business—all the kick-up over Phoebe's book!—tried her pretty high, and she wasn't in the best of humours when I saw her last. By now I should think she's in a rare tweak, but *you* could bring her round your finger. If we go back to England with you, and you tell the old lady it was due to Phoebe you were able to recover young Edmund, all will be tidy. But if I have to take Phoebe back alone, and all you care for is to keep the business secret, we shall be lurched. You won't be able to keep it secret, either. What about Swale? What about—'

'The only one of my servants who knows where I have gone is Keighley. Swale is not with me. I am not as green as you think, Thomas!'

A slow grin spread over Tom's face. 'I don't think you *green*, Salford!' he said. 'Touched in the upper works is what you are!'

Sylvester looked frowningly at him. 'What the devil are you at now? Do you think me dependent on my valet? You should know better!'

'Should I? Who is going to look after Edmund on the journey?'

'I am.'

'*Have* you ever looked after him?' enquired Tom, grinning more widely.

'No,' said Sylvester, very slightly on the defensive.

'You *will* enjoy the journey! You wait till you've had to wash him half a dozen times a day, my lord Duke! You'll have to dress him, and undress him, and tell him stories when he begins to feel queasy in the chaise, and see he don't eat what he shouldn't—and I'll wager you don't know, so the chances are you'll be up half the night with him!—and you won't even be able to eat your dinner in peace, because he might wake up, and start kicking up a dust. He don't like strange places, you know. And don't think you can hand him over to a chambermaid, because he don't like foreigners either! And if you're gudgeon enough to spank him for being an infernal nuisance he'll start sobbing his heart out, and you'll have every soul in the place behaving as if you was Herod!'

'For God's sake, Thomas—' Sylvester said, half laughing. 'Damn you, I wish I'd never met you! Is it as bad as that?'

'Much worse!' Tom assured him.

'My God! I ought to have brought Keighley, of course. But what you don't realize is that when I drew from my bank what I supposed I should need I didn't bargain for two more persons being added to my party. We should come to a standstill before we reached Calais!'

'I hadn't thought of that,' admitted Tom. 'Well, we shall have to pawn something, that's all.'

'*Pawn* something?' repeated Sylvester. 'Pawn what?'

'We must think. Have you got that dressing-case of yours with you?'

'Oh, it's I who must pawn something, is it? No, I am happy to say I didn't bring anything but a portmanteau!'

'It will have to be your watch and chain, then. It's a pity you don't sport diamond tie-pins and rings. Now, if only you had a spanking great emerald, like the one Fotherby's dazzling us with today—'

'Oh, be quiet!' said Sylvester. 'I'll be damned if I'll pawn my watch! Or anything else!'

'I'll do it for you,' offered Tom '*I* ain't so high in the instep!'

'What *you* are, Thomas, is a—' Sylvester stopped, as the door opened, and Phoebe came into the room.

She was looking so haughty that Tom nearly laughed; and her voice was more frigid than Sylvester's at its coldest. 'Excuse me, if you please! Tom—'

'Miss Marlow,' interrupted Sylvester, 'I understand that I did you an injustice. I beg you will accept my sincere apology.'

She threw him a disdainful glance. 'It is not of the slightest consequence, sir. Tom, I came to tell you that I meant what I said to you on the stairs, and have settled what I shall do. I mean to beg Lady Ianthe to allow me to accompany her as far as to Paris. Once there I can await Grandmama at the Embassy. I am persuaded Sir Charles and Lady Elizabeth will permit me to remain with them when I tell them who I am. If you will go back to Dover with his grace—'

'Yes, that's a capital scheme!' said Tom. 'What's more, I'd give my last coachwheel to see the Ambassador's face when you tripped in, and said you was Lady Ingham's granddaughter, and had come to stay because you'd mislaid her ladyship on the road, *with* all your baggage! For heaven's sake, don't be so shatterbrained! Do you want to set Paris talking as well as London?'

She flinched at this, and Sylvester, seeing it, said: 'That's enough! Miss Marlow, you must see that that scheme is quite ineligible. Pray accept my escort to England!'

'I had rather hire myself out as a cook-maid!' she declared. '*Anything* would be preferable to travelling in your company!'

Having expressed himself in much the same terms, Sylvester was instantly nettled, and retorted: 'You endured my company for a se'enight not so long since without suffering any ill-effect, and I daresay you will survive a few more days of it!'

'I wish with all my heart I had never gone aboard that ship!' said Phoebe, with deep feeling.

'So do I wish it! For a more ill-judged—I beg your pardon! I believe you meant well!'

'I shall never mean you well again!' she told him fierily. 'As for your *condescension,* my lord Duke—'

'Phoebe, take a damper!' commanded Tom sternly. 'And listen to me! I've gone along with you till now, but I'm going no farther. You'll do as I tell you, my girl. We shall go home with Salford, and you will *not* be beholden to him, if that's what frets you, because he needs you to look after Edmund. Yes, and let me remind you that you promised that boy you wouldn't leave him until he had his Button again!'

'He won't care for that *now!*' she said.

But as Edmund peeped into the coffee-room at that moment, and, upon being applied to by Tom, instantly said that he would not let Phoebe go away, this argument failed. She did suggest to Edmund that his uncle would suffice him, but he vigorously shook his curly head, saying: 'No, acos Uncle Sylvester is *damned* if he will be plagued with me afore breakfast.'

This naïve confidence did much to alleviate constraint. Phoebe could not help laughing, and Sylvester, wreaking awful vengeance on his small nephew, lost his stiffness.

But just as Edmund's squeals and chuckles were at their height the company was startled by a roar of rage and anguish from above-stairs. It seemed to emanate from a soul in torment, making Sylvester jerk up his head, and Edmund stop squirming in his hold.

'What the devil—?' exclaimed Sylvester.

24

'*Now* what's amiss?' said Tom, limping to the door. 'It sounds as if the Pink of the Ton has found a speck of mud on his coat.'

'Pett! Pett!' bellowed Sir Nugent, descending the stairs. 'Pett, where are you? *Pett*, I say!'

As Tom pulled the door wide Sylvester set Edmund on his feet, demanding: 'What in God's name ails the fellow?'

With a final appeal to Pett as he crossed the hall Sir Nugent appeared in the doorway, nursing in his arms a pair of glossy Hessians, and commanding the occupants of the coffee-room to look—only to look!

'Don't make that infernal noise!' said Sylvester sharply. 'Look at what?'

'That cur, that mongrel!' Sir Nugent shouted. 'I'll hang him! I'll tear him limb from limb, by God I will!'

'Oh, sir, what is it?' cried Pett, running into the room.

'Look!' roared Sir Nugent, holding out the boots.

They were the Hessians of his own design, but gone were their golden tassels. Pett gave a moan, and fell back with starting eyes; Tom shot one quick look at Edmund, tried to keep his countenance, and, failing, leaned against the door in a fit of unseemly laughter; and Phoebe, after one choking moment, managed to say: 'Oh, dear how very unfortunate! But p-pray don't be distressed, Sir Nugent! You may have new ones put on, after all!'

'New ones—! Pett! If it was you who left the door open so that that mongrel could get into my room you leave my service today! Now! *Now*, do you hear me?'

'*Never!*' cried Pett dramatically. 'The chambermaid, sir! the boots! *Anyone* but me!'

Balked, Sir Nugent rounded on Tom. 'By God, I believe it was you!

Laugh, will you? *You* let that cur into my room!'

'No, of course I didn't,' said Tom. 'I'm sure I beg your pardon, but of all the kick-ups only for a pair of boots!'

'*Only*—!' Sir Nugent took a hasty step towards him, almost purple with rage.

'Draw his cork, Tom, draw his cork!' begged Edmund, his angelic blue eyes blazing with excitement.

'Fotherby, *will* you control yourself?' Sylvester said angrily.

'Sir, there is no scratch on them! At least we are spared that!' Pett said. 'I shall scour Paris day and night, sir. I shall leave no stone unturned. I shall—'

'My own design!' mourned Sir Nugent, unheeding. 'Five times did Hoby have them back before I was satisfied!'

'Oh, sir, shall I ever forget?'

'What a couple of Bedlamites!' Sylvester remarked to Phoebe, his eyebrows steeply soaring, his tone one of light contempt.

'Gudgeon,' said Edmund experimentally, one eye on his mentor.

But as Tom was telling Sylvester the tale of Chien's previous assault on the Hessians this essay passed unheeded. Sir Nugent, becoming momently more like an actor in a Greek tragedy, was lamenting over one boot, while Pett nursed the other, and recalling every circumstance that had led him to design such a triumph of modishness.

Sylvester, losing all patience, exclaimed: 'This is ridiculous!'

'Ridicklus!' said Edmund, savouring a new word.

'You can say that?' cried Sir Nugent, stung. 'Do you know how many hours I spent deciding between a plain gold band round the tops, or a twisted cord? Do you—'

'I'm not amused by foppery! I shall be—'

'Ridicklus gudgeon!'

'—obliged to you if—*What* did you say?' Sylvester, arrested by Edmund's gleeful voice, turned sharply.

The question, most wrathfully uttered, hung on the air. One scared look up into Sylvester's face and Edmund hung his head. Even Sir Nugent ceased to repine, and waited for the answer. But Edmund prudently refrained from answering. Sylvester, with equal prudence, did not repeat the question, but said sternly: 'Don't let me hear your voice again!' He then turned back to the bereaved dandy, and said: 'I shall be obliged to you if you will bring this exhibition to a close, and give me your attention!'

But at this moment the Young Person arrived on the scene, with an urgent summons from Ianthe. Miladi, alarmed by the sounds that had reached her ears, desired her husband to come up to her room immediately.

'I must go to her!' announced Sir Nugent. 'She will be in despair when she learns of this outrage! "Nugent," she said, when I put them on yesterday—the first time! only once worn! "You will set a fashion!" she said. I must go to her at once!'

With that, he laid the boot he was still holding in Pett's arms, and hurried from the room. Pett, with a deprecating look at Sylvester, said: 'Your grace will forgive us. It is a sad loss—a great blow, your grace!'

'Take yourself off!'

'Yes, your grace! At once, your grace!' said Pett, bowing himself out in haste.

'As for you,' said Sylvester, addressing his sinful nephew, 'if ever I hear such impertinence from you again it will be very much the worse for you! Now go!'

'I won't do it again!' said Edmund, in a small, pleading voice.

'I said, *Go!*'

Scarlet-faced, Edmund fled. This painful interlude afforded Phoebe an opportunity to resume hostilities, and she told Sylvester that his conduct was brutal. 'It is extremely improper, moreover, to vent your own ill-temper on the poor child! It would have been enough for you to have given him a quiet reproof. I was never more shocked!'

'When I wish for your advice, Miss Marlow, be sure that I will ask for it,' he replied.

She got up quickly, and walked to the door. 'Take care what you are about!' she said warningly, as a parting shot. '*I* am not one of your unfortunate servants, obliged to submit to your odious arrogance!'

'One moment!' he said.

She looked back, very ready to continue to do battle.

'Since Fotherby appears to be unable to think of anything but his boots, perhaps you, Miss Marlow, will be good enough to inform Lady Ianthe of my arrival,' said Sylvester. 'Will you also, if you please, pack Edmund's clothes? I wish to remove from this place as soon as may be possible.'

This request startled her into exclaiming: 'You can't take him away at this hour! Why, it's past his bedtime already! It may suit you to travel by night, but it won't do for Edmund!'

'I have no intention of travelling by night, but only of removing to some other hôtel. We shall leave for Calais in the morning.'

'Then you will remove without me!' said Phoebe. 'Have you *no* thought for anyone's convenience but your own? What do you imagine must be *my* feelings—if you can condescend to consider anything so trifling? While I was one of Sir Nugent's party my lack of baggage passed unheeded, but in yours it will not! And if you think I am going to one of the fashionable hôtels in a travel-stained dress, and nothing but a small bandbox for luggage, you are very much mistaken, Duke!'

'Of what conceivable importance are the stares or the curiosity of a parcel of hôtel servants?' he asked, raising his brows.

'Oh, how like you!' she cried. 'How *very* like you! To be sure, the mantle of your rank and consequence will be cast over me, won't it? How delightful it will be to become so elevated as to treat with indifference the opinions of inferior persons!'

'As I am not using my title, and my consequence, as you are pleased to call it, is contained in one portmanteau, you will find my mantle somewhat threadbare!' Sylvester flung at her. 'However, set your mind at rest! I shall hire a private parlour for your use, so you will at least not be obliged to endure the stares of your fellow guests!'

At this point Thomas entered a caveat. 'I don't think you should do that, Salford,' he said. 'You're forgetting that the dibs aren't in tune!'

A look of vexation came into Sylvester's face. 'Very well! We will put up at some small inn, such as this.'

'The inns are most of 'em as full as they can hold,' Tom warned him. 'If we have to drive all over the town, looking for a small inn that has rooms for the four of us, we shall very likely be up till midnight.'

'Do you expect me to remain *here?*' demanded Sylvester.

'Well, there's plenty of room.'

'If there is room here there will be—'

'No, there will not be room elsewhere!' interpolated Phoebe. 'Sir Nugent is hiring the whole house, having turned out the wretched people who were here before us! And why you should look like that I can't conceive, when it is just what you did yourself, when you made Mrs Scaling give up her coffee-room for your private use!'

'And who, pray, were the people I turned out of the Blue Boar?' asked Sylvester.

'Well, it so happened that there weren't any, but I don't doubt you *would* have turned them out!'

'Oh, indeed? Then let me tell you—'

'Listen!' begged Tom. 'You can be as insulting to one another as you please all the way to Dover, and I swear I won't say a word! But for the lord's sake decide what we are to do first! They'll be coming to set the covers for dinner soon. I don't blame you for not wanting to stay here, Salford, but what with pockets to let and young Edmund on our hands, what else can we do? If you don't choose to let Fotherby stand the nonsense you can arrange with Madame to pay your own shot.'

'Well, I am going to put Edmund to bed!' said Phoebe. 'And if you try to drag him away from me, Duke, I shall tell him that you are being cruel to me, which will very likely set him against you. Particularly after your cruelty to him!'

On this threat she departed, leaving Sylvester without a word to say. Tom grinned at him. 'Yes, you don't want Edmund to tell everyone *you* are a Bad Man. He's got Fotherby regularly blue-devilled, I can assure you! Come to think of it, he's already set it about that you grind men's bones for bread.'

Sylvester's lips twitched, but he said: 'It seems to me that Edmund has been allowed to become abominably out of hand! As for you, Thomas, if I have much more of your damned impudence—'

'*That's* better!' said Tom encouragingly. 'I thought you were never coming down from your high ropes! I say, Salford—'

He was interrupted by the return of Sir Nugent, who came into the room just then, an expression of settled gloom on his countenance.

'Have you told Ianthe that I am here?' at once demanded Sylvester.

'Good God, no! I wouldn't tell her for the world!' replied Sir Nugent, shocked. 'Particularly *now*. She is very much distressed. Feels it just as I knew she must. You will have to steal the boy while we are asleep. In the middle of the night, you know.'

'I shall do nothing so improper!'

'Don't take me up so!' said Sir Nugent fretfully. 'No impropriety at all! You are thinking you would be obliged to creep into Miss Marlow's bedchamber—'

'I am thinking nothing of the sort!' said Sylvester, with considerable asperity.

'There you go again!' complained Sir Nugent. 'Dashed well snapping off my nose the instant I open my mouth! No question of creeping into her room: she'll bring the boy out to you. You'll have to take her along with you, of course, and I'm not sure that Orde hadn't better go too, because you never know but what her la'ship might bubble the hoax if he stayed behind. The thing is—'

'You needn't tell me!–Thomas, either you may stop laughing, or I leave you to rot here!–Understand me, Fotherby! I have no need to steal my ward! Neither you nor Ianthe has the power to prevent my removing him. Well, though I am going to do so I have enough respect for her sensibility as to wish not only to inform her of my intention, but to assure her that every care shall be taken of the boy. Now perhaps you will either conduct me to

Ianthe, or go to tell her yourself that I am taking Edmund home tomorrow!'

'No, I won't,' said Sir Nugent. 'You may have the right to do it—well, I know you have! asked my attorney!—but does her la'ship know it? What I mean is will she own she knows it? If you think she will, Duke, all I can say is that you don't know much about females! Which is absurd, because you don't bamboozle me into believing you didn't offer a *carte blanche*, not a year after your come-out, to—what was that little lightskirt's name? You know the one I mean! A regular high flyer, with yaller curls, and—'

'We will leave my affairs out of this discussion!' said Sylvester, rigid with anger.

'Oh, just as you wish! Not but what I've often wanted to ask you—However, I can see you'll fly up into the boughs, so never mind that! The thing is, if I was to tell her la'ship what was in the wind she'd expect me to stop you making off with the brat. And let alone I don't want to stop you, how the devil could I? You know what females are, Duke—no objection to my saying that, is there?—She'll think I ought to pull out a sword, and it wouldn't be a mite of use telling her I haven't got a sword, because the trouble with females is they ain't rational! And a pretty time I should have of it, while you were running off with the boy, as merry as cup and can! Why, I shouldn't wonder at it if she didn't forgive me for a twelvemonth!'

'That,' said Sylvester, 'is your affair!'

'Well, of all the scaly things to say!' gasped Sir Nugent. 'Here's me anxious to help you to the boy, and instead of—Oh, my God, haven't you gone to bed yet?'

This exclamation was caused by the appearance on the threshold of Master Rayne, bearing all the look of one who, having reached a painful decision, was not to be turned from it. He was followed by Phoebe, who said: 'Edmund wishes to speak to you before he does go to bed, Sir Nugent.'

'No, no, take him away!' said Sir Nugent. 'I've had a very unpleasant shock—not by any means in prime twig!'

'It isn't *wish,* ezzackly,' said Edmund, walking resolutely up to his chair, and standing before him with his hands behind his back. 'If you please, I beg your pardon for having called you a gudgeon, sir. *Ridicklus* gudgeon,' he added conscientiously.

Sir Nugent waved him peevishly away. 'Oh, very well!'

'And also,' said Edmund heroically, 'it wasn't Chien. It was me. And I'm sorry, and—and here they are!'

As he spoke he brought his hands from behind his back, and opening them disclosed two dishevelled tassels. Phoebe, unprepared for this gesture, gave a gasp of consternation; Sir Nugent after staring for a tense moment at the tassels, said chokingly: 'You—you—! By God, if I don't—'

'Fotherby!'

Sylvester's voice, ripping across the room, checked the infuriated dandy as he started up menacingly from his chair. Sylvester came quickly forward, and Edmund, though he had stood his ground, breathed more easily. 'You *dare!*' Sylvester said through his teeth.

'I was only going to give him a shake,' said Sir Nugent sulkily. 'Damn it, I'm his father-in-law, ain't I?'

Sylvester uttered a short, contemptuous laugh, and looked down at Edmund. 'Give me those tassels, brat, and be off to bed!'

Edmund relinquished them, but said dolefully: 'I thought you wouldn't be angry any more if I said I was sorry!'

'I'm not angry,' Sylvester said, tickling his cheek with one careless finger.

'Word of a Rayne! Good-night, you imp! Don't keep Miss Marlow waiting!'

'*You're* not angry!' exploded Sir Nugent. 'I wonder you don't *reward* the young viper!'

'I may yet,' replied Sylvester coolly. 'He has done what I could not: given you your own again! When you kidnapped that boy, Fotherby, you knew yourself safe from me, because I would not publish my affairs to the world! I doubt if anything I could have done would have caused you such anguish as Edmund has made you suffer! Bless him, he's full of pluck! *How* his father would have laughed!'

'I have a good mind to call you out! Upon my soul I have!' Sir Nugent threatened.

'I don't think you have!' Sylvester tossed at him. 'I am accounted a fair shot, my hero!'

'I fancy,' said Sir Nugent, fulminating, 'that Nugent Fotherby is as game a man as ever lived! I fancy, if you were to ask anyone, that would be the answer. The thing is her la'ship wouldn't like it. Must cherish her! But if she thinks I'm going to take that changeling of hers along with us—'

The very thought of Edmund seemed to choke him, for he broke off, his choler mounting again, snatched up the tassels, which Sylvester had dropped disdainfully on the table, and stormed out of the room.

Tom could not but feel that Edmund's confession had still further complicated matters; for the Poisson Rouge now seemed hardly big enough to hold both Sylvester and Sir Nugent. But Edmund's villainy was soon found to have exercised a good effect. Ianthe, when the story was poured into her ears, said that Edmund must be punished. Sir Nugent told her bitterly that Sylvester would not allow it. So the secret of Sylvester's arrival was out. Ianthe fell back on her pillows with a shriek; but Sir Nugent, forgetting his marriage vows, informed her (smiting her dressing-table with his clenched fist so that all the gold-topped bottles on it jumped) that she might there and then choose between him and her hell-born brat. This show of violence quite overawed her. She was also a good deal impressed, for it was clearly a proof of masculine superiority, to which she instinctively responded. Her protests, though maintained tearfully, began to lack conviction; and when Sylvester, taking the law into his own hands, knocked on her door, and entered the room hard upon his knock, his reception was less daunting than might have been expected. He was certainly greeted with reproaches, but these were largely directed against his having encouraged Edmund to behave badly. As she blamed him for not having punished Edmund her subsequent declaration that nothing would induce her to abandon her child to his unkindness sounded lame even in her own ears. She then burst into tears, and said that no one had any consideration for her nerves.

This outbreak of lamentation brought Phoebe into the room, to beg her to restrain herself for Edmund's sake. 'I am persuaded you cannot wish to distress him!' she said. 'Only think how disturbing for such a little boy to hear his mama crying!'

'You are as heartless as Sylvester!' wept Ianthe. 'None of you cares for my sufferings!'

'Not I, certainly,' said Sylvester.

'*Oh!*' gasped Ianthe, bouncing up in her bed. Indignation brought her sobs to an abrupt end; an angry flush reddened her cheeks; and her lovely eyes darted fire at Sylvester.

'Not the snap of my fingers!' said Sylvester. 'You see, I am quite honest with you, Ianthe. And before you resume this affecting display of sensibility listen to what I have to say to you! It has pleased you to remember for four years a foolish thing I once said to you. You have cast it in my teeth so often that you have come to believe I meant it. No, don't turn away your head! Look me in the face, and answer me! Do you think that I could treat with unkindness all that I have left to me of Harry?'

She said sulkily, picking at her handkerchief: 'I am sure *I* never thought you cared so very much for Harry! You didn't shed a tear when he died!' She stopped, frightened by the expression on his face.

It was a moment before he spoke. Watching him, Phoebe saw that he was very pale, his satyr-look pronounced, his lip tightly compressed. When he unclosed them it was to say in a curt voice: 'When Harry died—I lost a part of myself. We will not discuss that. I have only this to add: you are Edmund's mother, and you may visit him whenever you choose to do so. I have told you so many times already, but I'll repeat it. Come to Chance when you please—with or without your husband!'

Sir Nugent, who had been listening intently, exclaimed as the door shut behind Sylvester: 'Well, upon my soul, that's devilish handsome of him! Now, you must own, my love, it *is* devilish handsome! Damme if I ever thought he'd invite me to Chance! The fact is I had a notion he didn't like me above half. I shall go, I think. I don't say it won't be a dead bore: no fun and gig, and the company pretty stiff-rumped, I daresay. But visiting at Chance, you know! I'll tell you what I'll do: I'll invite him to drink a glass of wine with me! No, by Jove, I'll invite him to dine with me! Do you think I should change my dress, my love? No! might put him out of countenance. I shall put on a fresh neckcloth: that will exactly answer the purpose!'

Full of these amiable plans he hurried from the room. Ianthe dissolved again into tears, but showed signs of recovering her spirits when Phoebe assured her she would take every care of Edmund upon the journey back to London.

'Oh, dear Miss Marlow, were it not for your going I could not consent to his being taken from me!' Ianthe said, clasping Phoebe's hand. 'I am sure you will care for him as well as I could myself! And if anyone is so unjust as to say that I deserted my child *you* know it is untrue!'

'If anyone should say such a thing to me I shall reply that he was torn from your arms,' promised Phoebe. 'Excuse me! I must go back to him, and blow out his candle.'

But when she reached the bedchamber she shared with Edmund she checked on the threshold, for Sylvester was sitting on the edge of Edmund's crib. He got up at once, saying with some constraint: 'I beg your pardon! I should not be here, but Edmund called to me.'

'Of course! It's of no consequence!' she said, in a more friendly tone than she had yet used to him.

'Phoebe, Uncle Vester says my papa would have cut off one tassel, and he would have cut off the other!' Edmund told her, his eyes sparkling.

She could not help laughing. 'I wonder how he would like it if you cut the tassels from *his* boots!'

'Ah, I have explained to him that it is a thing which must on no account be done to uncles!' Sylvester said. He ruffled Edmund's curls. 'Good-night, vile brat!'

'You won't go away?' Edmund said, assailed by a sudden fear.

'Not without you.'

'And Phoebe? And Tom?'

'Yes, they will both come with us.'

'Good!' said Edmund, releasing his clutch on Sylvester's coat. 'I daresay we shall be as merry as grigs!'

25

The party reached Calais two days later, having broken the journey at Etaples, where they stayed in what Sylvester unequivocally described as the worst hostelry ever to have enjoyed his patronage. Only Tom might have been said to have fulfilled Edmund's expectations.

Sylvester's temper had been ruffled at the outset, for not even the pledging of Phoebe's little pearl brooch as well as his own watch and chain provided him with enough money to enable him to travel in the style to which he was accustomed. He was extremely vexed with Tom for suddenly producing the brooch in the pawnbroker's shop, which piece of folly, he said, would now make it necessary for him to send one of his people over to France to redeem it. He disliked haggling over the worth of his watch; he disliked still more to be in any way beholden to Phoebe; and he emerged from this degrading experience in anything but a sunny humour. He then discovered that the hire of two post-chaises and four would result in the whole party's being stranded half-way between Abbeville and Calais, and was obliged to make up his mind which of two evils was likely to prove the lesser: to cram four persons, one of whom was a small boy subject to travel-sickness, into one chaise and four; or to hire two chaises, and drive for well over a hundred and twenty kilometres behind a single pair of horses. The reflection that Edmund, before he succumbed to his malaise, would fidget and ask incessant questions decided the matter: he hired two chaises, and in so doing made the discovery that Mr Rayne, a man of modest means, did not meet with the deference accorded to his grace of Salford. The post-master was not uncivil: he was uninterested. Sylvester, accustomed his whole life long to dealing with persons who were all anxiety to please him, suffered a slight shock. Until he had landed at Calais he had never made a journey in a hired vehicle. He had thought poorly of the chaise supplied by the Lion d'Argent; the two allotted to him in Abbeville filled his fastidious soul with disgust. They were certainly rather dirty.

'Why hasn't this carriage got four horses?' demanded Edmund.

'Because it only has two,' replied Sylvester.

'Couple o' bone-setters!' said Edmund disparagingly.

They were found to be plodders; nor, when the first change was made, was there much improvement in the pace at which the ground was covered. There was a world of difference between a team and a pair, as Phoebe soon discovered. The journey seemed interminable; and although the more sober pace seemed to affect Edmund less than the swaying of a well-sprung chaise drawn by four fast horses, he soon grew bored, a state of mind which made him an even more wearing companion than when he was sick. She could only be thankful when, at Etaples, Sylvester, after one look at her, said they would go no farther that day. She desired nothing so much as her bed; but to her suggestion that some soup might be sent up to her room Sylvester returned a decided: 'Certainly not! Neither you nor Edmund ate any luncheon, and if you are not hungry now you should be.' He gave her one of his searching looks, and added: 'I daresay you will like to rest before you dine, Miss Marlow. Edmund may stay with me.'

She was led upstairs by the boots to a room overlooking a courtyard; and having taken off her dress and hung it up, in the hope that the worst of its creases might disappear, she lay down on the bed and closed her eyes. The suspicion of a headache nagged at her, but she soon discovered that there was little chance of being able to rid herself of it. To judge by the noises that came from beneath her window the kitchens had access on to the yard, and were inhabited by a set of persons who seemed all to be quarrelling, and hurling pots and pans about.

Just as she was about to leave her room again Tom came to see how she did. He was carrying a glass of wine, which he handed to her, saying that Salford had sent it. 'He says you are done-up. And I must say,' added Tom critically, 'you do look hagged!'

Having studied her reflection in the spotted looking-glass she was well aware of this, and it did nothing to improve her spirits. She sipped the wine, hoping that it might lessen the depression that had been creeping on her all day.

'What a racket these Frenchies make!' observed Tom, looking out of the window. 'Salford cut up stiff when he found this room gave on to the yard, but ours is directly above the *salle des buveurs*, and that wouldn't have done for you at all. There seems to a fair going on: the town's packed, and no room to be had anywhere.'

'Have you to share a room with Salford? He won't like that!'

'Oh, that ain't what's making him ride grub!' said Tom cheerfully. 'He don't care for the company, and he ain't accustomed to being told by waiters that he shall be served *bientôt!* I left him coming the duke in the coffee-room, to get us one of the small tables to ourselves. He'll do it too: the waiter was beginning to bow and wash his hands—and all for no more than his grace's high-bred air and winning smile!'

They found, on descending to the coffee-room, that Sylvester had indeed procured a small table near the door, and was awaiting them there, with Edmund, who was seated on an eminence composed of two large books placed on his chair. Edmund was looking particularly angelic and was exciting a good deal of admiration.

'A little more of this sort of thing,' said Sylvester in an undervoice, as he pushed Phoebe's chair in for her, 'and his character would be ruined!'

'Except that he doesn't care for it,' she agreed.

'No, thank God! I have ordered what I hope you will like, Miss Marlow, but there is very little choice. What we should call an ordinary, at home.'

He turned to speak to a harried waiter, and Edmund, apparently reconciled to the French language by his uncle's fluency, suddenly announced that he too could talk French.

'Oh, what a bouncer!' said Tom. 'What can you say?'

'I can say *words*,' replied Edmund. 'I can say *bonjour* and *petit chou* and—' But at this point he lost interest, the waiter having dumped in front of him the *plat* of his careful choice.

The dinner was good, and, although the service was slow, the meal might have passed without untoward incident had Edmund not been inspired to favour the assembled company with a further example of his proficiency in the French tongue. An enormously fat woman, seated at the end of the table that ran down the centre of the room, after incurring his displeasure by nodding and smiling at him every time he looked up from his plate, was so much ravished by his beauty that when she passed his chair on her way out of the coffee-room she not only complimented Phoebe on his seraphic countenance but was unable to resist the temptation of swooping down upon him and planting a smacking kiss on his cheek. '*Petit chou!*' she said, beaming at him.

'*Salaude!*' returned Edmund indignantly.

For this he was instantly condemned to silence, but when Sylvester, after explaining to the shocked lady that Edmund had picked the word up without an idea of its meaning, offering her his apologies, and enduring the hearty amusement of all those within earshot, sat down again and directed a look at his erring nephew that boded no good to him, Phoebe took up the cudgels in Edmund's defence, saying: 'It is unjust to scold him! He *doesn't* know what it means! He must have heard someone say it at the Poisson Rouge, when he was in the kitchen!'

'Madame says it to Elise,' said Edmund enigmatically.

'Well, it isn't a very civil thing to say, my dear,' Phoebe told him, in gentle reproof.

'I didn't think it was,' said Edmund, in a satisfied voice.

'It seems to me an extraordinary thing that he should have been allowed to keep kitchen company,' said Sylvester. 'I should have supposed that amongst the four of you—'

'Yes, and it has often seemed extraordinary to me that amongst I know not how many people he should have been allowed to keep stable company!' flashed Phoebe.

This was so entirely unanswerable that silence reigned until Tom, to relieve the tension, asked Sylvester some question about the next day's journey. As soon as they left the coffee-room Phoebe took Edmund up to bed, bidding Sylvester a chilly good-night, and Tom a very warm one.

At breakfast on the following morning punctilious civility reigned, Sylvester addressing suave remarks to Phoebe, and Phoebe replying to them with formal courtesy.

But formality deserted Phoebe abruptly when she discovered that instead of Edmund she was to have Tom for her travelling companion. She said at once: 'No, no! Please leave Edmund with me! It was to take care of him that I came with you, Duke, and I assure you I am very happy to do so!'

'You are very good, ma'am, but I will take him today,' he replied.

'But why?' she demanded.

He hesitated, and then said: 'I wish it.'

It was spoken in his indifferent voice. She read in it a reflection on her management of Edmund, arising possibly from his overnight solecism, and turned away that Sylvester might not have the satisfaction of seeing how mortified she was. When she next glanced at him she found that he was watching her, she thought with a shade of anxiety in his rather hard eyes. He moved towards her, and said: 'What did I say to distress you? I had no such intention!'

She put up her brows. 'Distress me? Oh, no!'

'I am taking Edmund with me because I am persuaded you have the head-ache,' he said bluntly.

It was true, but she disclaimed, begging him to let Edmund go with her. His thought for her disarmed her utterly; her constraint vanished; and when she raised her eyes to his face they were shyly smiling. He looked down at her for a moment, and then said almost brusquely, as he turned away: 'No, don't argue! My mind is made up.'

By the time Calais was reached her head-ache had become severe, a circumstance to which she attributed her increasingly low spirits. Edmund, when he heard of it, disclosed that Uncle Vester had the head-ache too.

'I?' exclaimed Sylvester. 'I've never had the head-ache in my life, brat!'

'Oh!' said Edmund, adding with a confiding smile: 'Just a bit cagged-like!'

Since Tom had had the forethought to consult Sinderby, the inn which housed them that night, though a modest establishment in the unfashionable quarter of the town, was both quiet and comfortable. A tisane, followed by a night's undisturbed sleep, cured Phoebe's head-ache. Her spirits, however, remained low, but as she opened her eyes to see wet window-panes and a sky of a uniform gray this was perhaps not to be wondered at.

'We are in for an intolerably tedious crossing,' Sylvester said, when he joined the rest of the party at breakfast. 'There is very little wind—which has this advantage, I suppose, that it will be better for one of our number. I have been able to procure a cabin for you, Miss Marlow, but I fear you will be heartily sick of the crossing—particularly if it continues to rain, as it shows every sign of doing.'

'Why,' demanded Edmund, 'am I not let have an egg? I do not want this bread-and-milk. Keighley says it is cat-lap.'

'Never mind!' said Phoebe, laughing. 'You may have an egg tomorrow.'

'I may not be hungry tomorrow,' said Edmund gloomily. 'I am hungry *now!*'

'Oh, dear! Are you?'

'Fair gutfoundered!' said Edmund.

Sylvester, who was glancing through a newspaper, lowered it, and said sternly: 'You never learned *that* from Keighley!'

'No,' admitted Edmund. 'Jem says it.'

'Who the devil is Jem?'

'The one with the spotty face. Don't you *know*, Uncle Vester?' said Edmund, astonished.

'One of the stable-hands?'

Edmund nodded. 'He tells me very good words. He is a friend of mine.'

'Oh, is he?' said Sylvester grimly. 'Well, unless you want to feel my hand, don't repeat them!'

Quelled, Edmund returned to his bread-and-milk. Over his head Sylvester said ruefully: 'I make his apologies, Miss Marlow. It is the fault of too old a nurse, and by far too old a tutor. I must find a younger man.'

'I don't think that would answer nearly as well as a sensible female,' said Phoebe. 'Soemone like my own dear governess, who doesn't get into a fuss for torn clothes, and likes animals, and collecting butterflies and birds' eggs, and—oh, *you* know, Tom!'

'My dear Miss Marlow, only furnish me with her name and her direction!' begged Sylvester.

'You have met her,' she reminded him. 'But I am afraid I cannot spare her to you. She and I mean to set up house together, as soon as I come of age.'

'Set up house together!' he repeated incredulously.

'Yes. *She* is going to keep house, and *I*—' She stopped suddenly, gave a little gasp, and continued defiantly: 'And I am going to write novels!'

'I see,' he said dryly, and retired to the newspaper again.

26

They went aboard the packet in a light drizzle, and with less opposition from Master Rayne than might have been expected. When it was borne in upon him that his all-powerful uncle was unable to waft him miraculously across the sea he did indeed hover on the brink of a painful scene, saying: 'No, no, no! I won't go on a ship, I won't, I *won't!*' on a rising note that threatened a storm of tears. But Sylvester said: 'I *beg* your pardon?' in such blighting accents that he flushed up to the ears, gave a gulp, and said imploringly: 'If you please, I don't want to! It will give me that dreadful pain in me pudding-house!'

'In your *what?*'

Edmund knuckled his eyes.

'I thought there was more steel in you,' said Sylvester contemptuously.

'There is steel in me!' declared Edmund, his eyes flashing. 'Keighley says I have good bottom!'

'Keighley,' said Sylvester, in a casual tone, 'is waiting for us at Dover. Miss Marlow, I must beg you won't mention to him that Edmund found he couldn't throw his heart over. He would be very much shocked.'

'I will go on that ship!' said Edmund in a gritty voice. 'We Raynes can throw our hearts over *anything!*'

His heart shyed a little at the gangway, but Sylvester said: 'Show us the way, young Rayne!' and he stumped resolutely across it.

'Edmund, you're a great gun!' Tom told him.

'Game as a pebble!' asserted Edmund.

For Phoebe the crossing was one of unalleviated boredom. Sylvester, wrapping his boat-cloak round Edmund, kept him on deck; and since there was clearly nothing for her to do, and it continued to rain, she could only retire to her cabin and meditate on a bleak future. The packet took nine hours to reach Dover, and never had nine hours seemed longer. From time to time she was visited by Tom, bringing her either refreshments, or the latest news of Edmund. He had been a little sick, Tom admitted, but nothing to cause alarm. They had found a sheltered spot on deck, and were taking it in turns to remain there with him. No, there was nothing for her to do: Edmund, having slept for a time, now seemed pretty bobbish.

Towards the end of the crossing the rain ceased, and Phoebe went on deck. She found Edmund in a boastful mood, and Sylvester civil but curt. It was the first time Sylvester had been called upon to look after his nephew, and he was devoutly hoping it would be the last.

When the packet entered the Tidal Harbour it was nearly eight o'clock, and all four travellers were tired, chilled, and not in the best of spirits. The sight of Keighley's face, however, exercised a beneficial effect on two of the party: Edmund fell upon him with a squeal of joy, and Sylvester said, with a perceptible lightening of his frown: 'Thank God! You may have him, John!'

'That's all right, your grace,' said Keighley, grinning at him. 'Now, give over, do, Master Edmund, till I have his grace's portmanteau safe!'

He was surprised to see Phoebe, and still more so when Tom hailed him; but he accepted with apparent stolidity Sylvester's explanation that he was indebted to Miss Marlow and Mr Orde for the recovery of Edmund's person. All he said was: 'Well, to be sure, your grace! And how do *you* do, sir? I see that leg's a bit stiff-like still.'

Keighley had engaged rooms for Sylvester at the King's Head. He seemed to think there would be no difficulty in securing two more, but Phoebe said that she must lose no time in rejoining Lady Ingham.

'It would be wiser to ascertain first that she is still there,' Sylvester said, his frown returning. 'May I suggest that you accompany us first to the King's Head while Keighley makes enquiries at the Ship?'

'No need to send Keighley,' Tom interposed. 'I'll go there. Take care of Phoebe till I get back, Salford!'

Phoebe was reluctant to let him go without her, for she felt it to be unfair that he should be obliged to bear the brunt of Lady Ingham's displeasure; but he only laughed, told her that he could stand a knock far better than she would ever be able to, and went off.

The King's Head was less fashionable than the Ship. Keighley thought that there was no one putting up there who was at all likely to recognize his grace. He had engaged a parlour, and was soon able to assure Phoebe that there was a good bedchamber to be had, if she should need it. Phoebe, was was sitting beside Edmund while he ate his supper, said: 'Thank you, but—oh, surely I shan't need it?'

'How can I tell?' Sylvester replied. 'It occurs to me that you have been absent above a se'ennight. I must own I shouldn't expect Lady Ingham to kick her heels in Dover for so long, but you should know her better than I.'

'I wrote to her,' she faltered. 'She must have known I should return. Or, if I could not, that Tom would.'

'Then no doubt she is awaiting his arrival,' he said.

It was his indifferent voice again; she said no more, but as Edmund finished his supper she took him away to put him to bed. A plump chambermaid came to offer her services and, as Edmund took an instant liking to her, Phoebe was able to leave him to her supervision. It seemed probable that he would detain her for a considerable period, entertaining her with his saga, for as Phoebe closed the door behind her she heard him say chattily: 'I am a great traveller, you know.'

She found, on re-entering the parlour, that Tom had returned from his mission. He was talking to Sylvester, and she saw at once that he was looking grave. She paused, an anxious question in her eyes. He smiled at her, but what he said was: 'She ain't there, Phoebe. Seems to have gone back to London.'

Her eyes went from his face to Sylvester's. Sylvester said; 'Come and sit down, Miss Marlow! It is disappointing for you not to find her here, but of no great consequence, after all. You will be with her by tomorrow evening.'

'To have gone back to London! She must be very vexed with me!'

'Nothing of that!' Tom said, in a heartening tone. 'She never had your letter. Here it is! You'd have thought the gudgeons would have forwarded it to London, but not they! Well, I never did think the Ship was half the place it sets up to be! Not since I found the boot-catcher's thumb-mark on my new top-boots!'

'Then she cannot know where I went! All these days—Oh, good God, what must she be thinking?'

'Well, she knows I was with you, so she can't have thought you'd fallen into the sea, at all events. I only hope she ain't thinking I've eloped with you!'

She pressed a hand to her temple. 'Oh, she must know better than that! Was she alarmed? Did she try to discover where we had gone, or–What did they tell you at the Ship?'

'Precious little,' confessed Tom. 'You know what it's like there! All hustle and bustle, with people arriving and leaving at all hours. What I did discover is that your grandmother had a spasm, or some such thing, and went back to London the day after we disappeared, in rather queer stirrups. They had a doctor to her, but she can't have been very bad, you know, or she couldn't have travelled.'

But Phoebe, quite appalled, had sunk into a chair, and covered her face with her hands.

'My dear Thomas,' said Sylvester, in an amused tone, 'Lady Ingham's spasms are her most cherished possession! She adopted them years ago, and must find them invaluable, for while they never interfere with her pleasures they always intervene to prevent her being obliged to engage in anything that might bore her. Depend upon it, she posted back to town to pour out her troubles to Halford.'

'I daresay that's exactly so,' agreed Tom. 'The lord knows I had the deuce of a time bringing her up to the scratch at all. It's plain enough what happened: I let go the rein, and she bolted back to the stable. No need to fall into a fit of the dismals, Phoebe.'

'How can I help but do so?' she said. 'I have been so troublesome to her—' She broke off, turning away her face. After a short pause she said more quietly: 'She left no message?'

'Well,' said Tom reluctantly, 'only about our baggage! Muker told them at the Ship that if anyone was to ask for it they were to be told it was at the coach-office.'

'Very sensible,' said Sylvester, walking over to the sideboard. 'Obviously she guessed you would be returning. Miss Marlow, I know your tastes too well to hope you will let me pour you out a glass of sherry, so ratafia it must be.'

She accepted the glass he handed her, and sat holding it. 'At the coach-office–to be called for! She thought, then–She believed me capable of deserting her?'

'More likely took a pet,' said Tom.

'Much more likely,' said Sylvester. 'Madeira or sherry, Thomas? Until we confront Lady Ingham, Miss Marlow, it must be all conjecture–and singularly profitless. I'll engage to convince her that without your aid Edmund would have been irretrievably lost to me.'

'You have said yourself, Duke, that I had nothing to do with his recovery,' she said, with a faint smile. 'It is quite true, moreover.'

'Oh, I shan't tell her that!' he promised.

'But I shall!'

'Thank the lord she didn't take our baggage back to Green Street!' said Tom somewhat hastily. 'I'm going with Keighley to collect it the first thing tomorrow morning, and I shan't be glad to be able to leave off the clothes I have on!'

'When I consider,' said Sylvester, 'that the shirt you are wearing is mine, not to mention the neckcloth, and that I could very ill spare them, I resent that remark, Thomas!'

Phoebe, recognizing an attempt to give her thoughts a more cheerful direction, dutifully laughed, and made no further reference to Lady Ingham. A waiter came to lay the covers for dinner; and a perfectly spontaneous laugh was drawn from Phoebe when Tom, as soon as the first course was laid before him, recommended his host to send it back to the kitchens at once.

'Send it back?' repeated Sylvester, taken off his guard. 'Why should I?'

'To puff off your consequence, of course. Ask the waiter if he knows who you are! And if you have any trouble, offer to buy the place. *We* are accustomed to being entertained in the first style of elegance, I can tell you!'

Fascinated, Sylvester demanded the whole history of the journey to Abbeville. He was so much amused by it that he retaliated with a graphic account of Sir Nugent Fotherby's warm welcome to himself, which he had not hitherto thought in the least diverting. Not only present anxieties were forgotten, but past quarrels too. The good understanding that had been reached at the Blue Boar seemed to have returned; and Tom, seeing how easily Phoebe and Sylvester were sliding into their old way of exchanging views on any number of subjects, was just congratulating himself on the success of his tactics when an unthinking remark destroyed all the comfort of the evening. 'Like the villain in a melodrama!' Sylvester said, wiping the mischievous smile from Phoebe's lips, bringing the colour rushing into her cheeks, transforming her from the gayest of companions into a stiff figure reminding Tom forcibly of an effigy. Constraint returned. Sylvester, after the tiniest of checks, continued smoothly enough, but the warmth had left his voice; he had withdrawn behind his film of ice, perfectly affably and quite unapproachably.

Tom gave it up in despair. He had a very fair notion how matters stood, but there seemed to be nothing he could do to promote a lasting reconciliation. He was pretty sure Sylvester had forgotten Ugolino when he had uttered that unfortunate remark, but it was useless to say that to Phoebe. She was so morbidly sensitive about her wretched romance that even the mention of a book was liable to overset her. And however little Sylvester had remembered *The Lost Heir* when he spoke of a villain, he was remembering it now.

Phoebe retired immediately she rose from the dinner-table, Sylvester merely bowing when she said that she was tired, and would bid them good-night. And when he had closed the door on her retreating form, Sylvester turned, and said, smiling: 'Well, what is to be, Thomas? Piquet? Or shall we try whether there is a chessboard to be had?'

It was really quite hopeless, thought Tom, deciding in favour of chess.

He ate a hasty breakfast next morning, and went off with Keighley to the coach-office. When he returned, he found Sylvester standing by the window and reading a newspaper, and Phoebe engaged in the homely task of wiping the egg-stains from Edmund's mouth. He said: 'I've got all our gear downstairs, Phoebe. Keighley's waiting to know which of your valises you wish him to take up to your room. And I found this as well: here you are!'

She took the letter from him quickly, recognizing Lady Ingham's writing. 'The smaller one, if you please, Tom. Edmund! where are you off to?'

'Must speak to Keighley!' Edmund said importantly, and dashed off in the direction of the stairs.

'Unfortunate Keighley!' remarked Sylvester, not looking up from the newspaper.

Tom departed in Edmund's wake, and Phoebe, her fingers slightly trembling, broke the wafer that sealed her letter, and spread open the single, crossed sheet. Sylvester lowered the newspaper, and watched her. She did not say anything when she had finished reading the letter, but folded it again, and stood holding it, a blind look in her eyes.

'Well?'

She turned her head towards the window, startled. She had never heard Sylvester speak so roughly, and wondered why he should do so.

'You may as well tell me. Your face has already informed me that it is not a pleasant missive.'

'No,' she said. 'She supposed me—when she wrote this—to have persuaded Tom to take me home. I think Muker must have encouraged her to think it, to be rid of me. She is very jealous of me. She may even have believed me to be running away with Tom. That—that was my fault.'

'Unnecessary to tell me that! You have a genius for bringing trouble upon yourself.'

She looked at him for a moment, hurt and surprise in her eyes, and then turned away, and walked over to the fire. It seemed so needlessly cruel, and so unlike him, to taunt her when he knew her to be distressed that she felt bewildered. It was certainly a taunt, but there had been no mockery in his voice, only anger. Why he should be angry, what she had done to revive his furious resentment, she could not imagine. She found it a little difficult to speak, but managed to say: 'I am afraid I have. I seem always to be tumbling into a scrape. Hoydenish, my mother-in-law was used to call me, and did her best to teach me prudence and propriety. I wish she had succeeded.'

'You are not alone in that wish!' he said savagely.

The harsh, angry voice was having its inevitable affect on her: she began to feel sick, inwardly shivering, and was obliged to sit down, digging her nails into the palms of her hands.

'You tumbled into a scrape, as you are pleased to call it, when I first made your acquaintance!' he continued. 'It would be more correct to say that you flung yourself into it, just as you flung yourself aboard that ship! If you choose to behave like a hoyden it is your own affair, but that is never enough for you! You don't scruple to embroil others in your *scrapes!* Thomas has been a victim, *I* have been one—my God, have I not!—and now it is your grandmother! Does she cast you off? Do you think yourself hardly used? You have no one but yourself to thank for the ills you've brought on your own head!'

She listened to this tirade, rigid with shock, scarcely able to believe that it was Sylvester and not a stranger who hurled these bitter accusations at her. The thought flitted across her brain that he was deliberately feeding his wrath, but it was overborne by her own anger, which leaped from a tiny spark to a blaze.

He said suddenly, before she could speak: 'No—no! It's of no use! Sparrow, Sparrow!'

She hardly heard him. She said in a voice husky with passion: 'I have one other person to thank! It is yourself, my lord Duke! It was your arrogance that caused me to make you the model for my villain! But for you I should never have run away from my home! But for you no one need have known I was the author of that book! But for you I should not have *flung* myself aboard that schooner! *You* are the cause of every ill that has befallen me! You say I ill-used you: if I did you are wonderfully revenged, for you have ruined *me!*'

To her astonishment, and, indeed, indignation, he gave the oddest laugh.

As she glared at him he said in the strangest voice she had yet heard: 'Have I? Well—if that's so, I will make reparation! Will you do me the honour, Miss Marlow, of accepting my hand in marriage?'

Thus Sylvester, an accomplished flirt, making his first proposal.

It never occurred to Phoebe that he had shaken himself off his balance, and was as self-conscious as a callow youth just out of school. Still less did it occur to her that the laugh and the exaggerated formality of his offer sprang from embarrassment. He was famed for his polished address; she had never, until this day, seen him lose his mastery over himself. She believed him to be mocking her, and started up from her chair, exclaiming: 'How *dare* you?'

Sylvester, burningly aware of his own clumsiness, lost no time in making bad worse. 'I beg your pardon! you mistake. I had no intention—Phoebe, it was out before I well knew what I was saying! I never meant to ask you to marry me—I was determined I would not! But—' He broke off, realizing into what quagmires his attempts to explain himself were leading him.

'That I *do* believe!' she said hotly. 'You have been so obliging as to tell me what you think of me, and I believe that too! You came to Austerby to look me over, as though I had been a filly, and decided I was not up to your weight! *Didn't* you?'

'What *next* will you say?' he demanded, an involuntary laugh shaking him.

'*Didn't* you?'

'Yes. But have you forgotten how you behaved? How could I know what you were when you tried only to disgust me? It wasn't until later—'

'To be sure!' she said scathingly. '*Later*, when I first made you a victim, embroiling you in my improper flight from Austerby, and next wounded your pride as I daresay it was never wounded before, *then* you began to think I was just the wife that would suit you! The fervent offer which you have been so flattering as to make to me springs, naturally, from the folly that led me to thrust myself into your affairs, and so make it necessary for you to undertake a journey under circumstances so much beneath your dignity as to be posively degrading! How green of me not to have known immediately how it would be! You must forgive me! Had I dreamt that my lack of conduct would attach you to me I would have assumed the manners of a pattern of propriety whenever you came within sight of me! You would then have been spared the mortification of having your suit rejected, and I should have been spared an intolerable insult!'

'There was no insult,' he said, very pale. 'If I phrased it—if it sounded to you as though I meant to insult you, believe that it was not so! What I said to you before, I said because the crazy things you do convinced me you were *not* the wife that would suit me! I wanted never to see you again after that night at the Castlereaghs'—I *thought* so, but it wasn't so, because when I did see you again—I was overjoyed.'

Not a speech worthy of a man who made love charmingly, but Sylvester had never before tried to make love to a lady seething with rage and contempt.

'Were you indeed?' said Phoebe. 'But you soon recovered, didn't you?'

Nettled, he retorted: 'No, I only *tried* to! Stop ripping up at me, you little shrew!'

'Phoebe, don't you mean to change your dress?' said Tom, entering the room at this most inauspicious moment. 'Keighley took your valise up—' He broke off, dismayed, and stammered: 'Oh, I b-beg pardon! I didn't know—I'll go!'

'Go? Why?' Phoebe said brightly. 'Yes, indeed I mean to change my dress, and will do so immediately!'

Tom held the door for her, thinking that if only Sylvester, interrupted in the middle of an obvious scene, would drop his guard, grant him an opening, he could tell him just how to handle her. He shut the door, and turned.

'Good God, Thomas! This sartorial magnificence! Are you trying to put me to the blush?' said Sylvester quizzingly.

27

They left Dover just after eleven o'clock, by which time Miss Marlow had quarrelled with both her escorts. Emerging from her bedchamber in the guise of a haughty young lady of fashion she encountered Tom, and instantly asked him whether he had recovered the money he had left in his portmanteau. Upon being reassured on this point she asked him if he would hire a chaise for their conveyance to London. 'No,' said Tom, never one to mince his words. 'I've got a better use for my blunt!'

'I will repay you, I promise you!' she urged.

'Much obliged! When?' said Tom brutally.

'Grandmama—'

'Mighty poor security! No, I thank you!'

'If she will not do it I'll sell my pearls!' she declared.

'That *would* make me cut a fine figure, wouldn't it?'

'Tom, I don't wish to travel at Salford's expense!' she blurted out.

'That's easily settled. Sell your pearls, and pay him!'

She said stiffly: 'If you won't do what I particularly wish, will you at least request the Duke to tell you how much money he has expended on my behalf since we left Abbeville?'

'When I make a cake of myself it will be on my own account, and not on yours, Miss Woolly-crown!' said Tom.

Two vehicles had been provided for the journey. One was a hired post-chaise, the other Sylvester's own phaeton, and to each was harnessed a team of four horses. They were job horses, but they had been chosen by Keighley, and therefore, as Master Rayne pointed out to his uncle, prime cattle. When Tom brought his haughty charge out of the inn he found Master Rayne seated already in the phaeton, and Sylvester standing beside it, drawing on his gloves. He went up to him, exclaiming: 'Are you driving yourself all the way to London, Salford?'

'I am,' replied Sylvester. 'I would offer to take you with me, but I'm afraid Keighley must have that seat.'

'Yes, of course, but you don't mean to take Edmund too, do you? Had you not better let him come with us in the chaise?'

'My dear Thomas, my only reason for telling Keighley to bring my phaeton to Dover was to save that brat as much travel-sickness as I could! He is invariably sick in closed carriages, and never in open ones. Will you accompany Miss Marlow? I hope she will not find the journey too fatiguing: we are a little late in starting, but we should reach town in time for dinner.'

Tom, though strongly of the opinion that Sylvester, in his present humour, would be happy to part with his nephew on any terms at the end of the first stage, raised no further demur, but went back to hand Phoebe up into the chaise.

For the first five miles not a word was uttered within this vehicle, but at Lydden, Phoebe (recovering a trifle, in her faithful friend's opinion, from the sullens) asked Tom where he meant to put up in London.

'At Salford's house. He has invited me to spend a few days there. As long as I choose, in fact.'

'Good gracious!' said Phoebe. 'What an honour for you! No wonder you were so unwilling to oblige me! I must be *quite* beneath your touch!'

'You'll precious soon wish you were beneath my *touch*, if you don't take care, my girl!' said Tom. 'If you've any more pretty morsels of wit under your tongue, reserve 'em for Salford! He's far too well bred to give you your deserts: *I* ain't!'

Silence reigned for the next mile. 'Tom,' said Phoebe, in a small voice. 'Well?'

'I didn't mean to say that. It was a *horrid* thing to say! I beg your pardon.'

He took her hand, and gave it a squeeze. 'Pea-goose! What's the matter?' He waited for a moment. 'I know I walked smash into a turn-up between you and Salford. What are you trying to do? Break your own silly neck?'

She withdrew her hand. 'Excuse me, Tom, if you please! It would be quite improper in me to repeat what passed between us. Pray say no more!'

'Very well,' said Tom. 'But don't *you* choke yourself with pride, Phoebe!'

At Sittingbourne a halt was called, and the travellers partook of refreshment at the Rose. When they came out of the inn again, and Tom was about to hand Phoebe into the chaise, Sylvester said: 'Do you care to tool the phaeton for a stage or two, Thomas?'

'By Jove, yes!–if you think I shan't overturn it!' Tom replied, with a rueful grin. 'And if—' he hesitated, glancing at Phoebe.

'Do just as you wish!' she replied at once. 'I can very well finish the journey in one of the Accommodation coaches!'

Sylvester turned, and strode towards the phaeton. 'Get in!' said Tom curtly. He added, as he took his seat beside Phoebe: 'That's the first time I've ever been glad you are *not* my sister!'

She returned no answer. Scarcely half a dozen sentences were exchanged during the remainder of the journey; but although Phoebe pretended to be asleep for the greater part of the way sleep was never farther from her, so torn was she by conflicting emotions. Beside her Tom sat gazing out of the window, wondering what Sylvester could have said to have made her so angry; and wishing that there was something he could do for Sylvester, even if it were no more than relieving him of Edmund's company.

But Keighley was shielding Sylvester from Edmund. 'Give over plaguing his grace, Master Edmund!' said Keighley, 'Now, that's quite enough, Master Edmund! There's no good to be got out of flying into one of your tantrums!' said Keighley, thinking what a pity it was that he could no longer say the same to Sylvester.

It was after six when the carriages drew up in Berkeley Square, before Salford House. 'Why do we stop here?' demanded Phoebe.

'To set down my portmanteau, of course,' replied Tom, opening the chaise-door. 'Also, I daresay, to allow Salford to take leave of you! Try for a little civility!'

He climbed down from the chaise as he spoke. The doors of the great house were already flung open, and several persons emerged. 'Reeth, Reeth,

I've been to France!' shouted Edmund, dashing up the steps. 'Where's Button? She'll be *'stonished* when she hears the things I've done! Oh, Button, I have *needed* you! Did you miss me, Button? Phoebe doesn't do things the right way. Do you know, I had to *tell* her, Button?'

'Repellent brat!' remarked Sylvester. 'Reeth, Mr Orde is staying with me for a few days: take care of him for me! Will you go in with him, Thomas? I'll escort Miss Marlow to Green Street.'

This scheme seemed so fraught with disaster that Tom could not help saying, in an urgent undervoice: 'I wouldn't, Salford! Leave her to come about!'

'Go in with Reeth, Thomas: I shall be with you presently,' replied Sylvester, as though he had not heard this advice.

He mounted into the chaise, and almost before the door was shut grasped Phoebe's hands, saying: 'Phoebe, you must listen to me! I know I made wretched work of it: I can't explain it to you now—there is too little time—but I won't let you go like this! You can't think I would ask you to marry me in *jest*, or to insult you!'

'You have told me already that you never meant to ask me,' she replied, trying to pull her hands away. 'I fancy you will be truly thankful, when you have recovered from the mortification of having your suit rejected, that I didn't snap at so brilliant an offer. Will you please to release me, my lord Duke?'

'But I *love* you!' he said, gripping her hands rather more tightly.

'You are very obliging, but I cannot return your affection, sir.'

'I'll make you!' he promised.

'Oh, no, you will not!' returned Phoebe, thoroughly ruffled. '*Will* you let me go? If you have no more conduct than to behave in this fashion in the middle of the street, I have! Make me love you, indeed! If I were not so angry, I could laugh to think how exactly I hit him off when I wrote of Ugolino that, try as he might to appear conciliating, he could not open his lips without betraying his arrogance!'

'Do you call it arrogance when I tell you that I love you, and wish to make you my wife?' he demanded.

'Yes, and folly too! You have never suffered a rebuff, have you, Duke? When any female has shown herself not to be disposed to like you it has been a sport with you to *make* her like you very much too well, I daresay, for her comfort. You even lay bets that where others have failed *you* will succeed!'

'What nonsense is this?' he exclaimed. '*I?*'

'Yes, *you!* Was there not an heiress who was called the *Citadel?* Or are your conquests too numerous to be remembered by you?'

'I remember,' he said grimly. 'You had that from Ianthe, did you? Did she also tell you that it was a piece of funning between my brother and me—discreditable, if you like, but never meant to go beyond the pair of us?'

'In fact, you *didn't* storm the Citadel, Duke?'

'For God's sake, Phoebe, must you throw in my face the follies I committed when I was a boy?'

'I would not if you had outgrown that conceit! But you haven't! Why did you make yourself so agreeable to me? You must have had a great deal of practice, I think, for you did it beautifully! If I had not known what your object was I am sure you must have succeeded in it! But I did know! Tom told you that I ran away from Austerby because the thought of becoming your wife was repugnant to me, and you were so piqued that you determined I should fall in love with you, and afterwards be sorry!'

He had so entirely forgotten that pettish resolve that he was thunder-struck.

'Well?' said Phoebe, watching him. 'Can you deny it Duke?'

He released her hands at last, and uttered his crowning blunder.

'No. I *was* piqued, I *did*, in a fit of—conceit—arrogance—anything you please to call it!—form some such contemptible scheme. I beg you to believe it was of very short duration!'

'I *don't* believe it!' declared Phoebe.

The chaise turned into Green Street. Miss Marlow, having discharged much of the wrath she had been obliged to keep bottled up for so many painful hours, had begun to feel very low. The Creature beside her, not content with humiliating her in public, and regarding all the disagreeable experiences she had undergone on his behalf with indifference and ingratitude, had stormed at her, and insulted her, and now, when any but a monster of cold-hearted self-consequence must have known how tired and miserable she was, and how desperately in need of reassurance, he sat silent. Perhaps he needed encouragement? She gave it him. 'Having become acquainted with your other flames, Duke—all diamonds of the first water!—I should have to be uncommonly green to believe that you preferred me! You asked me to marry you because you are so determined not to be obliged to own yourself worsted that you will go to any lengths to achieve your object!'

Now or never was the time for Sylvester to retrieve his character! He said very levelly: 'You need say no more, Miss Marlow. It would be useless, I realize, for me to attempt to answer you.'

'If you wish to know what I think of you,' said Phoebe, in a shaking voice, 'it is that you are a great deal *worse* than Count Ugolino!'

He was silent. Well! now she knew how right she had been. He was not in the least in love with her, and very happy she was to know it. All she wanted was a suitable retreat, such as a lumber-room, or a coal-cellar, in which to enjoy her happiness to the full.

The chaise drew to a standstill, and Sylvester got out, and with his own hands let down the steps. Such condescension! Pulling herself together, Phoebe alighted, and said with great dignity: 'I must thank you, Duke, for having been so kind as to have brought me back to England. In case we should not meet again, I should like, before we say goodbye, to assure you that I am not unmindful of what I owe you, and that I wish you extremely happy.'

This very beautiful speech might just as well have remained unspoken, for all the heed he paid to it. He said: 'I am coming in with you,' and sounded the knocker.

'I beg you most earnestly not to do so!' she said, with passionate sincerity.

He took her hand in his. 'Miss Marlow, let me do this one thing for you! I know Lady Ingham, and what her temper is. I promise you she shall not be angry with you, if only I may see her first.'

'You are very good, Duke, but I assure you I need no intervention!' she said proudly.

The door opened. Horwich ejaculated: '*Miss Phoebe!*' He then encountered a most unnerving stare from Sylvester, and bowed, and stammered: 'Your g-grace!'

'Have Miss Marlow's baggage carried into the house!' said Sylvester coldly, and turned again to Phoebe. It was clearly useless to persist in argument; so, knowing that Horwich was listening to every word he said, he held out his hand, and said: 'I will leave you now, Miss Marlow. I can never be sufficiently grateful to you for what you have done. Will you present my compliments to Lady Ingham, and inform her that I hope to call upon her shortly, when I shall tell her–for I know well that *you* will not!–how deeply indepted to you I am? Goodbye! God bless you!' He bent, and kissed her hand, while Horwich, consumed with curiosity, goggled at him.

To Phoebe, long past being able to recognize what his intention must be, this speech was the last straw. She managed to say: 'Certainly! I mean–you exaggerate, Duke! Goodbye!' and then hurried into the house.

'When the baggage has been taken off, drive back to Salford House!' Sylvester told the chief postilion. 'You will be paid there. I am going to walk.'

When Reeth presently opened the doors to his master he was a good deal shocked. He had rather suspected that something was wrong, and he perceived now that something was very wrong indeed. He had seen that look on his grace's face once before. It wouldn't do to say anything about it, but at least he could tell him something that would do him good to hear. As he helped Sylvester out of his driving-coat, he said: 'I didn't have time to tell your grace before, but—'

'Reeth, what the devil are you doing here?' demanded Sylvester, as though he had only just become aware of him. 'Good God, you don't mean to say my mother is here?'

'In her own sitting-room, your grace, waiting for you to come in,' beamed Reeth. 'And stood the journey very well, I am happy to be able to assure your grace.'

'I'll go to her at once!' Sylvester said, walking quickly to the great stair.

She was alone, seated on one side of the fireplace. She looked up as Sylvester came in, and smiled mischievously.

'Mama!'

'Sylvester! Now, I won't be scolded! You are to tell me that you are delighted to find me here, if you please!'

'I don't have to tell you that,' he said, bending over her. 'But to have set out without me—! I ought never to have written to tell you what had happened! I did so only because I was afraid you might hear of it from some other source. My dear, have you been so anxious?'

'Not a bit! I knew you would bring him back safely. But it was a little too much to expect me to stay at Chance when such stirring events were taking place in London. Now, sit down and tell me all about it! Edmund's confidences have given rise to the wildest conjectures in my mind, and that delightful boy you have brought home with you thinks that perhaps I shall like to hear the story better from your lips. My dear, who is he?'

He had turned aside to pull forward a chair, and as he seated himself the Duchess saw him for the first time in the full light of the candles burning near her chair. Like Reeth, she suffered a shock; like Reeth, she recognized the look on Sylvester's face. He had worn it for many months after Harry's death; and she had prayed she might never see it again. She was obliged to clasp her hands together in her lap, so urgent was her impulse to stretch them out to him.

'Thomas Orde,' he replied, smiling, as it seemed to her, with an effort. 'A nice lad, isn't he? I've invited him to stay here for as long as he cares to: his father thinks it time he acquired a little town bronze.' He hesitated, and then said: 'I daresay he may have told you–or Edmund has–that he is a friend of Miss Marlow's. An adopted brother, as it were.'

'Oh, Edmund was very full of *Tom* and *Phoebe!* But how they came to be mixed up in that imbroglio I can't imagine! Phoebe seems to have been very kind to Edmund.'

'Most kind. It is rather a long story, Mama.'

'And you are tired, and would rather tell it to me presently. I won't tease you, then. But tell me about Phoebe! You know I have a particular interest in her. To own the truth, it was to see her that I came to London.'

He looked up quickly. 'To see her? I don't understand, Mama! Why should you—?'

'Well, Louisa wrote to tell me that everyone believed her to be the author of that absurd novel, and that she was having a very unhappy time, poor child. I hoped I might be able to put a stop to such nonsense, but I reached London only to discover that Lady Ingham had taken her to Paris. I can't think why she shouldn't have written to me, for she must have known I would help Verena's daughter.'

'It's too late!' he said. '*I* could have scotched the scandal! Instead—' He broke off, and looked keenly at her. 'I can't recall. Was my busy aunt Louisa at the Castlereaghs' ball?'

'Yes, dearest.'

'I see.' He got up jerkily, and moved to the fireplace, standing with his head turned a little away from the Duchess. 'I am sure she told you what happened there.'

'An unfortunate affair,' said the Duchess calmly. 'You were naturally very angry.'

'There was no excuse for what I did. I knew her dread of—I can see her face now!'

'What is she like, Sylvester?' She waited, and then prompted: 'Is she pretty?'

He shook his head. 'No. Not a beauty, Mama. When she is animated, I believe you would consider her taking.'

'I collect, from all I have heard, that she is unusual?'

'Oh, yes, she's unusual!' he said bitterly. 'She blurts out whatever may come into her head; she tumbles from one outrageous escapade into another; she's happier grooming horses and hobnobbing with stable-hands than going to parties; she's impertinent; you daren't catch her eye for fear she should start to giggle; she hasn't any accomplishments; I never saw anyone with less dignity; she's abominable, and damnably hot at hand, frank to a fault, and—a *darling!*'

'Should I like her, Sylvester?' said the Duchess her eyes on his profile.

'I don't know,' he said, a suggestion of impatience in his voice. 'I daresay—I hope so—but you might not. How can I possibly tell? It's of no consequence: she won't have me.' He paused and then said, as though the words were wrung out of him: 'O God, Mama, I've made such a mull of it! What am I to *do?*'

28

After a troubled night, during which she was haunted, waking or dreaming, by all the appalling events of the previous day, which had culminated in a shattering scene with Lady Ingham, Phoebe awoke to find the second housemaid pulling back the blinds, and learning from her that the letter lying on her breakfast-tray had been brought round by hand from Salford House not ten minutes earlier. The housemaid was naturally agog with curiosity, but any expectation she had of being made the recipient of an interesting confidence faded before the seeming apathy with which Miss Phoebe greeted her disclosure. All Miss Phoebe wanted was a cup of tea; and the housemaid, after lingering with diminishing hope for a few minutes, left her sitting up in bed, and sipping this restorative.

Once alone, Phoebe snatched up the letter, and tore it open. She looked first at the signature. *Elizabeth Salford* was what met her eyes, and drew from her a gasp of fright.

But there was nothing in the letter to make her tremble. It was quite short, and it contained no hint of menace. The Duchess wished very much not only to make the acquaintance of a loved friend's daughter, but also to thank her for the care she had taken of her grandson. She hoped that Phoebe would be able, perhaps, to visit her that day, at noon, when she would be quite alone, and they could talk without fear of interruption.

Rather a gratifying letter for a modest damsel to receive, one would have supposed, but the expression on Phoebe's face might have led an observer to conclude that she was reading a tale of horror. Having perused it three times, and failing to detect in it any hidden threat, Phoebe fixed her attention on the words: *I shall be quite alone*, and carefully considered them. If they were meant to convey a message it was hard to see how this could be anything but one of reassurance; but if this were so, Sylvester must have told his mother—*what?*

Thrusting back the bedclothes Phoebe scrambled out of bed and into her dressing-gown, and pattered down the stairs to her grandmother's room. She found the afflicted Dowager alone, and held out the letter to her, asking her in a tense voice to read it.

The Dowager had viewed her unceremonious entrance with disfavour, and she at once said in feeble accents: 'Oh, heaven! what now?' But this ejaculation was not wholly devoid of hope, since she too had been told whence had come Miss Phoebe's letter. Poor Lady Ingham had slept quite as badly as her granddaughter, for she had had much to puzzle her. At first determined to send Phoebe packing back to Somerset, she had been considerably mollified by the interesting intelligence conveyed to her (as Sylvester had known it would be) by Horwich. She had thought it promising, but further reflection had sent her spirits down again: whatever might be Sylvester's sentiments, Phoebe bore none of the appearance of a young female who had either received, or expected to receive, a flattering offer for her hand. Hope reared its head again when a letter from Salford House was thrust upon her; like Phoebe, she looked first at the signature, and was at once dashed down. 'Elizabeth!' she exclaimed, in a flattened voice. 'Extraordinary! She must have come on the child's account, I suppose. I only trust it may not be the death of her!'

Phoebe watched her anxiously while she mastered the contents of the letter, and when it was given back to her said imploringly: 'What must I do, ma'am?'

The Dowager did not answer for a moment. There was food for deep thought in the Duchess's letter. She gazed inscrutably before her, and the question had to be repeated before she said, with a slight start: 'Do? You will do as you are bid, of course! A very pretty letter the Duchess has writ you, and why she should have done so—but she hasn't, one must assume, read that abominable book!'

'She has read it, ma'am,' Phoebe said. 'It was she who gave it to Salford. He told me so himself.'

'Then he cannot have told her who wrote it,' said the Dowager. 'That you may depend on, for she dotes on Sylvester! If only she could be persuaded to take you up—But someone is bound to tell her!'

'Grandmama, I must tell her myself!' Phoebe said.

The Dowager was inclined to agree with her, but the dimming of a future which had seemed to become suddenly so much brighter vexed her so much that she said crossly: 'You must do as you please! *I* cannot advise you! And I beg you won't ask me to accompany you to Salford House, for I am quite unequal to any exertion! You may have the landaulet, and, for heaven's sake, Phoebe, try at least to *appear* the thing! You must wear the fawn-coloured silk, and the pink—no, it will make you look hideously sallow! It will have to be the straw with the brown ribands.'

Thus arrayed, Miss Marlow, shortly before noon, stepped into the landaulet, as pale as if it had been a tumbrel and her destination the gallows.

Such was the state of her mind that she would not have been surprised, on arrival at Salford House, to have been confronted by a host of Raynes, all pointing fingers of condemnation at her. But the only persons immediately visible were servants, who seemed, with the exception of the butler, whose aspect was benevolent, to be perfectly uninterested. It was well for her peace of mind that she did not suspect that every member of the household who had the slightest business in the hall had contrived to be there to get a glimpse of her. Such an array of footmen seemed rather excessive, not to say pompous, but if that was the way Sylvester chose to run his house it was quite his own affair.

The benevolent butler conducted her up one pair of stairs. Her heart was thumping hard, and she felt unusually breathless, both of which disagreeable symptoms would have been much aggravated had she known how many interested persons were watching from hidden points of vantage every step of her progress. No one could have told whence had sprung the news that his grace had chosen a leg-shackle at last, and was finding his path proverbially rough; but everyone knew it, from the agent-in-chief down to the humblest kitchen-porter; and an amazing number of these persons contrived to be spectators of Miss Marlow's arrival. Most of them were disappointed in her; but Miss Penistone and Button found nothing amiss, one of these ladies being sentimentally disposed to think any damsel of dear Sylvester's choice a paragon, and the other regarding her in the light of a Being sent from on high to preserve her darling from death by shipwreck, surfeit, neglect, or any other of the disasters which might have been expected to strike down an infant of tender years taken to outlandish parts without his nurse.

Phoebe heard her name announced, and stepped across the threshold of the Duchess's drawing-room. The door closed behind her, but instead of walking forward she stood rooted to the ground, staring across the room at her hostess. A look of naïve surprise was in her face, and she so far forgot herself as to utter an involuntary: 'Oh—!'

No one had ever told her how pronounced was the resemblance between Sylvester and his mother. At first glance it was startling. At the second one perceived that the Duchess had warmer eyes than Sylvester, and a kinder curve to her lips.

Before Phoebe had assimilated these subtle differences an amused laugh escaped the Duchess, and she said: 'Yes, Sylvester has his eyebrows from me, poor boy!'

'Oh, I *beg* your pardon, ma'am!' Phoebe stammered, much confused.

'Come and let me look at you!' invited the Duchess. 'I daresay your grandmother may have told you that I have a stupid complaint that won't let me get out of my chair.'

Phoebe stayed where she was, clasping both hands tightly on her reticule. 'Ma'am—I am very much obliged to your grace for having—honoured me with this invitation—but I must not accept your hospitality without telling you—that it was I who wrote—that dreadful book!'

'Oh, you *do* look like your mother!' exclaimed the Duchess. 'Yes, I know you wrote it, which is why I was so desirous of making your acquaintance. Come and give me a kiss! I kissed you in your cradle, but you can't remember *that!*'

Thus adjured, Phoebe approached her chair, and bent to plant a shy kiss on the Duchess's cheek. But the Duchess not only returned this chaste salute warmly but said: 'You poor, foolish child! Now tell me all about it!'

To hear herself addressed so caressingly was a novel experience. Miss Battery was gruff, Mrs Orde matter-of-fact, and Lady Ingham astringent, and these were the three ladies who had Phoebe's interests most to heart. She had never met with tenderness, and its effect was to make her tumble down on her knees beside the Duchess's chair, and burst into tears. Such conduct would have earned her a sharp reproof from Lady Ingham, but the Duchess seemed to think well of it, since she recommended her unconventional guest to enjoy a comfortable cry, removed her hat, and patted her soothingly.

From the moment of discovering that Sylvester had lost his heart to Phoebe the Duchess had been determined to like her, and to put out of her mind all thought of the book she had written; but she had expected to find it hard to do either of these things. It was one thing to nourish private doubts about her son: quite another to find him depicted as a villainous character in a novel that had taken the ton by storm. But so sooner did she see Phoebe and read the contrition in her frank eyes than her heart melted. It rejoiced too, for although Sylvester had said that Phoebe was not beautiful she had not expected to find her a thin slip of a girl, with a brown complexion and nothing to recommend her but a pair of speaking gray eyes. If Sylvester, who knew his own worth, and had coolly made out a list of the qualities he considered indispensable in his bride, had decided that only this girl would satisfy him, he had fallen more deeply in love than his mother had thought possible. She could have laughed aloud, remembering all he had once said to her, for there seemed to her to be no points of resemblance between Phoebe and that mythical wife he had described. She thought there would be some lively fights if he married Phoebe: certainly none of that calm, rather bloodless propriety which he had once considered to be the foundation of a successful alliance.

Well, the marriage might prove a failure, but the Duchess, who had conceived a profound dislike of five unknown but eligible ladies of quality, was much inclined to think that it might as easily turn out to be the making of both parties to it; and by the time the whole history of *The Lost Heir* had been sobbed into her lap, and a passionate apology offered to her, she was able to assure the penitent author, with perfect sincerity, that on the whole she was glad the book had been published, since she thought it had done

Sylvester a great deal of good. 'And as for Count Ugolino's shocking conduct towards his nephew, that, my dear, is the least objectionable part of it,' she said. 'For as soon as you embroiled him in his dastardly plots, you know, all resemblance to Sylvester vanished. And Maximilian, I am afraid, is quite unlike my naughty grandson! From all Mr Orde told me I feel that Edmund would have very speedily put Ugolino in his place!'

Phoebe could not help giving a tiny chuckle, but she said: 'I *promise* you it was coincidence, ma'am, but *he*–the Duke–did not think so.'

'Oh, he knew it was, whatever he may have said! Nor did he care a button for it. Ianthe has been spreading far worse stories about him (because more credible) for years, and he has treated them with perfect indifference. What he cared for was the sketch you drew of him when you first brought Ugolino on to your stage. It is not too much to say that that almost stunned him. Oh, don't hang your head! It was a salutary lesson to him, I believe. You see, my dear, I have lately been a little worried about Sylvester, suspecting that he had become–to use your word for him–arrogant. Perhaps you will feel that I should have noticed it long ago, but he never shows that side of himself to me, and I don't now go into company, so that I've had no opportunity to see what he is to others. I am really grateful to you for telling me what no one else has liked to mention!'

'Oh, no, no!' Phoebe said quickly. 'It was a caricature, ma'am! His manners are always those of a well-bred man, and there is no appearance in him of self-consequence. It was very wrong of me: he had given me no real cause! It was only—'

'Go on!' the Duchess said encouragingly. 'Don't be afraid to tell me! I might imagine worse that the truth, you know, if you are not open with me.'

'It–it seemed to me, ma'am, that he was polite not to honour others but himself!' Phoebe blurted out. 'And that the flattery he receives he–he doesn't notice because he takes it for granted–his consequence being so large. I don't know why it should have vexed me so. If he had seemed to hold others cheap I should only have been diverted, and that would have been a much worse fault in him. I think–it is his indifference that makes me so often want to hit him!'

The Duchess laughed. 'Ah, yes, I understand that! Tell me: he's not above being pleased?'

'No, ma'am, never!' Phoebe assured her. 'He is always affable in company: not a bit stiff! Only–I don't know how to express it–*aloof*, I think. Oh, I didn't mean to distress you! Pray, pray, forgive me!'

The Duchess's smile went a little awry. 'You haven't distressed me. It distressed me only to know that Sylvester was still living in some desolate Polar region–but it was only for a moment! I don't think he *is* living there any longer.'

'His brother, ma'am?' Phoebe ventured to ask, looking shyly up into her face.

The Duchess nodded. 'His twin-brother. They were not alike, but the bond between them was so strong that nothing ever loosened it, not even Harry's marriage. When Harry died–Sylvester went away. I don't mean bodily–ah, you understand, don't you? I might have been sure you would, for I know you to have a very discerning eye. Sylvester has a deep reserve. He will not have his wounds touched, and *that* wound—' She broke off, and then said, after a little pause: 'Well, he kept everyone at a distance for so long that I believe it became, as it were, an engrained habit, and is why he gave you the feeling that he was aloof–which exactly describes him, I must tell you!' She smiled at Phoebe, and took her hand. 'As for his indifferent air, my dear, I know it well—I have been acquainted with it for many years, and not only in Sylvester! It springs, as you so correctly suppose, from pride. *That* is an inherited vice! All the Raynes have it, and Sylvester to a marked degree. It is inborn, and it wasn't diminished by his succeeding, when he was much too young, to his father's dignities. I always did think that the worst thing that could have befallen him, but comforted myself with the thought that Lord William Rayne—he is Sylvester's uncle, and was guardian to both my sons for the two years that were left of their minority—that William would quickly depress any top-loftiness in Sylvester. But unfortunately William, though the kindest man alive, not only holds himself very much up, but is also convinced that the Head of the House of Rayne is a far more august personage than the Head of the House of Hanover! I have the greatest affection for him, but he is what I expect you would call gothic! He tells me, for instance, that society has become a mingle-mangle, and that too many men of birth nowadays don't keep *a proper distance*. He would have given Sylvester a thundering scold for showing incivility to the humblest of his dependants, but I am very sure that he taught him that meticulous politeness was what he owed to his own consequence: *noblesse oblige*, in fact. So, what with William telling him never to forget how exalted he was, and far too many people looking up to him as their liege-lord, I am afraid Sylvester became imbued with some very improper notions, my dear! And, to be candid with you, I don't think he will ever lose them. His wife, if he loved her, could do much to *improve* him, but she won't alter his whole character.'

'No, of course not, ma'am. I mean—'

'Which, in some ways, is admirable,' continued the Duchess, smiling a little at this embarrassed interjection, but paying no other heed to it. 'And the odd thing is that some of his best qualities spring directly from his pride! It would never occur to Sylvester that anyone could dispute his hereditary right of lordship, but I can assure you that it would never occur to him either to neglect the least one of the duties, however irksome, that attach to his position.' She paused, and then said: 'The flaw is that his care for his people doesn't come from his heart. It was bred into him, he accepts it as his inescapable duty, but he hasn't the love of humanity that inspires philanthropists, you know. Towards all but the very few people he loves I fear he will always be largely indifferent. However, for those few there's nothing he won't do, from the high heroical to such tedious things as giving up far too much of his time to the entertainment of an invalid mother!'

Phoebe said, with a glowing look: 'He could never think that tedious, I am persuaded, ma'am!'

'Good gracious, of all the boring things to be obliged to do it must surely be the worst! I made up my mind not to permit him to trouble about me, too, but—you may have noticed it!—Sylvester is determined to have his own way, and never more so than when he is convinced he is acting for one's good.'

'I have frequently thought him—a trifle high-handed, ma'am,' said Phoebe, her eye kindling at certain memories.

'Yes, I'm sure you have. Harry used to call him The Dook, mocking his overbearing ways! The worst of it is that it's so hard to get the better of him! He doesn't *order* one to do things: he merely makes it impossible for one to do anything else. Some idiotish doctor once convinced him it would cure me to take the hot bath, and he got me to Bath entirely against my will, and without ever mentioning the name of the horrid place. The shifts he was put to! I forgave him only because he had taken so much trouble over the iniquitous affair! His wife will have much to bear, I daresay, but she will never find him thoughtless where *her* well-being is concerned.'

Phoebe said, flushing: 'Ma'am–you mistake! I–he—'

'Has he put himself beyond forgiveness?' enquired the Duchess quizzically. 'He certainly told me he had, but I hoped he was exaggerating.'

'He doesn't wish to marry me, ma'am. Not in his heart!' Phoebe said. 'He only wished to make me sorry I had run away from him, and fall in love with him when it was too late. He couldn't bear to be beaten, and proposed to me quite against his will–he told me so himself!–and then, I think, he was too proud to draw back.'

'Really, I am quite ashamed of him!' exclaimed the Duchess. 'He told me he had made a *mull* of it, and that, I see, is much less than the truth! I don't wonder you gave him a set-down, but I am delighted to learn that all his famous address deserted him when he proposed to you! In my experience a man rarely makes graceful speeches when he is very much in earnest, be he never so accomplished a flirt!'

'But he *doesn't* want to marry me, ma'am!' averred Phoebe, sniffing into a damp handkerchief. 'He told me he did, but when I said I didn't believe him–he said he saw it was useless to argue with me!'

'Good heavens, what a simpleton!'

'And then I said he was *w-worse* than Ugolino, and he didn't s-say anything at all!' disclosed Phoebe tragically.

'That settles it!' the Duchess declared, only the faintest of tremors in her voice. 'I wash my hands of such a ninny! After having been given all this encouragement, what does he do but come home in flat despair, saying you won't listen to him? He even asked me what he should do! I am sure it was for the first time in his life!'

'F-flat despair?' echoed Phoebe, between hope and disbelief. 'Oh, *no!*'

'I assure you! And very disagreeable it made him, too. He brought Mr Orde up to take tea with me after dinner, and even the tale of Sir Nugent and the button failed to drag more than a faint smile from him!'

'He–he is *mortified*, perhaps–oh, I know he is! But he doesn't even *like* me, ma'am! If you had heard the things he said to me! And then–the very next instant–proposed to me!'

'He is clearly unhinging. I daresay you had no intention of reducing him to this sad state, but I feel you ought, in common charity, to allow him at least to explain himself. Very likely it would settle his mind, and it won't do for Salford to become addle-brained, you know! Do but consider the consternation of the Family, my dear!'

'Oh, ma'am—!' protested Phoebe, half laughing.

'As for his not liking you,' continued the Duchess, 'I don't know how that may be, but I can't recall that he ever before described any girl to me as *a darling!*'

Phoebe stared at her incredulously. She tried to speak, but only succeeded in uttering a choking sound.

'By this time,' said the Duchess, stretching out her hand to the embroidered bell-pull, 'he has probably gnawed his nails down to the quick, or murdered poor Mr Orde. I think you had better see him, my dear, and say something soothing to him!'

Phoebe, tieing the strings of her hat in a lamentably lopsided bow, said in great agitation: 'Oh, no! Oh, pray—!'

The Duchess smiled at her. 'Well, he is waiting in anxiety my love. If I ring this bell once he will come up in answer to it. If I ring twice Reeth will come, and Sylvester will know that you would not even speak to him. Which is it to be?'

'Oh!' cried Phoebe, scarlet-cheeked, and quite distracted. 'I can't—but I don't wish him to—oh, dear, what shall I do?'

'Exactly what you wish to do, my dear—but you must tell him what that is yourself,' said the Duchess, pulling the bell once.

'I don't know!' said Phoebe, wringing her hands. 'I mean, he *can't* want to marry me! When he might have Lady Mary Torrington, who is so beautiful, and good, and well behaved, and—' She stopped in confusion as the door opened.

'Come in, Sylvester!' said the Duchess calmly. 'I want you to escort Miss Marlow to her carriage, if you please.'

'With pleasure, Mama,' said Sylvester.

The Duchess held out her hand to Phoebe, and drew her down to have her cheek kissed. 'Goodbye, dear child: I hope I shall see you again soon!'

In awful confusion, Phoebe uttered a farewell speech so hopelessly disjointed as to bring a smile of unholy appreciation into the eyes of Sylvester, patiently holding the door.

She ventured to peep at him for one anxious moment, as she went towards him. It was a very fleeting glance, but enough to reassure her on one point: he did not look at all distracted. He was perhaps a little pale, but so far from bearing the appearance of one cast into despair he was looking remarkably cheerful, even confident. Miss Marlow, assimilating this with mixed feelings, walked primly past him, her gaze lowered.

He shut the door, and said with perfect calm: 'It was most kind in you to have given my mother the pleasure of making your acquaintance, Miss Marlow.'

'I was very much honoured to receive her invitation, sir,' she replied, with even greater calm.

'Will you do *me* the honour of granting me the opportunity to speak with you for a few minutes before you go away?'

Her calm instantly deserted her. 'No—I mean, I must not stay! Grandmama's coachman dislikes to be kept waiting for long, you see!'

'I know he does,' he agreed. 'So I told Reeth to send the poor fellow home.'

She halted in the middle of the stairway. 'Sent him home?' she repeated. 'And, pray, who gave you—'

'I was afraid he might take a chill.'

She exclaimed indignantly: 'You never so much as thought of such a thing! And you wouldn't have cared if you had!'

'I haven't reached that stage yet,' he admitted. 'But you must surely own that I am making progress!' He smiled at her. 'Oh, no, don't eat me! I promise you shall be sent back to Green Street in one of *my* carriages—presently!'

Phoebe, realizing that he was affording her an example of the methods of getting his own way lately described to her by his mother, eyed him with hostility. 'So I must remain in your house, I collect, until it shall please your grace to order the carriage to come round?'

'No. If you cannot bring yourself even to speak to me, I will send for it immediately.'

She now perceived that he was not only arrogant but unscrupulous.

Wholly devoid of chivalry, too, or he would not have done anything so shabby as to smile at her in just that way. What was more, it was clearly unsafe to be left alone with him: his eyes might smile, but they held besides the smile a very disturbing expression.

'It—it is—I assure you—quite unnecessary, Duke, for you to make me any—any explanation of—of anything!' she said.

'You can't think how relieved I am to hear you say so!' he replied, guiding her across the hall to where a door stood open, revealing a glimpse of a room lined with bookshelves. 'I am not going to attempt anything of that nature, I assure you! I should rather call it *disastrous* than unnecessary! Will you come into the library?'

'What—what a pleasant room!' she achieved, looking about her.

'Yes, and what a number of books I have, haven't I?' said Sylvester affably, closing the door. 'No, I have not, I believe, read them *all!*'

'I wasn't going to say *either* of those things!' she declared, trying hard not to giggle. 'Pray, sir, what is it you wish to say to me?'

'Just *my darling!*' said Sylvester, taking her into his arms.

It was quite useless to struggle, and probably undignified. Besides, it was a well-known maxim that maniacs must be humoured. So Miss Marlow humoured this dangerous lunatic, putting her arm round his neck, and even going so far as to return his embrace. She then leaned her cheek against his shoulder, and said: 'Oh, Sylvester! Oh, Sylvester!' which appeared to give great satisfaction. 'Sparrow, Sparrow!' said Sylvester, holding her still more tightly.

Convinced by the great good sense of this reply that the Head of the House of Rayne had recovered his wits, Phoebe heaved a sigh of relief, and offered a further palliative. 'I didn't mean that *wicked* thing I said to you!'

'Which one, my precious?' enquired Sylvester, relapsing into idiocy.

'That—that you are worse than Ugolino. I wonder you didn't *hit* me!'

'You know very well I wouldn't hurt a hair of your head, Sparrow. I am sure that is a very smart hat, but do allow me to remove it!' he said, pulling the bow loose as he spoke, and casting the hat aside. 'That's better!'

'I *can't* marry you after writing that book!' she said, softening the blow, however, by clinging rather closer.

'You not only can, but must, if I have to drag you to the altar! How else, pray, is my character to be re-established?'

She considered this, and was suddenly struck by an inspiration. She raised her head, and said: 'Sylvester! I know the very thing to do! I will write a book about you, making you the hero!'

'No, thank you, darling!' he replied with great firmness.

'Well, how would it be if I wrote a *sequel* to *The Lost Heir* and made Ugolino become quite *steeped* in infamy, and end up by perishing on the scaffold?'

'Good God! Sparrow, you are, without exception, the most incorrigible little wretch that ever drew breath! *No!*'

'But then everyone would know he *couldn't* be you!' she pointed out. 'Particularly if I dedicated it to you—which I could do with perfect propriety, you know, if I were just to subscribe myself *The Author.*'

'Now, that *is* a splendid thought!' he said. 'One of those pompous epistles, with my name and style set out in large print at the head, followed by *My Lord Duke*—which you are so fond of calling me—and then by several pages interlarded with a great many *Your Graces*, and such encomiums as may occur to you, and—'

'*None* would occur to me! I should have to rack my brain for *weeks* to think of anything to say of you except that you are odiously arrogant, and—'

'Don't you dare to call me arrogant! If ever I had any arrogance at all—which I deny!—how much could I possibly have left after having been ridden over rough-shod by you and Thomas, do you imagine?' He stopped, and turned his head towards the door, listening. 'And that, if I mistake not, *is* Thomas! I think, don't you, Sparrow, that he deserves to be the first to offer us his felicitations? He *did* try so hard to bring us about!' He went to the door, and opened it, to find Tom, who had just been admitted into the house, about to mount the stairs. 'Thomas, come into the library! I have something of an interesting nature to disclose to you!' He added, as his eyes alighted on the tight posy of flowers in Tom's hand: 'Now, what's all this, pray?'

'Oh, nothing!' Tom replied, blushing, but very off-hand. 'I chanced to see them, and thought her grace might like to have them. She was saying last night that she missed the spring flowers at Chance, you know.'

'Oh, indeed! Dangling after my mother, are you? Well, don't think I'll have you for a father-in-law, for I won't!'

'I don't think that is at all a proper way to speak of her grace,' said Tom, with dignity.

'You are very right!' approved Phoebe, as he came into the room. 'And the flowers are a very pretty attention: exactly what Mrs Orde would say you ought to do!'

'Well, that's what I— Oh, by Jove!' Thomas exclaimed, looking from Phoebe to Sylvester in eager enquiry.

'Yes, that's it,' said Sylvester.

'Oh, that's famous!' Tom declared, shaking him warmly by the hand. 'I never was more glad of anything! After you were such a goose, too, Phoebe! I wish you excessively happy, both of you!' He then hugged Phoebe, recommended her to learn how to conduct herself with propriety, and said, with rare tact, that he would take himself off at once.

'You will find her in her drawing-room,' said Sylvester kindly. 'But you would be better employed, let me remind you, in making your peace with Lady Ingham!'

'Yes, I shall do so, of course, but later, because she don't like morning-callers above half,' replied Tom.

'What you mean,' retorted Sylvester, 'is that your nerves are losing their steel! Tell her that you left me on the point of writing to Lord Marlow, to request his permission to marry his daughter, and fear nothing! She'll fall on your neck!'

'I say, that's a dashed good notion!' exclaimed Tom, his brow clearing. 'I think, if you've no objection, I *will* tell her that!'

'Do!' said Sylvester cordially, and went back into the library, to find himself being balefully regarded by his love.

'Of all the arrogant things I've heard you say—'

'My lord Duke!' interpolated Sylvester.

'—that remark was the most insufferable!' declared Phoebe. 'What makes you so sure Grandmama will be pleased, pray?'

'Well, what else am I to think, when it was she who proposed the match to me?' he countered, his eyes full of laughter.

'*Grandmama?*'

'You absurd infant, who do you suppose sent me down to Austerby?'

'You mean to tell me you came at *Grandmama's* bidding?'

'Yes, but with the *utmost* reluctance!' he pleaded outrageously.

'*Oh*—! Then–then when you sent me to her–Sylvester, you are *atrocious!*'

'No, no!' he said hastily, taking her in his arms again. He then, with great presence of mind, put a stop to any further recriminations by kissing her; and his indignant betrothed, apparently feeling that he was too deeply sunk in depravity to be reclaimable, abandoned (for the time being, at all events) any further attempt to bring him to a sense of his iniquity.

The
Corinthian

Georgette
Heyer

I

The company, ushered by a disapproving butler into the yellow saloon of Sir Richard Wyndham's house in St James's Square, comprised two ladies and one reluctant gentleman. The gentleman, who was not much above thirty years of age, but sadly inclined to fat, seemed to feel the butler's disapproval, for upon that dignified individual's informing the elder of the two ladies that Sir Richard was not at home, he cast a deprecating glance at him, not in the least the glance of a peer of the realm upon a menial, but an age-old look of one helpless man to another, and said in a pleading tone: 'Well, then, don't you think, Lady Wyndham—? Louisa, hadn't we better—? I mean, no use going in, my love, is there?'

Neither his wife nor his mother-in-law paid any attention to this craven speech. 'If my brother is gone out, we will await his return,' said Louisa briskly.

'Your poor Papa was always out when one wanted him,' complained Lady Wyndham. 'It is very affecting to me to see Richard growing every day more like him.'

Her fading accents were so lachrymose that it seemed probable that she would dissolve into tears upon her son's doorstep. George, Lord Trevor, was uneasily aware of a handkerchief, clutched in one thin, gloved hand, and put forward no further objection to entering the house in the wake of the two ladies.

Declining all offers of refreshment, Lady Trevor escorted her parent into the Yellow Saloon, settled her comfortably upon a satin sofa, and announced her intention of remaining in St James's Square all day, if need be. George, with a very clear idea, born of sympathy, of what would be his brother-in-law's emotions upon returning to his residence to find a family deputation in possession of it, said unhappily: 'You know, I don't think we should, really I don't! I don't like it above half. I wish you would drop this notion you've taken into your heads.'

His wife, who was engaged in stripping off her lavender-kid gloves, threw him a look of indulgent contempt. 'My dear George, if *you* are afraid of Richard, let me assure you that *I* am not.'

'Afraid of him! No, indeed! But I wish you will consider that a man of nine-and-twenty won't relish having his affairs meddled with. Besides, he will very likely wonder what the deuce it has to do with me, and I'm sure I can't tell him! I wish I had not come.'

Louisa ignored this remark, considering it unworthy of being replied to, which indeed it was, since she ruled her lord with a rod of iron. She was a handsome woman, with a great deal of decision in her face, and a leavening gleam of humour. She was dressed, not perhaps in the height of fashion, which decreed that summer gauzes must reveal every charm of a lady's body, but with great elegance and propriety. Since she had a very good figure, the prevailing mode for high-waisted dresses, with low-cut bodices, and tiny puff sleeves, became her very well: much better, in fact, than skin-tight pantaloons and a long-tailed coat became her husband.

Fashion was not kind to George. He looked his best in buckskin breeches and top boots, but he was unfortunately addicted to dandyism, and pained his friends and relatives by adopting every extravagance of dress, spending as much time over the arrangement of his cravat as Mr Brummell himself, and squeezing his girth into tight stays which had a way of creaking whenever he moved unwarily.

The third member of the party, reclining limply on the satin sofa, was a lady with quite as much determination as her daughter, and a far more subtle way of getting her wishes attended to. A widow of ten years' standing, Lady Wyndham enjoyed the frailest health. The merest hint of opposition was too much for the delicate state of her nerves; and anyone, observing her handkerchief, her vinaigrette, and the hartshorn which she usually kept by her, would have had to be stupid indeed to have failed to appreciate their sinister message. In youth, she had been a beauty; in middle age, everything about her seemed to have faded: hair, cheeks, eyes, and even her voice, which was plaintive, and so gentle that it was a wonder it ever made itself heard. Like her daughter, Lady Wyndham had excellent taste in dress, and since she was fortunate enough to possess a very ample jointure she was able to indulge her liking for the most expensive fal-lals of fashion without in any way curtailing her other expenses. This did not prevent her from thinking herself very badly off, but she was able to enjoy many laments over her straitened circumstances without feeling the least real pinch of poverty, and to win the sympathy of her acquaintances by dwelling sadly on the injustice of her late husband's will, which had placed his only son in the sole possession of his immense fortune. The jointure, her friends deduced hazily, was the veriest pittance.

Lady Wyndham, who lived in a charming house in Clarges Street, could never enter the mansion in St James's Square without suffering a pang. It was not, as might have been supposed from the look of pain she always cast upon it, a family domicile, but had been acquired by her son only a couple of years before. During Sir Edward's lifetime, the family had lived in a much larger, and most inconvenient house in Grosvenor Square. Upon Sir Richard's announcement that he proposed to set up an establishment of his own, this had been given up, so that Lady Wyndham had been able ever since to mourn its loss without being obliged to suffer any longer its inconveniences. But however much she might like her own house in Clarges Street it was not to be supposed that she could bear with equanimity her son's inhabiting a far larger house in St James's Square; and when every other source of grievance failed her, she always came back to that, and said, as she said now, in an ill-used voice: 'I cannot conceive what he should want with a house like this!'

Louisa, who had a very good house of her own, besides an estate in Berkshire, did not in the least grudge her brother his mansion. She replied: 'It doesn't signify, Mama. Except that he must have been thinking of marriage when he bought it. Would you not say so, George?'

George was flattered at being thus appealed to, but he was an honest, painstaking person, and he could not bring himself to say that he thought Richard had had any thought of marriage in his head, either when he had bought the house, or at any other time.

Louisa was displeased. 'Well!' she said, looking resolute, 'he must be brought to think of marriage!'

Lady Wyndham lowered her smelling salts to interpolate: 'Heaven knows

I would never urge my boy to do anything distasteful, but it has been an understood thing for years that he and Melissa Brandon would seal the long friendship between our families with the Nuptial Tie!'

George goggled at her, and wished himself otherwhere.

'If he doesn't wish to marry Melissa, I'm sure I should be the last person to press her claim,' said Louisa. 'But it is high time that he married someone, and if he has no other suitable young female in his eye, Melissa it must be.'

'I do not know how to face Lord Saar,' bemoaned Lady Wyndham, raising the vinaigrette to her nose again. 'Or poor dear Emily, with three girls besides Melissa to dispose of, and none of them more than passable. Sophia has spots, too.'

'I do not consider Augusta hopeless,' said Louisa fairly. 'Amelia, too, may improve.'

'Squints!' said George.

'A slight cast in one eye,' corrected Louisa. 'However, we are not concerned with that. Melissa is an extremely handsome creature. No one can deny *that*!'

'And such a desirable connection!' sighed Lady Wyndham. 'Quite one of the best families!'

'They tell me Saar won't last another five years, not at the rate he's going now,' said George. 'Everything mortgaged up to the hilt, and Saar drinking himself into his grave! They say his father did the same.'

Both ladies regarded him with disfavour. 'I hope, George, you do not mean to imply that Melissa is addicted to the bottle?' said his wife.

'Oh no, no! Lord, no, I never thought of such a thing! I'm sure she's an excellent young woman. But this I will say, Louisa: I don't blame Richard if he don't want her!' said George defiantly. 'Myself, I'd as soon marry a statue!'

'I must say,' conceded Louisa, 'she is a trifle cold, perhaps. But it is a very delicate position for her, you'll allow. It has been understood since both were children that she and Richard would make a match of it, and *she* knows that as well as *we* do. And here is Richard, behaving in the most odious way! I am out of all patience with him!'

George rather liked his brother-in-law, but he knew that it would be foolhardy to defend him, so he held his peace. Lady Wyndham took up the tale of woe. 'Heaven forbid that I should force my only son to a disagreeable marriage, but I live in hourly dread of his bringing home some dreadful, low-born creature on his arm, and expecting me to welcome her!'

A vision of his brother-in-law crossed George's mind's eye. He said doubtfully: 'Really, you know, I don't think he'll do that, ma'am.'

'George is quite right,' announced Louisa. 'I should think the better of Richard if he did. It quite shocks me to see him so impervious to every feminine charm! It is a great piece of nonsense for him to dislike the opposite sex, but one thing is certain: dislike females he may, but he owes a duty to the name, and marry he must! I am sure I have been at pains to introduce him to every eligible young woman in town, for I am by no means set on his marrying Melissa Brandon. Well! He would not look twice at any of them, so if that is the mind he is in, Melissa will suit him very well.'

'Richard thinks they all want him for his money,' ventured George.

'I dare say they may. What has that to say to anything, pray? I imagine you do not mean to tell me that Richard is romantic!'

No, George was forced to admit that Richard was not romantic.

'If I live to see him suitably married, I can die content!' said Lady Wyndham, who had every expectation of living for another thirty years. 'His present course fills my poor mother's heart with foreboding!'

Loyalty forced George to expostulate. 'No, really, ma'am! Really, I say! There's no harm in Richard, not the least in the world, 'pon my honour!'

'He puts me out of all patience!' said Louisa. 'I love him dearly, but I despise him with all my heart! Yes, I do, and I do not care who hears me say so! He cares for nothing but the set of his cravat, the polish on his boots, and the blending of his snuff!'

'His horses!' begged George unhappily.

'Oh, his horses! Very well! Let us admit him to be a famous whip! He beat Sir John Lade in their race to Brighton! A fine achievement indeed!'

'Very handy with his fives!' gasped George, sinking but game.

'*You* may admire a man for frequenting Jackson's Saloon, and Cribb's Parlour! *I* do not!'

'No, my love,' George said. 'No, indeed, my love!'

'And I make no doubt you see nothing reprehensible in his addiction to the gaming table! But I had it on the most excellent authority that he dropped three thousand pounds at one sitting at Almack's!'

Lady Wyndham moaned, and dabbed at her eyes. 'Oh, do not say so!'

'Yes, but he's so devilish wealthy it can't signify!' said George.

'Marriage,' said Louisa, 'will put a stop to such fripperies.'

The depressing picture this dictum conjured up reduced George to silence. Lady Wyndham said, in a voice dark with mystery: 'Only a mother could appreciate my anxieties. He is at a dangerous age, and I live from day to day in dread of what he may do!'

George opened his mouth, encountered a look from his wife, shut it again, and tugged unhappily at his cravat.

The door opened; a Corinthian stood upon the threshold, cynically observing his relatives. 'A thousand apologies,' said the Corinthian, bored but polite. 'Your very obedient servant, ma'am. Louisa, yours! My poor George! Ah—was I expecting you?'

'Apparently not!' retorted Louisa, bristling.

'No, you weren't. I mean, they took it into their heads—*I* couldn't stop them!' said George heroically.

'I thought I was not,' said the Corinthian, closing the door, and advancing into the room. 'But my memory, you know, my lamentable memory!'

George, running an experienced eye over his brother-in-law, felt his soul stir. 'B'gad, Richard, I like that! That's a devilish well-cut coat, 'pon my honour, it is! Who made it?'

Sir Richard lifted an arm, and glanced at his cuff. 'Weston, George, only Weston.'

'George!' said Louisa awfully.

Sir Richard smiled faintly, and crossed the room to his mother's side. She held out her hand to him, and he bowed over it with languid grace, just brushing it with his lips. 'A thousand apologies, ma'am!' he repeated. 'I trust my people have looked after you—er—*all* of you?' His lazy glance swept the room. 'Dear me!' he said. 'George, you are near to it: oblige me, my dear fellow, by pulling the bell!'

'We do not need any refreshment, I thank you, Richard,' said Louisa.

The faint, sweet smile silenced her as none of her husband's expostulations had ever done. 'My dear Louisa, you mistake—I assure you, you mistake! George is in the most urgent need of–er–stimulant. Yes, Jeffries, I rang. The Madeira–oh, ah! and some ratafia, Jeffries, if you please!'

'Richard, that's the best Waterfall I've ever seen!' exclaimed George, his admiring gaze fixed on the intricate arrangement of the Corinthian's cravat.

'You flatter me, George; I fear you flatter me.'

'Pshaw!' snapped Louisa.

'Precisely, my dear Louisa,' agreed Sir Richard amiably.

'Do not try to provoke me, Richard!' said Louisa, on a warning note. 'I will allow your appearance to be everything that it should be–admirable, I am sure!'

'One does one's poor best,' murmured Sir Richard.

Her bosom swelled. 'Richard, I could hit you!' she declared.

The smile grew, allowing her a glimpse of excellent white teeth. 'I don't think you could, my dear.'

George so far forgot himself as to laugh. A quelling glance was directed upon him. 'George, be quiet!' said Louisa.

'I must say,' conceded Lady Wyndham, whose maternal pride could not quite be overborne, 'there is no one, except Mr Brummell, of course, who looks as well as you do, Richard.'

He bowed, but he did not seem to be unduly elated by this encomium. Possibly he took it as his due. He was a very notable Corinthian. From his Windswept hair (most difficult of all styles to achieve), to the toes of his gleaming Hessians, he might have posed as an advertisement for the Man of Fashion. His fine shoulders set off a coat of superfine cloth to perfection; his cravat, which had excited George's admiration, had been arranged by the hands of a master; his waistcoat was chosen with a nice eye; his biscuit-coloured pantaloons showed not one crease; and his Hessians with their jaunty gold tassels, had not only been made for him by Hoby, but were polished, George suspected, with a blacking mixed with champagne. A quizzing glass on a black ribbon hung round his neck; a fob at his waist; and in one hand he carried a Sèvres snuffbox. His air proclaimed his unutterable boredom, but no tailoring, no amount of studied nonchalance, could conceal the muscle in his thighs, or the strength of his shoulders. Above the starched points of his shirt collar, a weary, handsome face showed its owner's disillusionment. Heavy lids drooped over grey eyes which were intelligent enough, but only to observe the vanities of the world; the smile which just touched that resolute mouth seemed to mock the follies of Sir Richard's fellow men.

Jeffries came back into the room with a tray, and set it upon a table. Louisa waved aside the offer of refreshment, but Lady Wyndham accepted it, and George, emboldened by his mother-in-law's weakness, took a glass of Madeira.

'I dare say,' said Louisa, 'that you are wondering what we are here for.'

'I never waste my time in idle speculation,' replied Sir Richard gently. 'I feel sure that you are going to tell me what you are here for.'

'Mama and I have come to speak to you about your marriage,' said Louisa, taking the plunge.

'And what,' enquired Sir Richard, 'has George come to speak to me about?'

'That too, of course!'

'No, I haven't!' disclaimed George hurriedly. 'You know I said I'd have nothing to do with it! I never wanted to come at all!'

'Have some more Madeira,' said Sir Richard soothingly.

'Well, thank you, yes, I will. But don't think I'm here to badger you about something which don't concern me, because I'm not!'

'Richard!' said Lady Wyndham deeply, 'I dare no longer meet Saar face to face!'

'As bad as that, is he?' said Sir Richard. 'I haven't seen him myself these past few weeks, but I'm not at all surprised. I fancy I heard something about it, from someone–I forget whom. Taken to brandy, hasn't he?'

'Sometimes,' said Lady Wyndham, 'I think you are utterly devoid of sensibility!'

'He is merely trying to provoke you, Mama. You know perfectly well what Mama means, Richard. When do you mean to offer for Melissa?'

There was a slight pause. Sir Richard set down his empty wineglass, and flicked with one long finger the petals of a flower in a bowl on the table. 'This year, next year, sometime–or never, my dear Louisa.'

'I am very sure she considers herself as good as plighted to you,' Louisa said.

Sir Richard was looking down at the flower under his hand, but at this he raised his eyes to his sister's face, in an oddly keen, swift look. 'Is that so?'

'How should it be otherwise? You know very well that Papa and Lord Saar designed it so years ago.'

The lids veiled his eyes again. 'How mediæval of you!' sighed Sir Richard.

'Now, don't, pray, take me up wrongly, Richard! If you don't like Melissa, there is no more to be said. But you do like her–or if you don't, at least *I* never heard you say so! What Mama and I feel–and George, too–is that it is time and more that you were settled in life.'

A pained glance reproached Lord Trevor. '*Et tu, Brute?*' said Sir Richard.

'I swear I never said so!' declared George, choking over his Madeira. 'It was all Louisa. I dare say I may have agreed with her. *You* know how it is, Richard!'

'I know,' agreed Sir Richard, sighing. 'You too, Mama?'

'Oh Richard, I live only to see you happily married, with your children about you!' said Lady Wyndham, in trembling tones.

A slight, unmistakable shudder ran through the Corinthian. 'My children about me . . . Yes. Precisely, ma'am. Pray continue!'

'You owe it to the name,' pursued his mother. 'You are the last of the Wyndhams, for it's not to be supposed that your Uncle Lucius will marry at this late date. There is Melissa, dear girl, the very wife for you! So handsome, so distinguished–birth, breeding: everything of the most desirable!'

'Ah–your pardon, ma'am, but do you include Saar, and Cedric, not to mention Beverley, under that heading?'

'That's exactly what I say!' broke in George. '"It's all very well," I said, "and if a man likes to marry an iceberg it's all one to me, but you can't call Saar a desirable father-in-law, damme if you can! While as for the girl's precious brothers." I said, "they'll ruin Richard inside a year!"'

'Nonsense!' said Louisa. 'It is understood, of course, that Richard would make handsome settlements. But as for his being responsible for Cedric's and Beverley's debts, I'm sure I know of no reason why he should!'

'You comfort me, Louisa,' said Sir Richard.

She looked up at him not unaffectionately. 'Well, I think it is time to be frank, Richard. People will be saying next that you are playing fast and loose with Melissa, for you must know the understanding between you is an open secret. If you had chosen to marry someone else, five, ten years ago, it would have been a different thing. But so far as I am aware your affections have never even been engaged, and here you are, close on thirty, as good as pledged to Melissa Brandon, and nothing settled!'

Lady Wyndham, though in the fullest agreement with her daughter, was moved at this point to defend her son, which she did by reminding Louisa that Richard was only twenty-nine after all.

'Mama, Richard will be thirty in less than six months. For I,' said Louisa with resolution, 'am turned thirty-one.'

'Louisa, I am touched!' said Sir Richard. 'Only the deepest sisterly devotion, I am persuaded, could have wrung from you such an admission.'

She could not repress a smile, but said with as much severity as she could muster: 'It is no laughing matter. You are no longer in your first youth, and you know as well as I do that it is your duty to think seriously of marriage.'

'Strange,' mused Sir Richard, 'that one's duty should be invariably so disagreeable.'

'I know,' said George, heaving a sigh. 'Very true! very true indeed!'

'Pooh! nonsense! What a coil you make of a simple matter!' Louisa said. 'Now, if I were to press you to marry some romantical miss, always wanting you to make love to her, and crying her eyes out every time you chose to seek your amusements out of her company, you might have reason to complain. But Melissa—yes, an iceberg, George, if you like, and what else, pray, is Richard?—Melissa, I say, will never plague you in *that* way.'

Sir Richard's eyes dwelled inscrutably upon her face for a moment. Then he moved to the table and poured himself out another glass of Madeira.

Louisa said defensively: 'Well, you don't *wish* her to cling about your neck, I suppose?'

'Not at all.'

'And you are not in love with any other woman, are you?'

'I am not.'

'Very well, then! To be sure, if you were in the habit of falling in and out of love, it would be a different matter. But, to be plain with you, you are the coldest, most indifferent, selfish creature alive, Richard, and you will find in Melissa an admirable partner.'

Inarticulate clucking sounds from George, indicative of protest, caused Sir Richard to wave a hand towards the Madeira. 'Help yourself, George, help yourself!'

'I must say, I think it most unkind in you to speak to your brother like that,' said Lady Wyndham. 'Not but what you *are* selfish, dear Richard. I'm sure I have said so over and over again. But so it is with the greater part of the world! Everywhere one turns one meets with nothing but ingratitude!'

'If I have done Richard an injustice, I will willingly ask his pardon,' said Louisa.

'Very handsomely said, my dear sister. You have done me no injustice. I wish you will not look so distressed, George: your pity is quite wasted on me, I assure you. Tell me, Louisa: have you reason to suppose that Melissa expects me to—er—pay my addresses to her?'

'Certainly I have. She has been expecting it any time these five years!'

Sir Richard looked a little startled. 'Poor girl!' he said. 'I must have been remarkably obtuse.'

His mother and sister exchanged glances. 'Does that mean that you will think seriously of marriage?' asked Louisa.

He looked thoughtfully down at her. 'I suppose it must come to that.'

'Well, for my part,' said George, defying his wife, 'I would look around me for some other eligible female! Lord, there are dozens of 'em littering town! Why, I've seen I don't know how many setting their caps at you! Pretty ones, too, but you never notice them, you ungrateful dog!'

'Oh yes, I do,' said Sir Richard, with a curl of the lips.

'*Must* George be vulgar?' asked Lady Wyndham tragically.

'Be quiet, George! And as for you, Richard, I consider it in the highest degree nonsensical for you to take up that attitude. There is no denying that you're the biggest catch on the Marriage Mart–yes, Mama, that is vulgar too, and I beg your pardon–but you have a lower opinion of yourself than I credit you with if you can suppose that your fortune is the only thing about you which makes you a desirable *parti*. You are generally accounted handsome–indeed, no one, I believe, could deny that your person is such as must please; and when you will take the trouble to be conciliating there is nothing in your manners to disgust the nicest taste.'

'This encomium, Louisa, almost unmans me,' said Sir Richard, much moved.

'I am perfectly serious. I was about to add that you often spoil everything by your odd humours. I do not know how you should expect to engage a female's affection when you never bestow the least distinguishing notice upon any woman! I do not say that you are uncivil, but there is a languor, a reserve in your manner, which must repel a woman of sensibility.'

'I am a hopeless case indeed,' said Sir Richard.

'If you want to know what I think, which I do not suppose you do, you need not tell me so, it is that you are spoilt, Richard. You have too much money, you have done everything you wished to do before you are out of your twenties; you have been courted by match-making Mamas, fawned on by toadies, and indulged by all the world. The end of it is that you are bored to death. There! I have said it, and though you may not thank me for it, you will admit that I am right.'

'Quite right,' agreed Sir Richard. 'Hideously right, Louisa!'

She got up. 'Well, I advise you to get married and settle down. Come, Mama! We have said all we meant to say, and you know we are to call in Brook Street on our way home. George, do you mean to come with us?'

'No,' said George. 'Not to call in Brook Street. I daresay I shall stroll up to White's presently.'

'Just as you please, my love,' said Louisa, drawing on her gloves again.

When the ladies had been escorted to the waiting barouche, George did not at once set out for his club, but accompanied his brother-in-law back into the house. He preserved a sympathetic silence until they were out of earshot of the servants, but caught Sir Richard's eye then, in a very pregnant look, and uttered the one word: 'Women!'

'Quite so,' said Sir Richard.

'Do you know what I'd do if I were you, my boy?'

'Yes,' said Sir Richard.

George was disconcerted. 'Damn it, you can't know!'

'You would do precisely what I shall do.'

'What's that?'

'Oh–offer for Melissa Brandon, of course,' said Sir Richard.

'Well, I wouldn't,' said George positively. 'I wouldn't marry Melissa Brandon for fifty sisters! I'd find a cosier armful, 'pon my soul I would!'

'The cosiest armful of my acquaintance was never so cosy as when she wanted to see my purse string untied,' said Sir Richard cynically.

George shook his head. 'Bad, very bad! I must say, it's enough to sour any man. But Louisa's right, you know: you ought to get married. Won't do to let the name die out.' An idea occurred to him. 'You wouldn't care to put it about that you'd lost all your money, I suppose?'

'No,' said Sir Richard, 'I wouldn't.'

'I read somewhere of a fellow who went off to some place where he wasn't known. Devil of a fellow he was: some kind of a foreign Count, I think. I don't remember precisely, but there was a girl in it, who fell in love with him for his own sake.'

'There would be,' said Sir Richard.

'You don't like it?' George rubbed his nose, a little crestfallen. 'Well, damme if I know what to suggest!'

He was still pondering the matter when the butler announced Mr Wyndham, and a large, portly, and convivial-looking gentleman rolled into the room, ejaculating cheerfully: 'Hallo, George! You here? Ricky, my boy, your mother's been at me again, comfound her! Made me promise I'd come round to see you, though what the devil she thinks I can do is beyond me!'

'Spare me!' said Sir Richard wearily. 'I have already sustained a visit from my mother, not to mention Louisa.'

'Well, I'm sorry for you, my boy, and if you take my advice you'll marry that Brandon wench, and be done with it. What's that you have there? Madeira? I'll take a glass.'

Sir Richard gave him one. He lowered his bulk into a large armchair, stretched his legs out before him, and raised the glass. 'Here's a health to the bridegroom!' he said, with a chuckle. 'Don't look so glum, nevvy! Think of the joy you'll be bringing into Saar's life!'

'Damn you,' said Sir Richard. 'If you had ever had a shred of proper feeling, Lucius, you would have got married fifty years ago, and reared a pack of brats in your image. A horrible thought, I admit, but at least I should not now be cast for the rôle of Family Sacrifice.'

'Fifty years ago,' retorted his uncle, quite unmoved by these insults, 'I was only just breeched. This is a very tolerable wine, Ricky. By the way, they tell me young Beverley Brandon's badly dipped. You'll be a damned public benefactor if you marry that girl. Better let your lawyer attend to the settlements, though. I'd be willing to lay you a monkey Saar tries to bleed you white. What's the matter with you, George? Got the toothache?'

'I don't like it,' said George. 'I told Louisa so at the outset, but you know what women are! Myself, I wouldn't have Melissa Brandon if she were the last woman left single.'

'What, she ain't the spotty one, surely?' demanded Lucius, concerned.

'No, that's Sophia.'

'Oh, well, nothing to worry about then! You marry the girl, Ricky: you'll never have any peace if you don't. Fill up your glass, George, and we'll have another toast!'

'What is it this time?' enquired Sir Richard, replenishing the glasses. 'Don't spare me!'

'To a pack of brats in your image, nevvy: here's to 'em!' grinned his uncle.

2

Lord Saar lived in Brook Street with his wife, and his family of two sons and four daughters. Sir Richard Wyndham, driving to his prospective father-in-law's house twenty-four hours after his interview with his own parent, was fortunate enough to find Saar away from home, and Lady Saar, the butler informed him, on her way to Bath with the Honourable Sophia. He fell instead into the arms of the Honourable Cedric Brandon, a rakish young gentleman of lamentable habits, and a disastrous charm of manner.

'Ricky, my only friend!' cried the Honourable Cedric, dragging Sir Richard into a small salon at the back of the house. 'Don't tell me you've come to offer for Melissa! They say good news don't kill a man, but *I* never listen to gossip! M'father says ruin stares us in the face. Lend me the money, dear boy, and I'll buy myself a pair of colours, and be off to the Peninsula, damme if I won't! But listen to me, Ricky! *Are* you listening?' He looked anxiously at Sir Richard, appeared satisfied, and said, wagging a solemn finger: 'Don't do it! There isn't a fortune big enough to settle *our* little affairs: take my word for it! Have nothing to do with Beverley! They say Fox gamed away a fortune before he was twenty-one. Give you my word, he was nothing to Bev, nothing at all. Between ourselves, Ricky, the old man has taken to brandy. H'sh! Not a word! Mustn't tell tales about m'father! But run, Ricky! That's my advice to you: *run!*'

'Would you buy yourself a pair of colours, if I gave you the money?' asked Sir Richard.

'Sober, yes; drunk, no!' replied Cedric, with his wholly disarming smile. 'I'm very sober now, but I shan't be so for long. Don't give me a groat, dear old boy! Don't give Bev a groat! He's a bad man. Now, when I'm sober I'm a good man—but I ain't sober above six hours out of the twenty-four, so you be warned! Now I'm off. I've done my best for you, for I like you, Ricky, but if you go to perdition in spite of me, I'll wash my hands of you. No, damme, I'll sponge on you for the rest of my days! Think, dear boy, think! Bev and your very obedient on your doorstep six days out of seven—duns—threats—wife's brothers done-up—pockets to let—wife in tears—nothing to do but pay! Don't do it! Fact is, we ain't worth it!'

'Wait!' Sir Richard said, barring his passage. 'If I settle your debts, will you go to the Peninsula?'

'Ricky, it's you who aren't sober. Go home!'

'Consider, Cedric, how well you would look in Hussar uniform!'

An impish smile danced in Cedric's eyes. 'Wouldn't I just! But at this present I'd look better in Hyde Park. Out of the way, dear boy! I've a very important engagement. Backed a goose to win a hundred-yard race against a turkey-cock. Can't lose! Greatest sporting events of the season!'

He was gone on the words, leaving Sir Richard, not, indeed, to run, as advised, but to await the pleasure of the Honourable Melissa Brandon.

She did not keep him waiting for long. A servant came to request him to step upstairs, and he followed the man up the wide staircase to the withdrawing room on the first floor.

Melissa Brandon was a handsome, dark-haired young woman, a little more than twenty-five years old. Her profile was held to be faultless, but in full face her eyes were discovered to be rather too hard for beauty. She had not, in her first seasons, lacked suitors, but none of the gentlemen attracted by her undeniable good looks, had ever, in the cockfighting phrase of her graceless elder brother, come up to scratch. As he bowed over her hand, Sir Richard remembered George's iceberg simile, and at once banished it from his obedient mind.

'Well, Richard?'

Melissa's voice was cool, rather matter-of-fact, just as her smile seemed more a mechanical civility than a spontaneous expression of pleasure.

'I hope I see you well, Melissa?' Sir Richard said formally.

'Perfectly, I thank you. Pray sit down! I apprehend that you have come to discuss the question of our marriage.'

He regarded her from under slightly raised brows. 'Dear me!' he said mildly. 'Someone would appear to have been busy.'

She was engaged upon some stitchery, and went on plying her needle with unruffled composure. 'Do not let us beat about the bush!' she said. 'I am certainly past the age of being missish, and you, I believe, may rank as a sensible man.'

'Were you ever missish?' enquired Sir Richard.

'I trust not. I have no patience with such folly. Nor am I romantic. In that respect, we must be thought to be well suited.'

'Must we?' said Sir Richard, gently swinging his gold-handled quizzing glass to and fro.

She seemed amused. 'Certainly! I trust you have not, at this late date, grown sentimental! It would be quite absurd!'

'Senility,' pensively observed Sir Richard, 'often brings sentiment in its train. Or so I have been informed.'

'We need not concern ourselves with that. I like you very well, Richard, but there is just a little nonsense in your disposition which makes you turn everything to jest. I myself am of a more serious nature.'

'Then in *that* respect, we cannot be thought to be well suited,' suggested Sir Richard.

'I do not consider the objection insuperable. The life you have chosen to lead up till now has not been such as to encourage serious reflection, after all. I dare say you may grow more dependable, for you do not want for sense. *That*, however, must be left to the future. At all events, I am not so unreasonable as to feel the difference in our natures to be an impassable barrier to marriage.'

'Melissa,' said Sir Richard, 'will you tell me something?'

She looked up. 'Pray, what do you wish me to tell you?'

'Have you ever been in love?' asked Sir Richard.

She coloured slightly. 'No. From my observation, I am thankful that I have not. There is something excessively vulgar about persons under the sway of strong emotions. I do not say it is *wrong*, but I believe I have something more of fastidiousness than most, and I find such subjects extremely distasteful.'

'You do not,' Sir Richard drawled, 'envisage the possibility of–er–falling in love at some future date?'

'My dear Richard! With whom, pray?'

'Shall we say with myself?'

She laughed. 'Now you are being absurd! If you were told that it would be necessary to approach me with some show of lovemaking, you were badly advised. Ours would be a marriage of convenience. I could contemplate nothing else. I like you very well, but you are not at all the sort of man to arouse those warmer passions in my breast. But I see no reason why *that* should worry either of us. If *you* were romantic, it would be a different matter.'

'I fear,' said Sir Richard, 'that I must be very romantic.'

'I suppose you are jesting again,' she replied, with a faint shrug.

'Not at all. I am so romantic that I indulge my fancy with the thought of some woman—doubtless mythical—who might desire to marry me, not because I am a very rich man, but because—you will have to forgive the vulgarity—because she loved me!'

She looked rather contemptuous. 'I should have supposed you to be past the age of fustian, Richard. I say nothing against love, but, frankly, love matches seem to me a trifle beneath us. One would say you had been hobnobbing with the bourgeoisie at Islington Spa, or some such low place! I do not forget that I am a Brandon. I dare say we are very proud; indeed, I hope we are!'

'That,' said Sir Richard dryly, 'is an aspect of the situation which, I confess, had not so far occurred to me.'

She was amazed. 'I had not thought it possible! I imagined everyone knew what we Brandons feel about our name, our birth, our tradition!'

'I hesitate to wound you, Melissa,' said Sir Richard, 'but the spectacle of a woman of your name, birth, and tradition, cold-bloodedly offering herself to the highest bidder is not one calculated to impress the world with a very strong notion of her pride.'

'This is indeed the language of the theatre!' she exclaimed. 'My duty to my family demands that I should marry well, but let me assure you that even *that* could not make me stoop to ally myself with one of inferior breeding.'

'Ah, this is pride indeed!' said Sir Richard, faintly smiling.

'I do not understand you. You must know that my father's affairs are in such case as—in short—'

'I am aware,' Sir Richard said gently. 'I apprehend it is to be my privilege to—er—unravel Lord Saar's affairs.'

'But of course!' she replied, surprised out of her statuesque calm. 'No other consideration could have prevailed upon me to accept your suit!'

'This,' said Sir Richard, pensively regarding the toe of one Hessian boot, 'becomes a trifle delicate. If frankness is to be the order of the day, my dear Melissa, I must point out to you that I have not yet—er—proffered my suit.'

She was quite undisturbed by this snub, but replied coldly: 'I did not suppose that you would so far forget what is due to our position as to approach *me* with an offer. We do not belong to *that* world. You will no doubt seek an interview with my father.'

'I wonder if I shall?' said Sir Richard.

'I imagine that you most certainly will,' responded the lady, snipping her thread. 'Your circumstances are as well known to me as mine are to you. If I may say so bluntly, you are fortunate to be in a position to offer for a Brandon.'

He looked meditatively at her, but made no remark. After a pause, she continued: 'As for the future, neither of us, I trust, would make great demands upon the other. You have your amusements: they do not concern me, and however much my reason may deprecate your addiction to pugilism, curricle racing, and deep basset—'

'Pharaoh,' he interpolated.

'Very well, pharaoh: it is all one. However much I may deprecate such follies, I say, I do not desire to interfere with your tastes.'

'You are very obliging,' bowed Sir Richard. 'Bluntly, Melissa, I may do as I please if I will hand you my purse?'

'That is putting it bluntly indeed,' she replied composedly. She folded up her needlework, and laid it aside. 'Papa has been expecting a visit from you. He will be sorry to hear that you called while he was away from home. He will be with us again tomorrow, and you may be sure of finding him, if you care to call at—shall we say eleven o'clock?'

He rose. 'Thank you, Melissa. I feel that my time has not been wasted, even though Lord Saar was not here to receive me.'

'I hope not, indeed,' she said, extending her hand. 'Come! We have had a talk which must, I feel, prove valuable. You think me unfeeling, I dare say, but you will do me the justice to admit that I have not stooped to unworthy pretence. Our situation is peculiar, which is why I overcame my reluctance to discuss the question of our marriage with you. We have been as good as betrothed these five years, and more.'

He took her hand. 'Have you considered yourself betrothed to me these five years?' he enquired.

For the first time in their interview her eyes failed to meet his. 'Certainly,' she replied.

'I see,' said Sir Richard, and took his leave of her.

He put in a belated appearance at Almack's that evening. No one, admiring his *point-de-vice* appearance, or listening to his lazy drawl, could have supposed him to be on the eve of making the most momentous decision of his life. Only his uncle, rolling into the club some time after midnight, and observing the dead men at his elbow, guessed that the die had been cast. He told George Trevor, whom he found just rising from the basset table, that Ricky was taking it hard, a pronouncement which distressed George, and made him say: 'I have not exchanged two words with him. Do you tell me he has actually offered for Melissa Brandon?'

'I'm not telling you anything,' said Lucius. 'All I say is that he's drinking hard and plunging deep.'

In great concern, George seized the first opportunity that offered of engaging his brother-in-law's attention. This was not until close on three o'clock, when Sir Richard at last rose from the pharaoh table, and Sir Richard was not, by that time, in the mood for private conversation. He had lost quite a large sum of money, and had drunk quite a large quantity of brandy, but neither of these circumstances was troubling him.

'No luck, Ricky?' his uncle asked him.

A somewhat hazy but still perfectly intelligent glance mocked him. 'Not at cards, Lucius. But think of the adage!'

George knew that Sir Richard could carry his wine as well as any man of his acquaintance, but a certain reckless note in his voice alarmed him. He plucked at his sleeve, and said in a lowered tone: 'I wish you will let me have a word with you!'

'Dear George—my very dear George!' said Sir Richard, amiably smiling. 'You must be aware that I am not—quite—sober. No words tonight.'

'I shall come round to see you in the morning, then,' said George, forgetting that it was already morning.

'I shall have the devil of a head,' said Sir Richard.

He made his way out of the club, his curly-brimmed hat at an angle on his head, his ebony cane tucked under one arm. He declined the porter's offer to call up a chair, remarking sweetly: 'I am devilish drunk, and I shall walk.'

The porter grinned. He had seen many gentlemen in all the various stages of inebriety, and he did not think that Sir Richard, who spoke with only the faintest slurring of his words, and who walked with quite wonderful balance, was in very desperate straits. If he had not known Sir Richard well, he would not, he thought, have seen anything amiss with him, beyond his setting off in quite the wrong direction for St James's Square. He felt constrained to call Sir Richard's attention to this, but begged pardon when Sir Richard said: 'I know. The dawn is calling me, however. I am going for a long, long walk.'

'Quite so, sir,' said the porter, and stepped back.

Sir Richard, his head swimming a little from sudden contact with the cool air, strolled aimlessly away in a northerly direction.

His head cleared after a while. In a detached manner, he reflected that it would probably begin to ache in a short time, and he would feel extremely unwell, and not a little sorry for himself. At the moment, however, while the fumes of brandy still wreathed about his brain, a curious irresponsibility possessed him. He felt reckless, remote, divorced from his past and his future. The dawn was spreading a grey light over the quiet streets, and the breeze fanning his cheeks was cool, and fresh enough to make him glad of his light evening cloak. He wandered into Brook Street, and laughed up at the shuttered windows of Saar's house. 'My gentle bride!' he said, and kissed his fingers in the direction of the house. 'God, what a damned fool I am!'

He repeated this, vaguely pleased with the remark, and walked down the long street. It occurred to him that his gentle bride would scarcely be flattered, if she could see him now, and this thought made him laugh again. The Watch, encountered at the north end of Grosvenor Square, eyed him dubiously, and gave him a wide berth. Gentlemen in Sir Richard's condition not infrequently amused themselves with a light-hearted pastime known as Boxing the Watch, and this member of that praiseworthy force was not anxious to court trouble.

Sir Richard did not notice the Watch, nor, to do him justice, would he have felt in the least tempted to molest him if he had noticed him. Somewhere, in the recesses of his brain, Sir Richard was aware that he was the unluckiest dog alive. He felt very bitter about this, as though all the world were in league against him; and, as he branched off erratically down a quiet side street he was cynically sorry for himself, that in ten years spent in the best circles he had not had the common good fortune to meet one female whose charms had cost him a single hour's sleep. It did not seem probable that he would be more fortunate in the future. 'Which, I suppose,' remarked Sir Richard to one of the new gas lamps, 'is a—is a consummation devoutly to be wished, since I am about to offer for Melissa Brandon.'

It was at this moment that he became aware of a peculiar circumstance. Someone was climbing out of a second-storey window of one of the prim houses on the opposite side of the street.

Sir Richard stood still, and blinked at this unexpected sight. His divine detachment still clung to him; he was interested in what he saw, but by no means concerned with it. 'Undoubtedly a burglar,' he said, and leaned nonchalantly on his cane to watch the end of the adventure. His somewhat sleepy gaze discovered that whoever was escaping from the prim house was proposing to do so by means of knotted sheets, which fell disastrously short of the ground. '*Not* a burglar,' decided Sir Richard, and crossed the road.

By the time he had reached the opposite kerbstone, the mysterious fugitive had arrived, somewhat fortuitously, at the end of his improvised rope, and was dangling precariously above the shallow area, trying with one desperate foot to find some kind of a resting place on the wall of the house. Sir Richard saw that he was a very slight youth, only a boy, in fact, and went in a leisurely fashion to the rescue.

The fugitive caught sight of him as he descended the area steps, and gasped with a mixture of fright and thankfulness: 'Oh! Could you help me, please? I didn't know it was so far. I thought I should be able to jump, only I don't think I can.'

'My engaging youth,' said Sir Richard, looking up at the flushed face peering down at him. 'What, may I ask, are you doing on the end of that rope?'

'*Hush*!' begged the fugitive. 'Do you think you could catch me, if I let go?'

'I will do my poor best,' promised Sir Richard.

The fugitive's feet were only just above his reach, and in another five seconds the fugitive descended into his arms with a rush that made him stagger, and almost lose his balance. He retained it by a miracle, clasping strongly to his chest an unexpectedly light body.

Sir Richard was not precisely sober, but although the brandy fumes had produced in his brain a not unpleasant sense of irresponsibility, they had by no means fuddled his intellect. Sir Richard, his chin tickled by curls, and his arms full of fugitive, made a surprising discovery. He set the fugitive down, saying in a matter-of-fact voice: 'Yes, but I don't think you are a youth, after all.'

'No, I'm a girl,' replied the fugitive, apparently undismayed by his discovery. 'But, please, will you come away before they wake up?'

'Who?' asked Sir Richard.

'My aunt—all of them!' whispered the fugitive. 'I am very much obliged to you for helping me—and do you think you could untie this knot, if you please? You see, I had to tie my bundle on my back, and now I can't undo it. And where is my hat?'

'It fell off,' said Sir Richard, picking it up, and dusting it on his sleeve. 'I am not quite sober, you know—in fact, I am drunk—but I cannot help feeling that this is all a trifle—shall we say—irregular?'

'Yes, but there was nothing else to be done,' explained the fugitive, trying to look over her own shoulder at what Sir Richard was doing with the recalcitrant knot.

'Oblige me by standing still!' requested Sir Richard.

'Oh, I am sorry! I can't think how it worked right round me like that. Thank you! I am truly grateful to you!'

Sir Richard was eyeing the bundle through his quizzing glass. '*Are* you a burglar?' he enquired.

A chuckle, hastily choked, greeted this. 'No, of course I'm not. I couldn't manage a bandbox, so I had to tie all my things up in a shawl. And now I think I must be going, if you please.'

'Drunk I undoubtedly am,' said Sir Richard, 'but some remnants of sanity still remain with me. You cannot, my good child, wander about the streets of London at this hour of night, and dressed in those clothes. I believe I ought to ring that bell, and hand you over to your—aunt, did you say?'

Two agitated hands clasped his arm. 'Oh, *don't!*' begged the fugitive. '*Please* don't!'

'Well, what am I to do with you?' asked Sir Richard.

'Nothing. Only tell me the way to Holborn!'

'Why Holborn?'

'I have to go to the White Horse Inn, to catch the stagecoach for Bristol.'

'That settles it,' said Sir Richard. 'I will not set you a foot on your way until I have the whole story from you. It's my belief you are a dangerous criminal.'

'I am not!' said the fugitive indignantly. 'Anyone with the veriest speck of sensibility would feel for my plight! I am escaping from the most odious persecution.'

'Fortunate child!' said Sir Richard, taking her bundle from her. 'I wish I might do the same. Let us remove from this neighbourhood. I have seldom seen a street that depressed me more. I can't think how I came here. Do you feel that our agreeable encounter would be improved by an exchange of names, or are you travelling incognita?'

'Yes, I shall have to make up a name for myself. I hadn't thought of that. My real name is Penelope Creed. Who are you?'

'I,' said Sir Richard, 'am Richard Wyndham, wholly at your service.'

'Beau Wyndham?' asked Miss Creed knowledgeably.

'Beau Wyndham,' bowed Sir Richard. 'Is it possible that we can have met before?'

'Oh no, but of course I have heard of you. My cousin tries to tie his cravat in a Wyndham Fall. At least, that is what he says it is, but it looks like a muddle to me.'

'Then it is *not* a Wyndham Fall,' said Sir Richard firmly.

'No, that's what I thought. My cousin tries to be a dandy, but he has a face like a fish. They want me to marry him.'

'What a horrible thought!' said Sir Richard, shuddering.

'I told you you would feel for my plight!' said Miss Creed. 'So would you now set me on my way to Holborn?'

'No,' replied Sir Richard.

'But you must!' declared Miss Creed, on a note of panic. 'Where are we going?'

'I cannot walk about the streets all night. We had better repair to my house to discuss this matter.'

'No!' said Miss Creed, standing stock-still in the middle of the pavement.

Sir Richard sighed. 'Rid yourself of the notion that I cherish any villainous designs upon your person,' he said. 'I imagine I might well be your father. How old are you?'

'I am turned seventeen.'

'Well, I am nearly thirty,' said Sir Richard.

Miss Creed worked this out. 'You couldn't possibly be my father!'

'I am far too drunk to solve arithmetical problems. Let it suffice that I have not the slightest intention of making love to you.'

'Well, then, I don't mind accompanying you,' said Miss Creed handsomely. 'Are you really drunk?'

'Vilely,' said Sir Richard.

'No one would credit it, I assure you. You carry your wine very well.'

'You speak as one with experience in these matters,' said Sir Richard.

'My father was used to say that it was most important to see how a man behaved when in his cups. My cousin becomes excessively silly.'

'You know,' said Sir Richard, knitting his brows, 'the more I hear of this cousin of yours the more I feel you should not be allowed to marry him. Where are we now?'

'Piccadilly, I think,' replied Miss Creed.

'Good! I live in St James's Square. Why do they want you to marry your cousin?'

'Because,' said Miss Creed mournfully, 'I am cursed with a large fortune!'

Sir Richard halted in the middle of the road. 'Cursed with a large fortune?' he repeated.

'Yes, indeed. You see, my father had no other children, and I believe I am most fabulously wealthy, besides having a house in Somerset, which they won't let me live in. When he died I had to live with Aunt Almeria. I was only twelve years old, you see. And now she is persecuting me to marry my cousin Frederick. So I ran away.'

'The man with a face like a fish?'

'Yes.'

'You did quite right,' said Sir Richard.

'Well, I think I did.'

'Not a doubt of it. Why Holborn?'

'I told you,' replied Miss Creed patiently. 'I am going to get on the Bristol coach.'

'Oh! Why Bristol?'

'Well, I'm not going to Bristol precisely, but my house is in Somerset, and I have a very great friend there. I haven't seen him for nearly five years, but we used to play together, and we pricked our fingers—mixing the blood, you know—and we made a vow to marry one another when we were grown up.'

'This is all very romantic,' commented Sir Richard.

'Yes, isn't it?' said Miss Creed enthusiastically. 'You are not married are you?'

'No. Oh, my God!'

'Why, what is the matter?'

'I've just remembered that I am going to be.'

'Don't you want to be?'

'No.'

'But no one could force *you* to be married!'

'My good girl, you do not know my relatives,' said Sir Richard bitterly.

'Did they talk to you, and talk to you, and *talk* to you? And say it was your duty? And plague your life out? And cry at you?' asked Miss Creed.

'Something of the sort,' admitted Sir Richard. 'Is that what your relatives did to you?'

'Yes. So I stole Geoffrey's second-best suit, and climbed out of the window.'

'Who is Geoffrey?'

'Oh, he is my other cousin. He is at Harrow, and his clothes fit me perfectly. Is this your house?'

'This is my house.'

'But wait!' said Miss Creed. 'Will not the porter be sitting up to open the door to you?'

'I don't encourage people to sit up for me,' said Sir Richard, producing from his pocket a key, and fitting it into the lock.

'But I expect you have a valet,' suggested Miss Creed, hanging back. 'He will be waiting to help you to bed.'

'True,' said Sir Richard. 'But he will not come to my room until I ring the bell. You need have no fear.'

'Oh, in that case—!' said Miss Creed, relieved, and followed him blithely into the house.

A lamp was burning in the hall, and a candle was placed on a marble-topped table, in readiness for Sir Richard. He kindled it by thrusting it into the lamp, and led his guest into the library. Here there were more candles, in chandeliers fixed to the wall. Sir Richard lit as many of these as seemed good to him, and turned to inspect Miss Creed.

She had taken off her hat, and was standing in the middle of the room, looking interestedly about her. Her hair, which clustered in feathery curls on the top of her head, and was somewhat raggedly cut at the back, was guinea gold; her eyes were a deep blue, very large and trustful, and apt at any moment to twinkle with merriment. She had a short little nose, slightly freckled, a most decided chin, and a pair of dimples.

Sir Richard, critically observing her, was unimpressed by these charms. He said: 'You look the most complete urchin indeed!'

She seemed to take this as a tribute. She raised her candid eyes to his face, and said: 'Do I? Truly?'

His gaze travelled slowly over her borrowed raiment. 'Horrible!' he said. 'Are you under the impression that you have tied that–that travesty of a cravat in a Wyndham Fall?'

'No, but the thing is I have never tied a cravat before,' she explained.

'That,' said Sir Richard, 'is obvious. Come here!'

She approached obediently, and stood still while his expert fingers wrought with the crumpled folds round her neck.

'No, it is beyond even my skill,' he said at last. 'I shall have to lend you one of mine. Never mind; sit down, and let us talk this matter over. My recollection is none of the clearest, but I fancy you said you were going into Somerset to marry a friend of your childhood.'

'Yes, Piers Luttrell,' nodded Miss Creed, seating herself in a large armchair.

'Furthermore, you are just seventeen.'

'Turned seventeen,' she corrected.

'Don't quibble! And you propose to undertake this journey as a passenger on an Accommodation coach?'

'Yes,' agreed Miss Creed.

'And, as though this were not enough, you are going alone?'

'Of course I am.'

'My dear child,' said Sir Richard, 'drunk I may be, but not so drunk as to acquiesce in this fantastic scheme, believe me.'

'I don't think you are drunk,' said Miss Creed. 'Besides, it has nothing to do with you! You cannot interfere in my affairs merely because you helped me out of the window.'

'I didn't help you out of the window. Something tells me I ought to restore you to the bosom of your family.'

Miss Creed turned rather white, and said in a small, but very clear voice: 'If you did that it would be the most cruel–the most treacherous thing in the world!'

'I suppose it would,' he admitted.

There was a pause. Sir Richard unfobbed his snuffbox with a flick of one practised finger, and took a pinch. Miss Creed swallowed, and said: 'If you had ever *seen* my cousin, you would understand.'

He glanced down at her, but said nothing.

'He has a wet mouth,' said Miss Creed despairingly.

'That settles it,' said Sir Richard, shutting his snuffbox. 'I will escort you to your childhood's friend.'

Miss Creed blushed. 'You? But you can't!'

'Why can't I?'

'Because—because I don't know you, and I can very well go by myself, and—well, it's quite absurd! I see now that you *are* drunk.'

'Let me inform you,' said Sir Richard, 'that missish airs don't suit those clothes. Moreover, I don't like them. Either you will travel to Somerset in my company, or you will go back to your aunt. Take your choice!'

'Do please consider!' begged Miss Creed. 'You know I am obliged to travel in the greatest secrecy. If you went with me, no one would know what had become of you.'

'No one would know what had become of me,' repeated Sir Richard slowly. 'No one—my girl, you have no longer any choice: I am going with you to Somerset!'

3

As no argument produced the least effect on Sir Richard's suddenly reckless mood, Miss Creed abandoned her conscientious attempt to dissuade him from accompanying her on her journey, and owned that his protection would be welcome. 'It is not that I am afraid to go by myself,' she explained, 'but, to tell you the truth, I am not quite used to do things all alone.'

'I should hope,' said Sir Richard, 'that you are not quite used to travelling in the common stage either.'

'No, of course I am not. It will be quite an adventure! Have you ever travelled by stagecoach?'

'Never. We shall travel post.'

'Travel post? You must be mad!' exclaimed Miss Creed. 'I dare say you are known at every posting inn on the Bath road. We should be discovered in a trice. Why I had thought of all that even before you made up your mind to join me! My cousin Frederick is too stupid to think of anything, but my Aunt Almeria is not, and I make no doubt she will guess that I have run away to my own home, and follow me. That is one of the reasons why I made up my mind to journey in the stage. She will enquire for me at the posting houses, and no one will be able to give her the least news of me. And just think what a bustle there would be if it were discovered that we had been travelling about the country together in a post chaise!'

'Does it seem to you that there would be less impropriety in our travelling in the stage?' enquired Sir Richard.

'Yes, much less. In fact, I do not see that it is improper at all, for how can I prevent your booking a seat in a public vehicle, if you wish to do so? Besides, I have not enough money to hire a post chaise.'

'I thought you said you were cursed with a large fortune?'

'Yes, but they won't let me have anything but the most paltry allowance until I come of age, and I've spent most of this month's pin money.'

'I will be your banker,' said Sir Richard.

Miss Creed shook her head vigorously. 'No, indeed you will not! One should never be beholden to strangers. I shall pay everything for myself. Of course, if you are set against travelling by the stage, I do not see what is to be done. Unless—' she broke off as an idea occurred to her, and said, with sparkling eyes: 'I have a famous notion! You are a notable whip, are you not?'

'I believe I am accounted so,' replied Sir Richard.

'Well, supposing you were to drive in your own curricle? Then I could get up behind, and pretend to be your Tiger, and hold the yard of tin, and blow up for the change, and—'

'No!' said Sir Richard.

She looked disappointed. 'I thought it would be exciting. However, I dare say you are right.'

'I am right,' said Sir Richard. 'The more I think of it, the more I see that there is much to be said for the stagecoach. At what hour did you say that it leaves town?'

'At nine o'clock, from the White Horse Inn, in Fetter Lane. Only we must go there long before that, on account of your servants. What is the time now?'

Sir Richard consulted his watch. 'Close on five,' he replied.

'Then we have not a moment to lose,' said Miss Creed. 'Your servants will be stirring in another hour. But you can't travel in those clothes, can you?'

'No,' he said, 'and I can't travel with that cravat of yours either, or that abominable bundle. And, now I come to look at you more particularly, I never saw hair worse cut.'

'You mean the back, I expect,' said Miss Creed, unresentful of these strictures. 'Luckily, it has always been short in front. I had to chop the back bits off myself, and I could not well see what I was about.'

'Wait here!' commanded Sir Richard, and left the room.

When he returned it was more than half an hour later, and he had shed his evening dress for buckskin breeches, and topboots, and a coat of blue superfine cloth. Miss Creed greeted him with considerable relief. 'I began to fear you had forgotten me, or fallen asleep!' she told him.

'Nothing of the sort!' said Sir Richard, setting a small cloak bag and a large portmanteau down on the floor. 'Drunk or sober, I never forget my obligations. Stand up, and I will see what I can do towards making you look more presentable.'

He had a snowy white cravat over one arm, and a pair of scissors in his hand. A few judicious snips greatly improved the appearance of Miss Creed's head, and by the time a comb had been ruthlessly dragged through her curls, forcing rather than coaxing them into a more manly style, she began to look quite neat, though rather watery-eyed. Her crumpled cravat was next cast aside, and one of Sir Richard's own put round her neck. She was so anxious to see how he was arranging it that she stood on tiptoe to catch a glimpse of herself in the mirror hanging above the mantelpiece, and got her ears boxed.

'*Will* you stand still?' said Sir Richard.

Miss Creed sniffed, and subsided into dark mutterings. However, when he released her, and she was able to see the result of his handiwork, she was so pleased that she forgot her injuries, and exclaimed: 'Oh, how nice I look! Is it a Wyndham Fall?'

'Certainly not!' Sir Richard replied. 'The Wyndham Fall is not for scrubby schoolboys, let me tell you.'

'I am not a scrubby schoolboy!'

'You look like one. Now put what you have in that bundle into the cloak bag, and we'll be off.'

'I have a very good mind not to go with you,' said Miss Creed, glowering.

'No, you haven't. You are now my young cousin, and we are wholly committed to a life of adventure. What did you say your name was?'

'Penelope Creed. Most people call me Pen, but I ought to have a man's name now.'

'Pen will do very well. If it occasions the least comment, you will say that it is spelt with two N's. You were named after that Quaker fellow.'

'Oh, that is a very good idea! What shall I call you?'

'Richard.'

'Richard who?'

'Smith—Jones—Brown.'

She was engaged in transferring her belongings from the Paisley shawl to the cloak bag. 'You don't look like any of those. What shall I do with this shawl?'

'Leave it,' replied Sir Richard, gathering up some gleaming scraps of guinea-gold hair from the carpet, and casting them to the back of the fireplace. 'Do you know, Pen Creed, I fancy you have come into my life in the guise of Providence?'

She looked up enquiringly. 'Have I?' she said doubtfully.

'That, or Disaster,' said Sir Richard. 'I shall know which when I am sober. But, to tell you the truth, I don't care a jot! *En avant, mon cousin!*'

It was past midday when Lady Trevor, accompanied by her reluctant husband, called at her brother's house in St James's Square. She was admitted by the porter, obviously big with news, and handed on by him to the butler. 'Tell Sir Richard that I am here,' she commanded, stepping into the Yellow Saloon.

'Sir Richard, my lady, is not at home,' said the butler, in a voice pregnant with mystery.

Louisa, who had extracted from her lord a description of Sir Richard's proceedings at Almack's on the preceding night, snorted. 'You will tell him that his sister desires to see him,' she said.

'Sir Richard, my lady, is not upon the premises,' said the butler, working up to his climax.

'Sir Richard has trained you well,' said Louisa dryly. 'But I am not to be put off so! Go and tell him that I wish to see him!'

'Sir Richard, my lady, did not sleep in his bed last night!' announced the butler.

George was surprised into indiscreet comment. 'What's that? Nonsense! He wasn't as foxed as that when *I* saw him!'

'As to that, my lord,' said the butler, with dignity, 'I have no information. In a word, my lord, Sir Richard has vanished.'

'Good Gad!' ejaculated George.

'Fiddle-de-dee!' said Louisa tartly. 'Sir Richard, as I suppose, is in his bed!'

'No, my lady. As I informed your ladyship, Sir Richard's bed has not been slept in.' He paused, but Louisa only stared at him. Satisfied with the impression he had made, he continued: 'The evening attire which Sir

Richard was wearing yesterday was found by his man, Biddle, upon the floor of his bedroom. Sir Richard's second-best top boots, a pair of buckskins, a blue riding coat, his drab overcoat, and a fawn-coloured beaver, have all disappeared. One is forced to the conclusion, my lady, that Sir Richard was called away unexpectedly.'

'Gone off without his valet?' George demanded in a stupefied tone.

The butler bowed. 'Precisely so, my lord.'

'Impossible!' George said, from the heart.

Louisa, who had been frowning over these tidings, said in a brisk voice: 'It is certainly very odd, but there is no doubt some perfectly reasonable explanation. Pray, are you certain that my brother left no word with *any* member of his household?'

'None whatsoever, my lady.'

George heaved a deep sigh, and shook his head. 'I warned you, Louisa! I *said* you were driving him too hard!'

'You said nothing of the sort!' snapped Louisa, annoyed with him for talking so indiscreetly before a palpably interested servant. 'To be sure, he may well have mentioned to us that he was going out of town, and we have forgotten the circumstance.'

'How can you say so?' asked George, honestly puzzled. 'Why, didn't you have it from Melissa Brandon herself that he was to call—'

'That will do, George!' said Louisa, quelling him with a look so terrible that he quailed under it. 'Tell me, Porson,' she resumed, turning again to the butler, 'has my brother gone in his post chaise, or is he driving himself?'

'None of Sir Richard's vehicles, my lady, sporting or otherwise, is missing from the stables,' said Porson, relishing the cumulative effect of his disclosures.

'He is riding, then!'

'I have ascertained from the head groom, my lady, that none of Sir Richard's horses has been abstracted. The head groom has not seen Sir Richard since yesterday morning.'

'Good Gad!' muttered George, his eyes starting with dismay at the hideous thought which presented itself to him. 'No, no, he would not do that!'

'Be quiet, George! For heaven's sake, be quiet!' Louisa cried sharply. 'Why, what nonsensical notion have you taken into your head? I am sure it is most provoking of Richard to slip off like this, but as for—I won't have you say such things! Ten to one, he has gone off to watch some odious sporting event: prizefighting, I dare say! He will be home presently.'

'But he didn't sleep at home!' George reminded her. 'And I'm bound to say he wasn't cold stone sober when he left Almack's last night. I don't mean he was badly foxed, but you know what he's like when he's—'

'I am thankful to say that I know nothing of the kind!' retorted Louisa. 'If he was not sober, it would account for his erratic behaviour.'

'Erratic behaviour! I must say, Louisa, that is a fine way to talk when poor Ricky may be at the bottom of the river,' exclaimed George, roused to noble courage.

She changed colour, but said faintly: 'How can you be so absurd? Don't say such things, I beg of you!'

The butler coughed. 'I beg your lordship's pardon, but if I might say so, Sir Richard would hardly change his raiment for the execution of—of what I apprehend your lordship means.'

'No. No, very true! He would not, of course!' agreed George, relieved.

'Moreover, my lord, Biddle reports that Sir Richard's drawers and wardrobe have been ransacked, and various articles of clothing abstracted. Upon going to rouse Sir Richard this morning, Biddle found his room in the greatest disorder, as though Sir Richard had made his preparations for a journey in haste. Furthermore, my lord, Biddle informed me that a portmanteau and a small cloak bag are missing from the cupboard in which they are customarily kept.'

George gave a sudden croak of laughter. 'Bolted, by Gad! Yoicks! gone awa-ay!'

'*George!*'

'I don't care!' said George defiantly. 'I'm devilish glad he has bolted!'

'But there was no need!' Louisa said, forgetting that Porson was in the room. 'No one was constraining him to marry—' She caught Porson's eye, and stopped short.

'I should inform your ladyship,' said Porson, apparently deaf to her indiscreet utterance, 'that there were several other Peculiar Circumstances attached to Sir Richard's disappearance.'

'Good heavens, you talk as though he has been spirited away by magic!' said Louisa impatiently. 'What circumstances, my good man?'

'If your ladyship will excuse me, I will fetch them for your inspection,' said Porson, and bowed himself out.

Husband and wife were left to stare at one another in perplexity.

'Well!' said George, not without satisfaction, 'you see now what comes of plaguing a man out of his mind!'

'I didn't! George, it is unjust of you to say so! Pray, how could I force him to offer for Melissa if he did not wish to? I am persuaded his flight has nothing whatever to do with that affair.'

'No man will bear being teased to do something he don't want to do,' said George.

'Then all I have to say is that Richard is a bigger coward than I would have believed possible! I am sure, if only he had told me frankly that he did not wish to marry Melissa I should not have said another word about it.'

'Ha!' ejaculated George, achieving a sardonic laugh.

He escaped reproof by Porson's coming back into the room, bearing certain articles which he laid carefully upon the table. In great astonishment, Lord and Lady Trevor gazed at a Paisley shawl, a crumpled cravat, and some short strands of guinea-gold hair, curling appropriately enough into a shape resembling a question-mark.

'What in the world—?' exclaimed Louisa.

'These articles, my lady, were discovered by the underfootman upon his entering the library this morning,' said Porson. 'The shawl, which neither Biddle nor myself can remember to have seen before, was lying on the floor; the cravat had been thrown into the grate; and the—er—lock of hair—was found under the shawl.'

'Well, upon my word!' said George, putting up his glass the better to inspect the articles. He pointed his glass at the cravat. 'That tells its own tale! Poor Ricky must have come in last night in a bad state. I dare say his head was aching: mine would have been, if I had drunk half the brandy he tossed off yesterday. I see it all. There he was, pledged to call on Saar this morning—no way out of it—head on fire! He tugged at his cravat, felt as though he must choke, and ruined the thing—and no matter how far gone he was, Ricky would never wear a crumpled necktie! There he was, sitting in a chair, very likely, and running his hands through his hair, in the way a man does—'

'Richard never yet disarranged his hair, and no matter how drunk he may have been, he did not pull a curl of *that* colour out of his own head!' interrupted Louisa. 'Moreover, it has been cut off. Anyone can see that!'

George levelled his glass at the gleaming curl. A number of emotions flitted across his rather stolid countenance. He drew a breath. 'You're quite right, Louisa,' he said. 'Well, I never would have believed it! The sly dog!'

'You need not wait, Porson!' Louisa said sharply.

'Very good, my lady. But I should perhaps inform your ladyship that the under-footman found the candles burning in the library when he entered it this morning.'

'I cannot see that it signifies in the least,' replied Louisa, waving him aside.

He withdrew. George, who was holding the curl in the palm of his hand, said: 'Well, *I* can't call anyone to mind with hair of this colour. To be sure, there were one or two opera dancers, but Ricky's not at all the sort of man to want 'em to cut off their hair for him. But there's no doubt about one thing, Louisa: this curl was a keepsake.'

'Thank you, George, I had already realized that. Yet I thought I knew all the respectable women of Richard's acquaintance! One would say that kind of a keepsake must have belonged to his salad days. I am sure he is much too unromantic now to cherish a lock of hair!'

'And he threw it away,' George said, shaking his head. 'You know, it's devilish sad, Louisa, upon my word it is! Threw it away, because he was on the eve of offering for that Brandon iceberg!'

'Very affecting! And having thrown it away, he then ran away himself—not, you will admit, making any offer at all! And where did the shawl come from?' She picked it up as she spoke, and shook it out. 'Extremely creased! Now why?'

'Another keepsake,' George said. 'Crushed it in his hands, poor old Ricky—couldn't bear the recollections it conjured up—flung it away!'

'Oh, fiddle!' said Louisa, exasperated. 'Well, Porson, what is it now?'

The butler, who had come back into the room, said primly: 'The Honourable Cedric Brandon, my lady, to see Sir Richard. I thought perhaps your ladyship would wish to receive him.'

'I don't suppose he can throw the least light on this mystery, but you may as well show him in,' said Louisa. 'Depend upon it,' she added to her husband, when Porson had withdrawn himself again, 'he will have come to learn why Richard did not keep his engagement with Saar this morning. I am sure I do not know what I am to say to him!'

'If you ask me, Cedric won't blame Richard,' said George. 'They tell me he was talking pretty freely at White's yesterday. Foxed, of course. How you and your mother can want Ricky to marry into that family is what beats me!'

'We have known the Brandons all our lives,' Louisa said defensively. 'I don't pretend that—' She broke off, as the Honourable Cedric walked into the room, and stepped forward, with her hand held out. 'How do you do, Cedric? I am afraid Richard is not at home. We—we think he must have been called away suddenly on urgent affairs.'

'Taken my advice, has he?' said Cedric, saluting her hand with careless grace. '"You run, Ricky! Don't do it!" that's what I said to him. Told him

I'd sponge on him for the rest of his days, if he was fool enough to let himself be caught.'

'I wonder that you should talk in that vulgar way!' said Louisa. 'Of course he has not *run*! I dare say he will be back any moment now. It was excessively remiss of him not to have sent a note round to inform Lord Saar that he could not wait on him this morning, as he had engaged himself to do, but—'

'You've got that wrong,' interrupted Cedric. 'No engagement at all. Melissa told him to call on m'father; he didn't say he would. Wormed it out of Melissa myself an hour ago. Lord, you never saw anyone in such a rage! What's all this?' His roving eye had alighted on the relics laid out upon the table. 'A lock of hair, by Jove! Devilish pretty hair too!'

'Found in the library this morning,' said George portentously, ignoring his wife's warning frown.

'Here? Ricky?' demanded Cedric. 'You're bamming me!'

'No, it is perfectly true. We cannot understand it.'

Cedric's eyes danced. 'By all that's famous! Who'd have thought it, though? Well, that settles our affairs! Devilish inconvenient, but damme, I'm glad he's bolted! Always liked Ricky—never wanted to see him bound for perdition with the rest of us! But we're done-up now, and no mistake! The diamonds have gone.'

'What?' Louisa cried. 'Cedric, not the Brandon necklace?'

'That's it. Last sheet-anchor thrown out to the windward—gone like that!' He snapped his fingers in the air, and laughed. 'I came to tell Ricky I'd accept his offer to buy me a pair of colours, and be off to the Wars.'

'But how? Where?' gasped Louisa.

'Stolen. My mother took it to Bath with her. Never would stir without the thing, more's the pity! *I* wonder m'father didn't sell it years ago. Only thing he didn't sell, except Saar Court, and that'll have to go next. My mother wouldn't hear of parting with the diamonds.'

'But Cedric, how stolen? Who took it?'

'Highwaymen. My mother sent off a courier post haste to m'father. Chaise stopped somewhere near Bath—two fellows with masks and horse pistols—Sophia screeching like a hen—my mother swooning—outriders taken by surprise—one of 'em winged. And off went the necklace. Which is what I can't for the life of me understand.'

'How terrible! Your poor Mama! I am so sorry! It is an appalling loss!'

'Yes, but how the devil did they find the thing?' said Cedric. 'That's what I want to know.'

'But surely if they took Lady Saar's jewel case—'

'The necklace wasn't in it. I'll lay my last shilling on that. My mother had a hiding place for it—devilish cunning notion—always put it there when she travelled. Secret pocket behind one of the squabs.'

'Good Gad, do you mean to say someone divulged the hiding place to the rascals?' said George.

'Looks mighty like it, don't it?'

'Who knew of it? If you can discover the traitor, you may yet get the necklace back. Are you sure of all your servants?'

'I'm sure none of them—Lord, I don't know!' Cedric said, rather hastily. 'My mother wants the Bow Street Runners set on to it, but m'father don't think it's the least use. And now here's Ricky bolted, on top of everything! The old man will go off in an apoplexy!'

'Really, Cedric, you must not talk so of your Papa!' Louisa expostulated.

'And we don't know that Richard has—has *bolted*! Indeed, I am sure it's no such thing!'

'He'll be a fool if he hasn't,' said Cedric. 'What do you think, George?'

'I don't know,' George answered. 'It is very perplexing. I own, when I first heard of his disappearance—for you must know that he did not sleep in his bed last night, and when *I* saw him he was foxed—I felt the gravest alarm. But—'

'Suicide, by God!' Cedric gave a shout of laughter. 'I must tell Melissa that! Driven to death! Ricky! Oh, by all that's famous!'

'Cedric, you are quite abominable!' said Louisa roundly. 'Of course Richard has not committed suicide! He has merely gone away. I'm sure I don't know where, and if you say anything of the sort to Melissa I shall never forgive you! In fact, I beg you will tell Melissa nothing more than that Richard has been called away on an urgent matter of business.'

'What, can't I tell her about the lock of yaller hair? Now, don't be a spoilsport, Louisa!'

'Odious creature!'

'We believe the lock of hair to be a relic of some long-forgotten affair,' said George. 'Possibly a boy and girl attachment. It would be gross impropriety to mention it beyond these walls.'

'If it comes to that, old fellow, what about the gross impropriety of poking and prying into Ricky's drawers?' asked Cedric cheerfully.

'We did no such thing!' Louisa cried. 'It was found upon the floor in the library!'

'Dropped? Discarded? Seems to me Ricky's been leading a double life. I'd have said myself he never troubled much about females. Won't I roast him when I see him!'

'You will do nothing of the sort. Oh dear, I wish to heaven I knew where he has gone, and what it all means!'

'I'll tell you where he's gone!' offered Cedric. 'He's gone to find the yaller-haired charmer of his youth. Not a doubt of it! Lord, I'd give a monkey to see him, though. Ricky on a romantic adventure!'

'Now you are being absurd!' said Louisa. 'If one thing is certain, it is that Richard has not one grain of romance in his disposition, while as for adventure—! I dare say he would shudder at the mere thought of it. Richard, my dear Cedric, is first, last, and always a man of fashion, and he will never do anything unbefitting a Corinthian. You may take my word for *that*!'

4

The man of fashion, at that precise moment, was sleeping heavily in one corner of a huge green-and-gold Accommodation coach, swaying and rocking on its ponderous way to Bristol. The hour was two in the afternoon, the locality Calcot Green, west of Reading, and the dreams troubling the repose of the man of fashion were extremely uneasy. He had endured some waking moments, when the coach had stopped with a lurch and a heave to take up or set down passengers, to change horses, or to wait while a laggardly pike keeper opened a gate upon the road. These moments had seemed to him more fraught with nightmare even than his dreams. His head was aching, his eyeballs seemed to be on fire, and a phantasmagoria of strange, unwelcome faces swam before his outraged vision. He had shut his eyes again with a groan, preferring his dreams to reality, but when the coach stopped at Calcot Green to put down a stout woman with a tendency to asthma, sleep finally deserted him, and he opened his eyes, blinked at the face of a precise-looking man in a suit of neat black, seated opposite to him, ejaculated: 'Oh, my God!' and sat up.

'Is your head *very* bad?' asked a solicitous and vaguely familiar voice in his ear.

He turned his head, and encountered the enquiring gaze of Miss Penelope Creed. He looked at her in silence for a few moments; then he said: 'I remember. Stagecoach—Bristol. Why, oh why, did I touch the brandy?'

An admonitory pinch made him recollect his surroundings. He found that there were three other persons in the coach, seated opposite to him, and that all were regarding him with interest. The precise-looking man, whom he judged to be an attorney's clerk, was frankly disapproving; a woman in a poke bonnet and a paduasoy shawl nodded to him in a motherly style, and said that he was like her second boy, who could not abide the rocking of the coach either; and a large man beside her, whom he took to be her husband, corroborated this statement by enunciating in a deep voice: 'That's right!'

Instinct took Sir Richard's hand to his cravat; his fingers told him that it was considerably crumpled, like the tails of his blue coat. His curly-brimmed beaver seemed to add to the discomfort of his aching head; he took it off, and clasped his head in his hands, trying to throw off the lingering wisps of sleep. 'Good God!' he said thickly. 'Where are we?'

'Well, I am not quite sure, but we have passed Reading,' replied Pen, rather anxiously surveying him.

'Calcot Green, that's where we are,' volunteered the large man. 'Stopped to set down someone. They ain't a-worriting theirselves over the time bill, that's plain. I dare say the coachman's stepped down for a drink.'

'Ah, well!' said his wife tolerantly. 'It'll be thirsty work, setting up on the box in the sun like he has to.'

'That's right,' agreed the large man.

'If the Company was to hear of it he would be turned off, and very rightly!' said the clerk, sniffing. 'The behaviour of these stagecoach men is becoming a scandal.'

'I'm sure there's no call for people to get nasty if a man falls behind his time bill a little,' said the woman. 'Live and let live, that's what I say.'

Her husband assented to this in his usual fashion. The coach lurched forward again, and Pen said, under cover of the noise of the wheels and the horses' hooves: 'You kept on telling me that you were drunk, and now I see that you were. I was afraid you would regret coming with me.'

Sir Richard raised his head from his hands. 'Drunk I most undoubtedly must have been, but I regret nothing except the brandy. When does this appalling vehicle reach Bristol?'

'It isn't one of the fast coaches, you know. They don't engage to cover much above eight miles an hour. I think we ought to be in Bristol by eleven o'clock. We seem to stop such a number of times, though. Do you mind very much?'

He looked down at her. 'Do you?'

'To tell you the truth,' she confided, 'not a bit! I am enjoying myself hugely. Only I don't want you to be made uncomfortable all for my sake. I quite see that you are sadly out of place in a stagecoach.'

'My dear child, you had nothing whatever to do with my present discomfort, believe me. As for *my* being out of place, what, pray, are you?'

The dimples peeped. 'Oh, *I* am only a scrubby schoolboy, after all!'

'Did I say that?' She nodded. 'Well, so you are,' said Sir Richard, looking her over critically. 'Except for— Did I tie that cravat? Yes, I thought I must have. What in the world have you got there?'

'An apple,' replied Pen, showing it to him. 'The fat woman who got out just now gave it to me.'

'You are not going to sit there munching it, are you?' demanded Sir Richard.

'Yes, I am. Why shouldn't I? Would you like a bit of it?'

'I should not!' said Sir Richard.

'Well, I am excessively hungry. That was the one thing we forgot.'

'What was?'

'Food,' said Pen, digging her teeth into the apple. 'We ought to have provided ourselves with a basket of things to eat on the journey. I forgot that the stage doesn't stop at posting houses, like the mail coaches. At least, I didn't forget exactly, because I never knew it.'

'This must be looked to,' said Sir Richard. 'If you are hungry, you must undoubtedly be fed. What are you proposing to do with the core of that apple?'

'Eat it,' said Pen.

'Repellent brat!' said Sir Richard, with a strong shudder.

He leaned back in his corner, but a tug at his sleeve made him incline his head towards his companion.

'I told these people that you were my tutor,' whispered Pen.

'Of course, a young gentleman in his tutor's charge *would* be travelling in the common stage,' said Sir Richard, resigning himself to the rôle of usher.

At the next stage, which was Woolhampton, he roused himself from the languor which threatened to possess him, alighted from the coach, and showed unexpected competence in procuring from the modest inn a very tolerable cold meal for his charge. The coach awaited his pleasure, and the attorney's clerk, whose sharp eyes had seen Sir Richard's hand go from his pocket to the coachman's ready palm, muttered darkly of bribery and corruption on the King's Highway.

'Have some chicken,' said Sir Richard amiably.

The clerk refused this invitation with every evidence of contempt, but there were several other passengers, notably a small boy with adenoids, who were perfectly ready to share the contents of the basket on Pen's knees.

Sir Richard had good reason to know that Miss Creed's disposition was extremely confiding; during the long day's journey he discovered that she was friendly to a fault. She observed all the passengers with a bright and wholly unselfconscious gaze; conversed even with the clerk; and showed an alarming tendency to become the life and soul of the party. Questioned about herself, and her destination, she wove, zestfully, an entirely mendacious story, which she embroidered from time to time with outrageous details. Sir Richard was ruthlessly applied to for corroboration, and, entering into the spirit of the adventure, added a few extempore details himself. Pen seemed pleased with these, but was plainly disappointed at his refusal to join her in keeping the small boy with adenoids amused.

He leaned back in his corner, lazily enjoying Miss Creed's flights into the realms of fancy, and wondering what his mother and his sister would think if they knew that he was travelling to an unknown destination, by stagecoach, accompanied by a young lady as unembarrassed by this circumstance as by her male attire. A laugh shook him, as he pictured Louisa's face. His head had ceased aching, but although the detachment fostered by brandy had left him, he still retained a feeling of delightful irresponsibility. Sober, he would certainly not have set forth on this absurd journey, but having done so, drunk, he was perfectly willing to continue it. He was, moreover, curious to learn more of Pen's history. Some farrago she had told him last night: his recollection of it was a trifle hazy, but there had surely been something about an aunt, and a cousin with a face like a fish.

He turned his head slightly on the dingy squabs of the coach, and watched, from under drooping eyelids, the animated little face beside him. Miss Creed was listening, apparently keenly interested, to a long and involved recital of the illness which had lately prostrated the motherly woman's youngest-born. She shook her head over the folly of the apothecary, nodded wisely at the efficiency of an age-old nostrum compounded of strange herbs, and was on the point of capping this recipe with one in use in her own family when Sir Richard's foot found hers, and trod on it.

It was certainly time to check Miss Creed. The motherly woman stared at her, and said that it was queer-and-all to meet a young gentleman so knowledgeable.

'My mother,' said Pen, blushing, 'has been an invalid for many years.'

Everyone looked solicitous, and a desiccated female in the far corner of the coach said that no one could tell *her* anything about illness.

This remark had the effect of diverting attention from Pen, and as the triumphant lady plunged into the history of her sufferings, she sat back beside Sir Richard, directing up at him a look quite as mischievous as it was apologetic.

The lawyer's clerk, who had not yet forgiven Sir Richard for bribing the coachman, said something about the license allowed to young persons in these days. He contrasted it unfavourably with his own upbringing, and said that if he had a son he would not pamper him by giving him a tutor, but would send him to school. Pen said meekly that Mr Brown was very strict, and Sir Richard, correctly identifying Mr Brown with himself, lent colour to her assertion by telling her sternly not to chatter.

The motherly woman said that she was sure the young gentleman brightened them all up, and for her part she did not hold with people being harsh with children.

'That's right,' agreed her spouse. 'I never wanted to break any of *my* young 'uns' spirits: I like to see 'em up-and-coming.'

Several of the passengers looked reproachfully at Sir Richard, and, that no doubt of his severity might linger in their minds, Pen subsided into crushed silence, folding her hands on her knees, and casting down her eyes.

Sir Richard saw that he would figure for the rest of the journey as an oppressor, and mentally rehearsed a speech which was destined for Miss Creed's sole edification.

She disarmed him by falling asleep with her cheek against his shoulder. She slept between one stage and the next, and when roused by the coach's halting with its usual lurch, opened her eyes, smiled drowsily up at Sir Richard and murmured: 'I'm glad you came. Are you glad you came?'

'Very. Wake up!' said Sir Richard, wondering what more imprudent remarks might be hovering on her tongue.

She yawned, and straightened herself. An altercation seemed to be in progress between the guard and someone standing in the inn yard. A farmer, who had boarded the coach at Calne, and was seated beside Pen, said that he thought the trouble was that the would-be passenger was not upon the way bill.

'Well, he cannot come inside, that is certain!' said the thin woman. 'It is shocking, the way one is crowded already!'

'Where are we?' enquired Pen.

'Chippenham,' responded the farmer. 'That's where the Bath road goes off, see?'

She sat forward to look out of the window. 'Chippenham already? Oh yes, so it is! I know it well.'

Sir Richard cocked an amused eye at her. '*Already?*' he murmured.

'Well, I have been asleep, so it seems soon to me. Are you very weary, sir?'

'By no means. I am becoming entirely resigned.'

The new passenger, having apparently settled matters with the guard, at this moment pulled open the door, and tried to climb up into the coach. He was a small, spare man, in a catskin waistcoat, and jean-pantaloons. He had a sharp face, with a pair of twinkling, lashless eyes set deep under sandy brows. His proposed entrance into the coach was resolutely opposed. The thin woman cried out that there was no room; the lawyer's clerk said that the way the Company over-loaded its vehicles was a scandal; and the farmer recommended the newcomer to climb on to the roof.

'There ain't an inch of room up there,' protested the stranger. 'Lord, I don't take up much space! Squeeze up, coves!'

'Full up! Try the boot!' said the farmer.

'Cast your winkers over me, cull: I don't take up no more room than what a bodkin would!' pleaded the stranger. 'Besides, there's a set of flash young coves on the roof. I'd be mortal afraid to sit with 'em, so I would!'

Sir Richard, casting an experienced eye over the man, mentally wrote him down as one probably better known to the Bow Street Runners than to himself. He was not surprised, however, to hear Miss Creed offering to squeeze up to make room, for he had, by this time, formed a very fair estimate of his charge's warmheartedness.

Pen, edging close to Sir Richard, coaxed the farmer to see for himself that there was room enough for one more passenger. The man in the catskin waistcoat grinned at her, and hopped into the coach. 'Dang me if I didn't think you was a flash cull too!' he said, squeezing himself into the vacant place. 'I'm obliged to ye, young shaver. When coves do Jimmy Yarde a service he don't forget it neither.'

The clerk, who seemed to have much the same opinion of Mr Yarde as that held by Sir Richard, sniffed, and folded his hands tightly on the box which he held on his knees.

'Lord bless you!' said Mr Yarde, observing this gesture with a tolerant smile, '*I* ain't no boman prig!'

'What's a boman prig?' asked Pen innocently.

'There, now! If you ain't a werry suckling!' said Mr Yarde, almost disconcerted. 'A boman prig, young gentleman, is what I trust you'll never be. It's a cove as ends up in Rumbo—ah, and likely on the Nubbing Cheat afore he's much older!'

Much intrigued, Pen demanded a translation of these strange terms. Sir Richard, having pondered and discarded the notion of commanding her to exchange places with him, lay back and listened with lazy enjoyment to her initiation into the mysteries of thieves' cant.

A party of young gentlemen, who had been spectators of a cockfight held in the district, had been taken up at Chippenham, and had crowded on to the roof. From the sounds preceding thence, it seemed certain that they had been refreshing themselves liberally. There was a good deal of shouting, some singing, and much drumming with heels upon the roof. The motherly woman and the thin spinster began to look alarmed, and the lawyer's clerk said that the behaviour of modern young men was disgraceful. Pen was too deeply engaged in conversation with Jimmy Yarde to pay much heed to the commotion, but when, after the coach had rumbled on for another five miles, the pace was suddenly accelerated, and the top-heavy vehicle bounced over ruts and potholes, and swung perilously first to one side and then to the other, she broke off her enthralling discourse, and looked enquiringly at Sir Richard.

A violent lurch flung her into his arms. He restored her to her own seat, saying dryly: 'More adventure for you. I hope you are enjoying it?'

'But what is happening?'

'I apprehend that one of the would-be sprigs of fashion above has taken it into his head to tool the coach,' he replied.

'Lord ha' mercy!' exclaimed the motherly woman. 'Do you mean that one of they pesky, drunken lads is a-driving of us, sir?'

'So I should suppose, ma'am.'

The spinster uttered a faint shriek. 'Good God, what will become of us?'

'We shall end, I imagine, in the ditch,' said Sir Richard, with unruffled calm.

Babel at once broke forth, the spinster demanding to be let out at once, the motherly woman trying to attract the coachman's notice by hammering against the roof with her sunshade, the farmer sticking his head out of the window to shout threats and abuse, Jimmy Yarde laughing, and the lawyer's clerk angrily demanding of Sir Richard why he did not *do* something?

'What would you wish me to do?' asked Sir Richard, steadying Pen with a comfortingly strong arm.

'Stop the coach! Oh, sir, pray stop it!' begged the motherly woman.

'Bless your heart, ma'am, it'll stop of its own this gait!' grinned Jimmy Yarde.

Hardly had he spoken than a particularly sharp bend in the road proved to be too much for the amateur coachman's skill. He took the corner too wide, the near-hind wheels mounted a slight bank, and skidded down the farther side into a deep ditch, and everyone inside the vehicle was flung rudely over. There were screams from the women, oaths from the farmer, the cracking noise of split wood, and the shatter of broken glass. The coach lay at a crazy angle with sprigs of thorn hedge thrusting in through the broken windows.

Pen, whose face was smothered in the many capes of Sir Richard's drab driving coat, gasped, and struggled to free herself from a hold which had suddenly clamped her to Sir Richard's side. He relaxed it, saying: 'Hurt, Pen?'

'No, not in the least! Thank you so very much for holding me! Are you hurt?'

A splinter of glass had cut his cheek slightly, but since he had been holding on to the leather armrest hanging in the corner of the coach, he had not been thrown, like everyone else, off his seat. 'No, only annoyed,' he replied. 'My good woman, this is neither the time nor the place for indulging in a fit of the vapours!'

This acid rider was addressed to the spinster, who, finding herself pitchforked on top of the lawyer's clerk, had gone off into strong hysterics.

'Here, let me get my dabblers on to that there door!' said Jimmy Yarde, hoisting himself up by seizing the opposite armrest. 'Dang me, if next time I travel in a rattler I don't ride on the roof, flash culls or no!'

The coach not having collapsed quite on to its side, but being supported by the bank and the hedge bordering the ditch, it was not difficult to force open the door, or to climb out through it. The spinster had indeed to be lifted out, since she had stiffened all over, and would do nothing but scream and drum her heels, but Pen scrambled out with an agility which scorned helping hands, and the motherly woman said that provided every gentleman would turn his back upon her she would engage to get out by herself too.

It was now considerably after nine o'clock, but although the sun had gone, the summer sky was still light, and the air warm. The travellers found themselves on a deserted stretch of road, a couple of miles short of the little town of Wroxham, and rather more than thirty miles from Bristol. The most cursory inspection of the coach was enough to convince them that it would need extensive repairs before being able to take the road again; and Sir Richard, who had gone immediately to the horses, returned to Pen's side in a few moments with the news that one of the wheelers had badly strained a tendon. He had been right in thinking that the reins had been handed over to one of the outside passengers. To tool the coach was a common enough pastime among young men who aspired to be whips, but that any paid coachman could have been foolish enough to relinquish his seat to an amateur far gone in drink was incomprehensible, until the coachman's own condition had been realized.

Pen, who was sitting on Sir Richard's portmanteau, received the news of complete breakdown with perfect equanimity, but all the other inside passengers burst into vociferous complaint, and besieged the guard with demands to be instantly conveyed to Bristol, by means unspecified. Between his indignation at his colleague's gross misconduct, and his exasperation at being shouted at by six or seven persons at once, the unfortunate man was for some time incapable of collecting his wits, but presently it was suggested that if the travellers would only be patient, he would ride back on one of the leaders to Chippenham, and there try to procure some sort of a vehicle to convey them to Wroxham, where they would be obliged to remain until the next Accommodation coach to Bristol picked them up there early on the following morning.

Several persons decided to set forward on foot for Wroxham at once, but the spinster was still having hysterics, the motherly woman said that her corns would not permit of her tramping two miles, and the lawyer's clerk held to it that he had a right to be conveyed to Bristol that night. There was a marked tendency in one or two persons to turn to Sir Richard, as being plainly a man accustomed to command. This tendency had the effect of making Sir Richard, not in the least gratified, walk over to Pen's side, and say languidly, but with decision: 'This, I fancy, is where we part company with our fellow travellers.'

'Yes, do let us!' assented Pen blithely. 'You know, I have been thinking, and I have a much better scheme now. We won't go to Bristol at all!'

'This is very sudden,' said Sir Richard. 'Do I understand you to mean that you have made up your mind to return to London?'

'No, no, of course not! Only now that we have broken down I think it would be silly to wait for another coach, because very likely we should be overtaken by my aunt. And I never really wanted to go to Bristol, after all.'

'In that case, it seems perhaps a pity that we came so far upon the road to it,' said Sir Richard.

Her eyes twinkled. 'Stupid! I mean, my home is not in Bristol, but near to it, and I think it would be much better, besides being like a real adventure, to walk the rest of the way.'

'Where is your home?' demanded Sir Richard.

'Well, it is near Queen Charlton, not far from Keynsham, you know.'

'I don't,' said Sir Richard. 'This is your country, not mine. How far, in your judgment, is Queen Charlton from where we now are?'

'I'm not *entirely* sure,' replied Pen cautiously. 'But I shouldn't think it could be above fifteen, or, at the most twenty miles, going 'cross country.'

'Are you proposing to walk twenty miles?' said Sir Richard.

'Well, I dare say it is not as much. As the crow flies, I expect it is only about ten miles off.'

'You are not a crow,' said Sir Richard dampingly. 'Nor, I may add, am I. Get up from that portmanteau!'

She rose obediently. 'I think I could quite well walk twenty miles. Not all at once, of course. What *are* we going to do?'

'We are going to retrace our steps along the road until we come to an inn,' replied Sir Richard. 'As I remember, there was one, about a couple of miles back. Nothing would induce me to make one of this afflictive coach party!'

'I must own, I am a little tired of them myself,' admitted Pen. 'Only I won't go to a posting house!'

'Make yourself easy on that score!' said Sir Richard grimly. 'No respectable posting house would open its doors to us in this guise.'

This made Pen giggle. She put forward no further opposition, but picked up the cloak bag, and set out beside Sir Richard in the direction of Chippenham.

None of the coach passengers noticed their departure, since all were fully occupied, either in reviling the coachman, or in planning their immediate movements. The bend in the road soon shut them off from sight of the coach, and Sir Richard then said: 'And now you may give me that cloak bag.'

'Well, I won't,' said Pen, holding on to it firmly. 'It is not at all heavy, and you have your portmanteau to carry already. Besides, I feel more like a man every moment. What shall we do when we reach the inn?'

'Order supper.'

'Yes, and after that?'

'Go to bed.'

Pen considered this. 'You don't think we should set forward on our journey at once?'

'Certainly not. We shall go to bed like Christians, and in the morning we shall hire a conveyance to carry us to Queen Charlton. A private conveyance,' he added.

'But—'

'Pen Creed,' said Sir Richard calmly, 'you cast me for the rôle of bear leader, and I accepted it. You drew a revolting picture of me which led everyone in that coach to regard me in the light of a persecutor of youth. Now you are reaping the harvest of your own sowing.'

She laughed. 'Are you going to persecute me?'

'Horribly!' said Sir Richard.

She tucked a confiding hand in his arm, and gave a little skip. 'Very well, I will do as you tell me. I'm very glad I met you: we are having a splendid adventure, are we not?'

Sir Richard's lips twitched. Suddenly he burst out laughing, standing still in the middle of the road, while Pen doubtfully surveyed him.

'But what is the matter with you?' she asked.

'Never mind!' he said, his voice still unsteady with mirth. 'Of course we are having a splendid adventure!'

'Well, I think we are,' she said, stepping out beside him again. 'Piers will be so surprised when he sees me!'

'I should think he would be,' agreed Sir Richard. 'You are quite sure that you don't regret coming in search of him, I suppose?'

'Oh yes, quite! Why, Piers is my oldest friend! Didn't I tell you that we made a vow to be married?'

'I have some recollection of your doing so,' he admitted. 'But I also recollect that you said you hadn't seen him for five years.'

'No, that is true, but it doesn't signify in the least, I assure you.'

'I see,' said Sir Richard, keeping his inevitable reflections to himself.

They had not more than two miles to go before they reached the inn Sir Richard had seen from the window of the coach. It was a very small hostelry, with a weatherbeaten sign creaking on its chains, a thatched roof, and only one parlour, besides the common taproom.

The landlord, upon hearing of the breakdown of the stagecoach, accepted the travellers' unconventional arrival without surprise. It was growing dark by this time, and it was not until Sir Richard had stepped into the inn, and stood in the light of a hanging lamp, that the landlord was able to obtain a clear view of him. Sir Richard had chosen for the journey a plain coat and serviceable breeches, but the cut of the blue cloth, the high polish on his top boots, the very style of his cravat, and the superfluity of capes on his drab overcoat all proclaimed so unmistakably the gentleman of fashion that the landlord was obviously taken aback, and looked from him to Pen with considerable suspicion.

'I shall require a bedroom for myself, and another for my nephew,' said Sir Richard. 'Also some supper.'

'Yes, sir. Did your honour say you was travelling on the Bristol stage?' asked the landlord incredulously.

'Yes,' said Sir Richard, raising his brows. 'I did say so. Have you any objection?'

'Oh no, sir! no, I'm sure!' replied the landlord hastily. 'Your honour said supper! I'm afraid we—we aren't in the habit of entertaining the Quality, but if your honour would condescend to a dish of ham and eggs, or maybe a slice of cold pork, I'll see to it on the instant!'

Sir Richard having graciously approved the ham and eggs, the landlord bowed him into the stuffy little parlour, and promised to have the only two guest chambers the inn possessed immediately prepared. Pen, directing a conspiratorial look at Sir Richard, elected to follow the portmanteau and the cloak bag upstairs. When she reappeared, a slatternly maidservant had spread supper on the table in the parlour, and Sir Richard had succeeded in forcing open two of its tiny windows. He turned, as Pen came in, and asked: 'What in heaven's name have you been doing all this time? I began to think you had deserted me.'

'Desert you! Of course I wouldn't do anything so silly! The thing was, I could see the landlord had noticed your clothes, so I thought of a famous tale to tell him. That's why I went off with him. I knew he would try to discover from me why you were travelling on the stagecoach.'

'And did he?'

'Yes, and I told him that you had had reverses on 'Change and had fallen on evil times,' said Pen, drawing up her chair to the table.

'Oh!' said Sir Richard. 'Was he satisfied with that?'

'Perfectly. He said he was very sorry. And then he asked where we were bound for. I said, for Bristol, because *all* the family had lost its money, and so I had had to be taken away from school.'

'You have the most fertile imagination of anyone of my acquaintance,' said Sir Richard. 'May I ask what school you have been gracing?'

'Harrow. Afterwards I wished I had said Eton, because my cousin Geoffrey is at Harrow, and I don't like him. I wouldn't go to his school.'

'I suppose it is too late to change the school now,' Sir Richard said, in a regretful tone.

She looked up quickly, her fascinating smile crinkling the corners of her eyes. 'You are laughing at me.'

'Yes,' admitted Sir Richard. 'Do you mind?'

'Oh no, not a bit! No one laughs in my aunt's house. I like it.'

'I wish,' said Sir Richard, 'you would tell me more about this aunt of yours. Is she your guardian?'

'No, but I have had to live with her ever since my father died. I have no real guardian, but I have two trustees. On account of my fortune, you understand.'

'Of course, yes: I was forgetting your fortune. Who are your trustees?'

'Well, one is my uncle Griffin—Aunt Almeria's husband, you know—but he doesn't signify, because he does just what Aunt tells him. The other is my father's lawyer, and he doesn't signify either.'

'For the same reason?'

'I don't know, but I shouldn't wonder at it in the least. Everyone is afraid of Aunt Almeria. Even I am, a little. That's why I ran away.'

'Is she unkind to you?'

'N-no. At least, she doesn't ill-treat me, but she is the kind of woman who always gets her own way. Do you know?'

'I know,' Sir Richard said.

'She talks,' explained Pen. 'And when she is displeased with one, I must say that it is very uncomfortable. But one should always be just, and I do not blame her for being so set on my marrying Fred. They are not very rich, you see, and of course Aunt would like Fred to have all my fortune. In fact, I am very sorry to be so disobliging, particularly as I have lived with the Griffins for nearly five years. But, to tell you the truth, I didn't in the least want to, and as for marrying Fred, I could *not*! Only when I suggested to Aunt Almeria that I would much prefer to give my fortune to Fred, and *not* marry him, she flew into a passion, and said I was heartless and shameless, and cried, and talked about nourishing vipers in her bosom. I thought that was unjust of her, because it was a very handsome offer, don't you agree?'

'Very,' said Sir Richard. 'But perhaps a trifle—shall we say, crude?'

'Oh!' Pen digested this. 'You mean that she did not like my *not* pretending that Fred was in love with me?'

'I think it just possible,' said Sir Richard gravely.

'Well, I am sorry if I wounded her feelings, but truly I don't think she has the least sensibility. I only said what I thought. But it put her in such a rage that there was nothing for it but to escape. So I did.'

'Were you locked in your room?' enquired Sir Richard.

'Oh no! I daresay I should have been if Aunt had guessed what I meant to do, but she would never think of such a thing.'

'Then—forgive my curiosity!—why did you climb out of the window?' asked Sir Richard.

'Oh, that was on account of Pug!' replied Pen sunnily.

'Pug?'

'Yes, a horrid little creature! He sleeps in a basket in the hall, and he *always* yaps if he thinks one is going out. That would have awakened Aunt Almeria. There was nothing else I could do.'

Sir Richard regarded her with a lurking smile. 'Naturally not. Do you know, Pen, I owe you a debt of gratitude?'

'Oh?' she said, pleased, but doubtful. 'Why?'

'I thought I knew your sex. I was wrong.'

'Oh!' she said again. 'Do you mean that I don't behave as a delicately bred female should?'

'That is one way of putting it, certainly.'

'It is the way Aunt Almeria puts it.'

'She would, of course.'

'I am afraid,' confessed Pen, 'that I am not very well-behaved. Aunt says that I had a lamentable upbringing, because my father treated me as though I had been a boy. I ought to have been, you understand.'

'I cannot agree with you,' said Sir Richard. 'As a boy you would have been in no way remarkable; as a female, believe me, you are unique.'

She flushed to the roots of her hair. 'I *think* that is a compliment.'

'It is,' Sir Richard said, amused.

'Well, I wasn't sure, because I am not out yet, and I do not know any men except my uncle and Fred, and they don't pay compliments. That is to say, not like that.' She looked up rather shyly, but chancing to catch sight of someone through the window, suddenly exclaimed: 'Why, there's Mr Yarde!'

'Mr who?' asked Sir Richard, turning his head.

'You can't see him now: he has gone past the window. You *must* remember Mr Yarde, sir! He was the odd little man who got into the coach at Chippenham, and used such queer words that I could not perfectly understand him. Do you suppose he can be coming to this inn?'

'I sincerely trust not!' said Sir Richard.

5

His trust was soon to have been misplaced, for after a few minutes the landlord came into the room, to ask apologetically whether the noble gentleman would object to giving up one of his rooms to another traveller. 'I told him as how your honour had bespoke both bedchambers, but he is very wishful to get a lodging, sir, so I told him as how I would ask your honour if, maybe, the young gentleman could share your honour's chamber—there being two beds, sir.'

Sir Richard, meeting Miss Creed's eye for one pregnant moment, saw that she was struggling with a strong desire to burst out laughing. His own lips quivered, but before he could answer the landlord, the sharp face of Mr Jimmy Yarde peered over that worthy's shoulder.

Upon recognizing the occupants of the parlour, Mr Yarde seemed to be momentarily taken aback. He recovered himself quickly, however, to thrust his way into the parlour with a very fair assumption of delight at encountering two persons already known to him. 'Well, if it ain't my young chub!' he exclaimed. 'Dang me if I didn't think the pair of you had loped off to Wroxham!'

'No,' said Sir Richard. 'It appeared to me that Wroxham would be over-full of travellers tonight.'

'Ay, you're a damned knowing one, ain't you? Knowed it the instant I clapped my glaziers on you. And right you are! Says I to myself, 'Wroxham's no place for you, Jimmy, my boy!''

'Was the thin woman still having the vapours?' asked Pen.

'Lordy, young chub, she were stretched out as stiff as a corpse when I loped off, and no one knowing what to do to bring her to her senses. Ah, and mighty peevy I thought myself, to hit on the notion of coming to this ken—not knowing as you had bespoke all the rooms afore me.'

His bright face shifted to Sir Richard's unpromising countenance. 'Unfortunate!' said Sir Richard politely.

'Ah, now!' wheedled Mr Yarde, 'you wouldn't go for to out-jockey Jimmy Yarde! Lordy, it's all of eleven o'clock, and the light gone. What's to stop your doubling up with the young shaver?'

'If your honour would condescend to allow the young gentleman to sleep in the spare bed in your honour's chamber?' interpolated the landlord in an ingratiating tone.

'No,' said Sir Richard. 'I am an extremely light sleeper, and my nephew snores.' Ignoring an indignant gasp from Pen, he turned to Mr Yarde. 'Do you snore?' he asked.

Jimmy grinned. 'Not me! I sleep like a babby, so help me!'

'Then you,' said Sir Richard, 'may share my room.'

'Done!' said Jimmy promptly. 'Spoke like a rare gager, guv'nor, which I knew you was. Damme, if I don't drain a clank to your very good health!'

Resigning himself to the inevitable, Sir Richard nodded to the landlord, and bade Jimmy draw up a chair.

Not having boarded the stagecoach when Pen had announced Sir Richard to be her tutor, Jimmy apparently accepted her new relationship without question. He spoke of her to Sir Richard as 'your nevvy', drank both their healths in gin-and-water bespoken by Sir Richard, and seemed to be inclined to make a night of it. He became rather loquacious over his second glass of daffy, and made several mysterious references to Files, and those engaged on the Dub-lay, and the Kidd. Various embittered strictures on Flash Culls led Sir Richard to infer that he had lately been working in partnership with persons above his own social standing, and did not mean to repeat the experience.

Pen sat drinking it all in, with her eyes growing rounder and rounder, until Sir Richard said that it was time she was in bed. He escorted her out of the parlour to the foot of the stairs, where she whispered to him in the tone of one who has made a great discovery: 'Dear sir, I don't believe he is a respectable person!'

'No,' said Sir Richard. 'I don't believe it either.'

'But is he a *thief*?' asked Pen, shocked.

'I should think undoubtedly. Which is why you will lock your door, my child. Is it understood?'

'Yes, but are you sure you will be safe? It would be dreadful if he were to cut your throat in the night!'

'It would indeed,' Sir Richard agreed. 'But I can assure you he won't. You may take this for me, if you will, and keep it till the morning.'

He put his heavy purse into her hand. She nodded. 'Yes, I will. You will take great care, will you not?'

'I promise,' he said, smiling. 'Be off now, and don't tease yourself over my safety!'

He went back to the parlour, where Jimmy Yarde awaited him. Being called upon to join Mr Yarde in a glass of daffy, he raised not the slightest objection, although he very soon suspected Jimmy of trying to drink him under the table. As he refilled the glasses for the third time, he said apologetically: 'Perhaps I ought to warn you that I am accounted to have a reasonably strong head. I should not like you to waste your time, Mr Yarde.'

Jimmy was not at all abashed. He grinned, and said: 'Ah, I said you was a peevy cull! Knowed it as soon as I clapped my daylights on to you. You learned to drink Blue Ruin in Cribb's parlour!'

'Quite right,' said Sir Richard.

'Oh, I knowed it, bless your heart! 'That there gentry-cove would peel remarkable well,' I says to myself. "And a handy bunch of fives he's got." Never you fret, guv'nor: Jimmy Yarde's no green 'un. What snabbles me, though, is how you come to be travelling in the common rumble.'

Sir Richard gave a soft laugh suddenly. 'You see, I have lost all my money,' he said.

'Lost all your money?' repeated Jimmy, astonished.

'On 'Change,' added Sir Richard.

The light, sharp eyed flickered over his elegant person. 'Ah, you're trying to gammon me! What's the lay?'

'None at all.'

'Dang me if I ever met such a cursed rum touch!' A suspicion crossed his mind. 'You ain't killed your man, guv'nor?'

'No. Have you?'

Jimmy looked quite alarmed. 'Not me, guv'nor, not me! I don't hold with violence, any gait.'

Sir Richard helped himself to a leisurely pinch of snuff. 'Just the Knuckle, eh?'

Jimmy gave a start, and looked at him with uneasy respect. 'What would the likes of you know about the Knuckle?'

'Not very much, admittedly. I believe it means the filching of watches, snuffboxes, and such-like from the pockets of the unsuspecting.'

'Here!' said Jimmy, looking very hard at him across the table, 'you don't work the Drop, do you?'

Sir Richard shook his head.

'You ain't a Picker-up, or p'raps a Kidd?'

'No,' said Sir Richard. 'I am quite honest—what you, I fancy, call a Flat.'

'I don't!' Jimmy said emphatically. 'I never met a flat what was so unaccountable knowing as what you are, guv'nor; and what's more I hope I don't meet one again!'

He watched Sir Richard rise to his feet, and kindle his bedroom candle at the guttering one on the table. He was frowning in a puzzled way, clearly uncertain in his mind. 'Going to bed, guv'nor?'

Sir Richard glanced down at him. 'Yes. I did warn you that I am a shockingly light sleeper, did I not?'

'Lord, you ain't got no need to fear *me*!'

'I am quite sure I have not,' smiled Sir Richard.

When Jimmy Yarde, an hour later, softly tiptoed into the low-pitched bedchamber above the parlour, Sir Richard lay, to all appearances, peacefully asleep. Jimmy edged close to the bed, and stood watching him, and listening to his even breathing.

'Don't drop hot tallow on me, I beg!' said Sir Richard, not opening his eyes.

Jimmy Yarde jumped, and swore.

'Quite so,' said Sir Richard.

Jimmy Yarde cast him a look of venomous dislike, and in silence undressed, and got into the neighbouring bed.

He awoke at an early hour, to hear roosters crowing from farm to farm in the distance. The sun was up, but the day was still misty, and the air very fresh. The bed creaked under him as he sat up, but it did not rouse Sir Richard. Jimmy Yarde slid out of it cautiously, and dressed himself. On the dimity-covered table by the window, Sir Richard's gold quizzing glass and snuffbox lay, carelessly discarded. Jimmy looked wistfully at him. He was something of a connoisseur in snuffboxes, and his fingers itched to slip this one into his pocket. He glanced uncertainly towards the bed. Sir Richard sighed in his sleep. His coat hung over a chair within Jimmy's reach. Keeping his eyes on Sir Richard, Jimmy felt in its pockets. Nothing but a handkerchief rewarded his search. But Sir Richard had given no sign of returning consciousness. Jimmy picked up the snuffbox, and inspected it. Still no movement from the bed. Emboldened, Jimmy dropped it into his capacious pocket. The quizzing glass swiftly followed it. Jimmy went stealthily towards the door. As he reached it, a yawn made him halt in his tracks and spin round.

Sir Richard stretched, and yawned again. 'You're up early, my friend,' he remarked.

'That's right,' said Jimmy, anxious to be gone before his theft could be discovered. 'I'm not one for lying abed on a fine summer's morning. I'll get a breath of air before I have my breakfast. Daresay we'll meet downstairs, eh, guv'nor?'

'I dare say we shall,' agreed Sir Richard. 'But in case we don't, I'll relieve you of my snuffbox and my eyeglass now.'

Exasperated, Jimmy let fall the modest bundle which contained his nightgear. 'Dang me, if I ever met such a leery cove in all my puff!' he said. 'You never saw me lift that lobb!'

'I warned you that I was a shockingly light sleeper,' said Sir Richard.

'Bubbled by a gudgeon!' said Jimmy disgustedly, handing over the booty. 'Here you are: there's no need for you to go calling in any harman, eh?'

'None at all,' replied Sir Richard.

'Damme, you're a blood after my own fancy, guv'nor! No hard feeling?'

'Not the least in the world.'

'I wish I knew what your lay might be,' Jimmy said wistfully, and departed, shaking his head over the problem.

Downstairs he found Pen Creed, who had also awakened early. She bade him a cheerful good morning, and said that she had been out, and was of the opinion that it was going to be a hot day. When he asked her if she and her uncle meant to board the next stagecoach to Bristol, she replied prudently that her uncle had not yet told her what they were going to do.

'You are bound for Bristol, ain't you?' enquired Jimmy.

'Oh yes!' said Pen, with a beautiful disregard for the truth.

They were standing in the taproom, which, at that hour of the morning, was empty, and just as Pen was beginning to say that she wanted her breakfast, the landlady came through the door leading from the kitchen, and asked them if they had heard the news.

'What news?' Pen asked uneasily.

'Why, everyone's in quite a pucker up at Wroxham, us being quiet folk, and not used to town ways. But there's my boy Jim come in saying there's one of they Bow Street Runners come down by the Mail. What he may want, surely to goodness there's none of us knows! They do say as how he stopped off at Calne, and come on easy-like to Wroxham. And there he be, poking his nose into respectable houses, and asking all manner of questions! Well, what I say is, *we've* nothing to hide, and he may come here if he pleases, but he will learn nothing.'

'Is he coming here?' asked Pen, in a faint voice.

'Going to all the inns hereabouts, by what they tell me,' responded the landlady. 'Jem took the notion into his head it's all along of the stagecoach which you and your good uncle was on, sir, for seemingly he's been asking a mort of questions about the passengers. Our Sam looks to see him here inside of half an hour. "Well," I says, "let him come, for I'm an honest woman, and there's never been a word said against the house, not to my knowledge!" Your breakfast will be on the table in ten minutes, sir.'

She bustled into the parlour, leaving Pen rather pale, and Jimmy Yarde suddenly thoughtful. 'Runners, eh?' said that worthy, stroking his chin. 'There now!'

'I have never seen one,' said Pen, with a creditable show of nonchalance. 'It will be most interesting. I wonder what he can want?'

'There's no telling,' replied Jimmy, his lashless eyes dwelling upon her in a considering stare. 'No telling at all. Seems to me, though, he won't be wanting a flash young chub like you.'

'Why, of course not!' replied Pen, forcing a laugh.

'That's what I thought,' said Jimmy, transferring his gaze to the long coat which had been flung across one of the tables. 'Might that be your toge, young shaver?'

'Yes, but I didn't need it after all. It is much warmer outside than I thought it would be.'

He picked it up, shook out its folds, and gave it to her. 'Don't you go leaving things about in common taprooms!' he said austerely. 'There's plenty of files—ah, even in these quiet parts!—would be glad to get their dabblers on to a good toge like that.'

'Oh yes! Thank you! I'll take it upstairs!' said Pen, glad of an opportunity to escape.

'You couldn't do better,' approved Jimmy. 'Then we'll have a bit of food, and though I don't hold with harmen in general—which is to say, with Law officers, young shaver—why, I'm a peaceable man, and if any such be wishful to search me, they're welcome.'

He strolled into the parlour, with the air of one whose conscience is clean, and Pen hurried off upstairs, to tap urgently on Sir Richard's door.

His voice called to her to come in, and she entered to find him putting the finishing touches to his cravat. He met her eyes in the mirror, and said: 'Well, brat?'

'Sir, we must leave this place instantly!' said Pen impetuously. 'We are in the greatest danger!'

'Why? Has your aunt arrived?' asked Sir Richard, preserving his calm.

'Worse!' Pen declared. 'A Bow Street Runner!'

'Ah, I thought you were a housebreaker in the first place!' said Sir Richard, shaking his head.

'I am not a housebreaker! You know I am not!'

'If the Runners are after you, it is obvious to me that you are a desperate character,' he replied, slipping his snuffbox into his pocket. 'Let us go downstairs, and have some breakfast.'

'Please, dear sir, be serious! I am sure that my aunt must have set the Runner on to me!'

'My dear child, if there is any one thing more certain than another it is that Bow Street has never heard of your existence. Don't be silly!'

'Oh!' She heaved a sigh of relief. 'I do trust you are right, but it is just the sort of thing Aunt Almeria would do!'

'You are the best judge of that, no doubt, but you may take it from me that it is not in the least the sort of thing a Bow Street Runner would do. You will probably find that the man he wants is our friend Mr Yarde.'

'Yes, at first I thought that too, but he says the Runner is welcome to search him if he wants to.'

'Then it is safe to assume that Mr Yarde has disposed of whatever booty it was he ran off with. Breakfast!'

In considerable trepidation, Pen followed him down to the parlour. They found Jimmy Yarde discussing a plate of cold beef. He greeted Sir Richard with a grin and a wink, obviously quite unabashed by his previous encounter with him that morning, to which he referred in the frankest terms. 'When I meet up with a leery cove, I don't bear malice,' he announced, raising a tankard of ale. 'So here's to your wery good health, guv'nor, and no hard feelings!'

Sir Richard seemed to be rather bored, and merely nodded. Jimmy Yarde fixed him with a twinkling eye, and said: 'And no splitting to any harman about poor old Jimmy boning your lobb, because he never did, and you know well it's in your pocket at this wery moment. What's more,' he added handsomely, 'I wouldn't fork you now I has your measure, guv'nor, not for fifty Yellow Boys!'

'I'm glad of that,' said Sir Richard.

'No splitting?' Jimmy said, his head on one side.

'Not if I am allowed to eat my breakfast in peace,' replied Sir Richard wearily.

'All's bowman then!' said Jimmy, 'and not another word will you hear from me, guv'nor, till we gets to Bristol. Damme if I don't ride outside the rattler, just to oblige you!'

Sir Richard looked meditatively at him, but said nothing. Pen sat down facing the window, and watched the road for signs of the Bow Street Runner.

Contrary to the landlady's expectations, the Runner did not reach the inn until some little time after the breakfast covers had been removed, and Jimmy Yarde had strolled out to lounge at his ease on a bench set against the wall of the hostelry.

The Runner entered the inn by way of the yard at the back of it, and

the first person he encountered was Sir Richard, who was engaged in
settling his account with the landlord. Miss Creed, at his elbow, drew his
attention to the Runner's arrival by urgently twitching his coat sleeve. He
looked up, with raised brows, saw the newcomer, and lifted his quizzing
glass.

'Beg your pardon, sir,' said the Runner, touching his hat. 'Me not
meaning to intrude, but being wishful to speak with the landlord.'

'Certainly,' said Sir Richard, his brows still expressive of lanquid
surprise.

'At your convenience, sir: no hurry, sir!' said the Runner, retreating to a
discreet distance.

The sigh which escaped Miss Creed was one of such profound relief that
it was plain her alarms had not until that moment been allayed. Sir Richard
finished paying his shot, and with a brief: 'Come, Pen!' tossed over his
shoulder, left the taproom.

'He didn't come to find me!' breathed Pen.

'Of course he didn't.'

'I couldn't help being a little alarmed. What shall we do now, sir?'

'Shake off your very undesirable travelling acquaintance,' he replied
briefly.

She gave a gurgle. 'Yes, but how? I have *such* a fear that he means to go
with us to Bristol.'

'But we are not going to Bristol. While he is being interrogated by that
Runner, we, my child, are going to walk quietly out by the back door, and
proceed by ways, which I trust will not prove as devious as the tapster's
description of them, to Colerne. There we shall endeavour to hire a vehicle
to carry us to Queen Charlton.'

'Oh, famous!' cried Pen. 'Let us go at once!'

Five minutes later they left the inn unobtrusively, by way of the yard,
found themselves in a hayfield, and skirted it to a gate leading into a ragged
spinney.

The village of Colerne was rather less than three miles distant, but long
before they had reached it Sir Richard was tired of his portmanteau. 'Pen
Creed, you are a pestilent child!' he told her.

'Why, what have I done?' she asked, with one of her wide, enquiring
looks.

'You have hailed me from my comfortable house—'

'I didn't! It was you who *would* come!'

'I was drunk.'

'Well, that was not my fault,' she pointed out.

'Don't interrupt me! You have made me travel for miles in a conveyance
smelling strongly of dirt and onions—'

'That was the fat woman's husband,' interpolated Pen. 'I noticed it
myself.'

'No one could have failed to notice it. And I am not partial to onions. You
drew a portrait of me which led everyone in the coach to regard me in the
light of an oppressor of innocent youth—'

'Not the thin, disagreeable man. *He* wanted me to be oppressed.'

'He was a person of great discrimination. Not content with that, you
pitchforked me into what threatens to be a life friendship with a pickpocket,
to escape from whose advances I am obliged to tramp five miles, carrying a
portmanteau which is much heavier than I had supposed possible. It only
remains for me to become embroiled in an action for kidnapping, which I

feel reasonably assured your aunt will bring against me.'

'Yes, and now I come to think of it, I remember that you said you were going to be married,' said Pen, quite unimpressed by these strictures. 'Will she be very angry with you?'

'I hope she will be so very angry that she will wish never to see my face again,' said Sir Richard calmly. 'In fact, brat, that reflection so far outweighs all other considerations that I forgive you the rest.'

'I think you are a very odd sort of person,' said Pen. 'Why did you ask her to marry you, if you did not wish to?'

'I didn't. During the past two days that is the only folly I have not committed.'

'Well, why did you mean to ask her, then?'

'*You* should know.'

'But you are a man! No one could make you do anything you did not choose to do!'

'They came mighty near it. If you had not dropped out of the window into my arms, I have little doubt that I should at this moment be receiving the congratulations of my acquaintance.'

'Well, I must say I do not think you are at all just to me, then, to call me a pestilent child! I saved you—though, indeed, I didn't know it—from a horrid fate.'

'True. But need I have been saved in a noisome stagecoach?'

'That was part of the adventure. Besides, I explained to you at the outset why I was travelling on the stage. You must own that we are having a very exciting time! And, what is more, you have had more adventure than I, for you actually shared a room with a real thief!'

'So I did,' said Sir Richard, apparently much struck by this circumstance.

'And I can plainly see a cottage ahead of us, so I expect we have reached Colerne,' she said triumphantly.

In a few moments, she was found to have been right. They walked into the village, and fetched up at the best-looking inn.

'Now, what particular lie shall we tell here?' asked Sir Richard.

'A wheel came off our post chaise,' replied Pen promptly.

'Are you never at a loss?' he enquired, regarding her in some amusement.

'Well, to tell you the truth I haven't had very much experience,' she confided.

'Believe me, no one would suspect that.'

'No, I must say I think I was quite born to be a vagabond,' she said seriously.

The story of the faulty wheel was accepted by the landlord of the Green Man without question. If he thought it strange that the travellers should have left the main highway to brave the perils of rough country lanes, his mild surprise was soon dissipated by the announcement that they were on their way to Queen Charlton, and had attempted to find a shorter road. He said that they would have done better to have followed the Bristol road to Cold Ashton, but that perhaps they were strangers in these parts?

'Precisely,' said Sir Richard. 'But we are going to visit friends at Queen Charlton, and we wish to hire some sort of a vehicle to carry us there.'

The smile faded from the landlord's face when he heard this, and he shook his head. There were no vehicles for hire at Colerne. There was, in fact, only one suitable carriage, and that his own gig. 'Which I'd be pleased to let out to your honour if I had a man to send with it. But the lads is all out haymaking, and I can't go myself. Maybe the blacksmith could see what's to be done to patch up your chaise, sir?'

'Quite useless!' said Sir Richard truthfully. 'The wheel is past repairing. Moreover, I instructed my postilion to ride back to Wroxham. What will you take for lending your gig to me without a man to go with it?'

'Well, sir, it ain't that so much, but how will I get it back?'

'Oh, one of Sir Jasper's grooms will drive it back!' said Pen. 'You need have no fear on that score!'

'Would that be Sir Jasper Luttrell, sir?'

'Yes, indeed, we are going on a visit to him.'

The landlord was plainly shaken. Sir Jasper was apparently well known to him; on the other hand Sir Richard was not. He cast him a doubtful, sidelong look, and slowly shook his head.

'Well, if you won't let out your gig on hire, I suppose I shall have to buy it,' said Sir Richard.

'Buy my gig, sir?' gasped the landlord, staggered.

'And the horse too, of course,' added Sir Richard, pulling out his purse.

The landlord blinked at him. 'Well, I'm sure, sir! If that's the way it is, I don't know but what I could let you drive the gig over yourself—seeing as how you're a friend of Sir Jasper. Come to think of it, I won't be needing it for a couple of days. Only you'll have to rest the old horse afore you send him back, mind!'

Sir Richard raised no objection to this, and after coming to terms with an ease which led to the landlord's expressing the wish that there were more gentlemen like Sir Richard to be met with, the travellers had only to wait until the cob had been harnessed to the gig, and led round to the front of the inn.

The gig was neither smart nor well sprung, and the cob's gait was more sure than swift, but Pen was delighted with the whole equipage. She sat perched up beside Sir Richard, enjoying the hot sunshine, and pointing out to him the manifold superiorities of the Somerset countryside over any other county.

They did not reach Queen Charlton until dusk, since the way to it was circuitous, and often very rough. When they came within sight of the village, Sir Richard said: 'Well, brat, what now? Am I to drive you to Sir Jasper Luttrell's house?'

Pen, who had become rather silent during the last five miles of their drive, said with a little gasp: 'I have been thinking that perhaps it would be better if I sent a message in the morning! It is not Piers, you know, but, though I did not think of her at the time, it—it had occurred to me that perhaps Lady Luttrell may not perfectly understand . . .'

Her voice died away unhappily. She was revived by Sir Richard's saying in matter-of-fact tones: 'A very good notion. We will drive to an inn.'

'The George was always accounted the best,' offered Pen. 'I have never actually been inside it, but my father was used to say its cellars were excellent.'

The George was discovered to be an ancient half-timbered hostelry with beamed ceilings and wainscoted parlours. It was a rambling house, with a large yard, and many chintz-hung bedrooms. There was no difficulty in procuring a private parlour, and by the time Pen had washed the dust of the roads from her face, and unpacked the cloak bag, her spirits, which had sunk unaccountably, had begun to lift again. Dinner was served in the parlour, and neither the landlord nor his wife seemed to recognize in the golden-haired stripling the late Mr Creed's tomboyish little girl.

'If only my aunt does not discover me before I have found Piers!' Pen said, helping herself to some more raspberries.

'We will circumvent her. But touching this question of Piers, do you—er—suppose that he will be able to extricate you from your present difficulties?'

'Well, he will have to, if I marry him, won't he?'

'Undoubtedly. But—you must not think me an incorrigible wet blanket—it is not easy to be married at a moment's notice.'

'Isn't it? I didn't know,' said Pen innocently. 'Oh well, I dare say we shall fly to Gretna Green then! We used to think that would be a splendid adventure.'

'Gretna Green in those clothes?' enquired Sir Richard, levelling his quizzing glass at her.

'Well, no, I suppose not. But when Piers has explained it all to Lady Luttrell, I expect she will be able to get some proper clothes for me.'

'You do not entertain any doubts of Lady Luttrell's—er—receiving you as her prospective daughter-in-law?'

'Oh no! She was always most kind to me! Only I did think that perhaps it would be better if I saw Piers first.'

Sir Richard, who had so far allowed himself to be borne along resistless on the tide of this adventure, began to perceive that it would shortly be his duty to wait upon Lady Luttrell, and to give her an account of his dealings with Miss Creed. He glanced at that young lady, serenely finishing the last of the raspberries, and reflected, with a wry smile, that the task was not going to be an easy one.

A servant came in to clear away the dishes presently. Pen at once engaged him in conversation and elicited the news that Sir Jasper Luttrell was away from home.

'Oh! But not Mr Piers Luttrell?'

'No, sir, I saw Mr Piers yesterday. Going to Keynsham, he was. I do hear as he has a young gentleman staying with him—a Lunnon gentleman, by all accounts.'

'Oh!' Pen's voice sounded rather blank. As soon as the man had gone away, she said: 'Did you hear that, sir? It makes it just a little awkward, doesn't it?'

'Very awkward,' agreed Sir Richard. 'It seems as though we have now to eliminate the gentleman from London.'

'I wish we could. For I am sure my aunt will guess that I have come home, and if she finds me before I have found Piers, I am utterly undone.'

'But she will not find you. She will only find me.'

'Do you think you will be able to fob her off?'

'Oh, I think so!' Sir Richard said negligently. 'After all, she would scarcely expect you to be travelling in my company, would she? I hardly think she will demand to see my nephew.'

'No, but what if she does?' asked Pen, having no such dependence on her aunt's forbearing.

Sir Richard smiled rather sardonically. 'I am not, perhaps, the best person in the world of whom to make—ah—impertinent demands.'

Pen's eyes lit with sudden laughter. 'Oh, I do hope you will talk to her like that, and look at her just *so*! And if she brings Fred with her, he will be quite overcome, I daresay, to meet you face to face. For you must know that he admires you excessively. He tries to tie his cravat in a Wyndham Fall, even!'

'That, in itself, I find an impertinence,' said Sir Richard.

She nodded, and lifted a hand to her own cravat. 'What do you think of mine, sir?'

'I have carefully refrained from thinking about it at all. Do you really wish to know?'

'But I have arranged it just as you did!'

'Good God!' said Sir Richard faintly. 'My poor deluded child!'

'You are teasing me! At least it was not ill enough tied to make you rip it off my neck as you did when you first met me!'

'You will recall that we left the inn in haste this morning,' he explained.

'I am persuaded *that* would not have weighed with you. But you put me in mind of a very important matter. You paid my reckoning there.'

'Don't let that worry you, I beg.'

'I am determined to pay everything for myself,' Pen said firmly. 'It would be a shocking piece of impropriety if I were to be beholden for money to a stranger.'

'True. I had not thought of that.'

She looked up with her sudden bright look of enquiry. 'You are laughing at me again!'

He showed her a perfectly grave countenance. 'Laughing? I?'

'I know very well you are. You may make your mouth prim, but I have noticed several times that you laugh with your eyes.'

'Do I? I beg your pardon!'

'Well, you need not, for I like it. I would not have come all this way with you if you had not had such smiling eyes. Isn't it odd how one knows if one can trust a person, even if he is drunk?'

'Very odd,' he said.

She was hunting fruitlessly through her pockets. 'Where can I have put my purse? Oh, I think I must have put it in my overcoat!'

She had flung this garment down on a chair, upon first entering the parlour, and stepped across the room to feel in the capacious pockets.

'Are you seriously proposing to count a few miserable shillings into my hand?'

'Yes, indeed I am. Oh, here it is!' She pulled out a leather purse with a ring round its neck, from one pocket, stared at it, and exclaimed: 'This is not my purse!'

Sir Richard looked at it through his glass. 'Isn't it? It is certainly not mine, I assure you.'

'It is very heavy. I wonder how it can have come into my pocket? Shall I open it?'

'By all means. Are you quite sure it is not your own?'

'Oh yes, quite!' She moved to the table, tugging at the ring. It was a little hard to pull off, but she managed it after one or two tugs, and shook out into the palm of her hand a diamond necklace that winked and glittered in the light of the candles.

'*Richard!*' gasped Miss Creed, startled into forgetting the proprieties again. 'Oh, I beg your pardon! But look!'

'I am looking, and you have no need to beg my pardon. I have been calling you Pen these two days.'

'Oh, that is another matter, because you are so much older!'

He looked at her somewhat enigmatically. 'Am I? Well, never mind. Do I understand that this gaud does not belong to you?'

'Good gracious, no! I never saw if before in my life!'

'Oh!' said Sir Richard. 'Well, it is always agreeable to have problems solved. Now we know why your friend Mr Yarde had no fear of the Bow Street Runner.'

6

Pen let the necklace slip through her fingers on to the table. 'You mean that he stole it, and then—and then put it in *my* pocket? But, sir, this is terrible! Why—why, that Runner will next come after us!'

'I think it more likely that Mr Yarde will come after us.'

'Good God!' Pen said, quite pale with dismay. 'What are we to do?'

He smiled rather maliciously. 'Didn't you desire to meet with a real adventure?'

'Yes, but— Oh, do not be absurd and teasing, I beg of you! What shall we do with the necklace? Couldn't we throw it away somewhere, or hide it in a ditch?'

'We could, of course, but it would surely be a trifle unfair to the owner?'

'I don't care about that,' confessed Pen. 'It would be dreadful to be arrested for thieving, and I know we shall be!'

'Oh, I trust not!' Sir Richard said. He straightened the necklace, where it lay on the table, and looked down at it with a slight frown creasing his brow. 'Yes,' he said meditatively. 'I have seen you before. Now, *where* have I seen you before?'

'Do please put it away!' begged Pen. 'Only think if a servant were to come into the room!'

He picked it up. 'My lamentable memory! alas, my lamentable memory! Where, oh, *where* have I seen you?'

'Dear sir, if Jimmy Yarde finds us, he will very likely cut our throats to get the necklace back!'

'On the contrary, I have his word for it that he is opposed to all forms of violence.'

'But when he does not discover it in my pocket, where he placed it—and now I come to think of it, he actually had my coat in his hands—he must guess that we have discovered it!'

'Very likely he will, but I cannot see what profit there would be in cutting our throats.' Sir Richard restored the necklace to its leather purse, and dropped it into his pocket. 'We have now nothing to do but to await the arrival of Jimmy Yarde. Perhaps—who knows?—we may induce him to divulge the ownership of the necklace. Meanwhile, this parlour is very stuffy, and the night remarkably fine. Do you care to stroll out with me to admire the stars, brat?'

'I suppose,' said Pen defiantly, 'that you think I am very poor spirited!'

'Very,' agreed Sir Richard, his eyes glinting under their heavy lids.

'I am not afraid of anything,' Pen announced. 'Merely I am *shocked*!'

'A waste of time, believe me. Are you coming?'

'Yes, but it seems to me as though you have put a live coal in your pocket. What if some dishonest person were to steal it from you?'

'Then we shall be freed from all responsibility. Come along!'

She followed him out into the warm night. He appeared to have banished all thought of the necklace from his mind. He pointed various constellations out to her, and, drawing her hand through his arm, strolled with her down the street, past the last straggling cottages, into a lane redolent of meadowsweet.

'I suppose I was poor spirited,' Pen confided presently. 'Shall you feel obliged to denounce poor Jimmy Yarde to the Runner?'

'I hope,' said Sir Richard dryly, 'that Mr Piers Luttrell is a gentleman of resolute character.'

'Why?'

'That he may be able to curb your somewhat reckless friendliness.'

'Well, I haven't seen him for five years, but it was always I who thought of things to do.'

'That is what I feared. Where does he live?'

'Oh, about two miles farther down this road! *My* home is on the other side of the village. Should you like to see it?'

'Immensely, but not at the moment. We will now retrace our steps, for it is time that you were in bed.'

'I shan't sleep a wink.'

'I trust that you are mistaken, my good child—in fact, I am reasonably certain that you are.'

'And to add to everything,' said Pen, unheeding. 'Piers has got a horrid man staying with him! I don't know what is to be done.'

'In the morning,' said Sir Richard soothingly, 'we will attend to all these difficulties.'

'In the morning, very likely, Aunt Almeria will have discovered me.'

On this gloomy reflection, they retraced their steps to the inn. Its unshuttered windows cast golden gleams out into the quiet street, several of them standing open to let in the cool night air. Just as they were about to pass one of them on their way to the inn door, a voice spoke inside the room, and to her astonishment, Sir Richard suddenly gripped Pen's arm, and brought her to a dead halt. She started to enquire the reason for this sudden stop, but his hand across her mouth choked back the words.

The voice from within the house said with a slight stammer: 'You c-can't come up to C-Crome Hall I tell you! It's b-bad enough as it is. G-good God, man, if anyone were to see me sneaking off to meet you here they'd p-precious soon smell a rat!'

A more robust voice answered: 'Maybe I've been smelling rats myself, my young buck. Who was it foisted a partner on to me, eh? Were the pair of ye meaning to cheat Horace Trimble? Were ye, my bonny boy?'

'You fool, you let yourself be b-bubbled!' the stammerer said furiously. 'Then you c-come here—enough to ruin everything! I tell you I d-daren't stay! And don't come up to C-Crome Hall again, damn you! I'll m-meet you tomorrow, in the spinney down the road. 'Sblood, he can't have g-gone far! Why don't you go to B-Bristol if he didn't b-break back to London? Instead of c-coming here to insult me!'

'I insult you! By the powers, that's rich!' A full-throated laugh followed the words, and the sound of a chair being dashed back on a wooden floor.

'Damn your impudence! You've b-bungled everything, and now you c-come blustering to me! *You* were to arrange everything! *I* was to l-leave all to you! Finely you've arranged it! And n-now you expect m-me to set all to rights!'

'Softly, my buck! softly! You're crowing mighty loud, but I did my part of the business all right and tight. It was the man you were so set on that bubbled me, and that makes me think, d'ye hear? It makes me think mighty hard. Maybe you'd better think too—and if you've a notion in your head that Horace Trimble's a green 'un, get rid of it! See?'

'Hush, for G-God's sake! You d-don't know who may be listening! I'll meet you tomorrow, at eleven, if I c-can shake off y-young Luttrell. We must think what's to be done!'

A door opened and was hastily shut again. Sir Richard pulled Pen back into the shadows beyond the window, and, a moment later, a slight, cloaked figure came out of the inn, and strode swiftly away into the darkness.

The warning pressure on Pen's arm held her silent, although she was by this time agog with excitement. Sir Richard waited until the dwindling sound of footsteps had died in the distance, and then strolled on with Pen's hand still tucked in his arm, past the open window to the inn door. Not until they stood in their own parlour again did Pen allow herself to speak, but as soon as the door was shut behind them, she exclaimed: 'What did it mean? He spoke of "Young Luttrell"—did you hear him? It must be the man who is staying with him! But who was the other man, and what were they talking about?'

Sir Richard did not appear to be attending very closely. He was standing by the table, a frown between his eyes, and his mouth rather grim. Suddenly his gaze shifted to Pen's face, but what he said seemed to her incomprehensible. 'Of course!' he muttered softly. 'So *that* was it!'

'Oh, *do* tell me!' begged Pen. '*What* was it, and why did you stop when you heard the stammering man speak? Do you—is it possible that you know him?'

'Very well indeed,' replied Sir Richard.

'Good heavens! And it is he who is visiting Piers! Dear sir, does it seem to you that everything is becoming a trifle awkward?'

'Extremely so,' said Sir Richard.

'Well, that is what I thought,' said Pen. 'First we are saddled with a stolen necklace, and now we discover that a friend of yours is staying with Piers!'

'Oh no, we do not!' said Sir Richard. 'That young gentleman is no friend of mine! Nor, I fancy, is his presence in this neighbourhood unconnected with that necklace. If I do not mistake, Pen, we have become enmeshed in a plot from which it will take all my ingenuity to extricate us.'

'I have ingenuity too,' said Miss Creed, affronted.

'Not a scrap,' responded Sir Richard calmly.

She swallowed this, saying in a small voice: 'Very well, if I haven't, I haven't, but I wish you will explain.'

'I feel sure you do,' said Sir Richard; 'but the truth is that I cannot. Not only does it appear to me to be a matter of uncommon delicacy, but it is also for the moment—a little obscure.'

She sighed. 'If does not seem fair, because it was I who found the necklace, after all. Who is the stammering man? You may just as well tell me that, because Piers will, you know.'

'Certainly. The stammering man is the Honourable Beverley Brandon.'

'Oh! I don't know him,' said Pen, rather disappointed.

'You are to be congratulated.'

'Is he an enemy of yours?'

'An enemy! No!'

'Well, you seem to dislike him very cordially.'

'That does not make him my enemy. To be exact, he is the younger brother of the lady to whom I was to have been betrothed.'

Pen looked aghast. 'Good God, sir, can he have come in search of you?'

'No, nothing of that kind. Indeed, Pen, I can't tell you more, for the rest is conjecture.' He met her disappointed look, and smiled down at her, gently pinching her chin. 'Poor Pen! Forgive me!'

A little colour stole up to the roots of her hair. 'I do not mean to tease you. I expect you will tell me about it when–when it isn't conjecture.'

'I expect I shall,' he agreed. 'But that will not be tonight, so be off with you to bed, child!'

She went, but was back again a few minutes later, round-eyed and breathless. 'Richard! He has found us! I have seen him! I am certain it was he!'

'Who?' he asked.

'Jimmy Yarde, of course! It was so hot in my room that I drew back the curtains to open the window, and the moon was so bright that I stood looking out for a minute. And there he was, directly below me! I could not mistake. And the worst is that I fear he saw me, for he drew back at once into the shadow of the house!'

'Did he indeed?' There was a gleam in Sir Richard's eye. 'Well, he is here sooner than I expected. A resourceful gentleman, Mr Jimmy Yarde!'

'But what are we going to do? I am not in the least afraid but I should like to be told what you wish me to do!'

'That is very easily done. I wish you to exchange bedchambers with me. Show yourself at the window of your own room, if you like, but on no accout pull back the blinds in mine. I have a very earnest desire to meet Mr Jimmy Yarde.'

Her dimples peeped. 'I see! like the fairy story! Oh, Grandma, what big teeth you have!" *What* an adventure we are having! But you will take care, won't you, sir?'

'I will.'

'And you will tell me all about it afterwards?'

'Perhaps.'

'If you don't,' said Pen, with deep feeling, 'it will be the most unjust thing imaginable!'

He laughed, and, seeing that there was no more to be got out of him, she went away again.

An hour later, the candlelight vanished from the upper room with the open casements and the undrawn blinds, but it was two hours before Mr Yarde's head appeared above the window sill, and not a light shone in the village.

The moon, sailing across a sky of deepest sapphire, cast a bar of silver across the floor of the chamber, but left the four-poster bed in shadow. The ascent, by way of the porch roof, a stout drainpipe, and a gnarled branch of wistaria, had been easy, but Mr Yarde paused before swinging a leg over the sill. His eye, trying to penetrate the darkness, encountered a drab driving coat, hanging over the back of a chair placed full in the shaft of moonlight. He knew that coat, and a tiny sigh escaped him. He hoisted himself up, and noiselessly slid into the room. He had left his shoes below, and his stockinged feet made no sound on the floor, as he crept across it.

But there was no heavy leather sack purse in the pocket of the driving coat.

He was disappointed, but he had been prepared for disappointment. He stole out of the moonlight to the bedside, listening to the sound of quiet breathing. No tremor disturbed its regularity, and after listening to it for a few minutes, he bent, and began cautiously to slide his hand under the dimly seen pillow. The other, his right, grasped a muffler, which could be readily clapped over a mouth opened to utter a startled cry.

The cry, hardly more than a croak, strangled at birth, was surprised out of himself, however, for, just as his sensitive fingers felt the object for which they were seeking, two iron hands seized him by the throat, and choked him.

He tore quite unavailingly at the hold, realizing through the drumming in his ears, the bursting of his veins, and the pain in his temples, that he had made a mistake, that the hands crushing the breath out of him certainly did not belong to any stripling.

Just as he seemed to himself to be losing possession of his senses, the grip slackened, and a voice he was learning to hate, said softly: 'Your error, Mr Yarde!'

He felt himself shaken and suddenly released, and, being quite powerless to help himself, fell to the floor and stayed there, making odd crowing noises as he got his wind back. By the time he had recovered sufficiently to struggle on to one elbow, Sir Richard had cast off the coverlet, and sprung out of bed. He was dressed in his shirt and breeches, as Mr Yarde's suffused eyes saw, as soon as Sir Richard had relit the candle by his bed.

Sir Richard laid aside the tinderbox, and glanced down at Mr Yarde. Jimmy's vision was clearing; he was able to see that Sir Richard's lips had curled into a somewhat contemptuous smile. He began gingerly to massage his throat, which felt badly bruised, and waited for Sir Richard to speak.

'I warned you that I was a shockingly light sleeper,' Sir Richard said.

Jimmy cast him a malevolent look, but made no answer.

'Get up!' Sir Richard said. 'You may sit on that chair, Mr Yarde, for we are going to enjoy a heart-to-heart talk.'

Jimmy picked himself up. A glance in the direction of the window was enough to convince him that he would be intercepted before he could reach it. He sat down and drew the back of his hand across his brow.

'Don't let us misunderstand one another!' Sir Richard said. 'You came to find a certain diamond necklace, which you hid in my nephew's coat this morning. There are just three things I can do with you. I can deliver you up to the Law.'

'You can't prove I come to fork the necklace, guv'nor,' Jimmy muttered.

'You think not? We may yet see. Failing the Bow Street Runner–but I feel he would be happy to take you into custody–I fancy a gentleman of the name of Trimble–ah, Horace Trimble, if my memory serves!–would be even happier to relieve me of you.'

The mention of this name brought an expression of great uneasiness into Jimmy's sharp countenance. 'I don't know him! Never heard of any such cove!'

'Oh yes, I think you have!' said Sir Richard.

'I ain't done you any harm, guv'nor, nor intended any! I'll cap downright—'

'You needn't: I believe you.'

Jimmy's spirits began to lift. 'Dang me if I didn't say you was a leery cove! You wouldn't be hard on a cull!'

'That depends on the–er–cull. Which brings me, Mr Yarde, to the third course I might–I say, might, Mr Yarde–pursue. I can let you go.'

Jimmy gasped, swallowed, and muttered hoarsely: 'Spoke like the gentry-cove you are, guv'nor!'

'Tell me what I want to know, and I will let you go,' said Sir Richard.

A wary look came into Jimmy's eyes. 'Split, eh? Lord bless you, there ain't anything to tell you!'

'It will perhaps make it easier for you if I inform you that I am already aware that you have been working in—somewhat uneasy partnership—with Mr Horace Trimble.'

'Cap'n Trimble,' corrected Jimmy.

'I should doubt it. He, I take it, is the—er—flash cull—whom you referred to last night.'

'I don't deny it.'

'Furthermore,' said Sir Richard, 'the pair of you were working for a young gentleman with a pronounced stammer. Ah, for a Mr Brandon, to be precise.'

Jimmy had changed colour. 'Stow your whids and plant 'em!' he growled. 'You're too leery for me, see? Damme if I know what your lay is!'

'That need not concern you. Think it over, Mr Yarde! Will you be handed over to Captain Trimble, or do you choose to go as you came, through that window?'

Jimmy sat for a moment, still gently rubbing his throat, and looking sideways at Sir Richard. 'Damn all flash culls!' he said at last. 'I'll whiddle the whole scrap. I ain't a bridle cull, see? What *you* calls the High Toby. That ain't my lay: I'm a rum diver. Maybe I've touched the rattler now and then, but I never went on the bridle lay, not till a certain gentry-cove, which we knows of, tempted me. And I wish I hadn't, see? Five hundred Yellow Boys I was promised, but not a grig will I get! He's a rare gager, that gentry-cove! Dang me if I ever works with such again! He's a bad 'un, guv'nor, you can lay your last megg on that!'

'I am aware. Go on!'

'There's an old gentry-mort going to Bath, see? Lord love you, she was his own mother! Now, that's what I don't hold with, but it ain't none of my business. Me and Cap'n Trimble holds up the chaise by Calne, or thereabouts. The necklace is in a hiding place behind one of the squabs—ah, and rum squabs they was, all made out of red silk!'

'Mr Brandon knew of this hiding place, and told you?'

'Lord love you, he made naught of that, guv'nor! We was to snaffle the necklace, and pike on the bean, see?'

'Not entirely.'

'Lope off as fast as we could. Now, I don't hold with violence, any gait, not that stammering young chub neither. But Cap'n Trimble looses off his pops, and one of the outriders gets it in the wing. While the Cap'n's a-covering the coves with his pops, I dubs the jigger—opens the door—and finds a couple of gentry-morts, hollering fit to rouse the countryside. I don't take nothing but the necklace, see? I'm a peevy cove, and this ain't my lay. I don't like it. We pikes, and Cap'n Trimble he pushes his pop into my belly, and says to hand over the necklace. Well, I does so. I'm a peevy cove. I don't hold with violence. Now, the lay is that we take them sparklers to that flash young boman prig, which is taking cover down here, with a regular green 'un, which he gets to know at Oxford. All's Bob, then! But I'm leery, see? Seems to me I'm working with a flash file, and if he makes off with the sparklers, which I suspicion he will, my young chub don't tip me my earnest. I forks the cove. Bristol's the place for me, I thinks, and I gets on to the werry some rattler which you and your nevvy's a-riding. When that harman from Bow Street comes along, I thinks there's a fastener out for me, and I tips the cole to Adam Tiler, as you might say.'

'You placed the necklace in my nephew's pocket?'

'That's it, guv'nor. No harman won't suspicion a young shaver like him I thinks. But you and he lopes off unbeknownst, and I comes to this place. Oh, I knew you was a peevy cull! So I touts the case, see?'

'No.'

'Runs my winkers over the house,' said Jimmy impatiently. 'I see your young shaver at this werry window—I should have remembered that you was a peevy cove, guv'nor.'

'You should indeed. However, you have told me what I wish to know, and you are now at liberty to—er—pike on the bean.'

'Spoke like the gentry-cove you are!' said Jimmy hoarsely. 'I'm off! And no hard feelings!'

It did not take him long to climb out of the window. He waved his hand with cheerful impudence, and disappeared from Sir Richard's sight.

Sir Richard undressed, and went to bed.

The boots, who brought up his blue coat in the morning, and his top boots, was a little surprised to find that he had exchanged bedchambers with his supposed nephew, but accepted his explanation that he disliked his original apartment with only an inward shrug. The Quality, he knew, were full of whims and oddities.

Sir Richard looked through his glass at his coat, which he had sent downstairs to be pressed, and said he felt sure the unknown presser had done his best. He next levelled the eyeglass at his top boots, and sighed. But when he was asked if there were anything amiss, he said No, nothing: it was good for a man to be removed occasionally from civilization.

The top boots stood side by side, glossily black and without a speck upon them of dust, or mud. Sir Richard shook his head sadly, and sighed again. He was missing his man, Biddle, in whose ingenious brain lay the secret of polishing boots so that you could see your face reflected in them.

But to anyone unacquainted with the art of Biddle Sir Richard's appearance, when he presently descended the stairs, left little to be desired. There were no creases in the blue coat, his cravat would have drawn approval from Mr Brummell himself, and his hair was brushed into that state of cunning disorder known as the Windswept Style.

As he rounded the bend in the staircase, he heard Miss Creed exchanging friendly salutations with a stranger. The stranger's voice betrayed his identity to Sir Richard, whose eyes managed, for all their sleepiness, to take very good stock of Captain Trimble.

Sir Richard came down the last flight in a leisurely fashion, and interrupted Miss Creed's harmless remarks, by saying in his most languid tone: 'My good boy, I wish you will not converse with strangers. It is a most lamentable habit. Rid yourself of it, I beg!'

Pen looked round in surprise. It occurred to her that she had not known that her protector could sound so haughty, or look so—yes, so insufferably proud!

Captain Trimble turned too. He was a fleshy man, with a coarse, florid sort of good looks, and a rather loud taste in dress. He said jovially: 'Oh, I don't mind the lad's talking to me!'

Sir Richard's hand sought his quizzing glass, and raised it. It was said in *haut-ton* circles that the two deadliest weapons against all forms of pretension were Mr Brummell's lifted eyebrow, and Sir Richard Wyndham's quizzing glass. Captain Trimble, though thick-skinned, was left in no doubt of its blighting message. His cheeks grew dark, and his jaw began to jut belligerently.

'And who might you be, my fine buck?' he demanded.

'I might be a number of different persons,' drawled Sir Richard.

Pen's eyes were getting rounder and rounder, for it appeared to her that this new and haughty Sir Richard was deliberately trying to provoke Captain Trimble into quarrelling with him.

For a moment it seemed as though he would succeed. Captain Trimble started forward, with his fists clenched, and an ugly look on his face. But just as he was about to speak, his expression changed, and he stopped in his tracks, and ejaculated: 'You're Beau Wyndham! Well, I'll be damned!'

'The prospect,' said Sir Richard, bored, 'leaved me unmoved.'

With the discovery of Sir Richard's identity, the desire to come to blows with him seemed to have deserted the Captain. He gave a somewhat unconvincing laugh, and said that there was no offence.

The quizzing glass focused upon his waistcoat. A shudder visibly shook Sir Richard. 'You mistake—believe me, you mistake, sir. That waistcoat is an offence in itself.'

'Oh, I know you dandies!' said the Captain waggishly. 'You're full of quips. But we shan't quarrel over a little thing like that. Oh, no!'

The quizzing glass fell. 'I am haunted by waistcoats,' Sir Richard complained. 'There was something with tobine stripes at Reading, horrible to any person of taste. There was a mustard-coloured nightmare at—Wroxham was it? No. I fancy, if memory serves me. Wroxham was rendered hideous by a catskin disaster with pewter buttons. The mustard-coloured nightmare came later. And now, to crown all—'

'Catskin?' interrupted Captain Trimble, his eyes fixed intently upon that disdainful countenance. 'Catskin, did you say?'

'Pray do not keep on repeating it!' said Sir Richard. 'The very thought of it—'

'Look'ee, sir, I'm by way of being interested in a catskin waistcoat myself! Are you sure it was at Wroxham you saw it?'

'A catskin waistcoat on its way to Bristol,' said Sir Richard dreamily.

'Bristol! Damme, I never thought—I thank you, Sir Richard! I thank you very much indeed!' said Captain Trimble, and plunged down the passage leading to the stable yard at the back of the inn.

Sir Richard watched him go, a faint, sweet smile on his lips. 'There, now!' he murmured. 'An impetuous gentleman, I fear. Let it be a lesson to you, brat, not to confide too much in strangers.'

'I didn't!' said Pen. 'I merely—'

'But he did,' Sir Richard said. 'A few chance words let fall from my tongue, and our trusting acquaintance is already calling for his horse. I want my breakfast.'

'But why have you sent him to Bristol?' Pen demanded.

'Well, I wanted to get rid of him,' he replied, strolling into the parlour.

'I thought you were trying to pick a quarrel with him.'

'I was, but he unfortunately recognized me. A pity. It would have given me a good deal of pleasure to have put him to sleep. However, I dare say it has all turned out for the best. I should have been obliged to have tied him up somewhere, which would have been a nuisance, and might have led to future complications. I shall be obliged to leave you for a short space this morning, by the way.'

'Do, please, sir, stop being provoking!' begged Pen. 'Did you see Jimmy Yarde last night, and what happened?'

'Oh yes, I saw him! Really, I don't think anything of particular moment happened.'

'He didn't try to murder you?'

'Nothing so exciting. He tried merely to recover the diamonds. When he–er– failed to do so, we enjoyed a short conversation, after which he left the inn, as unobtrusively as he had entered it.'

'Through the window, you mean. Well, I am glad you let him go, for I could not help liking him. But what are we going to do now, if you please?'

'We are now going to eliminate Beverley,' replied Sir Richard, carving the ham.

'Oh, the stammering man! How shall we do that? He sounded very disagreeable, but I don't think we should eliminate him in a rough way, do you?'

'By no means. Leave the matter in my hands, and I will engage for it that he will be eliminated without the least pain or inconvenience to anyone.'

'Yes, but then there is the necklace,' Pen pointed out. 'I feel that before we attend to anything else we ought to get rid of it. Only fancy if you were to be found with it in your pocket!'

'Very true. But I have arranged for that. The necklace belongs to Beverley's mother, and he shall restore it to her.'

Pen laid down her knife and fork. 'Then that explains it all! I thought that stammering man had more to do with it than you would tell me. I suppose he hired Jimmy Yarde, and that other person, to steal the necklace?' She wrinkled her brow. 'I don't wish to say rude things about your friends, Richard, but it seems to me very wrong of him–most improper!'

'Most,' he agreed.

'Even *dastardly!*'

'I think we might call it dastardly.'

'Well, that is what it seems to me. I see now that there is a great deal in what Aunt Almeria says. She considers that there are terrible pitfalls in Society.'

Sir Richard shook his head sadly. 'Alas, too true!'

'And vice,' said Pen awfully. 'Profligacy, and extravagance, you know.'

'I know.'

She picked up her knife and fork again. 'If must be very exciting,' she said enviously.

'Far be it from me to destroy your illusions, but I feel I should inform you that stealing one's mother's diamonds is not the invariable practice of members of the *haut ton*.'

'Of course not. I know *that!*' said Pen with dignity. She added in persuasive tones: 'Shall I come with you when you go to meet the stammering man?'

'No,' answered Sir Richard, not mincing matters.

'I thought you would say that. I wish I were really a man.'

'I still should not take you with me.'

'Then you would be very selfish, and disagreeable, and altogether abominable!' declared Pen roundly.

'I think I am,' reflected Sir Richard, recalling his sister's homily.

The large eyes softened instantly, and as they scanned Sir Richard's face a slight flush mounted to Pen's cheeks. She bent over her plate again, saying in a gruff little voice: 'No you are not. You are very kind, and obliging, and I am sorry I teased you.'

Sir Richard looked at her. He seemed to be about to speak, but she forestalled him, adding buoyantly: 'And when I tell Piers how well you have looked after me, he will be most grateful to you, I assure you.'

'Will he?' said Sir Richard, at his driest. 'I am afraid I was forgetting Piers.'

———

7

———

The spinney down the road, referred to by Beverley in his assignation with Captain Trimble, was not hard to locate. A careless question put to one of the ostlers elicited the information that it formed part of the grounds of Crome Hall. Leaving Pen to keep a sharp look-out for signs of an invasion by her relatives, Sir Richard set out shortly before eleven o'clock, to keep Captain Trimble's appointment. The impetuous Captain had indeed called for his horse, and had set off in the direction of Bristol, with his cloak bag strapped on to the saddle. He had paid his shot, so it did not seem as though he contemplated returning to Queen Charlton.

At the end of a ten-minute walk, Sir Richard reached the outskirts of the spinney. A gap in the hedge showed him a trodden path through the wood, and he followed this, glad to be out of the strong sunlight. The path led to a small clearing, where a tiny stream ran between clumps of rosebay willow herb in full flower. Here a slightly built young gentleman, dressed in the extreme of fashion, was switching pettishly with his cane at the purple heads of the willow herb. The points of his collar were so monstrous as to make it almost impossible for him to turn his head, and his coat fitted him so tightly that it seemed probable that it must have needed the combined efforts of three strong men to force him into it. Very tight pantaloons of a delicate biscuit hue encased his rather spindly legs, and a pair of tasselled Hessians sneered at their sylvan surroundings.

The Honourable Beverley Brandon was not unlike his sister Melissa, but the classic cast of his features was spoiled by a pasty complexion, and a weakness about mouth and chin not shared by Melissa. He turned, as he heard the sound of approaching footsteps, and started forward, only to be fetched up short by the sight, not of Captain Trimble's burly figure, but of a tall, well-built gentleman in whom he had not the slightest difficulty in recognizing his prospective brother-in-law.

He let his malacca cane drop from suddenly nerveless fingers. His pale eyes stared at Sir Richard. 'W-w-what the d-devil?' he stammered.

Sir Richard advanced unhurriedly across the clearing. 'Good morning, Beverley,' he said, in his pleasant, drawling voice.

'W-what are *you* d-doing here?' Beverley demanded, the wildest surmises chasing one another through his brain.

'Oh, enjoying the weather, Beverley, enjoying the weather! And you?'

'I'm staying with a friend. F-fellow I knew up at Oxford!'

'Indeed?' Sir Richard's quizzing glass swept the glade, as though in search of Mr Brandon's host. 'A delightful rendezvous! One would almost suspect you of having an assignation with someone!'

'N-no such thing! I was j-just taking the air!'

The quizzing glass was levelled at him. Sir Richard's pained eye ran over his person. 'Putting the countryside to scorn, Beverley? Strange that you who care so much about your appearance should achieve such lamentable results! Now, Cedric cares nothing for his, but–er–always looks the gentleman.'

'You have a d-damned unpleasant tongue, Richard b-but you needn't think I'll put up with it j-just because you've known me for y-years!'

'And how,' enquired Sir Richard, faintly interested, 'do you propose to put a curb on my tongue?'

Beverley glanced at him. He knew quite as well as Captain Trimble that Sir Richard's exquisite tailoring and languid bearing were deceptive; that he sparred regularly with Gentleman Jackson, and was accounted one of the best amateur heavyweights in England. 'W-what are you d-doing here?' he reiterated weakly.

'I came to keep your friend Trimble's appointment with you,' said Sir Richard, removing a caterpillar from his sleeve. Ignoring a startled oath from Mr Brandon, he added: 'Captain Trimble–by the way, you must tell me sometime where he acquired that unlikely title–found himself obliged to depart for Bristol this morning. Rather a hasty person, one is led to infer.'

'D-damn you, Richard, you mean you sent him off! W-what do you know about Trimble, and why did—?'

'Yes, I fear that some chance words of mine may perhaps have influenced him. There was a man in a catskin waistcoat–dear me, there seems to be a fatal spell attached to that waistcoat! You look quite pale, Beverley.'

Mr Brandon had indeed changed colour. He shouted: 'S-stop it! So Yarde split, d-did he? Well, w-what the d-devil has it to do with you, hey?'

'Altruism, Beverley, sheer altruism. You see, your friend Yarde–you know, I cannot congratulate you on your choice of tools–saw fit to hand the Brandon diamonds into my keeping.'

Mr Brandon looked quite stupefied. 'Handed them to *you?* Yarde d-did that? B-but how d-did you know he had them? How *c-could* you have known?'

'Oh, I didn't!' said Sir Richard, taking snuff.

'B-but if you didn't know, why d-did you constrain him–oh, what the d-devil does all this m-mean?'

'You have it wrong, my dear Beverley. I didn't constrain him. I was, in fact, an unwitting partner in the crime. I should perhaps explain that Mr Yarde was being pursued by a Runner from Bow Street.'

'A Runner!' Mr Brandon began to look ashen. 'Who set them on? G-god damn it, I—'

'I have no idea. Presumably your respected father, possibly Cedric. In Mr Yarde's picturesque but somewhat obscure language, he–er–tipped the cole to Adam Tiler. Have I that right?'

'How the d-devil should I know?' snapped Brandon.

'You must forgive me. You seem to me to be so familiar with–er–thieves and–er–swashbucklers, that I assumed that you were conversant also with thieving cant.'

'D-don't keep on talking about thieves!' Beverley said, stamping his foot.

'It is an ugly word, isn't it?' agreed Sir Richard.

Beverley ground his teeth, but said in a blustering voice: 'Very well! I *did* t-take the damned necklace! If you m-must know, I'm d-done up, ruined!

But you n-needn't take that psalm-singing t-tone with me! If I d-don't sell it, my father will soon enough!'

'I don't doubt you, Beverley, but I must point out to you that you have forgotten one trifling circumstance in your very engaging explanation. The necklace belongs to your father.'

'I c-consider it's family property. It's folly to keep it w-when we're all of us aground! D-damn it, I was forced to take the thing! *You* don't know w-what it is to be in the p-power of a d-damned cent-per-cent! If the old m-man would have p-parted, this wouldn't have happened! I told him a m-month ago I hadn't a feather to fly with, but the old fox wouldn't c-come up to scratch. I tell you, I've no c-compunction! He lectured me as though he himself w-weren't under hatches, which, by God, he is! Deep b-basset's been *his* ruin; m-myself I prefer to g-go to perdition with a d-dice box.' He gave a reckless laugh, and suddenly sat down at the moss-covered stump of a felled tree, and buried his face in his hands.

'You are forgetting women, wine, and horses,' said Sir Richard unemotionally. 'They also have played not inconsiderable rôles in this dramatic progress of yours. Three years ago you were once again under the hatches. I forget what it cost to extricate you from your embarrassments, but I do seem to recall that you gave your word you would not again indulge in—er—quite so many excesses.'

'Well, I'm n-not expecting *you* to raise the w-wind for me this time,' said Beverley sulkily.

'What's the figure?' Sir Richard asked.

'How should I know? I'm n-not a damned b-banking clerk! T-twelve thousand or so, I dare say. If you hadn't spoiled my g-game, I c-could have settled the whole thing.'

'You delude yourself. When I encountered your friend Yarde he was making for the coast with the diamonds in his pocket.'

'Where are they now?'

'In my pocket,' Sir Richard said coolly.

Beverley lifted his head. 'L-listen, Richard, you're not a b-bad fellow! Who's to know you ever had the d-diamonds in your hands? It ain't your affair: give them to m-me, and forget all about the rest! I swear I'll n-never breathe a w-word to a soul!'

'Do you know, Beverley, you nauseate me? As for giving you the diamonds I have come here with exactly that purpose.'

Beverley's hand shot out. 'I d-don't care what you think of m-me! Only hand the n-necklace over!'

'Certainly,' Sir Richard said, taking the leather purse out of his pocket. 'But you, Beverley, will give them back to your mother.'

Beverley stared at him. 'I'll be d-damned if I will! You fool, how could I?'

'You may concoct what plausible tale you please: I will even engage myself to lend it my support. But you will give back the necklace.'

A slight sneer disfigured Beverley's face. 'Oh, j-just as you l-like! Hand it over!'

Sir Richard tossed the purse over to him. 'Ah, Beverley! Perhaps I should make it clear to you that if, when I return to town, it has not been restored to Lady Saar I shall be compelled to—er—split on you.'

'You won't!' Beverley said, stowing the purse away in an inner pocket. 'M-mighty pretty behaviour for a b-brother-in-law!'

'But I am not your brother-in-law,' said Sir Richard gently.

'Oh, you n-needn't think I don't know you're g-going to m-marry

Melissa! Our scandals will become yours too. I think you'll keep your m-mouth shut.'

'I am always sorry to disappoint expectations, but I have not the smallest intention of marrying your sister,' said Sir Richard, taking another pinch of snuff.

Beverley's jaw dropped. 'You d-don't mean she wouldn't have you?'

'No, I don't mean that.'

'B-but it's as g-good as settled!'

'Not, believe me, by me.'

'The d-devil!' Beverley said blankly.

'So you see,' pursued Sir Richard, 'I should have no compunction whatsoever in informing Saar of this episode.'

'You w-wouldn't split on me to my f-father!' Beverley cried, jumping up from the tree stump.

'That, my dear Beverley, rests entirely with you.'

'But, d'damn it, m-man, I *can't* give the d-diamonds back! I tell you I'm d-done up, fast aground!'

'I fancy that to have married into your family would have cost me considerably more than twelve thousand pounds. I am prepared to settle your debts—ah, for the last time, Beverley!'

'D-devilish good of you,' muttered Beverley. 'G-give me the money, and I'll settle 'em myself.'

'I fear that your intercourse with Captain Trimble has led you to credit others with his trusting disposition. I, alas, repose not the slightest reliance on your word. You may send a statement of your debts to my town house. I think that is all—except that you will be recalled to London suddenly, and you will leave Crome Hall, if you are wise, not later than tomorrow morning.'

'Blister it, I w-won't be ordered about by y-you! I'll leave w-when I choose!'

'If you don't choose to do so in the morning, you will leave in the custody of a Bow Street Runner.'

Beverley coloured hotly. 'By G-God, I'll p-pay you for this, Richard!'

'But not, if I know you, until I have settled your debts,' said Sir Richard, turning on his heel.

Beverley stood still, watching him walk away down the path, until the undergrowth hid him from sight. It was several minutes before it occurred to him that although Sir Richard had been unpleasantly frank on some subjects, he had not divulged how or why he came to be in Queen Charlton.

Beverley frowned over this. Sir Richard might, of course, be visiting friends in the neighbourhood, but apart from a house belonging to some heiress or other, Crome Hall was the only country seat of any size for several miles. The more Beverley considered the matter, the more inexplicable became Sir Richard's presence. From a sort of sullen curiosity, he passed easily to a mood of suspicion, and began to think that there was something very odd about the whole affair, and to wonder whether any profit could be made out of it.

He was not in the least grateful to Sir Richard for promising to pay his debts. He certainly wished to silence his more rapacious creditors, but he would have considered it a stupid waste of money to settle any bill which could possibly be held over to some later date. Moreover, the mere payment of his debts would not line his pockets, and it was hard to see how he was to continue to support life in the manner to which he was accustomed.

He took the necklace out, and looked at it. It was a singularly fine specimen of the jeweller's art, and several of the stones in it were of a truly formidable size. It was worth perhaps twice twelve thousand pounds. One did not, of course, find it easy to obtain the real value of stolen goods, but even if he had been forced to sell it for as little as twenty thousand pounds he would still have been eight thousand pounds in pocket, since there was no longer the least necessity to share the proceeds with Horace Trimble. Trimble, Beverley thought, had bungled the affair, and deserved nothing. If only Richard could be silenced, Trimble need never know that the necklace had been recovered from Jimmy Yarde, and it could be sold to the sole advantage of the only one of the three persons implicated in its theft who had a real right to it.

The more he reflected on these lines, and the longer he gazed at the diamonds, the more fixed became Beverley's conviction that Sir Richard, instead of assisting him in his financial difficulties, had actually robbed him of eight thousand pounds, if not more. A burning sense of injury possessed him, and if he could at that moment have done Sir Richard an injury, without incurring any himself, he would certainly have jumped at the chance.

But short of lying in wait for him, and shooting him, there did not seem to be anything he could do to Richard, with advantage; and although he would have been very glad to have heard of Richard's sudden death, and would have thought it, quite sincerely, a judgement on him, his murderous inclination was limited, to do him justice, to a strong wish that Richard would fall out of a window, and break his neck, or be set upon by armed highwaymen, and summarily slain. At the same time, there was undoubtedly something queer about Richard's being in this remote village, and it might be worth while to discover what had brought him to Queen Charlton.

Sir Richard, meanwhile, walked back to the village, arriving at the George in time to see a couple of sweating horses being led into the stable, and a post chaise being pushed into one corner of the roomy yard. He was therefore fully prepared to encounter strangers in the inn, and any doubts of their identity were set at rest upon his stepping into the entrance parlour, and perceiving a matron with an imposing front seated upon one of the oaken settles, and vigorously fanning her heated countenance. At her elbow stood a stockily built young gentleman with his hair brushed into a Brutus, mopping his brow. He had somewhat globular eyes of no particular colour, and when seen in profile bore a distinct likeness to a hake.

The same unfortunate resemblance was to be observed, though in a less pronounced degree, in Mrs Griffin. The lady was built on massive lines, and appeared to be feeling the heat. Possibly a travelling costume of purple satin trimmed with a quantity of sarsenet, and worn under a spencer, and a voluminous cloak of drab merino cloth, might have contributed to her discomfort. Her locks were confined in a round cap, and over this she wore a beehive bonnet of moss-straw, trimmed with enough plumes to remind Sir Richard forcibly of a hearse. The landlord was standing in front of her in an attitude of concern, and as Sir Richard stepped into the entrance parlour, she said in tones of strong resolution: 'You are deceiving me! I demand to have this—this youth brought before me!'

'But, Mama!' said the stocky young man unhappily.

'Silence, Frederick!' pronounced the matron.

'But consider, Mama! If the—the young man the landlord speaks of is travelling with his uncle, he could not possibly be–be my cousin, could he?'

'I do not believe a word of what this man says!' declared Mrs Griffin. 'I should not wonder if he had been bribed.'

The landlord regretfully said that no one had tried to bribe him.

'Pshaw!' said Mrs Griffin.

Sir Richard judged it to be the time to call attention to his own presence. He walked forward in the direction of the staircase.

'Here is the gentleman!' said the landlord, with a good deal of relief. 'He will tell for himself that what I've said is the truth, ma'am.'

Sir Richard paused, and glanced with raised eyebrows from Mrs Griffin to her son, and from Mr Frederick Griffin to the landlord. 'I beg your pardon?' he drawled.

The attention of the Griffins instantly became focused upon him. The gentleman's eyes were riveted to his cravat; the lady, taking in his air of elegance, was plainly shaken.

'If your honour pleases!' said the landlord. 'The lady, sir, is come in search of a young gentleman, which has run away from school, the same being her ward. I've told her that I have but one young gentleman staying in the house, and him your honour's nephew, and I'd be glad if you'd bear me out, sir.'

'Really,' said Sir Richard, bored, 'I don't know whom you have staying in the house besides myself and my nephew.'

'The question is, *have* you a nephew?' demanded Mrs Griffin.

Sir Richard raised his quizzing glass, surveyed her through it, and bowed slightly. 'I was certainly under the impression that I had a nephew, ma'am. May I ask in what way he interests you?'

'If he *is* your nephew, I have no interest in him whatsoever,' declared the matron handsomely.

'Mama!' whispered her son, anguished. 'Recollect, I beg of you! A stranger! No proof! The greatest discretion!'

'I am quite distracted!' said Mrs Griffin, shedding tears.

This had the effect of driving the landlord from the room, and of flustering Mr Griffin. Between trying to pacify his parent, and excusing such odd behaviour to the elegant stranger, he became hotter than ever, and floundered in a morass of broken phrases. The look of astonishment on Sir Richard's face, the pained lift of his brows, quite discomposed him, and he ended by saying: 'The truth is my mother is sadly overwrought!'

'My confidence has been betrayed!' interpolated Mrs Griffin, raising her face from her damp handkerchief.

'Yes, Mama: precisely so! Her confidence has been betrayed sir, by–by the shocking conduct of my cousin, who has—'

'I have nourished a viper in my bosom!' said Mrs Griffin.

'Just so, Mama. She has nourished–at least, not quite that, perhaps, but it is very bad, very upsetting to a lady of delicate sensibility!'

'All my life,' declaimed Mrs Griffin, 'I have been surrounded by ingratitude!'

'Mama, you cannot be surrounded by–and in any case, you know it is not so! Do, pray, calm yourself! I shall claim your indulgence, sir. The circumstances are so peculiar, and my cousin's behaviour has exerted so strong an effect upon my poor mother that–in short—'

'It is the impropriety of it which is worse than anything!' said Mrs Griffin.

'Exactly so, Mama. You see, it is the impropriety, sir—I mean, my mother is not quite herself.'

'I shall never,' announced the matron, 'hold up my head again! It is my belief that this person is in league with her!'

'Mama, most earnestly I implore you—!'

'Her?' repeated Sir Richard, apparently bewildered.

'Him!' corrected Mr Griffin.

'You must forgive me if I do not perfectly understand you,' said Sir Richard. 'I apprehend that you have—er—mislaid a youth, and have come—'

'Precisely so, sir! We mis—at least, no, no, we did not mislay him, of course!'

'Ran away!' uttered Mrs Griffin, emerging from the handkerchief for a brief instant.

'Ran away,' corroborated her son.

'But in what way,' enquired Sir Richard, 'does this concern me, sir?'

'Not at all, sir, I assure you! No such suspicion is cherished by me, upon my word!'

'What suspicion?' asked Sir Richard, still more bewildered.

'None, sir, none in the world! That is just what I was saying. I have no suspicion—'

'But I have!' said Mrs Griffin, in much more robust tones. 'I accuse you of concealing the truth from me!'

'Mama, do but consider! You cannot—you know you cannot insult this gentleman by insinuating—'

'In the execution of my duty there is nothing I cannot do!' responded his mother nobly. 'Besides, I do not know him. I mistrust him.'

Mr Griffin turned wretchedly to Sir Richard: 'You see, sir, my mother—'

'Mistrusts me,' supplied Sir Richard.

'No, no, I assure you! My mother is sadly put out, and scarcely knows what she is saying.'

'I am in the fullest possession of my faculties, I thank you, Frederick!' said Mrs Griffin, gathering strength.

'Of course, of course, Mama! But the agitation—the natural agitation—'

'If he is speaking the truth,' interrupted Mrs Griffin, 'let him summon his nephew to stand before me!'

'Ah, I begin to understand you!' said Sir Richard. 'Is it possible, ma'am, that you suspect my nephew of being your errant ward?'

'No, no!' said Griffin feebly.

'Yes!' declared his mother.

'But Mama, only consider what such a thought must imply!' said Mr Griffin in a frenzied aside.

'I can believe anything of that unnatural creature!'

'I should doubt very much whether my nephew is upon the premises,' said Sir Richard coldly. 'He was engaged to spend the day with friends, upon an expedition of pleasure. However, if he should not yet have left the house, I will engage to—er—allay all these heart burnings.'

'If he has run out to escape us, I shall await his return!' said Mrs Griffin. 'And so I warn you!'

'I admire your resolution, ma'am, but I must point out to you that your movements are of no possible interest to me,' said Sir Richard, stepping over to the bell, and jerking it.

'Frederick!' said Mrs Griffin. 'Will you stand by and hear your mother being insulted by one whom I strongly suspect of being a dandy?'

'But Mama, indeed, it is no concern of ours if he is!'

'Perhaps,' said Sir Richard, in arctic tones, 'it may be of service if I make myself known to you, ma'am. My name is Wyndham.'

Mrs Griffin received this information with every appearance of disdain, but its effect upon her son was staggering. His eyes seemed to be in danger of bursting out of their sockets; he started forward, and ejaculated in tones of deepest reverence: 'Sir, is this possible? Have I the honour of addressing Sir Richard Wyndham?'

Sir Richard bowed slightly.

'The celebrated Whip?' asked Mr Griffin.

Sir Richard bowed again.

'The creator of the Wyndham Fall?' pursued Mr Griffin, almost overcome.

Tired of bowing, Sir Richard said: 'Yes.'

'Sir,' said Mr Griffin, 'I am happy to make your acquaintance! My name is Griffin!'

'How do you do?' murmured Sir Richard, holding out his hand.

Mr Griffin clasped it. 'I wonder I should not have recognized you. Mama, we have been quite mistaken. This is none other than the famous Sir Richard Wyndham—the friend of Brummell, you know! You must have heard me—you must have heard him spoken of. It is quite impossible that he can know anything of my cousin's whereabouts.'

She seemed to accept this, though with obvious reluctance. She looked Sir Richard over with disfavour, and said paralysingly: 'I have the greatest dislike of all forms of dandyism, and I have ever deplored the influence exerted by the Bow-Window set upon young men of respectable upbringing. However, if you are indeed Sir Richard Wyndham, I dare say you would not object to showing my son how to arrange his cravat in what he calls the Wyndham Fall, so that he need no longer spoil every neckcloth in his drawer before achieving a result which I consider lamentable.'

'Mama!' whispered the unhappy Mr Griffin. 'I beg of you!'

The entrance of a servant in answer to the bell's summons came as a timely interruption. Upon being asked to discover whether Sir Richard's nephew were in the house, he was able to reply that the young nephew had left the inn some time previously.

'Then I fear there is nothing for you to do but to wait his return,' said Sir Richard, addressing himself to Mrs Griffin.

'We should not dream of—Mama, there can be no doubt that she—he—did not come here after all. Lady Luttrell disclaims all knowledge, remember, and *she* must certainly have known if my cousin had come into this neighbourhood.'

'If I could think that she had gone to cousin Jane, all would not yet be lost!' said Mrs Griffin. 'Yet is it possible? I fear the worst!'

'This is all very perplexing,' complained Sir Richard. 'I was under the impression that this mysterious truant was of the male sex.'

'Frederick, my nerves can stand no more!' said Mrs Griffin, surging to her feet. 'If you mean to drag me the length of England again, I must insist upon being permitted the indulgence of half an hour's solitude first!'

'But Mama, it was not I who would come here!' expostulated Mr Griffin.

Sir Richard again rang the bell, and this time desired that a chambermaid should be sent to him. Mrs Griffin was presently consigned to the care of an abigail, and left the room majestically, commanding hot water to wash with, tea, and a decent bedchamber.

Her son heaved a sigh of relief. 'I must beg pardon, Sir Richard! You must allow me to beg your pardon!'

'Not at all,' said Sir Richard.

'Yes, yes, I insist! Such an unfortunate misunderstanding! An explanation is due to you! A slip of the tongue, you know, but my mother is labouring under strong emotion, and does not quite heed what she says. You noticed it: indeed, no one could wonder at your surprise! The unhappy truth, sir, is that my cousin is not a boy, but—in a word, sir—a female!'

'This explanation, Mr Griffin, is quite unnecessary, believe me.'

'Sir,' said Mr Griffin earnestly, 'as a Man of the World, I should value your opinion! Concealment is useless: the truth must be discovered in the end. What, sir, would you think of a member of the Weaker Sex who assumed the disguise of a man, and left the home of her natural protector by way of the window?'

'I should assume,' replied Sir Richard, 'that she had strong reasons for acting with such resolution.'

'She did not wish to marry me,' said Mr Griffin gloomily.

'Oh!' said Sir Richard.

'Well, I'm sure I can't see why she should be so set against me, but that's it, sir. The thing is that here's my mother determined to find her, and to make her marry me, and so hush up the scandal. But I don't like it above half. If she dislikes the notion so much, I don't think I ought to marry her, do you?'

'Emphatically not!'

'I must say I am very glad to hear you say that, Sir Richard!' said Mr Griffin, much cheered. 'For you must know that my mother has been telling me ever since yesterday that I must marry her now, to save her name. But I think she would very likely make me uncomfortable, and nothing could make up for that, in my opinion.'

'A lady capable of escaping out of a window in the guise of a man would quite certainly make you more than uncomfortable,' said Sir Richard.

'Yes, though she's only a chit of a girl, you know. In fact, she is not yet out. I am very happy to have had the benefit of the opinion of a Man of the World. I feel that I can rely on your judgement.'

'On my judgement you might, but in nothing else, I assure you,' said Sir Richard. 'You know nothing of me, after all. How do you know that I am not now concealing your cousin from you?'

'Ha-ha! Very good, upon my word! Very good, indeed!' said Mr Griffin, saluting a jest of the first water.

8

The Griffins did not leave Queen Charlton until the cool of the afternoon, and by the time he saw their chaise off the premises of the George, Sir Richard was heartily sick of the company of surely one of his most devout worshippers. No sign was seen of Pen, who had no doubt fled the house upon the Griffins' arrival. What sustenance she had snatched up to bear her strength up through a long day, Sir Richard had no means of knowing.

Mrs Griffin, tottering downstairs to partake of light refreshments, found her son hanging upon Sir Richard's bored lips. Upon hearing that he had divulged the secret of Pen's identity, she first showed a dangerous tendency to swoon, but upon being supplied with a glass of ratafia by Sir Richard, revived sufficiently to pour out her wrongs into his ear.

'What, I ask myself,' she said dramatically, 'has become of that tiresome girl? Into what company may she have fallen? I see that you, Sir Richard, are a person of sensibility. Conceive of my feelings! What—I say, *what* if my unfortunate niece should have fallen into the hands of some *Man?*'

'What indeed!' said Sir Richard.

'She must marry him. When I think of the care, the hopes, the maternal fondness I have lavished—but it is ever so! There is no gratitude in the world today.'

Upon this gloomy reflection, she ordered her chaise to be got ready to bear her instantly to Chippenham. She would have remained at Queen Charlton for the night, she explained, only that she suspected the sheets.

Sir Richard, having seen her off, walked down the street, to cool his heated brow, and to consider the intricates of his position.

It was while he was absent that Miss Creed and the Honourable Beverley Brandon, approaching the George from widely divergent angles, but with identical circumspection, came face to face in the entrance parlour.

They eyed one another. A few moments' conversation with the tapster had put Beverley in possession of information which he found sufficiently intriguing to make him run the risk of perhaps encountering Captain Trimble in entering the inn, and prosecuting further enquiries about Sir Richard Wyndham. Sir Richard, the tapster had told him, was putting up at the George with his nephew.

Now, Sir Richard's nephew, as Beverley knew well, was a lusty young gentleman not yet breeched. He did not mention this circumstance to the tapster, but on hearing that the mysterious nephew in question was a youth in his teens, he pricked up his ears, and penetrated from the taproom into the main parlour of the inn.

Here Pen, entering the George cautiously from the stable yard, came plump upon him. Never having seen his face, she did not at once recognize him, but when, after an intent stare, he moved towards her, saying with a slight stammer: 'How d-do you do? I think you m-must be Wyndham's nephew?' she had no doubt of his identity.

She was no fool, and she realized at once that anyone well acquainted with Sir Richard must be aware that she was not his nephew. She replied guardedly: 'Well, I call him my uncle, because he is so much older than I am, but in point of fact we are cousins only. Third cousins,' she added, making the relationship as remote as she could.

A smile which she did not quite like lingered on Beverley's rather slack mouth. Mentally, he was reviewing Sir Richard's family, but he said with great affability: 'Oh, indeed? Ch-charmed to make your acquaintance, Mr-er-er?'

'Brown,' supplied Pen, regretting that she had not thought to provide herself with a more unusual surname.

'Brown,' bowed Beverley, his smile widening. 'It is a great p-pleasure to me to m-meet any connection of W-Wyndham's. In such a remote spot, too! Now d-do tell me! What b-brings you here?'

'Family affairs,' answered Pen promptly. 'Uncle Richard—Cousin Richard, I mean, only I have always been in the way of calling him uncle, you understand—very kindly undertook to come with me.'

'So it was on y-your account that he came to Queen Charlton!' said Beverley. 'That is most interesting!' His eyes ran over her in a way that made her feel profoundly ill at ease. '*M-most* interesting!' he repeated. 'P-pray present my c-compliments to Wyndham, and tell him that I perfectly understand his reasons for choosing such a secluded locality!'

He bowed himself out with a flourish, leaving Pen in a state of considerable trepidation. In the taproom, he called for paper, ink, a pen, and some brandy, and sat down at a table in one corner to write a careful letter to Sir Richard. It took time, for he was not apt with a pen, and much brandy, but it was finished at last to his satisfaction. He looked round rather owlishly for wafers, but the tapster had brought him none, so he folded the note into a screw, wrote Sir Richard's name on it in a flourishing scrawl, and told the tapster to give it to Sir Richard upon his return to the inn. After that he went away, not quite steadily, but full of chuckling glee at his own ingenuity.

The tapster, who was busy serving drinks, left the twisted note on the bar while he hurried to the other end of the room with beer for a clamorous party of countrymen. It was here that Captain Trimble, coming into the taproom from the stable yard, found it.

Captain Trimble, who had spent a fruitless day in attempting to discover some trace of Jimmy Yarde in Bristol, was hot, and tired, and in no very good temper. He sat down on a high stool at the bar, and began to wipe his face with a large handkerchief. It was as he was restoring the handkerchief to his pocket that the note, and its superscription, caught his eye. He was well acquainted with Mr Brandon's handwriting, and he recognized it at once. It did not at first surprise him that Mr Brandon should have written to Sir Richard Wyndham; he supposed them to be of the same fashionable set. But as he looked idly down at the screw of paper thoughts of the wild-goose chase upon which Sir Richard had sent him took strong possession of his mind, and he wondered, not for the first time during that exasperating day, whether Sir Richard could have had a motive in dispatching him to Bristol. The note began to assume a sinister aspect; suspicion darkened the already warm colour in the Captain's cheeks; and after staring at the note for a minute, he cast a quick look round, saw that no one was watching him, and deftly palmed it.

The tapster came back to the bar, but by the time he had recollected the note, Captain Trimble had retired to a highbacked settle by the empty fireplace, and was calling for a can of ale. At a convenient moment, he unscrewed the twist of paper, and read its contents.

My very dear Richard, *had written Mr Brandon*, I am desolated to find that you have gone out. I should like to continue our conversation. When I tell you that I have been privileged to meet your nephew, my dear Richard, I feel that you will appreciate the wisdom of meeting me again. You would not wish me to talk, but a paltry twelve thousand is not enough to close my mouth, which, however, I am willing to do, tho' not for a less sum than I have it in my power to obtain by Other Means. Should you wish to discuss this delicate matter, I shall be in the spinney at ten o'clock this evening. If you do not come there, I shall understand that you have Withdrawn your Objection to my disposing of Certain Property as I choose, and I fancy that it would be Unwise of you to mention our dealings in this matter to anyone, either now or later.

Captain Trimble read this missive twice before folding it again into its original twist. The mention of Pen he found obscure, and of no particular interest. There was apparently a disreputable secret in some way connected with Sir Richard's young nephew, but the Captain did not immediately perceive what profit was to be made out of it. Far more arresting was the thinly veiled reference to the Brandon necklace. The Captain's eyes smouldered as he thought this over, and his massive jaw worked a little. He had suspected Beverley's good faith from the moment that Jimmy Yarde had been thrust on him as an accomplice. The matter seemed as clear as crystal now. Beverley and Yarde had hatched a plot to cheat him of his share in the fortune, and when Beverley had been raving against him for blundering—very convincingly he had raved too—he had actually had the necklace in his pocket. Well, Mr Brandon would have to learn that it was not wise to try to bubble Horace Trimble, and still less wise to leave unsealed notes lying about in a common taproom, As for Sir Richard, the Captain found his part in these tortuous proceedings very difficult to fathom. He seemed to know something about the diamonds, but he was far too wealthy a man, the Captain considered, to have the least interest in their worth in terms of guineas. But Sir Richard had undoubtedly meddled in the affair, and the Captain wished with all his heart that he could discover a way to pay him in full for his interference.

Captain Trimble was naturally a man of violence, but although he would have liked very much to spoil Sir Richard's handsome face, he wasted no more than a couple of minutes over this pleasing dream. Sir Richard, if it came to fisticuffs, would enjoy the encounter far more than would his assailant. A more determined assault, on a dark night, by a couple of stout men armed with clubs, might have a better chance of success, but even this scheme had a drawback. Sir Richard had been set upon twice before, by hardy rogues who planned to rob him. He had not been robbed, and he had not been attacked again. He was marked down by every cut-throat and robber in the Rogue's Calendar as dangerous, one who carried pistols, and could draw and fire with a speed and a deadly accuracy which made him a most undesirable man to molest.

Regretfully, the Captain decided that Sir Richard must be left alone, for the present, at all events.

By this time the tapster had discovered the loss of Mr Brandon's note. Everyone in the room disclaimed all knowledge of its whereabouts. Captain Trimble drained his can, and carried it over to the bar. As he set it down, he said: 'Isn't that a bit of paper I see?'

No one could see anything, but that might have been because the Captain bent so quickly to pick it up. When he straightened himself, the screw of paper was between his fingers. The tapster took it with a word of thanks, and gave it to one of the waiters, who had come into the taproom for a pint of burgundy, and told him to deliver it to Sir Richard. Captain Trimble, quite as well pleased as Beverley had been, betook himself to the coffee room, and ordered a sustaining meal.

Sir Richard, meanwhile, had returned to the inn. He found Pen awaiting him in the parlour, curled up in a big chair and eating an apple. 'This passion for munching raw fruit!' he remarked. 'You look a very urchin.'

She twinkled at him. 'Well, I am hungry. Did you—did you have a pleasant day with my Aunt Almeria, sir?'

'I hope with all my heart,' said Sir Richard, eyeing her with some severity, 'that *you* spent the day in the greatest possible discomfort. I wish it had rained.'

'I didn't. I visited my home, and I went to all the *particular* places Piers and I used to hide in, when people wanted us to do our lessons. Only I hadn't anything to eat.'

'I am glad,' said Sir Richard. 'Do you know that I have not only found myself in a position where I was forced to lie, and dissemble, and practise the most shocking deceit, but I have also been obliged to consort for five hours with one of the most commonplace young cubs it has ever been my ill-fortune to meet?'

'I knew Fred would come with my aunt! Doesn't he look just like a fish, sir?'

'Yes, a hake. But you cannot divert me from what I wish to say. Half an hour's conversation with your aunt has convinced me that you are an unprincipled brat.'

'Did she say unkind things of me?' Miss Creed wrinkled her brow. 'I don't think I am *unprincipled*, precisely.'

'You are a menace to all law-abiding and respectable citizens,' said Sir Richard.

She seemed gratified. 'I didn't think I was as important as that.'

'Look what you have done to me!' said Sir Richard.

'Yes, but I don't think you are very law-abiding or respectable,' objected Pen.

'I was once, but it seems a long time ago.'

She finished her apple. 'Well, I am sorry you are feeling cross, for I think I should tell you something which you may not be pleased about.'

He looked at her with misgiving. 'Let me know the worst!'

'It was the stammering man,' said Pen, not very lucidly. 'Of course, I quite see that I should have been more careful.'

'You mean Beverley Brandon. What has he been doing?'

'Well, you see, he came here. And just at that very same moment, I chanced to walk into the inn, and—and we met.'

'When was this?'

'Oh, not long ago! You were gone out. Only he seemed to know me.'

'Seemed to know you?'

'Well, he said surely I must be your nephew,' Pen explained.

Sir Richard had been listening to her with a gathering frown. He said now, with a grim note which she had not before heard in his voice: 'Beverley knows very well that the only nephew I have is a child in short petticoats.'

'Oh, have you got a nephew?' enquired Pen, diverted.

'Yes. Never mind that. What did you reply?'

'Well, I think I was quite clever,' said Pen hopefully. 'Naturally, I knew who he must be, as soon as he spoke; and I guessed, of course, that he must know I am not your nephew. Because even if some people think I have no ingenuity, I am not at all stupid,' she added, with a darkling look.

'Does that rankle?' His countenance had relaxed a little. 'Never mind! go on!'

'I said that in point of fact you were not my uncle, but I called you so because you were a great deal older than I. I said that you were my third cousin. Then he asked me why we had come to Queen Charlton, and I said it was on account of family affairs, though I would rather have pointed out that is was extremely ill-bred and inquisitive of him to ask me such questions. And after that he went away.'

'Did he, indeed? Did he say what had brought him here in the first place?'

'No. But he gave me a message for you, which I did not quite like.'

'Well?'

'It sounded sinister to me,' said Pen, preparing him for the worst.

'I can well believe it.'

'And the more I think of it the more sinister it appears to me. He said I must present his compliments to you, and tell you that he perfectly understands your reason for coming to such a secluded spot.'

'The devil!' said Sir Richard.

'I was afraid you would not be excessively pleased,' Pen said anxiously. 'Do you suppose that it means that he knows who I am?'

'Not that, no,' Sir Richard replied.

'Perhaps,' suggested Pen, 'he guessed that I am not a boy?'

'Perhaps.'

She thought the matter over. 'Well, I don't see what else he could possibly have meant. But Jimmy Yarde never suspected me, and I conversed with him far more than I did with this disagreeable stammering man. How very unfortunate it is that we should have met someone who knows you well!'

'I beg your pardon?' said Sir Richard, putting up his glass.

She looked innocently up at him. 'On account of his being aware that you have no nephew or cousin like me, I mean.'

'Oh!' said Sir Richard, lowering the glass. 'I see. Don't let it worry you!'

'Well, it does worry me, because I see now that I have been imprudent. I should not have let you come with me. It has very likely placed you in an awkward situation.'

'That aspect of it had not occurred to me,' said Sir Richard, faintly smiling. 'The imprudence was mine. I ought to have handed you over to your aunt at our first meeting.'

'Do you wish you had?' asked Pen wistfully.

He looked down at her for an instant. 'No.'

'Well, I'm glad, because if you had tried to, I would have run away from you.' She lifted her chin from her cupped hands. 'If you are not sorry to be here, do not let us give it another thought! It is so very fatiguing to go on being sorry about something which one has done. Did you order any dinner, sir?'

'I did. Duck and peas.'

'Good!' said Pen, with profound satisfaction. 'Where has Aunt Almeria gone, do you suppose?'

'To Chippenham, and then to Cousin Jane.'

'To Cousin Jane? Good gracious, why?'

'To see whether you have taken refuge with her, I imagine.'

'With Cousin Jane!' Pen exclaimed. 'Why, she is the most odious old woman, and takes snuff!'

Sir Richard, who had just opened his own box, paused. 'Er—do you consider that an odious habit?' he asked.

'In a female, I do. Besides, she spills it on her clothes. Ugh! Oh, I did not mean you, sir!' she added, with a ripple of sudden laughter. 'You do it with such an air!'

'Thank you!' he said.

A waiter came in to lay the covers for dinner, and presented a small, twisted note to Sir Richard on a large tray.

He picked it up unhurriedly, and spread it open. Pen, anxiously watching him, could detect nothing in his face but boredom. He read the note through to the end, and consigning it to his pocket, glanced towards Pen. 'Let me see: what were we discussing?'

'Snuff,' replied Pen, in a hollow voice.

'Ah, yes! I myself use King's Martinique, but there are many who consider it a trifle light in character.'

She returned a mechanical answer, and upon the waiter's leaving the room, interrupted Sir Richard's description of the proper way to preserve snuff in good condition, by demanding impetuously: 'Who was it from, sir?'

'Don't be inquisitive!' said Sir Richard calmly.

'You can't deceive me! I feel sure it was from that hateful man.'

'It was, but there is no occasion for you to trouble your head over it, believe me.'

'Only tell me! Does he mean to do you some mischief?'

'Certainly not. It would, in all events, be a task quite beyond his power.'

'I feel very uneasy.'

'So I perceive. You will be the better for your dinner.'

The waiter came in with the duck at that opportune moment, and set it upon the table. Pen was, in fact, so hungry that her thoughts were instantly diverted. She made a very good dinner, and did not again refer to the note.

Sir Richard, maintaining a flow of easy conversation, seemed to be wholly devoid of care, but the note had annoyed him. There was very little fear, he considered, of Beverley's being able to harm Miss Creed, since he could have no knowledge of her identity; and this veiled threat of exposing Sir Richard was a matter of indifference to that gentleman. But he would certainly meet Beverley in the spinney at the proposed hour, for it now became more than ever necessary to dispatch him to London immediately. While he remained in the neighbourhood there would be no question of delivering Pen into Lady Luttrell's care, and although Sir Richard had not the least desire to relinquish his self-appointed guardianship of that enterprising damsel, he was perfectly well aware that he must do so, and without any loss of time.

Accordingly, he sent her to bed shortly after half past nine, telling her that if she was not tired she deserved to be. She went without demur, so probably her day spent in the open had made her sleepy. He waited until a few minutes before ten o'clock, and then took his hat and walking cane, and strolled out of the inn.

There was a full moon, and not a cloud in the sky. Sir Richard had no difficulty in seeing his way, and soon came to the track through the wood. It was darker here, for the trees held out the moonlight. A rabbit scuttled across the path, an owl hooted somewhere at hand, and there were little rustlings in the undergrowth, but Sir Richard was not of a nervous disposition, and did not find these sounds in any way disturbing.

But he was hardly prepared to come upon a lady lying stretched across the path, immediately round a bend in it. This sight was, indeed, so unexpected that it brought him up short. The lady did not move, but lay in a crumpled heap of pale muslin and darker cloak. Sir Richard, recovering from his momentous surprise, strode forward, and dropped on to his knee beside her. It was too dark under the trees for him to be able to distinguish her features clearly, but he thought she was young. She was not dead, as he had at first feared, but in a deep faint. He began to chafe her hands, and had just bethought him of the tiny stream which he had observed that morning, when she showed design of returning consciousness. He raised her in his arms, hearing a sigh flutter past her lips. A moan succeeded the sigh; she said something he could not catch, and began weakly to cry.

'Don't cry!' Sir Richard said. 'You are quite safe.'

She caught her breath on a sob, and stiffened in his hold. He felt her little hands close on his arm. Then she began to tremble.

'No, there is nothing to frighten you,' he said in his cool way. 'You will be better directly.'

'Oh!' the exclamation sounded terrified. 'Who are you? Oh, let me go!'

'Certainly I will let you go, but are you able to stand yet? You do not know me, but I am perfectly harmless, I assure you.'

She made a feeble attempt to struggle up, and succeeded only in crouching on the path in a woebegone huddle, saying through her sobs: 'I must go! Oh, I must go! I ought not to have come!'

'That I can well believe,' said Sir Richard, still on his knee beside her. 'Why did you come? Or is that an impertinent question?'

It had the effect of redoubling her sobs. She buried her face in her hands, shuddering, and rocking herself to and fro, and gasping out unintelligible phrases.

'Well!' said a voice behind Sir Richard.

He looked quickly over his shoulder. 'Pen! What are you doing here?'

'I followed you,' replied Pen, looking critically down at the weeping girl. 'I brought a stout stick too, because I thought you were going to meet that odious stammering man, and I feel sure he means to do you a mischief. Who is this?'

'I haven't the slightest idea,' replied Sir Richard. 'And presently I shall have something to say to you on the subject of this idiotic escapade of yours! My good child, can't you stop crying?'

'What is she doing here?' asked Pen, unmoved by his strictures.

'Heaven knows! I found her lying on the path. How does one make a female stop crying?'

'I shouldn't think you could. She's going to have a fit of the vapours, I expect. And I do *not* see why you should hug people, if you don't know who they are.'

'I was not hugging her.'

'It looked like it to me,' argued Pen.

'I suppose,' said Sir Richard sardonically, 'you would have had me step over her, and walk on?'

'Yes, I would,' replied Pen promptly.

'Don't be a little fool! The girl had fainted.'

'Oh!' Pen moved forward. 'I wonder what made her do that? You know, it all seems extremely odd to me.'

'It seems quite as odd to me, let me tell you.' He laid his hand on the sobbing girl's shoulder. 'Come! You will not help matters by crying. Can't you tell me what has happened to upset you so?'

The girl made a convulsive effort to choke back her hysterical tears, and managed to utter: 'I was so frightened!'

'Yes, that I had realized. What frightened you?'

'There was a man!' gasped the girl. 'And I hid, and then another man came, and they began to quarrel, and I dared not move for fear they should hear me, and the big one hit the other, and he fell down and lay still, and the big one took something out of his pocket, and went away, and oh, oh, he passed so close I c-could have touched him only by stretching out my hand! The other man never moved, and I was so frightened I ran, everything went black, and I think I fainted.'

'Ran away?' repeated Pen, in disgusted accents. 'What a poor-spirited thing to do! Didn't you go to help the man who was knocked down?'

'Oh no, no, no!' shuddered the girl.

'I must say, I don't think you deserve to have such an adventure. And if I were you I wouldn't continue sitting in the middle of the path. It isn't at all helpful, and it makes you look very silly.'

This severe speech had the effect of angering the girl. She reared up her head, and exclaimed: 'How dare you? You are the rudest young man I ever met in my life!'

Sir Richard put his hand under her elbow, and assisted her to her feet. 'Ah—accept my apologies on my nephew's behalf, ma'am!' he said, with only the faintest quiver in his voice. 'A sadly ill-conditioned boy! May I suggest to you that you should rest on this bank for a few moments, while I go to investigate the—er—scene of the assault you so graphically described? My nephew—who has, you perceive, provided himself with a stout stick—will charge himself with your safety.'

'I'll come with you,' said Pen mutinously.

'You will—for once in your life—do as you are told,' said Sir Richard, and, lowering the unknown on to the bank, strode on down the track towards the clearing in the wood.

Here the moonlight bathed the ground in its cold silver light. Sir Richard had no doubt that he would find Beverley Brandon, either stunned, or recovering from the effects of the blow which had felled him, but as he stepped into the clearing he saw not only one man lying still on the ground, but a second on his knees beside him.

Sir Richard trod softly, and it was not until he had approached to within a few feet of the little group that the kneeling man heard his footsteps, and looked quickly over his shoulder. The moonlight drained the world of colour, but even allowing for this the face turned towards Sir Richard was unnaturally pallid. It was the face of a very young man, and perfectly strange to Sir Richard.

'Who are you?' The question was shot out in a hushed, rather scared voice. The young man started to his feet, and took up an instinctively defensive pose.

'I doubt whether my name will convey very much to you, but, for what it is worth, it is Wyndham. What has happened here?'

The boy seemed quite distracted, and replied in a shaken tone: 'I don't know. I found him here—like this. I—I think he's dead!'

'Nonsense!' said Sir Richard, putting him out of his way, and in his turn kneeling beside Beverley's inanimate body. There was a bruise on the livid brow, and when Sir Richard raised Beverley his head fell back in a way that told its own tale rather horribly. Sir Richard saw the tree stump, and realized that Beverley's head must have struck it. He laid his body down again, and said without the least vestige of emotion: 'You are perfectly right. His neck is broken.'

The boy dragged a handkerchief out of his pocket, and wiped his brow with it. 'My God, who did it?—I—I didn't, you know!'

'I don't suppose you did,' Sir Richard replied, rising to his feet, and dusting the knees of his breeches.

'But it's the most shocking thing! He was staying with me, sir!'

'Oh!' said Sir Richard, favouring him with a long, penetrating look.

'He's Beverley Brandon—Lord Saar's younger son!'

'I know very well who he is. You, I apprehend, are Mr Piers Luttrell?'

'Yes. Yes, I am. I knew him up at Oxford. Not very well, because I—well, to tell you the truth, I never liked him much. But a week ago he arrived at my home. He had been visiting friends, I think. I don't know. But of course I—that is, my mother and I—asked him to stay, and he did. He has not been quite well—seemed to be in need of rest, and—and country air. Indeed, I can't conceive how he comes to be here now, for he retired to his room with one of his sick headaches. At least, that was what he told my mother.'

'Then you did not come here in search of him?'

'No, no! I came— The fact is, I just came out to enjoy a stroll in the moonlight,' replied Piers, in a hurry.

'I see.' There was a dry note in Sir Richard's voice.

'Why are *you* here?' demanded Piers.

'For the same reason,' Sir Richard answered.

'But you know Brandon!'

'That circumstance does not, however, make me his murderer.'

'Oh no! I did not mean—but it seems so strange that you should both be in Queen Carlton!'

'I thought it tiresome, myself. My errand to Queen Charlton did not in any way concern Beverley Brandon.'

'Of course not! I didn't suppose—Sir, since you didn't kill him, and I didn't, who—who did, do you suppose? For he did not merely trip and fall, did he? There is that bruise on his forehead, and he was lying face upwards, just as you saw him. Someone struck him down!'

'Yes, I think someone struck him down,' agreed Sir Richard.

'I suppose you do not know who it might have been, sir?'

'I wonder?' Sir Richard said thoughtfully.

Piers waited, but as Sir Richard said no more, but stood looking frowningly down at Beverley's body, he blurted out: 'What ought I to do? Really, I do not know! I have no experience in such matters. Perhaps you could advise me?'

'I do not pretend to any very vast experience myself, but I suggest that you should go home.'

'But we can't leave him here—can we?'

'No, we can't do that. I will inform the magistrate that there is—er—a corpse in the woods. No doubt he will attend to it.'

'Yes, but I don't wish to run away, you know,' Piers objected. 'It is the most devilish, awkward situation, but of course I don't dream of leaving you to—to explain it all to the magistrate. I shall have to say that it was I who found the body.'

Sir Richard, who knew that the affair was one of extreme delicacy, and who had been wondering for several minutes in what way it could be handled so as to spare the Brandons as much humiliation as possible, did not feel that the entry of Piers Luttrell into the proceedings would facilitate his task. He cast another of his searching looks over the young man, and said: 'Your doing so would serve no useful purpose, I believe. You had better leave it to me.'

'You know something about it!'

'Yes, I do. I am on terms of—er—considerable intimacy with the Brandons, and I know a good deal about Beverley's activities. There is likely to be a peculiarly distasteful scandal arising out of his murder.'

Piers nodded. 'I was afraid of that. You know, sir, he was not at all the thing, and he knew some devilish odd people. A man came up to the house, enquiring for him only yesterday—a seedy sort of bully: I dare say you may be familiar with the type. Beverley did not like it above half, I could see.'

'Were you privileged to meet this man?'

'Well, I saw him: I didn't exchange two words with him. The servant came to tell Beverley that a Captain Trimble had called to see him, and Beverley was so much put out that I—well, I fear I did rather wonder what was in the wind.'

'Ah!' said Sir Richard. 'The fact that you have met Trimble may—or may not—prove useful. Yes, I think you had better go home, and say nothing about this. No doubt the news of Beverley's death will be conveyed to you tomorrow morning.'

'But what shall I tell the constable, sir?'

'Whatever he asks you,' replied Sir Richard.

'Shall I say that I found Beverley here, with you?' asked Piers doubtfully.

'I hardly think that he will ask you that question.'

'But will he not wonder how it came about that I did not miss Beverley?'

'Did you not say that Beverley gave it out that he was retiring to bed? Why should you miss him?'

'Tomorrow morning?'

'Yes, I think you might miss him at the breakfast table,' conceded Sir Richard.

'I see. Well, if you feel it to be right, sir, I—I own I would rather not divulge that I was in the wood tonight. But what must I say if I am asked if I know you?'

'You don't know me.'

'No-no. No, I don't, of course,' said Piers, apparently cheered by this reflection.

'That is a pleasure in store for you. I came into this neighbourhood for the purpose of—er—making your acquaintance, but this seems hardly the moment to enter upon a matter which I have reason to suspect may prove extremely complicated.'

'You came to see *me?*' said Piers, astonished. 'How can this be?'

'If,' said Sir Richard, 'you will come to see me at the George tomorrow—a very natural action on your part, in view of my discovery of your guest's corpse—I will tell you just why I came to Queen Charlton in search of you.'

'I am sure I am honoured—but I cannot conceive what your business with me may be, sir!'

'That,' said Sir Richard, 'does not surprise me nearly as much as my business is likely to surprise you, Mr Luttrell!'

9

Having got rid of Piers Luttrell, who, after peering at his watch surreptitiously, and several times looking about him as though in the expectation of seeing someone hiding among the trees, went off, rather relieved but much bewildered, Sir Richard walked away to rejoin Pen and the unknown lady. He found only Pen, seated on the bank with an air of aloof virtue, her hands folded primly on her knees. He paused, looking her over with a comprehending eye. 'And where,' he asked in conversational tones, 'is your companion?'

'She chose to go home,' responded Pen. 'I dare say she grew tired of waiting for you to come back.'

'Ah, no doubt! Did you, by any chance, suggest to her that she should do so?'

'No, because it was not at all necessary. She was very anxious to go. She said she wished she had not come.'

'Did she tell you why she had come?'

'No. I asked her, of course, but she is such a silly little missish thing that she would do nothing but cry, and say she was a wicked girl. Do you know what I think, Richard?'

'Probably.'

'Well, it's my belief she came to meet someone. She seems to me exactly the sort of female who would feel romantic just because there is a full moon. Besides, why else should she be here at this hour?'

'Why indeed?' agreed Sir Richard. 'I apprehend that you have little sympathy to spare for such folly?'

'None at all,' said Pen. 'In fact, I think it's silly, besides being improper.'

'You are severe!'

'I can tell by your voice that you are laughing at me. I expect you are thinking of my climbing out of a window. But *I* was not going to meet a lover by moonlight! Such stuff!'

'Fustian,' nodded Sir Richard. 'Did she disclose the identity of her lover?'

'No, but she said her own name was Lydia Daubenay. And no sooner had she told me that than she went off into another taking, and said she was distracted, and wished she had not told me. Really, I was quite glad when she decided to go home without waiting for you.'

'Yes, I had rather gathered the impression that her company was not agreeable to you. I suppose it hardly signifies. She did not appear to me to be the kind of young woman who could be trusted to bear a still tongue in her head.'

'Well, I don't know,' said Pen thoughtfully. 'She was so frightened I quite think she may not say a word about the adventure. I have been considering the matter, and it seems to me that she must be in love with someone whom her parents do not wish her to marry.'

'That,' said Sir Richard, 'seems to be a fair conclusion.'

'So that I shouldn't be at all surprised if she conceals the fact that she was in the wood tonight. By the way, was it the stammering man?'

'It was, and Miss Daubenay was right in her suspicion: he is dead.'

Miss Creed accepted this with fortitude. 'Well, if he is, I can tell you who killed him. That girl told me all over again how it happened, and there is no doubt that the other man was Captain Trimble. And he did it to get the necklace!'

'Admirable!' said Sir Richard.

'It is as plain as a pikestaff. And now that I come to think of it, it may very likely be all for the best. Of course, I am sorry for the stammering man, but you can't deny that he was a very disagreeable person. Besides, I know perfectly well that he was threatening you. That is why I followed you. Now we are rid of the whole affair!'

'Not quite, I fear. You must not think that I am unmoved by your heroic behaviour, but I could wish that you had gone to bed, Pen.'

'Yes, but I find that most unreasonable of you,' objected Pen. 'It seems to me that you want to keep all the adventure for yourself!'

'I appreciate your feelings,' said Sir Richard, 'but I would point out to you that your situation is a trifle—shall we say irregular?—and that we have been at considerable pains to excite no undue attention. Hence that abominable stagecoach. The last thing in the world I desire is to see you brought forward as a witness to this affair. If Miss Daubenay does not disclose her share in it, you may yet escape notice, but, to tell you the truth, I place little dependence on Miss Daubenay's discretion.'

'Oh!' said Pen, digesting this. 'You think there may be a little awkwardness if it should be discovered that I am not a boy? Perhaps we had better leave Queen Charlton?'

'No, that would indeed be fatal. We are now committed to this adventure. I am going to inform the local magistrate that I have discovered a corpse in this spinney. As you have encountered Miss Daubenay, upon whose discretion we have decided to place no reliance, I shall mention the fact that you accompanied me upon my evening stroll, and we must trust that no particular notice will be taken of you. By the way, brat, I think you had better become my young cousin—my remote young cousin.'

'Ah!' said Miss Creed, gratified. 'My own story!'

'Your own story.'

'Well, I must say I am glad you don't wish to run away,' she confided. 'You cannot conceive how much I am enjoying myself! I dare say it is otherwise with you, but, you see, I have had such a very dull life up till now! And I'll tell you another thing, Richard: naturally I am very anxious to find Piers, but I think we had better not send any word to him until we have finished this adventure.'

He was silent for a moment. 'Are you very anxious to find Piers?' he asked at last.

'Of course I am! Why, that is why we came!'

'Very true. I was forgetting. You will see Piers tomorrow morning, I fancy.'

She got up from the bank. 'I shall see him tomorrow? But how do you know?'

'I should have mentioned to you that I have just had the felicity of meeting him.'

'Piers?' she exclaimed. 'Here? In the wood?'

'Over Beverley Brandon's body.'

'I thought I heard voices! But how did he come to be here? And why didn't you bring him to me directly?'

Sir Richard took time over his answer. 'You see, I was under the impression that Miss Daubenay was still with you,' he explained.

'Oh, I see!' said Pen innocently. 'Yes, indeed, you did quite right! We don't want her to be included in our adventure. But did you tell Piers about me?'

'The moment did not seem to be propitious,' confessed Sir Richard. 'I told him to come to visit me at the George tomorrow morning, and on no account to divulge his presence in the wood tonight.'

'What a surprise it will be to him when he finds me at the George!' said Pen gleefully.

'Yes,' said Sir Richard. 'I think it will be—a surprise to him.'

She fell into step beside him on their way back to the road. 'I am glad you did not tell him! I suppose he had come to look for the stammering man? I can't conceive how he could have had such a disagreeable person to visit him!'

Sir Richard, who had rarely, during the twenty-nine years of his existence, found himself at a loss, now discovered that he was totally incapable of imparting his own suspicions to his trusting companion.

Apparently, it had not occurred to her that the sentiments of her old playfellow might have undergone a change; and so fixed in her mind was a five-year-old pact of betrothal that it had not entered her head to question either its durable qualities, or its desirability. She evidently considered herself plighted to Piers Luttrell, a circumstance which had no doubt had much to do with her friendly acceptance of Sir Richard's companionship. Phrases of warning half formed themselves in Sir Richard's brain, and were rejected. Piers would have to do his explaining; Sir Richard could only hope that upon coming face to face with him after a lapse of years, Pen might discover that as he had outgrown a childhood's fancy, so too had she.

They entered the George together. Pen went up to bed at a nod from Sir Richard, but Sir Richard rang the bell for a servant. A sleepy waiter came in answer to the summons, and, upon being asked for the direction of the nearest magistrate, said that Sir Jasper Luttrell was the nearest, but was away from home. He knew of no other, so Sir Richard desired him to fetch the landlord to him, and sat down to write a short note to whom it might concern.

When the landlord came into the parlour, Sir Richard was shaking the sand off the single sheet of paper. He folded it, and sealed it with a wafer, and upon being told that Mr John Philips, of Whitchurch, was the nearest available magistrate, wrote this gentleman's name on the note. As he wrote, he said in his calm way: 'I shall be obliged to you if you will have this letter conveyed directly to Mr Philips.'

'Tonight, sir?'

'Tonight. Mr Philips will, I imagine, come back with your messenger. If he asks for me, show him into this room. Ah, and landlord!'

'Sir?'

'A bowl of rum punch. I will mix it myself.'

'Yes, sir! Immediately, sir!' said the landlord, relieved to receive such a normal command.

He lingered for a moment, trying to summon up sufficient resolution to ask the fine London gentleman why he wanted to see a magistrate thus urgently. Sir Richard's quizzing glass came up, and the landlord withdrew in haste. The waiter would have followed him, but was detained by Sir Richard's uplifted forefinger.

'One moment! Who gave you the note which you delivered to me this evening?'

'It was Jem, sir—the tapster. It was when I went up to the bar for a pint of burgundy for a gentleman dining in the coffee room that Jem gave it to me. It was Captain Trimble who picked it up off the ground, where it was a-laying. It got swep' off the bar, I dessay, sir, the taproom being crowded at the time, and Jem with his hands full.'

'Thank you,' said Sir Richard. 'That is all.'

The waiter went away considerably mystified. Sir Richard, on the other hand, felt that the mystery had been satisfactorily explained, and sat down to await the landlord's return with the ingredients for a bowl of punch.

Mr Philips' residence was situated some five miles from Queen Charlton, and it was consequently some time before the clatter of horses' hooves in the street heralded his arrival. Sir Richard was queezing the lemon into the punch bowl when he was ushered into the parlour, and looked up fleetingly to say: 'Ah, how do you do? Mr Philips, I apprehend?'

Mr Philips was a grizzled gentleman with a harassed frown, and a slight paunch.

'Your servant, sir! Have I the honour of addressing Sir Richard Wyndham?'

'Mine, sir, is the honour,' said Sir Richard absently, intent upon his punch.

'Sir,' said Mr Philips, 'your very extraordinary communication—I may say, your unprecedented disclosure—has, as you perceive, brought me immediately to enquire into this incredible affair!'

'Very proper,' said Sir Richard. 'You will wish to visit the scene of the crime, I imagine. I can give you the direction, but no doubt the village constable is familiar with the locality. The body, Mr Philips, is—or was—lying in the clearing in the middle of the spinney, a little way down the road.'

'Do you mean to tell me, sir, that this story is true?' demanded the magistrate.

'Certainly it is true. Dear me, did you suppose me to be so heartless as to drag you out at this hour on a fool's errand? Are you in favour of adding the juice of one or of two lemons?'

Mr Philips, whose eyes had been critically observing Sir Richard's proceedings, said, without thinking: 'One! One is enough!'

'I feel sure you are right,' said Sir Richard.

'You know, sir, I must ask you some questions about this extraordinary affair!' said Philips, recollecting his errand.

'So you shall, sir, so you shall. Would you like to ask them now, or after you have disposed of the body?'

'I shall first repair to the scene of the murder,' declared Philips.

'Good!' said Sir Richard. 'I will engage to have the punch ready against your return.'

Mr Philips felt that this casual way of treating the affair was quite out of order, but the prospect of returning to a bowl of hot rum punch was so agreeable that he decided to overlook any trifling irregularity. When he returned to the inn, half an hour later, he was feeling chilled, for it was now past midnight and he had not taken his overcoat with him. Sir Richard had caused a fire to be kindled in the wainscoted parlour, and from the bowl on the table, which he was stirring with a long-handled spoon, there arose a very fragrant and comforting aroma. Mr Philips rubbed his hands together, and could not refrain from ejaculating: 'Ha!'

Sir Richard looked up, and smiled. His smile had won more hearts than Mr Philips', and it had a visible effect on that gentleman.

'Well, well, well! I won't deny that's a very welcome smell, Sir Richard! A fire, too! Upon my word, I'm glad to see it! Gets chilly at night, very chilly! A bad business, sir! A very bad business!'

Sir Richard ladled the steaming brew into two glasses, and gave one to the magistrate. 'Draw up a chair to the fire, Mr Philips. It is, as you say, a very bad business. I should tell you that I am intimately acquainted with the family of the deceased.'

Mr Philips fished Sir Richard's note out of his pocket. 'Yes, yes, just as I supposed, sir. I do not know how you would otherwise have furnished me with the poor man's name. You know him, in fact. Precisely! He was travelling in your company, perhaps?'

'No,' said Sir Richard, taking a chair on the opposite side of the fireplace. 'He was staying with a friend who lives in the neighbourhood. The name was, I think, Luttrell.'

'Indeed! This becomes more and more— But pray continue, sir! You were not, then, together?'

'No, nothing of the sort. I came into the west country on family affairs. I need not burden you with them, I think.'

'Quite quite! Family affairs: yes! Go on, sir! How came you to discover Mr Brandon's body?'

'Oh, by accident! But it will be better, perhaps, if I recount my share of this affair from its start.'

'Certainly! Yes! Pray do so, sir! This is a remarkably good bowl of punch, I may say.'

'I am generally thought to have something of a knack with a punch bowl,' bowed Sir Richard. 'To go back, then, to the start! You have no doubt heard, Mr Philips, of the Brandon diamonds?'

From the startled expression in the magistrate's eyes, and the slight dropping of his jaw, it was apparent that he had not. He said: 'Diamonds? Really, I fear— No, I must confess that I had not heard of the Brandon diamonds.'

'Then, I should explain that they make up a certain famous necklace, worth, I dare say, anything you like.'

'Upon my word! An heirloom! Yes, yes, but in what way—?'

'While on my way to Bristol with a young relative of mine, a slight accident befell our coach, and we were forced to put up for the night at a small inn near Wroxham. There, sir, I encountered an individual who seemed to me—but I am not very well versed in these matters—a somewhat questionable character. How questionable I did not know until the following morning, when a Bow Street Runner arrived at the inn.'

'Good God, sir! This is the most— But I interrupt you!'

'Not at all,' said Sir Richard politely. 'I left the inn while the Runner was interrogating this individual. It was not until my young cousin and I had proceeded some way on our journey that I discovered in my pocket a purse containing the Brandon necklace.'

The magistrate sat bolt upright in his chair. 'You amaze me, sir! You astonish me! The necklace in your pocket? Really, I do not know what to say!'

'No,' agreed Sir Richard, rising and refilling his guest's glass. 'I was rather taken aback myself. In fact, it was some time before I could think how it came to be there.'

'No wonder, no wonder! Most understandable, indeed! You recognized the necklace?'

'Yes,' said Sir Richard, returning to his chair. 'I recognized it, but—really, I am amazed at my own stupidity!—I did not immediately connect it with the individual encountered near Wroxham. The question was then not so much how it came to be in my possession, as how to restore it to Lord Saar with the least possible delay. I could picture Lady Saar's dismay at such an irreparable loss! Ah—a lady of exquisite sensibility, you understand!'

The magistrate nodded his comprehension. The rum punch was warming him quite as much as the fire, and he had a not unpleasant sensation of mixing with exalted persons.

'Happily—or perhaps I should say, in the light of future events, *unhappily*,' continued Sir Richard, 'I recalled that Beverley Brandon—he was Saar's younger son, I should mention—was staying in this neighbourhood. I repaired instantly to this inn, therefore, and, being fortunate enough to meet Brandon just beyond the village, gave the necklace to him without further ado.'

The magistrate set down his glass. 'You gave the necklace to him? Did he know that it had been stolen?'

'By no means. He was as astonished as I was, but engaged himself to restore it immediately to his father. I considered the matter satisfactorily settled—Saar, you know, having the greatest dislike of any kind of notoriety, such as must accrue from the theft, and the subsequent proceedings.'

'Sir!' said Mr Philips, 'do you mean to imply that this unfortunate young man was murdered for the sake of the necklace?'

'That,' said Sir Richard, 'is what I fear may have happened.'

'But this is shocking! Upon my word, sir, I am quite dumb-founded!—what—who can have known that the necklace was in his possession?'

'I should have said that no one could have known it, but, upon consideration, I imagine that the individual who hid it in my pocket may well have followed me to this place, waiting for an opportunity to get it back into his possession.'

'True! very true! You have been spied upon! Yet you have not seen that man in Queen Charlton?'

'Do you think he would—er—let me see him?' enquired Sir Richard, evading the question.

'No. No, indeed! Certainly not! But this must be looked to!'

'Yes,' agreed Sir Richard, pensively swinging his eyeglass on the end of its ribbon. 'And I think you might, with advantage, look to the sudden disappearance from this inn of a flashy person calling himself Captain Trimble, Mr Philips.'

'Really, sir! This becomes more and more— Pray, what reason have you for supposing that this man may be implicated in the murder?'

'Well,' said Sir Richard slowly, 'some chance words which I let fall on the subject of—ah—waistcoats, sent Captain Trimble off hotfoot to Bristol.'

The magistrate blinked, and directed an accusing glance towards his half empty glass. A horrid suspicion that the rum punch had affected his understanding was dispelled, however, by Sir Richard's next words.

'My acquaintance at the inn near Wroxham wore a catskin waistcoat. A casual reference to this circumstance had the surprising effect of arousing the Captain's curiosity. He asked me in what direction the man in the catskin waistcoat had been travelling, and upon my saying that I believed him to be bound for Bristol, he left the inn—er—incontinent!'

'I see! yes, yes, I see! An accomplice!'

'My own feeling,' said Sir Richard, 'is that he was an accomplice who had been—er—bubbled.'

The magistrate appeared to be much struck by this. 'Yes! I see it all! Good God, this is a terrible affair! I have never been called upon to— But you say this Captain Trimble went off to Bristol, sir?'

'He did. But I have since learned, Mr Philips, that he was back at this inn at six o'clock this evening. Ah! I should, I see, say *yesterday* evening,' he added with a glance at the clock on the mantelpiece.

Mr Philips drew a long breath. 'Your disclosures, Sir Richard, open up—are in fact, of such a nature as to— Upon my word, I never thought— But the murder! You discovered this, sir?'

'I discovered Brandon's body,' corrected Sir Richard.

'How came you to do this, sir? You had a suspicion? You—'

'None at all. It was a warm evening, and I stepped out to enjoy a stroll in the moonlight. Chance alone led my footsteps to the wood where I found my unfortunate young friend's body. It is only since making that melancholy discovery that I have pieced together the—er—evidence.'

Mr Philips had a hazy idea that chance had played an over-important part in Sir Richard's adventures, but he was aware that the punch he had drunk had slightly clouded his intellect. He said guardedly: 'Sir, the story you have unfolded is of a nature which—in short, it must be carefully sifted. Yes, indeed. Carefully sifted! I must request you not to remove from this neighbourhood until I have had time—pray do not misunderstand me! There is not the least suggestion, I assure you, of—'

'My dear sir, I don't misunderstand you, and I have no intention of removing from this inn,' said Sir Richard soothingly. 'I am aware that you have, so far, only my word for it that I am indeed Richard Wyndham.'

'Oh, as to that, I am sure—no suggestion of disbelieving— But my duty is prescribed! You will appreciate my position, I am persuaded!'

'Perfectly!' said Sir Richard. 'I shall hold myself wholly at your disposal. You, as a man of the world, will, I am assured, appreciate the need of the exercise of—ah—the most delicate discretion in handling this affair.'

Mr Philips, who had once spent three weeks in London, was flattered to think that the imprint of that short sojourn was pronounced enough to be discernible to such a personage as Beau Wyndham, and swelled with pride. Native caution, however, warned him that his investigation had better be postponed to a more sober moment. He rose to his feet with careful dignity, and set his empty glass down on the table. 'I am obliged to you!' he pronounced. 'I shall wait upon you tomorrow—no, today! I must consider this affair. A terrible business! I think one may say, a terrible business!'

Sir Richard agreed to this, and after a meticulous exchange of courtesies, Mr Philips took his leave. Sir Richard snuffed the candles, and went up to bed, not dissatisfied with his night's work.

In the morning, Pen was first down. The day was fine, and her cravat, she flattered herself, very well tied. There was a suggestion of a prance about her gait as she sallied forth to inspect the weather. Sir Richard, no believer in early rising, had ordered breakfast for nine o'clock, and it was as yet only eight. A maidservant was engaged in sweeping the floor of the private parlour, and a bored waiter was spreading clean cloths over the tables in the coffee room. As Pen passed through the entrance parlour, the landlord, who was conversing in low tones with a gentleman unknown to her, looked round, and exclaimed: 'Here is the young gentleman himself, sir!'

Mr Philips, confronted with the biggest crime ever committed within the limits of his jurisdiction, had perhaps imbibed too strong a brew of rum punch on the previous evening, but he was a zealous person, and, in spite of awaking with a very bad head, he had lost no time in getting out of his comfortable bed, and riding back to Queen Charlton to continue his investigations. As Pen paused, he stepped forward, and bade her a civil good morning. She responded, wishing that Sir Richard would come downstairs; and upon Mr Philips' asking her, in a tone of kindly patronage, whether she was Sir Richard's young cousin, assented, and hoped that the magistrate would not ask for her name.

He did not. He said: 'Now, you were with Sir Richard when he discovered this very shocking crime, were you not, young man?'

'Well, not precisely,' said Pen.

'Oh? How is that?'

'I was, and I wasn't,' Pen explained, with an earnestness which robbed the words of flippancy. 'I didn't see the body.'

'No? Just tell me exactly what happened. No need to feel any alarm, you know! If you walked out with your cousin, how came you to have separated?'

'Well, sir there was an owl,' confided Pen unblushingly.

'Come, come! An *owl?*'

'Yes: my cousin said that too.'

'Said what?'

'Come, come! He is not interested in bird life.'

'Ah, I see! You collect eggs, eh? That's it, is it?'

'Yes, and also I like to watch birds.'

Mr Philips smiled tolerantly. He wondered how old this slim boy was, and thought it a pity the young fellow should be so effeminate; but he was a countryman himself, and dimly he could recall the bird-watching days of his youth. 'Yes, yes, I understand! You went off on your own to try to catch a glimpse of this owl: well, I have done the same in my time! And so you were not with your good cousin when he reached the clearing in the wood?'

'No, but I met him on his return, and of course he told me what he had found.'

'I dare say, but hearsay, my boy, is not evidence,' said Mr Philips, nodding dismissal.

Pen made for the door, feeling that she had extricated herself from a difficult situation with aplomb. The landlord ran after her with a sealed letter. 'If I was not forgetting! I beg pardon, sir, but a young person brought this for you not an hour ago. Leastways, it was for a young gentleman of the name of Wyndham. Would that be in mistake for yourself, sir?'

Pen took the letter, and looked at it with misgiving. 'A young person?' she repeated.

'Well, sir, it was one of the servant girls from Major Daubenay's.'

'Oh!' said Pen. 'Oh, very well! Thank you!'

She passed out into the village street, and after dubiously regarding the direction on the note, which was to: "Wyndham Esq.", and written in a round schoolgirl's hand, she broke the seal, and spread open the single sheet.

> Dear Sir, *the letter began, primly enough,* The Unfortunate Being whom you befriended last night, is in Desperate Case, and begs that you will come to the little orchard next to the road at eight o'clock punctually, because it is vital that I should have Private Speech with you. Do not fail. Your obliged servant,
>
> Lydia Daubenay

It was plain that Miss Daubenay had written this missive in considerable agitation. Greatly intrigued, Pen enquired the way to Major Daubenay's house of a baker's boy, and set off down the dusty road.

By the time she had reached the appointed rendezvous it was half past eight, and Miss Daubenay was pacing up and down impatiently. A thick, high hedge shut the orchard off from sight of the house, and a low wall enclosed it from the road. Pen climbed on to this without much difficulty, and was greeted by an instant accusation: 'Oh, you are so late! I have been waiting ages!'

'Well, I am sorry, but I came as soon as I had read your letter,' said Pen, jumping down into the orchard. 'Why do you wish to see me?'

Miss Daubenay wrung her hands, and uttered in tense accents:

'Everything has gone awry. I am quite distracted! I don't know what to do!'

Pen betrayed no particular solicitude at this moving speech, but critically looked Miss Daubenay over.

She was a pretty child, about the same age as Pen herself, but shorter, and much plumper. She had a profusion of nut-brown ringlets, a pair of fawn-like brown eyes, and a soft rose-bud of a mouth. She was dressed in a white muslin dress, high-waisted, and frilled about the ankles, and with a great many pale-blue bows of ribbon with long fluttering ends. She raised her melting eyes to Pen's face, and breathed: 'Can I trust you?'

Miss Creed was a literal-minded female, and instead of responding with promptness and true chivalry, she replied cautiously: 'Well, probably you can, but I am not sure till I know what it is that you want.'

Miss Daubenay seemed a little daunted for a moment, and said in a soft moan: 'I am in such a taking! I have been very, very silly!'

Pen found no difficulty in believing this. She said: 'Well, don't stand there wringing your hands! Let us sit down under that tree.'

Lydia looked doubtful. 'Will it not be damp?'

'No, of course not! Besides, what if it were?'

'Oh, the grass might stain my dress!'

'It seems to me,' said Pen severely, 'that if you are bothering about your dress you cannot be in such great trouble.'

'Oh, but I am!' said Lydia, sinking down on to the turf, and clasping her hands at her bosom. 'I do not know what you will say, or what you will think of me! I must have been mad! Only you were kind to me last night, and I thought I could trust you!'

'I dare say you can,' said Pen. 'But I wish you will tell me what is the matter, because I have not yet had any breakfast, and—'

'If I had thought that you would be so unsympathetic I would never, never have sent for you!' declared Lydia in tremulous accents.

'Well, it is very difficult to be sympathetic when a person will do nothing but wring her hands, and say the sort of things there really is no answer to,' said Pen reasonably. 'Do start at the beginning!'

Miss Daubenay bowed her head. 'I am the most unhappy creature alive!' she announced. 'I have the misfortune to be secretly betrothed to one whom my father will not tolerate.'

'Yes, I thought you were. I suppose you went to meet him in the wood last night?'

'Alas, it is true! But do not judge me hastily! He is the most unexceptionable–the most—'

'If he is unexceptionable,' interrupted Pen, 'why won't your father tolerate him?'

'It is all wicked prejudice!' sighed Lydia. 'My father quarrelled with his father, and they don't speak.'

'Oh! What did they quarrrel about?'

'About a piece of land,' said Lydia mournfully.

'It sounds very silly.'

'It is silly. Only *they* are perfectly serious about it, and they do not care a fig for *our* sufferings! We have been forced to this hateful expedient of meeting in secret. I should tell you that my betrothed is the *soul* of honour! Subterfuge is repugnant to him, but what can be do? We love each other!'

'Why don't you run away?' suggested Pen practically.

Startled eyes leapt to hers. 'Run where?'

'To Gretna Green, of course.'

'Oh, I could not! Only think of the scandal!'

'I do think you should try not to be so poor-spirited. However, I dare say you can't help it.'

'You are the rudest boy I ever met!' exclaimed Lydia, 'I declare I wish I had not sent for you!'

'So do I, because this seems to me a silly story, and not in the least my concern,' said Pen frankly. 'Oh, pray don't start to cry! There, I am sorry! I didn't mean to be unkind! But why *did* you send for me?'

'Because, though you are rude and horrid, you did not seem to me like other young men, and I thought you would understand, and not take advantage of me.'

Pen gave a sudden mischievous chuckle. 'I shan't do *that*, at all events! Oh dear, I am getting so hungry! Do tell me why you sent for me!'

Miss Daubenay dabbed her eyes with a wisp of a handkerchief. 'I was so distracted last night I scarce knew what I was doing! And when I reached home, the most dreadful thing happened! Papa saw me! Oh, sir, he accused me of having gone out to meet P— to meet my betrothed, and said I should be packed off again to Bath this very day, to stay with my Great-Aunt Augusta. The horridest, most disagreeable old woman! Nothing but backgammon, and spying, and everything of the most hateful! Sir, I felt myself to be in desperate case! Indeed, I said it before I had time to recollect the consequences!'

'Said what?' asked Pen, patient but bored.

Miss Daubenay bowed her head again. 'That it was not—not *that* man I had gone to meet, but another, whom I had met in Bath, when I was sent to Great-Aunt Augusta to–to cure me of what Papa called my *infatuation*! I said I had been in the habit of meeting this other man c-clandestinely, because I thought that would make Papa afraid to send me back to Bath, and might perhaps even reconcile him to the Real Man.'

'Oh!' said Pen doubtfully. 'And did it?'

'No! He said he did not believe me.'

'Well, I must say I'm not surprised at that.'

'Yes, but in the end he did, and now I wish I had never said it. He said if there was Another Man, who was it?'

'You ought to have thought of that. He was bound to ask that question, and you must have looked very silly when you could not answer.'

'But I did answer!' whispered Miss Daubenay, apparently overcome.

'But how could you, if there wasn't another man?'

'I said it was you!' said Miss Daubenay despairingly.

IO

The effect of this confession upon Pen was not quite what Miss Daubenay had expected. She gasped, choked, and went off into a peal of laughter. Affronted, Miss Daubenay said: 'I don't see what there is to laugh at!'

'No, I dare say you don't,' said Pen, mopping her eyes. 'But it is excessively amusing for all that. What made you say anything so silly?'

'I couldn't think of anything else to say. And as for its being *silly*, you may think me very ill favoured, but I have already had *several* suitors!'

'I think you are very pretty, but I am not going to be a suitor,' said Pen firmly.

'I don't want you to be! For one thing, I find you quite odiously rude, and for another you are much too young, which is why I chose you, because I thought I should be quite safe in so doing.'

'Well, you are, but I never heard of anything so foolish in my life! Pray, what was the use of telling your father such fibs?'

'I told you,' said Lydia crossly. 'I scarcely knew what I was saying, and I thought— But everything has gone awry!'

Pen looked at her with misgiving. 'What do you mean?'

'Papa is going to wait on your cousin this morning.'

'What!' exclaimed Pen.

Lydia nodded. 'Yes, and he is not angry at all. He is pleased!'

'Pleased? Now can he be pleased at your holding clandestine meetings with a strange man?'

'To be sure, he did say that that was very wrong of me. But he asked me your name. Of course I don't know it, but your cousin told me his name was Wyndham, so I said yours was too.'

'But it isn't!'

'Well, how was I to know that?' demanded Lydia, aggrieved. 'I had to say something!'

'You are the most unprincipled girl in the world! Besides, why should he be pleased just because you said my name was Wyndham?'

'Apparently,' said Lydia gloomily, 'the Wyndhams are all fabulously wealthy.'

'You must tell him without any loss of time that I am *not* a Wyndham, and that I haven't any money at all!'

'How can I tell him anything of the kind? I think you are most unreasonable! Do but consider! If I said now that I had been mistaken in your name he would suppose you to have been trifling with me!'

'But you cannot expect me to pretend to be in love with you!' Pen said, aghast.

Lydia sniffed. 'Nothing could be more repulsive to me than such a notion. I am already sorry that I mentioned you to Papa. Only I *did*, and now I don't know what to do. He would be so angry if he knew that I had made it all up!'

'Well, I am very sorry, but it seems to me quite your own fault, and I wash my hands of it,' said Pen.

She glanced at Miss Daubenay's flower-like countenance, and made a discovery. Miss Daubenay's soft chin had acquired a look of obstinacy; the fawn-like eyes stared back at her with a mixture of appeal and determination. 'You can't wash your hands of it. I told you that Papa was going to seek an interview with your cousin today.'

'You must stop him.'

'I can't. You don't know Papa!'

'No, and I don't want to know him,' Pen pointed out.

'If I told him it had all been lies, I do not know what he might not do. I won't do it! I don't care what you may say: I *won't*!'

'Well, I shall deny every word of your story.'

'Then,' said Lydia, not without triumph, 'Papa will do something dreadful to you, because he will think it is you who are telling lies!'

'It seems to me that unless he is a great fool he must know you well enough by now to guess that it is *you* who have told lies!' said Pen, with asperity.

'It's no use being disagreeable and rude,' said Lydia. 'Papa thinks you followed me to Queen Charlton.'

'You mean you told him so,' said Pen bitterly.

'Yes, I did. At least, he asked me, and I said yes before I had had time to think.'

'Really, you are the most brainless creature! Do you *never* think?' said Pen, quite exasperated. 'Just look what a coil you've created! Either your Papa is coming to ask me what my intentions are, or—which I think a great deal more likely—to complain to Richard about my conduct! Oh dear, whatever will Richard say to this fresh disturbance?'

It was plain that all this meant nothing to Miss Daubenay. For form's sake, she repeated that she was very sorry, but added: 'I hoped you would be able to help me. But you are a boy! You don't understand what it means to be persecuted as I am!'

This remark could not but strike a chord of sympathy. 'As a matter of fact, I do know,' said Pen. 'Only, if helping you means offering for your hand, I won't do it. The more I think of it, the more ridiculous it seems to me that you should have dragged me into it. How could such an absurd tale possibly be of use?'

Lydia sighed. 'One does not think of those things in the heat of the moment. Besides, I didn't really mean to drag you in. It—it just happened.'

'I don't see how it could have happened if you didn't mean it.'

'One thing led to another,' Lydia explained vaguely. 'Almost before I knew it, the whole story had—had grown up. Of course I don't wish you to offer for my hand, but I do think you might pretend you want to, so that Papa shan't suspect me of telling lies.'

'No!' said Pen.

'I think you are very unkind,' whimpered Lydia. 'I shall be sent back to Bath, and Great-Aunt Augusta will spy on me, and I shall never see Piers again!'

'Who?' Pen's head was jerked round. '*Who* will you never see again?'

'Oh, please do not ask me! I did not mean to mention his name!'

'Are you—' Pen stopped, rather white of face, and started again: 'Are you betrothed to Piers Luttrell?'

'You know him!' Miss Daubenay clasped ecstatic hands.

'Yes,' said Pen, feeling as though the pit of her stomach had suddenly vanished. 'Yes, I know him.'

'Then you will help me!'

Miss Creed's clear blue eyes met Miss Daubenay's swimming brown ones. Miss Creed drew a long breath. 'Is—is Piers indeed in love with you?' she asked incredulously.

Miss Daubenay bridled. 'You need not sound so surprised! We have been plighted for a whole year! Why do you look so oddly?'

'I beg your pardon,' apologized Pen. 'But how he must have changed! It is very awkward!'

'Why?' asked Lydia, staring.

'Well, it—it—you wouldn't understand. He has been meeting you in woods for a whole year?'

'No, because Papa sent me to Bath, and Sir Jasper forbade him to see me any more, and even Lady Luttrell said we were too young. But we love each other!'

'It seems extraordinary,' said Pen, shaking her head. 'You know, I find it very hard to believe!'

'You are the horridest boy! It is perfectly true, and if you know Piers you may ask him for yourself! I wish I had never clapped eyes on you!'

'So do I,' replied Pen frankly.

Miss Daubenay burst into tears. Pen surveyed her with interest, and asked presently in the voice of one probing mysteries: 'Do you always cry as much as this? Do you—do you cry at Piers?'

'I don't cry *at* people!' sobbed Miss Daubenay. 'And if Piers knew how horrid you have been to me he would very likely knock you down!'

Pen gave a hiccup of laughter. This incensed Lydia so much that she stopped crying, and dramatically commanded Pen to leave the orchard immediately. However, when she discovered that Pen was only too ready to take her at her word, she ran after her, and clasped her by the arm. 'No, no, you cannot go until we have decided what is to be done. You won't—oh, you *can't* be cruel enough to deny my story to Papa!'

Pen considered this. 'Well, provided you won't expect me to offer for you—'

'No, no, I promise I won't!'

Pen frowned. 'Yes, but it's of no use. There is only one thing for it: You will have to run away.'

'But—'

'Now, don't begin to talk about the scandal, and spoiling your dress!' begged Pen. 'For one thing, it is odiously missish, and for another Piers will never be able to bear it.'

'Piers,' said Miss Daubenay, with swelling bosom, 'thinks me Perfect!'

'I haven't seen Piers for a long time, but he *can't* have grown as stupid as that!' Pen pointed out.

'Yes, he—oh, I hate you, I hate you!' cried Lydia, stamping her foot. 'Besides, how can I run away?'

'Oh, Piers will have to arrange it! If Richard doesn't object, I daresay I may help him,' Pen assured her. 'You will have to escape at dead of night, of course, which puts me in mind of a very important thing: you will need a rope ladder.'

'I haven't a rope ladder,' objected Lydia.

'Well, Piers must make one for you. If he throws it up to your window, you could attach it securely, could you not, and climb down it?'

'I would rather escape by the door,' said Lydia, gazing helplessly up at her.

'Oh, very well, but it seems rather tame! However, it is quite your own affair. Piers will be waiting for you with a post chaise and four. You will leap up into it, and the horses will spring forward, and you will fly for the Border! I can see it all!' declared Pen, her eyes sparkling.

Lydia seemed to catch a little of her enthusiasm. 'To be sure, it does sound romantic,' she admitted. 'Only it is a great way to the Border, and everyone would be so cross with us!'

'Once you were married that wouldn't signify.'

'No. No, it wouldn't would it? But I don't think Piers has any money.'

'Oh!' Pen's face fell. 'That certainly makes it rather awkward. But I daresay we shall contrive something.'

Lydia said: 'Well, if you don't mind, I would prefer *not* to go to Gretna, because although it would be romantic I can't help thinking it would be very uncomfortable. Besides, I couldn't have any attendants, or a wedding dress, or a lace veil, or anything.'

'Don't chatter!' said Pen. 'I am thinking.'

Lydia was obediently silent.

'We must soften your father's heart!' declared Pen at length.

Lydia looked doubtful. 'Yes, I should like that of all things, but how?'

'Why, by making him grateful to Piers, of course!'

'But why should he be grateful to Piers? He says Piers is a young cub.'

'Piers,' said Pen, 'must rescue you from deadly peril.'

'Oh no, please!' faltered Lydia, shrinking. 'I should be frightened! And just think how dreadful it would be if he didn't rescue me!'

'What a little goose you are!' said Pen scornfully. 'There won't be any real danger!'

'But if there is no danger, how can Piers—?'

'Piers shall rescue you from me!' said Pen.

Lydia blinked at her. 'I don't understand. How can Piers—?'

'Do stop saying "How can Piers?"!' Pen begged. 'We must make your father believe that I am a penniless young man without any prospects at all, and then we will run away together!'

'But I don't want to run away with you!'

'No, stupid, and I don't want to run away with you! It will be just a Plot. Piers must ride after us, and catch us, and restore you to your Papa. And he will be so pleased that he will let you marry Piers after all! Because Piers has very good prospects, you know.'

'Yes, but you are forgetting Sir Jasper,' argued Lydia.

'We can't possibly be plagued by Sir Jasper,' said Pen impatiently. 'Besides, he is away. Now, don't make any more objections! I must go back to the George, and warn Richard. And I will consult with Piers as well, and I daresay we shall have it all arranged in a trice. I will meet you in the spinney this evening, to tell you what you must do.'

'Oh no, no, no!' shuddered Lydia, 'not the spinney! I shall never set foot there again!'

'Well, here, then, since you are so squeamish. By the way, did you tell your Papa the whole? I mean, how you saw Captain Trimble kill the stammering man?'

'Yes, of course I did, and he says I must tell it to Mr Philips! It is so dreadful for me! To think that my troubles had put it out of my head!'

'What a tiresome girl you are!' exclaimed Pen. 'You should not have said a word about it! Ten to one, we shall get into a tangle now, because Richard has already told Mr Philips *his* story, and I have told him mine, and now you are bound to say something quite different. Did you mention Richard to your papa?'

'No,' confessed Lydia, hanging her head. 'I just said that I ran away.'

'Oh well, in that case perhaps there will be no harm done!' said Pen optimistically. 'I am going now. I will meet you here again after dinner.'

'But what if they watch me, and I cannot slip away?' cried Lydia, trying to detain her.

Pen had climbed on to the wall, and now prepared to jump down into the road. 'You must think of something,' she said sternly, and vanished from Miss Daubenay's sight.

When Pen reached the George Sir Richard had not only finished his breakfast, but was on the point of sallying forth in search of his errant charge. She came into the parlour, flushed and rather breathless, and said impetuously: 'Oh, Richard, such an adventure! I have such a deal to tell you! All our plans must be changed!'

'This is very sudden!' said Sir Richard. 'May I ask where you have been?'

'Yes, of course,' said Pen, seating herself at the table, and spreading butter lavishly on a slice of bread. 'I have been with that stupid girl. You would not believe that anyone could be so silly, sir!'

'I expect I should. What has she been doing, and why did you go to see her?'

'Well, it's a long story, and *most* confused!'

'In that case,' said Sir Richard, 'perhaps I shall unravel it more easily if you do not tell it to me with your mouth full.'

Her eyes lit with laughter. She swallowed the bread-and-butter, and said: 'Oh, I'm sorry! I am so hungry, you see.'

'Have an apple,' he suggested.

She twinkled responsively. 'No, thank you, I will have some of that ham. Dear sir, what in the world do you suppose that wretched girl did?'

'I have no idea,' said Sir Richard, carving several slices of the ham.

'Why, she told her Papa that she had gone into the spinney last night to meet *me*!'

Sir Richard laid down the knife and fork. 'Good God, why?'

'Oh, for such an idiotic reason that it is not worth recounting! But the thing is, sir, that her Papa is coming to see you about it this morning. She hoped, you see, that if she said she had been in the habit of meeting me clandestinely in Bath—'

'In Bath?' interrupted Sir Richard in a faint voice.

'Yes, she said we had been meeting for ever in Bath, on account of her Great-Aunt Augusta, and not wishing to be sent there again. I quite understand *that*, but—'

'Then your understanding is very much better than mine,' said Sir Richard. 'So far I have not been privileged to understand one word of this story. What has her Great-Aunt Augusta to do with it?'

'Oh, they sent Lydia to stay with her, you see, and she did not like it! She said it was all backgammon and spying. I could not but feel for her over that, for I know exactly what she means.'

'I am glad,' said Sir Richard, with emphasis.

'The thing is, that she thought if she told her Papa that she had met me clandestinely in Bath, he would not send her there again.'

'This sounds to me remarkably like mania in an acute form.'

'Yes, so it did to me. But there is worse to come. She says that instead of being angry, her Papa is inclined to be pleased!'

'The madness seems to be inherited.'

'That is what I thought, but it appears that Lydia told her Papa that my name was Wyndham, and now he thinks that perhaps she is on the brink of making a Good Match!'

'Good God!'

'I knew you would be surprised. And there is another circumstance too, which turns everything topsy-turvy.' She glanced up fleetingly from her plate, and said with a little difficulty: 'I discovered something which—which quite took me aback. She told me whom she went to meet in the wood last night.'

'I see,' said Sir Richard.

She flushed. 'Did you—did you know, sir?'

'I guessed, Pen.'

She nodded. 'It was stupid of me not to suspect. To tell you the truth, I thought— However, it doesn't signify. I expect you did not like to tell me.'

'Do you mind very much?' he asked abruptly.

'Well, I—it— You see, I had it fixed in my mind that Piers—and I— So I daresay it will take me just a little while to grow accustomed to it, besides having all my plans overset. But never mind that! We have now to consider what is to be done to help Piers and Lydia.'

'We?' interpolated Sir Richard.

'Yes, because I quite depend on you to persuade Lydia's Papa that I am not an eligible suitor. That is most important!'

'Do you mean to tell me that this insane person is coming here to obtain my consent to your marriage with his daughter?'

'I think he is coming to discover how much money I have, and whether my intentions are honourable,' said Pen, pouring herself out a cup of coffee. 'But I daresay Lydia mistook the whole matter, for she is amazingly stupid, you know, and perhaps he is coming to complain to you about my shocking conduct in meeting Lydia in secret.'

'I foresee a pleasing morning,' said Sir Richard dryly.

'Well, I must say I think it will be very amusing,' Pen admitted. 'Because—why, what is the matter, sir?'

Sir Richard had covered his eyes with one hand. 'You think it will be very amusing! Good God!'

'Oh, now you are laughing at me again!'

'Laughing! I am recalling my comfortable home, my ordered life, my hitherto stainless reputation, and wondering what I can ever have done to deserve being pitchforked into this shameless imbroglio! Apparently, I am to go down to history as one who not only possessed a cousin who was a monster of precocious depravity, but who actually aided and abetted him in attempting to seduce a respectable young female.'

'No, no!' said Pen earnestly. 'Nothing of the kind, I assure you! I have it all arranged in the best possible way, and *your* part will be everything of the most proper!'

'Oh, well, in *that* case—!' said Sir Richard, lowering his hand.

'Now I know you are laughing at me! I am going to be the only son of a widow.'

'That unfortunate woman has all my sympathy.'

'Yes, because I am very wild, and she can do nothing with me. That is why you are here, of course. I cannot but see that I don't look quite old enough to be an eligible suitor. Do you think I do, sir?'

'No, I don't. In fact, I should not be surprised if Lydia's parents were to arrive with a birch rod.'

'Good gracious, how dreadful! I never thought of that! Well, I shall depend upon you.'

'You may confidently depend upon me to tell Major Daubenay that his daughter's story is a farrago of lies.'

Pen shook her head. 'No, we can't do that. I said just the same myself, but you must see how difficult it would be to persuade Major Daubenay that we are speaking the truth. Consider, sir! She told him that I had followed her here, and I must admit it looks very black, because I *was* in the spinney last night, and you know we cannot possibly explain the real story. No, we must make the best of it. Besides, I quite feel that we ought to help Piers, if he does indeed wish to marry such a foolish creature.'

'I have not the slightest desire to help Piers, who seems to me to be behaving in a most reprehensible fashion.'

'Oh no, indeed he cannot help it! I see that I had better tell you their whole story.'

Without giving Sir Richard time to protest, she launched into a rapid and colourful account of the young lovers' tribulations. The account, being freely embellished with her own comments, was considerably involved, and Sir Richard several times interrupted it to crave enlightenment on some obscure point. At the end of it, he remarked without any noticeable display of enthusiasm: 'A most affecting history. For myself, I find the theme of Montague and Capulet hopelessly outmoded, however.'

'Well, I have made up my mind to it that there is only one thing for them to do. They must elope.'

Sir Richard, who had been playing with his quizzing glass, let if fall, and spoke with startling severity. 'Enough of this! Now, understand me, brat, I will engage to fob off the irate father, but there it must end! This extremely tedious pair of lovers may elope tomorrow for anything I care, but I will have no hand in it, and I will not permit you to have a hand in it either. Do you see?'

Pen looked speculatively at him. There was no smile visible in his eyes, which indeed looked much sterner than she had ever believed they could. Plainly, he would not lend any support to her scheme of eloping with Miss Daubenay herself. It would be better, decided Pen, to tell him nothing about this. But she was not one to let a challenge rest unanswered, and she replied with spirit: 'You may do as you choose, but you have *no* right to tell me what I must or must not do! It is not in the least your affair.'

'It is going to be very much my affair,' replied Sir Richard.

'I don't understand what you can possibly mean by saying anything so silly!'

'I daresay you don't, but you will.'

'Well, we won't dispute about that,' said Pen pacifically.

He laughed suddenly. 'Indeed, I hope we shan't!'

'And you won't tell Major Daubenay that Lydia's story was false?'

'What do you want me to tell him?' he asked, succumbing to the coaxing note in her voice, and the pleading look in her candid eyes.

'Why, that I have been with my tutor in Bath, but that I was so troublesome that my Mama—'

'The widow?'

'Yes, and *now* you will understand why she is a widow!'

'If you are supposed to favour your mythical father, I do understand. He perished on the gallows.'

'That is what Jimmy Yarde calls the Nubbing Cheat.'

'I daresay it is, but I beg you won't.'

'Oh, very well! Where was I?'

'With your tutor.'

'To be sure. Well, I was so troublesome that my Mama sent you to bring me home. I expect you are a trustee, or something of that nature. And you may say all the horridest things about me to Major Daubenay that you like. In fact, you had better tell him that I am *very* bad, besides being quite a pauper.'

'Have no fear! I will draw such a picture of you as must make him thankful that his daughter has escaped becoming betrothed to such a monster.'

'Yes, do!' said Pen cordially. 'And then I must see Piers.'

'And then?' asked Sir Richard.

She sighed. 'I haven't thought of that yet. Really, we have so much on our hands that I cannot be teased with thinking of any more plans just now!'

'Will you let me suggest a plan to you, Pen?'

'Yes, certainly, if you can think of one. But first I should like to see Piers, because I still cannot quite believe that he truly wishes to marry Lydia. Why, she does nothing but cry, Richard!'

Sir Richard looked down at her enigmatically. 'Yes,' he said. 'Perhaps it would be better if you saw Piers first. People—especially young men—change a great deal in five years, brat.'

'True,' she said, in a melancholy tone. 'But *I* didn't change!'

'I think perhaps you did,' he said gently.

She seemed unconvinced, and he did not press the point. The waiter came in to clear away the covers, and hardly had he left the parlour than Major Daubenay's card was brought to Sir Richard.

Pen, changing colour, exclaimed: 'Oh dear, now I wish I weren't here! I suppose I can't escape now, can I?'

'Hardly. You would undoubtedly walk straight into the Major's arms. But I won't let him beat you.'

'Well, I hope you won't!' said Pen fervently. 'Tell me quickly, how does a person look depraved? *Do* I look depraved?'

'Not in the least. The best you can hope for is to look sulky.'

She retired to a chair in the corner, and sprawled in it, trying to scowl. 'Like this?'

'Excellent!' approved Sir Richard.

A minute later, Major Daubenay was ushered into the parlour. He was a harassed-looking man, with a high colour, and upon finding himself confronted by the tall, immaculate figure of a Corinthian, he exclaimed: 'Good Gad! You *are* Sir Richard Wyndham!'

Pen, glowering in the corner, could only admire the perfection of Sir Richard's bow. The Major's slightly protuberant eyes discovered her. 'And *this* is the young dog who has been trifling with my daughter!'

'*Again?*' said Sir Richard wearily.

The Major's eyes started at him. 'Upon my soul, sir! Do you tell me that this—this young scoundrel is in the habit of seducing innocent females?'

'Dear me, is it as bad as that?' asked Sir Richard.

'No, sir, it is not!' fumed the Major. 'But when I tell you that my daughter has confessed that she went out last night to meet him clandestinely in a wood, and has met him many times before in Bath—'

Up came Sir Richard's quizzing glass. 'I condole with you,' he said. 'Your daughter would appear to be a young lady of enterprise.'

'My daugher,' declared the Major, 'is a silly little miss! I do not know what young people are coming to! This young man—dear me, he looks no more than a lad!—is, I understand, a relative of yours?'

'My cousin,' said Sir Richard. 'I am—er—his mother's trustee. She is a widow.'

'I see that I have come to the proper person!' said the Major.

Sir Richard raised one languid hand. 'I beg you will acquit me of all responsibility, sir. My part is merely to remove my cousin from the care of a tutor who has proved himself wholly incapable of controlling his—er—activities, and to convey him to his mother's home.'

'But what are you doing in Queen Charlton, then?' demanded the Major.

It was plain that Sir Richard considered the question an impertinence. 'I have acquaintances in the neighbourhood, sir. I scarcely think I need trouble you with the reasons which led me to break a journey which cannot be other than—er—excessively distasteful to me. Pen, make your bow!'

'Pen?' repeated the Major, glaring at her.

'He was named after the Great Quaker,' explained Sir Richard.

'Indeed! Then I would have you know, sir, that his behaviour scarcely befits his name!'

'You are perfectly right,' agreed Sir Richard. 'I regret to say that he has been a constant source of anxiety to his widowed parent.'

'He seems very young,' said the Major, scanning Pen critically.

'But, alas, old in sin!'

The Major was slightly taken aback. 'Oh, come, come, sir! I daresay it is not as bad as that! One must make allowances for young people. To be sure, it is very reprehensible, and I do not by any means exonerate my daughter from blame, but the springtime of life, you know, sir! Young people take such romantic notions into their heads—not but what I am excessively shocked to learn of clandestine meetings! But when two young persons fall in love, I believe—'

'In love!' interpolated Sir Richard, apparently thunder-struck.

'Well, well, I daresay you are surprised! One is apt to fancy the birds always too young to leave the nest, eh? But—'

'Pen!' said Sir Richard, turning awfully upon his supposed cousin. 'Is it possible that you can have made serious advances towards Miss Daubenay?'

'I never offered *marriage*,' said Pen, hanging her head.

The Major seemed to be in danger of suffering an apoplexy. Before he could recover the power of speech, Sir Richard had intervened. Upon the Major's bemused ears fell a description of Pen's shameless precocity that caused the object of it to turn away hastily to hide her laughter. According to Sir Richard's malicious tongue, Bath was strewn with her innocent victims. When Sir Richard let fall the information that this youthful moral leper was without means or expectations, the Major found enough breath to declare that the whelp ought to be horsewhipped.

'Precisely my own view,' bowed Sir Richard.

'Upon my word, I had not dreamed of such a thing! Penniless, you say?.

'Little better than a pauper,' said Sir Richard.

'Good Gad, what an escape!' gasped the Major. 'I do not know what to say! I am aghast!'

'Alas!' said Sir Richard, 'his father was just such another! The same disarming air of innocence hid a wolfish heart.'

'You appal me!' declared the Major. 'Yet he looks a mere boy!'

Pen, feeling that it was time she bore a part in the scene, said with an air of innocence which horrified the Major: 'But if Lydia says I offered marriage it is not true. It was all mere trifling. I do not wish to be married.'

This pronouncement once more bereft the Major of speech. Sir Richard's forefinger banished Pen to the corner, and by the time the outraged parent ceased gobbling, he had once more taken charge of the situation. He agreed that the whole affair must at all costs be hushed up, promised to deal faithfully with Pen, and finally escorted the Major out of the parlour, with assurances that such depravity should not go unpunished.

Pen, who had been struggling with an overwhelming desire to laugh, went off into a peal of mirth as soon as the Major was out of earshot, and had, in fact, to grasp a chairback to support herself. In this posture she was discovered by Mr Luttrell, who, as soon as Sir Richard and the Major had passed through the entrance parlour, oblivious of his presence there, bounced in upon Pen, and said through shut teeth: 'So! You think it damned amusing, do you, you little cur? Well, I do *not*!'

Pen raised her head, and through brimming eyes saw the face of her old playmate swim before her.

Mr Luttrell, stuttering with rage, said menacingly: 'I heard you! I could not help but hear you! So you didn't intend marriage, eh? You—you *boast* of having t-trifled with an innocent female! And you think you c-can get off scot free, do you? *I'll* teach you a lesson!'

Pen discovered to her horror that Mr Luttrell was advancing upon her with his fists clenched. She dodged behind the table, and shrieked: 'Piers! Don't you *know* me? Piers, look at me! I'm *Pen!*'

Mr Luttrell dropped his fists, and stood gaping. 'Pen?' he managed to utter. '*Pen?*'

I I

They stood staring at one another. The gentleman found his voice first, but only to repeat in accents of still deeper amazement: '*Pen?* Pen Creed?'

'Yes, indeed I am!' Pen assured him, keeping the table between them.

His fists unclenched. 'But—but what are you doing here? And in those clothes? I don't understand!'

'Well, it's rather a long story,' Pen said.

He seemed slightly dazed. He ran his hand through his hair, in a gesture she knew well, and said: 'But Major Daubenay—Sir Richard Wyndham—'

'They are both part of the story,' replied Pen. She had been looking keenly at him, and thinking that he had not greatly changed, and she added: 'I should have known you anywhere! Have I altered so much?'

'Yes. At least, I don't know. It's your hair, I suppose, cut short like that, and—and those clothes!'

He sounded shocked, which made her think that perhaps he had changed a little. 'Well, I truly am Pen Creed,' she said.

'Yes, I see that you are, now that I have had time to look at you. But I cannot understand it! I could not help hearing some of what was said, though I tried not to—until I heard Miss Daubenay's name!'

'Please, Piers, don't fly into a rage again!' Pen said rather nervously, for she distinctly heard his teeth grind together. 'I can explain everything!'

'I do not know whether I am on my head or my heels!' he complained. 'You have been imposing on her! How could you do such a thing? *Why* did you?'

'I haven't!' said Pen. 'And I must say, I do think you might be a little more glad to see me!'

'Of course I am glad! But to come here, masquerading as a boy, and playing pranks on a defenceless— *That* was why she failed last night!'

'No, it wasn't! She saw the stammering man killed, and ran away, you stupid creature!'

'How do you know?' he asked suspiciously.

'I was there, of course.'

'With her?'

'Yes, but—'

'You *have* been imposing on her!'

'I tell you it's no such thing! I met her by the merest chance.'

'Tell me this!' commanded Piers. 'Does she know that you are a girl?'

'No, but—'

'I knew it!' he declared. 'And I distinctly heard the Major say that she had met you in Bath! I don't know why you did it, but it is the most damnable trick in the world! And Lydia–deceiving me–encouraging your advances–oh, my eyes are open now!'

'If you say another word, I shall box your ears!' said Pen indignantly. 'I would not have believed you could have grown into such a stupid, tiresome creature! I never met Lydia Daubenay in my life until last night, and if you don't believe me you may go and ask her!'

He looked rather taken aback, and said in an uncertain tone: 'But if you did not know her, how came you to be with her in the wood last night?'

'That was chance. The silly little thing swooned, and I—'

'She is not a silly little thing!' interrupted Piers, firing up.

'Yes, she is, very silly. For what must she do, upon reaching home, but tell her Papa that it was not you she had gone to meet, but me!'

This announcement surprised him. His bewildered grey eyes sought enlightenment in Pen's face; he said with a rueful grin: 'Oh Pen, do sit down and explain! You never could tell a story so that one could make head or tail of it!'

She came away from the table, and sat down on the window seat. After a pained glance at her attire, Piers seated himself beside her. Each took critical stock of the other, but whereas Pen looked Piers frankly over, he surveyed her rather shyly, and showed a tendency to avert his gaze when it encountered hers.

He was a well-favoured young man, not precisely handsome, but with a pleasant face, a good pair of shoulders, and easy, open manners. Since he was four years her senior, he had always seemed to her, in the old days, very large, far more experienced than herself, and quite worthy of being looked up to. She was conscious, as she sat beside him on the window seat, of a faint feeling of disappointment. He seemed to her little more than a boy, and instead of assuming his old mastery in his dealings with her, he was obviously shy, and unable to think of anything to say. Their initial encounter had of course been unfortunate, but Pen thought that he might, upon discovering her identity, have exhibited more pleasure at meeting her again. She felt forlorn all at once, as though a door had been shut in her face. A vague suspicion that what was behind the shut door was not what she had imagined only made her the more melancholy. To hide it, she said brightly: 'It is such an age since I saw you, and there is so much to say! I don't know where to begin!'

He smiled, but there was a pucker between his brows. 'Yes, indeed, but it seems so strange! Why did you say she had gone out to meet you, I wonder?'

It was apparent to Pen that Miss Daubenay possessed his thoughts to the exclusion of everyone else. Repressing a strong desire to favour him with her opinion of that young lady, she recounted as briefly as she could what had passed between her and Lydia in the orchard. Any expectation she might have had of his viewing his betrothed's conduct in the same light as she did was banished by his exclaiming rapturously: 'She is such an innocent little thing! It is just like her to have said that! I see it all now!'

This was too much for Pen. 'Well, I think it was a ridiculous thing to have said.'

'You see, she knows nothing of the world, Pen,' he said earnestly. 'Then, too, she is impulsive! Do you know, she always makes me think of a bird?'

'A goose, I suppose,' said Pen somewhat tartly.

'I meant a wild bird,' he replied, with dignity. 'A fluttering, timid, little—'

'She didn't seem to me very timid,' Pen interrupted. 'In fact, I thought she was extremely bold to ask a perfectly strange young man to pretend to be in love with her.'

'You don't understand her. She is so trusting! She needs someone to take care of her. We have loved one another ever since our first meeting. We should have been married by now if my father had not picked a foolish quarrel with the Major. Pen, you cannot think what our sufferings have been! There seems to be no end to them! We shall never induce our fathers to consent to our marriage, never!'

He sank his head in his hands with a groan, but Pen said briskly: 'Well, you will have to marry without their consent. Only you both of you seem to be so poor spirited that you will do nothing but moan, and meet in woods! Why don't you elope?'

'Elope! You don't know what you are saying, Pen! How could I ask that fragile little thing to do anything of the sort? The impropriety, too! I am persuaded she would shrink from the very thought of it!'

'Yes, she did,' agreed Pen. 'She said she would not be able to have attendants, or a lace veil.'

'You see, she has been very strictly reared–has led the most sheltered life! Besides, why should she not have a lace veil, and–and those things which females set store by?'

'For my part,' Pen said, 'I would not care a fig for such fripperies if I loved a man!'

'Oh, you are different!' said Piers. 'You were always more like a boy than a girl. Just look at you now! *Why* are you masquerading as a boy? It seems to me most peculiar, and not quite the thing, you know.'

'There were circumstances which–which made it necessary,' said Pen rather stiffly. 'I had to escape from my aunt's house.'

'Well, I still don't see why—'

'Because I was forced to climb out of a window!' snapped Pen. 'Moreover, I could not travel all by myself as a female, could I?'

'No, I suppose you could not. Only you should not be travelling by yourself at all. What a madcap you are!' A thought occurred to him; he glanced down at Pen with a sudden frown. 'But you were with Sir Richard Wyndham when I came in, and you seemed to be on mighty close terms with him, too! For heaven's sake, Pen, what are you about? How do you come to be in his company?'

The interview with her old playmate seemed to be fraught not only with disappointment, but with unforeseen difficulties as well. Pen could not but realize that Mr Luttrell was not in sympathy with her. 'Oh, that–that is too long a story to tell!' she replied evasively. 'There were reasons why I wished to come home again, and–and Sir Richard would not permit me to go alone.'

'But, Pen!' He sounded horrified. 'You are surely not travelling with him?'

His tone swept away adventure, and invested her exploit instead with the stigma of impropriety. She coloured hotly, and was searching her mind for an explanation that would satisfy Piers when the door opened, and Sir Richard came into the room.

One glance at Mr Luttrell's rigidly disapproving countenance; one glimpse of Pen's scarlet cheeks and over-bright eyes, were enough to give

Sir Richard a very fair notion of what had been taking place in the parlour. He closed the door, saying in his pleasant drawl: 'Ah, good morning, Mr Luttrell! I trust the–er–surprising events of last night did not rob you of sleep?'

A sigh of relief escaped Pen. With Sir Richard's entrance the reeling world seemed, miraculously, to have righted itself. She left the window seat, and went instinctively towards him. 'Sir, Piers says–Piers thinks—' She stopped, and raised a hand to her burning cheek.

Sir Richard looked at Piers with slightly raised brows. 'Well?' he said gently. 'What does Piers say and think?'

Mr Luttrell got up. Under that ironical, tolerant gaze, he too began to blush. 'I only said–I only wondered how Pen comes to be travelling in your company!'

Sir Richard unfobbed his snuffbox, and took a pinch. 'And does no explanation offer itself to you?' he enquired.

'Well, sir, I must say it seems to me–I mean—'

'Perhaps I should have told you,' said Sir Richard, drawing Pen's hand through his arm, and holding it rather firmly, 'that you are addressing the future Lady Wyndham.'

The hand twitched in Sir Richard's, but in obedience to the warning pressure of his fingers Miss Creed remained silent.

'Oh, I see!' said Piers, his brow clearing. 'I beg pardon! It is famous news indeed! I wish you very happy! But–but why must she wear those clothes, and what are you doing here? It still seems very odd to me! I suppose since you are betrothed it may be argued that— But it is most eccentric, sir, and I do not know what people may say!'

'As we have been at considerable pains to admit no one but yourself into the secret of Pen's identity, I hardly think that people will say anything at all,' replied Sir Richard calmly. 'If the secret were to leak out–why, the answer is that we are a very eccentric couple!'

'It will never leak out through me!' Piers assured him. 'It is no concern of mine, naturally, but I can't help wondering what should have brought you here, and why Pen had to get out of a window. However, I don't mean to be inquisitive, sir. It was only that–having known Pen all my life, you see!'

It was Miss Creed's turn now to give Sir Richard's hand a warning pinch. In fact, so convulsive was her grip that he glanced down at her with a reassuring little smile.

'I am afraid I cannot tell you our reasons for coming here,' he said. 'Certain circumstances arose which made the journey necessary. Pen's attire, however, is easily explained. Neither of us wished to burden ourselves with a duenna upon a mission of–er–extreme delicacy; and the world, my dear Luttrell, being a censorious place, it was judged expedient for Pen to pretend to be, instead of my affianced wife, my young cousin.'

'To be sure, yes! of course!' said Piers, mystified, but overborne by the Corinthian's air of assurance.

'By now,' said Sir Richard, 'we should be on our way back to London, had it not been for two unfortunate circumstances. For one of these, you, I must regretfully point out to you, are responsible.'

'I?' gasped Piers.

'You,' said Sir Richard, releasing Pen's hand. 'The lady to whom you, I apprehend, are secretly betrothed, has, in a somewhat misguided attempt to avert suspicion from the truth, informed her parent that Pen is the man with whom she had an assignation in the spinney last night.'

'Yes, Pen told me that. Indeed, I wish she had not done it, sir, but she is so impulsive, you know!'

'So I have been led to infer,' said Sir Richard. 'Unhappily, since I am for the present compelled to remain in Queen Charlton, her impulsiveness has rendered our situation a trifle awkward.'

'Yes, I see that,' owned Piers. 'I am very sorry for it, sir. But must you remain here?'

'Yes,' replied Sir Richard. 'No doubt it has escaped your memory, but a murder was committed in the spinney last night. It was I who discovered Brandon's body, and conveyed the news to the proper quarter.'

Piers looked troubled at this, and said: 'I know, sir, and I do not like it above half! For, in point of fact, *I* first found Beverley, only you told me not to say so!'

'I hope you did not?'

'No, because it is so excessively awkward, on account of Miss Daubenay's presence in the spinney! But if she has said that she went there to meet Pen—'

'You had better continue to preserve a discreet silence, my dear boy. The knowledge that you also were in the spinney would merely confuse poor Mr Philips. You see, I have the advantage of knowing who killed Brandon.'

'I think,' said Pen judicially, 'we ought to tell Piers about the diamond necklace, sir.'

'By all means,' agreed Sir Richard.

The history of the diamond necklace, as recounted by Miss Creed, made Mr Luttrell forget for a few moments his graver preoccupations. He seemed very much more the Piers of her childhood when he exclaimed: 'What an adventure!' and by the time had described to her his surprise at receiving a visit from Beverley, whom he had known but slightly up at Oxford; and had exchanged impressions of Captain Horace Trimble, they were once more upon very good terms. Sir Richard, who thought that his own interests would best be served by allowing Pen uninterrupted intercourse with Mr Luttrell, soon left them to themselves; and after Piers had once more felicitated Pen on her choice of a husband—felicitations which she received in embarrassed silence—the talk soon returned to his own difficulties.

She listened to his enraptured description of Miss Daubenay with as much patience as she could muster, but when he begged her not to divulge her sex to the lady for fear lest her nice sense of propriety might suffer too great a shock, she was so much incensed that she was betrayed into giving him her opinion of Miss Daubenay's morals and manners. A pretty squabble at once flared up, and might have ended in Piers' stalking out of Pen's life for ever had she not remembered, just as he reached the door, that she had engaged herself to further his pretensions to Lydia's hand.

It took a few moments' coaxing to persuade him to relax his air of outraged dignity, but when it was borne in upon him that Lydia had summoned Pen to her side that morning, he did seem to feel that such forward conduct called for an explanation. Pen waved his excuses aside, however. 'I don't mind that, if only she would not cry so much!' she said.

Mr Luttrell said that his Lydia was all sensibility, and deprecated, with obvious sincerity, a suggestion that a wife suffering from an excess of sensibility might prove to be a tiresome acquisition. As he seemed to feel that the support of Lydia was his life's work, Pen abandoned all thought of trying to wean him from his attachment to the lady, and announced her plans for his speedy marriage.

These palpably took Mr Luttrell aback. Lydia's refusal to elope with him he regarded as natural rather than craven, and when Pen's false-abduction scheme was enthusiastically described to him he said that she must be mad to think of such a thing.

'I declare I have a good mind to wash my hands of the whole affair!' said Pen. 'Neither of you has the courage to make the least push in the matter! The end of it will be that your precious Lydia will be married to someone else, and then you will be sorry!'

'Oh, don't suggest such a thing!' he begged. 'If only my father would be a little conciliating! He used to like the Major well enough before they quarrelled.'

'You must soften the Major's heart.'

'Yes, but how?' he asked. 'Now, don't, pray, suggest any more foolish abduction schemes, Pen! I daresay you think them very fine, but if you would but consider the difficulties! No one would ever believe we had not planned it all, because if she eloped with you she would not then wish to marry me, now, would she?'

'No, but we could say that I had forcibly abducted her. Then you could rescue her from me.'

'How should I know that you had abducted her?' objected Piers. 'And just think what a pucker everyone would be in! No, really, Pen, it won't answer! Good God, I should have to fight a duel with you, or something of that nature! I mean, how odd it would look if all I did was to take Lydia home!'

'Well, so we could!' said Pen, with eyes brightening, as new horizons swam into her ken. 'I could have my arm in a sling, and say that you had wounded me! Oh, do let us, Piers! It would be such a famous adventure!'

'You don't seem to me to have changed in the least!' said Piers, in anything but a complimentary tone. 'You are the most complete hand indeed! I cannot conceive how you came to be betrothed to a man of fashion like Wyndham! You know, you will have to mend your ways! In fact, I cannot conceive of your being married at all! You are a mere child.'

Another quarrel might at this point have sprung up between them, had not Sir Richard come back into the room just then, with Mr Philips in his wake. He was looking faintly amused, and the instant expression of extreme trepidation which transformed the countenances of the youthful couple by the window made his lips twitch involuntarily. However, he spoke without a tremor in his voice. 'Ah, Pen! Would you explain, if you please, your—er—owl story, to Mr Philips?'

'Oh!' said Pen, blushing furiously.

The magistrate looked severely across at her. 'From the information I have since received, young man, I am forced to the conclusion that your story was false.'

Pen glanced towards Sir Richard. Instead of coming to her rescue, he smiled maliciously, and said: 'Stand up, my boy, stand up, when Mr Philips addresses you!'

'Oh yes, of course!' said Pen, rising in a hurry. 'I beg pardon! My owl story! Well, you see, I did not know what to say when you asked why I had not been with my cousin last night.'

'Did not know what to say! You had only one thing to say, and that was the truth!' said Mr Philips austerely.

'I could not,' replied Pen. 'A lady's reputation was at stake!'

'So I am informed. Well, I do not say that I do not sympathize with your motive, but I must warn you, sir, that any further prevarication on your part may lead to serious trouble. Serious trouble! I say nothing of your conduct in meeting Miss Daubenay in a manner I can only describe as clandestine. It is no concern of mine, no concern at all, but if you were a son of mine— However, that is neither here nor there! Fortunately—' He cast a reproachful glance at Sir Richard–'fortunately, I repeat, Miss Daubenay's evidence corroborates the information that this shocking crime was perpetrated by a person corresponding with the description furnished me of the man Trimble. Were it not for this circumstance–for I will not conceal from you that I am far from being satisfied! Very far indeed! You must permit me to say, Sir Richard, that your presence in the spinney last night points to your having positively aided and abetted your cousin in his reprehensible— But I am aware that *that* is Major Daubenay's concern!'

'No, no, you have it wrong!' Pen assured him. 'My cousin was searching for me! In fact, he was very angry with me for going to the spinney, were you not, Richard?'

'I was,' admitted Sir Richard. 'Very.'

'Well, the whole affair seems to me very strange!' said Philips. 'I will say no more than that *yet!*'

'You behold me–er–stricken with remorse,' said Sir Richard.

The magistrate snorted, jerked a bow, and took himself off.

'My reputation! oh, my reputation!' mourned Sir Richard. 'Horrible and unprincipled brat, *why* the owl?'

'Well, I had to say something!' Pen pointed out.

'I am afraid,' said Piers, conscience-stricken, 'that it is a *little* Lydia's fault. But indeed, sir, she meant no harm!'

'I know,' said Sir Richard. 'She is so impulsive! I feel a hundred years old.'

He went out on the words, and Pen at once rounded on Mr Luttrell, saying in accusing accents: 'There! You see now what your precious Lydia has done!'

'She is no worse than you are! In fact, not as bad!' retorted Piers. '*She* would not masquerade about the country as a boy! I do not wonder at Sir Richard's feeling a hundred years old. If I were betrothed to you, I should feel the same!'

Miss Creed's eyes flashed. 'Well, I will tell you something, Piers Luttrell! I have got a cousin with a face like a fish, and *he* wants to marry me, which is why I escaped out a window. *But*–do you hear me?–I would a great deal rather marry him than you. If I had to marry you, I would drown myself! You are stupid, and rude, and spiritless!'

'Merely because I have a little common sense,' began Piers, very stiff, and rather flushed.

He was interrupted. A waiter came in with the news that a Young Person desired instant speech with Mr Wyndham.

Correctly divining this mythical being to be herself, Pen said: 'What can that nonsensical girl want now? I wish I had never come to Queen Charlton! Oh, very well! Show the young person in!'

'Good God, can it be Lydia?' exclaimed Piers, when the waiter had withdrawn.

The young person was not Miss Daubenay, but her personal maid, a rosy damsel, who appeared to be strongly imbued with her mistress's romantic ideals. She came in heavily veiled, and presented Pen with a sealed letter. While Pen tore it open, and read its agitated message, Piers besieged the girl with urgent questions, to which, however, she only replied with evasive answers, punctuated by giggles.

'Good gracious!' exclaimed Pen, deciphering Miss Daubenay's scrawl. 'Matters are now desperate! She says she will elope with you.'

'What?' Piers abandoned the servant, and strode to Pen's side. 'Here, give it to me!'

Pen warded him off. 'She says they are going to send her to the Wilds of Lincolnshire.'

'Yes, yes, that is where her grandmother lives! When does she go?'

'I can't read it—oh yes, I see! Tomorrow morning, with her Papa. She says I am to tell you to arrange for the elopement this evening, without fail.'

'Good God!' Piers snatched the letter from her, and read it for himself. 'Yes, you are right: she does say tomorrow morning! Pen, if she goes, it will be the end of everything! I never meant to do anything so improper as to elope with her, but I have now no choice! It is not as though her parents disapprove of me, or—or that I am not eligible. If *that* were so, it would be different. But until they quarrelled—however, talking is to no purpose!' He turned to the maidservant, who had by this time put back her veil, and was listening to him with her mouth open. 'Are you in your mistress's confidence?' he demanded.

'Oh yes, sir!' she assured him, adding with another giggle: 'Though the master would tear me limb from limb if he knew I was taking letters to you, sir.'

Piers ignored this somewhat exaggerated statement. 'Tell me, is your mistress indeed resolved upon this course?'

'Oh!' said the damsel, clasping her plump hands together, 'she was never more resolved in her life, sir! "I must Fly!" she says to me, clean distracted. "Lucy," she says, "I am Utterly Undone, for All is Discovered!" So I popped on my bonnet, sir, and slipped out when Cook's back was turned, "for," says my poor young mistress, with tears standing in her eyes fit to break anyone's heart, "if I am whisked off to Lincolnshire, I shall die!" And so she will, sir, no question!'

Pen sat down again, hugging her knees. 'Nothing could be better!' she declared. 'I always liked the notion of your eloping to Gretna Green. In fact, it was my suggestion. Only, Lydia told me that you have no money, Piers. Shall we make Richard pay for the post chaise?'

'Certainly not!' he replied. 'Of course I have enough money for *that*!'

'I think you ought to have four horses,' she warned him. 'Posting charges are very high, you know.'

'Good God, Pen, I'm not penniless! Lydia meant only that I am dependent upon my father. If he refuses to forgive us, I shall be obliged to find some genteel occupation, but I am persuaded that once the deed is done he will very soon come round. Oh, Pen! is she not an angel? I am quite overcome! Is it not affecting that she should trust me so implicitly?'

Pen opened her eyes at this. 'Why shouldn't she?' she asked, surprised.

'Why shouldn't she? Really, Pen, you don't understand in the least! Think of her placing her life, honour, all, in my care!'

'I don't see anything wonderful in that,' replied Pen contemptuously. 'I think it would be a great deal more extraordinary if she didn't trust you.'

'I remember now that you never had much sensibility,' said Piers. 'You are such a child!' He turned again to the interested abigail. 'Now, Lucy, attend to me! You must take a letter back to your mistress, and assure her besides that I shall not fail. Are you prepared to accompany us to Scotland?'

She gaped at him for a moment, but however strange the idea might have been to her it apparently pleased her, for she nodded vehemently, and said: 'Oh yes, thank you, sir!'

'Who ever heard of taking a maid on an elopement?' demanded Pen.

'I will not ask Lydia to fly with me without some female to go with her!' declared Piers nobly.

'Dear me, I should think she would wish the girl at Jericho!'

'Lydia is quite unused to waiting upon herself,' said Piers. 'Moreover, the presence of her maid must lend respectability to our flight.'

'Has she a little lapdog she would like to take with her too?' asked Pen innocently.

Piers cast her a quelling look, and stalked across the room to a small writing table near the window. After testing the pen that lay on it, mending it, and dipping it in the standish, he then sat while the ink dried on it, frowning over what he should write to his betrothed. Finally, he dipped the pen in the standish once more, and began to write, punctuating his labour with reminders to Lucy to see that her mistress had a warm cloak, and did not bring too many bandboxes with her.

'Or the parrot,' interpolated Pen.

'Lor', sir, Miss Lydia hasn't got any parrot!'

'If you don't hold your tongue, Pen—?'

'No little lapdog either?' Pen asked incredulously.

'No, sir, 'deed, no! There's only her lovebirds, the pretty things, and her doves!'

'Well, you will not have room in the chaise for a dovecot, but you should certainly bring the lovebirds,' said Pen, with an irrepressible chuckle.

Piers flung down his pen. 'Another word from you, and I'll put you out of the room!'

'No, you won't, because this is a private parlour, and you are nothing but a guest in it.'

'But will I tell Miss to bring the lovebirds?' asked Lucy, puzzled.

'No!' said Piers. 'Oh, do stop, Pen! You are driving me distracted! Listen, I have told Lydia that I will have a chaise waiting in the lane behind the house at midnight. Do you think that is too early? Will her parents go to her room as late as that?'

'No, sir, that they won't!' said Lucy. 'The Major does be such a one for retiring early! He'll be in bed and asleep by eleven, take my word for it, sir!'

'Fortunately, it is moonlight,' Piers said, shaking sand over his letter. 'Listen, Lucy! I depend upon you to see that your mistress goes early to bed; she must get what sleep she can! And you must wake her at the proper time, do you understand? Can I trust you to pack for her, and to bring her safely to me?'

'Oh yes, sir!' replied Lucy, bobbing a curtsey. 'For I wouldn't be left to face the Major, not for ever so!'

'You had best go back to the house with all possible speed,' Piers said, applying a wafer to the folded letter, and handing it to her. 'Mind, now! that letter must not fall into the wrong hands!'

'If anyone tries to take it from you, you must swallow it,' put in Pen.

'Swallow it, sir?'

'Pay no attention to my friend!' said Piers hastily. 'There! Be off with you, and remember that I depend upon your fidelity!'

Lucy curtseyed herself out of the room. Piers looked at Pen, still hugging her knees on the window seat, and said severely: 'I suppose you flatter yourself you have been helpful!'

Impish lights danced in her eyes. 'Oh, I have! Only think if you had had to turn back to fetch the lovebirds, which very likely you would have had to do if I had not reminded the abigail about them!'

He could not help grinning. 'Pen, if she does bring them, I'll—I'll turn back to wring your neck! Now I must go to arrange for the hire of a chaise, and four fast horses.'

'Where will you find them?' she asked.

'There is a posting house at Keynsham where they keep very tolerable cattle. I shall drive over there immediately.'

'Famous! Go where you are known, and let the news of your wanting a chaise for midnight spread all over the countryside within three hours!'

He checked. 'I had not thought of that! The devil! This means I must go into Bristol, and I can ill spare the time, with so much to attend to.'

'Nothing of the sort!' said Pen, jumping up. 'Now I will be helpful indeed! I will drive to Keynsham with you, and *I* will order the chaise.'

His brow cleared. 'Oh Pen, will you? But Sir Richard! Will he not object, do you think? Of course, I would take every care of you, but—'

'No, no, he will not object, I assure you! I shall not tell him anything about it,' said Pen ingenuously.

'But that would not be right! And I should not wish to do anything—'

'I will leave a message for him with the landlord,' promised Pen. 'Did you walk into the village, or have you a carriage here?'

'Oh, I drove in! The gig is in the yard now. I confess, if you feel it would not be wrong of you to go with me, I should be glad of your help.'

'Only wait while I get my hat!' Pen said, and darted off in search of it.

12

Miss Creed and Mr Luttrell, partaking of midday refreshment in Keynsham's best inn, and exhaustively discussing the details of the elopement, were neither of them troubled by doubts of the wisdom of the gentleman's whisking his betrothed off to Scotland at a moment when that lady had become entangled in a case of murder. Indeed, Mr Luttrell, a single-minded young man, was in a fair way to forgetting that he had ever had Beverley Brandon to stay with him. He had left his mother trying to write a suitable letter to Lady Saar, and if he thought about the unfortunate affair at all it was to reflect comfortably that Lady Luttrell would do everything that was proper. His conversation was confined almost exclusively to his own immediate problems, but he digressed several times to animadvert on Pen's unconventional exploits.

'Of course,' he conceded, 'it is not so shocking now that I know that you are betrothed to Wyndham, but I own it does surprise me that he—a man of the world—should have countenanced such a prank. But these Corinthians delight in oddities, I believe! I dare say no one will wonder at it very much. If you were not betrothed it would be different, naturally!'

Pen's clear gaze met his steadily. 'I think you make a great bustle about nothing,' she said.

'My dear Pen!' He gave a little laugh. 'You are such a child! I believe you haven't the smallest notion of the ways of the world!'

She was obliged to admit that this was true. It occurred to her that since Piers seemed to be well-informed on this subject she might with advantage learn a little from him. 'If I were not going to marry Richard, would it be very dreadful?' she asked.

'Pen! What things you do say!' he exclaimed. 'Only think of your situation, travelling all the way from London in Wyndham's company, without even your maid to go with you! Why, you *must* marry him now!'

She tilted her chin. 'I don't see that I must at all.'

'Depend upon it, if you do not, he does. I must say, I think it excessively strange that a man of his years and–and *milieu*–should have wished to marry you, Pen.' He realised his speech was scarcely complimentary, and hastened to add: 'I don't mean *that* precisely, only you are so much younger than he is, and such a little innocent!'

She pounced on this. 'Well, that is one very good reason why I need not marry him!' she said. 'He is so much older than I am that I dare say no one would think it in the smallest degree odd that we should have taken this journey together.'

'Good God, Pen, he is not as old as that! What a strange girl you are! Don't you wish to marry him?'

She stared at him with puckered brows. She thought of Sir Richard, of the adventures she had encountered in his company, and of the laughter in his eyes, and of the teasing note in his voice. Suddenly she flushed rosily, and the tears started to her own eyes. 'Yes. Oh, yes, I do!' she said.

'Well! But what is there to cry over?' demanded Piers. 'For a moment I quite thought— Now, don't be silly, Pen!'

She blew her nose defiantly, and said in somewhat watery accents: 'I'm not crying!'

'Indeed, I can't conceive why you should. I think Wyndham a very good sort of man–a famous fellow! I suppose you will become very fashionable, Pen, and cut the deuce of a dash in town!'

Pen, who could see no future beyond a life spent within the walls of her aunt's respectable house, agreed to this, and made haste to direct the conversation into less painful channels.

Although Keynsham was situated only a few miles distant from Queen Charlton, it was close on the dinner hour when Piers set Pen down at the George Inn again. By this time, a post chaise had been hired and four good horses chosen to draw it, the whole being appointed to arrive at a rendezvous outside the gates of Crome Hall at half past eleven that evening. Beyond a certain degree of anxiety concerning the extent of the baggage his betrothed would wish to bring with her, and some fears that her flight might be intercepted at the outset, Mr Luttrell had nothing further to worry about, as his guide and mentor frequently assured him.

Pen would have liked to have been present at the fatal hour, but this offer Piers declined. They bade each other farewell, therefore, at the door of the George Inn, neither suffering the smallest pang at the notion that each was about to be joined in wedlock to another.

Having waved a last goodbye to her old playmate, Pen went into the inn, and was met by Sir Richard, who looked her up and down, and said: 'Abominable brat, you had better make a clean breast of the whole! Where have you been, and what mischief have you done?'

'Oh, but I left a message for you!' Pen protested. 'Did they not give it to you, sir?'

'They did. But the intelligence that you had gone off with young Luttrell merely filled me with misgivings. Confess!'

She twinkled at him. 'Well, perhaps you will not be *quite* pleased, but indeed I did it all for the best, Richard!'

'This becomes more and more ominous. I am persuaded you have committed some devilry.'

She passed into the parlour, and went to the mirror above the fireplace to pat her crisp, dishevelled curls into order. 'Not *devilry*, precisely,' she demurred.

Sir Richard, who had been observing her in some amusement, said: 'I am relieved. Yes, I think the sooner you put on your petticoats again the better, Pen. That is a very feminine trick, let me tell you.'

She coloured, laughed, and turned away from the mirror. 'I forgot. Well, it doesn't signify, after all, for it seems to me that I have reached the end of my adventure.'

'Not quite,' he replied.

'Yes, I have. You do not know!'

'You look extremely wicked. Out with it!'

'Piers and Lydia are going to elope tonight!'

The laugh died out of his eyes. 'Pen, is this your doing?'

'Oh no, indeed it is not, sir! In fact, I had quite a different plan, only I dared not tell you, and, as a matter of fact, Piers did not think well of it. I wanted to abduct Lydia, so that Piers could rescue her from me, and so soften her Papa's heart. However, I dare say you would not have approved of that.'

'I should not,' said Sir Richard emphatically.

'No, that's why I said nothing to you about it. In the end Lydia decided to elope.'

'You mean that you bullied the wretched girl—'

'I did not! You are most unjust, sir! On my honour, I did not! I don't say that I didn't perhaps put the notion into her head, but it was all the Major's doing. He threatened to take her to Lincolnshire tomorrow morning, and of course she could not support life there! Oh, here comes the waiter! I will tell you the whole story presently.'

She retired to her favourite seat in the window while the covers were laid, and Sir Richard, standing with his back to the mighty fireplace, watched her. The waiter took his time over the preparations for dinner, and during one of his brief absences from the parlour, Pen said abruptly: 'You were quite right: he has changed, sir. Only you were wrong about one thing: he does not think I have changed at all.'

'I did not suspect him to be capable of paying you so pretty a compliment,' said Sir Richard, raising his brows.

'Well, I don't think he meant it to be a compliment,' said Pen doubtfully.

He smiled but said nothing. The waiter came back into the room with a laden tray, and began to set various dishes in the table. When he had withdrawn, Sir Richard, pulled a chair out for Pen, and said: 'You are served, brat. Hungry?'

'Not very,' she replied, sitting down.

He moved to his own place. 'Why, how is that?'

'Well, I don't know. Piers is going to elope with Lydia at midnight.'

'I trust that circumstance has not taken away your appetite?'

'Oh no! I think they will deal famously together, for they are both very silly.'

'True. What had you to do with their elopement?'

'Oh, very little, I assure you, sir! Lydia made up her mind to do it without any urging from me. All I did was to hire the post chaise for Piers, on account of his being well known in Keynsham.'

'I suppose that means that we shall be obliged to sustain another visit from Major Daubenay. I seem to be plunging deeper and deeper into a life of crime.'

She looked up enquiringly. 'Why, sir? You have done nothing!'

'I am aware. But I undoubtedly should do something.'

'Oh no, it is all arranged! There is truly nothing left to do.'

'You don't think that I—as one having reached years of discretion—might perhaps be expected to nip this shocking affair in the bud?'

'Tell the Major, do you mean?' Pen cried. 'Oh, Richard, you would not do such a cruel thing? I am persuaded you could not!'

He refilled his glass. 'I could, very easily, but I won't. I am not, to tell you the truth, much interested in the affairs of a pair of lovers whom I have found, from the outset, extremely tiresome. Shall we discuss instead our own affairs?'

'Yes, I think we ought to,' she agreed. 'I have been so busy today I had almost forgot the stammering man. I do trust, Richard, we shall not be arrested!'

'Indeed, so do I!' he said, laughing.

'It's very well to laugh, but I could see that Mr Philips did not like us at all.'

'I fear that your activities disarranged his mind. Fortunately, news has reached him that a man whom I suspect of being none other than the egregious Captain Trimble has been taken up by the authorities in Bath.'

'Good gracious, I never thought he would be caught! Pray, had he the necklace?'

'That, I am as yet unable to tell you. It is to be hoped that Luttrell and his bride will not prolong their honeymoon, since I fancy Lydia will be wanted to identify the prisoner.'

'If she knew that, I dare say she would never come back at all,' said Pen.

'A public-spirited female,' commented Sir Richard.

She giggled. 'She has no spirit at all. I *told* you so, sir! Will the—the authorities wish to see me?'

'I hardly think so. In any event, they are not going to see you.'

'No, I must say I feel it might be excessively awkward if I were forced to appear,' remarked Pen. 'In fact, sir, I think—I think I had better go home, don't you?'

He looked at her. 'To your Aunt Almeria, brat?'

'Yes, of course. There is nowhere else for me to go.'

'And Cousin Fred?'

'Well, I hope that after all the adventures I have gone through he will not want to marry me any more,' said Pen optimistically. 'He is very easily shocked, you know.'

'Such a man would not be at all the husband for you,' he said, shaking his head. 'You must undoubtedly choose someone who is not at all easily shocked.'

'Perhaps I had better mend my ways,' said Pen, with a swift unhappy smile.

'That would be a pity, for your ways are delightful. I have a better plan than yours, Pen.'

She got up quickly from the table. 'No, no! Please no, sir!' she said in a choking voice.

He too rose, and held out his hand. 'Why do you say that? I want you to marry me, Pen.'

'Oh Richard, I wish you would not!' she begged, retreating to the window. 'Indeed, I don't want you to offer for me. It is extremely obliging of you, but I could not!'

'Obliging of me! What nonsense is this?'

'Yes, yes, I know why you have said it!' she said distressfully. 'You feel that you have compromised me, but indeed you haven't for no one will ever know the truth!'

'I detect the fell hand of Mr Luttrell,' said Sir Richard rather grimly. 'What pernicious rubbish has he been putting into your head, my little one?'

This term of endearment made Pen wink away a sudden tear. 'Oh no! Only I was stupid not to think of it before. Really, I have no more sense than Lydia! But you are so much older than I am that it truly did not occur to me—until Piers came, and that you told him to save my face, that we were betrothed! *Then* I saw what a little fool I had been! But it does not signify, sir, for Piers will never breathe a word, even to Lydia, and Aunt Almeria need not know that I have been with you all the time.'

'Pen, will you stop talking nonsense? I am not in the least chivalrous, my dear: you may ask my sister, and she will tell you that I am the most selfish creature alive. I never do anything to please anyone but myself.'

'That I know to be untrue!' Pen said. 'If your sister thinks it, she doesn't know you. And I am not talking nonsense. Piers was shocked to find me with you, and you *did* think he had reason, or you would not have said what you did.'

'Oh yes,!' he responded. 'I am well aware of what the world would think of this escapade, but, believe me, my little love, I don't offer marriage from motives of chivalry. To be plain with you, I started on this adventure because I was drunk, and because I was bored, and because I thought I had to do something which was distasteful to me. I stayed in it because I found myself enjoying it as I have not enjoyed anything for years.'

'You did not enjoy the stagecoach,' she reminded him.

'No, but we need not make a practice of travelling by the stagecoach, need we?' he said, smiling down at her, 'Briefly, Pen, when I met you I was about to contract a marriage of convenience. Within twelve hours of making your acquaintance, I knew that no matter what might happen, I would not contract *that* marriage. Within twenty-four hours, my dear, I knew that I had found what I had come to believe did not exist.'

'What was that?' she asked shyly.

His smiled was a little twisted. 'A woman—no, a chit of a girl! An impertinent, atrocious, audacious brat—whom I am very sure I cannot live without.'

'Oh!' said Pen, blushing furiously. 'How *kind* of you to say that to me! I know just why you do, and indeed I am very grateful to you for putting it so prettily!'

'And you don't believe a word of it!'

'No, for I am very sure you would not have thought of marrying me if Piers had not been in love with Lydia Daubenay,' she said simply. 'You are sorry for me, because of that, and so—'

'Not in the least.'

'I think you are a little, Richard. And I quite see that to a person like you—for it is no use to pretend to me that you are selfish, because I know that you are nothing of the sort—to a person like you, it must seem that you are bound in honour to marry me. Now, confess! That is true, is it not? Don't—*please* don't tell me polite lies!'

'Very well,' he replied. 'It is true that having embroiled you in this situation I ought in honour to offer you the protection of my name. But I am offering you my heart, Pen.'

She searched feverishly for her handkerchief, and mopped her brimming eyes with it. 'Oh, I *do* thank you!' she said in a muffled voice. 'You have such beautiful manners, sir!'

'Pen, you impossible child!' he exclaimed. 'I am trying to tell you that I love you, and all you will say is that I have beautiful manners!'

'You cannot fall in love with a person in three days!' she objected.

He had taken a step towards her, but he checked himself at that. 'I see.'

She gave her eyes a final wipe, and said apologetically: 'I beg your pardon! I didn't mean to cry, only I think I am a little tired, besides having had a shock, on account of Piers, you know.'

Sir Richard, who had been intimately acquainted with many women, thought that he did know. 'I was afraid of that,' he said. 'Did you care so much, Pen?'

'No, but I thought I did, and it is all very lowering, if you understand what I mean, sir.'

'I suppose I do. I am too old for you, am I not?'

'I am too young for you,' said Pen unsteadily. 'I dare say you think I am amusing—in fact, I know you do, for you are for ever laughing at me—but you would very soon grow tired of laughing, and—and, perhaps be sorry that you had married me.'

'I am never tired of laughing.'

'Please do not say any more!' she implored. 'It has been such a splendid adventure until Piers came, and forced you to say what you did! I—I would rather that you didn't say any more, Richard, if you please!'

He perceived that his careful strategy in allowing her to meet her old playfellow before declaring himself had been mistaken. There did not seem to be any way of explaining this. No doubt, he thought, she had from the outset regarded him in an avuncular light. He wondered how deeply her affection had been rooted in the dream-figure of Piers Luttrell, and, misreading her tears, feared that her heart had indeed suffered a severe wound. He wanted very much to catch her up in his arms, overbearing her resistance and her scruples, but her very trust in him set up a barrier between them. He said, with the shadow of a smile: 'I have given myself a hard task, have I not?'

She did not understand him, and so said nothing. Not until Piers had shown her a shocked face, and Sir Richard had claimed her as his prospective wife, had she questioned her own heart. Sir Richard had been merely her delightful travelling companion, an immensely superior personage on whom one could place one's dependence. The object of her journey had obsessed her thoughts to such a degree that she had never paused to ask herself whether the entrance into her life of a Corinthian had not altered the whole complexion of her adventure. But it had; and when she had encountered Piers, it had been suddenly borne in upon her that she did not care two pins for him. Then Piers had turned the adventure into a faintly sordid intrigue, and Sir Richard had made his declaration, not because he had wanted to (for if he had, why should he have held his tongue till then?) but because honour had forced the words out of him. It was absurd to think that a man of fashion, nearing his thirtieth year, could have fallen head-over-ears in love with a miss scarcely out of the schoolroom, however easily the miss might have tumbled into love with him.

'Very well, Miss Creed,' said Sir Richard. 'I will woo you in form, and according to all the dictates of convention.'

The ubiquitous waiter chose this moment to come into the parlour to clear the table. Turning to gaze out of the window, Miss Creed reflected that in a more perfect world no servant would intrude upon his legitimate business at unreasonable moments. While the waiter, who seemed from his intermittent sniffs to be suffering from a cold in the head, shuffled about the room, clattering plates and dishes together on a tray, she resolutely winked away another tear, and fixed her attention on a mongrel dog, scratching for fleas in the middle of the street. But this object of interest was presently sent scuttling to cover by the approach of a smart curricle drawn by a pair of fine bays, and driven by a young blood in a coat of white drab cloth, with as many as fifteen capes, and two tiers of pockets. A Belcher handkerchief protruded from an inner pocket, and the coat was flung open to display an astonishing view of a kerseymere waist-coat, woven in stripes of blue and yellow, and a cravat of white muslin spotted with black. A bouquet was stuck in a button-hole of the driving coat, and a tall hat with a conical crown and an Allen brim was set at a rakish angle on the head of this exquisite.

The equipage drew up outside the George, and a small Tiger jumped down from the back of the curricle, and ran to the horses' heads. The exquisite cast aside the rug that covered his legs, and alighted, permitting Miss Creed, a glimpse of white corduroy breeches, and short boots with very long tops. He passed into the inn while she was still blinking at such a vision, and set up a shout for the landlord.

'Good gracious, sir, such an odd creature has arrived! I wish you could have seen him!' Pen exclaimed. 'Only fancy! He has a blue-and-yellow striped waistcoat, and a spotted tie!'

'I wear them myself sometimes,' murmured Sir Richard apologetically.

She turned, determined to keep the conversation to such unexceptionable subjects. 'You, sir? I cannot believe such a thing to be possible!'

'It sounds remarkably like the insignia of the Four-Horse Club,' he said. 'But what in the name of all that's wonderful should one of our members be doing in Queen Charlton?'

A confused sound of conversation reached them from the entrance parlour. Above it the landlord's voice, which was rather high-pitched, said clearly: 'My best parlour is bespoke by Sir Richard Wyndham, sir, but if your honour would condescend—'

'*What?*'

There was no difficulty at all in hearing the monosyllable, for it was positively shouted.

'Oh, my God!' said Sir Richard, and turned to run a quick eye over Miss Creed. 'Careful now, brat! I fancy I know this traveller. What in the world have you done to that cravat? Come here!'

He had barely time to straighten Miss Creed's crumpled tie when the same penetrating voice uttered: 'Where? In there? Don't be a fool, man! I know him well!' and hasty footsteps were heard crossing the entrance parlour.

The door was flung open; the gentleman in the fifteen-caped driving coat strode in, and, upon setting eyes on Sir Richard, cast his hat and gloves from him, and started forward, exclaiming: '*Ricky!* Ricky, you dog, what are you doing here?'

Pen, effacing herself by the window, watched the tall young man wring Sir Richard's hand, and wondered where she could have seen him before. He seemed vaguely familiar to her, and the very timbre of his reckless voice touched a chord of memory.

'Well, upon my soul!' he said. 'If this don't beat all! I don't know what the deuce you're doing here, but you're the very man I want to see. Ricky, does that offer of yours hold good? Damme, if it does, I'm off to the Peninsula by the first boat! There's the devil and all to pay in the family this time!'

'I know it,' Sir Richard said. 'I take it you have heard the news about Beverley?'

'My God, don't tell me *you've* heard it?'

'I found him,' Sir Richard said.

The Honourable Cedric clapped a hand to his head. 'Found him? What, *you* weren't looking for him, Ricky, were you? How many more people know about it? Where's that damned necklace?'

'Unless the law officers have now got it, I fancy it is in one Captain Trimble's pocket. It was once in my possession, but I handed it over to Beverley, to—er—restore to your father. When he was murdered—'

Cedric recoiled, his jaw dropping. 'What's that? Murdered? Ricky, not Bev?'

'Ah!' said Sir Richard, 'so you *didn't* know?'

'Good God!' Cedric said. His roving eye alighted on the decanter and the glasses which the waiter had left upon the table. He poured himself out a glass, and tossed it off. 'That's better. So Bev's been murdered, has he? Well, I came here with a little notion of murdering him myself. Who did it?'

'Trimble, I imagine,' Sir Richard replied.

Cedric paused in the act of refilling his glass, and looked up quickly. 'For the sake of the necklace?'

'Presumably.'

To Pen's astonishment, Cedric broke into a shout of laughter. 'Oh, by God, but that's rich!' he gasped. 'Oh, blister me, Ricky, that's hell's own jest!'

Sir Richard put up his eyeglass, surveying his young friend through it with faint surprise. 'I did not, of course, expect the news to prostrate you with grief, but I confess I was hardly prepared—'

'Paste, dear old boy! nothing but paste!' said Cedric, doubled up over a chair back.

The eyeglass dropped. 'Dear me!' said Sir Richard. 'Yes, I ought to have thought of that. Saar?'

'Years ago!' Cedric said, wiping his streaming eyes with the Belcher handkerchief. 'Only came out when I—I, mark you, Ricky!—set the Bow Street Runners on to it! I thought m' father was devilish lukewarm over the affair. Never guessed, however! There was m' mother sending messenger upon messenger up to Brook Street, and the girls nagging at me, so off I went to Bow Street. Fact is, my head's never at its best in the morning. No sooner had I set the bloodhounds on to the damned necklace than I began to think the thing over. I told you Bev was a bad man, Ricky. I'll lay you a monkey he stole the necklace.'

Sir Richard nodded. 'Quite true.'

'Damme, I call that going too far! M' mother had a secret hiding place made for it in her chaise. M' father knew. I knew. Bev knew. Dare say the girls knew. But no one else, d'ye mark me? Thought it all out at White's. Nothing like brandy for clearing the head! Then I remembered that Bev took himself off to Bath last week. Never could imagine why! Thought I'd better look into things m'self. Just made up my mind to take a little journey to Bath, when in walked m' father in a deuce of a pucker. He'd heard from Melissa that I'd been to Bow Street. Pounced on me, looking as queer as Dick's hatband, and wanting to know what the devil I meant by setting the Runners on to it. Now, Ricky, dear boy, would you say I was a green 'un? Give you my word I never guessed what was coming! Always thought m' father meant to stick to the diamonds! He sold 'em three years ago when he had that run of bad luck! Had 'em copied, so that no one was the wiser, not even my mother! He was as mad as Bedlam with me, and damme, I don't blame him, for if my Runner ran the necklace to earth there'd be the devil to pay, and no pitch hot! So that's why I'm here. But what beats me is, what in thunder brought *you* here?'

'You told me to run,' murmured Sir Richard.

'So I did, but to tell you the truth I never thought you would, dear boy. But why here? Out with it, Ricky! You never came here in search of Bev!'

'No, I didn't. I came upon purely–er–family affairs. I fancy you have never met my young cousin, Pen Brown?'

'Never knew you had a cousin of that name. Who is he?' said Cedric cheerfully.

Sir Richard made a slight movement, indicating Pen's presence. The room was deeply shadowed, for the waiter had not yet brought in the candles, and the twilight was fading. Cedric turned his head, and stared with narrowed eyes towards the window seat, where Pen had been sitting, half hidden by the curtains. 'Damme, I never saw you!' he exclaimed. 'How d'ye do?'

'Mr Brandon, Pen,' Sir Richard explained.

She came forward to shake hands, just as the waiter entered with a couple of chandeliers. He set them down upon the table, and moved across the room to draw the curtains. The sudden glow of candlelight for a moment dazzled Cedric, but as he released Pen's hand his vision cleared, and became riveted on her guinea-gold curls. A portentous frown gathered on his brow, as he struggled with an erratic memory. 'Hey, wait a minute!' he said. 'I haven't seen you before, have I?'

'No, I don't think so,' replied Pen in a small voice.

'That's what I thought. But there's something about you–did you say he was a cousin of yours, Ricky?'

'A distant cousin,' amended Sir Richard.

'Name of Brown?'

Sir Richard sighed. 'Is it so marvellous?'

'Damme, dear boy, I've known you from m' cradle, but I never heard of any relative of yours called Brown! What's the game?'

'If I had guessed that you were so interested in the ramification of my family, Cedric, I would have informed you of Pen's existence.'

The waiter, interested, but unable to prolong his labours in the parlour, slowly and sadly withdrew.

'Something devilish queer about this!' pronounced Cedric, with a shake of his head. 'Something at the back of my mind, too. Where's that burgundy?'

'Well, I thought at first I had met you before,' offered Pen. 'But that was because of your likeness to the stam–to the other Mr Brandon.'

'Don't tell me you knew him!' exclaimed Cedric.

'Not very well. We happened to meet him here.'

'I'll tell you what, my lad: he was not fit company for a suckling like you,' said Cedric severely. He frowned upon her again, but apparently abandoned the effort to recall the errant memory, and turned back to Sir Richard. 'But your cousin don't explain your being here, Ricky. Damme, what *did* bring you to this place?'

'Chance,' replied Sir Richard. 'I was—er—constrained to escort my cousin to this neighbourhood, upon urgent family affairs. Upon the way, we encountered an individual who was being pursued by a Bow Street Runner—your Runner, Ceddie—and who slipped a certain necklace into my cousin's pocket.'

'You don't mean it! But did you know Bev was here?'

'By no means. That fact was only revealed to me when I overheard him exchanging somewhat unguarded recriminations with the man whom I suppose to have murdered him. To be brief with you, there were three of them mixed up in his lamentable affair, and one of the three had bubbled the other two. I restored the necklace to Beverley, on the understanding that it should go back to Saar.'

Cedric cocked an eyebrow. 'Steady now, Ricky, steady! I'm not corkbrained, dear old boy! Bev never consented to give the diamonds back—unless he was afraid you were going to mill his canister. Devilish lily-livered, Bev! Was that the way of it?'

'No,' said Sir Richard. 'That was not the way of it.'

'Ricky, you fool, don't tell me you bought him off!'

'I didn't.'

'Promised to, eh? I warned you! I warned you to have nothing to do with Bev! However, if he's dead there's no harm done! Go on!'

'There is really very little more to tell you. Beverley was found—by me—dead, in a spinney not far from here, last night. The necklace had vanished.'

'The devil it had! Y'know, Ricky, this is a damned ugly business! And, the more I think of it the less I understand why you left town in such a hurry, and without a word to anyone. Now, don't tell me you came on urgent family affairs, dear boy! You were disguised that night! Never seen you so foxed in my life! You said you were going to walk home, and by what the porter told George you had it fixed in your head your house was somewhere in the direction of Brook Street. Well, I'll lay anyone what odds they like you did not go to serenade Melissa! Damme, what did happen to you?'

'Oh, I went home!' said Sir Richard placidly.

'Yes, but where did this young sprig come into it?' demanded Cedric, casting a puzzled glance at Pen.

'On my doorstep. He had come to find me, you see.'

'No, damn it, Ricky, that won't do!' protested Cedric. 'Not at three in the morning, dear boy!'

'Of course not!' interposed Pen. 'I had been awaiting him—oh, for hours!'

'On the doorstep?' said Cedric incredulously.

'There were reasons why I did not wish the servants to know that I was in town,' explained Pen, with a false air of candour.

'Well, I never heard such a tale in my life!' said Cedric. 'It ain't like you, Ricky, it ain't like you! I called to see you myself next morning, and I found Louisa and George there, and the whole house in a pucker, with not a man jack knowing where the devil you'd got to. Oh, by jupiter, and George would have it you had drowned yourself?'

'Drowned myself! Good God, why?'

'Melissa, dear boy, Melissa!' chuckled Cedric. 'Bed not slept in—crumpled cravat in the grate—lock of—' He broke off, and jerked his head round to stare at Pen. 'By God, I have it! *Now* I know what was puzzling me! That hair! It was yours!'

'Oh, the devil!' said Sir Richard. 'So that was found, was it?'

'One golden curl under a shawl. George would have it it was a relic of your past. But hell and the devil confound it, it don't make sense! You never went to call on Ricky in the small hours to get your hair cut, boy!'

'No, but he said I wore my hair too long, and that he would not go about with me looking *so*,' said Pen desperately. 'and he didn't like my cravat either. He was drunk, you know.'

'He wasn't as drunk as that,' said Cedric. 'I don't know who you are, but you ain't Ricky's cousin. In fact, it's my belief you ain't even a boy! Damme, you're Ricky's past, that's what you are!'

'I am not!' said Pen indignantly. 'It is quite true that I'm not a boy, but I never saw Richard in my life until that night!'

'Never saw him until that night?' repeated Cedric, dazed.

'No! It was all chance, wasn't it, Richard?'

'It was,' agreed Sir Richard, who seemed to be amused. 'She dropped out of a window into my arms, Ceddie.'

'She dropped out of—give me some more burgundy!' said Cedric.

13

Having fortified himself from the decanter, Cedric sighed, and shook his head. 'No use, it still seems devilish odd to me. Females don't drop out of windows.'

'Well, I didn't drop out precisely. I climbed out, because I was escaping from my relations.'

'I've often wanted to escape from mine, but I never thought of climbing out of a window.'

'Of course not!' said Pen scornfully. 'You are a man!'

Cedric seemed dissatisfied. 'Only females escape out of windows? Something wrong there.'

'I think you are excessively stupid. I escaped out of the window because it was dangerous to go by the door. And Richard happened to be passing at the time, which was a very fortunate circumstance because the sheets were not long enough, and I had to jump.'

'Do you mean to tell me you climbed down the sheets?' demanded Cedric.

'Yes, of course. How else could I have got out, pray?'

'Well, if that don't beat all!' he exclaimed admiringly.

'Oh, that was nothing! Only when Sir Richard guessed that I was not a boy he thought it would not be proper for me to journey to this place alone, so he took me to his house, and cut my hair more neatly at the back, and tied my cravat for me, and—and *that* is why you found those things in his library!'

Cedric cocked an eye at Sir Richard. 'Damme, I knew you'd shot the cat, Ricky, but I never guessed you were as bosky as that!'

'Yes, said Sir Richard reflectively, 'I fancy I must have been rather more up in the world than I suspected.'

'Up in the world! Dear old boy, you must have been clean raddled! And how the deuce did you get here? For I remember now that George said your horses were all in the stables. You never travelled in a hired chaise, Ricky!'

'Certainly not,' said Sir Richard. 'We travelled on the stage.'

'On the—on the—' Words failed Cedric.

'That was Pen's notion,' Sir Richard explained kindly. 'I must confess I was not much in favour of it, and I still consider the stage an abominable vehicle, but there is no denying we had a very adventurous journey. Really, to have gone post would have been sadly flat. We were overturned in a ditch; we became—er—intimately acquainted with a thief; we found ourselves in possession of stolen goods; assisted in an elopement; and discovered a murder. I had not dreamt life could hold so much excitement.'

Cedric, who had been gazing at him open-mouthed, began to laugh. 'Lord, I shall never get over this! *You*, Ricky! Oh Lord, and there was Louisa ready to swear you would never do anything unbefitting a man of fashion, and George thinking you at the bottom of the river, and Melissa standing to it that you had gone off to watch a mill! Gad, she'll be as mad as fire! Out-jockeyed, by Jupiter! Piqued, repiqued, slammed, and capotted!' He once more mopped his eyes with the Belcher handkerchief. 'You'll have to buy me that pair of colours, Ricky: damme, you owe it to me, for I told you to run, now, didn't I?'

'But he did not run!' Pen said anxiously. 'It was *I* who ran. Richard didn't.'

'Oh yes, I did!' said Sir Richard, taking snuff.

'No, no, you know you only came to take care of me; you said I could not go alone!'

Cedric looked at her in a puzzled way. 'Y'know, I can't make this out at all! If you only met three nights ago, you can't be eloping!'

'Of course we're not eloping! I came here on—on a private matter, and Richard pretended to be my tutor. There is not a question of eloping!'

'Tutor? Lord! I thought you said he was your cousin?'

'My dear Cedric, do try not to be so hidebound!' begged Sir Richard. 'I have figured as a tutor, an uncle, a trustee, *and* a cousin.'

'You seem to me to be a sad romp!' Cedric told Pen severely. 'How old are you?'

'I am seventeen, but I do not see that it is any concern of yours.'

'Seventeen!' Cedric cast a dismayed glance at Sir Richard. 'Ricky, you madman! You're in the basket now, the pair of you! And what your mother and Louisa will say, let alone that sour-faced sister of mine—! When is the wedding?'

'That,' said Sir Richard, 'is the point we were discussing when you walked in on us.'

'Better get married quietly somewhere where you ain't known. You know what people are!' Cedric said, wagging his head. 'Damme, if I won't be best man!'

'Well, you won't,' said Pen, flushing. 'We are not going to be married. It is quite absurd to think of such a thing.'

'I know it's absurd,' replied Cedric frankly. 'But you should have thought of that before you started jauntering about the country in this crazy fashion.

There's nothing for it now: you'll have to be married!'

'I won't!' Pen declared. 'No one need ever know that I am not a boy, except you, and one other, who doesn't signify.'

'But, my dear girl, it won't do! Take it from me, it won't do! If you don't know that, I'll be bound Ricky does. I daresay you don't fancy the notion, but he's a devilish fine catch, you know. Blister it, we were looking to him to bring our family fortunes about, so we were!' he added, with an irrepressible chuckle.

'I think you are vulgar and detestable!' said Pen. 'I have got a great deal of money of my own; in fact, I'm an heiress, and I have a very good mind not to marry anyone!'

'But only think what a waste!' protested Cedric. 'If you are an heiress, and you can't stomach the notion of marrying Ricky, for which I won't blame you, for the Lord knows he's no lady's man!—a hardened case, m' dear: never looked seriously at a female in his life!—I suppose you wouldn't make shift with your humble servant?'

'Your conversation, my dear Cedric, is always edifying,' said Sir Richard icily.

But Pen, instead of being offended, giggled. 'No, thank you. I shouldn't like to marry you at all.'

'I was afraid you wouldn't. You'll have to take Ricky, then! Nothing else for it! But you're too young for him: no getting away from that! Damme, if I know what maggot got into your heads to set you off on this crazy adventure!'

'You are labouring under a misapprehension, Cedric,' said Sir Richard. 'There is nothing I desire more than to marry Pen.'

'Well, of all things!' gasped Cedric. 'And here was I thinking you a hopeless case!'

'I am going to bed,' stated Pen.

Sir Richard moved across the door to open it for her. 'Yes, my child: go to bed. But pray do not let Cedric's artless chatter prejudice you! For addle-pated folly I have never met his equal.' He possessed himself of her hand, as he spoke, and lifted it to his lips. 'Pleasant dreams, brat,' he said softly.

She felt a lump rise in her throat, achieved a tremulous smile, and fled, but not before she had heard Cedric exclaim in tones of the liveliest surprise: 'Ricky, you ain't really in love with that chit, are you?'

'I think,' said Sir Richard, closing the door, 'that we shall be more usefully employed in discussing the circumstances which brought you here, Cedric.'

'Oh, by all means!' Cedric said hastily. 'Beg pardon! No intention of prying into your affairs, dear boy; not the least in the world! Now, don't get into a miff! You know how it is with me! Never could keep a discreet tongue in my head!'

'That is what I am afraid of,' Sir Richard said dryly.

'Mum as an oyster!' Cedric assured him. 'But that you of all men, Ricky—! That's what beats me! However, no concern of mine! What's all this you were telling me about Bev?'

'He's dead. That seems to be the most important thing.'

'Well, it's no good expecting me to pull a long face over it. He was a bad man, take my word for it! What was he doing in this spinney you talk of?'

'As a matter of fact, he went there to meet me,' said Sir Richard.

Cedric frowned at him. 'More in this than meets the eye. Why, Ricky?'

'To be plain with you, he had hit upon the notion of extorting money from me by threatening to make known the fact that my supposed cousin was a girl in disguise.'

'Yes, that's Bev all over,' nodded Cedric, quite unsurprised. 'Offered to pay his debts, didn't you?'

'Oh, I had offered that earlier in the day! Unfortunately Captain Trimble learned of my appointment with Beverley in the spinney, and went there before me. I fancy he had nothing more than robbery in mind. There was a witness to the meeting, who described how a quarrel sprang up, and how Trimble struck Beverley down, searched his pockets, and made off. Possibly he thought he had merely stunned him. When I found him his neck was broken.'

'Jupiter!' said Cedric, giving a whistle of consternation. 'It's worse than I thought, then! The devil! There will be no hushing this up. They don't suspect you of having a hand in it, do they, Ricky?'

'I am fast acquiring a most unsavoury reputation in this neighbourhood, but so far I have not been arrested for murder. What precise object had you in coming here?'

'Why, to choke the truth out of Bev, of course! Couldn't get it out of my head he was at the bottom of that robbery. He was badly dipped, y'know. M' father wants my bloodhound called off, too, but I'm damned if I can come up with any trace of him. If you met the fellow on the Bristol road, that would account for my missing him. I went to Bath. Last I heard of Bev was that he was there, with Freddie Fotheringham. Freddie told me Bev had gone off to stay with some people called Luttrell, living at a place near here. So I saw m' mother, got the full story of the robbery out of her, and came on here. *Now* what's to do?'

'You had better make the acquaintance of the local magistrate. A man who might well be Trimble was taken up in Bath today, but whether the necklace was on him I know not.'

'Must lay my hands on that plaguey necklace!' frowned Cedric. 'Won't do if the truth about that were to come out. But what are you going to do, Ricky? It seems to me you're in the deuce of a coil too.'

'I shall no doubt be able to answer that question when I have talked the matter over with Pen tomorrow,' Sir Richard replied.

But Sir Richard was not destined to have the opportunity of talking over any matter with Miss Creed upon the morrow. Miss Creed, going dejectedly up to bed, sat for a long time at the open window of her room, and gazed blindly out upon the moonlit scene. She had spent, she decided, quite the most miserable day of her life, and the sudden incursion of Cedric Brandon had done nothing to alleviate her heaviness of heart. It was apparent that Cedric considered her adventure only one degree less fantastic than the notion that she was to marry Sir Richard. According to his own words, he had known Sir Richard from the cradle, so that it was fair to assume that he was very well acquainted with him. He gave it as his opinion that she must marry Sir Richard, which was tantamount to saying, she reflected, that she had put Sir Richard into the uncomfortable position of being obliged to offer for her. It was most unjust, Pen thought, for Sir Richard had not been sober when he had insisted on accompanying her into Somerset, and he had, moreover, done it out of sheer solicitude for her safety. It had not occurred to her that a gentleman so many years her senior could be supposed to compromise her, or to engage his own honour so disastrously. She had liked him from the moment of setting eyes on him; she had plunged into terms of intimacy with him in the shortest possible time;

and had, indeed, felt as though she had known him all her life. She thought herself more stupid even than Lydia Daubenay not to have realized before ever they had reached Queen Charlton, that she had tumbled headlong in love with him. She had refused to look beyond her meeting with Piers, yet she could not but admit to herself now that she had been by no means anxious to summon Piers to her side when she had arrived at the George. By the time she did come face to face with him, he would have had to have been a paragon indeed to have won her from Sir Richard.

His conduct had been anything rather than that of a paragon. He had spoiled everything, Pen thought. He had accused her of impropriety, and had forced Sir Richard into making a declaration he had surely not wanted to make.

"Because I don't suppose he loves me at all," Pen argued to herself. "He never said so until Piers was so odious: in fact, he treated me just as if he really was a trustee, or an uncle, or somebody years and years older than I am, which I dare say was what made it all seem quite proper to me, and not in the least scandalous. Only then we fell into so many adventures, and he was obliged to fob off Aunt Almeria, and then the stammering man guessed I was a girl, and Piers was disagreeable, and I got into a scrape through Lydia's folly, and the Major came, and now this other Mr Brandon knows about me, and the end of it is I have placed poor Richard in the horridest situation imaginable! There is only one thing for it: I shall have to run away."

This decision, however, made her feel so melancholy that several large tears brimmed over her eyelids and rolled down her cheeks. She wiped them away, telling herself it was stupid to cry. "Because if he doesn't want to marry me, I don't want to marry him—much; and if he does, I dare say he will come to visit me at Aunt's house. No, he won't. He'll forget all about me, or very likely be glad that he is rid of a badly behaved, tiresome ch-charge! Oh dear!"

So sunk in these dismal reflections did she become that it was a long time before she could rouse herself sufficiently to prepare for bed. She even forgot the elopement she had helped to arrange, and heard the church clock strike midnight without so much as recalling that Lydia should now be stepping up into the hired post chaise, with or without a cage of lovebirds.

She spent a miserable night, disturbed by unquiet dreams, and tossing from side to side in a way that soon untucked all the sheets and blankets, and made the bed so uncomfortable that by six in the morning, when she finally awoke to find the room full of sunlight, she was very glad to leave it.

A considerable portion of her waking hours had been spent in considering how she could run away without Sir Richard's knowing anything about it. A carrier was used to go into Bristol on certain days, she remembered, and she made up her mind either to buy a seat on his wagon, or, if it was not one of his days, to walk to Bristol, and there book a seat on the London stagecoach. Bristol was not more than six or seven miles distant from Queen Charlton, and there was, moreover, a reasonable hope of being offered a lift in some conveyance bound for the town.

She dressed herself, and very nearly started to cry again when she struggled with the folds of the starched muslin cravat, because it was one of Sir Richard's. Once dressed, she packed her few belongings in the cloak bag he had lent her, and tiptoed downstairs to the parlour.

The servants, though she could hear them moving about in the coffee room and the kitchen, had not yet come into the parlour to draw back the blinds, and to set the room to rights. In its untidy, overnight state it looked dispiriting. Pen pulled the blinds apart, and sat down at the writing table to compose a letter of farewell to Sir Richard.

It was a very difficult letter to write, and seemed to entail much nose blowing, and many watery sniffs. When she had at last finished it, Pen read it through rather dubiously, and tried to erase a blot. It was not a satisfactory letter, but there was no time to write another, so she folded and sealed it, wrote Sir Richard's name on it, and propped it up on the mantelpiece.

In the entrance parlour she encountered the pessimistic waiter who had served them on the previous evening. His eyes seemed even duller than usual, and beyond staring in a ruminative fashion at her cloak bag, he evinced no interest in Pen's early rising.

She explained to him glibly that she was obliged to go into Bristol, and asked if the carrier would be passing the George. The waiter said that he would not be passing, because Friday was not his day. 'If you had wanted him yesterday, it would have been different,' he added reproachfully.

She sighed. 'Then I shall be obliged to walk.'

The waiter accepted this without interest, but just as she reached the door he bethought him of something, and said in a voice of unabated gloom: 'The missus is going to Bristol in the trap.'

'Do you think she would take me with her?'

The waiter declined to offer an opinion, but he volunteered to go and ask the missus. However, Pen decided to go herself, and, penetrating to the yard at the back of the inn, found the landlord's wife packing a basket into the trap, and preparing to mount into it herself.

She was surprised at Pen's request, and eyed the cloak bag with suspicion, but she was a stout, good-natured woman, and upon Pen's assuring her mendaciously that Sir Richard was well aware of her projected expedition, she allowed her to get into the trap, and to stow the cloak bag under the seat. Her son, a phlegmatic young man, who chewed a straw throughout the journey, took the reins, and in a few minutes the whole party was proceeding up the village street at a sober but steady pace.

'Well, I only hopes, sir, as I'm not doing wrong,' said Mrs Hopkins, as soon as she had recovered from the exertion of hoisting her bulk into the trap. 'I'm sure I was never one to pry into other folks' business, but if you *was* running away from the gentleman which has you in charge, I should get into trouble, that's what.'

'Oh no, indeed you won't!' Pen assured her. 'You see, we have not our own carriage with us, or—or I should not have been obliged to trouble you in this way.'

Mrs Hopkins said that she was not one to grudge trouble, and added that she was glad of company. When she discovered Pen had had no breakfast, she was very much shocked, and after much tugging and wheezing, pulled out the basket from under the seat, and produced out of it a large packet of sandwiches, a pie wrapped in a napkin, and a bottle of cold tea. Pen accepted a sandwich, but refused the pie, a circumstance which made Mrs Hopkins say that although the young gentleman would have been welcome to it, it was, in point of fact, a gift for her aunt, who lived in Bristol. She further disclosed that she was bound for the town to meet her sister's second girl, who was coming down on the London stage to work as a chambermaid at the George. The ball of conversation having been set rolling in this easy fashion, the journey passed pleasantly enough, Mrs Hopkins furnishing

Pen with so exhaustive an account of the various trials and vicissitudes which had befallen every member of her family, that by the time the trap drew up at an inn in the centre of Bristol, Pen felt that there could be little she did not know about the good lady's relatives.

The stage was not due to arrive in Bristol until nine o'clock, at which hour the coach setting out for London would leave the inn. Mrs Hopkins set off to visit her aunt, and Pen, having booked a seat on the stage, and deposited the cloak bag at the inn, sallied forth to lay out her last remaining coins on provisions to sustain her during the journey.

The streets were rather empty at such an early hour, and some of the shops had not yet taken down their shutters, but after walking for a few minutes, and observing with interest the changes which, in five years, had taken place in the town, Pen found a cookshop that was open. The smell of freshly baked pies made her feel hungry, and she went into the shop, and made a careful selection of the viands offered for sale.

When she came out of the shop, there was still half an hour to while away before the coach was due to start, and she wandered into the market-place. Here there were quite a number of people already busy about the day's business. Pen caught sight of Mrs Hopkins bargaining with a salesman over the price of a length of calico, but since she did not feel that she wanted to learn any more details about the Hopkins' family, she avoided her, and pretended to be interested in a clockmaker's shop. So intent was she on avoiding Mrs Hopkins' motherly eye, that she was blissfully unaware that she herself was being closely scrutinized by a thickset man in a duffle coat, and a wide-brimmed hat, who, after gazing fixedly at her for some moments, stepped up to her, and, laying a heavy hand on her shoulder, said deeply: 'Got you!'

Pen jumped guiltily, and looked round in sudden alarm. The voice sounded familiar; to her dismay she found herself staring up into the face of the Bow Street Runner who had overtaken Jimmy Yarde at the inn near Wroxham.

'Oh!' she said faintly. 'Oh! Are you not the—the man I met—the other day? Good—good morning! A fine day, isn't—isn't it?'

'That's so, young sir,' said the Runner, in a grim tone. 'And a werry complete hand you be, and no mistake! I've been wanting another touch at you. Ah, and when Nat Gudgeon wants a touch at a cove, he gets it, and no mistake about that neither! You come along with me!'

'But I haven't done anything wrong! Indeed I haven't!' said Pen.

'If you haven't, then there's no call for you to be scared of me,' said Mr Gudgeon, with what seemed to her a fiendish leer. 'But what I been thinking, young sir, is, that you and that fine gentleman what was with you loped off mighty quick from that there inn. Why, anyone might have thought, so they might, as how you had took an unaccountable dislike to me!'

'No, no, we didn't! But there was nothing to stay for, and we were already much delayed.'

'Well,' said Mr Gudgeon, shifting his grip to her arm, and grasping this firmly above the elbow, 'I've got a fancy to question you more particular, young sir. Now, don't you make the werry great mistake of trying to struggle with me, because it won't do you no good. Maybe you ain't never heard tell on a cove by the name o' Yarde: likewise you wouldn't reckernize a set o' sparklers if you was to see one. Lor'! if I had a brace of meggs for every green-looking young chub like you which I've took up—ah, and shut up in the Whit just as snug as you please!—I'd be a werry rich man, so I would. You come along with me, and stop trying to gammon me, because I've got a werry strong notion you know a deal more about a certain set o' sparklers nor what you're wishful I should get wind of.'

By this time, the attention of several persons had been attracted, and a small crowd was beginning to gather. Pen cast a hunted look round. She saw the aghast face of Mrs Hopkins, but no means of escape, and gave herself up for lost. Mr Gudgeon evidently meant to march her off to the gaol, or at any rate to some place of safe-keeping, where her sex, she suspected, would soon be discovered. Meanwhile, the crowd was swelling, several members of it loudly demanding to know what the young gentleman had done, and one knowledgeable individual explaining to his neighbours that that was one of they Bow Street Runners from London, that was. Nothing would serve her, Pen decided, but a certain measure of frankness. Accordingly, she made no attempt to break away from the Runner's hold, but said in as calm a tone as she was able to assume: 'Indeed, I do not mind going with you at all. In fact, I know just what you want, and I dare say I can furnish you with some very valuable information.'

Mr Gudgeon, who was not accustomed to be met with any appearance of sang froid, was not in the least softened by this speech. He said in a shocked voice: 'There's a sauce! Ay, you're a rare gager, young as you be! Why, you young warmint, and you with your mother's milk not dry on your lips! You come along, and no bamming, now!'

A section of the crowd showed a disposition to accompany then, but Mr Gudgeon addressed these gentry in such fierce accents that they dispersed in a hurry, and left him to escort his captive out of the market-place in lonely state.

'You are making a great mistake,' Pen told the Runner. 'You are searching for the Brandon diamonds, are you not? Well, I know all about them, and, as a matter of fact, Mr Brandon wishes you to stop searching for them.'

'Ho!' said Mr Gudgeon, with deep meaning. 'He does, does he? Dang me, if ever I see the equal of you for sauce!'

'I wish you will listen to me! I know who has the diamonds, and, what is more, he murdered the other Mr Brandon to get them.'

Mr Gudgeon shook his head in speechless wonder.

'He *did*, I tell you!' Pen said desperately. 'His name is Trimble, and he was in a plot with Jimmy Yarde to steal the necklace! Only it went awry, and the necklace was restored to Mr Beverley Brandon, and then Captain Trimble killed him, and made off with the diamonds. And Mr Cedric Brandon is searching for you high and low, and if you will only go to Queen Charlton you will find him there, and he will tell you that what I say is true!'

'I never heard the like!' gasped Mr Gudgeon, affronted. 'A werry thorough-going young rascal you be, and no mistake about that! And how might you come to know such a powerful deal about these sparklers, might I take the liberty of asking?'

'I know Mr Brandon well,' answered Pen. '*Both* Mr Brandons! And I was in Queen Charlton when the murder was committed. Mr Philips, the magistrate, knows all about me, I assure you!'

Mr Gudgeon was a little shaken by this announcement, and said more mildly: 'I don't say as I disbelieve you, nor I don't say as I believe you neither; but it's an unaccountable queer story you're telling me, young sir, and that's a fact.'

'Yes, I dare say it may seem so to you,' Pen agreed. She felt his grip slacken on her arm, and decided to press home her advantage. 'You had better come with me to Queen Charlton at once, because Mr Brandon wants to see you, and I expect Mr Philips will be very glad of your help in finding Captain Trimble.'

Mr Gudgeon looked at her sideways. 'Either I've been mistook,' he said slowly, 'or you're the most precious young warmint I ever did see. Maybe I will go to this place you talks about, and maybe while I'm gone you'll sit waiting for me where you won't do no harm.'

They had turned into a broad thoroughfare with streets leading off from it on either side. Pen, who had no intention of returning to Queen Charlton, or of being locked up in Bristol gaol, made up her mind, now that Mr Gudgeon's grasp on her arm had become little more than perfunctory, to try the chances of escape. She said airily: 'Just as you please, only I warn you, Mr Brandon will be excessively angry if he hears that you have molested me. Naturally, I do not wish to— Oh, look, look! Quick!'

They were abreast of one of the side streets by this time, and Pen's admirable start brought the runner to a dead halt. She clasped his arm with her free hand, and exclaimed: 'Over there, just turning into that road! It was he! Captain Trimble! He must have seen me, for he set off running at once! oh, do be quick!'

'Where?' demanded Mr Gudgeon, taken off his guard, and looking round wildly.

'*There!*' panted Pen, and tore herself free of his hold, and ran like a deer down the side street.

She heard a shout behind her, but wasted no time in looking back. A woman engaged in scrubbing her front doorstep set up a cry of Stop, thief! and an errand boy with a large basket on his arm, gave a shrill catcall. Pen reached the end of the street with the sound of the hue and cry behind her, turned the corner, saw an alley leading to a huddle of mean dwellings, and sped down it.

It led her into a labyrinth of narrow streets, with dirty gutters, and crazy cottages, and backyards noisome with the refuse left to rot in them. She had never penetrated into this part of the town before, and was soon quite lost. The circumstance did not trouble her much, however, for the noise of the chase had died away in the rear. She did not think that anyone had seen her dive into the alley so that she was able to entertain a reasonable hope of shaking off the pursuit. She stopped running, and began to walk, rather breathlessly, in what she trusted was an easterly direction. After traversing a number of unknown streets, she came at last to a more respectable part of the town, and ventured to enquire the way to the inn where she had left her cloak back. She discovered that she had overshot it, and, further, that the time was now a few minutes after nine. She looked so dismayed that her informant, a stout man in corduroys and a frieze coat, who was just preparing to climb into a gig, asked her whether she wanted the London stagecoach. Upon her admitting that she did, he said philosophically: 'Well, you've missed it.'

'Oh dear, what shall I do?' said Pen, foreseeing a day spent in skulking about the town to escape discovery by Mr Gudgeon.

The farmer, who had been looking her over in a ruminative fashion, said: 'Be you in a hurry?'

'Yes, yes! That is, I have paid for my seat, you see.'

'Well, I'm going to Kingswood myself,' said the farmer. 'You can get up alongside me in the gig, if you like. You'll likely catch up with the stage there.'

She accepted this offer gratefully, for she thought that even if she did not succeed in overtaking the stage she would be safer from Mr Gudgeon at Kingswood than in Bristol. Happily, however, the farmer was driving a fast-trotting young horse, and they reached the main London road before the heavy stage had drawn out of the town. The farmer set Pen down in Kingswood, at the door of the inn, and having ascertained that the coach had not yet called there, bade her a cheerful farewell, and drove off.

Feeling that she had escaped disaster by no more than a hair's breadth, Pen sat down upon the bench outside the inn to await the arrival of the stage. It was late in coming, and the guard, when Pen handed him her ticket, seemed to take it as a personal affront that she had not boarded it in Bristol. He told her, with malign satisfaction, that her cloak bag had been left behind at the Talbot Inn, but after a good deal of grumbling he admitted that she had a right to a seat in the coach, and let down the steps for her to mount into it. She squeezed herself into a place between a fat man and a woman nursing a peevish infant; the door was shut, the steps let up again, and the vehicle resumed its ponderous journey to London.

14

Sir Richard Wyndham was not an early riser, but he was roused from sleep at an unconscionably early hour upon the morning of Pen's flight by the boots, who came into his room with a small pile of linen, which had been laundered in the inn, and his top boots, and told him diffidently that he was wanted downstairs.

Sir Richard groaned, and enquired what time it was. With even greater diffidence, the boots said that it was not quite eight o'clock.

'What the devil?' exclaimed Sir Richard, bending a pained glance upon him.

'Yes, sir,' agreed the boots feelingly, 'but it's that Major Daubenay, sir, in such a pucker as you never did see!'

'Oh!' said Sir Richard. 'It is, is it? The devil fly away with Major Daubenay!'

The boots grinned, but awaited more precise instructions. Sir Richard groaned again, and sat up. 'You think I ought to get up, do you? Bring me my shaving water, then.'

'Yessir!'

'Oh, ah! Present my compliments to the Major, and inform him that I shall be with him shortly!'

The boots went off to execute these commands, and Sir Richard, surveying the beauty of the morning with a jaundiced eye, got out of bed.

When the boots came back with a jug of hot water, he found Sir Richard in his shirt and breeches, and reported that the Major was pacing up and down the parlour more like a wild beast in a circus than a Christian gentleman.

'You appal me,' said Sir Richard unemotionally. 'Just hand me my boots, will you? Alas! Biddle, I never realized your worth until I was bereft of you!'

'Beg pardon, sir?'

'Nothing,' said Sir Richard, inserting his foot into one of the boots, and pulling hard.

Half an hour later he entered the parlour to find his matutinal guest fuming up and down the floor with a large watch in his hand. The Major, whose cheeks were unbecomingly flushed, and whose eyes started quite alarmingly, stabbed at this timepiece with one quivering finger, and said in a suppressed roar: 'Forty minutes, sir! Forty minutes since I entered this room!'

'Yes, I have even surprised myself,' said Sir Richard, with maddening nonchalance. 'Time was when I could not have achieved this result under an hour, but practice, my dear sir, practice, you know, is everything!'

'An hour!' gobbled the Major. 'Practice! Bah, I say! Do you hear me, sir?'

'Yes,' said Sir Richard, flicking a speck of dust from his sleeve. 'And I imagine I am not the only one privileged to hear you.'

'You are a dandy!' uttered the Major, with loathing. 'A dandy, sir! That's what you are!'

'Well, I am glad that the haste with which I dressed has not obscured the fact,' replied Sir Richard amiably. 'But the correct term is Corinthian.'

'I don't care a fig what the correct term may be!' roared the Major, striking the table with his fist. 'It's all the same to me: dandy, Corinthian, or pure popinjay!'

'If I lose my temper with you, which, however, I should be loth to do—at all events, at this hour of the morning—you will discover that you are mistaken,' said Sir Richard. 'Meanwhile, I presume that you did not bring me out of my bed to exchange compliments with me. What, sir, do you want?'

'Don't take that high and mighty tone with me, sir!' said the Major. 'That whelp of yours has made off with my daughter!'

'Nonsense!' said Sir Richard calmly.

'Nonsense, is it? Then let me tell you that she has gone, sir! Gone, do you hear me? And her maid with her!'

'Accept my condolences,' said Sir Richard.

'Your condolences! I don't want your damned condolences, sir! I want to know what you mean to do!'

'Nothing at all,' replied Sir Richard.

The Major's eyes positively bulged, and a vein stood out on his heated brow. 'You stand there, and say that you mean to do nothing, when your scoundrel of a cousin has eloped with my daughter?'

'Not at all. I mean to do nothing because my cousin has not eloped with your daughter. You must forgive me if I point out to you that I am getting a little weary of your paternal difficulties.'

'How dare you, sir? how dare you?' gasped the Major. 'Your cousin meets my daughter by stealth in Bath, lures her out at dead of night here, deceives her with false promises, and now—*now*, to crown all, makes off with her, and you say—*you* say that you are weary of *my* difficulties!'

'Very weary of them. If your daughter has left your roof—and who shall blame her?—I advise you not to waste your time and my patience here, but to enquire at Crome Hall whether Mr Piers Luttrell is at home, or whether he also is missing.'

'Young Luttrell! By God, if it were so I should be glad of it! Ay, glad of it, and glad that any man rather than that vicious, scoundrelly whelp of yours, had eloped with Lydia!'

'Well, that is a fortunate circumstance,' said Sir Richard.

'It is nothing of the kind! You know very well it is not young Luttrell! She herself confessed that she had been in the habit of meeting your cousin, and the young dog said in this very room—in this very room, mark you, with you standing by—'

'My good sir, your daughter and my cousin talked a great deal of nonsense, but I assure you they have not eloped together!'

'Very well, sir, very well! Where then is your cousin at this moment?'

'In his bed, I imagine.'

'Then send for him!' barked the Major.

'As you please,' Sir Richard said, and strolled over to the bell, and pulled it.

He had scarcely released it when the door opened, and the Honourable Cedric walked in, magnificently arrayed in a brocade dressing gown of vivid and startling design. 'What the deuce is the matter?' he asked plaintively. 'Never heard such an ungodly racket in my life. Ricky, dear old boy, you ain't *dressed*?'

'Yes,' sighed Sir Richard. 'It is a great bore, however.'

'But, my dear fellow, it ain't nine o'clock!' said Cedric in horrified tones. 'Damme if I know what has come over you! You can't start the day at this hour: it isn't decent!'

'I know, Ceddie, but when in Rome, one—er—is obliged to cultivate the habits of the Romans. Ah, allow me to present Major Daubenay—Mr Brandon!'

'Servant, sir!' snapped the Major, with the stiffest of bows.

'Oh, how d'ye do?' said Cedric vaguely. 'Deuced queer hours you keep in the country!'

'I am not here upon a visit of courtesy!' said the Major.

'Now, don't tell me you've been quarrelling, Ricky!' begged Cedric. 'It sounded devilish like it to me. Really, dear boy, you might have remembered I was sleeping above you. Never at my best before noon, y'know. Besides, it ain't like you!'

He lounged, yawning, across the room to an armchair by the fireplace, and dropped into it, stretching his long legs out before him. The Major glared at him, and said pointedly that he had come to see Sir Richard upon a private matter.

This hint passed over Cedric's head. 'What we want is some coffee—strong coffee!' he said.

A maidservant in a mobbed cap came in just then, and seemed astonished to find the room occupied. 'Oh, I beg pardon, sir! I thought the bell rang!'

'It did,' said Sir Richard. 'Have the goodness to tap on Mr Brown's door, and to request him to step downstairs as soon as he shall have dressed. Major Daubenay wishes to speak to him.'

'Hey, wait a minute!' commanded Cedric. 'Bring some coffee first, there's a good girl!'

'Yes, sir,' said the maid, looking flustered.

'Coffee!' exploded Major Daubenay.

Cedric cocked an intelligent eyebrow. 'Don't like the notion? What shall it be? Myself, I think it's too early for brandy, but if you fancy a can of ale, say the word!'

'I want nothing, sir! Sir Richard, while we waste time in such idle fripperies as these, that young dog is abducting my daughter!'

'Fetch Mr Brown,' Sir Richard told the servant.

'Abduction, by Jupiter!' said Cedric. 'What young dog?'

'Major Daubenay,' said Sir Richard, 'is labouring under the delusion that my cousin eloped last night with his daughter.'

'Eh?' Cedric blinked. An unholy gleam stole into his eys as he glanced from Sir Richard to the Major; he said unsteadily: 'No, by Jove, you don't mean it? You ought to keep him in better order, Ricky!'

'Yes!' said the Major. 'He ought indeed! But instead of that he has— I will not say *abetted* the young scoundrel–but adopted an attitude which I can only decribe as callous, sir, and supine!'

Cedric shook his head. 'That's Ricky all over.' His gravity broke down. 'Oh lord, what the deuce put it into your head that your daughter had gone off with his cousin? I'll tell you what, it's the richest jest I've heard in months! Ricky, if I don't roast you for this for years to come!'

'You are going to the Peninsula, Ceddie,' Sir Richard said, with a lurking smile.

'You are amused, sir!' the Major said, bristling.

'Lord, yes, and so would you be if you knew as much about Wyndham's cousin as I do!'

The maidservant came back into the room. 'Oh, if you please, sir! Mr Brown's not in his room,' she said, dropping a curtsey.

The effect of this pronouncement was startling. The Major gave a roar like that of a baffled bull; Cedric's laughter was cut short; and Sir Richard let his eyeglass fall.

'I knew it! Oh, I knew it!' raged the Major. 'Now, sir!'

Sir Richard recovered himself swiftly. 'Pray do not be absurd, sir!' he said, with more asperity than Cedric ever remembered to have heard in his voice before. 'My cousin has in all probability stepped out to enjoy the air. He is an early riser.'

'If you please, sir, the young gentleman has taken his cloak bag with him.'

The Major seemed to be having considerable difficulty in holding his fury within bounds. Cedric, observing his gobblings with a sapient eye, begged him to be careful. 'I knew a man once who got into just such a taking. He burst a blood vessel. True as I sit here!'

The maidservant, upon whom the Honourable Cedric's charm of manner had not fallen unappreciated, smothered a giggle, and twisted one corner of her apron into a screw. 'There was a letter for your honour upon the mantelshelf when I did the room out,' she volunteered.

Sir Richard swung round on his heel, and went to the fireplace. Pen's note, which she had propped up against the clock, had fallen down, and so missed his eye. He picked it up, a little pale of countenance, and retired with it to the window.

> My dear Richard, *Pen had written.* This is to say goodbye to you, and to thank you very much for all your kindness. I have made up my mind to return to Aunt Almeria, for the notion of our being obliged to marry is preposterous. I shall tell her some tale that will satisfy her. Dear sir, it was truly a splendid adventure. Your very obliged servant, Penelope Creed.
>
> PS. I will send back your cravats and the cloak bag, and indeed I thank you, dear Richard.

Cedric, watching his friend's rigid face, dragged himself out of his chair, and lounged across to lay a hand on Sir Richard's shoulder. 'Ricky, dear boy! Now, what is it?'

'I demand to see that letter!' barked the Major.

Sir Richard fiddled the sheet, and slipped it into his inner pocket. 'Be content sir: my cousin has not eloped with your daughter.'

'I don't believe you!'

'If you mean to give me the lie—' Sir Richard checked himself, and turned to the abigail. 'When did Mr Brown leave this place?'

'I don't know, sir. But Parks was downstairs—the waiter, sir.'

'Fetch him.'

'If your cousin has not gone off with my daughter, show me that letter!' demanded the Major.

The Honourable Cedric let his hand fall from Sir Richard's shoulder, and strolled into the middle of the room, an expression of disdain upon his aristocratic countenance. 'You, sir—Daubenay, or whatever your name may be—I don't know what maggot's got into your head, but damme, I'm tired of it! For the lord's sake, go away!'

'I shall not stir from this room until I know the truth!' declared the Major. 'I should not be surprised if I found that you were both in league with that young whippersnapper!'

'Damme, there's something devilish queer about the air of this place!' said Cedric. 'It's my belief you're all mad!'

At this moment the gloomy waiter came into the room. His disclosure that Pen had gone to Bristol with Mrs Hopkins made Sir Richard's face assume a more mask-like expression than ever, but they could not fail to assuage one at least of the Major's alarms. He mopped his brow, and said gruffly that he saw that he had made a mistake.

'That's what we've been telling you,' Cedric pointed out. 'I'll tell you another thing, sir: I want my breakfast, and I'll be damned if I'll sit down to it with you dancing about the room, and shouting in my ear. It ain't restful!'

'But I don't understand!' complained the Major in a milder tone. 'She said she went out to meet your cousin, sir!'

'I have already told you, sir, that your daughter and my cousin both talked a deal of nonsense,' said Sir Richard, over his shoulder.

'You mean she said it to make me believe—to throw dust in my eyes? Upon my soul!'

'Now, don't start that again!' begged Cedric.

'She has gone off with young Luttrell!' exploded the Major. 'By God, I'll break every bone in his body!'

'Well, we don't mind that,' said Cedric. 'You go and do it, sir! Don't waste a moment! Waiter, the door!'

'Good God, this is terrible!' exclaimed the Major, sinking into a chair, and clapping a hand to his brow. 'Depend upon it, they are half way to the Scottish border by now! As though that were not enough! But there is Philips wanting me to take that wretched girl to Bath this morning, to see whether she can recognize some fellow they have caught there! What am I to say to him? The scandal! My poor wife! I left her prostrate!'

'Run back to her at once!' urged Cedric. 'You have not a moment to spare! Tell me, though, had this fellow the diamonds upon him?'

The Major made a gesture as of one brushing aside a gnat. 'What should I care for that? It is my misguided child I am thinking about!'

'I dare say you don't care, but I do. The man who was murdered was my brother, and those diamonds belong to my family!'

'Your brother? Good God, sir, I am astonished!' said the Major, glaring at him. 'No one—no one, believe me!—would credit you with having sustained such a loss! Your levity, your—'

'Never mind my levity, old gentleman! Has that damned necklace been found?'

'Yes, sir, I understand that the prisoner had a necklace in his possession. And if that is your only concern in this appalling affair—'

'Ricky, I must get my hands on that necklace. I hate to leave you, dear old boy, but there's nothing for it! Where the devil's that coffee? Can't go without my breakfast!' He caught sight of the waiter, who had reappeared in the doorway. 'You there! What the devil do you mean by standing gaping? Breakfast, you gaby!'

'Yes, sir,' said the waiter, sniffing. 'And what will I tell the lady, sir, *if* you please?'

'Tell her we ain't receiving—! What lady?'

The waiter proffered a tray with a visiting card upon it. 'For Sir Richard Wyndham,' he said lugubriously. 'She would be obleeged by the favour of a word with him.'

Cedric picked up the card, and read aloud: 'Lady Luttrell. Who the deuce is Lady Luttrell, Ricky?'

'Lady Luttrell!' said the Major, starting up. 'Here! Ha, is this some dastardly plot?'

Sir Richard turned, a look of surprise in his face. 'Show the lady in!' he said.

'Well, I always knew country life would never do for me,' remarked Cedric, 'but damme, I never realized one half of it till now! Not nine o'clock, and the better part of the county paying morning calls! Horrible, Ricky, horrible!'

Sir Richard had turned away from the window, and was watching the door, his brows slightly raised. The waiter ushered in a good-looking woman of between forty and fifty years of age, with brown hair flecked with grey, shrewd, humorous eyes, and a somewhat masterful mouth and chin. Sir Richard moved to meet her, but before he could say anything the Major had burst into speech.

'So, ma'am! So!' he shot out. 'You wish to see Sir Richard Wyndham, do you? You did not expect to meet me here, I dare say!'

'No,' agreed the lady composedly. 'I did not. However, since we shall be obliged, I understand, to meet one another in future with an appearance at least of complaisance, we may as well make a start. How do you do, Major?'

'Upon my word, you are mighty cool, ma'am! Pray, are you aware that your son has eloped with my daughter?'

'Yes,' replied Lady Luttrell. 'My son left a letter behind to inform me of this circumstance.'

Her calm seemed to throw the Major out of his stride. He said rather lamely: 'But what are we to do?'

She smiled. 'We have nothing to do but to accept the event with as good a grace as we can. You do not like the match, and nor do I, but to pursue the young couple, or to show the world our disapproval, will only serve to make us both ridiculous.' She looked him over with a rather mocking light in her eyes, but he seemed so much taken aback, that she relented, and held out her hand to him. 'Come, Major! We may as well bury the hatchet. I cannot be estranged from my only son; you, I am persuaded, would be equally loth to disown your daughter.'

He shook hands with her, not very graciously. 'I do not know what to say! I am utterly confounded! They have behaved very ill towards us, very ill indeed!'

'Oh yes!' she sighed. 'But did we perhaps behave ill towards them?'

This was plainly going too far for the Major, whose eyes began to bulge again. Cedric intervened hastily: 'Don't set him off again, ma'am, for the lord's sake!'

'Hold your tongue, sir!' snapped the Major. 'But you came here to see Sir Richard Wyndham, ma'am! How is this?'

'I came to see Sir Richard Wyndham upon quite another matter,' she replied. Her glance dwelled for an instant on Cedric, and travelled past him to Sir Richard. 'And you, I think, must be Sir Richard Wyndham,' she said.

He bowed. 'I am at your service, ma'am. Permit me to present Mr Brandon to you!'

She looked quickly towards Cedric. 'Ah, I thought your face familiar! Sir, I hardly know what to say to you, except that I am more deeply distressed than I am well able to express to you.'

Cedric looked startled. 'Nothing to be distressed about on my account, ma'am, nothing in the world! Must beg your ladyship to excuse my appearance! The fact is, these early hours, you know, put a man out!'

'Lady Luttrell refers, I apprehend, to Beverley's death,' said Sir Richard dryly.

'Bev? Oh, of course, yes! Shocking affair! Never was more surprised in my life!'

'It is a source of profound dismay to me that such a thing should have happened while your brother was a guest in my house,' said Lady Luttrell.

'Don't give it a thought, ma'am!' begged Cedric. 'Not your fault—always thought he would come to a bad end—might have happened anywhere!'

'Your callousness, sir, is disgusting!' proclaimed the Major, picking up his hat. 'I will not remain another instant to be revolted by such a display of heartless unconcern!'

'Well, damme, who wants you to?' demanded Cedric. 'Haven't I been trying to get you to go away this past half hour? Never met such a thick-skinned fellow in my life!'

'Escort Major Daubenay to the door, Ceddie,' Sir Richard said. 'I understand that Lady Luttrell wishes to see me upon a private matter.'

'Private as you please, dear boy! Ma'am, your very obedient! *After* you, Major!' He bowed the Major out with a flourish, winked at Sir Richard, and went out himself.

'What an engaging scapegoat!' remarked Lady Luttrell, moving forward into the middle of the parlour. 'I confess, I much disliked his brother.'

'Your dislike was shared by most of his acquaintance, ma'am. Will you not be seated?'

She took the chair he offered, and looked him over rather penetratingly. 'Well, Sir Richard,' she said, perfectly mistress of the situation, 'you are wondering, I dare say, why I have come to call upon you.'

'I think I know,' he replied.

'Then I need not beat about the bush. You are travelling with a young gentleman who is said to be your cousin, I understand. A young gentleman who, if my maid is to be believed, answers to the somewhat unusual name of Pen.'

'Yes,' said Sir Richard. 'We should have changed that.'

'Pen Creed, Sir Richard?'

'Yes, ma'am! Pen Creed.'

Her gaze did not waver from his impassive countenance. 'A trifle odd, sir, is it not?'

'The word, ma'am, should have been fantastic. May I know how you came by your information?'

'Certainly you may. I have lately supported a visit from Mrs Griffin and her son, who seemed to expect to find Pen with me. They told me that she had left their roof in her cousin's second-best suit of clothes, by way of the window. That sounded very like Pen Creed to me. But she was not with me, Sir Richard. It was not until this morning that my maid told me of a golden-haired boy who was putting up with his cousin—yourself, Sir Richard—at this inn. That is why I came. I am sure that you will appreciate that I felt a certain degree of anxiety.'

'Perfectly,' he said. 'But Pen is no longer with me. She left for Bristol this morning, and is now, I must suppose, a passenger on the London stagecoach.'

She raised her brows. 'Still more surprising! I hope that you mean to satisfy my curiosity, sir?'

'Obviously I must do so,' he said, and in a cool, expressionless voice, recounted to her all that had happened since Pen had dropped from her rope of sheets into his arms.

She heard him in attentive silence, and all the time watched him. When he had done, she did not say anything for a moment, but looked thoughtfully at him. After a pause, she said: 'Was Pen very much distressed to find my son head over ears in love with Lydia Daubenay?'

'I did not think so.'

'Oh! And my son, I think you said, showed himself to be shocked at the seeming impropriety of her situation?'

'Not unnaturally, though I could have wished that he had not shown his disapproval quite so plainly. She is very young, you see. It had not occurred to her that there was anything amiss.'

'Piers had never the least tact,' she said. 'I expect he told her that you were in honour bound to marry her.'

'He did, and he spoke no less than the truth.'

'Forgive me, Sir Richard, but did you offer for Pen because you felt your honour to be involved?'

'No, I asked her to marry me because I loved her, ma'am.'

'Did you tell her so, Sir Richard?'

'Yes. But she did not believe me.'

'Perhaps,' suggested Lady Luttrell, 'you had not previously given her reason to suppose that you had fallen in love with her?'

'Madam,' said Sir Richard, with a touch of impatience, 'she was in my care, in a situation of the utmost delicacy! Would you have expected me to abuse her confidence by making love to her?'

'No,' she said, smiling. 'From the little I have seen of you, I should have expected you to have treated her just as I imagine you did: as though you were indeed her uncle.'

'With the result,' he said bitterly, 'that that is how she regards me.'

'Is it indeed?' she said tartly. 'Let me tell you, Sir Richard, that men of twenty-nine, with your air, countenance, and address, are not commonly regarded by young females in the light of uncles.'

He flushed, and smiled a little wryly. 'Thank you! But Pen is not like other young females.'

'Pen,' said Lady Luttrell, 'must be a very odd sort of a female if she has spent all this while in your company and not succumbed to a charm of manner which you must be so well aware that you possess that I do not scruple to mention it. I consider that your conduct in aiding the chit to escape was disgraceful, but since you were drunk at the time I suppose one must overlook that. I do not blame you for anything you have done since you found yourself in the stagecoach: indeed, you have behaved in a manner that would, if I were twenty years younger, make me envy Pen exceedingly. Finally, if she did not spend the better part of last night crying her eyes out, I know nothing about my own sex! Where is the letter she left for you? May I see it?

He drew it from his pocket. 'Pray read it, if you wish. It contains nothing, alas, that may not be read by other eyes than mine.'

She took it from him, read it, and handed it back. 'Just as I thought! Breaking her heart, and determined you shall not know it! Sir Richard, for a man of experience, which I judge you to be, you are a great fool! You never kissed her!'

An unwilling laugh was dragged out of him at this unexpected accusation. 'How could I, situated as we were? She recoiled from the very thought of marriage!'

'Because she thought you had asked her to marry you out of pity! Of course she recoiled!'

'Lady Luttrell, are you serious? Do you indeed think—'

'Think! I know!' said her ladyship. 'Your scruples were very fine, I make no doubt, but how should a chit of Pen's age understand what you were about? She would not care a fig for your precious honour, and I dare say—indeed, I am sure!—that she thought your forbearance mere indifference. And the long and the short of it is that she has gone back to her aunt, and will very likely be bullied into marrying her cousin!'

'Oh no, she will not!' said Sir Richard, with a glance at the clock on the mantelshelf. 'I am desolated to be obliged to leave you, ma'am, but if I am to overtake that stagecoach this side of Chippenham, I must go.'

'Excellent!' she said, laughing. 'Do not waste a thought on me! But having caught the stage, what do you propose to do with Pen?'

'Marry her, ma'am! what else?'

'Dear me, I hope you do not mean to join my foolish son at Gretna Green! I think you had better bring Pen to Crome Hall.'

'Thank you, I will!' he said, with the smile which she privately thought irresistible. 'I am very much in your debt, ma'am.'

He raised her hand to his lips, and kissed it, and left the room, calling for Cedric.

Cedric, who had been partaking of breakfast in the coffee room, lounged out into the entrance parlour. 'The devil take you, Ricky, you're as restless as that plaguey friend of yours! What's the matter now?'

'Ceddie, were you driving your own horses yesterday?'

'Dear old boy, of course I was, but what has that to say to anything?'

'I want 'em,' said Sir Richard.

'But, Ricky, I've got to go to Bath to get hold of that necklace before it's discovered to be made of paste!'

'Take the landlord's gig. I must have a fast pair immediately.'

'The landlord's gig!' gasped Cedric, reeling under the shock. 'Ricky, you *must* be mad!'

'I am not in the least mad. I am going after the London stage, to recover that brat of mine. Be a good fellow, now, and tell them to harness the horses at once!'

'Oh, very well!' Cedric said. 'If that's the way it is! But I'll be satisfied with nothing less than a cavalry regiment, mind!'

'You shall have anything you like!' promised Sir Richard, already half way up the stairs.

'Mad, quite mad!' said Cedric despairingly, and set up a shout for an ostler.

Ten minutes later, the bays were harnessed to the curricle, and Sir Richard had stepped out into the yard, pulling on his gloves. 'Famous!' he said. 'I hoped you were driving your bays.'

'If you lame 'em—'

'Ceddie, are you–is it possible that you are going to tell me how to drive?' asked Sir Richard.

Cedric, who was still clad in his exotic dressing gown, leaned against the doorpost, and grinned. 'You'll spring 'em. *I* know you!'

'If I lame them, I will make you a present of my own greys!' said Sir Richard, gathering up the reins.

'Part with your greys?' exclaimed Cedric. 'No, no, you'd never bring yourself to do that, Ricky!'

'Don't disturb yourself: I shan't have to.'

Cedric made a derisive sound, and lingered to watch him mount on to the box seat. A commotion behind him distracted his attention, and he turned in time to see Mrs Hopkins enter the inn through the front door, closely followed by a thickset man in a frieze coat, and a broad-brimmed hat. Mrs Hopkins was labouring under great agitation, and sank immediately into a chair, volubly explaining to the bewildered landlord that she had never had such a turn in her life, and did not expect to recover from her palpitations for a twelvemonth. 'Took up by a Bow Street Runner, Tom!' she panted. 'And him so innocent-seeming as never was!'

'Who?' demanded her spouse.

'That poor young gentleman which is Sir Richard's cousin! Under my very eyes, Tom, and me not dreaming of such a thing! And then if he didn't break away, the which I can't but be glad of, whatever anyone may say, Mr Gudgeon not excepted, for a nicer-spoken young gentleman I never did see, and I'm a mother myself, and I have a heart, though others may not, naming no names, and meaning no offence!'

'My God, here's a pretty coil!' exclaimed Cedric, grasping with remarkable swiftness the gist of her remarks. 'Hi, Ricky, wait!'

The bays were dancing with impatience. 'Stand away from their heads!' commanded Sir Richard.

'And here's Mr Gudgeon himself, wishful to see Sir Richard and Mr Brandon very particular, which I was obliged to take him up in the trap, though little I want Bow Street Runners, or the like, in my house, as you well know, Tom!'

'*Ricky!*' shouted Cedric, striding out into the yard. 'Wait, man! That bloodhound of mine is here, and there's the devil to pay!'

'Fob him off, Cedric, fob him off!' called Sir Richard over his shoulder, and swept out of the yard into the street.

'Ricky, you madman, hold a minute!' roared Cedric.

But the curricle had bowled out of sight. The ostler enquired whether he should run after it.

'Run after my bays?' said Cedric scornfully. 'You'd need wings, not legs, to catch them, my good fool!'

He turned back to the inn, encountering in the doorway Lady Luttrell, who had come out to see what all the shouting was about.

'What is the matter, Mr Brandon?' she asked. 'You seem very much put out.'

'Matter, ma'am! Why, here's Richard gone off after the London stage, and that crazy girl of his taken up by the Bow Street Runner in Bristol!'

'Good God, this is horrible!' she exclaimed. 'Sir Richard must be recalled at all costs! The child must be rescued!'

'Well, by all accounts she seems to have rescued herself,' said Cedric. 'But where she may be now, the Lord only knows! However, I'm glad that Runner has arrived: I was getting deuced tired of hunting for him.'

'But is it impossible to stop Sir Richard?' she asked urgently.

'Lord, ma'am, he's half way to the London road by now!' said Cedric.

This pronouncement was not strictly accurate. Sir Richard, driving out of Queen Charlton at very much the same time as Miss Creed was boarding the Accommodation coach at Kingswood, chose to take the road to Bath rather than that which led to Keynsham, and thence, due north, through Oldland to join the Bristol road at Warmley. His experience of Accommodation coaches was not such as to induce him to place much confidence in their being likely to cover more than eight miles an hour, and he calculated that if the stage had left Bristol at nine o'clock, which seemed probable, it would not reach the junction of the Bath and Bristol roads until noon at the earliest. The Honourable Cedric's bays, drawing a light curricle, might be depended upon to arrive at Chippenham considerably in advance of that hour, and the Bath road had the advantage of being well known to Sir Richard.

The bays, which seemed to have been fed exclusively on oats, were in fine fettle, and the miles flashed by. They were not, perhaps, an easy pair to handle, but Sir Richard, a notable whip, had little trouble with them, and was so well satisfied with their pace and stamina that he began to toy seriously with the idea of making the Honourable Cedric a handsome offer for them. He was obliged to rein them in to a sedate pace whilst threading his way through the crowded streets of Bath, but once clear of the town he was able to give them their heads on the long stretch to Corsham, and arrived finally in Chippenham to learn that the Accommodation coach from Bristol was not due there for nearly another hour. Sir Richard repaired to the best posting inn, superintended the disposal of the sweating bays, and ordered breakfast. When he had consumed a dish of ham and eggs, and drunk two cups of coffee, he had the bays put-to again, and drove westward along the Bristol road, at a leisurely pace, until he came to a fork, where a weatherbeaten signpost pointed northward to Nettleton and Acton Turville, and westward to Wroxham, Marshfield, and Bristol. Here he reined in, to await the approach of the stage.

It was not long in putting in an appearance. It rounded a bend in the deserted road ahead, a green-and-gold monstrosity, rocking and swaying top-heavily in the centre of the road, with half a dozen outside passengers on the roof, the boot piled high with baggage, and the guard sitting up behind with the yard of tin in his hand.

Sir Richard drew the curricle across the road, hitched up his reins, and jumped lightly down from the box seat. The bays were quiet enough by this time, and except for some fidgeting, showed no immediate disposition to bolt.

Finding his way barred, the stagecoachman pulled up his team, and demanded aggrievedly what game Sir Richard thought he was playing.

'No game at all!' said Sir Richard. 'You have a fugitive aboard, and when

I have taken him into custody, you are at liberty to proceed on your way.'

'Ho, I am, am I?' said the coachman, nonplussed, but by no means mollified. 'Fine doings on the King's Highway! Ah, and so you'll find afore you're much older!'

One of the inside passengers, a red-faced man with very bushy whiskers, poked his head out of the window to discover the reason for the unexpected halt; the guard climbed down from the roof to argue with Sir Richard; and Pen, squashed between a fat farmer, and a woman with a perpetual sniff, had a sudden fear that she had been overtaken by the Bow Street Runner. The sound of the guard's voice, saying: 'There, and if I didn't suspicion him from the werry moment I set eyes on him at Kingswood!' did nothing to allay her alarms. She turned a white, frightened face towards the door, just as it was pulled open, and the steps let down.

The next instant, Sir Richard's tall, immaculate person filled the opening, and Pen, uttering an involuntary sound between a squeal and a whimper, turned first red, and then white, and managed to utter the one word: '*No!*'

'Ah!' said Sir Richard briskly. 'So there you are! Out you come, my young friend!'

'Well, I never did in all my life!' gasped the woman beside Pen. 'Whatever has he been and gone and done, sir?'

'Run away from school,' replied Sir Richard, without a moment's hesitation.

'I haven't! It isn't t-true!' stammered Pen. 'I won't go with you, I w-won't!'

Sir Richard, leaning into the coach, and grasping her hand, said: 'Oh, won't you, by Jove? Don't you dare to defy me, you—brat!'

'Here, guv'nor, steady!' expostulated a kindly man in the far corner. 'I don't know when I've taken more of a fancy to a lad, and there's no call for you to bully him, I'm sure! Dare say there's many of us have wanted to run away from school in our time, eh?'

'Ah,' said Sir Richard brazenly, 'but you do not know the half of it! You think he looks a young innocent, but I could tell you a tale of his depravity which would shock you.'

'Oh, how dare you?' said Pen indignantly. 'It isn't true! Indeed, it isn't!'

The occupants of the coach had by this time ranged themselves into two camps. Several persons said that they had suspected the young varmint of running away from the start, and Pen's supporters demanded to know who Sir Richard was, and what right he had to drag the poor young gentleman out of the coach.

'Every right!' responded Sir Richard. 'I am his guardian. In fact, he is my nephew.'

'I am not!' stated Pen.

His eyes looked down into hers, with so much laughter in them that she felt her heart turn over. 'Aren't you?' he said. 'Well, if you are not my nephew, brat, *what are you?*'

Aghast, she choked: 'Richard, you—you—*traitor!*'

Even the kindly man in the corner seemed to feel that Sir Richard's question called for an answer. Pen looked helplessly round, encountered nothing but glances either of disapproval, or of interrogation, and raised her wrathful eyes to Sir Richard's face.

'Well?' said Sir Richard inexorably. '*Are* you my nephew?'

'Yes—no! Oh, you are abominable! You wouldn't *dare!*'

'Yes, I would,' said Sir Richard. 'Are you going to get out, or are you not?'

A man in a plum-coloured coat recommended Sir Richard to dust the young rascal's jacket for him. Pen stared up at Sir Richard, read the determination behind the amusement in his face, and allowed herself to be pulled to her feet, and out of the stuffy coach.

'P'raps when you've quite finished, your honour, you'll be so werry obliging as to move that curricle of yourn!' said the coachman sardonically.

'Richard, I can't go back!' Pen said in a frantic undertone. 'That Runner caught me in Bristol, and I only just contrived to escape!'

'Ah, that must have been what Cedric was trying to tell me!' said Sir Richard, walking up to the bays, and backing them to the side of the road. 'So you were arrested, were you? What a splendid adventure for you, my little one!'

'And I have left your cloak bag behind, and it's no use trying to drag me away with you, because I won't go! I won't, I won't!'

'Why won't you?' asked Sir Richard, turning to look down at her.

She found herself unable to speak. There was an expression in Sir Richard's eyes which brought the colour rushing into her cheeks again, and made her feel as though the world were whirling madly round her. Behind her, the guard, having let up the steps, and shut the door, climbed, grumbling, on to the roof again. The coach began to move ponderously forward. Pen paid no heed to it, though the wheels almost brushed her coat. 'Richard, you—you don't want me! You *can't* want me!' she said uncertainly.

'My darling!' he said. 'Oh, my precious, foolish little love!'

The coach lumbered on down the road; as it reached the next bend, the roof passengers, looking back curiously to see the last of a very odd couple, experienced a shock that made one of them nearly lose his balance. The golden-haired stripling was locked in the Corinthian's arms, being ruthlessly kissed.

'Lawks a-mussy on us! whatever is the world a-coming to?' gasped the roof passenger, recovering his seat. 'I never did in all my born days!'

'Richard, Richard, they can see us from the coach!' expostulated Pen, between tears and laughter.

'Let them see!' said the Corinthian.

The Convenient Marriage

Georgette Heyer

I

Lady Winwood being denied, the morning caller inquired with some anxiety for Miss Winwood, or, in fact, for any of the young ladies. In face of the rumour which had come to her ears it would be too provoking if all the Winwood ladies were to withhold themselves. But the porter held the door fully open and said that Miss Winwood was at home.

Directing the coachman of her extremely smart town carriage to wait for her, Mrs Maulfrey stepped into the dim hall, and said briskly: 'Where is Miss Winwood? You need not be at the trouble of announcing me.'

All the young ladies, it seemed, were in the small saloon. Mrs Maulfrey nodded, and walked across the hall with a click of her high heels. As she ascended the stairs her armazine skirts, spread over very large *paniers à coudes*, brushed the banisters on either side of her. She reflected, not for the first time, that the stairway was too narrow, and the carpet positively shabby. She would be ashamed for her part of such oldfashioned furnishings; but although she claimed cousinship, she was not, she admitted to herself, a Winwood of Winwood.

The small saloon, by which name the porter designated a back sitting-room given over to the use of the young ladies, lay up one pair of stairs, and was well known to Mrs Maulfrey. She tapped with her gloved hand on one of the panels of the door, and entered on the echo of her knock.

The three Misses Winwood were grouped by the window, presenting an artless and agreeable picture. Upon a faded yellow satin sopha sat Miss Winwood and Miss Charlotte, their arms entwined about each other's waists. They were much alike, but Miss Winwood was held to be the greater beauty. Her classic profile was turned to the door, but upon Mrs Maulfrey's rustling entrance she looked round and displayed to the visitor a pair of melting blue eyes and a sweet, arched mouth that formed at the moment an O of mild surprise. A quantity of fair curls dressed without powder and threaded by a blue riband framed her face and tumbled on to her shoulders in several ordered locks.

Miss Charlotte was not seen to advantage beside the Beauty of the Family, but she was a true Winwood, with the famous straight nose and the same blue eyes. Her curls, not quite so fair as her sister's, owed their existence to hot irons, her eyes were of a shallower blue, and her colouring inclined towards the sallow; but she was allowed to be a very well-looking young lady.

Miss Horatia, the youngest of the three, had nothing that declared her lineage except her nose. Her hair was dark, her eyes a profound grey, and her brows, nearly black and rather thick, were quite straight, and gave her a serious, almost frowning, expression. No amount of careful training would induce an arch in them. She was quite half a head shorter than her sisters, and, at the age of seventeen, was obliged regretfully to admit that she was not likely to grow any taller.

When Mrs Maulfrey came into the room Horatia was seated on a low stool by the sopha, propping her chin in her hands, and scowling dreadfully. Or perhaps, thought Mrs Maulfrey, that was just a trick of those preposterous eyebrows.

All three sisters wore morning toilets of worked muslin over slight hoops, with tiffany sashes round their waists. Countrified, thought Mrs Maulfrey, giving her fringed silk mantle a satisfied twitch.

'My dears!' she exclaimed. 'I came the instant I heard! Tell me at once, is it true? Has Rule offered?'

Miss Winwood, who had risen gracefully to receive her cousin, seemed to droop and to grow pale. 'Yes,' she said faintly. 'Alas, it is quite true, Theresa.'

Mrs Maulfrey's eyes grew round with respect. 'Oh, Lizzie!' she breathed. 'Rule! A Countess! Twenty thousand a year, I have heard, and I daresay it may be found to be more!'

Miss Charlotte set a chair for her, observing with a reproving note in her voice: 'We believe Lord Rule to be a most eligible gentleman. Though no one,' she added, clasping Miss Winwood's hand tenderly, 'however genteel, could be worthy of our dearest Lizzie!'

'Lord, Charlotte!' said Mrs Maulfrey tartly, 'Rule's the biggest prize in the market, and you know it. It is the most amazing piece of good fortune ever I heard. Though I will say, Lizzie, you deserve it. Yes, you do, and I am quite enchanted for you. Only to think of the Settlements!'

'I find the thought of Settlements particularly indelicate, Theresa,' said Miss Charlotte. 'Mama will no doubt arrange with Lord Rule, but Lizzie cannot be supposed to concern herself with such sordid questions as the size of Lord Rule's fortune.'

The youngest Miss Winwood, who all the time had continued to sit with her chin in her hands, suddenly raised her head and delivered herself of one shattering word. 'S-stuff!' she said, in a deep little voice that just quivered on a stammer.

Miss Charlotte looked pained; Miss Winwood gave a rather wan smile. 'Indeed, I fear Horry is in the right,' she said sadly. 'It is just the Fortune.' She sank on to the sopha again, and gazed fixedly out of the window.

Mrs Maulfrey became aware that the steady blue eyes were swimming in tears. 'Why, Lizzie!' she said. 'One would think you had had dark tidings instead of a splendid Offer!'

'Theresa!' intoned Miss Charlotte, putting both arms about her sister. 'Is this worthy of you? Can it be that you have forgotten Mr Heron?'

Mrs Maulfrey had forgotten Mr Heron. Her jaw dropped slightly, but she recovered in a moment. 'To be sure: Mr Heron,' she said. 'It is very afflicting, but—Rule, you know! I don't say poor Mr Heron is not a very estimable creature, but a mere lieutenant, dearest Lizzie, and I daresay will soon have to go back to that horrid war in America—it's not to be thought of, my love!'

'No,' said Elizabeth in a suffocated voice. 'Not to be thought of.'

Horatia's dark gaze dwelled bodingly on her second sister. 'I think it would be a very good thing if Charlotte were to have R-Rule,' she pronounced.

'Horry!' gasped Charlotte.

'Lord, my dear, what things you say!' remarked Mrs Maulfrey indulgently. 'It's Elizabeth Rule wants.'

Horatia shook her head vehemently. 'No! Only a Winwood,' she said in the tense way she had. 'All arranged years ago. I d-don't believe he's set eyes on L-Lizzie upwards of half a d-dozen times. It can't signify.'

Miss Charlotte released her sister's hand, and said palpitatingly: 'Nothing—*nothing* would induce me to marry Lord Rule, even if he had offered for me! The very notion of Matrimony is repugnant to me. I have long made up my mind to be a Prop to Mama.' She drew a breath. 'If ever any gentleman could induce me to contemplate the Married State, I assure you, my dear Horry, it would be one far other than Lord Rule.'

Mrs Maulfrey had no difficulty in interpreting this announcement. 'For my part, I like a rake,' she observed. 'And Rule is so extremely handsome!'

'I think,' said Horatia obstinately, 'that M-Mama might have suggested Charlotte.'

Elizabeth turned her head: 'You don't understand, Horry dear. Mama could not do such an odd thing.'

'Does my Aunt force you to it, Lizzie?' inquired Mrs Maulfrey, pleasantly intrigued.

'Oh no, no!' Elizabeth replied earnestly. 'You know Mama's tenderness. She is all consideration, all sensibility! It is only my own consciousness of my Duty to the Family that leads me to take a step so—so disastrous to my happiness.'

'M-mortgages,' said Horatia cryptically.

'Pelham, I suppose?' said Mrs Maulfrey.

'Of course it is Pelham,' replied Charlotte with a touch of bitterness. 'Everything is his fault. Ruin stares us in the face.'

'Poor Pelham!' Elizabeth said, with a sigh for her absent brother. 'I am afraid he is very extravagant.'

'It's his gambling debts, I take it,' opined Mrs Maulfrey. 'My Aunt seemed to think that even your Portions . . .' She left the sentence delicately unfinished.

Elizabeth flushed, but Horatia said: 'You can't blame P-Pel. It's in the blood. One of us must m-marry Rule. Lizzie's the eldest and the p-prettiest, but Charlotte would do very well. Lizzie's promised to Edward Heron.'

'Not "promised", dearest,' Elizabeth said in a low voice. 'We only—hoped, if he could but get his Captaincy, perhaps Mama would consent.'

'Even supposing it, my love,' said Mrs Maulfrey with great good sense, 'what—what, I ask of you, is a Captain of a Line Regiment when compared with the Earl of Rule? And from all I hear the young man has the most meagre of fortunes, and who, pray, is to buy his promotion?'

Horatia said, quite undaunted: 'Edward t-told me that if he had the good fortune to be in another engagement there might be a ch-chance.'

Miss Winwood gave a slight shudder, and lifted one hand to her cheek. 'Don't, Horry!' she begged.

'It doesn't signify,' Mrs Maulfrey declared. 'I know you will say I am unfeeling, my dear Lizzie, but it would not do at all. Why, how would you contrive on the young man's pay? It is all horribly sad, but only think of the position you will fill, the jewels you will have!'

The prospect appeared to affect Miss Winwood with repulsion, but she said nothing. It was left to Horatia to express the sentiments of all three sisters. 'Vulgar!' she said. 'You are, you know, Theresa.'

Mrs Maulfrey blushed, and made a business of arranging her stiff skirts. 'Of course I know *that* would not weigh with Lizzie, but you can't deny it is a brilliant match. What does my Aunt feel?'

'Deeply thankful,' said Charlotte. 'As indeed we must all be, when we consider the straits Pelham has placed us in.'

'Where is Pelham?' demanded Mrs Maulfrey.

'We are not quite certain,' answered Elizabeth. 'We think perhaps in Rome now. Poor Pel is but an indifferent correspondent. But I feel sure we shall hear from him quite soon.'

'Well, he will have to come home for your wedding, I suppose,' said Mrs Maulfrey. 'But, Lizzie, you must tell me! Has Rule paid his addresses? I had not the least idea of anything of the kind, though, naturally, I had heard that it was in a way arranged. But he has been so very—' She apparently thought better of what she had been about to say, and broke off. 'But that's neither here nor there, and I daresay he will be a charming husband. Have you given him your answer, Lizzie?'

'Not yet,' said Elizabeth almost inaudibly. 'I–I too had no notion of it, Theresa. I have met him, of course. He stood up with me for the first two dances at the subscription-ball at Almack's, when Pelham was at home. He was–he has always been–all that is amiable, but that he intended offering for my hand I never dreamed. He waited on Mama yesterday only to–to solicit her permission to pay his addresses to me. There is nothing announced yet, you must understand.'

'Everything of the most correct!' approved Mrs Maulfrey. 'Oh, my love, I cannot help it if you say I have no sensibility, but only conceive of having Rule paying his addresses to one! I declare I would give my eyes–or, I would have,' she corrected herself, 'had I not married Mr Maulfrey. And so,' she added, 'would every other young lady in town! Why, my dears, you would not believe the caps that have been set at him!'

'Theresa, I must, I must request you not to talk in that odious way!' said Charlotte.

Horatia was looking at her cousin with interest. 'Why do you say "only c-conceive of Rule paying his addresses to one"? I thought he was quite old.'

'Old?' said Mrs Maulfrey. 'Rule? Nothing of the sort, my dear! Not a day above thirty-five, I'll stake my reputation. And what a leg! What an air! The most engaging smile!'

'I c-call that old,' said Horatia calmly. 'Edward is only t-twenty-two.'

There did not seem to be much to say after that. Mrs Maulfrey, perceiving that she had culled all the news that her cousins could at this present impart, began to think of taking her leave of them. Though sorry for Elizabeth's evident distress at the magnificent prospect ahead of her she could not in the least understand it, and considered that the sooner Lieutenant Heron was posted back to his regiment the better it would be. Therefore, when the door opened to admit a spare female of uncertain age, who informed Elizabeth with a flutter in her voice that Mr Heron was below and begged the favour of a word with her, she pursed her lips, and looked as disapproving as she could.

Elizabeth's colour fluctuated, but she rose up from the sopha, and said quietly: 'Thank you, Laney.'

Miss Lane seemed to share a little of Mrs Maulfrey's disapproval. She regarded Elizabeth in a deprecating way, and suggested: 'My dear Miss Winwood, do you think you should? Do you think your Mama would like it?'

Elizabeth replied with her gentle air of dignity: 'I have Mama's permission, dear Laney, to–to tell Mr Heron of the approaching change in my estate. Theresa, you won't I know, speak of Lord Rule's obliging offer until–until it is formally announced.'

'Too noble creature!' Charlotte sighed, as the door closed softly behind Miss Winwood. 'How very lowering it is to reflect upon the trials that afflict the Female Sex!'

'Edward is afflicted too,' said Horatia practically. Her penetrating eyes rested on her cousin. 'Theresa, if you ch-chatter about this you will be sorry. Something must be d-done.'

'What can be done, when our sweetest Lizzie goes a Willing Sacrifice to the Altar?' said Charlotte in a hollow voice.

'Trials! Sacrifice!' exclaimed Mrs Maulfrey. 'Lord, one would think Rule an ogre to listen to you! You put me out of all patience, Charlotte. A house in Grosvenor Square, and Meering, which I am told is quite superb, the park seven miles about, and three lodge-gates!'

'It will be a great position,' said the little governess in her breathless way. 'But who should fill it better than dear Miss Winwood? One has always felt that she was destined for a high place.'

'Pho!' said Horatia scornfully, and snapped her fingers '*That* for Rule's great p-position!'

'Miss Horatia, I beg of you, not that ungenteel gesture!'

Charlotte came to the support of her sister. 'You should not snap your fingers, Horry, but you are quite in the right. Lord Rule does very very well for himself in getting a Winwood for his bride.'

Meanwhile Miss Winwood, pausing only for a moment on the staircase to calm the agitation which the news of Mr Heron's arrival had induced, went down to the library on the ground floor of the house.

Here there awaited her a young man in a state of greater agitation than her own.

Mr Edward Heron, of the 10th Foot, at present in America, was stationed in England on Recruiting Service. He had been wounded at the Battle of Bunker's Hill, and sent home shortly afterwards, his wound being of a serious enough nature to preclude his taking further part—for a time at least—in the hostilities abroad. Upon his recovery gazetted, greatly to his chagrin, for Home Service.

The acquaintance between himself and Miss Winwood was of long standing. The younger son of a country gentleman whose estates marched with Viscount Winwood's, he had known the Misses Winwood almost from the hour of his birth. He was of excellent if impoverished family, and had he been the possessor of a rather large fortune might have been deemed an eligible though not brilliant match for Elizabeth.

When Miss Winwood entered the library he arose from a seat by the window, and came towards her with an anxious look of inquiry upon his countenance. He was a personable young man, and looked very well in his scarlet regimentals. He had height, and good shoulders, and a frank, open countenance, rather pale still from prolonged suffering. He carried his left arm a little stiffly, but declared himself to be in perfect health, and very ready to rejoin his regiment.

A glance at Miss Winwood's face informed him that the anxiety occasioned by her brief note had not been misplaced. Taking her hands in a strong clasp he said urgently: 'What has occurred? Elizabeth! something terrible?'

Her lips quivered. She drew her hands away, and put one of them out to grasp a chair-back. 'Oh, Edward, the worst!' she whispered.

He grew paler. 'Your note alarmed me. Good God, what is it?'

Miss Winwood pressed her handkerchief to her mouth. 'Lord Rule was with Mama yesterday–in this very room.' She raised her eyes imploringly to his face. 'Edward, it is all at an end. Lord Rule has offered for my hand.'

A dreadful stillness fell in the shadowed room. Miss Winwood stood with bowed head before Mr Heron, leaning a little on the chair-back.

Mr Heron did not move, but presently he said rather hoarsely: 'And you said—?' But it was hardly a question; he spoke it mechanically, knowing what she must have said.

She made a hopeless gesture. 'What can I say? You know so well how it is with us.'

He took a step away from her, and began to pace up and down the room. 'Rule!' he said. 'Is he very rich?'

'Very rich,' said Elizabeth desolately.

Words crowded in Mr Heron's throat, hurt, angry, passionate words, yet not one of them could he utter. Life had dealt him her cruellest blow, and all that he could find to say, and that in a numb voice which did not seem to belong to him, was: 'I see.' He perceived that Elizabeth was silently weeping, and at once came to her, and took her hands, and drew her to a couch. 'Oh, my love, don't cry!' he said, a catch in his own voice. 'Perhaps it is not too late: we can contrive something–we must contrive something!' But he spoke without conviction, for he knew that he would never have anything to set against Rule's fortune. He put his arms round Elizabeth, and laid his cheek against her curls while her tears fell on his gay scarlet coat.

After a while she drew herself away. 'I am making you unhappy too,' she said.

At that he went down on his knee beside her, and hid his face in her hands. She did not make any effort to pull them away, but said only: 'Mama has been so kind. I am permitted to tell you myself. It is–it must be good-bye, Edward. I have not strength to continue seeing you. Oh, is it wrong of me to say that I shall have you in my heart always–always?'

'I cannot let you go!' he said with suppressed violence. 'All our hopes–our plans–Elizabeth, Elizabeth!'

She did not speak, and presently he raised his face, flushed now and haggard. 'What can I do? Is there nothing?'

She touched the couch beside her. 'Do you think I have not tried to think of something?' she said sadly. 'Alas, did we not feel always that ours was nothing but a dream, impossible to realize?'

He sat down again, leaning his arm on his knee, and looking down at his own neat boot. 'It's your brother,' he said. 'Debts.'

She nodded. 'Mama told me so much that I did not know. It is worse than I imagined. Everything is mortgaged, and there are Charlotte and Horatia to think for. Pelham has lost five thousand guineas at a sitting in Paris.'

'Does Pelham never win?' demanded Mr Heron despairingly.

'I don't know,' she replied. 'He says he is very unlucky.'

He looked up. 'Elizabeth, if it hurts you I am sorry, but that you should be sacrificed to Pelham's selfish, thoughtless—'

'Oh, hush!' she begged. 'You know the Fatal Tendency in us Winwoods. Pelham cannot help it. My father even! When Pelham came into his inheritance he found it already wasted. Mama explained it all to me. She is so very sorry, Edward. We have mingled our tears. But she thinks, and how can I not feel the truth of it, that it is my Duty to the Family to accept of Lord Rule's offer.'

'Rule!' he said bitterly. 'A man fifteen years your senior! a man of his reputation. He has only to throw his glove at your feet, and you–Oh God, I cannot bear to think of it!' His writhing fingers created havoc amongst his pomaded curls. 'Why must his choice light upon you?' he groaned. 'Are there not others enough?'

'I think,' she said diffidently, 'that he wishes to ally himself with our Family. They say he is very proud, and our name is–is also a proud one.' She hesitated, and said, colouring: 'It is to be a marriage of convenience, such as are the fashion in France. Lord Rule does not–cannot–pretend to love me, nor I him.' She glanced up, as the gilt time-piece on the mantel-shelf chimed the hour. 'I must say good-bye to you,' she said, with desperate calm. 'I promised Mama–only half an hour. Edward—' She shrank suddenly into his embrace–'Oh, my love, remember me!' she sobbed.

Three minutes later the library door slammed, and Mr Heron strode across the hall towards the front door, his hair in disorder, his gloves and cocked hat clenched in his hand.

'Edward!' The thrilling whisper came from the stairhead. He glanced up, heedless of his ravaged face and wild appearance.

The youngest Miss Winwood leaned over the balustrade, and laid a finger on her lips. 'Edward, c-come up! I must speak to you!'

He hesitated, but an imperious gesture from Horatia brought him to the foot of the stairs. 'What is it?' he asked curtly.

'Come up!' repeated Horatia impatiently.

He slowly mounted the stairs. His hand was seized, and he was whisked into the big withdrawing-room that overlooked the street.

Horatia shut the door. 'D-don't speak too loud! Mama's bedroom is next door. What did she say?'

'I have not seen Lady Winwood,' Mr Heron answered heavily.

'Stupid! L-Lizzie!'

He said tightly: 'Only goodbye.'

'It shan't be!' said Horatia, with determination. 'L-listen, Edward! I have a p-plan!'

He looked down at her, a gleam of hope in his eyes. 'I'll do anything!' he said. 'Only tell me!'

'It isn't anything for you to do,' said Horatia. 'I am g-going to do it!'

'You?' he said doubtfully. 'But what can you do?'

'I d-don't know, but I'm g-going to try. M-mind, I can't be sure that it will succeed, but I think perhaps it m-might.'

'But what is it?' he persisted.

'I shan't say. I only told you because you looked so very m-miserable. You had better trust me, Edward.'

'I do,' he assured her. 'But—'

Horatia pulled him to stand in front of the mirror over the fireplace. 'Then straighten your hair,' she said severely. 'J-just look at it. You've crushed your hat too. There! Now, g-go away, Edward, before Mama hears you.'

Mr Heron found himself pushed to the door. He turned, and grasped Horatia's hand. 'Horry, I don't see what you can do, but if you can save Elizabeth from this match—'

Two dimples leapt into being; the grey eyes twinked. 'I know. You w-will be my m-most obliged servant. Well, I will!'

'More than that!' he said earnestly.

'Hush, Mama will hear!' whispered Horatia, and thrust him out of the room.

2

Mr Arnold Gisborne, lately of Queen's College, Cambridge, was thought by his relatives to have been very fortunate to have acquired the post of secretary to the Earl of Rule. He was tolerably satisfied himself, employment in a noble house was a fair stepping-stone to a Public Career, but he would have preferred, since he was a serious young man, the service of one more nearly concerned with the Affairs of the Nation. My Lord of Rule, when he could be moved thereto, occasionally took his seat in the Upper House, and had been known to raise his pleasant, lazy voice in support of a Motion, but he had no place in the Ministry, and he displayed not the smallest desire to occupy himself with Politicks. If he spoke, Mr Gisborne was requested to prepare his speech, which Mr Gisborne did with energy and enthusiasm, hearing in his imagination the words delivered in his own crisp voice. My lord would glance over the sheets of fine handwriting, and say: 'Admirable, my dear Arnold, quite admirable. But not quite in my mode, do you think?' And Mr Gisborne would have sadly to watch my lord's well-kept hand driving a quill through his most cherished periods. My lord, aware of his chagrin, would look up and say with his rather charming smile: 'I feel for you, Arnold, believe me. But I am such a very frippery fellow, you know. It would shock the Lords to hear me utter such energetic sentiments. It would not do at all.'

'My lord, may I say that you like to be thought a frippery fellow?' asked Mr Gisborne with severity tempered by respect.

'By all means, Arnold. You may say just what you like,' replied his lordship amiably.

But in spite of this permission Mr Gisborne did not say anything more. It would have been a waste of time. My lord could give one a set-down, though always with that faint look of amusement in his bored grey eyes, and always in the pleasantest manner. Mr Gisborne contented himself with dreaming of his own future, and in the meantime managed his patron's affairs with conscientious thoroughness. The Earl's mode of life he could not approve, for he was the son of a Dean, and strictly reared. My lord's preoccupation with such wanton pieces of pretty femininity as La Fanciola, of the Opera House, or a certain Lady Massey filled him with a disapproval that made him at first scornful, and later, when he had been my lord's secretary for a twelve-month, regretful.

He had not imagined, upon his first setting eyes on the Earl, that he could learn to like, or even to tolerate, this lazy, faintly mocking exquisite, but he had not, after all, experienced the least difficulty in doing both. At the end of a month he had discovered that just as his lordship's laced and scented coats concealed an extremely powerful frame, so his weary eyelids drooped over eyes that could become as keen as the brain behind.

Yielding to my lord's charm, he accepted his vagaries if not with approval at least with tolerance.

The Earl's intention to enter the married state took him by surprise. He had no notion of such a scheme until a morning two days after his lordship had visited Lady Winwood in South Street. Then, as he sat at his desk in the library, Rule strolled in after a late breakfast, and perceiving the pen in his hand, complained: 'You are always so damnably busy, Arnold. Do I give you so much work?'

Mr Gisborne got up from his seat at the desk. 'No, sir, not enough.'

'You are insatiable, my dear boy.' He observed some papers in Mr Gisborne's grasp, and sighed. 'What is it now?' he asked with resignation.

'I thought, sir, you might wish to see these accounts from Meering,' suggested Mr Gisborne.

'Not in the least,' replied his lordship, leaning his big shoulders against the mantelpiece.

'Very well, sir.' Mr Gisborne laid the papers down, and said tentatively: 'You won't have forgotten that there is a Debate in the House to-day which you will like to take part in?'

His lordship's attention had wandered; he was scrutinizing his own top-boot (for he was dressed for riding) through a long-handled quizzing-glass, but he said in a mildly surprised voice: 'Which I shall what, Arnold?'

'I made sure you would attend it, my lord,' said Mr Gisborne defensively.

'I am afraid you were in your cups, my dear fellow. Now tell me, do my eyes deceive me, or is there a suggestion—the merest hint—of a—really, I fear I must call it a bagginess—about the ankle?'

Mr Gisborne glanced perfunctorily down at his lordship's shining boot. 'I don't observe it, sir.'

'Come, come, Arnold!' the Earl said gently. 'Give me your attention, I beg of you!'

Mr Gisborne met the quizzical gleam in my lord's eyes, and grinned in spite of himself. 'Sir, I believe you should go. It is of some moment. In the Lower House—'

'I felt uneasy at the time,' mused the Earl, still contemplating his legs. 'I shall have to change my bootmaker again.' He let his glass fall on the end of its long riband, and turned to arrange his cravat in the mirror. 'Ah! Remind me, Arnold, that I am to wait on Lady Winwood at three. It is really quite important.'

Mr Gisborne stared. 'Yes, sir?'

'Yes, quite important. I think the new habit, the coat *dos de puce*—or is that a thought sombre for the errand? I believe the blue velvet will be more fitting. And the *perruque à bourse*? You prefer the Catogan wig, perhaps, but you are wrong, my dear boy, I am convinced that you are wrong. The arrangement of curls in the front gives an impression of heaviness. I feel sure you would not wish me to be heavy.' He gave one of the lace ruffles that fell over his hand a flick. 'Oh, I have not told you, have I? You must know that I am contemplating matrimony, Arnold.'

Mr Gisborne's astonishment was plain to be seen. 'You, sir?' he said, quite dumbfounded.

'But why not?' inquired his lordship. 'Do you object?'

'Object, sir! I? I am only surprised.'

'My sister,' explained his lordship, 'considers that it is time I took a wife.'

Mr Gisborne had a great respect for the Earl's sister, but he had yet to learn that her advice carried any weight with his lordship. 'Indeed, sir,' he said, and added diffidently: 'It is Miss Winwood?'

'Miss Winwood,' agreed the Earl. 'You perceive how important it is that I should not forget to present myself in South Street at–did I say three o'clock?'

'I will put you in mind of it, sir,' said Mr Gisborne dryly.

The door opened to admit a footman in blue livery. 'My lord, a lady has called,' he said hesitatingly.

Mr Gisborne turned to stare, for whatever Rule's amusements abroad might be, his inamoratas did not wait upon him in Grosvenor Square.

The Earl raised his brows. 'I am afraid–I am very much afraid–that you are–shall we say–a little stupid, my friend,' he said. 'But perhaps you have already denied me?'

The lackey looked flustered, and answered: 'The lady bade me tell your lordship that Miss Winwood begs the favour of a word with you.'

There was a moment's silence. Mr Gisborne had with difficulty checked the exclamation that rose to his lips, and now affected to arrange the papers on his desk.

The Earl's eyes, which had narrowed suddenly, to his servant's discomfiture, were once more bland and expressionless. 'I see,' he remarked. 'Where is Miss Winwood?'

'In the smaller saloon, my lord.'

'Very well,' said his lordship. 'You need not wait.'

The lackey bowed, and went out. My lord's gaze rested thoughtfully on Mr Gisborne's profile. 'Arnold,' he said softly. Mr Gisborne looked up. 'Are you very discreet, Arnold?' said his lordship.

Mr Gisborne met his look full. 'Yes, sir. Of course.'

'I am sure you are,' said his lordship. 'Perhaps even–a little deaf?'

Mr Gisborne's lips twitched. 'Upon occasion, amazingly deaf, sir.'

'I need not have asked,' said the Earl. 'You are a prince of secretaries, my dear fellow.'

'As to that, sir, you are very obliging. But certainly you need not have asked.'

'My maladroitness,' murmured his lordship, and went out.

He crossed the wide marble paved hall, observing as he passed a young woman, obviously an abigail, seated on the edge of a straight chair, and clutching her reticule in a frightened manner. Miss Winwood, then, had not come quite unattended.

One of the lackeys sprang to throw open the massive mahogany door that led into the small saloon, and my lord went in.

A lady, not so tall as he had expected to see, was standing with her back to the door, apparently inspecting an oil painting that hung on the far wall. She turned quickly as he came in, and showed him a face that certainly did not belong to Miss Winwood. He checked for a moment, looking down at her in some surprise.

The face under the simple straw hat also showed surprise. 'Are you L–Lord Rule?' demanded the lady.

He was amused. 'I have always believed so,' he replied.

'Why, I th-thought you were quite old!' she informed him ingenuously.

'That,' said his lordship with perfect gravity, 'was unkind in you. Did you come to see me in order to–er–satisfy yourself as to my appearance?'

She blushed fierily. 'P-please forgive m-me!' she begged, stammering dreadfully. 'It w-was very r-rude of m-me, only you s-see I was surprised just for the m-moment.'

'If you were surprised, ma'am, what can I be but deeply flattered?' said the Earl. 'But if you did not come to look me over, do you think you could tell me what it is I am to have the honour of doing for you?'

The bright eyes looked resolutely into his. 'Of c-course, you don't know who I am,' said the visitor. 'I'm afraid I d-deceived you a little. I was afraid if you knew it was not L-Lizzie you might not receive me. But it was not quite a lie to say I was Miss W-Winwood,' she added anxiously. 'B-because I am, you know. I'm Horry Winwood.'

'Horry?' he repeated.

'Horatia,' she explained. 'It is an odious name, isn't it? I was given it on account of Mr W-Walpole. He is my godfather, you understand.'

'Perfectly,' bowed his lordship. 'You must forgive me for being so dull-witted, but would you believe it?—I am still quite in the dark.'

Horatia's gaze faltered. 'It is—it is very difficult to explain it to you,' she said. 'And I expect you are horridly shocked. But I did bring my m-maid, sir!'

'That makes it far less shocking,' said his lordship reassuringly. 'But would it not be much easier to explain this very difficult matter to me if you were to sit down? Will you let me take your cloak?'

'Th-thank you,' said Horatia, relinquishing it. She bestowed a friendly smile upon her host. 'It is not anything n-near so difficult as I thought it would be. Before you came in my spirits quite f-failed. You see, my M-mama has not the smallest n-notion of my being here. But I couldn't think of anything else to do.' She gripped her hands together, and drew a deep breath. 'It is because of L-Lizzie—my sister. You have offered for her, haven't you?'

Slightly taken aback, the Earl bowed. Horatia said in a rush: 'C-could you—would you m-mind very much—having m-me instead?'

The Earl was seated in a chair opposite to her, absently swinging his eyeglass, his gaze fixed on her face in an expression of courteous interest. The eyeglass stopped swinging suddenly, and was allowed to fall. Horatia, looking anxiously across at him, saw a rather startled frown in his eyes, and hurried on: 'Of c-course I know it ought to be Charlotte, for she is the elder, but she said nothing would induce her to m-marry you.'

His lips quivered. 'In that case,' he said, 'it is fortunate that I did not solicit the honour of Miss Charlotte's hand in marriage.'

'Yes,' agreed Horatia. 'I am sorry to have to say it, but I am afraid Charlotte shrinks from the idea of m-making such a sacrifice, even for L-Lizzie's sake.' Rule's shoulders shook slightly. Have I said s-something I shouldn't?' inquired Horatia doubtfully.

'On the contrary,' he replied. 'Your conversation is most salutary, Miss Winwood.'

'You are laughing at me,' said Horatia accusingly. 'I d-daresay you think I am very stupid, sir, but indeed, it is most serious.'

'I think you are delightful,' said Rule. 'But there seems to be some misapprehension. I was under the impression that Miss Winwood was—er—willing to receive my addresses.'

'Yes,' concurred Horatia. 'She is w-willing, of course, but it makes her dreadfully unhappy. Th-that's why I came. I hope you don't m-mind.'

'Not at all,' said his lordship. 'But may I know whether I appear to all the members of your family in this disagreeable light?'

'Oh no!' said Horatia earnestly. 'M-mama is excessively pleased with you, and I myself d-don't find you disagreeable in the least. And if only you would be so v-very obliging as to offer for m-me instead of Lizzie I should like you very well.'

'But why,' asked Rule, 'do you want me to offer for you?'

Horatia's brows drew close over the bridge of her nose. 'It must sound very odd,' she admitted. 'You see, Lizzie must m-marry Edward Heron. Perhaps you do not know him?'

'I believe I have not the pleasure,' said the Earl.

'W-well, he is a very particular friend of ours, and he loves L-Lizzie. Only you know how it is with younger sons, and poor Edward is not even a Captain yet.'

'I am to understand that Mr Heron is in the Army?' inquired the Earl.

'Oh, yes, the T-tenth Foot. And if you had not offered for L-Lizzie I feel sure M-mama would have consented to him being contracted to her.'

'It was most lamentable of me,' said Rule gravely. 'But at least I can remedy the error.'

Horatia said eagerly: 'Oh, you will take m-me instead?'

'No,' said Rule, with a faint smile. 'I won't do that. But I will engage not to marry your sister. It's not necessary to offer me an exchange, my poor child.'

'B-but it is!' said Horatia vigorously. 'One of us m-must marry you!'

The Earl looked at her for a moment. Then he got up in his leisurely way, and stood leaning on the back of a chair.

'I think you must explain it all to me,' he said. 'I seem to be more than ordinarily dull this morning.'

Horatia knit her brows. 'Well, I'll t-try,' she said. 'You see, we're so shockingly poor. Charlotte says it is all P-Pelham's fault, and I dare say it may be, but it is no use blaming him, b-because he cannot help it. G-gambling, you know. Do you gamble?'

'Sometimes,' answered his lordship.

The grey eyes sparkled. 'So do I,' declared Horatia unexpectedly. 'N-not really, of course, but with Pelham. He taught me. Charlotte says it is wrong. She is l-like that, you know, and it makes her very impatient with poor P-Pel. And I m-must say I feel a little impatient myself when Lizzie has to be sacrificed. Mama is sorry too, b-but she says we must all feel d-deeply thankful.' She coloured, and said rather gruffly: 'It's v-vulgar to care about Settlements, but you are very rich, are you not?'

'Very,' said his lordship, preserving his calm.

'Yes,' nodded Horatia. 'W-well—you see!'

'I see,' agreed Rule. 'You are going to be the Sacrifice.'

She looked up at him rather shyly. 'It c-can't signify to you, can it? Except that I know I'm not a Beauty, like L-Lizzie. But I have got the Nose, sir.'

Rule surveyed the Nose. 'Undoubtedly, you have the Nose,' he said.

Horatia seemed determined to make a clean breast of her blemishes. 'And p-perhaps you could become used to my eyebrows?'

The smile lurked at the back of Rule's eyes. 'I think, quite easily.'

She said sadly: 'They won't arch, you know. And I ought to t-tell you that we have quite given up hope of my g-growing any taller.'

'It would certainly be a pity if you did,' said his lordship.

'D-do you think so?' Horatia was surprised. 'It is a great trial to me, I can assure you.' She took a breath, and added, with difficulty: 'You m-may have n-noticed that I have a– a stammer.'

'Yes, I had noticed,' the Earl answered gently.

'If you f-feel you c-can't bear it, sir, I shall quite understand,' Horatia said in a small, anxious voice.

'I like it,' said the Earl.

'It is very odd of you,' marvelled Horatia. 'But p-perhaps you said that to p-put me at my ease?'

'No,' said the Earl. 'I said it because it was true. Will you tell me how old you are?'

'D-does it matter?' Horatia inquired forebodingly.

'Yes, I think it does,' said his lordship.

'I was afraid it m-might,' she said. 'I am t-turned seventeen.'

'Turned seventeen!' repeated his lordship. 'My dear, I couldn't do it.'

'I'm too young?'

'Much too young, child.'

Horatia swallowed valiantly. 'I shall grow older,' she ventured. 'I d-don't want to p-press you, but I am thought to be quite sensible.'

'Do you know how old I am?' asked the Earl.

'N-no, but my cousin, Mrs M-Maulfrey, says you are not a d-day above thirty-five.'

'Does not that seem a little old to you?' he suggested.

'Well, it is rather old, perhaps, b-but no one would think you were as much,' said Horatia kindly.

At that a laugh escaped him. 'Thank you,' he bowed. 'But I think that thirty-five makes a poor husband for seventeen.'

'P-pray do not give that a thought, sir!' said Horatia earnestly. 'I assure you, for my p-part I do not regard it at all. In f-fact, I think I should quite like to marry you.'

'Would you?' he said. 'You do me great honour, ma'am.' He came towards her, and she got up. He took her hand, and raised it to his lips a moment. 'Now what is it you want me to do?'

'There is one very particular thing,' Horatia confided. 'I should not c-care to ask it of you, only that we are m-making a bargain, are we not?'

'Are we?' said his lordship.

'But you know w-we are!' Horatia said. 'You w-want to marry into m-my Family, don't you?'

'I am beginning to think that I do,' remarked his lordship.

Horatia frowned. 'I quite understood that that was why you offered for L-Lizzie.'

'It was,' he assured her.

She seemed satisfied. 'And you do not w-want a wife to interfere with you. Well, I p-promise I won't.'

His lordship looked down at her rather enigmatically. 'And in return?'

She drew closer. 'C-could you do something for Edward?' she begged. 'I have d-decided that there is only one thing for him, and that is a P-patron!'

'And—er—am I to be the Patron?' asked his lordship.

'Would you m-mind very m-much?'

A muscle at the corner of the Earl's mouth twitched, but he answered with only the suspicion of a tremor in his voice: 'I shall be happy to oblige you, ma'am, to the best of my poor endeavour.'

'Thank you very m-much,' said Horatia seriously. 'Then he and Lizzie can be m-married, you see. And you will tell Mama that you would just as soon have me, won't you?'

'I may not phrase it quite like that,' said the Earl, 'but I will endeavour to make the matter plain to her. But I do not entirely see how I am to propose this exchange without divulging your visit to me.'

'Oh, you need not m-mind that!' said Horatia cheerfully. 'I shall tell her m-myself. I think I had b-better go now. No one knows where I am, and perhaps they m-may wonder.'

'We will drink to our bargain first, do you not think?' said the Earl, and picked up a small gilt handbell, and rang it.

A lackey came in answer to the bell. 'You will bring me—' the Earl glanced at Horatia—'ratafia, and two glasses,' he said. 'And my coach will be at the door within ten minutes.'

'If—if the c-coach is for me,' said Horatia, 'it is only a step to South Street, sir.'

'But I would rather that you permitted me to convey you,' said his lordship.

The butler brought the ratafia himself, and set the heavy silver tray down on a table. He was dismissed with a nod, and went regretfully. He would have liked to see with his own eyes my lord drink a glass of ratafia.

The Earl poured two glasses, and gave one to Horatia. 'The bargain!' he said, and drank heroically.

Horatia's eyes twinkled merrily. 'I f-feel sure we shall deal f-famously together!' she declared, and raised the glass to her lips.

Five minutes later his lordship walked into the library again. 'Ah—Arnold,' he said. 'I have found something for you to do.'

'Yes, sir?' said Mr Gisborne, rising.

'You must get me a Captaincy,' said Rule. 'A Captaincy in the—in the 10th Foot, I think, but I am sure you will find out.'

'A Captaincy in the 10th Foot?' repeated Mr Gisborne. 'For whom, sir?'

'Now, what was the name?' wondered his lordship. 'Hawk—Hernshaw—Heron. I rather think it was Heron. For a Mr Edward Heron. Do you know a Mr Edward Heron?'

'No, sir, I don't.'

'No,' sighed Rule. 'Nor do I. It makes it very awkward for us, but I have great faith in you, Arnold. You will find out all about this Edward Heron.'

'I'll try, sir,' replied Mr Gisborne.

'I am afraid I give you a deal of trouble,' apologized his lordship, preparing to depart. At the door he looked back. 'By the way, Arnold, I think you may be under some slight misapprehension. It is the youngest Miss Winwood who does me the honour of accepting my hand.'

Mr Gisborne was startled. 'Miss Charlotte Winwood, sir? The youngest Miss Winwood, I believe, is scarcely out of the schoolroom.'

'Certainly not Miss Charlotte Winwood,' said the Earl. 'I have it on excellent authority that nothing would induce Miss Charlotte to marry me.'

'Good God, my lord!' said Mr Gisborne blankly.

'Thank you, Arnold. You comfort me,' said his lordship, and went out.

3

The youngest Miss Winwood's return to South Street was witnessed by both her sisters from the windows of the withdrawing-room. Her absence had certainly been remarked but since the porter was able to inform the rather agitated governess that Miss Horatia had gone out attended by her maid, no great concern was felt. It was odd of Horatia, and very wayward, but no doubt she had only stolen out to buy the coquelicot ribbons she had coveted in a milliner's window, or a chintz patch for a gown. This was Elizabeth's theory, delivered in her soft, peaceable voice, and it satisfied Lady Winwood, lying upon the sopha with her vinaigrette to hand.

The appearance of a town coach, drawn by perfectly matched bays with glittering harness, did not occasion more than a fleeting interest until it became apparent that this opulent equipage was going to draw up at the door of No. 20.

Charlotte exclaimed: 'Lord, who can it be? Mama, a caller!' She pressed her face against the window, and said: 'There is a crest on the panel, but I cannot distinguish—Lizzie, I believe it is Lord Rule!'

'Oh no!' Elizabeth fluttered, pressing a hand to her heart.

By this time the footman had sprung down, and opened the coach door. Charlotte grew pop-eyed. 'It's Horry!' she gasped.

Lady Winwood clutched the vinaigrette. 'Charlotte, my nerves!' she said in a fading voice.

'But, Mama, it is!' insisted Charlotte.

Elizabeth had a premonition. 'Oh, what can she have been doing?' she said, sinking into a chair, and growing quite pale. 'I hope nothing—nothing dreadful!'

Impetuous footsteps were heard on the stairs; the door was opened urgently, and Horatia stood before them, flushed and bright-eyed, and swinging her hat by its ribbon.

Lady Winwood's hands fumbled with her Medici scarf. 'Dearest, the draught!' she moaned. 'My poor head!'

'Pray, Horry, shut the door!' said Charlotte. 'How can you bounce so when you know how shattered Mama's nerves are?'

'Oh, I am sorry!' Horatia said, and carefully shut the door. 'I forgot. L-Lizzie, everything is settled, and you *shall* m-marry Edward!'

Lady Winwood was moved to sit up. 'Good God, the child's raving! Horatia, what—*what* have you been doing?'

Horatia tossed the cloak aside, and plumped down on the stool beside her mother's sopha. 'I've b-been to see Lord Rule!' she announced.

'I knew it!' said Elizabeth, in the voice of Cassandra.

Lady Winwood sank back upon her cushions with closed eyes. Charlotte, observing her alarming rigidity, shrieked: 'Unnatural girl! Have you no consideration for our dearest Mama? Lizzie, hartshorn!'

The hartshorn, the vinaigrette, and some Hungary Water applied to the temples restored the afflicted Lady Winwood to life. She opened her eyes and found just strength to utter: 'What did the child say?'

Charlotte, fondly clasping her mother's frail hand, said: 'Mama, do not agitate yourself, I beg of you!'

'You n-need not be agitated, M-mama,' Horatia told her penitently. 'It is quite true that I've b-been to see Lord Rule, but—'

'Then all is at an end!' said Lady Winwood fatalistically. 'We may as well prepare to enter the Debtors' Prison. I am sure I do not mind for myself, for my Days are Numbered, but my beautiful Lizzie, my sweetest Charlotte—'

'M-mama, if only you w-would listen to me!' broke in Horatia. 'I have explained everything to L-Lord Rule, and—'

'Merciful heavens!' said Elizabeth. 'Not—not Edward?'

'Yes, Edward. Of course I told him about Edward. And he is n-not going to marry you, Lizzie, but he p-promised he would be Edward's P-patron instead—'

Lady Winwood had recourse to the vinaigrette again, and desired feebly to be told what she had ever done to deserve such calamity.

'And I explained how n-nothing would induce Charlotte to m-marry him, and he did not seem to m-mind that.'

'I shall die,' said Charlotte with resolution, 'of Mortification!'

'Oh, Horry dear!' sighed Elizabeth, between tears and laughter.

'And I asked him,' concluded Horatia triumphantly, 'if he would marry m-me instead. And he is g-going to!'

Her relatives were bereft of speech. Even Lady Winwood apparently considered that the situation had gone beyond the powers of her vinaigrette to mend, for she allowed it to slip from her hand to the floor while she stared in a bemused way at her youngest-born.

It was Charlotte who found her voice first. 'Horatia, do you say that you had the Indelicacy, the Impropriety, the–the Forwardness, to ask Lord Rule to marry you?'

'Yes,' said Horatia staunchly. 'I had to.'

'And–and—' Charlotte groped for words–'he consented to–to marry you in place of *Lizzie?*'

Horatia nodded.

'He cannot,' said Charlotte, 'have noticed the Stammer.'

Horatia put up her chin. 'I s-spoke to him about the S-stammer, and he said he l-liked it!'

Elizabeth rose up from her chair and clasped Horatia in her arms. 'Oh, why should he not? Dearest, dearest, never could I permit you to sacrifice yourself for me!'

Horatia suffered the embrace. 'Well, to tell you the truth, Lizzie, I would like to m-marry him. But I c-can't help wondering whether you are quite sure you d-don't want to?' She searched her sister's face. 'D-do you really like Edward better?'

'Oh, my love!'

'Well, I c-can't understand it,' said Horatia.

'It is not to be supposed,' stated Charlotte flatly, 'that Lord Rule was in earnest. Depend upon it, he thinks Horry a Mere Child.'

'N-no, he does not!' said Horatia, firing up. 'He w-was in earnest, and he is c-coming to tell M-mama at three this afternoon.'

'I beg that no one will expect me to face Lord Rule!' said Lady Winwood. 'I am ready to sink into the ground!'

'Will he come?' demanded Charlotte. 'What irremediable harm may not Horry's impropriety have wrought? We must ask ourselves, will Lord Rule desire to ally himself with a Family one of whose members has shown herself so dead to all feelings of Modesty and Female Reserve?'

'Charlotte, you shall not say that!' said Elizabeth with unwonted stringency. 'What should he think but that our dearest is but an impulsive child?'

'We must hope it,' Charlotte said heavily. 'But if she has divulged your attachment to Edward Heron I fear that all is at an end. We who know and value dear Horry do not notice her blemishes, but what gentleman would engage to marry her in place of the Beauty of the Family?'

'I thought of that myself,' admitted Horatia. 'He s-says he thinks he will grow used to my horrid eyebrows quite easily. And I will t-tell you something, Charlotte! He said it would be a p-pity if I became any taller.'

'How mortifying it is to reflect that Lord Rule may have been amusing himself at the expense of a Winwood!' said Charlotte.

But it seemed that Lord Rule had not been amusing himself. At three o'clock he walked up the steps of No. 20 South Street, and inquired for Lady Winwood.

In spite of her dramatic refusal to face the Earl, Lady Winwood had been induced to await him in the withdrawing-room, fortified by smelling-salts, and a new polonaise with tobine stripes which had arrived from her dress-maker's just in time to avert a nervous collapse.

Her interview with his lordship lasted for half an hour, at the end of which time the footman was despatched to inform Miss Horatia that her presence in the withdrawing-room was desired.

'Aha!' cried Horatia, shooting a wicked glance at Charlotte, and springing to her feet.

Elizabeth caught her hands. 'Horry, it is not too late! If this arrangement is repugnant to you, for Heaven's sake speak, and I will throw myself upon Lord Rule's generosity!'

'Repugnant? S-stuff!' said Horatia, and danced out.

'Horry, Horry, at least let me straighten your sash!' shrieked Charlotte.

'Too late,' Elizabeth said. She clasped her hands to her breast. 'If I could be assured that this is no Immolation upon the Altar of Sisterly Love!'

'If you wish to know what I think,' said Charlotte, 'Horry is very well pleased with herself.'

Horatia, opening the door into the withdrawing-room, found her mother actually upon her feet, the smelling-salts lying forgotten on an ormolu table by the fire. In the middle of the room Rule was standing, watching the door, one hand, with a great square sapphire glowing on it, resting on a chairback.

He looked very much more magnificent and unapproachable in blue velvet and gold lacing than he had seemed in his riding habit, and for a moment Horatia surveyed him rather doubtfully. Then she saw him smile and was reassured.

Lady Winwood swam towards her and embraced her. 'My dearest!' she said, apparently overcome. 'My lord, let my treasured child answer you with her own lips. Horatia love, Lord Rule has done you the honour to request your hand in marriage.'

'I t-told you he was going to, M-mama!' said Horatia incorrigibly.

'Horatia—I beg of you!' implored the long-suffering lady. 'Your curtsy, my love!'

Horatia sank obediently into a curtsy. The Earl took her hand, as she rose, and bowed deeply over it. He said, looking down at her with a laugh in his eyes: 'Madam, may I keep this little hand?'

Lady Winwood heaved a tremulous sigh, and wiped away a sympathetic tear with her handkerchief.

'P-pretty!' approved Horatia. 'Indeed you m-may, sir. It is very handsome of you to give me the p-pleasure of having you p-propose for me.'

Lady Winwood looked round apprehensively for her salts, but perceiving that his lordship was laughing, changed her mind. 'My baby . . . !' She said indulgently: 'As you see, my lord, she is all unspoiled.'

She did not leave the newly plighted pair alone, and the Earl presently took his leave with equal correctness. The front door had barely closed behind him before Lady Winwood had clasped Horatia in a fond embrace. 'Dearest child!' she said. 'You are very, very fortunate! So personable a man! Such delicacy!'

Charlotte put her head round the door. 'May we come in, Mama? Has he really offered for Horry?'

Lady Winwood dabbed at her eyes again. 'He is everything that I could wish for! Such refinement! Such *ton!*'

Elizabeth had taken Horatia's hand, but Charlotte said practically: 'Well, for my part, I think he must be doting. And repulsive as the thought is, I suppose the Settlements . . . ?'

'He is all that is generous!' sighed Lady Winwood.

'Then I'm sure I wish you joy, Horry,' said Charlotte. 'Though I must say that I consider you far too young and heedless to become the wife of any gentleman. And I only pray that Theresa Maulfrey will have enough proper feeling to refrain from chattering about this awkward business.'

It did not seem at first as though Mrs Maulfrey would be able to hold her tongue. Upon the announcement of the betrothal she came to South Street, just as her cousins knew she would, all agog to hear the whole story. She was palpably dissatisfied with Elizabeth's careful tale of 'a mistake', and demanded to know the truth. Lady Winwood, rising for once to the occasion, announced that the matter had been arranged by herself and his lordship, who had met Horatia and been straightway captivated by her.

With this Mrs Maulfrey had to be content, and after condoling with Elizabeth on having lost an Earl only to get a lieutenant in exchange, and with Charlotte on being left a spinster while a chit from the schoolroom made the match of the season, she departed, leaving a sense of relief behind her, and a strong odour of violet scent.

Charlotte opined darkly that no good would come of Horatia's scandalously contrived marriage.

But Charlotte was alone in her pessimism. A radiant Mr Heron, fervently grasping both Horatia's hands, thanked her from the heart, and wished her happiness. Mr Heron had had the honour of meeting Lord Rule at an extremely select soirée in South Street, and his lordship had roused himself to take the young man aside and talk to him of his future. Mr Heron had no hesitation in declaring the Earl to be a very good sort of a man indeed, and no further remarks concerning his reputation or his advanced years were heard to pass his lips. Elizabeth, too, who had been forced to nerve herself to meet her erstwhile suitor, found the ordeal shorn of its terrors. My lord kissed her hand, and as he released it said with his slight, not unpleasing drawl: 'May I hope, Miss Winwood, that I am no longer an ogre?'

Elizabeth blushed, and hung her head. 'Oh—Horry!' she sighed, a smile trembling on her lips. 'Indeed, my lord, you were never that.'

'But I owe you an apology, ma'am,' he said solemnly, 'for I made you "dreadfully unhappy".'

'If we are to talk of apologies, sir—! You, who have been all kindness!' She lifted her eyes to his face, and tried to thank him for what he would do for Mr Heron.

Apparently he did not choose to be thanked; he put it aside with his lazy laugh, and somehow she could not go on. He stayed by her for a few minutes, and she had leisure to observe him. Later she told Mr Heron seriously that she thought Horry might be very happy.

'Horry is happy,' replied Mr Heron, with a chuckle.

'Ah yes, but you see, dearest, Horry is only a child. I feel—I feel anxiety, I won't conceal from you. Lord Rule is not a child.' She puckered her brow. 'Horry does such things! If he will only be gentle with her, and patient!'

'Why, love,' said Mr Heron, humouring her, 'I don't think you need to put yourself about. His lordship is all gentleness, and I don't doubt will have patience enough.'

'All gentleness,' she repeated. 'Indeed he is, and yet–do you know, Edward, I think I might be afraid of him? Sometimes, if you do but notice, he has a trick of closing his lips that gives to the whole face an air of–I must say inflexibility, quite foreign to what one knows of him. But if he will only come to love Horry!'

No one but Miss Winwood was inclined to indulge in such questionings, least of all Lady Winwood basking in the envy of her acquaintance. Everyone was anxious to felicitate her; everyone knew what a triumph was hers. Even Mr Walpole, who was staying at Arlington Street at the time, came to pay her a morning visit, and to glean a few details. Mr Walpole's face wore an approving smile, though he regretted that his god-daughter should be marrying a Tory. But then Mr Walpole was so very earnest a Whig, and even he seemed to think that Lady Winwood was right to disregard Rule's political opinions. He set the tips of his fingers together, crossing one dove-silk stockinged leg over the other, and listened with his well-bred air to all Lady Winwood had to say. She had a great value for Mr Walpole, whom she had known for many years, but she was careful in what she told him. No one had a kinder heart than this thin, percipient gentleman, but he had a sharp nose for a morsel of scandal, and a satiric pen. Let him but get wind of Horatia's escapade, and my Lady Ossory and my Lady Aylesbury would have the story by the next post.

Fortunately, the rumour of Rule's offer for Elizabeth had not reached Twickenham, and beyond wondering that Lady Winwood should care to see Horatia married before the divine Elizabeth (who was quite his favourite), he said nothing to put an anxious mother on her guard. So Lady Winwood told him confidentially that, although nothing was yet to be declared, Elizabeth too was to leave the nest. Mr Walpole was all interest, but pursed his lips a little when he heard about Mr Edward Heron. To be sure, of good family (trust Mr Walpole to know that!), but he could have wished for someone of greater consequence for his little Lizzie. Mr Walpole did so like to see his young friends make good matches. Indeed, his satisfaction at Horatia's betrothal made him forget a certain disastrous day at Twickenham when Horatia had shown herself quite unworthy of having the glories of his little Gothic Castle exhibited to her, and he patted her hand, and said that she must come and drink a syllabub at Strawberry quite soon. Horatia, under oath not to be *farouche* ('for he may be rising sixty, my love, and live secluded, but there's no one whose good opinion counts for more'), thanked him demurely, and hoped that she would not be expected to admire and fondle his horrid little dog, Rosette, who was odiously spoiled, and yapped at one's heels.

Mr Walpole said that she was very young to contemplate matrimony, and Lady Winwood sighed that alas, it was true: she was losing her darling before she had even been to Court.

That was an unwise remark, because it gave Mr Walpole an opportunity for recounting, as he was very fond of doing, how his father had taken him to kiss George the First's hand when he was a child. Horatia slipped out while he was in the middle of his anecdote, leaving her Mama to assume an expression of spurious interest.

In quite another quarter, though topographically hardly a stone's throw from South Street, the news of Rule's betrothal created different sensations. There was a slim house in Hertford Street where a handsome widow held her court, but it was not at all the sort of establishment that Lady Winwood visited. Caroline Massey, relict of a wealthy tradesman, had achieved her position in the Polite World by dint of burying the late Sir Thomas's connection with the City in decent oblivion, and relying upon her own respectable birth and very considerable good looks. Sir Thomas's fortune, though so discreditably acquired, was also useful. It enabled his widow to live in a very pretty house in the best part of town, to entertain in a lavish and agreeable fashion, and to procure the sponsorship of a Patroness who was easy-going enough to introduce her into Society. The offices of this Patroness had long ceased to be necessary to Lady Massey. In some way, best known (said various indignant ladies) to herself, she had contrived to become a Personage. One was for ever meeting her, and if a few doors remained obstinately closed against her, she had a sufficient following for this not to signify. That the following consisted largely of men was not likely to trouble her; she was not a woman who craved female companion-ship, though a faded and resigned lady, who was believed to be her cousin, constantly resided with her. Miss Janet's presence was a sop thrown to the conventions. Yet, to do them justice, it was not Lady Massey's morals that stuck in the gullets of certain aristocratic dames. Everyone had their own *affaires*, and if gossip whispered of intimacies between the fair Massey and Lord Rule, as long as the lady conducted her amorous passages with discretion only such rigid moralists as Lady Winwood would throw up hands of horror. It was the fatal taint of the City that would always exclude Lady Massey from the innermost circle of Fashion. She was not *bon ton*. It was said without rancour, even with a pitying shrug of well-bred shoulders, but it was damning. Lady Massey, aware of it, never betrayed by word or look that she was conscious of that almost indefinable bar, and not even the resigned cousin knew that to become one of the Select was almost an obsession with her.

There was only one person who guessed, and he seemed to derive a certain sardonic amusement from it. Robert, Baron Lethbridge, could usually derive amusement from the frailty of his fellows.

Upon an evening two days after the Earl of Rule's second visit to the Winwood establishment, Lady Massey held a card-party in Hertford Street. These parties were always well attended, for one might be sure of deep play, and a charming hostess, whose cellar (thanks to the ungenteel but knowledgeable Sir Thomas) was excellently stocked.

The saloon upon the first floor was a charming apartment, and set off its mistress to advantage. She had lately purchased some very pretty pieces of gilt furniture in Paris, and had had all her old hangings pulled down, and new ones of straw-coloured silk put in their place, so that the room, which had before been rose-pink, now glowed palely yellow. She herself wore a gown of silk brocade with great panniers, and an underskirt looped with embroidered garlands. Her hair was dressed high in a *pouf au sentiment*, with curled feathers for which she had paid fifty louis apiece at Bertin's, and scented roses, placed artlessly here and there in the powdered erection. This coiffure had been the object of several aspiring ladies' envy, and had put Mrs Montague-Damer quite out of countenance. She too had acquired a French fashion, and had expected to have it much admired. But the exquisite *pouf au sentiment* made her own *chien couchant* look rather ridiculous, and quite spoiled her evening's enjoyment.

The gathering in the saloon was a modish one; dowdy persons had no place in Lady Massey's house, though she could welcome such freaks as the Lady Amelia Pridham, that grossly fat and free-spoken dame in the blonde satin who was even now arranging her rouleaus in front of her. There were those who wondered that the Lady Amelia should care to visit in Hertford Street, but the Lady Amelia, besides being of an extreme good nature, would go to any house where she could be sure of deep basset.

Basset was the game of the evening, and some fifteen people were seated at the big round table. It was when Lord Lethbridge held the bank that he chose to make his startling announcement. As he paid on the *couch* he said with a faintly malicious note in his voice: 'I don't see Rule to-night. No doubt the bridegroom-elect dances attendance in South Street.'

Opposite him, Lady Massey quickly looked up from the cards in front of her, but she did not say anything.

A Macaroni, with an enormous ladder-toupet covered in blue hair-powder, and a thin, unhealthily sallow countenance, cried out: 'What's that?'

Lord Lethbridge's hard hazel eyes lingered for a moment on Lady Massey's face. Then he turned slightly to look at the startled Macaroni. He said smilingly: 'Do you tell me I am before you with the news, Crosby? I thought you of all people must have known.' His satin-clad arm lay on the table, the pack of cards clasped in his white hand. The light of the candles in the huge chandelier over the table caught the jewels in the lace at his throat, and made his eyes glitter queerly.

'What are you talking about?' demanded the Macaroni, half rising from his seat.

'But Rule, my dear Crosby!' said Lethbridge. 'Your cousin Rule, you know.'

'What of Rule?' inquired the Lady Amelia, regretfully pushing one of her rouleaus across the table.

Lethbridge's glance flickered to Lady Massey's face again. 'Why, only that he is about to enter the married state,' he replied.

There was a stir of interest. Someone said: 'Good God, I thought he was safe to stay single! Well, upon my soul! Who's the fortunate fair one, Lethbridge?'

'The fortunate fair one is the youngest Miss Winwood,' said Lethbridge. 'A romance, you perceive. I believe she is not out of the schoolroom.'

The Macaroni, Mr Crosby Drelincourt, mechanically straightened the preposterous bow he wore in place of a cravat. 'Pho, it is a tale!' he said uneasily. 'Where had you it?'

Lethbridge raised his thin, rather slanting brows. 'Oh, I had it from the little Maulfrey. It will be in the *Gazette* by to-morrow.'

'Well, it's very interesting,' said a portly gentleman in claret velvet, 'but the game, Lethbridge, the game!'

'The game,' bowed his lordship, and sent a glance round at the cards on the table.

Lady Massey, who had won the *couch*, suddenly put out her hand and nicked the corner of the Queen that lay before her. 'Paroli!' she said in a quick, unsteady voice.

Lethbridge turned up two cards, and sent her a mocking look. 'Ace wins, Queen loses,' he said. 'Your luck is quite out, my lady.'

She gave a little laugh. 'I assure you I don't regard it. Lose to-night, win to-morrow. It goes up and down.'

The game proceeded. It was not until later when the company stood about in little chatting groups, partaking of very excellent refreshments, that Rule's betrothal was remembered. It was Lady Amelia, rolling up to Lethbridge, with a glass of hot negus in one hand and a sweet biscuit in the other, who said in her downright way: 'You're a dog, Lethbridge. What possessed you to hop out with that, man?'

'Why not?' said his lordship coolly. 'I thought you would all be interested.'

Lady Amelia finished her negus, and looked across the room towards her hostess. 'Diverting,' she commented. 'Did she think to get Rule?'

Lethbridge shrugged. 'Why do you ask me? I'm not in the lady's confidence.'

'H'm! You've a trick of knowing things, Lethbridge. Silly creature. Rule's not such a fool.' Her cynical eye wandered in search of Mr Drelincourt, and presently found him, standing apart, and pulling at his underlip. She chuckled. 'Took it badly, eh?'

Lord Lethbridge followed the direction of her gaze. 'Confess, I've afforded you some amusement, my lady.'

'Lord, you're like a gnat, my dear man.' She became aware of little Mr Paget inquisitively at her elbow, and dug at his ribs with her fan. 'What do you give for Crosby's chances now?'

Mr Paget tittered. 'Or our fair hostess's, ma'am!'

She gave a shrug of her large white shoulders. 'Oh, if you want to pry into the silly woman's affairs—!' she said, and moved away.

Mr Paget transferred his attention to Lord Lethbridge. ''Pon my soul, my lord, I'll swear she went white under the rouge!' Lethbridge took snuff. 'Cruel of you, my lord, 'pon my soul it was!'

'Do you think so?' said his lordship with almost dulcet sweetness.

'Oh, positively, sir, positively! Not a doubt she had hopes of Rule. But it would never do, you know. I believe his lordship to be excessively proud.'

'Excessively,' said Lethbridge, with so much dryness in his voice that Mr Paget had an uncomfortable feeling that he had said something inopportune.

He was so obsessed by this notion that he presently confided the interchange to Sir Marmaduke Hoban, who gave a snort of laughter and said: 'Damned inopportune!' and walked off to replenish his glass.

Mr Crosby Drelincourt, cousin and hair-presumptive to my Lord of Rule, seemed disinclined to discuss the news. He left the party early, and went home to his lodging in Jermyn Street, a prey to the gloomiest forebodings.

He passed an indifferent night, and awoke finally at an uncommonly early hour, and demanded the *London Gazette*. His valet brought it with the cup of chocolate with which it was Mr Drelincourt's habit to regale himself on first waking. Mr Drelincourt seized the journal and spread it open with agitated fingers. The announcement glared at him in incontrovertible print.

Mr Drelincourt looked at it in a kind of daze, his nightcap over one eye.

'Your chocolate, sir,' said his valet disinterestedly.

Mr Drelincourt was roused out of his momentary stupor. 'Take the damned stuff away!' he shouted, and flung the *Gazette* down. 'I am getting up!'

'Yes, sir. Will you wear the blue morning habit?'

Mr Drelincourt swore at him.

The valet, accustomed to Mr Drelincourt's temper, remained unmoved, but found an opportunity while his master was pulling on his stockings to peep into the *Gazette*. What he saw brought a faint, sour smile to his lips. He went away to prepare a razor with which to shave Mr Drelincourt.

The news had shocked Mr Drelincourt deeply, but habit was strong, and by the time he had been shaved he had recovered sufficient mastery over himself to take an interest in the all-important question of his dress. The result of the care he bestowed upon his person was certainly startling. When he was at last ready to sally forth into the street he wore a blue coat with long tails and enormous silver buttons, over a very short waistcoat, and a pair of striped breeches clipped at the knee with rosettes. A bow served him for cravat, his stockings were of silk, his shoes had silver buckles and heels so high that he was obliged to mince along; his wig was brushed up *en hérisson* to a point in the front, curled in pigeons' wings over the ears, and brought down at the back into a queue confined in a black silk bag. A little round hat surmounted this structure, and to complete his toilet he had a number of fobs and seals, and carried a long, clouded cane embellished with tassels.

Although the morning was a fine one Mr Drelincourt hailed a chair, and gave the address of his cousin's house in Grosvenor Square. He entered the sedan carefully, bending his head to avoid brushing his toupet against the roof; the men picked up the poles, and set off northwards with their exquisite burden.

Upon his arrival in Grosvenor Square Mr Drelincourt paid off the chairmen and tripped up the steps to the great door of Rule's house. He was admitted by the porter, who looked as though he would have liked to have shut the door in the visitor's painted face. Mr Drelincourt was no favourite with Rule's household, but being in some sort a privileged person he came and went very much as he pleased. The porter told him that my lord was still at breakfast, but Mr Drelincourt waved this piece of information aside with an airy gesture of one lily-white hand. The porter handed him over to a footman, and reflected with satisfaction that that was a nose put well out of joint.

Mr Drelincourt rarely waited upon his cousin without letting his gaze rest appreciatively on the fine proportions of his rooms, and the elegance of their appointments. He had come to regard Rule's possessions in some sort as his own, and he could never enter his house without thinking of the day when it would belong to him. To-day, however, he was easily able to refrain from the indulgence of this dream, and he followed the footman to a small breakfast-room at the back of the house with nothing in his head but a sense of deep injury.

My lord, in a dressing-gown of brocaded silk, was seated at the table with a tankard and a sirloin before him. His secretary was also present, apparently attempting to cope with a number of invitations for his lordship, for as Mr Drelincourt strutted in he said despairingly: 'But, sir, you must surely remember that you are promised to her Grace of Bedford to-night!'

'I wish,' said Rule plaintively, 'that you would rid yourself of that notion, my dear Arnold. I cannot imagine where you had it. I never remember anything disagreeable. Good-morning, Crosby.' He put up his glass the better to observe the letters in Mr Gisborne's hand. 'The one on the pink paper, Arnold. I have a great predilection for the one writ on pink paper. What is it?'

'A card-party at Mrs Wallchester's, sir,' said Mr Gisborne in a voice of disapproval.

'My instinct is never at fault,' said his lordship. 'The pink one it shall be. Crosby, really there is no need for you to stand. Have you come to breakfast? Oh, don't go, Arnold, don't go.'

'If you please, Rule, I wish to be private with you,' said Mr Drelincourt, who had favoured the secretary with the smallest of bows.

'Don't be shy, Crosby,' said his lordship kindly. 'If it's money Arnold is bound to know all about it.'

'It is not,' said Mr Drelincourt, much annoyed.

'Permit me, sir,' said Mr Gisborne, moving to the door.

Mr Drelincourt put down his hat and his cane, and drew out a chair from the table. 'Not breakfast, no!' he said a little peevishly.

The Earl surveyed him patiently. 'Well, what is it now, Crosby?' he inquired.

'I came to,' said Mr Drelincourt, 'I came to speak to you about this—this betrothal.'

'There's nothing private about that,' observed Rule, addressing himself to the cold roast beef.

'No, indeed!' said Crosby with a hint of indignation in his voice. 'I suppose it is true?'

'Oh, quite true,' said his lordship. 'You may safely felicitate me, my dear Crosby.'

'As to that—why, certainly! Certainly, I wish you very happy,' said Crosby, put out. 'But you never spoke a word of it to me. It takes me quite by surprise. I must think it extremely odd, cousin, considering the singular nature of our relationship.'

'The—?' My lord seemed puzzled.

'Come, Rule, come! As your heir I might be supposed to have some claim to be apprised of your intentions.'

'Accept my apologies,' said his lordship. 'Are you sure you won't have some breakfast, Crosby? You do not look at all the thing, my dear fellow. In fact, I should almost feel inclined to recommend another hair powder than this blue you affect. A charming tint, Crosby: you must not think I don't admire it, but its reflected pallor upon your countenance—'

'If I seem pale, cousin, you should rather blame the extraordinary announcement in to-day's *Gazette*. It has given me a shock; I shan't deny it has given me a shock.'

'But, Crosby,' said his lordship plaintively, 'were you really sure that you would outlive me?'

'In the course of nature I might expect to,' replied Mr Drelincourt, too much absorbed in his disappointment to consider his words. 'I can give you ten years, you must remember.'

Rule shook his head. 'I don't think you should build on it,' he said. 'I come of distressingly healthy stock, you know.'

'Very true,' agreed Mr Drelincourt. 'It is a happiness to all your relatives.'

'I see it is,' said his lordship gravely.

'Pray don't mistake me, Marcus!' besought his cousin. 'You must not suppose that your demise could occasion in me anything but a sense of the deepest bereavement, but you'll allow a man must look to the future.'

'Such a remote future!' said his lordship. 'It makes me feel positively melancholy, my dear Crosby.'

'We must all hope it may be remote,' said Crosby, 'but you cannot fail to have observed how uncertain is human life. Only to think of young Frittenham, cut off in the very flower of his youth by the overturning of his curricle! Broke his neck, you know, and all for a wager.'

The Earl laid down his knife and fork, and regarded his relative with some amusement. 'Only to think of it!' he repeated. 'I confess, Crosby, what you say will add—er—piquancy to my next race. I begin to see that your succession to my shoes–by the way, cousin, you are such a judge of these matters, do, I beg of you, tell me how you like them?' He stretched one leg for Mr Drelincourt to look at.

Mr Drelincourt said unerringly: '*A la d'Artois*, from Joubert's. I don't favour them myself, but they are very well–very well indeed.'

'It's a pity you don't,' said his lordship, 'for I perceive that you may be called upon to step into them at any time.'

'Oh, hardly that, Rule! Hardly that!' protested Mr Drelincourt handsomely.

'But consider how uncertain is human life, Crosby! You yourself said it a moment back. I might at any moment be thrown from a curricle.'

'I am sure I did not in the least mean—'

'Or,' continued Rule pensively, 'fall a victim to one of the cut-throat thieves with which I am told the town abounds.'

'Certainly,' said Mr Drelincourt a little stiffly. 'But I don't anticipate—'

'Highwaymen too,' mused his lordship. 'Think of poor Layton with a bullet in his shoulder on Hounslow Heath not a month ago. It might have been me, Crosby. It may still be me.'

Mr Drelincourt rose in a huff. 'I see you are determined to make a jest of it. Good God, I don't desire your death! I should be excessively sorry to hear of it. But this sudden resolve to marry when everyone had quite given up all idea of it, takes me aback, upon my soul it does! And quite a young lady, I apprehend.'

'My dear Crosby, why not say a very young lady? I feel sure you know her age.'

Mr Drelincourt sniffed. 'I scarcely credited it, cousin, I confess. A schoolroom miss, and you well above thirty! I wish you may not live to regret it.'

'Are you sure,' said his lordship, 'that you won't have some of this excellent beef?'

An artistic shudder ran through his cousin. 'I never–positively never–eat flesh at this hour of the morning!' said Mr Drelincourt emphatically. 'It is of all things the most repugnant to me. Of course you must know how people will laugh at this odd marriage. Seventeen and thirty-five! Upon my honour, I should not care to appear so ridiculous!' He gave an angry titter, and added venomously: 'To be sure, no one need wonder at the young lady's part in it! We all know how it is with the Winwoods. She does very well for herself, very well indeed!'

The Earl leaned back in his chair, one hand in his breeches pocket, the other quite idly playing with his quizzing-glass. 'Crosby,' he said gently, 'if ever you repeat that remark I am afraid–I am very much afraid–that you will quite certainly predecease me.'

There was an uncomfortable silence. Mr Drelincourt looked down at his cousin and saw that under the heavy lids those bored eyes had entirely lost their smile. They held a very unpleasant glint. Mr Drelincourt cleared his throat, and said, his voice jumping a little: 'My dear Marcus—! I assure I meant nothing in the world! How you do take one up!'

'You must forgive me,' said his lordship, still with that alarming grimness about his mouth.

'Oh, certainly! I don't give it a thought,' said Mr Drelincourt. 'Consider it forgotten, cousin, and as for the cause, you have me wrong, quite wrong, you know.'

The Earl continued to regard him for a moment; then the grimness left his face, and he suddenly laughed.

Mr Drelincourt picked up his hat and cane, and was about to take his leave when the door opened briskly, and a lady came in. She was of middle height, dressed in a gown of apple-green cambric with white stripes, in the style known as *vive bergère*, and had a very becoming straw hat with ribands perched upon her head. A scarf caught over one arm, and a sunshade with a long handle completed her toilet, and in her hand she carried, as Mr Drelincourt saw at a glance, a copy of the *London Gazette*.

She was an extremely handsome woman, with most speaking eyes, at once needle-sharp, and warmly smiling, and she bore a striking resemblance to the Earl.

On the threshold she checked, her quick gaze taking in Mr Drelincourt. 'Oh—Crosby!' she said, with unveiled dissatisfaction.

Rule got up, and took her hand. 'My dear Louisa, have you also come to breakfast?' he inquired.

She kissed him in a sisterly fashion, and replied with energy: 'I breakfasted two hours ago, but you may give me some coffee. I see you are just going, Crosby. Pray don't let me keep you. Dear me, why will you wear those very odd clothes, my good creature? And that absurd wig don't become you, take my word for it!'

Mr Drelincourt, feeling unable to cope adequately with his cousin, merely bowed, and wished her good morning. No sooner had he minced out of the room than Lady Louisa Quain flung down her copy of the *Gazette* before Rule. 'No need to ask why that odious little toad came,' she remarked. 'But, my dear Marcus, it is too provoking! There is the most nonsensical mistake made! Have you seen it?'

Rule began to pour coffee into his own unused cup. 'Dear Louisa, do you realize that it is not yet eleven o'clock, and I have already had Crosby with me? What time can I have had to read the *Gazette*?'

She took the cup from him, observing that she could not conceive how he should care to go on drinking ale with his breakfast. 'You will have to put in a second advertisement,' she informed him. 'I can't imagine how they came to make such a stupid mistake. My dear, they have confused the names of the sisters! Here it is! You may read for yourself: "The Honourable Horatia Winwood, youngest daughter of—" Really, if it were not so vexing it would be diverting! But how in the world came they to put "Horatia" for "Elizabeth"?'

'You see,' said Rule apologetically, 'Arnold sent the advertisement to the *Gazette*.'

'Well, I never would have believed Mr Gisborne to be so big a fool!' declared her ladyship.

'But perhaps I ought to explain, my dear Louisa, that he had my authority,' said Rule still more apologetically.

Lady Louisa, who had been studying the advertisement with a mixture of disgust and amusement, let the *Gazette* drop, and twisted round in her chair to stare up at her brother in astonishment. 'Lord, Rule, what can you possibly mean?' she demanded. 'You're not going to marry Horatia Winwood!'

'But I am,' said his lordship calmly.

'Rule, have you gone mad? You told me positively you had offered for Elizabeth!'

'My shocking memory for names!' mourned his lordship.

Lady Louisa brought her open hand down on the table. 'Nonsense!' she said. 'Your memory's as good as mine!'

'My dear, I should not like to think that,' said the Earl. 'Your memory is sometimes too good.'

'Oh!' said the lady critically surveying him. 'Well, you had best make a clean breast of it. Do you really mean to marry that child?'

'Well, she certainly means to marry me,' said his lordship.

'What?' gasped Lady Louisa.

'You see,' explained the Earl, resuming his seat, 'though it ought to be Charlotte, she has no mind to make such a sacrifice, even for Elizabeth's sake.'

'Either you are out of your senses, or I am!' declared Lady Louisa with resignation. 'I don't know what you're talking about, and how you can mean to marry Horatia, who must be still in the schoolroom, for I'm sure I have never clapped eyes on her—in place of that divinely beautiful Elizabeth—'

'Ah, but I am going to grow used to the eyebrows,' interrupted Rule. 'And she has the Nose.'

'Rule,' said her ladyship with dangerous quiet, 'do not goad me too far! Where have you seen this child?'

He regarded her with a smile hovering round his mouth. 'If I told you, Louisa, you would probably refuse to believe me.'

She cast up her eyes. 'When did you have this notion of marrying her?' she asked.

'Oh, I didn't,' replied the Earl. 'It was not my notion at all.'

'Whose, then?'

'Horatia's, my dear. I thought I had explained.'

'Do you tell me, Marcus, the girl asked you to marry her?' said Lady Louisa sarcastically.

'Instead of Elizabeth,' nodded his lordship. 'Elizabeth, you see, is going to marry Mr Heron.'

'Who in the world is Mr Heron?' cried Lady Louisa. 'I declare, I never heard such a farrago! Confess, you are trying to take me in.'

'Not at all, Louisa. You don't understand the situation at all. One of them must marry me.'

'That I can believe,' she said dryly. 'But this nonsense about Horatia? What is the truth of it?'

'Only that Horatia offered herself to me in her sister's place. And that—but I need not tell you—is quite for your ears alone.'

Lady Louisa was not in the habit of giving way to amazement, and she did not now indulge in fruitless ejaculations. 'Marcus, is the girl a minx?' she asked.

'No,' he answered. 'She is not, Louisa. I am not at all sure that she is not a heroine.'

'Don't she wish to marry you?'

The Earl's eyes gleamed. 'Well, I am rather old, you know, though no one would think it to look at me. But she assures me she would quite like to marry me. If my memory serves me, she prophesied that we should deal famously together.'

Lady Louisa, watching him, said abruptly: 'Rule, is this a love-match?'

His brows rose; he looked faintly amused. 'My dear Louisa! At my age?'

'Then marry the Beauty,' she said. 'That one would understand better.'

'You are mistaken, my dear. Horatia understands perfectly. She engages not to interfere with me.'

'At seventeen! It's folly, Marcus.' She got up, drawing her scarf around her. 'I'll see her for myself.'

'Do,' he said cordially. 'I think—but I may be prejudiced—you will find her adorable.'

'If you find her so,' she said, her eyes softening, 'I shall love her—even though she has a squint!'

'Not a squint,' said his lordship. 'A stammer.'

4

The question Lady Louisa Quain longed to ask yet did not ask was: 'What of Caroline Massey?' Her brother's relations with the fair Massey were perfectly well known to her, nor was she, in the general way, afraid of plain speaking. She told herself that nothing she could say would be likely to have any effect on his conduct, but admitted that she lacked the moral courage to broach the subject. She believed that she enjoyed a good deal of Rule's confidence, but he had never discussed his amorous adventures with her, and would be capable of delivering an extremely unpleasant snub if she trespassed on forbidden ground.

Although she did not flatter herself that her influence had had very much to do with it, it was she who had urged him to marry. She said that if there was one thing she found herself unable to bear it was the prospect of seeing Crosby in Rule's shoes. It was she who had indicated Miss Winwood as a suitable bride. She liked Elizabeth, and was quick to value not only her celestial good looks, but the sweetness of her disposition as well. Surely the possession of so charming a wife would wean Rule from his odious connection with the Massey. But now it did not seem as though Rule cared whom he married and that augured very ill for his bride's future influence over him. A chit of seventeen too! It could not be more unpromising.

She waited on Lady Winwood and met Horatia. She left South Street later in quite another frame of mind. That black-browed child was no simpering miss from the schoolroom. Lord! thought her ladyship, what a dance she would lead him! It was better, far better than she had planned. Elizabeth's docility would not have answered the purpose near so well as Horatia's turbulence. Why, she told herself, he'll have not a moment's peace and no time at all for that odious Massey creature!

That Rule foresaw the unquiet future that so delighted his sister seemed improbable. He continued to visit in Hertford Street, and no hint of parting crossed his lips.

Lady Massey received him in her rose and silver boudoir two days after the announcement of his betrothal. She was dressed in a négligée of lace and satin, and reclined on a brocaded sopha. No servant announced him; he came into the room as one who had the right, and as he shut the door, remarked humorously: 'Dear Caroline, you've a new porter. Did you tell him to shut the door in my face?'

She held her hand to him. 'Did he do so, Marcus?'

'No,' said his lordship. 'No. That ignominious fate has not yet been mine.' He took her hand and raised it to his lips. Her fingers clasped his, and drew him down to her. 'I thought we were being very formal,' he said, smiling, and kissed her.

She retained her hold on his hand, but said half quizzically, half mournfully: 'Perhaps we should be formal—now, my lord.'

'So you did tell the porter to shut the door in my face?' sighed his lordship.

'I did not. But you are to be married, are you not, Marcus?'

'Yes,' admitted Rule. 'Not just at this moment, you know.'

She smiled, but fleetingly. 'You might have told me,' she said.

He opened his snuff-box and dipped in his finger and thumb. 'I might, of course,' he said, possessing himself of her hand. 'A new blend, my dear,' he said, and dropped the pinch on to her white wrist, and sniffed.

She pulled her hand away. 'Could you not have told me?' she repeated.

He shut his snuff-box and glanced down at her, still good-humoured, but with something at the back of his eyes which gave her pause. A little anger shook her; she understood quite well: he would not discuss his marriage with her. She said, trying to make her voice light: 'You will say it is not my business, I suppose.'

'I am never rude, Caroline,' objected his lordship mildly.

She felt herself foiled, but smiled. 'No indeed. I've heard it said you're the smoothest-spoken man in England.' She studied her rings, moving her hand to catch the light. 'But I didn't know you thought of marriage.' She flashed a look up at him. 'You see,' she said, mock-solemn, 'I thought you loved me—only me!'

'What in the world,' inquired his lordship, 'has that to do with my marriage? I am entirely at your feet, my dear. Quite the prettiest feet I ever remember to have seen.'

'And you've seen many, I apprehend,' she said with a certain dryness.

'Dozens,' said his lordship cheerfully.

She did not mean to say it, but the words slipped out before she could guard her tongue. 'But for all that you are at my feet, Marcus, you have offered for another woman.'

The Earl had put up his glass to inspect a Dresden harlequin upon the mantelpiece. 'If you bought that for a Kändler, my love, I am much afraid that you have been imposed upon,' he remarked.

'It was given me,' she said impatiently.

'How shocking!' said his lordship. 'I will send you a very pretty pair of dancing figures in its place.'

'You are extremely obliging, Marcus, but we were speaking of your marriage,' she said, nettled.

'You were speaking of it,' he corrected. 'I was trying to—er—turn the subject.'

She got up from the sopha and took an impatient step towards him.

'I suppose,' she said breathlessly, 'you did not think the fair Massey worthy of so signal an honour?'

'To tell you the truth, my dear, my modesty forbade me to suppose that the fair Massey would—er—contemplate marriage with me.'

'Perhaps I would not,' she replied. 'But I think that was not your reason.'

'Marriage,' said his lordship pensively, 'is such a very dull affair, you know.'

'Is it, my lord? Even marriage with the noble Earl of Rule?'

'Even with me,' agreed Rule. He looked down at her, a curious expression that was not quite a smile in his eyes. 'You see, my dear, to use your own words, you would have to love me—only me.'

She was startled. Under her powder a faint flush crept into her cheeks.

She turned away with a little laugh and began to arrange the roses in one of her bowls. 'That would certainly be very dull,' she said. She glanced sideways at him. 'Are you perhaps jealous, my lord?'

'Not in the least,' said the Earl placidly.

'But you think that were I your wife you might be?'

'You are so charming, my dear, that I feel sure I should have to be,' said his lordship bowing.

She was too clever a woman to press her point. She thought she had gone too far already, and however angry she might be at his marriage she had no wish to alienate him. At one time she had held high hopes of becoming the Countess of Rule, though she was perfectly aware that such an alliance would be deemed a shocking one by the Polite World. She knew now that Rule had baffled her. She had caught a glimpse of steel, and realized that there was something hidden under that easy-going exterior that was as incalculable as it was unexpected. She had imagined that she could twist him round her finger; for the first time she was shaken by doubt, and knew that she must tread warily if she did not wish to lose him.

This she certainly did not want to do. The late Sir Thomas had, in his disagreeable way, tied up his capital so fast that his widow found herself for ever in most unpleasant straits. Sir Thomas had had no sympathy with females who doted on pharaoh and deep basset. Happily the Earl of Rule was not afflicted by the same scruples, and he had not the smallest objection to assisting pecuniarily a distressed lady. He never asked uncomfortable questions on the vice of gambling, and his purse was a fat one.

He had startled her to-day. She had not thought that he dreamed of a rival; now it appeared that he knew very well, probably had known from the first. She would have to be careful; trust her to know how matters lay between him and Robert Lethbridge!

No one ever spoke of it, no one could tell how the story got about, but any number of people knew that once Robert Lethbridge had aspired to the hand of Lady Louisa Drelincourt. Louisa was now the wife of Sir Humphrey Quain, with no breath of scandal attaching to her name, but there had been a day, in her mad teens, when the town hummed with gossip about her. No one knew the whole story, but everyone knew that Lethbridge had been head over ears in love with her and had proposed for her hand, and been rejected, not by the lady herself but by her brother. That had surprised everybody, because although it was true that Lethbridge had a dreadful reputation ('the wildest rake in town, my love!'), no one could have supposed that Rule of all people would put his foot down. Yet he had certainly done so. That was common knowledge. Just what had happened next no one exactly knew, though everyone had his or her version to propound. It had all been so carefully hushed up, but a whisper of Abduction started in Polite Circles. Some said it was no abduction but a willing flight north to Gretna, across the Border. It may have been so, but the runaways never reached Gretna Green. The Earl of Rule drove such fleet horses.

Some held that the two men had fought a duel somewhere on the Great North Road; others spread a tale that Rule carried not a sword but a horse-whip, but this was generally allowed to be improbable, for Lethbridge, however infamous his behaviour, was not a lackey. It was a pity that no one had the true version of the affair, for it was all delightfully scandalous. But none of the three actors in the drama ever spoke of it and if Lady Louisa was reported to have eloped with Lethbridge one night, she was known twenty-four hours later to be visiting relatives in the neighbourhood of Grantham. It was quite true that Robert Lethbridge disappeared from society for several weeks, but he reappeared in due course without wearing any of the symptoms of the baffled lover. The town was agog to see how he and Rule would comport themselves when they met, as they were bound to meet, but once again disappointment awaited the scandalmongers.

Neither showed any sign of enmity. They exchanged several remarks on different subjects, and if it had not been for Mr Harry Crewe, who had actually seen Rule drive his racing curricle out of town at the extremely odd hour of ten in the evening, even the most inveterate gossip-mongers would have been inclined to have believed the whole tale a mere fabrication.

Lady Massey knew better than that. She was well acquainted with Lord Lethbridge and would have wagered her very fine diamonds that the sentiments he cherished towards the Earl of Rule were tinged with something more than a habitual maliciousness.

As for Rule, he betrayed nothing, but she was not inclined to run the risk of losing him by encouraging too openly the advances of Robert Lethbridge.

She finished the arrangement of her flowers and turned, a gleam of rueful humour in her fine eyes.

'Marcus, my dear,' she said helplessly, 'something much more important! Five hundred guineas at loo, and that odious Celestine dunning me! What am I to do?'

'Don't let it worry you, my dear Caroline,' said his lordship. 'A trifling loan, and the matter is settled.'

She was moved to exclaim: 'Ah, how good you are! I wish—I wish you were not to be married, Marcus. We have dealt extremely, you and I, and I have a notion that it will all be changed now.'

If she referred to their pecuniary relations she might have been thought to have reason for this speech. Lord Rule was likely to find himself with new demands on his purse in the very near future. Viscount Winwood was on his way home to England.

The Viscount, having received in Rome the intelligence of his youngest sister's betrothal, was moved to comply with his parent's desire for his immediate return, and set forward upon the journey with all possible speed. Merely halting a few days in Florence, where he happened to chance upon two friends, and spending a week in Paris upon business not unconnected with the gaming-tables, he made the best of his way home, and would have arrived in London not more than three days later than his fond mother expected him had he not met Sir Jasper Middleton at Breteuil. Sir Jasper, being on his way to the Capital, was putting up at the Hôtel St Nicholas for the night, and was in the midst of a solitary dinner when the Viscount walked in. Nothing could have been more providential, for Sir Jasper was heartily bored with his own company, and had been yearning this many a day to have his revenge on Pelham for a certain game of piquet played in London some months before.

The Viscount was delighted to oblige him; they sat up all night over the cards and in the morning the Viscount, absent-minded no doubt through lack of sleep, embarked in Sir Jasper's post-chaise and was so borne back to Paris. The game of piquet being continued in the chaise, he noticed nothing amiss until they arrived at Clermont, and since by that time there were only some seven or eight posts to go before they reached Paris, it needed no great persuasion to induce him to continue the journey.

He arrived eventually in London to find the preparations for Horatia's nuptials in full swing; and he expressed himself extremely well satisfied with the contract, cast a knowing eye over the Marriage Settlements, congratulated Horatia on her good fortune, and went off to pay his respects to the Earl of Rule.

They were naturally not strangers to each other, but since Pelham was some ten years the Earl's junior they moved in different circles and their acquaintanceship was slight. This circumstance did not weigh with the lively Viscount in the least; he greeted Rule with all the casual bonhomie he used towards his cronies and proceeded, by way of making him feel one of the family, to borrow money from him.

'For I don't mind telling you, my dear fellow,' he said frankly, 'that if I'm to appear the thing at this wedding of yours I must give my tailor a trifle on account. Won't do if I come in rags, you know. Girls won't like it.'

The Viscount was not exactly a fop, but anything less ragged than his slim person would have been hard to find. It did not require the efforts of two stout men to coax him into his coats, and he had a way of arranging his cravat askew, but his clothes were made by the first tailor in town, and of the finest stuffs, embellished with any quantity of heavy gold lacing. At the moment he sat in one of Rule's chairs with his legs stretched out in front of him, and his hands thrust into the pockets of a pair of fawn breeches. His velvet coat hung open to display a waistcoat embroidered in a design of exotic flowers and humming birds. A fine sapphire pin was stuck in the cascade of lace at his throat and his stockings, which represented a dead loss of twenty-five guineas to his hosier, were of silk with large clocks.

The Viscount nobly upheld the Winwood tradition of good looks. He had a reasonable height, and a slender build, and bore a resemblance to his sister Elizabeth. Both had golden locks, and deep blue eyes, straight and beautiful noses, and delicately curved lips. There the likeness ended. Elizabeth's celestial calm was quite lacking in her brother. The Viscount's mobile face was already rather lined, and his eye was a roving one. He looked to be very good-natured, which indeed he was, and appeared to survey the world with a youthful air of cynicism.

Rule received with equanimity the suggestion that he should pay for his prospective brother-in-law's wedding clothes. He glanced down at his guest with some amusement, and said in his bored way: 'Certainly, Pelham.'

The Viscount looked him over with approval. 'I'd a notion we should deal famously,' he remarked. 'Not that I'm in the habit of borrowing from my friends, y'know, but I count you one of the family, Rule.'

'And admit me to its privileges,' said the Earl gravely. 'Admit me still further and let me have a list of your debts.'

The Viscount was momentarily startled. 'Hey? What, all of 'em?' He shook his head. 'Devilish handsome of you, Rule, but can't be done.'

'You alarm me,' said Rule. 'Are they beyond my resources?'

'The trouble is,' said the Viscount confidentially, 'I don't know what they are.'

'My resources, or your debts?'

'Lord, man, the debts! Can't remember the half of 'em. No, it's no use arguing. I've tried to add 'em up a score of times. You think you've done it and then some damned bill you forgot years ago crops up. Never come to the end of it. Wiser to leave it alone. Pay as you go, that's my motto.'

'Is it?' said Rule, mildly surprised. 'I shouldn't have thought it.'

'What I mean,' explained the Viscount, 'is, when a fellow puts the bailiffs on to you, so to speak, then it's time to settle with him. But as for paying all my bills—damme, I never heard of such a thing! Wouldn't do at all.'

'Nevertheless,' said Rule, moving over to his desk, 'I believe you must oblige me in this. Your arrest for debt, perhaps even in the act of bestowing your sister's hand on me in marriage, would quite unnerve me.'

The Viscount grinned. 'Would it so? Well, they can't clap up a peer yet, y'know. Just as you please, of course, but I warn you, I'm in pretty deep.'

Rule dipped a quill in the standish. 'If I were to give you a draft on my bankers for five thousand? Or shall we say ten, as a rounder sum?'

The Viscount was moved to sit up. 'Five,' he said firmly. 'Since you're making a point of it, I don't mind settling up to five thousand, but give away ten thousand pounds to a lot of tradesmen I can't and I won't do. Damme, flesh and blood won't stand it!'

He watched Rule's quill move across the paper, and shook his head. 'Seems wicked to me,' he said. 'I've nothing to say against spending money, but blister it, I don't like to see it thrown away!' He sighed. 'You know, I could put it to better use, Rule,' he suggested.

Rule shook the sand off the paper and handed it to him. 'But somehow I feel sure you won't, Pelham,' he said.

The Viscount cocked an eyebrow intelligently. 'Like that, is it?' he said. 'Oh, very well! But I don't like it. I don't like it at all.'

Nor did his sisters like it when they heard of it. 'Given you five thousand pounds to pay your debts?' cried Charlotte. 'I never heard of such a thing!'

'No more did I,' agreed Pelham. 'Thought for a moment the man was queer in his head, but he don't seem to be.'

'Pel, I do think perhaps you might have waited,' Elizabeth said rather reproachfully. 'It seems almost—almost indecent.'

'And it will all go on gaming,' said Charlotte.

'Devil a penny of it, miss, so that's all you know,' replied the Viscount without rancour.

'Why n-not?' inquired Horatia bluntly. 'It usually d-does.'

Her brother threw her a look of scorn. 'Lord, Horry, if a man trusts you with a cool five thousand to pay your debts, there's no more to be said.'

'I suppose,' said Charlotte waspishly, 'Lord Rule requires to see your accounts.'

'I'll tell you what it is, Charlotte,' the Viscount informed her, 'if you don't sweeten that tongue of yours you'll never get a husband.'

Elizabeth intervened rather hastily. 'Will it meet them all, Pel?'

'It'll keep the blood-suckers quiet for a while,' replied his lordship. He nodded to Horatia. 'He'll make you a devilish good husband, I daresay, but you'd best be careful how you deal with him, Horry!'

'Oh,' said Horatia, 'you don't understand, P-Pel! We are not going to interfere with each other at all! It is j-just like a French marriage of c-convenience.'

'I'm not saying it ain't convenient,' said the Viscount, glancing at Rule's draft, 'but if you take my advice you won't play your tricks on Rule. I've a strong notion you might regret it.'

'I have felt that too,' Elizabeth said, an anxious note in her voice.

'S-stuff!' pronounced Horatia, unimpressed.

5

The wedding of the Earl of Rule to Miss Horatia Winwood passed off without any unseemly fracas, such as the arrest of the bride's brother for debt or a scene created by the bridegroom's mistress (an event not entirely unexpected by the hopeful), occurring to mar its propriety. The Earl arrived punctually, which surprised everyone, including his harassed secretary; and the bride seemed to be in excellent spirits. Indeed, there were those who considered her spirits too excellent for so solemn an occasion. She was not observed to shed a single tear. However, this lack of sensibility was more than made up for by the demeanour of Lady Winwood. Nothing could have been more proper than that lady's whole bearing. She was supported by her brother, and wept silently throughout the ceremony. Miss Winwood and Miss Charlotte as bridesmaids looked beautiful and behaved becomingly; Mr Walpole's sharp eyes took in everything; Lady Louisa Quain bore up very well, but had recourse to her handkerchief when my lord took Horatia's hand in his; Mr Drelincourt wore a new wig, and a look of saintly resignation; and the Viscount performed his part with careless grace.

It was understood that after a few days spent in the country, the bride and groom were bound for Paris, the choice of destination having been left to the bride. Elizabeth thought it an odd place for a honeymoon, but 'Pho!' said Horatia. 'We are not like you and Edward, w-wanting to make love all d-day long! I want to see things, and go to V-Versailles, and b-buy smarter clothes than Theresa Maulfrey's!'

This part at least of her programme was faithfully carried out. At the end of six weeks the noble pair returned to London, the bride's luggage, so it was rumoured, occupying an entire coach.

The nuptials of her youngest-born had proved to be too much for Lady Winwood's delicate constitution. The varied emotions she had sustained were productive of a fit of the vapours, and the intelligence that her son had signalized his sister's wedding-day by betting fifty pounds on a race between two geese in Hyde Park set the seal to her collapse. She withdrew with her two remaining daughters (one, alas, so soon to be reft from her) to the fastness of Winwood, and there built up her shattered nervous system on a diet of eggs and cream and paregoric draughts, and the contemplation of the Marriage Settlements.

Charlotte, who had thus early in life perceived the Hollowness of Worldly Pleasures professed herself very well pleased with the arrangement, but Elizabeth, though she would not have dreamed of urging Poor Dear Mama, would have preferred to be in London for Horry's homecoming. And this in despite of the fact that Mr Heron found it easily compatible with his not very arduous duties to spend a considerable portion of his time at his home, not two miles distant from Winwood.

Of course Horry journeyed into Hampshire to visit them, but she came without the Earl, a circumstance that distressed Elizabeth. She arrived in her own chaise, a high-sprung affair with huge wheels and the most luxurious blue velvet upholstery; was attended by her abigail, two postilions, and a couple of grooms riding behind the chaise. At first glance she seemed to her sisters to have changed out of all recognition.

Evidently the day of demure muslins and chip hats was done, for the vision in the chaise wore a gown of tobine stripes over a large hoop, and the hat perched on top of curls dressed *à la capricieuse* bore several waving plumes.

'Good gracious, it cannot be Horry!' gasped Charlotte, falling back a step.

But it was soon seen that the change in Horatia went no deeper than her clothes. She could hardly wait for the steps of the chaise to be let down before she sprang into Elizabeth's arms, and she paid not the slightest heed to the crushing of her stiff silk gown or the tilting of that preposterous hat. From Elizabeth she flew to Charlotte, words bubbling off her tongue. Oh, yes, it was the same Horry: no doubt of that.

She stayed one night only at Winwood, which, said Charlotte, was just as well for her Mama, whose state of health was still too precarious to enable her to bear so much chatter and excitement.

Had she enjoyed her honeymoon? Oh, she had had a famous time! Only fancy, she had been to Versailles and spoken with the Queen, and it was perfectly true, the Queen was the most ravishingly beautiful creature and so elegant that she set all the fashions. See, she herself was wearing shoes *cheveux à la Reine*! Whom else had she met! Why, everyone in the world! Such routs, such soirées, and oh, the fireworks at the Tuileries ball!

It was not until they had retired to bed that Elizabeth had an opportunity for a *tête-à-tête*. But no sooner did Horatia set eyes on her sister than she sent her maid away, and curled upon the sopha with Elizabeth beside her. 'I'm so g-glad you came, L-Lizzie,' she said confidingly. 'Charlotte disapproves d-dreadfully of me, doesn't she?'

Elizabeth smiled. 'I am sure you don't care a rap for her disapproval, Horry.'

'Of c-course I don't. I do so hope you will be m-married very soon, L-Lizzie. You have no n-notion how agreeable it is.'

'Quite soon now, we hope. But with Mama so poorly I don't think of it. Are you—are you very happy, dearest?'

Horatia nodded vigorously. 'Oh, yes! Only that I can't help f-feeling sometimes that I stole M-Marcus from you, Lizzie. But you do still prefer Edward, don't you?'

'Always,' Elizabeth answered, laughing. 'Is it very bad taste in me?'

'Well, I m-must say I can't understand it,' said Horatia candidly. 'But perhaps it is b-because you aren't horribly worldly, like m-me. L-Lizzie, even if it is odious of m-me, I must say it is delightful to have just what one wants, and to d-do as one pleases.'

'Yes,' agreed Miss Winwood rather doubtfully, 'I suppose it is.' She stole a glance at Horatia's profile. 'Lord Rule—could not accompany you on this visit?'

'As a m-matter of fact,' admitted Horatia, 'he would have come, only I w-wanted to have you all to m-myself, so he gave up the notion.'

'I see,' said Elizabeth. 'Don't you think, love, that you should have come together, perhaps?'

'Oh, no,' Horatia assured her. 'He quite understood, you know. I find too that fashionable p-people hardly ever do things together.'

'Horry dear,' said Miss Winwood with difficulty, 'I do not want to sound like Charlotte, but I have heard that when—when their wives are so very fashionable—gentlemen do sometimes look elsewhere for entertainment.'

'I know,' said Horatia sapiently. 'But you see I p-promised I wouldn't interfere with Rule.'

It was all very disturbing, Elizabeth felt, but she said no more. Horatia returned to town next day, and the Winwoods heard of her thereafter through the medium of the post and the *Gazette*. Her letters were not very illuminating, but it was apparent that she was enjoying a life full of social engagements.

Elizabeth heard more direct tidings of her from Mr Heron upon the occasion of his next visit into the country.

'Horry?' said Mr Heron. 'Well, yes, I have seen her, but not quite lately, my love. She sent me a card for her drum Tuesday se'nnight. It was a very brilliant affair, but you know I am not in the way of going out a great deal. Still, I did go there,' he added. 'Horry was in spirits, I thought.'

'Happy?' Elizabeth said anxiously.

'Oh, certainly! My lord too was all amiability.'

'Did he seem—could you tell whether he seemed fond of her?' Elizabeth asked.

'Well,' said Mr Heron reasonably, 'you would not expect him to display his affection in public, dearest. He was just as he always is. A little amused, I thought. You see, Horry seems to have become quite the rage.'

'Oh, dear!' said Miss Winwood, with deep foreboding. 'If only she does not do anything shocking!' A glance at Mr Heron's face made her cry out: 'Edward, you have heard something! I beg you will tell me at once!'

Mr Heron made haste to reassure her. 'No, no, nothing in the world, my love. Merely that Horry seems to have inherited the Fatal Tendency to gamble. But nearly everyone plays nowadays, you know,' he added soothingly.

Miss Winwood was not soothed, nor did an unexpected visit a week later from Mrs Maulfrey do anything to alleviate her alarms.

Mrs Maulfrey was staying at Basingstoke with her Mama-in-law, and drove over to Winwood to pay a morning call on her cousins. She was far more explicit than had been Mr Heron. She sat in a *bergère* chair in the saloon, facing Lady Winwood's couch, and, as Charlotte afterwards remarked, that that afflicted lady did not suffer an immediate relapse was due to her own fortitude rather than to any consideration shown her by her guest.

It was quite obvious that Mrs Maulfrey had not come on any charitable errand. Charlotte, always just, said: 'Depend upon it, Theresa tried to patronize Horry. You know her encroaching way. And really, I cannot altogether blame Horry for snubbing her, though I hope I am far from excusing Horry's excesses.'

Horry, it seemed, was becoming the talk of the Town. Lady Winwood, receiving this piece of news, was moved to recall with complacency a day when she herself had been a reigning toast.

'A Toast!' said Mrs Maulfrey. 'Yes, aunt, and I am sure no one need wonder at it, but Horry is not a Beauty, and if she is a Toast, which I never yet heard, it is certainly not on that account.'

'We ourselves think dear Horry very pretty, Theresa,' said Miss Winwood gently.

'Yes, my dear, but you are partial, as indeed I am too. No one is fonder of

Horry than I am, and I put her behaviour down to her childishness, I assure you.'

'We are aware,' said Charlotte, sitting very straight and stiff in her chair, 'that Horry is little more than a child, but we should find it hard to believe that the behaviour of a Winwood could be such as to call for that or any other excuse.'

Slightly quelled by that stern gaze, Mrs Maulfrey fidgeted with the strings of her reticule, and said with a light laugh: 'Oh, certainly, my dear! But I saw with my own eyes Horry strip one of the bracelets off her wrist at Lady Dollabey's card-party—pearls and diamond chips, my love! the most ravishing thing!—and throw it on to the table as her stake because she had lost all her money. You may imagine the scene: gentlemen are so thoughtless, and of course several must needs encourage her, staking rings and hair-buckles against her bracelet, and such nonsense.'

'Perhaps it was not very wise of Horry,' said Elizabeth. 'But not, I think, such a very great matter.'

'I am bound to say,' remarked Charlotte, 'that I hold gaming in any form in the utmost abhorrence.'

Lady Winwood unexpectedly entered the lists. 'Gaming has always been a passion with the Winwoods,' she observed. 'Your Papa was greatly addicted to every form of it. I myself, when my health permits it, am excessively fond of cards. I remember some very pleasant evenings at Gunnersbury, playing at silver pharaoh with the dear Princess. Mr Walpole too! I wonder that you can talk so, Charlotte: it is quite disloyal to Papa's memory, let me tell you. Gaming is quite in the mode; I do not disapprove of it. But I must say I cannot approve of the Winwood luck. Do not tell me my little Horatia has inherited that, Theresa! Did she lose the bracelet?'

'Well, as to that,' said Mrs Maulfrey reluctantly, 'it was not staked in the end. Rule came into the card-room.'

Elizabeth looked quickly across at her. 'Yes?' she said. 'He stopped it?'

'N-no,' said Mrs Maulfrey, with dissatisfaction. 'Hardly that. He said in his quiet way that it might be difficult to assess the worth of a trinket, and picked up the bracelet, and put it back on Horry's wrist, and set a rouleau of guineas down in its place. I did not wait to see any more.'

'Oh, that was well done of him!' Elizabeth cried, her cheeks glowing.

'Certainly one may say that he behaved with dignity and propriety,' conceded Charlotte. 'And if that is all you have to tell us of Horry's behaviour, my dear Theresa, I must confess I feel you have wasted your time.'

'Pray do not be thinking that I am a mere mischief-maker, Charlotte!' besought her cousin. 'And it is not by any means all. I have it on the best of authority that she had the—yes, positively I must call it the audacity—to drive young Dashwood's gig up St James's for a bet! Right under the windows of White's, my dear! Now don't mistake me: I am sure no one thinks anything but that she's a madcapchild—indeed, I understand she takes extremely, and people think her exploits vastly diverting, but I put it to you, is this conduct befitting the Countess of Rule?'

'If it befits a Winwood—which, however, I do not maintain,' said Charlotte with hauteur, 'it may certainly befit a Drelincourt!'

This crushing rejoinder put Mrs Maulfrey so much out of countenance that she found herself with very little more to say, and presently took her leave of the Winwood ladies. She left behind her a feeling of uneasiness which culminated in a suggestion, put tentatively forward by Elizabeth, that Lady Winwood should think of returning to South Street. Lady Winwood said in a failing voice that no one had the least regard for the frailty of her poor nerves, and if ever good had come of interfering between man and wife she had yet to hear of it.

However, the business was settled in the end by a letter from Mr Heron. Mr Heron had got his Captaincy, and was to go into the West Country in the further execution of his duties. He desired to make Elizabeth his wife without any more delay, and proposed an immediate wedding.

Elizabeth would have liked to be married quietly at Winwood, but her Mama, having no notion of allowing her triumph in getting two daughters respectably married within three months to pass unnoticed, arose tottering from her couch and announced that never should it be said that she had Failed in her Duty towards her loved ones.

The wedding was naturally not so brilliant an affair as Horatia's, but it passed off very well, and if the bride appeared pale she was allowed to be in great beauty for all that. The bridegroom looked extremely handsome in his Regimentals, and the ceremony was graced by the presence of the Earl and Countess of Rule, the Countess wearing for the occasion a gown that made every other lady blink with envy.

Elizabeth, in all the bustle of hurried preparation, had had few opportunities of being private with Horatia, and on the only occasion when she found herself alone with her sister she had realized with a sinking heart that Horatia was on her guard against too intimate a conversation. She could only hope to have more opportunity later in the year, when Horatia promised to come to Bath, which watering-place Captain Heron was to make his headquarters.

6

'Well, if you wish to know what I think,' said Lady Louisa stringently—'though I make not the smallest doubt that you don't—you're a fool, Rule!'

The Earl, who was still glancing over some papers brought to him by Mr Gisborne a few moments before his sister's arrival, said absently: 'I know. But you must not let it distress you, my dear.'

'What,' demanded her ladyship, disregarding this flippancy, 'are those papers? You need not put yourself to the trouble of telling me. I know the look of a bill, trust me!'

The Earl put them into his pocket. 'If only more people understood me so well!' he sighed. 'And respected my—er—constitutional dislike of answering questions.'

'The chit will ruin you,' said his sister. 'And you do nothing—nothing to avert calamity!'

'Believe me,' said Rule, 'I hope to have enough energy to avert that particular calamity, Louisa.'

'I wish I may see it!' she replied. 'I like Horry. Yes, I do like her, and I did from the start, but if you'd one grain of sense, Marcus, you would take a stick and beat her!'

'But think how fatiguing!' objected the Earl.

She looked scornfully across at him. 'I wanted her to lead you a dance,' she said candidly. 'I thought it would be very good for you. But I never dreamed she would make herself the talk of the town while you stood by and watched.'

'You see, I hardly ever dance,' Rule excused himself.

Lady Louisa might have replied with some asperity had not a light footstep sounded at that moment in the hall, and the door opened to admit Horatia herself.

She was dressed for the street, but carried her hat in her hand, as though she had just taken it off. She threw it on to a chair, and dutifully embraced her sister-in-law. 'I am sorry I was out, L-Louisa. I have been to see M-Mama. She is feeling very low, because of having l-lost Lizzie. And Sir P-Peter Mason, whom she quite thought was g-going to offer for Charlotte because he doesn't like L-levity in a Female, is promised to Miss Lupton after all. M-Marcus, do you think Arnold might like to m-marry Charlotte?'

'For heaven's sake, Horry,' cried Lady Louisa with foreboding, 'don't ask him!'

Horatia's straight brows drew together. 'N-no, of course not. But I m-might throw them together, I think.'

'Not, I beg of you,' said his lordship, 'in this house.'

The grey eyes surveyed him questioningly. 'N-not if you would rather I didn't,' said Horatia obligingly. 'I am not set on it, you understand.'

'I am so glad,' said his lordship. 'Consider the blow to my self-esteem if Charlotte were to accept Arnold's hand in marriage.'

Horatia twinkled. 'Well, you n-need not put yourself about, sir, for Charlotte says she is going to D-dedicate her Life to M-mama. Oh, are you going already, Louisa?'

Lady Louisa had risen, drawing her scarf round her shoulders. 'My dear, I have been here this age. I came only for a word with Marcus.'

Horatia stiffened slightly. 'I see,' she said. 'It was a p-pity I came in, perhaps.'

'Horry, you're a silly child,' said Lady Louisa, tapping her cheek. 'I have been telling Rule he should beat you. I doubt he is too lazy.'

Horatia swept a polite curtsy, and closed her lips firmly together.

The Earl escorted his sister out of the room, and across the hall. 'You are not always very wise, are you, Louisa?' he said.

'I never was,' she answered ruefully.

Having seen his sister into her carriage the Earl returned rather thoughtfully to the library. Horatia, swinging her hat defiantly, was already crossing the hall towards the stairs, but she paused as Rule spoke to her. 'Do you think you could spare me a moment of your time, Horry?'

The scowl still lingered on her brow. 'I'm g-going to luncheon with Lady M-Mallory,' she informed him.

'It is not yet time for luncheon,' he replied.

'No, but I have to change my g-gown.'

'That is naturally important,' agreed the Earl.

'Well, it is,' she insisted.

The Earl held the door into the library open. Up went Horatia's chin. 'I m-may as well tell you, my lord, that I'm feeling c-cross, and when I'm cross I don't talk to p-people.'

Across the wide stretch of hall the Earl's eyes met and held hers. 'Horry,' he said pleasantly, 'you know how much I dislike exertion. Don't put me to the trouble of fetching you.'

The chin came down a little, and the smouldering eyes showed a certain speculative interest. 'C-carry me, do you m-mean? I wonder if you would?'

The gravity of Rule's expression was dispelled by a slight look of amusement. 'And I wonder whether you really think that I would not?' he said.

A door at the end of the hall, leading to the servants' quarters, opened, and a footman came out. Horatia shot a triumphant glance at the Earl, set one foot on the bottom stair, hesitated, and then swung round and walked back into the library.

The Earl closed the door. 'You play fair, Horry, at all events,' he remarked.

'Of c-course,' said Horatia, seating herself on the arm of a chair and once more tossing her ill-used hat aside. 'I did not m-mean to be disobliging, but when you talk me over with your sister it makes me f-furious.'

'Are you not rather leaping to conclusions?' suggested Rule.

'Well, anyway, she said she had been t-telling you that you ought to beat me,' said Horatia, kicking her heel against the chair-leg.

'She is full of good advice,' agreed his lordship. 'But I haven't beaten you yet, Horry, in spite of it.'

Slightly mollified, the bride remarked: 'No, b-but I think when she says things about m-me you might defend m-me, sir.'

'You see, Horry,' said his lordship with a certain deliberation, 'you make that rather difficult.'

There was an uncomfortable pause. Horatia flushed to the roots of her hair, and said, stammering painfully: 'I'm s-sorry. I d-don't m-mean to behave outrageously. W-what have I done n-now?'

'Oh, nothing really very desperate, my dear,' Rule said non-committally. 'But do you think you could refrain from introducing a wild-animal into Polite Circles?'

A giggle, hastily choked, escaped her. 'I was afraid you'd hear about that,' she confessed. 'B-but it was quite an accident, I assure you, and–and very diverting.'

'I haven't the least doubt of that,' Rule replied.

'Well, it truly was, M-Marcus. It jumped on to Crosby's shoulder and p-pulled his wig off. But nobody m-minded at all, except Crosby. I'm afraid it isn't a very well-trained monkey.'

'I'm afraid it can't be,' said Rule. 'Some such suspicion did cross my mind when I found it had–er–visited the breakfast-table before me the other morning.'

'Oh dear!' Horatia said contritely. 'I am very sorry. Only Sophia Colehampton has one, and it goes everywhere with her, so I thought I would have one too. However, I d-don't really like it m-much, so I think I won't keep it. Is that all?'

He smiled. 'Alas, Horry, it is only the beginning. I think–yes, really I think you must explain some of these.' He drew the sheaf of bills out of his pocket and gave them to her.

On the top lay a sheet of paper covered with Mr Gisborne's neat figures. Horatia gazed in dismay at the alarming total. 'Are they–all mine?' she faltered.

'All yours,' said his lordship calmly.

Horatia swallowed. 'I d-didn't mean to spend as m-much as that. Indeed I c-can't imagine how it can have come about.'

The Earl took the bills from her, and began to turn them over. 'No,' he agreed, 'I have often thought it very odd how bills mount up. And one must dress, after all.'

'Yes,' nodded Horatia, more hopefully. 'You do understand that, d-don't you, Marcus?'

'Perfectly. But—forgive my curiosity, Horry—do you invariably pay a hundred and twenty guineas for a pair of shoes?'

'What?' shrieked Horatia. The Earl showed her the bill. She stared at it with dawning consternation. 'Oh!' she said 'I–I remember now. You s-see, Marcus, they–they have heels studded with emeralds.'

'Then the matter becomes comprehensible,' said his lordship.

'Yes. I wore them at the Subscription-ball at Almack's. They are called *venez-y-voir*, you know.'

'That would account, no doubt,' remarked Rule, 'for the presence of the three young gentlemen whom I found—er—assisting at your toilet that evening.'

'B-but there is nothing in that, Rule!' objected Horatia, lifting her downcast head. 'It is quite the thing for gentlemen to be admitted as soon as the under-dress is on. I know it is, b-because Lady Stokes d-does it. They advise one how to p-place one's p-patches, and where to bestow one's flowers, and what p-perfume to use.'

If the Earl of Rule found anything amusing in being instructed by his bride in the art of dalliance the only sign he gave of it was the very faintest quiver of the lips. 'Ah!' he said. 'And yet—' he looked down at her, half-smiling—'And yet I believe I might advise you in these matters to even better purpose.'

'B-but you're my husband,' Horatia pointed out.

He turned back to the bills. 'That is undoubtedly a handicap,' he admitted.

Horatia appeared to consider the subject closed. She peered over his arm. 'Have you f-found anything else dreadful?' she inquired.

'My dear, are we not agreed that one must dress? I don't question your expenditure—though I confess I succumbed to curiosity over the shoes. What—shall we say—puzzles me a trifle—'

'I know,' she interrupted, sedulously regarding her feet. 'You w-want to know w-why I haven't paid them myself.'

'My inquisitive disposition,' murmured his lordship.

'I c-couldn't,' said Horatia gruffly. 'That's w-why!'

'A very adequate reason,' said that placid voice. 'But I thought I had made provision. My lamentable memory must be at fault again.'

Horatia set her teeth. 'I m-may deserve it, sir, but p-please don't be odious. You know you m-made provision.'

He laid the bills down. 'Pharaoh, Horry?'

'Oh n-no, not all of it!' she said eagerly, glad to be able to produce an extenuating circumstance. 'B-Basset!'

'I see.'

The note of amusement had left his voice; she ventured to raise her eyes, and saw something very like a frown on his face. 'Are you d-dreadfully angry?' she blurted out.

The frown cleared. 'Anger is too fatiguing an emotion, my dear. I was wondering how best to cure you.'

'C-cure me? You can't. It's in the b-blood,' said Horatia frankly. 'And even Mama don't disapprove of gaming. I didn't understand it quite p-perfectly at first, and I d-daresay that is why I lost.'

'Quite possibly,' assented Rule. 'Madam Wife, I am constrained to tell you—in my character of indignant husband—that I cannot countenance excessive gaming.'

'Don't, oh *don't*,' implored Horatia, 'm-make me promise to p-play only whisk and silver pharaoh! I c-couldn't keep it! I will be m-more careful, and I'm sorry about those shocking bills!—Oh gracious, only look at the time! I must go, I p-positively must go!'

'Don't distress yourself, Horry,' recommended the Earl. 'To be the last arrival is always effective.' But he spoke to space. Horatia had gone.

His wife's gyrations, however much perturbation they might occasion Lady Louisa, were watched by others with very different feelings. Mr Crosby Drelincourt, whose world had assumed a uniformly dun hue from the moment of his cousin's betrothal, began to observe a ray of light breaking through the gloom, and Lady Massey, taking note of the young Countess's every exploit and extravagance, patiently bided her time. Rule's visits to Hertford Street had become more infrequent, but she was far too clever to reproach him, and took care to be her most charming self whenever she saw him. She was already acquainted with Horatia—a circumstance she owed to the kind offices of Mr Drelincourt, who made it his business to present her to the Countess at a ball—but beyond exchanging curtsies and polite greetings with Horatia whenever they chanced to meet she had not sought to increase the friendship. Rule had a way of seeing more than he appeared to, and it was unlikely that he would permit an intimacy between his wife and his mistress to grow up without interference.

It seemed to be Mr Drelincourt's self-appointed duty to make presentations to his new cousin. He even presented Robert Lethbridge to her, at a drum at Richmond. His lordship had been out of town when the Earl and Countess of Rule returned from their honeymoon and by the time he first clapped eyes on the bride she had already—as young Mr Dashwood so brilliantly phrased it—Taken the Town by Storm.

Lord Lethbridge saw her first at the drum, dressed in satin *soupir étouffe*, with a coiffure *en diadème*. A patch called the Gallant was set in the middle of her cheek, and she fluttered ribbons *à l'attention*. She certainly took the eye, which may have been the reason for Lord Lethbridge's absorption.

He stood against one wall of the long saloon, and his eyes rested on the bride with a curious expression in them, hard to read. Mr Drelincourt, observing him from a distance, ranged alongside, and said with a titter: 'You are admiring my new cousin, my lord?'

'Profoundly,' said Lethbridge.

'For my part,' shrugged Mr Drelincourt, never one to conceal his feelings, 'I find those eyebrows positively grotesque. I do not call her a beauty. Decidedly I do not.'

Lethbridge's glance flickered to his face; his lips curled imperceptibly. 'You ought to be delighted with her, Crosby,' he said.

'Pray allow me to present you to the Paragon!' said Mr Drelincourt crossly. 'But I warn you, she stammers hideously.'

'And gambles, and drives gigs up St James's,' said his lordship. 'I never hoped for better.'

Mr Drelincourt looked sharply round at him. 'Why—why—'

'What a fool you are, Crosby!' said Lethbridge. 'Present me!'

'Really, my lord, really! Pray how am I to take that?'

'I had not the least intention of being enigmatic, believe me,' replied Lethbridge acidly. 'Make me known to this excellent bride.'

'You are in a devilish humour, my lord, I protest,' complained Crosby, but he moved towards the group about Horatia. 'Cousin, permit me! May I present one who is all eagerness to meet you?'

Horatia had very little desire to meet any crony of Mr Drelincourt's whom she cordially despised, and she turned with obvious reluctance. But the man who stood before her was not at all like Crosby's usual companions. None of the absurdities of the Macaroni marred the elegance of his person. He was dressed with magnificence, and he seemed to be considerably older than Mr Drelincourt.

'Lord Lethbridge, my Lady Rule!' said Crosby. 'You perceive him quite agog to meet the lady about whom the whole town is talking, dear cousin.'

Horatia, spreading her skirts in a curtsy, flushed a little, for Mr Drelincourt's words stung. She arose swimmingly and extended her hand. Lord Lethbridge received it on his wrist and bent with incomparable grace to salute it. A flicker of interest awoke in Horatia's eyes: his lordship had an air.

'Our poor Crosby has always such a happy turn of phrase,' murmured Lethbridge, and won a glimpse of a dimple. 'Ah, precisely! Let me lead you to that couch, madam.'

She took his arm and went with him across the saloon. 'C-Crosby detests me,' she confided.

'But of course,' said his lordship.

She frowned, rather puzzled. 'That isn't very c-civil, sir. Why should he?'

His brows rose in momentary surprise; he looked critically at her, and laughed. 'Oh—because he has such execrable taste, ma'am!'

It did not seem to Horatia as though this was the reason he really had in mind, and she was about to inquire deeper into the matter when he changed the subject. 'I need hardly ask, ma'am, whether you are *ennuyée* to the point of extinction with such affairs as these?' he said, indicating with a wave of his hand the rest of the company.

'N-no, I am not,' replied Horatia. 'I l-like it.'

'Delightful!' smiled his lordship. 'You infect even such jaded spirits as mine with enthusiasm.'

She looked a little doubtful. What he said was excessively polite, but the tone he used held a tinge of light mockery which baffled while it intrigued her. 'J-jaded spirits usually seek the c-card-room, sir,' she remarked.

He was gently fanning her with the cabriolet-fan he had taken from her hand, but he paused, and said with a quizzical look: 'Ah—and so sometimes do enthusiastic ones, do they not?'

'S-sometimes,' admitted Horatia. 'You have heard all about m-me.'

'By no means, ma'am. But when I learn of a lady who never refuses a wager, why, I desire to know more of her.'

'I am certainly very p-partial to games of chance, sir,' said Horatia wistfully.

'One day you shall play your cards against me,' said Lethbridge, 'if you will.'

A voice spoke immediately behind them. 'Do not play with Lord Lethbridge, ma'am, if you are wise!'

Horatia looked over her shoulder. Lady Massey had entered the saloon through a curtain archway, and was standing leaning her hand lightly on the back of the couch. 'Oh?' Horatia said, glancing at Lethbridge with new interest. 'Will he f-fleece me?'

Lady Massey laughed: 'Why, ma'am, am I to tell you that you are talking to the most hardened gamester of our times? Be warned, I implore you?'

'Are you?' inquired Horatia, regarding Lethbridge, who had risen at Lady Massey's approach, and was watching her with an indefinable smile. 'Then I should l-like very m-much to play with you, I assure you!'

'You will need iron nerves, ma'am,' Lady Massey said banteringly. 'If he were not here I might tell you some shocking tales about him.'

At that moment Lord Winwood, who was strolling towards the doorway, caught sight of the group by the couch, and promptly bore down upon his sister. He executed a bow in Lady Massey's direction, and bestowed a nod on Lethbridge. 'Your very obedient, ma'am. Servant, Lethbridge. I've been looking all over for you, Horry. Promised to present a fellow to you.'

Horatia got up. 'Well, b-but—'

The Viscount took her hand to draw it through his arm, and as he did so pinched her fingers significantly. Understanding this brotherly nip to mean that he had something of importance to say to her, Horatia sketched a curtsy to Lady Massey, and prepared to walk away with the Viscount, only pausing to say seriously: 'P-perhaps we shall try a throw against each other some day, my lord.'

'Perhaps,' Lethbridge bowed.

The Viscount led her firmly out of earshot. 'Good God, Horry, what's all this?' he demanded, with pious intention but a complete absence of tact. 'Keep away from Lethbridge: he's dangerous. Damme, was there ever such a one for getting into the wrong company?'

'I sh-shan't keep away from him,' declared Horatia. 'Lady M-Massey says he is a hardened g-gamester!'

'So he is,' said the ill-advised Viscount. 'And you're no pigeon for his plucking, Horatia, let me tell you.'

Horatia pulled her hand away, her eyes flashing. 'And l-let me tell you, P-Pel, that I'm a m-married lady now, and I w-won't be ordered about by you!'

'Married! Ay, so you are, and you've only to let Rule get wind of this and there'll be the devil to pay. The Massey too! 'Pon my soul, if ever I met another to equal you!'

'W-well, and what have you against Lady M-Massey?' said Horatia.

'What have I—? Oh Lord!' The Viscount tugged ruefully at his solitaire. 'I suppose you don't—no, exactly. Now don't plague me with a lot of silly questions, there's a good girl. Come and drink a glass of negus.'

Still standing by the couch, Lord Lethbridge watched the departure of the brother and sister, and turned his head to observe Lady Massey. 'Thank you, my dear Caroline,' he said sweetly. 'That was vastly kind of you. Did you know it?'

'Do you think me a fool?' she retorted. 'When that plum drops into your hand, remember then to thank me.'

'And the egregious Winwood, I fancy,' remarked his lordship, helping himself to a pinch of snuff. 'Do you want that plum to fall into my hand, dear lady?'

The look that passed between them was eloquent enough. 'We need not fence,' Lady Massey said crisply. 'You have your own ends to serve; maybe I can guess what they are. My ends I daresay you know.'

'I am quite sure that I do,' grinned Lethbridge. 'Do forgive me, my dear, but though I have a reasonable hope of achieving mine, I'm willing to lay you any odds you don't achieve yours. Now is not that outspoken? You did say we need not fence, did you not?'

She stiffened. 'What am I to understand by that, if you please?'

'Just this,' said Lethbridge, shutting his enamelled snuff-box with a snap. 'I don't need your assistance, my love. I play my cards to suit myself, neither to oblige you nor Crosby.'

'I imagine,' she said dryly, 'we all of us desire the same thing.'

'But my motive,' replied his lordship, 'is by far the purest.'

7

Lady Massey, accepting Lethbridge's snub with tolerable equanimity, had no difficulty in interpreting his last cryptic speech. Her momentary anger gave place immediately to a somewhat cynical amusement. She herself was hardly of the stuff that could plan the undoing of a bride for no more personal reason than a desire for revenge on the groom, but she was able to appreciate the artistry of such a scheme, while the cold-bloodedness of it, though rather shocking, could not but entertain her. There was something a little devilish in it, and it was the devil in Lethbridge that had always attracted her. Nevertheless, had Horatia been any other man's wife than Rule's she would have thought shame to lend herself even passively to so inhuman a piece of mischief. But Lady Massey, prepared before she set eyes on Horatia to resign herself to the inevitable, had changed her mind. She flattered herself that she knew Rule, and who knowing him could think for a moment that this ill-assorted union could end in anything but disaster? He had married for an heir, for a gracious châtelaine, certainly not for the alarms and excursions that must occur wherever Horatia went.

Something he had once said to her remained significantly in her memory. His wife must care for him—only for him. She had caught then a glimpse of steel, implacable as it was unexpected.

Rule, for all his easy going, would be no complaisant husband and if this loveless marriage of convenience went awry, why then, divorce was not so rare in these days. If a Duchess could suffer it, so too might a Countess. Once free of his tempestuous wife, with her hoydenish flights and her gaming excesses, he would turn with relief to one who created no scenes and knew to a nicety how to please a man.

It suited Lady Massey very well to permit Lethbridge to work his mischief; she wanted to have no hand in it; it was an ugly business after all, and her provocative words to Horatia had been the malicious prompting of the moment rather than a concerted attempt to throw her into Lethbridge's arms. Yet finding herself beside Horatia at Vauxhall Gardens a week later, and seeing Lethbridge answer a beckoning gesture from a fair beauty in one of the boxes only with a wave of his hand, she could not resist the impulse to say: 'Alas, poor Maria! What a fruitless task to attempt Robert Lethbridge's enslavement! As though we had not all tried—and failed!'

Horatia said nothing, but her eyes followed Lethbridge with a speculative gleam in them.

It did not need Lady Massey's words to spur up her interest. Lethbridge, with his hawk-eyes and his air of practised ease, had at the outset attracted her, already a trifle bored by the adulation of younger sparks. He was very much the man-of-the-world, and to add to his fascination he was held to be dangerous. At the first meeting it had seemed as though he admired her; had he shown admiration more plainly at the second his charm might have dwindled. He did not. He let half the evening pass before he approached her and then he exchanged but the barest civilities and passed on. They met at the card table at Mrs Delaney's house. He held the bank at pharaoh and she won against the bank. He complimented her, but still with that note of mockery as though he refused to take her seriously. Yet, when she walked in the Park with Mrs Maulfrey two days later and he rode past, he reined in and sprang lightly down from the saddle and came towards her, leading his mount, and walked beside her a considerable distance, as though he were delighted to have come upon her.

'La, child!' cried Mrs Maulfrey, when at last he took his leave of them. 'You'd best have a care—he's a wicked rake, my dear! Don't fall in love with him, I beg of you!'

'F-fall in love!' said Horatia scornfully. 'I want to play c-cards with him!'

He was at the Duchess of Queensberry's ball, and did not once approach her. She was piqued, and never thought to blame Rule's presence for his defection. Yet when she visited the Pantheon in Lady Amelia Pridham's party, Lethbridge, arriving solitary midway through the evening, singled her out and was so assiduous in his attentions that he led her to suppose that at last they were becoming intimate. But upon a young gentleman's approaching to claim Horatia's attention his lordship relinquished her with a perfectly good grace and very soon afterwards withdrew to the card-room. It was really most provoking, quite enough to make any lady determined to plan his downfall, and it did much to spoil her enjoyment of the party. Indeed, the evening was not a success. The Pantheon, so bright and new, was very fine, of course, with its pillars and its stucco ceilings and its great glazed dome, but Lady Amelia, most perversely, did not want to play cards, and in one of the country dances Mr Laxby, awkward creature, trod on the edge of her gown of diaphanous Jouy cambric just come from Paris, and tore the hem past repair. Then, too, she was obliged to decline going for a picnic out to Ewell on the following day on the score of having promised to drive to Kensington (of all stuffy places!) to visit her old governess, who was living there with a widowed sister. She had half a notion that Lethbridge was to be at the picnic and was seriously tempted to bury Miss Lane in oblivion. However, the thought of poor Laney's disappointment prevented her from taking this extreme step, and she resolutely withstood all the entreaties of her friends.

The afternoon dutifully spent in Kensington proved to be just as dull as she had feared it would be and Laney, so anxious to know all she had been doing, so full of tiresome gossip, made it impossible for her to leave as soon as she would have liked to have done. It was very nearly half past four before she entered her coach, but fortunately she was to dine at home that evening before going with Rule to the Opera, so that it did not greatly signify that she was bound to be late. But she felt that she had spent an odious day, the only ray of consolation—and that, she admitted, a horridly selfish one—being that the weather, which had promised so well in the morning, had become extremely inclement, quite unsuitable for picnics, the sky being overcast by lunch-time, and some thunderous clouds gathering which made the light very bad as early as four o'clock. A threatening rumble sounded as she stepped into the coach, and Miss Lane at once desired her to remain on until the storm had passed. Luckily the coachman was confident that it would hold off for some time yet, so that Horatia was not obliged to accept this invitation. The coachman was somewhat startled at receiving a command from her ladyship to spring his horses, as she was monstrously late. He touched his hat in a reluctant assent and wondered what the Earl would say if it came to his ears that his wife was driven into town at the gallop.

It was, accordingly, at a spanking pace that the coach headed eastwards, but a flash of lightning making one of the leaders shy badly across the road, the coachman soon steadied the pace, which, indeed, he had had some trouble in maintaining, both his wheelers being good holders and quite unused to so headlong a method of progression.

The rain still held off, but lightning quivered frequently and the noise of thunder afar became practically continuous, while the heavy clouds overhead obscured the daylight very considerably and made the coachman anxious to pass the Knightsbridge toll-gate as soon as possible.

A short distance beyond the Halfway House, an inn mid-way between Knightsbridge and Kensington, a group of some three or four horsemen, imperfectly concealed by a clump of trees just off the road, most unpleasantly assailed the vision of both the men on the box. They were some way ahead, and it was difficult in the uncertain light to observe them very particularly. Some heavy drops of rain had begun to fall, and it was conceivable that the horsemen were merely seeking shelter from the imminent downpour. But the locality had a bad reputation, and although the hour was too early for highwaymen to be abroad the coachman whipped up his horses with the intention of passing the dangerous point at the gallop, and recommended the groom beside him to be ready with the blunderbuss.

That worthy, peering uneasily ahead, disclosed the fact that he had not thought proper to bring this weapon, the expedition hardly being of a nature to render such a precaution necessary. The coachman, keeping to the crown of the road, tried to assure himself that no highwaymen would dare to venture forth in broad daylight. 'Sheltering from the rain, that's all,' he grunted, adding rather inconsequently: 'Saw a couple of men hanged at Tyburn once. Robbing the Portsmouth Mail. Desperate rogues, they was.'

They were now come within hailing distance of the mysterious riders, and to both men's dismay the group disintegrated and the three horsemen spread themselves across the road in a manner leaving no room for doubt of their intentions.

The coachman cursed under his breath, but being a stout-hearted fellow lashed his horses to a still wilder pace in the hope of charging through the chain across the road. A shot, whistling alarmingly by his head, made him flinch involuntarily, and at the same moment the groom, quite pale with fright, grabbed at the reins and hauled on them with all his strength. A second shot set the horses swerving and plunging, and while the coachman and groom fought for possession of the reins a couple of the frieze-clad ruffians rode up and seized the leaders' bridles, and so brought the whole equipage to a standstill.

The third man, a big fellow with a mask covering his entire face, pressed up to the coach, shouting: 'Stand and deliver!' and leaning from the saddle wrenched open the door.

Horatia, startled, but as yet unalarmed, found herself confronted by a large horse-pistol, held in a grimy hand. Her astonished gaze travelled upwards to the curtain-mask and she cried out: 'Gracious! F-foot-pads!'

A laugh greeted this exclamation and the man holding the barker said in a beery voice: 'Bridle culls, my pretty! We bain't no foot-scamperers! Hand over the gewgaws and hand 'em quick, see?'

'I shan't!' said Horatia, grasping her reticule firmly.

It seemed as though the highwayman was rather at a loss, but while he hesitated a second masked rider jostled him out of the way and made a snatch at the reticule. 'Ho-ho, there's a fat truss!' he gloated, wresting it from her, 'and a rum fam on your finger too! Now softly, softly!'

Horatia, far more angry than she was frightened at having her purse wrenched from her, tried to pull her hand away, and failing, dealt her assailant a ringing slap.

'How dare you, you odious p-person!' she raged.

This was productive only of another coarse guffaw, and she was beginning to feel really rather alarmed when a voice suddenly shouted: 'Lope off! Lope off! or we'll be snabbled! Coves on the road!'

Almost at the same moment a shot sounded, and hooves could be heard thundering down the road. The highwayman released Horatia in a twinkling; another shot exploded; there was a great deal of shouting and stamping and the highwaymen galloped off into the dusk. The next instant a rider on a fine bay dashed up to the coach and reined in his horse, rearing and plunging. 'Madam!' the newcomer said sharply, and then in tones of the utmost surprise: 'My Lady Rule! Good God, ma'am, are you hurt?'

'W-why, it's you!' cried Horatia. 'No, I'm n-not in the least hurt.'

Lord Lethbridge swung himself out of the saddle and stepped lightly up on to the step of the coach, taking Horatia's hand in his. 'Thank God I chanced to be at hand!' he said, 'There is nothing to frighten you now, ma'am. The rogues are fled.'

Horatia, an unsatisfactory heroine, replied gaily: 'Oh, I w-wasn't frightened, sir! It is the m-most exciting thing that has ever happened to m-me! But I must say I think they were very cowardly robbers to run away from one m-man.'

A soundless laugh shook his lordship. 'Perhaps they ran away from my pistols,' he suggested. 'So long as they have not harmed you—'

'Oh, n-no! But how came you on this road my l-lord?'

'I have been visiting friends out at Brentford,' he explained.

'I thought you were going to the p-picnic at Ewell?' she said.

He looked directly into her eyes. 'I was,' he answered. 'But my Lady Rule did not join the party.'

She came aware that her hand was still reposing in his and drew it away. 'I d-didn't think you c-cared a rap for that,' she said.

'Didn't you? But I did care.'

She looked at him for a moment and then said shyly:

'P-please will you d-drive back with m-me?'

He appeared to hesitate, that queer twisted smile hovering round his mouth.

'Why n-not?' Horatia asked.

'No reason in the world, ma'am,' he replied. 'If you wish it of course I will drive with you.' He stepped down into the road again, and summoned up the groom, telling him to mount the bay horse. The groom, who was looking shamefaced from his late encounter with the coachman, hastened to obey him. Lord Lethbridge again climbed into the coach; the door was shut; and a few minutes later the vehicle began to move forward in the direction of London.

Inside it Horatia said with the frankness her family considered disastrous:

'I quite thought you d-did not like m-me very much, you know.'

'Did you? But that would have been very bad taste on my part,' said his lordship.

'W-well, but you p-positively avoid me when we meet,' Horatia pointed out. 'You know you d-do!'

'Ah!' said his lordship. 'But that is not because I do not like you, ma'am.'

'W-why, then?' asked Horatia bluntly.

He turned his head. 'Has no one warned you that Robert Lethbridge is too dangerous for you to know?'

Her eyes twinkled. 'Yes, any number of people. Did you g-guess that?'

'Of course I did. I believe Mamas all warn their daughters against my wicked wiles. I am a very desperate character, you know.'

She laughed. 'W-well, if I don't m-mind, why should you?'

'That is rather different,' Lethbridge replied. 'You see, you are—if you will let me say so—very young.'

'D-do you mean that I am too young to b-be a friend of yours?'

'No, that is not what I mean. You are too young to be allowed to do—unwise things, my dear.'

She looked inquiring. 'W-would it be unwise of me to know you?'

'In the eyes of the world, certainly it would.'

'I d-don't give a fig for the world!' declared Horatia roundly.

He stretched out his hand to take hers, and kissed her fingers. 'You are—a very charming lady,' he said. 'But were you and I to call friends, ma'am, the world would talk, and the world must not talk about my Lady Rule.'

'Why should people think odious things about you?' asked Horatia, indignation in her voice.

A sigh escaped him. 'Unfortunately, ma'am, I have made for myself a most shocking reputation and once one has done that there is no being rid of it. Now I feel quite sure that your excellent brother told you to have naught to do with Lethbridge. Am I right?'

She coloured. 'Oh, n-no one pays the least heed to P-Pel!' she assured him. 'And if you will l-let me be a friend of yours I w-will be whatever anyone says!'

Again he seemed to hesitate. A warm hand once more clasped his. 'P-please let m-me!' Horatia begged.

His fingers closed round hers. 'Why?' he asked. 'Is it because you want to gamble with me? Is that why you offer me your friendship?'

'N-no, though that w-was what I wanted, to begin with,' Horatia admitted. 'But now that you've told me all this I feel quite d-differently and I *won't* be one of those horrid p-people who believe the worst.'

'Ah!' he said, 'but I am afraid Rule would have something to say to that, my dear. I must tell you that he is not precisely one of my well-wishers. And husbands, you know, have to be obeyed.'

It was on the tip of her tongue to retort that she did not care a fig for Rule either, when it occurred to her that this was scarcely a proper sentiment, and she replied instead: 'I assure you, sir, Rule d-does not interfere with my f-friendships.'

They had come by this time to the Hercules Pillars Inn by Hyde Park, and only a comparatively short distance remained between them and Grosvenor Square. The rain, which was now coming down in good earnest, beat against the windows of the coach, and the daylight had almost vanished. Horatia could no longer distinguish his lordship with any clarity, but she pressed his hand and said: 'So that is quite decided, isn't it?'

'Quite decided,' said his lordship.

She withdrew her hand. 'And I will be v-very friendly and set you down at your house, sir, for it is raining much too hard for you to ride your horse. P-please tell my coachman your direction.'

Ten minutes later the coach drew up in Half-Moon Street. Horatia beckoned up her groom and bade him ride his lordship's horse on to its stable. 'And I n-never thanked you, my lord, for rescuing me!' she said. 'I am truly very much obliged.'

Lethbridge replied: 'And so am I, ma'am, for having been granted the opportunity.' He bowed over her hand. 'Till our next meeting,' he said, and stepped down on to the streaming pavement.

The coach moved forward. Lethbridge stood for a moment in the rain, watching it sway up the road towards Curzon Street and then turned with the faintest shrug of his shoulders and walked up the steps of his house.

The door was held for him by the porter. He said respectfully: 'A wet evening, my lord.'

'Very,' said Lethbridge curtly.

'I should tell your lordship that a—a person has called. He arrived but a short time ahead of your lordship, and I have him downstairs, keeping an eye on him.'

'Send him up,' Lethbridge said, and went into the room that overlooked the street.

Here he was joined in a few moments by his visitor, who was ushered into the room by the disapproving porter. He was a burly individual, dressed in a frieze coat, with a slouch hat grasped in one dirty hand. He grinned when he saw Lethbridge and touched his finger to his forelock. 'Hoping all's bowman, your honour, and the leddy none the worse.'

Lethbridge did not reply, but taking a key from his pocket unlocked one of the drawers of his desk and drew out a purse. This he tossed across the room to this guest, saying briefly: 'Take it, and be off with you. And remember, my friend, to keep your mouth shut.'

'God love yer, may I shove the tumbler if ever I was one to squeak!' said the frieze-clad gentleman indignantly. He shook the contents of the purse out on to the table and began to tell over the coins.

Lethbridge's lip curled. 'You can spare yourself the pains. I pay what I promised.'

The man grinned more knowingly than ever. 'Ah, you're a peevy cull, you are. And when I works with a flash, why, I'm careful, see?' He told over the rest of the money, scooped it all up in one capacious paw, and bestowed it in his pocket. 'Right it is,' he observed genially, 'and easy earned. I'll let myself out of the jigger.'

Lethbridge followed him into the narrow hall. 'No doubt,' he said. 'But I will give myself the pleasure of seeing you off the premises.'

'God love yer, do you take me for a mill ken?' demanded the visitor, affronted. 'Lordy, them as is on the rattling lay don't take to slumming kens!' With which lofty but somewhat obscure remark he took himself off down the steps of the house and slouched away towards Piccadilly.

Lord Lethbridge shut the door and stood for a moment in frowning silence. He was aroused from his abstraction by the approach of his valet, who came up the stairs from the basement to attend him and remarked with concern that the rain had wetted his lordship's coat.

The frown cleared. 'So I perceive,' Lethbridge said. 'But it was undoubtedly worth it.'

8

It was past five o'clock when Horatia arrived in Grosvenor Square, and upon hearing the time from the porter, she gave a small shriek of dismay, and fled upstairs. In the upper hall she almost collided with Rule, already dressed for the opera. 'Oh, my l-lord, such an adventure!' she said, breathlessly. 'I am horribly l-late, or I would tell you now. Do p-pray forgive me! I w-won't be above a moment!'

Rule watched her vanish into her own room, and proceeded on his way downstairs. Apparently having very little dependence on his wife's notions of time, he sent a message to the kitchens that dinner was to be set back half an hour, and strolled into one of the saloons to await Horatia's re-appearance. The fact that the opera began at seven did not seem to worry him in the least, and not even when the hands of the gilt clock on the mantelpiece stood at a quarter to six did he betray any sign of impatience. Below stairs the cook, hovering anxiously between a couple of fat turkey poults on the spits and a dish of buttered crab, called down uncouth curses on the heads of all women.

But by five minutes to six the Countess, a vision of gauze, lace, and plumes, took her seat at the dinner-table opposite her husband, and announced with a winning smile that she was not so very late after all. 'And if it is G-Gluck, I d-don't mind m-missing some of it,' she remarked. 'But I m-must tell you about my adventure. Only fancy, M-Marcus, I have been held up by highwaymen!'

'Held up by highwaymen?' repeated the Earl, somewhat surprised.

Horatia, her mouth full of buttered crab, nodded vigorously.

'My dear child, when and where?'

'Oh, by the Halfway House when I was c-coming home from Laney's. It was f-full daylight too and they t-took my purse. But there wasn't much in it.'

'That was fortunate,' said the Earl. 'But I don't think I entirely understand. Was this daring robbery effected without any opposition being offered by my heroic servants?'

'W-well, Jeffries had not brought his p-pistols, you see. The coachman explained it all to me afterwards.'

'Ah!' said the Earl. 'Then no doubt he will carry his goodness far enough to explain it all to me as well.'

Horatia, who was in the act of serving herself from a dish of artichokes, looked up quickly at that, and said: 'P-please don't be disagreeable about it, Rule. It was m-my fault for staying so long with L-Laney. And I don't think Jeffries could have d-done anything even with a b-blunderbuss because there were a n-number of them, and they all shot pistols!'

'Oh!' said Rule, his eyes narrowing a little. 'How many, in fact?'

'W-well, three.'

His lordship's brows rose. 'You begin to interest me rather profoundly, Horry. You were held up by three men—'

'Yes, and they were all m-masked.'

'I thought perhaps they might be,' said his lordship. 'But do you tell me that the only thing you lost to these–er–desperadoes–was your purse?'

'Yes, but one of them t-tried to pull a ring off my finger, I d-dare say they would have taken everything I had only that in the very n-nick of time I was rescued. W-was not that romantic, sir?'

'It was certainly fortunate,' said the Earl. 'May I ask who they were who performed this gallant deed?'

'It was Lord L-Lethbridge!' replied Horatia, bringing out the name with a slightly defiant ring.

For a moment the Earl did not say anything at all. Then he reached out his hand for the decanter of claret, and refilled his glass. 'I see,' he said. 'So he too was in Knightsbridge? What a singular coincidence!'

'Yes, w-wasn't it?' agreed Horatia, glad to find that her announcement had not provoked any signs of violent disapproval.

'Quite–er–providential,' said his lordship. 'And did he put all these armed men to flight single-handed?'

'Yes, quite. He c-came g-galloping up, and the highwaymen ran away.'

The Earl inclined his head with an expression of courteous interest. 'And then?' he said gently.

'Oh, th-then I asked him if he would d-drive home with me, and I must tell you, Rule, he was not at all inclined to at f-first, but I insisted, so he d-did.' She drew a breath. 'And p-perhaps I ought to tell you, also, that he and I have d-decided to be friends.'

Across the table the Earl's calm eyes met hers. 'I am of course honoured by this confidence, my dear. Am I expected to make any remark?'

Horatia blurted out: 'W-well, Lord Lethbridge t-told me you would not l-like it.'

'Ah, did he indeed?' murmured his lordship. 'And did he give any reason for my supposed dislike?'

'N-no, but he told m-me that he was not a p-proper person for me to know, and that m-made me excessively sorry for him, and I said I did not c-care what the world said, and I would know him.'

The Earl touched his lips with his napkin. 'I see. And if–let us suppose–I were to take exception to this friendship—?'

Horatia prepared for battle. 'W-why should you, sir?'

'I imagine that his lordship's rare foresight prompted him to tell you my reasons,' replied Rule a little dryly.

'They seem to m-me very stupid and–yes, unkind!' declared Horatia.

'I was afraid they might,' said Rule.

'And,' said Horatia with spirit, 'it is no g-good telling me I m-mustn't know Lord L-Lethbridge, because I shall!'

'Would it be any good, I wonder, if I were to request you–quite mildly, you understand–not to make a friend of Lethbridge?'

'No,' said Horatia. 'I l-like him, and I won't be ruled by odious p-prejudice.'

'Then if you have finished your dinner, my love, let us start for the opera,' said Rule tranquilly.

Horatia got up from the table feeling that the wind had been taken out of her sails.

The work being performed at the Italian Opera House, of which his lordship was one of the patrons, was *Iphigénie en Aulide*, a composition that had enjoyed a considerable success in Paris, where it was first produced.

The Earl and Countess of Rule arrived midway through the first act, and took their seats in one of the green boxes. The house was a blaze of light, and crowded with persons of fashion who, while having no particular taste for music, all flocked to the King's Theatre, some with the mere intention of being in the mode, others for the purpose of displaying expensive toilets, and a few, like the Earl of March, who sat with his glass levelled at the stage, in the hope of discovering some new dancer of surpassing attractions. Amongst this frippery throng were also to be seen the *virtuosi*, of whom Mr Walpole, comfortably ensconced in Lady Hervey's box, was of the most notable. In the pit a number of young gentlemen congregated, who spent the greater part of their time in ogling the ladies in the boxes. The Macaronis were represented by Mr Fox, looking heavy-eyed, as well he might, having sat till three in the afternoon playing hazard at Almack's; by my Lord Carlisle, whose round youthful countenance was astonishingly embellished by a patch cut in the form of a cabriolet; and of course by Mr Crosby Drelincourt, with a huge nosegay stuck in his coat, and a spy-glass set in the head of his long cane. The Macaronis, mincing, simpering, sniffing at crystal scent-bottles, formed a startling contrast to the Bucks, the young sparks who, in defiance of their affected contemporaries, had flown to another extreme of fashion. No extravagance of costume distinguished these gentlemen, unless a studied slovenliness could be called such, and their amusements were of a violent nature, quite at variance with your true Macaroni's notions of entertainment. These Bloods were to be found at any prize-fight, or cockfight, and when these diversions palled could always while away an evening in masquerading abroad in the guise of footpads, to the terror of all honest townsfolk. Lord Winwood, who was engrossed throughout the first act of the opera in a heated argument respecting the chances of his pet bruiser, the Fairy, against Mr Farnaby's protégé, the Bloomsbury Tiger, at Broughton's Amphitheatre next evening, was himself something of a Blood, and had spent the previous night in the Roundhouse, having been moved to join a party of light-hearted gentlemen at the sport of Boxing the Watch. As a result of this strenuous pastime his lordship had an interesting bruise over one eye, a circumstance that induced Mr Drelincourt to utter a squeak of horror on sight of him.

When the curtain presently fell on the first act the real business of the evening might be said to begin. Ladies beckoned from boxes, gentlemen in the pit went to pay their court to them, and a positive buzz of conversation arose.

Rule's box was very soon full of Horatia's friends, and his lordship, ousted from his wife's side by the ardent Mr Dashwood, suppressed a yawn and strolled away in search of more congenial company. He was presently to be seen in the parterre, chuckling at something Mr Selwyn seemed to have sighed wearily into his ear, and just as he was about to move towards a group of men who had hailed him, he chanced to look up at the boxes, and saw something that apparently made him change his mind. Three minutes later he entered Lady Massey's box.

Since his marriage he had not singled Lady Massey out in public, so that it was with triumph mixed with surprise that she held out her hand to him. 'My lord!–You know Sir Willoughby, I believe? And Miss Cloke, of course,' she said, indicating two of her companions. 'How do you like the *Iphigénie*, sir? Lord Lethbridge and I are agreed that Marinozza is sadly out of voice. What do you say?'

'To tell you the truth,' he replied, 'I only arrived in time to see her exit.'

He turned. 'Ah, Lethbridge!' he said in his soft, sleepy way. 'What a fortunate *rencontre*! I apprehend that I stand in your debt, do I not?'

Lady Massey looked sharply round, but the Earl had moved to where Lethbridge stood at the back of the box, and Sir Willoughby Monk's stout form obscured her view of him.

Lethbridge bowed deeply. 'I should be happy indeed to think so, my lord,' he said with exquisite politeness.

'Oh, but surely!' insisted Rule, gently twirling his eyeglass. 'I have been held quite spell-bound by the recountal of your—what shall I call it?—your knight-errantry this very afternoon.'

Lethbridge's teeth gleamed in a smile. 'That, my lord? A mere nothing, believe me.'

'But I am quite lost in admiration, I assure you,' said Rule. 'To tackle three—it was three, was it not? Ah yes!—to tackle three desperate villains single-handed argues an intrepidity—or should I say a daring?—you were always daring, were you not, my dear Lethbridge?—a daring, then, that positively takes one's breath away.'

'To have succeeded,' said Lethbridge, still smiling, 'in depriving your lordship of breath is a triumph in itself.'

'Ah!' sighed the Earl. 'But you will make me emulative, my dear Lethbridge. More of these deeds of daring and I shall really have to see if I cannot—er—deprive you of breath.'

Lethbridge moved his hand as though to lay it on his sword-hilt. No sword hung at his side, but the Earl, watching this movement through his glass, said in the most friendly way imaginable: 'Precisely, Lethbridge! How well we understand each other!'

'Nevertheless, my lord,' Lethbridge replied, 'you must permit me to say that you might find that task a difficult one.'

'But somehow I feel—not entirely beyond my power,' said his lordship, and turned back to pay his respects to Lady Massey.

In the box opposite the crowd had begun to grow thinner, only Lady Amelia Pridham, Mr Dashwood, and Viscount Winwood remaining. Mr Dashwood having borne the Viscount company on his adventures of the previous night, Lady Amelia was scolding them both for their folly when Mr Drelincourt entered the box.

Mr Drelincourt wanted to speak with his cousin Rule, and was quite put out to find him absent. Nor was his annoyance assuaged by the naughty behaviour of my Lady Rule, who, feeling that she had a score to pay off, chanted softly:

> 'The Muse in prancing up and down
> Has found out something pretty,
> With little hat, and hair dressed high—'

Mr Drelincourt, reddening under his paint, interrupted this popular ditty. 'I came to see my cousin, ma'am!'

'He isn't here,' said Horatia. 'C-Crosby, your wig is l-like the last verse of the song. You know, it runs like this: *Five pounds of hair they wear behind, the ladies to delight, O!*—only it doesn't delight us at all.'

'Vastly diverting, ma'am,' said Mr Drelincourt, a little shrilly. 'I quite thought I had seen Rule beside you in this box.'

'Yes, b-but he has walked out for a while,' replied Horatia. 'Oh, and you c-carry a fan! Lady Amelia, only see! Mr Drelincourt has a fan m-much prettier than mine!'

Mr Drelincourt shut the fan with a snap. 'Walked out, has he? Upon my word, you are monstrously used, cousin, and you a bride!' He peered through the glass in the head of his cane at the boxes opposite, and uttered a titter. 'What fair charmer can have lured him—Good God, the Massey! Oh, I beg pardon, cousin—I should not have spoken! A jest—the merest jest, I assure you! I had not the least intention—la, do but observe the creature in the puce satin over there!'

Viscount Winwood, who had caught something of this interchange, started up out of his chair with a black scowl on his face, but was restrained by Lady Amelia, who grasped the skirts of his coat without ceremony and gave them an admonitory tug. She got up ponderously, and surged forward. 'So it's you, is it, Crosby? You may give me your arm back to my box, if it's strong enough to support me.'

'With the greatest pleasure on earth, ma'am!' Mr Drelincourt bowed, and tittupped out with her.

Mr Dashwood, observing the bride's expression of puzzled inquiry, coughed, exchanged a rueful glance with the Viscount, and took his leave.

Horatia, her brows knit, turned to her brother. 'What did he m'mean, P-Pel?' she asked.

'Mean? Who?' said the Viscount.

'Why, C-Crosby! Didn't you hear him?'

'That little worm! Lord, nothing! What should he mean?'

Horatia looked across at the box opposite. 'He said he should not have spoken. And *you* said—only the other d-day—about Lady M-Massey—'

'I didn't!' said the Viscount hastily. 'Now don't for God's sake ask a lot of silly questions, Horry!'

Horatia said, with a flash of her eyes: 'Tell me P-Pelham!'

'Ain't nothing to tell,' replied the Viscount, wriggling nobly. 'Except that the Massey's reputation don't bear probing into; but what of that?'

'V-very well,' said Horatia, a singularly dogged look about her mouth. 'I shall ask Rule.'

The Viscount was seriously alarmed by this threat, and said rashly: 'No, don't do that! Damme, there's nothing to ask, I tell you!'

'P-perhaps Crosby will explain it then,' said Horatia. 'I will ask him.'

'Don't you ask that viper anything!' ordered the Viscount. 'You'll get nothing but a pack of scandal-mongering lies from him. Leave well alone, that's my advice.'

The candid grey eyes lifted to his face. 'Is R-Rule in love with Lady M-Massey?' Horatia asked bluntly.

'Oh, nothing like that!' the Viscount assured her. 'These little affairs don't mean being in love, y'know. Burn it, Horry, Rule's a man of the world! There's nothing in it, my dear gal—everyone has 'em!'

Horatia glanced across at Lady Massey's box again, but the Earl had disappeared. She swallowed before replying: 'I kn-know. P-please don't think that I m-mind, because I d-don't. Only I think I m-might have been told.'

'Well, to tell you the truth, I thought you must know,' said Pelham. 'It's common knowledge, and it ain't as though you married Rule for love, after all.'

'N-no,' agreed Horatia, rather forlornly.

9

It was not a difficult matter for Lord Lethbridge and Lady Rule to pursue their newly declared friendship. Both being of the *haut ton* they visited the same houses, met, quite by chance, at Vauxhall, at Marylebone, even at Astley's Amphitheatre, whither Horatia dragged the unwilling Miss Charlotte Winwood to see the still new wonder of the circus.

'But,' said Charlotte, 'I must confess that I can discover nothing to entertain or elevate the mind in the spectacle of noble horses performing the steps of a minuet, and I cannot conceal from you, Horatia, that I find something singularly repugnant in the notion that the Brute Creation should be obliged to imitate the actions of Humanity.'

Mr Arnold Gisborne, their chosen escort, appeared to be much struck by this exposition, and warmly felicitated Miss Winwood on her good sense.

At which moment Lord Lethbridge, who had quite by accident taken it into his head to visit the Amphitheatre on this particular evening, entered the box, and after a brief interchange of civilities with Miss Winwood and Mr Gisborne, took the vacant chair beside Horatia and proceeded to engage her in conversation.

Under cover of the trumpets which heralded the entrance into the ring of a performer who was advertised on the bill to jump over a garter fifteen feet from the ground, at the same time firing off two pistols, Horatia said reproachfully: 'I sent you a c-card for it, but you did not come to my hurricane-party, sir. That was not very friendly of you, now w-was it?'

He smiled. 'I do not think my Lord Rule would exactly welcome my presence in his house, ma'am.'

Her face hardened at that, but she replied lightly enough: 'Oh, you n-need not put yourself about for that, sir. My lord does not interfere with m-me, or—or I with him. Shall you be at the ball at Almack's Rooms on Friday? I have promised M-Mama I will take Charlotte.'

'Happy Charlotte!' said his lordship.

Almost any right-minded young female would have echoed his words, but Miss Winwood was at that very moment confiding to Mr Gisborne her dislike of such frivolous amusements.

'I own,' agreed Mr Gisborne, 'that this present rage for dancing is excessive, yet I believe Almack's to be a very genteel club, the balls not in the least exceptionable, such as those held at Ranelagh and Vauxhall Gardens. Indeed, I believe that since Carlisle House was given up the general *ton* of these entertainments is much raised above what it was.'

'I have heard,' said Charlotte with a blush, 'of masquerades and ridottos from which all Refinement and Decorum—but I will not say more.'

Happily for Miss Winwood no ball at Almack's Rooms was ever sullied by any absence of propriety. The club, which was situated in King Street, was in some sort an offshoot of Almack's in Pall Mall. It was so exclusive that no one hovering hopefully on the fringe of Society could ever hope for admittance. It had been founded by a *coterie* of ladies headed by Mrs

Fitzroy and Lady Pembroke, and for the sum of ten guineas, a very modest subscription, a ball and a supper were given once a week there for three months of the year. Almack himself, with his Scotch accent and his bag-wig, waited at supper, while Mrs Almack, dressed in her best saque, made tea for the noble company. The club had come to be known as the Marriage Mart, a circumstance which induced Lady Winwood to persuade Charlotte into accepting her sister's invitation. Her own indifferent health made it impossible for her to chaperon Charlotte herself at all the places of entertainment where a young lady making her début ought to be seen, so she was once more extremely thankful that Horatia was suitably married.

Lord Winwood and his friend Sir Roland Pommeroy, a very fine young buck, were chosen by Horatia as escorts to the ball. Sir Roland expressed himself to be all happiness, but the Viscount was less polite. 'Hang you, Horry, I hate dancing!' he objected. 'You've a score of beaux, all of 'em falling over themselves for chance of leading you out. Why the plague d'you want me?'

But it seemed that Horatia for some reason best known to herself did want him. Warning her that he had no notion of dancing through the night and would probably end in the card-room, the Viscount gave way. Horatia said, with truth, that she had not the least objection to him playing cards, since no doubt she would find partners enough without him. Had the Viscount realized what particular partner she had in mind he might not have yielded so easily.

As it was, he escorted both his sisters to King Street and performed his duties to his own satisfaction by leading Horatia out for the opening minuet, and going down one of the country dances with Charlotte. After that, seeing his sisters comfortably bestowed in the middle of Horatia's usual court, he departed in search of liquid refreshment and more congenial entertainment. Not that he expected to derive much enjoyment even in the card-room, for dancing and not gaming being the object of the club stakes would be low, and the company probably unskilled. However, he had caught sight of his friend Geoffrey Kingston when he first arrived, and had no doubt that Mr Kingston would be happy to sit down to a quiet game of piquet.

It was some time before Lord Lethbridge appeared in the ballroom, but he came at last, very handsome in blue satin, and Miss Winwood, who happened to catch sight of him first, instantly recognized the saturnine gentleman who had joined them at Astley's. When he presently approached Horatia, and Miss Winwood observed the friendly, not to say intimate, terms they seemed to be on, misgiving seized her, and she began to fear that Horatia's frivolity was not confined to the extravagance of her dress, whose great hoop and multitude of ribbons and laces she had already deplored. She contrived to catch Horatia's eye in a reproving fashion, just as her sister was going off for the second time on Lord Lethbridge's arm to join the dance.

Horatia chose to ignore this look, but it had not escaped Lethbridge, who said, raising his brows: 'Have I offended your sister? I surprised a most unloving light in her eye.'

'W-well,' said Horatia seriously, 'it was not very polite in you not to ask her to d-dance this time.'

'But I never dance,' said Lethbridge, leading her into the set.

'S-silly! you are dancing,' Horatia pointed out.

'Ah, with you,' he replied. 'That is different.'

They became separated by the movement of the dance, but not before

Lethbridge had marked with satisfaction the blush that mounted to Horatia's cheeks.

She was certainly not displeased. It was quite true that Lethbridge hardly ever danced, and she knew it. She had seen one or two envious glances follow her progress on the floor and she was far too young not to feel conscious of triumph. Rule might prefer the riper attractions of Caroline Massey, but my Lady Rule would show him and the rest of the Polite World that she could capture a very rare prize on her own account. Quite apart from mere liking, which she undoubtedly felt towards Lethbridge, he was the very man for her present purpose. Such easy conquests as Mr Dashwood, or young Pommeroy, would not answer at all. Lethbridge, with his singed reputation, his faint air of haughtiness, and his supposed heart of marble, was a captive well worth displaying. And if Rule disliked it—why, so much the better!

Lethbridge, perfectly aware of these dark schemes, was playing his cards very skilfully. Far too clever to show an ardency which he guessed would frighten Horatia, he treated her with admiration savoured with the mockery he knew she found tantalizing. His manner was always that of a man many years her senior; he teased her, as in his continued refusal to play cards with her; he would pique her being unaware of her presence for half an evening, and devoting himself to some other gratified lady.

As they came together again, he said with his bewildering abruptness: 'My lady, that patch!'

Her finger stole to the tiny square of black silk at the corner of her eye. 'W-why, what, sir?'

'No,' he said, shaking his head. 'Not the Murderous, I beg of you! It won't do.'

Her eyes twinkled merrily. As she prepared to go down the dance again, she said over her shoulder: 'Which then, p-please?'

'The Roguish!' Lethbridge answered.

When the dance ended, and she would have rejoined Charlotte and Sir Roland, he drew her hand through his arm and led her towards the room where the refreshments were laid.

'Does Pommeroy amuse you? He does not me.'

'N-no, but there is Charlotte, and perhaps—'

'Forgive me,' said Lethbridge crisply, 'but neither does Charlotte amuse me—Let me fetch you a glass of ratafia.'

He was back in a moment, and handed her a small glass. He stood beside her chair sipping his own claret and looking straight ahead of him in one of his abstracted fits.

Horatia looked up at him, wondering, as she so often did, why he should all at once have lost interest in her.

'Why the Roguish, my lord?'

He glanced down. 'The Roguish?'

'You said I must wear the Roguish p-patch.'

'So I did. I was thinking of something else.'

'Oh!' said Horatia, snubbed.

His sudden smile lit his eyes 'I was wondering when you would cease to call me so primly "my lord",' he said.

'Oh!' said Horatia, reviving. 'B-but indeed, sir—'

'But indeed, ma'am!'

'W-well, but what should I c-call you?' she asked doubtfully.

'I have a name, my dear. So too have you—a little name that I am going to use, with your leave.'

'I d-don't believe you c-care whether you have my l-leave or not!' said Horatia.

'Not very much,' admitted his lordship. 'Come, shake hands on the bargain, Horry.'

She hesitated, saw him laughing and dimpled responsively. 'Oh, very well, R-Robert!'

Lethbridge bent and kissed the hand she had put into his. 'I protest I never knew how charming my poor name could sound until this moment,' he said.

'Pho!' said Horatia. 'I am very sure any number of ladies have b-been before me with it.'

'But they none of them called me R-Robert,' explained his lordship.

Meanwhile, the Viscount, emerging briefly from the card-room, was obliged to answer a beckoning signal from Miss Winwood. He strolled across the room to her, and asked casually: 'Well, Charlotte, what's to do?'

Charlotte took his arm and made him walk with her towards one of the window embrasures. 'Pelham, I wish you won't go back to the card-room. I am uneasy on Horry's account.'

'Why, what's the little hussy about now?' inquired the Viscount, unimpressed.

'I do not say that it is anything but the thoughtlessness that we, alas, know so well,' said Charlotte earnestly, 'but to dance twice in succession with one gentleman and to go out on his arm gives her an air of singularity which I know dear Mama, or indeed Lord Rule, would deprecate.'

'Rule ain't so strait-laced. Whom has Horry gone off with?'

'With the gentleman whom we met at Astley's the other evening, I think,' said Charlotte. 'His name is Lord Lethbridge.'

'What?' exclaimed the Viscount. 'That fellow here? Odd rot him!'

Miss Winwood clasped both hands on his arm. 'Then my fears are not groundless? I should not wish to speak ill of one who is indeed scarcely known to me, yet from the moment I set eyes on his lordship I conceived a mistrust of him which his conduct to-night has done nothing to diminish.'

The Viscount scowled darkly. 'You did, eh? Well, it ain't my business, and I've warned Horry, but if Rule don't put his foot down mighty soon he's not the man I think him, and so you may tell Horry.'

Miss Winwood blinked. 'But is that all you mean to do, Pelham?'

'Well, what can I do?' demanded the Viscount. 'Do you suppose I'm going to go and snatch Horry from Lethbridge at the sword's point?'

'But—'

'I'm not,' said the Viscount definitely. 'He's too good a swordsman.' With which unsatisfactory speech he walked off, leaving Miss Winwood greatly disturbed, and not a little indignant.

The Viscount might seem to his sister to treat the matter with callousness, but he was moved to broach the subject to his brother-in-law in what he considered to be a very delicate manner.

Coming out of the card-room at White's he nearly walked into Rule, and said with great cheerfulness: 'Burn it, that's fortunate. The very man I want!'

'How much, Pelham?' inquired his lordship wearily.

'As a matter of fact I was looking for someone who might lend me some money,' said the Viscount. 'But how you rumbled it beats me!'

'Intuition, Pelham, just intuition.'

'Well, lend me fifty pounds and you shall have it back tomorrow. My luck's going to turn.'

'What makes you think so?' Rule asked, handing over a bill.

The Viscount pocketed it. 'Much obliged to you. I'll swear you're a good fellow. Why, I've been throwing out for the last hour, and a man can't go on throwing out for ever. Which reminds me, Rule, I've something to say to you. Nothing of moment, you understand, but you know what women are, rabbit 'em!'

'None better,' said his lordship. 'So you may safely leave the matter in my hands, my dear Pelham.'

'Blister it, you seem to know what I'm going to say before I've said it!' complained the Viscount. 'Mind you, I warned Horry he was dangerous at the outset. But then, women are such fools!'

'Not only women,' murmured Rule. 'Will you do me a favour, Pelham?'

'Anything in the world!' replied the Viscount promptly. 'Pleasure!'

'It is quite a small thing,' Rule said. 'But I shall stand greatly in your debt if you would refrain in future from—er—warning Horry.'

The Viscount stared. 'Just as you say, of course, but I don't care to see that fellow Lethbridge dancing attendance on my sister, and so I tell you!'

'Ah, Pelham!' The Viscount, who had turned to go back into the card-room, checked, and looked over his shoulder. 'Nor do I,' said Rule pensively.

'Oh!' said the Viscount. He had flash of insight. 'Don't want me to meddle, eh?'

'You see, my dear boy,' said his lordship apologetically, 'I am not really such a fool as you think me.'

The Viscount grinned, promised that there should be no meddling and went back to make up for lost time in the card-room. True to his word, he arrived in Grosvenor Square next morning and impressively planked fifty pounds in bills down on the table before Rule. His luck, it seemed, had turned.

Never one to neglect opportunity, he spent a week riotously following his rare good fortune. No less than five bets of his making were entered in the book at White's; he won four thousand in a night at pharaoh, lost six at quinze on Wednesday, recovered and arose a winner on Thursday, on Friday walked into the hazard-room at Almack's and took his seat at the fifty-guinea table.

'What, Pel, I thought you was done up!' exclaimed Sir Roland Pommeroy, who had been present on the disastrous Wednesday.

'Done up? Devil a bit!' replied the Viscount. 'My luck's in.' He proceeded to fix two pieces of leather round his wrist to protect his ruffles. 'Laid Finch a pony on Tuesday Sally Danvers would be the lighter of a boy by Monday.'

'Ecod, you're mad, Pel!' said Mr Fox. 'She's had four girls already!'

'Mad be damned!' quoth the Viscount. 'I had the news on the way here. I've won.'

'What, she's never given Danvers an heir at last?' cried Mr Boulby.

'An heir?' said the Viscount scornfully. 'Two of 'em! She's had twins!'

After this amazing intelligence no one could doubt that the signs were extremely propitious for the Viscount. In fact, one cautious gentleman removed himself to the quinze room, where a number of gamesters sat round tables in silence, with masks on their faces to conceal any betraying emotion, and rouleaus of guineas in front of them.

As the night wore on the Viscount's luck, which had begun by fluctuating in an uncertain fashion, steadied down. He started the evening by twice throwing out three times in succession, a circumstance which induced Mr Fox to remark that the gull-gropers, or money-lenders, who waited in what he called the Jerusalem chamber for him to rise, would find instead a client in his lordship. However, the Viscount soon remedied this set-back by stripping off his coat and putting it on again inside out, a change that answered splendidly, for no sooner was it made than he recklessly pushed three rouleaus into the centre of the table, called a main of five, and nicked it. By midnight his winnings, in the form of rouleaus, bills and several vowels, or notes of hand, fairly littered the stand at his elbow, and Mr Fox, a heavy loser, called for his third bottle.

There were two tables in the hazard-room, both round, and large enough to accommodate upwards of twenty persons. At the one every player was bound by rule to keep not less than fifty guineas before him, at the other the amount was fixed more moderately at twenty guineas. A small stand stood beside each player with a large rim to hold his glass or his teacup and a wooden bowl for the rouleaus. The room was lit by candles in pendent chandeliers, and so bright was the glare that quite a number of gamesters, the Viscount amongst them, wore leather guards bound round their foreheads to protect their eyes. Others, notably Mr Drelincourt, who was feverishly laying and staking odds at the twenty-guinea table, affected straw hats with very broad brims, which served the double purpose of shading their eyes and preventing their wigs from becoming tumbled. Mr Drelincourt's hat was adorned with flowers and ribands and was held by several other Macaronis to be a vastly pretty affair. He had put on a frieze greatcoat in place of his own blue creation, and presented an astonishing picture as he sat alternately sipping his tea and casting the dice. However, as it was quite the thing to wear frieze coats and straw hats at the gaming table, not even his severest critics found anything in his appearance worthy of remark.

For the most part silence broken only by the rattle of the dice and the monotonous drone of the groom-porters' voices calling the odds brooded over the room, but from time to time snatches of desultory talk broke out. Shortly after one o'clock quite a burst of conversation proceeded from the twenty-guinea table, one of the gamesters having taken it into his head to call the dice in the hope of changing his luck. Someone, while they waited for a fresh bale, had started an interesting topic of scandal and a shout of laughter most unpleasantly assailing the ears of Lord Cheston, a rather nervous gambler, caused him to deliver the dice at the other table with a jerk that upset his luck.

'Five-to-seven, and three-to-two against!' intoned the groom-porter dispassionately.

The laying and staking of bets shut out the noise of the other table, but as silence fell again and Lord Cheston picked up the box, Mr Drelincourt's voice floated over to the fifty-guinea table with disastrous clarity.

'Oh, my lord, I protest; for my part I would lay you odds rather on my Lord Lethbridge's success with my cousin's stammering bride!' said Mr Drelincourt with a giggle.

The Viscount, already somewhat flushed with wine, was in the act of raising his glass to his lips when this unfortunate remark was wafted to his ears. His cerulean blue eyes, slightly clouded but remarkably intelligent still, flamed with the light of murder, and with a spluttered growl of 'Hell and damnation!' he lunged up out of his chair before anyone could stop him.

Sir Roland Pommeroy made a grab at his arm. 'Pel, I say, Pel! Steady!'

'Lord, he's three parts drunk!' said Mr Boulby. 'Here's a pretty scandal! Pelham, for God's sake think what you're doing!'

But the Viscount, having shaken Pommeroy off, was already striding purposefully over to the other table, and seemed to have not the least doubt of what he was doing. Mr Drelincourt, looking round, startled to see who was bearing down upon him, let his jaw drop in ludicrous dismay, and received the contents of his lordship's glass full in his face. 'You damned little rat, take that!' roared the Viscount.

There was a moment's shocked silence, while Mr Drelincourt sat with the wine dripping off the end of his nose, and staring at the incensed Viscount as one bemused.

Mr Fox, coming over from the other table, grasped Lord Winwood by the elbow, and addressed Mr Drelincourt with severity. 'You'd best apologize, Crosby,' he said. 'Pelham, do recollect! This won't do, really it won't!'

'Recollect?' said the Viscount fiercely. 'You heard what he said, Charles! D'you think I'll sit by and let a foulmouthed—'

'My lord!' interrupted Mr Drelincourt, rising and dabbing at his face with a rather unsteady hand. 'I–I apprehend the cause of your annoyance. I assure your lordship you have me wrong! If I said anything that–that seemed—'

Mr Fox whispered urgently: 'Let it alone now, Pel! You can't fight over your sister's name without starting a scandal.'

'Be damned to you, Charles!' said the Viscount. 'I'll manage it my way. I don't like the fellow's hat!'

Mr Drelincourt fell back a pace; someone gave a snort of laughter, and Sir Roland said wisely: 'That's reasonable enough. You don't like his hat. That's devilish neat, 'pon my soul it is! Now you come to mention it, ecod, I don't like it either!'

'No, I don't like it!' declared the Viscount, rolling a fiery eye at the offending structure. 'Pink roses, egad, above that complexion! Damme, it offends me, so it does!'

Mr Drelincourt's bosom swelled. 'Sirs, I take you all to witness that his lordship is in his cups!'

'Hanging back, are you?' said the Viscount, thrusting Mr Fox aside. 'Well, you won't wear that hat again!' With which he plucked the straw confection from Mr Drelincourt's head and casting it on the floor ground his heel in it.

Mr Drelincourt, who had borne with tolerable composure the insult of a glass of wine thrown in his face, gave a shriek of rage, and clapped his hands to his head. 'My wig! My hat! My God, it passes all bounds! You'll meet me for this, my lord! I say you shall meet me for this!'

'Be sure I will!' promised the Viscount, rocking on the balls of his feet, his hands in his pockets. 'When you like, where you like, swords or pistols!'

Mr Drelincourt, pale and shaking with fury, besought his lordship to name his friends. The Viscount cocked an eyebrow at Sir Roland Pommeroy. 'Pom? Cheston?'

The two gentlemen indicated expressed their willingness to serve him.

Mr Drelincourt informed them that his seconds would wait upon them in the morning, and with a somewhat jerky bow withdrew from the room. The Viscount, his rage at the insult to Horatia slightly assuaged by the satisfactory outcome of the disturbance, returned to his table and continued there in the highest fettle until eight in the morning.

Somewhere about noon, when he was still in bed and asleep, Sir Roland Pommeroy visited his lodging in Pall Mall and, disregarding the valet's expostulations, pushed his way into my lord's room and rudely awakened him. The Viscount sat up, yawning, rolled a blear-eye upon his friend, and demanded to know what the devil was amiss.

'Nothing's amiss,' replied Sir Roland, seating himself on the edge of the bed. 'We have it all fixed, snug as you please.'

The Viscount pushed his nightcap to the back of his head and strove to collect his scattered wits. 'What's fixed?' he said thickly.

'Lord, man, your meeting!' said Sir Roland, shocked.

'Meeting?' The Viscount brightened. 'Have I called someone out? Well, by all that's famous!'

Sir Roland, casting a dispassionate and expert eye over his principal, got up and went over to the wash-basin and dipped one of his lordship's towels in cold water. This he wrung out and silently handed to the Viscount, who took it gratefully and bound it round his aching brow. It seemed to assist him to clear his brain, for presently he said: 'Quarrelled with someone, did I? Damme, my head's like to split! Devilish stuff, that burgundy.'

'More likely the brandy,' said Sir Roland gloomily. 'You drank a deal of it.'

'Did I so? You know, there was something about a hat—a damned thing with pink roses. It's coming back to me.' He clasped his head in his hands, while Sir Roland sat and picked his teeth in meditative patience. 'By God, I have it! I've called Crosby out!' suddenly exclaimed the Viscount.

'No, you haven't,' corrected Sir Roland. 'He called you. You wiped your feet on his hat, Pel.'

'Ay, so I did, but that wasn't it,' said the Viscount, his brow darkening.

Sir Roland removed the gold toothpick from his mouth, and said succinctly: 'Tell you what, Pel, it had best be the hat.'

The Viscount nodded. 'It's the devil's own business,' he said ruefully. 'Ought to have stopped me.'

'Stop you!' echoed Sir Roland. 'You flung a glass of wine in the fellow's face before anyone knew what you was about.'

The Viscount brooded, and presently sat up again with a jerk. 'By God, I'm glad I did it! You heard what he said, Pom?'

'Drunk, belike,' offered Sir Roland.

'There's not a word of truth in it,' said the Viscount with grim meaning. 'Not a word, Pom, d'you take me?'

'Lord, Pel, no one ever thought there was! Ain't one fight enough for you?'

The Viscount grinned rather sheepishly and leaned back against the bed-head. 'What's it to be? Swords or pistols?'

'Swords,' replied Sir Roland. 'We don't want to make it a killing matter. Fixed it all up for you out at Barn Elms, Monday at six.'

The Viscount nodded, but seemed a trifle abstracted. He discarded the wet towel and looked wisely across at his friend. 'I was drunk, Pom, that's the tale.'

Sir Roland, who had resumed the use of his toothpick, let it fall in his surprise, and gasped: 'You're never going to back out of it, Pel?'

'Back out of it?' said the Viscount. 'Back out of a fight? Burn it, if I don't know you for a fool, Pom, I'd thrust that down your gullet, so I would!'

Sir Roland accepted this shamefacedly, and begged pardon.

'I was drunk,' said the Viscount, 'and I took a dislike to Crosby's hat—Damn it, what's he want with pink roses in his hat? Answer me that!'

'Just what I said myself,' agreed Sir Roland. 'Fellow can wear a hat at Almack's if he likes. Do it myself sometimes. But pink roses—no.'

'Well, that's all there is to it,' said the Viscount with finality. 'You put it about I was in my cups. That's the tale.'

Sir Roland agreed that ought certainly to be the tale and picked up his hat and cane. The Viscount prepared to resume his interrupted slumber, but upon Sir Roland's opening the door, opened one eye and adjured him on no account to forget to order breakfast at Barn Elms.

Monday dawned very fair, a cool lifting mist giving promise of a fine day to come. Mr Drelincourt, accompanied in a coach by his seconds, Mr Francis Puckleton and Captain Forde, arrived at Barn Elms some time before six, this excessive punctuality being accounted for by the irregularity of the Captain's watch. 'But it's no matter,' said the Captain. 'Drink a bumper of cognac and take a look at the ground, hey, Crosby?'

Mr Drelincourt assented with rather a wan smile.

It was his first fight, for though he delighted in the delivery of waspish speeches he had never until that fatal Friday felt the least desire to cross swords with anyone. When he had seen the Viscount stalking towards him at Almack's he had been quite aghast, and would have been perfectly willing to eat the rash words that had caused all the bother had not the Viscount committed that shocking rape upon his hat and wig. Mr Drelincourt was so much in the habit of considering his appearance above anything else that this brutal action had roused him to a really heroic rage. At that moment he had quite genuinely wanted to spit the Viscount on the end of a small-sword, and if only they could have engaged there and then he had no doubt that he would have acquitted himself very well. Unfortunately etiquette did not permit of so irregular a proceeding, and he had been forced to kick his heels for two interminable days. When his rage had died down it must be confessed that he began to look forward with apprehension to Monday's meeting. He spent a great deal of the weekend perusing Angelo's *Ecole d'Armes*, a work that made his blood run quite cold. He had, of course, learned the art of fencing, but he had a shrewd notion that a buttoned foil presented a very different appearance from a naked duelling sword. Captain Forde congratulated him on having hit upon a worthy opponent in the Viscount, who, he said, though he was perhaps a trifle reckless, was no mean swordsman. He had already fought two duels, but one had been with pistols, with which weapon he was considered to be very dangerous. Mr Drelincourt could only be thankful that Sir Roland had chosen swords.

Captain Forde, who seemed to take a gruesome delight in the affair, recommended his principal to go early to bed on Sunday night and on no account to drink deep. Mr Drelincourt obeyed him implicitly, but passed an indifferent night. As he tossed and turned, wild ideas of inducing his seconds to settle for him crossed his brain. He wondered how the Viscount was spending the night and entertained a desperate hope that he might be drinking himself under the table. If only some accident or illness would befall him! Or perhaps he himself could be smitten by a sudden indisposition? But in the cold light of dawn he was forced to abandon this scheme. He was not a very brave man, but he had his pride: one could not draw back from an engagement.

Mr Puckleton was the first of his seconds to arrive in the morning, and while Crosby dressed he sat astride a chair sucking the knob of his tall cane and regarding his friend with a melancholy and not unadmiring eye.

'Forde's bringing the weapons,' he said. 'How do you feel, Crosby?'

There was an odd sensation in the pit of Mr Drelincourt's stomach, but he replied: 'Oh, never better! Never better, I assure you.'

'For myself,' said Mr Puckleton, 'I shall leave it all to Forde. To tell you the truth, Crosby, I've never acted for a man before. Wouldn't do it for anyone but you. I can't stand the sight of blood, you know. But I have my vinaigrette with me.'

Then Captain Forde arrived with a long flat case under his arm. Lord Cheston, he said, had engaged to bring a doctor with him, and Crosby had better make haste, for it was time they were starting.

The morning air struck a chill into Mr Drelincourt's bones; he huddled himself into his greatcoat and sat in a corner of the coach listening to the macabre conversation of his two companions. Not that either the Captain or Mr Puckleton talked about the duel; in fact, they chatted on the most mild subjects such as the beauty of the day, the quietness of the streets, and the Duchess of Devonshire's *al fresco* party. Mr Drelincourt found himself hating them for their apparent callousness, yet when the Captain did mention the duel, reminding him to meet so dashing a fighter as the Viscount with steadiness and caution, he turned a sickly hue and did not answer.

Arrived at Barn Elms they drew up at an inn adjacent to the meeting place, and there the Captain discovered that his watch was considerably in advance of the correct time. Casting a knowing glance at his pallid principal, he then made his suggestion they should drink a glass of cognac, for, said he in Mr Puckleton's ear: 'We'll never get our man on the ground by the looks of it.'

The brandy did little to restore Mr Drelincourt's failing spirits, but he drank it, and with an assumption of nonchalance accompanied his seconds out of the back of the inn and across a field to the ground, which was pleasantly situated in a sort of spinney. Captain Forde said that he could not have a better place for fighting. 'Upon my word, I envy you, Crosby!' he said heartily.

After that they walked back to the inn, to find that a second coach had driven up, containing Lord Cheston and a neat little man in black who clasped a case of instruments, and bowed very deeply to everybody. At first he mistook Captain Forde for Mr Drelincourt, but this was soon put right, and he bowed again to Crosby and begged pardon.

'Let me assure you, sir, that if it should chance that you are to be my patient you need have no alarms, none at all. A clean sword wound is a very different affair from a bullet wound, oh, very different!'

Lord Cheston offered his snuff-box to Mr Puckleton. 'Attended a score of these affairs, haven't you, Parvey?'

'Dear me, yes, my lord!' replied the surgeon, rubbing his hands together. 'Why, I was present when young Mr Ffolliot was fatally wounded in Hyde Park. Ah, before your time, that would be, my lord. A sad business–nothing to be done. Dead on the instant. Dreadful!'

'Dead on the instant?' echoed Mr Puckleton, turning pale. 'Oh, I trust nothing of that sort–really I wish I had not consented to act!'

The Captain gave a scornful snort and turned his shoulder, addressing Cheston. 'Where's Sir Roland, my lord?' he asked.

'Oh, he's coming with Winwood,' replied Cheston, shaking some specks of snuff out of his lace ruffle. 'Daresay they'll drive straight to the ground. Thought Pom had best go and make sure Winwood don't over-sleep. The very devil to wake up is Pel, you know.'

A faint, last hope flashed into Mr Drelincourt's soul that perhaps Sir Roland would fail to bring his principal to the meeting place in time.

'Well,' said the Captain, glancing at his watch, 'may as well go on to the ground, eh, gentlemen?'

The little procession started out once more, the Captain striding ahead with Lord Cheston, Mr Drelincourt following with his friend Puckleton and the doctor bringing up the rear.

Dr Parvey hummed a little tune to himself as he trod over the grass; Cheston and the Captain were talking casually of the improvements at Ranelagh. Mr Drelincourt cleared his throat once or twice and at last said: 'If—if the fellow offers me an apology I think I should let it rest at that, d-don't you, Francis?'

'Oh, yes, pray do!' agreed Mr Puckleton with a shudder. 'I know I shall feel devilish queasy if there is much blood.'

'He was drunk, you know,' Crosby said eagerly. 'Perhaps I should not have heeded him. I daresay he will be sorry by now: I don't—I don't object to him being asked if he cares to apologize.'

Mr Puckleton shook his head. 'He'd never do it,' he opined. 'He's fought two duels already, so I'm told.'

Mr Drelincourt gave a laugh that quivered uncertainly in the middle. 'Well, I hope he mayn't have sat up over the bottle last night.'

Mr Puckleton was inclined to think that even such a mad young buck as Winwood would not do that.

By this time they had reached the ground and Captain Forde had opened that sinister case. Reposing in a bed of velvet lay two shining swords, their blades gleaming wickedly in the pale sunlight.

'It still wants a few minutes to six,' observed the Captain. 'I take it your man won't be late?'

Mr Drelincourt stepped forward. 'Late? I give you my word I don't intend to wait upon his lordship's convenience! If he does not come by six I shall assume he does not mean to meet me, and go back to town.'

Lord Cheston looked him over with a certain haughtiness. 'Don't put yourself about, sir: he'll be here.'

From the edge of the clearing a view of the road could be obtained. Mr Drelincourt watched it in an agony of suspense, and as the moments dragged past began to feel almost hopeful.

But just as he was about to ask Puckleton the time (for he felt sure it must now be well over the hour), a gig came into sight, bowling at a fine rate down the road. It drew up at the gate which stood open on to the meadow and turned in.

'Ah, here's your man!' said Captain Forde. 'And six of the clock exactly!'

Any hopes that Mr Drelincourt still nursed were put to flight. The Viscount, with Sir Roland Pommeroy beside him, was driving the gig himself, and from the way in which he was handling a restive horse it was evident that he was not in the least fuddled by drink. He drew up on the edge of the clearing, and sprang down from the high perch.

'Not late, am I?' he said. 'Servant, Puckleton, servant, Forde. Never saw such a perfect morning in my life.'

'Well, you don't see many of 'em, Pel,' remarked Cheston, with a grin.

The Viscount laughed. His laughter sounded fiendish to Mr Drelincourt.

Sir Roland had picked the swords out of their velvet bed and was glancing down the blades.

'Nothing to choose between 'em,' said Cheston, strolling over to him.

The Captain tapped Mr Drelincourt on the shoulder. 'Ready, sir? I'll take your coat and wig.'

Mr Drelincourt was stripped of his coat and saw that the Viscount, already in his shirt-sleeves, had sat down on a tree-stump and was pulling off his top boots.

'Take a drop of cognac, Pel?' inquired Sir Roland, producing a flask. 'Keep the cold out.'

The Viscount's reply was clearly wafted to Mr Drelincourt's ears. 'Never touch spirit before a fight, my dear fellow. Puts your eye out.' He stood up in his stockinged feet and began to roll up his sleeves. Mr Drelincourt, handing his wig to Mr Puckleton's tender care, wondered why he had never before realized what sinewy arms the Viscount had. He found that Lord Cheston was presenting two identical swords to him. He gulped, and took one of them in a damp grasp.

The Viscount received the other, made a pass as though to test its flexibility, and stood waiting, the point lightly resting on the ground.

Mr Drelincourt was led to his place, the seconds stepped back. He was alone, facing the Viscount, who had undergone some sort of transformation. The careless good humour had left his handsome face, his roving eye look remarkably keen and steady, his mouth appallingly grim.

'Ready, gentlemen?' Captain Forde called. 'On guard!'

Mr Drelincourt saw the Viscount's sword flash to the salute, and setting his teeth went through the same motions.

The Viscount opened with a dangerous thrust in prime, which Mr Drelincourt parried, but failed to take advantage of. Now that the assault was begun his jumping nerves became steadier; he remembered Captain Forde's advice, and tried to keep a good guard. As for luring his opponent on, he was kept too busy keeping a proper measure to think of it. An opportunity offering he delivered a thrust in tierce which ought to have ended the affair. But the Viscount parried it by yielding the foible, and countered so quickly that Mr Drelincourt's heart leapt into his mouth as in the very nick of time he recovered his guard.

The sweat was rolling off his brow and his breath came in exhausted gasps. All at once he thought he saw an opening and lunged wildly. Something icily cold pierced his shoulder, and as he reeled the seconds' swords struck his wavering blade upwards. It flew out of his hand, and he sank back into the arms of Mr Puckleton, who cried out: 'My God, is he killed? Crosby! Oh, there is blood! I positively cannot bear it!'

'Killed? Lord, no!' said Cheston scornfully. 'Here, Parvey, neatly pinked through the shoulder. I take it you are satisfied, Forde?'

'I suppose so,' grunted the Captain. 'Damme, if I ever saw a tamer fight!' He looked disgustedly down at the prostrate form of his principal, and inquired of Dr Parvey whether it was a dangerous wound.

The doctor glanced up from his work and beamingly replied: 'Dangerous, sir? Why, not in the least! A little blood lost, and no harm done. A beautifully clean wound!'

The Viscount, struggling into his coat, said: 'Well, I'm for breakfast. Pom, did you bespeak breakfast?'

Sir Roland, who was conferring with Captain Forde, looked over his shoulder. 'Now, Pel, would I forget a thing like that? I'm asking Forde here if he cares to join us.'

'Oh, by all means!' said the Viscount, shaking out his ruffles. 'Well, if you're ready, I am, Pom. I'm devilish hungry.'

With which he linked his arm in Sir Roland's and strolled off to tell his groom to drive the gig round to the inn.

Mr Drelincourt, his shoulder bandaged and his arm put into a sling, was assisted to his feet by the cheerful doctor, and assured that he had merely received a scratch. His surprise at finding himself still alive held him silent for a few moments, but he presently realized that the dreadful affair was at an end, and that his wig lay on the ground beside his shoes.

'My toupet!' he said faintly. 'How could you, Francis? Give it to me at once!'

10

For several days after his encounter with the Viscount Mr Drelincourt kept his bed, a pale and interesting invalid. Having conceived a dislike of Dr Parvey, he rejected all that Member of the Faculty's offers to attend to him to his lodging, and drove home with only the faithful but shaken Mr Puckleton to support him. They shared the vinaigrette, and upon arrival in Jermyn Street Mr Drelincourt was supported upstairs to his bedchamber, while Mr Puckleton sent the valet running to fetch the fashionable Dr Hawkins. Dr Hawkins took a suitably grave view of the wound and not only blooded Mr Drelincourt, but bade him lie up for a day or two, and sent off the valet once more to Graham's, the apothecary's for some of the famous Dr James's powders.

Mr Puckleton had been so much upset by the fury of the Viscount's swordplay, so thankful that he had not stood in his friend's shoes, that he was inclined to look upon Mr Drelincourt as something of a hero, and said so often that he wondered how Crosby should have challenged Winwood so coolly, that Mr Drelincourt began to feel that he had indeed behaved with great intrepidity. He no less than Mr Puckleton had been impressed by the skill the Viscount displayed, and by dint of dwelling on his lordship's two previous encounters he soon talked himself into believing that he had been pinked by a hardened and expert duellist.

These agreeable reflections were put to flight by the appearance of the Earl of Rule, who came to visit his afflicted relative on the following morning.

Mr Drelincourt had not the smallest desire to meet Rule at the moment, and he sent a hasty message downstairs that he was unable to receive anyone. Congratulating himself on having acted with considerable presence of mind, he composed himself against a bank of pillows, and resumed his study of the *Morning Chronicle*.

He was interrupted by his cousin's pleasant voice. 'I am sorry you are too ill to receive me, Crosby,' said the Earl, walking into the room.

Mr Drelincourt gave prodigious start, and let the *Morning Chronicle* fall. His eyes goggled at Rule, and he said between alarm and indignation: 'I told my man I could not see visitors!'

'I know you did,' replied the Earl, laying his hat and cane on a chair. 'He delivered your message quite properly. Short of laying hands on me there was no stopping me, no stopping me at all, my dear Crosby.'

'I'm sure I don't know why you was so anxious to see me,' said Mr Drelincourt, wondering how much his lordship had heard.

The Earl looked rather surprised. 'But how would it be otherwise, Crosby? My heir desperately wounded, and I not at his side? Come come, my dear fellow, you must not believe me so heartless!'

'You are very obliging, Marcus, but I find myself still too weak to converse,' said Mr Drelincourt.

'It must have been a deadly wound, Crosby,' said his lordship sympathetically.

'Oh, as to that, Dr Hawkins does not consider my case desperate. A deep thrust, and I have lost a monstrous amount of blood, and had a deal of fever, but the lung is unharmed.'

'You relieve me, Crosby. I feared that I might be called upon to arrange your obsequies. A melancholy thought '

'Vastly ' said Mr Drelincourt, eyeing him with resentment.

The Earl pulled a chair forward and sat down. 'You see, I had the felicity of meeting your friend Puckleton,' he explained. 'His account of your condition quite alarmed me. My stupid gullibility, of course. Upon reflection I perceive that I should have guessed from his description of Pelham's swordplay that he was prone to exaggerate.'

'Oh,' said Mr Drelincourt, with a self-conscious laugh, 'I don't profess to be Winwood's match with swords!'

'My dear Crosby, I did not suppose you a master, but this is surely over-modesty?'

Mr Drelincourt said stiffly: 'My Lord Winwood is known to be no mean exponent of the art, I believe.'

'Well, no,' replied the Earl, considering the point. 'I don't think I should call him mean. That is being too severe, perhaps. Let us say a moderate swordsman.'

Mr Drelincourt gathered the scattered sheets of the *Morning Chronicle* together with one shaking hand. 'Very well, my lord, very well, and is that all you have to say? I am ordered to rest, you know.'

'Now you put me in mind of it,' said the Earl, 'I remember there was something else. Ah yes, I have it! Do tell me Crosby—if you are not too exhausted by this tiresome visit of mine, of course—why did you call Pelham out? I am quite consumed by curiosity.'

Mr Drelincourt shot a quick look at him. 'Oh, you might well ask! Indeed, I believe I should have made allowance for his lordship's condition. Drunk, you know, amazingly drunk!'

'You distress me. But continue, dear cousin, pray continue!'

'It was absurd—a drunken fit of spleen, I am persuaded. His lordship took exception to the hat I wear at cards. His behaviour was most violent. In short, before I could know what he would be at he had torn the hat from my head. I could do no less than demand satisfaction, you'll agree.'

'Certainly,' agreed Rule. 'Er—I trust you are satisfied, Crosby?' Mr Drelincourt glared at him. His lordship crossed one leg over the other. 'Strange how misinformed one may be!' he mused. 'I was told—on what I thought credible authority—that Pelham threw a glass of wine in your face.'

There was an uncomfortable pause. 'Well, as to that—his lordship was quite out of his senses, not accountable, you know.'

'So he did throw his wine in your face, Crosby?'

'Yes, oh yes! I have said, he was most violent, quite out of his senses.'

'One might almost suppose him to have been forcing a quarrel on you, might not one?' suggested Rule.

'I daresay, cousin. He was bent on picking a quarrel,' muttered Mr Drelincourt, fidgeting with his sling. 'Had you been present you would know there was no doing anything with him.'

'My dear Crosby, had I been present,' said Rule softly, 'my well-meaning but misguided young relative would not have committed any of these assaults upon your person.'

'N-no, c-cousin?' stammered Mr Drelincourt.

'No,' said Rule, rising, and picking up his hat and stick. 'He would have left the matter in my hands. And I, Crosby, should have used a cane, not a small-sword.'

Mr Drelincourt seemed to shrink into his pillows. 'I—I am at a loss to understand you, Marcus!'

'Would you like me to make my meaning even clearer?' inquired his lordship.

'Really, I—really, Marcus, this tone—! My wound—I must beg of you to leave me! I am in no fit state to pursue this conversation, which I protest I do not understand. My doctor is expected, moreover!'

'Don't be alarmed, cousin,' said the Earl. 'I shan't try to improve this time on Pelham's handiwork. But you should remember to render up thanks in your prayers for that wound, you know.' With which sweetly spoken valediction he went out of the room, and quietly closed the door behind him.

Mr Drelincourt might have been slightly consoled had he known that his late opponent had come off very little better at the Earl's hands.

Rule, visiting him earlier, had not much difficulty in getting the full story from Pelham, though the Viscount had tried at first to adhere to precisely the tale Mr Drelincourt told later. However, with those steady grey eyes looking into his and that lazy voice requesting him to speak the truth, he had faltered, and ended by telling Rule just what happened. Rule listened in patently unadmiring silence, and at the end said: 'Ah—am I expected to thank you for this heroic deed, Pelham?'

The Viscount, who was in the middle of his breakfast, fortified himself with a long draught of ale, and replied airily: 'Well, I won't deny I acted rashly, but I was a trifle in my cups, you know.'

'The thought of what you might have felt yourself compelled to do had you been more than a trifle in your cups I find singularly unnerving,' remarked the Earl.

'Damn, it Marcus, do you tell me you'd have had me pass it by?' demanded Pelham.

'Oh, hardly that!' said Rule. 'But had you refrained from taking it up in public I should have been greatly in your debt.'

The Viscount carved himself a slice of beef. 'Never fear,' he said. 'I've seen to it no one will talk. I told Pom to set it about I was drunk.'

'That was indeed thoughtful of you,' said Rule dryly. 'Do you know, Pelham, I am almost annoyed with you?'

The Viscount laid down his knife and fork and said resignedly: 'Burn it if I see why you should be!'

'I have a constitutional dislike of having my hand forced,' said Rule. 'I thought we were agreed that I should be allowed to—er—manage my affairs alone, and in my own way.'

'Well, so you can,' said the Viscount. 'I ain't stopping you.'

'My dear Pelham, you have—I trust—already done your worst. Until this lamentable occurrence your sister's partiality for Lethbridge was not such as to attract any—er—undue attention.'

'It attracted that little worm's attention,' objected the Viscount.

'Do, Pelham, I beg of you, allow your brain the indulgence of a little thought,' sighed his lordship. 'You forget that Crosby is my heir. The only sustained emotion I have ever seen him display is his violent dislike of my marriage. He has made the whole world privy to it. In fact, I understand he causes considerable amusement in Polite Circles. Without your ill-timed interference, my dear boy, I venture to think that his remark would have been considered mere spite.'

'Oh,' said the Viscount, rather dashed. 'I see.'

'I had hopes that you might,' said Rule.

'Well, but Marcus, so it was spite! Damned spite!'

'Certainly,' agreed Rule. 'But when the lady's brother springs up in a noble fury—you must not think I do not sympathize with you, my dear Pelham: I do, from the bottom of my heart—and takes the thing in so much earnest that he forces a quarrel on willy-nilly; and further issues a veiled challenge to the world at large—you did, did you not, Pel? Ah, yes, I was sure of it!—in case any should dare to repeat the scandal—why, then, there is food enough for speculation! By this time I imagine that there is scarcely a pair of eyes in town not fixed on Horry and Lethbridge. For which, Pelham, I have undoubtedly you to thank.'

The Viscount shook his head despondently. 'As bad as that, is it? I'm a fool, Marcus, that's what it is. Always was, you know. To tell you the truth, I was devilish set on fighting the fellow. Ought to have let him eat his words. Believe he would have.'

'I am quite sure he would,' agreed Rule. 'However, it is too late now. Don't distress yourself, Pelham: at least you have the distinction of being the only man in England to have succeeded in provoking Crosby to fight. Where did you wound him?'

'Shoulder,' said the Viscount, his mouth full of beef. 'Could have killed him half a dozen times.'

'Could you?' said Rule. 'He must be a very bad swordsman.'

'He is,' replied the Viscount with a grin.

Having visited both the principals in the late affair, the Earl dropped into White's to look at the journals. His entry into one of the rooms seemed to interrupt a low-voiced conversation which was engaging the attention of several people gathered together in one corner. The talk ceased like a snapped thread, to be resumed again almost immediately, very audibly this time. But the Earl of Rule, giving no sign, did not really suppose that horse-flesh was the subject of the first debate.

He lunched at the club, and shortly afterwards strolled home to Grosvenor Square. My lady, he was informed upon inquiry, was in her boudoir.

This apartment, which had been decorated for Horatia in tints of blue, lay at the back of the house, up one pair of stairs. The Earl went up to it, the faintest of creases between his brows. He was checked half-way by Mr Gisborne's voice hailing him from the hall below.

'My lord,' said Mr Gisborne. 'I have been hoping you might come in.'

The Earl paused, and looked down the stairway, one hand resting on the baluster rail. 'But how charming of you, Arnold!'

Mr Gisborne, who knew his lordship, heaved a despairing sigh. 'My lord, if you would spare only a few moments to glance over some accounts I have here!'

The Earl smiled disarmingly. 'Dear Arnold, go to the devil!' he said, and went on up the stairs.

'But, sir, indeed I can't act without your authority! A bill for a perch-phaeton, from a coach-maker's! Is it to be paid?'

'My dear boy, of course pay it. Why ask me?'

'It is not one of your bills, sir,' said Mr Gisborne, a stern look about his mouth.

'I am aware,' said his lordship, slightly amused. 'One of Lord Winwood's, I believe. Settle it, my dear fellow.'

'Very well, sir. And Mr Drelincourt's little affair?'

At that the Earl, who had been absorbed in smoothing a crease from his sleeve, looked up. 'Are you inquiring after the state of my cousin's health, or what?' he asked.

Mr Gisborne looked rather puzzled. 'No, sir, I was speaking of his monetary affairs. Mr Drelincourt wrote about a week ago, stating his embarrassments, but you would not attend.'

'Do you find me a sore trial, Arnold? I am sure you must. It is time I made amends.'

'Does that mean you will look over the accounts, sir?' asked Mr Gisborne hopefully.

'No, my dear boy, it does not. But you may—ah—use your own discretion in the matter of Mr Drelincourt's embarrassments.'

Mr Gisborne gave a short laugh. 'If I were to use my own discretion, sir, Mr Drelincourt's ceaseless demands on your generosity would find their way into the fire!' he said roundly.

'Precisely,' nodded the Earl, and went on up the stairs.

The boudoir smelt of roses. There were great bowls of them in the room, red and pink and white. In the middle of this bower, curled upon a couch with her cheek on her hand, Horatia was lying, fast asleep.

The Earl shut the door soundlessly, and trod across the thick Aubusson carpet to the couch, and stood for a moment, looking down at his wife.

She made a sufficiently pretty picture, her curls, free of powder, dressed loosely in the style the French called *Grèque à boucles badines*, and one white shoulder just peeping from the lace of her négligée. A beam of sunlight, stealing through one of the windows, lay across her cheek; and seeing it, the Earl went over to the window, and drew the curtain a little way to shut it out. As he turned Horatia stirred and opened drowsy eyes. They fell on him, and widened. Horatia sat up. 'Is it you, my l-lord? I've been asleep. Did you w-want me?'

'I did,' said Rule. 'But I did not mean to wake you, Horry.'

'Oh, that d-doesn't signify!' She looked up at him rather anxiously. 'Have you come to scold me for p-playing loo last night? I w-won, you know.'

'My dear Horry, what a very unpleasant husband I must be!' said the Earl. 'Do I only seek you out to scold you?'

'No-no, of course not, but I thought it m-might be that. Is it n-nothing disagreeable?'

'I should hardly call it disagreeable,' Rule said. 'Something a little tiresome.'

'Oh, d-dear!' sighed Horatia. She shot a mischievous look at him. 'You are g-going to be an unpleasant husband, sir. I know you are.'

'No,' said Rule, 'but I am afraid I am going to annoy you, Horry. My lamentable cousin has been coupling your name with Lethbridge's.'

'C-coupling my name!' echoed Horatia. 'W-well, I do think Crosby is the m-most odious little toad alive! What did he say?'

'Something very rude,' replied the Earl. 'I won't distress you by repeating it.'

'I suppose he thinks I'm in l-love with Robert,' said Horatia bluntly. 'But I'm n-not, and I don't c-care what he says!'

'Certainly not: no one cares what Crosby says. Unfortunately, however, he said it in Pelham's hearing, and Pelham most unwisely called him out.'

Horatia clapped her hands together. 'A d-duel? Oh, how f-famous!' A thought occurred to her. 'M-Marcus, Pelham isn't hurt?'

'Not in the least; it is Crosby who is hurt.'

'I am very glad to hear it,' said Horatia. 'He d-deserves to be hurt. Surely you d-did not think that would annoy me?'

He smiled. 'No. It is the sequel that I fear may annoy you. It becomes necessary for you to hold Lethbridge at arm's length. Do you understand at all, Horry?'

'No,' said Horatia flatly. 'I d-don't!'

'Then I will try to explain. You have made Lethbridge your friend—or shall I say that you have chosen to become his friend?'

'It's all the same, sir.'

'On the contrary, my dear, there is a vast difference. But however it is, you are, I believe, often in his company.'

'There is n-nothing in that, sir,' Horatia said, her brows beginning to lower.

'Nothing at all,' replied his lordship placidly. 'But—you will have to forgive me for speaking plain, Horry—since Pelham has apparently considered the matter to be of enough moment to fight a duel over, there are a very few people who will believe that there is nothing in it.'

Horatia flushed, but answered roundly: 'I d-don't care what people believe! You've said yourself you kn-know there's n-nothing in it, so if you don't mind I am sure no one else n-need!'

He raised his brows slightly. 'My dear Horry, I thought I had made it abundantly clear to you at the outset that I do mind.'

Horatia sniffed, and looked more mutinous than ever. He watched her for a moment, then bent, and taking her hands drew her to her feet. 'Don't frown at me, Horry,' he said whimsically. 'Will you, to oblige me, give up this friendship with Lethbridge?'

She stared up at him, hovering between two feelings. His hands slid up her arms to her shoulders. He was smiling, half in amusement, half in tenderness. 'My sweet, I know that I am quite old, and only your husband, but you and I could deal better together than this.'

The image of Caroline Massey rose up clear before her. She whisked herself away, and said, a sob in her throat: 'My l-lord, it was agreed we should not interfere with each other. You'll allow I d-don't interfere with you. Indeed, I've n-no desire to, I assure you. I won't cast R-Robert off just b-because you are afraid of what vulgar people may say.'

The smile had left his eyes. 'I see. Ah—Horry, has a husband any right to command, since he may not request?'

'If p-people talk it is all your fault!' Horatia said, disregarding this. 'If only you would be civil to R-Robert too, and—and f-friendly, no one would say a word!'

'That, I am afraid, is quite impossible,' replied the Earl dryly.

'Why?' demanded Horatia.

He seemed to deliberate. 'For a reason that has become—er—ancient history, my dear.'

'Very well, sir, and what is this reason? Do you m-mean to tell me?'

His mouth quivered responsively. 'I admit you have me there, Horry. I don't mean to tell you.'

She said stormily: 'Indeed, my lord? You won't tell me w-why, and yet you expect me to cast off R-Robert!'

'I confess it does sound a trifle arbitrary,' admitted his lordship ruefully. 'The story, you see, is not entirely mine. But even though I am unable to divulge it the reason is a sufficient one.'

'V-vastly interesting,' said Horatia. 'It is a p-pity I can't judge for myself, for I must tell you, sir, that I have no n-notion of deserting my friends only b-because a creature like your horrid c-cousin says odious things about me!'

'Then I very much fear that I shall have to take steps to enforce this particular command,' said the Earl imperturbably.

She rejoined hotly: 'You c-can't c-coerce me into obeying you, my lord!'

'What a very ugly word, my dear!' remarked the Earl. 'I am sure I have never coerced anyone.'

She felt a little baffled. 'Pray, what do you m-mean to do, sir?'

'Dear Horry, surely I told you? I mean to put an end to the intimacy between you and Robert Lethbridge.'

'W-well, you c-can't!' declared Horatia.

The Earl opened his snuff-box, and took a pinch in a leisurely fashion. 'No?' he said, politely interested.

'No!'

The Earl shut the snuff-box, and dusted his sleeve with a lace-edged handkerchief.

'W-well, have you n-nothing else to say?' demanded Horatia, goaded.

'Nothing at all, my dear,' said his lordship with unruffled good-humour.

Horatia made a sound rather like that of an infuriated kitten, and flounced out of the room.

II

No lady of spirit, of course, could resist the temptation of pushing matters further, and Horatia was a lady of considerable spirit. The knowledge that the eyes of the Polite World were on her invested her behaviour with a certain defiance. That anyone should dare to suppose that she, Horry Winwood, had fallen in love with Lethbridge was a ludicrous presumption to be treated only with scorn. Attracted by Lethbridge she might be, but there was a very cogent reason why she should not be in the least in love with him. The reason stood well over six foot in height, and was going to be shown, in vulgar parlance, that what was sauce for the goose could be sauce for the gander as well. And if the Earl of Rule could be roused to take action, so much the better. Horatia, her first annoyance having evaporated, was all agog to see what he would do. But he must be made to realize that his wife had no intention of sharing his favours with his mistress.

So with the laudable object of making his lordship jealous Horatia sought in her mind for some outrageous thing to do.

It did not take her long to hit upon the very thing. There was to be a ridotto held at Ranelagh, which, to tell the truth, she had given up all idea of attending, Rule having refused quite unmistakably to escort her. There had been a slight argument over the matter, but Rule had ended it by saying pleasantly: 'I don't think you would care for it, my dear. It won't be a very genteel affair, you know.'

Horatia was aware that public ridottos were looked upon by the select as very vulgar masquerades, and she accepted the Earl's decision with a good grace. She had heard all sorts of scandalous tales of the excesses committed at such affairs, and had really no wish, beyond a certain curiosity, to be present at one.

But now that battle was joined with the Earl a different complexion was put on the matter and it seemed all at once eminently desirable that she should attend the Ranelagh ridotto, with Lethbridge, of course, as her escort. There could be no fear of scandal, since both would be masked, and the only person who should know of the prank was my Lord of Rule. And if that did not rouse him, nothing would.

The next step was to enlist Lord Lethbridge. She had feared that this might prove a little difficult (since he was so anxious not to cast a slur on her good name), but it turned out to be quite easy.

'Take you to the ridotto at Ranelagh, Horry,' he said. 'Now, why?'

'B-because I want to go, and Rule wo-can't t-take me,' said Horatia, correcting herself hurriedly.

His oddly brilliant eyes held a laugh. 'But how churlish of him!'

'N-never mind that,' said Horatia. 'W-will you take me?'

'Of course I will,' replied Lethbridge, bowing over her hand.

So five evenings later Lord Lethbridge's coach drew up in Grosvenor Square, and my Lady Rule, in full ball dress, a grey domino over her arm, and a loo-mask dangling by its strings from her fingers, came out of the house, tripped down the steps, and got into the coach. She had thoughtfully left a message with the porter for Lord Rule. 'If his lordship should inquire for me, inform him that I am gone to Ranelagh,' she said airily.

Her first view of Ranelagh made her delighted to have come, quite apart from the original object of the exploit. Thousands of golden lamps arranged in tasteful designs lit the gardens. Strains of music floated on the air; and crowds of gay dominoes thronged the gravel walks. In the various rotundas and lodges that were scattered about the ground refreshments could be had, while in the pavilion itself dancing was going forward.

Horatia, observing the scene through the slits of her mask, turned impulsively to Lethbridge, standing beside her with a scarlet domino hanging open from his shoulders, and cried: 'I am so g-glad we came! Only see how pretty! Are you not charmed with it, R-Robert?'

'In your company, yes,' he replied. 'Do you care to dance, my dear?'

'Yes, of course!' said Horatia enthusiastically.

There was nothing to shock the primmest-minded person in the demeanours of those in the ballroom, but Horatia opened her eyes a little at the sight of a scuffle for the possession of a lady's mask taking place later beside the lily-pond under the terrace. The lady fled with most ungenteel shrieks of laughter, hotly pursued by her cavalier. Horatia said nothing, but thought privately that Rule might have reason for not wishing his wife to attend public ridottos.

However, to do him justice, Lord Lethbridge steered his fair charge carefully clear of any low-bred romping, and she continued to be very well pleased with the night's entertainment. In fact, as she said over supper in one of the boxes, it was the most delightful adventure imaginable, and only wanted one thing to make it perfect.

'Good God, Horry, what have I left undone?' asked Lethbridge, in mock dismay.

She dimpled. 'Well, R-Robert, I do think it would be quite the n-nicest party I have ever been to if only we c-could play cards together!'

'Oh, rogue!' Lethbridge said softly. 'You will shock the solitary gentleman in the next box, my dear.'

Horatia paid no heed to this, beyond remarking that it was ten to one the gentleman was a stranger.

'You don't like d-dancing, Robert, you know you d-don't! And I do want to try my skill against you.'

'Too ambitious, Horry,' he teased. 'I was playing cards when you were sewing samplers. And I'll wager I was playing better than you sewed.'

'L-Lizzie used to finish all my samplers for me,' admitted Horatia. 'But I p-play cards much better than I sew, I assure you. R-Robert, why won't you?'

'Do you think I would fleece so little a lamb?' he asked. 'I haven't the heart!'

She tilted her chin. 'P-perhaps I should fleece you, sir!' she said.

'Yes—if I let you,' he smiled. 'And of course I undoubtedly should.'

'L-let me win?' said Horatia indignantly. 'I am n-not a baby, sir! If I play, I play in earnest.'

'Very well,' said Lethbridge. 'I will play you—in earnest.'

She clapped her hands together, causing the man in the next box to glance round at her. 'You w-will?'

'At piquet—for a certain stake,' Lethbridge said.

'W-well, of course. I d-don't mind playing high, you know.'

'We are not going to play for guineas, my dear,' Lethbridge told her, finishing the champagne in his glass.

She frowned. 'R-Rule does not like me to stake my jewels,' she said.

'Heaven forbid! We will play higher than that.'

'G-good gracious!' exclaimed Horatia. 'For what then?'

'For a lock—one precious lock—of your hair, Horry,' said Lethbridge.

She drew back instinctively. 'That is silly,' she said. 'Besides—I c-couldn't.'

'I thought not,' he said. 'Forgive me, my dear, but you see you are not really a gamester.'

She reddened. 'I am!' she declared. 'I am! Only I c-can't play you for a lock of hair! It's stupid, and I ought not. B-besides what would you stake against it?'

He put his hand to the Mechlin cravat about his throat and drew out the curious pin he nearly always wore. It was an intaglio of the goddess Athene with her shield and owl, and looked to be very old. He held it in the palm of his hand for Horatia to see. 'That has come down in my family through very many years,' he said. 'I will stake it against a lock of your hair.'

'Is it an heirloom?' she inquired, touching it with the tip of her finger.

'Almost,' he said. 'It has a charming legend attached to it, and no Lethbridge would ever let it out of his possession.'

'And w-would you really stake it?' Horatia asked wonderingly.

He put it back in his cravat. 'For a lock of your hair, yes,' he answered. 'I *am* a gamester.'

'You shall n-never say that I was n-not!' Horatia said. 'I will play you for my hair! And to show I really d-do play in earnest—' she thrust her hand into her reticule, searching for something—'There!' She held up a small pair of scissors.

He laughed. 'But how fortunate, Horry!'

She put the scissors back in the reticule. 'You haven't w-won it yet, sir.'

'True,' he agreed. 'Shall we say the best of three games?'

'D-done!' said Horatia. 'P-play or pay! I have finished my supper, and I should l-like to play now.'

'With all my heart,' bowed Lethbridge, and rose, offering his arm.

She laid her hand on it, and they left the box together, wending their way across the space that lay between it and the main pavilion. Skirting a gaily chattering group, Horatia said with her pronounced stammer: 'Where shall we p-play, R-Robert? Not in that c-crowded card-room! It wouldn't be discreet.'

A tall woman in an apple-green domino turned her head quickly, and stared after Horatia, her lips just parted in surprise.

'Certainly not,' said Lethbridge. 'We shall play in the little room you liked, leading off the terrace.'

The green domino stood quite still, apparently lost either in surprise or meditation, and was only recalled to her surroundings by an apologetic voice murmuring: 'Your pardon, ma'am.'

She turned to find she was blocking the way of a large Black Domino, and stepped aside with a light word of apology.

Though there was plenty of music to be heard coming from various corners of the gardens, the fiddlers who scraped in the ballroom were temporarily silent. The pavilion was pretty well deserted, for the supper interval was not yet over. Horatia passed through the empty ballroom on Lethbridge's arm, and was just stepping out on to the moonlit terrace when someone in the act of entering almost collided with her. It was the man in the Black Domino, who must have come in from the gardens by the terrace steps. Both fell back at once, but in some inexplicable fashion the edge of Horatia's lace under-dress had got under the stranger's foot. There was a rending sound, followed by an exclamation from Horatia, and conscience-stricken apologies from the offender.

'Oh, I beg a thousand pardons, ma'am! Pray forgive me! I would not for the world—Can't think how I can have been so clumsy!'

'It does not signify, sir,' Horatia said coldly, gathering up her skirt in her hand, and walking through the long window on to the terrace.

The Black Domino stood aside for Lethbridge to follow her, and once more begging pardon, retreated into the ballroom.

'How horribly p-provoking!' Horatia said, looking at her hopelessly torn frill. 'Now I shall have to go and p-pin it up. Of course it is quite ruined.'

'Shall I call him out?' Lethbridge said. 'Faith, he deserves it! How came he to tread on your skirt at all?'

'G-goodness knows!' said Horatia. She gave a little chuckle. 'He was d-dreadfully overcome, wasn't he? Where shall I find you, R-Robert?'

'I'll await you here,' he answered.

'And then we p-play cards?'

'And then we play cards,' he concurred.

'I w-won't be above a m-moment,' Horatia promised optimistically, and vanished into the ballroom again.

Lord Lethbridge strolled towards the low parapet that ran along the edge of the terrace, and stood leaning his hands on it, and looking idly down at the lily-pond a few feet below. Little coloured lights ringed it round, and some originally minded person had designed a cluster of improbable flowers to hold tiny lamps. These floated on the still water, and had provoked a great deal of laughter and admiration earlier in the evening. Lord Lethbridge was observing them with a rather contemptuous smile twisting his lips when two hands came round his neck from behind, and jerked apart the strings that held his domino loosely together.

Startled, he tried to turn round, but the hands that in one lightning movement had ripped off his domino, closed like a flash about his throat, and tightened suffocatingly. He clawed at them, struggling violently. A drawling voice said in his ear: 'I shan't strangle you this time, Lethbridge. But I am afraid–yes, I am really afraid it will have to be that pond. I feel sure you will appreciate the necessity.'

The grip left Lord Lethbridge's throat, but before he could turn a thrust between his shoulder-blades made him lose his balance. The parapet was too low to save him; he fell over it and into the lily-pond with a splash that extinguished the lights in that cluster of artificial flowers which he had looked at so scornfully a minute before.

A quarter of an hour later the ballroom had begun to fill again, and the fiddlers had resumed their task. Horatia came out on to the terrace and found several people standing there in little groups. She hesitated, looking for the Scarlet Domino, and saw him in a moment, sitting sideways on the parapet and meditatively surveying the pond below. She went up to him. 'I w-wasn't so very long, was I?'

He turned his head, and at once stood up. 'Not at all,' he said politely. 'And now–that little room!'

She had half advanced her hand to lay it on his arm, but at that she drew back. He stretched out his own, and took hers in it. 'Is anything the matter?' he asked softly.

She seemed uncertain. 'Your v-voice sounds queer. It–it is you, isn't it?'

'But of course it is!' he said. 'I think I must have swallowed a morsel of bone at supper, and scraped my throat. Will you walk, ma'am?'

She let him draw her hand through his arm. 'Yes, b-but are you sure no one will come into the room? It would look very particular if anybody were to see me l-lose a lock of hair to you–if I d-do lose.'

'Who is to know you?' he said, holding the heavy curtain back from a window at the end of the terrace. 'But you need not be alarmed. Once we have drawn the curtains–like that–no one will come in.'

Horatia stood by the table in the middle of the small saloon, and watched the Scarlet Domino pull the curtains together. Suddenly, in spite of all her desire to do something outrageous, she wished that she had not pledged herself to this game. It had seemed innocent enough to dance with Lethbridge, to sup with him in full eye of the public, but to be alone with him in a private room was another matter. All at once he seemed to her to have changed. She stole a look at his masked face, but the candles on the table left him in a shadow. She glanced towards the door, which very imperfectly shut off the noise of the violins. 'The d-door, R-Robert?'

'Locked,' he said. 'It leads into the ballroom. Still nervous, Horry? Did I not say you were not a real gamester?'

'N-nervous? G-gracious no!' she said, on her mettle. 'You'll find I'm not such a poor g-gamester as that, sir!' She sat down at the table, and picked up one of the piquet packs that lay on it. 'D-did you arrange everything, then?'

'Certainly,' he said, moving towards another table set against the wall. 'A glass of wine, Horry?'

'N-no, thank you,' she replied, sitting rather straight in her chair, and casting yet another glance towards the curtained window.

He came back to the card-table, slightly moved the cluster of candles on it, and sat down. He began to shuffle one of the packs. 'Tell me, Horry,' he said, 'did you come with me tonight for this, or to annoy Rule?'

She gave a jump, and then laughed. 'Oh, R-Robert, that is so very like you! You always g-guess right.'

He went on shuffling the pack. 'May I know why he is to be baited?'

'No,' she replied. 'I d-don't discuss my husband, even with you, R-Robert.'

He bowed, ironically she thought. 'A thousand pardons, my dear. He stands high in your esteem, I perceive.'

'Very high,' said Horatia. 'Shall we c-cut?'

She won the cut, and electing to deal, picked up the pack, and gave a little expert shake of her arm to throw back the heavy fall of lace at her elbow. She was far too keen a gambler to talk while she played. As soon as she touched the cards she had never a thought for anything else, but sat with a look of serious, unwavering concentration on her face, and scarcely raised her eyes from her hand.

Her opponent gathered up his cards, glanced at them, and seemed to make up his mind what to discard without the smallest hesitation. Horatia, knowing herself to be pitted against a very fine player, refused to let herself be hurried, and took time over her own discard. The retention of a knave in her hand turned out well, and enabled her to spoil the major hand's repique.

She lost the first game, but not by enough points to alarm her. Once she knew she had thrown a guard she should have kept, but for the most part she thought she had played well.

'My game,' said the Scarlet Domino. 'But I think I had the balance of the cards.'

'A little perhaps,' she said. 'Will you cut again for d-deal?'

The second game she won, in six quick hands. She had a suspicion that she had been allowed to win it, but if her opponent had played with deliberate carelessness it was never blatant enough to warrant any remark. She held her tongue, therefore, and in silence watched him deal the first hand of the final game.

At the end of two hands she was sure that he had permitted her to win the second game. The cards had run very evenly throughout, and continued to do so, but now the more experienced player was ahead on points. She felt for the first time that she was up against a gamester immeasurably more skilled than herself. He never made a mistake, and the very precision of his play and judgment seemed to cast her own shortcomings into high relief. She played her cards shrewdly enough, but knew that her weakness lay in counting the odds against finding a desired card in the pick-up. Knowing him to be some forty points to the good, she began to discard with less caution, playing for a big hand.

The game had become for her a grim struggle, her opponent a masked figure of Nemesis; as she picked up her cards in the last hand her fingers quivered infinitesimally. Unless a miracle occurred there was no longer any hope of winning; the best she could expect was to avert a rubicon.

No miracle occurred. Since they were not playing for points it did not signify that she was rubiconed, yet, irrationally, when she added her score and found the total ninety-eight she could have burst into tears.

She looked up, forcing a smile. 'You win, sir. I f-fear rather l-largely. I d-didn't play well that last game. You l-let me win the second, d-didn't you?'

'Perhaps,' he said.

'I wish you had not. I d-don't care to be treated like a child, sir.'

'Content you, my dear, I had never the least notion of letting you win more than one game. I have set my mind on that curl. I claim it, ma'am.'

'Of c-course,' she said proudly. Inwardly, she wondered what Rule would say if he could see her now, and quaked at her own daring. She took the scissors out of her reticule. 'R-Robert, what are you g-going to do with it?' she asked rather shyly.

'Ah, that is my affair,' he replied.

'Yes. I kn-know. But—if anyone f-found out—horrid things would be said, and R-Rule would hear of it and I d-don't want him to, because I know I—I ought n-not to have done it!' said Horatia in a rush.

'Give me the scissors,' he said, 'and perhaps I'll tell you what I mean to do with it.'

'I c-can cut it myself,' she replied, aware of a tiny feeling of apprehensiveness.

He had risen and come round the table. 'My privilege, Horry,' he said, laughing, and took the scissors out of her hand.

She felt his fingers amongst her curls, and blushed. She remarked with would-be lightness: 'It will be a very p-powdery one, R-Robert!'

'And a charmingly scented one,' he agreed.

She heard the scissors cut through her hair, and at once got up. 'There! For g-goodness sake don't tell anyone, w-will you?' she said. She moved towards the window. 'I think it is time you took me home. It must be d-dreadfully late.'

'In a moment,' he said, coming towards her. 'You are a good loser, sweetheart.'

Before she had even a suspicion of his purpose he had her in his arms and with one deft hand nipped the mask from her face. Frightened, white with anger, she tried to break free, only to find herself held quite powerless. The hand that had untied her mask came under her chin, and forced it up; the Scarlet Domino bent and kissed her, full on her indignant mouth.

She wrenched herself away as at last he slackened his embrace. She was breathless and shaken, trembling from head to foot. 'How d-dare you?' she choked, and dashed her hand across her mouth as though to wipe away the kiss. 'Oh, how dare you *t-touch* me?' She whirled about, flew to the window, and dragging the curtain back, was gone.

The Scarlet Domino made no attempt to pursue her, but stayed in the middle of the room, gently twisting a powdered curl round one finger. An odd smile hovered about his mouth; he put the curl carefully into his pocket.

A movement in the window made him look up. Lady Massey was standing there, an apple-green domino covering her gown, her mask dangling from her hand. 'That was not very well contrived, surely, Robert?' she said maliciously. 'A vastly pretty scene, but I am amazed that so clever a man as you could make such a stupid mistake. Lord, couldn't you tell the little fool was not ready for kisses? And I thinking you knew how to handle her! You'll be glad of my help yet, my lord.'

The smile had quite vanished from the Scarlet Domino's mouth, which had suddenly grown very stern. He put up a hand to the strings of his mask, and untied them. 'Shall I?' he said, in accents utterly unlike Lord Lethbridge's. 'But are you quite sure, madam, that it is not you who have made—a very great mistake?'

12

Horatia partook of breakfast in bed some six hours later. She was too young for her troubles to deprive her of sleep, but though she had certainly slept she had had horrid dreams, and awoke not very much refreshed.

When she had fled from the little card-room at Ranelagh she had been so angry that she had forgotten that her mask was off. She had run right into Lady Massey, also maskless, and for one moment they had faced each other. Lady Massey had smiled in a way that drove the blood up into Horatia's cheeks. She had not spoken a word; and Horatia, dragging her domino closely round her, had slipped across the terrace, and down the steps into the garden.

A hackney coach had conveyed her home, and deposited her in the cold dawn in Grosvenor Square. She had half expected to find Rule sitting up for her, but to her relief there was no sign of him. She had told the tire-woman she might go to bed, and she was glad of that too. She wanted to be alone, to think over the disastrous events of the night. But when she had extricated herself from her gown, and made herself ready for bed, she was so tired that she could not think of anything, and fell asleep almost as soon as she had blown out the candle.

She awoke at about nine o'clock, and for a moment wondered why she should feel so oppressed. Then she remembered, and gave a little shudder.

She rang her silver hand-bell, and when the abigail brought in her tray of chocolate and sweet biscuits she was sitting up in bed, her curls, with the powder still clinging to them, tumbled all about her shoulders, and a deep frown on her face.

While the waiting-woman collected her scattered jewels and garments she sipped the chocolate, pondering her problem. What had seemed a mere prank twelve hours earlier had by now assumed gigantic proportions. There was first the episode of the curl. In the sane daylight Horatia was at a loss to imagine how she could ever have consented to play for such a stake. It was—yes, no use blinking facts, it was vulgar: no other word for it. And who could tell what Lethbridge might not do with it? Before that kiss she had had no fear of his discretion, but now he seemed to her monstrous, capable of boasting, even, that he had won the curl from her. As for the kiss, she supposed that she had brought that on herself; a reflection which gave her no comfort. But worst of all had been the meeting with Caroline Massey. If she had seen, and Horatia was certain that she had, the tale would be all over the town by to-morrow. And the Massey had Rule's ear. Depend upon it, if she refrained from telling anyone else she would be bound to tell him, only too glad of the opportunity to make mischief between him and his wife.

Suddenly she pushed the tray away from her. 'I'm g-going to get up!' she said.

'Yes, my lady. What gown will your ladyship wear?'

'It doesn't m-matter,' Horatia answered curtly.

An hour later she came down the stairs, and in a resolute voice inquired of a footman whether the Earl was in the house.

His lordship, she was told, had that instant come in, and was with Mr Gisborne.

Horatia drew a breath, as though in preparation for a dive into deep waters, and walked across the hall to Mr Gisborne's room.

The Earl was standing by the desk with his back to the door, reading a speech Mr Gisborne had prepared for him. He had evidently been riding, for he wore top-boots, a little dusty, and buckskin breeches, with a plain but excellently cut coat of blue cloth with silver buttons. He held his whip and gloves in one hand; his hat was thrown down on a chair. 'Admirable, my dear boy, but far too long. I should forget the half of it, and the Lords would be shocked, quite shocked, you know,' he said, and gave the paper back to the secretary. 'And Arnold—do you think—a little less impassioned? Ah yes, I thought you would agree! I am never impassioned.'

Mr Gisborne was bowing to Horatia; my lord turned his head, and saw her. 'A thousand pardons, my love! I did not hear you come in,' he said.

Horatia bestowed a rather perfunctory smile on Mr Gisborne, who accustomed to the friendliest of treatment from her, instantly wondered what could be the matter. 'Are you very b-busy, sir?' she asked, raising her anxious eyes to Rule's face.

'Arnold will tell you, my dear, that I am never busy,' he replied.

'W-well, could you spare me a m-moment of your time n-now?' Horatia said.

'As many as you desire,' he said, and held open the door for her to pass out. 'Shall we go into the library, ma'am?'

'I d-don't mind where we go,' said Horatia in a small voice. 'But I want to be p-private with you.'

'My dear, this is very flattering,' he said.

'It isn't,' replied Horatia mournfully. She went into the library, and watched him shut the door. 'I want to be p-private because there is something I m-must tell you.'

The veriest hint of surprise flickered for an instant in his eyes; he looked at her for a moment, rather searchingly, she thought. Then he moved forward. 'But won't you sit down, Horry?'

She stayed where she was, her hands gripping the back of a chair. 'No, I think I'll s-stand,' she answered. 'M-Marcus, I had better tell you at once that I've done something d-dreadful!'

At that a smile quivered at the corners of his mouth. 'I'm prepared for the worst, then.'

'I assure you, it isn't f-funny,' said Horatia tragically. 'In f-fact, I'm afraid you will be amazingly angry, and I m-must own,' she added in a rush of candour, 'I d-deserve it, even if you beat me with that whip, only I d-do hope you won't, M-Marcus.'

'I can safely promise you that I won't,' said the Earl, laying both whip and gloves down on the table. 'Come, Horry, what is the matter?'

She began to trace the pattern of the chair-back with one finger. 'Well, I—w-well, you see, I—M-Marcus, did they give you my m-message last night?' She raised her eyes fleetingly, and saw him gravely watching her. 'I desired the p-porter to tell you, if—if you asked that I was gone to Ranelagh.'

'Yes, I did get that message,' Rule answered.

'Well–w-well, I did go there. To the ridotto. And I w-went with Lord Lethbridge.'

There was a pause. 'Is that all?' Rule asked.

'No,' confessed Horatia. 'It's only the b-beginning. There's m-much worse to come.'

'Then I had better reserve my wrath,' he said. 'Go on, Horry.'

'You see, I w-went with Lord Lethbridge, and–and left the message, because–because—'

'Because you naturally wanted me to know that you had–shall we say?–thrown down the glove. I quite understand that part of it,' said Rule encouragingly.

She looked up again. 'Yes, that w-was the reason,' she admitted. 'It wasn't that I wanted very p-particularly to be with him, Rule. And I thought since everyone was to be m-masked that nobody would know, except you, so that I should just make you angry and n-not cause any scandal at all.'

'The matter is now perfectly clear,' said Rule. 'Let us proceed to Ranelagh.'

'W-well, at first it was very p-pleasant, and I liked it excessively. Then–then we had supper in one of the boxes, and I t-teased Robert to play cards with me. You must know, M-Marcus, that I wanted dreadfully to play with him, and he never would. At last he said he would, but–but not for money.' She knit her brows, puzzling over something, and suddenly said: 'Rule, d-do you think that perhaps I d-drank too much champagne?'

'I trust not, Horry.'

'Well, I c-can't account for it otherwise,' she said. 'He said he would p-play for a lock of my hair, and it's no use d-deceiving you, Rule, I agreed!' As no explosion of wrath greeted this confession she took a firm grip of the chair-back, and continued. 'And I l-let him take me to a p-private room–in fact, I wanted it to be p-private–and we played p-piquet, and–and I lost. And I m-must say,' she added, 'though he is the most odious m-man I ever met he is a very, very fine card-p-player.'

'I believe he is,' said the Earl. 'I need not ask, of course, whether you paid your stake.'

'I had to. It was a d-debt of honour, you see. I let him cut one of my c-curls off, and–and he's got it n-now.'

'Forgive me, my dear, but have you told me this because you wish me to get that curl back for you?' inquired his lordship.

'No, no!' Horatia replied impatiently. 'You c-can't get it back; I lost it in fair play. Something much, m-much worse happened then–though it w-wasn't the worst of all. He–he caught hold of me, and took my m-mask off, and–kissed me! And Rule, the m-most dreadful thing! I f-forgot about my mask, and I ran away, and–and Lady Massey was just outside the w-window, and she saw me, and I know she had been w-watching all the time! So you see, I've m-made a vulgar scandal, and I thought the only thing I could do was to t-tell you at once, because even if you are furious with me, you ought to know, and I couldn't b-bear anyone else to tell you!'

The Earl did not seem to be furious. He listened calmly to the whole of this hurried speech, and at the end of it walked forward across the space that separated them, and to Horatia's astonishment took her hand in his and raised it to his lips. 'My compliments, Horry,' he said. 'You have surprised me.' He released her hand, and went towards the desk that stood in the window. Taking a key from his pocket he unlocked one of the drawers and pulled it open. Horatia blinked at him, utterly at a loss. He came back to her, and held out his hand. In the palm of it lay a powdered curl.

Horatio gave a gasp, staring at it. Then she looked up, quite dumb-founded. 'M-mine?' she stammered.

'Yours, my dear.'

'But I—but—how did you c-come by it?'

He gave a little laugh. 'I won it.'

'Won it?' she repeated, uncomprehending. 'How *c-could* you? Who—Rule, whom did you win it from?'

'Why, from you, Horry. Whom else could I have won it from?'

She clutched his wrist. 'Rule, it—it was not *you*?' she squeaked.

'But of course it was, Horry. Did you think I would let you lose to Lethbridge?'

'Oh!' cried Horatia on a sob. 'Oh, I am so th-thankful!' She let go of his wrist. 'But I d-don't understand. How did you know? Where were you?'

'In the next box to yours.'

'The m-man in the black d-domino? Then—then it was you who trod on my g-gown?'

'You see, I had to contrive that you should be out of the way for a few moments,' he apologized.

'Yes, of course,' nodded Horatia, quite appreciating this. 'It was very c-clever of you, I think. And when I c-came back and thought your voice odd—*that* was you?'

'It was. I flatter myself I imitated Lethbridge's manner rather well. I admit that the noise those fiddles made helped me.'

She was frowning again. 'Yes, b-but I don't understand quite. D-did Robert exchange d-dominoes with you?'

A laugh lurked in his eyes. 'It was not precisely an exchange. I—er—took his, and hid my own under a chair.'

Horatia was regarding him keenly. 'D-didn't he mind?'

'Now I come to think of it,' said the Earl pensively, 'I am afraid I forgot to ask him.'

She came a little nearer. 'Marcus, did you m-make him give it to you?'

'No,' replied the Earl. 'I—er—took it.'

'T-took it? But why did he let you?'

'He really had no choice in the matter,' said his lordship.

She drew a long breath. 'You m-mean you took it by f-force? And didn't he do anything? What became of him?'

'I imagine that he went home,' said the Earl calmly.

'W-went home! Well, I n-never heard of anything so poor-spirited!' exclaimed Horatia, with disgust.

'He could hardly do anything else,' said the Earl. 'Perhaps I ought to explain that the gentleman had the—er—misfortune to fall into the lily-pond.'

Horatia's lips parted. 'Rule, d-did you push him in?' she asked breathlessly.

'You see I had to dispose of him somehow,' said his lordship. 'He was really quite *de trop*, and the lily-pond so conveniently situated.'

Horatia gave up all attempt to preserve her gravity, and went off into a peal of laughter. 'Oh, R-Rule, how famous! I w-wish I had seen it!' A thought occurred to her; she said quickly: 'He w-won't call you out, will he?'

'Alas, I fear there is no likelihood of that,' Rule replied. 'You see, Horry, you are my wife–a circumstance that makes Lethbridge's position a little awkward.'

She was not satisfied. 'R-Rule, suppose he tries to do you a m-mischief?' she said anxiously.

'I hardly think he would succeed,' said Rule, unconcerned.

'W-well, I don't know, but I wish you will take care, Marcus.'

'I promise you you need have no fear for me, my dear.'

She looked a trifle uncertain, but allowed the matter to drop. She said rather gruffly: 'And perhaps you will tell Lady M-Massey that it was you all the time?'

His mouth hardened. 'Lady Massey,' he said deliberately, 'need not trouble you–in any way, Horry.'

She said with difficulty: 'I think I would rather you told her, sir. She–she looked at me in a way that–in a way that—'

'It will not be necessary for me to tell Lady Massey anything,' said Rule. 'She will not, I think, mention what happened last night.'

She glanced up at him, puzzled. 'Did she know then that it was you?'

He smiled rather grimly. 'She did indeed know it,' he replied.

'Oh!' Horatia digested this. 'Were you going to t-tell me all this if I hadn't told you?' she asked.

'To be frank with you, Horry, no: I was not,' Rule answered. 'You will have to forgive my stupidity. I did not think that you would tell me.'

'W-well, I don't think I should have told you if Lady M-Massey hadn't seen me,' said Horatia candidly. 'And I d-don't suppose Robert would have explained it, because it m-makes him look quite ridiculous. And I w-wouldn't have spoken to him again. Now I see, of course, that he did not behave so very b-badly after all, though I must say I d-don't think he should have proposed that stake, do you?'

'Most certainly I do not.'

'No. Well, I won't have him for a friend, Rule!' said Horatia handsomely. 'You won't m-mind if I am civil to him, will you?'

'Not at all,' Rule replied. 'I am civil to him myself.'

'I d-don't call it civil to push a person into a p-pond,' objected Horatia. She caught sight of the clock. 'Oh, I said I would d-drive out with Louisa! Only look at the time!' She prepared to depart. 'There is one thing that makes me very c-cross,' she said, frowning at him. 'It was odious of you to l-let me win the second game!'

He laughed, and caught her hands, pulling her towards him. 'Horry, shall we consign Louisa to the devil?' he suggested.

'N-no, I must go,' Horatia answered, suddenly shy. 'B-besides, she hasn't seen my landaulet!'

The landaulet, the possession of which was enough to set any lady in the forefront of fashion, was glitteringly bright and new, having only just come from the coachmaker. Lady Louisa duly admired it, pronounced it to be extremely comfortable, and was so obliging as to say that she had not in the least minded being kept waiting over half an hour. Since she had shopping to do in Bond Street the coachman was instructed to drive there first, and the two ladies leaned back against the cushions and embarked on a discussion concerning the proper kind of ribbons to wear with a ball dress of green Italian taffeta for which Lady Louisa had just purchased two ells of stuff. By the time the rival merits of ribbons *à l'instant*, *à l'attention*, *au soupir de Vénus*, and a great many others had been fully weighed, the carriage drew up outside a fashionable milliner's, and the ladies went in to select a branch of artificial flowers with which Lady Louisa hoped to make bearable a hat she had bought two days ago, and quite detested already.

It was naturally impossible for Horatia to visit a milliner without purchasing something on her own account, so when the flowers had been selected, she tried on a number of hats, and bought finally an enormous confection composed chiefly of stiff muslin in Trianon grey, which was labelled, not without reason, '*Grandes Prétentions.*' There was a *collet monté* gauze scarf in the same delectable shade of grey, so she bought that as well. A cap *à la glaneuse* caught her eye as she was about to leave the shop, but she decided not to add that to her purchases, Lady Louisa having had the presence of mind to declare that it made her look rather prim.

Horatia was just a little nervous of her sister-in-law, whom she suspected of disapproving of her, but Lady Louisa was behaving quite delightfully, and had not suggested by so much as a look that she thought it extravagant of Horry to buy that hat. She had even said that it was ravishing, so when they stepped into the landaulet again Horatia was feeling more friendly towards Louisa than she ever remembered to have felt before.

This was precisely what Lady Louisa wanted. As the carriage moved forward she pointed her furled sunshade at the coachman's back, and said: 'My dear, how much does he hear of what one says?'

'Oh, n-nothing!' Horatia assured her. 'He is very d-deaf, you know. D-didn't you notice how I have to shout at him?'

'I fear it would take me an age to grow used to an open carriage,' sighed Lady Louisa. 'But if he is really deaf—my dear, there was something I wanted to say to you. That is—no, I don't want to say it at all, but I think I ought to, for I know Rule never would.'

Horatia's smile faded. 'Indeed?' she said.

'I detest people who interfere,' said her ladyship hastily, 'but I do feel you have a right to know why you shouldn't admit Lord Lethbridge to your friendship.'

'I am aware, L-Louisa,' said Horatia stiffly. 'His r-reputation—'

'It isn't that, my love. Only he, and Rule, and I know, and Rule won't tell you because he'd never give me away bless him!'

Horatia turned, round-eyed. 'G-give you away, Louisa?'

Lady Louisa sank her voice to a confidential murmur, and started bravely to tell her sister-in-law just what had happened in a mad spring-tide seven years ago.

13

At about the same moment that Lady Louisa was engaged laying bare her past history for Horatia's inspection, Lord Lethbridge was being admitted into a house in Hertford Street. Declining the footman's escort he walked up the stairs to the saloon overlooking the street, where Lady Massey was impatiently awaiting him.

'Well, my dear,' he said, closing the door behind him. 'I am flattered of course, but why am I summoned so urgently?'

Lady Massey was staring out of the window but she wheeled about. 'You had my billet?'

He raised his brows: 'If I had not, Caroline, I should not be here now,' he said. 'It is not my practice to pay morning calls.' He put up his glass and critically surveyed her through it. 'Allow me to tell you, my cherished one, that you are looking something less than your usual incomparable self. Now what can be amiss?'

She took a step towards him. 'Robert, what happened at Ranelagh last night?' she shot at him.

His thin fingers tightened perceptibly about the shaft of his quizzing glass, his eyes, narrowed to mere slits, stared across at her. 'At Ranelagh . . .' he repeated. 'Well?'

'Oh, I was there!' she replied. 'I heard you speak to that little fool. You went into the pavilion. What happened then?'

He had let his glass fall and drawn a snuff-box from his pocket. He tapped it with one finger and opened it. 'And pray what is that to you, Caroline?' he asked.

'Someone said a Scarlet Domino had gone into the smallest card-room. I saw no one there. I went out on to the terrace. I saw—you, as I thought—cut one of the bride's curls off—oh, that doesn't signify now! She ran out and I went in.' She stopped, pressing her handkerchief to her lips. 'My God, it was Rule!' she said.

Lord Lethbridge took a pinch of snuff, shook away the residue, and raised the pinch first to one nostril, then to the other. 'How very disconcerting for you, my love!' he said blandly. 'I'm sure you betrayed yourself.'

She shuddered. 'I thought it was you. I said—it makes no odds what I said. Then he took off his mask. I was near to swooning.'

Lord Lethbridge shut the snuff-box and dusted his ruffles. 'Very entertaining, Caroline. And I hope it will be a lesson to you not to interfere in my affairs. How I wish I had seen you!'

She reddened angrily, and moved towards a chair. 'You were always spiteful, Robert. But you were at Ranelagh last night, and you wore that scarlet domino. I tell you I saw no other there!'

'There was no other,' replied Lethbridge coolly. He smiled, not very pleasantly. 'What an instructive evening our dear Rule must have spent! And what a fool you are, Caroline! Pray, what did you say to him?'

'It's no matter,' she said sharply. 'Perhaps you lent him your domino? It would be so like you!'

'Now there you are wrong,' he replied with great affability. 'It would not be in the least like me. That domino was wrested from me.'

Her lips curled. 'You permitted it? You let him take your place with the girl? That is not very probable!'

'I had no choice in the matter,' he said. 'I was eliminated in the neatest possible way. Yes, I said "eliminated", Caroline.'

'You take it very calmly!' she remarked.

'Naturally,' he replied. 'Did you suppose I should gnash my teeth?'

She plucked at the folds of her gown. 'Well, are you satisfied? Do you mean to be done with the bride? Is it all over?'

'As far as you are concerned, my dear, I should imagine that it is certainly all over,' he said reflectively. 'Not, of course, that I was privileged to witness your meeting with Rule. But I can guess. I am quite acute, you know.'

She abandoned the sarcastic attitude she had adopted, and stretched out her hand. 'Oh, Robert, can you not see that I am upset?'

'Easily,' he answered. 'So are my plans upset, but I don't permit that to put me in a taking.'

She looked at him, wondering. He had an alert air, his eyes were bright and smiling. No, he was not one to give way to unprofitable emotion. 'What are you going to do?' she asked. 'If Rule means to stop the girl—'

He snapped his fingers. 'I said my plans were upset. I believe it to be quite true.'

'You don't seem to care,' she remarked.

'There are always more plans to be made,' he said. 'Not for you,' he added kindly. 'You may as well make up your mind to that. I am really distressed for you, my dear. Rule must have been so useful.' He eyed her for a moment, and his smile broadened. 'Oh, did you love him, Caroline? That was unwise of you.'

She got up. 'You're abominable, Robert,' she said. 'I must see him. I must make him see me.'

'Do, by all means,' Lethbridge said cordially. 'I wish you may plague him to death; he would dislike that. But you won't get him back, my poor dear. Very well do I know Rule. Would you like to see him humbled? I promise you you shall.'

She walked away to the window. 'No,' she said indifferently.

'Odd!' he commented. 'I assure you, with me it has become quite an obsession.' He came towards her. 'You are not very good company today, Caroline. I shall take my leave of you. Do make Rule a scene and then I will come to see you again, and you shall tell me all about it.' He picked up her hand and kissed it. '*Au revoir*, my love!' he said sweetly, and went out humming a little tune under his breath.

He was on his way home to Half-Moon Street when my Lady Rule's landaulet turned a corner of the road and came at a smart pace towards him. Horatia, seated alone now, saw him at once, and seemed undecided. Lethbridge swept off his hat and stood waiting for the carriage to draw up.

Something in that calm assumption that she would order her coachman to stop appealed to Horatia. She gave the necessary command and the landaulet came to a standstill beside Lethbridge.

One look at her was enough to assure Lethbridge that she knew just what had happened at Ranelagh. The grey eyes held a gleam of amusement. It annoyed him but he would not let that appear.

'Alas, the jealous husband came off with the honours!' he said.

'He w-was clever, wasn't he?' Horatia agreed.

'But inspired!' Lethbridge said. 'My damp fate was particularly apt. Make him my compliments, I beg of you. I was certainly caught napping.'

She thought that he was taking his humiliating defeat very well, and replied a little more warmly: 'We were b-both caught napping, and p-perhaps it was as well, sir.'

'I blame myself,' he said meditatively. 'Yet I don't know how I could have guessed. . . . If I had but been aware of Caroline Massey's presence I might have been more on my guard.'

The arrow struck home as he knew it would. Horatia sat up very straight. 'Lady Massey?'

'Oh, did you not see her! No, I suppose not. It seems that she and Rule laid their heads together to plan our undoing. We must admit they succeeded admirably.'

'It's n-not t-true!' Horatia stammered.

'But—' He broke off artistically, and bowed. 'Why, of course not, ma'am!'

She stared fiercely at him. 'Why did you say that?'

'My dear, I beg a thousand pardons! Don't give it another thought! Depend upon it, it was no such thing.'

'Who told you?' she demanded.

'No one told me,' he said soothingly. 'I merely thought that the fair lady knew a vast deal of what happened last night. But I am sure I was wrong.'

'You w-were wrong!' she said. 'I shall ask R-Rule!'

He smiled. 'An excellent notion, ma'am, if it will set your mind at rest.'

She said rather pathetically: 'You do think he will say it was n-nonsense, don't you?'

'I am quite sure he will,' said Lethbridge, laughing, and stood back to allow the coachman to drive on.

He flattered himself he was an adept at shooting tiny poisonous shafts; certainly that one had gone home. While she assured herself it was a lie Horatia could not help remembering, first Lady Massey's cruel little smile, and second, Rule's own words: *She did indeed know*. And of course now Lethbridge had put her in mind of it she realized that whether the tale was true or not Rule would be bound to deny it. She did not believe it, no, but she could not help thinking about it. She could not rid herself of the idea that as a rival to the beautiful Lady Massey she stood no chance of success. Crosby Drelincourt had been the first to tell her in his oblique fashion that Lady Massey was Rule's mistress, but it was to Theresa Maulfrey that she was indebted for further information. Mrs Maulfrey had never liked her young cousin very much, but she had made a determined attempt to cultivate her friendship as soon as she became a Countess. Unfortunately, Horatia had no more liking for Theresa than Theresa had for her, and perfectly understood the meaning of that lady's sudden amiability. As Charlotte had so shrewdly guessed, Mrs Maulfrey had tried to patronize Horatia and when the gay Countess showed plainly that she stood in no need of patronage she had found herself quite unable to resist the temptation of saying a great many spiteful things. On the subject of Rule and his loves she spoke as a woman of the world, and as such carried weight. Horatia was left with the impression that Rule had been for years the Massey's slave. And, as Mrs Maulfrey so sapiently remarked, a man did not change his mode of life for a chit in her teens. Mrs Maulfrey spoke of him admiringly as an accomplished lover: Horatia had no notion of swelling the ranks of his conquests. She supposed—for gentlemen were known to be strange in these matters—that he would be quite capable of making love to his wife in the interval between dalliance with widows and opera-dancers. However, since she had married him on the tacit understanding that he might amuse himself as he pleased, she could hardly object now.

So the Earl of Rule, setting out to woo his young wife, found her polite, always gay, but extremely elusive. She treated him in the friendliest way possible—rather, he thought ruefully, as she might treat an indulgent father.

Lady Louisa, considering that the state of affairs was unsatisfactory, took him roundly to task. 'Don't tell me!' she said. 'You're in a fair way to doting on that child! Lord, I'm out of all patience with you! Why don't you make her love you? You seem to be able to do it with any other misguided female, though why I don't know!'

'Ah!' said the Earl. 'But then you are only my sister, Louisa.'

'And don't try to turn it off!' said Lady Louisa wrathfully. 'Make love to the girl! Gracious heaven, why *isn't* she in love with you?'

'Because,' said the Earl slowly, 'I am too old for her.'

'Stuff and fiddle!' snapped her ladyship.

When the Earl went down to Meering a week later he suggested that Horatia should accompany him. Perhaps if Lady Massey had not chosen the previous evening to throw herself in his way Horatia might have wished for nothing better. But Rule and she had gone to Vauxhall Gardens with a snug party of their own contriving, and Lady Massey had gone there also.

It had all been mighty pleasant until after supper. There was music and dancing and everything had been very gay, the supper excellent and the Earl an ideal husband and host. And then it had all gone awry, for when she had tripped off with Mr Dashwood, and Pelham, and Miss Lloyd to look at the cascade, Rule too had left the box and wandered over to greet some friends. Horatia had seen him strolling down one of the paths with Sir Harry Topham, a racing crony. Twenty minutes later she had seen him again, but not with Sir Harry. He was in the Lovers' Walk (which made it worse) and standing very close to him and looking up at him in the most melting way was Lady Massey. Even as Horatia caught sight of them the Massey put up her hands to Rule's shoulders.

Horatia had whisked round and declared her intention of walking down quite another path. Miss Lloyd and Pelham had fallen behind; probably Mr Dashwood had not observed the Earl. She had him away from the fatal spot in a trice so that she did not see her husband remove Lady Massey's hands from his shoulders.

No one could have been in greater spirits than my Lady Rule for the rest of that horrid evening. Several people remarked on it, and Mr Dashwood thought her more entrancing than ever.

But when Rule visited her room next morning and sat down on the edge of her bed while she drank her chocolate he found her in a wayward mood. Go to Meering? Oh, no, she could not! Why, she had a hundred engagements and it would be dreadfully dull in the country.

'That is not very complimentary of you,' Rule said, half smiling.

'Well, but Rule, you are only g-going for a week, I daresay, and think how tiresome to pack for such a short stay! Of c-course I shall come with you after the Newmarket m-meeting, if we d-don't go to Bath.'

'I would very much rather you come with me now, Horry.'

'Very w-well,' Horatia said, in the voice of a martyr. 'If you say I m-must, I will.'

He got up. 'Heaven forbid, my dear!'

'R-Rule, if you feel cross about it, please tell me! I d-don't want to be a b-bad wife.'

'Do I look cross?' he inquired.

'N-no, but I never can tell what you think by l-looking at you,' said Horatia candidly.

He laughed. 'Poor Horry, it must be very difficult for you. Stay in town, my dear. You are probably quite right. Arnold will make me attend to business at Meering.' He put a finger under her chin, and tilted it up. 'Don't game all my fortune away while I am gone, will you?' he said teasingly.

'No, of c-course not. I will be very g-good. And you need not be afraid that I shall encourage Lord Lethbridge, for Louisa told me all about him and I quite see that I m-mustn't know him.'

'I am not afraid of that,' he answered, and bent and kissed her.

14

So the Earl of Rule went away to Meering accompanied only by Mr Gisborne, while his wife stayed in London and tried to convince herself that she did not miss him at all. If she was not successful in this, at least nobody could have suspected it from her demeanour. Since the big house in Grosvenor Square seemed unbearably empty without his lordship Horatia spent as much of her time as she could away from it. No one meeting her at all the card-parties, routs, drums, and picnics that she attended could have supposed her to be pining most unfashionably for her own husband. In fact, her sister Charlotte said severely that her frivolity was excessively unbecoming.

Lord Lethbridge she had no difficulty in keeping at arm's length. They naturally met at a great many parties, but his lordship, finding Horatia was civil but very formal, seemed to accept with equanimity his relegation to the ranks of her merest acquaintance and made no attempt to win her over again. Horatia put him out of her life without much regret. Glamour might still have clung to a rakehell who abducted noble damsels, but no glamour remained about a man who had been pushed into a pond in full ball-dress. Horatia, sorry only that she never had played cards with him, discarded him without a pang, and proceeded to forget about him.

She was succeeding admirably when he forced himself on her notice again in a manner as unexpected as it was outrageous.

A charming entertainment was held at Richmond House, with dancing and fireworks. Never was there so elegantly contrived a party. The gardens were brightly illuminated, supper spread in the apartments, and the fireworks let off from a platform of barges anchored in the river to the admiration of the guests and all the unbidden spectators who crowded every near-by house. At midnight a shower of rain came, but since by that time all the fireworks had been finished, it could not be thought to signify, and the guests retired to the ballroom for the dancing.

Horatia left the party early. It had been pretty to see the fireworks, but she found that she did not care to dance. For this a new pair of diamond-embroidered shoes was partly responsible. They pinched her abominably, and nothing, she discovered, could so effectually ruin one's enjoyment as an uncomfortable shoe. Her coach was called for shortly after twelve, and resisting all the entreaties of Mr Dashwood, she departed.

She decided she must have attended too many balls, for certainly she had found this one almost tedious. It was really very difficult to dance and chatter gaily when one was all the time wondering what a large, sleepily smiling gentleman was doing miles away in Berkshire. It was apt to make one *distraite*, and to give one a headache. She leaned back in the corner of the coach and closed her eyes. Rule was not coming back for a week. What if one were to take him by surprise, and drive down to Meering the very next day? No, of course one could not do any such thing . . . she would send these shoes back to the makers, and let them make her another pair. The coiffeur too—really, he had dressed her head abominably; there were dozens of pins sticking into her scalp, and the wretch should have known that the Quésaco style did not become her at all. All those heavy plumes bunched up made her look forty if she was a day. And as for the new Serkis rouge Miss Lloyd had induced her to use, it was the horridest stuff in the world, and so she would tell Miss Lloyd the very next time she saw her.

The coach drew up and she opened her eyes with a start. It was raining quite fast now, and the footman was holding an umbrella to protect his mistress's finery. The rain seemed to have extinguished the flambeaux that always burned in iron brackets at the foot of the steps leading up to the front door. It was quite dark, the clouds obscuring what had been a fine moon.

Horatia drew her cloak, an affair of white taffeta with a collar of puffed muslin, tightly round her, and holding her skirts up in one hand, stepped down on to the wet pavement. The footman held the umbrella well over her, and she sped quickly up the steps to the open door.

In her hurry she was over the threshold before she realized her mistake. She gave a gasp and stared round her. She was standing in a narrow hallway, not in her own house, nor any like it, and the lackey, even now in the act of shutting the door, was no servant of Rule's.

She turned quickly. 'There is a m-mistake,' she said. 'Open the d-door, please!'

A step sounded behind her; she looked over her shoulder and saw Lord Lethbridge.

'A thousand welcomes, my lady!' Lethbridge said, and flung open the door of the saloon. 'Pray enter!'

She stood perfectly still, dawning anger struggling with the bewilderment in her face. 'I don't understand!' she said. 'What does this m-mean, sir?'

'Why, I will tell you, ma'am, but pray come in!' Lethbridge said.

She was aware of the silent lackey behind her; one could not make a scene before servants. After a moment's hesitation she walked forward, and into the saloon.

It was lit by a great many candles, and at one end of the room a table was laid with a cold supper. Horatia frowned. 'If you are giving a p-party, sir, I assure you I was not invited, and d-don't mean to stay,' she announced.

'It is not a party,' he replied, shutting the door. 'It's for you and me, my dear.'

'You must be mad!' said Horatia, gazing at him in perplexity. 'Of c-course I would never c-come to supper with you alone! If you asked me, I vow I never knew of it, and I c-can't imagine why my coachman set me down here.'

'I didn't ask you, Horry. I planned it as a little surprise for you.'

'Then it was a great piece of impertinence!' said Horatia. 'I suppose you b-bribed my coachman? Well, you may escort me out to the coach again, sir, at once!'

He laughed. 'Your coach, my dear, has gone, and your coachman and groom are lying under a table in a tavern off Whitehall. My own men conveyed you here. Now, do you not agree that I planned it very neatly?'

Wrath blazed in Horatia's eyes. 'I think it was m-monstrous of you!' she said. 'Do you m-mean to tell me you had the audacity to overpower my servants?'

'Oh, no!' he answered lightly. 'That would have been unnecessarily violent. While you were at Richmond House, my love, what more natural than that the honest fellows should refresh themselves at the nearest tavern?'

'I d-don't believe it!' snapped Horatia. 'You d-don't know much of Rule if you think he keeps a coachman who gets d-drunk! You m-must have had him set upon, and I shall send for a c-constable in the morning and tell him! Then perhaps you will be sorry!'

'I expect I should be,' agreed Lethbridge. 'But do you think the constable would believe that one tankard of beer apiece could have so disastrous effect on your servants? For you see, I didn't have them overpowered quite as you think.'

'D-drugged!' Horatia cried hotly.

'Precisely,' smiled his lordship. 'Do, I beg of you, let me take your cloak!'

'No!' said Horatia. 'I w-won't! You are quite out of your senses, and if you have not the civility to summon me a chair, I will w-walk home!'

'I wish you would try and understand, Horry,' he said. 'You will not leave my house tonight.'

'N-not leave your house—oh, you *are* m-mad!' Horatia said with conviction.

'Then be mad with me, love,' Lethbridge said, and put his hand on her cloak to remove it.

'D-don't call me "love"!' choked Horatia. 'Why—why you are trying to ruin me!'

'That's as you choose, my dear,' he said. 'I'm ready—yes, I'm ready to run away with you, or you may return home in the morning and tell what tale you please.'

'You m-make a habit of running away with f-females, do you not?' said Horatia.

His brows contracted, but only for a moment. 'So you have that story, have you? Let us say that I make a habit of running away with the females of your family.'

'I,' said Horatia, 'am a W-Winwood, which you will find makes a vast d-difference. You can't force me to elope with you.'

'I shan't try,' he replied coolly. 'Yet I believe we might deal extremely together, you and I. There's something about you, Horry, which is infinitely alluring. I could make you love me you know.'

'N-now I know what is the m-matter with you!' exclaimed Horatia, suddenly enlightened. 'You're drunk!'

'Devil a bit,' answered his lordship. 'Come, give me your cloak!' He twitched it from her as he spoke, and threw it aside, and stood for a moment looking at her through half shut eyes. 'No, you're not beautiful,' he said softly, 'but—damnably seductive, my pretty!'

Horatia took a step backward. 'D-don't come near me!'

'Not come near you!' he repeated. 'Horry, you little fool!'

She tried to dodge away from him, but he caught her, and pulled her roughly into his arms. There was a wild struggle; she got one hand free and dealt him a ringing slap; then he had both her arms clamped to her sides, and kissed her suffocatingly. She managed to jerk her head away, and brought one sharp heel down full on his instep. She felt him flinch, and twisted herself free, hearing the lace at her corsage rip in his clutching fingers. The next moment the table was between them, and Lethbridge was nursing his bruised foot and laughing. 'Gad, you little spitfire!' he said. 'I never dreamed you would show such spirit! Damme, I believe I shan't let you go back to that dull husband of yours after all. Oh, don't scowl so, sweetheart, I'm not going to chase you round the room. Sit down.'

She was by now really frightened, for it seemed to her as though he must be out of his senses. She kept a wary eye on his movements, and decided that the only thing to do was to pretend to humour him. Trying to speak quite steadily, she said: 'If you sit down, so will I.'

'Behold me!' Lethbridge replied, flinging himself into a chair.

Horatia nodded, and followed his example. 'P-please try and be sensible, my l-lord,' she requested. 'It isn't the least use telling me that you are fallen in l-love with me, because I d-don't believe it. Why did you bring me here?'

'To steal your virtue,' he answered flippantly. 'You see, I am quite frank with you.'

'W-well, I can be frank too,' retorted Horatia, her eyes gleaming. 'And if you think you are g-going to ravish m-me, you quite mistake the m-matter! I'm much nearer the door than you are.'

'True, but it is locked, and the key'—he patted his pocket—'is here!'

'Oh!' said Horatia. 'So you don't even play f-fair!'

'Not in love,' he replied.

'I wish,' said Horatia forcefully, 'you would stop talking about l-love. It makes me feel sick.'

'My dear,' he said, 'I assure you I am falling deeper in love with you every moment.'

She curled her lip. 'Stuff!' she snorted. 'If you l-loved me the l-least little bit, you wouldn't do this to me. And if you did ravish me you would be p-put into prison, if Rule d-didn't kill you first, which I daresay he would do.'

'Ah!' said Lethbridge. 'No doubt I should be put into prison—if you had the courage to tell the world of this night's work. It would be worth it. Oh, it would be worth it, only to know that Rule's damned pride was in the dust!'

Her eyes narrowed; she leaned a little forward, her hands clenched in her lap. 'So that is it!' she said. 'F-fustian, my lord! It would d-do very well at Drury Lane, I d-daresay, but in life, n-no!'

'We can but try,' said Lethbridge. The mockery had vanished, leaving his face very harsh, the mouth set in grim lines, the eyes staring straight ahead.

'I can't imagine how ever I c-could have wanted you for a friend,' said Horatia, meditatively. 'You are d-dreadfully poor-spirited, I think. C-couldn't you find a way of revenge except through a woman?'

'None so exquisitely complete,' Lethbridge answered, unmoved. His gaze travelled to her face. 'But when I look at you, Horry, why, I forget revenge, and desire you for yourself alone.'

'You c-can't imagine how flattered I am,' said Horatia politely.

He burst out laughing. 'You adorable rogue, I believe a man might keep you a twelvemonth and not be tired of you!' He got up. 'Come, Horry, throw in your lot with mine! You were made for something better than to be tied to a man who don't care a rap for you. Come away with me, and I'll teach you what love can be!'

'And then Rule can divorce m-me, and of c-course you'll m-marry me?' suggested Horatia.

'I might even do that,' he concurred. He walked over to the table and picked up one of the bottles that stood on it. 'Let us drink to—the future!' he said.

'Very w-well, sir,' Horatia answered in a voice of deceptive mildness. She had risen when he did, and taken a step towards the empty fireplace. Now, as he stood with his back to her, she bent swiftly and picked up the heavy brass poker that lay there.

Lethbridge was filling the second glass. 'We will go to Italy, if you like,' he said.

'Italy?' said Horatia, tiptoeing forward.

'Why not?'

'B-because I wouldn't go to the end of the street with you!' flashed Horatia, and struck with all her might.

The poker fell with a rather sickening thud. Half horrified, half triumphant, Horatia watched Lethbridge sway a moment, and crash to the ground. The wine-bottle, slipping from his nerveless fingers, rolled over the carpet spilling its contents in a dark ruby flood.

Horatia caught her underlip between her teeth, and went down on her knees beside the limp form, and thrust her hand into the pocket he had patted so confidently. She found the key, and pulled it out. Lethbridge was lying alarmingly still; she wondered whether she had killed him, and shot a frightened look towards the door. No sound disturbed the silence; she realized with a sigh of thankfulness that the servants must have gone to bed, and got up. There was no blood on the poker, and none that she could see on Lethbridge's head, though his wig, gaping up from his forehead, might conceal that. She put the poker back in the grate, caught up her cloak and sped over to the door. Her hand shook so that she could scarcely fit the key into the lock, but she managed it at last, and the next moment was out in the hall, tugging at the bolts of the front door. They scraped noisily, and she cast a quick nervous glance behind her. She got the door open, and wrapping her cloak round her fled down the steps into the street.

There were large puddles in the road, and heavy clouds threatening to obscure the moon, but for the moment it had stopped raining. The road was eerily quiet; blank, shuttered windows on either side, and a little draughty wind sneaking up to whip Horatia's skirts about her ankles.

She set off, almost running in the direction of Curzon Street. She had never in her life been out alone on foot at this hour, and she prayed fervently that she would not meet anyone. She had nearly reached the corner of the street when, to her dismay, she heard voices. She checked, trying to see who these late wayfarers might be. There were two of them, and their progress seemed a little uncertain. Then one of them spoke in a quite unmistakable if slightly thick voice. 'I'll tell you what I'll do,' it said. 'I'll lay you a pony you're wrong!'

Horatia gave a tiny shriek of relief and hurled herself forward, straight into the arms of the astonished roysterer, who reeled under the impact. 'P-Pel!' she sobbed. 'Oh, P-Pel, take me home!'

The Viscount steadied himself by grasping at the railings. He blinked at his sister in a bemused fashion, and suddenly made a discovery. 'Burn it, it's you, Horry!' he said. 'Well, well, well! Do you know my sister, Pom? This is my sister, Lady Rule. Sir Roland Pommeroy, Horry—friend o' mine.'

Sir Roland achieved a beautiful leg. 'Your la'ship's most obedient!' he said.

'P-Pel, will you take me home?' begged Horatia, clasping his wrist.

'Permit me, ma'am!' said Sir Roland, gallantly presenting his arm. 'Should be honoured!'

'Wait a minute,' commanded the Viscount, who was frowning portentously. 'What's the time?'

'I d-don't know, but it m-must be dreadfully late!' said Horatia.

'Not a second after two!' Sir Roland said. 'Can't be after two. We left

Monty's at half past one, didn't we? Very well, then, call it two o'clock.'

'It's more than that,' pronounced the Viscount, 'and if it's more than that, what's bothering me is, what the devil are you doing here, Horry?'

'Pel, Pel!' besought his friend. 'Remember—ladies present!'

'That's what I say,' nodded the Viscount. 'Ladies don't walk about at two in the morning. Where are we?'

Sir Roland thought. 'Half-Moon Street,' he said positively.

'Very well, then,' said the Viscount, 'tell me this: what's my sister doing in Half-Moon Street at two in the morning?'

Horatia, who had listened impatiently to this interchange, gave his wrist a shake. 'Oh, don't stand there talking, P-Pel. I couldn't help it, indeed I couldn't! And I'm dreadfully afraid I've killed Lord Lethbridge!'

'What?'

'K-killed Lord Lethbridge,' shuddered Horatia.

'Nonsense!' said the Viscount.

'It isn't nonsense! I hit him with a p-poker as hard as I could, and he f-fell and lay quite still.'

'Where did you hit him?' demanded the Viscount.

'On the head,' said Horatia.

The Viscount looked at Sir Roland. 'D'you suppose she killed him, Pom?'

'Might have,' said Sir Roland judicially.

'Lay you five to one she didn't,' offered the Viscount.

'Done!' said Sir Roland.

'Tell you what,' said the Viscount suddenly. 'I'm going to see.'

Horatia caught him by the skirts of his coat. 'No, you sh-shan't! You've got to take me home.'

'Oh, very well,' replied the Viscount, relinquishing his purpose. 'But you've no business to go killing people with a poker at two in the morning. It ain't genteel.'

Sir Roland came unexpectedly to Horatia's support. 'Don't see that,' he said. 'Why shouldn't she hit Lethbridge with a poker? You don't like him. I don't like him.'

'No,' said the Viscount, acknowledging the truth of this statement. 'But I wouldn't hit him with a poker. Never heard of such a thing.'

'No more have I,' admitted Sir Roland. 'But I tell you what I think, Pel: it's a good thing.'

'You think that?' said the Viscount.

'I do,' maintained Sir Roland doggedly.

'Well, we'd better go home,' said the Viscount, making another of his sudden decisions.

'Th-thank goodness!' said Horatia, quite exasperated. She took her brother's arm, and turned him in the right direction. 'This way, you stupid, horrid c-creature!'

But the Viscount at that moment caught sight of her elaborate coiffure, with its bunch of nodding plumes, and stopped short. 'I knew there was something mighty queer about you, Horry,' he said. 'What have you done to your hair?'

'N-nothing, it's only a Quésaco. D-do hurry, Pel!'

Sir Roland, interested, bent his head. 'I beg pardon, ma'am, what did you say it was?'

'I s-said it was a Quésaco,' replied Horatia, between tears and laughter. 'And that's Provençal signifying "What does it mean?"'

'Well, what does it mean?' asked the Viscount reasonably.

'Oh, P-Pel, I don't know! Do, do, take me home!'

The Viscount permitted himself to be drawn onward. They traversed Curzon Street without mishap, and Sir Roland remarked that it was a fine night. Neither the Viscount nor his sister paid any heed to this. The Viscount who had been thinking, said: 'I don't say it ain't a good thing if you've killed Lethbridge, but what I can't make out is what brought you here at this time of night?'

Horatia, feeling that in his present condition it was useless to attempt to explain to him, replied: 'I went to the p-party at Richmond House.'

'And was it agreeable, ma'am?' inquired Sir Roland politely.

'Yes, th-thank you.'

'But Richmond House ain't in Half-Moon Street,' the Viscount pointed out.

'She walked home,' explained Sir Roland. 'We were walking home, weren't we? Very well, then. She walked home. Passed Lethbridge's house. Went in. Hit him on the head with the poker. Came out. Met us in the street. There you are. Plain as a pikestaff.'

'Well, I don't know,' said the Viscount. 'Seems queer to me.'

Sir Roland drew nearer to Horatia. 'Deeply regret!' he whispered hoarsely. 'Poor Pel not quite himself.'

'For m-mercy's sake, do hurry!' replied Horatia crossly.

By this time they had reached Grosvenor Square, and it had begun to rain again. The Viscount said abruptly: 'Did you say it was a fine night?'

'I may have,' said Sir Roland cautiously.

'Well, I think it's raining,' announced the Viscount.

'It is raining, and my f-feathers will be ruined!' said Horatia. 'Oh, now what is it Pel?'

The Viscount had stopped. 'Forgotten something,' he said. 'Meant to go and see whether that fellow Lethbridge was dead.'

'P-Pel, it doesn't matter, really it d-doesn't!'

'Yes it does, I've got a bet on it,' replied the Viscount, and plunged off in the direction of Half-Moon Street.

Sir Roland shook his head. 'He shouldn't have gone off like that,' he said severely. 'Lady on his arm—walks off, not a word of apology. Very cool, very cool indeed. Take my arm, ma'am!'

'Thank g-goodness we're there!' said Horatia, hurrying him along.

At the foot of the steps of her own house, she stopped and looked Sir Roland over dubiously. 'I shall have to explain it all to you, I suppose. C-come and see me tomorrow. I mean today. Please remember to c-come! And if I've really k-killed Lord Lethbridge, don't, don't say anything about it!'

'Certainly not,' said Sir Roland. 'Not a word.'

Horatia prepared to ascend the steps. 'And you will go after P-Pelham and take him home, won't you?'

'With the greatest pleasure on earth, ma'am,' said Sir Roland, with a profound bow. 'Happy to be of service!'

Well, at least he doesn't seem to be as drunk as Pelham, thought Horatia, as the sleepy porter opened the door to her knock. And if only I can make him understand how it all happened, and Pelham doesn't do anything foolish, perhaps Rule need never know anything about this.

Slightly cheered by this reflection, she went up the stairs to her bedroom, where a lamp was burning. Picking up a taper, she lit the candles on her dressing-table, and sat down before the mirror, quite worn out. The plumes in her hair were draggled and limp; her corsage was torn. She put her hand to it mechanically, and suddenly her eyes widened in horror. She had been wearing some of the Drelincourt jewels—a set of pearls and diamonds, ear-rings, brooch and bracelets. The ear-rings were there, the bracelets still on her wrists, but the brooch had gone.

Her mind flew back to her struggle in Lethbridge's arms, when her lace had been torn. She stared at her own image in the glass. Under the Serkis rouge she had turned deathly pale. Her face puckered; she burst into tears.

15

Nothing intervening to cause the Viscount to swerve from his purpose, he pursued a somewhat erratic course back to Half-Moon Street. Finding the door of Lethbridge's house open, as Horatia had left it, he walked in without ceremony. The door into the saloon was also ajar, and lights shone. The Viscount put his head into the room and looked round.

Lord Lethbridge was seated in a chair by the table, holding his head in his hands. An empty bottle of wine lay on the floor, and a Catogan wig, slightly dishevelled. Hearing a footfall his lordship looked up and stared blankly across at the Viscount.

The Viscount stepped into the room. 'Come to see if you was dead,' he said. 'Laid Pom odds you weren't.'

Lethbridge passed his hand across his eyes. 'I'm not,' he replied in a faint voice.

'No. I'm sorry,' said the Viscount simply. He wandered over to the table and sat down. 'Horry said she killed you, Pom said So she might, I said No. Nonsense.'

Lethbridge, still holding a hand to his aching head, tried to pull himself together. 'Did you?' he said. His eyes ran over his self-invited guest. 'I see. Let me assure you once more that I am very much alive.'

'Well, I wish you'd put your wig on,' complained the Viscount. 'What I want to know is why did Horry hit you on the head with the poker?'

Lethbridge gingerly felt his bruised scalp. 'With a poker was it? Pray ask her, though I doubt if she will tell you.'

'You shouldn't keep the front door open,' said the Viscount. 'What's to stop people coming in and hitting you over the head? It's preposterous.'

'I wish you would go home,' said Lethbridge wearily.

The Viscount surveyed the supper-table with a knowing eye. 'Card party?' he inquired.

'No.'

At that moment the voice of Sir Roland Pommeroy was heard, calling to his friend. He too put his head round the door, and, perceiving the Viscount, came in. 'You're to come home,' he said briefly. 'Gave my word to my lady I'd take you home.'

The Viscount pointed a finger at his unwilling host. 'He ain't dead, Pom. Told you he wouldn't be.'

Sir Roland turned to look closely at Lethbridge. 'No, he ain't dead,' he admitted with some reluctance. 'Nothing for it but to go home.'

'Blister it, that's a tame way to end the night,' protested the Viscount.

'Play you a game of piquet.'

'Not in this house,' said Lethbridge, picking up his wig and putting it cautiously on his head again.

'Why not in this house?' demanded the Viscount.

The question was destined to remain unanswered. Yet a third visitor had arrived.

'My dear Lethbridge, pray forgive me, but this odious rain! Not a chair to be had, positively not a chair nor a hackney! And your door standing wide I stepped in to shelter. I trust I don't intrude?' said Mr Drelincourt, peeping into the room.

'Oh, not in the least!' replied Lethbridge ironically. 'By all means come in! I rather think that I have no need to introduce Lord Winwood and Sir Roland Pommeroy to you?'

Mr Drelincourt recoiled perceptibly, but tried to compose his sharp features into an expression of indifference. 'Oh, in that case—I had no notion you was entertaining, my lord—you must forgive me!'

'I had no notion of it either,' said Lethbridge. 'Perhaps you would care to play piquet with Winwood?'

'Really, you must hold me excused!' replied Mr Drelincourt, edging towards the door.

The Viscount, who had been regarding him fixedly, nudged Sir Roland. 'There's that fellow Drelincourt,' he said.

Sir Roland nodded. 'Yes, that's Drelincourt,' he corroborated. 'I don't know why, but I don't like him, Pel. Never did. Let's go.'

'Not at all,' said the Viscount with dignity. 'Who asked him to come in? Tell me that! 'Pon my soul, it's a nice thing, so it is, if a fellow can come poking his nose into a private card party. I'll tell you what I'll do: I'll pull it for him.'

Mr Drelincourt, thoroughly alarmed, cast an imploring glance at Lethbridge, who merely looked saturnine. Sir Roland, however, restrained his friend. 'You can't do that, Pel. Just remembered you fought the fellow. Should have pulled his nose first. Can't do it now.' He looked round the room with a frown. ''Nother thing!' he said. 'It was Monty's card party, wasn't it? Well, this ain't Monty's house. Knew there was something wrong!'

The Viscount sat up, and addressed himself to Lord Lethbridge with some severity. 'Is this a card party or is it not?' he demanded.

'It is not,' replied Lethbridge.

The Viscount rose and groped for his hat. 'You should have said so before,' he said. 'If it ain't a card party, what the devil is it?'

'I've no idea,' said Lethbridge. 'It has been puzzling me for some time.'

'If a man gives a party, he ought to know what kind of party it is,' argued the Viscount. 'If you don't know, how are we to know? It might be a damned soirée, in which case we wouldn't have come. Let's go home, Pom.'

He took Sir Roland's arm and walked with him to the door. There Sir Roland bethought himself of something, and turned back. 'Very pleasant evening, my lord,' he said formally, and bowed, and went out in the Viscount's wake.

Mr Drelincourt waited until the two bottle-companions were well out of earshot, and gave a mirthless titter. 'I did not know you was so friendly with Winwood,' he said. 'I do trust I have not broken up your party? But the rain, you know! Not a chair to be had.'

'Rid yourself of the notion that any of you are here by my invitation,' said

Lethbridge unpleasantly, and moved across to the table.

Something had caught Mr Drelincourt's eye. He bent, and picked up from under the corner of the Persian rug a ring brooch of diamonds and pearls of antique design. His jaw dropped; he shot a quick, acute glance at Lethbridge, who was tossing off a glass of wine. The next moment the brooch was in his pocket, and as Lethbridge turned he said airily: 'I beg a thousand pardons! I daresay the rain will have stopped. You must permit me to take my leave.'

'With pleasure,' said Lethbridge.

Mr Drelincourt's eye ran over the supper-table laid for two; he wondered where Lethbridge had hidden his fair visitor. 'Don't, I implore you, put yourself to the trouble of coming to the door!'

'I wish to assure myself that it is shut,' said Lethbridge grimly, and ushered him out.

Some hours later the Viscount awoke to a new but considerably advanced day, with the most imperfect recollections of the night's happenings. He remembered enough, however, to cause him, as soon as he had swallowed some strong coffee, to fling off the bedclothes and spring up, shouting for his valet.

He was sitting before the dressing-table in his shirtsleeves, arranging his lace cravat, when word was brought to him that Sir Roland Pommeroy was below and desired a word with him.

'Show him up,' said the Viscount briefly, sticking a pin in the cravat. He picked up his solitaire, a narrow band of black ribbon, and was engaged in clipping this round his neck when Sir Roland walked in.

The Viscount looked up and met his friend's eyes in the mirror. Sir Roland was looking very solemn; he shook his head slightly, and heaved a sigh.

'Don't need you any longer, Corney,' said the Viscount, dismissing his valet.

The door closed discreetly behind the man. The Viscount swung round in his chair, and leaned his arms along the back of it. 'How drunk was I last night?' he demanded.

Sir Roland looked more lugubrious than ever. 'Pretty drunk, Pel. You wanted to pull that fellow Drelincourt's nose.'

'That don't prove I was drunk,' said the Viscount impatiently. 'But I can't get it out of my head that my sister Rule had something to do with it. Did she or did she not say she hit Lethbridge over the head with a poker?'

'A poker, was it?' exclaimed Sir Roland. 'Could not for the life of me remember what it was she said she hit him with! That was it! Then you went off to see if he was dead.' The Viscount cursed softly. 'And I took her la'ship home.' He frowned. 'And what's more, she said I was to wait on her this morning!'

'It's the devil of a business,' muttered the Viscount. 'What in God's name was she doing in the fellow's house?'

Sir Roland coughed. 'Naturally—needn't tell you—can rely on me, Pel. Awkward affair—mum's the word.'

The Viscount nodded. 'Mighty good of you, Pom. I'll have to see my sister first thing. You'd best come with me.'

He got up and reached for his waistcoat. Someone scratched on the door, and upon being told to come in, the valet entered with a sealed letter on a salver. The Viscount picked it up and broke the seal.

The note was from Horatia, and was evidently written in great agitation.

Dear Pel: The most Dredful thing has happened. Please come at once. I am quite Distracted. Horry.

'Waiting for an answer?' the Viscount asked curtly.

'No, my lord.'

'Then send a message to the stables, will you, and tell Jackson to bring the phaeton round.'

Sir Roland, who had watched with concern the reading of the note, thought he had rarely seen his friend turn so pale, and coughed a second time. 'Pel, dear old boy—must remind you—she hit him with the poker. Laid him out, you know.'

'Yes,' said the Viscount, looking a trifle less grim. 'So she did. Help me into my coat, Pom. We'll drive round to Grosvenor Square now.'

When, twenty minutes later, the phaeton drew up outside Rule's house, Sir Roland said that perhaps it would be better if he did not come in, so the Viscount entered the house alone, and was shown at once to one of the smaller saloons. Here he found his sister, looking the picture of despair.

She greeted him without recrimination. 'Oh, P-Pel, I'm so glad you've come! I am quite undone, and you must help me!'

The Viscount laid down his hat and gloves, and said sternly: 'Now, Horry, what happened last night? Don't put yourself in a taking: just tell me!'

'Of c-course I'm going to tell you!' said Horatia. 'I w-went to Richmond House to the b-ball and the fireworks.'

'Never mind about the fireworks,' interrupted the Viscount. 'You weren't at Richmond House, nor anywhere near it, when I met you.'

'No, I was in Half-Moon Street,' said Horatia innocently.

'You went to Lethbridge's house?'

At the note of accusation in her brother's voice, Horatia flung up her head. 'Yes, I did, but if you think I w-went there of my own choice you are quite odious!' Her lip trembled. 'Though w-why you should believe that I didn't, I can't imagine, for it's the stupidest tale you ever heard, and I know it d-doesn't sound true.'

'Well, what is the tale?' he asked, drawing up a chair.

She dabbed at her eyes with the corner of her handkerchief. 'You see, my shoes p-pinched me, and I left the b-ball early, and it was raining. My c-coach was called, and I suppose I never looked at the footman—indeed, why should I?'

'What the devil has the footman to do with it?' demanded the Viscount.

'Everything,' said Horatia. 'He w-wasn't the right one.'

'I don't see what odds that makes.'

'I m-mean he wasn't one of our servants at all. The c-coachman wasn't either. They were L-Lord Lethbridge's.'

'What?' ejaculated the Viscount, his brow growing black as thunder.

Horatia nodded. 'Yes, and they drove me to his house. And I w-went in before I realized.'

The Viscount was moved to expostulate: 'Lord, you must have known it wasn't your house!'

'I tell you I didn't! I know it sounds stupid, but it was raining, and the f-footman held the umbrella so that I c-couldn't see m-much and I was inside b-before I knew.'

'Did Lethbridge open the door?'

'N-no, the porter did.'

'Then why the devil didn't you walk out again?'

'I know I should have,' confessed Horatia, 'but then Lord Lethbridge came out of the s-saloon, and asked me to step in. And, P-Pel, I didn't understand; I thought it was a m-mistake, and I d-didn't want to make a scene before the p-porter, so I went in. Only n-now I see how foolish it was of me, because if Rule comes to hear of it, and m-makes inquiries, the servants will say I went in w-willingly and so I did!'

'Rule mustn't hear of this,' said the Viscount grimly.

'No, of c-course he mustn't, and that's why I sent for you.'

'Horry, what happened in the saloon? Come, let me hear the whole of it!'

'It was d-dreadful! He said he w-was going to ravish me, and oh, Pel, it was just to revenge himself on R-Rule! So I p-pretended I might run away with him, and as soon as he turned his back, I hit him with the p-poker and escaped.'

The Viscount drew a sigh of relief. 'That's all, Horry?'

'No, it isn't all,' said Horatia desperately. 'My g-gown was torn when he k-kissed me, and though I d-didn't know till I got home, my brooch fell out, and, P-Pel, he's got it now!'

'Make yourself easy,' said the Viscount, getting up. 'He won't have it long.'

Catching sight of his face, which wore a starkly murderous expression, Horatia cried out: 'What are you going to do?'

'Do?' said the Viscount, with a short, ugly laugh. 'Cut the dog's heart out!'

Horatia sprung up suddenly. 'P-Pel, you can't! For g-goodness' sake don't fight him! You know he's m-much better than you are, and only think of the scandal! P-Pel, you'll ruin me if you do! You can't do it!'

The Viscount checked in bitter disgust. 'You're right,' he said. 'I can't. Fiend seize it, there must be some way of forcing a quarrel on him without bringing you into it!'

'If you fight him everyone will say it was about m-me, because after you f-fought Crosby people t-talked, and I did silly things–oh, you mustn't, P-Pel. It's b-bad enough with Sir Roland knowing—'

'Pom!' exclaimed the Viscount. 'We'll have him in! He might have a notion how I can manage it.'

'Have him in? W-why, where is he?'

'Outside with the phaeton. You needn't mind him, Horry; he's devilish discreet.'

'W-well, if you think he could help us, he can c-come in,' said Horatia dubiously. 'But p-please explain it all to him, first, P-Pel, for he must be thinking the most d-dreadful things about me.'

Accordingly, when the Viscount returned presently to the saloon with Sir Roland, that worthy had been put in possession of all the facts. He bowed over Horatia's hand, and embarked on a somewhat involved apology for his inebriety the night before. The Viscount cut him short. 'Never mind about that!' he adjured him. 'Can I call Lethbridge out?'

Sir Roland devoted deep thought to this, and after a long pause pronounced the verdict. 'No,' he said.

'I m-must say, you've got m-much more sense than I thought,' said Horatia approvingly.

'Do you mean to tell me,' demanded the Viscount, 'that I'm to sit by while that dog kidnaps my sister, and do nothing? No, damme, I won't!'

'Devilish hard on you, Pel,' agreed Sir Roland sympathetically. 'But it won't do, you know. Called Drelincourt out. Deal of talk over that. Call Lethbridge out—fatal!'

The Viscount smote the table with his fist. 'Hang you, Pom, do you realize what the fellow did?' he cried.

'Very painful affair,' said Sir Roland. 'Bad *ton*. Must hush it up.'

The Viscount seemed to be bereft of words.

'Hush it up now,' said Sir Roland. 'Talk dies down—say three months. Pick a quarrel with him then.'

The Viscount brightened. 'Ay, so I could. That solves it.'

'S-solves it? It doesn't!' declared Horatia. 'I m-must get my brooch back. If Rule m-misses it, it will all come out.'

'Nonsense!' said her brother. 'Say you dropped it in the street.'

'It's no good saying that! I tell you Lethbridge means m-mischief. He may wear it, just to m-make Rule suspicious.'

Sir Roland was shocked. 'Bad blood!' he said. 'Never did like the fellow.'

'What sort of brooch is it?' asked the Viscount. 'Would Rule be likely to recognize it?'

'Yes, of course he would! It's part of a set, and it's very old—fifteenth century, I think.'

'In that case,' decided his lordship, 'we've got to get it back. I'd best go and see Lethbridge at once—though how I'll keep my hands off him I don't know. Burn it, a pretty fool I look, calling on him last night!'

Sir Roland was once more plunged in thought. 'Won't do,' he said at last. 'If you go asking for a brooch, Lethbridge is bound to guess it's my lady's. I'll go.'

Horatia looked at him with admiration. 'Yes, that would be m-much better,' she said. 'You are very helpful, I think.'

Sir Roland blushed, and prepared to set forth on his mission. 'Beg you won't give it a thought, ma'am. Affair of delicacy—tact required—a mere nothing!'

'Tact!' said the Viscount. 'Tact for a hound like Lethbridge! My God, it makes me sick, so it does! You'd better take the phaeton; I'll wait for you here.'

Sir Roland once more bowed over Horatia's hand. 'Shall hope to put the brooch in your hands within half an hour, ma'am,' he said, and departed.

Left alone with his sister, the Viscount began to pace about the room, growling something under his breath whenever he happened to think of Lethbridge's iniquity. Presently he stopped short. 'Horry, you'll have to tell Rule, Damme, he's a right to know!'

'I c-can't tell him!' Horatia answered with suppressed passion. 'Not again!'

'Again?' said his lordship. 'What do you mean?'

Horatia hung her head, and recounted haltingly the story of the ridotto at Ranelagh. The Viscount was delighted with at least one part of the story, and slapped his leg with glee.

'Yes, b-but I didn't know it was Rule, and so I had to confess it all to him next d-day and I won't—I won't make another c-confession! I said I w-wouldn't see anything of Lethbridge while he was away and I can't, I c-can't tell him about this!'

'I don't see it,' said the Viscount. 'Plenty to bear you out. Coachman—what happened to him, by the way?'

'D-drugged,' she replied.

'All the better,' said his lordship. 'If the coach came back to the stables without him, obviously you're telling the truth.'

'But it didn't! He was too clever,' said Horatia bitterly. 'I had the c-coachman in this morning. He thinks it was the b-bad beer, and the coach was taken back to the tavern. So I said I had been forced to get a link-boy to summon me a hackney. And I d-didn't think it was quite fair to send him off when I knew he and the footman had been d-drugged, so I said this time I wouldn't tell Rule.'

'That's bad,' said the Viscount, frowning. 'Still, Pom and I know you hit Lethbridge on the head, and got away.'

'It's no good,' she said mournfully. 'Of c-course you would be bound to stand by me, and that's what Rule would think.'

'But hang it, Horry, why should he?'

'Well, I—well, I w-wasn't very nice to him b-before he went away, and he wanted me to g-go with him and I wouldn't, and d-don't you see, P-Pel, it looks as if I p-planned it all, and hadn't really given up Lethbridge at all? And I l-left that horrid b-ball early, to make it worse!'

'It don't look well, certainly,' admitted the Viscount. 'Have you quarrelled with Rule?'

'No. N-not quarrelled. Only—No.'

'You'd best tell me, and be done with it,' said his lordship severely. 'I suppose you've been up to your tricks again. I warned you he wouldn't stand for 'em.'

'It isn't that at all!' flamed Horatia. 'Only I f-found out that he had planned the R-Ranelagh affair with that odious Lady M-Massey.'

The Viscount stared at her. 'You're raving!' he said calmly.

'I'm not. She was there, and she knew!'

'Who told you he planned it with her?'

'W-well, no one precisely, but Lethbridge thought so, and of course I realized—'

'Lethbridge!' interrupted the Viscount with scorn. 'Upon my word, you're a damned little fool, Horry! Lord don't be so simple! A man don't plot with his mistress against his wife. Never heard such a pack of nonsense!'

Horatia sat up. 'P-Pel, do you really think so?' she asked wistfully. 'B-but I can't help remembering that he said *she d-did indeed know* it was he all the t-time.'

The Viscount regarded her with frank contempt. 'Well if he said that it proves she wasn't in it—if it needs proof, which it don't. Lord, Horry, I put it to you, would he be likely to say that if she'd had a finger in the pie? What's more, it explains why the Massey's gone off to Bath so suddenly. Depend on it, if she found out it was he in the scarlet domino they had some sort of a scene, and Rule's not the man to stand that. Wondered what happened to make her go off in such a devil of a hurry. Here, what the deuce—?' For Horatia, with a sudden squeak of joy, had flung herself into his arms.

'Don't do that,' said the Viscount testily, disengaging himself.

'Oh, P-Pel, I never thought of that!' sighed Horatia.

'You're a little fool,' said the Viscount.

'Yes, I see I am,' she confessed. 'B-but if he has b-broken with that woman, it makes me more than ever decided not to tell him about l-last night.'

The Viscount thought this over. 'I must say it's a devilish queer story,' he said. 'Daresay you're right. If we can get that brooch back you're safe enough. If Pom don't succeed—' His lip tightened, and he nodded darkly.

Sir Roland, meanwhile, had arrived in Half-Moon Street, and was fortunate enough to find Lord Lethbridge at home.

Lethbridge received him in a gorgeous flowered dressing-gown. He did not look to be much the worse for the blow he had received, and he greeted Sir Roland with suave amiability. 'Pray sit down, Pommeroy,' he said. 'To what do I owe this unexpected honour?'

Sir Roland accepted the chair, and proceeded to display his tact. 'Most unfortunate thing,' he said. 'Last night–not quite myself, you know–lost a brooch. Must have dropped out of my cravat.'

'Oh?' said Lethbridge, looking at him rather hard. 'A pin, in fact?'

'Not a pin, no. A brooch. Family jewels–sometimes wear it–don't care to lose it. So I came round to see if I dropped it here.'

'I see. And what is it like, this brooch?'

'Ring brooch; inner circle pearls and openwork bosses, outer row pearls and diamonds,' said Sir Roland glibly.

'Indeed? A lady's ornament, one would almost infer.'

'Belonged to my great-aunt,' said Sir Roland, extricating himself from that predicament with masterly skill.

'Ah, no doubt you value it highly then,' remarked his lordship sympathetically.

'Just so,' said Sir Roland. 'Sentiment, you know. Should be glad to put my hand on it again.'

'I regret infinitely that I am unable to help you. May I suggest that you look for it in Montacute's house? I think you said you spent the evening there?'

'I didn't lose it there,' replied Sir Roland firmly. 'Naturally went there first.'

Lethbridge shrugged. 'How very unfortunate! I fear you must have dropped it in the street.'

'Not in the street, no. Remember having it on just before I came here.'

'Dear me!' said Lethbridge. 'What makes you remember so particularly?'

Sir Roland took a moment to think this out. 'Remember it because Pel said: "That's a queer tie-pin, Pom." And I said: "Belonged to my great-aunt." Then we came here. Must have had it on then.'

'It would certainly seem so. But perhaps you lost it after you left my house. Or do you remember that Winwood then said: "Where's your tie-pin?"'

'That's it,' said Sir Roland, grateful for the assistance. 'Pel said: "Why, what's become of your tie-pin, Pom?" Didn't come back–time getting on, you know. Knew it would be safe here!'

Lethbridge shook his head. 'I fear your recollection is not very clear, Pommeroy. I have not got your brooch.'

There was nothing for Sir Roland to do after that but to take his leave. Lord Lethbridge escorted him out into the hall, and sweetly bade him farewell. 'And do pray advise me if you succeed in finding the brooch,' he said with great civility. He watched his crestfallen visitor go off down the steps, and transferred his gaze to the porter's face. 'Send Moxton to me,' he said, and went back into the saloon.

In a few moments his butler appeared. 'My lord?'

'When this room was swept this morning, was a brooch found?' asked Lethbridge.

The lids descended discreetly over the butler's eyes. 'I have not heard of it, my lord.'

'Make inquiries.'

'Yes, my lord.'

While the butler was out of the room, Lethbridge stood looking out of the window, slightly frowning. When Moxton came back he turned. 'Well?'

'No, my lord.'

The frown lingered. 'Very well,' Lethbridge said.

The butler bowed. 'Yes, my lord. Your lordship's luncheon is served.'

Lethbridge went into the dining-room, still attired in his dressing-gown, still wearing a thoughtful, puzzled look on his face.

He sat for some time over his meal, absently sipping his port. He was not, as he had told Caroline Massey, the man to gnash his teeth over his own discomfiture, but the miscarriage of last night's plans had annoyed him. That little vixen wanted taming. The affair had become tinged, in his mind, with a sporting element. Horatia had won the first encounter; it became a matter of supreme importance to force a second one, which she would not win. The brooch seemed to present him with the opportunity he lacked—if only he could lay his hand on it.

His mind went back; his acute memory re-created for him the sound of ripping lace. He raised his glass to his lips, savouring the port. Ah, yes, undoubtedly the brooch had been lost then. No doubt a distinctive trinket, possibly part of the Drelincourt jewels. He smiled a little, picturing Horatia's dismay. It could be turned into a shrewd weapon, that ring-brooch—wielded in the right hands.

The brooch was not in his house, unless his servants were lying. He did not, for more than a fleeting moment, suspect any of them of theft. They had been with him some years; probably knew that he was an ill master to cheat.

The image of Mr Drelincourt's face flashed across his mind. He set down his glass. Crosby. Such a sharp-eyed fellow, Crosby. But had he had the opportunity to pick up a brooch from the floor unseen? He went over his movements during that brief visit. Crosby's arrival: no chance then. The departure of Winwood and Pommeroy. Had he taken them to the door? No. Still no chance for Crosby. Some talk he had had with him, not very much, for his head had been aching furiously, and then what? His fingers closed again around the stem of his glass, and instantly he remembered drinking a glass of wine to steady himself. Yes, certainly a chance for Crosby then. He had tossed off the wine, and turned. Now, had Crosby had one hand in his pocket? The picture lived again; he could see Crosby standing behind a chair, looking at him, withdrawing his hand from his pocket.

Really, it was quite amusing. There was no proof, of course, not a shadow of proof, but perhaps a visit to Crosby might be not unfruitful. Yes, one might hazard a guess that the brooch was an heirloom. Crosby—an astute fellow: quite needle-sharp—would recognize a Drelincourt heirloom. Decidedly a visit to Crosby was likely to repay one for one's trouble. Crosby, no doubt, was hatching a little plan to make mischief between Rule and his bride. Well, he would spare Crosby the pains. There should be mischief enough, but more mischief than the mere displaying of a brooch.

He got up from the table, and went in a leisurely fashion up the stairs, still revolving these delectable thoughts in his head. What a surprise for dear Crosby to receive a call from my Lord Lethbridge! He rang his hand-bell for his valet, and discarding his dressing-gown, sat down before the mirror to complete his elaborate toilet.

On his way, an hour later, to Mr Drelincourt's lodging, he looked in at White's but was told upon inquiry that Mr Drelincourt had not been into the Club that day. He went on towards Jermyn Street, twirling his ebony cane.

Mr Drelincourt lived in a house owned by a retired gentleman's gentleman, who himself opened the door to his lordship. He said that Mr Drelincourt was gone out.

'Perhaps,' said his lordship, 'you can give me his direction.'

Oh, yes, that could easily be done. Mr Drelincourt was gone out of town, and had taken a small cloak-bag with him.

'Out of town, eh?' said his lordship, his eyes narrowing. He drew a guinea from his pocket, and began to juggle gently with it. 'I wonder, can you tell me where, out of town?'

'Yes, my lord. To Meering,' replied Mr Bridges. 'Mr Drelincourt desired me to hire a post-chaise for him, and set off at two o'clock. If your lordship had come twenty minutes ago, you'd have caught him.'

Lethbridge dropped the guinea into his hand. 'I may still catch him,' he said, and ran lightly down the steps of the house.

Hailing a hackney, he had himself driven back to Half-Moon Street. His household found itself goaded into sudden activity; a footman was sent off to the stables to order my lord's light post-chaise and four to be brought round immediately, and my lord went upstairs, calling to his valet to bestir himself, and lay out a travelling dress. In twenty minutes his lordship, now clad in a coat of brown cloth, with his sword at his side, and top-boots on his feet, came out of the house again, gave his postilions certain pithy instructions, and climbed up into the chaise, a light carriage very like a sedan, slung on whip springs over very high wheels. As the equipage rounded the corner into Piccadilly, heading westwards, his lordship leaned back at his ease, calm in the knowledge that no hired post-chaise and four could hope to reach Meering, even with an hour's start, before being overtaken by him.

16

Mr Drelincourt, as it happened, had no idea that Lord Lethbridge could be on his heels.

Not dreaming that anybody, least of all my Lord Lethbridge, had discovered his theft of the brooch, he saw no need to make haste down to Meering, and put off starting on his journey until after luncheon. Mr Drelincourt, though lavish in dress and some matters, was very careful how he spent money on small items. The hiring of a chaise to carry him thirty-three miles into the country cost him a pang, and to pay, on top of that, possibly as much as four or five shillings for lunch at an inn would have seemed to him a gross extravagance. By lunching at his lodgings he would not be put to the necessity of baiting on the road at all, for he thought he would arrive at Meering in time to dine with his cousin. He would put up for the night there, and if Rule did not offer him one of his own carriages for his return it would be a shabby piece of behaviour, and one which he did not at all anticipate, for Rule, to do him justice, was not mean, and must be well aware that the charges for a post-chaise would be lightened if it made the return journey empty.

It was in a pleasurable frame of mind that Mr Drelincourt set forward upon his journey. The day was fine, quite ideal for a drive into the country, and after he had let down the window in the door in front of him to order the postilions not to ride at such a rattling pace, he had nothing to do but to lean back and admire the scenery or indulge his imagination in agreeable reflection.

It was not to be supposed that there was any portion of the Drelincourt inheritance unknown to Mr Drelincourt. He had recognized the brooch in a flash, and could have recited unerringly the different pieces which comprised that particular set of jewels. When he had stooped so quickly to pick it up he had had no very clear idea in his head of what he meant to do with it, but a night's repose had brought him excellent counsel. He had no doubt at all that Horatia had been concealed somewhere in Lethbridge's house; the brooch proved that to his satisfaction, and ought to prove it to Rule's satisfaction also. He had always thought Horatia a jade; for his part he was not in the least surprised (though shocked) to discover that she had taken advantage of Rule's absence to spend the night in her lover's arms. Rule, who was always too stupidly sleepy to see what was going on under his nose, would probably be greatly surprised, and even more shocked than his cousin, whose obvious and not too painful duty it was to appraise him of his wife's loose conduct at once. There could be only one course open to his lordship then, and Mr Drelincourt was inclined to think that after so disastrous a venture into matrimony, he would hardly risk another.

Altogether the world seemed a better place to Mr Drelincourt this mild September day than it had seemed for several months.

Not in the general way a keen student of Nature, he was moved today to admire the russet tints in the trees, and to approve from the well-sprung chaise the bursts of fine country through which he passed.

Meering being situated near Twyford, in the county of Berkshire, the road to it led out of town by way of Knightsbridge and Hammersmith to Turnham Green and Hounslow, where at the George Inn the chaise stopped to change horses. The two postilions, who had formed the poorest opinion of Mr Drelincourt from the moment of his commanding them not to drive too fast, were disgusted by his conduct at the George, for instead of getting down to drink a glass of Nantes brandy, and allowing them time also to refresh themselves, he sat tight in the chaise, and never gave the ostler so much as a groat.

The second stage was Slough, ten miles farther on. The chaise set forward again, drawing out of Hounslow on to the heath, a tract of wild land so ill-famed that for several unpleasant minutes Mr Drelincourt sat wishing that he had gone to the expense of hiring a guard to accompany the chaise. Nothing untoward happened, however, and he was soon being driven over Cranford Bridge in the direction of Longford.

At Slough Mr Drelincourt got down to stretch his legs, while the horses were changed. The landlord, who had come bustling out of the Crown Inn as a good landlord should on the approach of a gentleman's chaise, allowed the jolly smile to fade from his face at the sight of Mr Drelincourt, and abated a little of his welcoming civility. Mr Drelincourt was well known upon this road, and no favourite with honest landlords. Since he was my Lord of Rule's relative, Mr Copper went through the form of suggesting refreshment, but upon this being refused, he went back to his inn, remarking to his wife that the one thing in life that beat him was how a genial, open-handed gentleman like his lordship came to have such a mean worm as Mr Drelincourt for his cousin.

After Slough, the road ran by way of Salt Hill to Maidenhead. A mile farther on, at Maidenhead Thicket, it branched off from the Worcester way, and took the Bath Road to Hare Hatch and Twyford.

The chaise had passed through Maidenhead, and was bowling along at a respectable pace towards the Thicket, when one of the postilions became aware of a second chaise some way behind. A bend in the road enabled him to get a glimpse of it. He said over his shoulder to the other postilion: 'Lordy, that'll be the Quality, sure enough! Springing his horses, he is. No good racing him with our precious Missy squawking at the back of us.'

The lad riding one of the wheelers understood him to refer to Mr Drelincourt, and agreed, though regretfully, that they had better draw into the side and let the Quality go by.

The thunder of hooves galloping in the rear soon penetrated to Mr Drelincourt's ears and caused him to rap with his cane on the window, and upon the postilion's looking over his shoulder, to signal to him to draw in to the side of the road. Mr Drelincourt had had experience of good-for-nothing lads who raced their horses against other chaises, and he disapproved strongly of this pastime.

The second chaise rapidly overhauled the first and swung past in a little cloud of dust struck up by the galloping hooves. Mr Drelincourt had the briefest view of it, but caught sight of the flash of a crest on one of the panels. He felt much annoyed with the unknown traveller for driving at such a pace, and was uneasily hoping that his postilions were able to control their own horses (which showed signs of wishing to dash off after the other chaise) when he saw that the other chaise was pulling up ahead of them. That seemed very strange to him, for there was no apparent reason to account for it. It seemed stranger still when the horses wheeled and backed, and wheeled again, till the chaise lay right across the road, effectively barring the way.

Mr Drelincourt's postilions, also observing this manœuvre, supposed the other chaise to have overshot its objective, and to be about to turn round again. They reined their horses to a walk. But the crested chaise remained across the road, and they were forced to come to a standstill.

Mr Drelincourt, considerably astonished, sat forward to see more closely, and called to his postilions: 'What is it? Why don't they go on? Is it an accident?'

Then he saw Lord Lethbridge spring down from the other chaise, and he shrank back in his seat, his heart jumping with fright.

Lethbridge walked up to Mr Drelincourt's equipage, and that shivering gentleman pulled himself together with an effort. It would not do for him to cower in the corner, so he leaned forward and let down the window. 'Is it you, indeed, my lord?' he said in a high voice. 'I could scarce believe my eyes! What can have brought you out of town?'

'Why, you, Crosby, you!' said his lordship mockingly. 'Pray step down out of that chaise. I should like to have a little talk with you.'

Mr Drelincourt clung to the window frame and gave an unnatural laugh. 'Oh, your pleasantries, my lord! I am on my way to Meering, you know, to my cousin's. I—I think it is already five o'clock, and he dines at five.'

'Crosby, come down!' said Lethbridge, with such an alarming glitter in his eyes that Mr Drelincourt was quite cowed, and began to fumble with the catch of the door. He climbed down carefully, under the grinning stare of his postilions. 'I vow I can't imagine what you was wanting to say to me,' he said. 'And I am late, you know. I ought to be on my way.'

His arm was taken in an ungentle grip. 'Walk with me a little way, Crosby,' said his lordship. 'Do you not find these country roads quite charming? I am sure you do. And so you are bound for Meering? Was not that a rather sudden decision, Crosby?'

'Sudden?' stammered Mr Drelincourt, wincing at the pressure of his lordship's fingers above his elbow. 'Oh, not at all, my lord, not in the least! I told Rule I might come down. I have had it in mind some days, I assure you.'

'It has nothing to do, of course, with a certain brooch?' purred Lethbridge.

'A b-brooch? I don't understand you, my lord!'

'A ring-brooch of pearls and diamonds, picked up in my house last night,' said his lordship.

Mr Drelincourt's knees shook. 'I protest, sir, I—I am at a loss! I—'

'Crosby, give me that brooch,' said Lethbridge menacingly.

Mr Drelincourt made an attempt to pull his arm away. 'My lord, I don't understand your tone! I tell you frankly, I don't like it. I don't take your meaning.'

'Crosby,' said his lordship, 'you will give me that brooch, or I will take you by the scruff of your neck and shake you like the rat you are!'

'Sir!' said Mr Drelincourt, his teeth chattering together, 'this is monstrous! Monstrous!'

'It is indeed monstrous,' agreed his lordship. 'You are a thief, Mr Crosby Drelincourt.'

Mr Drelincourt flushed scarlet. 'It was not your brooch, sir!'

'Or yours!' swiftly replied Lethbridge. 'Hand it over!'

'I—I have called a man out for less!' blustered Crosby.

'That's your humour, is it?' said Lethbridge. 'It's not my practice to fight with thieves; I use a cane instead. But I might make an exception in your case.'

To Mr Drelincourt's horror, he thrust forward his sword hilt and patted it. That unfortunate gentleman licked his lips and said quaveringly: 'I shall not fight you, sir. The brooch is more mine than yours!'

'Hand it over!' said Lethbridge.

Mr Drelincourt hesitated, read a look in his lordship's face there was no mistaking, and slowly inserted his finger and thumb into his waistcoat pocket. The next moment the brooch lay in Lethbridge's hand.

'Thank you, Crosby,' he said, in a way that made Mr Drelincourt long for the courage to hit him. 'I thought I should be able to persuade you. You may now resume your journey to Meering—if you think it still worth while. If you don't—you may join me at the Sun in Maidenhead, where I propose to dine and sleep. I almost feel I owe you a dinner for spoiling your game so unkindly.' He turned, leaving Mr Drelincourt speechless with indignation, and walked back to his chaise, which had by this time drawn up to the side of the road, facing towards London again. He climbed lightly into it and drove off, airily waving his hand to Mr Drelincourt, still standing in the dusty road.

Mr Drelincourt gazed after him, rage seething up in him. Spoiled his game, had he? There might be two words to that! He hurried back to his own chaise, saw the looks of rich enjoyment on the postilions' faces, and swore at them to drive on.

It was only six miles to Meering from the Thicket, but by the time the chaise turned in at the Lodge gates it was close on six o'clock. The house was situated a mile from the gates, in the middle of a very pretty park, but Mr Drelincourt was in no mood to admire the fine oaks, and rolling stretches of turf, and sat in a fret of impatience while his tired horses drew him up the long avenue to the house.

He found his cousin and Mr Gisborne lingering over their port in the dining-room, which apartment was lit by candles. It might be broad daylight outside, but my lord had a constitutional dislike of dining by day, and excluded it by having the heavy curtains drawn across the windows.

Both he and Mr Gisborne were in riding-dress. My lord was lounging in a high-backed chair at the head of the table, one leg, encased in a dusty top-boot, thrown negligently over the arm. He looked up as the footman opened the door to admit Mr Drelincourt, and for a moment sat perfectly still, the look of good humour fading from his face. Then he picked up his quizzing-glass with some deliberation, and surveyed his cousin through it. 'Dear me!' he said. 'Now why?'

This was not a very promising start, but his anger had chased from Mr Drelincourt's mind all memory of his last meeting with the Earl, and he was undaunted. 'Cousin,' he said, his words tripping over one another. 'I am here on a matter of grave moment. I must beg a word with you alone!'

'I imagine it must indeed be of grave moment to induce you to come over thirty miles in pursuit of me,' said his lordship.

Mr Gisborne got up. 'I will leave you, sir.' He bowed slightly to Mr Drelincourt, who paid not the slightest heed to him, and went out.

Mr Drelincourt pulled a chair out from under the table and sat down. 'I regret extremely, Rule, but you must prepare yourself for most unpleasant tidings. If I did not consider it my duty to apprise you of what I have discovered, I should shrink from the task!'

The Earl did not seem to be alarmed. He still sat at his ease, one hand lying on the table, the fingers crooked round the stem of his wine-glass, his calm gaze resting on Mr Drelincourt's face. 'This self-immolation on the altar of duty is something new to me,' he remarked. 'I daresay my nerves will prove strong enough to enable me to hear your tidings with—I trust—tolerable equanimity.'

'I trust so, Rule, I do indeed trust so!' said Mr Drelincourt, his eyes snapping. 'You are pleased to sneer at my notion of duty—'

'I hesitate to interrupt you, Crosby, but you may have noticed that I never sneer.'

'Very well, cousin, very well! Be that as it may, you will allow that I have my share of family pride.'

'Certainly, if you tell me so,' replied the Earl gently.

Mr Drelincourt flushed. 'I do tell you so! Our name—our honour, mean as much to me as to you, I believe! It is on that score that I am here now.'

'If you have come all this way to inform me that the catch-polls are after you, Crosby, it is only fair to tell you that you are wasting your time.'

'Very humorous, my lord!' cried Mr Drelincourt. 'My errand, however, concerns you more nearly than that! Last night—I should rather say this morning, for it was long past two by my watch—I had occasion to visit my Lord Lethbridge.'

'That is, of course, interesting,' said the Earl. 'It seems an odd hour for visiting, but I have sometimes thought, Crosby, that you are an odd creature.'

Mr Drelincourt's bosom swelled. 'There is nothing very odd, I think, in sheltering from the rain!' he said. 'I was upon my way to my lodging from South Audley Street, and chanced to turn down Half-Moon Street. I was caught in a shower of rain, but observing the door of my Lord Lethbridge's house to stand—inadvertently, I am persuaded—ajar, I stepped in. I found his lordship in a dishevelled condition in the front saloon, where a vastly elegant supper was spread, covers, my lord, being laid for two.'

'You shock me infinitely,' said the Earl, and leaning a little forward, picked up the decanter and refilled his glass.

Mr Drelincourt uttered a shrill laugh. 'You may well say so! His lordship seemed put out at seeing me, remarkably put out!'

'That,' said the Earl, 'I can easily understand. But pray continue, Crosby.'

'Cousin,' said Mr Drelincourt earnestly, 'I desire you to believe that it is with the most profound reluctance that I do so. While I was with Lord Lethbridge, my attention was attracted by something that lay upon the floor, partly concealed by a rug. Something, Rule, that sparkled. Something—'

'Crosby,' said his lordship wearily, 'your eloquence is no doubt very fine, but I must ask you to bear in mind that I have been in the saddle most of the day, and spare me any more of it. I am not really very curious to know, but you seem anxious to tell me: what was it that attracted your attention?'

Mr Drelincourt swallowed his annoyance. 'A brooch, my lord! A lady's corsage brooch!'

'No wonder that Lord Lethbridge was not pleased to see you,' remarked Rule.

'No wonder, indeed!' said Mr Drelincourt. 'Somewhere in the house a lady was concealed at that very moment. Unseen, cousin, I picked up the brooch and slipped it into my pocket.'

The Earl raised his brows. 'I think I said that you were an odd creature, Crosby.'

'It may appear so, but I had a good reason for my action. Had it not been for the fact that Lord Lethbridge pursued me on my journey here, and by force wrested the brooch from me, I should lay it before you now. For that brooch is very well known both to you and me. A ring-brooch, cousin, composed of pearls and diamonds in two circles!'

The Earl never took his eyes from Mr Drelincourt's; it may have been a trick of the shadows thrown by the candles on the tables, but his face looked unusually grim. He swung his leg down from the arm of the chair leisurely, but still leaned back at his ease. 'Yes, Crosby, a ring-brooch of pearls and diamonds?'

'Precisely, cousin! A brooch I recognized at once. A brooch that belongs to the fifteenth-century set which you gave to your—'

He got no further. In one swift movement the Earl was up, and had seized Mr Drelincourt by the throat, dragging him out of his chair, and half across the corner of the table that separated them. Mr Drelincourt's terrified eyes goggled up into blazing grey ones. He clawed ineffectively at my lord's hands. Speech was choked out of him. He was shaken to and fro till the teeth rattled in his head. There was a roaring in his ears, but he heard my lord's voice quite distinctly. 'You lying, mischief-making little cur!' it said. 'I have been too easy with you. You dare to bring me your foul lies about my wife, and you think that I may believe them! By God, I am of a mind to kill you now!'

A moment more the crushing grip held, then my lord flung his cousin away from him, and brushed his hands together in a gesture infinitely contemptuous.

Mr Drelincourt reeled back, grasping and clutching at the air, and fell with a crash on to the floor, and stayed there, cowering away like a whipped mongrel.

The Earl looked down at him for a moment, a smile quite unlike any Mr Drelincourt had ever seen curling his fine mouth. Then he leaned back against the table, half sitting on it, supported by his hands, and said: 'Get up, my friend. You are not yet dead.'

Mr Drelincourt picked himself up and tried mechanically to straighten his wig. His throat felt mangled, and his legs were shaking so that he could hardly stand. He staggered to a chair and sank into it.

'You said, I think, that Lord Lethbridge took this famous brooch from you? Where?'

Mr Drelincourt managed to say, though hoarsely: 'Maidenhead.'

'I trust he will return it to its rightful owner. You realize, do you, Crosby, that your genius for recognizing my property is sometimes at fault?'

Mr Drelincourt muttered: 'I thought it was—I—I may have been mistaken.'

'You were mistaken,' said his lordship.

'Yes, I—yes, I was mistaken. I beg pardon, I am sure. I am very sorry, cousin.'

'You will be still more sorry, Crosby, if one word of this passes your lips again. Do I make myself plain?'

'Yes, yes, indeed, I—I thought it my duty, no more, to—to tell you.'

'Since the day I married Horatia Winwood,' said his lordship levelly, 'you have tried to make mischief between us. Failing, you were fool enough to trump up this extremely stupid story. You bring me no proof—ah, I am forgetting! Lord Lethbridge took your proof forcibly from you, did he not? That was most convenient of him.'

'But I—but he did!' said Mr Drelincourt desperately.

'I am sorry to hurt your feelings,' said the Earl, 'but I do not believe you. It may console you to know that had you been able to lay that brooch before me I still should not have believed ill of my wife. I am no Othello, Crosby. I think you should have known that.' He stretched out his hand for the bell, and rang it. Upon the entrance of a footman, he said briefly: 'Mr Drelincourt's chaise.'

Mr Drelincourt heard this order with dismay. He said miserably: 'But, my lord, I have not dined, and the horses are spent. I—I did not dream you would serve me so!'

'No?' said the Earl. 'The Red Lion at Twyford will no doubt supply you with a supper and a change of horses. Be thankful that you are leaving my house with a whole skin.'

Mr Drelincourt shrank, and said no more. In a short time the footman came back to say that the chaise was at the door. Mr Drelincourt stole a furtive glance at the Earl's unrelenting face, and got up. 'I'll—I'll bid you good night, Rule,' he said, trying to collect the fragments of his dignity.

The Earl nodded, and in silence watched him go out in the wake of the footman. He heard the chaise drive past the curtained windows presently, and once more rang the bell. When the footman came back he said, absently studying his finger-nails: 'I want my racing curricle, please.'

'Yes, my lord!' said the footman, startled. 'Er—now, my lord?'

'At once,' replied the Earl with the greatest placidity. He got up from the table and walked unhurriedly out of the room.

Ten minutes later the curricle was at the door, and Mr Gisborne, descending the stairs, was astonished to see his lordship on the point of leaving the house, his hat on his head, and his small sword at his side. 'You're going out, sir?' he asked.

'As you see, Arnold,' replied the Earl.

'I hope, sir—nothing amiss?'

'Nothing at all, dear boy,' said his lordship.

Outside a groom was clinging to the heads of two magnificent greys, and endeavouring to control their capricious movements.

The Earl's eye ran over them. 'Fresh, eh?'

'Begging your lordship's pardon, I'd say they were a couple of devils.'

The Earl laughed, and climbed into the curricle, and gathered up the reins in one gloved hand. 'Let them go.'

The groom sprang to one side, and the greys plunged forward.

The groom watched the curricle flash round a bend in the avenue and sighed. 'If I could handle them like that—' he said, and wandered back to the stables, sadly shaking his head.

17

The Sun at Maidenhead was a very popular posting inn, its appointments and kitchens being alike excellent.

Lord Lethbridge sat down to dinner in one of the private rooms, a pleasant apartment, panelled with old oak, and was served with a duck, a quarter of mutton with pickled mushrooms, a crayfish, and a quince jelly. The landlord, who knew him, found him to be in an unusually mellow mood, and wondered what devilry he had been engaged on. The reflective smile that hovered over his lordship's thin lips meant devilry of some sort, of that he was quite certain. For once in his life the noble guest found no fault with the food set before him, and was even moved to bestow a word of praise on the burgundy.

My lord Lethbridge was feeling almost benign. To have outwitted Mr Drelincourt so neatly pleased him more than the recovery of the brooch. He smiled to think of Crosby travelling disconsolately back to London. The notion that Crosby could be fool enough to carry an empty tale to his cousin never occurred to him; he himself was not one to lose his head, and although he had a poor opinion of Mr Drelincourt's intelligence such heights of folly were quite beyond his comprehension.

There was plenty of company at the Sun that evening, but whoever else was kept waiting for his dinner, the landlord saw to it that Lethbridge was served instantly. When the covers were withdrawn, and only the wine left on the table, he came himself to ask whether my lord required anything else, and closed the shutters with his own hand. He set more candles on the table, assured his lordship that he would find his sheets well aired, and bowed himself out. He had just told one of the abigails to be sure not to forget to take a warming-pan up presently, when his wife called to him from the doorway: 'Cattermole, here's my lord driven up!'

'My lord', in Maidenhead, could mean only one person, and Mr Cattermole sped forth at once to welcome this honoured guest. He opened his eyes rather at the sight of the racing curricle, but shouted to an ostler to come to the horses' heads, and himself hurried up all bows and smiles.

The Earl leaned over to speak to him. 'Good evening, Cattermole. Can you tell me if Lord Lethbridge's chaise changed horses here rather more than an hour ago?'

'Lord Lethbridge, my lord? Why, his lordship is putting up here for the night!' said Cattermole.

'How very fortunate!' said the Earl, and climbed down from the curricle, flexing the fingers of his left hand. 'And where shall I find his lordship?'

'In the oak-parlour, my lord, just finished his dinner. I will escort your lordship.'

'No, you need not do that,' replied the Earl, walking into the inn. 'I know my way.' At the foot of the shallow stairs he paused, and said softly over his shoulder: 'By the way, Cattermole, my business with his lordship is private. I feel sure I can rely on you to see that we are not disturbed.'

Mr Cattermole shot him a quick, shrewd glance. There was going to be trouble, was there? Not good for the house, no, not good for the house, but still worse for it to offend my Lord Rule. He bowed, his face a plump, discreet mask. 'Certainly, my lord,' he said, and drew back.

Lord Lethbridge was still sitting over his wine, still meditating over the events of the day, when he heard the door open. He looked up, and stiffened. For a moment they faced one another, Lethbridge rigid in his chair, the Earl standing silent in the doorway, looking across at him. Lethbridge read that look in an instant. He got up. 'So Crosby did visit you?' he said. He put his hand in his pocket and drew out the brooch. 'Is that what you came for, my lord?'

The Earl shut the door, and turned the key in the lock. 'That is what I came for,' he said. 'That, and one other thing, Lethbridge.'

'My blood, for instance?' Lethbridge gave a little laugh. 'You will have to fight for both.'

The Earl moved forward. 'That should afford us both gratification. You have a charming taste in revenge, but you have failed, Lethbridge.'

'Failed?' said Lethbridge, and looked significantly at the brooch in his hand.

'If your object was to drag my name in the mud, why, certainly!' said Rule. 'My wife remains my wife. Presently you shall tell me by what means you forced her to enter your house.'

Lethbridge raised his brows. 'And what makes you so sure that I had any need to employ force, my lord?'

'Merely my knowledge of her,' replied the Earl. 'You have a vast deal of explaining to do, you see.'

'I don't boast of my conquests, Rule,' Lethbridge said softly, and saw the Earl's hand clench involuntarily. 'I shall explain nothing.'

'That we shall see,' said Rule. He pushed the table down to one end of the room, against the wall, and blew out the candles on it, leaving only the pendant chandelier in the centre of the room to light them.

Lethbridge thrust the chairs back, picking up his sword from one of them, and drawing it from the scabbard. 'My God, how I have waited for this,' he said suddenly. 'I am glad Crosby went to you.' He put the sword down again, and began to take off his coat.

The Earl made no reply, but set about his own preparations, pulling off his top-boots, unbuckling his sword-belt, rolling up his deeply ruffled shirt-sleeves.

They faced one another under the soft candlelight, two big men in whom rage, long concealed, burned with a steady strength too great to admit of vain flusterings. Neither seemed to be aware of the strangeness of the scene, here in the upper parlour of an inn, with below them, penetrating faintly to the quiet room, the hum of voices in the coffee-room. With deliberation they set the stage, with deliberation snuffed a candle that was guttering, and divested themselves of coats and boots. Yet in this quiet preparation was something deadly, too deadly to find relief in a noisy brawl.

The swords flashed in a brief salute, and engaged with a scrape of steel on steel. Each man was an experienced swordsman, but this was no affair of the fencing-master's art, with its punctilious niceties, but a grim fight, dangerous in its hard swiftness. For each antagonist the world slid back. Nothing had reality but the other man's blade, feinting, thrusting, parrying. Their eyes were on each other's; the sound of their stockinged feet shifting on the boards was a soft thud; their breathing came quick and hard.

Lethbridge lunged forward on his right foot, delivering a lightning thrust in tierce, his arm high, the muscles standing out on it ribbed and hard. Rule caught forte on forte; the forcible glanced along his arm, leaving a long red slash, and the blades disengaged.

Neither checked; this was no quarrel to be decided by a single hit. The blood dripped slowly from Rule's forearm to the floor. Lethbridge leaped back on both feet and dropped his point. 'Tie it!' he said curtly. 'I've no mind to slip in your blood.'

Rule pulled a handkerchief from his breeches pocket, and twisted it round the cut, and dragged the knot tight with his teeth.

'On guard!'

The fight went on, relentless and untiring. Lethbridge attempted a flanconnade, opposing his left hand. His point barely grazed Rule's side; the Earl countered in a flash. There was a scuffle of blades, and Lethbridge recovered his guard, panting a little.

It was he who was delivering the attack all the time, employing every wile known to his art to lure Rule into giving an opening. Time after time he tried to break through the guard; time after time his blade was caught in a swift parry, and turned aside. He was beginning to flag; the sweat was rolling in great drops off his forehead; he dared not use his left hand to dash it from his eyes lest in that second's blindness Rule should thrust home. He thrust rather wildly in carte; the Earl parried it half-circle, and before Lethbridge could recover, sprang in, and seized the blade below the hilt. His own point touched the floor. 'Wipe the sweat from your eyes!'

Lethbridge's lips writhed in a queer, bitter smile.—'So—you are—quits?'

The Earl did not answer; he released the sword, and waited. Lethbridge passed his handkerchief across his brow and threw it aside.

'On guard!'

A change came; the Earl was beginning at last to press the attack. Hard driven, Lethbridge parried his blade again and again, steadily losing strength. Knowing himself to be nearly done, he attempted a *botte coupée*, feinting in high carte and thrusting in a low tierce. His blade met nothing but the opposition of Rule's and the fight went on.

He heard the Earl speak, breathlessly, but very clearly. 'Why did my wife enter your house?'

He had no struggle left to waste in attack; he could only parry mechanically, his arm aching from shoulder to wrist.

'Why did my wife enter your house?'

He parried too late; the Earl's point flashed under his guard, checked, and withdrew. He realized that he had been spared, would be spared again, and yet again, until Rule had his answer. He grinned savagely. His words came on his heaving breaths: 'Kidnapped–her.'

The swords rang together, disengaged. 'And then?'

He set his teeth; his guard wavered; he recovered it miraculously; the hilt felt slippery in his wet grasp.

'And then?'

'I do not–boast–of my–conquests!' he panted, and put forth the last remnant of his strength to beat back the attack he knew would end the bout.

His sword scraped on Rule's; his heart felt as though it would burst; his throat was parched; the ache in his arm had become a dull agony; a mist was gathering before his eyes. The years rolled back suddenly; he gasped out: 'Marcus–for God's sake–end it!'

He saw the thrust coming, a straight lunge in high carte aimed for the heart; he made one last parry too late to stop the thrust, but in time to deflect it slightly. Rule's point, sliding over his blade, entered deep into his shoulder. His own dropped; he stood swaying for an instant, and fell, the blood staining his shirt bright scarlet.

Rule wiped the sweat from his face; his hand was shaking a little. He looked down at Lethbridge, lying in a crumpled heap at his feet, sobbing for breath, the blood on his shirt soaking through, and forming a pool on the oak boards. Suddenly he flung his sword aside and strode to the table, and swept the bottle and the glass off it. He caught up the cloth and tore it with his strong teeth, and ripped it from end to end. The next moment he was on his knees beside Lethbridge, feeling for the wound. The hazel eyes opened, considering him. 'I believe–I shan't die–this time–either!' Lethbridge whispered mockingly.

The Earl had laid bare the wound, and was staunching the blood. 'No, I don't think you will,' he said. 'But it's deep.' He tore another strip from the cloth and made it into a pad, and bound it tightly round the shoulder. He got up and fetched Lethbridge's coat from a chair, and rolling it up placed it under his head. 'I'll get a doctor,' he said briefly, and went out, and from the head of the stairs shouted for the landlord.

Stout Cattermole appeared so promptly that it seemed as though he must have been waiting for that call. He stood with his hands on the banister, looking anxiously up at the Earl his brow puckered, his lips close-folded.

'Send one of your lads for a doctor,' said Rule, 'and bring up a bottle of cognac.'

The landlord nodded and turned away. 'And Cattermole!' said his lordship. 'Bring it yourself.'

At that the landlord smiled rather sourly. 'Be sure, my lord.'

Rule went back into the oak parlour. Lethbridge was lying where he had left him, with eyes closed. He looked very white; one of his hands lay limply on the floor beside him, the fingers curling upwards. Rule stood looking down at him, frowning. Lethbridge did not move.

Cattermole came in with a bottle and glasses. He put these down on the table, casting a worried appraising glance at the still figure on the floor. He muttered: 'Not dead, my lord?'

'No.' The Earl picked up the bottle, and poured some brandy into one of the glasses.

'Thank God for it! You do me no good by this, my lord.'

'I don't think you'll suffer,' replied the Earl, calmly, and returned to Lethbridge and knelt again.

'Lethbridge, drink this!' he said, slightly raising him.

Lethbridge opened his eyes; they were blank with exhaustion, but grew keener as he swallowed the cognac. He raised them to Rule's face a moment, made an odd little grimace, and looked beyond Rule at Cattermole, bending over him. 'What the devil do you want?' he said unpleasantly.

The landlord drew down the corners of his mouth. 'No, he's not dead,' he remarked under his breath. 'I'll be within call my lord.'

He went out and shut the door behind him.

The blood had soaked through the pad; the Earl tightened the bandage and stood up again. Picking up the sword he wiped it carefully, and put it back into the scabbard.

Lethbridge lay watching him with a look of cynical amusement on his face. 'Why mar what you have made?' he inquired. 'I was under the impression that you wished to kill me.'

The Earl glanced down at him. 'If I let you die, the consequences to myself might prove a trifle difficult to avoid,' he replied.

Lethbridge grinned. 'That is more in my manner than in yours,' he said. He raised himself on his elbow and tried to sit up.

'You had better lie still,' said the Earl, slightly frowning.

'Oh, no!' gasped Lethbridge. 'The position is—altogether—too lowly. Add to your humanity by assisting me to that chair.'

The Earl bent over him, and hoisted him up; he sank into the chair panting a little, and pressing his hand to his shoulder. A grey shade had crept into his face; he whispered: 'Give me the brandy—quite a deal to say to you.'

The Earl had already poured it out, and now held the glass to Lethbridge's lips, Lethbridge took it unsteadily in his own hands, saying with a snap: 'Damn you, I'm not helpless!' He drank it at a gulp, and lay back recovering his strength. The Earl began to unroll his sleeves. Presently Lethbridge spoke again.

'Sent for the doctor, did you? How magnanimous! Well, he'll be here any moment. I suppose. Let's be done with this. Your wife took no harm of me.' He saw the grey eyes lift quickly, and gave a faint laugh. 'Oh, make no mistake! I am all the villain you think me. She saved herself.'

'You interest me,' said Rule, moving towards a chair, and sitting down on the arm of it. 'I have always thought her a lady of infinite resources.'

'Resources,' murmured Lethbridge. 'Yes, decidedly. She used a poker.'

The Earl's lips twitched. 'I see. Your recollection of the subsequent events is no doubt a little—shall we say—imperfect?'

A laugh shook Lethbridge; he winced and pressed his hand to his shoulder again. 'I believe she thought she had killed me. Tell her the only grudge I bear her is for having left my front door open.'

'Ah, yes!' said Rule. 'The arrival of Crosby.'

Lethbridge had shut his eyes, but he opened them again at that. 'Is that all you know? I suppose Crosby did not tell you that he found Winwood and Pommeroy with me?'

'He did not,' said Rule. 'Perhaps he thought it irrelevant, or perhaps–who knows?–he considered it might spoil the effect of his story. I am sorry if it fatigues you, but I fear I must request you to tell me a little more. What, for instance, brought Winwood to your house?'

'Oh, the intelligence that I had been slain–with a poker.'

Rule drew a breath. 'You dismay me,' he said. 'I hardly dare to ask–what then?'

'Be at ease. He took my recovery in good part. You may pour me some more brandy. Yes, in quite good part. He even offered me a game of piquet.'

'Ah,' said Rule. 'Now I begin to understand. Is it too much to hope that Pommeroy was in the same condition?'

'I did not descry much difference. They were both induced to take their leave on the discovery that I was not–as they had apparently thought–giving a card-party.' He took his replenished glass and drained it. 'My relief was only equalled by Crosby's. Crosby then pocketed the brooch. This morning I sustained a second visit from Pommeroy. He came to get it back. The humour of that should appeal to you. I had not known till then of the brooch's existence. The rest I imagine you know. If Crosby had not been fool enough to carry his tale to you–there would be a hand still to play.' He put his empty glass down and drew the brooch from the pocket of his breeches. 'Take it. It is not worth while. Don't cheat yourself with the notion that you behold me repentant. Revenge–your wife called it fustian. I don't know. But had we met–thus'–he nodded to where his sword lay–'years ago–who shall say?' He moved, trying to ease his shoulder; he was frowning. 'Experience–leads me to admit–you may have been right to stop Louisa marrying me. I have none of the husbandly virtues. Is she happy with her country squire? I am sure she is; at best women are–dull creatures.' His face contracted with pain. He said irritably: 'Wipe my sword and sheath it. I shall use it again, believe me.' He watched Rule in silence for a moment, and as the sword slid back into the scabbard, he sighed. 'Do you remember fencing with me at Angelo's?'

'I remember,' Rule answered, half smiling. 'We were always very even-matched.'

'You have improved. Where's that damned leech? I've not the slightest desire to oblige you by dying.'

'Do you know, Robert, it would really not oblige me?'

Lethbridge looked up at him, the mockery back in his eyes. 'Memory is a damnably intrusive thing, eh? I shan't die.' His head sank a little on his chest; he lifted it with an effort, and leaned it against the upholstered chair-back. 'You'll admit it was clever of me to win Horry's friendship. I told her, by the way, that Caroline was in your Ranelagh plot.'

Rule said gently: 'You had always a poisonous tongue, Robert.'

'Oh, always,' Lethbridge agreed.

He heard the opening of the door and turned his head. 'At last! Pray take that look off your face, my good man; I suppose you have seen a sword-wound before.'

The doctor set down his bag on the table. 'I have seen many, sir,' he answered primly. His eye alighted on the brandy bottle. 'Cognac? That is not a remedy. I wish you may not end this night in a high fever.' He looked at the bloodstained bandage and sniffed. 'H'm! Some bleeding. Landlord, send up two of your lads to carry his lordship to his room. Pray sit still, sir. I shall not inspect your hurt till I have you in bed.'

Lethbridge gave a wry smile. 'I could not wish you a deadlier fate than to be in my shoes now, Marcus.' He held out his left hand. 'I've done with you.

You arouse the worst in me, you know. Your cut will heal quicker than mine, for which I am sorry. It was a good fight—I don't remember a better. Hatred lends a spice, doesn't it? If you want to add to your damned goodness, send word to my fool of a valet to join me here.'

Rule took his hand and gripped it. 'The only thing that ever made you tolerable, my dear Robert, was your impudence. I shall be in town to-morrow. I'll send him down to you. Good night.'

Half an hour later he strolled into the library at Meering, where Mr Gisborne sat reading a newspaper, and stretched himself on the couch with a long sigh of content.

Mr Gisborne looked at him sideways, wondering. The Earl had clasped his hands behind his head, and where the lace ruffle fell back from his right wrist the corner of a bloodstained handkerchief showed. The lazy eyelids lifted. 'Dear Arnold, I am afraid you will be disappointed in me again. I hardly dare tell you but we are going back to London to-morrow.'

Mr Gisborne met those twinkling eyes and bowed slightly. 'Very well, sir,' he said.

'You are—yes, positively you are—a prince of secretaries, Arnold,' said his lordship. 'And you are quite right, of course. How do you contrive to be so acute?'

Mr Gisborne smiled. 'There's a handkerchief round your forearm, sir,' he pointed out.

The Earl drew the arm from behind his head and regarded it pensively. 'That,' he said, 'was a piece of sheer carelessness. I must be growing old.' With which he closed his eyes and relapsed into a state of agreeable coma.

18

Sir Roland Pommeroy, returning empty-handed from his mission, found Horatia and her brother playing piquet together in the saloon. For once Horatia's mind was not wholly concentrated on her cards, for no sooner was Sir Roland ushered in than she threw down her hand and turned eagerly towards him. 'Have you g-got it?'

'Here, are you going to play this game, or not?' said the Viscount, more single-minded than his sister.

'No, of c-course not. Sir Roland, did he give it to you?'

Sir Roland waited carefully until the door was shut behind the footman and coughed. 'Must warn you, ma'am—greatest caution needed before the servants. Affair to be hushed up—won't do if it gets about.'

'Never mind about that,' said the Viscount impatiently. 'Never had a servant yet who did not know all my secrets. Have you got the brooch?'

'No,' replied Sir Roland. 'Deeply regret, ma'am, but Lord Lethbridge denies all knowledge.'

'B-but I know it's there!' insisted Horatia. 'You d-didn't tell him it was mine, d-did you?'

'Certainly not, ma'am. Thought it all out on my way. Told him the brooch belonged to my great-aunt.'

The Viscount, who had been absently shuffling the pack, put the cards down at this. 'Told him it belonged to your great-aunt?' he repeated. 'Burn it, even if the fellow was knocked out, you'll never get him to believe your great-aunt came tottering into his house at two in the morning! 'Tain't reasonable. What's more, if he did believe it, you oughtn't to set a tale like that going about your great-aunt.'

'My great-aunt is dead,' said Sir Roland with some severity.

'Well, that makes it worse,' said the Viscount. 'You can't expect a man like Lethbridge to listen to ghost stories.'

'Nothing to do with ghosts!' replied Sir Roland, nettled. 'You're not yourself, Pel. Told him it was a bequest.'

'B-but it's a lady's brooch!' said Horatia. 'He c-can't have believed you!'

'Oh, your pardon, ma'am, but indeed! Plausible story–told easily–nothing simpler. Unfortunately, not in his lordship's possession. Consider, ma'am–agitation of the moment–brooch fell out in the street. Possible, you know, quite possible. Daresay you don't recollect perfectly, but depend upon it that's what happened.'

'I do recollect p-perfectly!' said Horatia. '*I* w-wasn't drunk!'

Sir Roland was so much abashed at this that he relapsed into a blushful silence. It was left to the Viscount to expostulate. 'Now, that'll do Horry, that'll do! Who said you were? Pom didn't mean anything of the kind, did you, Pom?'

'N-no, but you were, b-both of you!' said Horatia.

'Never mind about that,' replied the Viscount hastily. 'Nothing to do with the point. Pom may be right, though I don't say he is. But if you did drop it in the street, there's no more to be done. We can't go all the way to Half-Moon Street hunting in the gutters.'

Horatia clasped his wrist. 'P-Pel,' she said earnestly, 'I d-did drop it in Lethbridge's house. He tore my lace and it was p-pinned to it. It has a very stiff catch and c-couldn't fall out just for n-no reason.'

'Well, if that's so,' said the Viscount, 'I'll have to go and see Lethbridge myself. Ten to one it was all that talk about Pom's great-aunt that made him suspicious.'

This plan did not commend itself to either of his hearers. Sir Roland was unable to believe that where tact had failed the Viscount's crude methods were likely to succeed, and Horatia was terrified lest her hot-headed brother should attempt to recover the brooch at the sword's point. A lively discussion was only interrupted by the entrance of the butler announcing luncheon.

Both the visitors partook of this meal with Horatia, the Viscount needing no persuasion, and Sir Roland very little. While the servants were in the room the subject of the brooch had necessarily to be abandoned, but no sooner were the covers withdrawn than Horatia took it up again just where it had been dropped, and said: 'D-don't you see, Pel, if you go to Lethbridge now that Sir Roland has already been, he m-must suspect the truth?'

'If you ask me,' replied the Viscount, 'he knew all along. Great-aunt! Well, I've a better notion than that.'

'P-Pel, I do wish you wouldn't!' said Horatia worriedly. 'You know what you are! You fought Crosby, and there was a scandal. I know you'll d-do the same with Lethbridge if you see him.'

'No, I shan't,' answered the Viscount. 'He's a better swordsman than I am, but he ain't a better shot.'

Sir Roland gaped at him. 'Mustn't make this a shooting affair, Pel. Sister's reputation! Monstrous delicate matter.'

He broke off, for the door had opened.

'Captain Heron!' announced the footman.

There was a moment's amazed silence. Captain Heron walked in, and pausing on the threshold, glanced smilingly round. 'Well, Horry, don't look at me as though you thought I was a ghost!' he said.

'Ghosts!' exclaimed the Viscount. 'We've had enough of them. What brings you to town, Edward?'

Horatia had sprung up out of her chair. 'Edward! Oh, have you brought L-Lizzie?'

Captain Heron shook his head. 'No, I'm sorry, my dear, but Elizabeth is still in Bath. I am only in town for a few days.'

Horatia embraced him warmly. 'Well, n-never mind. I am so very g-glad to see you, Edward. Oh, do you know Sir Roland P-Pommeroy?'

'I believe I have not that pleasure,' said Captain Heron, exchanging bows with Sir Roland. 'Is Rule from home, Horry?'

'Yes, thank g-goodness!' she answered. 'Oh, I d-don't mean that, but I am in a d-dreadful fix, you see. Have you had luncheon?'

'I lunched in South Street. What has happened?'

'Painful affair,' said Sir Roland. 'Best say nothing, ma'am.'

'Oh, Edward is perfectly safe! Why, he's my brother-in-law. P-Pel, don't you think perhaps Edward could help us?'

'No, I don't, said the Viscount bluntly. 'We don't want any help. I'll get the brooch back for you.'

Horatia clasped Captain Heron's arm. 'Edward, p-please tell Pelham he m-mustn't fight Lord L-Lethbridge! It would be fatal!'

'Fight Lord Lethbridge?' repeated Captain Heron. 'It sounds a most unwise thing to do. Why should he?'

'We can't explain all that now,' said the Viscount. 'Who said I was going to fight him?'

'You d-did! You said he w-wasn't a better shot than you are.'

'Well, he ain't. All I've got to do is to put a pistol to the fellow's head, and tell him to hand over the brooch.'

Horatia released Captain Heron's arm. 'I m-must say, that is a very clever plan, P-Pel!' she approved.

Captain Heron looked from one to the other, half laughing, half startled. 'But you're all very murderous!' he expostulated. 'I wish you would tell me what has happened.'

'Oh, it's nothing,' said the Viscount. 'That fellow Lethbridge got Horry into his house last night, and she dropped a brooch there.'

'Yes, and he wants to c-compromise me,' nodded Horatia. 'So you see, he won't give the brooch up. It's all d-dreadfully provoking.'

The Viscount got up. 'I'll get it back for you,' he said. 'And we won't have any damned tact about it.'

'I'll come with you, Pel,' said the crestfallen Sir Roland.

'You can come home with me while I get pistols,' replied the Viscount severely, 'but I won't have you going with me to Half-Moon Street, mind.'

He went out, accompanied by his friend. Horatia sighed. 'I d-do hope he'll get it this time. Come into the library, Edward, and tell me all about L-Lizzie. Why didn't she c-come with you?'

Captain Heron opened the door for her to pass out into the hall. 'It was not considered advisable,' he said. 'But I am charged with messages for you.'

'N-not advisable? Why not?' asked Horatia, looking over her shoulder.

Captain Heron waited until they had reached the library before he answered. 'You see, Horry, I am happy to tell you that Lizzie is in a delicate situation just now.'

'Happy to tell me?' echoed Horatia. 'Oh! Oh, I see! How famous, Edward! Why, I shall be an aunt! Rule shall take me to B-Bath directly after the Newmarket M-meeting. That is, if he d-doesn't divorce me,' she added gloomily.

'Good God, Horry, it's not as bad as that?' cried Heron, aghast.

'N-no, it isn't, but if I d-don't get my brooch back, I daresay he will. I am a b-bad wife, Edward. I see it now.'

Captain Heron took his seat beside her on the sopha, and possessed himself of her hand. 'Poor Horry!' he said gently. 'Will you tell me all about it, right from the start?'

The story that was haltingly told him was rather involved, but he unravelled it after a time, and gave it as his opinion that there would be no divorce. 'But I think one thing, Horry,' he said. 'You should tell Rule.'

'I c-can't, and I won't,' said Horatia vehemently. 'Who ever heard such a story?'

'It is an odd story,' he admitted. 'But I think he would believe you.'

'N-not after all the stupid things I've done. And if he d-did he would have to c-call Lethbridge out, or something, and that would m-make a scandal, and he'd n-never forgive me for having b-been the cause of it.'

Captain Heron held his peace. He reflected that there might well be more behind the story. He was not very well acquainted with Rule, but he remembered that Elizabeth had perceived the inflexibility about the Earl's mouth, and had owned to some misgivings. Captain Heron had great faith in his wife's judgment. It did not seem to him, from what Horatia unconsciously told him, that the pair were living in that perfect state of conjugal happiness which he and his fair Lizzie enjoyed. If there was already a slight coldness between them (which, since Horatia had declined going to Meering, there seemed to be) it was perhaps an ill moment to choose for the recounting of this improbable adventure. At the same time Captain Heron was not inclined to place much reliance on his brother-in-law's powers of persuasion. He patted Horatia's hand, and assured her it would all come right, but inwardly he was not very hopeful. However, he felt that he owed a great debt of gratitude to her for having given him his Lizzie, and it was with real sincerity that he offered to help her in any way that he could.

'I knew you w-would, Edward,' said Horatia, rather tremulously. 'But perhaps P-Pel will get it, and then everything will be all right.'

It was a long time before the Viscount, still accompanied by the faithful Sir Roland, returned to Grosvenor Square, and Horatia had begun to fret, picturing some hideous scene of combat, convinced that the Viscount's lifeless body would at any moment be borne in. When at last he walked in, she almost hurled herself on his chest. 'Oh, P-Pel, I made sure you were d-dead!' she cried.

'Dead? Why the deuce should I be dead?' said the Viscount, removing his elegant cloth coat from her clutch. 'No, I haven't got the brooch. The fellow wasn't in, blister him!'

'Not in? Then what are we to d-do?'

'Call again,' replied the Viscount grimly.

But the Viscount's second call, made shortly before dinner, proved as fruitless as the first. 'It's my belief he's keeping out of my way,' he said. 'Well, I'll catch him in the morning before he has a chance to go out. And if that damned porter tells me he's out then, I'll force my way in and see for myself.'

'Then I think I had better accompany you,' decided Captain Heron. 'If you try to break into another man's house there's likely to be trouble.'

'Just what I said myself,' nodded Sir Roland, still in attendance. 'Better all go. Call for you at your lodging, Pel.'

'Devilish good of you, Pom,' said the Viscount. 'Say nine o'clock.'

'Nine o'clock,' agreed Sir Roland. 'Nothing for it but to go to bed betimes.'

Captain Heron was the first to arrive at the Viscount's lodgings in Pall Mall next morning. He found the Viscount fully dressed, and busy with the loading of one of his silver-mounted pistols.

'There's a sweet little pistol for you,' said the Viscount, stopping the hammer at half-cock. 'Blew the pips out of a playing card with it once. Cheston laid me ten to one against. Why, you couldn't miss with this pistol! At least,' he added naïvely, 'I daresay you might, but I couldn't.'

Captain Heron grinned at this aspersion cast on his marksmanship, and sat down on the edge of the table, watching the Viscount pour in his powder. 'Well, all I beg of you is, don't blow Lethbridge's head off, Pelham!'

'Might have to wing him,' said the Viscount, picking up a piece of soft kid from the table and placing his ball in it. 'I won't kill him, though, damme, I'll be hard put to it not to!' He lifted the gun, and with his thumb over the touchhole gently rammed down the ball. 'There you are. Where's Pom? Might have known he'd oversleep.' He slipped the pistol into his pocket, and stood up. 'Y'know, Edward, this is the devil of a business,' he said seriously. 'No knowing how Rule would take it if it came to his ears. Rely on you to help me.'

'Of course I'm going to help you,' replied Captain Heron. 'If Lethbridge has the brooch, we'll get it.'

Sir Roland appearing at this moment, they picked up their hats, and set off for Half-Moon Street. The porter who opened the door to them once more denied his master.

'Not in, eh?' said the Viscount. 'Well, I think I'll step in and take a look.'

'But he's not in, my lord!' insisted the porter, holding the door. 'He went out yesterday in his chaise, and is not back yet.'

'Don't believe him, Pel,' counselled Sir Roland in the rear.

'But sir, indeed my lord is not in! There is another—well, a person, sir, asking for him besides yourself.'

Captain Heron set his sound shoulder to the door, and thrust it back.

'That's mighty interesting,' he said. 'We will step upstairs to be quite sure that his lordship has not come in unbeknown. In with you Pel!'

The porter found himself driven firmly backwards, and raised a shout for help. A burly individual in a frieze greatcoat and a dirty neck-cloth, who was sitting on a chair in the narrow hall, looked on grinning but offered no assistance. The butler came puffing up the stairs, but paused when he saw the company. He bowed to the Viscount, and said severely: 'His lordship is from home, my lord.'

'Perhaps you didn't look under the bed,' said the Viscount.

A hoarse laugh from the man in the frieze coat greeted this sally. 'Ah, you've hit it, your honour. He's a peevy cull, and so I allus said.'

'Eh?' said Sir Roland, regarding him through his eyeglass. 'Who's this fellow, Pel?'

'How the devil should I know?' demanded the Viscount. 'Now you stay where you are, what-ever-your-name is. I'm going up to have a little talk with his lordship.'

The butler placed himself at the foot of the stairs. 'Sir, his lordship is not in the house!' He saw the Viscount draw the pistol from his pocket, and gasped: 'My lord!'

'Stand out of my way, or you might get hurt,' said the Viscount.

The butler retreated. 'I assure your lordship—I—I don't understand, my lord! My master is gone into the country!'

The Viscount gave a snort, and ran up the stairs. He came back in a very few moments. 'True enough. He's not there.'

'Loped off!' ejaculated the burly man. 'Damn my blood if I ever deal with a flash cull again!' With which cryptic remark he drove his fist into his hat, and sat glowering.

The Viscount looked at him with interest. 'What do you want with him, hey? Who are you?'

'That's my business,' retorted the burly man. 'Twenty rum guineas, that's what I wants, and that's what I'll get if I stays here till tomorrow.'

Captain Heron spoke, addressing himself to the butler. 'Our business with his lordship is urgent—can you inform us of his direction?'

'His lordship,' said the butler stiffly, 'left no word, sir. Indeed, I wish that I were aware of his destination, for this—this person, sir, insists upon staying until his return, though I have warned him I shall send for a constable.'

'You don't dare send for no harman,' said the burly man scornfully. 'I knows what I know, ah, and I knows who'll sleep in Rumbo if I splits.'

Sir Roland, who had been listening intently to this speech, shook his head. 'Y'know, I don't follow what he says at all,' he remarked. 'Rumbo? Never heard of the place.'

'The likes of you calls it Newgate,' explained the burly man. 'I calls it Rumbo: See?'

The Viscount looked at him frowningly. 'I've a notion I've met you before,' he said. 'I don't know your face, but damme, I do know your voice!'

'Might have been masked,' suggested Sir Roland helpfully.

'Lord, Pom, don't be such a— Wait a bit, though! Masked?' The Viscount slapped his leg. 'That's given it to me! Blister it, you're the rogue that tried to hold me up on Shooter's Hill once!'

The burly man, who had changed colour, slid towards the door, muttering: 'No, I never did so! It's a lie!'

'Lord, I don't bear you any malice,' said the Viscount cheerfully. 'You got nothing from me.'

'A highwayman, is he?' said Sir Roland with interest. 'Devilish queer company Lethbridge keeps! Devilish queer!'

'H'm!' remarked Captain Heron, surveying the burly man with scant approval. 'I can guess what your business is with his lordship, my man.'

'Can you?' said Sir Roland. 'Well, what is it?'

'Use your wits,' said Captain Heron unkindly. 'I should like very much to give him up to the Watch, but I suppose we can't.' He turned to the butler. 'I want you to cast your mind back. The night before last a brooch was lost in this house. Do you recall finding it?'

The butler seemed pleased to be able to answer at least one question. 'No, sir, I don't. There wasn't a brooch found in this house. His lordship asked me particularly whether it had been picked up, just after that gentleman called yesterday.' He nodded towards Sir Roland.

'What's that?' ejaculated the Viscount. 'Did you say *after* he called?'

'I did, my lord. His lordship sent for me not more than a minute or so after the gentleman had left the house.'

Captain Heron grasped the Viscount's arm restrainingly. 'Thank you,' he said. 'Come Pelham, there's no more to be done here.'

He drew the unwilling Viscount towards the door, which the porter opened with alacrity.

The three conspirators descended the steps, and set off slowly towards Piccadilly.

'Dropped in the street,' said Sir Roland. 'Said so all along.'

'It begins to look like it,' agreed Captain Heron. 'Yet Horry is certain the brooch was lost in that house. I imagine the butler was speaking the truth. Could anyone else have found the brooch?'

The Viscount stopped short. 'Drelincourt!' he said. 'By the lord Harry, that little viper, that toad, that—'

'Are you talking of that Macaroni cousin of Rule's?' asked Captain Heron. 'What had he to do with it?'

Sir Roland, who had been staring at the Viscount, suddenly shook him by the hand. 'You've got it, Pel. You've got it,' he said. 'Lay you odds he took the brooch.'

'Of course he took it! Didn't we leave him with Lethbridge? By God, I'll wring his damned scraggy neck!' said the Viscount wrathfully, and plunged off at a great rate towards Piccadilly.

The other two hurried after him.

'Was Drelincourt there that night?' asked Captain Heron of Sir Roland.

'Came in because it was raining,' explained Sir Roland. 'Pel wanted to pull his nose. Daresay he will now.'

Captain Heron caught up with the Viscount. 'Pelham, go easy!' he said. 'If he hasn't got it and you accuse him, you'll only work a deal of harm. Why should he have taken the brooch?'

'To make mischief! Don't I know him!' replied the Viscount. 'If he's gone off with it to Rule already, we're finished.'

'That's so,' nodded Sir Roland. 'Yes, that's so, Pel. No getting away from it. Better finish Drelincourt too. Nothing else to do.'

'Pelham, you young madman, give me that pistol of yours!' commanded Captain Heron.

The Viscount shook him off, and strode on. Sir Roland plucked at the Captain's sleeve. 'Better let Pel deal with the fellow,' he said confidentially. 'Devilish fine shot, you know.'

'Good God, you're as mad as he is,' groaned Captain Heron. 'We mustn't let this come to a fight, man!'

Sir Roland pursed his lips. 'I don't see why not,' he said judicially. 'Trifle irregular, but there's two of us to see fair play. Do you know Drelincourt?'

'No, but—'

'Ah, that accounts for it!' nodded Sir Roland. 'If you knew him, you'd agree. Fellow ought to be killed. Thought so for a long time.'

Captain Heron gave it up in despair.

19

Mr Crosby Drelincourt had been much too shaken by his experiences to think of dinner when he left Meering. All he desired was to reach his own lodgings. He drove from Meering to Twyford, where he changed horses, and went to the grievous expense of hiring an armed guard to protect him from highwaymen. The journey home seemed to him interminable, but the chaise set him down in Jermyn Street not long after ten o'clock, by which time he had recovered a little from his adventures, and had begun to feel the pangs of hunger. Unfortunately, since he had not been expected to return that night, no supper had been provided, and he was forced to go out to an ordinary, so that he might just as well, he reflected bitterly, have dined on the road after all.

He slept late next morning, and was sitting down to breakfast in his dressing-gown when he heard a thundering on the front door, followed in a few moments by the sound of voices. He dropped his knife, listening. One voice was raised insistently, and Mr Drelincourt knew that voice. He turned quickly to his valet, who had just set the coffee-pot down before him: 'I'm not at home!' he said. 'Quick, don't let them come up!'

The valet said obtusely: 'Beg pardon, sir?'

Mr Drelincourt thrust him towards the door. 'Tell them I'm away, you fool! Stop them coming up! I'm not well; I can't see any one!'

'Very good, sir,' said the valet, hiding a smile.

Mr Drelincourt sank back into his chair, nervously wiping his face with his napkin. He heard the valet go downstairs to parley with the visitors. Then, to his horror, he heard someone come up, three steps at a time.

The door was rudely burst open. Viscount Winwood stood on the threshold. 'Away, are you?' he said. 'Now why are you so anxious not to see me, eh?'

Mr Drelincourt rose, gripping the edge of the table. 'Really, my lord, if—if a man may not be private when he chooses!' He perceived the face of Sir Roland Pommeroy peering over the Viscount's shoulder, and licked his lips. 'Pray—pray what's the meaning of this intrusion, sir?' he demanded weakly.

The Viscount advanced into the room, and sat down without ceremony on the corner of the table, one hand in his capacious coat-pocket. Behind him Sir Roland propped his shoulders against the wall, and began dispassionately to pick his teeth. Captain Heron ranged alongside the Viscount, ready to intervene at need.

Mr Drelincourt looked from one to the other with the deepest misgiving. 'I can't conceive what—what should bring you here, gentlemen!' he said.

The Viscount's angelic blue eyes were fixed on his face. 'What took you out of town yesterday, Drelincourt?' he inquired.

'I–I—'

'I have it from your man below that you went away in a chaise and four, and came home late—too late to be disturbed now. Where did you go?'

'I fail—I fail entirely to see how my movements should concern you, my lord!'

Sir Roland withdrew the toothpick from his mouth. 'Don't want to tell us,' he remarked. 'Black, very black!'

'Well, he's going to tell us,' said the Viscount, and got up.

Mr Drelincourt took a backward step. 'My lord! I—I protest! I don't understand you! I went into the country on private business—purely private business, I assure you!'

'Private, was it?' said the Viscount, advancing towards him. 'It wasn't on business connected with jewellery, I take it?'

Mr Drelincourt turned ashen-pale. 'No, no!' he gasped.

The Viscount whipped the pistol from his pocket, and levelled it. 'You lie, you little viper!' he said through his teeth. 'Stand still!'

Mr Drelincourt stood rooted to the floor, his fascinated gaze on the pistol. Sir Roland was moved to protest. 'Not out of hand, Pel, not out of hand! Must do the thing decently!'

The Viscount paid no heed. 'You picked up a ring-brooch in Lethbridge's house the other night, didn't you?'

'I don't know what you mean!' chattered Mr Drelincourt. 'A brooch? I know nothing about it, nothing!'

The Viscount pressed the muzzle of his pistol into the pit of Mr Drelincourt's stomach. 'There's a mighty light trigger on this pistol of mine,' he said. 'It only needs a touch to send it off. Don't move. I know you took that brooch. What did you do with it?'

Mr Drelincourt was silent, breathing rather fast. Sir Roland replaced his toothpick carefully in its gold case, and pocketed it. He strolled forward, and tucked his fingers into the back of Mr Drelincourt's neck-cloth, and twisted it scientifically. 'Take the pistol away, Pel. Going to choke it out of him.'

Mr Drelincourt, his throat already bruised from his cousin's crushing grip, gave a strangled shriek. 'Yes, I took it! I didn't know how it came to be there—indeed, I had no notion!'

'You carried it to Rule? Answer!' snarled the Viscount.

'No, no, I didn't. I swear I didn't!'

Captain Heron, watching him closely, nodded. 'Don't choke him, Pommeroy, I think he's speaking the truth.'

'If you didn't take it to Rule, where is it?'

'I haven't got it!' gasped Mr Drelincourt, his eyes on the Viscount's pistol.

'Can't expect us to believe that,' said Sir Roland, impersonally. 'Went off to Meering with it, didn't you?'

'Yes, I did, but I never gave it to Rule. Lord Lethbridge has it!'

Sir Roland was so surprised that he released him. 'Damned if I can make head or tail of this!' he said. 'How the deuce did he come by it?'

'He—he overtook me, and wrested the brooch from me. I couldn't stop him. I swear I'm telling the truth!'

'There, that's what all your talk of great-aunts brought about, Pom!' said the Viscount bitterly.

'It's a good thing,' said Sir Roland. 'Now we know who has got the brooch. Makes it simple. Find Lethbridge—get the brooch—whole affair settled.'

The Viscount turned to Mr Drelincourt. 'Where is Lethbridge?'

Mr Drelincourt said sullenly: 'I don't know. He said he should sleep the night in Maidenhead.'

The Viscount was thinking fast. 'Maidenhead? That's a matter of twenty-six or seven miles. Call it a three-hour run. We'll get him.' He slipped the pistol back into his pocket. 'Nothing more to be done here. As for you—' he rounded on Mr Drelincourt, who shrank perceptibly, '–the next time you cross my path will be the last. Come on, Pom; come, Edward.'

When they were once more in the street Captain Heron began to shake with silent laughter.

'What the devil's the matter with you?' said the Viscount, pausing to frown at him.

Captain Heron grasped the railings. 'His face!' he choked. 'You breaking in in the middle of his breakfast–oh lord!'

'Ha!' said Sir Roland. 'Middle of his breakfast, was he? Dashed amusing!'

Suddenly the humour of the situation dawned upon the Viscount. He went off into a crack of laughter. Mr Drelincourt, peering from between the curtains of his room, was infuriated by the sight of his three visitors doubled up with mirth on the pavement.

Captain Heron let go the railings at last. 'Where now?' he asked faintly.

'White's,' decided the Viscount. 'Won't be anyone there at this hour. We must think this one out.'

'I'm not a member, you know,' said Captain Heron.

'What's that matter? Pom ain't either. I am, though,' replied the Viscount, and led the way up the street.

They found the coffee-room in the club deserted, and took possession of it. The Viscount stretched himself in a chair, and thrust his hands into his breeches pockets.

'Say Lethbridge started from Maidenhead at ten,' he mused. 'He'll arrive about one. Maybe earlier. Drives fast horses.'

Sir Roland was inclined to cavil at this. 'Wouldn't start at ten, Pel. Too early.'

'What's to keep him?' asked the Viscount. 'Nothing to do in Maidenhead that I ever heard of.'

'There's a bed, ain't there? Do you ever get up before nine? Lay you odds he don't either. Call it eleven.'

'Does it signify?' inquired Captain Heron, adjusting his sash.

'Signify? Of course it signifies!' replied the Viscount. 'We've got to intercept the fellow. Does he take his luncheon on the road, Pom?'

'Takes his lunch at Longford–King's Head,' said Sir Roland.

'Or Colnbrook,' said the Viscount. 'They do you a very good dish of mutton and broiled mushrooms at the George.'

'No, no, Pel,' said Sir Roland gently. 'You're thinking of the Pigeons at Brentford.'

The Viscount devoted some thought to this, and came to the conclusion that his friend was right. 'Well, then, call it Longford. Lunches at noon. Won't get to London before two.'

'I wouldn't say that, Pel,' objected Sir Roland.

'Damme, you must give the fellow time to sit a bit over his wine!'

'Not at Longford,' said Sir Roland simply. 'He won't sit over his wine at the King's Head.'

'Well, if it's like that, he won't take his luncheon there,' said the Viscount. 'That puts us out.'

Captain Heron sat up. 'Stop talking about his luncheon!' he begged. 'He'll eat it somewhere, and that's all that concerns us. How are you going to intercept him?'

The Viscount let his chin sink into his cravat, and pondered deeply.

'Short of holding him up, you can't do it,' said Captain Heron. 'You can only wait for him at his house.'

The Viscount jerked himself in his chair. 'You've hit it, Edward! That's a devilish good idea of yours! We'll do it.'

'What, wait for him in Half-Moon Street? I don't say it's a good idea, but—'

'Lord no!' interrupted the Viscount. 'No sense in that. We'll hold him up.'

'Good God, that wasn't my idea!' said Captain Heron, alarmed.

'Of course it was your idea; you thought of it, didn't you? And one thing I will say, Edward, I never expected it of you. Always thought you too devilish respectable.'

'You were right,' said Captain Heron firmly. 'I am as respectable as can be. I won't be a party to any hold-up.'

'Why not? No harm in it. Shan't hurt the fellow—much.'

'Pelham, will you have some sense? Consider my uniform!'

Sir Roland, who had been pensively sucking the end of his cane, raised his head. 'Got a notion,' he said. 'Go home and change it. Can't hold a man up in regimentals. Wouldn't be reasonable to expect it of him, Pel.'

'Lord, you don't suppose we'll any of us do it dressed like this, do you? We want greatcoats and masks.'

'I've got a roquelaure,' said Sir Roland helpfully. 'Had it made for me last month by Grogan. Meant to show it to you, Pel. Pretty shade of grey—silver buttons, but I don't know about the lining. Grogan was all for a Carmelite silk, but I'm not sure I care for it, not at all sure.'

'Well, you can't hold up a chaise in a silk-lined roquelaure. We've got to have frieze coats and mufflers.'

Sir Roland shook his head. 'Can't be done, Pel. You got a frieze coat, Heron?'

'No, thank God, I haven't!' said Captain Heron.

'Nor have I,' said the Viscount, springing up. 'And that's why we must get hold of that fellow we left at Lethbridge's. Come along! We've no time to waste.'

Sir Roland rose, and said admiringly: 'Dashed if I should ever have thought of that. It's you who have the head, Pel, not a doubt of it.'

'Pelham, do you realize that in all probability it was that ruffian that kidnapped your sister?' demanded Captain Heron.

'Do you think so? Yes, by God, I believe you're right! Said he was waiting for twenty guineas, didn't he? Well, if Lethbridge can hire him so can we,' declared the Viscount, and strode out.

Captain Heron caught him up in the street. 'Pelham, it's all very well, but we can't do a hare-brained thing like that! If we're caught I'm like to be broke.'

'Well, it always beat me why you ever wanted to go into the Army,' said the Viscount. 'But if you want to rat, Pom and I can do it without you!'

Sir Roland, shocked, said: 'Pel, dear old boy, Pel! Think what you're saying! Heron ain't ratting. Only said he'd be broke if we was caught. Mustn't jump down a man's throat just because he makes a remark.'

'If it were for anyone but Horry, I would rat,' said Captain Heron. 'Why in thunder don't you wait for Lethbridge to come home, Pelham? If three of us can't get the brooch away from him without masquerading as highwaymen—'

'Because this is a better way!' said the Viscount. 'Great thing is to avoid scandal. If I put a pistol to the fellow's head, and he calls me out, where are we then? Worse off than ever! Affair's bound to come to Rule's ears, and if you think he won't suspect Horry's in it, you don't know him. This way, we'll have the brooch without a breath of scandal, and no one the wiser. Now, are you with me, or not, Edward?'

'Yes, I'm with you,' said Captain Heron. 'There is something in what you say, if it doesn't go awry!'

'It can't go awry, man—unless that rogue's left Lethbridge's house.'

'Can't have done that,' said Sir Roland. 'Said he was going to stay there till he had his twenty guineas. Lethbridge not back—can't have had 'em. Must be there still.'

Sir Roland proved to be right. When they arrived once more in Half-Moon Street, the burly man was still seated in the hall. The porter, as soon as he saw who it was on the doorstep, made a spirited attempt to slam the door. This was frustrated by Sir Roland, who hurled himself against it with great presence of mind, and nearly knocked the breath out of the porter by jamming him between the door and the wall. When he had extricated himself he found all three gentlemen inside the hall again, and groaned. However, as soon as it was explained to him that they only wanted to take away the burly man, he brightened considerably, and even permitted them to hail that worthy into the saloon for a little private conversation.

The burly man, confronted by the Viscount's pistol, flung up his hands. 'Don't you go for to let off that pop, your honour!' he said huskily. 'I ha'n't done you a mite o' harm!'

'Not a mite,' agreed the Viscount. 'What's more, I won't do you any harm if you behave yourself. What's your name? Come on, man, I've got to call you something, haven't I?'

'You call me Ned. Ned Hawkins,' replied the burly man. 'It ain't the name, but it's one I got a fancy for. Edward Hawkins, that's me, at your service, gen'lemen.'

'We don't want another Edward,' objected Sir Roland. 'Heron's name's Edward, and we shall only get 'em mixed up.'

'Well, I don't mind being Frederick—to oblige the company,' conceded Mr Hawkins.

'Hawkins will do,' replied the Viscount. 'You're on the High Toby, aren't you?'

'Me?' exclaimed Mr Hawkins virtuously. 'Cross me heart if—'

'That'll do,' interrupted the Viscount. 'Blew the hat off your head on Shooter's Hill six months ago. Now I've got a piece of work for you to do. What do you say to twenty guineas, eh?'

Mr Hawkins recoiled. 'Dang me if ever I works with a flash cull again, that's what I says!'

The Viscount lifted his pistol. 'Then I'll hold you, while my friend there goes for a constable.'

'You dassn't!' grinned Mr Hawkins. 'You get me put in the Whit, and I takes his peevy lordship with me—ah, and how'll you like that?'

'Pretty well,' said the Viscount. 'He's no friend of mine. Friend of yours?'

Mr Hawkins spat comprehensively. Sir Roland, his sense of propriety offended, interposed. 'Here, I say, Pel, can't have the fellow spitting all over another man's house. Bad *ton*, dear boy. Devilish bad!'

'Don't do that again!' ordered the Viscount. 'What's the use of it? Diddled you out of your money, hasn't he?'

'Ay, loped off,' growled Mr Hawkins. 'A boman prig, he is! When I gets my hands on him—'

'I can help you to do that,' said the Viscount. 'What do you say to holding him up?—for twenty guineas?'

Mr Hawkins looked suspiciously from one to the other. 'What's the lay?' he demanded.

'He's got something I want,' said the Viscount briefly. 'Make up your mind! The Watch, or twenty guineas?'

Mr Hawkins caressed his stubby chin. 'Who's in it? All of you coves?' he inquired.

'All of us. We're going to hold up his chaise.'

'What, in them toges?' said Mr Hawkins, indicating the Viscount's gold-laced coat.

'Of course not, you fool!' answered the Viscount impatiently. 'That's what we want you for. We must have three greatcoats like your own, and masks.'

A broad grin spread over Mr Hawkins's countenance. 'Damn my blood, but I like your spirit!' he announced. 'I'll do it! Where is this cull?'

'On the Bath Road, heading for London.'

'That'll mean the Heath, that will,' nodded Mr Hawkins. 'When's it for?'

'Any time after noon. Can't say precisely.'

Mr Hawkins pulled down his mouth. 'Dang me if I like it, then. I like to work when the tattler's up, see?'

'If there's one thing we don't want it's any tattlers,' replied the Viscount firmly.

'Lord love your honour, ain't you ever heard on the moon?'

'The moon! By the time that's up our man will be safe in this house. This is daylight or nothing.'

Mr Hawkins sighed. 'Just as you say, your honour. And you wants a set of toges and shaps? Bring your own nags?'

'Own horses, own pistols,' agreed the Viscount.

'You'll have to mount me, then, Pelham,' put in Captain Heron.

'Mount you with pleasure, my dear fellow.'

'Own pops?' said Mr Hawkins. 'Us bridle culls don't use them little pops all over wedge, your honour.'

The Viscount glanced down at his pistol. 'What's wrong with it? Devilish good pistol. Gave a hundred guineas for the pair.'

Mr Hawkins pointed a grimy finger at the silver mountings. 'All that wedge. That's what's wrong with it.'

'Oh, very well,' said the Viscount. 'But I like my own pistols, you know. Now where do we get these coats and mufflers?'

'You know the Halfway House?' said Mr Hawkins. 'That's where I'll be. There's a flash ken thereabouts, where I keeps my nag. I'll be off there now, and when you comes, why dang me if I don't have the toges and tyes ready for you!'

'And how do I know you will be there?' said the Viscount.

'Because I wants twenty guineas,' replied Mr Hawkins logically. 'And because I wants to get my hands on that boman prig. That's how.'

20

An hour later three gentlemen might have been observed riding soberly out to Knightsbridge. Captain Heron, bestriding a raking chestnut from the Viscount's stables, had changed his scarlet regimentals and his powdered wig for a plain suit of buff, and a brown tie-wig. He had found time, before joining the Viscount at his lodging, to call in Grosvenor Square again, where he had found Horatia in a fever of anxiety. When she learned of the new development in the affair, she first expressed herself as extremely dissatisfied that no one had killed the wretched Mr Drelincourt, and it was some few minutes before Captain Heron could induce her to speak of anything but that gentleman's manifold iniquities. When her indignation had abated somewhat he laid the Viscount's plan before her. This met with her instant approval. It was the cleverest notion she had ever heard of, and of course it could not fail.

Captain Heron warned her to keep her own counsel, and went off to Pall Mall.

He had not much expectation of finding Mr Hawkins either at the Half-way House or anywhere else, but it was obviously no use saying so to the optimistic Viscount. By this time his brother-in-law was in fine fettle, so that whether Mr Hawkins kept his appointment or not, it seemed probable that the plan would be carried out.

About a quarter of a mile before the Halfway House was reached, a solitary rider, walking his horse, came into view. As they drew closer he looked over his shoulder, and Captain Heron was forced to admit that he had misjudged their new acquaintance.

Mr Hawkins greeted him jovially. 'Dang me if you wasn't speaking the truth!' he exclaimed. His eyes ran over the Viscount's mare approvingly. 'That's a nice bit of horseflesh, that is,' he nodded. 'But tricksy—tricksy, I'll lay my life. You come along o' me to the boozing ken I told you of.'

'Got those coats?' asked the Viscount.

'Ay, all's bowman, your honour.'

The ale-house which Mr Hawkins had made his headquarters lay some little distance off the main road. It was an unsavoury haunt, and from the look of the company in the tap-room seemed to be frequented largely by ruffians of Mr Hawkins's calling. As a preliminary to the adventure the Viscount called for four bumpers of brandy, for which he paid with a guinea tossed on to the counter.

'Don't throw guineas about, you young fool!' said Captain Heron in a low voice. 'You'll have your pocket picked if you're not more careful.'

'Ay, the Capting's in the right of it,' said Mr Hawkins, overhearing. 'I'm a bridle cull, I am—never went on the dublay yet, no, and never will, but there's a couple of files got their winkers on you. We gets all sorts here—locks, files, common prigs, and foot-scamperers. Now, my bullies, drain your clanks! I got your toges up the dancers.'

Sir Roland plucked at the Captain's sleeve. 'You know, Heron,' he whispered confidentially, 'this brandy—not at all the thing! Hope it don't get into poor Pel's head—very wild in his cups—oh, very wild! Must keep him away from any dancers.'

'I don't think he meant "dancers",' soothed Captain Heron. 'I fancy that's a cant word.'

'Oh, that's it, is it,' said Sir Roland, relieved. 'It's a pity he don't speak English. Don't follow him at all, you know.'

Mr Hawkins's dancers proved to be a flight of rickety stairs, up which he led them to a malodorous bedroom. Sir Roland recoiled on the threshold, raising his scented handkerchief to his nose. 'Pel—no, really Pel!' he said faintly.

'Smells a bit of onions,' remarked the Viscount. He picked up a battered tricorne from a chair, and casting aside his rakish chapeau *à la Valaque*, clapped it over his fair, unpowdered locks. He surveyed the effect in the cracked mirror, and chuckled. 'How d'you like it, Pom?'

Sir Roland shook his head. 'It ain't a hat, Pel. You couldn't call it a hat.'

Mr Hawkins gave a guffaw. 'It's a rare shap, that one. Better nor yours.'

He handed the Viscount a muffler, and showed him how to tie it to conceal every vestige of his lace cravat. The Viscount's shining top-boots made him purse his lips. 'You could see your face in them stampers,' he said. 'Hows'-ever, it can't be helped.' He watched Sir Roland struggle into a large triple-caped overcoat, and handed him a hat more battered than the Viscount's. He eyed Sir Roland's elegant gauntlets disparagingly. 'Properly speaking, you don't want no famstrings,' he said. 'But I dunno. Maybe best keep them white dabblers o' yours covered. Now, you gen'lemen, stow these here masks away till I gives the word to put 'em on. Not till we gets to the Heath that won't be.'

Captain Heron pulled his muffler tight and jammed his beaver well over his eyes. 'Well, at all events, Pelham, I defy my own wife to recognize me in these clothes,' he remarked. 'I could only wish that the coat were not so tight round the chest. Are we ready?'

Mr Hawkins was pulling a wooden case from under the bed. This he opened, and displayed three horse pistols. 'I got two myself, but I couldn't come by no more,' he said.

The Viscount lifted one of these weapons, and grimaced. 'Clumsy. You can have it, Pom. I brought my own.'

'Not them little pops all over wedge?' asked Mr Hawkins, frowning.

'Lord, no! Horse pistols like your own. You'd best leave the shooting to me, Pom. No knowing what will happen if you let that barker off.'

'That gun,' said Mr Hawkins, offended, 'belonged to Gentleman Joe, him as went to the Nubbing Cheat a twelve-month back. Ah, and a rare buzz he was!'

'Fellow who robbed the French Mail about a year ago?' inquired the Viscount. 'Hanged him, didn't they?'

'That's what I said,' replied Mr Hawkins.

'Well, I don't care for his taste in pistols,' said the Viscount, handing the weapon over to Sir Roland. 'Let's be going.'

They trooped down the wooden stairs again, and out into the yard, where a couple of seedy-looking men were walking the horses up and down. These Mr Hawkins sent about their business. The Viscount tossed them a couple of silver pieces, and went to see that his pistols were still safe in the saddle holsters. Mr Hawkins told him he need not be anxious. 'Couple o' my own lads, they are,' he said, hoisting himself on to the back of a big brown gelding.

The Viscount swung lightly into the saddle, glancing over the brown horse's points. 'Where did you steal that nag?' he asked.

Mr Hawkins grinned, and laid a finger to the side of his nose.

Sir Roland, whose horse, apparently having as poor an opinion of the hostelry as his master, was sidling and fidgeting in a fret to be off, ranged alongside the Viscount and said: 'Pel, we can't ride down the high road in these clothes! Damme, I won't do it!'

'High road?' said Mr Hawkins. 'Lord love you, it ain't high roads for us, my bully! You follow me.'

The way Mr Hawkins chose was unknown to his companions, and seemed very tortuous. He skirted every village, took a wide detour round Hounslow and led them eventually on to the Heath shortly after one. Ten minutes' canter brought the main Bath Road into sight.

'You want to lie up where no one won't see you,' advised Mr Hawkins. 'There's a bit of a hill I knows of, with some bushes atop. Know the look of our man's rabler?'

'Do I know the look of his what?' said the Viscount.

'His rabler—his coach is what I mean!'

'Well, I do wish you'd say what you mean,' said the Viscount severely. 'He's driving a chaise-and-four, that's all I know.'

'Don't you know his horses?' asked Captain Heron.

'I know the pair he drives in his curricle, but that don't help us. We'll stop the first chaise we see, and if it ain't him, we'll stop the next.'

'That's it,' agreed Sir Roland, dubiously eyeing his mask. 'Daresay we'll need some practice. Look here, Pel, I don't at all like this mask. There's too much of it.'

'For my part,' said Captain Heron with an irrepressible laugh, 'I'm thanking God for mine!'

'Well, if I put it on it'll hang down all over my face,' objected Sir Roland. 'Shan't be able to breathe.'

They had come by this time to the hillock Mr Hawkins had mentioned. The bushes which grew on its slope afforded excellent protection, and it commanded a long view of the road, from which it was set back at a distance of about fifty yards. Reaching the top of it, they dismounted, and sat down to await their prey.

'I don't know if it has occurred to you, Pelham,' said Captain Heron, removing his hat, and throwing it down on the grass beside him, 'but if we stop many chaises before we chance on the one we're after, our first victims are likely to have plenty of time to inform against us in Hounslow.' He looked across the Viscount's sprawling person to Mr Hawkins. 'Ever had that happen to you, my friend?'

Mr Hawkins, who was chewing a blade of grass, grinned. 'Ah, I've had it happen. No scout-cull ain't snabbled me yet.'

'Burn it, man, how many chaises do you expect to see?' said the Viscount.

'Well, it's the main Bath Road,' Captain Heron pointed out.

Sir Roland removed his mask, which he had been trying on, to say: 'Bath season not begun yet.'

Captain Heron stretched himself full-length on the springy turf, and clasped his hands lightly over his eyes to protect them from the sun. 'You're fond of betting, Pelham,' he said lazily. 'I'll lay you ten to one in guineas that something goes wrong with this precious scheme of yours.'

'Done!' said the Viscount promptly. 'But it was your scheme, not mine.'

'Something coming!' announced Sir Roland suddenly.

Captain Heron sat up, and groped for his hat.

'That's no post-chaise,' said their guide and mentor, still chewing his blade of grass. He glanced up at the sun, calculating the time. 'Likely it's the Oxford stage.'

In a few moments the vehicle came into sight round a bend in the road, some way off. It was a great lumbering coach, drawn by six horses, and piled high with baggage. Beside the coachman sat an armed guard, and all over the roof such passengers who could only afford to pay half their fare perched and clung precariously.

'Don't touch stage rablers myself,' remarked Mr Hawkins, watching the coach lurch and sway over the bumps in the road. 'Nothing to be had but a rum fam or two, or a thin truss.'

The coach laboured ponderously on, and was presently lost to sight. The noise of the plodding hooves was borne back in the still air for long after it had gone, growing fainter and fainter until at last it died.

A solitary horseman bearing westwards passed next. Mr Hawkins sniffed at him, and shook his head. 'Small game,' he said scornfully.

Silence, except for the trill of a lark somewhere overhead, again fell over the Heath. Captain Heron dozed peacefully; the Viscount took snuff. The sound of a coach travelling fast broke the stillness after perhaps twenty minutes had elapsed. The Viscount nudged Captain Heron sharply, and picked up his mask. Mr Hawkins cocked his head on one side, listening. 'Six horses there,' he pronounced. 'Hear 'em?'

The Viscount had risen, and put his mare's bridle over her head. He paused. 'Six?'

'Ay, outriders, I dessay. Might be the Mail.' He looked his three companions over. 'Four on us—what do you say, my bullies?'

'Good God, no!' replied the Viscount. 'Can't rob the Mail!'

Mr Hawkins sighed. 'It's a rare chance,' he said wistfully. 'Ah, what did I tell you? Bristol Mail, that is.'

The Mail had swept round the bend, accompanied by two outriders. The horses, nearing the end of the stage, were sweating, and one of the leaders showed signs of lameness.

A wagon, going at a snail's pace along the white road, was the only other thing that relieved the monotony during the next quarter of an hour. Mr Hawkins remarked that he knew a cove who got a tidy living prigging the goods off tumblers, but he himself despised so debased a calling.

Sir Roland yawned. 'We've seen one stage, one mail, man riding a roan cob, and a wagon. I call it devilish dull, Pel. Poor sport! Heron, did you think to bring a pack of cards?'

'No,' answered Captain Heron sleepily.

'No, no more did I,' said Sir Roland, and relapsed into silence.

Presently Mr Hawkins put his hand to his ear. 'Ah,' he said deeply, 'that sounds more like it! You want to get your masks on, gen'lemen. There's a chaise coming.'

'Don't believe it,' said Sir Roland gloomily, but he put his mask on and got into the saddle.

The Viscount fixed his own mask, and once more crushed the hat on to his head. 'Lord, Pom, if you could see yourself!' he said.

Sir Roland, who was engaged in blowing the curtain of his mask away from his mouth, paused to say: 'I can see you, Pel. That's enough. More than enough.'

Mr Hawkins mounted the brown gelding. 'Now, my bullies all, take it easy. We ride down on 'em, see? You wants to be careful how you looses off them pops. I'm a peaceable cove, and we don't want no killing.' He nodded at the Viscount. 'You're handy with your pop; you and me'll do the shooting, and mind it's over their nobs!'

The Viscount drew one of his pistols from the holster. 'Wonder how the mare will take it?' he said cheerfully. 'Steady, Firefly! Steady, lass!'

A post-chaise drawn by four trotting horses came round the bend. Mr Hawkins snatched at the Viscount's bridle. 'Easy, easy!' he begged. 'Give 'em time to come alongside! No sense in letting 'em see us yet. You wait on me.'

The post-chaise came on. 'Nice pair of wheelers,' commented Sir Roland. 'Good holders.'

'Capting, you'll cover them postilions, see?' ordered Mr Hawkins.

'If we don't move soon, there'll be no postilions to cover!' snapped the Viscount. 'Come on, man!'

The post-chaise was almost abreast of them. Mr Hawkins released the Viscount's bridle. 'At 'em, then!' he said, and drove his heels into his horse.

'Yoiks! Forrard away!' halloed Sir Roland, and thundered down the slope, waving his pistol.

'Pom, don't you let that barker off!' shouted the Viscount, abreast of him, and levelling his own slenderer weapon. Rising in his stirrups, he pulled the trigger, and saw one of the postilions duck as the shot whistled over his head. The mare shied violently and tried to bolt. He held her head on her course, and came down like a thunderbolt across the road. 'Stand and deliver!—steady, lass!'

The postilions had dragged their frightened horses to a standstill. Captain Heron pressed up closer, covering them with his pistol. Sir Roland, a connoisseur of horseflesh, had allowed his attention to be diverted by the two wheelers, and was studying them closely.

The Viscount and Mr Hawkins had ridden up to the chaise. The window was let down with a bang, and an old gentleman with a red face pushed his head and shoulders out, and extending his arm fired a small pistol at the Viscount. 'Dastardly rogues! Cut-throat robbers! Drive on, you cowardly rascals!' he spluttered.

The shot sang past the Viscount's ear; the mare reared up in alarm, and was steadied again. 'Hi, mind what you're about, sir!' said his lordship indignantly. 'You devilish near got me in the head!'

Mr Hawkins on the other side of the chaise, thrust his pistol into the old gentleman's face. 'Drop your pops!' he growled. 'And step out, d'you see? Come on, out with you!' He let the reins fall on his horse's neck, and leaned sideways in the saddle, and wrenched open the door of the chaise. 'A rare gager, you are! Hand over your truss! Ah, and that pretty lobb o' yourn!'

The Viscount said quickly: 'Draw off, you fool! Wrong man!'

'Lordy, he's good enough for me!' replied Mr Hawkins, wresting a snuff-box from the old gentleman's grasp. 'A nice little lobb, this! Come on now, where's your truss?'

'I'll have the Watch on you!' raved his victim. 'Damnable! Broad daylight! Take that, you thief!' With which he dashed his hat at Mr Hawkin's pistol, and diving back into the coach seized a long ebony cane.

'Lord, he'll have an apoplexy,' said the Viscount, and rode round the chaise to Mr Hawkins's side. 'Give me that snuff-box,' he ordered briefly. 'Edward! Here, Edward! Take the fool away! We've got the wrong man.' He dodged a blow aimed at his head with the ebony cane, tossed the snuff-box into the chaise, and reined back. 'Let 'em go, Pom!' he called.

Sir Roland came round to him. 'Wrong man, is it? Tell you what, Pel—as nice a pair of wheelers as I've seen. Just what I've been looking for. Think he'd sell?'

The old gentleman, still perched on the step of the chaise, shook his fist at them. 'Murderous dogs!' he raved. 'You'll find I'm a match for you, you rogues! Don't like the look of this little cane of mine, eh? I'll break the head of the first man to come a step nearer! Robbers and cowards! White-livered scoundrels! Drive on, you damned shivering fools! Ride 'em down!'

Captain Heron, in charge of the baffled Mr Hawkins, said in a voice that shook with suppressed mirth: 'For God's sake come away! He'll burst a blood-vessel at this rate.'

'Wait a bit,' said Sir Roland. He swept off his abominable beaver, and bowed over his horse's withers. 'Haven't the honour of knowing your name, sir, but you've a very pretty pair of wheelers there. Looking for just such a pair.'

The old gentleman gave a scream of rage. 'Insolence! Steal my horses, would you? Postilion! I command you, drive on!'

'No, no! Assure you nothing of the sort!' protested Sir Roland.

Captain Heron bore down upon him, and seizing his bridle, dragged him away. 'Come away,' he said, 'you'll ruin us all, you young madman!'

Sir Roland allowed himself to be led off. 'A pity,' he said, shaking his head. 'Great pity. Never saw such a queer-tempered fellow.'

The Viscount, who was speaking a few pithy words to Mr Hawkins, turned his head. 'How the devil should he know you wanted to buy his horses? Besides, we haven't time to buy horses. We'd better get back to our ambush. Mare stood the firing pretty well, didn't you, sweetheart?'

Captain Heron watched the chaise rolling away up the road. 'He'll lay information in Hounslow, Pelham, you mark my words.'

'Let him,' said the Viscount. 'He won't get the Watch out against us. Why, we didn't take a thing!'

'Not a thing,' muttered Mr Hawkins sulkily. 'And him with his strong-box under the seat! Dang me if I ever works with flash culls again!'

'Don't keep on saying that,' said the Viscount. 'You can take what you like from the right man, but you don't rob anyone else while you're with me!'

They rode on up the slope, and once more dismounted. 'Well, if I'm broke for this, I think I'll take to the—what-do-you call it? Bridle-lay. I'd no notion it was so easy,' said Captain Heron.

'Yes, but I don't like the clothes,' said the Viscount. 'Devilish hot!'

Sir Roland sighed. 'Beautiful wheelers!' he murmured sadly.

The afternoon wore on. Another wagon lumbered past, three more horsemen, and one stage.

'Can't have missed the fellow, can we?' fretted the Viscount.

'All we missed was our luncheon,' replied Captain Heron. He pulled his watch out. 'It's on three already, and I dine in South Street at five.'

'Dining with my mother, are you?' said the Viscount. 'Well, the cook's damned bad, Edward, and so I warn you. Couldn't stand it myself. One reason why I live in lodgings. What's that, Hawkins? Heard something?'

'There's a chaise coming up the road,' said Mr Hawkins. 'And I hope it's the right one,' he added bitterly.

When it came into sight, a smart, shining affair, slung on very high swan's-neck springs, the Viscount said: 'That's more like it! Now then, Pom, we've got him!'

The manœuvre that had succeeded so well with the first chaise, succeeded again. The postilions, alarmed to find no less than four ruffians descending upon them, drew up in a hurry. Captain Heron once more covered them with his pistol, and the Viscount dashed up to the chaise, shouting in as gruff a voice as he could assume: 'Stand and deliver there! Come on, out of that!'

There were two gentlemen in the chaise. The younger of them started forward, levelling a small pistol. The other laid a hand on his wrist. 'Don't fire, my dear boy,' he said placidly. 'I would really rather that you did not.'

The Viscount's pistol hand dropped. He uttered a smothered exclamation.

'Wrong again!' growled Mr Hawkins disgustedly.

The Earl of Rule stepped unhurriedly down on to the road. His placid gaze rested on the Viscount's mare. 'Dear me!' he said. 'And—er—what do you want me to deliver, Pelham?'

21

Not long after four o'clock a furious knocking was heard on the door of the Earl of Rule's town house. Horatia, who was on her way upstairs to change her gown, stopped and turned pale. When the porter opened the door and she saw Sir Roland Pommeroy on the doorstep without his hat, she gave a shriek, and sped down the stairs again. 'Good G-God, what has happened?' she cried.

Sir Roland, who seemed much out of breath, bowed punctiliously. 'Apologize unseemly haste, ma'am! Must beg a word in private!'

'Yes, yes, of course!' said Horatia, and dragged him into the library. 'Someone's k-killed? Oh, n-not Pelham? Not P-Pelham?'

'No, ma'am, upon my honour! Nothing of that sort. Most unfortunate chance! Pel desired me to apprise you instantly. Rode home post-haste—left my horse nearest stables—ran round to wait on you. Not a moment to lose!'

'Well, w-what is it?' demanded Horatia. 'You found L-Lethbridge?'

'Not Lethbridge, ma'am, Rule!' said Sir Roland, and flicking his handkerchief from his sleeve, dabbed at his heated brow.

'Rule?' exclaimed Horatia in accents of the profoundest dismay.

'No less, ma'am. Very awkward situation.'

'You—you d-didn't hold Rule up?' she gasped.

Sir Roland nodded. 'Very, very awkward,' he said.

'Did he re-recognize you?'

'Deeply regret, ma'am—recognized Pel's mare.'

Horatia wrung her hands. 'Oh, was ever anything so unlucky? What d-did he say? What d-did he think? What in the world b-brings him home so soon?'

'Beg you won't distress yourself, ma'am. Pel carried it off. Presence of mind, you know—mighty clever fellow, Pel!'

'B-but I don't see how he could carry it off!' said Horatia.

'Assure your ladyship, nothing simpler. Told him it was a wager.'

'D-did he believe it?' asked Horatia, round-eyed.

'Certainly!' said Sir Roland. 'Told him we mistook his chaise for another's. Plausible story—why not? But Pel thought you should be warned he was on his way.'

'Oh, yes, indeed!' she said. 'But L-Lethbridge? My b-brooch?'

Sir Roland tucked his handkerchief away again. 'Can't make the fellow out,' he replied. 'Ought to be home by now, instead of which—no sign of him. Pel and Heron are waiting on with Hawkins. Have to carry a message to Lady Winwood. Heron—very good sort of a man indeed—can't dine in South Street now. Must try to stop Lethbridge, you see. Beg you won't let it distress you. Assure you—brooch shall be recovered. Rule suspects nothing—nothing at all, ma'am!'

Horatia trembled. 'I d-don't feel as though I can p-possibly face him!' she said.

Sir Roland, uneasily aware that she was on the brink of tears, retreated towards the door. 'Not the slightest cause for alarm, ma'am. Think I should be going, however. Won't do for him to find me here.'

'No,' agreed Horatia forlornly. 'No, I s-suppose it won't.'

When Sir Roland had bowed himself out she went slowly upstairs again, and to her bed-chamber, where her abigail was waiting to dress her. She had promised to join her sister-in-law at Drury Lane Theatre after dinner, and a grande toilette in satin of that extremely fashionable colour called Stifled Sigh was laid out over a chair. The abigail, pouncing on her to untie her laces, informed her that M. Frédin (pupil of that celebrated academician in coiffures, M. Léonard of Paris) had already arrived, and was in the powder-closet. Horatia said 'Oh!' in a flat voice, and stepping out of her polonaise, listlessly permitted the satin underdress to be slipped over her head. She was put into her powdering-gown next, and then was delivered into the hands of M. Frédin.

This artist, failing to perceive his client's low spirits, was full of enthusiastic suggestions for a coiffure that should ravish all who beheld it. My lady has not cared for the Quésaco? Ah, no, by example! a little too sophisticated! My lady would prefer her hair dressed in Foaming Torrents—a charming mode! Or—my lady being *petite*—perhaps the Butterfly would better please the eye.

'I d-don't care,' said my lady.

M. Frédin, extracting pins with swift dexterity, shaking out rolled curls, combing away a tangle, was disappointed, but redoubled his efforts. My lady, without doubt, desired something new, something *épatante*. One could not consider the Hedgehog, therefore, but my lady would be transported by the Mad Dog. A mode of the most distinguished: he would not suggest the Sportsman in a Bush; that was for Ladies past their first blush; but the Royal Bird was always a favourite; or, if my lady was in a pensive mood, the Milksop.

'Oh, d-dress it *à l'urgence*!' said Horatia impatiently. 'I'm l-late!'

M. Frédin was chagrined, but he was too wise in the knowledge of ladies' whims to expostulate. His deft fingers went busily to work, and in an astonishingly short space of time Horatia emerged from the closet, her head a mass of artlessly tumbled curls, dashed over with powder *à la Maréchale*, violet-scented.

She sat down at her dressing-table, and picked up the rouge-pot. It would never do for Rule to see her looking so pale. Oh, if it was not that odious Serkis rouge that made her look a hag! Take it away at once!

She had just laid down the haresfoot and taken the patch-box out of the abigail's hand when someone scratched on the door. She started, and cast a scared look over her shoulder. The door opened and the Earl came in.

'Oh!' said Horatia faintly. She remembered that she must show surprise, and added: 'G-good gracious, my l-lord, is–is it indeed you?'

The Earl had changed his travelling dress for an evening toilet of puce velvet, with a flowered waistcoat and satin small clothes. He came across the room to Horatia's side, and bent to kiss her hand. 'None other, my dear. Am I–now don't spare me–am I perhaps *de trop?*'

'No, of c-course not,' replied Horatia uncertainly. She felt a trifle breathless. At sight of him her heart had given the oddest leap. If the abigail had not been there–if she had not lost her brooch—! But the abigail, tiresome creature, was there, bobbing a curtsy, and Lethbridge had her brooch, and of course she could not fling herself into Rule's arms and burst into tears on his chest. She forced herself to smile. 'No, of c-course not,' she repeated. 'I am prodigiously g-glad to see you. But what brings you b-back so soon, sir?'

'You, Horry,' he answered, smiling down at her.

She blushed and opened the patch-box. Her thoughts jostled one another in her head. He must have broken with the Massey. He was beginning to love her at last. If he found out about Lethbridge and the brooch it would all be spoiled. She was the most deceitful wretch alive.

'Ah, but I beg you will let me show *my* skill,' said his lordship, removing the patch-box from her hand. He selected a tiny round of black taffeta, and gently turned Horatia's head towards him. 'Which shall it be?' he said. 'The Equivocal? I think not. The Gallant? No, not that. It shall be—' He pressed the patch at the corner of her mouth. 'The Kissing, Horry!' he said, and bent quickly and kissed her on the lips.

Her hand flew up, touched his cheek, and fell again. Deceitful, odious wretch that she was! She drew back, trying to laugh. 'My l-lord, we are not alone! And I–I m-must dress, you know, for I p-promised to g-go with Louisa and Sir Humphrey to the p-play at Drury Lane.'

He straightened. 'Shall I send a message to Louisa, or shall I go with you to this play?' he inquired.

'Oh–oh, I m-mustn't disappoint her, sir!' said Horatia in a hurry. It would never do to be alone with him a whole evening. She might blurt out the whole story, and then–if he believed her–he must think her the most tiresome wife, for ever in a scrape.

'Then we will go together,' said his lordship. 'I'll await you downstairs, my love.'

Twenty minutes later they faced one another across the dining table. 'I trust,' said his lordship, carving the duck, 'that you were tolerably well amused while I was away, my dear?'

Tolerably well amused? Good heavens! 'Oh, yes, sir–t-tolerably well,' replied Horatia politely.

'The Richmond House ball–were you not going to that?'

Horatia gave an involuntary shudder. 'Yes, I–went to that.'

'Are you cold, Horry?'

'C-cold? No, sir, n-not at all.'

'I thought you shivered,' said his lordship.

'N-no,' said Horatia. 'Oh, no! The–the Richmond House b-ball. It was vastly pretty, with fireworks, you know. Only my shoes p-pinched me, so I d-didn't enjoy myself m-much. They were new ones, too, with diamonds sewn on them, and I was so c-cross I should have sent them back to the m-makers only that they were ruined by the wet.'

'Ruined by the wet?' repeated the Earl.

Horatia's fork clattered on her plate. That was what came of trying to make conversation! She had known how it would be; of course she would make a slip! 'Oh, yes!' she said breathlessly. 'I f-forgot to tell you! The b-ball was spoiled by rain. Wasn't it a pity? I–I got my feet wet.'

'That certainly was a pity,' agreed Rule. 'And what did you do yesterday?'

'Yesterday?' said Horatia. 'Oh, I–I d-didn't do anything yesterday.'

There was a laugh in his eyes. 'My dear Horry, I never thought to hear such a confession from you,' he said.

'No, I–I did not feel very w-well, so I–I–so I stayed at home.'

'Then I suppose you haven't yet seen Edward,' remarked the Earl.

Horatia, who was sipping her claret, choked. 'Good gracious, yes! Now, however c-could I have come to forget that? Only f-fancy, Rule, Edward is in town!' She was aware that she was sinking deeper into the quagmire, and tried to recover her false step. 'B-but how did you know he was here?' she asked.

The Earl waited while the footman removed his plate, and set another in its place. 'I have seen him,' he replied.

'Oh–oh, have you? W-where?'

'On Hounslow Heath,' replied the Earl, putting up his glass to survey a pupton of cherries which was being offered to him. 'No, I think not. . . . Yes, on Hounslow Heath, Horry. A most unexpected rencontre.'

'It m-must have been. I–I wonder w-what he was doing there?'

'He was holding me up,' said the Earl calmly.

'Oh, w-was he?' Horatia swallowed a cherry stone inadvertently and coughed. 'How–how very odd of him!'

'Very imprudent of him,' said the Earl.

'Yes, v-very. P-perhaps he was doing it for a w-wager,' suggested Horatia, mindful of Sir Roland's words.

'I believe he was.' Across the table the Earl's eyes met hers. 'Pelham and his friend Pommeroy were also of the party. I fear I was not the victim they expected.'

'W-weren't you? No, of c-course you weren't! I mean–d-don't you think it is t-time we started for the p-play, sir?'

Rule got up. 'Certainly, my dear.' He picked up her taffeta cloak and put it round her shoulders. 'May I be permitted to venture a suggestion?' he said gently.

She glanced nervously at him. 'Why, y-yes, sir! What is it?'

'You should not wear rubies with that particular shade of satin, my dear. The pearl set would better become it.'

There was an awful silence; Horatia's throat felt parched suddenly; her heart was thumping violently. 'It–it is too l-late to change them n-now!' she managed to say.

'Very well,' Rule said, and opened the door for her to pass out.

All the way to Drury Lane Horatia kept up a flow of conversation. What she found to talk about she could never afterwards remember, but talk she did, until the coach drew up at the theatre, and she was safe from a *tête-à-tête* for three hours.

Coming home there was of course the play to be discussed, and the acting, and Lady Louisa's new gown, and these topics left no room for more dangerous ones. Pleading fatigue, Horatia went early to bed, and lay for a long time wondering what Pelham had done, and what she should do if Pelham had failed.

She awoke next morning heavy-eyed and despondent. Her chocolate was brought in on a tray with her letters. She sipped it, and with her free hand turned over the billets in the hope of seeing the Viscount's sprawling handwriting. But there was no letter from him, only a sheaf of invitations and bills.

Setting down her cup she began to open these missives. Yes, just as she had thought. A rout-party; a card-party; she did not care if she never touched a card again; a picnic to Boxhill: never! of course it would rain; a concert at Ranelagh: well, she only hoped she would never be obliged to go to that odious place any more! . . . Good God, could one have spent three hundred and seventy-five guineas at a mantua-maker's? And what was this? Five plumes at fifty louis apiece! Well, that was really too provoking, when they had been bought for that abominable Quésaco coiffure which had not become her at all.

She broke the seal of another letter, and spread open the single sheet of plain, gilt-edged paper. The words, clearly written in a copper-plate hand, fairly jumped at her.

> If the Lady who lost a ring-brooch of pearls and diamonds in Half-Moon Street on the night of the Richmond House Ball will come alone to the Grecian Temple at the end of the Long Walk at Vauxhall Gardens at midnight precisely on the twenty-eighth day of September, the brooch shall be restored to her by the Person in whose possession it now is.

There was no direction, no signature; the handwriting was obviously disguised. Horatia stared at it for one incredulous minute and then, with a smothered shriek, thrust her chocolate tray into the abigail's hands and cast off the bed-clothes. 'Quick, I m-must get up at once!' she said. 'Lay me out a w-walking dress, and a hat, and my g-gloves! Oh, and run d-downstairs and tell someone to order the l-landaulet—no, not, the l-landaulet! my town-coach, to c-come round in half an hour. And take all these l-letters away, and oh, d-do p-please hurry!'

For once she wasted no time over her toilet, and half an hour later ran down the stairs, her sunshade caught under her arm, her gloves only half on. There was no sign of Rule, and after casting a wary glance in the direction of the library door, she sped past it and was out in the street before anyone could have time to observe her flight.

The coach was waiting, and directing the coachman to drive to Lord Winwood's lodging in Pall Mall, Horatia climbed in and sank back against the cushions with a sigh of relief at having succeeded in leaving the house without encountering Rule.

The Viscount was at breakfast when his sister was announced, and looked up with a frown. 'Lord, Horry, what the devil brings you at this hour? You shouldn't have come; if Rule knows you've dashed off at daybreak it's enough to make him suspect something's amiss.'

Horatia thrust a trembling hand into her reticule and extracted a crumpled sheet of gilt-edged paper. 'Th-that's what brings me!' she said. 'Read it!'

The Viscount took the letter and smoothed it out. 'Well, sit down, there's a good girl. Have some breakfast . . . Here, what's this?'

'P-Pel, can it be L-Lethbridge?' she asked.

The Viscount turned the letter over, as though seeking enlightenment on the back of it. 'Dashed if I know!' he said. 'Looks to me like a trap.'

'B-but why should it be? Do you think p-perhaps he is sorry?'

'No, I don't,' said his lordship frankly. 'I'd say at a guess that the fellow's trying to get his hands on you. End of the Long Walk? Ay, I know that Temple. Devilish draughty it is, too. And it's near one of the gates. Tell you what, Horry: I'll lay you a pony he means to abduct you.'

Horatia clasped her hands. 'But, P-Pel, I must go! I must try and g-get the brooch b-back!'

'So you shall,' said the Viscount briskly. 'We'll see some sport now!' He gave back the letter and took a long drink of ale. 'Now you listen to me, Horry!' he ordered. 'We'll all go to Vauxhall to-night—you and I and Pom, and Edward too if he likes. At midnight you'll go to that temple, and the rest of us will lie hid in the shrubbery there. We shall see who goes in, never fear. If it's Lethbridge, we've got him. If it's another—though, mind you, it looks to me like Lethbridge—you've only to give a squawk and we'll hear you. We shall have that damned brooch by to-morrow, Horry!'

Horatia nodded. 'Yes, that's a very clever plan, P-Pel. And I'll tell Rule that I am g-going with you, and he w-won't mind that at all. D-didn't Lethbridge c-come to town yesterday?'

The Viscount scowled. 'Can't have done. Edward and that fellow Hawkins and I stayed till past nine on that cursed Heath, and never saw a sign of him. You know we stopped Rule's chaise?'

'Yes, of c-course. Sir Roland told me and Rule did too.'

'Gave me a devilish queer turn when I saw who it was,' confessed the Viscount. 'He's quick, is Rule. Must own he's quick, Horry. Recognized my mare the instant he clapped eyes on her.'

'B-but he didn't suspect, P-Pel? You're sure he d-didn't suspect?' she cried anxiously.

'Lord, no! How should he?' said the Viscount. He glanced at the clock. 'I'd best get hold of Pom, and as for you, you go home, Horry.'

Arrived once more in Grosvenor Square, Horatia discarded her hat and her gloves and went in search of Rule. She found him in the library, reading the *Morning Chronicle*. He rose at her entrance and held out his hand. 'Well, my love? You're up betimes.'

Horatia put her hand in his. 'It was such a f-fine morning,' she explained. 'And I am to d-drive in the park with M-Mama.'

'I see,' he said. He lifted her fingers to his lips. 'Is not to-day the twenty-eighth, Horry?'

'Yes. Yes, it is,' she replied.

'Then will you come with me to the ball at Almack's rooms?' suggested Rule.

Consternation spread over her face. 'Oh—oh, how d-delightful that would be!' she said. 'Only I c-can't! I've promised to go to Vauxhall with P-Pel.'

'I have always found,' remarked his lordship pensively, 'that most of one's engagements were only made to be broken.'

'I can't break this one,' Horatia said with real regret.

'Is it so important? You will make me jealous, Horry—of Pelham.'

'It's very, very important!' she said earnestly. 'That is to say, I m-mean—Well, P-Pel wants me to be there particularly, you see!'

The Earl was playing with her fingers. 'Do you think Pel would permit me to make one of this expedition?' he said.

'Oh, no, I am quite sure he w-wouldn't like that at all!' said Horatia, appalled. 'At least—I d-don't mean that, of course, but—but he is to present some people to me, and they are strangers, you see, and I daresay you would not c-care for them.'

'But I have a reputation for being the most friendly of mortals,' said the Earl plaintively. He let go her hand and turned to arrange his cravat in the mirror. 'Don't distress yourself on my account, my dear. If I don't care for these strangers I promise I will dissemble.'

Horatia gazed at him in complete dismay. 'I d-don't think you would enjoy it, M-Marcus. Really, I do not.'

He bowed slightly. 'At your side, Horry, I could enjoy anything,' he said. 'And now, my dear, if you will excuse me, I will go and attend to all the affairs which my poor Arnold wants me to deal with.'

Horatia watched him go out of the room, and straightway sat herself down at the desk in the window and scribbled a frantic note to her brother.

This missive, brought by hand, reached the Viscount's lodging just as he came back to it from his visit to Sir Roland. He read it, swore under his breath, and dashed off an answer.

'*The devil fly away with Rule,*' he wrote. '*I'll set Pom on to draw him off.*'

When this brief note was delivered to her Horatia read it rather doubtfully. Her experience of Sir Roland's tact was not such as to lead her to place very much reliance on his handling of an awkward situation. However, she herself had said all she dared to dissuade Rule from accompanying her to Vauxhall, and Sir Roland could hardly be less successful.

The Earl was still closeted with Mr Gisborne when a lackey came in to announce that Sir Roland Pommeroy desired to speak with him. He looked up from the paper he was about to sign, and Mr Gisborne, who happened to be watching him, was surprised to see a gleam of amusement in his eyes. The information that Sir Roland had called did not seem to warrant that particular gleam. 'Very well,' said his lordship. 'Tell Sir Roland that I will be with him immediately . . . Alas, Arnold, something always interrupts us, does it not? I am quite desolated, believe me, but I shall have to go.'

'Desolated, sir?' said Mr Gisborne, cocking an eyebrow. 'If you will permit me to say so, I thought that you looked rather pleased.'

'But that was not because the interruption drags me from your side, my dear boy,' said his lordship, putting down his quill and rising. 'I am enjoying myself this morning.'

Mr Gisborne wondered why.

Sir Roland Pommeroy had been shown into one of the saloons, and was standing by the window when the Earl came in. From the movement of his lips it might have been supposed that he was silently rehearsing a speech.

'Good morning, Pommeroy,' said the Earl, closing the door. 'This is an unexpected pleasure.'

Sir Roland turned and came forward. ''Morning, Rule, Beautiful day! Trust you reached home safely yesterday? Extremely distressed I should have mistaken your chaise for—er—for the other one.'

'Not at all,' replied his lordship with great civility. 'There was not the slightest need for you to put yourself to the trouble of calling, my dear fellow.'

Sir Roland tugged at his cravat. 'To tell you the truth—didn't come on that score,' he confessed. 'Felt sure you would understand how it was.'

'Quite right,' said the Earl, opening his snuff-box. 'I did understand.'

Sir Roland helped himself to a pinch and sniffed it up one nostril. 'Very good blend. I always have my own put up by my man in the Haymarket. Always use the same, you know. Plain Spanish.'

'Ah, indeed?' said the Earl. 'This is blended for me by Jacobs, in the Strand.'

Sir Roland perceived that he was being led into a discussion that had nothing whatsoever to do with his mission, and firmly abandoned it. 'Reason I called,' he said, 'was quite different. Hoping very much you will join a little card-party–my house–this evening.'

'Why, this is very kind of you,' said Rule, with the faintest inflexion of surprise in his pleasant voice.

This was not lost on Sir Roland, who, thrust out by the Viscount to 'draw off' his lordship, had protested feebly: 'Deuce take it, Pel, I hardly know the man! Years older than I am! Can't ask him to my house like that!' He sought once more to loosen his cravat, and said: 'Aware–devilish short notice–trust you'll forgive–very difficult to find a fourth. Last moment, you understand. Game of whisk.'

'Nothing,' said the Earl, 'would please me more than to be able to oblige you, my dear Pommeroy. Unfortunately, however—'

Sir Roland threw up his hand. 'Now don't say you cannot come! Pray do not! Can't play whisk with only three people, my lord. Most awkward situation!'

'I am sure it must be,' agreed his lordship sympathetically. 'And I expect you have tried everyone else.'

'Oh, everyone!' said Sir Roland. 'Can't find a fourth at all. Do beg of your lordship not to fail me!'

'I am extremely sorry,' said the Earl, shaking his head. 'But I fear I must decline your–er–very flattering invitation. You see, I have promised to join a party at Vauxhall Gardens with my wife.'

'Feel sure her ladyship would excuse you–almost bound to rain–very dull evening!' said Sir Roland feverishly. 'Apprehend it is Pel's party–not your taste at all, sir. Very queer people, Pel's friends. Wouldn't like them, I assure you.'

The Earl's lips twitched. 'You quite decide me, my dear Pommeroy. If they are like that I think I would rather be at her ladyship's side.'

'Oh, they are not!' said Sir Roland hastily. 'Oh, dear me, no, nothing of that sort! Very respectable people, but dull, you know–a set of company you would not like. Much better play whisk at my house.'

'Do you really think so?' The Earl appeared to meditate. 'I am, of course, very fond of whisk.'

Sir Roland breathed a sigh of relief. 'Knew I could count on you! Beg you will dine first–five o'clock.'

'Who are your other guests?' inquired his lordship.

'Well, to tell you the truth–not quite sure yet,' said Sir Roland confidentially. 'Bound to find someone glad of a game. Have it all fixed by five o'clock.'

'You tempt me very much,' said the Earl. 'And yet–no, I fear I must not yield. Some other evening, perhaps. You'll take a glass of madeira with me before you go?'

The crestfallen Sir Roland shook his head. 'Thank you, no–must get back to–that is to say, must get to Boodle's. Might find a fourth there, you understand. No chance of persuading your lordship?'

'I regret infinitely, but none,' Rule answered. 'I must–I positively must accompany my wife.'

Sir Roland went sadly back to Pall Mall, where he found the Viscount kicking his heels impatiently. 'No good, Pel,' he said. 'Did what I could–no moving him.'

'The devil fly away with the fellow!' said the Viscount wrathfully. 'What in thunder ails him? Here we have the whole affair planned out as snug as you please, and he must needs ruin all by taking it into his head to join my party! Damme, I won't have him in my party!'

Sir Roland rubbed his chin thoughtfully with the knob of his cane. 'Trouble is, Pel, you haven't got a party,' he said.

The Viscount, who had cast himself into a chair, said irritably: 'What the hell does that matter?'

'Does matter,' insisted Sir Roland. 'Here's Rule joining you to-night, and I told him he wouldn't like the party–said they were queer people–hoping to put him off, you know–and if you don't arrange a party–well, you see what I mean, Pel?'

'Well, if that don't beat all!' said the Viscount indignantly. 'It ain't enough for me to waste the whole day planning this damned affair, I have to get a party together as well just to fall in with your silly tale! Burn it we don't want a party! Where am I to find a lot of queer people? Tell me that!'

'Meant it for the best, Pel,' said Sir Roland placatingly. 'Meant it for the best! Must be any number of queer people in town–know there are–Club's full of them.'

'But they ain't friends of mine!' replied the Viscount. 'You can't go round the Club asking a lot of queer-looking strangers to come to Vauxhall with you. Besides, what should we do with them when we got 'em there?'

'Give them supper,' said Sir Roland. 'While they have supper we slip off–get the brooch–come back–ten to one no one notices.'

'Well, I won't do it!' said the Viscount flatly. 'We'll have to think of some way to keep Rule off.'

Ten minutes later Captain Heron walked in to find both gentlemen plunged in profound thought, the Viscount propping his chin in his hands, Sir Roland sucking the head of his cane. Captain Heron looked from one to the other, and said: 'I came to see what you mean to do next. You've heard nothing of Lethbridge, I suppose?'

The Viscount lifted his head. 'By God, I have it!' he exclaimed. 'You shall draw Rule off!'

'I shall do what?' asked Captain Heron, startled.

'I don't see how,' objected Sir Roland.

'Lord, Pom, nothing easier! Private affairs to discuss. Rule can't refuse.'

Captain Heron laid his hat and gloves down on the table. 'Pelham, do you mind explaining? Why has Rule to be drawn off?'

'Why, because of–oh, you don't know, do you? You see, Horry's had a letter from someone offering to give her back the brooch if she'll meet him in the temple at the end of the Long Walk at Vauxhall to-night. Looks like Lethbridge to me–must be Lethbridge. Well, I had it all fixed that she and I and Pom here and you should go to Vauxhall, and while she went to the temple we'd stand guard.'

'That seems a good idea,' nodded Captain Heron. 'But it's surely odd of—'

'Of course it's a good plan! It's a devilish good plan. But what must that plaguy fellow Rule do but take it into his head to come too! As soon as I heard that I sent Pom off to invite him to a card-party at his house.'

Sir Roland sighed. 'Pressed him as much as I could. No use. Bent on going to Vauxhall.'

'But how the deuce am I to stop him?' asked Captain Heron.

'You're the very man!' said the Viscount. 'All you have to do is to go off to Grosvenor Square now and tell Rule you've matters of importance to discuss with him. If he asks you to discuss 'em at once, you say you can't. Business to attend to. Only time you can spare is this evening. That's reasonable enough: Rule knows you're only in town for a day or two. Burn it, he can't refuse!'

'Yes, but, Pelham, I haven't anything of importance to discuss with him!' protested Captain Heron.

'Lord, you can think of something, can't you?' said the Viscount. 'It don't signify what you talk about as long as you keep him away from Vauxhall. Family affairs—money—anything!'

'I'm damned if I will!' said Captain Heron. 'After all Rule's done for me I can't and I won't tell him that I want to talk about money!'

'Well, don't tell him so. Just say you must have a private word with him to-night. He ain't the man to ask you what it's about, and dash it, Edward, you must be able to talk about something when it comes to the point!'

'Of course you must,' corroborated Sir Roland. 'Nothing simpler. You've been at this War in America, haven't you? Well, tell him about that. Tell him about that battle you was in—forgotten its name.'

'But I can't beg Rule to give me an evening alone with him, and then sit telling him stories he don't want to hear about the war!'

'I wouldn't say that,' temporized Sir Roland. 'You don't know he doesn't want to hear them. Any number of people take a deal of interest in this war. I don't myself, but that ain't to say Rule doesn't.'

'You don't seem to understand,' said Captain Heron wearily. 'You expect me to make Rule believe I've urgent business to discuss with him—'

The Viscount interposed. 'It's you who don't understand,' he said. 'All we care about is keeping Rule away from Vauxhall to-night. If we don't do it the game's up. It don't matter a ha'porth how you keep him away so long as you do keep him away.'

Captain Heron hesitated. 'I know that. I'd do it if only I could think of anything reasonable to discuss with him.'

'You'll think of it, never fear,' said the Viscount encouragingly. 'Why, you've got the whole afternoon before you. Now you go round to Grosvenor Square at once, there's a good fellow.'

'I wish to God I'd put off my visit to town till next week!' groaned Captain Heron, reluctantly picking up his hat again.

The Earl of Rule was just about to go in to luncheon when his second visitor was announced. 'Captain Heron?' he said. 'Oh, by all means show him in!' He waited, standing before the empty fireplace until the Captain came in. 'Well, Heron?' he said, holding out his hand. 'You come just in time to bear me company over luncheon.'

Captain Heron blushed in spite of himself. 'I'm afraid I can't stay, sir. I'm due in Whitehall almost immediately. I came—you know my time is limited—I came to ask you whether it would be convenient—in short, whether I might wait on you this evening for—for a talk of a confidential nature.'

The Earl's amused glance rested on him thoughtfully. 'I suppose it must be to-night?' he said.

'Well, sir—if you could arrange—I hardly know how I may manage tomorrow,' said Captain Heron, acutely uncomfortable.

There was a slight pause. 'Then naturally I am quite at your service,' replied his lordship.

22

The Viscount, resplendent in maroon velvet, with a fall of Dresden lace at his throat, and his hair thickly powdered and curled in pigeon's wings over the ears, came at his sister's urgent request to dine in Grosvenor Square before taking her on to Vauxhall. His presence protected her from a *tête-à-tête* and if Rule was minded to ask any more awkward questions he, she considered, was better able to answer them than she was.

The Earl, however, behaved with great consideration and conversed affably on most unexceptionable topics. The only bad moment he gave them was when he promised to follow them to Vauxhall if Captain Heron did not detain him at home too long.

'But we've no need to worry over that,' said the Viscount as he got into his coach beside Horatia. 'Edward's pledged himself to keep Rule in check till midnight, and by that time we shall have laid hands on that trumpery brooch of yours at last.'

'It isn't a trumpery b-brooch!' said Horatia. 'It's an heirloom!'

'It may be an heirloom,' replied the Viscount, 'but it's caused more trouble than any heirloom was ever worth, and I've come to hate the very mention of it.'

The coach set them down by the waterside, where the Viscount hired a boat to take them the rest of the way. They had three hours to while away before midnight and neither of them was in the mood for dancing. Sir Roland Pommeroy met them at the entrance to the gardens and was very punctilious in handing Horatia out of the boat on to the landing-stage, warning her against wetting her silkshod foot on a damp patch, and proffering his arm with a great air. As he escorted her down one of the walks towards the centre of the gardens he begged her not to be nervous. 'Assure your la'ship Pel and I shall be on the watch!' he said.

'I'm not n-nervous,' replied Horatia, 'I w-want very much to see Lord Lethbridge, for I have a great desire to tell him just what I think of him!' Her dark eyes smouldered. 'If it weren't for the scandal,' she announced, 'I d-declare I wish he would abduct me, I would make him sorry he d-dared!'

A glance at her fierce frown almost persuaded Sir Roland that she would.

When they arrived at the pavilion they found that in addition to the dancing and the other amusements provided for the entertainment of the company, an oratorio was being performed in the concert hall. Since neither the Viscount nor his sister wished to dance, Sir Roland suggested that they should sit for a while and listen to this. He himself had no great opinion of music, but the only distraction likely to find favour with the Viscount or Horatia was gaming, and he wisely dissuaded them from entering the cardroom, on the score that once they had sat down to pharaoh or loo they would entirely forget the real object of their expedition.

Horatia fell in with this suggestion readily enough: diversions were all alike to her until the ring-brooch was in her possession again. The Viscount said that he supposed it could not be more tedious than walking about the gardens or sitting in one of the boxes with nothing to do but to watch the other people passing by. Accordingly they made their way to the concert hall and went in. A play-bill handed them at the door advertised that the oratorio was *Susanna*, by Handel, a circumstance that nearly made the Viscount turn back at once. If he had known it was a piece by that fellow Handel, nothing would have induced him to come within earshot of it, much less to have paid half a guinea for a ticket. He had once been obliged by his Mama to accompany her to a performance of *Judas Maccabeus*. Of course he had not had the remotest notion what it would be like or not even filial duty would have dragged him to it, but he did know now and he was damned if he would stand it a second time.

A dowager in an enormous turban who was seated at the end of the row said 'Hush!' in accents so severe that the Viscount subsided meekly into his chair and whispered to Sir Roland: 'Must try and get out of this, Pom!' However, even his audacity failed before the ordeal of squeezing past the knees of so many musical devotees again, and after glancing wildly to right and left he resigned himself to slumber. The hardness of his chair and the noise the performers made rendered sleep impossible, and he sat in increasing indignation until at long last the oratorio came to an end.

'W-well, I think perhaps I d-don't care very much for Handel either,' remarked Horatia, as they filed out of the hall. 'Though now I c-come to think of it, I believe M-Mama said that *Susanna* was not a very good oratorio. Some of the singing was p-pretty, wasn't it?'

'Never heard such a din in my life!' said the Viscount. 'Let's go and bespeak some supper.'

Green goose and burgundy partaken of in one of the boxes did much to restore his equanimity, and he had just told Horatia that they might as well stay where they were in comfort until midnight, when Sir Roland, who had been studying the throng through his quizzing-glass, suddenly said: 'Ain't that Miss Winwood, Pel?'

The Viscount nearly choked over his wine. 'Good God, where?'

Horatia set down her glass of ratafia. 'Ch-Charlotte?' she gasped.

'Over there—blue sacque—pink ribbons,' said Sir Roland, pointing.

'I c-can't see, but it sounds very l-like,' said Horatia pessimistically. 'She will wear blue and it d-doesn't become her in the least.'

By this time the Viscount had perceived his elder sister, and gave a groan. 'Ay, it's Charlotte sure enough. Lord, she's with Theresa Maulfrey!'

Horatia caught up her cloak and her reticule and retired to the back of the box. 'If Theresa sees us she'll c-come and join us, and we shall n-never shake her off!' she said agitatedly. 'P-Pel, do come away!'

The Viscount consulted his watch. 'Eleven o'clock. What the deuce do we do now?'

'We shall have to w-walk about the gardens,' decided Horatia. 'D-dodge them, you know.'

Apparently Mrs Maulfrey's guests were also seized by an inclination to wander about the gardens. No less than five times did the two parties almost converge and the Viscount whisk his sister round to hurry off down a different path, and when the conspirators at last found a secluded seat in the Lovers' Walk the Viscount sank down upon it quite exhausted and declared that his sister might in the future lose every jewel in the Drelincourt collection before he would stir a finger to help her to recover them.

Sir Roland always gallant, protested. 'Pel, dear old boy, Pel!' he said reprovingly. 'Assure your la'ship—pleasure to be of assistance!'

'You can't say it's a pleasure to dodge round shrubberies and corners for the best part of an hour!' objected the Viscount. 'Not but what if we can but lay hands on Lethbridge I don't say it won't have been worth it.'

'What are you g-going to do with him?' inquired Horatia with interest.

'Never you mind!' replied the Viscount darkly, and exchanged a glance with Sir Roland. 'What do you make the time, Pom?'

Sir Roland consulted his watch. 'All but ten minutes to the hour, Pel.'

'Well, we'd best be moving,' said the Viscount, getting up.

Sir Roland laid a hand on his arm. 'Just thought of something,' he said. 'Suppose we find someone else in the temple?'

'Not at midnight,' replied the Viscount, having considered the matter. 'Everyone's at supper. Lethbridge must have thought of that. Are you ready, Horry? You ain't scared?'

'Of c-course I'm not scared!' said Horatia scornfully.

'Well, don't forget what you've to do,' said the Viscount. 'We'll leave you at the bottom of the Long Walk. Won't do to escort you any further. Fellow might be watching. All you have to do—'

'D-don't tell me all over again, P-Pel!' begged Horatia. 'You and Sir R-Roland will go to the temple the other way and hide and I am to g-go slowly up the Long Walk. And I'm not in the least afraid, except of meeting Charlotte.'

Several secluded paths led to the little temple at the end of the Long Walk, and since it was conveniently surrounded by flowering shrubs the Viscount and Sir Roland had no difficulty in concealing themselves hard by it. Sir Roland, indeed, was unfortunate enough to scratch himself on a particularly thorny rose-bush, but as there was no one within earshot at the moment this did not signify.

Meanwhile Horatia trod up the Long Walk, keeping a wary eye cocked for any sign of her sister. The Viscount had been right in supposing that most of the company would be at supper; Horatia met few people on the way. One or two couples were strolling down the Walk; near the lower end a party of young ladies were ogling in a very ill-bred manner every gentleman who passed; but towards the upper end the Walk grew more and more deserted. Encountering at first one or two stares from young bucks, Horatia felt rather conspicuous in being quite unattended, but her alarming frown stood her in good stead, and a rakish gentleman in puce satin who had taken a step in her direction retreated hastily.

The Walk was lit by coloured lamps, but a fine moon riding high in the sky made these almost superfluous, though pretty. At the end of the Walk Horatia could see the little temple, incongruously festooned with lanterns. She wondered where her faithful swains were lying in ambush and what Captain Heron was talking about in Grosvenor Square.

A few shallow steps led up to the temple. Feeling in spite of her brave words just a trifle apprehensive, Horatia paused at the foot of them and glanced nervously around. She thought that she had caught the sound of footsteps.

She was right. Someone was approaching down one of the smaller paths that led to the temple.

She drew her cloak closer about her shoulders, hesitated a moment, and then setting her lips firmly ran up the steps and into the temple.

The footsteps came nearer and she heard them on the steps and resolutely faced the pillared archway, secure in the knowledge that Pelham was within hail.

She was prepared for Lethbridge, or for a masked form, or even for a hired ruffian, but none of these sinister apparitions met her bemused gaze. It was the Earl of Rule who stood on the threshold.

'R-Rule!' she stammered. 'Oh, d-dear, whatever shall–I–I mean how you s-startled me! I was waiting for P-Pelham, I n-never expected to see you!'

The Earl came across the marble floor to her side. 'You see, I was able to–er–escape from Edward,' he said.

Outside, Sir Roland Pommeroy whispered aghast: 'Pel–Pel, dear fellow–did you see?'

'See?' hissed the Viscount. 'Of course I saw! Now what's to be done? The devil seize that fool Heron!'

Inside, Horatia said with a hollow little laugh: 'How–how d-delightful that you c-could come after all! Have–have you had s-supper?'

'No,' replied his lordship. 'I didn't come for supper, you know. I came to find you.'

Horatia forced a smile. 'That was very p-pretty of you, sir. But–but you should take some s-supper. Do pray g-go and bespeak a b-box and I will w-wait for P-Pel and bring him to join you.'

The Earl looked down at her whimsically. 'My dear, you are very anxious to be rid of me, are you not?'

Horatia's eyes lifted quickly to his, brimful of sudden tears. 'N-no, I am not! Only I–oh, I c-can't explain!' she said wretchedly.

'Horry,' said his lordship, gathering her hands into his, 'once I thought you trusted me.'

'I do–oh, I do!' cried Horatia. 'Only I've been such a bad wife, and I did m-mean not to get into a scrape while you were away, and though it w-wasn't my fault it n-never would have happened if I hadn't d-disobeyed you and l-let Lethbridge be a f-friend of mine, and even if you b-believe me, which I d-don't see how you can, because it's such an impossible story, you w-won't ever forgive me for having m-made another d-dreadful scandal!'

The Earl retained his hold on her hands. 'But, Horry, what have I done that you should think me such a bugbear?'

'You aren't a bugbear!' she said vehemently. 'But I know you'll w-wish you'd never m-married me when you hear what a scrape I am in!'

'It would have to be a very bad scrape to make me wish that,' said his lordship.

'W-well, it is,' replied Horatia candidly. 'And it's all in such a m-muddle I don't know how to explain it.' She cast an anxious glance towards the archway. 'I d-daresay you are wondering why I am in this place all by m-myself. Well—'

'Not at all,' said Rule. 'I know why you are here.'

She blinked at him. 'B-but you can't know!'

'But I do,' said Rule gently. 'You came to meet me.'

'No, I d-didn't,' said Horatia. 'In fact, I c-can't imagine how you knew I was here.'

His eyes were alight with amusement. 'Can't you, Horry?'

'N-no, unless—' her brows snapped together. 'Oh, surely Edward c-can't have b-betrayed me?' she exclaimed.

'Certainly not,' said his lordship. 'Edward made a most–really, a most praiseworthy–attempt to keep me at home. Indeed, I believe that if I had not taken him into my confidence he would have barred me into my own house.' He slipped his hand into his pocket and drew it out again. 'I came, Horry, to keep an assignation with a lady, and to restore to her—that.'

The ring-brooch lay in the palm of his hand. Horatia gave a choked cry. 'M-Marcus!' Her startled eyes flew to his and saw them smiling down at her. 'Then you—but how? Where did you f-find it?'

'In Lord Lethbridge's possession,' replied Rule.

'Then—then you know? You knew all the t-time? But how c-could you have? Who t-told you?'

'Crosby told me,' said the Earl. 'I am afraid I was rather rough with him, but I didn't think it would be good for him to know how deeply I was indebted to him.'

'Crosby!' said Horatia, her eyes kindling. 'Well, I don't care if he is your cousin, Rule, I think he is the m-most odious toad alive and I hope you strangled him!'

'I did,' said the Earl.

'I am very glad to hear it,' said Horatia warmly. 'And if it was he who t-told you, you c-can't possibly know the t-truth, because for one th-thing he wasn't there and d-doesn't know anything about it, and for another I am perfectly certain he made up some horrid t-tale just to put you against me!'

'That would be a task quite beyond Crosby's power,' said the Earl, pinning the brooch into her lace. 'I learned the true story from Lethbridge. But it did not need his or any man's word, Horry, to convince me that only force could have induced you to enter Lethbridge's house that night.'

'Oh, R-Rule!' Horatia quavered, two large tears rolling down her cheeks.

The Earl's hands went out to her, but a footstep outside made him turn. The Viscount came in, fluent words on his lips. 'Beg pardon to have kept you waiting, Horry, but Lady Louisa—Well, by all that's fortunate!' He executed a well-feigned start. 'Rule! Never thought to see you here tonight! What a lucky chance!'

The Earl sighed. 'Go on, Pelham. I feel sure you have some urgent message for me which will take me to the other end of the gardens.'

'Oh, no, not as far as that!' the Viscount assured him. 'Only to the boxes. Met Lady Louisa—looking for you all over, Marcus. She wants to see you very particularly.'

'What I chiefly admire in you, Pelham, is your resourcefulness,' said his lordship.

'Pel, it doesn't m-matter any longer!' said Horatia, drying her eyes. 'M-Marcus knew the whole time, and it was he who had the b-brooch, and wrote me that letter, and there's nothing to worry about any m-more!'

The Viscount stared at the brooch, then at Rule, opened his mouth, shut it again and swallowed violently. 'Do you mean to tell me,' he demanded, 'that Pom and I have been moving heaven and earth to get that damned brooch back when all the time you had it in your pocket? No, damme, that's too much!'

'You see, when you held me up on Hounslow Heath I found myself quite unable to resist the temptation—an over-mastering one, believe me, Pelham—of—er—leading you on a little,' apologized his lordship. 'You will have to try to forgive me, my dear boy.'

'Forgive you?' said the Viscount indignantly. 'Do you realize that I haven't had a spare moment since that brooch was lost? We've even had to drag a highwayman into it, not to mention poor old Pom's great-aunt!'

'Really!' said Rule, interested. 'I had the pleasure of meeting the highwayman, of course, but I was not aware that Pommeroy's great-aunt also had a hand in the affair.'

'She hadn't, she's dead,' said the Viscount shortly. A thought occurred to him. 'Where's Lethbridge?' he asked.

'Lethbridge,' said his lordship, 'is at Maidenhead. But I do not think you need concern yourself with him.'

'Need I not?' said the Viscount. 'Well, I've a strong notion I shall be on my way to Maidenhead in the morning.'

'You will, of course, do just as you please, my dear boy,' said Rule amiably, 'but I should perhaps warn you that you will not find his lordship in a fit condition to receive you.'

The Viscount cocked a knowing eyebrow. 'Ha, like that, is it? Well, that's something. Pom will be glad to know. I'll call him in.'

'Pray don't put yourself to the trouble!' besought his lordship. 'I do not wish to seem uncivil, Pelham, but I am constrained to tell you that I find you—shall we say a trifle *de trop*?'

The Viscount looked from Rule to Horatia. 'I take you,' he said. 'You want to be alone. Well, I think I'll be off then.' He nodded at Rule. 'If you take any advice, Marcus, you'll keep an eye on that chit,' he said severely, and walked out.

Left alone with her husband, Horatia stole a glance at him under her lashes. He was looking gravely down at her. She said, the stammer very pronounced: 'Rule, I truly w-will try to be the s-sort of wife you w-wanted, and not m-make any m-more scandals or get into any scrapes.'

'You are the sort of wife I wanted,' he answered.

'Am-am I?' faltered Horatia, lifting her eyes to his face.

He came up to her. 'Horry,' he said, 'once you told me that I was rather old, but in spite of that we married one another. Will you tell me now, my dearest—was I too old?'

'You're not old at all,' said Horatia, her face puckering. 'You are j-just the right age for—for a husband, only I was young and stupid and I thought—I thought—'

He raised her hand to his lips. 'I know, Horry,' he said. 'When I married you there was another woman in my life. She is not there now, my darling, and in my heart she never had a place.'

'Oh, M-Marcus, put m-me there!' Horatia said on a sob.

'You are there,' he answered, and caught her up in his arms and kissed her, not gently at all, but ruthlessly, crushing all the breath out of her body.

'Oh!' gasped Horatia. 'Oh, I n-never knew you could k-kiss like that!'

'But I can, you see,' said his lordship. 'And—I am sorry if you do not like it, Horry—I am going to do it again.'

'But I d-do like it!' said Horatia. 'I l-like it very m-much!'

GETTE HEYER G

ER GEORGETT

GETTE HEYER G

ER GEORGETT

GETTE HEYER G

ER GEORGETT

GETTE HEYER G

ER GEORGETT

GETTE HEYER G

ER GEORGETT

GETTE HEYER G